DOUBLE HELIX

STAR TREK
THE NEXT GENERATION®

DOUBLE HELIX

Infection
John Gregory Betancourt

Vectors
Dean Wesley Smith
&
Kristine Kathryn Rusch

Red Sector
Diane Carey

Quarantine
John Vornholt

Double or Nothing
Peter David

The First Virtue
Michael Jan Friedman
&
Christie Golden

Double Helix Concept by
John J. Ordover and Michael Jan Friedman

POCKET BOOKS
New York London Toronto Sydney Singapore

This book is a work of fiction. Names, characters, places and incidents are products of the authors' imagination or are used fictitiously. Any resemblance to actual events or locales or persons, living or dead, is entirely coincidental.

POCKET BOOKS, a division of Simon & Schuster Inc.
1230 Avenue of the Americas, New York, NY 10020

ISBN: 0-7434-1272-9

First Pocket Books printing October 2002

10 9 8 7 6 5 4 3 2 1

Printed in the U.S.A.

These titles were previously published individually by Pocket Books.

Contents

DOUBLE HELIX

INFECTION

JOHN GREGORY BETANCOURT

PART 1:

THE COMING OF THE PLAGUE

Prologue

WHEN HE REACHED the broad windows of his hotel room, Solomon paused in his security sweep. Fifty meters below, on the far side of the square, seethed an angry-looking mob of humans. He couldn't really make out faces in the growing twilight, but he knew their type. *Rabble-rousers. Troublemakers.* Fifth- and sixth-generation human settlers on Archaria III, gone back to a more primitive mindset. To a man they dressed in simple brown clothes—shirts, pants, and boots. All the men sported long bushy beards, shoulder-length hair, and smug attitudes of cultural and species superiority.

Solomon snorted. Superior? *Hardly.* Stubborn, closed-minded, and prejudiced against nonhumans . . . in a word, *fools.* He never had time for fools.

Still, he continued to watch. The mob continued to grow. He estimated their number now at more than a hundred. They milled about in the square, beyond the black marble fountains, and continued their angry posturing. As water jetted from the mouths of ten larger-than-life Earth lions, as gold and silver fish darted through the meter-deep series of oval pools, he heard their voices begin to chant: *"Veritas . . . Veritas . . . Veritas!"* loud enough to reach even where he stood.

He swung his gaze around the square, noting how dozens of shopkeepers—smooth-cheeked humans, gray-skinned Peladians, and even a couple of Ferengi—had already begun to trundle their wares inside to safety. Pottery, fruits, souvenirs, it didn't matter what they sold—they weren't taking chances. Solomon chuckled. They could read the signs as clearly as he. Another riot was brewing. As he watched, durasteel shutters snapped shut one by one across the stores' entrances and windows. He could imagine the merchants inside busily throwing bolts, latching latches, and retreating to the safest parts of their buildings. *Poor paranoid fools,* he thought. *Race riots are the least of your worries.* From the look of things, in five minutes every building facing the square would be locked up tighter than a Romulan clam. Not that it would save any of them in the end.

Still more bearded men streamed into the square from the side streets. Solomon leaned forward, searching for a leader, but saw no sign of the elusive man called "Veritas." The chanting built to a crescendo.

Snorting derisively, Solomon took a step back. *I really don't have time for this nonsense,* he thought. It was too easy to get swept up in the excitement. *Business calls.*

"Computer, engage privacy mode. Black out the windows. Filter extraneous noises." Civil unrest always made money for someone. *But not me, not today.* He sighed with regret. After all, he had bigger projects to finish before he even *thought* about fun.

The windows' glass darkened to the color of charcoal, and the room grew hushed. Not even the ventilators made a sound. Raising his tricorder, Solomon continued his security sweep. Good—no unexpected EM readings, no bugs, no monitoring devices. Business as usual on Archaria III; no one suspected him of being anything more than another buyer for the Interstellar Corn and Grain Combine. ICGC always made a great cover on farming planets like this one. He smiled a bit wryly. All he'd had to do was flash his business ID at the front desk and the hotel had rolled out the red-carpet treatment, complete with complimentary fruit basket and bottle of wine from a local vineyard. Second-rate stuff, of course, and he hadn't touched it; the best wines always came from Mother Earth.

Crossing to the bed, he lifted a small silver suitcase and gripped the handle long enough for the smartlock to scan his DNA. When it beeped acceptance, he flipped open the latches without triggering the small explosive device embedded in the handle. In fifteen years of illegal activities, he had never once lost his equipment . . . but the Orion Syndicate never believed in taking chances. And all due precautions were necessary on this particular job. The client had paid extra for them.

Nestled inside the case lay the pieces of a narrow-beam long-range subspace transmitter. He assembled it deftly, then used the tricorder to aim the short conelike antenna to the proper coordinates, about 20 degrees up and toward the square.

When he activated the device, a flickering holographic image filled the air before him: burning red eyes, a shock of long white hair, skin the color of milk: the General. *I hate this part.* Solomon blinked, but the General's features had already begun to change, thanks to the security scrambler: now the General had the prominent nose, black hair with blue highlights, and upswept eyebrows of a Vulcan. It would be this way throughout their whole conversation, as the scrambler shifted the General's features from one race to another. Solomon found it strangely disconcerting. *There's nothing like face-to-face meetings.* Next client. . . .

"Report!" the General barked, voice flat and artificial, revealing nothing about his species. Undoubtedly it had been so crunched and mangled by computers on his end that no trace of the original spoken words remained.

"Stage One has begun," Solomon said matter-of-factly. *Keep the client happy, the first rule of any service industry, even terrorism.* "All ten bombs are in place. The plague virus will be released per your timetable."

"Acceptable." The General nodded, the deep red wattles under his chin shaking to match his three antennae. He began to grow horns and ivory-colored tusks. "I will transmit the second third of your payment to your accounts on Ferenginar. The final installment will follow successful completion of this phase of the plan."

Solomon licked his lips. "General . . ."

"Speak."

"The vaccine—you're sure it will work?" If he was going to expose himself to some new genetically enhanced plague, he wanted every assurance that it wouldn't kill him.

"Yes."

"The Orion Syndicate does not tolerate damage to its membership," he added pointedly.

"I would not risk wasting talent such as yours. I will need it again." The General waved a puckered yellow tentacle as his gray-green face grew the cheek gills of an Eshashu. Then, with a brusqueness that matched his suddenly Klingon features, he severed the connection.

Solomon sat on the bed and chewed his lip for a second. He felt sweat trickling down his sides and back. Waiting always made his stomach churn. He felt control begin to slip away. It was one thing to belong to the Orion Syndicate, the most successful criminal organization in the Alpha Quadrant. Extortion, arson, blackmail, and even murder had long been a part of his life. But it was quite another thing to take a freelance job planting exotic diseases in unknown aliens and then sit calmly and wait for a virus to strike.

What if the cure didn't work? What if he *wasn't* immune? What if—

He drew a deep breath and forced himself to relax. *Steady, steady. No need to panic. I'm safe. Probably the safest man on the planet.* He didn't like invisible dangers, but at least he had been inoculated against them.

The Archarians must have done something to earn this strong a reaction from the General, he thought grimly. *Poor bastards.* Then he forced such thoughts from his mind. He couldn't allow himself to start to feel sympathy.

Business was business, after all, and he was getting paid more than amply. Even after the Syndicate took its cut, he'd be well ahead for the quarter. Risa was getting boring; perhaps a well-earned vacation on Lomax or Gentree or one of the other up-and-coming pleasure worlds would soothe his nerves.

He glanced at the chronometer on the tricorder, still counting down to the carefully timed release of the plague. Just a few ticks more. . . .

"Nothing personal," he murmured to the million-odd humans and Peladians on the planet as the counter reached zero. He felt his heart skip as the moment came and passed, but he heard no sounds, no thunderous explosions, no vast collection of voices raised in cries of pain or sorrow or anguish as the invisible virus entered the planetary atmosphere. In his mind's eye, he saw it riding into the city on soft breezes, drifting like a fine mist through every street, into every home and business, into every set of lungs.

"Poor bastards," he whispered again. What *had* they done to the General?

Calmly he began to pack up the transmitter. Now, to see to the final part of the plans . . . he had to monitor how quickly the disease spread—and how quickly planetary authorities and the Federation dealt with it.

Let it be fast, he thought.

Chapter One

Stardate: 41211.0 Captain's Log, Supplemental

The Enterprise *continues on its mission to Archaria III, a planet jointly colonized by humans and Peladians. A new disease has cropped up, terrifying the inhabitants. So far, more than five thousand cases have been confirmed.*

The only drug at all effective in treating this disease is a rare compound called Tricillin PDF, which seems to prolong life, though only for a week at most. The Enterprise *will deliver a supply of the drug, quarantine the planet, then stay to oversee research into finding a cure.*

"—AND RENDER WHATEVER AID the Archarians require until the emergency is over," Captain Picard said, leaning forward at the conference table and gazing at each of his senior staff in turn.

William Riker, Geordi La Forge, and Worf looked uncomfortable at the mention of the plague, and he didn't blame them; he had always felt ill at ease when faced with intangible dangers. Deanna Troi looked deeply concerned, and Dr. Crusher looked . . . intrigued? *She has dealt with plagues before,* Picard reminded himself. *She knows how to contain them.*

The persistent low rumble of a starship at maximum warp filled the room. None of his crew spoke. *They feel the tension building already,* he thought.

"Captain," Dr. Crusher finally said, "I may have to bring samples of this virus aboard the *Enterprise* for study, and perhaps a few patients."

"Understood, Doctor. So long as all necessary security precautions are maintained, I see no problem. In the meantime"—he slid a data padd across the conference table to her—"the doctors of Archo City Hospital have prepared a full report, which you may find useful."

"Thank you." She pulled the padd in front of herself and began skimming the opening remarks.

"Something else is troubling you, sir," Deanna Troi said softly.

Picard hesitated, then gave a curt nod. Best to get it out in the open. "What disturbs me most is the thought that this whole problem may be of our own manufacture . . . a biological weapon."

"Impossible—how could that be?" Riker said, shaking his head dismissively. "Legalities aside, it's against everything the Federation stands for!"

"We do have treaties with most sentient races which prevent the development and use of biological weapons," Data said. "With all due respect, sir, the deployment of a genetically designed plague on a remote agricultural world such as Archaria III seems highly unlikely."

"Not necessarily," Picard said. He cleared his throat. "Archaria III is in many ways a throwback to human civilization two or three hundred years ago. It was settled by religious zealots early in the twenty-second century, and although they have largely come into the Federation's fold, old prejudices and resentments still bubble to the surface from time to time." The room was quiet for a moment while Picard allowed his point to sink in.

Riker finally broke the silence. "Sir, if I may ask, what is it that leads you to conclude this disease is a weapon?"

"*Might* be a weapon, Number One. A radical political group called the Purity League claims the plague is an act of God against 'blasphemous unnatural unions.' "

Riker gave him a blank stare. "Sir?"

Picard cleared his throat. *How to phrase this delicately.* He said, "The Purity League is opposed to interspecies mating—'mixers' as they call such people."

Again the rumble of the ship's engines filled the room. *They can't believe it, either,* he thought. *Humanity is supposed to be beyond such prejudices.*

He noticed that Deanna Troi, half human and half Betazoid herself, hid her inner feelings behind a mask of professional calm. He would have given a lot to know her true reaction. Undoubtedly she was even more shocked and horrified than he had been. *To think that some humans are still capable of such petty resentments. . . .*

He forced himself back to the problem at hand. "Mixers—or anyone else suspected of adulterating the purity of the human race—are treated as second-class citizens in many places on Archaria III," he continued. "Officially such prejudices are prohibited, of course, but in the backwater towns discrimination apparently still runs rampant. Only in the half-dozen large cities do humans and Peladians work and live together with something approaching harmony. In the country, things have apparently become so bad that most full-blooded Peladians now live in isolated enclaves surrounded by their own kind."

Riker said, "That sounds like a ghetto system."

"It is. Those of mixed heritage are even less fortunate, since they belong fully to neither the human nor the Peladian world. They were relocating to the cities in record numbers—until the plague struck. Now they're fleeing into the countryside once more, living like vagabonds in tent camps." Picard looked down at his clenched, interlaced fingers resting uneasily on the table. He didn't bother to feign relaxation. Sometimes it was good for the crew to see him share their anger.

Deanna Troi asked, "How many people of mixed blood are on the planet?"

"Nobody is quite sure. Estimates range from between 150,000 and 200,000 people. Obviously, those mixers who most closely resemble humans hide the truth to avoid conflict with the Purity League."

Data said, "I am aware of the Purity League, sir. The Federation has monitored their activities for many years, but has deemed them a minor nuisance with little actual influence."

"Their influence is growing," Picard said firmly. The private reports he had read gave alarming statistics; according to confidential surveys, fully half of the planet's human population harbored feelings of support for the Purity League, though the League's actual membership numbers were open to conjecture. It was certainly in the tens of thousands if not the hundreds of thousands.

He went on. "The Purity League's leader, Father Veritas, is using the plague as a rallying point for anti-alien sentiment. Apparently Veritas is responsible for inciting dozens of race riots in the last few months. The whole planet is in turmoil. The nonhuman population—and especially the partly human population—is running scared. The plague's growth has only served to make the situation worse." *"Veritas," indeed,* he thought, grimacing. *If ever there was a misnomer. . . .*

"Sir," said Deanna Troi, "Archaria III has a long history of interspecies problems, including wars, assassinations, and racism. Its history is part of several planetary evolution courses at the Academy. I believe everyone here has studied it to some degree."

A general murmur of agreement came from the rest of his senior staff. Picard found himself surprised—it hadn't been part of the curriculum when he had studied at the Academy—but he was pleased. *They're keeping up with the times.*

"That is correct, sir," said Data. "It was settled in 2102 by a human sect of religious fundamentalists called the Brotherhood. Seven years later, these human settlers encountered Peladian settlers, who had colonized the planet almost simultaneously."

Picard had never seen a Peladian and knew little about them, beyond the fact that they were humanoid, militant about privacy, and generally considered pacifists . . . except when provoked.

Data went on, "After a series of small wars, as the two sides got to know each other, peaceful relations and coexistence began. According to the information I have accessed, with the increasing agricultural importance of Archaria III their differences were largely put aside, in favor of economic cooperation."

"That is the public story," Picard said. He folded his arms and frowned a bit. "There have always been tensions. Until Father Veritas and the Purity League burst onto the scene sixteen years ago, the planetary government managed to contain most of the problems before they escalated. Over the past few years, though, there has been an increase in terrorism on Archaria III aimed at Peladians, at humans who have married them, and especially at their children—all in the name of human racial purity. That's another reason why the Federation suspects the plague may be genetically engineered."

"I'm sorry, sir," Riker said. "I'm still not quite clear on what leads you to that conclusion."

Picard looked at Dr. Crusher. "Doctor?"

She looked up from scanning her report. "All the victims are of mixed genetic origins," she said flatly. "Not just human-Peladian, but several other genetic mixes have been affected as well. Human-Vulcan, human-Etrarian, and human-Bajoran crossbreeds are all reported susceptible to infection. Pure human and pure Peladian genetic stock appear to be immune. I would strongly suggest that no one of mixed heritage be allowed access to the planet."

The news cooled the room. Worf glared. Riker folded his arms and frowned pensively, though he kept glancing almost surreptitiously at Deanna Troi. And Deanna herself gave the slightest hiss of anger—she was the most threatened of those present, Picard knew, since she was half human and half Betazoid.

He looked pointedly in her direction. She returned his gaze, but whatever emotion had escaped her tight control had been suppressed once more behind that professional, clinical wall.

Counselor, counsel thyself, he thought.

Dr. Crusher continued, "The symptoms come on very quickly. Apparently the virus enters the mouth or nasal passages and primary multiplication occurs in lymphoid tissues. Small amounts of virus reach the blood and are carried to other sites in the reticuloendothelial system, where they multiply quickly. High fever and severe abdominal cramping are part of the first stage. Then small white fever blisters begin to cover the body, especially the face, neck, and under the arms. This second stage lasts from one to three days. Infected patients lapse into comas by this point—and it's probably just as well. The pain would be extreme as the muscle cramping worsens and fever blisters form in their mouths, throats, and lungs. Victims begin to suffocate. Next comes stage three, when blood begins to ooze from the gums, nose, and ears. Rapid cellular degeneration follows. Total systemic collapse is inevitable and occurs within a week of infection—often within three to four days."

Picard swallowed. Her matter-of-fact tone did not mitigate the gruesome truth about the disease. *Pain. Unconsciousness. Suffocation. Cellular degeneration. Death.* He had long harbored a secret fear of death by disease, by something slow and insidious worming its way through his body millimeter by millimeter. He liked enemies he could see, touch, and outsmart.

"Could such a disease be genetically engineered?" he asked her. No sense avoiding the inevitable question.

"Could someone create such a disease? Yes, I can think of half-a-dozen research labs capable of cobbling it together with a few months of hard work. I think the real question is, *did* someone. It's much too soon to say whether this disease has been genetically engineered. . . . It could just as easily be a virus which has mutated to attack some previously unknown weakness in the immune system of genetic crosses."

"How likely is *that?"* Riker asked her.

"I don't know." She hesitated. "I really can't comment until I get a sample of the virus and break it down with a microscanner."

"Our mission is to find out," Picard said. He looked at each of his senior staff in turn. "If this plague is a biological weapon, it must be contained, an antidote must be found, and the designers must be brought to justice before more damage can be done."

Dr. Crusher nodded. *Set her on course,* Picard thought, *and she'll work wonders.*

"I'll begin work with Archarian doctors at once," she said, "to try to find a cure. With so many people infected, that must be my first priority. I'll beam down with my team and begin work immediately."

"Agreed," said Picard. "Unless you have an objection, Doctor, I want an away team to beam down to investigate the Purity League. If they are responsible, they might already have a cure."

"That shouldn't be a problem, as long as no member of the away team is of mixed genetic heritage. And of course anyone who leaves must be fully decontaminated and possibly even quarantined before resuming normal duties aboard the *Enterprise.*"

"Very good."

"I'd like to head up that away team," Riker said.

"My thoughts exactly, Number One. Take two people with you. Use native costumes. This will be a strictly undercover mission. No one, not even the planetary governor, must know about it."

"Understood, sir," said Riker. "With your permission, I'll take Lieutenant Yar and Lieutenant Commander Data."

Picard nodded. "Very well, Number One. Any other questions?" He glanced around the table one last time, but nobody spoke. They knew their jobs, just as he knew he could depend on them.

Chapter Two

"NOW ENTERING ORBIT around Archaria III, Captain," Geordi La Forge reported from the helm, his voice rising above the electronic whirs, beeps, and chirps that signified that all systems were operating at full efficiency. When the young lieutenant glanced over his shoulder, Picard saw the bridge lights gleam across the metallic visor that covered his eyes.

"On the viewscreen." Picard leaned forward, anxious to see this troubled little world. "Standard orbit, Mr. La Forge."

"Aye, sir."

Archaria III appeared on the main viewscreen at the front of the bridge. It was a lush planet, half water and half land, with swirls of white clouds covering the northern hemisphere. The three main continents—colored in rich browns and greens, dotted with picturesque lakes and long flowing rivers—looked like a paradise to him. *And what have they done with it,* he thought bitterly. *They busy themselves squabbling over genetic purity.*

Sometimes he just wanted to grab planet-bound people by the scruff of the neck, drag them into orbit, and force them to gaze in wonder at the worlds they called home. If they could only see the hugeness of the universe, or realize just how insignificant they were in the greater cosmic vastness, it might well knock some sense into them.

The comm system beeped urgently. Beside Lieutenant La Forge, Ensign Cherbach touched his controls and reported, "We are being hailed, sir. Governor Sekk wishes to speak with you."

So it begins. With a mental sigh, Picard dragged himself back from his reverie. Standing, he pulled his uniform straighter and took a step forward.

He wasn't looking forward to this conversation, but it had to be done.

"On screen," he said.

"Aye, sir."

The controls beeped softly in response, and the image of a balding, stocky man with a chest-length gray beard replaced the splendid view of the planet. Dark circles lined Governor Sekk's eyes, and deep worry lines creased his forehead. His ceremonial robes appeared rumpled and unkempt; several slight but noticeable food stains marked the front. *A good man pushed too hard,* was Picard's immediate reaction. *I don't think he's slept in days.* Clearly Sekk took the plague, the Purity League, and all the attendant problems quite seriously.

As does Starfleet, Picard thought grimly. *As do we all.*

Even in the midst of crisis, protocol had to be observed. Picard inclined his head and got the niceties under way: "I am Captain Jean-Luc Picard of the *Enterprise.* Governor Sekk, I presume?"

"Yes, Captain." Sekk's voice was hoarse, Picard noticed. Too many orders over too many hours? Too many speeches to try to keep up morale? "Thank you for coming so quickly."

"Not at all, Governor. I understand the situation is still quite dire."

Sekk nodded. "Our morgues and hospitals are overflowing. There are fifteen thousand reported cases of the plague to date, with more being reported by the hour. Officially we now have more than ten thousand dead. Our cities are being abandoned. There are riots in the streets." His voice rose an octave. "We must have immediate help!"

"Of course, Governor. We have sufficient supplies of Tricillin PDF aboard to last your doctors for several weeks. The *Constitution* is bringing additional supplies and should arrive shortly. If your people will provide the necessary coordinates, our transporter rooms will begin beaming the drug down immediately."

"Of course, Captain." He motioned urgently to someone Picard couldn't see. "One of my aides will get the information for you."

"My ship's medical staff is standing by to work with your doctors," Picard went on. "Any help they can provide will be given immediately. I believe Dr. Crusher, my chief medical officer, is already in contact with Dr. Tang at Archo City Hospital. I understand he is in charge of your efforts to find a cure."

"That's right, Tang is a good man. A very good man. Our best researcher."

Picard licked his lips. Now came the delicate part. The part he knew Sekk wouldn't like . . . and which he himself hated to have to do.

"Governor Sekk," he began, "as you can well imagine, the virulent nature of this disease has alarmed many of your neighboring star systems as well as Starfleet. All outbound ships have been ordered back to Archaria III. I am afraid I must place your planet under a quarantine, at least for the time being. No one may enter or leave."

Sekk seemed to shrink a little into himself. To an agricultural planet like Archaria III, quarantine would be viewed as nothing short of an economic death sentence; unless their grains and other foodstuffs were shipped out to market promptly, Archaria III's economy would begin to stagger and fail.

But the protests Picard expected never came. Governor Sekk only nodded wearily, as if he had been expecting it all along. "Very well, Captain. I will inform our spaceport at once. No more ships will be allowed to depart without Starfleet's approval."

Picard nodded. "Good." *Perhaps this won't be so difficult after all. If this is the level of cooperation I can expect, we should have the situation well in hand in just a few days.*

"Is there anything else you need?"

"I want to see a log of all outbound ships for the last three months, Governor, with flight plans. Plus passenger lists and complete cargo manifests. If any ships have to be chased down, we had best get started."

"Of course. The information is online with our spaceport's computers. I will make certain you have immediate access."

"Thank you." Picard hesitated a second. Sekk clearly *was* a good man, and his cooperation would undoubtedly come at a high personal price: after such a series of disasters—plague, planetary quarantine, economic ruin—he would stand little chance of being reelected planetary governor again. At least he could throw the man one little sop . . . something that might lead to a position within Starfleet's bureaucracy if Sekk followed up on it.

"I want you to know," Picard finally said, "that your assistance in this matter will not go unnoticed. I will personally see to it that your name is mentioned prominently in my reports to Starfleet."

Sekk nodded. "Thank you, Captain. But I would prefer your attentions go where they are most needed. Find a cure for the plague. Get the quarantine lifted. Help my people. That's all I really need." His smile was that of a kindly, benevolent ruler.

And a dozen red flags went up in Picard's mind. *He's hiding something.*

Picard returned that winning smile. "Understood, Governor. Thank you for your assistance. Picard out."

Returning to his command seat, he sat back and crossed his legs. *He's lying to me. Somehow, some way, he thinks he's pulled the wool over my eyes.*

He paused and thought, focusing not on the governor but on the people around him, trying to dredge some unvoiced suspicion from his subconscious. Officers hurried from station to station, scanning the planet and the rest of the system. The doors whooshed open as two more science officers came onto the bridge. The familiar chirps and beeps of the bridge filled his ears, along with the softer underlying bass vibration of a ship in orbit.

Picard retraced his conversation word by word, detail by detail. It *seemed* straightforward enough. Yet Sekk's all-too-convenient cooperation suddenly smelled wrong. *Why?*

The answer suddenly came to him: *So we won't suspect the data he provides.* Clearly the governor wanted to hide something. *But what?*

"Any thoughts, Number One?" he asked suddenly. He glanced at his second in command, still seated to his immediate right.

"I think he's playing us for fools, sir."

Picard covered his inner smile. *Riker will make a good captain someday. He's got the instincts for it.* "Fools, eh?" he said. "Would you care to elaborate?"

Riker hesitated. "I'm not sure, sir. I can't quite put my finger on it. . . ."

"Well, *I* can. I'll wager the governor sent his family off-planet in a private ship and doesn't want them sent back here. And I will be *very* surprised if we find a single reference to it in the spaceport's records."

Riker looked puzzled. "How did you know—"

"No career politician would surrender power so easily, Number One, and then refuse to take credit for it." He smiled a little grimly, thinking about the first time he had negotiated with the governor of a planet. He had been a lieutenant then, and Governor Silas Jones of the Rigel Colony had eaten him alive. "Sekk made one fatal mistake when he gave that stirring little speech about putting his people first."

Riker shook his head sadly. "Which is, of course, what a leader is supposed to do."

"Yes, but it was too easy, as if he would have turned things around so it looked like *he* gave us the records—in the best interest of his people, of course. Instead, he let me do all the work, then distanced himself from it. This way he hasn't lied or obstructed us in any way if the truth *does* come out."

"There's always one bad apple," Riker sighed. "Still, hopefully there are other people on this planet who can focus on more than their own interests."

It's nice to have an idealist for a first officer, Picard thought. *I know the Federation's philosophy will always be supported.*

"Sir," said La Forge, swiveling in his seat. "I have an idea of where we can find that extra ship."

"Oh?"

"Yes, sir."

Slowly Picard nodded. He liked initiative, and Geordi La Forge was another crewman who had the right instincts . . . and almost certainly could look forward to a long and distinguished career in Starfleet.

"Then it's your baby, Mr. La Forge," he said, settling back in his seat. "Proceed when ready."

"Thank you, sir."

Picard glanced at Riker again. "And now, Number One, don't you have an away mission to plan?"

Riker said, "It's well in hand, sir. Most of the Purity League's activities take place under the cover of darkness. We will be beaming down at dusk, and Lieutenant Yar is currently scouting the most likely spot to encounter them. I have already ordered native garb for the three of us. We will be ready on schedule."

"Excellent." Picard took a deep breath. *Like clockwork,* he thought with satisfaction. *A good ship runs like clockwork.*

An ensign appeared at his elbow holding a duty roster. After scanning the list of names, he signed off on it.

"Sir," said La Forge. "We have the spaceport's departure records now. Request permission to use the computer station in astrometrics for my research."

"Astrometrics?" Picard raised his eyebrows slightly. It seemed an odd request. "Is there some reason you need access to interstellar charting, Mr. La Forge?"

"I have a theory about the governor's secret ship, sir. Call it . . . a hunch."

Picard thought it over a heartbeat. *Give him a chance. Let him prove himself.*

"Very well," he said. Hunches often had a grain of logic to them, even if the conscious mind couldn't always pin it down. "Carry on, Mr. La Forge."

"Thank you, sir." All business, the lieutenant rose and strode from the bridge with apparent confidence and determination. Ensign Charles Ehrhart moved forward to take La Forge's place at the navigator's station.

Like clockwork, Picard thought, leaning back and smiling to himself. *Excellent.*

Chapter Three

It wasn't Dr. Tang's appearance that alarmed Dr. Crusher—a week's growth of reddish-brown beard, pasty skin, puffy eyes, and wild unkempt red hair sometimes went with the territory when you where a doctor or a research scientist working in an emergency. Rather, it was what she could see behind him: hundreds of patients lying side by side on the floor in the hospital's lobby.

Plague victims, she knew without having to ask. *They must have run out of beds in the wards. This is the best they can do.*

It was a grim image, yet to her it painted a more accurate picture of the planet's situation than a host of dry reports and nameless, faceless statistics. Things had to be bad indeed if they had resorted to putting people on floors.

Her call to Dr. Tang had been routed to a public comm stand in the lobby of the Archo City Hospital. Tang had replied within five minutes of being paged. And when he answered, he cut through the usual niceties abruptly. "How soon can we get that Tricillin PDF beamed down here, Doctor?"

"The drugs are being prepared for transport now," she said. "The first fifty crates should reach your location in less than five minutes. If you can find a place to put them, that is," she added, peering over his shoulder. "You do look a little full."

Tang turned and called to someone Dr. Crusher couldn't see: "We need more room! The Tricillin PDF is here! . . . Right!" He turned back to her.

"It will be taken care of. You can beam it down to these coordinates as soon as it's ready."

"Good." Dr. Crusher continued to stare at the hundreds of men and women and children beyond him. Something about them bothered her. They all lay curiously still despite being mashed in shoulder to shoulder and hip to hip. *Is this the comatose stage?* she wondered.

"Is there anything else you need?" She forced herself to focus on Dr. Tang. Brusque though he might be, he was still in charge of the hospital.

He snorted. "More doctors. A bigger hospital. A cure for the plague. Half a dozen tactical nuclear missiles lobbed at this city from orbit. Any combination of those will do."

Nuclear missiles? Was that an attempt at humor? If so, she didn't find it particularly funny—and Tang didn't seem to be laughing, either.

"If you need more help, I will be glad to have some of my people beam down to assist—"

"No!" He almost screamed the word. "Keep your people off this planet! They'll be infected, too!"

"We have biofilters aboard—"

"Don't you understand? Didn't you read my report? They just *don't work!"* He sucked in a deep breath. "This virus isn't like anything you've seen before, Doctor. It . . . it's *smart."*

She blinked. *Smart?* That didn't make any sense.

"Very well," she said coolly. "We can work from the *Enterprise* just as well, with your assistance."

He turned and paced away, then came back. His face was red, and he seemed to be struggling to keep his temper in check.

"Is something bothering you, Doctor?" she demanded, letting a professional mask hide her intense distaste for him. His appearance, his manner, his attitude—it all rubbed her the wrong way.

"Let me be blunt, Doctor," Tang finally said in a low voice. "We're not just losing the battle, we're losing the war. I have more than six thousand dead in my own hospital. Men, women, children, babies—" He gave a frustrated wave. "All die within a week . . . two weeks, with massive doses of Tricillin PDF. We haven't had *one* survivor. *Not one.* Do you know what that means?"

"I am well aware of the mortality rate." Beyond him, Dr. Crusher watched a dozen men dressed in white containment suits burst into the lobby from a side corridor. They began picking up the comatose patients and tossing them aboard a low motorized cart—stacking them one on top of another like so much deadwood.

Bodies, she thought with growing horror. *They haven't run out of beds, they've run out of slabs in the morgue.* A few limbs jutted out grotesquely from the growing pile on the cart. The big toe on every left foot held an identification tag, she saw now. *They're all dead. Not just dozens, but hundreds of them.*

As she gave an involuntary shiver, she met Dr. Tang's gaze again. He grinned at her now, widely, wolfishly, like a predator closing in on his next meal. *He's enjoying this,* she realized—and that horrified her almost as much as the bodies.

"Yes, Doctor," he said almost mockingly. "You start to understand the real situation now, don't you? It's not pleasant."

"How can you be so cold about it—"

He snapped back, "Don't judge us unless you've been in the same situation. You don't know how terrible it's been here. I—"

He paused and seemed to be trying to rein in his anger. Dr. Crusher didn't know what to say. She hadn't been in a situation like this before—and she hoped she never would be again.

In a calmer voice, Tang went on: "I know it's not a pretty little sickbay like you have aboard the *Enterprise,* but as you can see, we have room for that Tricillin now. Please get it down here as soon as possible, Doctor. We still have three thousand living patients who need it."

Dr. Crusher swallowed. "Immediately."

As a doctor, she had seen death many times and in many ways over the years, but even so, the cold unfeeling way these people were being tossed about still went against every grain of her moral and medical principles. She believed a certain dignity ought to come with death. The men in contamination suits might have been janitors cleaning up after a party instead of medical caregivers.

And Tang's rictus grin bothered her. Maybe it covered up a terrified interior, or maybe he had been pushed to the breaking point and beyond by the horrible tragedy unfolding around him, but she couldn't help how she felt.

He hasn't just lost his healing touch, he's lost his ability to feel empathy. He isn't a doctor, he's a . . . a body processor. The thought left her cold. *No matter how bad things get, I won't let it happen to me.*

"—and here is the access code for our medical computer's database," Dr. Tang was saying almost cheerfully, as though turning over the keys to a beach house. "You're going to need it." He entered it into the comm unit, and Dr. Crusher recorded it more by reflex than conscious thought. "It contains every scrap of information we have been able to gather about the virus. Precious little good it's done us. Thankfully, though, it's your problem now. *Starfleet's* problem, I mean. Good luck."

"Wait!" she said as he started to end the transmission. *That's it? He's just going to abandon me to my research? What kind of a madman is he?*

"What is it, Doctor?"

"I will begin reviewing your data at once." She swallowed at the lump in her throat. "In the meantime, I need a vial of contaminated blood beamed up. After that, I'll need a patient in the earliest stages of the disease."

Tang's eyes narrowed only the slightest bit. "I do not recommend that, Doctor," he said bluntly.

"Why not?" she demanded.

"The plague leaps through biofilters like they weren't there. For the first week, we kept them up around our quarantine wards, but it didn't help. Nothing stopped it."

"That's impossible," she said. "Nothing as big as a virus can get through a biofilter."

He shrugged. "Maybe we made a mistake. Maybe the plague virus was already loose everywhere on the planet simultaneously. Or maybe it's just smarter than we are. I just *don't know* anymore." He ran one hand through his unruly red hair. "But I still wouldn't risk it. Not aboard a starship. If it gets loose in a confined space like that, with your ventilator systems—well, I wouldn't want to be part of your crew. You'll end up spending the rest of your lives quarantined down here with the rest of us."

"We have air purifiers—"

"Not good enough." He shook his head. "Not even *close* to good enough. Why don't you *listen?"*

She sucked in an angry breath. *Count to ten. He's not deliberately trying to provoke you. Count to ten, and don't forget to breathe.*

"What *do* you recommend, then?" she managed to say in something approaching her normal tone.

He leaned forward, his expression growing even more intent. "I don't think this plague *can* be cured." His voice lowered to a whisper, as though taking her into his confidence. "Archaria III has one of the finest hospital systems in the Federation. All our equipment is new and top-of-the-line. Maybe not as good as you have aboard the *Enterprise,* but damned close. We haven't found an answer, and I've had a hundred people working on it for the last three weeks. We're not *going* to find an answer, Doctor. This is *it* for us."

"I refuse to accept that," Dr. Crusher said. With such a negative attitude, no wonder his people hadn't made any progress. "In human history alone, people have claimed that everything from polio to AIDS to cancer to Stigman's disease wasn't curable, and each time we've beaten the odds. There's *always* an answer. We just have to find it."

Tang leaned forward. "You want to know what I *really* think, Doctor? Do you want the best advice I can give?"

"Yes."

"Archaria III *must* be completely and forever isolated to keep the plague from spreading. Quarantine the planet, yes, that's a start. Post guards in orbit. Hell, *mine* the whole system! Shoot down any ship that tries to enter or leave. Cut us off from the galaxy, and never let anyone set foot here again! And pray—just pray—that the virus didn't jump planet with any of the dozens of starships that have already left."

Starships have been leaving? she thought with alarm. *Are they crazy?* Well, Jean-Luc would have to put a stop to that. She'd let him know as soon as she finished her conference with Dr. Tang.

"We *will* contain the plague," she said in her most reassuring tone. "This isn't the first disease Starfleet has faced, and it won't be the last."

Tang shook his head sadly. "Smug, arrogant Starfleet—you people always know better than the experts. Listen to me. This is the worst disease humanity has ever faced. It's airborne. There are *no survivors.* It kills everyone it infects. If it ever mutates . . . if it ever attacks nonmixers . . . Archaria will be a graveyard planet within a month."

Dr. Crusher swallowed again. *Some bedside manner.* Tang certainly wasn't pulling his punches.

"I must reserve judgment until I've had a chance to study your reports," she said flatly. "Have that blood sample prepared for transport. I'll let you know when I'm ready for a patient."

"Very well." He gave her a hopeless shrug. "It's your funeral. And others'. Check the video I sent. Tang out."

Taking a deep breath, Dr. Crusher sat back in her chair and chewed her lip thoughtfully. Around her, nurses and doctors bustled about their duties, setting up equipment, tending to a sprained ankle or a burned arm, conducting the routine physical exams that Starfleet required of every crew member.

Dr. Crusher ordered the computer to begin displaying the visual record Dr. Tang had sent. It showed a ten-year-old girl lying next to an older woman who, from the way she reached out to the little girl despite her own horrifying condition, could only have been her mother. They were dressed only in thin white smocks, although profuse sweating had turned the young girl's smock almost transparent and her devastated body showed through clearly. A cure would be found, and Crusher knew it, but it would come too late for this child and her mother. She had not even begun her work, but already Crusher felt that she had failed.

It can't be that bad. Nothing is ever hopeless. We will find a cure. She had to believe in herself and her people. How could she go on with her work if she didn't think they would succeed?

For a second, she thought about calling off the away team's trip to the planet. But no, she knew with 100 percent certainty that the *Enterprise*'s biofilters could remove anything as large as a virus, despite Dr. Tang's histrionics. He had made a mistake somewhere. *It's a scientific fact. Nothing as large as a virus can make it through unless we want it to.* Commander Riker's mission could prove the key to unraveling this whole medical mystery and finding a cure.

She tapped her combadge. "Crusher to Picard." *One last duty to attend to.*

"Picard here," he answered immediately.

"Captain, Dr. Tang informs me that starships have been leaving the planet since the plague broke out."

"I am aware of it, Doctor. We are using their flight plans to track them and order them back here."

"Good. Thank you. Crusher out."

Reassured, she accessed the Archo City Hospital's computer, tapped in the access codes Tang had given her, and found herself in the records section . . . looking at thousands upon thousands of recent files, all marked "Deceased."

On a sudden hunch, she called up Tang's personal records. *I want to see how well you do your job,* she thought. *Since you think you're so good—let's see you prove it!*

To her surprise, Ian Tang, M.D., Ph.D, had received dozens of awards, commendations, and citations for a career filled with exemplary work, community service, and medical leadership. Not only was he the finest virologist on Archaria III, he had headed up half-a-dozen ground-breaking studies on Plimpton's disease—including several she'd read. His name hadn't registered at first, but now she recognized it.

According to this file, he's just a few ticks short of sainthood, she realized. *Maybe he isn't exaggerating after all.*

Brilliant researcher or not, the official records seemed quite a contrast to the man with whom she had just spoken. If everyone from the planetary governor to Starfleet's Admiral Zedeker spoke so highly of Dr. Tang's abilities, what could make him so determinedly pessimistic? *It's almost as though he* wants *us to abandon the planet,* she thought grimly.

A horrible thought came to her. *Abandon it* . . . maybe that *was* the answer. After all the mixers had been killed off by the plague, why not use the plague as an excuse to cut ties with the Federation?

It might just work, she thought. *If he can persuade enough people that there will never be a cure, the Federation may well post a permanent quarantine around the planet. And then the Purity League would be free to take over and run things exactly as they want, with their humans-first philosophy, devil take the Peladians.*

She shivered. He was a virologist. He said they had state-of-the-art facilities. Could Tang be part of the Purity League? Could he have engineered the virus? What figures did Jean-Luc cite? Wasn't half the planet supposed to be part of or at least in support of the Purity League? Why not a doctor, too. Why not Tang? She shook her head violently, as if to toss away the very thought.

Just because I don't like him doesn't make him a killer, she told herself.

Despite all his dire warnings, Tang proved true to his word. Within ten minutes the transporter chief hailed Dr. Crusher on the comm system.

She tapped her badge. "Crusher here."

"O'Brien in Transport Room One, ma'am. I have a medical shipment for you from Dr. Tang at the Archo City Hospital. He told me to leave it in the transporter buffer until you had a secure facility to hold it."

Dr. Crusher heard a note of hesitation in the man's voice. He wasn't telling her everything.

"Is there something else?" she asked.

"Doctor . . . is this whatever-it-is safe? If you want, I can rig up a couple of extra biofilters and run it through them before we materialize it—"

"No! Don't filter it!" she cried. That was the sort of help she *didn't* need. She still remembered one overefficient medical student in her class who tried to cut corners by beaming medical specimens from the lab to his research station. The biofilters had automatically filtered out the contaminants he was supposed to study, leaving him with useless tissue samples.

"Yes, ma'am!" She heard him jump.

She sighed. *Tang really got to me. No need to take it out on O'Brien.*

"I'm sorry," she said. "I didn't mean to snap at you, O'Brien. Just hold everything in the transporter buffer for now. Make sure you disable the biofilters—these are medical specimens, and I need the contaminants. I'll have a secure containment field ready for you in about sixty seconds."

"Right, Doctor."

"Crusher out."

She stood. "Computer, create a level-one containment field half on top of workbench one. Make it half a meter square on all sides. Tie in with Transporter Room One. The medical samples presently in the transporter's buffer must materialize inside the containment field. Do not run any biofilters!" She wasn't taking any chances.

"Acknowledged," the computer said. A forcefield began to shimmer faintly around the workbench. Dr. Crusher knew it would flicker out of existence just long enough for her samples to beam in, then the computer would make sure nothing got in or out. *"Level-1 containment field has been activated."*

She tapped her badge. "Crusher to Transporter Chief O'Brien."

"O'Brien here," he responded instantly.

"We're ready. Energize."

Lights twinkled around the workbench, and as they faded, she saw the small rack of a dozen tiny vials. Dark blood filled each one.

Now, my good doctor, she thought, *let's take a look at this plague virus of yours.*

Chapter Four

GEORDI LA FORGE FOUND a skeleton crew on duty in Astrometrics: three young ensigns, all hard at work updating the ship's navigation logs and starcharts with new files uploaded from Starbase 40 the day before. All three snapped to attention as he strode in.

"At ease," he said. It was obvious they were fresh from the Academy, all spit-and-polish and ready to impress superior officers. "I'm just borrowing a computer console for a little while. Carry on with your work."

"Yes, sir," they all said, and they turned back to their tasks with noticeably stiffer spines.

Geordi knew they felt his presence keenly: they worked with more speed, precision, and more professional demeanors—and far less banter—than was normal for ensigns. He chuckled a bit, thinking back to his own days as a raw ensign. It felt like an eternity ago . . . and a different lifetime.

As the ensigns worked, they began calling off the new charts smartly. *They're trying to impress me.* Every few seconds, when they thought he wasn't looking (of course through his visor he saw it all, down to the 3-centimeter-long string that had unraveled from Ensign Barran's left sleeve), they glanced in his direction to see if their attention to detail was being duly noted.

Geordi focused on his own work instead. *First things first.* . . . He manually logged into the spaceport's computer system, then ran a quick search through the list of ships that had departed from the Archo City Spaceport in the last thirty days. One hundred and seventy-four in all, he counted, according to official records. He matched ships to ID codes and came up with a mix of 62 freighters and 112 passenger ships. A quick cross-check with the *Enterprise*'s records showed all the freighters had already been contacted and were supposedly en route back to Archaria III. *Simple enough.* The Federation moved quickly when a plague threatened.

Several of the freighters had already landed at the Archo City spaceport. He chuckled a bit to himself when he checked their status: it seemed their crews refused to disembark. They preferred the sealed environment of a starship to the open—and possibly plague-infected—air of the planet. *Call it self-imposed quarantine,* he thought. Even so, it wouldn't be good enough for Starfleet. The crews of those freighters wouldn't be leaving anytime soon, not until someone found a cure.

He moved on to the passenger ships. All ran commercially between Archaria III and a dozen nearby systems. And, as expected, all 112 had already been turned back to port here. Sixty-two had already landed again, and of those it appeared that most had also chosen to keep their hatches sealed. *More quarantines. And good luck to them.*

All right, the official ships were accounted for. Now came the fun part.

"Computer," he said. "Access service records at Archo City Spaceport."

"Accessing," the computer said. *"Ready."*

"How many starships have been serviced for departure at the Archo City spaceport within the last thirty days?"

"Two hundred and sixty-three," the computer replied.

He gave a low whistle. So many? He now had eighty-nine starships unaccounted for. Obviously quite a few must never have left the spaceport—once the quarantine order came down, they would have been stuck in their berths.

"List all the starships alphabetically and state their present location."

"The Alpha Queen, *en route back to Archaria III. The* Aspen, *parked in Berth 669-B. The* Belgrade, *parked in Berth 205-A. The* Brillman's Dream, *en route back to Archaria III—"*

The computer droned on through the names. Geordi listened with interest until they reached *Zythal's Revenge,* a Klingon freighter.

"End of list," the computer reported.

Geordi frowned. Nothing seemed out of the ordinary. And yet, one ship had to be missing, if the captain's theory were right. *And I know it is,* he thought.

Where would you hide a starship? *Out in the open. You just change the computer records.* If the Archo City spaceport's records listed a ship as parked in its berth, the spaceport computer would perpetuate the lie when accessed by the *Enterprise*'s computer. It was a simple rule as old as computer programming itself, best known as GIGO: garbage in/garbage out. If you fed a computer faulty information, you got faulty information out.

Well, you might fool a computer, but you couldn't fool a security camera. At least not as easily.

"Computer," he said. "Access security cameras at the Archo City Spaceport. List all ships presently berthed there, and show me a current security camera image of each one. Begin alphabetically."

"The Aspen, *parked in Berth 669-B. The* Belgrade, *parked in Berth 205-A—"*

Within sixty seconds, he found the missing starship: a small five-passenger planet-hopper called the *Event Horizon* had vanished from its berth without tipping off the spaceport computers. His smile grew to a wide grin.

"Got you!" he said.

"Sir?" called one of the ensigns.

"Nothing." He cleared his throat and tried to sound officious. "Carry on."

The *Event Horizon* was originally a Vulcan vessel, he saw: a tiny T'Poy-class starship, capable of warp 2. The *Enterprise*'s computer had a schematic of that model on file, so he accessed it and looked it over quickly to refresh his memory: yes, warp capabilities . . . five passengers . . . slow but reliable. It would be perfect for sneaking off-world.

He could think of half a dozen ways to get such a small starship off-planet without leaving a record or setting off the spaceport's alarm systems. Methods ranged from the heavy-handed (bribing a clerk at the spaceport to make fraudulent file entries) to the daring (chasing a larger ship as it lifted off, and hiding in the shadow of its propulsion wake).

The most likely seemed bribery . . . even though it left one or more witnesses in place. After all, what starship pilot would risk colliding with a larger vessel when a simple bribe or two would do the trick?

Still, he had a little more work to do, just to make sure he had the right vessel. He hadn't yet established a link from the *Event Horizon* to Governor Sekk.

"Computer," he said, "where and to whom is the *Event Horizon* registered?"

"Accessing. The Event Horizon *is registered on Parvo IV to the Clayton-Dvorak Consortium."*

Who? Geordi scratched his chin in puzzlement. *The Clayton-Dvorak Consortium? Must be a farmers' combine or some sort.* Which meant Governor Sekk's family had hitched a ride with friends . . . or the Consortium might be a front of some kind for the governor. . . .

"Locate the offices of the Clayton-Dvorak Consortium," he told the computer.

"Records indicate that the Clayton-Dvorak Consortium is no longer in business on Archaria III."

"Then where are they?"

"No information is available."

Could he have made a mistake? He stared at the empty berth where the *Event Horizon* should have been. *Starships don't just vanish.*

Even though Vulcans weren't known for building flashy starships, he knew they produced this particular model for export. It could be outfitted so opulently that a Roman emperor would have felt at home inside. It would have been perfect for a governor. No, Sekk wasn't off the hook yet.

Hmm. I'll come back to it. Geordi copied the information on the *Event Horizon* to a separate file. Maybe inspiration would strike after he finished looking through the rest of the records. First things first.

"Proceed with the display," he said. "Show me the next ship that's supposed to be in its berth."

And ten seconds later, he had his second match: the *Falcon's Talon,* a Klingon freighter that was supposed to be picking up five hundred metric tons of grain. And twenty seconds after that, the *Halibut* turned up gone. Followed shortly by its sister ship, the *Hemlock,* then the *Langley,* the *Middlemarch,* the *Nesfa,* the *Prushnikov,* and ten more. Geordi logged their absences with growing disbelief. All told, sixteen ships had disappeared from their berths in the spaceport without leaving any records of their departure.

Captain Picard is not *going to be happy,* he thought. *At least, not with the governor or the spaceport's security officers.*

He began checking ship's registries. As the captain had anticipated, one had been registered in the name of Armand Sekk, the planetary governor: the *Nesfa.*

"Computer," Geordi said, "locate Captain Picard."

"Captain Picard is in his ready room."

Geordi loaded the information on the missing ships into a data padd, then rose and hurried toward the turbolift. He had quite a report to make . . . and unless he'd missed his guess, the fireworks were just about to begin.

Chapter Five

DR. CRUSHER RAISED her medical tricorder and took a quick scan of the vials of contaminated blood: yes, her plague specimens had arrived intact; that overeager transporter chief hadn't run them through the biofilter after all.

According to the readings, nothing—literal vacuum—now surrounded the rack within the containment field. Not a single stray oxygen or hydrogen atom, let alone any virulent microbes, existed outside of the vials. She planned on there being no chance of the virus being let loose on the *Enterprise.*

"Computer, shut down forcefield," she said. It collapsed with the inevitable sharp snap of air rushing in to fill a suddenly exposed void. "Activate the microscanner."

"Microscanner ready."

Dr. Crusher picked up the first vial and swirled it slowly. Inside, the tainted blood looked just the same as any other human's. *If only it were so simple,* she thought with a sigh. *If only we could see the virus with our naked eyes, it would be so much easier to defend against it.*

She slipped the vial into the microscanner. The machine made the faintest of whirring sounds as—all within its self-contained unit—it unsealed the vial, loaded a sample, and initialized its diagnostic computer.

"Show display."

"Display activated."

A holographic image of the sample appeared in front of her: a three-dimensional pink field swarming with microscopic activity. Normal red and white blood cells swirled in and out of view, followed by oddly shaped T-cells, Y-cells, J-cells, and all the other components of a half-human, half-Peladian blood sample. Fortunately, Dr. Tang's notes had prepared her as to what she would find in a "normal" mixer's blood.

There! she spotted the invading virus . . . an almost triangular gray puff, with dozens of tiny tendrils radiating from its core. It really did look like the Rhulian flu, she thought.

The microscanner focused in on it at once, expanding until the virus took up the whole projection.

"Virus found."

"Begin comprehensive analysis of virus sample," she said. "Start with TXA sequencing and protein-strand breakdown. I want a level-one analysis."

The computer responded: *"A level-one analysis will take approximately fifty-two minutes."*

"Proceed. Display tests as they are completed."

"Working."

The image of the virus split down the middle as the microscanner began to take it apart protein strand by protein strand. Of course Dr. Tang had already run this test, but true research always began with an independent analysis.

Dr. Crusher watched the microscanner work for a moment, then stood and stretched. *This is going to be a two-cup job,* she thought. She headed for the replicator unit and the tea Jean-Luc Picard had recently introduced her to, Double Bergamot Earl Grey.

Captain Jean-Luc Picard kept his face neutral while Lieutenant La Forge made his report. Inside, though, he seethed with anger. *Sixteen missing ships! This is an outrage—how could Sekk possibly think he could get away with it?*

It certainly warranted an immediate call to the governor . . . and the immediate dispatch of alerts to every planet and starship in the sector. Those ships would be sent back to Archaria III on the double, and under armed escort, or they would face the consequences of defying Federation law.

"Very good, Mr. La Forge," he said. "Well done."

"Thank you, sir." La Forge handed him the data padd, and Picard glanced over the names of the ships once more. *Sixteen!* He couldn't believe it.

After downloading the information into his private log, he handed the data padd back. "Post an immediate alert to all ships, planets, and star-bases in the sector. Anyone spotting one of these ships is to report it at once—and avoid making direct contact. The nearest Federation ship will provide armed escort back here. If they ran once, we don't want to risk them running again."

"Understood, sir." La Forge turned smartly and hurried from the ready room.

Picard leaned back and rubbed his eyes with the palms of his hands for a second. He had no choice but to make a second call to the governor, and he looked forward to this one even less than the first. For a second he wished for the authority to remove Sekk from his elected job, but then he thought better of it. He didn't want to bog himself down with the onerous administrative chores of running a planet if he could possibly avoid it. Bad as he might be, Sekk at least understood the job.

"Computer," he said. "Get me Governor Sekk."

The computer bleeped, and a second later an even more harried-looking Governor Sekk appeared on the smaller monitor on the captain's desk.

Sekk gave a cursory nod, then asked, "What is the problem, Captain—this really isn't a good time. I am in the middle of a dozen crises here—"

"I'm afraid you're going to have to make time, Governor. Have you ever heard of a ship called—" he consulted the list. "The *Nesfa?"*

Sekk paled suddenly. He turned and bellowed, "Clear the room!" to his assistants. "I need to talk to Captain Picard alone! *Out!* All of you!"

They scrambled for the doors. The moment he was alone, Sekk turned back to the comm. Picard saw new lines of worry crease the man's face.

"If I claimed I hadn't heard of the *Nesfa,* it would be a lie. You know that. Let's not play games, Captain. You caught me; I confess. I need to know—is there something wrong with the *Nesfa?* It hasn't . . . met with an accident, has it?"

"Not that I know of, Governor. But I think it's time you told me the whole truth about what's going on here. I don't like being lied to—even if it's a lie of omission!"

Sekk sucked in a deep breath. "My wife and children are on board the *Nesfa.* My eldest son, Derek, took everyone off-planet the day the hospital reported the first plague cases. I wanted them safe. Is that a crime?"

"No, Governor. It's perfectly natural. Unfortunately, we're going to have to bring them back. This system is now under quarantine . . . and that applies to everyone, even your family."

"But you don't understand . . . my wife, Mira . . . she's half Peladian. If she comes back here, it's a death sentence for her. And for our four innocent children, Derek, Robin, Eric, and Denny. Denny is only two,

Captain. Bringing any of them back is nothing short of murder."

Picard swallowed. "Decisions like this one are never easy. But I can't make exceptions, even for you."

"I realize that, Captain. But you don't have to, at least not in this case. You see, they are still technically on Archaria III."

"Enough games, Governor. I need to know where they are. *Exactly* where."

Still Sekk hesitated. "You understand, of course, that I had to weigh my duties carefully. And this time I'm afraid my family won."

Picard frowned. Sekk certainly wasn't making this easy. "How do you know your family wasn't exposed to the plague?" he asked. "How do you know they aren't passing it on to others right now?"

"They left thirty-two days ago—on the day the first victims began flooding our hospitals, as I told you. Since the first symptoms appear within a few hours of exposure, and I talked to them not ten days ago, I know they're well." Sekk swallowed. "At least, I think so. I just haven't been able to raise them on the comm since then."

"Where are they?" he asked again.

"On Delos—our smallest moon. There's a research base there. It's been deserted for years. I don't think many people know about it any more . . . but the equipment is still functioning." He twisted his hands together. "I thought they would be safe there, Captain. And technically they *haven't* left Archaria III."

Picard frowned. A game of semantics . . . but true, in a manner of speaking. Starfleet classified moons as part of the planets they orbited.

"Governor . . . far be it from me to doubt your word, but I'm going to have to check your story. If your family *is* there, then we will be glad to render whatever assistance they may need, from repairing their comm systems to an emergency evacuation to the *Enterprise.* However, if they are *not* there . . ." He left the threat hanging.

"Understood, Captain. And if there *is* something wrong, I need to know immediately. I . . . I almost told you about them earlier. But I couldn't bring myself to do it. I hope you understand."

All too well. You didn't want to jeopardize your own position. Never mind that your family could be dead or dying and you wouldn't know about it.

Picard said: "I will keep you up to date. Next, I need you to look over this list of ships. What can you tell me about them?"

Picard transferred the whole list of missing ships to the comm unit. He knew Sekk would be seeing it on his end of the channel.

The governor read it over slowly, then shook his head. "I don't understand. What about them?"

"They are missing. Like the *Nesfa,* they have disappeared from their berths at *your* spaceport seemingly without a trace. I need to know what happened to them. Where did they go, Governor? How big *is* your family?"

Sekk bristled a little at that jab. "I don't know anything about these ships. But I *will* find out." From his tone and expression, Picard actually believed him this time. *His security system has as many holes as a sieve.*

He asked, "Is two hours sufficient time?"

"It should be." Sekk paused and licked his lips. "Captain . . . let me thank you in advance for not mentioning how my family left the planet to anyone else here. The situation is . . . *delicate* right now. Such news might well tip the scales toward the Purity League and chaos."

"I won't lie about it, Governor, and all the details *will* be in my report to Starfleet. But I have no intention of making any public proclamations, if that's any reassurance."

The new look on Sekk's face spoke more clearly than words: the governor was hardly satisfied. Even with the information buried in an official Starfleet report, dozens of eyes would see it on Archaria III. And some of those eyes undoubtedly would belong to the governor's political enemies, Picard knew.

I know how to play this game, too, Picard thought with a twinge of self-satisfaction. *You won't pull the wool over my eyes a second time and get away with it, Governor.*

"Thank you," Sekk finally said, sounding strangled.

"You're welcome, of course." Picard gave him the same warm smile he normally reserved for unsavory diplomatic functions. "Picard out."

The screen went blank. Taking a deep breath and dropping his phony expression, Picard rose and strode out onto the bridge again. The low rumble of the engines and the beeps and whirs of the controls proved a tonic for his nerves, and he let out his breath with a sigh, starting to relax again. La Forge had reclaimed the navigator's station and Riker had vanished . . . probably finalizing preparations for his away mission. *Like clockwork,* he thought. The mechanism of the ship continued to run without him.

Yet their problems had only just begun. *Fifteen more ships to find . . . and a moon base to uncover,* he thought. This job was not getting any easier.

"Mister Worf," he said, taking his command seat.

"Sir?" came the low Klingon growl.

"Please initiate surface scans of the planet's smaller moon, Delos. According to the governor, there is a small research base there. I want it found. There should be a starship and hopefully five life forms."

"Scanning . . . I have it, sir."

That was fast. "On screen."

The pock-marked face of the little moon appeared. Nestled within a large crater lay a complex of perhaps a dozen white-domed buildings, all interconnected by silver tubes—walkways of some sort, Picard assumed. Lights gleamed from all the windows. *At least they still have power.*

His gaze drifted to the base's landing pad—located on the far side of the crater and presently half masked in shadow. It contained not one, but threc ships. It seemed the governor's family was entertaining at their private hideout, he thought. He narrowed his eyes. One ship had almost Klingon lines. Could it be one of the two missing Klingon freighters?

Klingons might well explain the silence, he thought. *If they decided to move in and take over, I can see them smashing all the communications equipment.*

Unfortunately, he could also see them killing everyone in sight if sufficiently provoked.

But we mustn't jump to conclusions, he thought. *Nothing is wrong until we prove it wrong.*

"Can you identify those ships?" he asked Worf.

"Not yet, sir. They do not respond to hails."

"How many life forms are on the base?"

"Sensors pick up thirty-six," Worf reported. He looked up. "Ten are Klingon!"

Picard nodded with satisfaction: it had to be the missing freighter. That meant one less ship to worry about. Possibly two, if the third ship proved to be one of the missing vessels.

"Hail the base. And hail those ships again."

". . . Still no response, sir."

Blast. Why did everyone on this wretched planet have to make things more difficult? Picard stood and began to pace, arms behind his back, thinking. *One starship isn't enough to police a whole planet. If only the* Constitution *were here, we could split up duties.*

"Sir," said La Forge. He had been adjusting the controls for the viewscreen. "I believe you should take a look at this."

Picard turned. Under extreme magnification, one of the windows of the research station looked into a room . . . and on the floor of that room lay a human body . . . a man. His face was turned away from the window, but Picard could just make out the edge of his beard. *Could that be Derek Sekk? Or is it someone else?* A dark liquid—it looked like blood—had pooled around the man.

That settled things. If violence had broken out on the research station, he had no choice but to investigate. More lives might be at stake.

"Mr. Worf, coordinate with Lieutenant Yar before she leaves for her away mission. I want a team assembled from available security officers." *Klingons are down there.* "You will lead them, Mr. Worf. Heavy weapons, full contamination suits, and all due caution. Please bear in mind that this is a fact-finding mission, not a military assault."

"Yes, sir!"

Picard thought he detected a note of near glee in Worf's voice.

"Remember," he went on, "we do not know the situation on that base. I don't want to start a firefight if we can avoid it. But if anyone there needs medical or other care, we must be prepared to provide it."

Two cups of tea would not be enough, Dr. Crusher thought. She drank; she paced; she fretted; she stared at the unfolding computer model of the virus, still being mapped out in all its minuscule glory.

The rest of the medical team began to gather around the workbench. They, too, stared at the display, mesmerized: the nurses, the doctors, and even the biologists currently aboard the *Enterprise* all came in to watch. She had alerted anyone who might have an insight into the origin, treatment, or cure for the virus.

The talk around her grew hushed and subdued. *They feel it, too,* she thought. *We have barely begun work on the virus, and already the strain shows. No wonder Dr. Tang is at the end of his mental rope.*

Still, it was hard to feel sorry for Tang. Under the worst circumstances, that's when a person's true spirit showed. *And here I am, calmly sipping my tea, waiting for the computer to beep and say my cake is ready for frosting.* Reminded of her drink, Dr. Crusher took another sip—*feh, getting cold.*

Her thoughts turned back to her conversation with Dr. Tang. *What if he's right and we can't find a cure? What about all those people dying down there?*

An old saying came to her: Time resolves all problems. *Not this problem,* she thought.

She drained her tea, rose, and got another cup. *Five more minutes.* A three–cup solution.

It seemed an eternity, but finally the microscanner finished and beeped. She jumped, startled, and spilled a few drops onto her knees. *I should have seen that coming,* she thought. A hush fell over the room.

"Analysis completed," the computer proclaimed.

"Display the report." She leaned forward. Everyone around her did, too. She felt them holding their collective breath, just as she held her own.

"Virus appears to be a previously unknown variation of Rhulian influenza." A model of the triangular virus appeared, turning slowly before them. The computer began its breakdown: *"This virus consists of a single*

molecule of RNA surrounded by a 27-mm-diameter protein capsid and a buoyant density in CsCl of 1.39 g/ml. This molecular breakdown shows 36 percent carbon atoms, 21 percent oxygen atoms, 20 percent hydrogen atoms, 17 percent—"

"We already know that," Dr. Crusher muttered to herself. "We all know what Rhulian flu is made of!" More loudly, she added: "Show the protein and NXA strands. Compare and contrast to Rhulian flu, type one."

Twisted lines of interlocking RNA strands appeared before her, rotating slightly. The NXA sequences were almost identical . . . though she immediately spotted several differences in key strands, especially the T-cell inhibitors. And some of the strands just didn't seem to belong . . . as though they had mutated . . . *or been grafted on from some other virus,* she thought uneasily.

Assuming it's engineered, she thought, *whoever made it did a good job.*

She glanced at Ian McCloud, the ship's microbiologist. "What do you think?" she asked him.

He frowned. "I am a little disappointed," he said in his slightly lilting accent. "It would appear to be a fairly simple virus. The Rhulian flu NXA strands were catalogued thirty years ago—I see only a few minor differences." He pointed. "Here, here, and here. And—*hello!* What's this?"

"What?" Dr. Crusher demanded.

McCloud said, "Computer—stop the projection. Turn it back three seconds. There, Doctor!" His finger jabbed at one NXA sequence. "Do you see it?"

Dr. Crusher leaned forward. She didn't see anything out of the ordinary. And then it all but leaped out at her . . . the virus had a strange little hook on the very end of one NXA protein strand . . . an extra NXA code. She felt a surge of excitement. She had never seen anything like it before on a virus. *This could be it! The key to the mystery!*

"Yes!" she breathed. "What *is* that?"

"If I recall the Rhulian flu correctly, it's attached to the NXA strand that controls the shape of the virus." McCloud frowned. "I would need to look it up to make certain."

"You're right," Dr. Crusher said, disappointed. *I should know not to get my hopes up. It's too soon in our research.* "I remember it, too."

"Oddly enough, despite that change, the virus looks the same . . . exactly like type-one Rhulian flu. I find that odd. *Very* odd. A mutation large enough to show up in the NXA strands should be visible."

"That's right." Dr. Crusher sighed. It was puzzling. A dead end? Still, anything unusual gave them a starting point.

To the computer, she said: "Run a full development sequence on NXA protein strand—what's its designation?"

"445-J3," McCloud said.

"445-J3. *Build it!"*

"Working," the computer said. The display went blank, and then, in extreme closeup, it began to assemble one of the tendrils. The hook appeared to add a slight texture to the underside, as far as Dr. Crusher could tell. A new genetic sensor of some kind? Something to detect a flaw in the cells of a person with mixed human-alien heritage?

The computer finished rendering segment 445-J3. The texture curved down, then up in a winding, almost snakelike pattern. She had never seen anything quite like it before.

A shudder went through her as a horrible inspiration struck. *It's not a random pattern.*

"Freeze image," she said. The computer diagram paused. The textured curves rolled gently down then up, a valley and a hill . . . or a letter lying on its side?

She said, "Rotate ninety degrees counterclockwise."

The tendril turned slowly. The curves suddenly became the letter "S." No one could have mistaken it. The texture extended to the right after a slight separation . . . another letter? The initials of its designer, perhaps?

A hush fell over the room. *They see it, too,* she realized. *I'm not crazy.*

She brushed back her red hair with one hand. *One letter could easily be a fluke of nature,* she told herself. It proved nothing. *Unless . . .*

She didn't want to give the command. Its potential repercussions were too great. But it had to be given: "Pull back slowly."

More of the tendril began to appear. S—M—I—

People around her gasped. She felt her heart skip a beat. *A message. It's a message.*

Letters continued to appear: L—E—Y—O—

Dr. Crusher found herself mouthing the syllables.

U—A—R—E—D—E—A—D

Smile. You are dead.

It felt like a knife puncturing her stomach.

That's why it looked so much like Rhulian flu. It *was* Rhulian flu, but modified to carry out a very specific and a very deadly attack.

She exchanged a glance with Ian McCloud and found an expression of horror equal to her own on his face . . . and on the faces of everyone around them.

"The bastards . . ." Nurse Icolah breathed. "Those *bastards!"*

"Now we know what we're up against," Dr. Crusher said flatly. "This is actually good news. If someone made this virus, we can unmake it."

Deep inside, she knew it was the merest accident that she had stumbled onto the message, one chance in a million. If Ian McCloud hadn't spotted the odd hook, if she hadn't sequenced it, if the shape hadn't struck her as odd—if any of a thousand variables hadn't happened to come together just right—the twisted conceit of whatever bioengineer was responsible for the plague never would have been uncovered.

She regarded the computer model thoughtfully. The letters had been programmed into the virus on a protein level. That took some doing. And she wasn't quite sure *how* it had been done.

At least I'll have something new to tell Dr. Tang now, she thought with a morbid mental grin. *And it's something sure to wipe that smug look off his face.*

The truth hadn't quite sunk in yet. *They left a message on the protein level.* Who would want to sign a genetically designed virus? *Someone vain. Someone smart. Someone crazy.*

As for who . . . Starfleet's research centers could do it. But they wouldn't. She racked her brain for other possibilities. Vulcans, of course . . . and certainly the Romulans and the Cardassians. But not the Klingons . . . they wouldn't bother, even if they understood the underlying technology. Klingon medicine had barely advanced beyond leeches, in her opinion. *And an attack on innocent half-breed humans would be incredibly dishonorable,* she reminded herself. No, it couldn't be the Klingons.

Who else? Perhaps half-a-dozen other races had the technology, from the Tholians to the Praxx.

But why bother? Why would *anyone* bother to create a virus that only attacked this specific genetic weakness, then let it loose on Archaria III?

The Purity League had a motive. After all, they had embraced the plague as an easy way to rid their planet of the "mixer influence." Why not push it a little farther? Why not *create* the plague to do the dirty work?

Smile. You are dead.

Much as she tried to deny it, those four words spoke volumes. They were written in standard English. *That means humans did it. Or at least one human.*

Dr. Tang? She didn't know. How many other brilliant virologists could there be on Archaria III? And yet without proof, she wouldn't dare accuse him. *So how do I get proof? Confront him? Beam down and ransack his office? Send in my spies?*

She stared at the virus. *Smile. You are dead.* The message had to be a private joke, since no one else could have been expected to find it. A mocking little tag line, petty as a schoolyard bully's taunting.

So much for the transcendent nature of man, she thought bitterly. Those four little words kicked the legs out from under her belief system. *We think we've come so far. And yet we are still capable of* this.

She stood. Her doctors and nurses all looked stunned. The biologists looked stricken. McCloud had gotten over his terror and now looked intrigued. Grudgingly, she admitted the person responsible for the virus showed some real creativity. *McCloud wants to know how they did it.*

And, she realized, *so do I.*

And, she realized, the signature gave her more hope. Anything one human could do another human could undo.

First things first, though. Rumors about the virus would sweep the ship if she didn't put a stop to them now.

"This message is hereby classified top secret," she said, looking from face to face. Her people began to nod; they understood. *Loose lips sink ships.* "I don't want a whisper of what we've found getting out to anyone," she said firmly. "We don't want to create a panic . . . or a war." The Peladians might well adopt a hard stance if they knew humans had created this plague.

Of course, they would find out eventually, but right now didn't seem like a particularly good time. *Their children are dying, too,* she thought. *It's easy to lose control when it's your loved ones whose lives hang in the balance.* She didn't know what she'd do if Wesley came down with a disease like this plague virus.

One person had to be informed immediately, however. Tapping her combadge, she said, "Crusher to Captain Picard."

"Picard here, Doctor," he answered.

"I . . . think you'd better come to sickbay. I have something for you to see."

"Doctor, I'm rather occupied right now—"

"Captain, *it's important.* I need you here *now.*" She had never used that tone with him before, her Voice of Authority—usually reserved for Wesley on his bad days. *Not that he has many of them anymore.*

Captain Picard seemed to pick up on the importance of her request. He sighed, but said, "On my way, Doctor."

Chapter Six

THE DOOR TO TASHA YAR'S CABIN whisked open at her command, and Worf poked his head inside. "Lieutenant?" he called.

"I said come in!" She was in the next room. "I'll be right there."

He stepped inside, already ill at ease. Though he had been raised among humans, he felt his Klingon heritage most keenly in one-on-one meetings and social situations. It happened more and more as he ran up against what he considered the "human mysteries" . . . the little social nuances he never quite seemed to pick up on. *It should not matter to a warrior,* he thought. But somehow it always did.

What do you do when you are inside a human female's cabin and she isn't dressed yet? Should he try to make light conversation? Should he wait in silence? *It's business,* he told himself. *I'm supposed to be here to discuss a mission. The captain sent me. If I stick to business, nothing will go wrong.*

"Make yourself at home," Tasha called. "I'll be right out."

At home. He gave a mental snort. His every nerve was on edge. *If only I knew her better. I . . . could use a friend here.*

Perhaps it was his prickly Klingon nature, but it took him a long time to warm up to strangers. He could tell the rest of the ship's officers were trying their best to get to know each other, to form a real team, and eventually he knew they would all come together. But for now he still felt like an outsider among them, even when they went out of their way to include him in their social banter.

Water splashed. *Is she bathing?* He narrowed his eyes and almost left. *What is she doing in there?*

"If this is a bad time," he began, "I can come back later—"

"No, wait. I'll be right out. Really."

He glanced around her cabin to take his mind off the awkward position he was in. Tasha Yar had brought very few personal effects with her: a scattering of small holographic pictures—planets he didn't recognize, some with Tasha posing next to people he didn't know. In the far corner sat a small Vulcan kinetic sculpture, its thin wire strands dipping faintly in the breeze from the air vents. There was nothing here, nothing special and unique, that proclaimed, *"I am Tasha Yar."*

Perhaps she feels as alone as I do, he thought suddenly. *Perhaps—*

"Sorry about that," Tasha said, emerging from her bedroom and interrupting his thoughts. She wore a slate-gray robe and had a gray towel wrapped around her head. "I was getting ready for my away mission . . . I'm having trouble with my hair. What brings you here?"

"I—" Worf began. He stared as she pulled the towel off her head. Long, straight blond hair spilled out. Hair that didn't belong on her head. "What happened to you—" he burst out.

Instantly he regretted it. It was not an appropriate comment.

"Like it?" She made a face. "It's silly and impractical, if you ask me. I prefer it short."

"But—how—?"

"I borrowed a follicle stimulator from Dr. Crusher." She swept her hair back and out of her eyes with one hand. "Archarian women wear their hair long, unfortunately. Since we're supposed to be going in disguised as natives, I needed to grow it longer to fit in. What do you really think?" She turned a quick pirouette and gave an impish grin. "Stylish?"

"It is . . . *long.*"

She cocked her head quizzically. "I guess that's a compliment."

He swallowed and felt too hot suddenly.

"Wait until you see Commander Riker," she went on with an even broader grin. "Archarian men wear beards . . . long, bushy beards. That's something I'm really looking forward to seeing! He's normally so stiff and formal all the time."

"Unh. Yes. But there is nothing wrong with formality."

"Almost as bad as you."

"Uh—"

"That's supposed to be a joke." She grew more businesslike. "This isn't a social call, is it? What's wrong?"

"Lieutenant . . . we have a situation on the planet's smaller moon." Taking refuge in duty, he began to fill her in on the details. "The captain wants me to lead an away team on a recon mission," he concluded. "He thought it best for me to coordinate with you."

"I see." She nodded somberly. "Worf, you and I both know you're more than capable of dealing with this situation on your own. I'm going to leave it up to you. This is a good chance to impress the captain—don't blow it."

"I have no intention of—*blowing* it." He bristled at the very idea.

"Sorry, sorry, poor choice of words." She hesitated. "Let me suggest a team for you. Take Schultz, Detek, and Wrenn. They've been pulling a lot of extra duty shifts together since Farpoint, and they seem to work well as a team."

"I have already assigned them to this mission—as well as Ensign Clarke."

She raised her eyebrows. "Angling for my job, Worf? I couldn't have picked a better team."

Again he felt the heat rush to his face. "I—uh—"

"Relax, they're good choices. Go with my blessing. Bust some skulls. I know that's what you really want to do."

He gave a curt nod. *My people. Yes, I would like to meet more of my people . . . and bust some skulls!* He felt his blood surge at the thought of combat.

"Thank you—Tasha."

"Don't mention it." She grinned again. "We're all in this together, right?"

Dr. Crusher had her people carefully stationed at all corners of sickbay when Captain Picard strode in with all the subtlety of a hurricane. He did not look pleased at being summoned to sickbay.

"What is so important, Doctor," he said curtly. "We have a possible combat situation developing. My place is on the bridge right now."

"Just this." She took his arm and led him to the virus display. She hadn't changed the image since revealing the hidden message. "Look."

"Smile . . . you are dead?" He frowned. "What is this, Beverly? A joke?"

"That's exactly what I think it is." She nodded at the display. "A private joke. That message is written on the bottom of every single virus. It's been coded into the NXA protein strands."

He frowned. "Then it *is* artificial—"

"Created from Rhulian flu, and almost certainly by a human."

"I don't want to believe it. I—" He licked his lips. "I think—"

It was the first time she had seen him this way in years. *Since Jack died,* she thought. *Since that awful, awful day when my husband died.*

"We don't know who did it. He didn't sign his name. But I have a suspicion."

"Tell me."

"Dr. Tang, the head of Archo City Hospital. His specialty is virology, and to all indications he's very, very good . . . cutting-edge good."

"Do you have evidence of this?"

"No. It's just a feeling I have from talking with him—a feeling that he's doing his best to stonewall my research. I think he has some serious mental instabilities, and judging from his comments, he would fit right in with the Purity League. He wants the planet quarantined and left on its own permanently."

"These are very serious charges."

"I know. And I don't have any proof yet."

He hesitated, staring at the virus, at the letters on its underside. "Does the technology necessary to create this virus exist anywhere else on Archaria III *besides* Dr. Tang's hospital?"

"I doubt it. You would need a state-of-the-art research lab . . . and advanced knowledge of human and nonhuman virology."

Slowly Picard nodded. "You may be right. It would certainly help explain why Tang hasn't made any progress toward a cure."

Dr. Crusher nodded. *He wants them dead. Why create a cure for your own plague?*

"I'll alert Commander Riker to your suspicions—he may be able to turn up more information on Tang during his away mission." He cleared his throat. "Who else knows about this message?"

"So far, just the people here. I ordered them to keep it to themselves."

"Good. We don't want a panic on the planet. Are you any closer to a cure?"

"We're just starting to unravel the NXA protein threads holding the virus together. There's no telling what nasty little tricks our genetic programmer tucked into it."

Captain Picard gave a pensive nod. "Thank you, Doctor. You did the right thing. Keep me up to date on your progress." He paused. "You *can* cure it, can't you?"

"I think so, eventually. It's just a matter of time. Unfortunately, that's the one thing we're short of."

"Keep at it. Thousands are counting on you." Turning, he headed for the door.

As if we don't have enough pressure already.

After the doors whisked shut, Dr. Crusher took a deep breath. "All right," she called to her people. "Gather around. We have a lot of work to do."

She started handing out assignments: NXA sequencing, tests with antiviral compounds, analyses of the protein strands within the virus.

We will *get to the bottom of this mess,* she told herself. *And it's going to be sooner rather than later—Dr. Tang and his stonewalling be damned!*

Chapter Seven

FIFTEEN MINUTES AFTER his conversation with Tasha Yar, Worf met the four members of his away team in Transporter Room 3. Like them, he had changed into a full containment suit. The bulky white garment felt suffocating, but it covered him completely from head to heel. No virus would get through it. *I might as well be in a full spacesuit,* he thought.

He felt an itch starting in the middle of his back and gave a growl of displeasure. *Klingons are not meant for containment suits.* And as he continued to breathe, his faceplate fogged over. What had his instructor at the Academy told him to do when that happened? *Practice your breathing—keep it slow and steady.* Hyperventilating caused it.

He nudged the comm bar with his chin. A channel opened up to the other members of his away team.

"Since we will be beaming into potentially hostile territory," he said, letting a grim note creep into his voice, "you must be on your guard at *all* times. Watch your backs, no matter what you see or hear. And remember . . ." He paused for emphasis. "This *is* a good day to die!"

That did it. The ensign swallowed noticeably.

Worf gave a mental snort. *Humans.* It really *was* a good day to die. If you went into combat fearing nothing, you walked the path to glory.

He had already selected their beam-in coordinates: an unoccupied dome on the far edge of the research station. La Forge's last sensor scans had placed all the humans and Klingons a safe distance away, in the buildings nearer to the station's landing pad, so their arrival should go unnoticed. His plan called for securing the dome, then using it as a base of operations as they made their way through the complex slowly and methodically, searching for victims. Their first priority would be reaching the man La Forge had spotted.

"Take your positions for transport!" he barked.

His team scrambled onto the transporter pad. They arranged themselves in a semicircle, leaving the middle pad open for him. He took it, turned, and faced the ensign on duty at the transporter controls.

"Energize!" he said, loud enough to be heard even through his helmet.

As lights began to sparkle around him, the *Enterprise* disappeared . . . and was replaced by a dimly lit room perhaps twenty meters high and forty meters across. The white ceiling arched overhead in a huge dome.

Artificial gravity was on; it felt just under Earth normal to Worf. He dropped to a crouch, phaser rifle up and ready. Scans might show a room empty . . . but shields had been known to hide ambushes, and he never took unnecessary chances.

There was no ambush this time. Around him lay jumbles of boxes, huge wooden packing crates, and discarded machinery. The crates rose in teetering stacks; some of them nearly reached the ceiling.

No danger. Or nothing that leaped out with fangs bared and claws ready, he thought. Diseases were far more insidious than that.

"Guard duty." He motioned Schultz to the rear hatch and Clarke to the front. "Secure the dome," he said. "Shout if anyone tries to get in. Do not shoot unless fired upon or I give the word."

"Yes, sir!" They hurried to take up their positions. Only then did Worf relax enough to take his finger off his own phaser's firing button.

Wrenn had his tricorder out. Turning slowly, the ensign scanned the dome.

"No other life forms within thirty meters," he reported over the open channel. "The nearest life signs are from two humans located exactly thirty-two meters due north—that way." He pointed toward the front of the dome, just to the right of Clarke's position.

"Are they moving?" Worf asked.

"No, sir. From their life signs, I think they're either asleep or unconscious."

Or dying from the plague, Worf thought. He sucked in a deep breath. *Do not hyperventilate.*

"Keep monitoring them," he said. "Let me know if their status changes. And keep watch for anyone else moving in our direction."

Perhaps this would be easier than he had first thought. If everyone was sick, they would not offer resistance to the rescue mission. The Klingons here would not be affected by the plague, he reminded himself. Nor would any full-blooded humans.

First, he had to address the problem at hand: securing this dome. Frowning a little, he regarded the stacks of boxes and crates all around him. Clearly the people in charge of this base had used this chamber as their storage area . . . or their dump. The crates bore labels like "Thermo-entogram Modulator B-6" and "Dioxymosis Converter (F)," whatever those were. To the left, a few of the boxes made more sense: "Vegetable Concentrate 64" and "2400 Citric Protein Bars" sounded almost sensible in comparison, if not exactly appetizing. Sometimes he thought humans would eat anything, if it came in an attractive package.

First things first, though. The jumble of crates might conceal anything from a cloaked Romulan death squad to a the lost treasures of *Fret'vok.* If they planned on using this dome as a base of operations, they were going to have to search it fully—you couldn't cover your back if you didn't know what was behind you.

"Look behind the boxes on that side of the room," he told Detek and Wrenn. "If you see anything unusual, let me know immediately. Do not investigate yourselves."

"Yes, sir!"

Turning with a sigh, Worf squeezed between a pair of tall "Emulsion Generator" crates. His containment suit snagged for a second on a nail, but since the material couldn't be punctured by anything as soft as mere steel, he pulled sharply and felt himself snap free.

Whoever had packed all this junk into the dome had left less-than-adequate access corridors between the piles of crates. He edged down the nearest one and felt himself treading on things that crunched underfoot.

His phaser rifle had a small but powerful light mounted on top; he flicked it on, then swept the beam up and down the floor. Loose cables, discarded circuit relays, food wrappers, and other trash littered the floor here. From the thick layer of dust on everything, he knew no one had been back here in many years.

He had just turned to go back when Wrenn's excited voice squealed his name: *"Lieutenant Worf!"*

"What is it?" he demanded. Had the Klingons from the freighter detected them and launched an attack?

"Sir!" he heard Wrenn call. *"We found something! Blood—and according to my tricorder, it's human!"*

"Hold your position. I will be right there."

Somehow he managed to squeeze back out into the center of the dome without tumbling any of the piles of crates. He spotted Wrenn about halfway to the front door and sprinted over to join him.

The ensign pointed to dark stains on the floor. "According to my tricorder, that's human blood," he said. "It's dry, but fresh—about twelve hours old!"

Worf bent to examine the blood spatters. A trail of blood wound off between crates on that side of the dome. He hesitated, trying to decide how best to handle it.

"Is it fully human?" he finally asked. "Or is it a human-Peladian mix?" *One of the symptoms of the disease is uncontrollable bleeding,* he reminded himself.

Wrenn had to check. "Uh . . . fully human, sir. Not a trace of Peladian genetic material."

So we have the trail of a wounded human. Hefting his phaser rifle, Worf eased between crates of "Endochronic Thiotimoline Pumps" and "Phase Resonance Detectors." His heart began to pound with growing excitement. Shining his light at the floor, he studied the footprints and the blood. The drips became noticeably larger, and bloody handprints smeared the crates to either side where someone had rested or leaned to steady himself.

When the passageway opened up a little, he spotted at least three—and possibly as many as five—different sets of footprints that had disturbed the decades' worth of accumulated dust . . . whoever had come through here made no effort to conceal the trail. *They could not all be dead or dying,* Worf thought with growing unease. His eyes narrowed. *What happened here?*

He continued to follow the trail, winding between the crates and boxes. At last he reached the far wall.

The trail ended with a pool of sticky, half-congealed blood. And lying in that blood he found the bodies of six adult human males. Acharian settlers, he decided, noting their chest-length beards. He remembered what Tasha Yar had told him about the men on Archaria III all wearing long, bushy beards.

These six had been stabbed and cut repeatedly. The blood came from their wounds. But they had not died here—someone had carefully arranged the bodies. Eyes closed, hands neatly folded across their chests, they looked almost peaceful now. The trail he had followed must have been left by a burial party, he decided.

Better to die in honorable combat than to succumb to a disease, he thought with a nod. Unless they had been murdered. . . .

He moved closer and began to study the bodies with the dispassionate attention of a born predator. Death had been sudden, but not unexpected, he decided. He pulled their shredded tunics open to study their wounds. Two had numerous stab wounds.

Those cuts—

He leaned forward, studying the long, clean sweep of the death blows. A strong arm had delivered those cuts. The wounds looked exactly like the marks left by a mek'leth. *Or in this case, several mek'leths.*

Only Klingons used that particular type of short sword, he knew, with its razor-sharp edge and deadly point—perfect for slashing and thrusting. He liked to use one himself. Unlike disruptors, it made combat a personal experience . . . but it also made for messy corpses. *Exactly like these.*

Lights wavered behind him as the ensigns followed. Over the open comm channel he heard gasps of shock from Wrenn and Detek.

"Control yourself," he snarled. "You must have seen death before."

"Not like this," Wrenn gasped.

"All that blood," Detek said.

"What's going on?" Clarke demanded from his post by the front hatch. *"Do you need assistance? Lieutenant? Anybody?"*

"Quiet on the channel." Worf rose and pivoted on the balls of his feet, furious with the breaches in protocol. *This is going in their personal files,* he vowed. Simpering over a little blood!

He found Wrenn, pale-faced, two meters away, just standing there and staring open-mouthed at the bodies.

"Back to the center of the dome!" he said.

The ensign began to stammer in shock or fear.

"Go on!" Worf grimaced with distaste. *No stomach for a little blood!* He switched off his rifle's light, hiding the gruesome details. Perhaps that would help. *They are only humans,* he reminded himself. *They cannot help their weaknesses.* Still, he had expected more from them. After all, he was leading this mission.

"Go back to the center of the dome," he ordered a little more gently. "Wait there and keep it clear in case we have to return."

Worf clicked his comm bar back to the first setting so that he could talk to the "survivors" of his mission.

"Detek," he said, voice a low growl.

"Sir!" The ensign's voice quavered noticeably.

"Get the tricorder and medical supplies. You are now our rear guard."

Turning, he headed for the front hatch without a backward glance. *The other three will pull together and pick up the slack,* he thought. He hoped.

Chapter Eight

DR. CRUSHER PASSED OUT ASSIGNMENTS, and as her people scrambled to work on unraveling the secrets of the virus, she took a minute to page Dr. Tang at Archo City Hospital. *This should prove interesting,* she thought. *Let's see how he reacts to news of that hidden message.* Maybe it would force his hand . . . or surprise him into an admission of guilt.

Tang finally answered the page. "What is it?" he growled. *Still practicing Dracula's bedside manner, I see,* Dr. Crusher thought. *Only this time I know your real motive.*

She said: "Dr. Tang, I have isolated the virus and done a complete TXA breakdown. In the process, I found something quite disturbing—not only is the virus man-made, but its designer left a message."

"What!" He stared at her, to all appearances shocked. "What's the message?"

"Smile, you are dead." She gave him the NXA strand number. "Sequence it yourself. When you pull back the view, watch the bottom of the tendril. The modified texture spells it out clearly."

He sucked in a deep breath. "Doctor—I can't believe it! The Purity League claimed responsibility for the plague, but I never thought . . . I never dreamed . . . they actually had the resources to do it!"

If he was acting, he deserved a commendation for it. She hadn't seen a better job since the time she saw Sir Edmund Deere in *Hamlet* on Earth.

I should have asked Deanna to join me for this conference, she realized with a pang of disappointment. *Deanna would have sensed if he told us the truth.* She felt foolish for wasting the call. *I'll do it next time,* she vowed. *Until I know differently, you are still my prime suspect, Doctor!*

"Our captain wants this information kept strictly confidential," she said.

"Of course—I do understand."

He appeared humbled by the revelation, she thought. But then, if as he claimed he really *had* been working on the virus for weeks, he hadn't found that hidden message . . . and she turned it up within the hour. *Don't get too cocky,* she told herself. *It was luck. But luck is what you sometimes need.*

Tang went on, "I must tell the governor, though . . . but of course he won't dare release the information to anyone else. The repercussions would be disastrous. As your captain must already realize."

She nodded. Riots. Open warfare. And the pure-blooded Peladians would almost certainly get involved; how could they not? The next custom-made virus might well target *them.*

She said, "Getting back to our real problem—curing the plague—I'm ready to bring an infected test subject aboard."

"You have a vaccine already?" He leaned forward eagerly. "How does it work—can I get a sample—"

"No, we don't have a vaccine yet," she said quickly. She was finding it increasingly difficult to believe he was guilty. His every response seemed genuine and correct. "We have some other tests to run first. The virus appears to be a simple variant of Rhulian flu. We have some antiviral treatments specifically designed for that disease which might prove effective."

He sighed and shook his head. "The virus does appear simple at first glance, Doctor." *Back to stonewalling and doomsaying,* she thought. *How true to form.* "However, it cannot be cured by any traditional means—we tried all the Rhulian flu vaccines as well as every other antiviral agent known to the Federation. The virus resisted every treatment—it's all in the research notes I sent you. Every time we thought we had it licked, it flared up again."

"Yes, I read your report. But I have a clean environment here, and I have a crew working on modifying the biofilters in the transporters." *At least, I will as soon as this call is done.* "An aggressive program using several different treatments should prove successful."

"I hope so—for your sake." Tang shook his head. "We had no luck there, either, Doctor. But perhaps the *Enterprise*'s biofilters are more advanced than our own."

"Undoubtedly." Crusher hoped O'Brien knew what he was doing. "We have some . . . *creative* engineers aboard. If they can see the virus, they can eliminate it. It's that simple."

Tang shrugged helplessly. "I hope so, Doctor," he said. "I will have that test patient standing by. Please—for your own sake, maintain a quarantine field at all times. This virus really does jump the strongest forcefields."

"Of course," she said. "I intend to use every security measure at my disposal."

"Then I will await news of your ultimate success." He hesitated. "And Doctor . . ."

"Yes?" she said.

"I know how I must seem to you. You must think I'm a crackpot a . . . a medical *alarmist,* since I keep trying to poke holes in every theory and plan you come up with. Believe me when I say I *do* want a cure—I want it more desperately than you can possibly imagine! But I don't want to risk the lives of anyone healthy to get it, and that includes your crew."

"Thank you for your concern," she said. *I bet it gets even more heartfelt every time he tells that story.* "I do appreciate your advice. I have no intention of placing this crew at risk. Now, please get that patient ready. I'll want to beam him up within the hour."

"You will have him," he said, almost humbly.

"Crusher out."

Now to make sure we live up to our reputation, she thought. She tapped her combadge.

"Crusher to Transporter Chief O'Brien."

"O'Brien here, ma'am," came his answer.

"About those biofilters you mentioned this morning. How long will it take you to chain them together?"

She heard a distinct gulp on the other end of the comm channel. *Good,* she thought with satisfaction.

"No problem, ma'am!" O'Brien said.

"That's the kind of answer I like, O'Brien. Crusher out!"

On the bridge, Captain Picard faced the forward viewscreen and watched the *Constitution* enter the solar system with a measure of relief. Captain van Osterlich's ship had arrived not an hour too soon, he thought. With a second Galaxy-class starship to help keep order, he felt a little more relaxed. *We can go chasing after rogue ships now, if we have to,* he thought. There was no longer any need to worry about leaving the planet unguarded.

"Hail the *Constitution,"* he said.

"Captain van Osterlich is standing by," La Forge said.

"On screen."

The view of Archaria III disappeared, replaced by the smiling face of

Jules van Osterlich, its captain. Van Osterlich had broad cheekbones and thin hair so pale it looked almost white.

Picard grinned back. They had known each other the better part of twenty years. Though their careers kept them half a galaxy apart most of the time, they never passed up an opportunity to get together and talk about the good old days.

"Jean-Luc!" van Osterlich said. "The new ship suits you. I always knew you'd end up with one of the big ones. But the *Enterprise!* Quite a plum."

"Thank you, Jules. The *Constitution*'s looking pretty good, too. A fine ship."

"That she is."

"How long has it been . . . three years? Four? How are you?"

"I can't complain. So, I hear we have quite a situation developing below. Why don't you fill me in. My transporter crews are ready to beam medical supplies down, but we have a few minutes before we enter orbit."

"Dinner tonight? Bring your senior staff."

"Delighted."

"Good." Picard frowned. "We'll talk more then," he said. "In the meantime, you should know that things below are not quite what they appear. Governor Sekk has, ah, held out on us. And we suspect some of the hospital staff may be hindering the development of a cure for the plague in support of the Purity League. My chief medical officer is spearheading the research aboard the *Enterprise.*"

"And what is happening with the plague?"

"Latest reports indicate forty thousand victims. Three quarters of them are already dead. It isn't a pretty situation."

Van Osterlich whistled. "It's a disaster!" He glanced over his shoulder. "Governor Sekk is hailing me," he said. "We'll talk more tonight."

Picard nodded. "I'll break out the Saurian brandy."

Chapter Nine

"SECURE THE AREA!" Worf barked.

After kicking open the hatch to the next dome—it housed a research station complete with humming, beeping, chirping weather-monitoring equipment—he led the charge inside. Detek's tricorder showed two humans lying in the center of a cluster of three rooms. Asleep? Unconscious? Lying in ambush? He intended to find out.

He pointed: Schultz left, Clarke right. He went straight up the middle, treading as softly as a Klingon could.

He reached the door to the next room, pressed up beside it, and reached out to the handpad, which was unlocked. He pressed lightly, and it zipped to one side.

Taking a glance in, he spotted two figures lying in semi darkness . . . both women. He switched on the lights, but neither one moved.

Plague. White blisters covered their faces. *That's one of the first signs.*

"Sir, is it—?" Clarke asked over the comm.

"Yes." His voice came as a growl. "They have the plague. That means the whole base is contaminated."

For the first time since beaming down, he was thankful they were inside containment suits. Like Wrenn, they would have to be beamed out of them when they were evacuated.

He clicked the comm bar.

"Worf to Dr. Crusher. . . ."

"Crusher here," she replied an instant later. *"What is your situation?"*

"The plague is loose in here. We have found two victims so far. Both women."

"What are their symptoms?"

"White blisters on their faces. Low life signs. They are both unconscious."

He heard a slight hesitation in her voice. *"Mark their coordinates. We are almost ready to try beaming a patient through the ship's biofilters. We'll try your women if it works on our first subject."*

"Good." He felt a brief surge of pride. By coming here, they had already made a difference—these two women would have a chance for survival now.

"Are there any other plague victims?"

"Not yet," he said. "We will continue to investigate the base."

"Keep me up to date. Crusher out."

Worf turned to Ensign Detek. "Send the coordinates for these two to sickbay," he said. "And scan for more survivors."

"Yes, sir."

Detek raised his tricorder and turned slowly, scanning. "Five more humans are in the dome immediately to our left," he said. "The Klingons are still forty meters to the right."

Worf hesitated. Which group to contact first? *The humans,* he thought. *They are the most threatened by the plague.*

"We will investigate the humans first," he announced. "Let us go!"

He led the way to the back of the dome, opened the hatch into the ten-meter-long connective walkway, and advanced cautiously to the next hatch.

He pressed the handpad, but although it beeped, it stubbornly refused to open . . . locked from the inside, he decided.

"What is the status of the humans inside?" he asked.

"They are . . . alive and moving, sir. I believe they have detected us. They are taking up positions around the door."

Around the door? *Ambush!*

"Get down!" he ordered. "Rifles up!"

He clicked the comm bar and called the *Enterprise.* "I need an emergency site-to-site transport!" he yelled. "Put us inside the dome we're facing! On the farthest side!"

"Ready, sir," he heard an unfamiliar voice say.

The hatch started to open.

"Energize!"

As the transporter beam picked them up, he saw the flash of energy weapons being fired—

—and suddenly he and his men were materializing inside the dome, facing a curving white wall. He whirled. They hadn't gone far—twenty meters at the most—but they were in a different room now.

He charged the half-shut door. Bursting through, he launched himself into the main chamber.

Five people stood with their backs to him, and two of them had disruptors pointed out toward the open hatch. He recognized the corridor where he and his men had been standing seconds before.

The men with the disruptors started to turn. *Too late!* Worf thought with the glee of a predator closing in for the kill. He felt the roar of his blood. He voiced a wordless battle cry, *"A-a-a-a-r-h—"*

Before they could shoot him, he fired from his hip. *Heavy stun*—first the two men with the weapons, the one on the left, then the one on the right.

Even as they began to crumple, he closed the distance between in a heartbeat, still yelling, *"—a-a-a-a-h—"*

The other three—two men, a woman—were not armed. His Starfleet training took over and Worf dragged himself back from the berserker's abyss. It would have been easy to let himself go in the fury and passion of the moment, to kill and kill again while his blood sang the music of violence in his ears.

Panting, he halted before them. "Arms up!" he bellowed. He knew his voice carried through his faceplate when he shouted—it would be a little muffled, but clearly audible.

The three standing humans gaped at him, too shocked to move. They did not seem to be armed.

"Arms up, I said! I *will* shoot!"

This time they raised their arms.

Bending at the knees, he scooped up the disruptors dropped by the two men. *Set to kill,* he noticed. His ensigns took guard positions.

"Identify yourselves!" he snapped.

"My name is Newkirk," one of the men snarled. He was an older human with short gray hair. *No beard. Not from Archaria III.* "I am first officer of the *Middlemarch.* You just killed the captain, you Klingon bastard!"

Worf glared. "I am Lieutenant Worf of the Federation starship *Enterprise,"* he snapped back. "Your captain is stunned."

"You're a Klingon!" the other man said suspiciously. "What kind of trick is this?"

"I am a Starfleet officer. Identify yourself!"

"Macus Onetree," he said flatly, "second officer of the *Middlemarch.* About time you got here, Starfleet. We've needed rescue for three days. Those Klingons have attacked us twice."

"Explain."

Onetree hesitated. "Plague broke out on the planet, so we bugged it up to orbit. Captain Gorman"—he indicated one of the men Worf had shot—"thought we should ride out the problems here. He remembered this deserted base, so . . ." He snorted. "Between Klingons sniping at us, half our crew dropping dead from the plague, and our warp drive breaking down—what else can possibly go wrong?"

Worf gave a nod and lowered his phaser rifle. "How many dead from plague?" he asked.

"All but us five now. The others are in the next dome."

He nudged the comm bar with his chin. *That is easy enough to check,* he thought.

"Worf to La Forge."

"La Forge here," came the answer.

"How many life signs are now on this base?"

"Hold on . . . twenty-two."

Ten Klingons, five humans here, two in the other dome—that's only seventeen. The other five must be the governor's family. He gave a nod. That accounted for everyone.

"Have you met anyone else here besides the Klingons?" he asked.

"There are more humans holed up in one of the domes . . . they sealed the doors and they won't come out. They threatened to shoot anyone who came near, so we haven't bothered them. Since the Klingons smashed the base's comm equipment, we haven't been able to reach them."

They are better off locked in their dome, Worf thought. *These people may be immune because they are full humans, but they are carrying the virus.*

"You will stay here," he told them. "When your captain wakes up, inform him that he is under house arrest pending an investigation. Attacking Federation officers is still a crime."

"You're not going to leave us here!" Onetree cried.

Now he wants to be rescued. Worf snorted.

"You are welcome to come with me," he said. "I am going to see the Klingons next."

Chapter Ten

ONLY THE TRANSPORTER CHIEF'S LEGS remained visible as he crawled into the transporter's console. *Does he know what he's doing?* Dr. Crusher wondered, and not for the first time. This seemed a highly irregular way to adjust the biofilters. As she watched, his knees bent. His feet pointed, twitched, pointed again. And he crawled another twenty centimeters into the console.

"Are you sure you should be doing that?" Dr. Crusher asked. She had always been told to bring power off-line before adjusting relays. *It's got to be dangerous.*

"I've done it a thousand times before, ma'am," O'Brien said, sounding put-upon. "There are so many safety features and redundancies built in, it's physically impossible for me to get hurt—*Ow!"*

"Are you all right?"

"YES!" he bellowed. Then she heard him swear under his breath as something thumped loudly inside the console. *"Get in there!"*

Dr. Crusher wavered between calling for help and crawling in after him.

She jumped when an electric sizzle sounded and a curl of acrid black smoke rose from the control pads. She took a step back in alarm. *He doesn't know what he's doing!* she thought. *He's crazy!*

Another thump came, even louder than the first. The transporter chief gave another yelp and jerked back, feet spasming, and then he crawled out, alternately waving his fingers in the air and sucking on them.

"Are you all right?" she asked, one hand reaching instinctively for her medical tricorder. "Maybe I should take a look at that—"

"No need, Doc." He grinned up at her. "My own bloody stupidity. I touched the wrong relay."

Muttering to himself, he stuck his head under the console again. The sizzle came again, then disappeared as he undid whatever he had done before. A second plume of black smoke rose. She caught a whiff of something burning. *I really ought to call for backup—*

"Just an overloaded circuit," he said, as if that explained everything. "No need to worry."

"Oh." Dr. Crusher leaned over, trying to see what he was doing under there. *How can he see in there? It's pitch black. If he electrocuted himself—*

"Almost got it." One hand suddenly stuck out toward her. "Pass me that magnetic lock, will you, ma'am?"

"Coming." It sat on top of the control panel with half a dozen other tools. She grabbed it and smacked it into his palm like a nurse handing a doctor a medical instrument. *Ten years since I've done that!* She raised her tricorder and tried to scan those burned fingers, but he pulled his hand back under the console again before she caught more than a glimpse. *Probably a minor flash burn. He may have brushed a live EM conduit,* she thought, trying to dredge up old equipment-maintenance lessons from memory. *It's painful, but not serious. I'll send him some ointment later.*

Something creaked alarmingly under the console, like bones about to break. It sounded worse than anything else O'Brien had yet done.

"Unh . . . almost . . . there!"

The lights on the control panel flickered, then went out.

"Bloody hell!"

"Maybe I should call someone from engineering to assist you—" she began.

He stuck his head out and positively glared at her. *"Don't.* Ma'am. Beggin' your pardon, but I'd never hear the end of it! I've got my *pride,* you know."

"Lives are at stake here—"

"I know, and the sooner I shut up and get back to work, the sooner you'll get 'em saved." He disappeared into the console again.

Territorial, these engineering types. She sighed. At this point, it was probably best to let him do his work.

"Why don't they build these things to standard specs?" she heard O'Brien mutter to himself. "You'd think a Galaxy-class starship would use the same C-22a transporter-buffer configuration as the rest of the fleet, wouldn't you? But *no,* that's not good enough. Some bright kid decides it's better to start over from scratch and reinvent the wheel, and we're the ones who suffer for it. . . ."

Something creaked again. The lights flickered, came on, died, flickered, and died again. And then they didn't come on at all.

Dr. Crusher sighed. *Twelve minutes. Three more, then I call Engineering.*

"How's that?" he asked from inside. "Everything look okay?"

"It's completely dead."

"Eh? *Still?*" he called. Something made a banging sound, like steel on steel. Dr. Crusher winced. *He's insane. I'm trusting my patient—and the safety of the crew—to a madman.*

"Just a minute more!" he called.

"Are you *sure* this is going to work?"

"Of course." He grunted again. He pounded on something. He cursed. But finally the console lights came back on and a familiar hum of power filled the room.

"That does it." The transporter chief pulled his red-haired head out and gave her a winning smile. "Knew I'd get it in the end. I've manually cross-chained two transporter buffers, so you'll get a double-strength biofilter. No virus is going to make it through there unless *we* want it to. Just give the word, Doc, and I'll start the transport."

"Okay." Something made her hesitate, though. She still had her doubts about jerry-rigged transporters. It might do in a true emergency, but when the safety of the crew lay at stake, when a potentially lethal virus might make it on board, she wanted something extra. Strange creaking noises and flickering power supplies did *not* engender confidence, she thought.

That's why we're beaming into a level-1 containment field, she thought. Even if he screwed up the biofilters, nothing would get loose on the ship.

"Let's give it a try."

She tapped her badge. "Crusher to Dr. Tang."

"Tang here," he replied almost instantly. *He must have been waiting for my call.*

"Do you have that patient ready?"

"Yes. Lock onto the other person at these coordinates—"

Crusher glanced at O'Brien, who nodded.

"Bring him aboard," she said.

"He's in the pattern buffer," Transporter Chief O'Brien said. "Now . . . applying the first set of biofilter algorithms . . . now the second set . . . done!"

It's too easy, she thought. *If this worked, Dr. Tang would have cured all his patients by now.* Unless he only managed to reinfect them. Unless he sabotaged his own work to help the Purity League. *No virus can make it through the biofilters,* she thought. *It has to work. It's medically impossible for it* not *to work.*

"Leave him in the pattern buffer until I have the containment field set up," she said, starting for sickbay. "I'll let you know when we're ready."

"Got it, ma'am!"

Five minutes later, the hum of a transporter beam filled the sickbay. Dr. Crusher and her staff gathered around biobed 1 and the forcefield now shimmering there.

A woman materialized on the bed. She had long, flowing black hair, an elongated Peladian skull, and white blisters covering her face, neck, and hands.

Dr. Crusher raised her tricorder and began a quick scan. The virus was gone. *So much for Dr. Tang,* she thought. As far as she was concerned, this proved he had been lying all along. *Now, all we have to do is find an antiviral agent that works,* she thought, *and begin mass-producing it.*

"We have a winner," she announced. "The virus is gone."

Her staff let loose a cheer.

Smiling, she lowered her tricorder. "All we need is a vaccine and we'll be set. How is it coming?"

"I think we'll have something in a few hours. We're running cultures now. All indications are positive—we'll have that cure by the end of the day. It's only Rhulian flu, after all."

Dr. Crusher nodded. "Prepare two more biobeds," she said to her nurses. "We have patients on the moon to bring across."

It looked like the start of a very busy afternoon.

She continued to monitor her plague patient, listening to the steady beat of her heart on the biobed's monitor. Within twenty minutes, the woman's fever was gone. Within an hour, the fever blisters on her face had begun to shrink noticeably. Blood tests, sensor scans, and every medical instrument in sickbay revealed her to be a healthy young adult female in every way.

Too bad we can't beam every patient on the planet through our biofilters, she thought. *But even with all our transporters working around the clock—even if you count the* Constitution*—we would barely get one or two percent of the victims processed. And we would have to start beaming them back down to the planet because we'd run out of room here . . . and they would be reinfected immediately.*

No, they needed a real cure. That was the only solution.

Even so, Dr. Crusher found it hard to restrain her jubilation. It wasn't every day she had such immediate and gratifying results from a treatment. So much for Dr. Tang and all his dire warnings.

"Get back to work on the vaccine," she said.

Deanna Troi strolled in shortly thereafter. "I heard you have a new patient, Beverly," she said. "I can tell by the glow on your face that the news is good. Is she awake yet?"

"Not yet . . . but soon." Smiling, Dr. Crusher led the way to biobed 1. The white fever blisters had almost all vanished on the woman's face. "As you can see, she's still unconscious. I didn't want to administer a stimulant yet . . . rest is the best thing for her right now."

Deanna leaned close to the forcefield. "She's dreaming. I sense some very turbulent emotions . . . do you have a case history on her? I'd like to read it before we talk."

"No—and I'm sure the Archo City Hospital doesn't have one, either. They've been overwhelmed by the thousands of plague victims. They didn't even bother sending paperwork up with her—we don't even know her name."

Deanna sighed, but nodded. "All right. I want to be here when she wakes up, though. She's going to need counseling to deal with her trauma. Promise you'll call me?"

"Of course." That was the least they could do for their patient. Mental as well as physical health—a doctor had to worry about both.

Deanna gazed silently at the woman. "Is that forcefield still necessary?" she asked.

"For now. It's a standard safety procedure." *And I promised Dr. Tang—he insisted the virus leaped through biofilters. But when there isn't a virus present, it can't leap through anything, can it?* She gave a mental snort. *All those lies . . . I wonder how he sleeps at night. First things first. Once the plague is under control, I'll make sure charges are pressed against him . . . if not on Archaria III, then on a Federation world in a Federation court.*

The Federation took charges of genocide very seriously.

PART 2:

THE PLAGUE ESCAPES

Interlude

SUNSET OVER ARCHO CITY dazzled the eyes with brilliant fingers of red and pink and gold. Solomon studied the spectacular colors as he waited impatiently for his ground transportation to arrive. *No pollution. No air traffic. Not a person in sight . . . I might be the last person in this whole world,* he thought.

Faint in the distance, a truck rumbled somewhere behind him, breaking the spell. He sighed and glanced around impatiently. Where was his car? It should have been here by now.

I'm a grain buyer. Even in the midst of panic and chaos, they bend over backwards to serve me. He found a certain irony in the fact that he had pretty much destroyed the social fabric of their world. *Not that it was particularly worth saving.*

"Aren't you afraid of the plague?" the elderly desk clerk had asked him that afternoon when he came down for an early supper. He saw not another soul in the lobby, nor were any patrons eating in the hotel restaurant. *Rats leaving a sinking ship,* he thought with an inward chuckle. *Only with the planet quarantined, they have no place to go.*

"The plague? Not really," Solomon told him matter-of-factly. "I haven't had a sick day in my life, and I'm not going to start now."

"We have begun relocating most of our off-world guests to rural inns. We think they will be safer there, between the plague and the Purity League unrest. If you'd like, we can have your baggage packed while you're out—"

"No, thank you. I prefer to stay here."

"But the plague—"

"A minor inconvenience, that's all." He gave a dismissive gesture. "I'm sure either the Federation or your own excellent hospital system will soon have it sorted out. Besides, I thought only mixers were affected by it. I'm certainly not half Peladian!"

"Obviously, sir. So far, only those damn mixers have caught it, lucky for us humans."

"Oh?" *I know where your sympathies lie, poor old fool.* Feigning interest, Solomon asked, "Have you heard anything else about the plague? Like who's really responsible?"

"Not really . . . just a few rumors." The clerk licked his lips and leaned forward, voice dropping to a conspiratorial whisper. "They say the Federation is terrified that the disease is going to mutate and take us humans next. The Peladians made it, you know, in their secret laboratories."

Solomon stared at him incredulously. "No!" It was all he could do to keep from bursting out laughing. *The Peladians!* Oh, it was too funny. The Purity League certainly moved swiftly to put its own spin on the plague virus. *Everyone wants to take credit for it but me.*

"Yes, sir. It's true. That's exactly what I heard."

"Well, until I catch it myself, I'm not going to believe it. Now, can you check on my transport? It was supposed to be here by now."

And you really don't *want to see me when I'm annoyed,* he added mentally.

"At once, sir." Turning, the clerk hurried to a comm terminal in the back office.

Solomon leaned on the counter, listening with half an ear as the clerk yelled at some poor dispatcher. He hadn't realized how quickly a planet's infrastructure could collapse. *Less than 5 percent of the planet is susceptible to the virus, and everyone's acting like it's the end of the universe.*

A moment later, the clerk returned. "All the drivers called in sick today," he reported. "When I explained how important you were, Joshua Teague himself—Teague's the owner—promised to send his son with a vehicle for you. Best they have, he said. His son, Berke, is a good boy. I've known him for years. He won't let you down."

"Thank you."

"Best of all," the clerk went on, "they're only going to charge you the economy rental rates—to make up for your inconvenience, sir."

"It doesn't matter. I'm on an expense account." *The General is paying for it, after all,* Solomon thought. "I appreciate the trouble Mr. Teague is going to on my behalf. Please make sure he bills the full amount to my room here."

"Of course, sir!" The clerk looked overjoyed. *He'll probably take half of it for his own services,* Solomon thought with amusement. He had never been one to begrudge lowly employees their share of graft. *After all, that's what keeps the universe afloat.*

"How long will it take?" he asked. "It's getting dark, and I *am* in something of a hurry."

"It will be here momentarily, sir. Would you care for a complimentary drink while you wait? If you like, I can have it brought out to the lobby for you—"

"No, thank you. I think I'll wait outside."

"If you must, sir." The clerk didn't seem to like that idea, but Solomon didn't particularly care. After all, what could possibly happen?

He strolled through the deserted lobby and out to the deserted sidewalk and looked around the deserted square. None of the shops had opened today. But the black marble fountains burbled happily, and small grayish birds—real Earth pigeons, by their look—strutted happily this way and that. He watched, and studied the magnificent sunset as it colored the west with a brilliant palette.

At last a small luxury aircar settled to the ground in front of the hotel. It was a Praxx Cruiser, a couple of years old but once the very top of their line. Ten meters long and three meters high, its body had been elegantly sculpted along aerodynamic lines. Its shiny black paint job gleamed with fresh polish.

Not bad, Solomon decided, ambling over to inspect it. The last aircar they'd sent him had been a twenty-year-old Junco Jett. *Certainly much better than I expected.* If the Cruiser handled half as well as it looked, he would be one happy customer.

A bearded young man opened the side doors and climbed out. He did *not* look happy, though. He kept glancing around the square as though half expecting mobs of screaming Peladians to attack at any moment.

"You must be Buck Teague." Solomon smiled cheerfully and offered his hand. "Thanks for coming."

"It's Berke, sir." Berke shook hands, looking even unhappier. *Probably terrified he's going to catch something from me,* Solomon thought with growing amusement. *Everyone deals with a plague differently.*

Berke turned and pointed into the driver's compartment. "Autopilot, navigator console, manual controls, computer controls. Everything checked out this morning. Are you familiar with Praxx aircars?"

"Of course. I own several."

Berke nodded. "Just park it in the hotel lot when you're done. We'll have someone pick it up tomorrow."

"Thanks."

"No problem, sir. Thank you for using Teague Luxury Aircars, the best on Archaria III. Enjoy your trip." It sounded like a well-rehearsed script.

Solomon didn't waste any time. He climbed in, took the controls manually, and lifted off. The engine purred. The computer came on-line automatically as soon as he cleared the hotel's roof.

"Destination, sir?" it asked in its richly timbered Praxx voice.

Solomon released the controls. "Archo City Library, 5562 Vista Place." He had stationed the first of his fifty atmospheric monitoring stations there, on the rooftop.

"Very good, sir." The aircar banked to the left and began to accelerate. *"We will arrive in approximately five minutes."*

Solomon leaned back in his soft padded chair, which began to vibrate faintly, massaging his muscles. *Ah. Nothing like a Praxx vehicle,* he thought.

"Watch for aircars following us. If anyone takes a parallel course, inform me immediately."

"Of course, sir."

Solomon turned his head to gaze out the window. Nobody had reason to suspect him of any unlawful activities, of course, but with so few aircars out and about tonight, he knew he might catch some unwanted attention.

To the far north, he spotted a couple of official-looking troop transports flying quickly toward the spaceport. People could be so foolish, he thought, shaking his head. In a real plague situation, the *last* place you'd find him would be in a crowded public place. And yet half the planet seemed to be at the Archo City spaceport, trying desperately to get passage off Archaria III.

That very morning, he had watched a live broadcast from the spaceport terminal—the vid showed scenes of utter chaos, with flight counters closed, screaming masses of humans and Peladians fighting for space in nonexistent lines, children shrieking, mothers crying, fathers and brothers and cousins all on the verge of murder. And all just to escape a plague which couldn't possibly infect them.

Humans are crazy, he decided, and not for the first time in his life. The Peladians didn't seem much better.

"Hundreds of mixers trying to flee the planet have been collapsing in the spaceport terminal," the vid reporter said. *"Peace officers cart them off to a makeshift hospital as fast as they fall. Too bad they can't die at home."*

The makeshift hospital turned out to be a requisitioned circus tent erected on the landing pads between two parked starships. The vid showed a bright red-and-yellow striped tent as tall as the largest freighter, with dragon-shaped pennants fluttering from every peak and pinnacle. It looked ridiculous.

"That's right, Bob. With so many full-blooded humans here, the peace

officers have enough problems keeping order without having to bother with mixer trash—"

Solomon shook his head. *Utter stupidity!* He thought. They all, human and Peladians alike, needed to go home and wait it out. With all off-world traffic halted by the Federation, nobody would be leaving Archaria III anytime soon . . . not until the plague ran its course and burned itself out, or somebody found a cure, whichever came first.

He knew a cure wouldn't be long in coming. The General had a whole timetable set up around the plague. If events unfolded according to schedule, the Federation would find a cure for the plague virus within three weeks of their arrival here . . . but only after 98 percent of the planet's half-breed population were dead.

Solomon still had no idea *why* the General wanted to kill off so many innocent people. Not that it was his problem. But secretly, he half-wished the Federation would find the cure a little faster. He might be a member of the largest criminal organization in human space, but he didn't consider himself a murderer. *And that's what this is,* he thought. *Cold, calculated murder.*

He coughed a bit and fought a half-second of panic. But the General wouldn't have infected him. *He's not done with me yet. Phase Two has just begun. He still needs my reports.*

The aircar circled down toward the roof of a giant building complex: the Archo City Library. Its roof held parking spaces for hundreds of vehicles. Now, however, it lay completely deserted.

"This is your destination, sir," the aircar told him. It began landing procedures, flashing bright yellow lights and sounding an insistent beep to alert anyone who might be directly underneath them. *"Will you be staying here long, sir? If so, I can power down and recharge my energy cells."*

"No, not long." He leaned to the side and studied the hundreds of empty parking spaces on the library's roof. *It must be closed for the emergency,* he thought. It was probably just as well. He didn't want anyone to see him checking his monitoring stations. Though that was hardly an illegal activity, he never liked explaining himself to strangers . . . or peace officers.

His aircar landed beside the lift.

"Thank you for using Teague Luxury Aircars, the best on the planet. Please enjoy your stay."

"I'll be back in just a second," he said. "Keep the engines fully powered up."

"Of course, sir."

Solomon popped open the side door, hopped out, and hurried to the lift. It looked like a small square building with double doors. The doors didn't open for him this time as he approached, not that it mattered—he had no intentions of going inside.

He went around to the back of the structure. A week ago he had installed an atmospheric monitoring station here. It was a small innocuous-looking silver box about the size of a small loaf of bread. Vents on all three exposed sides allowed air to pass through freely.

Pulling a small tricorder from his pocket, he snapped it into a data port on the front of the station. A red light turned green as the tricorder downloaded all the data.

Easy enough. Tucking the tricorder back into his pocket, he jogged back to the Praxx aircar. *One down, forty-nine more to go,* he thought. He would be lucky to finish by midnight.

He didn't know what atmospheric conditions the General's scientists needed to monitor, but then he didn't need to. *As long as they get their data and I get my pay, we'll all be happy.*

As he slid back into the pilot's seat, the computer said, *"Thank you for using Teague Luxury Aircars, the best on Archaria III!"*

Solomon rolled his eyes. *Forty-nine more monitoring stations . . . that message is going to get* very *annoying,* he thought.

"What is your next destination, sir?"

"225 Altair Place, Convent Gardens." He had a monitoring station set up amid the tangle of purple rosebushes along the Rose Walk.

Chapter Eleven

DUSK FALLS BELOW. *The magic hour is here.*

In his cabin, Commander Riker stroked his long black beard and stared at himself in the mirror. He had never worn a beard before, and he had to admit he rather liked the effect. The follicle stimulator had given him a bushy growth in the style of a native Archarian. When he shrugged on a loose-fitting brown shirt and laced it up the front, then brown pants and soft brown boots, he barely recognized himself.

"Well, let's get going," he told himself.

He strode to the door and out into the corridor. Several crewmen did a double-take. Grinning, he nodded to them and said, "Carry on!"

"Sir." Data's voice came from behind, and Riker paused long enough for the android to catch up. Data too wore loose brown clothing and sported a thick brown beard. Flesh-colored makeup hid the metallic gold of his face and hands; only his slitted yellow eyes still marked him as other than human.

"Your eyes—"

"I have inserts to change their color and appearance, sir. However, since they impair my vision by 1.0037 percent, I have elected not to wear them until we actually beam down to the planet."

Riker nodded. "Other than that, you look good, Data. Truly human . . . and ready to rebel."

"Thank you, sir. You also look substantially different."

"I'll take that as a compliment."

"That is how I intended it, sir."

They reached the turbolift, which hissed open promptly. Deanna Troi stood inside. She stared at them, then broke out in giggles. *That better not be the reaction we get on the planet,* Riker thought. He stepped inside, folded his arms, and gave her a long stare. Oddly, her giggles grew louder, but at least this time she tried to stifle them a bit.

"Transporter Room Three," he said.

"Bill—" Deanna gasped. "You should see yourself!"

"I rather liked the effect." He stroked his beard and struck a new and even more heroic pose, one arm curled up and back with the first against his forehead. "I am a true planetary pioneer!"

"Sir," said Data, "very few human space pioneers actually wore beards. A comprehensive analysis starting with John Glenn in the mid-twentieth century shows—"

"Uh, that's not really what I meant, Data," said Riker.

"I'll leave you two to sort it out," Deanna said as the turbolift came to a stop. The doors shushed open and she stepped into the corridor, probably heading toward sickbay, Riker thought. She added over her shoulder, "Don't get too carried away, Bill."

"Thanks, Deanna—I think!" Riker called after her.

"May I ask you a question, sir?" Data said as the turbolift resumed its ascent.

"Certainly."

"Why does Counselor Troi call you 'Bill' when the rest of your fellow officers call you 'Will'?"

"I've known Deanna quite a bit longer than anyone else aboard. I used to go by Bill at the Academy—but then I dated a woman named Bili Beller, so we mutually decided I'd use Will." That conjured up images of her in his mind—tall and slender Bili, with her sea-green eyes, full pouting lips, and high cheekbones. He sighed and wondered what had happened to her.

He found Data staring inquiringly at him, so he cleared his throat and added, "Bill Riker and Bili Beller doesn't have the proper sound for a couple, so I went by Will. After we went our separate ways, I decided I liked Will better."

"The difference between two consonants seems inconsequential. Surely the measure of a man is determined by his actions, not his designation."

"Yes—and no. In some situations, the right name *can* make all the difference."

"And Will Riker is preferable to Bill Riker?"

"Or Billy-the-Kid Riker, a nickname I was also unfortunate enough to get stuck with at the Academy. So I had another reason to change it besides my girlfriend Bili."

Slowly Data nodded. "I believe I do see, sir. It is the difference between a shark and spark. Or a joke and a poke. Or a rose and a nose. Or—"

"Yes, exactly, Data."

"Is there a reason why you have not yet told Counselor Troi your new preference?"

"I, ah, haven't had a chance." *How do you tactfully explain the awkwardness of working with an old lover to an android?*

They reached the transporter room. As the doors slid open, Riker was pleased to find Lieutenant Yar already present. She, too, wore brown pants and shirt, but with a hooded cape slung almost casually across her shoulders. And like him, she had used a follicle stimulator; her suddenly long blond hair had been pulled back into a severe bun that accentuated the sharp lines of her jaw, cheekbones, and nose. She also wore no makeup . . . plain as a churchmouse, wasn't that the old saying? It fit this throwback racist zealot planet.

Yar turned to face him with a noticeable stiffening of her spine. *A month on board together and she hasn't relaxed once in my presence,* Riker thought. He had never seen anyone wound up so tight. *With the probable exception of Data. And with him it really is clockwork that's wound so tight.*

"Sir," Yar said. "I have your weapon. And Data's." She held out her left hand, revealing two small, gray, egg-shaped phasers of a design fit for civilians.

Riker and Data each accepted one. Riker turned his over, noting all the standard controls—pushbutton trigger, safety switch, and three degree settings—low, medium, and high. They would correspond to light stun, heavy stun, and kill, he knew. The lightly indented grips felt slightly different from standard Federation issue, as he wrapped his fingers around them . . . oddly soft and yielding, but still comfortable. He knew he could use the weapon with no difficulty.

The first rule of any away mission—drummed into every student at Starfleet Academy from day one—was to check your equipment personally. The phaser control had been set on light stun. When he tried to thumb it over to a higher setting, the switch jumped back. He thumbed it again with the same result.

"It's defective, Lieutenant," he said, offering it to her.

"No, sir," she said. "It's not unusual for civilians to bear arms on Archaria III, but local laws stipulate that any setting higher than 'light stun' must be permanently disabled on any weapon in civilian hands."

Riker nodded. "Have you selected a beamdown site?"

"Yes, sir. It's a small alley near Archo City Hospital. Civilian news broadcasts show an antimixer rally taking place there. It should start with speeches, chants, and the consumption of a lot of free alcoholic beverages. After that, it's anyone's guess—previous rallies have ended in everything from riots to lynch mobs chasing down mixers. Of course, a few have also ended peacefully." She grinned and he saw a little bit of a mischievous gleam in her eye. It was good to see her loosen up. "But that's not very likely tonight, from what I hear. Father Veritas wants Archo City Hospital destroyed, so I think we can pretty much count on some action."

Riker gave a nod. "Let's get moving," he said. He led the way onto the transporter platform, and Data and Yar took their positions to either side.

"Just a second, sir." Yar pulled up her hood and fastened a small silver chain under her chin. With her face suddenly hidden in shadow, only the faint glint of her icy blue eyes seemed alive. "It's traditional for Archarian woman to wear hoods in public," she said as if in reply to his scrutiny.

Data bent at the waist and pressed something to his face. When he rose, eyes as blue as Tasha Yar's met Riker's own. Riker blinked in sudden amazement. He would never have been able to pick Data out of a crowd of strangers. Not a single trace of the android's usual appearance remained.

"You would fool even your own mother, Data," he said in surprise. He gave a nod to Ensign Norman. "Energize!"

"Actually, sir," Data began, "I have no mother. Nevertheless, I view Dr. Soo—"

The transporter room shimmered, disappeared, and suddenly Riker found himself standing in a dark alley. The stench of decaying vegetation, raw sewage, old smoke, and several other even less savory smells hit him like a blow. Gagging, he steadied himself against a red-brick wall. Slowly his eyes grew accustomed to the dimness.

What little light spilled in from the streetlights in the street at the other end of the alley revealed nothing more than the vague outlines of abandoned crates and garbage bins around him. Every now and then humans passed the alley's mouth without so much as a glance in their direction, their silhouettes giving little clue about who they were and what they were up to. *Probably too busy hurrying away from the alley's stench,* Riker thought wryly.

"Yar, take point," he said.

"On it, sir." She glided up the alley as furtively as a shadow. If she hadn't been silhouetted against the light, he never would have seen her.

Riker started after her, but slipped on something slick and skated forward, off balance. Strong hands seized his shoulders and steadied him.

It was Data. "Careful, sir," the android said. "The ground offers little traction here."

"Thanks, Data."

"Actually, sir, given your thoughts on the matter, I have been reconsidering my name. It conveys a sense of information rather than purpose. It is also not a name commonly associated with Archarians."

"Or humans."

"Precisely. Which is why I thought taking the name Bret might be a better choice—at least for the duration of this mission."

"Bret?" Riker shook his head a little. "How did you pick that one—no, never mind. I'm sure it's a well-researched and thought-out selection."

Data tilted his head slightly. "Thank you, sir."

"And you had better call me Will from now on, too. First names for everyone, like we're old friends out for fun at the Purity League rally."

"Acknowledged—Will."

Tasha Yar had reached the mouth of the alley. She paused and looked back, motioning them forward. Riker hurried to join her, with Data at his heels.

"Sir," she said softly, "there are peace officers posted at the both intersections to our left and right. I don't think we can get out without being seen."

Riker peeked out and spotted the two uniformed officers. Both stood beneath spotlights, looking conspicuous. *Probably what they want . . . an obvious authority presence to deter rioters and looters.* The planet wasn't under martial law yet, but the government had to be getting close to station peace officers so blatantly.

Yar went on, "There is still some pedestrian traffic—I spotted a couple of people who looked like they might be factory workers hurrying home. The peace officers didn't even glance at them."

Riker said, "I don't think we'll have any trouble getting past them as long as we act like we belong here. Follow my lead. We'll bluff it through."

He took a deep breath and stepped out into the street with a little bit of a swagger, like he owned Archo City. With his beard and native garb, he knew he more than looked the part. To any casual observer, he *was* an Archarian.

Without hesitation Data and Yar joined him and matched his pace. *Just three friends out for an evening's fun at the Purity League rally,* Riker thought as they headed up the broad sidewalk. *We belong here. No need to question us.*

Yar said, "If my directions are correct, we need to turn right at the next intersection. Archo City Hospital is only a few blocks away."

"Excellent," Riker said. More loudly, he went on, "I think our harvest *will* be up ten percent this quarter."

"What harvest, Will?" Data said, sounding bewildered.

"Act like you belong here, Data!" Yar whispered fiercely at him. "Talk about farm stuff as we walk past the peace officers! Something innocuous!"

Data nodded woodenly, and suddenly he plastered a fake grin across his face. "Very well, Tasha," he said. "Since we are up to nothing more than business as usual, this seems like the perfect opportunity for me to practice humorous banter."

"Lucky for us it's dark!" Riker muttered half to himself. Data stood out like a Cardassian in Starfleet Headquarters when he tried too hard to be human.

"Will?" Data paused a millisecond, then went on, "So the farmer's daughter said to the traveling salesman—"

"Sorry, Bret, I've heard that one," Riker said.

"Bret?" Yar asked. "Did I miss something, sir?"

Riker sighed. "Long story, Tasha. In the alley, Bret here persuaded me that we should only use first names for the duration of the mission. Bret blends in better than Data. Proceed with your banter, Bret."

"Thank you, Will." Data paused a millisecond. "How about the one—"

"Heard it," Tasha said flatly.

Data frowned. "But how can you say you have heard it if I have not yet had a chance to relate the humorous part of the story?"

"I'll explain later," Riker told him.

They neared the intersection. Like all the other men on this planet, the peace officer waiting there wore his beard at chest length. He straightened a bit, looked them up and down, then started toward them at an amble.

Riker felt a jolt of panic and tried not to show it. *He's suspicious. What have we done wrong?*

His thoughts raced through the possibilities, and he studied his team from the corner of his eyes, but both Data and Tasha Yar looked the part of natives. Feigning indifference, they kept strolling toward the corner. To all appearances they *were* three Archarians out for a walk. *So why is he heading our way?*

"Hey!" the peace officer called. "Hold up there. Wait a second!"

Riker stopped and turned reluctantly to face him. The man wore a black one-piece uniform with bulging pockets at the hips, thighs, and chest. In one hand he carried an old-fashioned billy club; clipped to his belt were a phaser, an old-fashioned communicator, and several other objects which Riker could not readily identify.

"Yes, officer?" Riker called. He felt a rush of adrenaline. *Fight or flight,* he thought, but he shoved those instincts to the back of his mind. They hadn't done anything wrong; they had no reason to be concerned.

"Do you want me to stun him, sir—Will?" Yar subvocalized. Casually she eased one hand toward her concealed phaser. "If we can get him into the alley before the other officer notices—"

"Let's see what he wants first," Riker replied. "Maybe we can talk our way through it. Volunteer no information."

"Yes, sir. Will."

Reaching them, the peace officer drew to a halt and said, "Father Veritas be with you, friends."

Was he a member of the Purity League? Or an overly diligent officer trying to trap them into a confession? *Better to play it cautiously,* Riker thought. *Father Veritas hasn't done anything illegal here. At least, not that we know of. There's no reason not to respond in kind.*

"And with you," Riker said. "Are you a member?"

"Of course I belong. Don't let the uniform fool you." He stuck out his hand. "Kirk Jordan."

"Will Riker." They shook briefly. Riker turned to Yar and Data. "These are a couple of my friends—Bret and Tasha."

Jordan gave them both nods. "Going to the rally?" he asked.

"Yes. We got a little held up."

"They've already started." Jordan seemed to be accepting their story at face value, Riker thought. The peace officer went on, "You're a bit turned about. Archo City Hospital's that way." He pointed to the right.

"Really?" Pointedly Riker glanced the way they had been headed and feigned surprise. "But I thought—"

"Nope." Jordan turned and pointed to the corner. "Turn right and then head straight. You can't miss it. And if you do get lost, just ask one of us. Peace officers *are* here to help, after all!"

Riker forced a grin. "Thanks!" he said. *No wonder the planetary government can't get a handle on their Purity League problem,* he thought. *The peace officers are part of it.*

Jordan grinned back. "Have fun. I only wish I could join you, but I pulled crowd control tonight."

"That's a shame," Tasha said. "I heard Father Veritas might actually speak tonight."

"Don't count on it. That's what the rumors always say before a big rally, but nobody *I* know has ever laid eyes on the Father." With a quick wave, he jogged back to his post. "Have fun!" he shouted over his shoulder. "Death to mixers! Humans first and always!"

"Humans first!" Riker echoed. If this was the sort of reception the Purity League gave newcomers, it looked more and more like they would have no trouble fitting in. He turned back to Yar and Data. "Let's go!"

Chapter Twelve

THIS TIME, IT WAS Dr. Tang who called *her.*

He must be starting to panic, Dr. Crusher thought. *I'm getting close to a cure, and now he's running scared. He knows he's going to be exposed.*

This time, though, she kept him waiting on the comm channel long enough to call Deanna Troi into the room, too. When she slid behind her desk and faced Tang, Deanna stood beside her, watching and evaluating.

"What can I do for you, Doctor?" she asked, using her best poker face. *One hundred percent virus-free!* she thought. Every test on her patient checked out perfectly. *We have a cure. And now we're going to catch you in your lies.*

"I had hoped to get a status update on the patient you sent through the biofilters."

"Well, I have good news. Our patient is cured."

He raised his eyebrows. "Completely? Are you sure?"

"It's been four hours since we beamed her through our modified biofilters, and we have run every test ever devised on her. She passed them all with flying colors. The virus is gone. She's well."

Tang nodded. "That is what I feared. I *knew* it would appear successful. However, it's too soon to judge."

"Doctor," she said, "this is getting silly. The virus is *gone.* The symptoms have disappeared. If she weren't still sedated, our patient would be up and dancing a jig. I don't know how much healthier she needs to be to prove she's cured."

Tang folded his arms stubbornly. "We had the same initial success with our own experiments with biofilters. Unfortunately, the disease always returned within twenty-four hours . . . it returned—and it was nastier than ever."

"It must have been reinfection."

"We thought so at first . . . but it happened even in clean rooms set up with level-1 containment fields. The same containment fields you are using."

"That's not possible. There is no way for anything as big as that virus to get through a containment field."

"Nevertheless," Tang insisted, "you must monitor the patient for at least two days before making any such rash claims of a cure. We don't want to raise false hopes. Check my reports. I documented everything that happened in my biofilter experiments in excruciating detail. No, Doctor." Tang shook his head firmly. "As much as I want to believe in your cure, based on my *significantly* greater experience with the disease you must maintain that quarantine for at least forty-eight more hours. If the disease does not return within that period, I will be the first one to celebrate."

That did it. Dr. Crusher felt her professional resolve melt in a white hot fury.

"Listen to me!" she snapped. "I don't know what kind of game you're trying to pull, Tang, but I'm sick of it!"

He blinked in surprise. "What the—"

"I know you're behind the virus," she said. "You designed it for your Purity League friends, didn't you? That's why you're trying to block everyone else's research. Well, it's not going to work! It's just Rhulian flu with a few extra kinks—and not only have we cured *our* patient, we're going to have a vaccine within the day!"

"You're mad!" he said, staring at her with a horrified expression. "How—how can you even *think* that of me?"

"Then you deny it?"

"Yes—yes, absolutely!" He was almost speechless.

Dr. Crusher glanced up at Deanna Troi, who hesitated. *She's not sure. I have to push him further.*

"Knock it off, Tang," she said coldly. "Do yourself a favor and confess. If you turn over your research notes and the cure, maybe the courts will go easier on you."

"Doctor," he said urgently. "You are *wrong.* Everything in my notes *is* the truth. I would kill myself before taking another human life!"

"He's telling the truth," Deanna said suddenly.

"What?" Dr. Crusher took a deep breath. She felt as if her legs had just

been kicked out from under her. She would have staked her job on Tang's guilt.

The sounds of a muffled explosion carried over the connection, and the room behind Dr. Tang seemed to shake. Dust sifted down from the ceiling and Tang steadied himself against the comm unit.

"What's going on down there, Doctor?" Deanna demanded. "Are you under attack? Do you need assistance?"

"The hospital has been under periodic attack for almost two weeks now. Every few hours someone lobs a grenade at our front door. We have force-fields up. Nobody can get inside if we don't want them to."

"That's horrible!"

"The Purity League wants my hospital burned, to 'purify' the diseased mixers inside. I get dozens of death threats every day—I don't dare leave the hospital anymore. Does that sound like the life of someone working *for* the Purity League?"

"No," Dr. Crusher said. She looked at Deanna Troi again.

"Yes, I really am sure," Deanna said in answer to her unasked question. "He is on the verge of a nervous breakdown. He is under incredible stress. And he is innocent of everything you accused him of."

Tang was staring at her. "Who are you?" he demanded.

"I am the ship's counselor," she said. "Deanna Troi. I am pleased to meet you, sir."

"You're Betazoid—"

"*Half* Betazoid."

He swallowed. "Then you're going to be susceptible to the virus."

"I am . . . prepared to face that possibility."

"Ah." He blinked at them. "Ah, yes, I think I understand now. You two confronted me deliberately—you had to raise the possibility of my involvement with the Purity League to gauge my reaction, just in case I *was* involved."

"That's right," Dr. Crusher said. *I really put my foot in my mouth this time,* she thought with embarrassment. *At least I've got an out he can accept.* "Please—allow me to extend my apologies—"

"It is not necessary, I assure you. If I *had* been guilty, I'm sure I would have confessed!"

Dr. Crusher relaxed. *At least he isn't going to hold it against me,* she thought. She said, "About those attacks—are your patients safe?"

"Fortunately our security measures are more than capable, and the governor has troops posted at all entrances, so the truly needy can always get inside." He said it so matter-of-factly Dr. Crusher could scarcely believe it—Tang *accepted* a state of siege as the status quo.

"Do you need *any* assistance at all?" Deanna said. "I'm sure Captain Picard would beam down security forces to protect a hospital—"

"Not necessary. Our peace officers will suffice. And I do not wish to expose any of your crew to the dangers of infection. Now, if you'll excuse me, Doctor and Counselor, I have to work on finding a *real* cure."

How swiftly he took control of the conversation again and put her work down, Dr. Crusher thought. She found her teeth grinding in frustration, as Dr. Tang severed the link.

Incompetent, arrogant fool! she thought. *I have a patient cured here, and he won't even admit it!*

Deanna patted her shoulder. "If it helps, he really *does* think he's right. You might want to follow his advice about that woman—just in case."

Chapter Thirteen

JEAN-LUC PICARD ARRIVED at the transporter room just in time to see Captain Jules van Osterlich and two of his senior staff beam aboard. Jules had changed little in the three years since they had last seen each other . . . hair a little thinner, paunch a little bigger, but otherwise the same old friend from their days together at the Academy.

"Jules!" Picard said, stepping forward with a grin.

"Jean-Luc! You old spacedog!" Van Osterlich had been calling him that for the last thirty years.

They clasped arms and pounded each other on the back. It felt good to see Jules again, Picard thought. Command was often a lonely position, and he had learned to cherish his old friends all the more because of it.

"I'd like you to meet my senior officers," van Osterlich said. "This is Solack, my first officer—" Solack was a reed-thin Vulcan of perhaps eighty years . . . for a Vulcan, still in the prime of life. Solack inclined his head slightly in greeting. "—and Dr. Benjamin Spencer. Benny is my chief medical officer."

"Solack, Doctor." Picard gave them both polite nods. "I would like to give you a quick tour of our sickbay first, so Dr. Crusher can bring you up to date on her research."

"I would appreciate that, Captain," Dr. Spencer said.

Picard led the way out to the turbolift, trying to make polite small talk along the way. And yet he sensed something bothering his old friend. Jules seemed . . . distracted somehow. Not his usual self.

As they reached sickbay and the door whooshed open, Solack and Dr. Spencer went in first. Picard hooked his old friend's arm and held him back.

"What's bothering you?" he asked.

He licked his lips. "Jean-Luc . . . this whole setup stinks. I know the plague is man-made. Benny and your Dr. Crusher have been comparing notes since we reached orbit, and I've seen the message written on it. I have a theory."

Picard folded his arms. "Let's hear it." Jules had an almost uncanny knack for putting his finger on the heart of any problem.

"I don't know who created the plague, but I'll wager it wasn't done here or to the Purity League's order."

"Why not? Dr. Crusher suspects one of the staff at Archo City Hospital, a virologist named Tang. She's quite adamant about his guilt. He *has* been trying to hinder her research."

"I know. And she's wrong."

A pair of crewmen passed them, and Picard gave them a nod. Only when they were out of earshot did he turn back to his friend.

"Explain."

"I've known Ian Tang almost as long as I've known you. He's a good man, and he's 100 percent dedicated to his work . . . to healing. He would never be a party to mass murder!"

Picard frowned. "If so . . . then who *is* responsible?"

"I don't know yet. But I have a feeling sooner or later he'll tip his hand. You don't play games on a planetary scale unless something larger is at stake."

Picard nodded. "I agree. But until our culprit does reveal himself, we must proceed as though the virus is our sole concern. Let's see what progress Dr. Crusher has made."

They are still drinking, Worf thought with growing apprehension. From ahead came a new bout of boisterous Klingon song—a popular old drinking tune with a rousing chorus:

Comrades in death, in death we live!
Drink up, my brothers, tomorrow we give!
Death to the humans! Death to our foe!
Death to the Romulans! Strike a deadly blow!

He knew it well. Legions of Klingon warriors had sung that song for more than a hundred years, drinking to victory in their wars with Earth and Romulus. On "blow" they would drain their tankards of blood wine, then slam them down.

From the way they slurred their words, Worf knew the celebration had been going on a long time . . . a very long time indeed. And there was nothing more dangerous than a drunken Klingon.

He paused and looked back at his three young ensigns. Knowing the dangers, he couldn't let them face these Klingons. They were too inexperienced. Look at how Wrenn had handled a few corpses.

"Stay back," he said. "I must face these Klingons alone."

"Alone, sir? But, Sir . . . " Clarke began.

Worf glared. "These are Klingons!" he said. "They are singing songs about killing humans and Romulans. Do not question my orders again."

"Yes sir. I mean, no sir." Clarke blushed.

Worf stopped listening.

Taking a deep breath, he turned and strode up to the open hatch, stuck his head inside, and saw all ten Klingons in various stages of drunkenness. They were lounging on chairs, benches, and the floor holding tankards aloft, singing at the top of their lungs. A large keg of blood wine sat before them . . . and it was more than half gone.

The singing trailed off as they began to notice him. Several fumbled for mek'leths. One—their leader?—staggered to his feet.

"Put down your weapons," Worf said in Klingon.

"You—you are Klingon!" their leader said, his words slurring.

Worf glared. "And you are a disgrace to our people!"

"I am Krot of the House of Mok! No one insults me!"

Worf took three quick steps forward and backhanded Krot across the face. The Klingon crashed back into a weather-monitoring station. The equipment sparked and died.

"I am Worf, son of Mogh!" he roared through his helmet, "and I serve aboard the Starfleet vessel *Enterprise!* You have violated Federation law. You have killed humans here. What do you have to say for yourselves?"

Krot staggered to his feet, grinning. "Worf? I have never heard of you . . . and a Klingon serving aboard a *Federation* ship? I spit on you and your house, you simpering would-be human!"

Worf backhanded him again, but this time Krot was ready. Shrugging off the blow, he punched Worf in the head with the full strength of a Klingon warrior.

Worf staggered. His faceplate had cracked a dozen ways, he saw. As he shook off the blow, Krot reached forward, snagged his helmet, and *pulled.*

The helmet came off with a tearing sound. The seals hadn't held—not that it really mattered after the faceplate had shattered.

Roaring in rage, Worf tried a head-butt. He caught Krot by surprise, and the Klingon leader reeled back, this time laughing like a demon. A thin line of blood ran from a cut over his left eye. Worf glared his rage.

"Join us, Worf!" Krot shouted. "Maybe you are a real Klingon!" He picked up a tankard, dipped it into the keg of blood wine, and held it out. "Drink up! Sing the old songs! Let us know what kind of warrior you are!"

What have I done? Worf thought. He had exposed himself to the plague virus. *I cannot return to the* Enterprise.

He swallowed. Somehow, the thought did not alarm him. *Perhaps that is what I wanted,* he thought. *To see my own kind. At least for a day or two, until Dr. Crusher finds her cure.*

He accepted the tankard from Krot and raised it high in the air. "To the Emperor!" he cried.

"To the Emperor!" the others roared. They chanted as he raised the tankard to his lips. He drained it in a few deep gulps, and when he slammed it down and wiped his mouth with the back of his arm, they cheered.

Chapter Fourteen

AS CAPTAIN PICARD ENTERED SICKBAY, he paused in surprise. He had never seen it this busy before. Strange new equipment beeped or hummed on every workbench. Doctors, nurses, and scientists hustled around one another, carrying data padds, tricorders, and other devices. The bustle reminded him more of the training hospital at Starfleet Academy, with its dozen-interns-to-one-patient ratio. Dr. Crusher clearly had everyone working double or triple shifts. Every doctor, every nurse, and as far as he could tell every biologist aboard had been co-opted into the research.

And their case at hand . . . he took a moment to study the woman lying on the biobed in the middle of the room, the eye of the storm. A forcefield shimmered faintly around her. She had curiously smooth features and a slightly elongated skull, with wide dark eyes and pale skin. A flood of black hair spilled around her head. Despite being deathly ill, she had the sort of ethereal beauty of which poets speak.

"Doctor Crusher!" he called when he spotted Beverly on the far side of sickbay, examining microcellular readouts on the wall scanner. The machine bleeped as she entered new data. "May we see you for a minute."

She turned and noticed him. "Captain! And this must be Captain van Osterlich."

"That's right. I believe you already know Dr. Spencer, and this is Mr. Solack, the *Constitution*'s first officer. Gentlemen, may I present my chief medical officer, Dr. Beverly Crusher."

"I'm pleased to meet you." She turned toward the unconscious woman on the biobed. "We were just about to wake our test subject. She went through our transporter and a series of modified biofilters about five hours ago. We have been monitoring her condition, and I'm glad to report things look promising. The virus appears to be gone from her system."

"Do I hear a 'but'?" Picard asked.

"I'm afraid so. On Dr. Tang's advice, I am going to keep the containment field up and monitor her condition for another day or two to make absolutely sure."

Deanna Troi joined them, and once more Picard made the round of introductions.

"Have you told them yet?" Deanna asked Dr. Crusher.

"Told us what?" Picard demanded.

"Dr. Tang is innocent," Dr. Crusher said with a sigh. "I confronted him with Deanna present to monitor his reactions, and I'm afraid he passed. He isn't responsible for the disease."

Picard shot a glance at van Osterlich, who returned an I-told-you-so shrug.

"Go on," Picard told her. "You still don't look happy. Now that you know you can trust his data, I would think you would find him a valuable resource."

"That's the problem—his data are crazy! He insists the virus leaps level-one containment fields. And we all know that's impossible."

"Is it?" van Osterlich said. He glanced at his own chief medical officer. "Benny?"

"I'm afraid it sounds crazy to me, too. The containment field keeps out particulate matter. Its field's screen is set so fine that oxygen gets through but nothing else—no dust, no bacteria, no viri. Dr. Crusher has isolated the plague virus, and it's clearly a simple variation of Rhulian flu. It's simply *too large* to get through any containment field—you can't alter the laws of physics just because they're inconvenient!"

Dr. Crusher said, "Let me show you our patient." She led the way toward the biobed. "This is Jenni Dricks. She is one-quarter Peladian. We beamed her through that modified transporter field I mentioned—using two sets of biofilters—and to all appearances it worked perfectly. Not a trace of the plague virus remains in her body. But that's only half the problem."

"Why?" Picard asked.

"We eliminated the virus from her body, but she's still going to be susceptible to it once she beams back down to the planet."

Solack raised one eyebrow. "She cannot go home."

"Not until a real cure is found. Nor can anyone leave the planet who might be carrying the virus. We haven't found a cure so much as . . . a delaying tactic. Of course, we can beam people up and pass them through biofilters, such as our away team, but with a planet as large as this one with a population in the millions, it's a task that will take years. And we still won't have eliminated the virus in the wild."

"But surely it's a good start," Picard said. As long as they could contain the disease, that would buy its victims time until a real cure could be found and they could return to their old lives.

Dr. Crusher shook her head. "Unfortunately, it's going to be a drop in the bucket, so to speak. There isn't room on the *Enterprise* to rescue more than a fraction of the plague victims. The latest estimates—and that's all Dr. Tang can give me at this point—indicate roughly thirty-five *thousand* people have died of the disease. Another twenty thousand are infected. It would take weeks to beam them all through our biofilters using both ships and working around the clock. And we don't have enough room here to house a *tenth* of that number, even if we use the shuttlebays and cargo holds."

"I see your point," Picard said. The situation truly was disastrous, he thought. "But at least we have some good news—with the biofilters working, we can come and go as necessary."

"But everyone who leaves the planet will still have to go through a quarantine period," Dr. Crusher said. "Just to make sure. Dr. Tang's data may be crazy, but I don't want to take any chances."

"Agreed." He turned to van Osterlich. "Are you ready for dinner? I have some other ideas I wish to discuss with you. And that Saurian brandy I promised!"

"Of course," van Osterlich said with a grin. "Lead the way, Jean-Luc!"

"If you don't mind," Dr. Spencer said, "I would prefer to remain here and work on the virus."

"And I should return to the *Constitution,*" Solack said in a flat voice.

"Of course," van Osterlich said.

"This way," Picard said, heading for the door.

Deanna Troi crossed to Jenni's biobed and gazed at her through the shimmering forcefield. "You said you were going to wake her?"

"Yes, I think it's time. I no longer see any medical reason to keep her unconscious. The worst of the plague symptoms are gone."

Deanna turned to look at the patient on the biobed again. Up close, you could still see the ravages of the disease in the woman, Deanna thought. Small white scars covered her face and hands, but those would undoubtedly fade away in time. For someone who had been at death's door less than twelve hours ago, the change in her appearance could only be described as miraculous.

She reached out with her mind, feeling the turbulent emotions of a dreaming mind . . . a mix of fear and dread and horror. *Nightmares,* she realized.

"What can you tell me about her?"

"According to her file, Jenni is a quarter Peladian. Her husband was half-human, half-Peladian, and they had three children. Due to their genetic human-Peladian mix, all five proved highly susceptible to the plague."

"You're using the past tense. Is there something I should know?"

Dr. Crusher shrugged helplessly. "I don't know. I haven't been able to find out if the rest of her family is still alive. It's highly unlikely, since she was apparently the last of them to fall ill, and death counts are still rising rapidly all over the planet."

Deanna regarded the woman on the biobed. "Go ahead," she said. "I'll do what must be done."

Since Dr. Crusher could not reach through the containment field, she had the computer administer the stimulant directly through the biobed. In a few seconds, Jenni took a deep breath, opened her eyes, sat up—and screamed.

"It's all right," Deanna said soothingly. She felt the terror surging through their patient.

"Where am I?"

"You're on board the *Starship Enterprise.* You were fortunate enough to be a test subject—we are trying to cure the plague. And we think it worked on you."

"Then—I'm well?" She looked from face to face.

"That's right," Deanna said. "This is Dr. Crusher. She's the one who cured you."

"Hi, Jenni." Dr. Crusher smiled. "How do you feel?"

"Terrible—but much better!"

"Good."

"Jenni," Dr. Crusher said, "I'd like you to meet a friend. This is Deanna Troi, the ship's counselor. Deanna, this is Jenni Dricks."

"What about my children—my husband—" she asked.

"We don't know what happened to them," Deanna said. "The hospital record system has completely broken down."

"You have to find them—cure them, too—"

"We're working on it as fast as we can," Dr. Crusher said. "We hope to have a vaccine sometime tomorrow."

Jenni gave a sigh and sank back down. "They're dead," she said. Deanna felt despair come from her in waves.

"We don't know that—"

"I know it." She stared straight at the ceiling, and as Deanna watched, a tear rolled down her cheek, then another. Her emotions turned dark with an almost suicidal undertone.

Deanna drew Dr. Crusher aside. "Are you sure you don't know anything?" she asked softly.

"I tried to locate them, but I haven't been able to find their records." Dr. Crusher shook her head. "The support system in the hospital has completely broken down. It's impossible to get any queries answered. I would have gotten them all beamed up here if I could have."

"I'll try to find out what happened, then. That's my job, and I know how busy you are." Deanna never liked being the bearer of tragic news, but sometimes it could not be helped. At least she could make a few calls down to the hospital.

She returned to the biobed. Jenni turned and regarded her through dark, half-closed eyes.

"I'm feeling well enough to get up," the woman said, and she managed a wan smile. "I'm ready to return home. Can you beam me back down to the hospital?"

"You're in no condition for that," Deanna said. "I will try to locate your family. Dr. Crusher says we can beam them up for treatment. You have to understand that the doctors on your planet are so overwhelmed with treating the plague that they've stopped keeping accurate records—everything except plague research. It's not as simple as looking up their names in the computer's database anymore."

She turned to Dr. Crusher again. "Beverly, can you release the containment forcefield yet? I feel awkward standing outside—especially since Jenni is cured."

Dr. Crusher said, "I'm afraid not. We have to keep that two-day quarantine to make sure you're really well."

Deanna dragged over a chair and sat. "I'm going to need to know the names of your other family members. I don't know how easy it's going to be, but I promise you this—I will do my best to find out where they are."

"Thank you." She sank back with a little shiver and her large brown eyes seemed to droop. "My husband is Derek Dricks. My children are Vera, Thomas, Jason, and David."

She just needed a little reassurance, Deanna thought. She sensed a rising contentment within Jenni. *Someone to take over the responsibility of finding things out. Now that it's my job, she can rest.*

She did not look forward to discovering the truth about Jenni's family. She had to admit, their chances of survival were slim. Telling someone their loved ones were gone had to be the hardest task for any ship's counselor. It was the one part of her job she truly hated.

But I don't really know, she told herself. *We delivered the Tricillin PDF ahead of schedule. They could be holding on. There's a chance it kept them alive.*

At least a slight chance.

She glanced at Dr. Crusher. *Beverly thinks they're dead.* Beyond the raw hurt coming from Jenni, she sensed Dr. Crusher's true feelings: regret, remorse, sadness, and a touch of wistful nostalgia for her own lost husband.

"I'll tell you what I'll do," Deanna said suddenly, trying to sound a little more cheerful. "I'll go now and see what I can find out. With any luck, I'll have word by midnight. Is that acceptable?"

"Yes, thank you." Jenni smiled.

"Try to get some sleep," Deanna said as she stood. She felt a faint rumble in her stomach. *But I just had dinner,* she thought. "I'll take care of everything. If I have news, I promise I'll wake you."

"You look pale," Jenni said as she sat up. Deanna could hear the sudden alarm in her voice. "Are you all right? *Are you all right?"*

"I should be asking you that ques—"

Deanna gasped soundlessly. What felt like the blade of a knife turned in her guts. The pain, as sharp and hot as a real wound, cut through her so fast she couldn't breathe. Unable to do more than gasp, she half doubled over, clutching her stomach.

Dr. Crusher steadied her arm. "What is it—Deanna?"

And just as suddenly as it started, the pain disappeared. Taking a deep shuddering breath, Deanna met the doctor's gaze.

"It's the plague—" Jenni wailed. She had a terrified expression on her face.

"Nonsense," Deanna said firmly. It simply wasn't possible. "I must have pulled a muscle. I had a strenuous workout on the holodeck just a couple of hours ago."

"Oh. For a second, I thought you had it, too!" Jenni sank back with a nervous laugh. Her face looked as white as chalk to Deanna.

"I think I'd better take a look at you, anyway," Dr. Crusher said. "Hop up on biobed two."

She felt another rumble in her intestines. *It's probably nothing—something I ate. Maybe the replicators are acting up . . .*

That had to be the solution.

She took a step, and suddenly sickbay wobbled and the deck seemed to slide out from under her feet. She felt herself falling and grabbed for an instrument tray. Clattering loudly, medical devices scattered across the floor, and she pitched after them, coming to rest against biobed 2.

"Ah-h-h-h-h!" she heard herself cry. It sounded like the death cry of a wounded animal.

New pains blossomed in her stomach. Molten steel burned through her veins, seared to the lengths of her arms and legs, shot down her spine, radiated from her bones.

The universe spun around her. The pain grew even worse. Lancets sliced through her bones. Fires coursed through her limbs. *Please, make it stop, make it stop!* She couldn't move, couldn't think—

Suddenly feet appeared in front of her eyes. Dr. Crusher rolled her onto her back. She had a medical tricorder in hand and Deanna heard its low whir.

"Deanna—Deanna—can you hear me?" Dr. Crusher demanded. She turned Deanna's face toward her own and skinned back her left eye, then her right.

She tried to talk but only a raw moan of pain came out.

And then, as suddenly as a door slamming shut, the pain vanished. Deanna lay there panting and soaked in sweat. *What's wrong with me?*

Her hands shook when she raised them to her face. Softly she began to sob. She had never felt anything so horrible, so excruciatingly painful, in her entire life.

"Deanna—talk to me!" Dr. Crusher pried her hands away from her face. "Tell me what's wrong!"

Deanna forced herself to meet the doctor's gaze. *What happened?* She wondered. *Was it a seizure?* Her teeth began to chatter. Dr. Crusher was staring at her with a half-terrified, half-worried expression. A cold wind swept through her body.

"S-so c-col—c-cold!" She felt her whole body begin to shake, and she couldn't stop no matter how hard she tried.

"Give me a hand! Get her on a biobed!" Dr. Crusher said to Dr. Spencer.

Together they seized Deanna's limbs, lifted on the count of three, and bustled her over to a biobed. Deanna gasped as new pains shot through her chest and stomach. She had never felt this sick before in her life—sick and out of control. She felt her eyes rolling back.

"Ahhhh-nahhh-hh—" she heard a distant voice cry. *It's me,* some part of her realized. *I'm starting to dissociate from my body.*

That only happened in severe traumas or in cases where the pain became too great for a patient to deal with rationally. *So the mind starts to float free, apart from the body, an observer to the terror within.*

She tried to relax as the two doctors set her down on the biobed. Her shaking grew worse. She couldn't breathe, couldn't think. Distantly, she felt them strapping down her arms and legs. No matter how hard she tried, she couldn't make her body cooperate. She felt helpless and panicked.

"It's the plague!" she heard Jenni wail from across the room. "That's how it starts! I saw it in my husband and children!" She began to weep hysterically.

Deanna tried to sit up as the pain faded again. *I ought to comfort her,* some part of her realized—but on second thought, she knew she was in no condition to do much of anything. She needed someone to comfort *her.*

"Quiet!" Dr. Crusher barked at Jenni over her shoulder. *The first rule of triage,* Deanna thought, *is to treat the most critically wounded. Hysterical but otherwise well patients get shoved to the rear of the line.*

"It can't be the plague!" Dr. Spencer said.

But it is! Deanna thought. *Somehow, some way, I have it.* She knew; she had read the reports. There couldn't be any mistaking these symptoms. *It leaped the containment field. Dr. Tang was right—*

She pressed her eyes shut as new pains welled up in her belly. *And there's no time for bedside manners,* she thought.

This time as the white-hot irons pierced her innards, she began to scream, and nothing could make her stop.

Dr. Crusher worked frantically. *It can't be the plague,* she told herself over and over, as she reconfigured the biobed for a half-Betazoid, half-human biology. *Her symptoms be damned, it's impossible.* Impossible! *Our plague victim is cured. She and Deanna weren't in direct contact. No virus moves through a containment field—*

Still Deanna screamed. Then her breath came in rapid pants—then suddenly she went limp, unconscious from the pain. *Best thing for her,* Dr. Crusher thought with dismay.

"Her fever is still climbing rapidly," Nurse Anders said urgently.

That was another one of the plague's first signs. *But it can't be,* Dr. Crusher thought. *There's no way she could possibly be infected.*

"Doctor?" the nurse asked.

"Almost done . . . there!" The biobed was reconfigured. It began its automatic scanning process. Charts began to appear: heart, respiration, blood pressure, white blood cell count.

As Dr. Crusher studied the readouts, her mouth went dry. *Viral infection. Similar to Rhulian flu.*

It can't be.

But there couldn't be any doubt—Deanna *was* infected with the plague virus. The green graph that mapped microorganism activity showed it multiplying at a dizzying rate. From the genetic signature, it couldn't be anything else *but* the plague.

But how? It was a medical impossibility. Nothing can get through a containment field. There must be another answer.

She exchanged a quick glance with Dr. Spencer. From their startled reaction, she knew he had reached the same conclusion.

"It's crazy. Just like Dr. Tang's report," she growled, her fists clenched in frustration.

"Maybe not so crazy," he said. "Maybe he missed something. Maybe *we* missed something."

"Back to basics. Contain and control."

"Exactly."

She glanced around sickbay. Everyone present—seventeen humans, a Vulcan, a Bolian—was of pure genetic heritage. *Good.* They wouldn't have anyone else dropping in the middle of their work.

"Staff meeting!" she called. They had all been watching; they knew what had happened. They all gathered around in record time.

"We must contain this outbreak," she said, meeting their gazes one by one. "We have all—every one of us in this room—been exposed to the plague virus. Chances are good we're carriers; however, it's not going to affect us. We're going to have to work under strict quarantine restrictions until we can assess the damage. Anders, seal the doors. Smith, draw a blood sample from Counselor Troi. Everyone else—keep working. We need to find that vaccine!"

Dr. Spencer touched her arm. "Our captains—and Mr. Solack!" he said with a groan.

She winced. They were loose on the ship—and Solack had beamed back to the *Constitution.* A disaster on all fronts.

"Call Solack," she told him. "Maybe it can still be contained on your ship. I'll take care of our captains."

"A toast—" Captain Picard said, raising his goblet. He heard a strange hum and paused. *Transporter beam*—he realized as he saw his hand dissolve in a shimmer of colored light.

And the next thing he knew, he stood in sickbay facing Dr. Crusher. She had her hands on her hips. Around her, the medical staff scrambled with panicked expressions.

"What the hell are you doing?" he demanded.

"Sorry, Captain," she said. "Time was pressing. Deanna has come down with the plague virus." She pointed to biobed 2.

Picard stared. *Her face*—it had broken out in what looked like small white pustules.

"That's impossible!" Captain van Osterlich said.

"But it happened. Did you come into contact with anyone on the way back to your cabin?"

"An ensign—Ensign Clarke, who wanted to see me about a complaint, and I put him off until tomorrow morning. And I introduced Lieutenant La Forge to Captain van Osterlich."

"And there was the Vulcan—"

"Yes, Ensign T'Pona. And we shared a turbolift with several people—the Praxx whose name I can't pronounce and Ensign Crane."

"Tr'grxl-gn'ta," Crusher said, naming the Praxx. "He's letting people call him Tray now."

"That's the one." He frowned. "I believe that's all."

Dr. Crusher shook her head. "Too many. Too damn many. We'll never get this genie stuffed back in the bottle." She glanced at Dr. Spencer, who was talking urgently to someone over the comm link in the corner. "Let's hope Spencer has better luck."

Van Osterlich paled. "Solack—"

"Beamed back to the *Constitution* as soon as you left," Dr. Crusher finished.

He sprinted to join Dr. Spencer, and the two of them held an animated conversation.

Picard began to pace. *How many crewmen are going to prove susceptible? How many people of mixed genetic heritage are actually serving onboard the* Enterprise*?*

Deanna stirred and moaned a bit. Picard trailed Dr. Crusher to her side and watched as she administered a sedative hypospray. *No need for containment fields now,* he thought. Small comfort.

"I've already given her a shot of Tricillin PDF," she said. "That will help."

Deanna settled down and lay quietly. *Rest. That's the best thing for her right now,* he thought. *Let the doctors do their work. They'll find a cure.*

Picard chewed his lip, thinking through the possibilities. He glanced at his friend.

"Jules?" he called.

Shaking his head, van Osterlich rejoined him. "They had a staff meeting in my absence," he said. "It seems they were going to hold a surprise party for one of my lieutenants. It's too late. Half the crew must have been exposed at this point."

Picard heard sobbing. He turned and found Dr. Crusher's original patient—the beautiful woman who had been asleep—now sitting up on her bed.

"What's wrong?" he asked her.

"It's my fault," she said. "I brought the plague here!"

"Nonsense," he said. "That wasn't your fault. We'll lick this thing yet."

"Hang on," Dr. Crusher said. She brought her medical tricorder over and began to run scans on her first patient. "How are you feeling?"

"Like I just had my stomach kicked." Her lower lip trembled.

"This is very interesting." Dr. Crusher raised her tricorder and began a second scan. "Very interesting indeed."

"What?" Picard asked.

"I'm picking up the virus in Jenni's blood . . . it's the very first stage of infection." She shut off the tricorder with a snap. "I don't think you've been infected longer than an hour. Which means you didn't infect Deanna—she infected *you.* Her case is at least eight hours old."

"How is that possible?" Picard demanded. "You were supposed to have a level-one containment field up around her at all times—"

"Yes, Captain, we did. We *still do*—nobody bothered to take it down."

Picard turned to look at Jenni. "It's still up . . . run a full diagnostic. It must be malfunctioning!"

"It's not. These events match what Dr. Tang told us. Somehow, somewhere, our quarantine procedure failed."

Think! Picard told himself. *That's the problem here—we're being outwitted. Whoever designed that virus is laughing at us. What have we missed?*

This wasn't like any other virus humanity had ever encountered, despite its resemblance to Rhulian flu.

Nurse Anders ran up. "Doctor," she said urgently. "We have two more suspected cases of the plague. They're on their way to sickbay now. Shall we lift the quarantine on sickbay?"

Two more cases . . . that confirmed it, Picard thought. Deanna Troi had been spreading the virus through the ship all day.

"Yes," he said. "Speed is of necessity here. Have a site-to-site transport beam them directly here."

"Get them started on Tricillin PDF," Dr. Crusher said. "That's about all we can do right now."

"Yes, Doctor."

Turning, Picard studied Deanna's readouts. Her vital signs appeared to have stabilized, at least for the moment.

"We can't look at this as a tragedy," Dr. Crusher said. "Three more plague victims means three more test subjects . . . and a better chance of finding a cure."

"That's the attitude," Picard said. Never mind that the plague was loose on the *Enterprise.*

Chapter Fifteen

PEACE OFFICER JORDAN'S DIRECTIONS proved unnecessary—you would have had to be blind and deaf to miss the demonstration going on, Riker thought.

The noise reached deafening levels from three blocks away. As they followed the chanting, shouting, screaming, and out-and-out war-whoops to their source, they came to a broad parklike square where five streets came together. In the center of the square, atop a small grassy knoll, blazed a huge bonfire. Hundreds had gathered around it chanting *"Veritas! . . . Veritas! . . . Veritas!"* Others screamed antimixer slogans, waved angry fists at the hospital complex on the far side of the bonfire, or just talked, shouted, or jeered, all at the top of their lungs. The noise reached deafening levels. Riker began to worry about damage to their eardrums.

Tasha touched his arm and pointed, mouthing, "The hospital!"

He nodded and began to follow her as she picked her way through the crowds of revelers. They passed more uniformed peace officers, none of whom looked happy. *They're missing the party,* Riker realized. *They're all members of the Purity League, or Purity League sympathizers . . . wolves watching the sheep.* Hopefully whatever oaths they had sworn to do their duty will keep them in line . . . *They would rather join in than keep the peace.* Not that there was much peace to keep in this bedlam.

Men and women gave him friendly nods and waves and pats on the back, and he reciprocated. *Look like you're having fun,* he thought. *Blend in. We're all one big family here, united in our fear and paranoia.*

Reaching the fringes of the crowd, Lieutenant Yar circled slowly to the left. A couple of people gave her too-friendly slaps on the back and shoulder and rump, and he could tell it took all her restraint to keep from breaking their arms. Here he could see open kegs of liquor—people were passing cups of it everywhere.

Yar turned and shouted something he couldn't quite make out over the thunderous tumult around them. He shrugged helplessly and pointed to his ears. She nodded, accepted a couple of cups of liquor from one of the Purity Leaguers, and handed him one. Data, too, took one—*That's right,* Riker thought, *he's capable of eating and drinking. Practically human in every way physically.* Though of course Data couldn't metabolize food—he would eject it later.

Following the lead of the men around him, Riker raised one fist in the air and began to shout. Of course, nobody could hear him. Data and Yar began to shout, too—and to Riker's eye they all looked like dutiful members of the League.

Slowly they began to work their way around toward the far side of the bonfire, closer to Archo Hospital. Riker had a feeling, somehow, that when violence erupted, it would be in that direction. He wanted them . . . if not in the middle of it, at least close enough for firsthand observation.

At one point Riker turned to Data and mouthed: "How many people are here?"

Data used his fingers to flash a quick number: 5-5-0-0. *Fifty-five hundred.* Riker had estimated three or four thousand, but Data's number had to be closer to the truth. The android could count samples and extrapolate far better than he could.

On the far side of the bonfire they found a crude wooden platform already set up before the entrance of the Archo Hospital complex. A few men stood on the platform, shouting slogans he couldn't hear and periodically pointing at the line of six bored-looking peace officers who stood on the hospital's steps. The peace officers all wore riot gear, complete with shields, masks, and billy clubs.

"I thought you said this was going to be a riot!" he said slowly to Tasha, mouthing the words carefully so she could read his lips. It wasn't so much a riot as a boisterous demonstration, he decided. The six peace officers could be overwhelmed in seconds if a crowd this size turned violent.

"Wait!" she answered. "It will get worse!"

Riker turned his attention back to the platform. It seemed to be the center of protest activity. In front of it, several dozen men and women passed out pamphlets, flyers, and even banner signs with antimixer slogans printed on them:

ARCHARIA IS FOR HUMANS
WE WELCOME THE PLAGUE!
DEATH TO MIXERS

These had to be the demonstration's organizers . . . or at least a step closer to them. Riker approached, and a girl of perhaps sixteen pressed a flyer into his hands, smiling broadly at him. A redheaded young man with a full red beard pressed a banner on him—"Better Dead Than Impure!" He motioned for Riker to wave it.

Riker handed the sign to Data and turned back, but the girl and the redheaded man had moved on. He started for the platform, hoping to find someone in charge . . . when suddenly a bell began to toll.

The clear ringing tone cut through the noise of the demonstration. Everyone froze for a second, and between peals Riker could hear the crackle and hiss of the giant bonfire. The whole crowd seemed to be holding its breath in anticipation. Everyone began to turn toward the platform.

Spotlights went on, illuminating the stage in a soft, warm glow. Slowly, carefully, an old man in white robes climbed the steps to stand before them. He had to be seventy or eighty years old, Riker thought, and his steel-gray beard stretched nearly to his waist. Could this be the mysterious Father Veritas? Could this really be the secretive leader of the Purity League? Riker felt his pulse quicken.

A whispering sound came from the multitude: "Father Veritas!" most of them seemed to be saying.

"Friends." The old man's voice held a slight quaver, but it still boomed across the square—amplified by some hidden speaker system, Riker assumed. *"Friends, I am Brother Paul, a close friend of Father Veritas. Tonight I bring you a message from the Father himself. He bids me to thank you all for your support. The day of human freedom is at hand. Death to mixers!"*

"Freedom is ours!" the crowd shouted back.

So this wasn't Father Veritas, Riker thought, but one of his inner circle, sent out to speak the gospel to the multitudes.

"Are you with the League?" Brother Paul demanded.

"Freedom is ours!" the crowd roared.

"Do you love your freedom?"

"Freedom is ours!" the crowd roared again.

"Will you follow the Father to pure human salvation?"

"Freedom is ours!" the crowd screamed. *"Death to mixers! Death to mixers! Death to mixers!"*

Riker thought it sounded like a litany—everyone around them seemed to expect the questions and know the proper response. The Purity League certainly had draped itself in the trappings of a religion, he decided . . . complete with Fathers and Brothers.

"You know what must be done!" Brother Paul shouted. *"Now is the time for human freedom!* Now! **Now!** *Now!"*

Cheering, the crowd rushed the hospital's front steps. The peace officers holding the riot gear—all smirking with ill-concealed glee—simply stepped aside for them.

Riker gaped in shock. The mob raced past the peace officers, up the broad marble steps, between the tall black marble columns, and straight to the hospital's front door. They began to pound on the glass doors with their fists.

"Death to mixers!" they continued to shout. "Death to mixers! Death to mixers!"

Riker let one hand fall to his concealed phaser. If the crowd burst into the hospital and went on a killing spree, the three of them would have no choice but to reveal themselves and try to stop the rioters—without the help of the peace officers, if necessary. *If only we had real phasers,* he thought with frustration. A single hit on light stun might render a lightly built man unconscious for a few minutes, but burly men like so many of these—men with their adrenaline already pumped up—would hardly notice it.

Suddenly a forcefield crackled to life. It stretched across the whole front façade of the hospital . . . and slowly it began to extend outward, pushing all the attacking men and women away from the doors and windows, then down the steps toward the street. Riker let himself relax. It seemed the hospital had prepared for Father Veritas and his followers after all—and had a safe, nonviolent solution to the problem. He couldn't have come up with a better answer himself.

Relieved, he turned his attention back to the platform. Several people with old-fashioned megaphones had taken Brother Paul's place—and Brother Paul was nowhere to be seen now. *Spirited off to Purity League Headquarters, no doubt,* Riker thought with dismay. *If only I had a minute to talk to him.*

He squinted, but the floodlit glow that had surrounded Brother Paul was gone, making it difficult to see. Since the men now on the platform all wore shorter beards and plain clothes, in the semidarkness he didn't think he was seeing them well enough to be able to identify them again.

Shouting "A pure race is a good race!" and "Mixers must never be tolerated," they exhorted the audience to rise up and take back their planet. But the moment had passed; Brother Paul's magic no longer worked, at least not for these pedestrian rabble-rousers. The crowds began to disperse, streaming off down the five convergent streets in knots of ten or twenty at a time.

"Sir," Data said, "perhaps we should try to follow one of the groups."

Riker nodded. He had just been thinking the same thing. He turned slowly, looking at the crowd still around the podium.

The assembled people liked what they were hearing. Some cheered, while others continued to chant "Veritas!" over and over.

And just as suddenly as the riot had begun, the whole demonstration seemed to end. Men and women streamed away from the square, heading up the five streets that led away. The people with the megaphones hopped down and fled.

"Which way, Will?" Data asked.

Riker hesitated, turning slowly. Some of the rioters had begun to smash windows, throw stones, and try to overturn ground cars along the various streets. The peace officers had given up their posts and joined in.

But he had a feeling these people were, if not innocent, at least not clued in to the ringleaders. Cattle, easily manipulated, sent to do the Purity League's dirty work.

He made his decision: "This way." And he started up the street after the men with the megaphones.

Chapter Sixteen

AFTER HIS THIRD TANKARD of blood wine, Worf felt himself getting as plastered as the rest of his new-found Klingon friends. His tongue kept tripping over itself, but between bouts of song, fistfights, and bragging matches, he managed to piece together most of the details of what had brought Captain Krot and his men to this place.

Captain Krot had realized his ship would be caught on Archaria III as soon as the plague broke loose if he did not move quickly. Their cargo—fifty thousand tons of grain, destined for the qagh farms on Kra'togh IV—had already been delivered. They just had a few repairs to make to their warp drive.

"If we had left one day sooner," Krot said, "we never would have known about the plague. Bah! Bad luck follows me."

After cunningly bribing the docking clerk in charge of their vessel, they'd lifted off. "Your life will be spared if you delete our departure record!" Krot had said. He burst out laughing when he tried to describe the clerk's horrified expression when faced with a mek'leth at his throat!

Unfortunately, their emergency warp-drive repairs had not held up. Due to primary warp-core failure, they had only gotten as far as orbit.

It was then that they picked up a transmission to the *Enterprise.* Immediately Krot ordered a landing on one of the moons . . . and they were fortunate enough to spot this old base. It already had two ships parked here—they figured they would wait out the plague while they made repairs.

"We did not know that Klingons ran the *Enterprise!"* Krot proclaimed.

Worf silently congratulated himself on discreetly returning his human away team to the *Enterprise* shortly after his first cup of blood wine. The captain raised his tankard. "To Klingons everywhere!"

"To Klingons!" Worf echoed.

The rest of Krot's crew began to chant, again, and Worf drained his blood wine in two long gulps.

The world swam fuzzily before dropping back into focus.

"What will you do now?" Worf asked. "The system is under quarantine. You may not leave."

"Why should I care about a human quarantine? This plague does not affect Klingons!"

"It is better to cooperate," Worf said sagely.

"Have another drink!" Krot passed him a tankard. "And tell me more about this great Captain Picard of yours! Perhaps he will listen to reason—or a mek'leth, eh?"

"You must meet him! He is a great leader. Do not pull a mek'leth on him, though, or I will have to kill you!"

"Just try!"

Worf struggled to his feet. He couldn't quite get them to work. *Too much blood wine,* he realized. *Maybe—maybe I have said enough.*

Krot was laughing.

That was the last thing he remembered.

Chapter Seventeen

AS THEY TRAILED THE MEN AND WOMEN responsible for organizing the rally at the hospital, Riker tried to get as close to them as he could without attracting their attention. Luckily they seemed too preoccupied . . . they never looked back to see if anyone was following. They simply assumed they were safe. *Amateurs,* Riker realized thankfully. *They really have no idea what they're doing, do they?*

Perhaps a hundred other rally-goers had taken this street away from the square. With all their talk and chatter—mixed in with more chanting and slogan-shouting—Riker had a hard time trying to eavesdrop on the people he was following.

He caught bits and pieces:

". . . mixers must be purged soon, or—"

". . . save our families before the next plague—"

". . . across the bridge, you know—"

None of it made much sense, though a lot of it offered tantalizing hints. The next plague? What did they know about the virus?

He quickened his pace, closing the gap, straining to hear more.

They left the commercial part of the city, crossed a small bridge, and entered a residential area. Tall houses now surrounded them, pressing close to each other.

Unfortunately, they chose that moment to pause in front of one of the houses. He almost walked into them and had to step around and keep going to avoid attracting their attention. He cursed his luck, and caught another fragment of dialog:

". . . can't be trusted tonight. Maybe tomorrow, if—"

Then they all entered the house and the door slammed shut. He heard a deadbolt slam home. Just when it had started to get interesting! "So much for that—" he said.

He turned to Yar and Data. "Did you hear any more of what they were saying than I did?"

"I heard everything, sir," Data replied.

That's right—Data had far keener hearing than a human, as well as a photographic memory.

"Summarize," he said. "What did they say? I caught something about a second plague—are they planning to wipe out the Peladians next?"

"No, sir. They believe the Peladians are responsible for the first virus, and that a second one is coming to finish the job. It is supposed to wipe out all the humans on the planet."

Riker shook his head. "Then they don't know anything about it."

"Apparently not."

He had chosen the wrong group to follow.

He turned around and found the street deserted. "And we lost the rest of the rioters."

"Perhaps we should return to the hospital," Data suggested. "It might be possible to pick up Brother Paul's trail. Someone might have seen which way he went."

"That's our best hope," Riker agreed. "Let's go!"

They set off at a jog, and fifteen minutes later they reached the hospital complex once more. Most of the people had left, but several hundred had stayed behind. They all stood around the bonfire, drinking, singing protest songs, and watching the flames. It seemed rather pathetic to Riker.

He searched the faces in the crowd but did not recognize anyone. *Another dead end,* he thought bitterly. This mission was not going well.

"Sir." Data pointed to the left, and Riker squinted into the darkness at several shapes moving along the hospital's wall behind the bushes. They moved like phantoms, keeping low to the ground.

"What are they doing?" he asked Data softly. "Your eyes are better than mine."

"They appear to be planting explosive charges. However, from the looks of the devices they are not powerful enough to do any real damage. The hospital's forcefield will protect it."

Riker sucked in a deep breath. "Terrorists . . . this is what we've been waiting for. Keep an eye on them—we're going to chase them all the way to Father Veritas if we have to!"

The shapes suddenly sprinted away from the hospital. A heartbeat later, a series of brilliant flashes and thunderous explosions sounded. Bushes flew and clods of dirt started to rain down. The people around the bonfire began to scream and run for cover.

"Now!" Riker shouted, sprinting. Data and Tasha Yar followed.

Together, they pounded up the street, gaining steadily on the terrorists. These men had a little more sense than the rally organizers—they kept glancing back, and clearly knew they were being followed.

At a five-way intersection, they split up. Riker picked the middle terrorist and kept chasing him. From behind, he heard sirens begin to ring. *Here comes the cavalry,* he thought, tucking down his head and speeding up his gait.

The man seemed to know he was about to be caught, since he abruptly stopped, turned, and raised his arm.

"Phaser!" Riker shouted. He dove to the side a heartbeat ahead of the beam of brilliant blue light that lashed out at him. He rolled to his feet and darted into an alley for cover.

The terrorist's weapon had been set on kill, he realized. Its beam played across the building behind him, blowing out part of the second-floor wall. Bits of bricks and mortar began to thud to the ground around him.

Riker scrambled for cover. The terrorist fired again, taking out a shop window. Flames leaped inside the building, and more alarms began to ring.

Riker ducked into an alley as a third shot nearly took off his head.

Panting, Riker pulled out his own phaser. He counted to three, leaned out, and fired. Years of target practice paid off—he caught the man square in the side.

But the terrorist seemed to shrug off the light stun setting. *I knew using local weapons was a mistake,* Riker thought. Next time he'd follow his instincts.

Raising his phaser, the terrorist fired at Riker again. Riker staggered back as the corner of the building exploded into debris. When he peeked out again, the man had taken off at a dead run.

Sirens wailed. Stepping out, Riker aimed his phaser and fired a second time. Once more he hit the mark—but once more the weak light-stun setting had little effect.

"Data! Yar!" he shouted.

"Here, sir!" came both voices.

That's one good thing. They're both still alive and safe.

After counting to ten, he peeked around the corner. Two buildings were on fire and a third had a hole in its second floor big enough to fly one of the *Enterprise*'s shuttles through. *The peace officers are not going to be happy,* he thought. *Not to mention the shopkeepers.*

"I think he's gone!" Riker shouted. "Join me in the alley!"

Yar dashed over, and a second later Data followed. Yar was disheveled and out of breath. Data looked a mess. Even by the dim, flickering light of the fires, Riker could see that Data's human makeup had been rubbed off along the whole left side of his face, revealing his golden skin. And one of his eyepieces had fallen out.

"I hear aircars closing in on our position," Data said. "I strongly suggest we move away from this alley, sir, before we are arrested."

"Right. We still have that terrorist to catch." He stepped out onto the street—but a couple of phaser shots lashed out at him. He wheeled back as bits of masonry blasted loose, peppering his face and hands. *That wasn't a stun setting,* he realized.

"I thought you said they didn't have kill settings enabled on their weapons!" he said to Yar, rubbing at the stinging little wounds. He was lucky they hadn't blinded him.

"That's only the civilians, sir. The peace officers have fully functioning phasers."

"Now you tell me!"

One of the burning buildings suddenly collapsed with a shower of sparks and an avalanche of duracrete slabs. Dust rose in a cloud—that would provide them with cover for a few minutes, he thought. They had to get out of here.

He glanced behind him, but the alley dead-ended. There was only one way out—the way they had come in.

"I don't think they saw you two," he said. "I'll draw their fire, then do an emergency beamout. Get past them and try to catch up with our terrorist friend."

"Where will we meet up?" Yar demanded.

"Back at the alley where we beamed in. Be there in one hour."

She gave a nod. "Got it."

Riker leaped from hiding with his phaser in hand, blasting at every figure he saw. *Just like target practice,* he thought.

Light stun certainly worked better at close range. One man fell, then another, then a third. Riker rolled, landed behind a pile of duracrete slabs and paused, listening. *Let them think I'm wounded.* He felt his heart pounding like a battering ram. *I'll catch them when they least expect it.*

On the count of ten, he leaped out again—but headed back the way he had come instead of making for the next natural hiding place. His tactic caught two more peace officers by surprise. They had been trying to sneak up behind him. A pair of perfectly executed shots took them down.

That's five. How many are there?

They would have caught him if he'd behaved like a sensible terrorist and tried to get away. *Too bad I'm neither sensible nor a terrorist. I'm not interested in getting away—at least, not on foot.*

He started counting again. *One more volley, then I'll have the* Enterprise *beam me to safety,* he thought.

Licking his lips, he tensed to spring—but a sudden intense burst of phaser fire struck the building directly behind and above him. Bricks blasted outward, and he felt several strike his back, throwing him to the ground. Moaning in pain, he reached for his combadge—but it had come off. *Where?* His fingers scrabbled in the dirt and debris, searching.

"Riker to *Enterprise,"* he said urgently, hoping it had somehow activated. "Emergency beamout—"

Then something struck the back of his head, and he knew no more.

Chapter Eighteen

TASHA YAR RAN until she thought her lungs would burst, and she still saw no sign of the terrorist in black. He must have turned off somewhere. They must have lost him.

She drew to a halt. Data paused, looking back at her. "Tasha?"

"I have to rest," she panted. She put her hands on her knees and bent over, feeling sick and dizzy.

Since leaving Commander Riker, they hadn't had any luck. The peace officers had spotted them and given chase, and it seemed an alert had been raised. Everywhere they went, they spotted uniformed men in riot gear.

"This is not the place for a rest," Data said.

She nodded. "I know. But there's nothing I can do about it. I can't go any farther!"

A line of peace officers rounded the corner several blocks up. They wore helmets and carried heavy shields and phasers in their hands—and for Tasha Yar, it brought back a flood of terrible memories. As a fist of panic clutched her heart, she felt herself start to shake. *I'm not home. This isn't a rape gang. If things get bad, all we have to do is beam back to the* Enterprise.

"This way, Tasha," Data said urgently, grabbing her arm and pulling her up a narrow street.

Her legs felt like deadwood, but Yar forced them to move. Data had better eyesight than she did; he must have spotted something, she thought—some way of escape short of an emergency beamout.

At least this alley smelled better than the first; hulking shapes of discarded packing material and machinery blocked her way, but she darted around them.

Suddenly Data pulled her into a deeply recessed doorway. "Shh!" he said.

Behind them, she heard footsteps entering the alley. Bright lights swung up and down the length. *Great. We're trapped.*

"I have bad news," he told her in a soft voice.

"It can't get any worse!"

"This appears to be a dead end."

"What!" She turned and looked at him. "You've got to be kidding! I thought you knew where you were going!"

"It seemed the logical place to run."

She bit her lip, then turned and tried the door behind them. It had an old-style round knob, smooth and hard and cold. And, of course, it was locked. And, of course, a phaser set on stun wouldn't open it. *I should have insisted we bring live weapons,* she thought. *What was I thinking? Never again!*

"Data . . . can you force this door open?" she asked.

"That would be an illegal act," he said. "Federation code 44.1.6 clearly states—"

"Circumstances warrant it! *Open the door!*"

"Very well." He gripped the knob and turned it sharply. Metal inside the knob broke. Then he pushed, but the door still didn't move.

"It appears to be bolted from the inside."

"So push!"

Using the flat of his hand, Data gave the door a sharp jab perhaps twenty centimeters above the knob. The wood splintered.

Yar glanced toward the street. Lights continued to sweep the length of the alley. The peace officers were making their way through boxes fifteen meters away.

"Hurry!"

Data rammed his fist through the hole with a loud bang, and as she watched with growing fear, he felt around inside.

One of the peace officers shouted, "I think they're ahead of us!"

"Ah. A simple deadbolt," Data said.

He slid it aside, withdrew his arm, and pushed the door open. *Finally!* Yar ducked inside, and Data followed, closing the door with a slight squeak.

Pitch darkness surrounded her. She paused, listening to the pounding of her heart, waiting for cries of *"There they are!"* from the peace officers.

"Shall I brace the door closed in case they try to break it down?"

"With what?"

"There is sufficient lumber on the floor."

"Then do it!"

Outside, someone tried the doorknob.

"I am holding it," Data whispered. "They will not pass."

Something heavy—a pair of shoulders?—thumped against the wood. Evidently Data's strength convinced them that entry wasn't possible; they moved on, talking in low voices.

"How well can you see?" she asked.

"Well enough," said Data. "There is sufficient infrared radiation for me to navigate the warehouse."

She hesitated. "Don't take this the wrong way. But I want you to take my arm and lead me to another exit."

"I have a better idea, Tasha." Picking her up in his strong arms, he carried her on a twisting course through the length of the warehouse. At last he stopped and set her down.

"Where are we?"

"The other side of the warehouse. This door is marked 'Exit.' "

She heard him undo a couple of bolts, then he opened a heavy steel fire door half a centimeter. A blade of light fell inside—she blinked, then realized it wasn't that bright, just spillover from the street. They were looking out onto a small side street.

Tasha put her eye to the crack and peeked out. The peace officers had moved on, apparently. The street was deserted.

She opened the door and eased out. Pressed up against the building, she made her way to the main street at the front of the building, peeked around the corner, and gave a sigh of relief. She saw the peace officers' backs—they were moving up the street quickly.

Then she froze in place. Movement on a nearby rooftop had caught her eye. A sniper?

"Data," she whispered. "Get up here! Who is that?"

She pointed across and up twenty meters to the roof of another warehouse. A man stood silhouetted against the larger moon. He was gazing at the peace officers. And he held something dark in his hands. *A phaser?*

"I believe he is taking atmospheric samples," Data said. "The device he is holding is a Starfleet tricorder of the type used on planetary surveys. It collects data from monitoring stations."

That puzzled her. "What's he doing out at this hour? It has to be past midnight!"

"It is 1:07 A.M., according to the local clock. The man appears to be waiting for the peace officers to leave. His expression appears nervous."

Interesting. He's doing something illegal. She felt a rising suspicion. "Something isn't right here," she said.

"I agree. He does not appear to be wearing a Starfleet uniform. Nor do I recognize him as one of the *Enterprise*'s crew. He should not be carrying Starfleet equipment."

"I meant he doesn't belong on top of a warehouse in the middle of the night," Yar said. "He's up to something. He might be one of the terrorists."

"Unlikely," Data said. "His build does not match that of any of the three men we chased. However, I agree that his presence and actions do appear suspicious. What course of action do you suggest?"

"Simple. Let's question him."

"How?"

She drew her phaser and passed it to him. "You're the expert marksman. If you hit him with both our phasers, it should stun him, even at this distance. Then it's just a matter of picking him up and interrogating him."

"What if he has legitimate business?"

"Then we apologize and buy him a drink at the nearest bar."

"Very well." Data accepted her phaser with his left hand, then pulled out his own with his right. He stepped forward, raised both arms, and fired both phasers simultaneously.

Both beams struck the man's chest. *Perfect shot!* Yar thought. Without a sound, he collapsed and lay still.

It took them five minutes to get across the street and up to the roof. A large and rather flashy aircar waited there with its door open and its powerful engines idling. Yar switched on its lights, and their glow lit up the whole rooftop.

"It would appear he landed here to watch the peace officers," Data said.

"Not with this tricorder." She picked it up and handed it to him. "What do you make of it?"

"Starfleet issue. A current model. It should not be in civilian hands."

"Then what was he doing with it?"

Data turned slowly. "There—that is the atmospheric monitoring station he must have been checking." He crossed to the small silver box and pulled it off the wall. When he flipped open the top, he read something inside. "As I expected, it is set to monitor particle content in the air."

"Do you mean dust?"

"Any particulate matter—dust, pollution, and pollen are three examples."

"How about . . . an airborne virus?"

"Like the plague virus?"

"Exactly."

"It would count that, too."

The man began to stir and moan. Tasha regarded him suspiciously. "I think we've just found the key to the puzzle," she said. "Keep him covered."

Crossing to where he lay, she began searching through his pockets. Not one but two phasers, a knife, and three sets of identification cards . . . all very interesting. One ID claimed he was a grain buyer, another an engineering-supply salesman, and the third a missionary priest. *A priest?* She knew they were fake; a grain-buying engineering-sales missionary-priest might conceivably exist, but each of the three IDs gave different names and home planets.

He stirred and moaned. *He'll be awake soon. Might as well get it over with.*

"Wake up!" she said, giving his shoulder a shake.

He opened his eyes suddenly and gasped. "What—where—"

"That's what I want to know," she said with an unkind smile. Phaser stuns left people disoriented; she meant to take advantage of it. "Who are you—really—and what can you tell me about this plague?"

"Let go of me!"

She released him. With Data standing there, he wouldn't get away.

"I work for the Archo City Hospital," he said, sitting up and rubbing his head. "What happened?"

"Uh-uh. Not with these ID cards, you don't. And you don't have a beard; you're no Archarian." She fanned the identification cards out in front of his face. "And I'll stake my job none of these is you. Care to try again?"

He climbed to his feet, brushed himself off, and adjusted his collar. An almost mocking smile came over his face. "Not this time."

Lights shimmered, and he began to disappear as a transporter beam energized around him.

"No you don't!" Yar cried.

She leaped into the beam with him—and the next thing she knew, they were standing on a single transporter pad in a small, nearly dark room—a spaceship?

She grabbed his shirt and flung him into the bulkhead. He hit with a bone-jarring crunch and an "oof" of pain.

"Give up," she said.

"You'll die!" he snarled and grabbed for something on the wall. *A phaser?*

She leaped forward and kicked him in the stomach, then gave him a chop to the back to the neck when he doubled over in pain. He collapsed, shuddered once, and didn't move.

"Computer—more light!" she called.

The room brightened. She turned slowly, taking stock of the situation . . . she was in a cramped little cabin stuffed to overflowing with equipment. And a lot of it looked like Starfleet property.

I've hit the jackpot, she thought. *If he isn't involved with the plague, I'm a Vulcan princess.*

Three huge metal cylinders, stamped with tiny print, stood along the back wall. She crossed to examine one. The pressure gauge read 0.004. Whatever had been inside wasn't there now.

Turning, she looked at the racks of assault rifles, phasers, and other weapons covering the second wall, the one to which she had him pinned. Shivering, she realized how lucky she had been. *If he'd gotten one of those, I would be toast now.*

She folded back the collar of her shirt, revealing her combadge, and tapped it once. "Yar to *Enterprise,*" she said.

"*Enterprise.* Habbib here," came an ensign's voice.

"Locate Commander Riker and Lieutenant Commander Data and beam them to these coordinates."

"Lieutenant Commander Data has been located . . . Commander Riker is not wearing his combadge, however."

That didn't sound like Riker. *He'll be all right,* she told herself. *He's a survivor. Like me.*

"Thanks," she said. "If you locate Commander Riker, let me know."

"Yes, Lieutenant. *Enterprise* out."

The shimmer of a transporter beam appeared next to her, and Data materialized an instant later. He turned slowly, looking around the cabin, then bent to examine the unconscious man.

"He is dead," Data announced.

"What! That's impossible!" She stared incredulously at his body. "I didn't hit him that hard!"

"Nevertheless, he *is* dead."

Quickly she bent and rolled him over. She got a whiff of something acrid—*pentium xolinate.* It was a Cardassian drug, invariably fast and fatal.

"Suicide," she said, frowning. "He took poison. He must have had it hidden in a tooth."

Data moved to the cylinders. "We need to analyze these," he said suddenly.

"Could they hold something biological?" she asked.

"Like a virus?" Data asked. "It is a possibility. Biological agents are usually seeded into the atmosphere of a planet at least half a kilometer above the surface, however, to allow a wide dispersal through wind currents."

"He had a transporter."

Data paused. "It is theoretically possible to beam compressed gasses; they would expand immediately upon transport. That might be a highly effective method of seeding an atmosphere."

That's how he did it, Yar thought. *I know that's how he did it!*

Data continued to examine the cylinders. "They are marked 'Agricultural Prions.' However, a label does not always adequately represent a container's true contents."

"The expression is 'Don't judge a book by its cover.' "

"I believe that is what I said."

"We have to get them up to the *Enterprise.*" Frowning, she moved to the front of the ship and gazed out the viewport at a vast duracrete landing field. The morning twilight had just begun. In the thin gray predawn light, she saw dozens of larger starships surrounding their little ship. *We're in the Archo City Spaceport,* she thought.

"Let's fly her up to one of the shuttle bays," she said suddenly, sliding into the pilot's seat. "We can get a security team aboard and strip her down to her bulkheads, if necessary. Our friend there must be involved in the plague, somehow."

"That would seem a logical conclusion," Data said.

The ship's controls hadn't been locked or encrypted, Yar saw. With the hatches dogged, he must have considered his ship secure. He hadn't counted on her beaming aboard with him.

Powering up the impulse engines, she studied the layout of the controls. Basic operations appeared straightforward. She knew she wouldn't have any trouble flying this ship.

An intercom crackled: "This is Archo Spaceport Control. Power down your engines, *Paladium.* This planet is quarantined—you may not lift off."

"Negative, Control," Yar said. "This is Lieutenant Yar. I am bringing this vessel up for a rendezvous with the *Enterprise.*"

"Permission to lift off is expressly denied," the voice insisted. "Power down, *Paladium,* or we will be forced to take drastic action!"

She glanced at Data. "Drastic action? What are they capable of, putting us on report? They don't have any pursuit ships or missile batteries. This is an agricultural planet."

"I believe they are bluffing," Data said.

"That's all I need to know." Tasha Yar brought the engines to full life. A low but powerful vibration spread through the hull. She initiated the liftoff sequence.

"Paladium!" Control said. *"Power down! Now!"*

"Negative," she replied. "You have our flight plan. We'll see you in orbit."

She lifted off smoothly, and the landing field began to dwindle away below.

Next she tapped her combadge. "Yar to *Enterprise,"* she said.

"Enterprise. Habbib here."

"We are aboard a small starship called the *Paladium,"* she said. "We are bringing it up now. Slap a level-one forcefield around this ship as soon as we land in the shuttle bay."

"No containment field is necessary," Habbib said. "Restrictions on travel to and from the planet to the *Enterprise* have been lifted."

"Then we have a cure for the plague?" She felt a brief surge of elation.

"Negative, *Paladium.* The virus is on the *Enterprise* as well. We are now under the same quarantine restrictions as Archaria III."

Yar exchanged a look with Data. *How—* She shook her head. *Someone was sloppy,* she thought.

She said to Habbib, "I want a security detail standing by when we land. And alert sickbay. We may have the cause of the plague on board."

"Understood, *Paladium,"* Habbib said. "Security will be standing by. *Enterprise* out."

"That's it!" Control snarled over the intercom. *"We are fining your account one hundred thousand credits,* Paladium*!"*

"Go ahead," Yar replied. She severed the connection and accelerated toward the *Enterprise.*

Chapter Nineteen

THE ANNOYING BUZZ in the back of Will Riker's head slowly materialized into the murmur of voices. He opened one eye to the smallest of slits. *Big mistake.* Fireworks seemed to go off inside his skull, flares and starbursts and supernovas all mixed up together. He groaned despite himself and pressed his eye shut again. *Everything hurts.* Even breathing was a chore. He couldn't remember feeling this bad since his big second-year survival drop at the Academy. *A week alone on a jungle planet with only a knife, a compass, and my wits. Why did I ever elect to take Advanced Survival before I was really ready for it?* The raw elements—including a six-day hurricane to beat anything ever seen on Earth—had defeated him utterly when a tree blew over and pinned him down. He had lain there in the muck and mud, feeding the alien equivalent of giant leeches, for three days until rescuers arrived. He had counted himself lucky to survive.

This time, it had been a building.

At least I am *waking up,* he thought, trying to feel optimistic. There was a faint ringing sound in his ears just a few octaves below the chatter of voices. An outside noise? An inside noise? Hallucination? *Better hurt than dead.* That's what his instructor, Dr. Neelam, had told him when he limped in to give his oral report on his failure. *Kindly Dr. Neelam.* The image of his instructor's beaming face appeared in his mind, Dr. Neelam saying: "The sloppiest job I've ever seen, but you lived through it, Bill."

"I'm called Will now," he told Dr. Neelam.

"Hey, pal," a rough voice beside him said. "Ready to try sitting up?"

"Huh?" Riker opened both eyes, and after the world stopped moving, he managed to focus on the speaker—a man about his own age, tall and broad-shouldered, dressed all in shades of brown right down to a long dark shag of brown beard. He was grinning—a friendly grin, Riker decided after a minute's hesitation.

Archaria III. Away team. Right.

"The sleeper wakes!" the man went on. Offering his hand, he said, "Want me to help you sit up, pal? I hear your name is Will."

"Was I talking out loud?"

"Yep. Need a hand?"

"Uh . . . give me a minute. Where am I?"

"Some detention center. I'm not quite sure which one yet. Probably East Quadrant. That's where they nabbed us."

"Oh." Gingerly he felt his scalp. Assorted lumps, bumps, cuts, and abrasions—perhaps even a mild concussion, from the ringing in his ears. *I'll ask Dr. Neelam to look me over first thing. No, I mean Dr. Crusher.*

Wait. That was back on the ship. He paused, frowning. The *Enterprise.* Where was he? *Under a building. No. In a detention center.* He tried to focus on his newfound friend, the beaming man with the beard. What was the fellow's name? Had he said?

"Where—" he said again. *No, I already asked that.*

"Say, you are fuzzed out, aren't you? Dee-ten-shun Cen-ter. East Quadrant. They got a hundred and twelve of us in the roundup." The man gave a low chuckle and offered his hand. Riker took it, and the man pulled him to a sitting position.

That was a mistake. The world swirled like a whirlpool around him.

"You have a family name, Will?"

"Riker."

"Don't know 'em, sorry." He stuck out his hand again. "Mine is Clarence Darling."

"Clarence *Darling?*"

"Yes, sweetheart." Clarence rolled his eyes. "Old name. First settlers, so we're supposed to be proud. Nothing to do about it now."

At least Clarence had a sense of humor. Riker gave a low chuckle as he turned his head—not too quick!—to look around. Despite his caution, the room rolled like a ship on high seas, the floor rising up, the walls moving in. He tasted bile and gulped hastily. The ringing in his ears grew worse, louder and more shrill, a perfect bell tone had it come from a bell.

He pressed his eyes shut again. *I should have been a doctor. I could have healed myself.*

"Hope you don't mind," Darling said, "but I kind of appointed myself your watchdog. While you were unconscious, I mean. The pos picked you clean, but at least *our* side left you alone."

Pos? Oh . . . PO's—peace officers. He hadn't heard that slang term in years; it figured that it would still be circulating on a backwater planet like Archaria III. *Picked me clean . . . ?* Riker pulled himself up on his elbows—*Slowly! Don't rush it!*—and noticed his boots were missing. He still had his slightly fuzzy brown socks, though. They looked a little silly, and he wiggled his toes and took a perverse delight in noting *they* didn't hurt. They were the only thing in his whole body without their own private aches and pains.

Then more urgently he felt his pockets. *All gone. Phaser, combadge, everything.* He really had been cleaned out. Everything of any potential value had been removed. *Great. Humanity is supposed to be beyond racial prejudice, let alone petty thievery.*

"The pos roll everyone who comes in unconscious. Must be the Ferengi in them." Darling frowned suddenly. "You don't look so good all of a sudden. I think you need a doctor, Will. Better lie down till we can get out of here." He put one hand on Riker's chest and pushed him gently back onto the bench where he had been lying. "That's an order, soldier!"

Riker stiffened. *Soldier. Does he know I'm from the Federation? No, can't be, I'm not a soldier, anyway. Never mind that Bili used to call me that.* It had to be just a slang term of affection for a newfound friend, like "pal." *And I need a friend here. No combadge, no rescue. Dr. Neelam would approve. It's my survival test all over again.*

He focused his eyes on a water stain on the ceiling tiles directly overhead. The ringing in his head let up a little. The burble of voices rose around him. *What I wouldn't give for a minute of perfect silence. Or a doctor. Or a combadge—*

"I don't think we'll be here much longer," Darling said suddenly. "It's nearly dawn."

Riker felt something run down his cheek and gave a little shudder. *Bugs.* He hated bugs. But when he touched the spot, his fingers came away wet. *Not bugs. Blood.* He stared at the crimson smear. *A doctor. I'd better call Dr. Crusher. Time for the cavalry to rescue me. So much for Billy-the-Kid Riker, boy hero.*

What would Captain Picard do? *The captain wouldn't split up or lose his combadge or let a building fall on his head.* This was going to make one hell of a bad report. One *hell* of a bad report. *At least Data and Yar got away.* Rescue? He could have laughed—they wouldn't even know where to look. He'd have to find them . . . if they hadn't already reported him missing to the *Enterprise.*

The alley . . . perhaps they would be waiting for him there.

He levered himself up on his elbows again. And just like before, the universe began to tilt alarmingly. He felt himself starting to slide off the world, almost as though gravity weren't working quite right here. But that was ridiculous, wasn't it?

With a "Mph!" he lay back down. "Do I get to make a call, or am I stuck here?" he asked Darling. He forced the words out slowly. "What's the, ah, protocol for being arrested these days?"

"You *are* new to this rabble-rousing stuff, aren't you?" Darling chuckled. "There are too many of us. The most they're going to do is charge us with misdemeanors, issue citations, and chuck us out on our ears. And they probably won't even bother with the citations because nobody's going to pay them. Most of the pos are members of the League anyway. If they weren't on duty, they'd all be with us in the streets. After all, we all want the same thing, right?"

"Yeah." He had definitely gotten the impression that the peace officers supported the League. Had it only been last night? It seemed an eternity away.

Riker took a deep breath, shuddering a bit at a new stabbing pain in his left shoulder. *What's the first thing you do after a disaster? Take inventory.* No boots, no possessions. Easy enough. He slowly flexed his muscles. *Focus,* he told himself. Fingers, hands, arms; feet, legs, neck, and spine. All extremities in place. Lots of small pains, a couple of larger cuts and abrasions on his hands where he had fallen. Plus the assorted injuries to his head and that stabbing pain in his shoulder. Bruised but not broken, by and large, he decided. *I'd give anything for those bells to stop ringing.* If only he could think clearly. *A plan. I need a plan. What would Dr. Neelam do? "Survival first," he always said in class. "Worry about the civilized niceties later."*

Darling said, "So, spill the details. What happened to you, Will?"

"I got in a firefight with the pos and a building fell on me." He turned his head to look around the room more carefully. This time at least it stayed on an even keel. "Rather, the pos blasted it down on top of me."

"They used phasers set on high?" Darling gave a low whistle. "First I've heard of them using deadly force against us! Well, almost deadly force. You must have really gotten them angry."

"Afraid so. It was my own damn fault. We didn't want to be arrested and stunned two of them."

"Ever been picked up before?"

"No."

"I thought so. I tried to fight it my first time, too—and got my skull bashed with a billy for my troubles. This is my fifth time. Peaceful cooperation, that's the only way, once they've made the pinch."

"But what about . . ." He lost his train of thought for an instant and floundered. "You know?"

Darling seemed to pick up on it. "If you're in here with us, that means they didn't write you up. You're just another drunk-and-disorderly Leaguer they arrested for disturbing the peace. And with things the way they are . . . they don't have enough prisons to hold us all, even if they wanted to." He shrugged. "They can't lock up half the planet, after all!"

"The human half, you mean."

Darling grinned wolfishly. "The human *majority.*"

For a second Riker saw the true nature of the League in his rescuer's eyes. *Not a friend.* It was insidious, these racist beliefs. And yet he knew he needed Darling—needed the decent human inside him who would go out of his way to help a stranger.

Doors on the far side of the room banged open, and a short man in a black uniform strolled in, frowning. Unlike the others, he was clean-shaven and there was something odd about the shape of his skull . . . too elongated, too pointy on top.

Hisses, boos, and jeering catcalls greeted him. "Mixer!" Riker heard Darling snarl under his breath. So that was it—this was a Peladian.

"Listen up!" the Peladian peace officer said in a loud voice. He thumped the data padd he held with one slender finger. "All prisoners are being released on their own recognizance. Take advantage of this little learning experience and stay indoors tonight. The governor has declared a curfew, and anyone caught on the streets after dark will face the full force of the law!"

Darling chuckled. So did most of the others in the room. Riker looked around in bewilderment. Were they insane as well as prejudiced?

"What's so funny?" he finally whispered.

"That's the same speech he's given every morning for the last week!" Darling replied.

The smooth-cheeked officer glared until the laughter died down. "That's better," he finally said. "Now, form a line and make your way outside in an orderly manner. If you cooperate, you'll be home for breakfast."

Turning, he stalked out the door with the data padd slapping against his thigh. More mocking laughter trailed him, and jeering cries of, "Get off the planet, mixer!"

"Damn arrogant bastard," Darling snarled under his breath. "Thinks he's better than us!"

Riker held his tongue, but couldn't stop the thought: *He* is *better than all of you.* Cordial as Darling seemed, the underpinnings of his Purity League beliefs left no doubt about his true nature: xenophobe, human-supremacist, and violent-terrorist. *I must not forget that,* Riker told himself. *He thinks I'm one of them. That's the only reason he's behaving so well toward me.*

Chapter Twenty

WORF WOKE SLOWLY and groaned. *My head!* If felt like a split melon. Sitting up, he looked blearily around the room.

Klingons lay sprawled everywhere around him, snoring. Krot—Skall—Karqq—all the others . . .

It was the blood wine, he thought with growing horror. He had forgotten to check in with the *Enterprise* and make his report. He knew a human captain wouldn't kill him for such an oversight, but he felt he deserved execution.

He had lost track of his mission. He had neglected his duty. . . .

Never again, he thought. Even though he had been exposed to the plague virus and could not return to the *Enterprise,* he should have made his report. They could have been depending on him.

Struggling to his feet, he staggered a bit as his center of balance shifted. He searched for his lost helmet and finally spotted it in the corner, where Krot had flung it. Picking it up, he fitted it back on his head. Luckily the comm unit still worked. He clicked it on with his chin.

"Worf to *Enterprise,*" he said.

"Enterprise, Habbib here," came the reply.

"I wish to make a report," he said. "I have been exposed to the plague virus and will be remaining on this moon until a cure is found."

"Negative, sir," came the reply. "The whole ship has been exposed to the plague virus. There is no longer a quarantine situation. Captain Picard left orders for you to be transported back the minute you report in."

Worf frowned. *That is not good news,* he thought. Something terrible must have happened aboard ship—a medical disaster—for the disease to be loose on board.

"Energize," he said.

He had a very bad feeling inside.

Dr. Crusher rubbed bleary, burning eyes. *Sixteen cases,* she thought. Between the *Enterprise* and the *Constitution,* they now had *sixteen* confirmed cases of the plague. *This is a nightmare.*

The medical teams of both ships had combined aboard the *Enterprise.* And they still weren't making any progress.

And Dr. Tang, whenever they consulted him, seemed more depressed than ever. He continued to recommend quarantining the planet forever.

We need luck. And inspiration, Dr. Crusher thought. *We're missing something . . . something obvious.*

Not for the first time, she went back to the very core of the problem. *We have a virus that can squeeze through a level-1 containment field. How?* She studied its diagram on the monitor. *What are the possibilities?*

Teleportation? *Impossible!*

Changing its shape to something smaller? *Possible?* They had seen no sign of any metamorphic properties, however, and they had been watching live samples for hours. *Not likely,* she finally decided. *It's a form of Rhulian flu. It doesn't change shape.*

What else? *It needs a Trojan horse,* she thought. *Some way to sneak through a containment field without being caught or identified.* But it couldn't do that in its present form. It would have to be broken down and reassembled.

It's modular! Suddenly she had a horrible vision of how it might work. *Two or five or ten smaller parts, all coming together to form a virus . . . airborne miniparticles, drifting in the air until they meet up, then uniting to become the plague virus!*

She had never heard of any organism working in such a manner. But that didn't mean it wasn't possible. The added hooks on the NXA protein strands—those could be assembly instructions.

But it would have to be alive in its component parts, too. *What's alive but smaller than a virus?*

Nanotechnology? No, it couldn't possibly be mechanical in origin. Noroids? Sondarian frets? Prions? It could be any of those—or any of several dozen other obscure but normally innocuous life forms. *Things we don't screen out with biofilters because they're harmless,* she thought. *Things small enough to slip through a level-1 containment field.*

"Computer," she said. "Begin a new analysis of blood sample 76-B."

That was the most recent specimen drawn from Deanna Troi. "Find and catalog every life form and ever matter particle smaller than a virus."

The computer spoke. *"There are an estimated two hundred thousand subviral particles. Analysis will take approximately forty-one minutes."*

Dr. Crusher sighed. More delays. But she didn't see any alternatives. They certainly weren't making any progress with standard techniques or antiviral drugs.

"Begin analysis," she said. This looked like another two-cup problem.

She headed for the replicator and made her first cup of tea. Just as she was about to settle down to wait out the computer report, Captain Picard and Captain van Osterlich strode into sickbay. Behind them, waiting in the hall, she saw half a dozen security officers.

She stood. "What's happened?" she asked.

"Yar and Data are on their way up," Picard said. "They have stolen a starship. They claim it belongs to the man responsible for setting the plague loose on Archaria III."

Dr. Crusher felt her breath catch in her throat. *This could be the break we need,* she thought.

"What's on board?" she demanded. "Are there any cultures or samples . . . or a cure?"

"They weren't specific—but they have something they want analyzed immediately in xenobiology."

"Let's go," she said, grabbing a medical tricorder.

Yar piloted the *Paladium* into the *Enterprise*'s shuttle bay 2, then set the little ship down. After she had powered down the impulse engines, she unsealed the hatches, rose, and hurried into the main compartment.

Data had been busy taking down weapons, she saw. She whistled at the rack of ten Federation heavy assault phaser rifles he had uncovered.

"I haven't seen any of these since the war with Cardassia," she said, taking one down and turning it over in her hands.

"They are probably war surplus," he said. "This particular model was decommissioned seven years ago."

She turned hers over and examined the handle. The serial number had been neatly and methodically burned off with a phaser. No way to trace it back to whoever legally bought or sold it last. *Just another sign our unknown friend was up to no good,* she thought.

She put the phaser back into the rack, then glanced down at the man who had committed suicide rather than get caught. Everything seemed to point to his involvement in something big. And yet she saw no sign of anything to do with the virus . . . except those cylinders.

"Status report!" Captain Picard called, as he led Dr. Crusher and half-a-dozen others aboard.

Yar filled him in while Dr. Crusher hurried to the cylinders and began taking tricorder scans.

"This is it!" Crusher announced, and excitement made her voice crack. "These cylinders contain the three different elements that make up the plague virus! I want them beamed to xenobiology—we've got to start taking them apart to see how these prions work."

"Prions?" Captain Picard asked, looking puzzled.

"Yes—I figured it out in sickbay this morning. The virus is a composite organism. It consists of three prions. When they come together, they interlock, rewrite each other's RNA, and a virus cell is born. Individually the prions are harmless. We have hundreds of different ones in our bodies, and they don't do anything. Our transporter doesn't filter them out, and they are small enough when airborne to pass through a level-one containment field!"

"And that's how it got loose on my ship," Picard said, nodding. "It makes sense."

Data said, "We believe our suspect beamed the prions directly over the city, seeding the air. That's how it managed to disperse so quickly."

"I've got to get back to sickbay," Dr. Crusher said. "This is the best development we could have had. I know we'll have a cure soon."

Chapter Twenty-one

THEIR RELEASE WENT BETTER than Riker could have hoped. Darling spotted a couple more of his League pals and drafted them into helping get Riker out the door. They were burly, bearded men, strong as oxen, and when they draped Riker's arms across their shoulders for support, his feet barely touched the ground.

Darling signed all their names in an arrest record book, and five seconds later they were out on the street. The morning thoroughfares bustled with activity, and Riker sensed at once that something had happened—something big. An almost electric undercurrent ran through everyone in sight.

Darling grabbed a bearded man and demanded, "What happened? What's all the excitement?"

"Haven't you heard? They caught the man responsible for the plague! And Starfleet says they'll have a cure for it by nightfall!"

"Who was responsible?" Riker demanded.

"Some crazy off-worlder! Can you believe it? He wasn't even one of *us!*"

Pulling away, the man hurried down the street.

So much for the Purity League theory, Riker thought. He exchanged a glance with Darling. *I've spent the night chasing phantom terrorists, having buildings fall on my head, and getting locked up with racist crackpots—for nothing!*

"Well," Darling said, "that's quite a development. It *wasn't* the Peladians after all."

The man holding Riker's right arm let go. "You take him!" he said to Darling. "I have to get home—I want to see the news!"

"Me, too!" said Darling's other friend. He ducked out from under Riker's other arm and sprinted up the street.

Riker wobbled a bit, but Darling steadied him. "Hey, I'll still look out for you, pal," Darling said. "I've come this far. I'll see you safely home."

"If you can get me to a comm station," Riker said, "I'll call for transportation."

"Easily done!" Turning, Darling pointed to a public comm unit on the corner across from them. "Come on!"

He helped Riker hobble across the street, then stood watching while Riker activated the unit.

"This is William Riker," he said to the computer. "I need to talk to the duty officer aboard the *Starship Enterprise.*"

Darling gaped at him. "The *Enterprise?* Are you crazy? What do you want with Starfleet scum?"

"Just a second and I'll show you," Riker said.

In ten seconds Geordi La Forge appeared on the screen.

"What happened, sir?" La Forge said. "You look terrible. We've had half the peace officers in the city searching for you since midnight!"

"The peace officers arrested me," Riker said. "It's a long story. I need transportation to sickbay . . . I think I have a mild concussion . . . and maybe a couple of cracked bones."

"Right," La Forge said. "Stay there, sir. I'll trace the comm signal back to your location."

"Thanks." Riker turned to Darling, who was staring at him incredulously.

"You—you *lied* to me!" Darling said.

"No I didn't," Riker said. He grinned. "You made a lot of assumptions about me based on my appearance. Think about it the next time you see a mixer . . . or a Peladian!"

He hated to go out with a lecture, but somehow it seemed fitting. Darling certainly needed his myopic racist worldview expanded.

A transporter beam began to shimmer around him.

"People aren't always what they seem . . . and if you look, you'll find new friends in the *oddest* places!"

Chapter Twenty-two

"THIS IS HOW the virus works," Dr. Crusher said to the assembled senior officers of the *Enterprise* and the *Constitution.* The meeting room fell silent.

"The virus begins life as three different prions." A computer simulation showed the three different microorganisms. "Separately these prions are harmless. But when they meet up—in the air or in a human body—they join together to form a more complex organism . . . a multiprion."

The holographic projection showed all three prions integrating themselves into one larger cell.

"Their protein strands hook together, and a new multiprion is born. Its first task is to rewrite its own RNA. In effect, it turns itself into a virus cell. Now, imagine it happening with thousands of prions at once and you'll see how quickly people can become infected."

Captain Picard stepped forward. "Thanks to Dr. Spencer, Dr. Tang, and Dr. Crusher, we now have a cure—a fourth prion, one we designed ourselves. We have already begun seeding Archaria III's atmosphere with it. This fourth prion hunts for the other three, attaches itself to them, and disables the multiprion genetic codes. In short, they are turned back into harmless prions once more."

"Sir, who is responsible?" Geordi La Forge asked.

"Good question." Picard cleared his throat. "Officially, Starfleet and the planetary governor are assigning blame to the Purity League. That organization has been officially outlawed and disbanded, so some good has come out of this disaster."

"And unofficially?" Worf asked.

Van Osterlich rose. "Unofficially . . . we don't know. The one suspect we have is dead, and he doesn't seem to exist in any official Starfleet databases. His identity cards are fake. His starship's registration is fake. Nothing aboard his ship has a serial number or identification mark of any kind. He is simply a blank—officially, he doesn't exist. Whether he worked for himself or someone else is still open to conjecture. However, I think it's safe to say that this is the work of some outside party with significant resources . . . an organization that took advantage of the Purity League's racist attitudes to test a new type of weapon."

"The big question is motive," Captain Picard said. He looked from face to face, and his expression grew even more serious. "It can't be racial purity. It can't be the Purity League. In fact, Starfleet has only been able to come up with one possible motive. . . . *Practice.*"

In sickbay, William Riker lay on a biobed next to Deanna Troi, resting and listening to the almost jubilant hubbub around them. *They have their cure. Everything is going to work out.* He smiled.

"A penny for your thoughts," Deanna said.

He turned his head to face her. "You look terrible," he said. It was the first thing that popped into his mind. The white blisters that had covered her face were gone, but she still had a deathly white pallor.

"So do you, Bill. I'm just happy to be alive."

He chuckled. "You know I go by 'Will' these days, don't you."

"Yes . . . I wondered if you were going to tell me. Don't you feel comfortable enough with me to just talk anymore?"

He reached out his hand and took hers, then gave it a soft squeeze. "Of course I do, Deanna. Let down your guard. Listen to my emotions. You know how I truly feel."

She smiled. "You're naughty!"

He laughed. "You don't have to be an empath to sense *that!*"

Epilogue

THE GENERAL SAT in the command seat aboard his palatial ship, hugging his knees and gently rocking back and forth. *No, no, no!* he thought. All the news today was bad. *Solomon dead. The plague cured. Archaria III on the verge of racial peace for the first time in generations.* The Federation had turned disaster into triumph.

He snarled. He wanted to smash something. *Anything.*

Solomon had failed him. His scientists, whose best genetic weapon fizzled when put to the test, had failed him. *All this time, all this money. And for nothing!*

No, not for nothing. *It's a learning experience.* The speed with which the Federation had acted to contain his plague was commendable. Clearly his people would have to modify the disease further.

Two days, he thought. *It only took them two days!*

DOUBLE HELIX

VECTORS

DEAN WESLEY SMITH
&
KRISTINE KATHRYN RUSCH

For Jim and his great crew—
Ken, Debbie, Chris & Kathy

Chapter One

TEROK NOR. Its name was as dark as its corridors. He actually found himself seeking the light, but carefully. Oh, so carefully. Sometimes his cloak malfunctioned, and he was seen. Partially, like a heat shimmer across desert sand, or an electronic memory buried in an old computer. But he was seen.

He didn't dare make that mistake here. The General didn't tolerate mistakes from his agents.

He stood in the shadows just to the left of the main entrance to a place called Quark's Bar. The area the Ferengi bartender had called the Promenade lay before him, turning away to the right, bending with the shape of the station design. The walls were gray, the floors gray, everything was gray. The Cardassians had made no effort to decorate this place. Even the bar seemed dismal.

He shuddered and drew his cape around his body. He was glad he wouldn't have to stay here too long. This Terok Nor reminded him of his prison cell. He had lost too many years of his life there. He had spent too much time staring at gray metal walls, dreaming of escape. The metal walls, the ringing sound of boots against hard surfaces, the stench of fear—impossible to hide, even though the Cardassians kept their Bajoran prisoners separate from the rest of the population—permeated the place. If he shut his eyes, his other senses would find nothing to distinguish Terok Nor from that hideous cell, from that prison he had finally left. The prison had changed him—made him bitter, made him wiser, made him more careful.

Oh, so careful.

Two Cardassian guards walked the wide passage. Their gray skin matched the depressing decor. The only thing that seemed wrong to him was the heat. By rights this station should have been as cold as its walls, but it wasn't. The heat was thick and nearly unbearable. He didn't know how anyone could stand being here for long. The heat also accentuated the smells: the processed air, the unwashed bodies, the Rokassa juice wafting out from the bar. The sensations were almost too much for him.

He reminded himself that Terok Nor was the perfect testing ground. Two races, living in close proximity, with others coming and going. Their petty differences didn't matter. That one race kept the other prisoner, that one made the other labor in uridium processing were merely details. The important factor was much larger.

Terok Nor was the perfect testing ground for the General. A closed system, for the most part. But anyone entering the system—or departing the system—would leave a record. A trail he could follow, should he so choose.

He didn't choose at the moment.

Now he was most interested in Terok Nor itself.

To his right in the bar, crowds of uridium freighter pilots and crews shouted and laughed, the sounds echoing off the high ceilings. A few moments before, he'd been in there sitting at the bar, watching.

Waiting.

Trying to stay cool and block out the uridium smell with the odor of one of the pilots' Gamzian wine. But it hadn't helped, and besides, he couldn't see that well or hear that clearly with his cloak on.

A clang from the far end of the Promenade caught his attention. One of the Cardassian guards had dropped his phaser pistol, then grabbed the wall as if for support. The other guard bent over him, then glanced from side to side, as if worried that a Bajoran might see and take advantage.

He was too far away to hear their words. The first guard shrugged the other off. The second guard picked up the pistol and spoke on his communicator. Two guards who had apparently been patrolling just out of his line of sight ran toward the far end of the Promenade.

The first guard put an arm around the second, who again shrugged him off. The second tried to stand, and nearly collapsed. The first guard supported him, and together they walked along the walls, keeping as far out of sight as possible.

He felt excitement flash through him, and he tamped it down. He couldn't let his emotions interfere with his observations. This might be nothing. It was a bit early to see results. He hadn't expected anything so soon.

The guards passed him. He had to press himself against the gray metal so that they wouldn't brush him. They weren't conversing, although he wished they would. He wanted to know exactly what had happened.

He needed to know.

He had moved to follow the guards, but the Promenade gave him no cover. So he remained in the shadows.

He would wait here, in the heat and the stench, just as he had done in his cell. He was good at waiting, especially when he knew it would end. And it would end.

Soon he would get his answer.

Chapter Two

"I TELL YOU, BARTENDER," the drunk Cardassian freighter pilot was saying, none too softly, "someone has been sniffing my Gamzian wine."

"You don't sniff Gamzian wine," Quark said for the eighteenth time. He loaded up another tray, carefully balancing the Saurian brandy bottle in the center so that Rom wouldn't drop the whole thing. As if training his brother weren't enough of a headache, Quark had a bar full of pilots and crew—mostly Cardassian, all of them drunk, and none of them more annoying than the pilot at the very edge of the bar, nearest the door. He had been complaining about hearing sniffing sounds, which, Quark had to admit, he had thought he had heard too. But they had been coming from an empty chair beside the pilot. They were probably an acoustical trick, caused by loud voices and even louder laughter, not to mention—

A crash echoed through the bar, and all the noise stopped as everyone looked at the table closest to the Dabo game. Quark couldn't see what was going on, but he knew. He knew even before his brother Rom pushed his way out of a group of Cardassians, looking like a misbehaving child trying to find his way past a group of annoyed grownups. Rom was bowing and apologizing and moving quicker than Quark had ever seen him move.

Rom darted behind the bar, just as a Cardassian stood, drenched in Romulan ale. The blue liquid coated his neck ridges, making him look as if some fanciful person had decided that he needed a spot of color.

"Ferengi!" he barked.

Rom was cringing behind the bar, clinging to Quark's legs. Quark kicked him off.

"It wasn't my fault, brother," Rom said.

"Sure looks like it to me," Quark said.

Rom peeked over the bar, then ducked quickly, narrowly missing the tray Quark had just filled. The Cardassian was heading toward them. He looked bigger than most Cardassians, if that was possible, and meaner too.

Quark shook his leg, but Rom wouldn't let go.

The Cardassian shoved two patrons aside as he reached the bar. "You!" he said, grabbing Quark's collar and lifting him against the bar itself. Rom was still clinging to his leg, and Quark felt as if he were being stretched so hard that he might actually snap.

"Me?" he asked, trying to sound innocent.

"You!" The Cardassian pulled harder. Quark shook his foot desperately. They were going to break something or worse—he'd be tall as a Bajoran when they were done.

"Me?" Quark said again, still shaking that foot. Rom was like a tube grub.

"You!" the Cardassian said, and yanked. Quark's foot slipped through Rom's grasp, and he overbalanced the Cardassian, who fell backwards, pulling Quark with him. Quark grabbed at the bar, then a customer, then a table to catch his balance. Instead, he bounced on the Cardassian's chest.

The man smelled so fiercely of Romulan ale that Quark nearly sneezed. He apologized and rolled off the Cardassian, resisting the urge to scramble behind the bar as Rom had done. Quark had learned, in his years on Terok Nor, that the best way to handle Cardassians—usually—was to act as if their most unreasonable behavior were normal.

He braced himself on a chair, got to his feet, and tugged his shirt in place. The Romulan ale smell had followed him, and he resisted the urge to glance down. Once that stuff was on someone's clothing, it never came off. He didn't want to add a ruined shirt to Rom's list of errors this night.

"Much as I enjoyed our game," Quark said to the Cardassian, "I must get back to work. Is there anything I can get you?"

The Cardassian held a hand to his head. Quark couldn't tell if that was because the man had hit it or because the liquor he had consumed was finally making itself felt.

"Get me the Ferengi weasel whom you use as a serving wench."

"Wench?" Quark heard Rom's voice from behind the bar. This was the wrong time for Rom to take offense, at anything.

"You must mean my brother," Quark said, trying to think of a way to placate the Cardassian. "He's filling in tonight. He has never worked in a bar before—"

"That's obvious," someone said from behind Quark.

"—so if he's offended you in some way, let me make it up to you. I could refill your ale, or give you a half hour in one of my holosuites, or find someone to clean and press your uniform—"

"I want the Ferengi," the Cardassian said. He was sitting up on one elbow, his face grayer than Quark had ever seen Cardassian skin look.

Quark glanced at the bar. Rom would pay for this. All of it. The entire day. The entire *week.*

"I'm a Ferengi," Quark said.

"I'm not blind," the Cardassian said. "I want the other one!"

Quark closed his eyes for a moment. He would never get into the Divine Treasury. Never. Certainly not with Rom on Terok Nor.

"He's behind the bar," Quark whispered.

"What?" the Cardassian said.

"Behind. The. Bar." Quark opened his eyes. His eleven-year-old nephew Nog was watching him from the stairs, the boy's round face filled with a mixture of sadness and anger.

The Cardassian got to his feet. "You, you, and you," he said pointing to three other Cardassians. He certainly wasn't big on names. "Get that little maggot out here."

Quark held up his hands. "I really don't approve of bloodshed in my bar."

"I am not interested in blood," the Cardassian said.

The three Cardassian crewmen pulled Rom out from behind the bar. He was kicking, shaking his head, and apologizing all at the same time.

"Hold him there." The Cardassian pointed at the chair Quark was standing near. Quark took a few steps back, sneaking another glance at Nog.

The bar was silent except for Rom's protests. Nog mouthed, *Help him,* to Quark, who promptly turned away.

The Cardassians did as they were bid, placing Rom on the chair. Their ale-covered leader grabbed the Saurian brandy off the tray.

"Wait! Wait!" Quark said. "That's rare and precious and—"

The Cardassian was staring at him, the stench of Romulan ale coming off him in waves. "And?"

Quark bowed slightly so the Cardassian couldn't see his expression. "And I hope you enjoy it very much."

"I will." The Cardassian uncorked the brandy and poured it slowly, lovingly, over Rom's head. A roar of laughter went up in the bar, and then all the other Cardassians piled forward to pour their drinks on Rom.

Quark scuttled through the crowd and made it back to the relative safety behind the bar. He used a napkin to mop the ale off his shirt, and winced as another roar of laughter filled the place. The mixed drinks were turning purple on Rom's skull. He was spluttering, using his free hand to wipe at his nose and mouth.

"Stop them." Somehow Nog had found his way behind the bar. If Quark had thought his brother annoying, he had been mistaken. Annoying was this kid who seemed to think he knew everything, even though he believed his father was worthy of respect.

"After all the glasses Rom has broken today," Quark said, "I think I owe him one."

"You owe him one," Nog said. "They do not. They're making a fool of him."

"He made a fool of himself," Quark said, and moved to the edge of the bar.

The lone Cardassian pilot still sat there, staring at his Gamzian wine. He was muttering. Quark hurried away.

Laughter again rose from the group.

"Why aren't you doing anything?" Nog asked.

"I am doing something," Quark said. "I'm making more drinks. Everyone will be out in a moment."

"How can you?" Nog said. "He's your brother."

"Don't I know it," Quark said. Rom was still standing on that chair. No one was holding him anymore. His head was covered with a sickly yellow liquid; his clothing was drenched; and it looked like his shoes were melting, even though they couldn't be. The drinks, even mixed together, weren't toxic enough.

But the shoes could be cheap enough.

The Cardassians were standing around him, shouting and laughing each time someone poured a drink on Rom, but more and more the Cardassians were noticing that they were running out of liquor. A few were already bellying up to the bar to order more. Then a few more came.

And a few more.

Suddenly, he was swamped. "Nog?"

He turned. The boy was gone. Nog was as bad as his father and as worthless, too.

Quark moved faster than he had in a long time, mixing drinks, trying to keep the drunken Cardassians from tearing up his bar further. Rom would have to clean up those drinks before anyone fell. Quark didn't want to think about the damage that a falling Cardassian could cause. He didn't want to think about money at all. Right now, all it would do was make him mad.

Even though he was raking it in at the moment. Maybe he should hold a "Drench the Ferengi" contest once a month. The only catch would be that the customers would have to buy the drinks that they poured on Rom. And it would have to be on Rom. He wasn't good for anything else.

He had been that way since he was a boy. Useless. No business sense. Quark had sold Rom's birthday presents, swindled him in his school ventures, even made Rom pay a toll to get into his own room, and still Rom had not learned.

Not even by example.

Not even when he was young.

Quark shivered. And now he was stuck with his brother. His brother *and* his nephew, both of whom managed to inherit Quark's father's business sense, or rather his lack of it.

The traffic at the bar was slowing down. Quark looked up. Nog was helping Rom off the chair. Rom was shaking himself like a wet dog, drenching customers on either side. Fortunately, they were still too pleased with themselves to care.

With Nog's assistance, Rom squished his way to the bar. Quark slid a pile of towels across the bar. "Go clean up your mess," he said to his brother.

"My mess? Brother, they assaulted me and you did nothing."

Quark set his lower lip. He had had enough of Rom's whining. If this new relationship were to work—and part of him truly wished it wouldn't—then Rom would have to learn a few things.

"Nog," Quark said. "Clean up the spill before someone slips."

"No," Nog said. "My father—"

"Nog," Quark said with some force.

Nog glared at him, then picked up the towels and headed back to the sodden chair.

"Come back here," Quark said to Rom.

Rom squished his way around the bar, leaving prints. A few Cardassians watched, still chuckling. The rest had gone back to their drinks and their Dabo game.

When Rom made it to the side of the bar, Quark grabbed him by the ear and dragged him toward the stairs leading to the holosuites. The tables were empty, and no one was looking at them.

"Ow!" Rom said. "What was that for?"

"For being stupid enough to dump Romulan ale on a Cardassian pilot. I'm lucky you didn't dump it on Gul Dukat. He'd close us down."

"It was a simple mistake, brother. I—"

"If I had a strip of latinum for each stupid mistake you've made since you arrived on the station, I'd be a rich man," Quark said. He had been quiet as long as he could. "You brought this on yourself, and you're lucky it wasn't worse."

"Worse? Didn't you see what they did? The Visscus vodka and the Itharian molé turned into a fizzing powder that—"

"I saw what they did," Quark said, lowering his voice so that Rom had to lean forward to hear. "And if you had dumped that ale on Gul Dukat, you'd be in the brig now. Or worse."

"Worse?"

"Worse." Quark crossed his arms. "I let them pick on you for your own good. Maybe you'll learn to be more careful. This is a dangerous place. You can't go around being your happy-go-lucky self. You have to watch everything you do."

"Yes, brother," Rom said, meekly. Then he added, "And here I thought you were just mad at all the glasses I broke."

"That too," Quark said. "I'm going to start deducting the price of everything you break from your salary."

"But brother—"

Quark held up a hand. "I'm doing you a lot of favors, Rom. I didn't have to give you a home and a job when Prindora's father swindled you out of all your money."

"You weren't going to bring that up again," Rom said, glancing over his shoulder for Nog. The boy was still wiping the floor. Those Cardassians had poured a lot of liquid on Rom.

"It's kind of hard to forget, Rom. What kind of idiot fails to read the fine print in a contract?"

"It was a marriage contract," Rom said.

"So?" Quark asked. "How is that different from a regular contract?"

"It was even an extension of the marriage contract. I read the first one."

"Twelve years ago," Quark said. "And I'll bet you forgot the terms, didn't you?"

Rom swallowed and looked down.

"You loved Prindora, so you trusted her."

Rom nodded.

"She's a female, Rom."

"She was my wife," Rom said miserably.

"At least she remembered the Sixth Rule of Acquisition."

"That's not fair," Rom said.

"What is it?" Quark asked. "Do you even know?"

Rom straightened his shoulders. " 'Never allow family to stand in the way of opportunity.' "

"Good," Quark said. "Then you should understand why I let the Cardassians pour drinks on you. I made money, and that's more than I've done since you showed up."

"I'm sorry, brother," Rom said.

"You should be. Now go put on some clean clothes and get back out here. There's a lot of work to do." Quark glanced over at Nog. "And your son isn't a very good substitute."

"He's just a boy," Rom said.

"Go," Quark said, and Rom ran for their quarters. Quark shook his head and returned to the bar. Sometimes even he forgot the Sixth Rule of Acquisition. If he had remembered it, he wouldn't have allowed Rom here in the first place. But Rom had looked so pathetic when he arrived, dragging Nog behind him. Quark had actually felt sorry for them, although that emotion was quickly fading now. Every time he heard the sound of shattering glass.

"Nog!" he yelled. "When you finish that, I have some other things for you to clean."

The boy looked at him for a long moment. There was something in Nog's eyes, something a bit too rebellious for Quark, but then it disappeared as if it had never been.

"Yes, uncle," Nog said.

Quark nodded curtly, then leaned back and surveyed the bar. The Cardassian freighter crews were thinning. Drink had forced some of them to leave. The remaining ones weren't as rowdy as they had been earlier. The muttering pilot at the far end of the bar was still staring at his Gamzian wine. The glass was as full as it had been before the trouble started, but the Cardassian was an odd shade of green.

"And I thought the gray looked bad," Quark murmured. He frowned. A few of the Cardassians around the Dabo table were also faintly greenish. He had seen a lot of drunk Cardassians in his day, but he had never seen them turn vaguely green before. He had always thought that a hu-man trait.

Maybe they were all from the same ship. Or maybe the greenish tinge was being caused by something they'd eaten. Or maybe they were from a part of Cardassia Prime that made them look that way naturally.

"Or maybe that's how Cardassians look when they tan."

"What, uncle?"

Quark jumped. He hadn't realized Nog was beside him. "Do those Cardassians look strange to you?"

Nog peered at them. "They all look strange to me."

Quark nodded. Nog had a point. Maybe Quark had been here so long that everything abnormal was beginning to look normal.

What a frightening thought. He shuddered one more time, and then went back to work.

Chapter Three

THE LIGHTS IN THE MEDICAL LAB seemed dimmer than usual. Gul Dukat stepped inside, hands clasped behind his back. He was used to being here when colleagues and subordinates were wounded, but he felt uncomfortable here in cases like this. Illness. Especially unrecognized illness. The very idea made his skin crawl.

The displays were flashing, the monitors constantly recording various bits of information. In the main section, the physician assigned to Terok Nor, Narat, sat at his desk studying a screen before him. On beds hooked up to the monitors were two of Dukat's guards. Their skin was an odd greenish color, almost the color of a body shortly after it begins to decay.

Dukat raised his head slightly. Through the door of the second, smaller room, he could see the blanket-covered feet of the two Bajoran patients. Their doctor, Kellec Ton, stood beside them studying a Cardassian padd as if it were in a strange language. It looked odd to Dukat to see Bajorans here. They belonged in the medical part of the Bajoran area. It wasn't as well appointed as this, but then, they were workers. They didn't need all of this equipment.

He wouldn't have allowed them up here if Narat didn't believe that the disease the Bajoran workers had was related to the disease these two guards seemed to have.

Dukat took another step into the medical lab. Narat turned. He was slight, and his neck scales were hardly prominent. His eyes almost disappeared into his thin face. They were always bloodshot, but they seemed worse now. His thinning hair was cut short, almost too short, and stood straight up.

He wore a lab coat over his uniform, and it gave him a scholarly air.

"Ah, Gul Dukat. I appreciate you coming here so quickly."

Dukat glanced at the patients on the bed. He felt uncomfortable, so he wasn't going to give any leeway to Narat. "I don't like to have Bajorans up here."

"We have a forcefield at the doors, just as you recommended," Narat said. "But they're not going anywhere. They will die here, probably within a few hours."

He sounded certain.

"I'd like you to see them."

Dukat frowned, glancing again at the guards. One of them moaned and thrashed, clutching at his stomach. Narat uttered a small curse, then found a hypospray and shut off the quarantine field around the bed. He stepped inside, restarted the quarantine field, and administered hypo to the man's neck. The guard calmed slightly.

"What about them?" Dukat asked.

"In a moment," Narat said, as he let himself out of the quarantine field. "Let me tell you this in my own way."

He led Dukat to the second room. They stopped at the door. The forcefield Dukat had insisted on was more for the Bajoran doctor than it was for the patients, but Dukat didn't tell Narat that. Dukat wanted Narat and Kellec Ton to work together as best a Cardassian and a Bajoran could. He just wasn't going to take any chances.

As if he knew that Dukat was thinking of him, Kellec Ton looked up from his padd. He had the wide dark eyes that Dukat found so compelling in Bajorans. His nose ridge set them off. His face was long, but didn't give an impression of weakness like Narat's did. On Kellec, the length accented his bone structure and gave him a suggestion of power.

Dukat had been careful around this Bajoran doctor, and had limited his access to the Cardassians. Women found him attractive, and Dukat didn't like that. Kellec Ton had the kind of charisma that could be dangerous if allowed to run free.

Dukat couldn't study him any longer. He had to look at the patients.

The Bajorans on the table were not a strange shade of green. In fact, their color was normal. Better than normal. If he hadn't known better, Dukat would have thought them the picture of perfect health.

It was the stench that made their illness clear. The pervasive odor of rot clung to everything, as if there were food spoiling along the floors and walls of the room—food and unburied bodies decaying in a powerful sun.

He resisted the urge to bring his hand over his face. Kellec Ton was watching him, as if measuring Dukat's response. "Disgusting, isn't it?"

Kellec said. "You should go into the Bajoran section. The smell is so overpowering there I have no idea how anyone can eat." Then he tilted his head slightly. "Not that there's much to eat in the first place."

Dukat would not get into political discussions with this man. He was on Terok Nor because Dukat cared for his Bajoran workers. He was here because a healthy worker was a strong worker. The more uridium the Bajorans processed, the better for all concerned.

"What is this disease?" Dukat asked.

"If I knew, I might be able to help them." There was a controlled frustration in Kellec's voice. "So far, we've lost twenty Bajorans, and these two aren't far behind. They look good, don't they?"

Dukat nodded, then asked, "What is the odor?"

Kellec glanced at Narat, who nodded that he should continue. Kellec set the padd down on the instrument table. "Exactly what you think it is. Their bodies are decaying internally. I keep them sedated, but this disease, whatever it is, is incredibly painful. Some of the others broke through the sedatives before they died—I couldn't give them enough medication to ease the suffering."

Somehow, he made that sound like Dukat's fault. But Dukat had done nothing to cause this disease. Some Bajoran had brought it onto the station. He had left it to the Bajorans to cure. They handled their own health. That was why he allowed them Kellec Ton. If they needed specific supplies, Kellec Ton was supposed to act as liaison with the Cardassians.

"You should have notified us sooner. Perhaps Narat has something that will—"

"No, I don't," Narat said.

"Well," Dukat said, "I don't like diseases that destroy my workers. You should have brought this to me before it got out of control."

"The disease first showed up a day and a half ago," Kellec said. "I've been a bit busy since then."

"And it will only get worse," Narat said.

Dukat turned to him. Narat's face looked even more pinched than it had moments ago. "Why is that?"

He took Dukat's arm and led him to the edge of the nearest guard's bed. Up close, the greenish color was mottled. The ridges around the guard's eyes and down his neck were flaking, and a pale gray liquid lined his mouth and nostrils.

Dukat kept his distance, even though he knew the guard was surrounded by a quarantine field.

"This does not look like the same disease to me," Dukat said. Narat had told him earlier, when asking permission to have Kellec and two Bajorans brought to the medical lab, that the Cardassians were now infected with the disease that was killing the Bajorans.

"It doesn't look like the same disease," Narat said, "because you are looking at the symptoms. If you were looking at the disease itself on microscopic level, you would see that it is the same virus—even though it attacks Cardassians differently than it attacks Bajorans."

"So you'll be able to cure them," Dukat said.

Narat shook his head. "Not unless we discover something quickly."

"But if you know its cause," Dukat said, "then you should be able to find a counteragent."

"Should," Narat said, "and probably will." He glanced at Kellec Ton, who was standing near the door. Neither of them seemed as certain as doctors usually did.

"But?" Dukat asked.

"But we don't have the time," Kellec said.

"The disease progresses rapidly," Narat said. "That's a trait it shares in both Barjorans and in Cardassians. These guards came in complaining of dizziness and lack of coordination. Now they cannot sit on their own. The mucus that you see"—and he pointed to thc grayish fluid leaking out of their eyes, noses, and mouths. Dukat grimaced in spite of himself—"is filling their lungs. They will drown by tomorrow if we do not find a way to stop this."

"Drown?" Dukat repeated. He couldn't imagine anyone drowning on Terok Nor. If he had to predict a way his people might die here, it would not be by drowning.

"That's the net effect," Narat said.

"This is not possible," Dukat said. "Bajorans and Cardassians cannot contract the same diseases. We have known that—" he caught himself. Kellec Ton looked at him, eyes sharp. The Bajoran doctor did not need to know how much information the Cardassians had gathered on the Bajorans. "We have known that for a long time."

"We have," Narat said. "But this is something new."

"Brand new," Kellec said.

There was something in his voice that annoyed Dukat, a faint accusation. Dukat approached the door. The stench seemed to have grown.

"What are you suggesting?" Dukat asked.

"I'm not suggesting anything." Kellec's expression was mild, but his eyes were not. They were intense, filled with something that Dukat recognized.

Hatred.

Good. Let the Bajoran hate him. He wasn't competing in any popularity contests.

"But," Kellec continued, "I have heard rumors that this disease is the result of a Cardassian experiment, designed to rid the universe of Bajorans. What better way to get our planet than to destroy us all?"

Dukat felt rage rush through him, but he did not move. He waited until the first wave of anger had passed before responding. He didn't want the Bajoran to know that his comment had hit the mark.

"If that were the case," Dukat said, making certain he sounded calm, "then this disease would not be killing Cardassians."

"It would if someone made a mistake," Kellec said.

Their gazes met for a moment. They both knew the Cardassians were capable of this. Then Dukat said, "Your job is to find a cure for this disease—both versions, Cardassian and Bajoran."

"You're feeling compassion for Bajorans?" Kellec asked, with great sarcasm.

"I prefer to have my Bajorans alive and working," Dukat said. "Not straining the medical resources of Terok Nor."

He turned away from Kellec, no longer willing to look at the man. "If this disease progresses as rapidly as you say," he said to Narat, "then we have to isolate it. We don't want it spreading through the station."

"I'll do what I can," Narat said. "But we have a problem here. We are, essentially, in a floating tin can, sharing the same air. I can have the computers filter for an airborne version of this virus in the life-support system and neutralize it, but the disease might not be spread that way. We don't know enough about it."

"Isolate anyone who comes in contact with it," Dukat said. "I don't want this spreading."

"I won't be able to do that, treat these patients, and find a cure," Narat said. "You'll have to issue the order."

He had a point. "All right," Dukat said.

"It's probably too late," Kellec Ton said.

They turned to him.

Kellec shrugged. "If this disease has a long incubation period, then it could have been spreading all over the station long before any symptoms appeared."

"Then we'd all have it," Narat said softly.

Dukat felt his skin crawl again. He couldn't help himself; he shot another look at the ill guards. He would do anything not to end up like that.

Then the door to medical lab swished open. Two Cardassians Dukat didn't recognize entered. They were wearing the uniform of the uridium freighter crews. The woman was hanging on the man, barely able to walk. Her skin was green.

"You the doctor?" the man asked.

Dukat took a step backwards even though they hadn't come near him yet. He was standing near the second door.

"No," he said, and he sounded alarmed, even to his own ears. "I'm not the doctor."

"I am," Narat said, walking toward them as if this thing didn't bother him at all. "Quarantine protocol."

The quarantine field went up around the newcomers. Dukat let out a small sigh.

"Don't relax yet," Kellec said to him softly. "All it takes is a moment to get infected. One small breath of air. A touch."

Dukat whirled.

The Bajoran was watching him, that maddeningly calm expression on his face.

"Then find the cure," Dukat said.

"I plan to," Kellec said. "For my own people."

"I command you to find it for both." Dukat raised his voice. The new patient and his companion were looking at him, along with Narat.

"Why should I help your people?" Kellec asked.

"Why should I help yours?" Dukat asked.

They stared at each other for a moment. Then Kellec said, "You want our services and our planet."

"You cannot survive without us," Dukat said. "Not anymore."

"We could survive just fine," Kellec said.

There was a crash behind them. Dukat turned. The woman had collapsed. The man who had brought her was clutching the wall as if it gave him strength.

"I need some help over here," Narat said.

Dukat remained where he was.

"Open the force field," Kellec said.

Dukat looked at him.

"Open it, and I will help them," Kellec said.

Dukat brought the force field down. Kellec hurried to the others, demanding that Narat drop the quarantine field on that end as well. Both doctors picked up the female patient, helping her to a bed. Then they helped the male patient. They bent over the patients, lost in their work.

Dukat watched them for a moment, feeling itchy and cold. He glanced at his hand. The skin was its normal grayish color. Healthy. He was healthy.

For the moment.

Kellec wasn't looking at him, and Dukat didn't want to go any closer to taunt him. But Dukat knew Kellec, knew his kind. The man was a doctor first. He would heal a patient and then look to see the patient's race. That was why Dukat had Kellec brought to Terok Nor. For all his Bajoran patriotism, Kellec would save Cardassians if he had to.

In fact, he had just demanded to be allowed to. They would work together to solve this, Cardassian and Bajoran, because they had no other choice.

Chapter Four

DOCTOR KATHERINE PULASKI stood in the sickbay of the *Enterprise.* She was alone. The four medical staff members who were supposed to be in the area had honored her request and granted her the last few moments here alone.

She sighed. The instruments were on their trays, just as she liked them. The monitors were in their off positions. The desk was neat, but all of her personal experiments were gone. Sickbay was tidied up and ready for the new doctor.

Or the old doctor, as it were. Pulaski was being replaced by the doctor she'd replaced, Beverly Crusher. Which was as it should be. Dr. Crusher's presence had never entirely left this sickbay. No matter what Pulaski did, she had a sense of Beverly Crusher's presence. Part of it was the very layout of the bay. Of course, much was standard on each starship—and Pulaski had served on a number. But there were items left to each doctor's discretion—where to put the experiments, for example, or the way the desk was situated in the office. Pulaski had always meant to move the pieces around, to make the sickbay more efficient for her type of medicine. But the demands of being the chief medical officer on a starship—particularly an active starship like the *Enterprise,* a ship with a demanding captain—had never allowed her enough free time to reorganize.

That wasn't entirely true. There had been down periods where she had had some free time—once she had even helped Data in his Sherlock Holmes holodeck program—but she had generally used those times for resting. Making big changes like rearranging sickbay would have required a lot of effort, not just in moving of furniture but in retraining the staff. Effort she was now relieved she hadn't expended.

She tugged at her blue shirt and glanced at her travel bags. She had already removed personal items from her quarters, and all of her experiments and notes were already on the shuttle that would take her to Deep Space Five. She wasn't sure what her new assignment would be—Starfleet was being cagey about it, as always, which usually meant they were considering her for several missions and that she would get the one that rose to the top.

Still, she would miss the *Enterprise.* She loved starships and the challenges they presented. On starships she saw diseases no one else had seen; injuries whose treatment required a knowledge of the most current techniques or the most primitive, depending on whether she was aboard ship or on a hostile planet; aliens whose physiology was so strange that she didn't know what they looked like well, let alone if anything was wrong with them.

She hoped she would get reassigned to a starship, but she doubted that she would. If Starfleet Medical had its way, she would be heading to some starbase where she would squire newly minted doctors through their residencies.

If the truth be told, she'd rather stay on Deep Space Five than do that.

Her combadge chirruped.

She sighed. She would have to leave now. She wasn't ready. But she pressed the badge anyway.

"Pulaski."

"Doctor, sorry to bother you before you leave, but we have an emergency." Geordi La Forge sounded all business. "One of the crewmen got caught in an explosion in Jefferies Tube Three. There was a localized fire. We put it out, but he's severely burned."

Burns. She hated them. The trauma to the skin could continue long after the fire was actually put out.

"Beam him directly to sickbay," she said. She hated the transporter, thought it an infernal device, but it had its uses. Right now, she needed speed more than she needed caution.

The crewman shimmered into place on one of the biobeds. His blue shirt was in charred ruins around his badly burned skin. He was human, which made her task just a bit harder. Vulcans and Klingons handled burns—indeed all pain—better than humans.

He wasn't conscious, for which she was grateful, but he was moaning. Burn pain was excruciating. She hurried to the biobed, with the fleeting thought that the sickbay wouldn't be in order for Dr. Crusher. Ah, well. Reorganization simply wasn't Pulaski's strong suit. Dr. Crusher would understand.

The smell of burned skin filled the sickbay. The biobed was giving his vitals, but she wanted more information. She picked up her medical tricorder and ran it over him, watching the readouts confirm the information she was already receiving.

No deep trauma, no internal injuries. Just burns. The crewman would live. But she didn't slow down. First she eased his pain and put him into a deep, restful sleep. Then, for the next five minutes she carefully repaired the burned skin, one area at a time.

Skin repair was delicate work, but something she had done all of her career. She was quicker at it than most, but that was partly because she disliked it so much. Burns, she often thought, were the worst injury of all.

After she had finished, she stood, brushing a strand of hair from her face, and checked his readings again. Still resting comfortably. She'd keep him that way for a few hours to give that new skin time to heal. And to give his mind time to deal with the memory of the pain. Sometimes in cases like this, the memories were the hardest to heal. Much harder than the skin. She'd have to let Counselor Troi know before she left.

"Nice work, Doctor."

Pulaski started. No one was supposed to be here, and she didn't recognize the voice. Had someone beamed in with the crewman? She had been too preoccupied to notice.

She turned.

Beverly Crusher stood in the center of the bay, where Pulaski had been just minutes earlier. Her long red hair cascaded around her face. She looked thinner than Pulaski remembered.

"Very nice work," Dr. Crusher repeated.

"Thank you, Doctor." Pulaski smiled. The compliment meant a lot. Dr. Crusher was one of the best doctors in the fleet. Picard had told her she would always have a berth on the *Enterprise,* so when she decided that heading Starfleet Medical wasn't for her, she requested her old job back. Picard gave it to her without hesitation, even though—as he had solemnly told Pulaski—their current chief medical officer was one of the most talented physicians he had worked with. Picard was a diplomat, so Pulaski knew he might be exaggerating slightly, but he was also the captain of a starship, and he didn't give out idle praise.

Dr. Crusher looked around the main area of the sickbay as if she were a blind woman just recovering her sight. "You know, there were days at Starfleet Medical when I never thought I would ever see the inside of one of these again."

Pulaski smoothed her hair with one hand.

"I missed it a great deal."

"I imagine you did," Pulaski said. She felt her shoulders stiffen. She would miss it too.

"I'm sorry, Katherine," Dr. Crusher said. "You were doing an exceptional job here. I wouldn't have asked to come back to the *Enterprise* if it weren't for Wesley."

Pulaski nodded. "I had a feeling from the first that I was merely keeping this place warm for you."

"It looks like you did more than that." Dr. Crusher nodded at the crewman. His vitals were closer to normal than they had been just a few moments before. "I've never seen such quick work on a burn patient. I doubt I could have done as well."

"I've studied your logs," Pulaski said. "You've done as well or better."

Their gazes met, and an awkwardness that had been reflected in their words seemed to grow. Finally Dr. Crusher tossed her long hair back—such a girlish move from such an accomplished woman—and laughed.

"I'm sorry about this," she said. "I didn't realize it would be so uncomfortable."

Pulaski frowned just slightly. If Dr. Crusher was referring to their meeting, she should have known. It was an unwritten rule among chief medical officers that they never share a sickbay—at least not on a starship. The new officer replacing the old officer would wait until his or her predecessor was off the ship before entering sickbay.

But Pulaski said nothing. An unwritten rule was a tradition, yes, but it wasn't as if Dr. Crusher had done much more than been slightly impolite. It was something easily overlooked.

Apparently Pulaski's silence went on too long. Dr. Crusher's smile faded.

"There is a reason that I'm here early," she said.

Pulaski felt some of the tension leave her. The breach of etiquette had bothered her, even though she had just been trying to convince herself that it hadn't. She felt Dr. Crusher's returning as a slight rebuke, almost as if she weren't important enough to remain on the ship. She had known that the feeling was irrational and, in her better moments, had forgotten all about it. But it had been a thread, an undercurrent, during the whole last month, since she'd finally learned that she would be leaving.

"I hope it's not too serious," Pulaski said.

Dr. Crusher's mouth formed a thin line. "Starfleet Medical wanted me to tell you there's a problem on Bajor."

Whatever Pulaski had expected, it wasn't that. She fought to keep her face impassive, not to let her emotions show. Dr. Kellec Ton, after all, was her ex-husband, and as much as she cared about him, she had known that this moment could come. She had urged him to leave Bajor, knowing that with his temperament, he couldn't be safe under the Cardassian occupation. But he had refused, just as he had always refused to do the sensible thing during their marriage, citing his loyalty to his homeland and its great need for him in time of crisis.

"Why did Starfleet Medical believe they needed to inform me of this?"

Dr. Crusher's gaze held hers. "There are rumors that a plague on Bajor is killing both Cardassians and Bajorans."

Pulaski threaded her fingers together and held her hands over her stomach, as if the pressure would keep her nerves from getting worse.

"That's not possible," Pulaski said. "Their systems are too different. Viruses cannot be spread from Bajoran to Cardassian and back again."

"I thought the same thing," Dr. Crusher said softly. "But Starfleet Medical is taking the rumors seriously."

Rumors. If they only had rumors, they wouldn't know who died. For all they knew, Kellec was just fine.

Suddenly Pulaski knew why Dr. Crusher was telling her this. "They want me to contact Kellec for them, don't they?"

Dr. Crusher nodded. "A message from Starfleet might put him in jeopardy. A message from you—"

"Would seem normal. Or somewhat normal." Pulaski let her hands drop to her sides. She was on good terms with Kellec, as she was with her other two ex-husbands. But she didn't like talking with him. She had loved him a great deal, but his stubbornness had frustrated her—and it continued to frustrate her, even now.

"Starfleet Medical believes that Dr. Kellec Ton can confirm or deny the rumors."

Pulaski nodded. "As long as I present my questions in a way that won't put him in any danger."

"From what I understand of Kellec Ton," Dr. Crusher said, "he's probably already in danger, at least the political kind."

"He never could remain quiet about things that bothered him," Pulaski said.

"When was the last time you spoke with him?"

"A month ago." They had fought, as they often did. Kellec had agreed to go to a Cardassian space station to take care of their Bajoran workers. He hadn't explained his motives—he didn't dare on the unscrambled channels he could get out of Bajor—but he didn't have to. He would take care of the workers' ill health, document the atrocities he saw, and do what he could to promote the resistance movement from the inside—maybe even destroy the station, if it were within his power.

She had argued against the assignment, attempting to use medical arguments that couched her larger objections. But they had both known what she was talking about. And the argument had ended, as they all had, with Kellec shaking his head.

Katherine, my love, he had said. *Our fundamental problem is, and has always been, your unwillingness to let me make my own mistakes.*

She was letting him make his own mistakes. But she'd had to divorce him to do so.

"Can you contact him again?" Dr. Crusher asked.

Pulaski nodded. "I believe I know where to find him."

"Good," Dr. Crusher said. "I'm sorry to bother you with this, especially now. But it is the best way for us to handle this potential crisis."

There was something that Dr. Crusher wasn't telling her, something that Starfleet Medical was very interested in, something that they were willing to risk a high-profile contact with Bajor over. But Pulaski had been military for a long time. She knew better than to ask for information that she had not been given. If it had been something she needed to know, Dr. Crusher would have told her.

"Well," Pulaski said, "I guess it's time."

She glanced at her last patient on the *Enterprise.* The crewman's readings were mostly normal, his new skin looking pink and healthy. She went over to him and drew a blanket across him. He was sleeping peacefully. He wouldn't even remember his treatment. He would think Dr. Crusher had taken care of him, and even though she would probably correct him, he would never really know what had happened here.

But Pulaski would.

"I'm sorry it's such a mess. I had planned to leave it tidy for you."

Dr. Crusher smiled. "Medicine is rarely tidy."

Pulaski nodded. That was a fact she knew all too well.

Chapter Five

A MIST HAD FORMED at the base of the mountains. Gel Kynled felt the chill, even though he stood in the shadow of what had once been an excellent restaurant. It was Cardassian now, with the former restaurant owner working as a waiter and forced to suffer daily humiliation from the occupying army. Gel hated watching that. He hated so many things about Bajor these days. So many Bajorans simply took the Occupation as their lot in life. They looked away when their friends disappeared, mourned when their families died, but did nothing.

He couldn't stand doing nothing.

He had his arm wrapped around the waist of Cadema Hyle. She was too thin for him. Her clothing was baggy and barely hid the signs of starvation that had been so prominent a few months ago. Cadema had managed to escape from one of the camps—probably because the Cardassian guards had left her for dead. She had climbed out of the mountains, surviving on roots and berries before she made it back to their resistance cell. She never spoke of the experience, not after that first day, but it had changed her.

Like him, she was willing to do anything to get rid of the Cardassians. Anything at all.

It was nearly curfew. Most of the Bajorans who were on the streets were hurrying toward their homes. The people left in this area had nominal freedom, all of them knowing they could lose it with a single error. Staying out past curfew could be that error.

The Cardassians passing him were no longer on duty, but they weren't in a hurry either. Gel resisted the urge to check the time. He and Cadema were standing casually, looking younger than they were—because they had always looked younger than they were—and pretending to be in love. Idle youth, not caring about deadlines or curfews or Cardassian soldiers. But it was getting late, and Gel didn't dare call attention to himself. He needed his freedom, and so did Cadema. In fact, Cadema said she would do anything she could, anything, to prevent being captured by the Cardassians again.

He felt her shift ever so slightly. Her movement wasn't noticeable to anyone watching, but it was a sign that she was getting nervous too.

"A few more moments," he said softly.

She smiled at him, tilting her head upward, a lovesick look that didn't make it to her eyes. He smiled back, so fond. Lovers, taking the last few minutes of precious daylight to be together.

Someone coughed a few meters away, a loud, honking cough. It was their signal. Cadema tensed. Gel slid his left hand behind his back. His fingers rested lightly on a stolen Cardassian phaser tucked into a belt, holding it against his spine. He could draw and fire the pistol faster than a Cardassian could raise his arm. Gel had killed at least ten Cardassian guards with that pistol over the last few months. He planned on killing a lot more.

A Jibetian trader walked past, still coughing. He was long and lean, like most of his people, and his ridged cheeks were very pronounced. Gel had never seen him before.

"You need to do something for that cough," Cadema said, her voice gentle, as if giving advice to a friend.

The trader stopped, his cloak flowing around him. The movement was fluid and powerful. It also revealed the weapons at his waist. A pistol like Gel's and something Gel didn't recognize.

The trader's pale green eyes took both of them in. Nothing in his expression changed, but he seemed to recognize them as a team.

He stepped closer, so close that his words were audible only to Gel and Cadema. "My boss does not like being summoned."

Gel didn't move. He kept one hand on his weapon, the other casually draped over Cadema. As he spoke, he smiled, so that anyone watching would think they were still discussing cold remedies.

"Bajorans are dying," he said.

The trader shrugged. "You were warned there might be some casualties."

"Some," Cadema said. "We thought that meant only those initially involved. Your boss misled us."

The trader's gaze flickered toward the street and then back to them.

They were the last Bajorans out, and there were no more Cardassians. Curfew had started. In a few moments, they all would be in trouble.

"People in your business," the trader said, "should not be soft."

Gel's grip on the pistol tightened. He knew he was being goaded, and he would not let the trader get to him. All of the people he had dealt with, everyone who worked for the person—or persons—who had theoretically developed this perfect biological weapon to fight the Cardassians had been as cold and unfeeling and cruel as this trader. All of them. They were only in it for the money. Gel's resistance cell had spent the last of its reserves getting this weapon, and now it was backfiring on them.

"Soft, weak," Gel said, "those are all subjective terms. We're not talking about our ability to fight, or our own willingness to die for our beliefs. But this disease has spread beyond our cell, to the innocents. Our children have been dying. It's not a pretty death."

"You didn't buy a pretty death," the trader said. "You bought something a bit more destructive than that."

"My people are getting sicker faster than the Cardassians." Gel had to struggle to keep his voice down. Cadema was looking to make sure they were still alone on the street. They were.

So far.

"The disease incubates longer in Cardassians."

"Not good enough," Gel said. "You owe us more than that."

"We owe you nothing."

"You lied."

"What are you going to do? Turn us in? Which government will prosecute us for violating the local commerce laws? What remains of the Bajoran government? Or the Cardassian warlords?"

Cadema put a hand on Gel's chest. She knew how close he was to killing this bug.

"We have done what we promised," the trader said. "You wanted to get rid of the Cardassians. We offered you a way, and now they are dying. What more do you want?"

"The Bajoran antidote for the plague," Gel said.

The trader smiled. It was a cruel, empty smile.

"What if we turn you in to the Cardassians and tell them you're working for the person who started this plague?" Gel asked.

"And who's going to tell them? You, the great rebel leader killing his own people?" The trader laughed again, this time louder, his voice echoing down the empty street.

"We have kept complete documentation of all of our dealings with you, including surveillance of all of our meetings."

"You have never dealt with the same person."

"It doesn't matter. We have the conversations and the promises. We have it all."

"All except the names of the people you've really been dealing with," the trader said.

"That's not hard to find," Gel said. He was bluffing, but it was getting dark. He was getting desperate. He had thought this meeting would go better. "Give me the Bajoran antidote."

The trader smiled. "You think you are so courageous." He crossed his arms. "You believe you are so powerful, so smart. You don't like the idea that you've been tricked."

Cadema glanced at Gel. He knew what she was thinking, and he shook his head slightly, but she spoke anyway. "We will pay for it," she said.

The trader's ridged cheeks puffed out. Gel had worked with enough Jibetians to know that to be an expression of surprise. "Really?" he asked.

She nodded.

"You have no money. You used it all to pay us."

Gel felt cold. Perhaps they had been dealing out of their league.

Cadema let go of him and grabbed the trader by his long cloak. She pulled him close. She had surprising strength in those thin hands.

"We are losing our children, our families, the very reasons we are fighting the Cardassian dogs."

The trader stared at her for a moment. Cadema had let the veneer of civility drop. She had let him see their desperation. Gel thought he saw pity in the Jibetian's eyes.

"There is no antidote," the trader said.

"What?" Cadema let him go. "There has to be."

It hadn't been pity Gel had seen. It had been disgust. The look intensified. The Jibetian straightened his lapels. "My boss hates weakness. If you couldn't stomach the deaths, you should not have bought our services."

Gel brought out his laser pistol, aiming and firing as he moved. But he didn't get to see whether or not his shot hit its target. The Jibetian already had his pistol out. A shot caught Gel in the chest, smashing him back against the wall. His own pistol fell out of his grasp.

He didn't feel any pain, not yet anyway. He knew, somehow, that wasn't good.

Cadema dove out of the way, but the Jibetian turned toward her. The street was still empty. Why wasn't there anyone on the street? Why didn't anyone see this?

He tried to reach for the pistol, but he couldn't move his arms.

A second shot hit Cadema. She twitched once, and then didn't move, arms splayed, legs at an unnatural angle. The Jibetian pushed at her with his booted foot. She didn't respond.

Gel couldn't. His body wasn't obeying his commands. It had slumped down the wall until he was lying on his back, his neck shoved uncomfortably against the brick. Odd that the only discomfort he felt was in his neck. But he really couldn't feel much at all. And he seemed to have control of nothing more than his face. His breathing was short and uneven. He couldn't really take a deep breath at all. The pistol the Jibetian had used had scrambled Gel's systems. If he didn't get help soon, he would die here, on this street, just like Cadema.

Without the antidote. Without being able to tell his resistance cell there was no antidote.

All those deaths, on his shoulders.

The Jibetian leaned over him. That look of disgust was in his eyes again. He nudged Gel with his booted foot, and like Cadema, Gel didn't move.

"Trust me," the Jibetian said softly. "I've done you a favor."

"No," Gel whispered.

"Ah, but I did," the Jibetian said. "I gave you the only antidote to the plague."

And then he laughed. Gel closed his eyes, and the laugh followed him as he felt himself slip away into final blackness.

Chapter Six

THE BAJORAN MEDICAL SECTION of Terok Nor lacked everything the Cardassian medical section had. No quarantine fields, no biobeds, nothing except field medicine kits set up in corners, half a dozen of them, many of them without the most important equipment. Kellec Ton had been negotiating with Gul Dukat for more equipment when this plague hit, and then it became a minor consideration. Ton could barely keep up with the patients, finding them beds, making them comfortable. He couldn't worry about the lack of equipment.

He didn't have time.

The stench in this area was so foul he could almost touch it. The uncomfortable Cardassian heat, combined with the poor environmental systems, made the smell even worse. He tried to do an old-fashioned quarantine field: separate the sick from the healthy by placing the sick in a large room away from everything, but he had a hunch he was doing too little too late.

He bent over a teenage girl in the last stages of the disease. She lay on a cot he had found in one of the sleeping sections. She was moaning and clutching her stomach. All he could do was ease the pain, but even with the highest doses the pain slipped through. It was all he could do not to overdose these victims. He had to cling to some kind of hope that he would find a way to cure the disease before they all died.

His medical assistants, also people he'd had to fight for with Gul Dukat, had all been exposed. Kellec Ton had a hunch it was only a matter of time before they fell prey to this thing too. Before he did.

He had no idea what the incubation period was for this virus, but he knew it was longer than he had initially suspected. What research he had been able to do—mostly by word of mouth with the people who had fallen ill—revealed that they had felt fine for the last few weeks, and the illness had caught them by surprise. It was the secondary wave he was looking for, the people who had been infected by the earlier carriers. He had only spoken to a few—too many of them hadn't come in when they first noticed they weren't feeling well.

All of his training in the psychology of serious illness had prepared him for that, but he hadn't really expected it. If he knew something serious was happening on the station, and he felt poorly, he would have gone to get help immediately. Most people, however, entered a serious denial phase based on fear. *Yes,* the reasoning went, *my best friend has this disease, and I took care of her, but I'm strong. I never get sick. I am just out of sorts, making things up. I really can't be ill.*

By the time most of the second wave had come to him, they were so ill they couldn't talk. In fact, someone usually carried them in. All he could do now was watch them die.

He hated this.

He hated it as much as he hated the thick metal walls and the dim lighting, as much as he hated the way the Cardassians penned the Bajorans into these sections as if they were animals instead of people. Most of the Bajorans on Terok Nor already had weakened immune systems. They had been worked so hard that they were half dead on their feet. Their rations were meager, their hygiene poor. The close quarters made the spread of easily curable disease rampant. He knew that a virulent virus, like this one, would probably have found its way through the entire population already.

Now it was only a matter of time.

What he wanted was all that equipment in the Cardassian medical bay. The bright lights, the quarantine fields, the *chance* for his people to survive. Instead of working down here in the worst possible conditions, on the worst possible disease.

At least he had access to the station's computer system. Not all of it, of course, not even most of it, but Narat had made the medical files—the official medical files—available to him. What Kellec wanted was the unofficial files. He had heard that the Obsidian Order had done experiments on Bajorans, and it seemed likely to him that this was one of those experiments gone awry. Not in its treatment of Bajorans, but in the fact that it had somehow spread to the Cardassians.

Gul Dukat hadn't eased Kellec's mind on that, even though he had tried to. The fleeting look that had crossed his face when Kellec had accused the

Cardassians of this acknowledged the possibility. If this were a Cardassian experiment to destroy the Bajorans that had gotten out of control, then Kellec needed to know. He was better at solving puzzles when he had all of the relevant information.

He pulled a blanket across the poor girl. The disease accented her natural beauty, flushed her thin cheeks. Her hands were permanently dirt-stained and callused, but with them covered, she looked as she should have looked at this age, a young girl who had just finished flirting with a young man, a girl with no cares at all.

Just by looking at her no one would be able to guess that she would probably be dead before the day was out.

The comm link that Narat had given him beeped. That was the third time in less than an hour. Kellec supposed he should answer it. He had been trying to ignore it. The Cardassians believed that Kellec should be using his considerable brain power to help them, not his own people.

He hit the comm link so hard that he hoped he'd shattered it. But no such luck. Instead Narat said, "Why haven't you been answering my hails?"

"Because I've been treating dying patients down here," he snapped. "I got fifteen new patients in the last hour. Thirteen in the hour before that. I've forgotten how many came in the hour before that. So my hands are a bit full. What do you want?"

"Gul Dukat wants you to come up here. He believes you can't get work done down below."

Kellec clenched a fist, and then glanced around the room. People everywhere, holding their stomachs, rolled in fetal positions. The moans were so soft and so prevalent that he had to focus on them to hear them. And the smell. . . .

Kellec shook his head. His assistants were doing what they could. A handful of others, brave volunteers, were sitting at bedsides, holding hands, comforting, even though they knew they were staring in the face of death.

"Work?" Kellec asked. "What kind of work?"

"Finding a solution to this thing. We need—"

"We need some understanding. My people are dying. Or has Gul Dukat forgotten how sympathetic he believes he is toward the Bajorans?"

Narat was silent for a moment. A long moment. Then he said, "I presented this wrong. I know you're working below. But you and I must solve this thing together, and that takes research, I'm afraid. I have patients too, and they're dying—"

"Are they?" Kellec said. "Well, they're dying in better rooms than my people are, and so far they're dying in fewer numbers. I don't see what I'll gain from working with you."

"Then you're not the man I thought you were," Narat said.

Kellec took a deep breath. He did know what he'd gain. He had lied. It was precisely what he had been hoping for a few minutes ago. Better equipment. More access. Hope.

His assistants couldn't do the research. Only he could do that. And he was essentially useless here.

"You're wasting time, man," Narat said. "And we both know how precious time is."

"Yes, we do," Kellec said. He sighed. It wasn't that he hated the Cardassians. He did, in theory, although Dukat had been right when he said that Kellec would save a life before he'd take one. Any life, even a Cardassian life. No. His hesitation was more complex than that. He feared that his work with Narat would help the Cardassians at the expense of his own people.

"Kellec," Narat said into his silence. "You are the better researcher."

How much that must have cost the proud Cardassian doctor. To admit that he was less talented at medicine—*at his job*—than a Bajoran. To admit he needed a Bajoran's help.

"I tell you what," Kellec said. "If Gul Dukat is so set on needing my services then he must pay for them."

"I don't have the ability to authorize payment," Narat said, just as Kellec expected him to. But Kellec didn't give him time to say anything more.

"I want to move all of my people, both the sick and those who were exposed, to your medical area. I don't want them held in place like prisoners, although I do want quarantine fields so that we can do proper work. I want them to die with dignity if they're going to die, Narat, and if we find a way to save them, I want to make sure my people get treatment as fast as your people do. I also want my assistants up there, at my side, helping with all the work."

"Done," Narat said. His answer was too fast. He apparently had been going to promise that anyway.

Kellec paused. He wanted more. Some other concession, something that would make him feel like he wasn't being pulled by the Cardassians.

"If Gul Dukat wants to keep his prisoners alive and working in uridium processing," Kellec said, "he needs to increase the food rations. And he can't keep up production at its current rate. We have too many sick down here, and if he pushes the remaining people, the illness will just get worse. I want a mandatory eight-hour sleep period for all Bajorans, and a decrease in production."

"You know I'm not authorized—"

"Yes," Kellec said. "I know you're not authorized. But Gul Dukat is.

He's the one who makes the rules. Have him make this one. If he does, I'll come up."

"I'll do what I can," Narat said. "But you're wasting time."

Narat signed off.

Perhaps Kellec was wasting time, but he didn't think so. He needed to take care of his people first. It would only take Narat a few moments to get Dukat to agree to the concessions.

In the meantime, he stood and stretched. He needed some nourishment himself. He had some food and vitamin supplies in the tiny room the Cardassians had allotted him. It would do his people no good if he succumbed to this disease too. He had to do what he could to fend it off, and part of that was remembering to eat.

He slipped out of the medical area, and hurried down the corridor to his room. He suspected his room had once been some kind of storage closet. There was barely space for his bed. There was no replicator, no real bathroom—only a makeshift one with an old and malfunctioning sonic shower—and no porthole. Still, it was personal space, which was greatly lacking for Bajorans on Terok Nor.

He reached into his kit for a supplement, and saw instead that his personal link was blinking. He felt cold. He had brought the system up from Bajor, and so far the Cardassians hadn't tampered with it. Or if they had, they hadn't said anything. On it, he kept all his medical notes, and an open line to Bajor itself, since he theoretically was not a prisoner here.

His people on the surface were not to send him messages unless it was urgent. He had received several messages in the last few days about the plague, messages he had forwarded to Narat, partly as information, partly to prove he wasn't hiding anything from the Cardassians. Most of the messages requested that he return home. The plague had struck there, too, and was running through areas of Bajor the way it was running through Terok Nor.

He had sent carefully worded messages back, saying that he would remain on Terok Nor. Gul Dukat might see that as a twisted form of loyalty when, in fact, it was prudence. Kellec had not received word that the Cardassians on the surface had been affected. They had been here. That, plus the promise of using the Cardassian medical files, was enough to keep him here, for the moment. He had a better chance of finding the solution on Terok Nor.

With a shaking hand, he reached for the message button. It was a notification transmission. Once he responded, the person on the other end would be alerted, and they could have a conversation. He sat down and waited.

To his surprise, Katherine's face appeared on the small viewscreen. Her brown hair was tangled about her face, and her blue eyes were filled with compassion.

She looked very, very good.

And very far away.

"Ton," she said.

"Katherine."

"I was worried about you."

He smiled tiredly. "You always worry about me."

She nodded. "I'm hearing very bad things about your part of the quadrant."

"We're at war, Katherine," he said.

"No," she said. "I'm hearing more than that."

He frowned. She was asking about the plague. Had word reached the Federation then? He didn't dare ask her directly.

"Why are you calling me now, Katherine?"

"I'm surprised to find you still on Terok Nor. I would have thought they needed you on Bajor."

"They've been requesting my services on Bajor," he said. "But I'm too busy here. I haven't slept in two days, Katherine. I'm sorry, but I don't have time for small talk. Otherwise I'd ask about you and the *Enterprise* and all your various adventures. But I'm needed desperately elsewhere. Gul Dukat has demanded that I work in the Cardassian sickbay as well. It seems that my expertise is now considered to extend to Cardassians."

"It sounds serious," she said.

"It is." Then he paused and looked at her. They had always been attracted, and incompatible. He missed that soft, calm manner of hers. She had never been as intense as he was, but she was as driven, perhaps more so. She simply believed in conserving her energy for important things.

"Are you all right?" she asked softly.

"Tired," he said, "and distracted. There's too much I don't know, Katherine, and I have no time to learn it."

"Well," she said in that slow way of hers. "I wanted to tell you that I am no longer on the *Enterprise.* If you need to reach me, I'll be on Deep Space Five for a short time. I'll let you know when I go elsewhere. I haven't gotten my new duty assignment yet."

So that was her ostensible reason for this contact. Brilliant, Katherine. "Thank you," he said. "I always appreciate knowing what's happening with you."

She smiled. He loved that smile still, and missed it more than he wanted to admit. "Please," she said. "Take care of yourself."

And then she signed off. He sat in front of his system for a moment and forced himself to breathe. The Cardassians would find nothing amiss with that message, and yet he heard an entirely different conversation than the one they had in words. That was the benefit of having once been married; he and Katherine had a language all their own.

What she had really done was ask him about the plague. She had heard it was on Bajor, and was surprised he wasn't there treating it. He told her that it was bad, and that it wasn't just affecting Bajorans. The Cardassians had it too, which was why he was on Terok Nor. He also told her, as best he could in that limited conversation, that he had no solutions. Katherine was an excellent physician. She would know what that meant.

He sighed and ran a hand through his hair. That might be the last time he talked with her. Ever. If he got this thing.

But he couldn't think that way.

He didn't dare.

He stood. What he wouldn't give to have her here, now. She was the best researcher he knew, and she was up on all the current information. Her position at Starfleet gave her access to medical information from almost everywhere. He knew that the Federation had dealt with this sort of cross-species contamination, but he didn't remember where, and he didn't have the resources to find out. Katherine would.

She had one other asset that he couldn't discount. The most important one. She was one of the most creative physicians in the quadrant. She had discovered and neutralized all sorts of alien viruses, and she had a knack for discovering the right solution at the right time. If Katherine were here, she would look at that virus and the way it affected Cardassians versus the way it affected Bajorans, and she would know the detail he was missing. She would know, or she would do everything she could to find out.

Just as he was doing.

He sighed. Even if Narat wouldn't meet his terms, he would go to the Cardassian medical section. He had to. Discovering how to neutralize this virus was the only chance they had.

And maybe the only chance his people had.

Chapter Seven

DUKAT CONSTANTLY LOOKED at his skin. It was still gray. But he was rubbing it all the time. It had been crawling since the last time he had been in the medical area. He wasn't sick yet, but he had a hunch he was infected. He had a hunch they all were.

He didn't want to return to the medical area, but he had to. Narat hadn't reported since Kellec Ton had made his demands. Lower production. Eight-hour sleep schedules for Bajorans. Kellec's people were strong. They didn't need such precautions. Kellec Ton was taking advantage of Dukat, and Dukat was letting him.

It wouldn't last long. When this disease was cured he would make the Bajorans work double and triple shifts to make up for the lost production. He had to. He had quotas to fill. If he fell behind, he would lose his position here on Terok Nor. And that was the last thing he wanted.

The second-to-last thing. The last thing he wanted was to be the gul who watched an entire space station succumb to an incurable plague.

He stepped inside the medical area. It was jammed with patients. All the biobeds were full. Cardassians and Bajorans lay side by side, apparently not noticing each other. Bajoran and Cardassian medical workers examined the sick, carrying pads, studying readouts, administering pain medication.

The stench in the area was worse than before. Dukat put a hand over his mouth and nose. He couldn't help himself. The smell was so powerful, he doubted it would ever leave him. He would have to destroy his clothes.

If the odor was that strong, did that mean the quarantine fields weren't working? The crawling sensation in his skin grew worse.

He was a soldier. He had seen death countless times. He could handle this as well.

But he knew, deep down, that this was different. This was the kind of death every soldier feared. Impossible to resolve. Death by weakness, by illness, not in the course of battle, not for some important cause, but because something microscopic managed to defeat the body because the body wasn't strong enough to handle it.

Dukat made his way through the rows of moaning people to the office. He stopped at the door. Narat sat at one terminal, Kellec Ton at another. Above them, holographic images of the virus spun in slow circles. Computer readouts scrolled on each side, one readout in Cardassian, the other in Bajoran. The office was dark except for the light near the terminals themselves and whatever light was given off by the holographic image.

Dukat stared at it for a moment. Enlarged, the virus looked like an alien species, vibrant and alive. He didn't know much about biology—he didn't know the terminology for the prongs, or the fat center of the thing, or the ladder-like connectors on the sides. All he knew was that he would see the thing in his dreams. If he ever had time to sleep again.

"Are you finding anything?" he asked.

Both men jumped. Neither had heard him arrive. At least they were working hard. Narat turned to him. Kellec took another sample vial and placed it in the scope. He didn't bother to turn at all.

"Not enough," Narat said.

"We have found several things," Kellec said.

"We're just not finding out what we need quick enough," Narat said.

Kellec still hadn't turned. Dukat closed the door. "What things?"

"Well," Narat said, even though Dukat had directed the question at Kellec. "We have been able to confirm that this virus was created."

"Created?"

"By someone," Kellec said. "It doesn't occur in nature."

"We had suspected as much when we knew that it affected both Bajorans and Cardassians, but the virus's structure confirms it," Narat said. "See the—"

"I trust your opinion," Dukat said. "What does this mean?"

"Someone created it," Kellec snapped. "Someone targeted us intentionally, either both of our peoples or one of them."

Dukat suppressed a sigh. He had sent word to Central Command and to his contacts in the Obsidian Order. No one knew the cause of this virus, or if they did they weren't admitting it.

"If we could find who did this," Narat said, "we'd probably find a solution."

"But we don't have any time," Kellec said.

"I know," Dukat said. The casualties throughout the station were growing.

"No, you don't know," Kellec said.

Narat put a hand on Kellec's arm, but Kellec shook it away. He faced Dukat.

"This virus is extremely lethal." Kellec slid his chair back and pointed to the image above him. This time it showed small round blobs that appeared to be floating in something. "These are normal Bajoran cells. Now watch what happens when I introduce just one virus."

The virus was darker and flatter than the cells. It had a nonsymmetrical shape, accentuated by the precision of the cells themselves. It looked like a scout for an invading army.

Dukat stepped farther into the office, fascinated in spite of himself. The virus latched on to the nearest cell. Then the virus destroyed the cell and moved to another. If a cell happened to divide, the virus did too. The process was repeated cell by cell.

"The incubation period, at least in Bajorans, is fairly long for a virus of this type," Kellec said. "We don't know how it's introduced to the body, but we do know that once the virus has infiltrated the system, the disease progresses very rapidly."

Very rapidly. As Dukat watched, the virus destroyed the last remaining healthy cell.

He shuddered.

"I don't know if we can reverse the virus's path," Kellec said. "It completely destroys any cells it touches. But I suspect that we could stop it in the incubation phase—if we could only find it."

"This is the Bajoran version," Dukat said. "What about the Cardassian?"

"The virus seems to be the same, with slight differences; but it reacts the same way to Cardassian cells," Narat said. "It's as I told you before. Only the symptoms are different. But I am having no more luck than Kellec in discovering the way the virus is spread."

Kellec turned in his chair. His face seemed thinner than it had before, and he had deep shadows under his eyes. The disease was taking something from him as well, and he wasn't even sick.

"Actually," he said. "We're not being entirely accurate. You saw what happened in my sample. If I were to take the virus and touch you with it, either through fluid or saliva, you would get sick and die within the day. That is happening to some of our people. But they are not the ones who hold the secret. The ones who hold the secret are the ones who have incubated the disease for days or weeks. We do not know how many people are incubating it now. I'm testing my own blood to see if I am, but so far I have found nothing."

"We do know," Narat said, "that the virus itself can be spread by touch and through bodily fluids, but not through the air. But it has moved into too many people to be spread simply that way, so something else is spreading it. We just don't know what."

Dukat tensed.

"We have been cautioning everyone, but I suspect it's too late. We must not allow anyone to leave Terok Nor, and no one should come here." Narat bowed his head. "We have to remain completely isolated until the disease has passed."

Dukat straightened his shoulders. He had stopped all departures from Terok Nor already, and he wasn't allowing most arrivals. But the ore shipments continued, and he had been planning to allow the ore ships that were docked, waiting for processed material, to leave when they reached their quotas. To fail at this would mean admitting to Central Command that Terok Nor was crippled.

But it *was* crippled—perhaps dying.

"You haven't done that already?" Kellec sounded shocked. "We explained how important quarantine was."

"I've done what was needed," Dukat said. He wasn't about to admit that he hadn't done a full quarantine on Terok Nor.

"Do more," Kellec snapped.

"You're out of line, Bajoran," Dukat said.

Kellec tilted his head. "What are you going to do to me? Kill me?"

Dukat froze, then forced himself to breathe, hoping Kellec hadn't seen the expression on his face. Kellec had hit something Dukat hadn't realized: If the surviving Bajorans believed they had nothing left to lose, if they believed they would die anyway, they might rebel in ways that the Cardassians couldn't stop, particularly if his people were ill. He would become the gul not just of a station that succumbed to a plague, but a station in which all the Cardassians were overthrown before the plague took everyone out.

"I wouldn't be so smug, Kellec," Dukat said. "You blame my people for this disease, but yours could just as easily be responsible. Your rebels are sometimes willing to die for what they believe in. They might think: If a few Bajorans die to rid the universe of the Cardassians, that is not such a great price."

"My people aren't the ones attempting genocide," Kellec said. "Yours are."

"If we were attempting genocide," Dukat said, "your people would all be dead by now. Don't you see that Cardassian rule is better for you than leaving you to your own devices?"

"I'm sure it is," Kellec said. "My people are so happy processing your precious uridium."

"Please," Narat said. "Please. Both our peoples are dying. Can't we stop recriminations for a few moments and just concentrate on saving lives?"

"It is not in Gul Dukat's nature to save lives," Kellec said.

"That's right," Dukat said sarcastically. "That's why you're on the station. Because I have not a thread of compassion in my system."

"Stop this!" Narat shouted. "Now!"

Both Dukat and Kellec turned to him. Dukat had never seen Narat so flustered. Not even when his medical section was filled with casualties all needing his attention did Narat look this distressed.

"We have to find a way to destroy this disease," Narat said, "or we will all die. Bajoran, Cardassian, it doesn't matter. The virus doesn't seem to care. And neither can we. We have to work together."

He stood. He was of the same height as Dukat, but his back was hunched after years of studying and researching, bending over computers and lab specimens. Narat had served as a field medic, but he had never been a soldier. His body lacked the rigid discipline that Dukat's had.

"I know you realize how serious this is," Narat said to Dukat, "but I don't think you realize the scale. People are dying on Bajor as well. It will only be a matter of time before this spreads to Cardassia Prime. *We* may have spread it there in our ore freighters. Kellec and I do not know, and we can't even hazard a guess. We don't know how long this thing incubates. We may have contracted this disease from Bajor months ago, and may have been spreading it to Cardassia Prime all this time. Or even farther. We don't know."

Dukat took a deep breath. He hadn't thought of that. "I can't do anything about that," he said. "Central Command knows we have sick Bajorans here, and that the disease has spread to our people. They know the extent of the disease on Bajor. They will have to work out the rest of it themselves."

"I'm not telling you this so that you do anything about Cardassia Prime," Narat said, "although if I knew of something you could do, I would tell you. No. I'm telling you this because Kellec and I need help. We have been treating sick patients and trying to find a cure for this disease. We are making progress, but it's not enough, and it's not fast enough. The more minds we have working on this, the better."

"You can link with doctors and researchers all over Cardassia," Dukat said.

"It's not enough," Kellec said. "We've contacted Bajor as well, and the physicians there are as tired and as stumped as we are."

Dukat sensed they already had a solution. They were simply preparing him to hear it. Which meant he wouldn't like it.

"I have heard rumors," Kellec said, "that the Federation dealt with a virulent cross-species disease recently, and found a way to contain it."

"You heard this—what, a few hours ago, when you received that wonderfully sweet message from your ex-wife?"

Kellec flushed. Good, Dukat thought. The doctor had gotten a bit too arrogant for Dukat's tastes. It was good to give him a bit of his own medicine.

"No." Kellec was obviously struggling to maintain his composure. "I knew of this before."

"So why didn't you ask her about it?"

"Because I thought someone might be listening in," Kellec snapped.

"But," Narat said quickly, "the contact did give us an idea."

So, Narat was going to present this idea. And he was going to present it as his own as well as Kellec's.

"I'm waiting," Dukat said.

"Kellec's ex-wife, Dr. Katherine Pulaski, is one of the Federation's best doctors. She is currently not assigned anywhere."

"If she's one of the best, why doesn't she have an assignment?"

"She will," Kellec said. "The Federation is arguing within itself. There's too much demand for her services."

"So how does this apply to us?" Dukat asked.

"We'd like to bring her here. Have her work with us, and focus on the research itself," Narat said.

"No," Dukat said. "I will not have the Federation here."

"She wouldn't come as part of the Federation," Kellec said. "I could ask her to come for a family emergency."

"No," Dukat said again. "She's Federation. And I will not have them here." How many times did he have to repeat himself?

"Don't say no yet, Dukat," Narat said. "There's another, quite compelling, reason I think we should go with this plan."

Dukat crossed his arms. All he needed was the Federation to get its hooks into this place. They'd been looking for ways for years to discredit the Cardassians. This would be a first step. "What's your compelling reason?"

"She's human," Narat said.

Dukat shrugged.

"Chances are, she will not get this plague."

"So?" Dukat asked.

Narat put a hand on Dukat's arm. "Think of it. Right now, you have Kellec and me working on a cure for this disease. We can't keep up with both the research and caring for the patients. If one of us succumbs or, even worse, if both of us do, that's effectively signing a death warrant for you, Terok Nor, and all of Bajor."

Dukat stared at Narat's hand until Narat moved it. "We'll send for someone from Cardassia Prime, then," Dukat said.

"But would they come?"

Narat's question hung between them for a moment. Dukat didn't have an answer. Or maybe he did and didn't want to face it. What would he do, if he were on Cardassia Prime and making decisions from there? He wouldn't see the death, wouldn't smell it. The lives here would be statistics, except for the handful of people he knew, and even then, he would have to evaluate their importance to Cardassia. Coldly.

He closed his eyes. In that situation, he would ask himself: Is it worth sending a needed doctor or medical researcher off Cardassia Prime on a mission that may or may not succeed? Or would he be better off letting everyone die and letting the plague die with them? Then, after some time had elapsed and someone had discovered a cure, sending in a cleaning crew and beginning all over again?

He knew the answer to that. He knew it. He would do the most efficient job he could, the one that would bring the best results. If Central Command saw what this disease did, they would do anything they could to keep it from coming to Cardassia Prime. They would help from the surface, but they would not send help. It would be too dangerous to send help.

Dukat sighed and opened his eyes. "All right," he said. "Send for the woman. But do it unofficially, as a family emergency, just as you suggested."

"Can she bring assistants?" Kellec asked.

Dukat glared at him. Kellec was never satisfied, always wanting more. Always wanting too much.

"Assistants would be a doctor's first request," Narat said. "It would be yet another guarantee."

Dukat was being manipulated and he knew it. But he couldn't see any way out of this. He couldn't see any way at all. At least, not a way he liked. Not a way that ended in success. This felt like one of his only chances.

"I want no more than five Federation people here, less if possible," he said.

"Good," Narat said.

"You may not say 'good' after a moment," Dukat said, "because I have conditions."

Kellec tilted his head back. Narat held his position, waiting, like the good Cardassian that he was.

"First," Dukat said, "they will have access only to our medical files. Second, they shall be restricted to the medical areas of Terok Nor only. Third—"

"That's not possible," Kellec said. "What if the illness spreads so fast that we can't get the patients here?"

"We'll deal with it then," Narat said.

"Third," Dukat said as if he hadn't been interrupted, "they shall have no contact with the outside while they're here."

"But what if they need information they didn't bring?" Kellec asked.

Dukat glared at him. "I will not negotiate these terms."

"We can deal with special requests on a case-by-case basis, I assume," Narat said, more to Kellec than Dukat. "Am I right?"

Dukat wasn't even willing to make that promise, although he knew it was probably sensible. "Fourth, if I suspect even one of them is spying for the Federation, none of them will leave here alive. Is that clear?"

"Very," Kellec said.

"If your ex-wife is willing to come here under those conditions, then we will be happy to have her," Dukat said. "But I do not want a Federation ship docking at Terok Nor. I do not want one in Cardassian space."

"Then how will she get here?" Kellec asked. "You've just quarantined the station, so no ships can come here."

Good question. The man was always thinking.

"I'll have one of the freighter pilots trapped here on Terok Nor take his ship to meet the Federation vessel at the border. I'll send a few of my men along to make sure nothing untoward happens."

"Make sure they're all pilots," Narat said softly.

Dukat felt himself go cold. Narat was right. There was no guarantee the pilot would live long enough to ferry their Federation passengers back to Terok Nor.

"Tell your ex-wife to get here as quickly as possible," Dukat said. "I'll handle the travel arrangements personally. And Kellec?"

"Yes?" Kellec said.

"Don't see this as a victory for the Bajoran people. I meant what I said about spies. Your Federation help had better be on their best behavior. I will give no second chances."

Kellec had the good sense to only nod.

Chapter Eight

FOR THE SECOND TIME in a few days, Katherine Pulaski was packing her bags. She was in her quarters on Deep Space Five. All of her possessions were scattered about. She had just unpacked, and hadn't had time to hang her favorite paintings or to place her few sculptures. Her hardcopy books stood on a single shelf, including the first edition of Sir Arthur Conan Doyle's Sherlock Holmes stories that Data had given her upon her departure. It was a sentimental gift, and it had surprised her coming from Data. Apparently that surprise had shown on her face because he had tilted his head in that slightly robotic way he had, and asked, "Is the giving of parting gifts not a human custom, especially when the recipient will be missed?"

"It is, Data," she had said, and then hugged him, to his surprise and (she had to admit) to her own.

She stared at that book for a moment, but it would only add weight. Better to keep it here until she returned.

If she returned.

She had only a few more items to add to her bag, and very little time in which to do it. Her assistants would be reporting here before they went to the docking area to reboard the *Enterprise.* How strange it would be to be a guest on the very starship she had just served on.

Her hands were shaking, but it was not from fear. It was a release of tension. Her meeting with Starfleet Medical had been dicey. Thank heavens the *Enterprise* was still in dry dock. She had needed Beverly Crusher's help.

Kellec's request had come in a few hours before. It was less than

Starfleet had hoped for. They wanted to send in a large team to study the problem, perhaps work on Bajor. They wanted to use it so that they could gather more information on both the Bajorans and the Cardassians, as well as find a solution to this plague.

But some Cardassian official had anticipated this. The restrictions were severe. Pulaski wasn't sure she could do the work with only a handful of assistants. At first Starfleet wanted her to wait until they could get four specialists in plagues and alien diseases to go with her, but it would take days for the specialists to arrive from their various posts. She didn't have days. That was the one thing Kellec had made very clear.

He wasn't sure he would survive this. The Cardassian doctor who was looking over his shoulder as Kellec contacted Pulaski didn't look very confident either. The information she had gotten from them, purposely sketchy, was awful. They did give her the death rate on their space station, and it was climbing by the hour.

She played the message for Starfleet Medical. Then she asked that Beverly Crusher accompany her, as well as the three other ranking medical officers currently on Deep Space Five.

Starfleet Medical turned her down. This was a risky mission, they said. They didn't dare send that many valued officers.

Meaning they could sacrifice researchers but military medical staff was in short supply.

Meaning there was a good chance Pulaski and her team might not come back.

Starfleet Medical was going to try to negotiate with the Cardassians—after all, they reasoned, this was a medical emergency, and working together could benefit everyone—but Pulaski knew that wouldn't work. She had asked Crusher to come with her to argue for the high-ranking personnel, which hadn't worked. But Crusher had argued against negotiation, and on this Starfleet Medical had listened to their former director. They decided—and the Federation representatives agreed—to let Pulaski go in with lower-ranking assistants.

The next argument was about whether to bring in sophisticated equipment that would help send information back—not medical information, but information on the Cardassians and the Bajorans. Crusher had proved her worth here too, arguing that such equipment would jeopardize the lives of those being sent it.

"This is a mission of mercy," she had said. "We need to treat it like one. If Dr. Pulaski and her colleagues gain information on the Cardassians and Bajorans as a result, they can be debriefed when they return."

If they return. The last sticking point had been travel arrangements. They were going to use the Cardassians' plans to get them to Terok Nor, the space station that Kellec was on, but Pulaski had no idea how they would be able to leave. She was supposed to contact the Federation from Terok Nor when she was ready to go, but she had a hunch that sounded too easy. And what if she wanted to leave and they didn't want her to? They had to have a fail-safe for this, and so far no one had suggested one that seemed workable.

Pulaski finished the last of her packing. Amazing how she could bring her life down to two little suitcases—one a sophisticated medical kit with everything she hoped she would need. The other contained basics like clothing and Kellec's favorite—hot chocolate. He couldn't get it anymore on Bajor.

She closed the case just as someone hit the chime outside her door. "Come in," she said.

The door slid open and a woman entered. She was human—all of the team was, a precaution that Kellec had mentioned and Starfleet Medical had agreed with. She had blondish brown hair and compassionate eyes. She wore street clothes, just as she had been ordered to do. They were flowing garments of a gauze-like material, in a pale blue that became her fair skin.

"You must be Crystal Marvig," Pulaski said. "Welcome."

"Thank you," Marvig said. She glanced around the quarters, her gaze falling on the books. "I didn't know you collected real books."

"I don't," Pulaski said. "But each of these is personal to me, in its own way."

"I love books," Marvig said. "Particularly twentieth-century literature—you know the kind. The stuff that predicts the future."

Pulaski laughed. "I've seen it. It's amazing what they believed would happen."

"And how right they could be," Marvig said. She clasped her hands behind her back. The military posture didn't go with her relaxed attire.

"You've been briefed on this mission, I assume," Pulaski said.

"They told me it was a need-to-know."

Pulaski cursed under her breath. She had wanted her assistants to know what they were getting into. "And what did Starfleet Medical believe you need to know?"

"That this is a highly sensitive mission, and that it's quite dangerous."

"Brief and vague," Pulaski said. "How like them." She sighed. "Let's wait until Ensign Governo gets here, and then I'll brief you both."

"Edgar Governo? He's been assigned to this as well?" Marvig asked.

Pulaski nodded. "Do you know him?"

"We've been serving together here on Deep Space Five. He's never been on an away mission."

"Well, this is more complicated than an away mission," Pulaski said. "I trust they told you to pack lightly."

"And to keep suspicious items from my single piece of luggage, whatever that means."

Pulaski recited a list of items she believed could cause them problems on Terok Nor. Marvig shook her head at each item. As Pulaski was finishing, the door chime rang again.

"Come in," she said.

Ensign Governo entered. He was a thin young man with dark hair and intense eyes. He wore his regulation boots beneath black pants, and over a cotton T-shirt he wore a leather jacket. The effect was retro, and more stylish than Pulaski had expected. Seeing Starfleet personnel out of uniform was always a surprise.

She had met Governo just after her conference with Starfleet Medical. He was younger than she had would have thought from his record. He had an amazing gift for understanding alien physiology; it had gained him awards and accolades at medical school, and he had graduated at about the same time as Marvig, who was older.

Governo had a small bag slung over his shoulder. "I'm ready when you are, Doctor." Then, before she could respond, he saw Marvig standing near the books. "Crystal!"

"Edgar." She smiled. It was a warm smile, just the kind a patient needed to see. Pulaski was glad to see it too. Compassion and empathy were probably lacking at Terok Nor. "It looks like we're going on an adventure."

"Yes," Pulaski said, "you are."

"Only the three of us?"

"No. Alyssa Ogawa will join us on the *Enterprise.* She's one of the best nurses in the fleet, and I'm pleased to have her. She'll outrank both of you, and I want you to listen to her."

The two of them nodded.

"Were you briefed at all?" Pulaski asked Governo.

"I was told that this mission would be difficult and dangerous," he said, "and that if I had any qualms about working with infectious disease, I could back out now without a black mark on my record."

"That's more than I was offered," Marvig said.

"Well, I'm offering you more," Pulaski said. "I want you to know exactly what you're getting into."

She explained the situation to them, including the rules the Cardassians placed on their visit. She also explained the danger, the difficulties they would have on a station owned by a people who were not affiliated with the Federation, and the Federation's conflicting motives in sending them there.

"I do not want you to spy," Pulaski said. "You will be debriefed when you return. Remember all you can. I'm not even sure you should record anything in your personal logs—aside from the things you did that day, or medical notes. We have to be very cautious. *Very* cautious."

"Why are the Cardassians even allowing us to come?" Governo asked.

"They didn't say," Pulaski said, "and neither did Kellec. But I have a guess."

They waited, staring at her.

She took a deep breath. "I think they think this disease is so contagious none of them will be able to avoid it. I think they're gambling on it not affecting us, that we'll have a chance of curing it before everyone dies."

"Wow," Marvig said. "That's a dark view."

Pulaski nodded. "They wouldn't have sent for us otherwise. The Bajorans have no power over the Cardassians, and the Cardassians have repeatedly rebuffed Federation overtures in the past. I think this request smacks of desperation."

"I thought we were in negotiations with the Cardassians," Marvig said.

"We are," Pulaski said, "but they're not going well, and there are rumors they will fail. For whatever reason, the Cardassians do not trust the Federation, and we are representatives of the Federation. That's why we're going in an unofficial capacity, and that's what makes this mission even more dangerous."

"How's that?" Governo asked.

"If we run into trouble," Pulaski said, "we're on our own. The *Enterprise* will be just outside of Cardassian space, but she cannot enter it without Cardassian permission, permission they did not give in this emergency to get us to Terok Nor. I can't imagine that they would give it to get us out."

Marvig's face grew pale. "But what if we need to escape?"

"We have to be creative," Pulaski said. She stared at both of them. They were so young. Alyssa Ogawa was young too, but more experienced. A starship did that for its crew. "But we have to understand the risks. The greatest risk for all of us here is that we will not come out alive."

"What do you think the chances are of that?" Governo asked.

"High," Pulaski said. "I won't lie to you about that. I think at best we have a fifty-fifty chance of survival."

"I don't understand," Marvig said. "If we're in negotiations with the Cardassians, then why would they kill us?"

"We don't know what this disease is," Pulaski said. "And we've never seen the inside of one of their ore-processing stations. If one of us inadvertently comes across information that the Cardassians see as sensitive, we could all be punished for it."

They were staring at her as if it were her fault the mission was dangerous. Perhaps it was. Perhaps this wouldn't be happening at all if it weren't for her relationship with Kellec. But that didn't matter. What mattered were all those lives being lost.

"You may back out now," she said, "as long as you keep what I've told you confidential."

Governo seemed to be considering what she was saying, but Marvig jutted out her chin.

"I joined Starfleet so that I could do more than practice general medicine in some human colony. I joined it for the risks," she said. "It wouldn't do my oath any good to back out now, just when things get really difficult."

Governo looked at her as if he were surprised at what she said. "You're right." He nodded, a crisp, military move. "I'm a healer first."

"All right," Pulaski said. "Let's hope that all my warnings were merely an overreaction to the Cardassians' conditions."

But in her heart, she knew they weren't. And she wondered, as she gathered up her things, whether she had misrepresented the odds to the two before her.

If anything, she had overestimated their chances of survival. If all the stories Kellec had told her were to be believed, she would be surprised if they got off the station at all.

Chapter Nine

KIRA NERYS STOOD in the heat, sweat plastering her filthy shirt to her back, her feet swollen inside her boots. A blister rubbed against the inside of her heel. These boots were too small, even without the swelling. She had taken them—a gift really—from a dying friend. Amazing, that all they had to give each other anymore were items of clothing, bits of food, things that they had once taken for granted.

Her earring tinkled in the breeze. She had been wishing for a breeze not too long ago, but it only seemed to make things hotter. She was outside a rebel cell, and it wasn't even her cell. That's why they kept her here, waiting, until they made some decision about her.

She stared at the makeshift tents. Whoever ran this cell didn't plan things real well. They were in a hidden valley, one that was not on the maps but was pretty well known in this part of Bajor. The tents were pitched near a small creek, bone dry in the summer heat. If she had been in charge of this cell, she would have had them pitch their tents on the mountainside, where scraggly trees and boulders would have provided cover. As it was, if the Cardassians found this valley now, they would have found the cell.

Not that she was in any position to give advice.

She was here chasing rumors. She had heard of serious illness to the south, and had actually seen some of the bodies in a message sent to her by Shakaar. The problem was that neither she nor Shakaar had seen them die. There was talk of a disease, there was talk of a plague, but—so far—no one in her part of Bajor had seen evidence of it.

Not that she doubted that it existed.

She was told that Javi's cell knew more about it, and she had set up a meeting with one of her contacts. It had brought her here, a long trip through areas that weren't friendly to people like her. She was known as a member of the resistance, and even before last year's escapade on Terok Nor the Cardassians had been watching for her. They didn't know she had been to Terok Nor—the station's constable, Odo, had seen to that—but they suspected her. They suspected her of everything, but could never catch her.

Not for want of trying.

She sighed and ran a hand through her short hair. She could feel the sweat at the roots. She wished Javi would hurry. She didn't like waiting in this heat.

Finally, a woman slipped out of one of the tents. She wore a ripped dark dress, stained with sweat and dirt. The poverty here—even among the resistance—broke Kira's heart.

"Javi will see you now," the woman said.

Kira wasn't sure she wanted to go inside the tent. It had to be even hotter in there. But she climbed up the small incline to the creekside where the tent was, and slipped inside.

She had been right. It was hotter here. The heat felt old and oppressive, as if it had been accumulating for days instead of hours. Javi sat cross-legged near his portable computer system—the heart and soul of each resistance cell, Shakaar had once called those things. Javi was thinner than he had been the last time Kira saw him. His skin had the look of malnutrition, but his eyes were still bright.

Near him sat Corda, his second in command. She was taller than Kira and too thin as well. But on her it looked tough, as if the dry air and the heat and the lack of food had hardened her skin and made her more resilient.

"Sorry to keep you waiting, Nerys." Javi spoke slowly, as he always had. He had been part of Shakaar's cell for a brief time, and he had always irritated Kira with his cautious consideration of each decision. Apparently he had annoyed Shakaar too, because one day Kira heard that Javi had left with some of his own people to form a new cell. They were on speaking terms, though, and still had the same goals, unlike some of the resistance cells Kira had come into contact with. There were some that frightened even her, with their talk of noble suicide and total destruction.

"If I had known what it was like in here, Javi," Kira said, "I would have insisted you keep me waiting longer."

Javi shrugged. "You get used to the heat."

"Maybe you can get used to this heat. I certainly couldn't."

"Don't start, Kira," Corda said. "You're not here to criticize us."

"And it's a good thing, too, because I think your campsite is too exposed—you're putting your entire cell in jeopardy."

"But you're not here to tell us that," Corda said sarcastically.

"No," Kira said, "I'm not. I'm here because I'm supposed to confirm some rumors."

"About the plague," Javi said.

Kira went cold despite the heat. "They're calling it a plague now?"

"Hundreds dead, Nerys." Javi's voice was solemn. "Everyone who comes in contact with this thing gets ill."

"Everyone?" Kira asked.

"In time," Corda said.

"How have you gotten your information?"

"Do you mean were we exposed?" Corda asked. "No. We've been getting it the same as you have, in messages sent through sanitary computers."

Kira had never liked Corda. And the heat wasn't improving Kira's mood. "I'm not here to talk to you."

"You get to talk to me whether you like it or not," Corda said. "I'm the one who has been following this thing and reporting to Javi."

Kira glared at her for a moment. Corda glared back, not at all intimidated.

"This isn't helping us," Javi said. "We need to work together. Nerys has come to us for information, the kind, I believe, that isn't easily sent."

"But Corda just said that you haven't heard anything that we haven't heard," Kira said.

"I did not," Corda said. "We've gotten that, and we've gotten reports from other sources."

"Others?"

"Non-Bajorans. Some of the relief teams not tied to the Federation. They seem to be unaffected."

The relief teams were from charitable organizations that went to planets they considered not as developed to help with basics: food, medicine, clothing. Sometimes Kira appreciated their presence, sometimes she resented them more than she could say. What she wanted was Federation intervention, to stop this occupation by the Cardassians. But the Federation had rules and regulations, things she had never bothered to understand, and those rules and regulations didn't seem to apply to Bajor, although some people were telling her to be cautious with her tongue, that some day the Federation might come through.

She would believe that when she saw Bajorans move around unfettered on their own planet.

"What are they doing to stop this thing?" Kira asked.

"What they can," Corda said.

"Most of them are volunteers, Nerys, with no more medical training than we have." Javi sounded tired. Kira wondered how much power he had ceded in this cell to Corda, and how long it would be before she took the group too far. "They provide comfort where they can, but they can't do much."

"They are sure it's a disease, then?" Kira asked. "Shakaar wasn't. He thought maybe it was a Cardassian trick to get us focused in the wrong direction."

"It's a disease, all right," Javi said. "But it might also be a Cardassian trick."

Kira frowned. "What do you mean?"

"The disease is too virulent." Javi's words hung between them.

Kira's chill grew deeper. She wiped sweat off her forehead. "Not even the Cardassians would do something this monstrous," she said.

"Do you actually believe that?" Corda asked.

Kira wasn't sure. "If we're talking about a disease that infects everyone who comes in contact with it—"

"We are," Corda said.

"—then we're talking genocide." Kira swallowed. "The Cardassians have always made it plain that they see us as a lesser species, as people who 'benefit' from their rule, as slaves to work in their various mines and processing plants. But not as creatures to be wiped out of existence."

"They've always wanted Bajor," Corda said.

"Yes—but with its Bajoran population." Kira wiped the sweat off her face.

"Get her something to drink," Javi said to Corda.

"But—"

"Now," Javi said.

Corda sighed and got up, sliding past Kira.

"I'm sorry, Nerys," Javi said. "I know you don't much like Corda. But you must listen to her. She has run this cell, for the most part, since last fall."

Kira glanced over her shoulder. Corda was out of the tent. "I'm just worried, Javi," Kira said. "She didn't always understand the complexities of the Occupation."

Javi smiled. "Once I could have said that about you."

Kira looked at him. "Why is she running everything, Javi? What's going on?"

"The Cardassians had me for a while, Nerys. We're just beginning to bring me back to health. The tents are here not because Corda thinks it's a good spot, but because my body can hardly tolerate thin air at the higher elevations. Even this valley is difficult for me. We should really move on, now that the creek is dry, but the cell has opted to stay with me. I've tried to order them to leave, but they won't."

Kira threaded her hands together.

"Corda loves me," he said.

"And is making the wrong decisions for the cell because of it," Kira said.

Javi nodded. "We agree on that. But they're not life-threatening. Not yet, anyway. And I'm nearly mobile—I think we can get out of here soon. But do me a favor, Nerys. Listen to her. And don't fight her. This Cardassian threat is too great for us to be fighting amongst ourselves."

Kira let out the breath she hadn't realized she had been holding. Javi was right, of course, and she knew it. But she had disliked Corda for a very long time. It was hard to set aside that kind of antipathy, even now.

"All right," Kira said.

"Good." Javi placed his hands on the ground behind him and rested his weight on them. "I hope she brings me something as well. You're giving me an appetite again, Nerys. That's a good thing."

Kira laughed. "I've been accused of worse, I guess."

"What's he accusing you of?" Corda asked as she came in. She was carrying a tray with three mugs. She handed one to Kira. It was moba fruit juice, and somehow they had found a way to keep it cool in all this heat.

Kira took a sip, and relished the bittersweet coldness. Corda handed Javi his mug, and he sat forward, taking it in both hands as if it weighed too much for him. Kira wondered if his prediction was wrong, if he wasn't getting better at all.

"He's been yelling at me to listen to you," Kira said. "He says you've changed."

Corda glanced at Javi as if he had betrayed a confidence. He was looking at the mug he was drinking from and didn't seem to notice.

"Whether I've changed or not shouldn't matter," Corda said. "What does matter is what's happening. You don't believe the Cardassians can commit genocide. I do."

"I didn't say that," Kira said. "I said it's not in their best interest to kill us all."

Corda sat down, cradling her own mug in one hand. "But what if it is now? What if they no longer need us for all those jobs Cardassians refuse to do? What if they've finally found a way to automate the most dangerous tasks?"

Kira stared at her. It was possible. It was even probable.

"Now tell her the rest," Javi said.

Corda set her mug down. "We don't know for certain."

"Tell her," Javi said. "If you're going to do this right, tell her all you know. In every case."

Maybe Corda hadn't changed after all. Maybe Javi only believed she had. Maybe he had no other choice. Kira waited for whatever "the rest" was.

"We've heard," Corda said, "through less reputable sources, that Cardassians are dying of this also."

"That's not possible," Kira said. "They've always lorded their superior physiology over us, saying they're not vulnerable to Bajoran diseases. How could that change?"

"Do you believe all Cardassian lies?" Corda asked.

"That one I do," Kira said. "I've seen Bajorans die of horrible diseases, and never once have I seen a Cardassian get sick like that."

"Maybe they don't allow their people to get sick."

"And maybe it's the truth," Kira said. "If they got sick, we would have seen it. I've been in places where I know I would have seen it." She set her mug down as well, although she was reluctant to give up the last of the juice. "Maybe you're the one who is believing the lie. Maybe the Cardassians are the ones spreading the rumors that Cardassians are getting sick. That would make this illness look like an innocent virus instead of something the Obsidian Order dreamed up."

Javi smiled slightly. He was still the only one drinking. "See why we needed to hear from Kira?" he asked Corda. "Neither of us thought of that."

Corda's lips thinned. "We can't operate on supposition."

"I agree," Kira said.

"What we have heard is that a few Cardassians here have gotten ill, but they've been spirited away so fast that no one can confirm that it's the same disease. A few of the rumors say it's not. The Cardassians turn green and their scales flake off—or so they say. And Bajoran victims look even healthier than they did before they got sick, so maybe it's not related at all."

"But we don't know," Kira said.

"That's right," Corda said. "We don't know. And I have no idea how we could find out."

"Where were the Cardassians taken ill?" Kira asked.

"In the same regions where the Bajorans were sick," Corda said. "And a Ferengi said that he saw some green Cardassians on Terok Nor."

"Ferengi can't be trusted," Kira said. "They can be paid to give false information."

Corda nodded. "The problem is that, if my sources on Bajor are right, the sick Cardassians here have already been sent away."

"To Cardassia Prime?"

"I don't think so. But it doesn't matter. We have no idea where they've gone."

Kira frowned. "Just before I came here, I'd heard that Gul Dukat just gave an order that no outside ships were to arrive on or leave Terok Nor."

Corda's gaze met hers. Javi set down his mug. "Now we're getting somewhere."

"I didn't think much of it, until you mentioned the station."

"Dukat wouldn't care about his Bajoran prisoners," Corda said. "But he would care if Cardassians were getting ill."

"And even if he didn't, Central Command would order him to shut down operations if the Cardassians had a disease that spreads the way you described."

They stared at each other.

"What if it's a different disease?" Corda asked.

"What if it's not?" Javi asked.

"It doesn't matter," Kira said. "I'd been thinking of going to Terok Nor anyway."

"What? Nerys, what are you talking about?"

She turned to him and took his hand. It was cold from the mug, but the skin was dry and his bones felt thin beneath her fingers. He had lied to her. She had seen starvation victims before—the ones who survived but were never really healthy again. He wouldn't live long, and it wouldn't take a designer virus to kill him. A simple cold would do it.

"I've been to Terok Nor before, Javi," she said. "Just last year, I was there getting information for the resistance. It's dangerous, but it's possible to get around."

"Why would you go?"

"I was planning to go for a completely different reason," she said. "If the rumors of the disease among the Bajorans proved to be true, and now after talking with you I believe they are, I was going to Terok Nor to bring Dr. Kellec Ton home."

"What's Ton doing there?" Corda asked.

Kira glanced at her. She hadn't expected Corda to be familiar with Kellec Ton.

"Apparently, Gul Dukat sent for him a month ago. Dukat claimed his precious workers needed better health care, which I think is unlikely. Dukat has never cared for anyone. His production must have been down or something."

"Or perhaps this disease started on Terok Nor," Javi said, "and that's why he sent for Kellec."

"Maybe," Kira said. "But it didn't sound like that. I talked to Kellec before he went. He was going to see what he could do to further the resistance on Terok Nor. He was also going to use his free time to find weaknesses in the station, maybe a way for the resistance to get the Bajoran workers out of there."

"We don't have the ships for that," Corda said.

Kira shook her head. "You need to choose someone else to lead this cell after you, Javi."

"I don't appreciate all your insults, Kira," Corda said.

"I shouldn't have to tell you about the benefits of a quick and dirty surprise operation. We may not have big, powerful ships like the Cardassians, but we can slip in and out of any place, and with the right plan, we could get workers off Terok Nor."

Corda's smile was cruel. "Just don't pick Kira to relieve me, Javi," she said. "Kira has no idea about the realities of war."

"You don't know—"

"Ladies!" Javi said tiredly. "We fight Cardassians, not each other." He ran that thin hand along the side of his face, tugging at his earring. "Maybe that wouldn't be a bad mission, Nerys. Going to Terok Nor. You could find out if the Cardassians were ill, and if they were you could report back. But bring Kellec home."

"If he wants to come."

Javi nodded. "One more thing. I've been studying the information we've received. It's only a matter of time before everyone on Bajor gets ill if this is as bad as it seems. And so far, whoever has gotten ill has died."

Even in the heat, Kira couldn't suppress a shiver.

Chapter Ten

NOG WAS SITTING on the bar, his feet dangling over the edge. He was kicking the front with one heel, then the other, with no apparent rhythm at all. Quark didn't know what was worse, the boy's idleness, his disregard for the bar's rules, or the constant *bang, bang, bang* echoing in his ears.

"Do something useful," Quark said, shoving Nog as he passed. "And get off my bar."

"There's nothing useful to do, uncle," Nog said.

"There's always something useful." Quark picked up a dirty glass off one of the empty tables. Three groups of Cardassians sat at various tables, but they certainly didn't look as if they were celebrating. They were at least drinking—to excess, always a problem with Cardassians. Not that Quark could blame them. If there was really a disease going around that was going to make him turn green (which was only one step down from that hideous Cardassian gray), he'd probably start drinking too.

Or leave. Sneak off. Find somewhere else where the threat of death wasn't hanging over everything. He might do that anyway. He'd hardly had any customers in the last few days.

"But *what,* uncle?" Nog asked, still on the bar.

"For one thing," Quark said, "you can get off my bar. Then you can polish it from top to bottom with an earbrush."

"You're not serious."

"I've never been more serious," Quark said. "And remember, you'll do that every time you sit on my bar."

"You could have told him that sitting on the bar wasn't allowed, brother." Rom had apparently come out of their quarters. He wore a hat the Volian dressmaker had made him. It was made of some stretchy black material and molded itself to Rom's skull. It made his head look smaller, but at least it hid his ears.

"I would have thought sitting on the bar would be an obvious mistake, wouldn't you?" Quark asked.

"Actually, no," Rom said. "Rules are easier to follow if they're clear."

"Like not spilling things on the customers?"

"Are you ever going to forget that?" Rom asked.

"Not as long as you wear that silly hat." Quark brought the glass around back and set it beside Nog. "And wash this too, while you're at it."

Nog jumped off the bar, picked up the glass and started for their quarters.

"I want that bar shiny within the hour!" Quark called after him.

Nog didn't respond. He disappeared into the darkness as if he hadn't heard.

"I mean it, Rom," Quark said. "I want that bar cleaned in the next hour—"

"I'll do it," Rom said.

"—by Nog. He has to learn too." Quark sighed and surveyed the bar. He hated this quiet. The Cardassians were panicked and Gul Dukat had ordered that no more ships of any type could dock on Terok Nor. So not only were the Cardassians dwindling, thanks to disease and general fear, but the others who came through here, the suppliers, traders, and shadier types weren't appearing either. Quark's supply of Saurian brandy was getting low, and so were some of his more popular but hard-to-find items.

Rom scratched the top of his head. "Brother, do I have to wear this hat? It itches."

"Yes, you have to wear the hat," Quark snapped. Then he lowered his voice. "I can't have you serving customers with that blister on your ear."

Rom's hand went involuntarily to his right ear and Quark turned away in disgust. Nothing, ever, would get the memory of that out of his brain. Rom said it didn't hurt, but it was the ugliest thing Quark had ever seen. It served Rom right for the mistakes he had made earlier—and for not telling Quark that he was allergic to Jibetian beer.

Who knew what that horrible mixture of fluids had done to Rom's ears, anyway? The ears of Ferengi were their most sensitive spot. If an allergic reaction was going to start, it would start there. And Rom's allergy to Jibetian beer was bad enough, apparently, to have put him in sickbay on a freighter when he was a young man. Of course, Quark had been long gone by then and hadn't known about it. And Rom, typically, hadn't bothered to tell him, even when he knew he'd be working around the stuff.

"There aren't that many customers, brother," Rom said. "Perhaps it would be better if you waited on them yourself."

"You're right," Quark said. "Perhaps it would be better. Then I wouldn't have to pay you."

"But brother, how will Nog and I live?"

"Good question," Quark said. "And the answer is not very well if you refuse to do the work you're assigned. Now, go see if those tables need refills."

Rom tugged the hat. Quark could see the blister as an added lump on Rom's ear. Quark grimaced in distaste. How the Volian had managed to make a hat while looking at that ear was beyond Quark. And of course, Quark had had to pay for it. Rom didn't have any latinum yet; Quark was keeping track of all of these expenses in his ledger, but he had no idea how expensive the whole proposition was going to be. Rom had arrived—with Nog—and then the bar's business had dropped off. Who knew how much an eleven-year-old would eat? And constantly. It was as if he was going to grow as tall as a Cardassian. Or more likely, as if Rom hadn't fed him well before.

Rom reached the first table. Three Cardassians sat there, bent over their glasses as if their posture would protect them from the virus floating around the station. One of the Cardassians shook his head as Rom spoke to him. Rom smiled and bobbed a little, then backed away.

He stopped at the second table. There the Cardassian, one of the pilots who had poured liquor on Rom, said in a loud voice, "If you're trying to protect your skull from getting drenched, you'd better make sure that hat is waterproof."

"No, actually," Rom said. "I'm allergic to Jibetian beer and—"

"Rom!" Quark shouted.

"—I break out—"

"Rom!"

"—so I'm wearing this hat—"

"Rom!"

Rom looked up. "Brother, I—"

"One more word," Quark said, "and I will fire you."

Rom put a hand to his mouth. The Cardassian laughed. Rom made his way through the tables and leaned across the bar.

"I'm sorry, brother," he whispered. "But if I can't talk, how can I take orders?"

"One more word about the ear," Quark said slowly, as if he were speaking to a child. "Make up a story about the stupid hat. A story that doesn't involve pus."

"Sorry, brother," Rom said.

Nog came out of the quarters, clutching an earbrush in his left hand. Quark's earbrush. His best earbrush, the one with the real scagsteeth bristles.

"Nice try," Quark said, "but you use your own brush."

"He doesn't have one, brother."

"Then he can use yours," Quark said.

"He does anyway."

That was it. That was all it took. Quark's stomach actually somersaulted.

"Or I did," Nog said, "until Dad got that—"

"Enough!" Quark shouted. "Enough! No one is ever going to mention that again. Do you hear me? No one!"

All of the Cardassians stared at him as if he had gone crazy. The second group, the one that included the pilot that had been harassing Rom, seemed a bit bleary-eyed, and Quark realized they were drunker than he had initially thought they were. Getting them out of the bar would be difficult. Not that it mattered. He hardly had anyone in the bar as it was.

"I heard you, brother," Rom said.

That brought Quark back to himself. He turned toward Nog. "You, young man, you put my earbrush back and never touch it again. I don't share earbrushes with anyone, and I don't let just anyone touch them." Then he glared at Rom. "How could you? Not buying your own son an earbrush."

"He had one," Rom said. "He forgot it when we left Ferenginar, and I—"

"Didn't have enough latinum to buy him a new one, I know," Quark said. "Believe me, I know."

He shook his head. How did it always end up that *he* was the one who paid for everything? He sighed.

"Get yourself an earbrush, Nog, but for now, use your Dad's." Then Quark thought of that blister, and all the germs it carried. "Never mind. Don't after all. Get a cleaning cloth. But I still want the bar spit-polished. You understand?"

"You want me to spit on it?" Nog asked.

"No," Quark said. "It's a military term. I just want it so polished that it shines. Is that clear?"

Nog nodded. Why did everything become an impossible task with these two? Running the bar was suddenly three times harder.

The first group of Cardassians got up and left their tables, mumbling something about sleep. The second group was still huddled over their drinks. He could barely see the third group, but they seemed to be deep in conversation.

Customers leaving and none entering. Things couldn't get any worse.

Quark took a padd. He would inventory his alcohol one last time, and hope it lasted—of course, with this drop in business, it would last easily. He glanced at Rom.

"Just go away," he said.

"But brother, I haven't asked the other table if they wanted more to drink."

"Ask them, and then go away."

"Where are the cleaning cloths, uncle?" Nog asked.

Five times more work, Quark thought. At least.

Rom walked over to the last table. The drunken Cardassians at the second table catcalled him in soft tones. Quark didn't pay attention to what they were saying. He told Nog where the cloths were and was about to get back to his inventory when a Cardassian at the third table stood up.

He was green, like so many others had been in the last few days. Quark knew now that that was the beginning of the disease. He had been denying service to anyone who was green, but apparently the Cardassian had changed shades while he was in here.

The Cardassian raised a hand, looked at Rom, and toppled over backwards. His companions didn't seem to notice. Neither did the drunks at the next table.

Quark walked over. The Cardassian was on his back, moaning, a hand on his stomach. The other three at his table had passed out but they, at least, were a normal gray.

"Brother," Rom said. "We need to call for help."

"Oh no we don't," Quark said.

"But, he's—"

Quark put a hand over Rom's mouth. "I'm going to ban you from ever speaking in this place again."

"Bashender?" One of the Cardassians at the other table said. "You got any blood wine?"

"Yes," Quark said, even though what he had probably wasn't any good. He just didn't want the Cardassian looking at him.

"Get me shome," the Cardassian said.

"Nog!" Quark shouted. "Blood wine?"

"What?" Nog asked.

"Blood—oh, never mind." Quark turned to Rom and said very softly, "Stay right here, and cover his face."

"With what?" Rom asked, but by then Quark was already gone. He got the blood wine, and brought it back to the drunks.

"You know," he said to them, "you gentlemen look like you could use a free hour in a holosuite. Why don't you come with me?"

"Free?" Rom asked. "Brother, have you lost your mind?"

"What did I say to you about talking?" Quark snapped. He helped the Cardassians up, and guided them away from the sick Cardassian. He was careful to keep their backs to him, by talking to them the whole way, expounding the virtues of the various programs, hoping that Nog wasn't listening too closely to some of the programs.

He got them up the stairs and into one of the suites, the door closed behind them. Then he came back down the stairs.

The Cardassian's companions had well and truthfully passed out.

"What should we do?" Rom asked.

"Take his feet," Quark said.

"We're carrying him to the medical section?"

"Are you nuts?" Quark asked. "That's what medical people do."

"Then why aren't you calling them?"

"Why are you still talking?" Quark asked. "Pick up his feet."

Rom walked to the Cardassian's booted feet. "Can we get this disease?"

"If anyone can, you can," Quark mumbled.

"What?" Rom asked.

"No, we can't," Quark said.

"How do you know?"

"Because we would have had it by now."

"They don't have it," Rom said, looking at the three passed out at the table.

"Ferengi don't get Cardassian diseases," Quark said, although he had no idea if that was true.

"Oh," Rom said. "Are you sure?"

"Positive."

"All right, then," Rom said, and crouched. He grabbed the Cardassian's feet and lifted them.

"Nog," Quark said. "Keep a lookout. Let me know if you see any Cardassians or Odo."

"Odo?" Nog asked.

"The obnoxious shape-shifter who has been harassing me"—then Quark realized that Odo hadn't been in the bar in almost a week. "Never mind. Just let me know if you see anyone."

"All right," Nog said, and bent over the bar, continuing his polishing.

"At the door, Nog," Quark said. "Go to the door. Like a lookout."

"Oh," Nog said. "You didn't say that."

"What do I have to do? Put it in writing?"

"That might help," Rom said.

"Shut up."

Nog scrambled to the door. He stood there like a small sentry, looking just like Rom had at that age. Sincere, honest, clueless. Quark sighed. He hoped Nog understood what he was looking for.

"Brother . . ." Rom said, still holding the Cardassian's feet.

Quark nodded. He picked up the Cardassian by the armpits, and nearly staggered under the weight. Who knew that Cardassians were so heavy? Or that they smelled like this? Up close, the Cardassian's green skin looked even more noxious. His scales were flaking. Quark's stomach, already queasy thanks to Rom's ear blister, threatened to revolt.

"I don't know how much longer my back can take this, brother," Rom said.

Quark didn't know how much longer his stomach could take it either. "All right," he said, "here goes."

He stumbled backward, kicking a chair as he went. The Cardassian's butt dragged on the ground, his uniform leaving a polished streak mark on the dirty floor.

"Everything I do creates more work," Quark mumbled.

"What?" Rom said.

"Nothing. Just lift him higher."

"I can't, brother."

"You could if you weren't holding his feet."

"What do you suggest?" Rom asked. "His knees?"

They were halfway to the door. Quark wanted this guy out of the bar as quickly as possible. If he made Rom switch positions, quickly might not happen.

"No," Quark said. "Let's just keep going."

At that moment he backed into another table. Pain ran along his spine and he bit back a curse.

"Are you all right, brother?" Rom asked.

"Fine," Quark said, and moved around the table. Why did he have so much furniture in here in the first place? What had he been thinking?

The strain on his arm muscles was almost too much. He felt sweat run down the side of his face, get caught on his lobe, and work its way into his ear. It was his own fault for thinking the day couldn't get any worse.

He glanced over his shoulder. Nog was still at the door, looking out into the Promenade. Apparently he didn't see anything, or he would have said so. Right?

"Nog," Quark whispered. "Is it clear?"

"What?"

"The Promenade. Is there anyone there?"

Nog took a step farther out, which did nothing to bolster Quark's confidence. Then he turned back to Quark. "Yes."

Quark nodded at Rom. "This is the last leg," Quark said.

"I hope so," Rom said. "Is it my imagination or is he beginning to smell worse?"

It wasn't Rom's imagination. The Cardassian was beginning to smell like a Klingon meal made by a bad cook. Quark moved as fast as he could. He was still looking over his shoulder as he went through the doors. It wasn't that he didn't trust Nog. Or maybe it was.

The Promenade was mostly empty. The doors to the restaurants and stores were open, but there were no clients. The Volian sat in the window of his tailor's shop, working on an outfit, but he didn't appear to be looking up. Quark thought he saw something shimmer near the door to the bar, but when he focused on it, he saw nothing at all.

"Clear," he whispered.

"What?" Rom asked.

"Is that blister making you deaf?" Quark snapped.

"I hope not." Rom brought a hand to his ear, and the Cardassian tipped sideways. The Cardassian's foot bounced loudly on the floor. Quark nearly collapsed under his weight.

"Will you do your job?" Quark snapped. "Pick up the foot. Pick it up."

"Where are we going with him?"

"Just behind that post," Quark said, nodding in the opposite direction from the Volian's store. They were getting close to the second floor balcony, but he didn't see anyone there either. And he would have to take the risk.

They also couldn't leave a polished streak running from the Cardassian to the interior of the bar.

"Wait!" Quark said. "Nog, grab the Cardassian."

"Me?"

"Do you see anyone else named Nog?"

Nog came over, rubbing his hands together. His small face was squinched in an expression of disgust. "Where do you want me to hold him?"

"Where do you think?" Quark asked. "He can't be touching the ground."

Nog gave him the most pitiful expression Quark had ever seen. "I can't."

"You will or I'll make you clean the bar with your head skirt every day this week."

"You can't do that!" Nog said. "It isn't sanitary."

"Then I'll make you sanitize it after you're done."

"Don't underestimate him, son," Rom said. "Remember the drinks." And he reached for his ear.

"No!" Quark said too late. The foot bounced again, but this time Nog had grabbed the Cardassian's midsection.

"I want to go back to Ferenginar," Nog said. "Maybe I can live with Moogie."

Rom struggled to reach the foot without dropping the other one. Quark thought his arms would break.

"Moogie wouldn't treat me like this."

"Moogie would hide you in a closet," Quark said. "She has dreams of finding a better mate, and the last thing she needs is a grandson hanging around so that people know her age."

Rom got the foot. He nodded. "I promise I won't drop it again."

"Good," Quark said. "Or Narat will think broken ankles are part of this disease."

"You think I broke his ankle?" Rom said. "I didn't mean to. I mean—"

"No, I don't think you broke his ankle," Quark said. "But I might break yours soon."

They carried the Cardassian into the Promenade. Their footsteps echoed on the floor. Quark had never heard the Promenade echo before.

It was only a few meters to the post Quark had seen, but it felt like they had to travel light-years. When they reached it, and Quark gave the okay, all three dropped him at the same time. It sounded as if something exploded on the Promenade.

"Come on!" Quark said and ran for the bar.

"But, brother, what about the medical staff?" Rom was keeping up with him. So was Nog.

"You call them," Quark said. "But you will not mention the bar, got that? Tell them—oh, never mind. I'll do it."

They got inside and Quark slipped behind the bar. Before he contacted anyone, he was going to wash his hands. They felt sticky with sweat, and something else. Germs, probably. Virus. Possible infection.

He grimaced. He had a hunch things were going to continue to get worse. Much, much worse. And he doubted they would ever get better again.

Chapter Eleven

THE CARDASSIAN CREW piloting the freighter didn't mix with its passengers. Pulaski, Governo, Marvig, and Ogawa were confined to a small area that had once served as the crew's mess. The tables were bolted to the floor. The walls were a gunmetal gray, undecorated, and the room smelled of stale food Pulaski couldn't identify. There were no portholes, so she couldn't see the stars, but the freighter ran relatively smoothly, so she also couldn't feel the hum of the engines. It felt as if she were in a room on Cardassia Prime instead of in a freighter heading toward Terok Nor.

Her team was already working. Governo was bent over his research padd, reading about infectious diseases. Marvig was studying Cardassian physiology. Ogawa was supposed to be looking in the files to see if there was any previous history of cross-contamination between these two species, but she wasn't. She was staring at the walls, much as Pulaski was doing.

Alyssa Ogawa was slender, with dark hair and dark eyes, as human as the rest of them. Pulaski hadn't planned on putting together a completely human team, but Starfleet Medical thought it for the best. The less the Cardassians had to object to—and they would probably object to every species that arrived on Terok Nor—the better.

Pulaski was glad to have Ogawa for several reasons. The first and most important was that they had worked well together on the *Enterprise.* The second was that Ogawa was familiar with Bajoran physiology. The third was that she was the best nurse Pulaski had served with in her entire time in Starfleet.

Ogawa was also fairly level emotionally, and Pulaski would need that. Kellec wasn't, and even though Pulaski usually was, one of the things that had caused their marriage to dissolve was that Kellec could pull her into his moods. Ogawa would help Pulaski keep her own sense of self. She wasn't sure about the other two; since she had never worked with them before, she didn't know if they would be calm or highly volatile. Nothing in their personnel histories suggested any problems along those lines, so the best Pulaski could do was hope.

The group had managed the trip well so far. Captain Picard had strained the *Enterprise*'s engines getting her to the border of Cardassian space within sixteen hours of Pulaski's appointment. He would continue to patrol the area, waiting for her signal, for the next two weeks. If she didn't come out by then, another starship would take its place. The area would be patrolled indefinitely—or so Pulaski had been told. She doubted that Starfleet would continue to expend such resources for four officers, albeit good and valuable ones, much longer than a month. She had mentioned that to Captain Picard and he had looked away from her ever so briefly, as he had done when he told her that Beverly Crusher was returning to the *Enterprise*.

I am afraid I have been told the plan for the next two weeks. The other starship will wait at least as long, but you know as well as I do, Doctor, that things change within our universe in an instant. Should something happen and the Enterprise *must leave ahead of schedule, I shall get a message to you, and we shall make certain you have a way off Terok Nor.*

She had thanked him, of course, but they both knew that she was taking a great personal risk. Starfleet could only support that risk so far, and then she was on her own.

She sighed and stood up. She had forgotten how warm Cardassians liked their ships. She had forgotten a lot about them. How big they were, on average, and how disconcerting it was to see that gray skin—a color she associated with illness. Governo mentioned how reptilian he thought they were; she had forgotten that he had never seen a Cardassian before. That was why she gave him the assignment to study their physiology.

The room they placed the group in was getting smaller by the minute. Pulaski hated waiting. The Cardassian pilot had told her the trip would only take a few hours. She took that to mean three. It had been four, and she felt that was too long. She did know the freighter was operating at its highest speed, trying to get her to Terok Nor.

The Cardassians on board, the pilot and the handful of others, whom she could only think of as guards, had obviously been instructed not to talk to the group. The pilot had looked uncomfortable just telling Pulaski their arrival time. When she had asked for information on the plague, he had stared at her. When she pushed, he had said, "I'm sorry, ma'am. I'm a pilot, not a doctor."

She had let the topic drop after that. She would find out all the pertinent information soon enough.

The door to the mess opened. She turned. One of the Cardassian guards stood in the doorway.

"We're about to dock on Terok Nor. Gather your things."

As he spoke, the entire freighter rumbled ever so slightly. Ogawa glanced over at Pulaski. They were the two used to being on board ship, and they both recognized the sensation. The freighter wasn't about to dock. It had docked.

Governo put his padd in his duffel. Marvig closed her research. Ogawa's was already put away. The three of them stood. Pulaski grabbed her two bags and walked to the Cardassian. "I guess it's time," she said.

He nodded.

He led them down a dark and dirty corridor, with dim lighting that made the gunmetal-gray walls seem black. Even the air here seemed thick and oily. Pulaski had to walk swiftly to keep up with him.

"Have you been to Terok Nor since the plague started?" she asked.

"No one's calling it a plague," he said.

That was more than she got out of the pilot.

"Have you?" she asked.

"We were told we were quarantined on Terok Nor. We were surprised to be assigned to pick you up." His voice was flat. He wasn't speaking softly, but the net effect, from his tone to his demeanor, was one of secrecy. For some reason he had decided to talk with her.

"How long have you been trapped on Terok Nor?"

"A week." He ducked into another dark corridor. It felt to Pulaski as if they were going in circles, but she knew they weren't.

"That's not very long."

"It is when most of your friends are dying."

Ah, so there it was. The reason he was speaking to her. "And you don't have the disease?"

"I probably do," he said. "I'm going to die like the rest of them."

"Surely you can't believe that," she said. "One must always have hope."

"Hope?" he said. "You'll forget the meaning of the word after you've spent a day on Terok Nor."

He opened one last door, and pointed. Through the airlock, she saw a series of huge, round doors, shaped like giant gears in an ancient machine. The Cardassian pressed a button and the doors rolled back, clanging as they did so, one at a time.

Her door opened first. She stepped through the airlock onto the docking platform, and then another door rolled back, and she was in Terok Nor.

The heat didn't surprise her, but a faint odor of rot did. Space-station filtration systems should take care of smells, unless the odor was so pervasive nothing could be done about it.

She resisted the urge to glance over her shoulder at her Cardassian guide, but his warning rang in her ears like an old Earth curse: *Abandon hope all ye who enter here.*

She did look around her for her team. Governo was at her side, Ogawa and Marvig were behind her. They looked as serious as she felt.

Pulaski stepped out the final door into the corridor. The ceiling was higher here than on the freighter, and the place was clean. It was still decorated in Cardassian gray, however. Didn't they understand the value of a well-placed painting? Or even a nicely designed computer terminal?

The corridor did seem to extend forever, however, despite the branches off it. Another feature of Cardassian design, she assumed. At least poor lighting wasn't part of the design here. The lights were bright enough in this corridor to show that these walls were clean.

Behind her someone cleared his throat. She turned. Three Cardassians blocked the corridor. She had been so intent on her destination that she hadn't looked both ways when she came out the door, and she had turned in the wrong direction.

Two of the Cardassians stood a few steps behind the Cardassian in the middle. He was taller than the others, his shoulders broader, and his face thinner. His eyes had an intelligence that made her wary. With his strange ridges, that sickly gray color to his skin, and those bright eyes, he looked like a particularly charming reptile, the kind that smiled before inflicting its poisonous bite.

In fact, he was smiling now. "Doctor Katherine Pulaski?" he asked. He had a warm, seductive voice that seemed, to her, completely at odds with his appearance.

"Yes," she said.

"I'm Gul Dukat. I run Terok Nor. We're pleased you could come here on such short notice." As if she were coming for a dinner party or to give a speech.

"If you'll point the way, my assistants and I will get right to work."

"First," he said, "I thought we'd get you to your quarters and give you a short tour of our facility. Then we'll take you to the medical section."

She drew a sharp breath. No wonder the Bajorans hated the Cardassians. How insensitive was this man? And then she realized what he was doing. He saw her as a representative of the Federation first, a doctor second. He didn't want her first impression of his station to be one of illness and death.

Governo stepped up beside her, and was about to speak. She put a hand on his arm, and shoved him backwards. Out of the corner of her eye, she saw Marvig take him and hold him back. That answered one question. Governo would be her impulsive assistant.

"Mr. Dukat," she said, purposely making a mistake on his title. "I—"

"Gul Dukat," he said in those dulcet tones. "Gul is my title."

"I'm sorry," she said. "I didn't know." She took a step closer to him. The three Cardassians were so tall, it felt as if she were stepping toward a forest.

He watched her as if he had never seen a human before.

"I would love to see the station," she said, "but I was led to believe the medical situation here is urgent. Perhaps if we get this thing under control, you can give me a tour. Right now, though, my assistants and I would like to put our things in our quarters and report for our duties."

Dukat inclined his head toward her. "What you will see in our medical section isn't normal for Terok Nor."

She smiled at him. It would be another part of her job, she realized, to charm the snake. "It isn't normal anywhere." She glanced up at him, making her look purposefully vulnerable. "Perhaps Kellec didn't tell you about me. I'm a doctor. I have no interest in politics. I'm here as a favor to Kellec."

"And your assistants?"

"Are here because they have leave and they volunteered."

His smile was just a bit jaded. "And that's why the *Starship Enterprise* brought you to the rendezvous, because you're a simple doctor, volunteering your time."

"No," she said. "Until a few days ago, I served on that ship. I am between assignments. Captain Picard gave my position to his former chief medical officer, so he owed me a favor."

Dukat clearly wasn't buying that, so she sighed.

"And besides, having a starship escort me was the only way we could convince Starfleet to let us come. They worry about having valuable personnel so close to the Cardassian border."

"You're inside Cardassian space."

"I know," Pulaski said. "And with luck, we'll be able to make your people well. Please, let us work first."

"As you wish," he said.

"In fact," she said, "it would probably be best to show my assistants to their quarters and lead me to the medical area. I'm sure Kellec and your doctor could use the relief."

"All right." Dukat turned to his guards. "I'll take Dr. Pulaski to the medical section. You escort her assistants to their quarters, and when they're settled, bring them to the section as well."

"Forgive me, Doctor," Marvig said, "but perhaps one of us should come with you. We can both get right to work."

"Good suggestion, Crystal, but I'm used to field medicine. None of you are. Trust me, it's better for you to get your bearings and then come. It will prevent burnout later." Pulaski turned to Dukat. "Shall we go?"

He nodded and then, to her surprise, he took her hand and placed it on his arm. Such a courtly gesture, and one that would certainly rile Kellec if he saw it. Still, she let Dukat do it.

His uniform was softer than she expected from its design, and his skin was cooler. She wondered if the heat in the Cardassian ship and now here, on Terok Nor, was because Cardassians had cold blood, just like the Earthly creatures they resembled. She was surprised she didn't remember, and made a mental note to brush up on her own Cardassian physiology when she had a free moment. Every detail was important, and things she had studied years ago that were now lost to the sands of time might be more crucial than she had initially thought.

Dukat led her through the maze of corridors. "What have they told you of Terok Nor?" he asked as they walked.

"Only that it's an ore-processing plant," she said.

"Ah, such an oversimplification," he said. "Terok Nor is more than a simple factory. We are a very large station, and many ships come through here on their way to Cardassia Prime. Did you see the station as you came in?"

"No," she said. "We were restricted to the crew's mess."

A dark, troubled look crossed his face, and that hint of danger she had felt from the beginning returned. This was not a man to be trifled with. "They should have treated you better. After all, you've come here as a favor to us."

"I assumed that they made room for us where they could," she said.

He nodded. "Well, if you had seen us as you came in, you would have noted the difference in design from your space stations. We have a docking ring, and a habitat ring, and we are at the cutting edge of Cardassian technology—perhaps of technology all through the sector."

She didn't know if he wanted her to ask questions or not.

"We've put your quarters in the best section of our habitat ring. If there's anything you need, you come directly to me."

"I'll do that," she said.

"I wanted to show you the heart of the station," he said. "It's our Promenade. We have restaurants, stores, even a Ferengi-run bar, if your tastes run to alcohol, Dabo, and questionable holosuite programs."

"I hope I will get a chance to sample all three," she said. "I'm sure I'll need them when we have everything under control."

"You sound confident that you can cure this disease," Dukat said. "Is there something you know that my people don't?"

"Perhaps it's ignorance on my part," she said, thankful that her year with Picard had helped her brush up on her diplomacy. "I do not know as much as Kellec or your doctor about this disease, and they refused to send me the specs before I arrived. But it's my nature to be optimistic. If I weren't, I wouldn't be a doctor. We're all a bit egotistical, you know."

"I hadn't realized that," he said with all the smoothness of a lie.

These corridors seemed to go on forever. She wanted to remove her hand from his arm, but felt she didn't dare, not yet.

"Yes," she said. "We are. I think it a necessary skill. It leads us to places that aren't safe, to try things others wouldn't think of, and never to accept failure."

"Have you ever accepted failure?" Dukat said.

"Accepted it?" she asked. "No. Experienced it? Yes."

"Ah, yes, your marriage to Kellec." He didn't miss much. Her sense of him was correct.

"I wasn't thinking of that," she said. "I was thinking of death. We all lose patients, and we're never happy about it."

"You're bringing that attitude to my station," he said.

"I am, and so are my assistants. We'll do everything we can to stop this thing."

He paused. The corridor opened onto a larger area. It must have been the area he had called the Promenade. Ahead she saw lights and advertisements in Cardassian. A group of Cardassian guards were crowded around a post. She saw that catch Dukat's attention, and then saw him pretend that it didn't matter.

"I believe you will do everything you can to stop this disease," he said, and he sounded a bit surprised. She frowned. Was this the real Dukat? Beneath that reptilian coolness, was there a worried leader beneath? He would have to be stupid not to be. If the disease were half as bad as she had heard, he had to be worried about dying himself.

"Just be careful, Doctor," he said. "Kellec Ton is a bitter man. Do not believe everything he says."

She smiled, even though she had never felt less like doing so. "I know," she said. "I was married to him, remember?"

Dukat laughed. The sound echoed in the wide-open space and the huddle of guards near the post all turned in his direction. He led her into the Promenade. There were shops with windows opening onto the walk area. In one window, a Volian sat at a table, hand-stitching a shirt. Another door opened and a strange-looking man slipped through it. He wore a brown uniform, and he crossed his arms over his chest as she walked by. His face seemed half-formed, or imperfectly formed. She had never seen anyone from a species like that before.

Dukat was explaining what all the places were, but she wasn't really listening. The guards had lifted a man from the floor and were carrying him without a gurney in the direction she and Dukat were walking.

"And this is Quark's," he said, sweeping a hand toward a nearly empty bar.

She peered inside. There was a lot of light and color, but no customers. A Ferengi stood behind the bar. He looked nervous, but then they all did to her.

This would probably be her only opportunity to let go of Dukat. She slipped her hand from his arm, and went inside the bar. The Ferengi looked at her in surprise.

"Care for a drink?" he asked.

Three Cardassians were passed out at a back table, and another Ferengi was trying in vain to wake them up. She frowned at them.

"A bit of hot water on the back of the neck usually wakes up a Cardassian," she said to the bartender.

"Really?" he asked.

Dukat came inside. "I thought you were in a hurry to get to the infirmary."

"I am," she said. "I just thought—well, I had the impression that this would be the hub of the station."

"It is," the Ferengi said. "When no one's dying."

"Quark." That menacing tone was buried in Dukat's voice again. He sounded so threatening and yet so nice. How did he manage that?

"Have we far to go?" Pulaski asked, walking out of the bar ahead of him.

"Um, no," Dukat said.

"And I take it the infirmary is this way?" She headed in the direction the guards had walked.

"Yes," Dukat said.

She couldn't look too knowledgeable or he would get suspicious, so she slowed down just enough for him to catch up to her.

"What I've seen of the station," she said, "is already impressive."

He smiled at her, and then turned a small corner. "Here is the medical section." A door to her right slid open, and instantly the stench of rot overwhelmed her. She gagged involuntarily and put a hand to her mouth.

"She's turning green!" Dukat said, a hand on her shoulder, trying to push her further inside.

She shook him off. "It's a normal human reaction," she said, barely keeping control of her voice, "when faced with a smell like that."

His call, though, had brought a Cardassian to the front, and behind him, Kellec.

Kellec. Too slim by half. He hadn't been eating again. His hair was messy and his earring was caught on the top of his ear. He had deep circles under both eyes, and lines around his mouth she had never seen before.

And he looked dear. Very dear.

"Katherine?" he asked. "Are you all right?"

"I just don't care for the local perfume," she said, and wrapped him in a great hug. He was thin, so thin he felt fragile in her arms.

He returned the hug, but she could feel him looking over her shoulder at Dukat. So she had been right. They were in a pissing match, and Dukat had tried—and failed—to turn her into an issue.

She stepped back and surveyed the room. There were cots everywhere, and makeshift beds, all filled with green Cardassians, many of them holding their stomachs and moaning despite obvious sedation. The green color was startling. No wonder Dukat had panicked when he saw her get nauseous from the smell. It showed that he was a lot more panicked than his let-me-give-you-a-tour-of-the-station demeanor let on.

She made herself turn to him, even though she didn't want to. "Thank you for your kindness, Gul Dukat," she said. "I do hope we'll be able to finish our tour later."

He bowed his head slightly. "It would be my pleasure, Doctor. And remember, if you need anything, anything at all, come to me."

"I will."

Dukat glanced at the Cardassian who stood to the side, and then his gaze met Kellec's. There was pride in that look, and measuring, and something else, some sort of challenge. And then Dukat left.

"Tour?" Kellec asked. "He took you on a tour of the station instead of bringing you here?"

"He's afraid I'm going to send a bad report to Starfleet," Pulaski said. "But I made him bring me here directly."

"No one makes Dukat do anything," Kellec said.

"Oh, I don't know," Pulaski said. "You managed to get him to bring me here." She put a hand through her hair, wishing now that she had had a chance, a very brief one, to stop in her quarters. Kellec always made her feel like that.

"Dr. Pulaski," the Cardassian who had rushed to the door said. "I'm Dr. Narat."

He was hunched over more by the demands of his profession than with age. His dark eyes were sharp as well, but his face wasn't as reptilian as

Dukat's. There was a softness to Narat, a compassion that seemed built into him. Even though she had never met him before, she got a sense from him that he, too, was exhausted.

"Thank you for coming," he said. "You are alone?"

"I brought three assistants. I sent them to their quarters to drop off their things before coming here. I wanted to assess the situation alone."

Narat nodded. He swept a hand toward the beds. "This is just one area, only the Cardassians. We have two other rooms full in the medical section and we've had to take over an empty business space right next door."

"My heavens," Pulaski said.

Kellec nodded. "If it weren't for all the deaths," he said, "we would need even more room."

She glanced at him. She wasn't used to him being so blunt. At least not about losing patients. So things were awful here. Only doctors who had seen a lot of death in a short period of time had that flat affect, that way of speaking about terrible things as if they were commonplace.

And apparently they were.

"How many have died?" she asked.

"Everyone who has been sick for longer than two days," Narat said.

Her gaze met Kellec's. It wasn't just exhaustion she saw in his eyes. It was deep, overwhelming sadness, and more—a frustration and anger so strong that he had to fight to keep it held back. He knew as well as she, as well as any doctor, that anger only blinded. He needed to remain level.

"How many is that?" she asked gently. "How many have died?"

Kellec shook his head. "We've been too busy to keep track of the numbers, and we have no real assistants. It's not a relevant statistic at the moment."

"But how have you notified the families?"

"Niceties are gone, Katherine," he said. "We haven't done anything except triage, palliative measures, and research. We haven't had time."

"Maybe now," Narat said. "Now that you're here, we can do some of those things again."

Pulaski nodded. It wasn't like Kellec to let go of the small details. For any reason. "You said everyone who contracts the disease dies?"

"Everyone," Kellec said. "Within two days."

She glanced around the room. If something weren't done, a solution wasn't found, all of these people would be dead soon. And all of the patients in the next room, and the next.

"Cardassian and Bajoran?" she asked. "No one has survived?"

"No one."

She shook her head. "I've never heard of a plague like that," she said. "The black plague on Earth, in the days when medicine consisted of trickery and leeches, left one-quarter of the population alive. The Triferian flu on Vulcan only killed half. The worst plague I've ever heard of, the Nausicaan wort virus, which struck a thousand years ago, killed 95 percent of the Nausicaan population. No plague kills one hundred percent. Someone always survives."

Kellec shook his head. "If you contract this thing," he said, "you die."

"And that's why you believe this is a designer virus?" she asked.

"That, and several other factors. Its precision, for one thing. And the way it works. Let us show you what we've found so far. It would be nice to have a fresh eye on things." He took her arm and started to lead her toward the office.

She stopped though, and gazed at all the moaning patients. One hundred percent death rate. No wonder Kellec didn't want to talk about it. That made their job a thousand times harder. The best way to beat a viral infection was to discover what was different within those patients who were exposed and didn't get sick. Or those who got sick and survived. Often their systems produced antibodies that worked against the virus, and those antibodies could be replicated and placed in those patients who didn't manufacture them naturally.

But a 100-percent death rate completely cut the traditional options out. The solution had to be a lab-devised one, just like the virus itself. And that required researchers, not medical doctors. She did research, yes, but her main focus had always been her patients. Maybe Starfleet had been right in trying to send the viral experts here.

Maybe. But to do so would have meant at least a hundred more deaths in the time it took those experts to arrive. At least she was here now. Her assistants could look after the patients, and she could work with Kellec and Narat to find a cure.

The confidence she had spoken of to Dukat had vanished. In her entire career, she had never faced odds like this. Terok Nor had a small population. In order to save any of it, she and her colleagues had to find a solution fast.

The problem was that all the shortcuts had been blocked off. They had to do the impossible, and she wasn't even sure how to begin.

Chapter Twelve

HE STOOD IN THE SHADOWS next to Quark's bar, marveling at the difference a few days had made. Before there had been laughter and shouting, games and relaxation, but now there was silence. The Ferengi, Quark, was complaining about the silence, still worrying about his business, not realizing that soon, everything on Terok Nor would come to an end.

He had found it amusing when Quark had carried the ill Cardassian outside the bar before allowing his brother to report the illness. Quark still believed everything would turn around, things would get better, his bar would come back to life, and he would continue to earn his precious latinum.

Soon latinum wouldn't be important at all.

He had had a bad moment, though, as Quark, his brother, and his nephew had passed, carrying the Cardassian. For an instant, his shield had fizzled. He had caught it in time, but Quark had turned his head, almost as if he had seen the shimmer the malfunction caused. Fortunately, the Ferengi was so self-involved that he apparently thought nothing of it.

Ever since, though, he had kept close watch on the shield. It was his only protection here, allowing him to go undiscovered. Not that there were many left to discover him. The sick Cardassians had made their way, one by one, to the medical section. The well ones were staying away from populated areas, keeping themselves in their rooms unless they had duties—and sometimes even then.

Humanoids all shared an attitude toward disease. No matter how sophisticated the society, humanoids still feared tiny little microbes that attacked the body unseen. From Cardassians and Bajorans to Trills and Klingons, the fear of illness was uniform. And all the more amusing in societies like Cardassia's. Soldiers seemed to fear disease most of all.

He had enjoyed watching Terok Nor's leader, Dukat, when he felt he was alone. The constant washing of the hands. His reluctance to touch other Cardassians or Bajorans. His nervous movements every time he was about to enter the medical section. All of them were tiny gestures, but they were oh, so telling. And if Dukat felt that way, so did all the other Cardassians. He almost wished the symptomatic part of the disease lasted longer. It brought out the fear in the unaffected—or the not-yet-symptomatic, to be more accurate—so much better.

He made a mental note about that, not certain if he were going to use it or not.

But he was here to observe, and since he had arrived, he had observed a lot. The way the Cardassians simply kept going until they lost control; the resigned futility among the Bajorans; the added calls to the Prophets who, of course, were not listening: All of this intrigued him. And pleased him, if he had to be honest. Things were progressing better than he had expected.

Although that could change. Dukat's mood seemed lighter since he escorted the human woman across the Promenade and into the medical section. She looked vaguely familiar, with her brown hair and calm demeanor. He had a moment of panic when she excused herself from Dukat and walked into Quark's. For a moment, he thought she was going to walk over to him. It was as if she saw him, as if she knew he was there.

Instead, she had asked the Ferengi a question or two, and then had gone on.

He hadn't expected humans on Terok Nor. He hadn't expected anyone associated with the Federation. He had purposely chosen Cardassians and Bajorans because they had no official ties with the Federation and so wouldn't request Federation help.

What this woman was doing here baffled him, but she had obviously been brought in to help find a cure. Fortunately, a cure would prove extremely difficult. If not impossible. Diseases did not act the way this one did. Most doctors weren't creative enough to understand something so different, so fundamentally *alien.*

A single human woman would make no difference in this laboratory. He would worry only when teams of scientists came in. Federation scientists.

And by the time they arrived, it would be too late. No matter how light Gul Dukat's mood, the fact was that Terok Nor was doomed.

He had done the projections before he came, a timetable assuming everything went according to plan—which it had, much to his surprise. It was now time for him to leave. His cloaked ship would pick him up shortly.

And probably just in time. According to his projections, Terok Nor had very little time left.

Chapter Thirteen

SHE WAS CRAZY to have come back to Terok Nor. What had she been thinking when she offered to come here? Certainly she hadn't been thinking very clearly.

It no longer seemed like the risks that she took getting here in her small rebel ship, keeping it hidden from Cardassian scans, and then beaming aboard, were going to be worth it. It had been harder this time, because Terok Nor was closed to almost all ships. She wasn't sure if the beam-in had been detected; she doubted anyone was scouting for security breaches in the middle of this internal crisis.

Kira stood in the center of the Bajoran section. It looked nothing like it had a few months ago, when she had come here to get a list of Bajoran collaborators from a chemist's shop. She didn't like to think about that visit, and how close she had come to becoming a true prisoner of the Cardassians.

She ran her hands over her arms. She had goosebumps despite the warmth. This place smelled like rot, and if she hadn't known better, she would have thought it like one of the prisoner-of-war camps on Cardassia. Dukat had always prided himself on keeping a clean, well-run station, where he treated the Bajorans "fairly."

There was nothing fair about this place any longer. Not even the most delusional could miss that.

Ill Bajorans lay on the floor, their cheeks rosy, their eyes too bright. They held their stomachs and moaned, while family members tried to take care of them. Others were on blankets or coats that someone had given up.

There were no Cardassian guards in sight—it was as if the guards had forgotten the Bajorans were here.

Not that it mattered. The Bajorans were too busy dying to think of revolution.

She had had no idea the disease was this bad. If she had to guess, she would estimate that half of the Bajorans she saw were in some stage of illness.

And she saw no sign of Kellec Ton at all. No sign of any doctors, no sign of any help. How could Dukat allow this? How could anyone?

There had to be someone that the Bajorans looked to for leadership, someone who took control of various situations. But she didn't even know where to look. The fine web of corridors and large rooms that had served as the Bajoran section no longer had any order to it at all. The sick lay everywhere, even in the eating areas, and there were a few bodies stacked near the entrance to the processing plants.

Bodies. Stacked. She had never expected to see this.

She didn't even know where to begin.

She wanted to roll up her sleeves and help, but she knew nothing about medicine, at least this kind of medicine. Give her a patient with a phaser burn and she could treat it, or a broken arm and she could set it, but to die like this, moaning in excruciating agony while everyone around was busy with their own deaths, was something completely beyond her.

Two Cardassian guards walked through the corridor. They stepped over the ill and dying Bajorans as if they were simply rocks lying in their path. They were talking in low tones, their conversation impossible to hear.

Kira tensed. If they saw her, they might bring her to Dukat. And that was the last thing she needed.

She slid down the wall, and buried her face in her knees. She couldn't bring herself to moan, to feign the illness so many others were dying of. But she kept herself immobile.

As the Cardassians passed, their conversation became clearer.

". . . so desperate that he's allowing the Bajoran doctor to work on Cardassian patients."

"That's not what I've heard. I've heard the illnesses are related, and if they find a cure for one, they find a cure for both."

"It's a Bajoran trick."

"What makes you think that?"

"They designed this virus to kill us, but it backfired. It makes them sick as well."

"Surely if that were true, Dukat wouldn't let that Bajoran anywhere near the medical section."

"Dukat is smarter than you think. Perhaps he wants Narat to catch the Bajoran infecting Cardassians . . ."

Their voices faded. Kira raised her head just enough to be able to watch them leave out of the corner of one eye. So the rumor about the Cardassians was true; they were dying of this disease as well.

And of course, the lower-level guards believed that the Bajorans were behind the illness, not realizing that the Bajorans no longer had the capability to do anything like this. Bajorans were struggling just to stay alive.

She hadn't expected it to be so easy to discover where Kellec Ton was, though. He was in the Cardassian medical section, helping save Cardassians. She would never have believed it of him. He had to have some other plan in mind. But she wasn't sure what that would be, nor was she certain how to reach him. It would mean leaving the Bajoran section. Some Bajorans did, she knew, but very few. And they were usually collaborating somehow.

She had been outside the Bajoran section last year, when she went to the chemist's to steal that list of collaborators, but everything had gone wrong. She had had to kill the chemist, and she had gotten caught. She managed to lie her way out of it, though, and escape with her life.

She wasn't sure she'd be that lucky this time.

But if the Cardassians were sick too, and the guard levels down here were any indication, she might have an easier time of it. The entire station seemed to be preoccupied with itself, turned inward, not outward. Maybe no one cared any longer about collaborators and the resistance. Maybe all anyone on Terok Nor cared about was surviving from moment to moment.

She waited until she was certain the guards were long gone. Then she rose ever so slowly, looking both ways. As she did, the wall at her back moved.

She gasped and turned. What she had thought to be a small beam attached to the wall turned into a liquid, then formed itself into a man.

The security chief. Odo.

She swallowed. He had caught her the last time, and nearly tried her for murder. But she had convinced him that she hadn't killed that Cardassian chemist and he had helped her escape. She hadn't expected to see him again.

"Kira Nerys, isn't it?" Odo said, as his shape solidified.

She didn't answer him, just watched him.

"I wondered who would be foolish enough to beam aboard a quarantined station."

She swallowed hard, but lifted her chin in a defiant movement.

"Or didn't you know that everyone is dying here?" He tilted his head. He was such a strange creature. His features weren't completely formed, and yet she could see something in those eyes. A sadness, perhaps.

"You're not dying," she said.

"I'm not Bajoran or Cardassian." Odo crossed his arms. "You do realize that I should tell Gul Dukat of your arrival."

"I thought you said everyone is dying."

"It was only a slight exaggeration. Dukat, so far, seems fine."

"That's no surprise," Kira said.

"What does that mean?"

"It means those guards had this whole thing backwards. The Cardassians designed this plague to kill Bajorans, and now it's backfired on them."

"Do you actually believe that?" Odo asked. "You always struck me as such an intelligent woman before."

She felt herself flush. "So you believe the Cardassian version?"

"Actually, I have a feeling that there's something else going on entirely. Your people and the Cardassians are so focused on your hatred for each other that you can't see beyond yourselves."

She frowned. "What do you know?"

"Nothing, really. It's just a hunch." He tilted his head toward her. "Just like my hunch says it's no coincidence that you're here, now. What are you coming to do? Start a rebellion now that the Cardassians are weak?"

She swept her hand across the floor, indicating all the ill people. "As if that would do any good. Why isn't anyone taking care of them?"

"Believe it or not," Odo said, "someone is. It's just there is so much sickness on the station that each patient can only expect a moment or two of personal attention a day."

It was sadness she saw in his eyes. He was as helpless as she was. "Kellec Ton?" she asked. "He has been coming down here?"

"Is that why you're here? To check up on him?"

She couldn't answer that. Much as this shape-shifter's demeanor made her feel like trusting him, she had been in this situation too many times to trust anyone in authority. "Is he still alive?"

"I thought you overheard those guards," Odo said. "He's in the Cardassian section, trying to find a cure."

"Is he having any luck?"

"I'm not privy to the medical discussions, but from what I've seen, no. If anything, the plague has gotten worse."

She shivered ever so slightly. Kellec hadn't gone crazy, had he? He hadn't started the plague, as those guards accused him of doing?

Of course not. What was she thinking? Kellec Ton wasn't that kind of man. No matter what circumstances drove him to, he would never voluntarily take a life, let alone hundreds of lives.

"Is it as bad as they say?" she asked, not able to help herself.

"What do they say?"

"That anyone who catches this disease dies."

He looked away from her, at the moaning people around them. He seemed smaller than the last time she saw him, as if the suffering had diminished him somehow. Or perhaps everyone seemed smaller in the face of this kind of anguish.

"From what I have observed," he said slowly, "any Cardassian or Bajoran who is exposed to this disease eventually gets the disease. And anyone who gets it, dies."

"So I'm at risk," Kira said.

"I'm afraid so," Odo said.

They stared at each other for a moment. Then he said, "I'm going to have to locate your ship and warn its crew away from here."

She almost told him that she was in a scout ship, and that she had come alone, but he didn't need that information.

"They left anyway," she lied, "just after they brought me here."

"I'm going to check anyway," he said. "Because you made the biggest mistake of your life coming here."

"Are you threatening me?" she asked.

He shook his head. "I wish it were that easy. But this station is under quarantine. Anyone who comes here cannot leave, not until the quarantine is lifted, and I doubt it will be lifted anytime soon."

She looked at him.

"I will keep an eye out for any illegal transportation devices, and in fact, I think I'll recommend to Gul Dukat to raise the station's shield so that no one can leave via transporter."

"Then I will die here," she said.

"You chose to come," he said. "It was a bad decision." Then he gave her a compassionate look. "If you stay in the Bajoran section, you'll be all right."

"And if I choose not to?"

"I can't vouch for what happens to you."

"Why should I care what happens to me?" she asked. "From what you say, I'm dead anyway."

He sighed. "I have hope," he said, although his tone belied his words, "that someone will find a way to end this thing."

"You don't seem like an optimistic man."

He inclined his head toward her as a sort of acknowledgement. "I'm usually not. But your friend has brought his ex-wife aboard, and it took some doing. I have to believe she has the skills to help with all of us."

Kellec Ton's ex-wife? What had Kira heard about her? Not much, except—she was Starfleet. The Federation. That had to take some doing.

"What makes you think one person will make a difference?" Kira asked.

"I'm looking at it from a practical standpoint," he said. "She's not Bajoran or Cardassian."

"And so has no stake in developing the disease further?"

"Actually, no," he said. "She has a chance of staying alive long enough to develop a cure."

Chapter Fourteen

PULASKI'S EYES ACHED from the strain of staring at the Cardassian computer monitors. The LTDs here were set on a different frequency than the Federation mandated. These settings were not designed for human eyes, and were creating a serious version of eyestrain. She leaned back in her chair and with her thumb and forefinger massaged the bridge of her nose.

Ten hours of work, and it felt like only a moment. Ten hours. She thought she might have something, but she wanted to rest for just a second, to allow the hope to diminish.

The mood on Terok Nor, the hopelessness, had infected her more than she wanted to admit. She had tried to get Kellec to leave the medical section, but he refused to go. She thought of actually giving him a sedative so that he could sleep, but she couldn't do that. They might need his clear thinking.

At least she had convinced Narat to rest. What she wanted to do was to place the three main doctors on a rotating schedule, two on and one off at all times. This might continue for days, and it would do no good for Narat and Kellec to court illness by shorting themselves on sleep.

When Narat returned, she would convince Kellec to go. No matter what it took.

She would be doing the same in their shoes, though. One of the reasons she wanted to set up the new system was so that she ensured she would get some rest. Right now, she was the fresh one, seeing things with a new perspective, but over time that would change. She wanted all of them to have an advantage.

She sighed and stood, stretching. Even the chairs were poorly designed, at least for her human form. Apparently Cardassians had the assumption of height working for them. She had to rest her feet on the base of the chair instead of the floor, and that was playing havoc with her back. She turned and looked out the office door at the medical section's patient areas.

Ogawa was taking care of the Bajorans in the medical section, offering kind words and comfort. Marvig was below, in the Bajoran section, working in the corridors with the people too sick to make it here. Eventually, they would switch places. Pulaski had seen the Bajoran section on one of her short breaks, and it had been the worst thing yet on Terok Nor. Dozens of sick and dying people, with no one to care for them except their own families—if they had any families left.

Some of them were already weakened from years spent as Cardassian prisoners or as workers in the ore-processing area. Pulaski had no idea what working with uridium did to the immune system, but if uridium was like any other ore, it weakened everything it came into contact with.

Governo was ministering to the Cardassians. His bedside manner was gruffer and blunter than either Ogawa's or Marvig's, and the Cardassians seemed to appreciate that. They were the kind of patients who wanted the unvarnished truth—rather like Klingons in that respect—so that they could make decisions from there. Only the Cardassians were too sick to attempt to die with honor, as a Klingon would have done. Or perhaps it wasn't part of their culture. She didn't know. She had never really made a point of studying Cardassian social habits.

"Are you all right?" Kellec was behind her, his voice soft in her ear.

She nodded. "I needed to think."

"Staring out there helps you think?"

"There's nowhere else to look," she said.

"Up on the Promenade, there are windows that look out to the stars," Kellec said. "I go there if I need a moment alone."

"I'll remember that," Pulaski said. "But that wasn't the kind of thinking I needed to do."

"You've found something," Kellec said. He knew her so well. They had spent years apart, and it felt as if they had only been away from each other for a few hours.

"I think so." She turned away from the door and came back to her chair. She put her hands on it instead of sitting in it, more out of courtesy to her back than any other reason. "Let me show you."

She ran her fingers across the flat control board, punching up two holographic images. They were of the virus, its perfect form sinister to her, as if it had already imprinted itself in her subconscious as something evil.

Kellec stood beside her, staring at the images. "You see something here that I've missed."

"Yes," she said. She lowered her voice. "These are not the same virus."

"Katherine," Ton said. "I've been studying them for days. They're exactly the same."

"No," she said. "I double-checked your work and Narat's. You examined the viruses at first and thought they were the same. The computer reported that they were as well. From that point on, you've only been working with one form of the virus, pulled from the same culture."

He frowned at her, then peered at the images. He touched the control pad, making the images larger. "I don't see the difference."

"It's subtle," she said, "and this system, sophisticated as it is, isn't calibrated for such tiny differences. Apparently, Cardassian medicine is a lot more straightforward than the types we practice in the Federation."

He glanced at her, obviously not following.

"These systems," she said, "are designed for Cardassian physiology only. And why shouldn't they be? Even though several species come through Terok Nor, most everything here is geared toward Cardassians. On starships, and throughout the Federation, we're dealing with a wide variety of species all the time. Small things—infinitesimal things—can sometimes mean the difference between life and death."

"All right," he said. "What infinitesimal thing have I missed?"

She pointed to the image on the left. "This is Virus B, the virus that's killing the Bajorans." She punched in a label that ran across the bottom. Then she pointed to the image on the right. "This is Virus C, the one that's killing the Cardassians."

Kellec peered at both screens. Then he made them larger. "I must be tired," he said. "I can't see the difference."

"You are tired," she said. "This is why I want us all to have a few hours of sleep a day. But that's beside the point. Look here."

She pointed to a single strand on Virus B's DNA.

"Now," she said, "compare it to the same strand on Virus C's DNA."

He closed his eyes and brought the heel of his hand to his forehead. "How could I have missed that?"

"You weren't looking for it," she said. "They look so much alike—'"

"Don't make excuses for me, Katherine. I should have caught it."

"Why? You thought the viruses were the same."

"But they manifested differently."

"Yes," she said, "and that's completely logical given the differences between Cardassian and Bajoran physiology."

"But Cardassians and Bajorans don't get the same diseases. We all know that."

It wasn't like Kellec to go into recriminations. He was exhausted. She had to get him focused on something else. "You brought me in here for a new perspective."

"Yes," he said. "I did."

"Well, I have more."

He frowned. "This is the part you were reluctant to tell me."

She nodded. "And frankly, I'm relieved Narat isn't here. Are you sure we can talk here without being overheard?"

"No one out there is listening," Ton said.

"And Dukat?"

Kellec shrugged. "I don't know. I don't think he would be. It's not the way he usually does things."

"Good," she said.

"Why?"

She took a deep breath. "Because Virus B, found in the Bajorans, is mutating into Virus C and killing Cardassians."

Instantly Kellec's face went white; then he did the same thing she had been doing. He quickly checked around him to make sure no Cardassians had heard. If this information got out, Pulaski didn't know what Dukat would do with the news. But from the reports she had heard, she doubted he would stop short at wiping out most of the Bajoran people to stop this.

"How can you be sure it's not the other way around?" Kellec asked.

She punched up a different image. "Watch," she said.

She had a time-lapsed image of the Bajoran cultures that Kellec and Narat had been using. Over a period of a few days, the Bajoran virus mutated. She highlighted the new viruses in red.

"What made you look for that?" he asked.

"I saw how closely they were related. I knew we weren't dealing with a coincidence. Kellec, you and Narat are right. This is an artificially created virus."

"You mean it's designed to go from Bajoran to Cardassian?"

She nodded.

He gripped the back of the nearest chair. "If the Cardassians find out about this—"

"They'll wipe out every Bajoran they can find," she said. "And it will kill the Cardassian source of infection."

"You can't condone that!" he said.

"Of course not. But the Cardassians strike me as the kind of people who can justify such a thing."

Kellec sank into his chair. "I don't know what we do now, Katherine. We need this information to find a cure. But I want to wipe it all off the system."

"I already have," she said. "These are my files, coded to me only."

"That's precisely the thing that will get you in trouble with Dukat."

"I know." She touched the screen and the images disappeared. "But since I destroyed the material, he can't accuse me of spying, now can he?"

"Katherine, we needed that."

She shook her head. "It's enough to know it. The comparisons are gone, that's all. We have the knowledge. Now we have to use it."

"Swear to me you won't tell Narat."

"I wish we could," she said. "He has a keen mind."

"It's also a Cardassian mind."

"I know that too. And for that reason, I won't say a word."

Kellec squeezed her arm. "Thank you, Katherine."

"Don't thank me yet," she said. "We haven't found a cure."

"But we're one step closer than we were before you arrived. Narat and I never would have found that."

"You would have," she said.

"Just not in time." Kellec pushed his chair closer to the console. "At least now I have a bit of hope."

She prayed that that was enough to sustain him. Because the mutation of the virus worried her. She would have expected it to go the other way. She had actually been looking to see if the Cardassian form mutated into the Bajoran form when she found that she had the process exactly reversed.

She wasn't sure what that meant yet, besides the obvious results that Kellec envisioned, should the Cardassians discover how the virus traveled. But she didn't like what she was thinking, and she didn't know how to clear the suspicions from her brain.

Were an oppressed people wrong in doing anything they could to get rid of their oppressors?

She turned back toward the patients in the outer rooms, and got her answer.

Yes, they were. Some prices were too high, no matter what the cause.

Chapter Fifteen

QUARK RUBBED HIS LEFT EAR with the back of his left hand. It felt as if something were tickling the edge of his lobe, and not in a pleasant way. He leaned across the bar and surveyed his business.

His empty business.

He hadn't had a customer in hours. At this rate, he would be broke within the month, faster if Nog and Rom continued to spend all his latinum. No wonder Prindora left Rom. He could go through money faster than anyone Quark had ever seen.

Quark peered into the Promenade. There was no one there either. The Volian's shop was still open, but he hadn't had a customer since Rom needed his new hat. Several of the restaurants had closed, and most of the stores were closed as well. No one even wandered the Promenade, as if just moving around the station made a person vulnerable to disease.

Quark rubbed his ear again. All of this worry was making him break out. And of course, it would happen on the most sensitive spot on his body.

He heard a clang above him and he glanced up. Nog came out of the first holosuite, a bucket in his left hand. He set the bucket down, scratched his ear, and then picked up the bucket.

Quark felt cold.

He turned and leaned toward the mirror behind the bar. It wasn't a pimple that he was scratching. He hadn't broken out since he was a young Ferengi just hitting puberty. He leaned closer. The reddened area on his left ear looked more like . . . a blister.

"Nog!" he shouted.

"It's an infection that your carelessness has spread. And we're going to stop it." Quark dragged them down the hall. The stench coming from the medical area was stronger than he had expected. He had been smelling the rot for a week now and ignoring it, like he did in butcher shops on Ferenginar, but here it was nearly impossible to ignore.

"I don't think I'm going in there," Rom said.

"Yeah," Nog said. "They probably won't have time for us."

"They'll probably be happy to have something they can solve," Quark said with more bravado than he felt. If his ear didn't itch so badly that he wanted to scratch it off the side of his head, he wouldn't go into that place either. But he couldn't stand itching, especially on as sensitive a place as his ear.

He shoved Rom and Nog ahead of him, and the door to the medical lab opened. The smell was even worse. A hundred voices moaned.

Rom shook his head. "Brother, I—"

And Quark pushed him forward. Nog followed him in, and then Quark brought up the rear.

"Whatever it is," Dr. Narat said as he passed, "it will have to wait."

"It can't wait," Quark said.

"Are you dying?"

"No."

"Then it can wait." And Narat disappeared through a door.

"See?" Rom said. "We have to wait. Which means we should leave."

Quark caught him by the sleeve. Quark wasn't too happy about being here either—he'd never been in a room filled with green Cardassians before—but he wasn't about to leave now. For one thing, he might never make it back. And then he'd have to scratch until his ear bled, and the infection would grow worse, and his lobes would—

He couldn't allow himself to follow that train of thought. He shuddered and headed toward the office.

"I wouldn't go in there," a human woman said. She had long dark hair and beautiful eyes.

"Who are you?" Quark asked.

"Alyssa Ogawa," she said. "I'm helping here."

"We have a problem, and it needs some attention."

"Let me see what I can do," she said.

She slipped through the office door, and Rom turned to Quark. "She's beautiful, brother."

"She's hu-man, Brother," Quark said. "You can't trust a hu-man."

"Ah, but you can look at them," Rom said.

"Women are not your strong suit," Quark said. "Stop thinking about her."

She came out the door with Kellec Ton. He looked exhausted. "I don't have much time," he said. "What do you need?"

Quark leaned forward, pointing to his ear. "Look at this. *Look* at this. My brother got—"

"Couldn't this have waited?" Kellec Ton asked. "We have a real crisis here."

"We know and we're sorry," Rom said. "We'll leave now."

Quark pulled him closer. "No, we won't." He glanced around the room. "I admit, our problem is nothing like theirs—" and he shuddered a little at the very thought "—but it is uncomfortable."

"You can live with discomfort," Kellec Ton said. "Now, if you'll excuse me."

"No," Quark said. "I won't. Don't you understand? This itches."

"And I'm very sorry," Kellec said. He was holding the door like it was a lifeline. "But I don't have time—"

"These are our *ears,"* Quark said, his voice going up. "It would be like you getting an infection on your—"

"Brother!" Rom said, breathless with shock. "Remember Nog."

"I know about their—" Nog started to say, but Rom clapped a hand over his mouth.

"I'm sure the good doctor will help us when he has time," Rom said. "Now let's go."

Kellec Ton let out a small laugh and shook his head. "All right," he said. "You made your point. Let me look at that."

He bent down and turned on a small, handheld light. "It's an infection all right," he said, looking at Quark's ear. Then he examined Nog's and then Rom's. "And it's clearly transmittable, probably through the pus. Let me give you some antibacterial cream that should ease the itching and clear this right up."

"Thank you," Quark said.

"Yes," Rom said. "Thank you very much."

The doctor went into the office, and rummaged through a drawer. Rom leaned over to Quark. "I still think we shouldn't have bothered him."

"Shut up," Quark said. "We're getting help, aren't we?"

"Yes," Rom said. "But he's right. There are people *dying* here."

Quark nodded. He had to admit that he did agree with Rom, but for entirely different reasons. He wished they hadn't come here. Before it had seemed entirely personal. The Cardassians got sick and no one came to the bar. But it wasn't personal. In fact, it was so impersonal that it hurt. No one came to the bar because everyone was afraid of this—turning green, scaly, and the stench! And then dying.

Quark shuddered. He would have to start planning his future, a future that didn't include Terok Nor. He wasn't sure what he'd do, because once the word got out that Terok Nor was the site of a plague, Quark wouldn't be able to work anywhere—at least not have a bar. Customers didn't like hearing about contagious diseases in their bartender's past.

"Here you go," Kellec said, placing a tube in Quark's hand. "Follow the instructions. Your problems should ease by the end of the day."

"Thank you," Quark said. "We didn't mean to interrupt. If we had known—"

"No," Kellec said. "It's all right. You did me a favor. You reminded me that there's an entire universe out there. Even if things on Terok Nor and Bajor . . ." He shook his head. "Anyway. I needed to remember that life does go on."

"Yes, it does," Rom said. "And—"

Quark kicked him. He shut up.

"We do appreciate it," Nog said. "We won't bother you again." He scurried for the door. Quark followed a bit more slowly, the tube cool against his right hand. He was staring at the Cardassians on the beds and makeshift cots. He recognized a number of them, had served them drinks, listened to their problems. And they would all be gone soon, if something didn't change.

He sighed and slipped outside, where Rom and Nog were waiting for him.

"Well, brother," Rom said. "You did the right thing. Now all we have to do is apply that cream to our ears—"

"No," Quark said. "I'll apply it to my ears, and I'll give you your own dab of it. I'm not touching anything you touch ever again. Is that clear?"

"Perfectly," Rom said.

"Does this mean I get your earbrush?" Nog asked.

Quark stared at him for a moment, and then he sighed, unwilling to fight them anymore. "I guess it does," he said.

Chapter Sixteen

NEARLY TWENTY-FOUR HOURS without sleep. Pulaski felt it in the grit of her eyes, the sluggishness in her arms and legs. She had pulled all-nighters hundreds of times from college on, and she'd hated each and every one of them. Of course, she had to admit that this one she didn't mind, because the work needed to be done.

She bent over the culture she had been working on. She took a dropper and placed a small sample of solution on it, then glanced at the screen. Narat stood beside her. They watched as the solution moved through the viral cells, destroying them. It left all the other cells alone.

"I think we've got it," Narat said.

Part of it, anyway, Pulaski thought—but didn't add. She and Kellec hadn't told Narat about Virus B and Virus C and how that discovery had led them to this formula, which might actually be a cure. Kellec was testing a slightly different form of solution on Virus B, although what she and Kellec had told Narat was that Kellec was merely doing a double check.

Narat trusted them. He hadn't looked too closely at either experiment.

"The next step is to use test subjects," Pulaski said. She wiped a hand over her forehead. "But we don't have any."

"Just the patients," Narat said.

"I hate injecting an untried solution into someone," Pulaski said.

"I have to agree with Narat on this one, Katherine," Kellec said. "They're going to die anyway. We have to see if we can stop it."

She nodded. She knew. She had done the same several times in crisis situations, the last time on the *Enterprise.* But each time her scientist's brain warned that one day they would inject the wrong substance into the wrong patient, and that that patient would die too soon.

"Why don't you and Narat try the Cardassians?" Kellec said. "I'll try the Bajorans."

"It might not work on one group or the other," Narat said.

"We'll deal with that when it happens," Pulaski said. She took a deep breath. "Let's at least try a couple of patients before we inject everyone."

Narat nodded. "That much caution I can accept. Let's take three: one who is nearly gone, one in the middle of the disease, and one at the beginning."

"Get Edgar to help you find the patients," Pulaski said. "And Alyssa is among the Bajorans."

She sat down. Something was bothering her about the cure, she wasn't sure what. But it would come to her. Eventually.

Kellec was working among the Bajorans, moving beds so that they were closer to the office, injecting hypospray on the three patients. In the cultures, the results had happened quickly. Pulaski wasn't sure what would happen in an actual body.

Narat was doing the same with the Cardassians.

Ogawa looked excited. A strand of hair had fallen from her neat bun, and she was smiling for the first time since they had reached Terok Nor.

Governo seemed solemn. He probably wasn't certain this would work. The entire trip had been hard on him—first-time away missions often were for medical personnel, and this one was particularly difficult. Failure here would be worse than anything any of them had ever faced before, except Pulaski, and right now even she would be hard-pressed to remember an occasion worse than this.

Kellec finished with his few patients and sat down beside her. "How long do you think this will take?"

"If we're lucky, twenty minutes," she said.

They both knew what would happen if they were unlucky. They watched Narat work with the Cardassians.

"If this works," Kellec said, "it's only going to work on the virus. People will still catch it."

"I know." He had put his finger on what had been bothering her. "Maybe, though, it'll be like catching a cold—not anything to worry about."

"Maybe," he said. "But it bothers me that we haven't found how this thing incubates. You know how pernicious viruses are."

She did. Viruses mutated, often after medicine was introduced. She shivered. "Don't even think it."

"I have to," he said. "I'm worried."

"Dr. Kellec?" Nurse Ogawa called from the Bajoran section. "You need to come here."

Kellec cursed. "It backfired. We should have known better than to try this untested—"

Pulaski put her hand on his arm. "Shhh. You're jumping to conclusions."

They both went into the next room. The patient nearest the door, a young Bajoran girl, looked tired, her skin sallow. She sat up, with a hand on her head. "I'm hungry," she said with a bit of surprise.

Pulaski opened her tricorder and ran it over the girl. There wasn't a trace of the virus in her system. Kellec was confirming the information on the biobed readouts.

"She's cured," Pulaski said.

He examined the readings another time.

"Which one was she?" Pulaski asked Ogawa.

"The least sick," Ogawa said. Her smile had grown bigger. "And look, the next is losing some of that healthy color."

How odd that they were celebrating the fact that their patients were looking less healthy, but it was part of the disease to look that way. And part of the cure to go back to the way they had looked before, when they were subjected to all the difficulties of Terok Nor.

"Katherine," Kellec said softly. "We did it." And then he flung his arms around her, pulling her close. "We did it!"

She hugged him back and let him dance her around the room. Finally, she put a hand on his arm. "Kellec, we have a lot of people to inject with this cure."

"Yes," he said. "You make up a large batch, and I'll get going on injections."

"I'll take some down to Crystal in the Bajoran section," Ogawa said.

"Help her down there," Kellec said. "She'll need it."

Ogawa smiled and left. Pulaski went into the office. The Bajorans were cured, but she didn't know about the Cardassians. Her heart stopped when she saw Narat.

He was standing over a bed, his hands covering his face, his body so hunched that he looked as if he were in pain.

"My god," she whispered. What had saved the Bajorans had killed the Cardassians. And she had been so careful to make sure they had the slightly different injection.

She went to the other room and put a hand on Narat's shoulder. He was shaking.

"Narat?" she asked.

He raised his head. "I didn't think we'd—I didn't think—Look!" He pointed down. The Cardassian on the bed, whom Pulaski recognized as one of the guards, was his usual gray. His scales still flaked, but they didn't look as irritated as they had. And his eyes were bright.

She ran her tricorder over him as well. The virus was gone.

"Narat," she said. "You gave me quite a scare. I thought it hadn't worked."

"Oh, but it did, Dr. Pulaski. Thanks to you, we're all going to survive."

"I think we all had a part in it," she said. She put an arm around him and felt him lean against her. He wasn't a Cardassian to her anymore. He was simply a fellow doctor who had given up hope and didn't know what to do now that hope had been restored.

"Edgar," she said to Governo. "Start injecting our Cardassian patients. Dr. Narat will help you in a moment."

Governo nodded. He took the hypospray out of Narat's shaking hands. Pulaski led him into the office and helped him to a chair.

"I should be helping," he said. "I should—"

"You have enough to do," she said. "Edgar can handle things for the moment."

Narat looked at her. "What do you mean I have enough to do?"

"You need to reach Gul Dukat," she said. "We have to get this cure to Bajor." It was time to explain one thing to him. Otherwise nothing would work. She crouched. "Narat, I made a slightly different antidote for the Cardassians than for the Bajorans. It had to take into account the differences in physiology. I was afraid the Bajoran cure would make the Cardassians sick."

"It worked," he said, and she let out a small sigh of relief. He didn't ask any more questions.

"I'm going to continue to make up batches of the antidotes," she said. "The Cardassian version will be in the blue vials."

He nodded. Then he took a deep breath. "I didn't expect to react this way. I've never reacted like this—"

"Have you ever been faced with something like this before?"

He shook his head.

"Then give yourself a moment," she said. "Doctors have feelings too, even though we pretend not to."

She stood. Governo was injecting Cardassians all over the medical section. It was nice to see two of them back to their normal gray. The other test case wasn't bright green either. His skin color was a greenish gray that she assumed would become gray in a short period of time.

Kellec was smiling as he worked his way through the Bajorans. She had forgotten how good-looking he was when he smiled.

Out of the corner of her eye, she saw Narat stand. He went to the console and pressed a section with his palm. Dukat appeared on the small screen.

"I have good news," Narat said. "We found a cure."

Dukat closed his eyes and turned his head. Pulaski moved so that she could watch the entire interaction without being seen. Dukat let out a breath and then seemed to regain control of himself. He again faced the screen.

"If we move quickly," Narat said, ignoring Dukat's reaction, "we can save every life."

"Then what are you talking to me for?" Dukat said. "Do it."

"I don't just mean on the station," Narat said.

Dukat sucked in his breath. Pulaski threaded her fingers together. This was the key point.

"We need to get the information to Bajor, and Cardassia Prime, in case the plague gets there. The faster we do it, the better off we'll be."

"Can they manufacture this antidote themselves or must we make it for them?"

"Both," Narat said. "Some areas may not have anyone with the skills. I figure we take care of Terok Nor first and then send supplies to the planet below. Before that, though, I'll need to send the information to both planets."

"All right," Dukat said. He looked visibly relieved. "Is there anything else?"

Narat shook his head, but Pulaski stepped forward, and put her hand on his arm. "If I might intrude, Gul," she said.

Dukat looked surprised to see her. So, in truth, did Narat. He had apparently forgotten she was there.

"Did you find the antidote?" Dukat asked.

"All three of us did," she said.

"We wouldn't have found it without her," Narat said. "She brought a fresh perspective to the work."

Dukat templed his fingers and rested the tips against his mouth. He was contemplating her through the screen. It made her as uncomfortable as he had when they first met.

"We have found the cure for the virus," she said, "but we don't know how long the virus incubates. People will still catch it, until we figure out a way to stop it before the symptoms appear."

"But they won't die?" Dukat asked.

She nodded. "They will no longer die."

"Good. Then what do you need?"

"This is a designer virus," she said. "Someone made it. If we could find out where it first appeared, then we might be able to find who created it. Or at least, figure out how it is transmitted in its nonviral state."

"I'm afraid I'm not a doctor," Dukat said. "I didn't follow that."

"You see," Pulaski started, but Narat put his hand on her arm.

"The virus has several stages," Narat said. "We've caught it in all but the first stage. We're looking for that one still. If we find that one, we can prevent this virus from ever infecting us again."

"So what do you need from me?" Dukat asked.

"Permission to search for the source of the virus," Pulaski said.

"And you believe that it's on Bajor?" Dukat asked.

"I believe nothing," she said. "It could easily be here. But we must cover all of our bases."

"I believe it is on Bajor," Dukat said. *"I* believe the Bajorans infected themselves so that they could pass the disease onto us. They just didn't realize how lethal it would be."

"In my experience of the Bajoran people," Pulaski said, "I have never seen such behavior. It violates all of their beliefs."

"Forgive me, Doctor," Dukat said, "but your experience of the Bajoran people is of one rather eccentric Bajoran doctor."

"It seems you haven't read my file as carefully as I thought you had," Pulaski said.

Dukat shrugged. "I will not give you or your assistants permission to go to Bajor."

"If we find the source—"

"I said, I will not give your people permission to go to Bajor. I'm bending the rules to allow you here."

She took a deep breath. "It's important—"

"I understand that," Dukat said. "Narat will send a Cardassian team to Bajor in the next day or two. That will suffice."

No, it wouldn't. It wouldn't suffice at all. They would be looking for the wrong things. They would be looking for proof of Dukat's theory, that the Bajorans started this disease.

"I think an impartial observer would be best," she said.

"And we have none, as you have just indicated, Doctor. You and your people seem closer to the Bajorans than I'm comfortable with." He smiled at her. "I am very pleased with your work so far. Don't spoil it."

Narat's grip on her arm was firm. "We'll do what you say, Gul Dukat," Narat said. "I'll have a team ready."

"Good. Prepare my announcement. I want to send those messages to Bajor and Cardassia Prime within the hour," Dukat said.

Narat nodded.

"One more thing," Dukat said. "I don't mean to sound insensitive."

He paused and as he did, Kellec entered the room, but remained outside of Dukat's sight range. "But I am getting pressure about the decreased ore production. When do you believe we can get our Bajorans back to work?"

The question was directed at Narat, but Pulaski felt herself start to answer. Narat's fingers dug so hard into her arm that she nearly cried out in pain.

"A few days," Narat said.

"A few days is a long time, Narat," Dukat said. "We're already disastrously far behind."

Narat smiled. "Look at it this way," he said. "Just an hour ago, you were worried about surviving. Now you're worried about your future. Things have improved."

Dukat laughed. "So they have," he said, and signed off.

"Cardassian dog!" Kellec said, closing the door behind him. "All they think about is how much slave labor they can get out of us."

Narat stiffened beside Pulaski.

"Not all of them, Kellec," Pulaski said gently. "Narat has a different perspective."

"If you had a different perspective," Kellec said, "you wouldn't have made that promise."

"And what would you have had me do?" Narat said. "Tell him nothing and let him make the decision?"

They stared at each other for a moment. Finally, Kellec looked away. "Katherine," he said, "I need more of the antidote. I'm going to help with the work below."

"You've finished here?"

"For now," he said.

She nodded. "I have a batch already made up. I'll have another by the time you get back."

He picked up the vials she indicated, and then shook his head. "If there weren't lives at stake, I wonder if I would be doing this. I certainly don't want to be the agent that forces our people back into slave labor." And then he let himself out the door.

"He talks a big game," Pulaski said. "But he'll do what's right."

Narat nodded. "He's a good doctor."

They were both silent for a moment and then Pulaski said, "I'm afraid I don't think a Cardassian team will do us any good."

"It's all you're going to get," Narat said. "We can be impartial, you know."

She didn't know that. She didn't believe it either. That comment Gul Dukat made had angered her as well. She hadn't realized that she was closer to Kellec's beliefs than Narat's. But she said nothing. She made herself smile at him. "Well, then," she said, "I guess we have work to do."

"Good work," Narat said. "We're back in the business of saving lives."

"Thank heavens," Pulaski said. She wasn't sure how much more death she could take.

Chapter Seventeen

THE STENCH IN THE BAJORAN SECTION seemed worse than it had just a few hours before. Kellec entered the main corridor. The nightmare he had alleviated above still existed down here, the sick people all over the floors, the awful moaning, the heightened skin color. He wished it all would end.

He was carrying his kit with him. In the mess area, Ogawa and Marvig were inoculating the sickest patients first. Bajorans who had no symptoms or who had very few were helping find the sickest patients and getting them treatment first. It looked like an efficient system and Kellec wasn't going to interfere with it.

Instead, he went as far from that area as he could, to a room he wasn't even supposed to know existed. The Cardassian guards never came here; they thought it was a supply closet, not knowing that the Bajorans had long ago taken over the closet and made it a base.

There were sick people lining the corridors here, too. He bent over the nearest person—a young man, barely into puberty, and gave him a hypospray. It didn't take long for an older man to crouch beside him.

"Kellec," the man said.

"Rashan," Kellec said. "Is Ficen Dobat still well?"

"Well enough," Rashan said.

"Could you find him for me?"

Rashan nodded and disappeared down the corridor. Kellec went from patient to patient, inoculating each one, working as fast as he could. Soon he would have to go back to the med lab to get more of the antidote. He wasn't sure how he could look at Narat.

Katherine was right, of course. Narat was a good man who did what he could within the system. But Kellec believed a man should do more than "what he could within the system." If the system was flawed, a man had to work outside it. But Kellec said nothing to Narat. It would do no good.

Katherine didn't know that yet. Kellec wished he had arrived at the office just moments earlier. He had been too far away when he saw her step near the monitor. He had hurried to the office and held the door open ever so slightly, hearing her every word.

If only she had spoken to him first, perhaps Dukat might not have noticed if she disappeared off the station for a while. Kellec might have been able to smuggle her to Bajor, for her and her crew to witness the horrible conditions on the planet. Dukat would never agree to that. And Kellec wished Katharine hadn't told him her suspicions—all of their suspicions actually—that the disease had originated on Bajor.

Dukat chose to look at that as a sign that the Bajorans were infecting themselves so that they could make the Cardassians ill. But Katherine was right; the majority of Bajorans would find such a practice abhorrent. Though there were deviants in every group—he'd met a few in the resistance—they were always dealt with by the group leader. The crazies never got the upper hand.

No. Kellec understood what had happened. It was subtle and it was scary. The Cardassians had planted the virus, just as he had always suspected, and had done it on Bajor to make sure it would look like the Bajorans had created the disease. He found it suspicious that the disease hadn't made its way to Cardassia Prime. It was just like the Cardassians—but not the Bajorans—to sacrifice a few of their people for the good of all of them. If only he could get to Bajor, or if he could get someone there he could trust, he would be able to prove this.

At least Katherine had seen Dukat's true colors. He wasn't worried about losing Bajorans. He was worried about the drop in production. If Terok Nor failed to meet its quotas, Dukat could lose his comfortable position. And once the threat of death was removed, that was all he cared about.

He had moved far from the corridor he had started in. He was almost out of the antidote. He would have to go back to the medical lab in a moment. He couldn't stall much longer. He didn't see any Cardassian guards, but he couldn't assume that there weren't any. The Cardassians would leave guards down here until they were all dead. There just weren't as many as usual, because the sickness had depleted the Cardassian ranks as well.

Kellec stood and put a hand against his back. The moaning had quieted, and a few of the patients were looking brighter-eyed than they had a short time before. He smiled. At least he had been able to do this. His work rarely gave him satisfaction anymore—he was always repairing wounds that would never happen if the Cardassians didn't occupy Bajor—but this did satisfy him. Just that morning, he had thought everyone on Terok Nor would die. Everyone but Katherine, her team, and those silly Ferengi.

Rashan reappeared, silently, a talent of his. He put his hand on Kellec's shoulder. "Is there anything I can do?" he asked.

"Check on the patients near the area where I started," Kellec said.

Rashan nodded. As he passed, he said under his breath, "There are three Cardassian guards at the mouth of the corridor. Have a care."

And then he was gone.

Kellec resisted looking in the direction Rashan had indicated. Instead, he examined his kit to see how much more antidote he had. Enough to stall for a few more minutes.

But he wouldn't have to. As he looked, he realized that someone was standing beside him. He turned, and found himself face to face with Ficen Dobat.

"I understand you need a bit of help," Ficen said. He was a small man, the kind who disappeared easily in a crowd. Even when he was noticed, most people couldn't describe him well—a Bajoran of average height, brown hair, brown eyes, not very remarkable. But Ficen *was* remarkable. He currently led the resistance on Terok Nor, and he frequently accomplished the impossible.

Kellec smiled. "We found an antidote."

"Not a moment too soon," Ficen said. "We've already lost some good people."

They crouched near the kit. Kellec found a second hypospray and pretended to fill it. He didn't dare let Ficen use it—the man was untrained—but if those Cardassians poked their heads in this corridor, it would look as if he were helping Kellec.

"I have a favor to ask," Kellec said.

"Anything," Ficen said. "You've saved us, once again."

"Remember that when I make this request," Kellec said.

Ficen frowned.

"I need someone to go to Bajor for me. I need to find the source of this disease."

"The source?"

"Where it was first reported."

"And you think that was on Bajor?"

Kellec met Ficen's gaze. "I need to know, to clear this completely from all of us."

"Our people—" Ficen began, but Kellec held up a hand.

"I think the Cardassians started this and tried to make it look like we did it," Kellec said. "That probably means it started in a resistance cell somewhere, probably a place that's fairly centrally located."

"No resistance cell could be infiltrated by the Cardassians," Ficen said.

"Are you implying that we did this, just like the Cardassians say? Do we have cells that desperate?" Kellec said.

Ficen frowned. "Desperate times call for desperate measures."

"But this?" Kellec said. "Surely we wouldn't do this." He swept his hand over the corridor.

Ficen shook his head. "Of course not," he said. "But we know what it's like here, and it's easy even for us to contemplate the idea. Imagine how easy it is for the Cardassians."

"The ones who aren't already in the know," Kellec said.

Ficen sighed. "I don't think sending one of our people there is a good idea."

"I don't see any other choice," Kellec said. "Dukat is sending a team of his own to Bajor to investigate this. You know what he'll find."

Ficen cursed. "If they believe we did this, they'll retaliate."

"That's why we need real information, gathered by our own people." Kellec glanced over his shoulder. No guards so far. "But it has to be people we can trust."

Ficen nodded. "I'll see what I can do."

"Not good enough," Kellec said.

Ficen stood and handed the hypospray back to Kellec. "All right then," he said. "I'll let you know as soon as our team leaves Terok Nor."

Kellec smiled. "That's better," he said.

Chapter Eighteen

KIRA WAS VIOLATING HER AGREEMENT with Odo, but she had to. Ever since she had heard that a representative of the Federation was on Terok Nor, she'd been trying to figure out a way to make contact. And if Odo's report was accurate, she had to do so quickly. She had been exposed to the virus, and didn't have a lot of time left before she would have to seek out medical attention. She had heard that Kellec and his team had found a cure to the disease, but only after someone already had symptoms.

She wasn't looking forward to that.

She was in the habitat ring, near the quarters assigned to newcomers. It had taken her most of the evening to find where their rooms were located; she couldn't ask anyone, and her computer skills, while good, weren't good enough to find all of the alarm triggers the Cardassians had built into the system.

The only thing she had working for her was that as many Cardassians were sick as Bajorans. There were very few guards, and the ones she had seen were more preoccupied with the state of their own good health than with keeping an eye on Bajorans. Kira made sure she was wearing tattered old clothes, and she kept her hair tousled, so that she looked as if she were struggling—either with ore production or keeping her family alive somewhere.

She *was* struggling; that much was true. All of her contacts here were either ill or dying. She still hadn't found Ficen and she didn't know how to ask for him. Most of the Bajorans in the Bajoran section were preoccupied with their own families; they couldn't keep track of anything else.

Since she had arrived, she had been uneasy, frightened. She wished she could see Kellec Ton, but that was clearly becoming impossible. She thought of approaching the Federation assistants who were working in the Bajoran section. She had even come close to them once, close enough to overhear their discussions and to realize they weren't in charge of this mission. They were all on their first assignment outside Federation space, and were as baffled by it all as new recruits always were when brought into their first resistance cell.

No. She was in this corridor because she had no other choice. She hoped no one had found her tracks yet in the computer system. She had looked up several things, just in case someone was trying to find her, and had buried her request among half a dozen others. She figured it would give her time.

It had also given her the access code to the visitors' quarters' door. She hoped the Federation doctor wasn't paranoid enough to change her locks when she arrived. This would be the test.

Kira moved away from the wall and turned to the door. She punched the access override code into the lock—and heard the door shush open. One more step completed.

The quarters were dark. Apparently the doctor liked to sleep in total blackness. Kira stood completely still for a moment, letting her eyes adjust.

They did.

She listened, and heard deep, even breathing from the next room.

This was her first opportunity with the Federation doctor. The woman hadn't come to her quarters until very late. As Kira's eyes got used to the light, she saw clothing scattered on a nearby chair. Kira had heard that the woman had been awake for thirty-five hours straight. When she got to the room, she probably couldn't wait to get to sleep.

Well, Kira had no choice but to interrupt that sleep. She knew the layout of the quarters. It was like all others in this side of the habitat ring: a large main room, with a sleeping room to the right, replicators and the bathroom to the left. Kira slipped into the bedroom, and said softly, "Computer, low-level ambient light."

She wasn't sure if that gambit would work, but it did. Apparently the computer was programmed in the guest quarters to accept commands from any voice. The lights came up just a little, relieving the complete darkness and adding a very faint golden glow to the room.

The bed was in the center of everything. The woman who had been sleeping there was older than Kira had expected, and she wasn't particularly beautiful—which struck Kira as odd. With Kellec Ton's natural charm and good looks, she would have assumed he would have found a gorgeous mate. Apparently he was attracted to nice-looking women with a lot of brains.

"Who're you?" the woman—Pulaski, wasn't it?—asked. She was amazingly calm, given that she had just awakened to find a stranger in her bedchamber.

"My name doesn't matter," Kira said. "And I don't have a lot of time, so please listen to me."

Pulaski sat up in bed, adjusted the blankets around her, and pushed brown hair out of her eyes. "Computer," she said, as if Kira hadn't spoken, "how long have I been asleep?"

"One hour, three minutes, and forty-five seconds."

She sighed and leaned her head against the headboard. "One hour, three minutes, and forty-five seconds. I was hoping for at least two hours." She looked up at Kira. "This had better be good."

"I would like you to come with me to Bajor," Kira said.

Pulaski frowned, just a little. "I've already been through this with Gul Dukat. I'm afraid I can't leave the station."

"He doesn't have to know," Kira said. "I'll smuggle you down there and I'll bring you back."

"How is that possible?" Pulaski asked.

"I was on Bajor just two days ago. There are ways," Kira said. Her hands were damp. She was nervous. "I understand you've found a cure. They don't need you up here right now—"

"On the contrary," Pulaski said. "They do need me. The cure is only effective if someone is symptomatic. That means this disease can still spread all over the quadrant because we haven't found a way to take care of it in its incubation phases."

"But that's not urgent," Kira said. "Taking you to Bajor is."

"And why is that?" Pulaski asked. "We've already sent them the formula for the antidote, and we're sending some live cure down in shuttles. I'm not needed."

"You are," Kira said. "Not as a doctor. As an observer. We've been trying to get Federation representatives to Bajor for a long time, to see the conditions the Cardassians have imposed on us during the Occupation. Please. I'll take you to a few places, and we can do it quickly. No one will know you're gone. There are rumors of Federation negotiations with the Cardassians. We—"

Pulaski held up her hand. "I'm sorry," she said.

"No." Kira clenched her fists. "I won't take no for an answer. I won't. We need you."

Pulaski closed her eyes for a moment, then leaned her head back. It seemed as if she were making a decision. Finally she opened her eyes and looked at Kira.

"Now it's your turn to listen to me," Pulaski said softly. "The Cardassians didn't want us here. We had to agree to a lot of terms before we could arrive."

"One of them was turning your back on Bajoran suffering?" Kira asked.

"That's not fair," Pulaski said. "We're here because of Bajoran suffering."

"And Cardassian. I guess those rumors were correct. You are working with the Cardassians."

Pulaski shook her head. "I am here as a consultant on this disease only. I have strict orders to stay out of the political fights. In fact, I have to."

"Have to." Kira took a step forward. How many times had she heard that argument before? "Of course. You have to. So you won't see the atrocities being committed under your nose. So that you have deniability."

"I didn't say that." Somehow Pulaski's voice was still calm . . . what would it take to get this woman riled up? "What I did say was that in order to come here, we had to agree to terms. Or we wouldn't have been able to come at all."

"What does that have to do with me?" Kira said.

"Everything." Pulaski got out of bed. She was wearing a nightshirt, and her feet were bare. She grabbed a robe from her suitcase. She apparently hadn't even had time to unpack. "If the Cardassians find out that I was meeting with a Bajoran in my quarters, I would be reprimanded at best."

"You're afraid of a reprimand from Gul Dukat?" Kira couldn't keep the sarcasm from her voice.

Pulaski shook her head. "One of the terms we agreed to was that if one of my team got caught spying—or there was a suspicion of spying—we would all be killed."

"That's traditional Cardassian rhetoric," Kira said.

"You don't believe they'd do it?" Pulaski asked.

"Oh, they would if they caught you. But right now they're not going to catch anyone. So many of the Cardassians are sick, and those that aren't are concerned about staying well. It's a perfect scenario. Like I said, they won't miss you."

Pulaski's smile was small. "I wish I had your confidence in that. But I'm responsible for three other lives, and I'm not willing to risk them."

"How Starfleet of you," Kira said. "Your lives are so much more important than ours."

"You have quite a temper, don't you?" Pulaski asked.

Kira felt a flush build.

"It prevents you from seeing clearly." Pulaski took a step closer to Kira. They weren't that far apart now. Pulaski was slightly taller, but Kira was in better shape. She could kidnap the lady doctor and get her on that shuttle with no trouble at all.

"I see clearly enough," Kira said.

"Then you understand why I don't risk my team," Pulaski said.

"Because you are afraid of violating an agreement with the Cardassians." Kira spit out that last.

Pulaski shook her head. "We've had the privilege of coming to Terok Nor. As far as I know, no other Federation group—official or unofficial—has come here. I have spent most of my time in the medical lab, but my assistants have been all over the station, caring for Cardassians and Bajorans. The majority of the work two of my team members have done has been in the Bajoran section."

Pulaski stopped there. The words hung between them. Kira was beginning to understand where Pulaski was going, but wasn't sure she wanted to join her.

Pulaski's face was filled with compassion. "The Cardassians have worked hard to keep up their little fiction that everything is going well. But they've been having trouble doing so. As you said, there are very few guards and very little security right now. And my teams have had to venture into areas that I'm sure would have been off-limits otherwise."

"It's not the same as seeing Bajor," Kira said.

"No," Pulaski said. "It's not. But it will have to do. We'll be debriefed when we leave. And we'll be honest. We won't have to make anything up."

"You're trying to pretend that you sympathize with us when you make agreements with the Cardassians."

Pulaski's shoulders sagged. "If I were a Cardassian sympathizer, do you think I would have been married to Kellec Ton?"

"But you aren't any longer."

"That's right," Pulaski said. "Yet he's the one who asked for my help. There are many qualified doctors in Starfleet—and many unaffiliated ones all over the quadrant. Why do you think he asked for me?"

Kira crossed her arms and turned away. The woman had a point. A good point. Kira was letting her own disappointment blind her. She wanted the Federation group to come to Bajor so badly. She needed someone there. She felt if there were outside observers, things would change. They had to change—

She felt a hand on her shoulder. She looked back to see Pulaski's calm eyes measuring her.

"You could do us a favor, though."

"Us?" Kira said.

"Kellec and me."

Kira frowned. "How?"

"I tried to get permission to go to Bajor today. Gul Dukat refused, understandably. He's as afraid of letting me go down there as you are desirous of it. And probably for the same reason. He's worried about what information I'd take back to the Federation."

"I know," Kira said. "If you—"

"Please," Pulaski said. "Let me finish. We need to find the source of the virus."

"I thought you had a cure."

"We do, but it's not as effective as we'd like. We'd like a cure that destroys this virus completely. I don't know if you've been told, but this is a designer virus—"

"I know," Kira said.

"Then you understand that someone created it and someone planted it somewhere, we're not sure where. I wanted to go to Bajor to search for the source of the disease, but Dukat said no. He assigned a Cardassian team to conduct the search."

"Cardassians!" Kira pulled away. "You know what kind of search they'll do. They'll search until they have enough to prove that Bajorans did this thing, and then they'll use it as an excuse to slaughter hundreds of us."

"That's what I'm afraid of," Pulaski said. "So we need a pre-emptive strike. If you would go to Bajor and get this information on where the virus started *before* the Cardassians do, then we have two chances. The first is to find a solution that neutralizes this disease completely, and the second is to prevent the very scenario you're describing. If I can go to Dukat with proof that the virus started somewhere and it was brought in—or, even better, we can find the virus's designer—he'll have to call off his team. He wouldn't dare slaughter Bajorans in revenge. Not in front of a Federation observer."

"No," Kira said bitterly. "He'll wait until you're gone."

"And by then, the Bajorans at risk will have disappeared, won't they?" Pulaski asked.

Kira frowned. She had completely misjudged this woman. No wonder Kellec Ton had been attracted to her. Beneath that calm exterior, she had the courage of a Bajoran.

"Yes," Kira said slowly. "They could disappear."

"Good," Pulaski said.

"Before I go, I'd like to check with Kellec Ton, see if he agrees with the plan."

"Then do so," Pulaski said.

Kira shook her head. "It's not that easy. I can't move about freely in the Cardassian sections."

"Then I'll make certain he's in the Bajoran section in—what?—forty-five minutes?"

Kira should be able to make it back by then. "That'll do."

"Good," Pulaski said. She headed back toward the bed. "I understand your need to check up on me. But you'll find I'm on the level. I'm sure Kellec will have no objections to your trip to the surface."

"If you send Cardassian guards, I'll shoot them," Kira said.

"If I send Cardassian guards," Pulaski said, "you have every right to shoot me."

"Don't think I won't."

Pulaski smiled. "I know better than to double-cross a person like you," she said. "After all, I was once married to one. Now, if you'll excuse me, I'll contact Kellec, and then try to catch at least another hour of sleep."

Kira nodded. She couldn't quite bring herself to thank Pulaski—things hadn't gone as well as Kira had hoped. But they were still moving forward. And Kira felt as if she were being useful for the first time since this plague began.

And for her, being in the fight was always better than standing on the sidelines watching.

Chapter Nineteen

"I DON'T KNOW WHAT WENT WRONG," Kellec said. He was in the office staring through the door at the green Cardassians staggering in and the Bajorans brought up from below. Pulaski was at his side. She had never felt so discouraged in her life.

"Obviously something did," Narat said, and Pulaski could hear the blame in his voice. The two of them got along fine when things were moving well, but now they weren't getting along at all. They were taking the problems out on each other.

Reports of illness had started to come in only an hour ago. Now they had an official run on the med lab. Patients who had been cured ten hours ago were coming back, the sickness obviously in its early stages. A few had waited until the early stages were long past, and so, Pulaski believed, continued passing the disease on to others.

"Something did go wrong," she said without turning around. Governo was handling the Cardassians as he did before. She had instructed him to give them another dose of the antidote. Marvig was still in the Bajoran section, but Nurse Ogawa had come up with some of the sicker Bajorans to get them better treatment in the med lab.

"You know what it is?" Narat asked.

Pulaski nodded. Kellec was looking at her too. She let the door between the office and the main room close.

"If you think about it, you know just as well as I do," she said. "We haven't found how the virus starts. We have succeeded in preventing these patients from dying, but they're clearly reinfecting themselves."

"Or picking up the virus elsewhere," Narat said.

She shook her head. "I don't think so. Even when a patient caught the disease from the virus—and could prove that it wasn't incubating—that patient took at least two days to show signs of illness. These patients are coming back within ten to twelve hours."

"That means," Kellec said, "that the infecting agent isn't the virus."

Pulaski nodded. "Perhaps if we run some cultures, we can imitate the course of this reinfection in the lab."

"It should work," Kellec said.

"We should examine some of our older cultures as well," Narat said, his irritation with Kellec obviously forgotten.

"Good idea," Kellec said.

"It's not quite as hopeless," Pulaski said. "At least we have a point to work from."

The office door opened. Governo peeked in. "May I see you for a moment?" he asked Pulaski.

She walked over to him.

"I'm doing what you said," he said softly, "but I'm a little worried about reinjecting these Cardassians with the antidote. I mean, we don't know what this will do in high quantities in the body."

"The boy has a good point," Narat said.

"Yes, he does," Pulaski said. She put a hand on Governo's shoulder. "Just continue for now, Edgar. Whatever happens, it's better than dying for these poor people."

He nodded and went back into the main room. Pulaski closed the door again and leaned on it. The exhaustion she had been trying to fight was coming back, worse than before. "We're going to have to notify Bajor and Cardassia Prime."

"I suspect they already know," Ton said. "Let's not waste our time on that."

"No," she said. "We have to. What if they've sent patients away, thinking they were cured, and they can't get back to a medical facility?"

"They would have done it twelve hours ago, Katherine," Kellec said. "We have to focus our efforts here."

"Kellec is right," Narat said. "At this moment, everything we do should go toward finding the correct solution."

Pulaski nodded. But something was flitting around at the edge of her consciousness. Something she vaguely remembered—

"One of us should be doing as your assistant implied, Katherine." Kellec was standing near his console. "One of us should see if there are detrimental effects from too much antidote. We have to know where our limits are."

She looked at him. She knew he was going to suggest that Narat do it.

"You two found the cure in the first place," Narat said. "I'm not the researcher that you both are. You continue your search for the virus's origins. I'll investigate the effect of the antidote."

Pulaski let out a breath she hadn't even known she was holding. She made herself look away from Kellec, afraid that she would show her relief too clearly.

"All right." She walked over to the console. "Still, something more is bothering me. Something I feel I should know—"

"There were rumors," Kellec said, "that the Federation dealt with a similar plague, but I don't know the details."

"Of course," Pulaski said. "That's why this is bothering me."

"That was one of the reasons I asked permission to get you to come here. I figured you would know."

"I do know," she said. "The *Enterprise,* the ship I was on, dealt with it. But I never read the files. I always meant to—in fact, I was supposed to go through all of Crusher's logs, but I simply didn't have time. I looked at the overview and went on with my day-to-day work."

"That's not going to help us, Katherine," Kellec said. "You—"

"What is the meaning of this?" The office door crashed open and Dukat strode inside followed by three guards. One of them could barely stand. He was a light gray-green.

All three doctors glanced at each other. They had agreed moments ago to stall telling Dukat as long as possible.

"We told you, sir," Narat said, "that we can only treat a patient once the symptoms appear."

"Do I look like an idiot to you?" Dukat asked. His voice was lower than it had been a moment ago, and seemed a lot more menacing. "I have sent newly infected people back to the med lab for their shots. Those people are fine. But Linit here nearly died yesterday of this disease, and now he's got it again! You told me this was a cure."

"I know," Narat said. "But—"

Pulaski put a hand on his arm to quiet him. Narat seemed panicked by Dukat's anger, and panic would not do in this circumstance.

"When we told you about the cure," she said, "we also told you that it wasn't complete."

"You didn't tell me this would happen," Dukat said.

"We didn't know. We hoped the cure would hold once it killed the virus. But our patients seem to be reinfecting themselves."

"Themselves?"

"Yes," she said. "It's coming from within. That may sound bad to you—and I must admit, none of us are too happy about this turn of events—but it is good news in a way. It gives us something to base our new research on. It gives us hope."

"Hope! We had hope when we thought we'd gotten rid of this disease."

"We can get rid of it," Narat said. "For a few hours anyway."

"What good will that do?" Dukat asked.

"It'll prevent anyone from dying," Kellec said.

Dukat's lips thinned. He turned away from Kellec. "I'm very unhappy about this," Dukat said.

"We all are," Pulaski said.

"Yeah," Kellec said. "You would save us a lot of grief if you would just ask your people what the source of the virus was."

"Kellec!" Pulaski said.

"No," Dukat said. "That's fine. He can accuse us all he wants. It covers his Bajoran tracks. You're reinfecting everyone, aren't you, Kellec? That way no one gets off this station alive, and the Cardassians get the blame."

"You know better—" Kellec started forward, but Pulaski grabbed him.

"Both of you, stop it," she said. "You're acting like children."

She glanced at Narat for help but he hadn't moved. He was looking terrified.

"Fighting won't get us anywhere." She kept her hands on Kellec, but stepped between him and Dukat. "I've been with Kellec all day, and he hasn't done anything to reinfect your people. He hasn't had the opportunity. And you," she said, turning to Kellec, "can't you see how terrified he is? If he knew how this thing started, he wouldn't be this afraid."

"I am not afraid," Dukat said.

Kellec had the common sense to say nothing. Only grunt.

Dukat's eyes narrowed, but he also said nothing. Narat's gaze met Pulaski's. "She's right, you know," he said. "This is a time when we have to put aside our differences."

"It's getting very hard to do," Dukat said. "You gave us all hope yesterday and today it's gone. That's worse than having no hope in the first place."

"But I already explained what this means," Pulaski said. "It means we have a chance."

"I don't see it," Dukat said.

"There's one option we haven't tried," Kellec said. He eased himself away from Pulaski's hand. "Katherine and I were discussing it when you so nicely knocked and asked if you could come in."

"Kellec," Pulaski said warningly.

"And what's that?" Dukat asked, obviously choosing to ignore Kellec's tone.

"Katherine says the *Enterprise* dealt with something similar over a year ago. Remember when I asked you if she could come aboard, I told you there were rumors about this?"

Dukat turned his flat gaze to Pulaski. "So you have records of this?"

"No," she said, "and that's the problem. What I do know of it is very sketchy. But it wouldn't take long to get the information. The *Enterprise* is the ship that's waiting to pick us up, just outside Cardassian space."

"What a wonderful opportunity to bring a starship to Terok Nor," Dukat said, and to Pulaski he sounded just like Kellec. She took a deep breath, forcing herself to remain calm. They deserved each other. All this fighting and lack of reason. No wonder no one knew how to solve the problems between their two planets.

"I wasn't suggesting that," she said, working very hard to keep her voice level. "I would like to contact the *Enterprise* and have them send the records here."

Dukat frowned, as if her response surprised him. Then he said, "I will contact the *Enterprise.*"

"I'm sorry, Gul," she said, slipping back into her diplomatic mode, "but they won't give this information to you. You're not a doctor."

"Then Narat—"

"They'll wonder why I haven't asked," she said. "It's a simple request, really. You can monitor it."

Dukat's reptilian smile filled his face. "That would work. You may make the request, from my office."

"Katherine, I don't think that's a good idea," Kellec said.

"Do you want the information or not?" Dukat asked.

"I think we need it," Kellec said. "I just don't see why she can't send the message from here."

"Because," Dukat said, "it will interfere with your work. Yours and Narat's. You may come up with a solution on your own, while she's gone."

"It's all right, Kellec," she said. "I'll be fine."

"You don't know what this man is capable of," Kellec said.

She sighed. "I think, at the moment, we all have the same goals."

Dukat tilted his head, and smiled mockingly at Kellec. "I think your wife—"

"Ex-wife," Kellec said.

"—is telling us we can resume our loathing of each other when the crisis is past."

Kellec crossed his arms. "Thanks, but I plan to continue my loathing all the way through the crisis."

"Then I'll remove you and place you back in the Bajoran section," Dukat said.

"Oh," Kellec said. "I promise the loathing won't get in the way of my work. But, unlike you, I can't shut off my emotions when dealing with others. I see the consequences of each action."

Pulaski put her hand on Dukat's arm and started to lead him out of the office. "Each moment we delay is a moment that we need," she said to him.

He let her guide him into the main room. Cardassians were returning at a rate of two or three a minute. He grimaced at their green skin, the flaking scales, and she felt a shudder run through him.

"I would hope," she said, because she couldn't keep silent, "that you watch Kellec's actions, instead of listening to his words."

"I'm keeping a close eye on his actions," Dukat said. "I know what kind of a man he is."

They stepped into the Promenade and Dukat relaxed visibly.

"What surprises me," he continued, "is why you married him."

She smiled. "He's brilliant man."

"He's a fool."

"He hates witnessing pain. The Cardassians have caused a lot of pain on Bajor."

"The Bajorans brought it on themselves," Dukat said.

"I don't think the Bajorans would agree with that."

"What do you know?" Dukat asked. "You haven't observed our people."

"No," she said, "and I'm not trained in the subject. All I see is hatred on both sides. One day that will hurt you all."

"If we live through this plague," he said.

"That's my responsibility," she said. "I plan to see that you do."

Chapter Twenty

THE IMAGE OF DOZENS OF DEAD bodies piled on top of a cart like so much deadwood came back again, superimposed on the image of the stars she was gazing at through the Ten-Forward window, and pushing the voices of the *Enterprise* crew into the background. But this time Beverly Crusher didn't try to push the image away the way she usually did. She let herself remember the limbs jutting awkwardly, the tags on their toes, and just the sheer *number* of dead piled high in the Archarian hospital because there was no more room in the morgue.

That was Crusher's first view of the plague on Archaria III and the image that stayed burned in her mind. Thousands more died before she had found a cure.

But the image of those bodies never went away.

Neither did the memory of sixteen of her crewmates, including Deanna Troi, suffering the intense, crippling pain that seemed to twist from the inside, eating them alive like a monster Crusher couldn't see. And at the time couldn't fight.

It had taken Crusher some months to stop having nightmares.

But now the nightmares were back. The situation on Bajor seemed so similar to Archaria III. And she had helped Dr. Pulaski to walk into it basically alone. If only she had been able to go along, that would have been better than waiting here. But her request had been denied.

And she had been relieved. . . . She didn't want to face another plague. Not again. Not so soon. She didn't think she could handle another roomful of bodies piled on top of one another.

A gentle touch on her arm brought her back to the stars and the muffled conversation in the lounge. She turned and smiled at Captain Jean-Luc Picard, whose hand was resting comfortably on her arm.

"She's a good doctor," he said. He could still read her clearly. She had been annoyed at that a year ago. Then she discovered, in her short stint at Starfleet Medical, that she missed it.

Crusher nodded. Dr. Pulaski was. But even the best needed help at times. And it felt so frustrating not to be able to be there giving that help, instead of sitting here sipping Earl Grey tea.

"I know she's good," said Crusher. "That's not the problem. The problem is me. I hate waiting."

"Don't we all," the Captain said.

He was waiting too, waiting to hear from Pulaski. And he had served with the woman for the last year. He had to be worried. But in typical Jean-Luc fashion, he didn't say anything. He was willing to listen to her.

Over the last few days Ten-Forward had become Crusher's haven. Dr. Pulaski had left the medical areas in better shape than they'd been in a year ago, and it had only taken Crusher a day to get settled back in. Since the *Enterprise* was simply standing by on the Cardassian border, waiting for two weeks, there was very little for her to do. Being alone just wasn't what she needed at the moment, so she often sought company from whomever she found in the lounge. She didn't always talk. Sometimes she just let the buzz of conversation flow over her while she drank tea.

And thought of that pile of bodies on Archaria III.

She smiled at the captain, then took a sip of her tea, letting its perfumy flavor push the image of death back for a moment. "Thanks for joining me," she said.

He shrugged slightly. "We missed you last year. I missed you. I thought we might take this opportunity to get caught up."

She laughed. "And so I sit staring out the window."

"Sometimes," the captain said, "that's the best kind of catching up."

She smiled at him. She had missed him and the *Enterprise* a great deal. She had used Wesley as her main reason for returning, but in truth, there were many reasons.

"Dr. Crusher," Data's voice broke into the moment over the comm link. "You have an emergency incoming call from Dr. Pulaski on Terok Nor."

She was on her feet and headed for the screen built into the wall of Ten-Forward before she answered. "Put it through to here."

A moment later she had dodged around two tables and was at the screen as Dr. Pulaski's face appeared. Behind her stood a stern-looking Cardassian.

Crusher managed not to gasp at what she saw. In just a few short days

Pulaski looked as if she'd lived a dozen years, all without sleep. A week before, a neat, polished doctor had turned the medical area over to her; now Pulaski had deep circles under her eyes, her hair looked like it hadn't been combed in years, and a dark smudge of something streaked her neck.

And her eyes seemed almost haunted, as if she were seeing things no human should ever see.

"Dr. Crusher," Pulaski said, her voice level as always, "I need your help."

"Anything," Crusher said as Captain Picard moved up behind her.

"I need your records from the plague on Archaria III. It seems we may be dealing with something similar here."

Crusher nodded. "I was afraid of that."

"Can you send the records?" Pulaski asked. She was wasting no time. Crusher knew exactly how that felt.

Crusher glanced around at the captain, even though he would have nothing to do with this decision. The records of the plague on Archaria III were classified and under the direct control of Starfleet Medical. And since she was no longer in charge of Starfleet Medical, it was no longer her decision as to whether or not to release those records.

"How bad is it?" Crusher asked, trying to buy herself a little time to think. To get a message to Starfleet Medical from this distance could take a day, maybe more. And there was always a chance—a strong chance, considering the location of the plague—that they might turn her request down.

"It's bad," Pulaski said. "I wouldn't be making this request if I didn't think those records might help."

"Understood," Crusher said. "I'll need to—" The image of the bodies on Archaria III floated back to her mind. She had been about to say she would have to get clearance from Starfleet Medical, but in that time how many on Bajor would die?

How many deaths would it cost for her to follow the rules exactly?

Even one was too many.

She would get permission from Starfleet Medical after the records were sent. She had a few favors she could call in yet. She'd make them understand.

But that would take time. Time Dr. Pulaski didn't have.

She faced Pulaski directly. "Doctor, the encoded records will be downloaded to you within the next minute. Please stand by on this channel."

Pulaski's relief was obvious. "Thank you."

"Is there anything more we can do?" she asked, half-hoping Pulaski would invite her to Terok Nor. Crusher wanted to be busy. She could always say that the situation forced her to disobey the initial orders from Starfleet Medical.

"This just might be enough," Pulaski said. "Standing by."

The image went blank.

Crusher tapped her combadge. "Data, please download on the open line to Terok Nor all medical information from the Archaria III incident. Medical only. Let me know when you are finished."

"Understood," Data said.

She turned to the captain.

"I know I didn't follow procedure. I'll make it right with Starfleet Medical, though. It won't be a problem for you, Jean-Luc."

"I'm not worried about that, Beverly." His tone was warm. "I would have suggested you take the course of action you chose. It's clearly very bad there."

"How can you tell?" she asked.

"The Cardassian behind Dr. Pulaski," the captain said. "That was Gul Dukat himself."

Crusher instantly knew what the captain was saying. The image of the Archarian bodies came back. Crusher hadn't been able to save her, but maybe this time the bodies wouldn't be so numerous that they'd have to pile them in Terok Nor's infirmary.

"Data to Dr. Crusher."

"Go ahead," she said.

"All records have been sent."

"Thank you," she said.

She looked at the captain. "Now I guess it's time I faced the music with Starfleet Medical."

"We face the music," he said, taking her arm and heading her toward the door. "I was on Archaria III also. Remember?"

The image of the dead bodies came back again. Crusher squeezed the captain's hand in thanks. "How could I forget?"

Chapter Twenty-one

AH, THE SOUND OF CONVERSATION and laughter in his bar. Quark leaned against the back wall and closed his eyes. How he had missed this. It wasn't just the sound of the Dabo wheel and the silly girl's voice crying "Dabo!" or the clink of glasses, or even the silent accumulation of latinum as it made its way from his patrons' hands to his pockets. No. It was the feeling that he was in a viable business once more.

He was almost grateful to the plague. It had been such a traumatic experience that those who felt they had dodged it were coming into Quark's, wanting to drink themselves into oblivion. He was going to let them.

"Brother."

Of course Rom *would* interrupt Quark's reverie. Any time Quark felt that things were going his way, he had to be reminded of the presence of his stupid brother.

"What?" Quark asked, opening his eyes. Five more Cardassians were coming into the bar, laughing and slapping each other on the back.

"Brother, I have something to tell you."

"Well, it can wait," Quark said. "See those five? They're new customers and they need to buy drinks."

"Brother—"

"This is about making profits, Rom," Quark said. "Remember. 'A Ferengi without profit is no Ferengi at all.' "

"Brother, please don't quote the rules to me," Rom said. "I have something to tell you."

Quark leaned forward. "I'll make you recite every one of the rules if you don't get to work."

"Ah, yes, brother." Rom scurried toward the center of the bar, balancing a tray precariously on one hand.

Quark shook his head and began to make drinks. He already knew what three of those Cardassians would have. They were regulars, at least when they were well. And they were well now.

A Cardassian stood up in the back. Quark frowned. He had seen this before. He had a sinking sensation in his stomach. Maybe the lighting was bad. Maybe the Cardassian had spilled his drink. Maybe. There had to be some other explanation for the green color of his skin and the way he was swaying.

Quark slid out the side of the bar and hurried toward the Cardassian. If he got the Cardassian out of here before the man collapsed, there might be a chance that no one else would notice. Some kind of chance.

Any kind of chance.

Quark was halfway there when the Cardassian fell backwards.

All noise in the bar stopped. The Cardassian's companion stood and looked down at his fallen friend.

"This can't be right," he said. "He just got over the plague."

It was enough to start a stampede to the door. Quark grabbed at customers. "Don't believe them," he said. "I'm sure they misunderstood. Maybe he had been misdiagnosed. Surely—"

But no one was listening to him. They streamed out as if they were afraid they would suddenly topple over backwards, their skin a lovely shade of lime green. Even the Dabo girl had disappeared.

"Brother," Rom said.

Quark held up a hand. "Don't say a word to me. I don't want to hear it."

He headed back to the bar. It had taken five hours to fill the place up again, and only two minutes to empty it out. Except for the Cardassian on the floor. Moaning.

"Call a med team, would you, Rom?"

Rom gaped at him. "But brother, last time you made us—"

"I know what I did last time," Quark said. "There was no one in the bar then. Unless it was my imagination, we had a full bar this time. There's no hiding this one."

"All right, brother." Rom let his tray drop as he stared at the Cardassian.

Quark stared at Rom.

More specifically, Quark stared at Rom's ear.

On the lobe was a shiny pimple, with a whitehead that looked as if it could burst at any moment.

"Tell me, Rom," Quark said slowly. "A Cardassian dumped a case of Jibetian beer on your head."

"No, brother," Rom said, turning to him. "Well, not since the last time. No one has dumped anything on me."

"Then do you want to tell me where that pimple came from?" Quark asked, pointing.

Rom clapped a hand over the offending lobe. "I was trying to tell you."

"You were trying to tell me in a full bar. Now we have an empty bar. How did you get that—pustule—on your ear?"

Rom shrugged. "It grew there."

"Like hair."

"Or skin."

Quark nodded slowly. "And you're comfortable with that?"

"No," Rom said. "It itches. I was going to ask you if you had any cream left."

"I have some cream left," Quark said.

"I would like to borrow it," Rom said formally.

"And after you've applied it to your ear, you'll what? Scrape it off so that you can return it to me?"

"No," Rom said, obviously flustered. "I mean, I would—"

"You want me to give it to you," Quark said.

"Yes," Rom said. "But not all of it. Since you need it too."

"I don't need it," Quark said.

"Yes, you do," Rom said.

"No, I don't," Quark said. "I healed days ago. That's why I'm wondering what happened to you."

"The same thing that happened to you, brother. It came back."

Quark reached both hands up slowly and clapped his ears. Beneath his right hand, he felt a lump.

A pimple.

A pustule.

"What did you do to cause this?" Quark asked.

"Nothing," Rom said. "Maybe the cream didn't work."

"Obviously the cream didn't work," Quark said. He sank into a chair. "Not that it matters." He stared at the moaning green Cardassian on his floor. "No one will ever come here again."

Rom stared at him for a moment, then sat down beside him. "Things are bad, aren't they?"

Quark nodded. "And they're getting worse."

Chapter Twenty-two

PULASKI WAITED UNTIL KELLEC and Narat were seated in the small medical office's only two chairs. Governo and Marvig stood against the wall, and Ogawa was just coming in. The room was hot and stuffy, like almost everything on Terok Nor. With six of them, it was going to do nothing but get worse before this short meeting was over.

"Leave that door open," she said to Ogawa.

"Thank you," Governo said. Pulaski could see he was already sweating.

She had called this meeting the instant she got back to the medical area with the information from the *Enterprise.* It had taken fifteen minutes for them all to gather from different parts of the station, enough time for her to go over the data quickly. She didn't like what she saw, especially the final conclusion Dr. Crusher had put in the notes after the crisis was over.

"Ready?" She glanced at everyone.

"Do it, Katherine," Kellec said.

She nodded to him. In all the years she had known him, she'd never seen him this worried. Or this tired. The human faces around her all had deep worry carved in them, and Narat was now starting to look more afraid than anything else. But Kellec looked so strained she would have thought him seriously ill if she hadn't known what he had been through.

"Here's what the *Enterprise* was dealing with on Archaria III." She brought up the information supplied by Dr. Crusher on the screen in front of them. The three-dimensional image of a virus slowly spun, showing all its sides.

"That's very different from what we're dealing with," Kellec said.

And it was. Its shape bore no resemblance at all to the viruses she had spent the last week studying.

"Completely," Narat said.

"At a glance, I agree," Pulaski said. "This particular virus would be harmless to any Cardassian or Bajoran—or human, for that matter. This one wasn't designed for Cardassians or Bajorans or humans. It was designed to strike at cross-species breeds."

"Designed?" Narat asked.

"Designed," Pulaski said, "just as the virus we're dealing with was designed."

"Did they ever discover who created that one?" Governo asked.

"No," she said. "They didn't."

"Too bad," Marvig said.

"So why is this important?" Kellec said. "I see no possible connection."

Pulaski knew when her ex-husband was getting impatient and might just rudely leave.

"I'll get to that in a moment, Kellec," she said. "There is a tie, believe me."

He made a face, but remained in his chair.

She took a deep breath and then touched the console. "This is how the Archaria virus was formed." She set the screen in reverse motion.

The screen showed a computer image of the DNA of the virus shifting, breaking apart, until finally all that was left was three prions, the smallest life-form known to science. Prions were so tiny that not even transporter biofilters could remove them, so light they could blow on a slight breeze, and strong enough to live through freezing cold.

"The three prions are harmless separately," Pulaski said, "but when all three were present in the body of a cross-species humanoid, they merged and somehow rewrote their own DNA to form a deadly virus. Watch again."

She set the screen in forward motion and the three prions joined, changed, and formed the deadly Archaria virus.

"Amazing," Kellec said.

"So if the virus was killed," Narat said, "but the three prions remained in the body, the patient was reinfected."

"Almost at once," Pulaski said.

"Which is what we're dealing with here," Kellec said.

"This is pure evil," Marvig said.

"Again," Pulaski said, "I need to caution you all that our patients getting reinfected is just a similar symptom. There might be a completely different cause, we don't know yet. But at least this gives us a starting place we didn't have before."

"So our next step is what?" Governo asked.

Pulaski pointed at the tables where the sick were. "We take a few patients, both Cardassian and Bajoran, and cure them of the virus. Then we watch the prions in their blood to see if this pattern, or something similar, occurs. Once we know that, we might be on the track to a permanent cure."

"We can hope," Kellec said.

"You'd better do more than hope, Doctor."

The voice spun Kellec and Narat around.

Marvig stepped further away from the door.

Pulaski had seen Dukat come in just a second before Kellec spoke. The Gul now stood in the doorway of the medical office. He nodded to her.

"Fighting has broken out in a dozen places on Bajor," Dukat said, not waiting for a response from Kellec. "If it spreads here I don't have enough healthy guards to contain it. And if I can't contain it, the Cardassian fleet will."

"They're getting afraid back on Cardassia Prime," Kellec said. "I thought the mighty Cardassian warrior never showed fear."

"Kellec!" Pulaski said, making her voice take on the command authority she'd learned over the years. "Now is not the time."

Dukat nodded to her. He didn't even bother to smile. He was worried now, and not at all interested in baiting Kellec.

"You'd better listen to her, Bajoran," Dukat said. "At the moment I am the best friend you have. Find the final cure and find it fast. The Cardassian government will not allow this to reach Cardassia Prime."

Dukat turned and strode from the room.

Pulaski turned to say something to her ex-husband, but then stopped. His face was as white as she'd ever seen it. Narat was hunched so far over that he looked as if he were going to be sick.

Kellec glanced at Narat. "He means it, doesn't he?" Kellec asked.

Narat nodded.

"Means what?" Governo asked.

"Yeah," Marvig said, "what was that all about?"

"The Cardassian fleet will destroy this station and everyone on it—and all of Bajor—to stop this," Kellec said.

Again the Cardassian doctor nodded, as if destroying an entire planet's population was something they talked about every day.

For all Pulaski knew, maybe around here they did.

Chapter Twenty-three

KIRA SLIPPED INTO THE SECURITY OFFICE, looking both ways before closing the door. No one saw her go in, which was good. Very good.

The office was empty, of course. The constable was everywhere except where he was supposed to be. She didn't know how to summon him. Create a ruckus on the Promenade? Who would notice now that the disease was back? Only it wasn't really back—at least that's what one of the human medical assistants had told her.

It had never really left.

At least they had found a way to keep everyone from dying. That was a step in the right direction.

She made her way behind the desk and stared at the security console. Cardassian design, of course; but there had been modifications, modifications she didn't entirely understand. She threaded her fingers together, then eased them forward, cracking the knuckles. Since Odo wasn't here, she would just play with the console until he arrived. That would get his attention, and she might learn a few things in the process.

She placed a hand over the screen, wondering where to start.

"Touch that," Odo's gravelly voice said, "and you will spend the rest of your life in the brig."

"Oh, you frightened me," she said, but she moved her hand. Then she looked up. He was standing before her, his brown uniform trim as always. The door was closed, just as she had left it. Had he slid in under it? Or hadn't she heard him enter?

"You like to take chances, don't you?" he asked.

She gave him a half smile and shrugged. "One gets used to a certain level of danger."

"Maybe you do," he said. "But people who play dangerously around here more often than not get killed."

"Is that a threat?"

"From me, no," Odo said. "But if Dukat were to know you were here, then it would be. You need to be more cautious."

"Actually," she said. "That's why I'm here."

"You want me to teach you to be more cautious?" He actually sounded surprised. And then she realized he was making a joke. Not a very funny one, but it was at least an attempt.

"No," she said. "I need your help."

"Well," he said. "Isn't that an interesting turn of events."

She wasn't used to being a supplicant, especially with someone in a position of authority in a Cardassian government. "I need to get off the station."

"I thought we discussed that," he said.

"We did," she said. "That's why I'm here. I need your help to leave."

"Why should I do that?"

"Because," she said. "Kellec Ton has asked me to go to the surface to help him with the research."

"Kellec Ton?"

"And his ex-wife Pulaski."

"Why would they want you to go, when Dukat has already sent a team below?"

She stared at him for a moment. He worked for the Cardassians but he had always struck her as different. How different, she didn't know. And she couldn't rely on a guess.

"They need independent confirmation of the Cardassian findings."

"They don't trust the Cardassian findings, you mean," Odo said.

"And with cause," Kira said. "The Cardassians started this thing."

"It seems to me," Odo said, "they shouldn't trust the Bajoran findings either."

She stared at him.

"But then, it would be the prudent course to get information from both sides and compare. Somewhere in the middle they would find the truth." He tilted his strange head at her. "Do you have written permission from Kellec Ton to leave the station?"

He was playing with her again. Why did this shape-shifter always make her feel off-balance? Because she had never encountered anyone like him before? Or because he knew how to get to her when no one else did?

"Of course I don't have written permission," she said.

"Then how do I know you're not making this up?" Odo asked.

"Why would I make it up?"

"Why indeed." He frowned, musing. "I suppose I'll just have to check with Kellec."

"Okay," she said. "And Dr. Pulaski."

"And Dr. Pulaski," he said.

He didn't move, though; he didn't try to use his console or leave the room, either. He just watched her for a moment and then, to her surprise, he attempted a smile. It looked as if he didn't make that expression very often. It came out as half a grimace.

"All right," he said. "You may go."

"As easy as that?" she asked.

"As easy as that," he said.

"It's too easy."

"It's what you wanted."

"Yes, but you didn't check."

"You weren't worried about it. That's confirmation enough for me."

"What about the quarantine?" Kira asked. "Aren't you worried I'll fly off somewhere else?"

"Why should I worry about that?" he asked. "Even if Cardassian space weren't so heavily patrolled, you would never try anything like that."

"Just two days ago, you were worried that I might leave here and infect someone else."

"Two days ago, there wasn't a Cardassian fleet surrounding Terok Nor and Bajor. You couldn't go anywhere besides Bajor if you were the most cunning pilot in the quadrant."

Kira sank into the constable's chair. "The Cardassian fleet? What are they doing?"

"Think about it," Odo said. "The plague is back."

"And they don't want it to spread to Cardassia Prime." Kira pounded a fist on the console. "Those bastards!"

Something beeped beneath her hand.

"I would prefer it if you take your anger out on something a little less sensitive," Odo said.

"Well, then, I guess my mission becomes even more urgent," Kira said.

"It would seem so." Odo rounded the desk. "I'll give you clearance. Then the fleet won't give you any trouble."

She looked at him. Those eyes. So sad. She wondered why she always thought of him as sad.

"That's the second time you've done me a favor. Why?"

He shrugged. "Maybe I'll ask for repayment one day."

"Maybe." She slipped from behind the desk. "Anyway, thanks."

"You're welcome," he said. "But be careful. If this disease is a designer virus, like they're saying, finding information about it won't be easy."

She nodded. "Thanks for the warning."

"And it might also be dangerous."

"That one I figured out on my own." She glanced at the door. Two Cardassian guards walked through the Promenade. "I hate to impose on you one more time," she said, "but do you think you could beam me to my ship from here?"

He sighed. "What's one more violation among friends?" he asked, and pressed the console a few times.

As the transporter beam caught her, she saw him look up. His expression was unguarded—and worried? No. That had to be her imagination. She vowed to shut that imagination off while she conducted her investigation on Bajor. She couldn't afford to indulge in speculation.

Especially since that's all her Cardassian counterparts would be doing.

Chapter Twenty-four

DISTANT PHASER FIRE ECHOED throughout the station. Quark had the doors to the business shut and bolted and was still hiding behind the bar. His ear was swollen and covered with blisters. It itched so bad he couldn't think, and he was doing everything he could with his hands to keep them from scratching.

"That's the last of it, brother," Rom said as he came out of their quarters. His right ear was bleeding again. Quark shook his head. If the bar had been open, if he had had any customers, if he had still been serving drinks, he would have forbidden Rom to come out in public. But none of that mattered anymore.

The Bajorans had started rebelling in the Bajoran section, shooting the remaining Cardassian guards. Gul Dukat didn't have the forces to keep the Bajorans in check. It would only be a matter of time before they overran the station—and then Quark *really* didn't know what he'd do. The Bajorans weren't well known for having a lot of latinum.

Nog entered the bar behind his father. He was wearing the cap the Volian had made for Rom, attempting to follow Quark's edict not to scratch.

Quark sighed. He had hidden away all of the latinum, and had made Rom and Nog hide the expensive liquor. Now there was nothing he could do except—

"Aeeiieee!" He clapped a hand over his left ear and fell backwards. The itching suddenly got so intense that it was painful. Rom hurried to his side.

"Let me see, brother."

"You're not touching me with those infected hands," Quark said and rolled over, pressing his ear against the floor.

"I'll wash them first," Rom said.

"Just let us see, uncle," Nog said, crouching beside him.

Slowly Quark rolled the opposite direction so that they could see his left ear.

"Oh, my," Rom said.

"Oh, my?" Quark asked.

"Oh, my, my, my," Rom said.

"Oh, my, my, my, what?"

"Oh, my, my, my, my, my."

With his free hand, Quark shoved his brother. "Stop it! What do you see?"

"They're too big to be blisters," Nog said.

"What are?"

"The lumps, with pus, traveling toward your ear canal."

"Brother, you know how sensitive ear canals can be. If one of those gets down there and bursts . . ."

They all stared at each other. Then Quark got to his feet.

"I don't care who is shooting at whom, we have to get to the infirmary."

"People are dying, brother," Rom said.

"They're not dying anymore, stupid," Quark said. "They're just sick. And they aren't threatened with—" he couldn't suppress the shudder—"loss of ear function."

Rom's eyes got bigger. Nog put a hand on his hat. "That won't happen, will it, uncle?"

"Yes, it will," Quark said, "and it'll happen to me first. Let's go."

They walked to the door of the bar and peered through the glass design. The Promenade was empty.

"I think you should stay here, Nog," Rom said.

"Why?"

"It might be dangerous out there."

"No more dangerous than in here," Nog said, tugging on the hat.

"I want him treated too," Quark said. "I don't want to be reinfected."

He hit the door release and the glass doors opened. The silence was short-lived. He heard more shots and a few screams coming from far away.

"Follow me," he whispered. He motioned them out and let the doors close and lock behind them. He kept to the wall and crouched; at this level, no one would mistake them for Cardassians. Or Bajorans for that matter.

It took only a few moments to reach the infirmary.

The stench was as bad as it had been before. Maybe worse. Quark let himself inside, and saw patients everywhere, mostly Cardassians, leaning against the wall in a semblance of a line. At the end of it, the male hu-man assistant was attacking them all with a hypospray.

A few Cardassians sat on beds, clutching limbs with phaser burns. Dr. Narat came out of the office and his gaze met Quark's.

"I don't have time for Ferengi nonsense," he said.

"Look," Quark said, shoving his ear in Narat's direction. "The infection has gotten worse. It's heading for the ear canal and when it gets there—"

"I don't care," Narat said. "You can wait. It's not life-threatening."

"Well, that depends," Quark said. "If this continues, my quality of life will be dramatically lowered."

"It's a minor problem," Narat said. "Go back to your bar. When things settle down, we'll worry about your ear infection."

"Ear infection?" The hu-man female stood in the office door. She wore clothes and looked much too efficient for a female.

"Yes," Narat said. "I'm trying to get rid of them."

"Let me see," she said. She walked over to Quark, who tilted his head up so that she could examine his ear.

Her fingers were gentle on his lobes. If he weren't in so much pain—

"Kellec," she said. "Come see this."

Kellec Ton came out of the office and frowned at her. "What?" he said. "It's just an ear infection. I treated it before."

"You did?" she asked.

"Yes, with some antibacterial cream."

"How long ago was that?"

"A few days."

"And it's come back, worse," Quark said.

"When did this start?" the female asked.

"When the Cardassians poured drinks all over me," Rom said, a bit too eagerly.

"When was that?" the female asked.

Rom frowned. "About the time that Cardassian turned green and—"

"About the time the plague started," Quark said. He didn't want Rom to admit they had carried a sick Cardassian out of the bar. Hu-mans, Bajorans, and particularly Cardassians wouldn't take well to that.

"Really?" the female said. She bent over his ear again. "Was it this bad when you saw it, Kellec?"

"No," he said.

Narat joined them. "What you're thinking is not possible," he said.

"What are you thinking?" Quark asked.

"A third species," the female said, not to him, but to the other doctors. "And of course it manifests differently. And not as seriously."

"That we know of," Kellec said. "This could just be the early stages."

"Are you saying we have the plague?" Quark asked.

"Come into the office and let's find out," the female said. She sounded remarkably cheery about the whole thing.

Rom grabbed Quark's arm. "Brother, I don't want to die."

"It's not high on my list either," Quark said.

"It's better than being green for the rest of your life," Nog said, looking around. Rom shushed him, and shoved him forward.

"We won't die, will we?" Quark asked Narat as he followed him into the crammed office.

"Oh, you'll die," Narat said. Then he smiled. "Someday, anyway. You just probably won't die of this."

"Some bedside manner," Quark mumbled, and clenched his fists so that he wouldn't scratch his extremely itchy ears.

Chapter Twenty-five

THE SOUNDS OF PHASER FIRE off in the distance echoed through the heat and choking stench of the Bajoran section. Kellec Ton had never thought he would ever hear the sounds of battle here. Clearly a few Bajorans had managed to get Cardassian guns and were holding off the Cardassian guards. All the Cardassian guards had been driven from the Bajoran section of the station. For all he knew, the fighters might even be making headway into the Cardassian section. But it wasn't a headway that was taking them anywhere except closer to their own deaths.

And his too.

He had no doubt that if the final cure wasn't found quickly, the Cardassians would destroy the station. And possibly even Bajor.

Yet he wasn't going to tell the fighters that. They were Bajorans, fighters against Cardassian rule. As long as there was one of them left to fight, there was still hope.

Kellec moved quickly from one sick Bajoran to another, inoculating them with the temporary cure. It would get them back on their feet for at least ten hours. Then they'd be back sick again as the virus reformed and tore them apart. But at this point, ten hours was a very long time.

With luck Katherine and her people would find a final cure by then.

He checked his hypospray as he leaned over a young boy whose mother held him in her lap. She looked as flushed and sick as her son. He injected her first, then the boy. He had enough injections for a few more hours at this pace. He had brought supplies from the Cardassian medical lab, and his Bajoran assistants were helping him make more serum in the Bajoran medical area. But down here the process was much slower, the equipment nowhere near as good. There was no way they could keep making enough to maintain all the Bajorans alive until a final cure was found.

Since he'd come into the Bajoran section, the fighting had expanded from isolated sections and now covered the entire area. Most of it was between his position and the Cardassian medical lab. He doubted he could get through at this point; he'd face that problem when he completely ran out of serum.

Again, phaser fire echoed through the wide corridor as two Bajorans carrying another headed toward him.

"Doctor," one of them said, "can you help him?"

For an instant Kellec didn't realize the man they were carrying wasn't sick. He was wounded. A phaser had caught him in the left shoulder.

"Stretch him out here," Kellec said, motioning to an open place in the hallway beside the woman and her son.

They did as they were told, and quickly he inspected the wounded soldier. Phaser burn. Shock. But he would live, given a little time and care, assuming the entire station lived through this.

Kellec quickly gave the wounded soldier a shot against the virus just to be sure, then glanced up at the other soldiers. "Get him to the medical area. He's going to be fine. I'll check in on him in an hour or so."

"Thanks," the soldier said.

Kellec watched them carry him off. How crazy was this? He was temporarly curing his people of a deadly desease so they could keep fighting and dying. Sometimes it was hard to keep straight just why he was doing this.

The young boy took a deep shuddering breath, and then started to cry softly.

Kellec glanced at him. Both he and his mother were clearly recovering quickly, regaining the pale, hungry look of a normal Bajoran worker here on Terok Nor. More than likely, they were recovering for the second time.

He watched the mother comfort the child, then nodded. There was one of his reasons. The child. Kellec was fighting for a future for that child beyond working in an uridium-processing plant for a Cardassian dog. He'd keep his people alive long enough to see the Cardassians beaten, even if he had to die along with many others trying.

He moved on, injecting the temporary cure into Bajoran after Bajoran scattered along the wide hallway. And with each patient, he tried not to think about the fact that their only real hope for survival and winning this battle was Katherine and her crew.

They had to find the final cure and find it fast. But if there was anyone he trusted to do it, it was Katherine.

Chapter Twenty-six

IT HAD TAKEN KIRA LONGER than she expected to set up this meeting. She had been back on Bajor for more than a day, and three times she'd had to scramble for her life. The fighting here was intense and getting worse by the hour. The Bajorans saw weakness in the Cardassians and were fighting more and more directly, facing Cardassian guards head-on. She had never seen such ferocity in her own people—and she had always thought of them as extremely fierce—nor had she seen such desperation.

She had been feeling a bit desperate herself. Every time she stumbled, every time she felt even the slightest bit light-headed, she worried that she was getting sick. But so far, the disease had eluded her. She hoped it would continue to do so. There was no guarantee she would survive it if she caught it.

The plague was moving too swiftly. Too many people were dying. They either didn't have access to the temporary cure, or they hadn't initally believed the cure was temporary and had disappeared back into the hills. Cardassian guards had taken to haunting medical areas, looking for resistance leaders, hoping to arrest them when they came in for the cure, and that was stopping people from seeking help as well.

The farther away from a city center she got, the less frequently she encountered anyone with a cure at all.

So many Bajorans believed their faith would protect them. So many thought this plague was a lie invented by the Cardassians. And so many more believed that if they just stayed away from other Bajorans while the contagion was on the planet they would be all right. All of that served only to increase the death rate.

And now Kira was a little too far away from the medical facilities for her own comfort. But she had been tracking information on the origin of this disease, and she had come here.

She loathed this part of Bajor. It was barren scrub land, so unlike most of the planet that sometimes she felt as if she weren't on Bajor at all. If she squinted she could see mountains in the distance—or perhaps she just imagined them and their comfort.

The resistance cell that operated out of this area was known for attempting to organize the other cells. It didn't work, but it did mean that the information that flowed here was usually reliable.

"Nerys?"

She turned. An old man stood behind her, his arms open. She slipped into them and hugged him hard. "Chamar," she said. "It's been a long time."

"Too long." He backed out of the hug. "You're looking well."

"For now," she said. "But I don't like what I'm hearing."

He nodded. "The plague. It is the final sin the Cardassians will commit against us."

She took his hands in hers. "Where are the others?"

His eyes were sad. "They have scattered. Some to their families in this time of need, and others to fight a more direct war against the Cardassians. There are only a few of us left here, and I am the one who offered to come meet you."

"You're well?" she asked.

"For now," he said, echoing her words. He took her arm and led her down a thin path into a copse of dying trees. Behind them was a sturdy hut that had been there as long as she remembered. And the nice thing about it was that unless you knew it was there, you couldn't see it.

He pushed open the door. The interior was neat. A single room with a table and some comfortable chairs, and a small area set aside for sleeping.

"Would you like something?" he asked.

"Whatever you have," she said, knowing she didn't dare push him. Chamar did things in his own time.

"You have been traveling."

"All over Bajor," she said, deciding not to mention Terok Nor. "I'm helping in the medical effort."

"You have become a doctor since I saw you last, Nerys?"

She laughed. "No," she said. "I'm doing research for them, which is why I'm here."

"To the point so quickly," he said, setting a mug of juice in front of her. "You young people can wait for nothing."

So even in attempting to wait, she hadn't taken long enough. "I'm sorry, Chamar. It's just that every moment this disease lingers, we lose more Bajorans."

He nodded, looking tired. Then he closed his eyes. There was something he knew, something he didn't want to say. "What have you learned, Nerys?"

"That the first outbreaks happened at three different places on Bajor. The only things those places had in common were their space ports, the fact that they routinely sent ships to Terok Nor, and their high concentrations of Cardassians."

Chamar opened his eyes. "What else?"

"I heard rumors that Gel Kynled was behind this," she said. "I can't believe it. A Bajoran wouldn't do this."

He stared at her for a long time.

"I've met Gel," she said, "have you?"

"Once," Chamar said. "He wanted to serve in our cell. We threw him out."

"Why?"

"Because he walked up to a Cardassian guard and shot him at point-blank range—in front of witnesses. We had to risk good people to get him out of here. He was reckless."

"Yes," Kira said. "He was reckless. And he was dumb—he didn't have the ability to start anything of this magnitude."

"That's right," Chamar said. "If he were to spread a disease, he couldn't have created it. He would have had to buy it."

Kira felt as if someone slapped her. "You mean the Cardassians sold him the virus and he released it? Not even Gel is that dumb."

"Was that dumb," Chamar said. "Some of the earliest reported deaths were in his cell."

"So he died of this thing?"

"No," Chamar said. "He was shot at curfew by a Jibetian trader about two weeks ago."

"A Jibetian?" Kira said. "I didn't know the Cardassians worked with the Jibetians."

"Some Jibetian traders are little better than mercenaries, Nerys. They sell both sides against the other."

"Do we know who this trader is?"

"No," Chamar said. "And we've tried to find out. I don't think we're going to be able to find the creator of the disease, at least not this way."

"And the Cardassians won't give him up."

"If he is, indeed, a Cardassian," Chamar said.

"Why do you doubt it?" Kira asked.

Chamar shrugged. "I believe the Cardassians are evil, and a threat to our people. But I also believe they are the most self-centered people in the quadrant. They would never sacrifice themselves to a greater cause."

"But what if it was an accident? What if they didn't know it would affect them?"

"Nerys, from what I've heard, this virus is insidious. Would someone who devised a killing machine like that not first make sure it wouldn't kill him?"

She leaned back in her chair. "I don't like what you're saying."

"I don't either," he said. "It's easier to believe the Cardassians would do this. And that is what we will tell our people, once this is solved."

"I had hoped I would be able to give the doctors more information than this," Kira said.

"If they are true researchers, each piece of information helps," Chamar said.

Kira shook her head. "You think someone sold Gel a biological weapon against the Cardassians and he actually chose to use it?"

Chamar stared at her for a long time. "Nerys, if I gave you a weapon, and told you that with only one use you could destroy the Cardassians forever, that Bajor would be at peace forever, would you use it?"

"I'd like to think not," she said. "That's genocide."

"Is it?" Chamar asked. "What lengths would we go to in order to get rid of the Cardassian menace? How many Cardassians have you killed for the cause?"

Kira flinched.

"What's a few more?"

She hadn't touched her juice. Now she pushed the glass away. "Are you saying Gel was right in what he did?"

"Gel wasn't a man who understood subtlety, Nerys. And he was given an opportunity. I don't know how many of us, having seen our loved ones die horribly and knowing that everyone we love might suffer the same fate, would let such an opportunity pass us by."

Kira stood slowly. "You're scaring me, Chamar."

"I scare myself sometimes, Nerys. But I have had years to think on this, and every time I do, I realize that we are not as noble as we believe."

"I would never kill my own people to get rid of the Cardassians," Kira said.

"I don't think Gel would have either," Chamar said. "Which is why I believe there was an outside agent. Think on it, Nerys. The promise of no Cardassians, a fanatic like Gel, and a weapon. Only what the creator of that weapon doesn't say is that it is a two-pronged weapon, which kills both sides."

"That's too hideous to contemplate," Kira said.

"Yes, it is," Chamar said. "Which is why I hope you—or someone—finds the creator of this disease."

She nodded. "First we have to stop it. I need to get a message to Kellec Ton on Terok Nor. Do you still have communication equipment?"

"In a safe place," he said. "Let me take you there."

He got up slowly. Kira watched him. The information she got wasn't much, and yet it felt like a lot. Almost too much. She thought she was used to the lengths people went to, used to the cruelty in the world. And then she was surprised, like this afternoon, when she discovered that someone could go a step further.

Chamar made his way to the door. Kira followed him. She would send the message to Terok Nor, and then she would go back to her own work. Before she joined the fighting, though, she had one more task. She needed to round up the sick and get them closer to the medical areas, to make sure they got treatment when treatment was available. And she knew the treatment would become available. She had to believe Pulaski and Kellec Ton would find a solution. They had to.

She sighed. Why was it so easy to destroy? And so very hard to rebuild?

She didn't know, and she doubted she ever would.

Chapter Twenty-seven

PULASKI STOOD AND FORCED HERSELF to move a little, loosening tight and tired muscles. She was sweating slighty in the heat of the contained room, and her eyes felt strained from far too many hours staring at data. "Got to pace yourself," she said to herself.

She did a few slow stretches, then moved over toward the door. Through the window of the office she could see most of the medical section. Her team had been the only ones still working in the area since Kellec and Narat had left, a few hours before. Pulaski hadn't wanted them to, but they'd both felt it was important to distribute the temporary cure to their people, keeping each side at least going for the short term.

But that left all the research on her. And she had felt the weight of it the moment Kellec left.

Ensign Marvig bent over a Bajoran, carefully monitoring the progress of the three prions with a medical tricorder. Her hair was pulled back and Pulaski could see a rip in one leg of her uniform. Marvig hadn't had time to go back to her quarters in the last thirty-six hours. None of them had. And with the fighting going on around the station, Pulaski doubted they could even make it now.

After getting the information from the *Enterprise,* it had taken them only a few hours to discover that it was three prions forming the virus that had cause this epidemic, too. Pulaski knew that was too much of a coincidence. More than likely, the same virus designer who had created the Archaria III plague had created this one. Who this designer was had to be solved later, although she wished it could happen now.

Who would do such a thing?

And why?

But she couldn't focus on that. Right now the focus had to be on stopping the virus's formation here and now.

Nurse Ogawa moved from Cardassian patient to Cardassian patient, doing basically what Ensign Marvig was doing—monitoring the progress of the three prions to see if they formed the virus again. Just twenty minutes ago they had decided to try the same idea Dr. Crusher and the *Enterprise* crew had come up with at Archaria III. They would know shortly if the *Enterprise* cure, as they were calling it, was going to work or not. For some reason she didn't think it would this time, since this was the work of the same designer. If she were designing a virus, and she hoped she would never go that crazy, she would make certain it didn't fall prey to the same cure a second time.

Still, she had to try. Maybe this one had been unleashed at the same time, but took longer to incubate.

Or longer to reach Bajor.

Although she doubted it.

Two of the Ferengi were still in the medical area, sitting on a lab table. The older one, named Rom, looked nervous while his young son seemed both defiant and very interested in everything around him. Ensign Governo was monitoring them for the same prion reformation. Somehow, Pulaski knew the answer was with the Ferengi. She just didn't know how they were involved. She knew the Bajorans infected the Cardassians with the prions that caused the virus. But who had infected the Ferengi? And why did it only give them blisters instead of killing them?

She shook her head and then stretched again. Too many unaswered questions.

A faint explosion lightly shook the floor, and Marvig glanced up, a look of fear in her eyes. Pulaski nodded at her in a reassuring way and Marvig half smiled and went back to work. Too bad it wasn't that easy with all these patients.

She just hoped Kellec was all right. She had no idea how bad it was out there, but at the moment, as long as the fighting didn't come in here, she didn't care. None of it was going to matter unless she found the cure for this virus.

Nurse Ogawa glanced over at her and shook her head no.

Pulaski moved out into the patient area. "Not working?"

"Virus is forming. The *Enterprise* cure isn't stopping it or even slowing it down."

"I'm afraid it's the same with the Bajorans," Marvig said.

"And the Ferengi," Governo said. But he didn't take his eyes off his medical tricorder.

"You mean we're still sick?" the older Ferengi asked, clearly panicked. He put his hand to his ears, as if he could protect them from the infection. The younger Ferengi put a hand on his father's leg to calm him down.

"I'm afraid so," Governo said, still studying the tricorder intently. "But just stay put and don't worry. We'll find the cure."

Pulaski wished she could be as sure as Governo sounded.

"Dr. Pulaski," Governo said, his voice sounding unsure, "this is really odd."

"What is?"

She was about to step toward Governo and the Ferengi when Narat stumbled through the door of the medical area, another Cardassian slumped over his shoulder.

Narat looked faintly green and very weak. And it took her a moment to understand who the other greenish-tinted Cardassian was.

Gul Dukat.

Acting like a well-trained trauma unit, her crew sprang into motion. She and Governo went to help Narat and Dukat while Marvig and Ogawa helped two Cardassians who were not as sick off the biobeds.

She took Dukat and levered him over and onto his back on the bed. He tried to help, but was clearly so weak his effort almost made it more difficult. Cardassians were heavy enough.

Governo grabbed Dukat's legs and lifted them onto the bed as Pulaski started the scan. The virus was throughout his system, extrememly far advanced.

"Why didn't you come in here earlier?" she asked.

The look of terror in Dukat's eyes surprised her, but he said nothing.

"Have you been injected with any of this cure before?"

He shook his head no, then closed his eyes for a moment at the effort.

She upped the dosage slightly and injected him. "Now stay still and try to rest."

His hand came up and grabbed her sleeve. "The permanent cure?"

"I'll find it if you let go of my sleeve," she said. "Now rest. And that's an order."

For a moment she thought he was going to get angry, then he nodded, let go of her, and closed his eyes.

On the bed beside Dukat, Narat had just gotten his injection of the temporary cure from Nurse Ogawa. He looked up at Pulaski. "Anything?"

She shook her head.

He sighed. "I was hoping." Then he closed his eyes.

She stared at the two Cardassians for a moment, then turned to Ogawa.

"Monitor them closely. I want to know the moment the virus is clear from their systems."

"Understood," Ogawa said.

"Crystal, you continue monitoring the Bajorans."

"Yes, Doctor," Marvig said.

Pulaksi did a quick medical scan of Dukat. The temporary cure was already attacking the virus. In fifteen minutes he'd be back to his normal, overbearing self. But that gave her fifteen minutes of time in which to work.

She turned to Governo. "Okay, what were you going to show me with the Ferengi?"

On the lab table, the older Ferengi actually flinched.

Chapter Twenty-eight

PULASKI WATCHED THE MEDICAL MONITOR as if it might blow up at any moment. The Ferengi named Rom squirmed on the biobed, even though no one was actually touching him. She was instead looking at what was happening in his body. Governo had noticed an odd reaction just before Dukat had come in. But with the disruption of the now sleeping Dukat, they had missed the timing on whatever Governo had seen.

So they got the quivering Ferengi's permission to reinfect him and then heal him again. It had taken both the younger Ferengi and Governo a good twenty minutes to convince him it would be safe. It wasn't until the boy Ferengi offered to do it that the older one caved in.

"Dukat's starting to come around," Ogawa said.

"Give him a light sedative," Pulaski said. "I want him resting for at least another thirty minutes." Plus she wanted that long until she had to deal with him again.

"See it?" Governo said, his voice excited. He too was monitoring the ongoing prion activity in the Ferengi body.

"I did," Pulaski said. But she wasn't sure exactly what she had seen. It had happened so fast. But this time it was recorded, visual and all other data.

They both continued to monitor the forming of the virus until it was at its full stage, then she said, "Let's watch this on the screen in the office."

"Um," the Ferengi said.

Pulaski turned to him. She had learned in the last few moments that Rom was not very assertive.

"Um, would you mind curing me first?" he asked.

"Of course not," Pulaski said.

She nodded toward Governo, who hyposprayed the Ferengi. "There," he said when he was done. "All better."

The Ferengi's hands immediately went to his ears. His grin was wide enough to split his face. "Thanks."

Pulaski glanced at Narat. He was standing beside Dukat, monitoring his sleeping commander. Narat's color had returned to its normal healthy gray, just as Dukat's had. But Narat's stage of the infection had been nowhere near as advanced as Dukat's. With the gul, she was going to be safe.

"Narat, are you up to seeing something?"

"I think I should remain here," he said.

"All right." She was a bit relieved that he wasn't coming. She had kept so much from him in this research that she didn't want to blurt it out at the last minute. Still, she had to offer.

She followed Governo into the office. Right now Pulaski wished that Kellec were here. This was just the kind of thing she could use his knowledge on. But at the moment she was going to have to go it alone.

She quickly set the screen to start right before the strange event in the Ferengi virus formation, then started it slowly forward. Nothing seemed different. Three different and harmless prions were drawn together, just as in the other two races.

"Coming up right about now," Governo said.

As the prions started to join and alter their DNA, something different suddenly happened. The virus was formed, but also a fourth prion was formed and quickly expelled.

She froze the image on that prion, quickly isolated it and ran a computer diagnostic. The moment the data appeared, she glanced out the office window at the Cardassian doctor. Thank heavens he hadn't accepted her invitation.

"Amazing," Governo said, staring at the data. "That means what I think it means, doesn't it?"

She nodded. "That prion is the key prion in the Bajoran virus, which then mutates into the Cardassian virus."

"The Ferengi are carrying the catalyst prion that restores viral functioning even after it's cured," Governo said.

"Don't say that too loud," she said, glancing at where the nervous Ferengi and his calm son sat on the biobed, then at where Dukat still slept, with Narat standing beside him.

"Sorry," Governo said, his face white at what she was suggesting by the warning.

She stared at the data again. Her hunch had been right about the Ferengi being critical elements in this. But that still didn't answer the question of how to stop the prions from forming the virus.

Out of the corner of her eye she could see Dukat starting to stir.

"Ensign," she said to Governo, "I want you to remain in here going over this data again and again. We need to find a way to stop those prions from coming together in the first place. No one else is to see this unless I give permission. Understand?"

"Yes," he said.

She headed out toward Dukat, who was now sitting up.

"Are we going to live or not?" the Ferengi asked.

"You're going to be fine," she said. "Just stay there and keep calm."

Then she turned to Dukat. "And how are you feeling, Gul?"

"I've been better," he said. His voice was raspy and his eyes were bloodshot. Some of his scales were still flaking, but he didn't seem to notice. "How's the research going?"

"We're making progress, but we haven't found a final cure yet."

He dropped down off the biobed and stood up straight, towering over her. For a moment he tested his own balance, then took a deep breath and nodded. Finally he looked at her. "Doctor, I need to talk with you for a moment. Alone."

She nodded and indicated the door of the medical area leading out into the wide hallway beyond. Normally she'd have escorted him into the office, but Governo was working in there, and she didn't want to disturb the ensign.

Dukat glanced at Narat, then turned toward the main door, leaving the Cardassian doctor looking puzzled.

Pulaski followed Dukat, watching his steps gain confidence with each stride.

In the corridor he turned to face her. Then with a quick glance around to make sure no one was close by, he said, "Doctor, I'm not sure how much longer I can contain this situation."

"I'm not sure I follow you," Pulaski said.

"Before I fell ill I managed to hold off the Cardassian fleet, saying we were on the verge of a final cure. They are expecting it soon."

"And if we can't come up with it we die," Pulaski said.

"I'm afraid so, Doctor," he said. "All of us. And more than likely all of Bajor."

For an instant the corridor seemed to spin. She took a deep breath and it stopped. "I had better get back to work and you had better try to buy me a little more time."

He nodded and without another word turned and headed off down the corridor, his stride long and sure.

She watched him for a moment, doing her best to keep her entire body from shaking. She had known coming here that she and her team might not get back alive. She had accepted that. But she had never expected also to have to save an entire planet.

Finally, she turned and headed back toward the medical office, ignoring Narat's stares. That extra prion in the Ferengi held the secret to the cure. And as Dukat had just made very clear, she didn't have much time to find it.

Chapter Twenty-nine

BAJOR FILLED THE VIEWPORTS of the docking ring as the sounds of fighting echoed down the corridor. Kellec Ton knelt in the hallway and quickly wrapped the burned arm of a Bajoran fighter, then injected him with a quick painkiller.

"You'll be all right," Kellec said, patting the man on the leg.

The man nodded weakly, as Kellec moved and crouched next to the woman leaning against the bulkhead two steps away. Plague, in its middle stage. The woman looked to be about Kellec's age and her skin had the rosy glow of the disease. Her face was dirty and she was starting to smell of rot. He quickly injected her with the temporary cure, and then monitored her as the medicine started to work. She was going to make it, at least for another ten hours or so.

"Rest here as long as you can," he said, and she nodded.

He stood and checked the level of his hypospray. He had enough for another thirty or so, then he'd be forced to try to make his way through the fighting to one of the medical labs.

Down the hall to his right the fighting was raging, as the Cardassian guards tried to retake this area of the docking ring. So far his people had held them off, but it didn't look as if that would last long. He'd been forced here by following the wounded and sick workers. It was like following a never-ending road of blood and death.

With the fighting echoing behind him, he moved down the large hall. A low moan caught his attention, coming from an alcove. Three Bajoran workers lay in the dark, against the wall. The smell in the small area made it seem as if they'd been dead for a week, but he could tell that two of them were still breathing. Barely.

He scanned them quickly. The two who were still alive both needed to be in one of the medical areas, but at the moment that wasn't possible. With all the fighting there was no one to take them there and no way to get there.

He gave both survivors full plague shots, then quickly checked them again. They might make it. He didn't have much choice but to leave them and keep helping others. At this point he'd done everything he could for them. They were so far gone that if they did recover they wouldn't even remember him being here.

He went back out into the main hallway, as a group of seven Bajoran workers moved past and turned into one of the docking-bay corridors. Two of them carried Cardassian weapons, while the others carried iron bars. Three of them looked as if they were in the early stages of the plague.

"Hold on," Kellec shouted. He ran up behind them and quickly injected one of the men who he could tell was quickly getting sick.

"You Kellec Ton?" A man with a bloody rag wrapped around his arm stepped forward.

"I am," Kellec said. Kellec pointed at the other one clearly coming down with the plague. "You need this." He held up his hypospray.

The man nodded and moved up to where Kellec could inject him.

Then Kellec looked at the rest of them. "Have the rest of you been given the plague cure in the last four or five hours?"

All of them nodded.

"We're getting out of here," the man with the bloody arm said. "Heading for Bajor. Help with the fighting there. You want to come along?"

"You won't make it," Kellec said, shaking his head.

"Sure we will," the man said. "That's a Cardassian ore freighter right there, and we have two pilots among us."

"And there's a very large Cardassian fleet surrounding the station," Kellec said, pointing out the viewport.

"That's what the Cardassians want us to think," the man said, laughing. "We'll just drop right straight down and be on Bajor before what ships there are out there even know we've moved."

Kellec shook his head. "Don't waste all your lives."

The man with the bandaged arm stepped right up into Kellec's face. "We're going home and no Cardassian sympathizer is going to stop us."

The blow caught Kellec squarely in the stomach, sending him backward onto the deck gasping for breath. He couldn't believe the man had hit him.

"See you, Doctor," the man said, motioning for the men to turn around and head into the freighter.

Kellec tried to shout no, but there was no breath left in him. His stomach felt as if it were holding his lungs in a death grip. No air was going in or out. His shout came out as more of a choking gag.

By the time Kellec could even get his lungs to take in a small amount of air, the men were in the freighter and the lock had rolled closed.

Kellec stumbled to his feet and moved over to a viewport just as the freighter disengaged itself from the station and turned toward Bajor. The planet looked so close, so large.

Maybe they would make it.

Maybe he had been wrong.

Three seconds later the ship exploded as two shots from Cardassian warships blew it apart like a child's balloon against a pin.

"No!" Kellec shouted, then dropped down onto the deck, his head in his hands.

He sat there for a few moments, until the sounds of fighting grew in the corridor to his right. He had to keep going, to keep curing people for as long as he could.

He pulled himself back to his feet, facing Bajor and the expanding cloud of wreckage from the ore ship.

"Stupid fools," he said.

Beyond the wreckage, against the blackness of space, he could see three Cardassian warships. He knew, without a doubt, there were a lot more than that surrounding the station at this moment. He knew, without a doubt, those warships would blast this entire station if a cure wasn't found soon.

He picked up his hypospray and checked it to make sure it was still working, then headed in the direction away from the sounds of the fighting.

"Hurry, Katherine," he said to the walls and to the image of Bajor below him. "Hurry."

Chapter Thirty

PULASKI STARED AT THE IMAGE of the three prions on the screen. They seemed so harmless. The smallest living things known. She'd studied them in medical school. Everyone had. They were mostly of interest only because they were so small. Yet these three prions in front of her could mutate into a deadly virus when joined. They were far from harmless.

And one of them had been created by a biologically manufactured mutation in a Ferengi's body. It was no wonder the incubation period for this plague had taken so long. That special prion had had to travel through air or fluids from the Bajorans, then to a Ferengi, and then to a Cardassian, where it combined with two other naturally occurring prions to form a deadly virus.

Then that virus mutated into a deadly virus for Cardassians. Amazingly complex.

Yet it was an elegantly simple way to wipe out two races.

And so far impossible to stop.

Whoever had designed this had thought of almost everything. Even if the Ferengi were removed from the station and Bajor, the special prion was already here and multiplying in Cardassian and Bajoran bodies. She had no doubt that with the long incubation period it had already traveled to Cardassia. The Ferengi had been the start, but they were now no longer needed in the final deadly result.

She stared at that fourth prion. It revealed nothing.

She shoved her chair back and rubbed her eyes. She couldn't remember the last time she had slept or even eaten much more than a handful of nuts and a glass of water. But from her conversation in the hallway with Dukat two hours ago, she might not need to eat or sleep ever again. She didn't know how much time they had left, but she bet it wasn't much.

Behind her Governo, at another monitor, let out a long sigh.

"Nothing?" she asked.

"Nothing," he said. "I just don't understand what draws the three prions together. There has to be some sort of molecular attraction."

Pulaski looked at her assistant for a moment, letting what he had said sink in. He was right. There had to be something working between the prions that drew them together. And if she had to wager, she would bet that attraction was in that special prion created by the Ferengi mutation.

She'd been focusing all her energy on trying to find a way to kill the prions, not on why they went together. It hadn't even occurred to her to look in that area. It was lucky Governo had.

"There's just no way to isolate what that attraction might be at such a small, microscopic level," Governo said, "at least not without months of trial and error."

"We don't have months," she said. She doubted they even had hours left.

"I know," Governo said.

She stared over Governo's shoulder at the image of the prions on the screen. They were slowly working their way toward each other in the solution.

"I think the attraction comes from this one," Governo said, highlighting the prion with a red glow. Suddenly, staring at that red glow, Pulaski had the solution.

"What happens if we coat it?" she said.

"What?" Governo said, turning to stare at her.

"See the red highlight you have on that prion?"

He glanced around at it. "Yes?"

"You said you think the special prion is attracting the others in some unseen way. Right?"

He nodded.

"So what would happen if we coated all the prions somehow, and try to block the attraction, whatever it might be."

Governo nodded. "It might work. But first we have to find something that will stick to them."

Pulaski moved quickly to the door and out into the lab area. Narat was working over a sick Cardassian. Ogawa and Marvig huddled over a badly injured Bajoran.

"Listen up everyone," Pulaski said to her team. "I need at least a dozen blood cultures from all three races, virus-free but full of prions, set up at once. And then I need another dozen being set up right behind the first dozen. Make it fast."

"Did you find a cure?" Narat asked.

"We don't know yet," she said, heading for the nearest Cardassian to start drawing samples of blood. "And until we get these cultures set up, we won't know. You want to help?"

Narat had the common sense not to say anything more. But he instantly went to work beside her.

It took them thirty minutes to get everything set and ready to go for the first tests.

And another twenty minutes and seven failures before they found a molecular cousin of an iodine derivative that actually stuck to the prions, turning all of them the same shade of sickly brown. It was as if the prions had been dipped in dye.

"Now," Pulaski said, staring at the monitor in the office, "we need to find something that will ride on the iodine carrier, something that will block the attraction."

"I don't think we're going to need to," Governo said, his voice an octave higher than she had ever heard it. "Look at this!"

She watched the monitor where he was pointing. The sickly brown prions in the solution were moving past each other, not seeming to even notice. The attraction between them seemed to be gone.

"Color?" Pulaski said. "Could the attraction have been something as simple as color?"

"Or maybe they hate the derivative," Governo said. "At such a microscopic level, anything is possible."

They both stared at the prions for a few more long moments. But unlike what had been happening in previous tests, these prions were no longer interested in each other. And without that interest, they wouldn't form the deadly virus.

Governo looked up at her, his smile filling his face. "It's working. It's actually working."

Pulaski stepped back quickly into the medical lab. "How many more cultures from all three races are set up?"

"Six each," Ogawa said.

"I want to use all of them to test the iodine derivative. Quickly. Everyone monitor the cultures and put the computer on them as well. We don't want any prions to join."

Ten minutes later the tests, with the entire team watching closely, seemed to be conclusive. But she had to be sure—and at this point all normal medical procedures were long out the airlock.

"Now we try it in patients," she said.

Narat looked at her. That hesitation was built into both of them. But they had to get past it. They had to work quickly, or they would lose every chance they had. If the Cardassians blew up Terok Nor and then killed everyone on Bajor, they still wouldn't have stopped the plague. They would have committed genocide and a few days later gotten sick on Cardassia Prime.

And they would have unknowingly killed off their best chance to a solution.

Narat nodded.

Pulaski quickly mixed the iodine derivative with the cure and injected it into two Cardassians and two Bajorans, plus the older Ferengi.

Eighteen minutes later she had enough faith in their cure to call Dukat.

His face appeared on the screen. He wasn't the strong, confident Cardassian leader he'd been when she'd arrived. Now he looked more like a tired street fighter. And when he saw her he didn't even smile.

"We have it," she said.

"And you're sure it's permanent this time?"

"As sure as I can be under these conditions."

He nodded. "Get some to Narat and start the distribution. I'll see what I can do to convince the ships outside."

"I will," she said.

He cut the connection.

Behind her Governo said, "Not even a thank-you."

She dropped down into the chair and took a deep breath. "Not yet," she said, staring at the blank screen. "If we survive the next few hours, then he might thank us."

She glanced at the Cardassians who were getting this new version of the cure, and the Bajorans, who were walking around again, and the Ferengi, who was clapping his ears and jumping up and down, clearly gleeful that he felt better.

Governo followed her gaze. She smiled at him tiredly, and said, "I think we have all the thanks we need right here."

Epilogue

IT TOOK TWO WEEKS. They were smarter than he thought. His observers had reported back, saying the virus had been defeated yet again.

He was glad he was doing test cases. He had underestimated the intelligence of his foes. But he wouldn't do that again. He would be very careful next time. And, if it took a few more attempts, he would make them. He wanted to do this right. He would do this right.

And one day soon, he would succeed.

When someone said lack of pain was the best experience in the world, Quark had never understood them. But after this week, he did. His ears no longer itched and, more important, the pustules were gone from his ear canal. The female doctor had pronounced him well before she left—and her casual fingering of his lobes had proven that he still had ear function.

His ears were operating in another capacity now. They were reveling in the sound of a full bar. The fighting had stopped, which was too bad for the Bajorans but did ensure that Quark's black-market business would kick back up soon. Cardassians crowded the Dabo table, spending hard-earned latinum. They were drinking to wonderful excess, and a few were so happy to be alive they were splurging on expensive liquors, many of which Rom did not even know the names of.

Rom would come back to the bar, tray in hand, and mangle an order, often so badly that Quark would have to go to the table himself to clarify. But he was in too good a mood to be angry. He'd let Rom get away with his incompetence today. Tomorrow would be another story. Tomorrow, Rom and Nog had to start saving their salaries for another gold-plated ear brush, one Quark had had his eye on for a long, long time.

They would give him the funds, of course, or even better, he would never pay them and use the money for that brush. Which he would then keep locked up—and he would wear the key around his neck. He didn't want to risk cross-contamination again.

No matter what that female doctor and Kellec Ton had said. They believed that someone, or something, had actually brought the virus to the bar. They believed that the Ferengi had been infected first. Quark had begged them and even tried to bribe them to prevent them from sharing that insight with Narat, and in the end they had agreed. Kellec Ton, to Quark's surprise, negotiated the bribe: He wanted Quark to help with the Bajoran resistance on the station. In small ways. Funneling in messages or supplies, or helping someone escape Odo's eye. Quark refused, until Kellec Ton reminded him that they could easily reinfect the Ferengi—and make certain the virus didn't spread beyond Quark, Rom, and Nog.

Quark didn't believe the threat. He didn't think Kellec Ton was that sort of man (and the hu-man female's attempt to hide her laughter reinforced that) but, on the off-chance that the threat was real, Quark agreed to those terms, for a time of limited duration. He suggested a week. Kellec suggested a month. They had compromised on two weeks.

Which was good enough for Quark. It protected his bar, his livelihood, and, much as he hated to admit it, his family. For it looked like Rom and Nog weren't going anywhere soon. And that meant that Quark had to teach them to be at least mildly competent.

"Brother," Rom said. "Gul Dukat would like a vodtini twisted."

"A what?" Quark asked, turning toward his brother.

"A vodtini twisted."

"And what is that?" Quark asked.

"A hu-man drink, suggested by the good doctor. Apparently she said that generations of hu-mans drank it after their workday was over to relax."

"A vodka martini with a twist?" Quark asked.

"That's it!" Rom said.

Quark looked over his brother's head at Gul Dukat. He was sitting at a center table, looking exhausted, but he was managing to laugh with a few of the guards. "Does he know what vodka does to Cardassians?" Quark asked.

"How should I know?" Rom asked.

"Tell him that if he wants to drink it, he has to take it outside. Tell him that the fumes are too much for my other patrons." Quark shook his head. "Who'd have figured the hu-man was a practical jokester."

Rom frowned. "Jokes, brother?"

Quark nodded. "Vodka and Cardassians," he said. "If they've never had it before, it turns them green."

"That doesn't seem very funny to me," Rom said, and went back to Gul Dukat's table.

Quark watched him. What he didn't want to explain to his idiot brother was that sometimes the point of practical jokes wasn't humor. Sometimes the point was to teach someone a lesson.

Apparently the lady doctor believed Gul Dukat had some lessons to learn.

How many times would she have to say good-bye to the *Enterprise?* Pulaski leaned back in her chair in the captain's ready room. The fish were swimming in their aquarium, and Captain Jean-Luc Picard had a clear glass on his desk filled with perfectly brewed Earl Grey tea. The faintly flowery smell of the liquid permeated the room.

Picard was standing behind his desk, looking out the portholes to the stars. The ship was heading back to Deep Space Five at full warp. Apparently someone there had a new assignment for Pulaski and wanted her to arrive on the double.

Just what she needed. More work.

Beverly Crusher sat beside her, nursing an old-fashioned cup of coffee. Pulaski was having one as well. It wasn't Cardassian or Bajoran. It was an Earth beverage, with a taste of home.

She couldn't believe she was leaving. Even when she, Ogawa, Governo, and Marvig had boarded a Cardassian transport ship she hadn't believed she was going home. The trip to the *Enterprise* had been very different from the trip bringing them to Terok Nor. They were being treated like royalty, each with large cabins even though they weren't staying long enough to sleep in them, and the captain was treating them to a lengthy meal filled with things Pulaski had never seen before.

It all made her feel vaguely guilty about her parting recommendation to Gul Dukat. Even Kellec had given her a funny look when she gave it.

And it all sounded so innocent: a vodka martini with a twist. But she had done so because Dukat had annoyed—no, perhaps the correct term was angered—her, with his insistence on quotas and returning the station to normal. She had overheard him ordering double shifts and punishment for any Bajoran who still claimed weakness from the illness. He had also ordered harsh measures for the prisoners who had instigated the fighting.

He was putting Terok Nor back together the old way, ignoring Kellec's contribution and refusing to see that Bajorans were people, just like Cardassians.

It had riled her temper. And so she had sweetly told Dukat of a way he could rest at the end of his day.

At least she could be sure he wouldn't get sleep for one night. Maybe more. And if she ever saw him again, she could claim ignorance of vodka's effects on Cardassians.

"Are you sure you've told us everything?" Crusher was saying, her tone sympathetic. She had been through one of these plagues too and she had said, when Pulaski got off the transporter pad, that she would be there any time Pulaski needed to talk. "You have a strange expression on your face."

Pulaski smiled just a little. She wouldn't admit to the vodka remark, not in front of Captain Picard, but she did say, "I guess I am a bit surprised by the level of hatred between the Cardassians and the Bajorans."

"I think I can understand the Bajorans' reaction," Picard said, returning to his chair. "After all, the Cardassians have been occupying their planet for some time now."

"Yes, but they worked together on Terok Nor for a brief time, and then even that fell apart." Pulaski sighed. Not even the coffee was helping her bone-deep exhaustion. "And now both sides are blaming the other for the plague. The situation has grown worse instead of better."

"I can't help but wonder if that wasn't the designer's intent," Crusher said.

"What do you mean?" Picard asked.

"Well, we can assume that this plague is related to the one we dealt with on Archaria III," Crusher said. "It almost seems like a second trial of an experiment."

Pulaski looked at her. She had had the same thoughts.

"After all, it didn't respond to the same solution, and the stakes were escalated. There were three species involved. There was a new method of delivery. And"—Crusher paused to look first at Pulaski, then Picard "—this one had the added benefit of destabilizing a precarious region. So if this second trial failed, perhaps the designer saw a benefit in worsening the Cardassian-Bajoran situation."

Picard picked up his glass cup. "Who would do such a thing?"

"A monster," Pulaski said.

"But why?"

"I don't know," Crusher said. "And I'm not sure I want to find out."

"Surely you want to catch this person or persons," Picard said.

"I do," Crusher said, "but on my terms."

"Terms?" Picard asked.

Crusher nodded. But before she could respond, Pulaski spoke. "I understand what Dr. Crusher is saying. We weren't able to track the designer from the scant information we received from our sources on Bajor, and I take it, you had no more success on Archaria III."

"That's right," Picard said.

"Which means that the only way we'll be able to track this monster down . . ." Crusher said.

"Is if there's another plague," Pulaski said tiredly. "Let's hope that his experiment is over and he leaves us in peace."

"Unpunished?" Picard asked.

Pulaski nodded. "Unless we can find him before he causes more deaths." She closed her eyes. "I don't want to see any more death."

She felt a hand on her arm. She opened her eyes to see Crusher looking at her with concern. "You really should rest before you go to your next assignment. If you want, I'll contact Starfleet Medical and ask them for a leave—"

"No." Pulaski smiled. "Work is always better for me. But if you both will excuse me, I do think I'll go to my quarters now. I hope you won't be offended if I sleep most of the way back to Deep Space Five."

"Not at all," Picard said.

"We'll wake you so that you'll have enough time to get your notes together before the briefing with Starfleet Command on Deep Space Five," Crusher said.

"No need." Pulaski stood. "They're already together. I like to finish my tasks before going to bed. I sleep better that way. Good night all."

She heard them say good night as she stepped from the ready room to the bridge. Commander Riker sat in the captain's chair, and he smiled at her as she walked past. Data said hello and Geordi, who was at the engineering station on the bridge, asked her if she was doing all right.

"I'm fine," she said, and stepped into the turbolift. What she didn't tell them was how much she'd miss them, just like she would miss Kellec. It seemed as if her life was about moving away from the people she cared about.

She sighed. If there was one thing she had learned in all her years in Starfleet, it was that every time she left one group behind, she found another—different but just as good—ahead. She knew that. But it seemed as if she would never find a group quite like this one again.

Or perhaps she was just tired. Things always seemed better after she got a little sleep.

DOUBLE HELIX

RED SECTOR

DIANE CAREY

Chapter One

"ATTENTION! THIS IS A STARFLEET SPECIAL SECURITY FORCES EVACUATION SQUAD! WE ARE ABOUT TO LAND A DIPLOMATIC COACH AND FIVE FIGHTER ESCORTS. ALL CIVILIANS MUST CLEAR THE COURTYARD IMMEDIATELY! ANYONE REMAINING WILL BE STUNNED AND REMOVED TO A SECURITY BRIG! ALL PERSONS . . . ATTENTION! . . . THEY'RE NOT CLEARING OUT. CAN THEY EVEN HEAR ME? PERRATON, IS THE TRANSLATOR ON? PECAN, GET YOUR WING BACK INTO FORMATION! WHERE'S THE BROADCAST GREENLIGHT? WHAT KIND OF DUNSELS INSTALLED THIS SYSTEM?"

"AH, PERRATON HERE . . . STILES, BE AWARE THE BROADCAST SYSTEM IS GREEN AND TRANSLATING. YOU JUST CALLED THE WHOLE PLANET A BUNCH OF DUNSELS."

"SHUT IT DOWN!"

"OAK ONE, THIS IS BRAZIL. FORMATION'S SHIFTING STARBOARD. THE EMBASSY'S GOT A BIG GARGOYLE ON IT AND I'M ABOUT TO CLEAN ITS TEETH."

"LATERAL THRUST. ABORT LANDING PATTERN—PERRATON, WOULD YOU RED THE P.A. BEFORE I COUGH UP A LUNG?"

"Copy that. Public address speakers are shut down. Fighter formation's still too cramped for diamond grid, Stiles. Acorn just bumped a water tower."

"All wings, pull up! We'll modify formation and try our approach again. Did the whole city hear us arguing?"

"They heard *you* arguing."

"Ahhh, I should've become a medic . . . Nuts, Oak One. Go to Ruby formation. Pecan, move two degrees port. Brazil, get off his tail. Acorn, keep your wings trim. Why can't you people hold a hover grid?"

"Oak One, Acorn. It's not us. Stiles, it's you. You have to put the coach down and vertical your stabilizers to give us enough room to land in that courtyard."

"Stabilizers . . . I hate stabilizers . . . I was supposed to go in for multi-vehicular flight school this week, but nooo, I had to grab a mission. Listen up! I'll land the coach first, then all wings settle around me five seconds later. Keep it sharp!"

"What's the matter with you, Stiles?" Pilot Andrea Hipp's German accent seemed crisp over the comm. *"This isn't synchronized swimming, you know."*

"I said no chatter! The ambassador's watching!"

A prattle of aye-ayes settled the issue for the moment, but did nothing for Eric Stiles's stomach, or his icy fingers, or his tingling feet. This command stuff left a lot to be wished for. And his hair was in his eyes . . . he was looking through a blond curtain. Didn't help.

On the screens of his fully carpeted cockpit, Stiles saw the platinum glitter of the Federation Embassy at PojjanPiraKot seem to rise up to meet him. Actually, he and the coach he piloted were descending into the brick city courtyard, but the illusion of a floating building disoriented him briefly. On the secondary side monitors, the five fighter escorts regrouped into Ruby formation and found the space to wiggle into the brick court, settling around the main coach vessel like baby ducks crowding a drake.

"Doesn't look like I expected it to," he commented. "What are those metal bands on all the buildings?"

"The city's all reinforced." Ensign Travis Perraton's blue eyes peered with fresh curiosity at a smaller monitor as he adjusted the coach's shields to let them land, irritating Stiles with his eternal good mood. "They've got some kind of gravitational problem on this planet. All the buildings have had to be structurally rebuilt over the past few years since it started."

"What kind of gravitational trouble?"

"Something like high tides or earthquakes, I guess. That's what I've heard, anyway."

Stiles wanted to comment, but was busy settling the coach onto its extender pads. The fantasy of brilliant artisanship in moving spaceborne vessels into an atmosphere and landing them in a surefooted, graceful manner had shriveled in his hands. At least that part was over. He trembled with irritation as the system's check barberpoled. Perraton had managed to clear the belly shields. Otherwise, the coach would've sat in the air like a beachball on the water—and probably rolled over.

"You're down," Perraton confirmed. "You can unclench now."

"I'm fine!"

"Yeah, sure you are. You worried about coming in shielded for the whole twenty hours it took us to get here from the starbase."

Stiles bristled at the suggestion that he wasn't in control. "Emergency diplomatic evacuations have certain *regulations* attached. Not getting a second chance is just *one* of the assumptions. Evac regs *assume* the situation is hostile and precautions have to be—"

"Don't quote the book."

"Give me a view of the whole courtyard."

Screens around the cockpit flashed views of all six lander pads with irritated civilians scooping dirt out of huge potted plants and dumping it on the ship's pads. So much for respect.

"Are they throwing rocks?" Stiles asked.

"It's garbage." Eying the same screen, Perraton stood up and pulled on his torso armor, buckling the padded vest over his chest. "Some of 'em are throwing balls of mud from those pots."

Stiles straightened. "Secure the coach and scramble the evac squad. Nuts, Oak One. Remain in your cockpits. Do not get out, understood? Sit tight and let Oak Squad flush the dignitaries. I'll escort Ambassador Spock personally."

"They're pushing on my struts. Our light-stun phasers can—"

"Negative!" Stiles broiled. "Let 'em crowd you. Keep finger shields activated in case they touch the wings. And all of you shut up! I don't want the ambassador to hear the slightest disrespect."

"Oh, we respect you. Don't you respect him, Cashew?"

"I drip respect."

"As you were!"

"As I was? Did I change? I like me this way. Did you change, Acorn?"

"Animals," Stiles grumbled. "I'd like to get you disrespectful slugs on starship duty for five minutes, just five minutes. . . ." He buried himself in padded insulation as he pulled his flak vest over his head, then slipped into his gauntlets, adjusted his sidearm, and led Perraton out into the coach's main seating area.

Here, six other members of Oak Squad were already suited up and looking at him from inside their red-tinted helmet shields. Travis Perraton, Jeremy White, Bill Foster, Dan Moose, Brad Carter, Matt Girvan—their names and faces swam before his eyes like a manifest, and for a moment he thought the blood was rushing out of his head. Midshipmen and ensigns, all in training for what would eventually become specialties, for now they were assigned to Starbase 10 in the Security Division, under their senior ensign—Stiles. At twenty-one, Eric Stiles was the old man of the outfit. Perraton was next, at twenty years old and forty-two days junior to Stiles' ensign stripes. Knowing that they had heard the ribbing he took from the wings, Stiles felt his face flush. He had to lead the mission. He'd gotten himself into this on purpose. He had to address them as a commander. Nobody to hide behind. They'd seen the landing. His dream of a crisp textbook military approach and regulation landing had gone up in an ugly puff. Now the squad members were blushing and snickering, burying grins, trying not to look right at him—that was hard to take!

"Heads up." His voice cracked. "There's a riot going on outside. Some kind of local political trouble. The embassy is beam-shielded, so we have to go in the security door. As we approach, the guard will drop the door shields. We'll have to go in and come out in single file. We're going to put the dignitaries between us, at two or three in a row. There are about twenty of these people, so the seven of us'll be just about right. I'll go last, with the ambassador right in front of me. He's the primary person to guard, and if he gets so much as a hangnail, somebody's gonna answer to me in a dark alley. After we get—shut up, Foster!"

"I didn't say anything!" Bill Foster protested.

"Quit snickering! This is . . . this is—"

"Serious," Perraton supplied.

"I know, Eric," Foster muttered.

"You call me 'Ensign,' mister!"

"Aye aye, Ensign Mister."

"I want this mission to go like clockwork! I don't want a single twitch that isn't in the rule book! Don't snicker, don't slip, don't do anything that isn't regulation!"

A hand was pressed to his shoulder and drew him backward a step on the plush carpet.

"Everything'll go fine, Eric," Perraton mildly interrupted. "We're ready when you are." His short dark hair was buried under a white helmet with Starfleet's Delta Shield printed on the forehead, now obscured by the raised red visor. The shield glowed and sang at Stiles. Starfleet's symbol.

And Stiles had to make it look good. In the wake of Perraton's mental leashing, the symbol now lay heavily upon him. If he couldn't yell at his men, how would he keep them in shape?

He huffed a couple of steadying breaths, but didn't lower his voice. Now that he'd gotten up to a certain level of volume, it was hard to reel in from that. He took a moment to survey the squad—bright white helmets, black leggings, white boots, red chest pads against the black Starfleet jumpsuits, and the bright flicker of a combadge on every vest. Elbow pads, chin guards, red visors . . . looked fair. Good enough.

Time to go.

"There are riots going on," he repeated, "but so far nobody's tried to breach the embassy itself. Our job is to clear a path between the coach and the embassy and get all Federation nationals out. These people don't have a space fleet, but their atmospheric capabilities are strong enough to cause a few problems. I won't consider the mission accomplished until we're clear of the stratosphere. When we get out of the coach, completely ignore the people swarming around unless they come within two meters or show a weapon. Clear?"

"Clear, sir!" Carter, Girvan, Moose, and Foster shouted. Perraton nodded, and White raised his rifle. Had they accented the "sir" just a little too much?

Stiles stepped between them and the hatch. "Mobilize!"

Perraton took that as a cue, and punched the autorelease on the big hatch. The coach's loading ramp peeled back and lay neatly across the brick before them. Instantly, the stench of burning fuel flooded the controlled atmosphere inside the coach. At Stiles's side, Perraton coughed a couple of times. Other than that, nobody's big mouth cracked open. Stiles led the way down, his heavy boots thunking on the nonskid ramp.

They broke out onto a courtyard of grand proportions with colonnades flanking it on three sides and the diplomatic buildings on the fourth side—a battery of fifteen embassies, halls, and consulates. Most of them were empty now. The Federation was the last to evacuate. Two of the colonnades were in ruins; part of one was shrouded in scaffolding while being rebuilt. Most of the buildings showed signs of structural damage, but generally the Diplomatic Court of PojjanPiraKot was a stately and bright place, providing a sad backdrop for the ugliness of these protests.

A quick glance behind showed him the positions of the five fighters landed around the coach. Their glistening bodies, streamlined for both aerodynamics and space travel, shined in the golden sunlight. There was Air Wing Leader Bernt Folmer, their best pilot, code "Brazil," parked like a big car in front of Greg "Pecan" Blake. Behind the coach the tail fin of Andrea Hipp's "Cashew" fighter caught a glint of sun. On the other side, hopefully parked nose to tail, were Acorn and Chestnut, brothers Jason and Zack Bolt—but Stiles didn't bother to check their position. He only hoped they were in sharp order.

All around were angry people waving signs, some in a language he didn't understand, others scrawled in English, Vulcan, Spanish, Orion Yrevish, and a few other languages familiar from courtesy placards all over Starfleet Command where multitudes wandered.

The ones in English jumped out instantly before Stiles's racing mind. OUT ALIENS . . . LEAVE OUR PLANET . . . GET OUT STRANGERS . . . ALIENS UNWELCOME . . . CURSE ALIENS ALL. . . .

Some of the people were calling out in English, too, though clumsily and without really understanding the arrangement of nouns and verbs. The anti-alien message, though, arrowed directly through to the team.

To the music of enraged shouts from the people rattling gates and creating a din by banging small silver knives on the iron posts, Oak Squad broke into a jog and flooded into a broad shield of sunlight glaring between the embassy and the consulate next door. The doorways and lintels were heavily reinforced with titanium T-girders, and titanium bands swept around every building, two on each story, like shiny ribcages. Stiles glanced around at his squad, making sure nobody pulled ahead of the formation. This had to be crisp. The ambassador was watching from some window inside that embassy. Everybody was watching.

Fifty meters . . .

Oak Squad thundered forward relentlessly, their phaser rifles tight against their chests. As Stiles led his men across the patterned brick, he saw that just the raw heat from the coach's VTOL thrusters had scorched some of the bricks nearly black and pitted them beyond repair, destroying the geometric design in the historic courtyard.

His boots felt secure and thick as he crunched over the litter of broken glass, smashed fruit, and rocks that had been thrown by the rioters, who were now milling around the fighters and the coach. These Pojjan people were stocky and thick, with strong round cheekbones and bronze complexions tinged with an olive patina, reminding Stiles of Aztec paintings seen under a green filter. They wore various clothing, from the men's ordinary shirts and pants or the women's shiftlike dresses to the brightly beaded tribal tunics and leggings he'd seen on travel posters.

The travel agencies might as well rip those posters up. Nobody was going to want to come to this dump anymore.

He cast the rioters a threatening glance or two, but although some were touching the ships' landing struts they weren't doing anything destructive. Not yet anyway. If anything happened, the escort pilots would zap them. So he kept moving forward at a pace, letting the natives swerve out of his way. He led the squad manfully through a large puddle of fuel, some of which was still gulping out of a discarded and dented container. Their boots splattered it and freshened the stench.

Thirty meters.

Cries of anger, protest, and insult at Starfleet's intrusion into their courtyard grew louder, as the squad jogged across the brick plateau. Stiles didn't understand the Pojjan language, but some of these people were shouting in

English or Vulcan and waving get-out-of-town banners in English, apparently smart enough to know how to get to the Federation personnel.

It's getting to me. I'm allowing it to shake me. Just do the job, get the people out of the embassy, into the coach, and lift off. Ignore the crowd. Just ignore them.

At his right elbow, Travis Perraton was watching a gang of Pojjan teenagers on the other side of the embassy fence. A flash of flame—the teenagers were lighting up a fuel-soaked towel.

"They can't throw that this far, can they?" Blake asked from behind Stiles.

"They don't have to," Perraton said. "We're jogging toward puddles of kerosene."

"Gasoline," Midshipman Jeremy White corrected from the flank.

"Stinks," Dan Moose added, then cast to the man on his left, "Make room, Foster."

"Sorry."

"Bag the noise," Stiles snapped, turning his head briefly to the right. "Don't splash through the gas. If we get it on our uniforms, we're in big trouble."

And that was his error—that one glance over his shoulder. A stunning force struck his left shin just below the kneepad, driving his entire leg out behind him. Blown forward by the force of his own movement, Stiles let out a single strangled yell, leaped forward over a slick of gasoline, and crashed to the bricks just beyond the slick. Though he evaded the gas, he slid sidelong into a pile of garbage dumped on the courtyard. Managing to thrust his arms out, he somehow kept from landing on his phaser rifle, which instead clattered to the brick and butted him in the face shield, then scratched across his bared jaw. If his visor had been up, the rifle would've taken out his teeth.

A blunt force rammed into his lower back—a boot—as Carter tumbled over Stiles, crumpling to the bricks on top of the garbage. Carter rolled and ended up on one knee.

With his jaw and knee throbbing, Stiles tightened his body, twisted onto his side, and brandished his weapon at the laughing crowd as his face flushed with humiliation. They were laughing at him. His fantasy of a clockwork mission had just cracked and blown up before his eyes.

Bile rose in his throat, a rashy heat down his legs. His lungs tightened as he felt slimy garbage soak into his uniform and the stench of petroleum knot his innards. The sky wheeled above him, cluttered with white helmets and flashing red visors reflecting the afternoon sun.

Smiling, Perraton reached to pull him to his feet. "Nice going, lightfoot."

"Don't help me!" Stiles blurted.

As if bitten, Perraton retracted his hand. Stiles rolled to his feet, now smudged with the gummy remains of garbage and mudballs.

When he got to his feet, Stiles staggered a few steps in the wrong direction and was forced to endure the foolish chickenscratch of turning around and struggling back to the front of his squad, and the further embarrassment of realizing his men were deliberately slowing down so he could get in front. He slammed his way between them, elbowing Perraton and White cruelly out of his path. He didn't need their charity!

At the gates, two Pojjan guards immediately opened the iron grid and let them in without a word. The embassy's medieval-looking carved wooden door, three guys wide and set between two gargoyles, also opened automatically.

No, not automatically—this door was manual. Another guard or servant of some nationality Stiles didn't recognize was now peeking around the door's iron rim like a shy cow peeking out of a barn. He was an elderly man, with bent shoulders and bright green eyes set in a jowly dark face with stripes painted on it. More tribal weirdness.

Moving further into the heavily tiled foyer, Stiles suddenly felt ridiculously out of place. The foyer was splendid, its mosaics of gold-and-black chipped stone and glossy ceramics portraying some kind of historic battle scene and the coronation of somebody. Must be from way back, because this wasn't a monarchical culture anymore.

Was it?

The guard pushed the big door shut and swung a huge titanium bolt into place to lock them safely inside, then turned to the clutch of evac troopers and gasped, "One minute! I'll get the ambassador's assistant!"

And he disappeared into a wide archway that was two stories tall.

Oak Squad stood in the middle of the gorgeous tile floor, their uniforms scuffed and stinking, and looked around.

"I'd hate to be the guy who cleans the grout," Perraton commented.

White grunted as he scanned the mosaic on the ceiling. "How long you think we'll have to wait?"

"Not long," Stiles filled in. "They called for us to come get them, so they're probably ready to leave. And they're Vulcans, so you know they're efficient."

"How do you know they'll be stiffs?" Moose asked.

"Because Ambassador Spock's a st—a Vulcan. They like to have their own kind around. They understand each other better than we do."

"Oh, right," White drawled. "They do everything better than we do."

Stiles scoured him with a glare. "Don't start on me, Jeremy."

He turned away, but in his periphery he noted Perraton's quick motion to White, erasing any further annoying comments.

Though they stood in this wide foyer feeling dirty and small, they were not alone. Sounds of footsteps and voices leaked from the depths of the embassy halls, and twice Stiles saw ethereal forms slip from one office to another. Did they trust him to get them out safely? Had they seen the botched choreography of the landing? Did they wonder whether the ensign in command was competent enough to handle this?

He gripped his phaser rifle until his hands hurt and shifted from foot to foot, halting only when a young woman—a human—skittered through the grand main door and into the huge foyer. Stiles didn't pay attention. . . . The small-boned woman, with tightly wrapped brown hair, tiny pearl earrings, and a twitch in her left eye, went directly to the tallest of them—Jeremy White—and breathily said, "I'm Miss Karen Theonella, Ambassador Spock's deputy attaché. Are you Ensign Stiles?"

She had a tight foreign accent that sounded Earth-based, but Stiles couldn't pinpoint the country.

"He's over there, ma'am," White told her, and gestured.

Stiles stepped through the cluster of Starfleeters and took his helmet off, revealing his sweat-plastered blond hair. "Eric Stiles, ma'am. I'm here to evacuate the entire embassy. Nobody should be left behind."

"We understand." Miss Theonella rubbed her tiny pink palms as if kneading bread dough between them. "All embassy envoys, functionaries, ministers, delegates, and clerks will be going, as well as four Pojjana defectors who lost their homes in the last Constrictor. They're being given asylum here and we have clearance for them to be evacuated with us. In all there are thirty-five of us."

"Thirty-five!" Perraton blurted. Then he instantly clammed up, but the number twenty kept flashing in his eyes like beacons.

How could seven of them safely escort thirty-five dignitaries through fifty meters of rioting?

"We're prepared, ma'am," Stiles shoved in, more loudly than necessary, before anyone else could speak up. "About the landing . . . the ambassador is probably wondering why we were so . . . out of formation. . . ."

"What?" Miss Theonella's white temples puckered and her brows came together like pencil points. "We can't see the courtyard from here. There are only reception rooms on the court side of the building. Was there some reason you wanted us to be watching you? Was there a signal?"

He stared at her, caught between relief and disappointment that nobody had been watching. "Uh . . . no, no signal."

Preoccupied, the thin young woman simply said, "Continue to wait here, please, Ensign. I'll get the ambassador."

Again the evac squad stood alone, holding their rifles, standing in the middle of the gleaming tile floor, listening to the drumming chants of angry people outside in the square and trying to imagine how they were going to hustle thirty-five dignitaries through that. The unpleasant possibility of rushing half of them out to the coach, then coming back for the second group—Stiles winced. Two trips through that courtyard full of alien-haters? Was that safer than one big rush? If he ordered two separate groups, would the angry people see that as their last chance to get them and attack the second group?

"Wonder why they hate aliens," Dan Moose voiced.

Stiles noted that his men were looking at the windows and doors, but his own eyes were focused on the long hall of offices into which Miss Theonella had disappeared. The ambassador was in there somewhere.

All the men turned to face the hall to their left as a crowd of elegant dignitaries bobbed toward them. In the midst of them was the tall, instantly recognizable figure of the famous Ambassador Spock.

Bow? Kneel? Handshake?

"Don't faint! Eric, stand at attention!"

Perraton's anxious whisper boomed in Stiles's ear like a foghorn.

"Stand at attention!"

"Attention. . . ." Stiles planted his boots on the tile, but wasn't able to get them together. He squared his shoulders, raised his chin, held his breath, clutched his rifle, and forced an appearance of adept steadiness and control. Cool. Calm. Military. Crisp. In control. In charge. Confident. Smelly.

The ambassador and his party approached them, but Spock wasn't looking at them. Instead his dark head was bowed as he spoke to Miss Theonella, who was clipping along at his side. The ambassador listened, nodded, then spoke again while a male attendant slipped a glossy blue Federation Diplomatic Corps jacket onto the boss's shoulders.

The sight was a shock—Stiles had expected the flowing ceremonial robes that Vulcan seniors were usually seen wearing, but now that he saw Spock in the trim gray slacks and dark blue jacket with the UFP symbol on the left side, that outfit seemed to make more sense for a spaceborne evacuation. Robes might be harder to handle on boarding ramps and in tight quarters.

Why hadn't he thought of that?

Though Spock—tall, narrow, controlled—possessed all the regal formality common to his race, his famous form was somehow less imperious in person than Stiles had anticipated, his angular Vulcan features more animated, and framed by the fact that he was the only Vulcan in the bunch. Of course, Stiles had only seen still photos or staged lecture tapes. Seeing Spock in real life was very different—he wasn't stiff at all.

As they approached, he could hear Miss Theonella's thready voice.

". . . and the provincial vice-warden will be sending his prolocutrix as proxy to speak for the entire hemisphere at Federation central. Also, sir, the consul general's wife and children are waiting in the Blue Room, and Chancellor De Gaeta's wife is in his office."

Miss Theonella finished her sentence just as she and the ambassador and their party came into the foyer.

"Thank you, Karen, very good work," Ambassador Spock said gently, countering her quivering report with his silky baritone voice. "Suggest to the Sagittarian military attaché that he post a Pojjana communications sentry, and that person must speak both Bal Quonnot and Romulan."

That voice! That famous voice! Stiles had been hearing it all his life! Historical documentaries, training tapes, mission interactives, holoprograms—now he was here, in person, right in the same room with that voice!

"This is Ensign Stiles," Miss Theonella added with a gesture. "And the evacuation escort men, sir."

The ambassador scanned the team, then fixed his gaze at Stiles. Directly *at* him. Right in the eyes! He was looking right at him!

Those eyes—like blades! Black blades!

Stiles tried to take a breath, but all he got was a gulp of garbage fumes from his soaked trouser leg. As his lungs seized up, he felt the boink-boink of Perraton's finger poking him in the back.

Report, you idiot!

"Ev . . . Evacuation Squad reporting as you requested, sir! Ensign Eric J. Stiles, Starfleet Special Services reporting, sir! One G-rate transport coach, evacuation team, and five fighter escorts, sir!"

The ambassador's black-slash brows went up like bird's wings. The chamber fell to silence. Stiles' fervid report echoed absurdly.

Calmly Spock said, "At ease, Ensign."

His deep mellow voice took Stiles utterly by surprise.

"Aye aye, sir!" Stiles choked.

"We'll be ready within five minutes," the ambassador told him fluidly, then turned to the attendant who'd put the jacket on him. "Edwin, please bring out the consul general's family and Mrs. De Gaeta and turn them over to Ensign Stiles."

"Right away, Ambassador."

As the man left, Spock turned again to Miss Theonella. "You have our records and diplomatic pouches? The legal briefs and service files? Personnel manifests?"

She held up a stern black pilot's case with a magnetic lock, hanging from a strap on her shoulder. "All here, sir."

"Very well. We should also bring the jurisdictional warrants. They could be confiscated and used to gain passage into restricted areas."

"I'll get them, sir."

"No, I'll get them." The ambassador turned to leave, then paused and gazed briefly at the tiled floor, thinking. "Stiles . . ."

"Here, sir!"

Spock looked up at the inflamed response. Coolly he repeated, "At *ease,* Ensign."

Stiles shivered, glanced at Travis Perraton, and again met the ambassador's eyes. "Yes, sir. . . ."

"Are you by chance related to—"

"Yes, sir, I am, sir! Starfleet Security Commander John Stiles, Retired, is my grandfather, sir! He served with you under Captain James T. Kirk, Stardates 1709 to 1788 point 6 as Alpha-Watch navigator aboard the *U.S.S. Enterprise,* NCC 1701, commissioned stardate—"

"I recall the ship, Ensign."

"Oh . . . oh . . . aye, sir. . . ."

"You have a long line of Starfleet service officers in your family heritage, I also recall."

"Yes, sir! Several active-duty servicemen lost in the Romulan Wars, sir! A captain, two lieutenants, two—"

"Commendable, Mr. Stiles. Carry on." Spock turned to the little gaggle of people behind him and said, "All of you please stand by until everyone else arrives. Then you'll take your instructions from Ensign Stiles as to how you will arrange yourselves during the actual evacuation. As you know, the building is beam-shielded, and therefore we must go out the door and board the transport coach on foot. Unfortunately, our general safety compromises our safety during emergency evacuation. Karen, keep them in order. I will return momentarily."

With that he disappeared down a different hallway and into an office, leaving a confused clutch of embassy persons standing here in the foyer, wide-eyed and obviously frightened. By nature, the two groups divided to opposite sides of the foyer, embassy folks over there, Oak Squad over here.

Stiles let himself be tugged aside, and barely registered the low mutters of his men around him through the afterglow of his meeting with Spock.

"Beam-shielding," Matt Girvan grumbled. "There's planning. What if they had to get out under more dangerous conditions than mudballs and molotovs?"

"It's beam-shielded so assassins or terrorists can't beam *in.*"

"Why couldn't they make it one-way?"

"Too unstable. Sucks too much energy to maintain over time."

"Doesn't matter. We'll get 'em out. Eric'll carry them all on his back if he has to."

"If he doesn't choke up a lung first."

"We'll be lucky if he doesn't make us bow backward out of the room."

The team laughed. A cluttered sound, muffled . . . like a storm coming.

Beside Stiles, Perraton raised his helmet visor and smiled with genuine sympathy.

"You okay, Eric?" he asked.

Stiles felt his lips chapping as he breathed in and out, in and out, like a landed fish. He'd just met his hero and he didn't know if he'd liked it.

And it wasn't over. In fact, it was just beginning. He'd have to do everything perfectly from now on. No more botched formations. No more stammering. He had to be perfect. Smooth.

"Ease up, lightfoot," Perraton suggested privately. "He's just a guy."

"Just a guy," Stiles rasped. "He's a hero, Travis . . . a Starfleet icon . . . the first Vulcan in Starfleet . . . Captain James Kirk's executive officer . . . I've heard every story a hundred times all my life—do you know how many times he participated in saving the *whole* Federation? And even the Klingon Empire?"

"Doesn't matter now. Anyway, the hard part's over. You met him, you survived, and the experience didn't suck out your brains. He was a Starfleet man for half a century. He knows the drill. So get a perspective. Here he comes."

Do the job. Do the job.

The ambassador flowed back into the foyer, now carrying a slim red folder and followed by more than a dozen people and his attendant Edwin. Suddenly the foyer was swarming with civilians. At least they were mostly adults, a few teenagers—Stiles didn't relish the prospect of herding toddlers through that mess out there. He stiffened as the ambassador came directly to him.

"We're ready, Mr. Stiles."

"Yes, sir . . . how would you like to do this?"

Spock handed the folder to Miss Theonella. "Pardon me?"

"I . . . I figured you'd have some preference about . . . what order you want them in and . . . how to do it."

The ambassador thought about that briefly, his dark eyes working, as if he hadn't considered such an option. After a moment he vocally shrugged. "Your mission, Ensign."

Over Spock's shoulder, Perraton smiled and gave Stiles a thumbs-up.

Sustained by that, Stiles forced himself to rise to the demand. "Uh . . . if you people would form a line, two by two, and Oak Squad situate yourselves between them, uh, one every . . . uh—"

He paused, tried to do the math, but couldn't remember how. His brain *had* been sucked out!

Maybe he wouldn't have to count and add and divide—his men were already arranging themselves into position. Perraton was taking the lead, and motioning the others into the queue at intervals.

"I'll take the rear guard," Stiles said. "Ambassador, would you mind coming back here with me, sir?"

"Thank you, Ensign, I will."

"All right, let's—no, no, you can't do the door." Stiles motioned to the funny-looking butler who was still standing his post at the door, waiting to open it for everybody. "Travis, put that man in line behind Girvan and you do the door. Then fall in."

"Copy that."

"Okay, phaser rifles ready."

"Ready!" his men shouted.

"Rifles up!"

"Up!"

"Very well!"

Stiles took one more look at Ambassador Spock's steady form in line before him, at the large UFP shield printed on the back of the blue jacket. The stars of the United Federation of Planets swam before his eyes.

He drew a breath. His voice echoed under the high tiled ceiling.

"Mobilize!"

Chapter Two

BRASH SUNLIGHT BLARED into Stiles's eyes, smashing his dream of frictionless success. The sun courted the horizon now, directly ahead of them, as they charged the protesters crowding the courtyard. Curtains of fire roiled around them where the gasoline puddles had been ignited by molotovs. On the other side of the licking flames stood the coach and fighters and a half-dozen unconscious rioters. Apparently Brazil had needed to enable his stun phasers to back them off.

Now the rest of the protesters were giving the fighters a wider berth, and turned instead on the jogging queue of embassy personnel and their six Starfleet guards trying to wend through the pockets of stenchy flame.

A fist shook in his face—and Stiles rammed his rifle butt into somebody's chest. Mudballs slogged through the line, striking the civilians. One caught Moose in the helmet. He staggered, but got back in line before Stiles could react.

Crack!—a molotov bottle smashed in front of the ambassador. New flames broke out, flooding the bricks, dividing Spock, Stiles, and one woman from the rest of the line. Spock instantly veered sideways, caught the woman in front of him, and steered her around the flames and back behind Moose's protective form.

"Oak Squad!" Stiles shouted over the noise. "Phasers on stun, fire at will!"

He didn't know whether or not they heard him until White and Perraton opened fire on a group of protesters blocking the way to the coach. The rifles blanketed the area with a red bulb of energy, and the rioters went down in a heap.

"Wish we could just toast 'em," Stiles grumbled, tactlessly boiling with contempt for this civil unrest. Why couldn't they just follow rules and stick within the law? Why'd they have to cause trouble?

"Stiles Oak-One! Ramp!"

The coach's automatic ramp opened before them with a whine. Perraton led the frantic evacuees right to it, then angled to one side and shouted warnings to the crowd as the diplomatic people clomped up the ramp. Luckily nobody had to yell at them to stay in line. They were perfectly satisfied running for the cover offered by the coach's maw. Just as the middle of the line was swallowed by the coach, Jeremy White veered away from the queue to drive back the same herd of angry teenagers that had harassed them on the way in. Now those teenagers were armed with iron bars—and the bars were red hot. White held back on firing his weapon, instead using it to bash away the iron bars threatening him.

"Jeremy!" Stiles called. "Stun 'em!"

But White couldn't get enough room to turn his phaser rifle barrel down and take aim. He tried twice, and each time was pummeled by a hot iron bar—the teenagers were too close, surrounding him so he couldn't move forward or back. If he tried to stun them at hand-to-hand range, he'd end up stunning himself too. And White was getting angry. Stiles could hear his furious grunts and barks as adrenaline took over and defensive/offensive training got a grip on him. Step by step he drove the teenagers back, inch by inch, but not enough for rifle stun. And they were hitting him with their hot bars until his protective padding smoked and sparked.

"On board, on board!" Stiles shouted to the civilians. He couldn't help White until these people were all present and accounted for in the safety of the coach. When Ambassador Spock was finally on the ramp, Stiles wheeled around, jumped off the footboard, and rammed through the enraged teenagers. He drove one of them to the ground, then rammed his rifle butt into the ribs of another, until he could see White's scratched helmet and smell the burning padding of his uniform.

"Jeremy! You're covered! About face!"

White tried to turn, but was caught in the neck by a vicious blow and tumbled to the brick at Stiles's feet. Stiles stepped over him, aimed his rifle, and fired.

A burst of bright energy engulfed four of the teenagers, so close that Stiles felt his skin go numb even under the protective gear.

"Get up!" he ordered, kicking White uncharitably. "On your feet! Board the ship!"

White rolled out from under him, possessing the presence of mind to keep a grip on his weapon, because they sure didn't dare leave it here, and stumbled to the ramp. Perraton skidded down and caught him, then shoved him into the coach and shouted, "All clear, Stiles! Stiles! Eric!"

"Acknowledged! Power up!"

"Aye aye!"

"Nuts, Oak One, power up for liftoff!"

"*Copy, Oak One.*"

Instantly the fighters began humming with power buildup. Perraton disappeared back inside, and Stiles was two steps behind him, scrambling up the ramp on two feet and a hand, his weapon clutched in his other hand. Perraton was there to yank him inside, and backhanded the ramp control. The ramp whined upward and clacked shut, then the hatch bolts slammed into place.

Inside, Bill Foster was collecting the phaser rifles and slamming them back into their wall rack while the other men dumped their helmets into the reception locker.

"We're secure," Perraton reported. "Dan's powering up for you." He hit the hatch lock for takeoff, turned to Stiles and shrugged. "Wasn't so hard."

"It wasn't?" Stiles gasped, scanning the crowd of frightened evacuees. "Is anybody hurt?"

They all looked at each other, but no one spoke up. They were bruised, dirty, coughing, no longer the prim bunch he'd seen in the embassy, and one woman was sobbing, but most of them were in their seats and belted in. Now he saw that Ambassador Spock was buckling up two of the family members. So Spock was responsible for the organization. No surprise there.

Stiles dumped his helmet on the carpet and peeled out of his flak vest. "Where's Jeremy?"

"I'm over here."

Jeremy White's lanky form, smeared with dirt now, was sprawled in one of the crew seats, pressing a hand to his neck. His helmet was off too, and his uniform was still smoldering. Stiles stuffed his vest into Perraton's hands and hurried forward to Jeremy White.

"You all right?" he asked.

White blinked up at him. "Affirmative, more or less."

"Why'd you break formation?"

White's glare roughened. "Gosh, Eric, I got this irresistible crush on a girl way over there and figured to ask her out if I could just get through those terrorists with the hot irons and broken bottles—what the hell kind of a question is that?"

"You follow orders from now on, have you got that?"

Slumping back a little more, White grimaced. "Put a leash on it, will you? We're doing everything you say!"

Stiles almost snapped a reprimand, but what good would that do? And all the dignitaries were looking at him. Should he throw a tantrum?

Instead he surveyed White's dirt-flecked face and sandy hair, and decided on a better choice.

"You're all right, though?" he asked. "Not burned?"

The anger flowed out of White's heat-blotched cheeks. "Except that now I have to tell my mother I scratched the little body she cooked for nine months."

"Then take the portside defense guns. Let's get off this planet."

"Aye aye." White pushed out of his seat and made sure his neck wasn't bleeding.

"Girvan, starboard gun."

"Starboard, aye."

"Travis, navigate. We got a mountain range in our liftoff path."

"Right."

The three men went in three different directions, two to the defense pods and Perraton to the cockpit. A second later, Dan Moose came out of the cockpit and said, "We're powered up. I can't pilot this thing, though. You're the only one who can fly it in an atmosphere."

"I know, I'm coming. Sir, are you comfortable?" He paused before the ambassador on his way to the cockpit and asked a silly question. What difference did comfort make?

"I'm sorry about the trouble out there, sir," Stiles babbled. "If it were up to me, we'd sweep the whole courtyard with wide stun. Why do people have to behave that way?"

Spock straightened from helping Edwin buckle up. "Those people are frightened, Ensign, and disheartened. The political situation here is volatile. This was our last chance to evacuate Federation personnel. Prudence dictated that we get out while we can. The Pojjana have abandoned any overtures toward Federation membership, despite our efforts to help them protect themselves. This is an interplanetary squabble between them and the Bal Quonnot now, lacking clear rights and wrongs. Federation policy will now be hands off. The sector will be declared 'red.' "

"Then why were they trying to stop us from leaving? If they don't want us here—"

"A number of factions on this planet may find advantage in preventing our leaving. I should warn you," Spock added, and lowered his voice, "they never attacked the embassy itself because that would have been an act of war according to the Articles of Confederation. The embassy building is Federation soil. However, once we're in the atmosphere, they can shoot us down and claim any number of scenarios. We must be on our guard and ready to fight."

"We're ready, sir! I've got five fully armed fighter escorts, and this coach has two defense guns and a detachable midwing utility jump-plane."

Spock raised one eyebrow and drawled, "Yes . . . of course it does."

Now what did that mean?

Stiles was about to ask, then realized that all these innocent civilians were looking at the two of them, hanging on every word. From the ambassador's expression, Stiles got the idea he wouldn't get any answers even if he did ask. He shouldn't have asked anything. Gum stuck on your shoe doesn't ask, "Where are we going?"—it just sticks to the shoe.

Spock, having been around humans all his life, seemed to recognize the look. Stiles was instantly mortified that the ambassador had read the questions in his eyes. Why hadn't he taken the time to study the political climate here? Wasn't that his job as mission leader? Thirty-five diplomatic persons including the famous adventurer Ambassador Spock—killing them would send vibrations across the quadrant. Kidnapping them would be an even bigger coup—for somebody. A shipload of diplomatic hostages, and Stiles had to make a fool of himself by needing the most elementary facts explained to him.

Shriveled like a prune, he glanced around at all the people watching him, judging him, and croaked, "Prepare for lift-off."

"Very well." Spock simply took a seat in the first row, next to Miss Theonella and Edwin.

Feeling completely shrunken, Stiles threw off his gauntlets and stepped through the hatch to the cockpit and into the pilot's seat. Stinking of garbage, his jaw swelling up like a melon, he kicked the foot controls and threw the coach into antigrav so abruptly that the fighters were left below. Too bad. They'd catch up.

On his cockpit screens he noted all five Nuts coming up quickly on his flanks.

"Nuts, Oak One, I want some maneuvering room out of the city. Spread out. Attempt Emerald formation."

They each acknowledged with a green light, and he knew he was free to maneuver the bulky craft out over the countryside and toward the mountains. It would take the coach about five miles to reach escape velocity and make it up to an altitude at which they could veer up and out of the atmosphere. Soon the city pulled away beneath them, and he steered around two water towers and a radio antenna and was clear. Now for the mountains.

Since the mountain range surrounded the city on all sides, there was no way to avoid them. Coming in for a landing was less of a problem than accelerating to escape velocity, especially since they had to get up to speed as quickly as possible. This planet had an air force. He knew that much.

"Several Pojjan fighter aircraft just scrambled on an intercept course, Eric," Perraton reported.

"Behind us?"

"Angle two-five zero, port side and closing. Spreading out across our aft flanks."

"I'm increasing speed. As the atmosphere gets thinner, we'll get faster. They'll never catch us."

"Don't you want some defense back there?"

"Yes—yes, I do. Nuts, Oak One. Take up Diamond formation. Guard our aft flanks. Fall back, repeat, fall back. Acknowledge as you take position."

In his side ports he saw Pecan and Brazil fall away toward the aft, and soon all five green lights flashed in acknowledgement.

"Nothing'll get by our guys," he muttered with satisfaction.

"The Pojjan planes are trying to come around, Eric," Perraton warned. "All four of them coming around on the starboard side."

"Moving to port," Stiles accepted, and steered the coach out of the way so the nuts on the starboard flank could deal with the encroaching Pojjan fighters. "I don't know why they're even trying. In two minutes they won't be able to catch up with space-ready vessels."

"Oak One, Chestnut."

"Oak One. Go ahead, Zack."

"The Pojjans aren't firing on us yet, but they're trying to slip by us. Don't they know what our weapons can do?"

"Maybe not," Stiles said. "They don't have a space fleet."

"I don't know—it's like they're touring or something here. Should we open fire?"

Determined not to ignite a situation the ambassador already described as volatile, Stiles tried to use reserved judgment. He'd looked idiotic enough already. He had to make Spock proud of him.

"As long as they're not shooting," he said, "just stay between me and them. They can't catch me now."

"Understood."

"Ensign?"

Stiles glanced over his shoulder at the chilling sound of that voice. Ambassador Spock stood at the hatchway, gripping the rims and peering through to the wide forward screen.

"Yes, sir?" Stiles responded. "Is there a problem? We're almost to flank speed. The mountains are coming up under us. We'll be in space in about ninety seconds. I've positioned all my fighters in a rearguard, between us and the pursuit fleet, just in case the bad guys have more speed than they seem to. Nobody can catch us now, sir."

"Unlikely," Spock accepted, deliberately not stepping into the cockpit. "Ensign, may I make an observation?"

Stiles almost fainted with the depth of that question. An "observation" from Science Officer/Captain/Ambassador Spock? A Starfleet superior for as long as Stiles and his whole team had collectively been alive? That was virtually a direct order!

Stiles steered the coach through the first mountain peaks that reached toward them from a skirt of low snowclouds. "Of course you can, sir!"

Spock now stepped through the hatchway and knelt beside Stiles to get a better view of the mountains.

Why was he looking at the mountains?

"As I am sure you know," Spock began, "it is unlikely those planes pose any danger to us."

"Yes, sir. I mean, no, sir."

"And it is likely that the Pojjana know their planes cannot overtake us."

"Well . . . they might know it, sir. . . ."

"Then perhaps you should consider," the ambassador quietly advised, "that while the Pojjana do not possess strong spacefaring, their atmospheric capabilities are formidable. Those planes behind us could be diversionary."

Stiles heard the words, but for a moment they made no sense. Then, gradually, the picture of reality crystallized in his mind and he abruptly understood the ugly mistake he was making.

"Oh . . . oh!" Stiles's mouth suddenly went completely dry, and he gripped his controls. "Oh, God!"

Suddenly Travis Perraton tensed at his own console. "Tactical display shows something in front of us! Coming up through the clouds! It's an A/I! They've got an A/I blocking our way! There are mountains on both sides! Eric, can we climb?"

By not taking any chances, by pretending to be a topnotcher who knew how to do his job and going for finesse instead of humility, Stiles had left everything wide open. Eric Stiles, man about town, citizen of the galaxy, had left the ship without forward protection. No vanguard!

Now he was coming into the targeting sights of whatever the Pojjans wanted to throw in his way—he'd let those planes steer him into its firing range, and all his defensive fighters were five miles behind him, guarding him from planes that couldn't catch up. The Pojjan planes didn't have a chance of catching him, but they sure had a chance of steering the coach toward an assault net hidden in the mountains!

Stiles felt his throat close up around the realization that he'd been completely duped. Spock hadn't interfered until it became obvious that Stiles was being suckered into a vulnerable position.

And no, he couldn't climb yet. Not that high—not yet.

He stared at the forward screen as a huge, nasty-looking assault/interceptor moved merrily through the mountain pass, essentially a giant gun platform, on an intercept course with the coach. And certainly that would happen, because in this short space there was no way to gain enough velocity to rise any higher, and there were mountains funneling them on both sides. All that Pojjan A/I had to do was move toward them in the sky and let the cricket fly into the web.

There were only moments left before the two craft would intersect. Seconds—

Stiles bolted to his feet, driven by a rash decision.

"Ambassador, can you pilot this coach? Ah—what am I saying! I'm so—I'm such—of course you can!"

As Stiles stepped through the hatch, Spock stood aside as if he were clairvoyant about Stiles' intentions.

"I understand, Ensign," the ambassador said as he slid into the pilot's seat. "You know your nominal weapons will be ineffective against an assault/interceptor."

Stiles yanked open the equipment locker and pulled out an air mask and gloves. Dry-mouthed and ashamed, he rasped, "It's my duty to try, sir."

"Commendable."

Perraton twisted around in his seat. "What's going on? Eric? What're you doing? Where do you think you're going?" Then his blue eyes flashed with shock. "You're not going out in the Frog!"

Harnessed by his failure to master the savoir-faire of command, Stiles didn't respond. He yanked on his gloves and slipped the air mask's strap over his head.

"Oh, no!" Thrusting to his feet, Perraton grasped Stiles's arm, forcing Stiles to shake him off in order to yank on a thermal jacket. "Eric, you're not serious!"

"As you were, Mr. Perraton," Spock advised, steering the coach masterfully through the angry mountains.

Perraton shrank back into his seat, cold with astonishment, his lips working as he tried to think of something to say.

Spock adjusted his pitch controls, but continued speaking to Stiles. "The midwing is unlikely to be able to divert a craft of that mass," he attempted again.

Was he trying to talk Stiles out of going?

"I know that, sir," Stiles said. "But by my calculations you only need an additional fifteen seconds to get up enough speed to break out of the atmosphere over that thing."

"Eleven seconds."

"Oh . . . well, I'll try to get it for you. Good luck, sir."

Even in the midst of piloting the heavy coach, Spock bothered to turn and give him the gift of eye-to-eye contact, a deeply meaningful effort that Stiles didn't miss.

"And to you, Mr. Stiles," he said.

Stiles closed his thermal jacket around his chest as he ran down the aisle through the glances of frightened passengers. He wanted to forget about the jacket, but training had kicked in. If he didn't have the jacket, he'd been too cold to be effective inside the uninsulated midwing.

As he passed the side-gunner pods, Jeremy White cranked around with surprise. "Eric, where do you think you're going? Who's piloting?"

Stiles ran past him. "Mind your gun, Jeremy."

Spock hadn't tried to stop him. Why not? Travis was right—this was hopeless. A twelve-foot one-man defense plane against a hundred-foot assault/interceptor?

As Stiles crawled into the Frog, the smallness of the utility craft struck him like a club. The little detachable was a holdover from previous technology, just something people expected to see on a transport coach and could be used now and then to scout a landing area or as a spotter. It had phasers, yes, but hardly more powerful than a hand phaser, and not very useful against large targets. It was amphibious, hence its nickname, but was almost never used in water; mostly it gave passengers the illusion of safety and options which it really couldn't deliver. It hung from the belly of the big coach, more of a wart than anything useful in a battle situation.

And he was about to launch himself in this crackerbox and pretend he could do something about a hundred-foot A/I platform.

He had to do *something*. This was something.

They didn't need him anyway. Spock could pilot the coach, probably better than Stiles could, so he was useless here. Might as well take a wild shot at clearing the coach past the platform out there. The A/I was big, but not maneuverable. It was made to do exactly what it was doing—hover out there, block the path, and pounce on whatever those planes funneled through to it. If the coach could just get past it, the A/I couldn't chase them.

One chance . . . one chance. . . .

He dropped into the pilot's seat, which accepted his backside like a big hand, and didn't bother buckling himself in. No—better buckle in, just in case he had to spiral or yaw hard. Wouldn't help to fall out of the seat onto his head, would it?

The belts were hard and stiff over his shoulders and around his chest. His feet fell upon the lower trim controls. His gloved hands gripped the yoke. The Frog's comm system would automatically tie in with his combadge . . . he could still communicate with his team, with the ambassador . . . they'd be able to both see and hear him making a further fool of himself.

Though it seemed minutes were going by, in fact it was only seconds before he had yanked the release and the Frog had drifted away from the coach, instantly going to its own power once it felt itself let go.

Stiles rammed the throttle, and was suddenly rushing out from under the belly of the big gray-white transport as if bursting out of a cloud.

"Mr. Stiles, Spock here."

The voice in his ear startled him.

"Stiles, sir," he responded automatically.

"*You are at full throttle. You realize that the Frog will burn itself out quickly at that speed. In less than three minutes, you'll have nothing left.*"

"I know that, sir. I figure there won't be much point in doing any less."

"*Your choice, Ensign.*"

"I'm coming into range, sir. I'm opening fire. I'll try to distract them enough that you can get by."

"*Understood.*"

Oh, that was charity. What were the chances his little popgun phasers could do any damage to the enormous assault craft rushing toward him between the snowy crags of the mountain belt?

He opened fire anyway.

Shoot! Shoot! Again! Direct hit!

Bolts of red energy cut through the mist and skittered across the big gunladen maw of the A/I. He was way ahead of the coach now, in range of those guns, but they weren't firing at him. Why not? He was firing on them, so why weren't they returning fire?

No point. They knew the Frog wasn't worth the trouble, couldn't pose a threat to them, couldn't possibly stop them from taking down the coach.

And judging by the way his phaser energy sparked and fizzled on that ship's shielded skin, they were right. In seconds he wouldn't have any power left, at this speed, this effort.

The Frog rocketed over the top of the A/I, treating Stiles to a vision of bristling guns just waiting to skin the coach to death. All he had to do was distract them for eleven seconds, but they weren't playing. His last chance to be a hero was fizzling just like his phaser shots. They were ignoring him.

"They're ignoring me," he muttered. "Sir, how close are you to escape velocity?"

"*Twenty-five seconds, Ensign.*"

"Sir . . . they're not paying any attention to me. How can I get them to chase me instead of you?"

"*It's unlikely that you can,*" Spock bluntly told him.

Oh, why not? He'd come this far into the valley of the stupid. One more step couldn't do any worse.

"Sir," Stiles began, "I need a suggestion. I'll do anything for that eleven seconds."

"*Very good, Ensign. Consider this—that interceptor is not a space vessel. It depends upon lift.*"

"Thank you, sir!"

"*You'll be in extreme danger, Ensign.*"

"Doesn't matter, sir. In a couple of minutes, the Frog won't have anything left anyway. Here I go. . . ."

Spock didn't respond to that. Stiles waited for the zing of heroism to strike him, but nothing happened. He was too laden with the silliness of his mistakes to take much credit for what he was about to do. Pulling back on the Frog's steering mechanism, he vectored full about and once again streaked toward the interceptor when he heard the decisive Dutch accent of Fighter Wing Leader Bernt Folmer.

"*Oak One, Brazil. Stiles, what're you doing? You can't fight that thing off with a Frog!*"

"Maintain position, wing leader," Stiles told him. "Never mind me."

"*Eric, you're making the wrong decision.*"

"No, it isn't. Cut the chatter."

Before him he saw the A/I piercing the clouds on its way down the natural path formed by mountains on both sides, and beyond that the rushing coach heading directly toward him, its nose up slightly as it tried to reach up and over the A/I and gain escape velocity. Not being a fighting craft of any kind, rather the kind of vessel that would be protected rather than protect itself, it did nothing fast, nothing fierce. Everything was slow and steady—eleven seconds too slow.

In just a moment the coach would be in range of the blunt force of the A/I's guns, and be driven down with its precious payload.

Stiles aimed the nose of his Frog downward, directly at the A/I's tail fins. A slave to lift . . . to the air it rode upon. Not a space vessel . . . why hadn't he thought of that himself?

Like a mosquito buzzing a raven, he shot downward from the high peaks until all around him became a spiky blur. The A/I's big black body grew before him with stunning speed until it filled his forward canopy and he could see nothing but the interceptor and the nearing form of the coach beyond it. All he could see of the coach was the gleaming underbelly—what an angle Spock was piloting! The stresses—could the coach take that?

"Didn't know it could do that," he gasped, but there was hardly any sound. "Ambassador, this is Stiles. If I disable that interceptor, the five fighters can drive it out of your way. Do you copy?"

"*Understood. Three fighters would probably be sufficient, Ensign. The other two can effect rescue—*"

"No," Stiles said. "Not again. Keep them in formation, all five of them."

"*Explain your plan.*"

"I'm gonna clip that thing."

He was surprised when Spock didn't argue. Stiles found himself both gratified and humiliated by his hero's silence.

Then, abruptly, a giant hand reached out and slapped him blind. A crash like thunder deafened him.

Collision!

Chapter Three

THE FROG RAKED its port wing hard across the A/I's tail pectoral, shearing the fin off halfway down. With a sickening pitch, the tiny defender skidded over the metal top of the interceptor, then scraped off to one side like water sheeting off, now hopelessly damaged, and for a silly moment hung side by side in the sky with its enemy. As Stiles watched, the big interceptor almost casually yawed and lost altitude, falling away beneath the coach and rolling almost on its side, which prevented it from firing its forward guns at anything but the nearest mountain. The A/I took a couple of shots, but missed the coach entirely.

As if in a dream, Stiles listened to the reactions of his fighter pilots.

"The interceptor's falling off! All wings, attack formation! Get under the coach and drive the A/I down!"

"Affirmative. Formation Attack-Alpha."

Brazil's voice—giving the strike order.

Falling apart around Stiles, the Frog shook violently and rattled enough to make a man insane. Nothing responded as Stiles fought for trim—hopeless. The big interceptor was veering out of control, but unfortunately so was he.

"I'm going down!" he shouted, more to himself than anyone listening. He was glad when Spock didn't try to give him last-minute instructions. The Frog was croaking and there was nothing to be done about it.

"The A/I is veering off. They've got no control. Beautiful . . . Stiles, you did it. Eric?"

"I can't see him anymore! Bernt, have you got visual?"

"That's negative. He's off my screens. No visual."

"No visual, Travis."

"Oak One, do you copy? Do you copy!"

"Pecan, Chestnut—stay in formation! We're not out yet!"

Then, Spock's voice, like an oasis amid the youthful cries of the others. *"Coming to flank speed. All wings maintain formation."*

Without control he skimmed through the mountains, past knives of rock and white slopes of snow, scratching and plowing through whatever scooped up into his path, buffeted fiercely by winds and the force of his own fall. Around him the Frog cracked, broke, screamed, until finally an insurmountable crag caught the starboard wing and whipped him into a snow drift.

"Formation Emerald, all wings."

"I saw where he went. Right into the snow crest on the sun-side of mountain on the starboard beam. Permission to break formation and effect search."

"Negative. Maintain formation."

Spock's voice. Stiles clung to the low steady tone. It was the last thing he heard as his craft smashed into a snowy crevasse, as if the boot of a giant had scuffed a sandcastle. As the Frog plowed through fresh snow at flight speed, the impact knocked Stiles roughly left and right, held in place by the straps he almost hadn't bothered putting on. He saw only a spray of white pitted with rocks as the Frog's nose drove itself into the mountainside. The din of contact with mountainous matter and hard-packed snow muffled his helpless shouts and gasps. He crammed his eyes closed and waited to die. Pain raced up his left arm so hard, so sharp that he tried to turn away from it. His left arm tingled, went numb. Had it been cut off?

And suddenly, sharply, like a flat stone dropping, there was silence.

No . . . not quite. He could still hear the skitter of bits of ice and rock settling outside. He opened his eyes.

Nearly dark . . . the Frog was completely buried in snow. Entombed . . . and where? On top of an Alp? Even if he could get out, he could never survive.

Blood ran down the side of his face. Into his eye . . . and stung a little.

He was lying nearly on his back, with his knees up before him and the cockpit controls where the open sky should be. Just lucky to have landed on his ass instead of his head . . . could've been worse, could be hanging here upside down with the blood rushing to his head, looking dopey and unable. . . .

"Spock to Stiles. Can you hear me, Ensign?"

The voice from the comm unit jolted him as if he'd been stricken bodily. He flinched. "What . . . ?"

"*Ensign Stiles, this is Spock. We've reached escape velocity. Sensors indicate you've crashed and are stationary, but intact. Is that true? Are you down?*"

Stiles coughed and tried to focus his aching on the instrument panel. Yes, he could still see . . . tiny emergency lights cast a soft red glow, just enough to see by.

"Yes, I, uh . . . I'm crashed," he muttered, coughed again, then winced at the searing pain in his arm. "Down behind the lines. . . ."

"*Are you stable?*"

"No idea."

Above him, the canopy was completely darkened to a severe gray by a ton of snow and ice and dirt, only the tempered windshield preventing him from being crushed or suffocated.

How much fallout was he buried under? No way to know. Should he try to push out? Would it hold him here or let him slip down into a fissure? Was snow heavier than soil?

"Snow . . . ," he murmured, perplexed. Then a gurgling laugh rose in his throat. "I'm from Port Canaveral."

The sound of his voice drummed in his ears. Should he be doing something? Trying to get out?

There was no getting the canopy open under that much weight, and he sure couldn't do it with only one arm.

Still numb?

Yup.

"*All wings, come to stratospheric formation. Transfer to space thrust.*"

"*Coach, Brazil. Copy that. All wings comply.*"

"*But I can still get down there. I can land on that mountain—*"

"*Don't take action until I get a fix on him. These readings aren't steady.*"

That was Travis's voice. He sounded strange. . . .

Several seconds went by, long ones. Almost a minute. Well past the time when the coach should've been clear of the mountains. What was happening?

Then Ambassador Spock's smooth words broke through the crackling sounds of the pilots. "*The pursuit aircraft are moving away. They have given up. The coach is no longer in danger, Mr. Stiles.*"

Stiles cleared his throat and muttered, "Thanks for telling me, sir."

"*One of the wings can now break formation and effect rescue with relative dispatch.*"

"Rescue? . . . oh . . . me. . . ."

With a grunt, Stiles pushed off his helmet, surprised to see a crack in it, and realized his head had been driven into the canopy's side support strut. No wonder his head hurt.

"They may want us to try that," he decided. "There might be other hostiles out there. One ensign against five pilots and thirty-five dignitaries . . . Leave the fighters where they are, sir. I'll just . . . stay here."

It was all bravado. If Spock insisted, Stiles knew he wouldn't stand up to him. He could feel his friends listening, see Travis Perraton's friendly face blanked with astonishment that they were leaving a man behind, see Perraton's European features turn ruddy, his blue eyes widen. Suddenly Perraton—and all of them, really—seemed too young for this job. Maybe Stiles was fooling them, but he wasn't fooling the ambassador.

No one said anything. Nobody wanted to interrupt with the ambassador talking.

Glad they didn't say anything . . . that would've been even harder. Hearing their voices . . .

Spock . . . a half-dozen Starfleet officers rolled into one. An ambassador of high standing and galactic respect. A name known in the farthest reaches, on the tiniest colonies, on the lips of every Federation enemy. Spock and Starfleet were almost the same word. He could've insisted on a rescue attempt. Stiles would've backed down, let himself be rescued. Looked like a dopey kid being pulled out of the water because he'd showed off and fallen in.

Was he refusing rescue to avoid that moment?

Spock didn't press him. Stiles knew what that meant—he was being given something. Spock wasn't countermanding Stiles's decision to sacrifice himself. Ensign or not, Stiles was in charge, even if only in a token way. Nobody thought this would be a hard mission. He felt a little silly that Spock was giving in to him, handing him some kind of lollipop. On the other hand, was Spock going out of the way not to take something away from him? Maybe . . .

A hard bump made the mountainside vibrate. He felt it, through the Frog's skin, through the snow, through his jacket.

"There's somebody outside," he spoke up. "Something just landed near me . . . it's got to be them! They're here—they found me!"

"*Yes, we have them on sensors. A Pojjana jump-jet just settled on the mountain near you.*"

Stiles's mouth went suddenly dry. "How long . . . do you think they'll take to get through to me?"

Spock didn't answer him. Maybe he was busy up there, steering that coach into space, avoiding the three Pojjan moons that looped the planet so far away, so much farther than Earth's moon.

"I didn't know the coach could take that much stress," he sighed. "You put a lot of angle on it. Why didn't it stall? How do you do that?"

"Simply, but the Academy prefers not to teach the trick. I forced the P/T levels over tolerance so the thrusters had more power."

"Why didn't the tanks blow from the extra pressure?"

"Tolerance levels are standardized at point of safety. Going over tolerance only means that measurement becomes unreliable."

"You mean you were just taking a chance?"

"Exactly."

"Wow . . ."

Listening to thumps and thuds from the deep outside, Stiles saw a picture in his mind of the transport coach, piloted by Spock instead of himself, angling more steeping into the late-day sky than Stiles thought it possibly could. He never guessed a ship like that could take so much lift stress. He wouldn't have known to take the chance of added stress, wouldn't have been able to get the coach up fast enough to make use of the eleven seconds.

"I can hear them outside." He gazed up, only seven inches, to the snowed-over canopy. "They're looking for me in the snow. They're digging through . . . I hear the shovels . . . Maybe they're putting explosives on me. Maybe they're not going to dig me out at all. Why should they?"

"Steady, Ensign. You will not be killed."

"Respectfully suggest you don't know that, sir."

"Of course not. Ensign, this sector is now red. Some time may pass before the Federation can negotiate for your release. Do you understand?"

A tremor ran down Stiles's spine. "You mean . . . it might take a couple of months?"

"Or longer."

"Well . . . six months?" His hands chilled even beyond the cooling temperature in the cockpit. Sweat broke out on his brow in spite of the chill.

Spock didn't answer him. That meant something. Longer than six months?

"Sir, tell my family . . . tell them I didn't . . . or just say . . ."

"I will, Mr. Stiles. Be assured of that."

With a sudden groan, Stiles shut his eyes. His request suddenly seemed silly, melodramatic. But more than anything else it was pointless. He reviewed in his mind the faces of his father and grandfather, his aunts and uncles, the wide extended legacy of Stiles service to Starfleet and several other notable planetary corps within the structure of the Federation. Wherever they lived, wherever they were, the Stiles family made a show for themselves.

He shifted this way and that, but there was no room for movement. He was denied even that pitiful comfort and was forced to sit here and look back.

"Sir," he began again, "never mind about my family. Don't tell them anything. Just tell them I'm . . . not around anymore."

There was a brief silence, heavy and notable, like the pause between movements of a symphony. The baton remained in the air, the audience didn't applaud, the instruments were up.

"I shall tell them you performed your duty most admirably, young man," Spock slowly promised. *"You rose to an unforeseen challenge."*

A mirthless chuckle broke from Stiles's chest. More charity. Good words for a pathetic slob, so he wouldn't feel so pathetic.

Too late.

"Rose to it? I caused it. It was only unforeseen because I didn't foresee it." He shivered deeply, to his bones. "Don't bother with my family. Starfleet'll send them the official report. Don't tell them anything else . . . they won't be impressed. This story isn't that good. Doing duty's not enough for them. I'd be better off just lost at sea. No stories."

"Ensign," Spock began again, *"you needn't cheat yourself. You fit into an age-old tapestry of military valor. Even the small deeds are knightly."*

"Oh, please, sir, I've heard that since I was six. We take an oath . . . we wear uniforms . . . we take action . . . when there's trouble, we go toward it instead of away from it. We're military. Can't argue with that. It's got to mean something. If it means I stay here, then that's what it means."

A mechanical whine, muffled by the snow, found its way down to him. Drilling. Or cutting, maybe. He must be trapped under rocks or—were there trees up this high? He hadn't bothered looking.

His cold face cracked with a sorry smile as he reviewed the last few seconds. "I hope the other guys can't hear you talking to me this way."

Spock's voice crackled. Growing more faint. Distant. *"I sent Ensign Perraton to tend to the passengers. I have no need of a navigator. We are quite alone."*

Overhead, the scratching sound was louder now, more deliberate. The diggers weren't searching anymore. They were purposefully digging. They'd pinpointed this spot. Maybe a fin or wing was sticking out of the snow. Or maybe they had sensors that had caught him. They'd sure found him fast. Things sure could change suddenly.

Stiles let his head fall against the high seat back. "So . . . how'd you know I wanted to be alone? All my life I've heard how Vulcans don't have intuition . . . y'know, no . . . hunches. No emotional anchors, like us fallibles do."

"And you have believed the stories," Spock said.

Stiles touched a swelling on the side of his head and laughed minimally. "Oh, you're making fun of me now."

"With you, Ensign," the ambassador offered gently, *"not of you."*

"Everybody always says Vulcans can't joke."

"*Of course not. Nor do we love, fear, lie, or doubt.*"

Stiles laughed again. Strange that he could laugh . . . strange that this particular person could make him feel better when none of his friends had been able to.

The shovels, diggers, drills . . . getting closer now. Something scratched the nose of the Frog. Stiles saw a finger of golden sunlight appear in front of his left knee. They were almost here. In minutes, he'd be in the hands of the enemy. Would they kill him?

They had a lot of options. He had none. Here he was, trapped in his capsule, probably about to die, and even though his mission was successful, he crashed because of his own lack of foresight. His family was going to be disappointed in him . . . all those commanders, captains, lieutenants, heroes of the Romulan Wars—and one kid who never made it past ensign because he made a mistake on his first mission and got himself shot down.

He'd blown it. Allowed himself to be distracted. Put all his fighters behind him and figured nobody would think to come up in front. He was ashamed that Spock had been forced to point out something so obvious. That's what would go in the report, and on top of it all, after everything else, Spock was seeing that he was afraid.

"It's hard to breathe," he wheezed. Life support off?

"*The blue marker dot on the upper left of your emergency grid, ensign. Push it upward.*"

"Blue dot . . . oh. Got it—I hear the fan now. That's better . . ."

Fresh air, siphoned from outside. Not warm, though. In fact, the incoming air was frigid. But air was air and it cleared his head.

At the very least, he'd be captured now. Maybe tortured. Maybe killed. Would it be better to get killed right now, here on this mountain?

A crawling aneurysm of mortal fear moved through his brain, infecting his body until he was cold and shuddering. He felt it working on him even as he tried to keep it in check. It tightened his throat and changed the timbre of his voice. Could Spock hear that in his voice? Hear that he was afraid?

The sound of shovels scratched the top of his packed snow prison.

"It's getting cold. . . ."

Stiles shuddered through a sigh and this time saw his breath, as the chill from outside permeated the cockpit.

Another scratch—broader, brighter. They'd have him in a minute or two. Now he could hear voices above. Bootsteps. Shouts.

"Sir . . ."

"*Yes?*"

"I don't know . . . how well I'm going to do," he admitted.

"This is hardly routine for you," Spock offered. *"You are twenty-two."*

"Twenty-one." Miserable now, beginning to feel the pain in his shoulder through fading numbness, he tried to shift his feet but failed even to do that.

What did Spock mean? So he was twenty-one. So what?

Old enough to control simple fears. Old enough to put fear aside. What was a veteran like Spock really thinking of him?

He sank more deeply into his seat, let his legs go limp, flexed his good hand, and touched the frosted canopy near his face. "I guess this is where you tell me everything'll be all right eventually, and I'm brave and ought to be proud of myself."

"I hesitate to quote poetry," Spock said, and Stiles could almost see the hint of a smile.

So he smiled too. "Sir, I wouldn't know what to do with it if you did. I don't even read the insides of my birthday cards."

For a moment there was no sound from the now-distant coach, no response, no coddling. The comm unit crackled, struggling to pull in the spaceborne signal through systems that were probably broken or fried.

"I'm losing you, sir," Stiles said.

"Yes, your reception signal is thready."

"Should I try to boost?"

"Distance is a factor. No need to strain yourself. I'll boost from here."

Stiles's hand fell back to his side and he let himself go limp, trying to ease the ache in his head. A little shaving of frost fell from the canopy where he'd touched it. The flakes landed on his right cheek and stuck there, like a frozen tear. His face was too cold even to melt it.

"The Federation will negotiate for your freedom," Spock told him placidly. *"I'll see to it personally."*

"Don't make a spectacle," Stiles grumbled. "I don't want to be known as the little goof with the big rescue. Then somebody else'll be the hero and I'll just be the jerk who crashed in enemy territory and cost a mint to get back. I don't need that . . . God, my shoulder hurts . . . think they know how to set a human arm?"

"Yes, they know how."

Spock's voice was small now, but clear of static, patient and gentle, laden with understanding of what he was feeling. How could that be?

"I have worked with many humans in my lifetime. There is great comfort for me among them, and much to admire. Above all traits, I believe, I most admire their resilience. Be pliant, Eric. Once you survive this, you'll be a more valuable officer. And a better man."

Stiles heard the words, but it was as if he were listening to wind. Substantial, effective . . . but he didn't understand what made it happen.

An instant later he could barely remember what Spock had just said—all he remembered was the sound of his own name spoke so adaptably by that famous voice.

"What do you think I should do?" he asked simply. His throat was raw now. There were fumes in here. "If they don't kill me . . . what do I do to change? I already try so hard . . . how can I be better?"

Now that the question was asked, he steeled himself to listen, to remember a long sermon, the kind his grandfather used to lay on him when there was some lesson to be learned or some grave social gaffe to be corrected. All the way home from wherever they were, talk, talk, talk, preach, preach, preach.

And that was why he was surprised. As sunlight broke through above his face and the snow was scraped away from the cockpit's canopy, as he saw the faces of Pojjana soldiers peel back the rocks and crud from his Starfleet coffin, Stiles absorbed Spock's final word. Only one word . . . it echoed and echoed, rolled and settled, it chimed a resonant bell tone. He would hear it for the rest of his life.

"*Relax.*"

Chapter Four

HARD TO BREATHE. Stuffy.

Metal banging against metal. The whine of mechanical treads. Lower pitch than the aircraft. A hatch breaking open—and Stiles fell inelegantly forward and landed on a stone floor.

His head throbbed, his left shoulder and arm ached . . . at least the paramedics, or whatever they were, had bandaged the arm before stuffing him into the brig box on their plane. He'd thought it might've been broken, but it wasn't. His shoulder had been jammed into the side of the cockpit, numbing his whole arm. They'd given him a drug he thought might be poison, but turned out only to be a pain pill. For some reason, probably leverage, they didn't want him dead. Not yet.

Now he was here. He knew a prison cell when he saw one. Unlike Starfleet's fancy bright brigs, this one just had the old-fashioned titanium bars. Sure. Why use expensive energy beams to hold prisoners in when plain metal would do the same job and couldn't be shorted out?

Pressing his right hand to the stone floor, Stiles pushed himself from his knees to a sitting position. Tile, not stone. Big squares of rough-glazed tile. What was it his mother had called that color? Terra cotta.

Over his shoulder, the oval door or hatch or whatever it was that he'd come through clanked shut and barked loudly as it was locked from outside. Nobody had talked to him, nobody had counseled or advised him, nobody had told him what was going on or how long he would be here, or what the legal process would be. Did the Pojjans even have a legal process? How much of a coup was going on here? Was there a government in place at all?

Ashamed of his failure to do simple mission homework, Stiles realized he had no idea what to expect or any way to judge what had happened to him. The Pojjan soldiers had pulled him off the top of the mountain, bandaged his arm, run some kind of scanner over him, flown him back and dumped him into this cell. Was this a prison? Or just a holding cell? Would he be here for six months, or moved to a trial, a sentence, a hotel room?

"I'm not a criminal," he murmured, trying to sort all this out. "Not a rebel or terrorist . . . so what am I?"

With notable effort, he stood up on shaky legs. His head throbbed relentlessly. The cell was dry at least, and warm enough. Well, at least they weren't barbarians. And there was light. Not much—enough to see by, not enough to disturb sleep. All the lights were outside his cell, beyond the titanium bars. Probably they had learned that light fixtures could be cannibalized into lock-blowing bombs. He remembered that from the Academy alternative-energy course.

A bunk and mattress, a woolly blanket, a toilet, a sink.

"Welcome to Alcatraz," he grumbled with a sigh. "Hope they feed me."

"You'll be fed."

Stiles flinched back a step. His heart drummed.

"Who's talking?" he yelped. "Where are you?"

"In the next cell."

Stiles pressed against the bars, trying to see, but the cells were side by side and there was no doing it. The bars were cold against his cheek.

"Are you a prisoner?" he asked.

"Seems obvious."

A male voice. Sounded young. Not old, anyway. Sounded like it could be one of his own team.

"Are you a criminal?"

"My incarceration is political."

"Political . . . so's mine, I think. What're they going to do to us? Have they got courts on this planet? Are there laws?"

"Yes, they have laws."

"How soon will they—"

"Not soon. They're in turmoil here. The Federation is leaving."

"Yeah, I've heard that rumor . . ."

This was getting him nowhere. He couldn't see the other guy, and if he asked too many questions, that guy would be justified in asking questions also and Stiles would feel obliged to answer.

Then again, why not?

"Who are you? What's your name?"

"Zevon."

"Just 'Zevon'?"

"Yes. Who are you?"

"Eric Stiles."

"Human?"

"Uh-huh."

"Starfleet, then."

"How do you know that?"

"The only humans on this planet are either Starfleet personnel or Federation diplomatic corps workers. The Pojjana would never put diplomatic staff in prison."

"Ah . . . they'll harass the military but not the civilians. There's brainy."

"The military understands that capture is part of the job. The Pojjan know that."

Stiles shuffled to his cot and sat stiffly down, then sank back against the wall. "Are you saying that if I weren't Starfleet, they wouldn't put me wherever we are?"

"That's correct. They wouldn't have captured you at all. The Federation would be hostile if civilians were made political pawns. Starfleet is fairer game."

"Oh, that's great. . . ."

Lying back as he was, Stiles gazed at his uniform, at the black field of shirt and pants, the ribbed waistband, and the poppy-red shoulder band under his chin. It looked strange with the combadge missing. They'd taken it. So they knew it wasn't just jewelry.

"But wait a minute," he began. "I was guarding a coach full of civilians and the Pojjana tried to shoot us down. Why would they do that? Isn't that making them political pawns?"

"The Pojjana could have claimed the coach crashed. If they gained possession of the civilians alive, they probably would have put them back in the embassy and claimed some delay or other."

"Buying time?"

"Most likely. The Pojjana are clumsy with politics. They do things without knowing why."

"Just hedging their bets?"

"Perhaps. The lingering of a thousand civilians is easier to justify than the disappearance of one soldier."

Stiles flexed his legs and winced at the stiffness. "What you're saying is that I'm small potatoes."

"I would suspect so," Zevon confirmed quietly. "If that means what I infer."

"Yeah . . . mmm . . . ow . . ."

From the other cell, the man called Zevon quietly asked, "Are you injured?"

"My ship crashed. I got knocked around. I thought my shoulder was broken, but it's not. Mission was simple . . . if headquarters . . . if they'd just cued me in to the situation, none of this would've happened. They should've briefed me. I'm just an ensign. I'm not supposed to know everything. Somebody should've known this would happen . . . so they can have it. They don't come and get me? Fine. I'll stay here. I don't need Starfleet if they don't need me." Staring at the floor tiles between the frame of his bent knees, he sighed. "I have a date tomorrow night. . . ."

Prison. Prisoner of war? But there was no war. Why was he a prisoner? Did a cold war have prisoners? How long?

Ambassador Spock hadn't told him how long this might last. Now Stiles understood—the ambassador had just not known. He had deliberately evaded answering. The answer was bad. More than six months?

How long would it be before his hair got long enough to braid? How much longer before he actually started braiding it, just for something to do?

Staring ahead at the next few minutes, with an aching shoulder and a throbbing head, somehow the concept of months eluded him. Right now even the concept of lunch was eluding him. How long before he got hungry? Would they feed him? Was deprivation part of the torture regime? How much did this Zevon really know about Pojjan habits? If Zevon himself was Pojjan, he might not really know how they'd treat a human prisoner.

I'm on my own.

"I wouldn't be here if I'd had a better team," he complained. "Travis was the only one with any off-station experience. It's not my fault what happened."

"You were in command of a landing party?"

"It wasn't my fault!"

The other prisoner fell to silence. Stiles's own protest echoed briefly, then died. Ashamed and angry, he sat up and stared at the floor tiles, memorizing the grout. As if framed in each octagonal tile, scuffed and scratched, he saw his teammates' faces.

"Sorry . . ." he whispered. The faces all merged into one face, his own—scarred and shriveled like the picture of Dorian Gray sitting in the attic, hidden, corrupted with excesses.

He pressed a moist palm to his forehead, brushed back his hair, now gritty and sweat-matted, closed his eyes. Thoughts tumbled. Blames and guilts blended into a single nauseous mass.

"I shouldn't. . . ."

His voice pierced the tomblike quiet, then dissolved. He clamped his lips shut before he lost control of what popped out of them. Didn't know whether Zevon could hear him. Hoped not.

Hot in here. It hadn't been hot when he'd been dumped here. Was somebody playing with the temperature controls? Trying to break him down?

"It won't work!" He vaulted to his feet, skidding on the tile. When nothing changed, he paced. Across the cell, around the perimeter, along the bars, to the toilet, back to the bunk. There, he faced himself again.

He turned and continued pacing. His arms and legs ached. Why was he hurting more now than when he'd crashed?

"Do you feel anything?"

"I feel insulted. I feel like I'm being laughed at. I feel—"

"That's not what I mean. Do you feel anything unusual—anything physical?"

Stiles paused at Zevon's sudden return to the conversation. "Like what?"

"Pressure . . ."

"I've got a headache, if that's what you're asking."

"No! Are you standing?"

"What?"

Suddenly his eyes began to sting fiercely, his head to throb horridly, as if he'd fallen into a vat of acid. Had he been shot? Phasered? Some kind of Pojjan weapon? Cramps gripped his midsection and he grabbed the titanium bars of his cell, contracting against them until his knees couldn't fit between them anymore and he began to slip toward the floor. The floor was shaking! The walls were rumbling!

As he forced his eyes open, he saw the stone wall across from his cell now tattered and flaking before his astonished gaze.

Over a whine in his ears he shouted, "What's happening! What is this? An earthquake?"

"Lie on the floor! Quickly!" The other prisoner called over the increasing roar of collapsing stone and cracking mortar. "Lie face up! Put your arms flat at your sides! Breathe deeply!"

"What is this? What is this! Why is this happening!"

"It's the Constrictor! Lie down!"

Stiles pushed off the bars and rushed to the hatch through which he'd been dumped in here. He pounded until his fist rang with numbness. "Hey! Let us out of here! The building's coming down on us! Let us out of here!"

"Lie down, you fool," the other man said one more time.

"Ow—ah—ah—!" Grasping at his ringing head with both hands, Stiles staggered across the tiled floor, insane with new agony. As if iron bars were hanging from his limbs, brute force, like sheer invisible tonnage, pushed him to his knees. The floor came up to meet him and he collapsed forward, pressed physically to the cold tile as if crushed by a giant's palm.

With one last effort he dragged his right arm under him and managed to turn halfway over, then partially onto his back. After that he gave in to the rule of sheer might. He gasped as his flesh flattened against the tiles with such duress that he could feel the edges of the tile and the shape of the grout lines creasing his body. He stared, consumed with fear, at his own arms stretching out before him.

As his face lay against a tile, he saw a crack develop in the floor, small at first and then larger, running through the bars and out into the corridor, then up the wall. The building—

Trapped on his side, Stiles tried to raise his head, to follow the crack with his eyes, but his skull alone weighed a hundred pounds. His arms, sprawled out before him, actually began to bow into the shape of the floor over the indentation of a drain he hadn't even noticed until now. Insane with shock, he witnessed the surreal horror of his right arm breaking, his unsupported limb molding itself to the squared-off shape of the drain. His lips peeled back with sheer agony.

There, where his right arm lay shattered and compressed into the shape of the drain, a fissure opened in the floor, swallowing the drain's metal grate, dismembering the tiles, uncoupling the titanium bars as shriveling compression took over and the planet opened up.

Stiles felt himself fall, deadweight, strong-armed through a cracking floor, and saw in his last glance the mangled building unravel itself and cleave down upon him.

Beneath the grind and roar of utter demolition, he listened as if disconnected to the echo of his own cries.

Chapter Five

"CAN YOU HEAR ME?"

"You don't have to yell, Eric."

"We're doing whatever you say."

"Stiles?"

"The Federation will negotiate for your freedom. I'll see to it personally."

"Wasn't so hard."

"This is hardly routine for you. You needn't cheat yourself."

"Eric Stiles! Can you hear me?"

"Relax."

Voices pumped through a haze of agony. Had to answer them. How else would they find him?

Cold stuffy air lay against tons of crushed stone and the sharktoothed edges of cracked and disrupted floor tile that now formed more of a wall, bracing one side of a deep fissure.

Faint light swam above, dusty shafts of light, offering no comfort but instead framing the ugliness of what lay above and around.

Water dripped somewhere nearby. Hear it, smell it.

Feel it—his left thigh was soaked.

At least I've still got a leg.

Eric Stiles tried to raise the leg he'd just rediscovered. The knee came up a few inches, which forced him to balance by raising his head and shoulders—agony searing through his right arm, shoulders, and right side. He threw his head back and gritted his teeth. The effort drove him all the way to consciousness, suddenly, like hitting a rock, and his eyes shot open. The light he had seen as a blur now focused far overhead. It must be . . . forty feet up. Had that been the cell, up there? Was that the same light in the corridor outside his bars?

"I hear you. I'm trying to reach you."

Who was that?

Until he heard the other voice, this one clear and not far away, Stiles hadn't been aware that he was moaning, wincing out the sheeting pain in his right arm. Broken. He remembered now. It had been sucked into the shape of the tile drain, broken in at least two places.

Were the bones popping through the skin? Would he bleed to death from a broken arm?

"Eric Stiles, speak if you can."

No, leave me alone. I'm almost dead. Let me finish. Complete one thing. Follow through on this one thing.

Slowly, more slowly than the trickling of thought or water, his body adjusted to the constant pain. As he stopped struggling, stopped trying to lift himself, gradually his arm settled from searing mind-numbing agony to an acceptable throb with his fingers numb. The numbness itself hurt, but after a time he was able to concentrate on the hazy light far overhead and play mental games with it. He endured its mockery, accused it of fickleness, fielded its insults, and claimed it was impotent. Surging in and out of awareness, he conducted a conversation with the faint light and imagined that it was singing to him.

At that point, the fleeting thought that he might be delirious finally settled home and he cleared his throat just to hear his own voice. Just as he began to drowse again, something crashed—the sound of brick and tile falling.

Stiles flinched bodily and raised his head. "Who's there?"

"Zevon."

"Where are you?"

"Making my way to you. Can you come toward me?"

"My leg," Stiles gasped roughly, "it's pinned under something."

Only now did he comprehend that his leg was caught, only when he actually heard the words, even though he'd spoken them himself. Was the leg cut off? Just an imagined sensation? He could feel his toes. Was that important?

"Did the building collapse?" he asked. His words echoed slightly, enough to offer a sensation of cave dwelling.

Zevon's response filtered uneasily from far away. "A sinkhole has opened beneath the jail building. We fell into it. It may have saved our lives by relieving the stress at the critical moment."

"What stress?"

"The Constrictor. A particularly harsh one this time."

Stiles paused and concentrated on breathing. He'd heard that Constrictor word before. Where?

Resting his left hand on his chest, he felt himself breathe. In, out, in, and a sigh.

"This is . . . this is really . . . what's the word—ironic?"

"What is?" Zevon sounded closed-in, muffled.

"I pulled rank to get this mission."

"How did you?"

"The ensign who was up for duty that night, he was on my watch rotation. When I heard about somebody getting a chance to evac Ambassador Spock . . . what an opportunity! I rotated the other guy to an escort mission off the starbase. When the name for duty officer came up, it was mine."

Glancing around his jagged stone prison, Stiles noted with clearing eyes the truly freakish surroundings which would now only in the most generous of mists have resembled a building. Twisted pipes and structural supports lay in tatters around him, the walls of former street-level chambers now fractured in dozens of places, so that plasterwork, concrete sections, brackets, lathe, joists, and support rods showed their gory broken edges. His jail cell had been on the street level. Now he was forty feet below the street, in what could be described as a wide well-shaft walled in on all sides by the remains of the floors above.

"Still in the cell," he muttered.

Stone and metal collided somewhere in the dimness, behind a huge slab of concrete that must be the remains of the wall between his cell and Zevon's. How much of the broken building had wedged itself between them?

"Is there anybody else in here?" Stiles raised his head. "Wish I could move . . . I'm so . . . cold . . ."

"Can you see your bunk?"

Bunk? Oh—Stiles blinked and forced himself to figure out his surroundings. There was the toilet, standing on its head with a piece of support rod piercing the bowl. What if he had landed over there? What would that rod have done to his body?

"Has your bunk fallen somewhere near you?" Zevon asked again, more forcefully despite the muffling of the wall material between them.

Stiles turned his head to the left. "It's right next to me."

"Pull the blanket or the mattress on top of you. Cover yourself with it."

"Why?"

"Because you're going into shock."

"Oh, I'm just . . . it's just that my leg's stuck and . . . I can't. . . ."

"You're getting cold. The temperature down here is still—"

"Look, I don't even know you! You could be some kind of a murderer or a criminal. Why should I listen to you? You're coming over here to kill me, aren't you?"

"Pull the blanket over you. Cover your body."

"You just don't want me to see what you're going to do to me."

"Cover yourself, Stiles. Do it immediately. This is an order!"

His right arm shivered violently, transferring the shivering to his chest, his neck, and he suddenly tensed. The collapsed cell around him echoed with a grievous moan. He couldn't disobey orders. Starfleet officers had an obligation. Set a good example. He was older than all the others.

His left hand cramped briefly, shifted—he forced it upward. The bunk lay on his left, tipped up on one of its points and leaning against whatever was behind it. Supported by something he couldn't see . . . supported, as he had been by Travis, Bernt, Andrea, the Bolt brothers, the whole team. The Evac Team.

"Come on, Eric, lift your hand. You can do it."

Travis Perraton stood up behind that bunk, holding the metal rim, edging the bunk toward his hand until Stiles's fingers touched the blanket.

"Pull it down." Jeremy was there too.

The woolly fabric was cool, but warmed almost immediately as he clutched it. Looking down at him, Travis and Jeremy detached the blanket from where it was tucked under the thin mattress, and the blanket fell onto his arm and shoulder with just a tug.

"Thanks," he murmured. "I knew you'd get here."

Travis nodded and looked at Andrea Hipp and Bernt Folmer. They reached down through the rubble and pulled the blanket over Stiles's chest.

Jeremy White's hand floated forward and tucked the blanket around Stiles's right ribs. "There you go, chief."

"What took you guys so long?" Stiles grumbled, smiling. "My right arm's broken . . . you guys really butchered this building. What'd you have to hit it so hard for? You could've just blown one wall. I could've walked right out. I guess you didn't want to take any chances. What a team . . . you're so great to me . . . I'm sorry I yelled at you."

"You always yell," Travis told him. "We quit listening a long time ago."

"*Long* ago," Andrea Hipp agreed with a grin.

"I'm glad to see you," Stiles told them. "There's some guy in the next cell . . . I think he's going to kill me."

"Why should he?" Andrea asked.

Bernt Folmer shook his head. "You're just nervous. Don't worry about him."

"But he's a criminal or something," Stiles protested.

"How do you know?"

"He's in jail, isn't he?"

Travis smiled and jiggled Stiles's knee. "So are you, lightfoot."

Heartened by the presence of his team, Stiles raised his head again and surveyed the sheared-off slab of wall that pinned his right leg. "Why don't you lift this off me? I think I can stand up if you do. My toes are moving."

Uneasily Jeremy White glanced at Bernt. "Well . . . we can't."

"Why not?" Stiles blinked at him, then looked at Andrea and Bernt, then finally at Travis, from whom he would get the straight answer. "What's wrong?"

Travis Perraton leaned against a jagged rock piercing a crack in the wall. "We didn't make it."

"We tried to get you," Andrea added. "But they got us instead."

"What?" Shoving up on his one good elbow, Stiles almost immediately collapsed in a surge of shock and misery. "Aw, Travis . . . how'd you and Jeremy get out of the coach? Why'd you leave? Bernt, the fighters were guarding the coach! You were the Wing Leader . . . you had your orders. . . ."

"We didn't want to leave you," Bernt said.

"You're such a bag of emotions, Eric," Travis commented.

Jeremy splayed his hands in a shrug. "So we're ghosts. Could be worse. Eric, you're going into shock."

"Stay awake, Eric." Travis knelt beside him. "Eric, stay with me, lightfoot. Don't go to sleep. Are you listening? Open your eyes."

"Cover up," Andrea reminded.

"Okay, I've got my own orders, I get it." Pulling the blanket over his chest again, Stiles felt a series of moans run through his body. The sound was detached, as if made by a wheezing wind or a sighing pipe deep in the plumbing.

"Stay awake, Eric," Bernt warmly repeated. "That's an order."

"Aye aye," Stiles murmured. "I feel better now. I'm warming up. Thanks for looking after me."

Travis offered his continental maitre-d' smile. "Sure, lightfoot."

"We've got to go," Bernt said.

Stiles forced his eyes open again. "So soon?"

Andrea shrugged. "It's just that they hate aliens."

"See ya," Jeremy threw in.

Stiles sighed. "See ya. Hey, what about my arm?"

"I can set your arm, ensign." Another voice. Soothing and stable.

He turned his head to his right, and there in the haze of feeble light saw the one person who could sustain him in any crisis.

"Ambassador . . . you came," he rasped, as if thanking the famous man for dropping in at a party. "And I'm just gum on your shoe. . . ."

Spock tilted his elegant head accommodatingly and with his long hands caressed Stiles's demolished arm. "You're under great strain, ensign. I shall set your arm before I go. I have a splint here, but the arm will have to be lifted briefly. Relax."

The words were clear and inspired confidence. Stiles closed his eyes, understanding that there would be terrific pain and he would do better if he relaxed as ordered. Spock pressed a reassuring hand to Stiles's chest, as comfortingly as Travis or Jeremy might have done, then cradled Stiles's shattered limb. His expression became studious and determined.

Stiles closed his eyes tighter, turned his face away, and braced for punishment. When it came, the gripping anguish took him completely by surprise despite his preparation. To a young man in the prime of youth who had never had a broken bone, pain's sheer overdrive utterly disemboweled him. His head cranked back into the stone, his teeth gritted, and he was dimly aware of his body as it wrung and twisted. With every shred of self-control he possessed, he forced his right shoulder to relax and his arm to disengage from the cruelty as he felt his own bones grating.

A disembodied voice phasered gasps into the cool cellar, but he barely registered the sound as his own. Why was it taking so long? Did it take hour to set a bone? Why didn't Spock just cut the arm off? Stiles dealt with the loathsome pain and the sudden heaving of his stomach at this, his first taste of dynamic physical torment.

"Another moment . . ." Spock's voice was his lifeline, but for the first time he didn't believe the hollow reassurance. "Almost finished, ensign."

"Why do you have to hurt me?" Stiles moaned. "You're the only one I ever respected. . . ."

"One more wrap . . . relax now. Let me secure this. Your arm will adjust in a few minutes. Relax, Ensign . . . relax."

A gentle hand pressed to the hollow of his shoulder, poised there, and beneath the steadiness and reassurance of that contact Stiles let his neck and shoulders go limp, and finally convinced his legs to lie quiet. Then the nausea set in. His brow furrowed and his lips clamped against the surging in his stomach and throat. Moans shuddered through his body. He heard them, felt them, but could no more control them than harness the shattered building that now cradled him so far below the street.

His own groans wakened him from the drowse brought on by pain. The first concrete thing he noticed was that the searing jab of broken bones in his arm had drained to a manageable ache. Or perhaps it hurt more than he thought it did, but he was conditioned now to the racking and this was better than that. Desolation of spirit sank in on him, and he opened his eyes and looked to his right.

A narrow form stood over him, plucking at the wrappings on his arm. The slick dark hair seemed so familiar . . . the features somewhat less angular than he remembered, but close enough . . . soft light from overhead dipping into the curves of those famous pointed ears, which had come to represent such style and trust to anyone in the Federation. . . .

Stiles blinked his eyes clear and moved his right leg. The knee came up where he could see it. Torn pants.

His right leg? Wasn't it pinned under a rock?

"Did you move that by yourself?"

"With a lever," the other man said. The voice was different. "A piece of rod from the broken wall." He held up a three-foot remnant of wall rod, then set it down again. "It broke, but it did serve to move the slab from your leg. You're free now. Don't move, however. You're injured."

"I'll be fine," Stiles protested. "Takes more than an earthquake to get a Starfleeter down."

"Of course. Try not to move. I've splinted your arm with two bent pieces of linoleum and strips of my blanket. I hope it holds. Does it seem to pinch at all?"

"Where's everybody else?" Stiles asked, ignoring the other question. "Where'd they go?"

"Who?"

"The Evac Team. They were here . . . sit me up, will you, sir?" Stiles drew a full breath, the first one in a long time that wasn't cramped and tight. Oxygen surged into his body, clearing his head.

"You need not call me 'sir.' "

"But I can't just . . ."

"You may call me Zevon. I don't care for the other."

Stiles gazed briefly at the long fingers holding him gently in place. Now that his eyes were adjusted to the dimness and no longer blurred by pain, he surveyed that hand, the long dark red sleeve, the velvety padded jacket of gunmetal gray and with a turtleneck collar of the same dark red, and above that a stranger's face with somehow familiar features. The upswept eyebrows, dark eyes, becalmed face—but a young face. And the hair was not cut in the typically Vulcan slick helmet, but instead a rather roughly cut shag of cordovan brown, longer than Spock's, less orderly, tucked behind the lovely shell-shaped ears, the left of which had a small but noticeable scar, a slight nip out of the side edge. So he'd been through something, some time in the past.

Young, though. Not a hundred-plus-year-old ambassador with a stunning history spanning back to the first openings of deep space—someone else. Stiles struggled briefly with trying to figure Zevon's age, but in his condition he couldn't compute human years against anybody else's.

"Did I lose consciousness?" Stiles asked.

"Briefly," Zevon admitted. "I have no anesthetic to give you, nor any pain medication. Sad thing, for a scientist to be unprepared."

His expression was efficient, as one might expect, yet somehow unashamedly sympathetic. Odd . . .

"I guess we've been down here alone the whole time." Stiles glanced past Zevon, just to make sure he wasn't seeing Travis or Jeremy anymore. Or even the ambassador he so deeply revered. Somehow they'd gotten him through the worst, and retired.

"In fact," Zevon confirmed, "I believe we were alone in the jail building when the Constrictor came."

"Constrictor . . . so what are you doing here, anyway?"

"I am a political prisoner. I was hunted and kidnapped."

"You personally? They wanted you?"

"No. Anyone of my race."

"Why? I mean, I'm just here because my ship crashed. That's how they got me. Nobody hunted me down. Why would they hunt you down? Is it just because they hate aliens?"

"Some, but I command a particular kind of ship. They thought my presence here would give them leverage."

"You command a ship? You said you were a scientist, not a captain!"

"Primarily I am a scientist. The command is a position of royal favor."

With a small shake of his head, Stiles frowned. "I never heard of anything like that in the Vulcan fleet."

"Not Vulcan." Zevon passively adjusted the position of Stiles's right arm. "Romulan."

Stiles drew one breath, sharply, and heaved himself to a partially sitting position, up on his right hip. The blanket slipped from his body and fell to one side. He reached over his own form, fished for the piece of rod he knew was here. His fingers struck the rod, knocked it a few inches, and he found it again. In a single swipe he raised the rod, knocked the Romulan along the side of his face, drove him away, and pointed the sharp end of the rod.

"You get away from me!" he shouted. "Stay away from me!"

Chapter Six

From across the ragged remains of their two crushed cells, Zevon pressed a hand to his face where Stiles had struck him.

"I am not your enemy," he said. "I have no reason to hurt you. We'll both die if you hold me off like this for long."

"All Romulans are our enemies," Stiles blistered. "You just keep your distance!"

"But I freed you from the stone. I set your arm."

"To use me as some kind of hostage! I've been stupid enough for one day! I'm not being stupid again. You stay back. I'm getting out of here."

Zevon lowered his hand. His face showed a single bruised cheekbone, but no open wound. "We must help each other. The prisoners are the last ones they'll dig out. You can't possibly climb out of here, ensign. I doubt you can take a single step."

"I'll take all the steps I need." Stiles held the metal rod between them like a club or sword, ready to use it either way. His right shoulder and arm pumped fiercely now as he exerted himself, throbbing inside the splinted wrapping. Zevon had managed to splint the arm with the elbow bent instead of straight at Stiles's side, and that would prove an advantage as he tried to get out of this hole.

The nasty pit of broken rock wall and plaster sheets and plumbing spun around him suddenly, jagged edges and smooth sheets blending into a single blue-gray cylinder.

"Lie down," Zevon suggested, "before you pass out."

"I don't listen to Romulans!"

His chest heaving with effort, Stiles let his body rest slightly on the edge of a folded bolt of linoleum flooring. He had no idea where the flooring had come from—there had been nothing like this in the holding area. Probably from one of the floors above. How many stories had collapsed on them? Since he had never seen the building from the outside, he had no way of knowing.

Thinking of something else, he looked at his right arm. One irregularly cut sheet of linoleum had been formed around his lower arm and another around the upper arm, held in place by strips of wool. A single wedge of metal slat, some kind of corner brace, had also been strapped there, and was holding his arm in a bent position. By resting the arm on his lap, he could relieve the strain in his shoulder.

"We'll just wait," he gasped. "Somebody'll come to rescue us. They'll come for us . . . they'll get here."

"Ensign Stiles," Zevon attempted slowly, "we are prisoners. There's been a Constrictor, a bad one. The Pojjana will be cleaning up for months. They'll be digging the survivors and bodies out for at least two weeks. Two of your weeks, I should specify. While we may live that long, certainly you can't hold that rod against me for so long. Is there a point in holding it now?"

"There is," Stiles forced through a tight throat. "You're a Romulan. I'm Starfleet. I don't have to believe a thing you say. Maybe this wasn't an earthquake at all. Maybe you bombed the building, you or your people. The Pojjans could dig us out in an hour."

"And so a standoff begins?" Zevon folded his arms, shook his head, and offered a parental gaze. "You make yourself suffer for nothing. I am no soldier."

"I know what you are." His hand and arm shuddering under the weight of the metal bar, Stiles drew his legs up under him and tried to maneuver to a better position. The effort exhausted him, made his head spin. A dark tunnel formed on either side of his vision and he realized he was passing out. With a single heave he rearranged himself. Fighting a sudden clutching muscle spasm in his back, he twisted sideways and managed to shift until he could lean back against the tilted mattress on the bunk he had never yet slept upon.

Sleep . . . sounded so nice right now . . . deliberately he drew long, steady breaths until his head cleared and the tunnel-vision faded back. "We'll starve in here, like this."

Zevon nodded. Had he just said something like that? Stiles thought the conversation sounded familiar.

"I hear water," the Romulan said. "If we have water, we can survive."

"Yeah? How long's a week on your planet?" Stiles blinked to focus his eyes. He saw his bandaged left arm shiver as it held the metal rod toward Zevon. One arm bandaged, the other broken and splinted.

Tightening his folded arms, Zevon leaned back against the cracked wall behind him. "I'm counting in your weeks. I know how humans think."

Stiles raised his head from where he had allowed it to rest back on the upright mattress. "Oh? And how is that? Just how do we think? Since you know us so well, you who've never met one of us before, how do humans all think? For your information, soldier, humans are the least like each other of all the races around. That's what my grandfather told me, and he got it from nobody less than Captain James Kirk himself. So you just tell me again how all humans think."

"I meant no insult."

"Stay away from me."

Zevon held up a peaceable hand and nodded. "You must pull the blanket back over yourself. You'll go into shock again if you fail to stay warm."

"I'll take care of myself, thanks." Trying to appear in control, Stiles held the rod higher between himself and the Romulan, doing his best to convey an ongoing threat. "Spock expects me to act right . . . get along here and . . . be an officer. I won't let him down. Somehow he'll know how I did. I've got to make him proud. . . ."

Tilting his head, Zevon asked, "The ambassador? Is that who you were evacuating?"

"Sure was. Did it, too. He's out and you can't have him."

"We don't want him, ensign. Please try to relax and put that—"

"Don't you tell me to relax! Don't you say that word to me! That isn't your word."

"Very well . . . I'll find another word . . . with whom did you have a date tomorrow night?"

"Huh?" Stiles narrowed his eyes. Was this man telepathic? "How'd you know . . . her name's Ninetta. Ninetta Rashayd. She works down in atmospheric control at the starbase. Y'know, the base life support. Air. Took me two weeks to pronounce her name right so she wouldn't give me that look when I asked her out. Not that it matters much now. . . ."

"What kind of look?"

"Well . . . *that* look. The one that tells you to keep your mouth shut and don't even ask." His quivering left arm sagged a little, the rod now resting on his knee. "Travis used to rib me about it. Jeremy used to imitate the look. He was really good at it . . . really funny. I wonder if they're really dead. . . ."

"I beg your pardon?"

"I shouldn't have yelled at them," Stiles murmured, scouring the recent past, smelling his mistakes. "They were doing everything I said to do . . .

they were with me. And I gave them hell because I couldn't take a little ribbing."

"Hardly matters now. Please put the blanket back on yourself. Your face is going pale—"

"What did you say made this Constrictor thing happen? Did you tell me? If you did, I forgot it all."

"Graviton waves," Zevon patiently explained. Clearing a place for himself, he sat down on something Stiles couldn't see. "They originate in space and bathe the planet. A recurring disaster for the Pojjana. As unpredictable as lightning-lit wildfires. When the waves strike the planet, everything suddenly gets two, three, or even five hundred percent heavier. What you felt was the pressure of yourself suddenly weighing several hundred pounds. Blood trying to slog through compressed veins, muscles screaming for relief. . . ."

"I remember that part."

"The Constrictor causes massive shifts in tectonic plates, tidal waves, earthquakes, as you call them. Buildings collapse, air vehicles crash . . . some people suffocate if it lasts more than a few seconds . . . elderly people are crushed to death by their own weight. . . ." Waving his hand at their surroundings, Zevon glanced up into the cylindrical pit that trapped them. "Sinkholes and fissures open up under people while they're pinned helplessly to the ground. . . ."

The rod sagged a little more, finally resting against Stiles's leg with his limp hand upon the close end. He gazed at Zevon, listening to the ghastly narrative just as he had listened all his life to the stories of trial and triumph with Captain Kirk and Mr. Spock at the helm of their legendary starship. This story, though, had a glaze of the horrific. It was real. He'd just been through it.

How many other people out there were suffering? What had happened to those rioters in the courtyard? The people in the other embassies lining that brick area?

"How long's this been going on?"

"Nine years," Zevon said. "The first Constrictor wiped out a fifth of the planet's population. Nearly a billion people died."

"A *billion?*" The word pulsed in Stiles' head, cooling down the throbbing of his arm and back. How many million was a billion? Why couldn't he do the mathematics? He was a pilot . . . he could multiply figures . . . do the trigonometry for atmospheric . . . for . . . landing. . . .

A *billion.* The number grew and grew, pressing him down beneath the utter oppression of its swelling. If so many could die, he could endure some discomfort. A broken arm abruptly seemed surmountable, his moans and winces petty.

"Yes," Zevon said. "At first I could scarcely absorb such a number. Now I can put a face to each one."

"Why would you care so much about this Constrictor thing?" Stiles asked.

But Zevon did not answer that. "Half the buildings were destroyed," he continued instead. "Countless trillions of tons of planetary material suddenly heavier for a few critical, deadly moments . . . even the most stoic among us was disturbed to his core. The people of the planet worked valiantly to rebuild. Then it came again, and we knew it was a recurring phenomenon. After the second time, they gave up rebuilding and concentrated on structural shoring of the buildings and bridges which had been strong enough to survive the first two. They've constructed pressure-tolerant housing and connected buildings so the structures could hold each other up . . . I could liken this to a meltdown in a nuclear plant. Now the Pojjana hate all aliens, who brought this thing upon them. If they could put the aliens off the planet, perhaps the Constrictor would go with them. They've scrubbed their planet clean of all who were not native, and still the blight from space has struck on. It will continue to strike, and they will continue to hate you and me and all aliens for what we have done to them. Periodically the Constrictor will send out a roaring burp of radiation into subspace, which causes waves of gravitons. There is no turning it off . . . it will go on indefinitely now. Our meager lifetimes will never see the end of it."

Something in the Romulan's voice, something in his bearing and the set of his shoulders caught Stiles with an unexpected wave of empathy. Zevon's arms were still folded, as if to protect himself, and he gazed not at Stiles but at a nearby pile of russet tiles that no longer resembled a floor. He seemed resigned to the facts, but troubled by hearing them so clinically reviewed in his own voice.

Again, with a different tone, Stiles raised the question that his clearing mind insisted needed asking.

"How do you know so much about this?"

In a clear silence that now fell, moisture dripped from an unseen pipe, draping its solemn percussion on Stiles's question and Zevon's answer.

"I caused it."

"Nobody told me the Romulan Empire was at war with these people!"

At such a declaration, the walls crackled and vibrated, pebbles shivered down the tilted slabs into the sinkhole that had trapped the two unfortunate prisoners.

Across the well, the young Romulan's brows rose at Eric Stiles's abrupt statement. "War? Oh . . . no, no, there is no war. This was . . . utterly unintentional."

Curbing a lifetime of parochialism for the moment, Stiles reined in his assumptions. "Well . . . what happened, then?"

"This sector is run by the Bal Quonnot, on another planet in this system. They allowed us to conduct quantum-warp experiments here."

"Us? The . . . Romulan Empire?"

"Yes."

"You?"

"Yes. The Pojjana have been struggling for identity amid the Bal Quonnot administration. The Pojjana did not want to deal with the Empire."

"I don't think I'd deal with you either," Stiles said. "If you caused this thing."

Zevon actually nodded, perhaps in agreement, but certainly in understanding. "The Pojjana let the Federation court them for membership, to see if an alien science could retract what another alien science had done to them. The Federation went so far as to establish a planetary outpost."

"How many of these things have happened?"

"Six, now. In nine years. Not in predictable intervals. The Pojjana led the Federation along, but avoided committing to membership, hoping you would help. They wanted the benefits but not the obligations."

"It's happened before," Stiles confirmed. "I've heard of planetary governments trying to get the best of both worlds, refusing to make the decision but still accepting Federation protection and help."

"The Federation is disappointed," Zevon went on. "To your credit, you practice what you preach. The sector is red now."

Stiles paused to fill his lungs with a full breath. His shoulders squeezed in a muscle spasm, and he closed his eyes briefly. "That's what Spock said . . . red sector. I don't know what it means. . . ."

"It means many things. Many banishments, many edicts, many restrictions."

Stiles cleared his throat, and the effort made his ribs ache. "How do you know so much about . . . stuff I'm supposed to know?"

"All Imperial royal family members are well-schooled in astral politics."

Raising his head sharply, Stiles blurted, "Royal family!"

"Yes."

He stared, but Zevon did not meet his eyes. "How close . . . how high . . ."

"The Emperor is my mother's brother. I am fourteenth in line for the throne."

"Is that . . . close?"

"In a population of two hundred billion inhabiting ninety planets, it is considered very close. However, it's unlikely that I shall ever actually take the throne. Certainly I have no desire to take it."

A cold rock formed in Stiles's chest as he digested the fact that he was involved in something with far more depth than he had first imagined. What moments ago had been two minor players in somebody else's huge drama now became something entirely different.

"How did they capture you?" he asked. "If you're so . . . royal."

"I made the error of accompanying a landing party to take measurements of—not that it matters. I forgot I'd been declared a public enemy. There were bounty hunters. They turned me over to the government. That riot out there . . . it was sparked by my presence here in the city."

"And the government is holding you here? Sounds like they wanted the riots to spark. Why else would they keep you here?"

With a nod, Zevon congratulated him. "Very possibly. This is not a usual holding area for political prisoners. They're usually held in the mountains."

"So we're hostages?"

"Certainly we carry some incendiary value for leverage," Zevon contemplated, "but neither the Empire nor the Federation can cavalierly enter a sector declared red by any major power. That is one of the few agreements between the Federation, the Empire, the Klingons, Orions, Centaurans, and others that has in fact stood the test of time and trouble. Compromise of that is considered irremediable. Relations, friendly or strained, would change instantly. The Pojjana may hope to tempt all that, but . . ." The young Romulan shook his head, a gesture of clear understanding of the situation. "You and I . . . we are on our own here for some time, I should think."

"Alone," Stiles echoed, "on a planet full of people who hate everybody who isn't them."

Shift the legs again. He forced himself to adjust. His shoulders seemed like water now. In his hand the metal rod was like ice and suddenly heavy. His elbow quivered as he tried to continue holding the rod up.

"You're a captain?" he asked, fighting for concentration.

"Centurion. I have . . . I had command of a science vessel. My command was a royal favor. It's common to give lower royalty command of royal barges. I thought myself very lucky not to be carting one of my own relatives about in a barge. I always remained aware that I hadn't earned command. I ceded most ship responsibility to my subcommander. The crew understood . . . they never spoke ill of me. What I earned was status as a fully qualified astrophysicist. I was supervising the unit conducting quantum-warp experiments that set up a sympathetic subspace vibration of free-floating gravitons. Now the Constrictor breaks on the shores of the Pojjan planet. And no one will ever stop it."

Zevon dropped his gaze to the messy excuse for a floor. He didn't look up anymore.

"I'm something of an embarrassment to my family," he went on, so quietly that Stiles could barely hear him. "I'm not . . ."

"A 'leader of men'?" Stiles supplied.

As odd as it now seemed to see someone who looked like Zevon return a smile, the Romulan did in fact grin mildly. "Just to prove it, if you said that to any of my uncles or brothers, they would kill you just to prove differently."

Returning the grin, Stiles chuckled. "Call my mother a sow, but don't tell me I'm no leader of men?"

"Something like that."

As Stiles felt his small troubles shrink to inconsequence, he gazed at Zevon and absorbed what he had heard. A hundred questions—none good—crackled in his mind.

"Well, here we are then," Stiles groaned. "A senior duty ensign who finagled his way into command of a landing party because of a family connection with Ambassador Spock. Big me, I thought I could distinguish myself. You know what I see when I look up the ladder? Captain Stiles, Lieutenant Stiles, Lieutenant Commander Stiles, heroes of the Romulan wars, officers on starship service . . . and little Ensign Stiles, who died in the pit after botching a simple evac." He let his head drop back and gazed up, far up, to the patch of dim light at the top of the hole. "I wish I were Ensign Anybody Else."

"Surrounded by giants," Zevon offered. "No wonder you could barely see."

Registering only slightly the favor just done him, Stiles clung instead to the sorrow and shame. "So here I am," he trudged on, "trapped in a sinkhole with a Romulan duke who doesn't want the command he's got, and a collapsed building's about to come down on us. Aren't we pathetic? If you had any emotion, you'd probably cry."

Sharply Zevon kicked at a plank that lay between them, sending it clacking into another position. His eyes hardened. "I am not Vulcan," he snapped, and instantly looked away again.

The reaction was so sincere that Stiles almost reached out physically to yank back his words. "Sorry," he offered. "You can pretty much count on me to say the wrong thing. Look, if you were in the sector conducting experiments—everybody does that. Quantum warp . . . that's tricky business. There's nobody who knows everything about that. It's almost not even science. It's practically magic. If something went wrong, it's not your fault."

"It was my fault," Zevon insisted. He pressed a hand to his left thigh and seemed to hurt himself with his own touch. "I should've stood up to my superiors when I first saw what the result might be. The graviton impulses were too erratic. I knew that. I knew it before we started. I should never have condoned the switch-on. As senior scientist, I had the right to postpone."

"Why didn't you, then?"

"I was . . . timid. Yes, I was the senior authority, but only because of my bloodline. There were other scientists who were more qualified quantum specialists. They warned me . . . but I was afraid to fail."

So familiar. Why did everybody have to go through this? Just doing their jobs, and all this had to happen. Sitting here in the near-darkness, three levels below the street, cradled in wreckage and out of the line of sight of any judgmental forces, Eric Stiles released himself from the bondage of prying eyes and pointless opinions. How foolish did he have to be to keep holding this weapon on Zevon?

If only he could put it down.

With a cleansing sigh, he muttered, "Listen, I . . . I feel. . . ." In his left hand, the metal rod wobbled between them, stubbornly holding its position. "Do me a favor, will you? Come over and . . . hold this for me."

Across the wreckage, Zevon blinked, stood up stiffly, and moved toward him.

Stiles parted his lips and started to say something else, but in sudden punctuation of Zevon's dire prophesy, a loud crumbling noise erupted over their heads. Buried in a gray cloud burping from above, Zevon disappeared as several large chunks of building material and a gout of rubble shattered through the hole in the floors above them, chittering like a rockslide, and came sheeting down into their chamber. The rain of rock and pebbles hissed furiously and crashed in a million pieces onto the desk of their little area. Stiles threw his working arm over his face and bent to one side, but he couldn't move far enough to avoid being painted with dust and grit. The metal rod he had claimed as a weapon flew out of his hand and clanked somewhere in the dimness. Cold, stinging debris sheeted his body. The Pojjan guards had taken away his padded vest, gloves, and knee pads, leaving only his daywear uniform to fend off the sharp bits. He felt himself being cut in a hundred tiny places.

As soon as the sound faded, he shoved himself up on his left elbow and twisted around. "Zevon? Where are you?"

In response, he only heard the sound of Zevon coughing somewhere in the cloud of dust. Alive, at least.

Stiles pushed up on his elbow. "Are you okay?"

Out of the puff of stone dust, shimmering paint fragments and insulation, Zevon finally and slowly came to his feet. Rock bits sheeted off his back and shoulders as he stood and limped over the jagged wreckage to Stiles's side, where he braced himself on the thing Stiles was sitting upon.

"You okay?" Stiles asked again.

Zevon wiped dust from his face. "What is 'okay'?"

"You don't know? Something tells me you speak English, right?"

"Classroom English."

"Oh. I guess it got started with two alphabetical letters, O and K. It means . . . agreement. All right. Well. No idea why it would mean that."

"I see . . . yes, then, I am both O and K."

"But you're limping."

"A piece of this rod went through my thigh. I pulled it out."

"What? You got speared by a piece of that stuff?"

"Yes, when we first fell—"

"Come here! You could be bleeding to death! Let me see your leg."

Turning to show Stiles a crudely bandaged part of his thigh above the knee, Zevon winced and tolerated Stiles's tucking the strips of blanket which now bound each of them. "A few moments ago you were willing to spear me with a piece of this material."

"Well, never underestimate the capacity of Eric Stiles to make a dunderhead of himself. You're still bleeding here. That stuff's blood, isn't it? The green, uh—"

"Yes. I thought it had stopped."

"It hasn't. Let me—come a little closer. Your pant leg is soaked with blood. God . . . we gotta stop this. Pad the wound with something . . . just a minute."

As Zevon gripped a standing slab and winced, Stiles ripped apart the edge of the mattress near him and pulled out a wad of stuffing. He folded the stuffing into a crude pad, then worked it between the blanket strip and the wound on Zevon's leg, unfortunately causing considerable pain, until Zevon could barely stand when it was over.

"That'll help," Stiles hoped. "Come here. Take the weight off it. Sit here next to me."

He smoothed a place on his slab and pulled Zevon to his side. They sat leg to leg, facing each other, as Stiles adjusted the knot on Zevon's bandage. "It didn't pierce through your leg, did it? You could be bleeding in two places. I can't tell—"

"No," Zevon told him, his voice weak now. "No . . . a simple puncture . . ."

Stiles looked at him and paused. "You dragged yourself all the way from your cell to mine, through that wreckage, with your leg impaled like this?"

"I thought you would die if I didn't come." As pebbles continued to trickle around them, Zevon dug through the rubble to the blanket that had fallen off Stiles. Without meeting Stiles's eyes, he pressed the blanket back around the ensign's chest and hips and tucked it as well as possible. "We must keep you warm. You could still go into shock."

Surveying his companion, Stiles allowed himself to be cared for by these unlikely hands. "Don't take this wrong," he began a moment later, "but why would you care? We don't know each other. I could've been just a garden-variety criminal. Why would it matter so much to you if I died?"

For many moments Zevon was silent, though obviously troubled. He tucked and retucked the blanket two or three times before the ringing question demanded attention.

"Because the count is crushing me," he said.

Stiles frowned. "What count?"

Settling his hands in his lap, Zevon sat suddenly still. He sighed roughly, and his expression took on a shield of burden. His eyes crimped. He couldn't look at Stiles.

Again he sighed.

"Tyrants have made names for themselves by murdering a thousand people," he slowly said. "Ten thousand, a hundred thousand . . . a million. I have surpassed them all. There are no Hitlers, no Yum Nects, no Stalins or Li Quans who can compete with me. Among all the men and women of the galaxy, you have the privilege of sitting with someone who is utterly unique. You see, I'm the only person, anywhere, on any world, living or dead . . . who has killed a billion people."

As he sat on his rock, gazing at Zevon and hearing the echo of true burden, feeling as if he had known this man all his life, Eric Stiles grew up ten years in ten seconds. The urge to say something, to trowel away the grief with mere words, failed him entirely. There were no words for this. Not this.

Rather than flapping his gums as usual, he was completely disinclined to speak at all. Instead he shifted his good hand a few inches and gripped Zevon's forearm in a sustaining way, and did not shrink from the contact. Empathy flowed through the simple touch. The concept of billions of people dead at a single sweep overcame them both and seemed oddly tangible. For an instant or two, critical instants, Stiles totally comprehended the number.

Then, as all huge things do, the grasp of such volume fled and he was left only with the tremendous drumming regret that Zevon must have borne all these years. It wasn't the kind of thing that got better with time. Some things didn't.

There had to be another effort, a different one. One that looked forward for a change.

And that view was tricky for Eric Stiles, but for the first time in his life he didn't care what had happened in the past. For the first time, the future was everything.

With his hand still pressed to Zevon's arm, Stiles spoke quietly, firmly.

"I'm here now. This is where I am. Things are going to be different for both of us. We're getting out of here eventually, and when we do, everything's changing. You and I have both been dragged along by our situations like being caught in a river current or something. It's all we've been able to do just keeping our faces up out of the water all our lives. This . . . it's got to stop. We have to get our own grip on things."

Zevon gazed at him with all the fascination and confusion of a child looking into a kaleidoscope. "How can we?"

"By making sure that things are different because we're here." Stiles hitched himself up to a better position, still holding firmly to Zevon's arm. "When they pull us out of this hole, we're going to still be alive. Then we're going to go to work. We're gonna pay back the universe for all the goofs and gaffes we've made before. We're not going to think about escaping or fighting. This is our planet now. We have a lot to do before the next Constrictor hits."

Mystified, perhaps wondering if his companion were delirious, Zevon narrowed his eyes. "What?"

Heartened by his own words and by the new determination welling in his heart, Stiles willed his conscience into line and saw the future as a clear tunnel of purpose.

"I'll tell you what," he said. "We're going to save a billion people."

Chapter Seven

Four Years Later, Federation Standard Time

"ZEVON, I THINK WE'VE GOT something this time! Look at this!"

"If I'd had the right equipment, this could've been found months ago."

"It reads like a Richter scale! We're actually picking up spaceborne disruption. Watch this."

"But not focused. No way to tell if we have minutes or hours, or even days."

"But we know this time that it's coming. That's something!"

"There hasn't been a Constrictor in more than two years. We've predicted it twice before. The first time we predicted the Constrictor would come in three weeks. It came in three hours. The second time, nothing happened at all."

"But we learned from those mistakes!"

"They won't believe us, Eric."

"But this time we know!"

"They won't believe us."

The lab smelled of a burning circuit. Off to Stiles's right, in the corner, the tired dust collector clacked and whirred, creating a sense of action where in fact there was little.

His taxed back muscles shuddered as he sank back in his chair. "How can we convince them? What do you think we should do? It's not like we can threaten Orsova, and he's got the keys to all the telephones."

Beside him in the only other chair, Zevon seemed more troubled than vindicated by their good work today and the breakthrough they'd been waiting for, which now blinked before them on the overworked spectrometer, its flickering screen data reflected in the cold contents of their two soupbowls.

"You need to eat," Zevon said, his voice a rasp of fatigue and frustration.

Only now did Stiles realize that his partner was looking not at the glimmering jewels on the screen, but at the filmy soup.

Stiles pressed back and stretched his arms. "Four years of horse-drool soup. So I skip it once in a while. So what? *Limosh t'rui maloor.*"

Zevon looked at him. *"Telosh li cliah maheth."*

Stiles felt abruptly self-conscious and guilty about his appearance. He almost never looked in the mirror over the sink back in their cell anymore—he even trimmed his beard without looking. If he didn't look, he could convince himself from moment to moment that his cheeks were not so sunken beneath the scruffy yellow beard he'd allowed to grow there, his eyes not dull, he could imagine the fullness of youth and the sheen of health he had once possessed and not even noticed in those days. He could ignore the bruises on his temples and the black blotches under the sleeves of his sweater. At least they'd given him a sweater.

He'd stopped looking in mirrors a long time ago, right about when the beard had stopped helping him hide his deteriorating physical condition. All he could tell from the beard was that he was still blond and hadn't gone prematurely gray from the daily stress and struggle.

Over the past four years the Pojjana behavior had been frequently baffling, inconsistent, sometimes maddening, sometimes solicitous, as political temperatures surged or chilled. Things changed every few months—except for a couple of things. The most consistent parts of his life and Zevon's were this lab and the prison's assistant warden, who unfortunately did not have enough to do.

"They've let us come to the lab almost every day," he voiced, shifting from just thinking to also speaking his thoughts. "Why wouldn't they listen to what we find out?"

Weary, Zevon simply gazed at him, seeing something other than the problem of convincing the Pojjana that there might be a way to save lives from the Constrictor. Lately Zevon had had more trouble concentrating, and Stiles was worried. They needed this breakthrough, not just for the billion, but for the two of them. They needed sanity and purpose, some reason to rise above the endless sense of being broken down and dull as barbells. After four years, they needed a win.

Stiles shifted uneasily under Zevon's toil-worn gaze, knowing that the Romulan saw him clearly and hated the sight. A shaft of burning pain ran through Stiles's innards, but he battled to keep it out of his face. He knew Zevon didn't miss it, though. He wasn't fooling anybody.

"Stop watching me," he protested when he could speak again.

"You're in pain, aren't you?"

"No."

"You should eat. It always helps."

"It helps because it makes me throw up, and then I'm too weak to feel anything. Typical Romulan logic."

"Typical Eric defiance," Zevon muttered, his eyes deeply solicitous and sad.

For a moment they simply looked at each other. Eventually, in his mind Stiles stopped seeing his own demolished physical condition and started seeing Zevon's. Zevon had started out typically lean, as was natural for his genetics, but four years ago he'd been strong and well-nourished, with good muscle tone in his arms and shoulders and a glow of privilege in his face. Now his complexion was sallow and his arms were thin. His hair had lost its mahogany luster and had grown below his shoulders. He kept it out of his way by simply pushing it behind his ears. Being Vulcanoid ears, they did the job very well. He was less inclined to bother cutting his hair, though Stiles occasionally offered a trim when he was cutting his own. Strange—Stiles, so used to Starfleet spit-and-polish, had made a silly effort to cling to neatness during their four years as political prisoners, even trimming his nails and cuticles just to have something to do. He was the one who did their laundry and mended the rips in their clothing.

He would've expected the same, even more, from a prince of the Romulan royal line, but Zevon didn't really care what he looked like. His long-suffering uniform, stained and tired, would've dissolved from his shoulders if Stiles hadn't bothered keeping the seams stitched. The only echo of civilization offered them here was their privilege to use the lab, and the fact that every couple of days they got showers. The Pojjana hadn't built a new jail. They'd just pushed the old one back up from the pit and nailed it together. A concrete floor now replaced the tiled one Stiles had first seen when he'd been thrown in here. Generally speaking, though, the food stunk, the quarters were dank, the mattresses sagged, the floor was cold, and the light was bad. Otherwise, home sweet home.

"I wish I had a communicator," Stiles mentioned. "Just one, and I could broadcast this new information to the whole planet. *Somebody'd* listen." Shifting his weakened legs, he added, "I don't miss home very often, but at moments like this I do."

Zevon rubbed his chilly hands. "The silence from home is an old story now. The royal family must not know I'm here, or they would have come by now. They must think me dead. The Pojjana must not be communicating with the Romulan government, or word of my presence would filter out."

"The Pojjana aren't about to tell the empire you're here. You're their trump card. Why should they stir up trouble? And if it comes, they want you here as leverage."

Uneasy with this line of talk, Zevon grew irritable. "My people would come if they knew. We've discussed this enough before."

"Well, mine wouldn't," Stiles concluded. "Obviously. Because they sure as hell know I'm here."

"The Federation declared the sector red, so they have to observe it or they can't expect anyone else to. It has nothing to do with you personally, Eric. Ambassador Spock would've had you out of here if influence mattered."

"If they made it away from the planet alive. They could all be cosmic dust for all we know."

Zevon turned to him. "Eric, you must cling to better hopes. I've had to watch you deteriorate physically, it's taken its toll on us both, but I refuse to watch your hopes turn to dust. Spock expects you to behave like an officer and a gentlemen. I expect that also."

Stiles grinned. "Talk, talk." He gestured at the vibrations playing out on the data screen. "Look at that . . . here we sit with information that could save the billion, and we can't figure out how to get the word to anybody farther up than Orsova. He'll eat it, probably choke, then hit me."

"He is a victim of alien backlash. The Pojjana no longer know whom to trust. You and I are convenient representatives of all the trouble brought down upon these people by the Constrictor. If they knew it was I personally who had—"

Defying the numbness in his legs and shoulders, Stiles launched forward and grasped Zevon's arm. "Quiet! Shut up. Don't take chances."

Zevon's gaze fell. "I wish, now and then, just to tell them and be done with it. I deserve whatever they do."

"You keep your alien mouth shut. You want to risk these plush surroundings? If they knew, they might put us someplace . . . oh . . . tacky."

Now Zevon looked up, and his expression tightened. "We have to risk a change, Eric. You can't stay here much longer. You can't stay on this planet, much less in this prison complex—"

He was interrupted by the sharp clack of the lab door lock. They both tensed visibly, though Stiles was too weak to do much more than uncross his legs.

"Uh-oh—"

Assistant Warden Orsova came in first, as he always did. He was a typical Pojjana northern-hemisphere male, built like a brick, a head shorter than Stiles or Zevon, but nearly as wide. His coppery complexion shimmered in the lab light. His eyes were black as the drawer knobs around the lab. Following him was one of the guards of the lower ranks, with an infantry symbol emblazoned on his uniform front and the colors of an unfamiliar unit.

"Hello, you men." Orsova slurred the words as he drawled his way through his own language.

He was drunk. They recognized the signs. Orsova held his liquor well, but there was a certain lingering odor, and his behavior would change, submerged anger bubbling behind his eyes. On days like this, his frustrations and boredom fluttered to the surface, and he would eventually come to act on them.

The soldier, though, seemed perfectly sober. His dark eyes glowed with anticipation, and his fists were clenched.

Orsova looked at Stiles and Zevon. "What are you doing today?"

Fighting his nerves, Stiles fiddled with the spectrometer, making sure not to do anything by mistake that could wipe out their newfound readings. "Just sitting here making up my mind that zebras are white with black stripes instead of the other way around."

"Get up," Orsova ordered.

Suddenly icy, Zevon turned to the clutter of equipment on the lab table. "We have twenty more minutes."

"Not you, ears," Orsova corrected, and looked at Stiles. "Just him."

Stiles chuckled and shook his head. "Orsova, your timing smells to Tarkus. So does your breath, by the way."

"Get up."

"He can't get up," Zevon protested, but too quietly.

Orsova buried his wide hands in Stiles's collar and dragged him to his feet. Holding Stiles with one hand, he held the other hand out to the soldier. "Pay."

Grinding his teeth, the soldier dug into his thigh pouch and came up with several of the thin minted chips the Pojjana used as a medium of exchange and piled them into Orsova's hand.

Without ceremony Orsova handed Stiles over to the soldier, who by now was fairly gasping with the thrill.

Zevon said nothing, did nothing as the soldier hauled Stiles to the middle of the floor, reeled back his muttonlike arm, and backhanded Stiles across the jaw. Lacking the strength to counter the sheer force, Stiles whirled into the far wall. As he slid down, a streak of blood smeared the dirty plaster.

As he landed on his knees, Stiles pressed the back of his hand to his cut lip and hoped the blood would clot. He didn't want to die of a slap. That'd be so stupid.

He turned and slipped farther down, but looked up as Orsova's barn-wide shoulders blocked the bare light from the ceiling. "Picked a weakling this time," he choked. "No loose teeth."

"He'll try again," Orsova said.

"Sure. I can't feel much these days anyway."

Beyond the soldier's balled fists, Stiles could see Zevon seated at the lab table, both hands pressed to the edge of the table. As the soldier's fist plunged into Stiles's gut and the familiar lights of agony flashed, Stiles let his mind go blank. That little trick was getting easier as the months and years drained away the defiance Zevon somehow still saw in him. He was glad he was on his knees already, for he could never have stayed on his feet and he didn't want to be seen falling again. His lungs cried for air. If Orsova's soldier hadn't been holding him by the collar again, he'd be on the deck, shriveled up like a jellyfish.

"You aren't afraid anymore," Orsova commented from over there.

Stiles blinked at him, still seeing only the flash and pop of pain's decorations. "Well, what's another pound to an elephant? So you hire me out again. So what? One of these days you ought to beat me up yourself instead of auctioning me off. Or can't you handle it?"

Furious, the soldier heaved his victim to his feet, then rammed his thick elbow into Stiles's ribs and flung him into the wall again. Stiles tried to go limp, but this particular soldier didn't fall for the trick. Some did, but this guy knew to drive the air out of his plaything's body before flinging him, assuring that Stiles was tense as he struck the wall. Worked.

Shuddering, helpless, Stiles writhed like an unlicked cub on the cold cement. His own moans rattled from his throat, but he had no connection to them nor any control, and was blinded by the lights popping behind his eyes, so familiar he'd started to name them. He was up to Louise when they began finally to fizzle and he blinked back to the apparition of Orsova's left boot near his nose, as the big warden pulled the rabid soldier off and held him to one side.

"Let me finish him!" the soldier bellowed. "He's an alien! There's no other alien anywhere!"

"No," Orsova flatly refused.

"Then let me kill the Romulan!"

"No."

"You dumb drunken mule," Stiles struggled. "You're blowing a—chance to—save half the planet. We've found a way to—predict the Constrictor. Pound me all you want—but get a message to the—authorities. We've finally—done it!"

"Done it," Orsova echoed. "You know we're tired of keeping you. There's talk of just executing you."

"Fine," Stiles grunted. "Execute me. But bury me deep. I don't want to come heaving up when the big one hits."

Orsova's reddened eyes turned hard. "There hasn't been a Constrictor in two years. Maybe it won't come again. Why should we feed and keep aliens here, and give you a lab and let you work, after what you gave to us?"

"It wasn't him," Zevon said without turning. "It was—"

"Shut up, Romulan," Stiles barked from the floor. "I don't need your—pointy help."

"And it will come again," Zevon persisted, looking now at Orsova. "Like seismic activity, it doesn't go away. It builds up to something worse. The two of us have used our time learning to read the spaceborne graviton pulses—"

"You two aren't as much fun as you used to be." Orsova cast a furious glance at Zevon and added, "I know the game. Pretending."

Stiles wiped blood from his mouth with a shaking hand. "Not—pretending. We just don't—give a damn anymore. You've had two—two years of good crops . . . that haven't been squooshed . . . two years of—"

"I paid you!" the soldier roared, shoving at Orsova's arm.

Orsova held him back. "Less and less reason to let enemies work on our equipment," he said to Stiles. "We should put you on trial and execute you now. It isn't enough that we stop taking care of you when you're sick."

Might as well talk to the wall.

"Take the message," Stiles attempted one more time. "There's another Constrictor coming. The planet . . . can get ready. Save the billion—"

The effort of speaking coiled Stiles into a knot and apparently gave Orsova the idea that this was the best satisfaction he would get today.

"I paid!" the soldier shouted.

"You paid to beat an alien," Orsova said, "not to kill one. Go out now. Go."

Orsova yanked the door open and shoved the soldier out, then left the lab and shut the door behind him.

That was the paradigm of their life—Orsova sold opportunities to beat up the human alien, while he got his own jollies from watching the effects on the Romulan alien.

Zevon watched the frosted glass door, saw something that held him in his place—Stiles couldn't see the door from where he lay, but knew to simply lie gasping and wait. Ultimately a shuffle in the corridor spared him, and Zevon broke from the table and rushed to his side.

"Curses," Stiles wheezed, "foiled again."

"Eric . . ." Zevon sorrowfully turned him enough to raise him to a nearly sitting position and held him there. Stiles could never have held himself, but would simply have slumped back into a supine position and probably suffocated on the deck. "Look at you. . . ."

"What a way to—live—aw, God—I hate that son of a bitch. . . ."

"Orsova is a walking symptom. He lost his children in the last Constrictor. Now he tortures us to ease his bitterness. The soldiers he brings here . . . they're the same."

Zevon got to one knee, then hoisted Stiles up and deposited him on the only cot in the lab. The Romulan's face was creased with misery, overlaid by a firm mask of bottled rage.

"Hey," Stiles gasped. "Your emotions are showing."

"I keep telling you—I am *not* Vulcan." Zevon angrily snatched a beaker of purified water from a shelf, soaked a rag, and pressed the cool compress to Stiles's bleeding lip.

"We'll never convince him to let us talk to the chief warden or anybody," Stiles murmured. "How can we convince them that this is their chance?"

"We're not that certain of our readings," Zevon reminded. "The prediction might be off by months. Stop moving."

"I'm not moving . . . I'm writhing in agony."

"Exercise some self-control."

"But *you're* not a Vulcan."

Obviously troubled, Zevon frowned. "All we know is that another Constrictor, a very strong one, has been building for two years and will certainly strike. The phenomenon hasn't gone away at all."

"But we *know,* Zevon, that's something. Help me—"

With Zevon's help, Stiles jerkily shifted onto his side as his aching ribs and stomach muscles cramped again. His eyes clutched shut as he bore through the spasm, feeling worse for Zevon than himself. Zevon could do nothing more than grasp him and wait until the torment worked its way out. Stiles paced himself, breathing chunkily, until he could finally count through ten long breaths and his face and hands stopped involuntarily flinching.

"Orsova and his kind," he began when he could speak again, "they think we're just stalling to avoid execution . . . we've got to convince them somehow. Or go over them to the consul general."

"They will be convinced when the Constrictor comes."

"And we can laugh in their faces, if Orsova or some other anti-alienite doesn't find a way to kill us first."

Zevon sat down on the cot beside him and gazed at the dirty floor. "I can hardly blame them. A billion people dead . . . what would we do to anyone who caused that on our planets?"

"If we can predict the Constrictors," Stiles muttered, "then it's only a matter of time before we can reduce the effects."

"A thousand years of time, perhaps, between those two miracles."

"But if we can just predict them, then planes can be landed, people can put on compression suits, get into reinforced buildings, put the babies and old people in antigrav chambers—you know how to build those. Why won't they listen?"

"I don't know."

Stiles managed a sustaining sigh, let the lungful of oxygen flow through him and clear his head a little more. When he could relax a little more, he gazed at Zevon. "You think I can't feel what's happening to me? I know how sick I am. My muscles are deteriorating. I can feel my innards slowly dissolving. When Orsova's customers kick me now, it doesn't heal anymore. I won't survive the Constrictor when it comes. You don't have to pretend. Even without the Constrictor I don't have that long. Orsova'll have me beaten up once too often, or I'll fall down and my heart'll collapse . . . I can't have more than a few more weeks."

"If I hadn't caused the Constrictor, you would be somewhere else today. Probably a lieutenant." His sharp features creasing, Zevon pressed the heels of his hands into his thighs as if the mental torture caused him some physical pressure too. Several seconds passed before he could finally say, "Now my great mistake has killed my only friend."

Stiles gazed at him, feeling supremely wise. The inner peace would've knocked him over like phaser stun if he'd been standing. He was completely content, as if lying in a hammock under a bower of autumn leaves. Zevon's grief actually amused him, and he smiled.

"Jesus, do you do Irish tragedies too?" he chided. "Zevon of the Sorrows . . . Listen, clown, you gave me four extra years. My own mistake killed me that night, the night we met. I was in the hole. I died there. You crawled through the wall and gave me four years I wasn't gonna get."

Irritated by the compliment, Zevon shook his head. "You wouldn't have been here at all—"

"Yeah, well, flog yourself again. Gimme that broom over there to hit you with. If I could get up, I'd beat your ass blue."

"It's already green."

Stiles laughed, despite the fact that his midsection had cramped again. He stiffened and moaned, but then he laughed again. Zevon smiled as he stuffed a rolled lab apron under Stiles's head. For a moment they retired into peaceable silence. Over the years, they had learned to be silent together. In fact, they seldom talked like this anymore. Seldom needed to.

They knew each other so well, and what a great feeling it was to be silent, silent together.

The lab seemed quiet, but now as they sat together Stiles focused on the chitter of the computer as it doggedly worked on the last problem fed into it, the burble of chemical processors trying to separate molecules for identification of spaceborne particles brought to them by the Pojjana Air Patrols, and the plink of the faucet in the sink dripping. Plink . . . plink . . . plink. . . .

Nice sound.

He dared to draw a longer breath, which forced him to cough convulsively. When that cleared, he wiped spittle from his beard and tried to relax.

"I was pointless back in Starfleet," he wandered on. Why did he feel like talking? Oh, well. "There were a thousand of me. Ensigns by the carton. Probably most of 'em officers by now. Wouldn't have happened to me . . . botched the mission like I did . . . might as well be here, distracting somebody like Orsova. I mean, if he wasn't hitting me he'd just be . . . hitting you."

"Quiet."

"After I die, you go on without me. Don't you quit. You don't need me. Don't let Orsova slow you down. If you can predict the Constrictor within days, you can save thousands. Within hours, you can save millions. If you can get the Pojjana to listen, they can save ten million this time, maybe a half billion the next—"

"Without you, I have no wish to keep working."

"You don't need me." Stiles raised his head and grasped Zevon's arm with a ferocity of strength he didn't think he still had. "I've never been anything much more than raw material anyway. Starfleet tried to whip me into something worth having, and I thought they'd succeeded, but twenty-one-year-olds never think they're young. They'll go out and hoe a row of stumps before they realize they forgot to bring seed. That was me . . . was it ever me."

"Eric," Zevon pointlessly admonished, but had nothing new to say about that.

"You think you can do it, right? Whether I'm here or not, you can do it, right?"

"I can improve the predictions . . . if this first one is accurate within days, I can learn to fine-tune it. Bring it to hours. After the first one, I'll know how. If they let me continue—"

"They'll let you. You'll convince them. Don't you stop trying, right? If you stop trying, I'll be dead for nothing. I don't mind being dead, but dead for nothing stinks."

Inexpressibly disturbed, Zevon nodded. "I promise, Eric."

Scarcely were the prophetic words out than the door suddenly rattled and both men flinched—they hadn't even noticed the sound of footsteps in the hall. Abruptly aware of the great serviceability of silence and how much they sacrificed if they talked too long, Stiles willed himself to a sitting position and shifted until his legs hung over the end of the cot and Zevon was sitting almost beside him. They didn't stand. That would've been taken as threatening. They'd learned that too, a long time ago, the hard way.

Orsova rolled in, a little less drunk than before, his bulky guard uniform somewhat askew and a bundle under his arm.

Desperate at the prospect of two beatings in a single day, Zevon bolted to his feet between the big Pojjana and Stiles, standing out of the way of Stiles's grasping hand. "Leave him alone! If you want me to beg, Orsova, this time I will."

But the big assistant warden skewed a glance at him, then said, "I didn't come to beat him. I came to give him clean clothes."

The astounding claim literally drove Zevon back a step, enough that Stiles could get a grip on his arm.

"Why?" Stiles asked.

Orsova dumped the bundle of clothing onto Stiles's lap. "Because a deal's been made. They're coming to get you. You're going home."

"Starfleet's coming?"

"Somebody is," Orsova confirmed without commitment. "The orders to free you come all the way from Consul Bellinorn, and he hates everybody."

At the name of the chief provincial judiciary consul, Stiles felt the air fly from his lungs. "We're . . . we're going home?"

Orsova shrugged. "Just you."

"What? What about Zevon!"

"He's Romulan."

Stiles used his grip on Zevon to yank himself up despite the protests of his body and rage gave him the strength to be there. "You're kidding! I'm not going without him!"

"Yes."

"No! You're doing this on purpose!"

"Stop, Eric." Zevon pulled him back.

Orsova blinked his reddened eyes, peered with something like sentimental regret at the bundle of clothing, shrugged again, and simply left the room, bothering to clunk the door shut behind him, as if to give them a few final minutes alone. Courtesy? Since when?

Shuddering like an old man, Stiles stood beside Zevon, and the two of them stared at the door. They couldn't look at each other. Not yet.

"He's lying," Stiles rasped. "He's tricking us for some reason . . . he wants something. That's got to be it, Zevon. He's telling lies. This is Red Sector. Starfleet wouldn't come in here. It's a lie."

"Perhaps something has changed," Zevon suggested reasonably. "If the sector has been declared green, how would we know it, here in prison?"

"We'd hear about it . . . somebody would say something. We'd hear rumors."

Slowly shaking his head, Zevon stood with his arms at his sides and common sense on him like a cloak. "No, Eric. No."

"We'd hear about it. . . ."

"No."

Barely aware of where his legs were, Stiles sank back onto the cot. The metal frame squawked under his weight and the sound nearly knocked him unconscious. His head drummed, hearing the squawk again and again. Before him, Zevon's legs seemed to be surrounded by a slowly closing tunnel.

After a moment, Zevon came to sit beside him. Together they stared at the lab, still not looking at each other. Their world, this lab, this prison, this planet, turned inside out for them both in the next ten seconds. Suddenly everything was changed, heaving as if in some kind of earthquake, and for a ridiculous moment there seemed to be a Constrictor holding them both to this cot, to this floor, to the bedrock beneath the building.

Who was coming? If the Sector had turned green, they probably would've heard about it, and there hadn't been a whisper. Not a thing had changed, not a flicker of instability—nothing. Who was strong enough to come through Red Sector after Eric Stiles?

"It must be the ambassador," Zevon said, as if reading Stiles's mind. "He must finally have found a way to bring you out."

"I don't care if God Himself is coming," Stiles uttered. The words gagged in his throat. "I don't want to go."

"You must go," Zevon told him firmly.

"I don't *have* to go. Nobody can make me . . . I won't go. Not even for Ambassador Spock . . . no, not even for him. Everything I've done, I did so he'd be proud of me. If I go back, everything'll fall apart. If I die here, he can be proud of me. I'll be lost in the line of duty. If I'm alive, I'm headed back to disgrace. Court-martial. Home to humiliation. Zero purpose . . . complete uselessness. I cheated my dopey destiny for four years. Now I'm twenty-five and dying, about to be crushed in name as well as in body . . . and you and I . . . Zevon . . . we'll never see each other again. I don't want to go. I'm not going."

Without really turning to face him, Zevon glanced down at his side, at his own arm pressing against Stiles's, and he moved enough to clasp Stiles's hand. Still, they did not look at each other.

"You must go," Zevon told him firmly. "They can save you. The Federation will cure you. You will go."

Despite the physical abuse, the sickness, the deterioration, the pain, Stiles found himself looking fondly back upon the years of working side by side with Zevon, at first concentrating on keeping each other alive, later on the goal of deciphering the erratic Constrictor pattern. Their discoveries—that there was no pattern, but that waves did build before a Constrictor and could be measured . . . the possibility of predicting the disasters before they hit . . .

"Y'know, I didn't mind the pain or the beatings, or anything," he said. "I didn't mind the chance to stay here and do what I perceived as my duty. It's better for me to die here than go back and die humiliated. You understand, you're Romulan—it's better for my family to believe that I died in battle."

"That is often best," Zevon conditionally agreed, "but not always. Not this time."

He squeezed Stiles's hand, careful of his own strength and the possibility of actually crushing the weakened muscles and the thready bones.

Stiles gazed at their clasped hands, and sucked each breath as if it were his last.

"You're the only friend I've got," he uttered. "I'm dying and they're taking me away from my only friend."

"They'll cure you. You'll live."

"I don't want to live humiliated. I want to die here. At least I died trying, instead of going back disgraced and a failure, court-martialed—"

"No, Eric. You must go."

"Why? Why do I have to go? I'd rather die here."

"You must go for the billion."

"Huh?"

"You forget, as usual, that others are involved who are not looking at you or judging you."

"Who?"

"The billion we can save."

"You son of a bitch . . . don't do this to me."

"And me, Eric. You'll save me too."

For the first time, the idea of going home seemed less prickly. "How?" he demanded.

In a measured tone, Zevon explained, "If you go back and they cure you, you can get word to the Romulan Empire that I am here, that I'm alive. The royal family will have no choice but to breach Red Sector and get me out. My people don't think I'm alive, or they would have come already. They can find resources to make a deflection system. Look what I'm working with—ancient trash, chips and coils and conductors, a spectrograph the age of my mother, and still we've found a way to predict. Look at those copper wires! On my ship, I had more facilities in my cabin than we have here. Mathematics based on assumptions of certain things happening at the same time—think what I could do with real technology!"

Zevon paused, seemed to dream briefly, then leaned back until he could rest against the wall. He had to tip his head forward a little to avoid scuffing the points of his ears against the wall when he turned his head to glance at Stiles.

"I am still royal family, Eric. If they know I'm here, they'll get me out. They'll negotiate, they'll threaten, but they'll gain my freedom. And I will come back—I'll wring cooperation out of my people for what we've done here. The Pojjana will finally believe, when I come back with resources. I know what can be done. You must go out of Red Sector, Eric. Go out and get cured, and tell my people. And they will come. This is the greatest favor you can do, of all the good you have done here."

Stiles blinked, surprised. "Me? What'd I do? I'm barely an assistant. Don't treat me like that."

"I would never bother to patronize you," Zevon said, giving him a glare of inarguable clarity and conviction. "You are nothing like the young man in the pit. That boy, yes, he died there. But the boy in us always fades, Eric, if we're fortunate. Now you're a different man, a better man. Look at what you've learned in four years. I know technical things, but you're the one who had the breakthrough with the flux meter. You're the one who told me to check for invisible phase shifts in the infrared. I told you how ridiculous that was, but you insisted I check, and you were right. Look what you and I have done here, with tricks and dirt and screwdrivers. I explain what I'm doing, and you provide the leap of imagination that sends us to the next step. We . . . Romulans and Vulcans, even Klingons, we were all in space before Terrans, but look at you. Look how fast your progress has been . . . You've caught up in a century and charged beyond us. You are the people who see things the rest of us miss. One day together, with real facilities . . . your people and mine, working together . . . some day we'll stop shooting at each other, and think what we can do then!"

Now Stiles did look at him, and did not look away. Zevon's dark umber hair had long ago lost its polished-wood gloss, his complexion its glow of youth, and his face was creased now with weariness, starvation, physical stress, and the unending worry that their time would run out, yet still his brown eyes held a glimmer of purpose and hope that had never once flagged in all these years. Zevon had been in the pit with Stiles. Together they had crawled from the lowest place a man can go, the place of worthlessness and damage, and they had made something of it. They had made a bond with each other, and they had achieved a breakthrough that could save a billion people.

If things went right . . . just a little more right.

"If I go," Stiles murmured, "we'll never see each other again."

The words struck them both with the force of a physical blow. It was the one thing they'd never mentioned. Excuses, platitudes, hollow reassurances dodged through his head. The Federation would make peace with the Romulans. There'd be a treaty. Most Favored Systems status. Mail. Visits. The curtain rising so the two of them would be able to . . . see each other.

No matter how the story played in his mind, the final scene was the same. None of that would happen. He and Zevon would never see each other again.

He held on to Zevon in mute torment, the light touch becoming a sustaining grip, and he didn't know what in the universe to say.

"You must go," Zevon quietly insisted, "because you must live. You must live because I have to get off this planet so I can save these people even against their will. If I leave, I will come back. If you leave . . . you must never come back."

The faucet dripped, the computer clicked, and with a palpable crack Eric Stiles's heart broke in half for the second time in his life. In Zevon's angular features he saw the blurred echo of the face of Ambassador Spock, calling him from the distant past, beckoning one more act of Starfleet honor from the carved-out gourd of failure.

Zevon squeezed Stiles's hand again and thumped it placidly against the edge of the cot in punctuation, as if instructing a child about something which must, absolutely must, be the choice of the day.

"Go home, Eric," he summoned. "Go home, and live."

Chapter Eight

"THAT'S NOT A STARFLEET SHIP. What is this? Who in hell's coming for me?"

Stiles wrestled back against the grip of Orsova and one of the prison guards. They had him by the elbows, and there was no breaking away. He was too weak to do more than protest with anger and suspicion in his voice.

Orsova clapped a wide hand to Stiles's chest and said, "Stand still or I'll be happy to take you back to your cell."

"Take me back, then! Fine!"

"Stand still."

There was no chance to run, even if he could. The landing field was dotted with Pojjana soldiers, their red-and-brown jackets flashing in the landing lights, their coppery faces flinching at the approach of the unwelcome craft. Alien spacecraft hardly ever landed on the planet anymore. They just weren't welcome. This was a bizarre occasion and Stiles still didn't know what he was watching.

His head swimming with regrets, fears, and rough-edged anguish, Stiles begged the stars to put things back the way they'd been this morning, but no miracle came his way. The clanky-looking merchant trader, bulbous and utilitarian, with its exhaust hatches flapping and its hull plates chattering, continued its inartistic approach.

"If that's a Federation ship, it's second-hand," he commented. "No Federation spaceport ever built anything like that."

Unable to wrestle Orsova or the other guard, Stiles condemned himself to watch the landing. Port fin was high . . . too much pitch . . . not squared on the strip markings . . . lateral thrusters going too long.

Ah, the echoes almost hurt, echoes of another landing, not so far from here. He'd come to this planet an outclassed hotfoot who let haste get the better of him, overwhelmed by proximity to greatness, the approval of his hero, whose face he'd seen in the back of his mind all these many, many months, urging him to rise above the mangled messes he'd made. His life had imploded, his preconceptions defoliated, his internal fortitude hammered to a fine edge by circumstances he'd never anticipated, and he'd been preparing himself for a long time to die. Now living was a lot more scary than dying of whatever was eating his muscles. Strange . . . he and Zevon didn't really even know what illness Stiles had. The Pojjana doctors hadn't been able to identify it. Of course, since the patient was a prisoner and an alien, they hadn't tried all that hard.

So Stiles had gotten ready, over the months, to pass away. Now he was suddenly afraid not to go. Today, once again, the universe turned on its edge for him. He stood now at the municipal landing field, barely an echo of that feckless and slapdash boy, but he was still trembling like a kid, so fiercely that Orsova and the other guard had to hold him up. Would Ambassador Spock himself step down the black ramp of the unfamiliar vessel landing out there?

"I don't want to go," he muttered in his throat.

Beside him, Orsova watched the ship settle. "I'll miss you, too."

This time there was no Zevon to talk sense into him. Zevon was back in the prison. For him, nothing had changed. Except, now, he would be alone.

Terrible guilt racked Stiles's chest. All the words of sense and reason from the lab suddenly seemed to leak like cheesecloth. How could he leave Zevon like this? Here in this dump, alien and hated, alone, powerless, with another Constrictor coming and nobody to believe him about it? Before this, they'd at least always had each other.

"Who's doing this?" he demanded as the ship settled and its thrusters shut down with a wheeze. "Who're you giving me to, Orsova? This is your doing, isn't it? You weren't getting anything out of watching Zevon while you tortured me anymore, so now you're up to something else, aren't you?"

"You're going home," Orsova drably said. "I would enjoy keeping you, but you're going."

"Why?" Stiles glared at him. "Why would you let anybody shove you around? Who are you afraid of?"

"You're an alien. Your own filthy kind have come to get you. Shut your mouth and go with them."

"What about Zevon?"

"He's mine from now on."

Summoning his last threads of energy, Stiles raised his elbow and rammed it laterally into Orsova's round face. The big guard staggered, but never let go of Stiles's arm. Before even regaining his balance, Orsova shoved Stiles viciously sideways, into the rocky substance of the other guard, who pivoted to provide a backboard for whatever Orsova wanted to do.

Stiles tried to brace himself, but he might as well be skinned alive as drum up a vestige of physical superiority—hell, he could barely keep standing. Orsova reeled back a thick arm like a cannon, poised to turn Stiles into mashed oats.

Refusing to close his eyes, Stiles winced and prepared for pain and flash.

"Stop!"

Though he attempted to turn toward the sound, Stiles found his head reeling and comprehended that somehow Orsova had gotten a lick in there someplace. He shook his head, squeezed his eyes shut briefly, and fought to focus.

When he could see again, he frowned at a clutch of odd-looking aliens he didn't recognize, yellow in the face with some kind of green growth on their heads that might be their idea of hair. Their cheeks were smooth as babies' butts, they had no recognizable nose, and two eyes pretty far apart. Their clothing was a mishmash, obviously not uniform in any way, so this wasn't anybody's military unit, just a ship's crew from some ungodly where. Sure wasn't Starfleet. Why were yellow aliens coming for him?

From the middle of the clutch came the sharp voice again. "Stop that. Get away from that man."

Abruptly—and that was the shock—Orsova flinched back, and *so did the other guard.*

And so did about a dozen other Pojjana soldiers who were standing within flinching distance.

What?

Stiles found himself struggling to stand up all alone, without even the assistance of his daily tormenter to help.

An old man strode bonily up to him, right up until there wasn't even a foot between them. Human. Old, darn old. Over a hundred, maybe, with a full head of frost-white hair, a simple flight suit framing his narrow body. The old man flicked a medical scanner between them. Piercing blue eyes watched the instrument's indicator lights.

"You Eric Stiles?"

"Who wants to know?"

"I'm your new granddad, son. Grew a beard, huh? I had one of those once. Itched." The ancient man turned to the yellow aliens who flanked him and said, "Get him aboard, boys."

Stiles backed up a clumsy step as two of the yellow aliens stepped toward him. "Who are you? Where are you taking me? You're not Starfleet. There's nobody like them in the Federation—what do you want?"

From behind, Orsova and two other Pojjana guards shoved him forward again roughly, but the narrow old man snapped his fingers and his blue eyes flashed with confidence and he barked, "Hands off him!"

So abruptly that Stiles almost collapsed between them, the guards—even Orsova—relaxed their threat.

The old man approached and leered at Orsova. "Don't get any ideas, butch. I'm old, but I'm ornery."

Amazing! The burly Pojjana all backed away again, so fast that the suction almost dragged Stiles off his feet.

"What the hell—" Stiles glanced at them, then glared at the frail white-haired codger. "Who are you that you can make them flinch like quail?"

The old man was completely unimpressed by the lines of Pojjana soldiers, and indeed they shied away from him. "Let's just say that once upon a time I removed a thorn from the lion's paw. Now the lion thinks I'm powerful. Of course, he's right."

Weird—somehow this old man's voice . . . it sounded familiar. The way he snapped at those men—

"What's all that mean?" he asked. "What thorn?"

But the codger, without taking his eyes off Stiles, waved at the yellow guys, who moved forward again. "Don't look back, son," he said. "It doesn't pay."

As the yellow aliens pressed toward him, Stiles stumbled back. "You keep your alien paws off me!" He slapped at them as they attempted to get a grip on him. "I don't want to go without Zevon! Orsova, I'll get you for this someday! All of you get away from me!"

"Hypo."

"I don't want to go! I don't want to go . . . I don't . . . want. . . ."

Familiar voices. How secure they sounded, how wondrous! The anchorage of life, those voices. All the hours upon hours, watching historic mission tapes, memorizing the fiery defiance of Captain James Kirk during the M5 experiments, the Nomad occurrence, the incident at Memory Alpha, sinking into Mr. Spock's baritone warble explaining where the probe came from, listening to the counterpoint of Dr. McCoy's perplexed and concerned protests, the voice less of an officer than a humanitarian trying to expand his humanity beyond natural limits . . . those men, they always pushed themselves, teased every limit, never backed away. . . .

Wish I'd been there, with those men in those times, taking those orders. I could've followed those orders and given them ten cents change! Just imagine—First Officer Spock saying, "These are your orders, Ensign Stiles." Imagine. . . .

Their voices were more familiar than his own family's, more familiar than Travis Perraton's calming tone behind him making sure he didn't make quite as much a fool of himself as he otherwise might, or Jeremy White taunting him while the others laughed. But it had been a good laugh . . . he hadn't appreciated it back then. They were having fun, enjoying themselves all because he was with them. That was worth being laughed at. It never hurt so much, except that he let it hurt. If they were enjoying themselves, then the existence of Eric Stiles was doing some good.

He wanted to wake up. Usually he could will himself out of unconsciousness after a short struggle. Orsova commonly knocked him into a dither, and he had learned to claw his way out of the tunnel to the light place where Zevon would be waiting for him, usually stitching a cut or stanching a nosebleed. Wounds could actually heal without a tissue-bonding beam.

That medical scanner, it looked like a super satellite to him after four years in a culture backed off a hundred fifty years from what he'd grown up with. Funny how quickly he'd gotten used to the downteching. Before, he'd never thought a person could get through a day without Federation flash and spark. He'd gotten through a day.

"At a time."

Oh—his own voice this time. Didn't sound so bad. Come on, fight out of the hole. Zevon would be at the top of the tunnel, pressing a wet cloth to Stiles's head.

"Mmmm . . ."

"That's it, son, wake up. You're bound to have a headache, Don't fight it."

Stiles fought anyway. He defied the thrum in his skull and finally found the power to force his eyes open when he sensed there was some kind of light on the other side of the lids. Zevon would be there when he got them open.

Red lights? Familiar too . . . shipboard lights in an alert situation. Red, so the eyes could still adjust. Most eyes, anyway. Human eyes . . .

"Let me get the lights."

That gravelly, homespun voice again. The codger.

"Where's Zevon?"

Stiles registered his own voice and clung to the sound, which brought him all the way up to consciousness. When he could see, he realized the lights weren't red anymore, but were a soft golden light, shining in small, obviously ship-built quarters rigged as some kind of sickbay. He saw a shelf with rows of bottles, piles of folded cloth, several pieces of medical scanning equipment, hyposprays, and a dozen other recognizable and somehow foreign contraptions. He knew what they all were, yet they were foreign to him, and unwelcome.

"So I'm out," he managed.

"You are," the old man said.

Forgetting himself for just a moment, Stiles fixed upon the old man's face and tried to register that voice. He felt like a computer with a new search order—*identify, identify.*

"Who are these people running this ship?"

"Smugglers."

"Why would a human ride with them? And why'd you come into Red Sector? Are you an expatriate or something?"

The old man's icy blue eyes flickered and one brow arched. "I came because of typical pointed-eared hardheadedness, that's why."

"Huh?"

"And once in a while a man's got to slip into forbidden territory. Inoculations, contraband chemicals, antitoxins . . . makes the stars spin."

"But . . . if you . . . why would they. . . ."

"Why don't you just relax, Ensign?"

"Ensign . . . haven't heard that in a while. You better call me something else."

The doctor tilted his snowy head. "Why should I? You haven't surrendered your commission, have you?"

"It got surrendered for me. I'm not that kid anymore. Starfleet gave up on me. I gave up on them."

"You're here, aren't you?"

"Look, don't you think I know pity when I see it? Guilt? It's not Eric Stiles they came after. It's their own reputation for not leaving a man behind." Stiles huffed. "I grew up back there. I *did* leave Starfleet behind. I could handle myself. I didn't want to be rescued. Starfleet can't just fly in and order me to leave when I don't want to go."

"Well, actually, Ensign, they can. You're still on the duty roster."

"What do I care? And I told you not to call me ensign. All this is just a joke on you anyway. I don't care how many famous people they send after me, Starfleet's not getting its pound of flesh out of Eric Stiles. I'll never make it home."

"Oh? Why not?

"Because I'm dying. There's hardly a pound of flesh left. Can this boat turn around? Do these yellow guys have a reverse button?"

The old man wiped his pale, gnarled hands on a blue towel. "You're not dying, boy. I just cured you."

Stiles rolled his head on the pillow and challenged the codger with a glower. "I'm too far gone for that."

"Not too far for me. You had a viral infection of operational tissue. Your heart, your muscles, intestinal walls, a few internal organs . . . it's just something that hits humans on that planet. We had to watch out for it back when we maintained an embassy. To the Pojjana, it's barely a common cold, but to humans, it eats muscle. In five or six months, with some physical therapy, your tissues will be rebuilt. You'll be young again, kid. Just call me the fountain of youth."

"Starfleet sent us on a mission to a planet with a human-killer virus?"

"They had a vaccine, but didn't bother to vaccinate the evacuation team. You boys weren't supposed to come in contact with any native Pojjana during the evac mission, and that virus requires twelve weeks of repeated exposure. Nobody expected any of Oak Squad to stay there for four years. You probably got it from the food supply at the prison."

Stiles stared at him. "How do you know so much about me?"

"Ambassador Spock sent me. Ring a bell?"

Taken unaware by the dropping of that name, Stiles heaved up on his elbows—and then the second shock came. He was up on his own elbows!

"What's wrong?" the old man asked.

"I haven't been able to sit up by myself for . . ." All at once Stiles dropped back on his pillow, but not from weakness. He stared at the old man and watched decades peel away before his eyes as he suddenly realized—

"Ambassador Spock sent you . . . of course! You're—you're—my God, you're—"

"Yes, that's who I am. The Supreme Surgeon. The Mighty Medicine Man. The Hypo-Hero. The Real—"

"McCoy! Doctor McCoy!"

"You can have an autograph later." The elderly man snapped the top back onto a bottle and placed it back on the nearest shelf. "Now relax before you have a bacterial flareup. Where'd I put that sedative?"

"Are you Doctor Leonard McCoy? *The* Doctor McCoy?"

"Betcha."

"Then it *is* an official rescue?"

"No. I convinced the consul general to remand you into my custody. When we cross into Federation territory, you'll be officially handed over to Starfleet."

"You gave the Pojjana some kind of medical help?"

"That's the short version, yes."

"Then you broke the Prime Directive?"

"Sure did," the esteemed elder proudly confirmed. "You would've too. The P.D.'s been through so many incarnations and reinterpretations in my lifetime you'd think the thing was written on rubber. In a changing galaxy, you've got to have that."

"But you're a Starfleet surgeon—"

"Retired. If I come into Red Sector, it's my own affair. I'm a free agent. Took me a year and a half to get the Pojjana to owe me enough to get you out. It's a damned shame what happens to you kids who get caught in the crossfire—"

"I'm not that kid anymore," Stiles bristled. "I'm an old man now. I can stick up for myself."

Leonard McCoy lasered him a scolding glower that cut him off in mid-thought. "Boy," the doctor said, "I got socks older than you."

Perfectly intimidated, Stiles settled back and shut his mouth. He'd have to keep it shut until he figured things out. How much had changed out there? Four years in prison was an eternity. Stiles knew he'd broken Federation rules by helping Zevon try to learn how to predict the Constrictor. And he'd have done more to help those people, done anything he could to curb the results of all-encompassing natural disaster. Plain decency didn't allow a man to sit by and watch. What other rules had he broken in his distance and ignorance?

He didn't care. Even after a lifetime of family conditioning, Starfleet had been surprisingly easy to leave behind. Now, this force in his life that had faded to an echo, something he could ignore and forget, now it held ultimate sway over him. Four years ago, though restricted in a jail, Stiles had taken control over his own life. That control was about to be wrested from him again. He was an ensign again, a man in uniform. Today he was free—but more imprisoned than ever.

Then he thought of something else and pushed himself up again. "Can you get Zevon out?"

"Who?"

"Another prisoner. We were together the whole time. We kept each other alive."

"Not another Starfleet man. I'd have known about that."

"No, he's . . . he. . . ."

As the doctor waited for the word Stiles was about to unthinkingly spit, Stiles held himself back. For four years he'd said whatever popped into his mind, careless of consequences because there weren't any consequences, heedless of hurt feelings because he and Zevon endured so much hurt that feelings stopped making any difference a long time ago.

He'd made a promise to Zevon to inform the Romulan Empire that their prince was a captive, not dead as they probably suspected. Was it a good idea to tell anybody else Zevon was Romulan?

I'll get the message to them myself, somehow. I'll figure out a way.

"One miracle at a time," McCoy told him. "We can make a report on your friend, see if Command has a process—"

"I'll take care of it." Stiles lay back again, enjoying the sensation of getting a lungful of air without pain, entertaining thoughts of breaking away and running back to the Pojjana and continuing his work with Zevon now that he was cured. Cured . . . the idea of dying was easier to grasp.

But how would that be? The sector was still red. Zevon was right—he'd be better served to tell the Romulans and let them get Zevon out, then let Zevon pressure his own people into helping the Pojjana. It's the least they owed . . . and the Pojjana still saw both Stiles and Zevon as evil aliens. They might have to be forced to accept help.

The Constrictor was coming, he was sure of it. Zevon would be caught in the middle of it, maybe even killed if the Pojjana wouldn't listen to him.

"I've got to fight my way to somebody with influence," Stiles grumbled aloud, gazing at the scratched brown wall of the small quarters. When he realized he'd spoken aloud, he turned to the elderly surgeon, but the famous old man was busy with something medical and apparently hadn't heard him or didn't care.

"They're going to court-martial me, aren't they?"

"Hmm?" McCoy glanced at him. "I wouldn't know. Why would they?"

"I botched a critical mission."

"Did you?"

"I thought I knew everything."

"Show me a twenty-one-year-old who doesn't." McCoy pulled a hypo off his shelf and fitted it with a newly loaded—whatever that thing was called that held the medicine. "I'll give you something to make you sleep. Tomorrow we'll start your physical therapy. You might as well relax for a while. It's a long ride back from Red Sector to whatever Starfleet's got waiting for you."

Chapter Nine

"ORSOVA."

"Mffbuh . . . muh?"

"*You're not unconscious. Stand up.*"

"Huh? Stand up?"

"*You're not dead. Stand up and shake off the daze. Find your feet.*"

"Who . . . who . . . r'you?"

"*This mechanism distorts my voice. Forget trying to recognize me. You will never know me.*"

"Where is this? Where have you brought me to?"

"*You're on a space vessel.*"

"Space? Space! . . . Prove it."

"*Look out that portal. See your planet, your moons.*"

Disoriented, nauseated, Orsova tripped over his bootlace and stumbled from the cool floorspace to a carpeted area where there was a hole in the wall. There he fingered the porthole ledge and peered out three layers of thick window.

Breath stuck in his throat. He choked and wobbled. There, before him, near enough to touch, hung planetary bodies he had seen hanging in the distant night since he was a child. He had seen them as egg-sized eternalities, and today they were in his lap. Crisp sunlight and shadows like hats rode the bold sandy satellites.

"Oh!" he gasped. "Oh—moons! Too close! How did you make me come here! How did I come here! Oh . . . those moons are close. . . ."

"*Beautiful, aren't they? You were transported here with an energy beam.*"

"A beam . . . through space . . ."

He tried to remember, but there was only the hazy idea of being trapped in his tracks, of looking down to see his knees dissolving and his boots disappearing. He had heard of those transport beams, but thought they might be myths.

But he was here, and he had not walked or flown here. Something had flickered and brought him here. He accepted that.

The buzzing mechanical voice spoke again.

"*Now you know you are really in space.*"

Where was the buzzing voice coming from? It was speaking fluent enough Pojjana, but with an accent. Machines didn't have accents. Somewhere, there was a person talking.

Nothing familiar in the voice. No accent he'd heard before.

"Who are you?"

"*These are the conditions. You will not try to look at me. We will speak through this device.*"

"Where are you? Are you in this ship with me?"

"*Nearby. Stop trying to find me. Take your hand from that latch or you die here! . . . Yes, back away. Remain in that chamber.*"

Orsova chose silence for a moment, to think. Failing that, he asked, "Why do you come here? And why now?"

"*The Federation has come here,*" it went on. "*Why did they come?*"

"To get their man," Orsova told it. "How did you know they came?"

"*I follow the medical trail,*" the voice said. '*The old doctor came here. I kept watch.*"

"Why would you keep watch on doctors?"

Stepping foot by foot, toe by toe around the dim cabin, Orsova looked at every panel of the glossy interior plating. Was the metallic surface thin? Was he seeing shadows of a living form? Just a haze? Or were these echoes of his own reflection deep in the polished surface?

As he moved around, pressing his fingers to each panel, leaving prints on the sheen, he asked, "What do you want?"

"*I want to help you.*"

"We accept no help from aliens. How did you get past our mountain defense?"

"*We are nowhere near your defenses. We have beamed you far out. You can see how far.*"

The strange mechanically disguised voice reminded Orsova of the growling of awakened rezzimults in the swamps near the capitol city.

"What do you want?" he asked, abruptly nervous, as if someone had turned off the heat. "Why did you bring me to space? What do you need me for?"

"Tell no one that I spoke to you, and you will have greatness beyond your dreams. I will help you gain influence, become powerful. You will find my friendship wondrous. When I need you, you will be here."

"I don't even know who you are."

"You will never know me. I must not be known. You are one of many pawns throughout the galaxy. I tend many fronts, light many candles. Do as I say, and we will see what the years may bring."

Chapter Ten

SEVENTEEN WEEKS LATER, after a blur of physical therapy, drug treatments, rebreaking and re-fusion of his old fractures—so they'd be somewhat recognizable as human bones to the archaeologists of the distant future—and a flurry of puzzling comments from Dr. McCoy, Eric Stiles stood in the loading area of a smelly livestock transport ship that stocked colonies with cows or sheep or something. After weeks of treatment, a trim of the beard he couldn't quite yet bear to shave off, and fresh clothing—blessedly not a uniform—he felt as if someone had cut off his head and spliced it onto a new body. He could stand here by himself for a long time before even feeling the first shivers of weakness. He was far from rosy health yet, but a lot further from the death he'd been passively anticipating.

He and McCoy had transferred nine times in the past seventeen weeks, in a flurry of passage notices, manifests, bribes, seamy personages, and shady deals. Stiles scarcely had an idea of what ship he was on, except that this one had obvious Federation markings—and stank. Generally the ships were hardly distinguishable one from the other, and he and the doctor had remained relatively confined, to keep from "seeing" anything, whatever that meant.

Seventeen weeks of physical therapy and quaint tales. No matter how many times Stiles asked what was going to happen to him, Dr. McCoy always played old and swerved into some tall story about the glorious past, or the irritating past, or the past that could've been done better if only so-and-so had listened to him. Stiles got the idea. The doctor didn't want to be the one to tell him what was coming.

Now they were about to rendezvous with the first Starfleet ship Stiles had seen since he'd been dragged out of his fighter. On one of the courtesy screens, he and Dr. McCoy watched the brand new Galaxy-class *Starship Lexington* pull up to docking range. Then a transport pod came out of the starship and made its way toward the livestock transport.

"Why don't they just get it over with and beam us over?" Stiles complained. "The sooner this is done, the better for me. I can take my dishonorable discharge and vanish."

"Discharge?" McCoy didn't look at him. The lights of the airlock flashed on his papery face.

"It's the only way to get out of a long, drawn-out court-martial. I don't care if they put me on trial, but I don't have the time to waste. I've got a message to deliver. They'll offer me a deal. Dishonorable discharge. And I'll take it."

"Don't blame you."

The vessel around them endured a slight physical bump, and a moment later the nearest airlock clacked and rolled open. Two Starfleet security men stepped out, with holstered phasers and full helmets. One of them stepped forward.

"Dr. Leonard McCoy and Ensign Eric Stiles?"

McCoy stepped forward. "That's us, son."

"Ensign Pridemore, sir, and Ensign Moytulix, here to escort you to the starship. If you don't mind my saying so, sir, I'm honored to have this duty."

"Thank you, Ensign," McCoy allowed with a practiced nod. "Carry on."

"Yes, sir. If you'll both follow me—"

The security officers parted, and Pridemore led the way back into the pod. Stiles let McCoy go first, though he was feeling the bristling power of strong legs again and nearly plowed into the pod just on the hope of getting this misery over with sooner. There was no getting around the next few days. He'd have to face the music, take the stain on his record, plead guilty to whatever they threw at him, and get out so he could find a way to notify the empire about Zevon. That was everything, Zevon was everything, and Stiles was in a perfect panic of worry for him.

His head was swimming. Yes sir, no sir, carry on . . . all the common phrases he'd abandoned so easily . . . they spun him like coins on a table. He felt as if he were reliving somebody else's life, detached from any real involvement of his own.

"Right over here, sir." Ensign Pridemore gestured Stiles to a seat in the cramped back of the transport pod.

"I'd rather stand and look out the viewport."

"Sorry, sir. Regulations."

Stiles stepped to the seat. "You don't have to 'sir' me. I don't outrank you."

"It's my honor, sir." Pridemore took off his helmet, hung it on the bulkhead hook, and turned toward the piloting console.

"Yeah, yeah." Stiles dropped into his seat and slumped into the cushions.

McCoy sat across from him. The other security ensign, his helmet obscuring his face, stood at the airlock hatch at full attention. Seemed kind of silly.

Within twelve minutes, they were landing in the bay of the starship. The pattern of approach and responses from the baymaster seemed like echoes of his past, as Stiles eavesdropped on the cockpit action and imagined himself in the pilot's seat.

As the interior lights of the starship's hangar bay flooded the pod, Dr. McCoy clapped his knees with those gnarled white hands and said, "Ready to get this over with?"

Stiles sighed. "Do elephants have four knees?"

McCoy stepped over and helped Stiles to his feet, which seemed bizarre and distorted. Being helped by a man well over a hundred—and needing it—reminded Stiles that he had a few months of recovery yet to go.

Ensign Pridemore got up and stepped to the hatch. "This way, gentlemen," the young man said.

Young . . . yes, Pridemore seemed young to Stiles. A long time since he'd seen a person younger than himself in any authority. He felt a sudden pang of sympathy for the two ensigns here with him today. So much was expected of them—

"If you'll stand here, Mr. Stiles," Pridemore said, motioning him to the middle of the hatch entrance, only then motioning to McCoy. "Doctor? Here, sir."

Without comment the old surgeon came to stand beside Stiles. The staging was mysterious, but Stiles assumed a security team was stationed outside the door and would be escorting him to quarters under guard. The brig? Probably not. He wasn't a criminal, after all. Just a turkey being led to the slaughter.

"Ready, sir?" Pridemore asked.

"We're ready," the doctor confirmed. "Open'er up."

Pridemore, curiously, stepped aside then instead of leading them down the ramp that must be out there, and punched the hatch controls.

The hatch swung open and for a moment Stiles was blinded, after weeks of dim smugglers and tramp ships, by an unfortunately placed spotlight somewhere in the hangar bay that plunged instantly into his eyes and made him blink.

Then a sound rushed up the ramp and engulfed him. Was something exploding?

He moved slightly to one side, enough to get out of the direct beam of that one culprit light, and let his eyes adjust. As he blinked, he identified that unfamiliar sound. Applause.

He stepped forward to see what was happening, and saw sprawled out before him a field of Starfleet crewmen, officers, civilian guests and dignitaries, all knocking their hands together and looking up the ramp at him and McCoy.

"Sorry!" Stiles gasped. He was standing right in the way. Careful of his new physical coordination, he stepped quickly to one side, faced the famous Leonard McCoy, and began to politely applaud also.

"What're you doing?" Dr. McCoy asked.

Stiles kept applauding. "I was in the way."

The doctor's leathery face crumpled in disapproval and he grasped Stiles by the arm and pulled him back to the middle of the ramp. "They're not applauding me, hammerhead!"

"Honor Guard! Atten-HUT!"

The sharp disembodied order echoed in the huge hangar bay, answered by the crack of heels on the deck as a tunnel of uniformed men and women came abruptly to attention, flanking the red carpet which stretched out from the end of the ramp to the edge of the crowd.

"What?" Stiles stumbled a few steps down the ramp, baubling drunkenly as he realized Dr. McCoy wasn't following him down the ramp. He stopped in the middle of the slope and stared at the throng of people applauding before him.

And there was music—trumpet fanfare in vaulting military tradition. He hadn't heard music in years.

A stimulating cheer rose now above the continuing applause, and some of the people in the crowd were jumping and waving, calling, "Eric! Eric! Eric!"

Stiles turned halfway around and looked back up the ramp at Leonard McCoy. The doctor wagged a scolding hand at him, waving him the rest of the way down the ramp.

Spreading his hands perplexedly, Stiles complained, "I don't get this. . . ."

But he barely heard his own voice over the cheering. As he turned back to the crowd, confused and overwhelmed, a flicker of sense came into the picture—Ambassador Spock now stood at the end of the tunnel of uniforms. The senior Vulcan now looked more ambassadorial than the one time Stiles had met him. That day four years ago, the ambassador had been wearing a jacket and slacks. Today he wore a ceremonial robe of glossy purple quilted fabric and a royal blue velvet cowl. Apparently this was some kind of ceremony. With him stood a captain and some officers and a couple of dignitaries. They continued applauding as Stiles meandered down the red carpet, entertaining ideas of slipping between a couple of these guards at attention and maybe getting out of here somehow without anybody noticing.

He stopped five feet short of the end of the runway, staring like a jerk at the ambassador and the captain and all those other spiffy dressers.

The ambassador waited a few seconds, then came forward into the honor guard tunnel. The other dignitaries just followed him in there.

Ambassador Spock's weathered face shone every crease in the harsh hangar bay lights, but under the Vulcan reserve there was an unmistakable sheen of pride and delight. In fact, a hint of a grin tugged at his bracketed mouth and his slashed brows were slightly raised. As he stood flanked by the captain and the dignitaries, all facing Stiles like a vast wall of phaser stun, the applause tapered off and then suddenly stopped in deference and respect.

"Welcome home, ensign," the ambassador said warmly. The soft knell of victory rang in his words and triggered a whole new wave of applause and cheering. As he turned toward the captain beside him, the applause almost instantly fell off again. "I am honored to present Captain James Turner of the *U.S.S. Lexington.*"

"Ensign Stiles, I'm pleased to finally meet you in person," the thin officer said, smiling broadly and pumping Stiles's hand. "I first heard about you when I was in command of the *Whisperwood.* Your story was very compelling to me, and I used it to train my fighter squadrons. I admit to pulling some strings so the *Lexington* could be the ship to meet you today."

"Oh . . . I . . . thanks." Stiles leaned closer and urgently told him, "This is some kind of mistake!"

The captain grinned again and took Stiles's elbow and turned him slightly. "My first officer, Commander Audrey."

"Welcome aboard, Ensign," the smiling woman said, "and welcome home."

The captain turned him a little more, while Ambassador Spock watched in passive approval despite the desperate glance Stiles tossed him. In a whirl he was introduced to a half dozen other people.

"Federation Ambassador Whitehead . . . Provincial Ambassador Oleneva . . . Chief Adjutant Kuy, representing Admiral Ulvit . . . Governor Ned Clory from your home state of Florida . . . Port Canaveral's Mayor Tino Griffith, Princess Marina from the Kingdom of Palms on our host planet here in this star system. . . ."

They each greeted him and pumped his hand and patted his arms, some even hugged him, but he scarcely caught a syllable, registering only the mention of an honors breakfast in the ward room.

"You've—got the wrong guy," he protested again as Captain Turner steered him back to Ambassador Spock. By now, Dr. McCoy had shuttled down the ramp and was standing beside Spock, and for an instant as Stiles turned the years peeled back and he saw them as they had been so many decades ago. Spock, streamlined and subdued in his blue Science Division tunic, his black hair glossily reflecting a single horizontal band of light from the hangar ceiling. Leonard McCoy, in a short-sleeved medical smock, strong arms casually folded, his thick brown hair glistening in a much more raucous way, his supremely human expression enjoying a proud and friendly grin, cirrus-blue eyes set in a square face now famous throughout the settled galaxy. Two legends, standing together, for Eric Stiles.

This couldn't be happening. They had something so wrong.

He was whisked to a podium mounted at the far end of the hangar bay while a team taxied the pod into its cubicle and the crowd closed in on the hole it made. Somebody ushered him to a row of chairs and put him between Ambassador Spock and Dr. McCoy—good thing, too, because then he had a buffer from those adoring grins. As Captain Turner and those other ambassadors stood up to make speeches—heroism, selflessness, sacrifice, fortitude, survival, strength, pride of Starfleet, son of Federation dynamism—Stiles caught only the odd word or phrase, none of which struck him as applying to himself, and he leaned slightly toward Dr. McCoy. Through his teeth he implored, "Will you please *tell* them?"

"Just smile and nod a lot," McCoy wryly advised. "Let 'em have their ceremony. Next week the president's giving you the Federation Medal of Valor."

Stiles stared at him briefly. How could anybody be so casual with a sentence like that coming out of his mouth?

"The m—" Nope, couldn't get it out of his own. "God . . . I don't get it . . . I just don't get this at all. . . ."

"Indeed?" Ambassador Spock offered a solemn gaze. He *did* look amused! "A hero's welcome is a mystery to you after your great sacrifice, Ensign?"

"I didn't sacrifice anything," Stiles argued, keeping his voice way down while the speaker's boomed over the P.A. system. "I crashed into a mountain, and sat there about to wet my pants because I was afraid of the big bad aliens. I must've looked like a kid to you!"

"You *were* a kid," the ambassador blithely told him, startlingly familiar with the vernacular.

Dr. McCoy leaned forward a little. "My eighth psychology textbook, Spock," he explained, speaking from the corner of his mouth. "Chapter Four."

The ambassador looked past Stiles to the doctor, and they communicated with a few eye movements.

After a moment of this, Spock leaned back. "I see."

They were both silent for several minutes while listening—or pretending to listen—to the princess of somewhere happily welcoming the famous survivor Ensign Stiles and all the various dignitaries to her star system. Stiles heard part of her words as if listening to a training tape. The words bore no attachment to himself, except that he had the feeling he was getting into deeper and deeper trouble. When they found out what really happened—

"Stiles."

Maybe he should stand up and just explain what occurred and the mistakes he made and then offer to quietly retreat while they went on with their party. Would it be a good idea to compromise Starfleet's perception, point out this big mistake, right here in front of all these people? He'd hardly spoken to anybody but Zevon for so long . . . get up and talk to this crowd? His knees started shaking.

"Kid. Psst."

"Huh?"

McCoy still didn't turn to speak to him, and kept his voice barely above a whisper. "Now, listen and listen good. You did all right four years ago. Some deskbound paperpusher sent a bunch of kids into a tricky, dangerous political powderkeg without an experienced senior officer—"

"Without briefing them about what they could be facing," Spock took over, very quietly, "to rescue some very important personnel—"

"With Romulans all over the place and riots going on," McCoy interrupted. "They took a pack of untried kids barely out of officer school, with no black space experience at all, and sent you into a civil war and said, 'Go, do.' "

"Without a second thought," Spock added, "you took the initiative, sacrificed yourself, and allowed everyone else to get out alive. Then you kept yourself alive in an untenable situation long enough to be rescued. You are a hero, young man, by any measure."

Stiles felt his legs quiver, his hands grow cold as they spoke to him of these indigestibles as if telling tales of some unconfirmed legend. The crowd of dress uniforms, court gowns, and Sunday best shifted before his eyes and swam with applause as the speaker handed over the podium to the next one.

"Twenty-one-year-olds fail to see themselves as young," the ambassador explained, able to speak up now in the cover of the applause. "They lack the perspective of experience. In Starfleet, they are frequently older than everyone else around them. That is the curse of being a 'senior in high school,' if you will."

"You're one of the older kids," Dr. McCoy said, "so you figure you're not a kid at all. I'm bigger than everybody, so I'm big. Kids feel as if they should know everything. Starfleet handed you a situation that should've gone to a lieutenant. You improvised. You did what you thought was right. We don't damn people for inexperience."

"To you," Spock added, "your mistakes looked like crashing failures. To me, they simply looked like inexperience."

Now the ambassador did turn and fix him with those eyes nobody could look away from. "All these people are proud of you."

"And you deserve it," the doctor finished. "So shut up."

Another round of applause. Another speech, more appreciation, more applause, cheering. They were as insubstantial as dust. All he heard was the ambassador's words and the doctor's over and over in his head, like some musical echo or siren song drawing him along. His memories were of a butter-fingered ensign crowing his own authority and trying to win his spurs, fumbling every ball and landing ass-backward in a flat failure. He balked at any other explanation. They were being kind to him, he knew, and to themselves for their part of the mistake. Starfleet was better at admitting its errors than Eric Stiles ever had been.

He *had* been young then, too young to know it was okay not to already have all the experience of life. It was all right not to know everything. Or much of anything. It was okay . . . it was okay.

I'm okay, Zevon. Don't worry.

In a flush of emotion and self-examination he endured the next half hour of applause and honors without really registering much of it. By the time Spock took his arm and drew him to his feet, Stiles was humbled beyond description. He collected his only pleasure from knowing his survival was making so many people feel good about themselves. That was pretty good, really. When they teased him and spoke poorly, he'd at least been giving them something to converse about. Today he was doing the same sort of thing, deserve it or not. He shook hands and denied his way across the platform, then down to the crowd as the people smiled and then left him alone. They seemed to understand that he was overwhelmed, and the crowd funneled politely to the exits, heading for the ship's mess and ward rooms where the banquets were waiting. Music played again over the PA, and everyone was laughing and cheery, all because of him. On this astonishing day, he had everything he'd once thought he ever wanted.

And now he didn't want it.

"If you'll come this way," Ambassador Spock was saying, "there are some other people who've been waiting a long time to meet you."

"Not more," Stiles moaned. He lowered his eyes. Maybe whoever it was would just get the idea he'd had too much and leave him alone. The ship's captain had gotten the message and corralled the princess and the mayor and governor and were waiting with them about halfway to the exit, giving Stiles a few minutes to breathe. They were conversing with each other, obviously waiting for him, but also deliberately not looking at him.

He needed the time too. He stood at the side of the slowly emptying hangar bay, with Spock and McCoy providing a welcome buffer between himself and the throng.

"Eric!"

"Hey, Eric!"

With a notable wince, he turned away from the sound. If he kept his back to the masses, maybe they'd think he just didn't hear.

"Lightfoot!"

Something sparked in his head. Now he turned toward the calls. Not twenty steps away, held back by a couple pillars of meat in security uniforms, were the last people in the universe he had expected to see alive, never mind here.

"Travis?" Stiles's voice caught in his throat.

At his side, McCoy gave him a little push. "Go ahead, son. Go see 'em."

Behind Travis Perraton, also crowding the guards, were Jeremy White, Matt Girvan, Greg Blake, Dan Moose, and both the Bolt twins. At the front of the group, Travis Perraton's dark hair was grown out from the Starfleet junior-officer close-clip, and his blue eyes gleamed and bright smile flashed like a star as he reached between the guards and said, "They won't let us through!"

"Security guard," Ambassador Spock smartly ordered, "stand down."

In unison the four guards snapped, "Aye, sir!" and came to at-ease, allowing Perraton, White, Blake, Girvan, Moose, and the Bolts to flood into the reception area. All at once Stiles was engulfed in a coil of embraces, until finally he was clinging to Travis Perraton and getting his back slapped by everybody else.

Spock and McCoy graciously moved away, leaving the young men together without interference. The row of guards between them and everyone else would assure that the former evac team would have a few private moments before all the ringing and tickertaping started again.

Stiles shook like a scarecrow as he clutched at the physical reality of Travis and Jeremy and the Bolts.

"Thought you were all dead!" he gasped, tears flowing freely down his balanced face.

"Dead?" Jeremy White repeated. "Where'd you get that idea?"

"You showed up in the . . . I heard you . . . you said . . . the anti-aircraft guns—"

"We got clear, Eric," Travis said. "You gave us the extra seconds we needed to get away."

"You gotta be kidding," Matt Girvan protested. "He knows. He's just making us say it over and over."

Zack Bolt laughed. "And he'll never let us forget it. Wait and see."

"What is this?" Jason Bolt reached out and grasped Stiles's beard and shook it warmly. "Nonregulation Stiles! Since when!"

Dan Moose poked at Stiles's ribs. "And he's skinnier than Jeremy!"

His eyes blurring as he shuddered under the coil of Travis's arm, Stiles blinked from one face to the other, then ran the route again. Without a bit of the shame he would've once felt, he wiped tears from his cheeks. "Where . . . where are . . ."

Typically, Jeremy took over with a clinical explanation. "Well, Bernt and Andrea left Starfleet and went back to Holland, but they send their good wishes and demand a crew reunion as soon as you feel up to it. Bill Foster got promoted, and he's stationed on Alpha Zebra Outpost. Brad Carter's a civilian now too, and he's coming in tomorrow. He's just finishing exam week at college, so he couldn't be here today."

Only now did Stiles register that Travis, Greg, and Matt were not wearing Starfleet uniforms.

Civilians?

Jason held up a stern finger. "But they're all waiting for a communique on when and where we're having a crew reunion. Those of us still in the service have been given special dispensation from our current duties just so we can attend. The dope civvies among us, who shall remain rankless, are being offered free transportation and hotel, as if they deserve it."

"Troublemaker," Travis said with a laugh.

Greg Blake shrugged. "So I'll re-enlist," he tossed off. "Eric's bound to need a new wing leader. Can't do without me, can you?"

"He can't do without any of us," Zack said. "Who'd pick him up when he trips?"

Matt laughed. "Who'd stop him from putting his hand in front of a phaser?"

"Who'd he have to shout at when things didn't happen fast enough?"

"You need us, Lightfoot," Jeremy punctuated.

"Not so fast." Travis protected Stiles from them and held up his free hand judiciously. "Don't be a tidal wave. Eric made it through four years in prison on a hostile planet without anybody to help him keep from making a jerk of himself. Maybe he doesn't need our help for that anymore."

Stiles laughed with them. The ribbing that would've unsettled him once today felt like cool pond water.

Travis gave him a comradely squeeze. "Maybe he doesn't even want to stay in Starfleet."

"I sure wouldn't," Jason commented.

The other twin added, "He's done his duty."

"Twice over," Matt agreed. "They owe *him* now."

"What a life," Travis went on. "Speaking engagements all over the Federation—"

"Scholarships," Dan Moose said.

Blake made an exaggerated bow. "Honorary degrees—"

"Ceremonial dinners," Matt fed in.

"Starring in training films, have books written about you—hell, write your own book! Any idiot with a pen can do that!" Perraton looked at him admiringly. "You're gonna get rich and fat, Eric. Wish to the devil it could've been me!"

Until this moment Stiles had been lost in a daze, but Travis's latest sentence snapped him into biting clarity. He straightened his shoulders—a miracle in itself—and slipped abruptly back in command. Escaping from Travis's cordial embrace, he took hold of his friend's arm and control over the moment.

"No, you don't," he said. "I'm glad it wasn't you and you're glad too, and don't forget it, Travis. I'm so happy I could cry to see all of you, but I'm not the kid you knew."

Their faces changed, subtly, though even after all this time he could still read them. Perhaps even better than before. Some were arguing with him in their minds. Others were realizing they may have made a mistake to say what they'd been saying, perhaps even to be here today.

From the captain's group nearby, Ambassador Spock and Dr. McCoy finally breached the bubble of intimacy encircling Stiles and his crewmates.

"Mr. Stiles," the ambassador began, "excuse me. As soon as you're ready, the captain and dignitaries are ready to go to the wardroom for the honors banquet. We have a table set aside for you and your friends."

"Yes!" Travis beamed, and shook hands victoriously with one of the Bolts.

"You're most welcome, gentlemen," Spock allowed. "And Dr. McCoy has something for Mr. Stiles."

"Me?" Stiles rubbed his clammy hands on his thighs as Dr. McCoy stepped past Spock.

"Here you go, son." The doctor handed him a leatherbound packet with a Starfleet seal.

"What is it?" Stiles asked, as he took the plush folder with its satin ribbon and official wax seal.

"It's your way out," the doctor said. "Clean and legal. A medical discharge, issued directly from the surgeon general, with a retroactive field promotion. You'll go out as a full lieutenant, with commensurate pension."

Stiles looked up. "But you cured me. I don't have a legitimate medical claim."

"I cured your body," McCoy told him. Those active and ancient blue eyes flared. "Your soul is still scarred."

As the moment turned suddenly solemn beneath the doctor's prophetic words, the men around Stiles fell silent and stopped shifting. Their hands fell away from him and they made clear by their demeanor that he was once again in charge, once more the man who would make the important decision of the moment for them all.

A man, making decisions . . .

He glanced at them, saw the civilian clothes on some of them, Starfleet uniforms on others, and his two worlds suddenly collided. They looked young to him, young and unscarred and inexperienced.

"Thank you, sir." He handed the pouch back to Dr. McCoy and straightened his shoulders. "But I've got too much to do. My soul's just gonna have to heal."

His friends erupted into silly cheers around him, as if they understood something he wasn't registering at all. Over there Captain Turner, the princess, the governor and mayor were all looking at him, and now they had started applauding politely. Not the cheers of the huge crowd this time, but something much more substantial and wise.

How come everybody knew what he had just thought of?

Ambassador Spock reached out and took Stiles's hand. "Congratulations, Lieutenant. And welcome back to Starfleet."

Chapter Eleven

Eleven Years Later . . .

U.S.S. Enterprise, Starfleet Registry NCC1701-D

"THERE HAVE BEEN over fifty major outbreaks of raids or attacks on the Neutral Zone by angry Romulan commanders who before this made no violent overtures at all—and with no apparent reason. We've got to get some better intelligence."

Captain Jean-Luc Picard's comment would generally not have traveled beyond the ears of his first officer and the physician who stood at his side on the command deck, but Ambassador Spock's Vulcan hearing brought the private conversation to him as he stepped from the turbolift. These were troubled times. Despite them, reverie clouded his thoughts.

To step from a turbolift, to hear the sibilance of the door and sense anticipation, the murmur of a starship's bridge electrical systems softly working—these were mighty memories.

For a brief moment in a frozen pocket of his mind, the carpet changed texture, the bulkheads drained from tan to blue-gray, the rail turned glossy red, lights dimmed, and there were crisp shadows over his head. More blue, more black, and at the center that oasis of mesa-gold. The center of his universe, that dot of gold.

Memories only. He dismissed them, but they pursued.

He failed to escape them, as he stepped down to the command deck, also failing to understand—until his foot struck the lower carpet—that he was treading the sacred ground of officers aboard a starship, of the captain and his chosen few: and that he was no longer among them. For decades he had not been among them. How swiftly these automatic impulses flooded back! Perhaps this was why he spent so little time aboard ships anymore.

He nearly stepped back and waited to be invited, but by now Captain Picard had risen and turned to greet him.

"Ambassador, welcome aboard," the captain began, his deep theatrical voice communicating undisguised delight, and he even smiled.

Spock took his hand, a gesture he had come over the years to find suspiciously comforting, and thus held it longer than necessary for courtesy. When embarking on difficult missions, especially those couched in mystery, he had come to depend upon the sustenance of the human tendency to get to know one another quickly and with a speck of intimacy. Few races in the galaxy had that talent. He had come to cherish it.

"You know Mr. Riker," the captain invited pleasantly.

"Ambassador, hello!" William Riker, yes—the ship's first officer. A bright smile, and no attempt to subdue his pride that a distinguished Federation identity had come aboard his starship.

"Good evening, Mr. Riker," Spock offered, and also took Riker's hand.

"And Dr. Crusher, of course," the captain added, turning.

Only the ship's doctor, Beverly Crusher (in fact the person he had come here to meet), restrained herself from offering to shake a Vulcan's hand.

She was a stately woman, tall, reedy, and red-haired, with a sculpted face that echoed a Renaissance painting Spock had once seen in the Manhattan Museum of Art. He found it a credit to Dr. Crusher that he remembered the painting now for the first time in nearly nine decades, but recalled also his thoughts at the time that the woman in the picture was pale and too thin. Understanding that humans' emotional condition frequently communicated itself to their physical appearance, he surmised that the doctor was strained and troubled. She did not smile as did her captain and first officer, and that he also found suggestive.

"Good evening, Doctor. I'm gratified to have you involved."

"Now you'll get some answers, Beverly," Captain Picard told her with a placating smile.

She glanced at him, then stepped closer to Spock.

"I'd like to say it's my pleasure, Ambassador," the woman said, "but unfortunately I doubt any of us will enjoy the next few weeks."

"That will depend upon the outcome, as always."

Spock slipped his traveling cloak from his shoulders and let his attending yeoman take it from him, leaving his arms a little cool with unencumberment. Though he felt obliged by tradition to wear the Vulcan robes and plastiformed emblems when moving among the public or visiting Starfleet localities, such dress aboard a ship seemed provincial. Among these men and women, he could feel comfortable in simple black slacks and his cowl-necked daywear tunic. The cobalt-and-purple quilted strips running from his shoulders to his thighs were the only jewel-tones on the bright tan bridge, excepting only the shoulder yoke of medical blue on Beverly Crusher's uniform.

Again, he found himself wading in memories unbidden.

And a few he had dismissed freely—the officers here on this bridge were people he knew, had encountered in a previous mission, and since allowed to fade from his mind. He had learned long ago to remember the names of ships, captains, and some officers—but that cluttering one's mind with lieutenants, yeomen, and others tended only to inaccuracy. Eventually those crewmen and officers either disappeared into the mists of service or civilian life, or became commanders and captains themselves, in which case their names and ranks and ships turned into a long roster he would just have to amend later.

He remembered Captain Picard's senior security officer, the noted Klingon who defied so much to be here, but he could not summon the name. The android at the science station, however, had a name that no mathematician could forget—Data.

"There've been two more skirmishes this morning, Ambassador," Captain Picard reported. "The Starfleet ships *Ranger* and *Griffith* were set upon just outside the Crystal Ball Nebula, and the *Ranger* was actually boarded."

"Is everyone all right?" Spock asked.

"No fatalities, sixteen casualties, and apparently one of their passengers was kidnapped. The details are hazy so far."

Troubled by these unpredictable rashes, so obviously driven by emotion rather than by tactical plans, Spock paused a moment to gather his thoughts.

"Unfortunately, events are moving forward with the rapidity typical of a national crisis. We can now officially call the disease an epidemic." Spock lowered his voice and significantly added, "Captain, the proconsul of the Senate died yesterday."

"Uh-oh," Riker opined.

Picard grimaced. "That means instability at the top of the empire."

"Dr. McCoy should be arriving soon," Spock told them, "with current information about the medical aspects of the Romulan crisis. You should shortly be receiving a signal from a Tellarite grain ship upon which he's traveling at the moment."

"Leonard McCoy," Dr. Crusher observed, "is the only man I've ever known who can shuttle in and out of nontreaty cultures as easily as the rest of us visit the stores in a shopping promenade. He can charm his way past border guards and squirm past warrants like some kind of spirit."

"Hardly charm," Spock commented. "In any case, we should shortly have fresh information. The massive sickness is causing havoc throughout the empire."

"We've been feeling the effect," Captain Picard validated. "These border eruptions are like wildcat strikes. Isolated leaders are finding excuses to attack Federation outposts and ships, staging incidents on purpose, hoping one of them will flame into all-out conflict. Nothing that smacks of coordination, however, not so far."

"They are not coordinated attacks at all," Spock concurred. "As certain members of the royal family die, their followers—and sometimes the family members themselves—are flaring up in frustration and anger."

"And fear," Crusher added. "The royal family is spread all over, and they're all in charge. And they're all terrified. They're not only dying themselves, but also watching their children die. It's not a gentle disease, Ambassador . . . it attacks quickly, painfully, then inflicts a slow death. It behaves like a curse. Some people think that's what it is. Terrified people do terrible things."

"We've got a reason to be terrified too," her captain said. "As more and more of the royal family die, others who have had no chance for power are seeing an opportunity for upheaval. The Federation's managing to handle these spurts without considering any one of them an act of war, but how long can we hold out? If the structure breaks down too much—"

"Could that happen?" Dr. Crusher asked. "Could the empress really be deposed because she and her whole family are sick?"

Riker looked at Crusher. "If the empress dies, all the hungry near-orbiters who never had a shot at the throne will start smelling velvet."

"With too many decisive defeats of Romulan flare-ups by Starfleet crews," Picard added, "the empress could be deposed very quickly and someone more hungry for war could take over. No matter how you look at it politically, there's every reason to stir up trouble and virtually no reason not to. So our goal in these skirmishes is to prevail, but not so decisively that the Romulan commanders are deeply humiliated or destroyed. We try to push them back without squashing them, stalling for time, seeking a biological solution. If the empress falls and her relatives are all infected too, there could be decades of instability on one of the Federation's longest borders. We have a stake in restoring the status quo."

"True," Spock agreed, relieved that they shared his hopes. "Better to have a stable empire as a neighbor than anarchy at our gates."

"Well, we've done a good job so far," Will Riker injected, "of keeping these flare-up attacks from turning into acts of war."

"As the family breaks down," Spock said, "some dissident elements are striking out at the Federation, even though the core of the royal family is not yet ready to do that. Some of these elements are in control of ships."

Spock turned a fraction toward him, careful not to turn his back on the captain. "Those closest to power—the empress, her immediate relatives, and their immediate relatives—seem more concerned about stopping this biological attack than using it as leverage to foment trouble."

"Wouldn't you, sir? They see a chance that they might not have to die."

"Not everyone craves havoc, Mr. Riker. As Dr. Crusher pointed out, many of these victims wish only to live and see their children live, and to do so in a fairly stable civilization. Unfortunately, the empress must walk a very thin tightrope. For her own survival as a ruler, after nearly two hundred years of anti-Federation propaganda, she must not be seen as cowardly or complacent toward the Federation. The Romulan people on the outskirts, including those in command of ships, have been told all their lives to distrust the Federation. Now all the Romulan leadership is suddenly dying. What would you expect them to think?"

"Yes . . ." Riker's eyes widened. "How much of a leap would it be to assume the Federation is doing this?"

Spock rewarded him with a nod. "The propaganda is turning on them."

"And now they need our help." Dr. Crusher folded her long arms. "It figures. Has it occurred to anyone that this may be a genetic anomaly?"

"Isolated to the royal family?" Picard protested. "How likely is that?"

"Pretty damned likely, Jean-Luc." Crusher held out a hand. "The Romulans used to do genetic experiments—about a century ago, a little more. Those experiments could just now have incubated to mutancy and be coming back to bite them. It could be completely incurable. In that case, are we getting involved just to prove we *didn't* do it? I'm not sure I can prove a negative that big. If that's what the Federation expects, I've got an impossible mission here."

Wondering if indeed all physicians were necessarily cantankerous, Spock found himself sympathetic to her dilemma. The ball she had been cast was a familiar one to medical specialists with deep-space exploration, for they had the most experience dealing with the unknown, the foreign, and the unheard-of as commonplace. He had in his long life seen this firsthand, seen that expression in the eyes of many doctors into whose hands a monumental task had been shoved.

"Like myself, Doctor," he placated, "I know you prefer clarity to choices. However, choices are the more frequent curse of authority. The Romulans are advanced, but the Federation is much more advanced in the medical field. We've had to deal with so wide an array of alien members."

Will Riker cocked a hip and leaned against the navigation station, drawing a glance from the crewman manning the helm. "They might as well accept our help. They can always kill us tomorrow."

"Whatever the sociopolitical ramifications," Spock added, "they simply need our help."

"Captain, short-range emergency sensors," the fierce voice of Picard's Klingon officer erupted suddenly. As they all turned to look up at him, towering there over the tactical station at the back of the wide bridge, the surly lieutenant raised his eyes from the board and glared at the forward screen. "A Romulan Scoutship just decloaked off our bow!"

"Shields up, Mr. Worf. Red alert. Battle stations. Helm, hold position."

Lieutenant Worf watched the incoming angular feather-painted Romulan wing on the wide forward screen. "Should I arm photon torpedoes also, sir, considering their duophasic shields?"

"Ah, certainly."

Spock turned. "Captain, may I suggest—"

"I understand, Ambassador, but no Romulan commander expects less and I don't intend to show squeamishness."

Retreating, and somewhat embarrassed at this change in himself, Spock instantly acceded, "Forgive me."

"Captain, they are hailing," Data reported.

"Ship to ship, Mr. Data."

"Frequencies open, sir."

"This is Captain Jean-Luc Picard, *U.S.S. Enterprise,* Starfleet. Identify yourself, please."

"*Subcommander Cul, Captain, Imperial Reconnaissance Scout Tdal.*"

"You're in violation of the Neutral Zone treaty by several light-years, Subcommander. Explain your presence here."

"*Our weapons are cold, Captain. We have a passenger.*"

Picard paused, then glanced at Spock.

Spock was careful to keep his expression subdued, although this was probably a fruitless attempt, for even that subtle effort belied involvement.

"Yes," Picard drawled. "Mr. Worf, shields down. Subcomander, prepare for beaming."

"*We are prepared.*"

Impressed, Spock once again looked at Picard. "How did you know, Captain? Even I was not sure."

"Because it's logical, Ambassador," the captain responded, his dark eyes glinting. "Mr. Data, please scan for human physiology and beam their passenger directly to the bridge."

"Understood, captain. Transporter room, this is the bridge."

The android relayed the captain's orders, and in 4.9 seconds the shaft of glittering energy appeared as expected on the portside deck ramp leading to the captain's ready room. Spock noted the angle of the ramp and hoped it would cause no trouble or surprise.

As the column of lights coagulated into familiar form, he stepped toward it, then again restrained himself, not wishing to appear too custodial. He was relieved when Mr. Riker stepped to the ramp and put out an assisting hand in anticipation. Another two seconds brought the white-haired, pin-thin form of Leonard McCoy fully onto the bridge, shouldering a simple canvas satchel. The work of the Romulan wing was done.

"Sir, the Tdal is bearing off," Worf reported immediately. "They are vectoring back toward Romulan space at emergency high warp."

"Very good—and I don't blame them," Picard said. "Stand down from general quarters. Welcome to the Enterprise, Dr. McCoy."

"Captain Picard, nice to be aboard," the doctor's elderly voice scratched. "Can you turn the heat up in here? That Romulan shoebox was cold as a coffin nail. Hi, Spock."

"Doctor."

"You're looking stiff."

"Thank you."

"Back trouble?"

"If you like."

"I brought a big hypodermic needle from my medical antiques collection."

"A display which ideally fits your personality, I have always reflected."

"I . . . ah . . . all right, I owe you one. Morning, Beverly."

"Leonard," the other physician chuckled. "And it's evening here."

"Dammit. Why can't the galaxy just go to Federation Standard Time?"

William Riker smiled again and took McCoy's sticklike arm in his to escort him down the ramp. Spock resisted the urge to reach out and stop Riker's robust grip—McCoy's spidery limbs seemed so frail—then chided himself for his absurdity.

"That was hardly a Tellarite grain ship, Doctor," he commented instead.

"So I lied. It was the only way I could get a ship with high warp to bring me all the way back. Anything else would've taken ten weeks. We don't have ten weeks."

"No, we don't," Crusher endorsed. "The Romulan royal family is not a dozen people. It's over a thousand, installed in positions of power all over the empire. How close you are to the current ruler causes a lot of jockeying and marrying and even assassinations, but there's never been anything like this. This certainly isn't just some jealous cousin maneuvering for the crown." She turned specifically to McCoy. "What have you concluded?"

"Concluded? Oh, I did say that in my message yesterday, didn't I? What

I came up with is that the Romulans are right. The infection is definitely man-made. Not an accident."

"How did you come to this?" Spock asked, careful to phrase the question in a way that would dodge McCoy's still-youthful barbed humor.

"I've made some progress. What else do you expect from a man old enough to call Moses by his first name? Anyway, that's why I need Beverly's help."

"You need *my* help?" Dr. Crusher asked.

"Hell, yes, I need help. I'm old, all right? Besides, you're the one who worked on this mess before."

She regarded him with a gaze startlingly similar to the way Captain Kirk used to regard McCoy. "You mean this Romulan disease is the same multiprion nightmare—?"

"That's right. The same thing you and Dr. Spencer of the *Constitution* encountered back on Archaria III. It's mutated or been artificially mutated. That's why you haven't recognized it. It's been targeted to the genetics of the Romulan royal family."

Clearly irritated that her victory was being compromised, Crusher scowled. "How did you recognize it if it's mutated?"

McCoy's white head bobbed in a nod. "My dear, you remember the line 'Methinks he doth protest too much'? Well, me have begun to think this infection doth show up too much. Prion-based infections just don't appear randomly this often, and certainly not in a pattern that leaps from one planet to another, infecting a vastly different DNA makeup. Somebody's forcing mutations, combining prions that would never hook up naturally, then targeting whole races for infection. This biological terrorism smacks to me of experimentation."

"My God!" Riker blurted.

Spock heard the exclamation, but was himself focused on the doctor's unexpected declaration. "Someone is working toward a larger goal? The Romulan royal family is not the target?"

"I don't think so," McCoy said. "I don't think the goal is to kill off the royal family at all. I think they're being used as an incubation test site. I think the goal is to develop a bioagent that can be neither cured nor treated."

"Upon what do you base this?"

The doctor's gravelly voice took on a surge of confidence. "On the same multiprion sickness popping up all over the place, sometimes in isolation, other times in populated areas, but each time with some new aberration. A plague here, a flu there, an infection yonder, a couple of them leaping racial boundaries . . . until now, nobody's tied the incidents together; but I've seen this kind of thing before on a smaller scale, and I got suspicious. So I started ordering some quiet information gathering about three years ago. And, folks, this isn't just an epidemic. It's a *pandemic.*"

The word sent a chill through the bridge that Spock found nearly palpable. Even he discovered his hands suddenly clenched and forced himself to control his reaction. Ever since the first armies began forming and moving in the first civilizations on the earliest planets, pandemics had been a far more insidious scourge than any war.

Dr. McCoy paused long enough to see his revelation run its course of shock and nervousness, then enjoyed center stage again.

"When the Romulan royal family popped up with this deadly strain," he went on, "I started gathering the results of tests all over the quadrant, and sure enough they've got enough common characteristics to eliminate either the idea of coincidence or the idea of any other cause. These aren't dozens of isolated biological occurrences—they're all mutations of a single strain."

"So it couldn't be remnants of genetic testing?" Riker jabbed, leaning a little toward Dr. Crusher.

McCoy swiveled to him. "Genetics? Whoever said that?"

"Nobody said that," Crusher injected quickly. Her face masked a cold and bottled fury, as a knight's who had just been told the dragon is still alive. "Did you bring the results of all these tests? I'd like to examine them."

He patted his satchel. "Along with a cache of Scaffold Mints for the wardroom."

"As ever," Spock commented, "you keep your eye on the future."

"Watch it, pal, or I'll sit on you and give you a lecture on how long two cockroaches can live off the glue on the back of a postage stamp."

Dr. Crusher clasped her hands in a manner of controlled anxiety. "Who ever heard of 'two cockroaches'? Doctor, have you isolated the matrix on this Romulan mutation?"

McCoy's ancient blue eyes fixed on hers with the zeal of youth. "First thing. And, bless us all, it's a DNA strain, not RNA, which mans we can beat it with one medication if we can come up with the right one. Healthy blood cells can replace the atrophied cells. All I need is a continuing source of uninfected royal blood for about a week to generate healthy plasma. But first, we've got to keep the members of the royal family who're still alive from dying. That's going to be your job. Keep them alive long enough to throw the infection off or for me to synthesize a cure."

"Treat the symptoms."

"But treat them in the right order. It might not be the right thing to do to lower a fever. The fever's something that I think helps. You're going to be treating the empress herself and over twenty of her family members on the home planet. You'll be communicating with physicians all over the empire, telling them how to treat the family members they've got. Meanwhile, I'll be trying to find a cure for the mutation. I've had my network of spies quietly sifting through information on the whole empire and the Federation—even through the Klingon Empire—for weeks now. So far, we haven't found a single family member who's not infected."

"Ripple-effect contamination," Crusher breathed. "God, that's a new twist. . . ."

"What's that mean?" Riker asked.

Spock almost answered, but restrained himself. He was curious to hear Dr. McCoy's analysis of what was happening to the Romulans, and forced himself to remember that his role on a starship was no longer to provide information and move events along.

"Means we can't synthesize a cure without an uncontaminated family member. I need clear blood, and I can't find anybody. Also means this is no accident. Somebody's doing this on purpose. Somebody planned this plague in such a way as to make sure it can't be cured. That's why," McCoy added, now turning to Picard, "I arranged to have this rendezvous on board the *Enterprise.*"

"I beg your pardon?" Picard asked.

"Three years ago, Captain, you picked up a Romulan defector. He left the empire in disgrace after leading a coup against the empress. When that failed, he fled to the Federation and you offered sanctuary. Correct?"

"Oh . . . yes, a minor incident for us. We gave him sanctuary and resisted the extradition police on the planet where we found him. What was his name, Mr. Riker, do you remember?"

"Uh . . . believe it was Renn something, wasn't it, sir?"

"Check on the man, would you, please?"

"Aye, sir." Riker moved to the science station and looked over the android's shoulder. "Check ship's log and all ancillary documentations for Stardates 41099.1 through the ensuing six months. It's in there somewhere."

"Checking, sir."

"Then link into the archivist's computer at Starbase Ten. We're still in range, aren't we?"

While they worked, McCoy said, "Disgraced blood's as good as any. This defector's the third cousin to the empress on her mother's side, so it'll be undiluted blood and give us a strong base for immunological work."

"That must be what the message means," Picard said, glancing at Spock. "The admiralty gave me orders to cooperate with you both and transport you to any location in Federation space that you specified.

They must mean for us to take you to this Rekk person, once we find where he is."

Spock nodded. "Rather than risk transporting him from station to station, we hoped to use the starship, for safety and security reasons."

"We're at your disposal, of course," Picard assured.

"If I can't find any uncontaminated plasma," McCoy contemplated, "then it's all over. Ninety-five percent of the infected people are going to die and there's no way to stop it. You get this thing, you are dead."

His flat statement had a chilling effect.

"The next trick," McCoy added, "is getting us in there."

"What?" Crusher asked. "Why don't we just go in? They know why we're coming, right?"

"They'll give special access to Dr. McCoy and to you," Riker told her, "but not to the starship. Medical access is a little different from military access."

"Correct," Spock said. "If any starship moves through the Neutral Zone and into Romulan space, the imperial leadership will be forced to act against us. Their own people will stand for nothing less. The empress knows Federation medical science may be their only chance, no matter who concocted this attack, but she would be forced to respond against a ship of the line or she could lose power before she loses her life."

"That's why we're not going," Picard explained. "At least, *we* are not." And he looked worriedly at Beverly Crusher.

"Arrangements will be made," Spock assured her, and felt suddenly remiss in having delayed securing passage. In fact, permission for passage into Romulan space had been secured, but not the method of passage.

"It's a problem," Captain Picard said. From the captain's expression, Spock could tell that the blueblooded commander of this *Enterprise* thoroughly understood the ramifications of secured space, and when a starship could and could not be of service.

"Yes," Spock reluctantly admitted. "Even the UFP diplomatic corp cannot breach imperial space. This time, the royal family wants us in, but no one else does. Perhaps . . . secrecy required concessions I should not have made this time."

"Sir?" Riker straightened at Data's side. "We've got something here."

The android touched his controls and read off, "The Romulan defector Rekk Devra Kilrune is no longer living in the Federation."

"Where is he, then?" Picard asked. "We'll go get him."

Data swiveled around in his chair, his expression particularly childlike. "No, sir . . . he is no longer *living* in the Federation."

Riker held out a hand that stopped what seemed to be turning into a debate of unclarity, and looked at his captain. "Rekk Devra was murdered, Captain . . . fifteen months ago, during a visit to Deep Space Nine."

A mantle of chill descended upon the bridge, as winter cloaks northern hills. Spock felt it, and saw that all the others also felt it. Shoulders tightened, pensive glances traveled, fists clenched, lips pressed. Strange how a revelation could be so tangible, so very present.

The last living uncontaminated royal family member, dead. Whoever was driving the force of this plague was a critical step ahead.

And now . . . what?

Chapter Twelve

Combat Support Tender Saskatoon,
Starfleet Registry CST 2601

"DAMAGE CONTROL, TOP DECK!"

"Take some of the new midshipmen up there with you."

"Right. You and you, and your friend over there, come with me."

"And this one."

On the severely angled bridge deck of the *Saskatoon,* Eric Stiles hooked the nearest midshipman and handed him to Jeremy White as Jeremy rushed past him, dragging the other three kids.

"Did it hit us or just skin us?" Stiles tossed as an afterthought as he brushed hot bits of plastic from his shoulders. "Mr. Perraton, have somebody trim the deck gravitational compensators, please. Rafting hands, man umbilicals one, two, and four."

"Direct hit, midships upper quadrant, lateral shield, port side."

"Did you say upper quadrant?"

"Upper. At least I think it's there—" Jeremy's words became garbled as he disappeared into the bulky body of the CST, jumping through hatch after hatch until he got to the tubular companionway that would take him to the operational deck above the middle of the ship. Smoke rolled freely from chamber to chamber through the body of the CST, a ship built on lateral lines to avoid transfer of equipment up and down ladder wells. Despite its 200-meter LOA, the tender only had three decks. Factories didn't need stairways.

"Rats," Stiles muttered, surveying the shattered trunk housing that had just been blown all over the deck. "Ship to ship."

To his right, at the comm station, Midshipman Zelasko controlled a cough and squeaked, "Ship to ship, sir."

Nearly choking on the acrid smoke from fried circuits in the deck and sparks on the smoldering carpet, Stiles held onto the helm stanchion as the CST rolled noticeably under him. "Captain Sattler, I've got to be able to get closer than this. If both our ships can't move off as a unit, you've got to kick those fighters off harder when they come into range. I know you've never done this before, but—"

"Sorry, Commander—Fire!" The captain's voice from the Destroyer *Lafayette* crackled back at him through the electrical charges of phaser and disruptor fire in open space. *"Sorry again. Two units got past us. I can't move off with a kinked nacelle, not even on impulse, without knowing what else is damaged up there."*

"The arbitrariness of battle is for you to worry about, Captain, thank the god of problems."

"He said cheerily," Travis Perraton edited from the other side of the narrow horseshoe-shaped bridge, where he was dodging from station to station coordinating the next few moves. To somebody on the upper deck, he spoke into a comm unit. "Just control the damage, Adams, don't repair it yet. We don't come first out here, remember?"

Spitting dust from his neatly trimmed moustache, Stiles turned forward again and wrapped up his communication with the destroyer. "We'll have your external diagnostic in a minute, Captain."

"Are you damaged? You're venting something off your upper hull."

"Yes, we've got some damage, but we'll repair it later. Your ship comes first. Keep the comm lines open if possible. You'll have to drop your shields while we raft up and do the work. That'll be the tricky part. You'll want to have one of the other Starfleet ships run a cover grid."

"I'll contact the Majestic *and—tactical, broad on the bow—fire! Deflectors, shift double starboard! Hail the* Majestic*—fire at will, Samuels!* Majestic, *Sattler here—"*

"She's got her hands full." Stiles turned and called back into the scoped hatchways, not bothering with the comm. "Tell me when you know something, Jeremy! Those Romulans can see we're vulnerable, so work faster."

Jeremy's disembodied voice trailed back through three sections. *"Scanning . . . nacelle hasn't been breached . . . not on the outside, anyway . . . could be internal feedback from a hit someplace else, though. The main injector's secure . . . there's a crack in the sliding bulkhead. Let me follow it down . . . I got it, Eric, I see a fractured buckler. It's not the nacelle. It's the strut."*

"Great!" Stiles clapped his hands once, and startled the socks off his new helmsman. "That's a relief. Ship to ship—Captain Sattler, good news. It's not the nacelle that's kinked. It's only the strut. We'll raft up right here and square it, but you've got to keep those stingers off us for a solid fifteen minutes. I have to put extravehicular crew on the skin of your ship and I don't want anybody barbecued on your hull."

"*Commander, you fix my nacelle in fifteen minutes in the middle of this mess and I'll owe you a big sloppy kiss and a crystal decanter of your favorite. We'll put out the warning pennant and anybody who comes near your workers will feel the heat. There's nothing like a movable starbase when we need one!*"

The charming—oh, yes—and sultry voice of the destroyer's captain made Stiles smile again. For a moment, he had trouble imagining her in a uniform. "I'll take the kiss and send the decanter to my grandfather. Maintain standby communications and let us handle the rafting. Drop your shields on our mark."

"*Pennant's flashing. Standing by for rafting approach. Do you intend to use tractors or umbilicals?*"

"Both," Stiles told her.

"*Aren't tractors faster?*"

"Usually, but if we get hit and there's a power failure, our ships would just drift away from each other and we couldn't help each other. With umbilicals, we'll be netted together no matter what happens."

"*Good thinking. Ready when you are.*"

"Three . . . two . . . one . . . mark."

"*Affirmative, shields down. Approach when ready.*"

Glancing at his bridge crew, Stiles said, "Okay, boys, we've got fifteen minutes! That's two to raft up and thirteen to effect repair. Let's clone that destroyer a new nacelle strut. Sound off."

From deep through the body of the combat support tender, team leaders and section masters called off.

"Internal repair squad ready, sir!"

"Rafting hands ready. Umbilicals one, two, and four manned, magnetic tethers hot."

"Rivet squad suited and ready, sir."

"Caissons ready."

"Gun team?"

"Weapons armed and ready!"

"Where are the evil twins?"

"Already in the airlock, Eric."

"Beautiful. Lateral thrusters one half. Let's move in."

"All hands, brace for action rafting! Shields down!"

Ah, the chatter of activity. What a good noise.

Out there, not far away on the cosmic scale, a half dozen Romulan fighters darted around two Starfleet destroyers, one patrol cutter, and three merchant ships caught in the crossfire. Bursts of phaser fire, disruptor streams, glancing hits and direct detonations lit the fabric of black space like flashing jewels. There was a startling beauty about it, stitched firmly into the crazy quilt of hazard and excitement.

"Okay, you lot—tea time! Battle Cook Woody reportin' f'duty, sah!"

Stiles rolled his eyes and groaned. What timing.

At the port entryway, Ship's Mess Officer Alan Wood came rolling in as he always seemed to in moments of critical action, or did critical action always happen at teatime?

Stiles didn't argue, as their in-house real-live London butcher distributed cookies, tea, and coffee to an obviously busy crew.

"There y'go. Two sugars, Trav. Told y'I wouldn't f'get. Eric, sir, no caffeine for you, double cream, honey, and ye olde ginger snaps."

"You always know what calms me down, Alan. And don't call me 'honey.' "

"Aye aye, dear."

"Put the tray down and take over Jason's driver coil balance, Battle Cook."

"You got it."

They were completely vulnerable now. Both the CST and the destroyer were shields down. These were the crucial minutes during which any enemy shot could cut all the way through any bulkhead or hull plate and take out anything inside, man or machine.

He glanced around at the bridge crew, peeked back through the infinity mirror of hatchways leading into the depths of the *Saskatoon* and its work areas, saw the unit leaders looking back at him from their various places, and satisfied himself that all segments were ready to work. He turned now to watch the two main screens, one always viewing forward, one always aft, and the sixteen auxiliary screens around the horseshoe. On the screens, shown from a dozen different angles, there was a hot battle going on at this edge of a small solar system. He stood beside the command chair, so seldom used that it held parts and charts and anything else they needed handy at any given time. He almost never sat in it. Should have it removed altogether.

"Watch your aft swing," he told the helmsman. "There's a solar current here."

"I can do it manually, I think," the helmsman boldly claimed.

"You think, *sir.*" Travis turned at the brash helmsman's statement, reached across the auxiliary board on the upper controls, and tapped one of the pads. "I've got it. Stabilizers on."

The young helmsman fumed, but said nothing.

Stiles glanced at Travis and shrugged. Kids.

He stepped a little closer to the helm, just to intimidate at the right level. If only he could remember the kid's name.

"Okay, junior," he decided, "this is your first battle rafting. Let's do it right."

The midshipman gritted his teeth. "Aye, sir."

"Adjust to starboard on the transverse axis . . . watch your amplitude of pitch . . . not bad. Don't let the roll go . . . quarter reverse on the port lateral. More thrust to port . . . less underthrust . . . never mind the bumpers, don't try to be graceful. . . ."

On the starboard deck, Travis clamped his lips to keep from laughing at the helmsman's obvious annoyance with help he clearly needed. Stiles saw the effort, but any possibility of amusement for himself was lost in the sheer danger of what they were about to do. An action rafting was never routine, no matter how well-drilled the crew could possibly become.

When the CST and the destroyer were snugged up beam-to-beam and in line, and the CST had been raised to near-touching level with the *Lafayette*'s starboard nacelle, Stiles called, "Pass line two."

"Pass two!" the response came from amidships.

On one of the small monitors, umbilical number two snaked out and grappled the attraction bracket on the high side of the destroyer.

"Capture two!" the line handler called.

Suddenly the destroyer heaved up on its port nacelle as a Romulan fighter veered in too close and opened fire. Bright light washed Stiles and everyone around him from all the starboard screens, a fierce shining glitter of destruction and raw heat.

"Whoa," Stiles murmured, shielding his eyes. "Close one."

Travis flinched at the proximity of death. "*Lafayette,* steady your position, can you?"

"*We're attempting to hold as steady as possible,* Saskatoon," the other commanding officer responded. "*That current came up under us just as that Romulan fired on us. Double whammy.*"

"I know you're taking fire," Stiles interrupted, "but we only need thirty seconds to finish this. Hold still that long."

"*Understood.*"

"Spring in closer now," he said to the helm trainee. "Keep us trim. Work a little faster. Don't overcompensate. Let the gravitational umbilicals do the heavy lifting."

"Closing," the kid said. "Twenty meters . . . fifteen meters . . ."

"Pass one."

"Passing one!"

"Hold two."

"Two holding."

"Capture one!"

"Forward starboard thruster one quarter and shift down port bow 10 degrees."

"Forward one quarter, port bow down ten, aye."

"Pass four, hold one."

"Passing four!"

"Hold one, aye."

"Two and four, haul away."

"Haul away two!"

"Haul away four!"

Music, music. The church chimes of efficient rafting. Thirty seconds to spare. Snuggling his CST up to a big, powerful, scarred, smoldering battleship in the middle of a flashing firefight—ah! The chunky hull of the CST didn't fit well against the streamlined multihulled destroyer, so he had to pick and choose which umbilicals would line up best, then cast one and pivot in on it. What a gorgeous process.

"I love skirmishes," he effused happily. "That's good! Cut thrust. Engine crew, stand by. Mr. Blake! Scan for stress."

"Scanning, sir."

As disruptor fire flashed on some of the smaller monitors, showing the ongoing space battle between another destroyer and those Romulan buzz-saws, Stiles nodded in satisfaction, even though Blake couldn't see him. Greg Blake had known him since they were both fifteen years old. The "sir" was almost silly in that regard, but he knew his long-time crew threw it in for effect at moments like this. There were always impressionable midshipmen and junior officers serving on the CST, most of whom would move on after the grueling training they would receive here.

On the screen to his left, the streamlined body of the Destroyer *Lafayette* drew close to the lumbering CST, in fact close enough to touch if that viewport had been a window they could open. He saw the gleaming hull plates and the buttonhead rivets as clearly as his own fingernails.

"What a great way to live," he muttered. "She gets all the glory and the headaches, she has to guess what the enemy's doing—and on top of that she has to protect us in the middle of a battle. This is the best damn duty around."

"You could ask for a date," Travis suggested. "I bet she'd go, the way she sounds when she talks to you. Maybe if you grow your beard back—"

"I'm not dating anybody who outranks me," Stiles commented, aware of the glances from Midshipman Zelasko at the comm station and the two little ensigns over at the engineering board. "Bad enough having a cocky Canadian first officer around. And the beard itched."

Outside, close enough to smell the gunpowder, seven other ships were engaged in a spark battle, a border skirmish with hotheaded Romulans. These eruptions had been going on for months now, sparks of aggression that seemed like temper tantrums from isolated Romulan units. The empire kept claiming nothing was wrong, that these were just dissatisfied commanders venting their frustration, but Stiles didn't believe it. Something was going on in the Romulan Empire that was causing rogue attacks. The Federation wanted to be prudent. Ignore acts of war. Avoid any one of these bursts turning into a lit fuse that couldn't be put out by anything other than full-out conflict.

"Okay, Travis," Stiles said when he was satisfied that the ships were as close as possible and the umbilicals were taut. "Go do that voodoo that you do so well."

"Ten seconds and counting," Travis responded, and hit a comm button. "Rivet team, hit open space. Signal when you're on the davit boom."

"*Acknowledged,*" one of the Bolt brothers responded. "*Ready.*"

"Launching." Travis hit his controls.

The hiss of the airlock shot through the whole ship. There was no place on the CST to get away from that big sound as the lock depressurized and the repair crew sprayed out from the tender on a spiderweb of cables from the swinging davit, two men to a cable, a total of twelve men in spaceworthy suits, each fully armed with a trapeze harness and a tool vest. Their job wasn't to fight the enemy—it was to fight the enemy's results.

The interior of the CST fell oddly silent, giving way to the bleeps and whirs of shipboard mechanical redundancy, and a symphony of eyes swept the wall-wide grid of screens. Dozens of angles, each fixed on some aspect of the repair job—only a few were dedicated to the fight that was still going on within phaser-striking distance of this oddly protectionless refuge.

Stiles settled back on his heels and listened to the critical exchange between Jeremy White, back in the engineering control room, and Travis here on the bridge, whose job it was to manage the rivet squad. In less than a minute, the two men had the rivet squad swung over on the external davits to the nacelle of the *Lafayette,* crawling all over it with their magnetic boots like a tidy infestation.

The open comm lines brought in the work as if it were happening right at his feet, bits of dialogue overlapping others as the squad split up to do a half dozen jobs in a matter of minutes.

"*Got some burnoff plating infecting this binding strake.*"

"*I'll help you.*"

"*Stand clear.*"

"*Two more centimeters.*"

Travis talking at the same time: "Don't crowd him, Zack. You're too close to the welding stream."

"*I'm Jason.*"

"Clone."

"*I need the spreader over here.*"

"*—swing that caisson under me, will you?*"

"*—and engage the thrusters so you've got balance—*"

Then Jeremy's voice from two sections back: "Mr. Evans, countersink those outer rivets before you caulk them in."

"*You sure, sir?*"

"We always countersink. Maintains a flush surface."

"*What difference—*"

"A big one at hyperlight. Morton, what are you doing? Move your arm so I can see."

"*Chocking the vertical bracket stringers?*"

Stiles touched his comm button and interrupted. "Chock 'em in under the shell plating, Mr. Morton. Then caulk it with foam."

"*Won't hold more than a week.*"

"It only has to hold a day. Just double-secure the center of effort and wrap it up. You got nine minutes left."

"*Thank you.*"

"Welcome."

"Mr. Lightcudder?"

Startled by a completely unfamiliar voice only inches from his shoulder, Stiles cranked around and found himself face to face with a total stranger. Total! Never seen the guy before. Right here on the working deck!

Civilian. No uniform, no identifying patches or badges. Work clothes.

How could this happen?

It couldn't, but here he was, grinning like a Halloween pumpkin. No escort, no nothing.

Oh—actually there was a nervous ensign standing at the bridge hatchway, evidently having just brought the man in. Why hadn't the ensign done the officer approach? The ensign shrugged as Stiles raked him with a glare.

The civilian was stocky, wearing a bulky tan jacket with big round buttons and a heavy neck scarf, which gave the man an illusion of being short. Actually Stiles looked him nearly in the eye, so he was at least five feet nine. He had a round face with flush-dots on the puffy cheeks, a halo of metal-shaving hair mounted behind his balding forehead, round brown eyes, round shoulders—the guy was round.

"Are you Mr. Lightcudder?" the round guy asked.

"What?" Stiles stepped back and got a better look. "Who are you? How'd you get on my bridge?"

The odd newcomer kept his eyes fixed on Stiles. "They just put me on board from the *Lafayette.* I was told to report to Mr. Lightcudder. My name's Ansue Hashley and I'm *so* grateful for—"

"A civilian is transferred to my CST and this is the first I hear of it?"

Greg Blake strode by and handed him a padd on the way past. "Nobody likes to talk to you."

"We avoid it," Matt Girvan said from the engineering support station.

"Any of you know about this?" Stiles asked, swiveling a glance around the bridge.

Nobody did.

"Well, Mister—"

"Hashley. Ansue Hashley. I'm—"

"You'll have to stand by a few minutes. We're in the middle of an operation. Just park right there and don't do anything and don't touch anything."

"I will, Mr. Lightcudder, I mean I won't, and I'll stand right here." Hashley planted both feet and pointed a sausage finger at his boots.

Stiles glanced at Travis, who frowned and muttered, "Lightcudder . . ."

"*Stiles, Jason. There's some kind of Charlie Noble sticking up here and it's actually hot.*"

Turning back to his job, Stiles twitched at the proximity of the stranger. "Hot? Electrically?"

"*No, it's actually radiating heat. In fact, it's glowing.*"

"That can't be right. . . ."

"*No kidding. I don't want to touch it.*"

"No, don't touch it. Jeremy!"

"Copy that," Jeremy called from two hatches back. "Pretty weird, Eric. You want me to suit up?"

"Talk to the destroyer's CE first. Have him tell you what that thing is and turn it off if he can. I don't want a hole burned in somebody's EVS."

"*Closing the breach now . . . two more centimeters . . . one more . . . hold!*"

"*Hold the crane!*"

"*Holding.*"

"What's all that they're talking about?" Hashley asked.

Annoyed, Stiles quickly said, "Just shortcuts we take, Mr. Hashley. We have to get the *Lafayette* back into action so they can press the Romulans back."

"Are they going to kill the Romulans?"

"Not if they can avoid it."

"Isn't this a battle?"

"No, it's just a commercial blockade. Some hothead venting off at us."

"But the Romulans attacked your patrols, didn't they? Isn't that an act of war?"

"It's more complicated than that."

"I thought we were having a war and that's why they wanted me."

"No war yet." With his demeanor Stiles did his best to communicate that he was preoccupied.

"Rig a gantline over here. We'll just horse the strut with brute force and tribolt it."

"I love brute force. Gives me a sense of superiority."

"—the magnetic coupling?"

"No, the spreader. I'll hand it—"

"—the only way you'll ever get any respect."

"What kind of a ship is this?" Ansue Hashley looked all around. "It's not a starship—"

Stiles watched the screens, told himself that he should ignore the man, then decided he would enjoy showing off a little. "No, not a starship."

"Cruiser?"

"No."

"Battleship."

"Hardly. Jason, Stiles. Pull that spreader all the way out of the bridle and discard it. Don't be tidy. Six minutes."

"Six, aye."

"What kind of ship are you, then?" Hashley asked again.

"We're a combat support tender. Some people call us a 'floating starbase.' We're a heavy-laden, multipurpose vessel made to support more specialized Starfleet vessels. We carry structural and weapons-repair specialists, materiel, fuel, ammunition and dry stores. We can resupply a ship on the fly or right in the middle of active engagement, like we're doing now. One of our jobs is to quickly make operational any ready-reserve ships on standby. We did that to *Lafayette* last week."

"And now she needs you again!" Hashley's eyes flew wide. "Right in the middle of a fight! How do you do something like that!"

"With step-by-step processes. Being fast is a matter of survival, not just success."

"You must've been busy lately, with all the trouble that's been erupting."

"We've been nonstop for months," Stiles agreed. "Wish we knew why all these skirmishes were erupting—"

"I know why! Do you want me to tell you? I know all about it!"

Stiles leered briefly at the man, sure he didn't actually know more than Starfleet frontliners, but disturbed by Hashley's confident claim.

"Crossfire! Incoming!" Ensign Ashikaga shouted from the tactical sensors.

"Detonate!" Stiles authorized, and the shots lanced out before the sound his words had died.

At the weapons console, Matt Girvan fell on his controls instantly, obviously expecting the authorization to fire while there were extravehicular crew out there. He'd been ready to defend the CST, despite the attempts by *Lafayette* and *Majestic* to protect the wounded destroyer and her rafted repair ship. Phaser fire blew from the *Saskatoon,* cutting across the paths of two streams of disruptor fire that actually were meant to hit the *Majestic* but had missed. The shots detonated in mid-space—good work, though the power wash and the stress of opening fire rocked the CST and caused the umbilicals to sing through their hull mounts. The inside of the ship whined freakishly, buffeted by the power wash.

"Oh, what happened?" Ansue Hashley's arms flew wide as the deck rocked. "Did we get shot?"

Not a direct hit, but the wash did enough damage to fritz several of the monitors. Two went completely dark, and a half dozen flashed and became garbled, losing the view of the rivet team on the destroyer's nacelle strut.

His ears aching, Stiles crossed to the portside monitors and called over the whine. "Check the men!"

Horrified by the shouts and calls rattling over the comm from the repair team, he fixed on the nearest monitor, which showed a closeup flurry of elbows and parts of suits, but didn't give a clear view of any one person.

Frantic for a wide view, Stiles muttered, "I'd really like a look."

"I'm getting green on all the life-support signals," Travis said with undisguised relief. "The body of the ship deflected the wash."

"Lucky angle. I hate to fire when I've got men out." No one paid any attention except Ansue Hashley, whose eyes somehow got even wider at the declaration. Stiles punched the nearest comm link. "Rivet squad, running out of time. Minute and thirty left."

"Shouldn't you be out there, Mr. Lightcudder?" Hashley asked. "If you're in command?"

"No, they don't need me out there."

"Maybe there's something I can do. . . ."

"Not right now, thanks."

"*Stiles, Bolt. Strut cradle's secure, riveted, and caulked. Main injector's flowing and the sliding bulkhead is jury-rigged over the cofferdam and—Monks, is it glazed? Yes, it's glazed and chemical-bonded. Ready to retract the caissons and the davit.*"

"A whole minute early!" Stiles whooped. "You guys are singing! Back inside before we get another visitation."

He stood back to listen to the tumble of orders as the rivet team handled their own reshipping. This was when all the hours of brain-frying drills paid off.

"*Mr. Stiles, this is Sattler. We saw the crossfire. Do you need assistance?*"

"Don't worry about us, Captain. Your ship's the important one here, not ours. Soon as I get my men aboard, we'll shove off and you can do your job with those Romulans. Congratulations on your first combat rafting."

"*You're a piece of work, Mr. Stiles. Now I know where you get your reputation.*"

"All lies. Stand by, please."

Travis met his questioning gaze as if cued in psychically. "The caissons are boarded, davits coming back in, and all hands will be aboard in another few seconds."

"Ready on the umbilicals. Prepare to shove off," he called through the ship, not bothering with the comm.

"Ready one!"

"Ready on two!"

"Ready four!"

"Release four."

"Release four, aye!"

"Slack one. Helm, swing out on number two." Yikes, he sure had to find out that kid's name soon. Always happened when they got a new batch of trainees. "Hey, I said slack one!"

"Slacking one!"

"Haul away, four."

"Hold it!" Jeremy suddenly called from three compartments back. "Four's fouled."

"Hold all lines!" Stiles poked his head through the hatch, but didn't actually leave the bridge. "What's the story?"

"Looks like the retractor's jammed. Must've taken a hit we didn't notice."

"Disengage the line."

"Cut and run from our end?"

"Right, let it float. We'll pick it up later if we can. It's not fouled onto *Lafayette,* is it? Because we'll have to go out again if it is. They can't trail a line into battle."

"No, line's free. It's our retractor housing."

"Cut it."

"Aye aye . . ." They all waited until a loud *chunk* boomed through the ship's body. Then Jeremy spoke again. "Line's detached. We're clear, Eric."

"Ship to ship." He watched while the communications kid tapped in, then looked at the screen displaying the nearby plates of the destroyer. "We're clear of rafting, *Lafayette.* Bear off laterally. When you've cleaned up the mess out there, we'll reprovision you and the *Majestic.*"

"*Excellent job,* Saskatoon. *Bearing off. Shields up. And thanks again, double trouble.*"

"No problem. Good work, Mr. Perraton, Mr. White, everybody."

He turned to the main screen as, with nothing less than heart-stirring dynamism, the great shining gray form of the destroyer peeled off at quarter impulse and drove into the swarm of Romulans.

"This is wondrous!" Ansue Hashley hopped on his toes and spread his hands wide. "You should be in the headlines!"

"Nah, no headlines. This is nuts-and-bolts duty."

"But you should get recognition for this kind of wonderful thing!"

"Do without food and bandages for a while. Helm, hard over. Come full about and give them room to fight. I don't want the destroyers to have to protect us."

"Hard over, sir."

"I could write an article!" Ansue Hashley insisted. "I know some people where I could send it! You do such a vital, glorious thing!

Stiles watched the screens, deliberately not looking at him. "It's vital, not glorious. Headlines are for the *Lafayette* and the *Majestic.*"

Shuddering as its great engines vibrated, the muscular combat tender turned on an axis and hummed away from the center of the dispute, leaving the cloud of Romulans and the two Federation ships behind in a sparkle of weapons fire.

"Secure the ship, Travis," he said casually, knowing that the actual activities were hardly casual. Punching the comm, he added, "Clones, Stiles."

"*Bolt and Bolt, Ship Riveters-at-Large. Would you like an appointment, sir?*"

"Great work, rivet squad, excellent. You get an 'A' for speed and an extra minute to sleep tonight."

"*Wow.*"

"Bailiff, shoot that man."

As the laughter of relief and satisfaction rippled through the CST, Stiles turned like an old-time gunfighter and hooked his thumbs in an imaginary holster belt.

"Okay, Mr. Hashley . . . what's your story?"

"Oh! Me—yes!" Ansue Hashley stuck out a computer cartridge. "I watched while they composed this. It says right on here to report to Mr. Lightcudder and give this to you. Is it all right to?"

Stiles pushed the card into the nearest terminal, which clicked, and flipped, but nothing came up on the monitor above it.

"Where is it?" he wondered.

From the tool alley, Greg Blake called, "It's back here, Mr. Lightcudder."

"Uh . . . yeah, would you pass it back up here, please?"

"Certainly, Mr. Lightcudder."

The screen flickered once, then a message came up on it—printed, not vocal. Obviously somebody didn't want this read aloud by anybody, including the ship's systems.

"Mmm . . . explains . . . almost nothing." Stiles looked at the printed message, sensing Travis and the bridge guys looking from behind him. "You don't deal much with Starfleet, do you, Mr. Hashley?"

ATTENTION MR. LTCDR
EYES ONLY DO NOT BROADCAST
HOLD ITEM TOP SECURITY

"Not even the name of the ship in the message," Travis said as he came up behind Stiles. "What item?"

Stiles cocked a hip and glared at him until Travis uttered, "Oh . . . right."

They both turned to Hashley, who looked back and forth between them again and again.

"Smuggling?" Stiles asked.

"Oh, transporting. I'm an agricultural broker. Usually, anyway. Well, I used to be. Sometimes I take other cargo. Well, most of the time. Well—"

"What other cargo?"

"Anything anybody wants. Mostly stuff the Romulans want. Most of the time I don't even know what's in the crates and casks. I don't ask much. I've been running the same twenty-light-year relay for the past seven years. The Romulans had laws that said I shouldn't be doing it, but they were liking what I did. They could've stopped me any time, but they bought what I had and paid me to move more. If the patrols stopped me, they usually settled for a quarter of my cargo." Ansue Hashley smiled, and suddenly looked like a carved pumpkin. "I give very generous bribes."

How could you hate a jack-o-lantern?

"First of all, 'Lightcudder' isn't anybody's name. Those letters mean 'Lieutenant Commander.' "

Hashley blinked as if he'd been slapped. "But aren't you . . . the captain? Oh, no, did I make a terrible mistake?"

"No, you didn't make a mistake. Combat support tenders are piloted by lieutenant commanders, officered by lieutenants, and crewed by chief, ensigns, midshipmen, and able crewmen. Most of these young people are here for experience and training. CST duty is considered good experience because of the active labor, tactical judgment, and hands-on ship handling. You also get a taste of battle situations without actually having to fight. Not usually, anyway. So I'm not 'Captain Lightcudder.' I'm Lieutenant Commander Stiles."

"Oh . . . oh, goodness, oh, my goodness, I made such a big mistake. . . . Stiles, Stiles, I won't forget again. Oh, I'm so sorry. . . ."

"No, no."

"But I feel just awful, horrible—"

"It's not important. What *is* important is how you got transferred here without my knowing about it, and why the *Lafayette* would do that."

"Oh, I'm top secret! At least, my location is."

"Why?"

"Because the Romulans are trying to kidnap me."

As Travis finished his immediate duties and came down to the center of the squatty bridge to stand behind him, Stiles folded his arms and insisted again, *"Why?"*

"Because I know too much. I'm the one who knows why the Romulans have been skirmishing with the Federation on all the border fronts. You said you didn't know, remember? But I do."

Stiles glanced at Travis, who made a subtle shrug with just his eyes.

"The *Lafayette* slipped you on board here to sort of shuffle the cards so the Romulans wouldn't know which ship you're on?"

"Yes! Also to get me out of the line of fire. The Federation doesn't want me to be a scraping goat."

"Well, how do you feel about telling me this big secret that suddenly makes my ship a target?"

"Oh, I feel fine about it! I know everything. I know why the Romulans are panicking."

Hashley stepped closer and poked Stiles in the folded forearm, and his eyes got big as golf balls.

"Poison! The whole Romulan royal family! Every single member of the emperor's bloodline, no matter where they are, all over the empire. They're all dying!"

"What?"

Astonished, Eric Stiles sank back on the edge of the helm. His feet felt molded to the deck. His arms wouldn't unfold.

"We haven't heard anything about that!" Travis blurted, glancing custodially at Stiles, then back at the funny agricultural broker who had been dropped on them.

"It's a big, huge secret," Hashley went on. "The Romulan royal family is trying to keep it secret. They don't want anybody to know their empire's leadership could all be dying, one by one. It'll be just a mess if such a big weakness gets discovered, even if only by people inside the empire."

Behind Stiles's shoulder, Travis asked, "And they think the Federation's behind the . . . the whatever's killing them?"

"Poisoning," Hashley said. "Or maybe an engineered virus—anyway, it's something definitely artificially constructed. A hundred and ten members of the royal family have died already, and all the others are infected. I'm the only Federation citizen running the Neutral Zone, so they know I'm smart and I know why they're attacking Federation ships."

Stiles swallowed a hard lump and registered that his feet were suddenly blocks of ice. That didn't sound right. Nobody cared that much about one Federation guy running cargo, and Hashley sure wasn't the only one.

"What's this thing they've got?" he asked. "How does it manifest itself?"

"They've got a blood disease. First they get real weak, real suddenly. Then their arms and legs start hurting. Pretty soon they can hardly walk and breathe. It's infected every single member of the emperor's bloodline. It's specialized to the blood of the royal family, so they know this is a mass-assassination attempt. It's supposed to be a secret, but I found out about it, so they tried to kidnap me."

"The Romulans?"

"That's right. And the *Majestic* came in and rescued me, and they were trying to get back to Federation space with me when the Romulans attacked them. They beamed me to the *Lafayette* to confuse the Romulans, and now the *Lafayette* beamed me to you, to keep confusing them. Now they don't know where I am."

The bridge fell to an uneasy silence.

"Aren't you kind of . . . blabbing a lot, Mr. Hashley?"

"Oh, yes! That way I'm never the only one to know anything!"

"Pretty cavalier about it, aren't you?" Travis commented.

Hashley shrugged his round shoulders and showed the palms of his hands, then abruptly clapped them together and drew a sharp breath. "Stiles! Are you Eric John Stiles?"

"Well—"

"I remember you! You're Eric John Stiles the Hero! You got the Medal of Valor eight years ago!"

"Ten," Stiles mumbled.

"Eleven," Travis corrected, and he took Hashley by the arm in a stern manner. "We don't talk about that around here very much, Mr. Hashley. He's just our lightcudder and that's how we keep it."

"Oh, I'm so happy to be here and meet him, though!"

"Mr. Hashley," Stiles interrupted, "is there anything you're not telling us?"

"Me? No! I'd tell you anything I knew. I don't want to know any secrets, not ever. Secrets can get you killed. I never want to be the only one—"

"Okay, okay." Stiles pushed himself off the helm and uncracked his tingling arms from around his ribs. "I'll keep you in protective custody until I can communicate with somebody about you . . . if you'll just . . . quiet down a little. We'll assign you a bunk . . . Travis, uh . . . get some crew up here to clean up all this broken plastic and chips."

"Oh, I'll do it!" Hashley dropped to his knees right where he was standing and began swiftly plucking the residue of damage off the deck and stuffing it into his pockets. "I love to help. Sitting in quarters while everybody else is working, that's just not for me. I'm an action kind of man."

"Yeah . . . Travis, take us back over the Neutral Zone border and . . . hold position in case they need us again. I'll be in my quarters."

With icy hands clenched, Stiles paused in the dimness of his quarters and closed his eyes. The computer had clicked and whirred, but it had provided only poor answers. A thousand memories shot back as if rocketing from yesterday instead of—what was it, now, fourteen, almost fifteen years ago? Didn't seem so long.

The door chime sounded.

For a moment, he thought of not answering.

"Yeah."

The panel opened and Travis looked in. "Hey, Lightcudder. Can I interrupt?"

"Sure."

Travis came all the way in, carrying a steaming cup of hot chocolate and a particularly concerned expression he was trying to disguise as something else. He stood at the door for a moment as it closed behind him.

"You all right, Eric?" he asked.

Warmed by the solicitous effort, Stiles tried to appear relaxed by brushing the remains of his breakfast toast off his desk chair. "Eh, I guess so. Sit down, Travis. And I, in my infinite wisdom, shall sit also."

He slumped into the chair, and put one boot up on the edge of a drawer that wasn't quite closed and his elbow up on the desk.

Depositing the hot chocolate on the desk near Stiles' resting hand, Travis sat down on the bunk. The quarters were too small for two chairs, so the bunk was almost constantly rumpled, being used more often as a couch than a place to sleep. "Ship's secure. Jeremy's handling the damage we took—it should be repaired in about twenty minutes. And Ansue Hashley's crawling around the chambers sucking up damage with the shoulderheld vac."

"You guys are getting the process down fast with these new kids."

"That's what we do. The fight's still going on, but the destroyers seem to have it locked up. The Romulan fighters are trickling away one by one. I think they'll leave us alone."

"Good," Stiles muttered. "I need to be left alone." As Travis planted both feet and leaned forward, Stiles quickly amended, "No, no, I don't mean you."

The door chimed and Greg Blake poked in when the panel opened. "Eric, okay if we shut down the warp injection system so we can flush the lines?"

"How many of the Romulan fighters are still in the vicinity?"

"Only about four now."

" 'About' four?"

"Guess I better check."

"Guess you better. But listen, hail Captain Sattler and make sure we're not pressuring her by staying in the vicinity. If she needs us to bear off, we'll move out before we shut anything down. Be nice about it."

"Will do. Sorry to interrupt."

The door panel slid shut again.

"You never try to push, do you?" Travis observed. "That's why all the captains appreciate you so much."

"It's just that I'm sweet and polite and I know my place."

"Know your *place . . . ?"*

"Sure, think about it. CST's are usually commanded by the guys who couldn't qualify to run the glory machines, so they get out among the starshippers and try throwing their weight around. They're impolite. They take it out on the captains, who they think surpassed them. I'm just not like that. I try to be accommodating and patient and helpful without being ub—ob—what's that word you used last week?"

"Obsequious?"

"That's it. I'm satisfied with what I'm doing. Remember when we got assigned the CST duty? The team was depressed and down because they thought we'd get something fancier, but they all adjusted, and it's turned out to be great work."

"They adjusted because you packed 'em off to special training for combat-ready missions. You made sure we all had skills in hands-on operations management, not just Academy certificates in theories and simulators. Then you juggled us around until you found our strengths. You even pushed Brad and Bill back out to the private sector."

"I had to push them. We had a good relationship going among all of us, and nobody wanted to be the first to leave. They were ready to go. Starfleet couldn't make as much use of them as free enterprise could. Not everybody flourishes in uniform. CST duty didn't make good use of their natural abilities. For others, this is the best they'll do, or this is where they're most useful. Better this than have them go out and try to be hotshots and wash out. Maybe cost some lives."

Travis grinned coquettishly. "What about me?"

"You? You're a bum. I just keep you here as my first officer out of charity. And me . . . this is perfect for me."

"Eric?" One of the evil twins knocked on the door, not bothering with the chime. "You asleep?"

"No, come on in."

One of the Bolts appeared and stuck his tousled blond head around the doorframe. "Permission to put a team outside and patch the PGV meter?"

"As long as Jeremy says it's safe to go out."

"Right. And do either of you know where the cylinder punch went? As my mother used to say, 'You had it last.' "

Travis spoke up before Stiles could bother saying he didn't know. "It's in the aft locker in the tool alley, Zack, on the inboard side, underneath the conduction paper."

"Thanks. Sorry to interrupt."

When they were alone again, Stiles regarded Travis with quizzical respect. "How do you tell those two apart so fast? Fifteen years, and it still takes me half a conversation."

"Just doing what any good exo does. So . . . what do you think of Hashley?"

"I think he's into something a lot more complicated than he believes," Stiles said. "I checked the Bureau of Shipping records just before you came in. Ansue Cabela Hashley, human, Federation citizenship, most of the right licenses, skirts the law now and then but not much, originally from Rigel system, nothing much worth putting on record. He's been running the same patch of space back and forth for years like a bug, shuttling minor contraband into Romulan space. The Romulans have pretty much encouraged him by not enforcing their own laws in his case. He probably brings in things they can't get, and they like it. He hasn't been hurting anybody and more people like him than not, so he's been considered small potatoes."

"Till now."

Stiles nodded. "He's a cosmic worker-insect. Now he's stepped in goo and he's stuck. Probably he doesn't even realize that the reason he's been safe is that things haven't been too tense with the Romulans over the past twenty years. Now that they're tensing up, well, he *has* been breaking

Romulan law right along. I'm guessing the Federation doesn't have good cause to protest. Then he stumbled on this poison thing and suddenly the small potato is a hot potato."

"What do you think the connection is between the blood thing and Hashley?"

"No idea."

"It's got to be more than he thinks," Travis surmised. "More than just his 'knowing' about the poisoning, or whatever it is. Nobody would try to kidnap him just because he knew about it."

"He said it could be an engineered virus. Some kind of assassination plot. If a hundred or so imperial relatives have died, I can't believe Starfleet's not working on it already. We're a day late and a dollar short to make it our problem."

Stiles sank deeper into his chair, rocked back some, and rested his head on the worn neckrest. As the chair protested with a squawk, the hot chocolate finally drew him with its rich scent, and he scooped up the cup and blew across the milky warmth.

Watching the steam rise, Travis smiled. "You're a contented man, Eric."

"Oh, Travis . . . I lived for four years at the mercy of whim. Would they decide to beat me up? Would they feed us today? Would the Constrictor come? We had no control. After that, even a little control seems terrific to me. I love the day-to-day activities of being alive. Walking freely to and from my cabin, my friends around me, going all over space, meeting alien races, a new batch of trainees every few months . . . I meet all kinds of people and I talk to and like most of them. I kind of enjoy getting through things. People are a lot less prickly when you don't return it."

"You sure don't talk like a man who did the heroic deed and got awarded the Medal of Valor," Travis observed. "What a dismal example for all those punks out there who're shooting for the braids and brass, know that? They want glory."

"Not all it's cracked up to be." Stiles sipped his hot chocolate again and breathed into the steam. "I didn't get the MV for any deeds. I got it for sitting on my bruised ass for four years and not dying quite fast enough."

Leaning sideways, Travis lounged on an elbow and huffed disapprovingly. "What's Romulan for 'crappola'?"

"I think it's 'enushi.' 'Enushmi.' "

"Figures you'd know."

Allowing himself a little smile, Stiles drew a deep breath and sighed also. "I washed my hands of Red Sector nine years ago, Travvy, when I was finally sure the message about Zevon had gotten all the way back to his family. It took me a year to get the message through, and another year to make sure there hadn't been any snags and that his immediate family and the empress definitely knew he was there. He was sure they'd come get him. I made sure he got back home, and now I find out it might have been his death sentence."

"You acted above and beyond the call," Travis tried to confirm, obviously relieved they'd broken through to the real reason he'd come in here. "It's not even in the widest perimeter of imagination your fault, and you flipping well know it."

Stiles nodded. "In my three rational brain cells, I know it. But in the rest of them . . . he's dying because I made sure he got home."

"That's nutty."

Taking a long draw on the hot chocolate, Stiles gazed with growing sentiment into the thick warm drink and saw in there all the wonders of freedom. The foam turned like ebb tide, the swirling dark cream like clouds and wind.

"You ever been a prisoner of war?"

His question moved softly between them as if made of music. Travis had no reason to supply an answer.

Stiles watched the foam bubbles pop in his mug.

"You live together in a way that no two other people ever do. You mop the other guy's blood and bind his wounds, listen to his dreams and watch his hopes decay . . . you can't get away from the smells, the sweat, the fears crawling on you like cancer . . . after a while you run out of words to hold each other's brains inside, so you just stop talking. You start communicating without words. Just a look, or a touch . . . or you just sit there together. The intimacy can't be described. You see each other so raw, so demolished . . . more than you ever wanted anybody to see you. Weak, sick, scared, sobbing . . . crushed by loneliness like a plague, till you finally turn to each other and pray the other guy's lonely too."

He raised his eyes. Deeply moving to the point of sorrow was the expression on Travis's face, a shivering guilt that threaded its way from the distant past and prevented forgetting.

"I survived because of two forces moving in my life," Stiles continued softly. "One was the ghost of Ambassador Spock in my mind, telling me I could survive, I could rise above all this, that he'd be proud of me if I did . . . I heard his voice every night for the whole four years, narrating the plan for how I would behave and what he expected of me. I don't have any idea if it was all in my mind and I was making it up in some kind of hero-worship fantasy, but Travis, I swear to eternity it kept me alive. Just knowing what he expected of me and hearing his voice from the other side of the snow . . . calling me by my first name . . . he kept me alive by making me believe it was my duty and that I could prevail. The other force," he added softly, "was Zevon. Whenever the ambassador's image faded and that leash started to fray, Zevon would be there in the haze, some kind of echo of Spock, holding himself above the trouble we were in, always reminding me without even saying it that something bigger was expected of me. I needed him and he needed me, and together we worked for a common purpose. He gave me a reason to struggle out of my cot morning after morning. If I didn't come, he came to get me and made me get up. If he's out there somewhere, sick, maybe dying . . . I can't let him face it without me."

Travis looked at him and a moment later sat bolt upright. "You mean—you don't mean try to make another contact! The last one took you a year!"

"Zevon might not have a year this time, Travis."

"Oh, my God! This is a little sudden—" Breathing in gulps, Travis glanced around the quarters as if looking for the writing on the wall. "My God . . . I'll contact Starbase Fourteen . . . get another CST out here to cover the precinct . . . I'll have to give them some kind of excuse."

The fact that Travis Perraton so quickly absorbed and didn't question the moral imperative came to Stiles as a compliment, a vote of loyalty, and it bolted into place his flickering plan.

"I'll come up with something," he said.

Travis pressed his hands to his face, shook his head, then let his hands fall to his lap and sighed. "You and your causes. Just when I think you're settling down, you come up with some lofty goal."

"I don't have any lofty goals," Stiles told him. "I've got my goal. Save Zevon if I can, and if I can't, be with him when he dies. That's my goal."

"What about averting an interstellar conflict? If we can make a solid contact in the royal family, somebody inclined to trust us the way Zevon and you trust each other, maybe Starfleet can help the Romulans with this poison thing they've got going."

"That's not my problem. If it's in the cards, great. We're one ship with limited influence and we're better off keeping a leash on our aspirations. If there's a conflict, somebody else'll handle it. If we're there, we'll help. We can only do so much in life. Things change. Then they change again. I've been a hero. Got what I thought I wanted, and it was nice, but how long can you keep that up? Once the handshaking and the medals are done with, the heroness just fades. You can't strut around for the rest of your life being heroic. *I* can't, anyway. I'm not James Kirk. The good thing is that I don't want to be. I'm gonna do *my* part, not his part."

Travis leered at him with narrowed eyes. "That's the most depressing nobility I've ever heard."

"Works, though. You prepared for the hard part?"

"I'm always prepared, Eric."

"That's it then. Ready about."

"Ready about, aye."

Chapter Thirteen

NOW WHAT?

The last living Romulan royal family member, the last chance at uncontaminated blood, was no longer living.

Riker's profound words tolled through the silence on the bridge.

Spock was particularly aware of Dr. McCoy's expression and longed to have a few private moments, but that would not come today. Decades ago, Leonard McCoy had lost his ability—or even desire—to hide his feelings. Now his bent shoulders further sagged, his wrinkled eyes crimped, his dry lips pursed, and he seemed to weaken. This news portended a grueling struggle for the physicians, with no possible short cuts. Spock knew McCoy had seen many failures in his long life, and together they had fielded many fears and changes, and yet somehow McCoy had never lost his hope to alter one more arrow of fate before the years finally caught up to him. Failure this time might mean failure in his last attempt to make the galaxy better.

"Captain," Mr. Worf interrupted, "another ship on long-range, sir."

Picard looked up at him. "The *Tdal* returning for some reason?"

"No, sir. Starfleet encryption."

"Identify her as soon as you can, Mr. Worf."

"Sensors are reading the vessel now, sir," the Klingon obliged. "Heavy keel . . . double hull . . . multipurpose configuration . . . It's a tender, sir, combat support. The . . . *Saskatoon.*"

Picard turned to the forward screen, but nothing was visible yet. "Signal recognition and render salute pennants as we pass."

"Aye, sir."

Instantly shedding despair of Riker's news, McCoy came to life and found the nimbleness in his ancient fingers to poke Spock in the arm. "A CST! Give you any ideas, Spock, ol' man?"

"I beg your pardon?"

"Double-hulled, industrial, strong enough to defend herself, but doesn't attract much attention? Get it?"

"Ah—" Spock felt his brows flare. Decades ago he may have been embarrassed, but such social pressures were long withered from disuse. "Yes . . . conveniently unprovoking, yet combat-ready . . . possibly, Doctor!"

McCoy turned gingerly to Picard. "See if you can get 'em to stop! Pull 'em over on a traffic violation or something!"

"I don't think that'll be necessary, Doctor," the captain said as he watched the helm console from where he stood. "The CST is on an approach vector. They're reducing speed."

"Captain," Data reported, "*Saskatoon* is hailing us."

"Mr. Data, go ahead and give us ship to ship," Picard ordered.

"Aye, sir. Frequencies open."

"This is Captain Picard, *Saskatoon.* Do you have a problem?"

"*What a relief that we found you before you moved on! I've got to speak to Ambassador Spock.*"

Spock wondered if he had heard incorrectly, though he knew that was unlikely. He had been cautious to keep his whereabouts private. Who was this CST commander that he could pierce top security?

Glancing at Spock, obviously surprised that anyone else knew, Picard sedately required, "Identify yourself, please."

"*This is Lieutenant Commander Eric Stiles. Is Ambassador Spock there? It's an emergency.*"

Chapter Fourteen

COMMANDER STILES APPEARED in the turbolift within ten minutes of the first message, instantly flooding Spock with nostalgia for the young man he had once counseled, for today there appeared on the upper bridge another kind of young man altogether. His blond hair slightly darkened to an ashy shade, and the beard he had grown while in captivity was missing. His face had lengthened to a manful form, lacking the baby-fat of the twenty-one-year-old, and his hairline had changed. He looked like a wizened echo of the boy who had stormed the embassy.

Hesitating only an instant, as if unsure whether to come down the starboard ramp or the port ramp, Eric Stiles virtually ran to the command deck.

"Commander Stiles," Captain Picard greeted. "It's a pleasure."

Stiles said. "Sorry, Captain. I'm sorry to barge in. . . ."

Riker reached for Stiles's hand and shook it. "I remember your return from captivity, Mr. Stiles. I was in the audience on board the *Lexington.* It's a privilege to have a Medal of Valor winner visit us—"

"Thanks." Stiles turned instantly to Spock, and it was as if they had spoken only yesterday. "I've got a problem. And I think I can help you with yours. Can we talk alone?"

How odd.

Stiles's eyes were filled with complexity. The years sheared away between them and once again Spock was speaking candidly with the frightened boy who so needed the lifeline of an experienced voice sounding around him. Yet there was more.

Captain Picard gestured to the port side. "My ready room, Ambassador. Help yourselves."

"Manna from heaven," McCoy uttered, staring. "Spock! A Romulan royal nowhere near any other Romulans! And you don't believe in luck!"

"Yes, I do," Spock fluidly contradicted. "This is most startling. You remain certain that your cellmate was a member of the Romulan royal family?"

"Absolutely. And if he's still alive and you help me go get him, you'll have an uncontaminated member of the royal family."

"How the devil do you know about *that?"* McCoy raved.

Stiles blinked. "Well . . . you've had your contacts searching all over the Romulan Empire for an isolated member of the family . . . I've got a few contacts too . . . y'know, Medal of Valor and all . . . you get some connections, even if you don't want them. . . ."

McCoy blew a breath out his nostrils. "What's it take to keep a secret in this galaxy!"

Spock turned to him. "This is troubling. It means the news is leaking out."

"This is the part that hasn't leaked out!" Stiles quickly told them. "I haven't told anybody about Zevon. The only people who know are me and my first officer and a couple members of my original evac squad who stayed with me. And now the two of you."

"How is it possible that nobody else knew?" McCoy asked. "Ten years ago when I pulled you out of there, Starfleet debriefed you thoroughly—"

"Eleven years."

"Ten, eleven, twenty, what's the difference?"

"I was debriefed for weeks," Stiles agreed. "I told them I had a Romulan cellmate and they notified the Romulans. At the time there weren't any formal relations, no exchange of ambassadors. . . . I made sure the message got through to the precinct governor, who would have to report directly to the Senate, and they'd have to report to the—well, back then it was the emperor. So I thought the royal family would take it from there."

Spock had listened to these words with growing trepidation, but certainly also with a rising sensation of possibility. "This is a profound blessing in disguise, both for Zevon and for the Romulan Empire. If he is indeed still in Red Sector, isolated, still alive, then he presents a distinct ray of hope."

McCoy pointed a crooked finger. "I'll send Dr. Crusher to the Romulan royal family to treat them and try to keep them alive. In the meantime, I need to get to this Zevon and synthesize a vaccine from his blood, *before* anybody else gets to him."

"Who else could get to him?" Stiles asked. "Why would anybody want to?"

"Whoever's inflicted this biological attack, that's who. You don't think this is accidental, do you?"

"I thought it was just a plague! Something natural!"

"Nope."

His face a pattern of fears and troubles, Stiles frowned with consternation. "That's just what Hashley tried to tell us . . . all his talk about viral terrorism and mass-assassination . . . I thought he was exaggerating."

At that name, Spock felt his back muscles tighten. He glanced at McCoy, who, if possible, was more pale than usual at the casual mention of a key figure. Stiles clearly did not understand the full ramifications of how the puzzle pieces fit into place.

"Hashley again," McCoy complained. "He's as bad as the infection."

Stiles squinted. "Huh? What's that mean?"

"Ansue Hashley," Spock said, "is important to maintaining stable relations between the Federation and the Romulan Empire, Commander. How recently did you speak to him?"

Stiles's eyes widened, and he swiveled his gaze between them. "You mean the same Hashley I'm talking about? An ag broker? That guy?"

"Yes, that guy."

"You've got to be kidding! He didn't seem capable of being part of a mass-assassination scheme. Starfleet captains had been tossing him from ship to ship like a hot potato to keep the Romulans from knowing where he was. I couldn't figure why he'd be so important. I thought they just didn't want to bother with him!"

McCoy explained, "The Romulans tracked the royal infection back to his cargo. That's why they think the Federation started it. The Romulans wanted him so they could have a scapegoat and tell their people they'd caught the culprit, that the Federation was definitely to blame for the deaths of their royal family."

"Where is Hashley now?" Spock asked. "Aboard *Saskatoon?*"

Stiles shrugged hopelessly. "No, I don't have him. I didn't want him. He's safe, though. We remanded him to the custody of the first Starfleet law-enforcement ship we found."

"Which ship?"

"The *Ranger.*"

Spock immediately turned and depressed the keypad of the bridge comm unit. "Captain Picard, do you know the name of the passenger who was kidnapped from the *Ranger* this morning?"

"I'll pull the report, ambassador. One moment."

"I'll put Dr. Crusher on it," McCoy said. "They want her help. They'll treat Hashley well."

"It's my fault," Stiles said. He had left the conversation they were having and was having one with himself. "I never checked . . . never confirmed that Zevon had been rescued. He was so sure his family would get him out—he made me sure too. Until five days ago I was completely convinced that he was back home. Now I find out he never . . . they just didn't bother to go get him. All these years he's been trapped in Pojjana space, by himself, without me . . . because of me. When I found out they'd left him, the only thing I could think to do was try to get your help."

In all his years Spock had witnessed many examples of human fidelity and found he appreciated them all. At first he had looked down his nose at such demonstrations. Later he had learned to accept them with some curiosity, and even to accept that part of himself.

Spock moved to stand near Stiles, to make sure he had all the attention he needed.

"You and Zevon were friends," he began. "I deeply appreciate that. You depended upon each other in the worst of times. Today you still understand what happened to you, the forces that worked upon your lives. Time has not dulled your decency. Today, as I watch you in your effort and your torments, I cross yet another barrier to fondness. I enjoy the humanity I see in you, this childlike sense of justice that defies all forces. Like a whirlpool you draw us all into your devotion. We will go to save the Romulans, yes. But because of you will we go also to save Zevon."

McCoy watched them both with a charming softness. Spock noticed the doctor's gaze, but did not meet it.

Stiles clearly battled the pressure of tears behind his eyes. Solemnly he murmured, "Every time I see you . . . you rescue me in some way."

A swelling sensation of completeness satisfied Spock deeply. While before this there had been only a duty, a mission, now there was a quieter and more profound purpose. Crossing the quadrant to save a nation had its appeal. Crossing to save a friend had even more.

"Well, Spock," McCoy interrupted, "you and I seem to have a mission in Pojjan space."

Stiles came abruptly to life as a balloon suddenly fills with air, apparently afraid that they would make some other choice for some reason he failed to see. "Let me take you! We've got a thick hull, nonaggressive configuration, support registry—completely unprovoking in nature, just a big industrial muscle. We've got full regulation defensive weapons, and we all know what *that* really means. Let me take you through Romulan space in the CST. It's perfect! It's a good option. And I know the way!"

McCoy raised his frosty brows. "Imagine never thinking of that. Silly us."

Stiles took that as a threat. "If you don't clear me to go with you, I'll go anyway."

McCoy looked at Spock. "Remind you of anybody?"

Chapter Fifteen

"ORSOVA."

"What do you want now? Why do you bring me to space this time? You always call at bad times for me! I was busy!"

"*The Pojjana lion of science. Genius savior of the planet. Engineer of the Constrictor meter. Conqueror of the Constrictor. Still amazed to see open space. You know nothing about science.*"

"I know everything. I have power now."

"*You have Zevon now.*"

Picking himself up from the strange carpet where he had fallen after the dizzying effect of a transporter beam, Orsova bristled and tried to appear confident. "Zevon works for me."

"*Zevon does all the work you take credit for. I know the difference. I helped make it happen. Now I want something from you. A Federation ship is coming your way.*"

"Federation? Why! This is Red Sector! How can they come here!"

"*They have new business here. They have visited Romulan space.*"

"Romulan? Why would they go there? They have no treaty! Have they . . . ?"

As the Voice summoned him again, Orsova felt the sting of being completely out of touch with the space-active civilizations of the quadrant for so many years. All this time Red Sector had been a huge favor for him, a sanctuary where a prison guard could rise to power if he knew how to play on public opinion—and if he had a Voice to tell him each step.

That had been easy. Play to the hatred. The Pojjana had been ready, eager, to despise and distrust. The Voice was right. Orsova had used that. Found it easy. Surrounded himself with those eager to hate most, happy to have their distrust bring them also to power, and learned how to nurture the distrust even when there was no one around to hate anymore.

Making them accept Zevon, an alien . . . that had taken time. But it had been the most important part.

Now this ghost, this Voice, came to him when he no longer needed it. Orsova knew in his gut that this speaking person was an alien.

"Why would the Federation come again after all these years?" he asked. "What do they want here? We have no Federation people in Red Sector."

"*They have their reasons. You will have to be prepared to stop them. Crash their ship, destroy it, or drive them off. Kill them if you can.*"

"But why are they coming?"

"*Can your planetary defense destroy a Starfleet ship? This is not a starship, but a utility vessel—*"

"You don't know why they're coming, do you?" Suddenly emboldened, Orsova blurted his revelation. "You don't know, do you, Voice?"

"*Information is diaphanous. It changes.*"

"Means, you don't know why they're coming."

"*When I need you again, I will beam you to me.*"

"In space?"

"*Wherever I must be.*"

"Means, you have to hide from them."

"*Go back now. Go now, and get ready to face the Federation. Make them go from here, and there will be even bigger rewards for you.*"

Chapter Sixteen

The Imperial Palace, Romulan Star Empire

"My name is Beverly Crusher, Commander, Medical Corps, Starfleet. I'm here to treat the empress."

"Yes, Dr. Crusher, we have agreed to give you cooperation. I am Sentinel Iavo."

"Sentinel? Not Centurion?"

"I am a member of the Royal Civil Attaché to the Imperial Court, not part of the Imperial Space Fleet. We discovered long ago that military titles for our civil officials only caused dangerous confusion. Where is your ship docked? At the municipal spaceport?"

"No. We were dropped off. The ship has left. It's just the two of us now."

"The two of you? No guards? No Starfleet security?"

"I don't need them, do I? We have an agreement . . . don't we?"

Standing before Beverly Crusher, Sentinel Iavo was a very handsome Romulan with typically dark brown hair but remarkably large and pale green eyes. He wore his Imperial Court uniform with a certain casualness, and his clothing indeed was not like that of the military guards stationed in the hallways they'd passed through. She couldn't guess his age—that was tricky with Romulans—though he didn't strike her as particularly young. He stood in the expected Vulcanlike posture, straight and contrived, the only clue to any nervousness his constant rubbing of the fingernails of one hand against the palm of the other hand.

The palace was a four-century-old monolith, its stone walls dressed in tapestries and heavy draperies like any Austrian castle, except the rooms and corridors were lit by modern fixtures—not a torch in sight. Funny—she'd expected torches.

And there was music playing. Harp-like music, backed sometimes by the hollow beat of a tenor drum and a hint of something similar to a cello in the background. No musicians visible—nope, it was a sound system.

She smelled incense, too, faintly. Or dinner.

The Sentinel gave her a moment to look around, then asked, "What would you like first?"

"I want you to close up the palace completely," she began. "Total security. Nobody in or out without high clearance, nobody at all. You're the highest advisor?"

"Correct, Doctor, I am the empress's senior civil authority. I have held this post since before the emperor died, and my brother before me, and our father before him."

"Oh, isn't that nice . . . then you have the authority to enact my terms. No changes of personnel from now on. Whoever's in the kitchen will stay there and keep working. The same maids, the same servants, the same everybody. These same guards will stay on duty here. They can sleep here if they have to, but I don't want to see anybody new. When you have your security in place, I'd like everything and everybody cleared through my lovely assistant here."

Crusher made what she hoped was a graceful half-turn and held out a hand. At her side and a polite couple of steps behind, Data offered her the medical tricorder. He also held their two duffel bags and Crusher's hospital-in-a-bag medical satchel, full of all the instruments, medications, and a computer with both an immunological database and a general medical lexicon. The load was a little cumbersome because she'd packed everything she could think of. There was going to be no calling for supplies.

Data said nothing. The only expression of personality was the poignant lack of it, and perhaps the sheen of soft lightning, reflected off the velvet, casting a glow that turned his metallic complexion herbal.

"You needn't have brought so many medical supplies, Dr. Crusher," Iavo told her as he took one of the duffels from Data. "We have eight major hospital complexes in the city, which will bring anything you require to treat the empress."

"Mr. Iavo, when I say I want security, I mean absolute security. I want nothing delivered from anywhere as of right now. Nothing comes into the palace. Not medicine, not food, not people, not weapons."

"There are no weapons here, madam," the Sentinel assured. "The palace is completely energy-secure. Our security office constantly monitors any active energy, and would instantly identify an armed disruptor or phaser—"

"Hmm. I wondered why all your guards carried daggers," Crusher recalled. "I thought it was just traditional. Where's the empress?"

"This way, please."

Another corridor. An obviously private series of chambers, more guards, one more short corridor . . . finally, Iavo cleared Crusher and Data into the empress's bedchamber.

And what a place it was. Draped in soft green velvet embossed with ancient symbols, softly lit by unseen fixtures, carpeted with something that seemed like rabbit fur, the room was warm and thick with the scent of burning herbs. In the center of the room was a sitting area with a generous couch and an oblong blackwood table with a single chair.

There were two female attendants hovering near the bed, and four imperial guards, each in a uniform and helmet, standing near the bed posts. The bed had six posts, each as thick as a full-grown man's body and carved with angular features of hands and faces, each hand holding one of the faces and pushing it toward the ceiling. Each face grimaced hellishly, and in its teeth held a carved skewer that stuck out from the totem, so that the bedposts bristled like a bottle brush with wooden spikes. Some of the spikes were broken off, yet the blunt ends darkened and showing no wounded wood, hinting that the bed was very old. The wood had never been stained, it had just blackened with sheer age.

And in the bed, bundled in velvet and fur, was the young empress. Her eyes were closed, but not in rest. Her hair was meticulously combed yet lusterless, almost crispy from her long fight to stay alive, as her body sapped whatever healthy cells it could draw back into itself in its last desperations.

All over the empire, members of the royal family looked like that, or had, or soon would.

Crusher approached the bed, aware that Data was right behind her, maintaining a student-like silence. She listened briefly to the empress's respiration, looked at her complexion, noted her skin color, an obscene russet—*very* wrong—but did not touch her.

"Communications relays have been set up all over the empire for you. Attending physicians are standing by for your instructions."

"Are they willing to cooperate with a Federation physician?" she asked.

Iavo seemed embarrassed, or perhaps hopeless. "They have tried everything they know."

Crusher folded her arms. "Yes . . . I suppose they have."

And she simply stood there, a hip cocked, said nothing more, and did nothing, while the harp music plucked the draperies.

Data's amber eyes flicked between her and Iavo, but he also said, as she had instructed, nothing.

Iavo watched as his empress moaned softly, unattended. The two female attendants peered uneasily. The helmeted guards remained at attention, but their eyes shifted.

"Are you going to treat her?" Iavo finally asked.

"Yes, but I'll need something from you," Crusher said.

"What do you want from us?" Iavo asked.

Now he got it.

She took one step toward him, then locked her stance. "I want Ansue Hashley. Bring him here, alive."

"All right, Mr. Hashley, I've heard enough."

"But I want to finish telling you about—"

"No, that's enough talking. Sit still while I finish sealing this."

Crusher stood over Ansue Hashley's ragged bulk and shook her head in disgust. He was bruised, cut, flushed, nicked in a hundred places, and pale from loss of blood, yet somehow that mouth kept running and running.

"You know, Sentinel Iavo," she began as her seamer's beam sketched closed the last cut on Hashley's face, "you people didn't have to torture this man. If you'd open up your borders and deal with humans more, you'd know after talking to this man for ten minutes that he doesn't have it in him to organize a mass-assassination plot. And we would've told you about the prion-based epidemic we've been fighting. Imperial isolationism has hurt you this time."

Near the empress's bed, Iavo rubbed his forefingernail against his other hand's thumb knuckle and protested with his expression. "The infection was imported on his vessel. We tracked it back to a low-level medication in his cargo bound for—"

"He's a busy little gossip, not a biological terrorist," Crusher insisted as Hashley's big sopsy eyes blinked up at her. "That medicine has been coming in here for more than forty years from a pharmaceutical company sympathetic to Romulans. All Mr. Hashley did was bring it in. Somebody else engineered the tainting of the shipment and then the delivery of the tainted stuff to all the royal family members. Hashley here is just a dupe."

"Whose dupe?"

Crusher shook her head and let herself rattle on, spilling her thoughts. "Nobody clever enough to distribute this infection would run a little trade route for ten years. If you knew more about humans—it's kind of obvious this man's not biding his time to take over the universe. Romulans might be that tenacious, but humans don't have the patience. Or a two-hundred-year lifespan. Why do you think we're always in such a damn hurry? Gotta get things done before we die."

Pacing uneasily nearby, Sentinel Iavo switched fingernails and leered doubtfully at Ansue Hashley, who sat like a bruised puppy. "Whose dupe was he?"

"We're not sure," Crusher admitted. "Dr. McCoy's right, though. It's got all the earmarks of a series of cross-racial multiprion plagues. Until recently, nobody put them together. The first clue was just three years ago at Deep Space Nine. Well—then the station was called Terok Nor."

"I remember that!" Hashley offered. "Cardassians, Bajorans, and Ferengi all got the same sickness! They were all accusing—"

"Oh, I missed a scratch right next to your lip," Crusher cut off. "Here—let me seal it up. Don't move, now. . . . The Cardassians suspected a Bajoran rebel group of manufacturing the disease, and they were partly right. The rebels were happy to make sure the Cardassians caught the disease, until they found out that Bajorans could get it too. And there was no way the Bajorans at that time had the resources or the science infrastructure to develop something as advanced as cross-species viral infection. They can't even do it now, and back then they were subjugated. Not only the Deep Space Nine infection, but we also found out that two years earlier several human-alien hybrids were infected with an unidentified virus, and that's unheard-of in nature. This thing's being systematically mutated, targeted, and delivered."

Iavo stopped pacing briefly. "I take it those were not all human and the same alien hybrids."

"No, they were all mixed up. People with that kind of genetics just can't 'catch' the same thing naturally. There you go, Mr. Hashley, all patched up. You'll be sore, but you'll live. Now, I want you to just stay right here with me and Data and help us do what we have to do." She straightened, handed Data the sealer to put back in the med-pack, then turned to Iavo. "All right, Sentinel, I'm ready to start treating the empress. Are you ready to help?"

The tall imperial official glanced at the two female servants, then met the gaze of one of the four guards. They seemed to be communicating, but not in the way one would expect of a senior government official and a clutch of underlings from way, way under. Iavo clutched his hands before him, flexed them, stretched his fingers, looked at the furry carpet for a moment then raised his eyes again at the nearest guard.

Such a simple step took a very long time, as choices go. Finally, seeming to make a decision or part of one, Iavo turned his back to the guards as if deeply troubled by their presence. "What do you need from us?"

Crusher watched the guards for a moment. Were they averting their eyes on purpose? "First of all, I want these women out of here. Data and Mr. Hashley can be my assistants. And I'd like you to cool it off by fifteen degrees in here. Clear that incense or whatever's burning out of the chamber and circulate some fresh air."

"But this is how we always—"

"If 'always' was working, you wouldn't need me here, would you? Cool, and air, please."

Iavo paused, seemed to be deciding between being insulted and some other reaction Crusher couldn't make out.

Once again the Sentinel met the eyes of the guard nearest to him.

"We'll do as you instruct, Doctor," he agreed, speaking slowly. Hypnotically he rubbed a single fingernail. "Do you think you can save her?"

Chapter Seventeen

STILES'S HANDS SHOOK as he stood beside the *Saskatoon*'s command chair. On the other side of the chair, Ambassador Spock placidly standing, the elderly Leonard McCoy sitting in a console chair—both men watched the approach of a forbidden planet in a forbidden sector. Stiles had offered the doctor the command chair, but McCoy had demurred, saying that only the "golden boy" should sit there. Stiles hadn't been able to sit in their presence, so the chair went empty through the entire voyage. Even when Alan brought tea.

Every regulation in several civilizations prevented their coming here, yet here they flew. The hoops of outposts, stations, guard ships, patrols, and bureaucratic drumbeating they'd had to jump through had left Stiles with a headache that was still here days and days later. The tension of moving into Romulan space to drop off Dr. Crusher and Data had been enough to peel fruit, and now *Saskatoon* was deep inside Red Sector, trailing deals and bribes and threats and name-dropping that had gotten them all the way here.

For Stiles, though, this was the door of purgatory. He couldn't keep his hands warm anymore. The self-examination was no fun either. Why was he so nervous? He had these heavy hitters with him, didn't he?

Why was his stomach twisted up into a spiral? The absence of foolish cockiness should've been reassuring and mature, but the fact was he wished he still had it. That zing of thinking he knew everything had protected him from a whole lot of scared. Wishing he could feel his fingers, he wondered if those two men over there had ever preferred to pull their own teeth out than go in someplace they had to go. Duty, cause, purpose, rank, ability—all those things fell short of the driving force he needed to overcome what he felt. There was only one thing drawing him forward, against all the forces pushing him back.

Gripping one hand with the other to hide the trembling, he looked briefly to portside, to Travis and Alan. Alan winked reassuringly, and Travis gave him a thumbs-up. They were willing to go.

Embarrassed, he puckered his shoulders. His friends were reassuring him, supporting him into the unknown. It should be the other way around.

"Hero," he muttered.

No one heard. He barely heard himself.

Spock glanced at him.

The planet of his dread swelled on the main screen and six of the ancillary monitors.

"Approach, Eric?" Travis prodded from the port side.

"Hm? Oh . . . sorry. Helm—let's see . . . come to point nine, equatorial approach vector, angle four one. No—four two. There's a constant thermal over that big canyon."

"May I ask what you're reading on the planet's surface?" Ambassador Spock asked. "Anything unfamiliar? Any sign of destruction by the Constrictor?"

"I'm picking up airstrips," Jeremy reported, "a couple of things that might be missile deployment facilities . . . heliports . . . some satellites . . . pretty typical. Maybe mid- or late-twenty-first-century equivalent or so. I could be all wrong, though."

At tactical, Zack Bolt commented, "You get to a certain level of atmospheric aeronautics and yours is as good as anybody's."

Stiles waved an icy hand toward Spock. "Why don't you have a look for yourself, sir? You were here too, and I'm sure you knew the layout a lot better than I ever did. After all . . ."

If Spock's dark eyes saw through the layers of reasons and excuses, he made no hint of that, except perhaps for the hesitation before accepting.

"Very well," he said, and took the place at the science station as Jeremy moved out of his way. He bent over the readout hood, tapped some of the controls, causing monitors to flicker and change, focus or choose new subjects.

Stiles knew what Spock expected—a devastated planet, a civilization crushed nearly out of existence, the people who'd managed to survive suffering in the few remaining caves and wreckage that hadn't been smashed, hardly any old people, hardly any kids. . . .

But that's not what came up.

Maps of the planet's cities, boundaries in some places marked off by electronic border markers readable from space. Stiles recognized some of what he saw from that first approach all those years ago, and he was stirred by new apprehensions. He recognized the mountains showing up on geographical long-range, and flinched. The idea of returning in triumph, healthy, alive, in command of a ship, dissolved and crumbled away. Suddenly he was twenty-one and out of control.

The hum of the ship around him as thrusters moved them toward orbit pounded like blood in his head. He was grateful when Travis quietly took over the approach orders, doing so smoothly enough that nobody seemed to notice. Or at least they pretended they didn't.

Stiles wasn't much for putting on airs, but he'd have liked to give them a little command puff-up right about now, just for Christmas. Couldn't find it, though. Just couldn't find it.

"Cities seem intact. No signs of catastrophic damage," Spock commented as he clicked his way through the scanner's offerings. "I recognize several of the buildings at the main city complexes on the primary continent. . . ." Now he leaned closer and seemed almost to frown. "Although . . . the architectural style has changed significantly. Many of the old constructions are missing, replaced by complexes with only one or two stories." He turned his head, without straightening up, to look at Stiles. "During your incarceration, did you hear any word of so broad a cultural change?"

"Me? Zevon and I used to talk about what could be done to help buildings survive the Constrictor . . . elastic brackets and joints, different construction materials—either much heavier so they could withstand the pressure, or much lighter so they wouldn't be crushed . . . but nobody ever paid attention to us. That was just us, just talking."

"They seem to have implemented many changes," Spock commented, looked at what he saw on the screens. "Even the colors of the cities are different now. I believe they may have changed materials significantly. They seem to be primarily using quarried granite rather than timber and brick. And I'm reading quintotitantium and dutronium reenforcement members rather than conventional steel and iron. When I evacuated, they were incapable of such a development at their industrial level."

"Granite . . ." Stiles sifted his memory. "Dutronium . . . Zevon and I used to design—we used to think up all kinds of things. Maybe the Pojjana just figured out some of them on their own. It doesn't take that much to figure out how to build a spandex house, y'know . . . most of our ideas just made basic sense. It's not like we had much to work with or anything. . . ."

McCoy watched the continent slowly turn on the large forward screen. "Do you think he's still alive and influencing their development?"

"I hope so, I sure hope so," Stiles said with his heart squeezing fearfully. "Zevon doesn't have a prime directive. But I don't know how he could get anybody to listen to him. We could never get past the assistant warden. And I don't know if . . . they turned on him after I got pulled out or . . . maybe they just . . ."

No one said anything to comfort or refute his tortured suppositions or stem the racing of his imagination.

"There's only so much he could do," Stiles grumbled, his thoughts taking on a life of their own. "After all, the sector's been red for years. Nobody's been in or out, right?"

"We watch the sector constantly," Spock undergirded. "There has been extremely little breaching, give or take the odd delinquent shaman."

Dr. McCoy's white brows danced. "Or the occasional sublime wise-ass. Other than that, a skinny bird couldn't slip in and out of Red Sector without somebody's noticing. Mr. Stiles, you think your friend could be somewhere other than the capital city? Running some process that engineers those new buildings?"

"Even Zevon couldn't make industries all by himself, even if he were in charge of the whole planet, never mind a prisoner. Besides, he wasn't an architect. Is eleven years long enough to make sweeping changes on a whole planet? Nah . . . probably not. He'd have to get all the way up to somebody trusting him first, and, believe me, on a planet of people who *really* don't like aliens, that could take . . . well, more doing than either of us could manage from a prison cell or our lab. Travis, adjust the trim, will you?"

"Trim, aye. Give it another three degrees level, Stinson."

"Aye aye, sir, three degrees starboard."

"We must not assume," Spock mentioned, "that anything is the same after eleven years."

Stiles strode around to the other side of the bridge, where Spock was still scanning the readouts of the planet below. "Are you saying you think he's dead?"

Spock glanced at him. "You spare yourself by accepting the likelihood. You nearly died yourself."

"I was sick."

"And ill-treated, poorly fed, ignored, imprisoned—"

"Zevon's Romulan. He's stronger than—"

"Not stronger enough," the ambassador cautioned, now standing straight and looking right at him. "The odds . . . are troubling."

McCoy was watching him. Stiles could sense it.

He could sense—and see—the fretful averted attention of everybody around him. They all knew his past. He was too close to this. Maybe it was a mistake not sending somebody completely impassive. There was more at stake than just Zevon. Was he thinking clearly enough?

"What do we do?" Stiles wondered. "Just . . . approach?"

"Almost to the atmosphere, Eric," Travis reported. "What do you want to do?"

"I don't know yet."

"We've got to have an order either to enter or veer off. At this point we can't hover."

"No doubt the planetary monitoring system has already noticed us," Spock told him. "Although they had no spaceborne fleet, they were perfectly able to effect short-range scans of the immediate area, for defensive purpose. I'm sure they have identified your ship as a Starfleet unit. If you don't mind my suggesting we broadcast a—"

A shriek cut him off as the CST bellowed around them and the whole ship was jaw-kicked. The deck canted to an instant 30-degree list, as if they'd struck something out in the middle of space. Were they too low? Had they hit a mountain?

Pinned to the side of the helm for a terrible few seconds, Stiles gritted his teeth and fought against the thrust. He heard the cries of his crew as they were thrown violently against the side of the tender, crammed into bulkheads and equipment and each other in a tangle of pressure and shock.

"What is it!" he called. "Did we hit a satellite?"

Jeremy clung to the console one chair down from where Spock was pressed to the science ledge. "Energy funnel! It's pulling us down!"

Dr. McCoy clasped his chair and grimaced. "I *hate* this kind of thing—"

"Is it coming from the planet?" Twisting, Stiles jabbed at the helm over the shoulder of the flabbergasted trainee pilot. "Oh, no, I *know* they shouldn't have this! They didn't have anything like this! Not that could pull in a CST! We can tow a starship!"

Travis scrambled for the engineering mainframe to see if there was an answer there, but when he turned again his face was a mask of bafflement. "It's as if the planet itself has grabbed us!"

The Imperial Palace

Cool air, finally, moved through the ancient halls of the crown family's traditional home. The soft harp music played eternally over the sound system, just sweet enough to drive anybody crazy after the first twenty hours. The tape had looped a few times, and by now Ansue Hashley had taken to humming harmony to the tunes he recognized.

This, in bitter contrast to the suffering empress, who was roused now and then by Crusher's ministrations and wakened to relentless agony because from time to time medical tests required her cooperation. Even when the young woman was allowed to sink back into unconsciousness, her struggle just to breathe provided a pathetic percussion to the damned harp music. It had been a difficult two days.

"Mr. Hashley, please take these two instruments and clean them thoroughly, the way I showed you yesterday, and then bring them back," Crusher instructed. She'd only caught a few catnaps and was feeling the stress of fatigue. This was like being a resident again.

"I just love helping you," Hashley said. "Maybe when we get out of this, I can join Starfleet and come to the *Enterprise* and be your assistant."

"You could certainly do something like that," she said. "No reason you couldn't take a few paramedical courses and start a new career. I'm thinking of switching to professional wrestler, myself. Whew . . . could you bring me that pillow and put it behind my back? I can't let go of this IV pump right now. I've almost got a result . . . stand by, Data."

In her periphery, Crusher saw Data look up from his communications center, formerly the empress's dressing-room vanity. "Standing by, Doctor."

The imperial communications relays were tied in to over six hundred stations throughout the empire. Data had taken nearly three hours to confirm, through codes, geological information, and star-mapping devices, that the relays were actually working and in contact with a spiderweb of stations on several planets. After all, what good would it be if they were just talking to a con artist next door?

Her head swam as she took a moment to relax her brain, while her hands worked under the blue light of the portable sterile field she'd set up. She even indulged in closing her eyes for a few moments, until the field readings bleeped. Sounded like a cannon going off.

Crusher forced her eyes open and blinked a couple of times, focusing on the readings rushing across the miniature monitor screen. "Good, very good . . . I was right. Data, confirm that the physicians should stop fighting the fever. Let it run its course—it stresses the attacking prions."

"Relaying that, doctor. Your progress is remarkable for only two days."

"That's me—Remarkable Bev. Look at that! I knew it was there . . . add that they shouldn't inject supplements of kelassium, no matter how low the levels get."

Data stopped working the console and looked at her. "Doctor, is it not true that Vulcanoids can suffer irreparable intestinal scarring from lack of kelassium?"

"Absolutely, but this test is hinting to me that the kelassium's not leaving the body at all. Look . . . see these protovilium levels? Those only show up when there's a repository of kelassium. They shouldn't be reading this way if she is really K-deficient."

Hashley looked up from organizing the medical instruments. "I've heard of that kind of thing! When I was delivering industrial incendiaries to Carolus, one of the company medics told me about how the body defends itself with some really weird stuff."

Crusher only half-registered what he said. She had learned over the past hours to pick on a word or two without really committing herself to listening. "Mmm, this is weird, all right . . . if these chemical bonds are leading me down the right track, the kelassium's being stored in the second liver. That tells me the attacking prions feed on kelassium. At least partially—Data, are you getting this?"

"Yes, Doctor."

"Storing kelassium deprives the infection of an energy source. I think low kelassium's part of the body's natural fortification. Let's take a chance."

"Is that wise?" the android asked. "Some of these patients are dangerously ill already."

Crusher leaned closer to her patient and checked the moaning young woman's temperature in a particularly unscientific yet somehow instinctive way—with the back of her hand. "Mmm . . . brink of death's a prickly place, Data. Sometimes you gotta dance to keep standing there."

Even though she wasn't looking at him, she could still somehow see, perhaps only in her mind, the android's perplexed expression. He didn't counter her comment, though, or question the risk she was taking. Instead he turned back to the portable comm console and relayed the latest thread of hope.

She wished she could speak more freely, venture some opinions about the crassness of hereditary rulership, mutter a few truths about how it always compromised freedom somewhere down the line—and not usually that far down either—but the four guards were always there, and one of the two women. The guards took turns standing watch every six hours, never leaving the immediate chambers or sitting rooms. And Sentinel Iavo floated in and out . . . at the moment he was floating back in.

"Any success, Doctor?"

Crusher looked up and took the moment to stretch her back and shoulders. "A little. Nominal. Enough to give us an idea that we might eventually beat some of this."

Iavo went to the fireplace, which until now had been stone cold, and turned the head of an unrecognizable carved creature on the mantel; a hissing sound was heard, as flames jumped up in the fake logs, rose to a certain height, adjusted themselves, and settled as if they'd been burning all night. The royal chamber was instantly haunted, medieval.

"The empress may live because of your ministrations," Iavo gauged. All across the empire, the royal family members are beginning to slowly outlive their symptoms."

"So," Crusher said, "you've been listening in on our relays, Sentinel?"

He paused. After a moment, he admitted, "Yes, of course."

Still he did not turn from the fire. Turning in her chair, Crusher surveyed his tall form, narrow and dark against the flickering golden glow from beyond it, and marveled—not for the first time—that no matter where she traveled in the stars, no matter what strange forces she witnessed or what bizarre life forms she encountered, what twisted trees grew or weeds crawled, all over the galaxy fire was always the same color.

And also the same was the smell from the cauldron of ambition.

Sentinel Iavo held his hands toward the fire. Crusher saw them spread before him and slightly to the side, framed in paint-by-number fireglow.

Stretching one arm out, Crusher snapped her fingers once, quietly, toward Data. Flinching as if awakened, the android swiveled away from his console and sat watching. With her other hand, she waved Ansue Hashley into the corner behind her, then put a finger to her lips and gave him the evil eye. The man paled, his eyes widened, and with some wisdom garnered from years running an illegal route, he measured the sense of not arguing or even speaking.

Crusher leaned over the empress and touched the pallid cheek whose changes of color and heat had been the cusp of the doctor's life for many hours. The empress moaned softly. A tear appeared in the corner of the quiet girl's eye. Perhaps she knew.

The two standing guards moved away from the end of the bed. The two who had been resting now stood up.

"I suppose," Crusher began quietly, "you've never had a problem like this come your way, Sentinel."

Iavo gazed into the fire. "Nothing like this."

"How does temptation taste to someone who has been loyal all his life?"

For a moment he was silent. He sighed. "It has a certain bitter spice."

"Are you enjoying the chance?" she asked him. "Or are you cornered by other pressures?"

This time Iavo did not answer. The guards stood now in a line, three on one side of him, one on the other, all four facing Crusher, Data, Ansue Hashley, and the dying empress in her bed.

"It must be frustrating," Crusher said, "always to be on the periphery of glory, nearly able to touch it, always condemned to taste but never swallow . . . and now to see yourself within a step of supreme power . . . and your followers to see themselves jumping all the obstacles in one leap—advisors, attendants . . . Sentinels . . . they all see an opportunity that otherwise would never have occurred. The murder of the empress would be hard for the people to accept, I'm sure, but no one here will care if a Federation doctor and her party suddenly turn up missing. *Enterprise* officers aren't exactly on the empire's favorite-people list, are we? Therefore, the empress and her family will die without continued treatment."

Despite the fact that there was no real wood, the fire was engineered to crackle and snap—even to put forth the scent of burning autumn leaves. Still with his back to her, Sentinel Iavo lowered his head as if watching her words spin inside some kind of crystal ball in his mind.

Barely above a whisper, he told her, "You came here with no guards, madam."

Crusher turned fully in her seat and rubbed her hands on her knees. "Now that you know I might save her, you have to go through with it, don't you?"

The guard at Iavo's right drew his ceremonial dagger. A second guard did the same while the others watched and gripped the handles of their own weapons.

Crusher stood up.

Sensing the change, Iavo now turned around to face her. Now the line of Romulans and the threat they posed clicked gracefully into place. For a brief moment Beverly Crusher stood in awe of this elegant race, so Vulcan in their stature, so human in their passion.

The last two guards pulled their knives. Firelight played upon the blades. And Iavo himself touched the still-sheathed ceremonial dirk that was the symbol of the highest nonroyal office in the Romulan Star Empire.

Data came to her side. Ansue Hashley stood behind them.

Crusher pressed back her shoulder-length hair, steadied herself, lowered her weaponless hands to her sides, and looked directly at Iavo.

"How are we going to do this?"

Chapter Eighteen

"WHAT'VE WE GOT?"

Jeremy White responded with typically terse calm. "We've got thirteen minutes before we crash."

"Yellow alert, everybody," Stiles ordered.

"Yellow, aye!"

The CST shifted its manner substantially, as certain lights and meters went dark and others popped on, systems deciding which were important and which could wait. The din was maddening—the ship screamed and strained, engines howling right through the bulkheads, setting up harmonic vibrations in every member.

On the main screen and all the other exterior visual monitors, black space and a planet gave way to the filtering gauze of clouds. They were entering the atmosphere!

While he tried to keep control over his voice, to keep from shouting or sounding excited, it was necessary to speak up over the tin bray of the engines fighting to keep them in space.

"Veer out!" he ordered. "Get us some kilometers."

Both hating and loving the fact that Ambassador Spock and the irascible Leonard McCoy were watching him through a dangerous moment, he forced himself to concentrate on anything but the two of them. For a second he thought Spock might stay at the science-readout station, where he so obviously and eternally belonged, where he fit so well on a starship or any ship, but the famous officer subtly stepped aside for Jeremy White to take that position.

Stiles hesitated an instant, soon accepting the appropriateness and grandeur of the sacrifice. Spock was letting them handle their own destiny without interference. How did he know to do that? How could he hold himself in check like this?

His stomach turning, Stiles stepped to the starboard side. "Come on, Jeremy, analyze it."

Jeremy's usually sedate expression was screwed into annoyance, possibly because of Spock's presence. "It's some kind of hybrid of a tractor beam and a graviton ray. I've never seen energy combined this way. If a CST can tow a starship, how can they be holding us?"

Travis asked, "Did they have this tech when you were here, Eric?"

"No, hell, no! Matt, can we—"

Realizing he couldn't be heard five sections back over the scream, of the engines, he struck the nearest comm.

"Matt, can we effect any kind of a fair-lead landing?"

From section five, Girvan called over the mechanical scream, *"Not at seven thousand feet per second at this angle we can't!"*

"Okay, let's come up with something else. How long before the beam pulls us into the mountain?"

"Calculating," Jeremy said. "Draw is increasing incrementally with our thrust ratios. They're pouring the coals to it."

"Let's pour our own," Stiles said. "Let's try impulse point zero five, helm."

"Point zero five!"

"Don't shout."

Stiles shrugged at the kid, a simple gesture that had a visible effect on the young terrified teenagers, who were all watching him to measure how many points they should go on the panic meter. Going into a battle situation, with rules to follow and procedures to rely on, had been something they could handle after Starfleet training. Having the ship tilt and scream under them as a planet sucked at it—that was something nobody'd ever trained for. Of course, having it smash into a planet's surface would be hard to come back from, too.

Stiles found orders popping from his lips and responses coming from the crew in a step-by-step manner that had saved thousands of spacefarers in the past, a protocol upon which he now relied.

"Let's have all the rookies to support positions. Primary crew take your emergency stations. Alan, watch the gyro display and tell me personally if it starts jumping. Let's have red alert."

"Red alert!" Travis echoed.

A dozen changes erupted with that order. The lighting all over the CST shifted to muted cherry. The hatches between sections slammed shut and pressure locked—*sssschunk.*

"Keep up the thrust." Stiles knew they were doing that already. Just wanted to make sure nobody pushed the wrong button. The ship's sublight engines whined valiantly. "Let's see what we've got to fight with. Give me some numbers and colors."

Immediately Travis called into the comm. "Engine thrust control, give us numbers and colors."

Almost immediately section leaders' voices from all over the ship started bubbling through the comm system to the bridge, because now all the hatches were closed. Travis, Zack Bolt, and Greg Blake relayed what he needed to know and left out what he didn't.

"Six GCG, sir."

"Red over yellow on the plasma injectors, Eric."

"Green on the pellet initiators."

"We're nine points overbudget on the MHD. They're trying to equalize."

To his shipmates across the bridge Jeremy called, "Just compensate when it spikes!"

"Hear that, Jason? Compensate the spike only! Jason!"

The engine noise swelled to a howl, as if a hurricane were transferring itself from section to section right through the sealed hatches. Beneath the engine noise squealed the grind of real physical stress, as the ship twisted and cranked against the planetary force hauling on them. It was as if they were towing some great body that insisted upon moving in the opposite direction. And they were losing. . . .

"Thrust increasing!" Greg Blake called. "No effect, sir! We're slipping down even faster!"

"Put more power to it, then."

What else could they do?

Stiles glanced sideways at Leonard McCoy, glad the doctor was sitting down. He didn't want to be responsible for the famous elderly physician being scratched, spindled, or mutilated from falling down in the *Saskatoon.* Spock, too, seemed stable enough, despite the ravaged tilt of the deck and the slow spin that tore at the artificial gravity.

Travis punched at the controls with one hand while holding himself in place with the other. "Maybe we can twist out sideways—use the lateral—"

"We'd gulp too much fuel," Jeremy argued. "We're already burning the deuterium at fail-safe rate! It's all we can do to hold position. Ten more minutes and we won't have anything left at all. We've got nothing to twist with."

Pulling himself bodily upward to Jeremy's side, Stiles tried to make sense of what he saw on the maps and visual analyses of the planet below. "What's the source of this beam? Anybody reading the surface?"

Greg Blake was the one to answer. "Reading an energetic pulse station at the northern foot of the valley. It's east of the . . . looks like a swamp. No lifesigns. It must be automated."

"Yes, there's a swamp. Zack, target that facility."

"Targeted," Zack Bolt responded. "Phasers armed."

"Fire phaser one," Stiles ordered.

A single phaser beam broke from the ship's weapon array and bolted down toward the planet, but hadn't made it a half second away before suddenly bending sharply and bouncing like a ricocheted bullet off an invisible field between them and the planet.

Alan Wood covered his head, as hot sparks and bits of melting metal blew into the bridge from section two.

"Insulate!" Stiles yelled at the same time. From where he stood he could see his experienced shipmates grab the trainees and yank them to the interior areas of the CST.

Sure enough, the phaser beam lanced around, bending every time it hit the egg-shaped energy field and shooting back past the ship, until finally, inevitably, it struck hull.

An explosion ripped through the midsection electronics, blowing sparks, hissing—and somebody cried out in pain. Shouted orders and desperate measures shot forward, audible even through the closed hatches.

"So much for phasers . . ."

"Rupture! Section four, starboard PTC! Automatic sealant nozzle heads are fused—"

"Tell 'em to do it manually," Stiles called. "Is everyone okay?"

Jeremy looked at him grimly. "It's a reflector envelope! Our own phaser hit us! We can't fire out!"

"Pardon me . . . would you take a suggestion?"

Spock!

The voice jolted Stiles. He spun around and looked up to the grand figure on the starboard deck. "Are you *kidding?"*

The stately Vulcan kept a grip on the buffer edge of the science console and somehow made his awkward position look graceful on the wickedly tilted deck. "Quicksand. If we struggle, the beam sucks us down at a commensurate rate, drawing upon our own energy to exert more pull than we can exert thrust. If we hold still, all it may do is hold us in place."

While the engines howled and the hull peeved, Stiles gazed at the ambassador and Spock back at him as if they had all week. Doubt and illogic spun through Stiles's training and experience, then jumped the gully to irrational trust.

He looked at the readouts, at Jeremy's face skewed with doubt, at Travis desperately trying to make sense of what the ultrascience officer had just suggested . . . as precious seconds slipped away, Stiles found himself adding up the crazy numbers.

His eyes flipped again to Spock, and he shook his head and winced. "I was about to fall for something again, wasn't I?"

"Literally."

"Sir . . . I hope you're everything I think you are." Without turning away from Spock's steady eyes, Stiles tossed over his shoulder, "Cut thrust."

"That can't be right!" the panicked trainee at the helm protested, his eyes swiveling wildly. "We'll get pulled into the planet!"

Stiles started to explain, then cut himself off and waved. "Travis!"

Perraton instantly yanked the midshipman from the helm and slid into the seat himself. "Cutting thrust. Sorry, kid. Go sit down till we see how dead we are."

His own order eating at his stomach, Stiles leered at Spock as if to share the burden. His mind raced, as he scoured his memory of all those recorded missions on the first *Starship Enterprise,* when Spock faced the worst mysteries of the cosmos as Captain Kirk's unswerving sidekick.

The whine of the engines depleted noticeably, like howling wolves running over a hill and disappearing into the mist.

"Is it working?" Stiles dared to ask.

Quiet with victory, Travis half-turned to confirm with a good glance. "We're slowing down. . . ."

"We've just bought ourselves about twenty more minutes," Jeremy assessed. "I wouldn't bet on more."

"Keep measuring."

Irritated with the knowledge that he wouldn't have been able to save his ship if Spock hadn't been here, Stiles bristled with selfconsciousness, fighting to think with a divided mind.

"Can't fire out . . . can we beam through the reflector bubble?"

"I don't know that!" Zack Bolt rebelled at the idea. "I know for sure I could never beam you back up through that thing!"

"That doesn't make any—"

"Beam out?" Travis swung around. "Then what? Find the beam housing and kick it down? That thing can take hand phaser fire!"

"We'll use the nacelle charges," Stiles told him.

"Those are only five-minute charges," Travis explained, with sudden fear in his eyes. "They'll take out a mile and a half. You'll never get away in time."

"We'll do something," Stiles shabbily assured. "Let's try it. Ready the transporter."

"Are you nuts?" Jeremy grabbed at Stiles's arm, keeping one hand on his controls. "Give me time to analyze the reflector envelope! Maybe you can't beam through it."

"How long before it pulls us down, did you say?"

His face sheeting to white, Jeremy shook his head. "All right, all right."

Some inner checklist rang in Stiles's head, and he turned to Spock, prepared to use all the resources he had at his disposal—and this was one dynamite resource. "Can we?"

Now that he'd been invited, Spock leaned to look at Jeremy's science monitors that gave them the energy analysis of that beam. Even after several seconds of study and two significant frowns, Spock could only postulate, "Possibly."

Stiles's leg muscles knotted. "Let's try beaming through."

On his other side, Jeremy protested, "Let me beam something solid out first."

"You got thirty seconds. Somebody get me a jacket. I'm going myself."

"*You* are?" McCoy asked. "Damn! Another hotshot!"

The comm button was hot under Stiles's finger. "Jason, bring me two of the shaped charges we use to blow off nacelles. Meet me in the transporter section." He accepted and yanked on a jacket somebody handed him from the aft bridge locker. "I've got to find Zevon. Nobody else knows—"

"Neither do you know the way around the city," Spock pointed out. He stood squarely before Stiles. "You were a prisoner. But I do."

That's what he needed—a super-shadow.

But he couldn't think of any reason that didn't make absolute sense. Pushy, pushy Vulcan . . .

"What about me?" Dr. McCoy made a rickety effort to stand up.

Stiles gaped at him, instantly in a bind. His mouth opened, closed again, opened—what could he say? McCoy couldn't possibly run or fight, but if he stayed here . . . and what about the others? Offer to beam a hundred-and-some-year-old man down to save his life and leave the entire young crew behind with their lives dangling?

McCoy's ice-blue eyes sharpened. "Are you going to refuse one of the greatest explorers and pioneers in Starfleet history?"

Choking on what he hoped was damage smoke and not something else, Stiles uttered, "I . . . I . . . uh. . . ."

"Eric," Jeremy interrupted, "We're slipping. They're not pulling us down with our energy now, but it's still pulling us with whatever energy it can muster itself. We're slipping deeper into the atmosphere. Sixteen minutes till we hit the surface."

Travis looked at him. "Can we turn so we don't hit engines-first?"

"No chance."

Spock stripped out of his ceremonial robe and dumped it on the deck. "We should go, Commander."

But Stiles was still gawking at McCoy without knowing what to say.

The aged physician leered back at him with singular determination.

Spock snapped up the front of his formal jacket—it turned out the big clunky Vulcan molded jewels also had a clasping mechanism—and simply preempted, "Doctor, please."

Leveling a finger at Stiles, McCoy huffed, "If you don't come out of transport with your arms sticking out of your head and you find that Romulan, you bring me the whole package, not just a sample of his blood. I've got to have a constant, warm, living source for several days to do what I need to do. I need him, got it? Not a sample. Him, himself."

"Thank you," Spock said. "We shall do our utmost."

"You'd better."

And McCoy stepped aside, out of the way of everybody who was working to keep the CST in the atmosphere.

"Travis, come here." Stiles grasped his friend's arm and held it fiercely. "Backup plan three, got it?"

"Really?"

"Yes, really. Got it?"

"Got it."

"Travis . . . don't let my ship sink."

Somehow Travis found a smile. "We'll do what we have to, Eric."

Stiles started to respond, but his words stuck in his throat. Travis assured him by returning the grip, and said nothing more.

Drawing a tight breath, Stiles jumped to the hatchway and grasped the hatch handle, then looked back for Spock. "Mr. Ambassador? Let's fly or fry."

"After you, Mr. Stiles."

The Imperial Palace

What had begun as a complex and troubling medical mission had first metamorphosed into the glimmerings of success—a chance to save a thousand royal family members and shore up the stability of the Federation's closest and most dangerous neighbor on this side of the street—and had now once again altered its form and function. Now Crusher, Data, and the hapless merchant named Hashley were about to fight for their own lives. As abruptly as wind shifts, they had become the targets of an assassination plan that had seemed as distant to them as stars were apart.

As her stomach muscles spun into spirals, Beverly Crusher thought fast, conjuring up a half-dozen alternatives before settling on one. She couldn't sedate them all. She couldn't seduce them all . . . there had to be something better.

"Allow me to play to your sense of honor," she began, with a bluntness she hoped Romulans would appreciate. "If your men can take my man, Sentinel, I'll pack up my instruments and leave, and let the empress and her family die. You won't even have to kill me."

Sentinel Iavo tipped his head as if he hadn't quite heard her right. He nodded once at Data after deciding she couldn't possibly be talking about Hashley.

"Him?"

"Yes," Crusher said. "Him."

"A duel?"

"If you have the integrity."

Iavo glanced at the sergeant of his guards. The sergeant frowned in suspicion, but said nothing.

"How is it honorable," Iavo parried, "for five men to do battle with one man?"

Crusher shrugged. "Well, he works out a lot. You know Starfleet."

The five Romulan men, warriors all, looked at Data and saw a lanky, wiry human who carried Crusher's medical bags.

Crusher held her breath. Come on, men, think . . . how do we spell Romulan chivalry?

"He has no weapon," one of the other guards protested as he finally drew his own blade.

"You told us no active phasers or disrupters could get through the palace's security screen," Crusher said, "so you can either give him a dagger, or fight him like he is."

Despite being obviously intrigued by the wager, Iavo's expression hardened. "There is no integrity in sacrificing everything on a game. I refuse, Doctor. I cannot afford to let you leave here now. You will die today."

Crusher shrugged. "Have it your way. You still have to fight him."

Data stood alone in the middle of the carpet, calm and waiting, seeming very small. Perfect—the Romulans didn't like this at all. Whether they won or not, they were petty about fighting and too chicken to bet on themselves. And she'd piqued their sense of fair play. Conscience could be such a burden, couldn't it? She hadn't expected them to take a silly wager, but now they were ashamed to fight Data in what appeared to be a no-win for Starfleet.

The Romulans glanced at each other in waves of hesitation, doubt, suspicion—and a flash of guilt?

Over her shoulder, Crusher heard the faint voice of Ansue Hashley. "I . . . I can fight . . . a little. . . ."

"Shh," the doctor murmured. "Go ahead, Data."

Without verbal acknowledgement, Data moved forward. Crusher pressed Hashley back, and the line of battle drew itself across the fur carpet. There before her, like a museum painting on a wall, stood the stirring vision of four distinguished Romulan charioteers and their Sentinel in rebellion, and thus they descended to the ranks of hatchet men.

Between the two factions in the bedchamber stood the couch and the oblong table and its chair. For a moment these three objects seemed as insurmountable as any moat. The recorded harp lyricals continued mindlessly to play, the fire to skitter and glow, the empress to suffer through her next breaths.

Ultimately the tension in the room became tangible, breakable—or maybe it was just the accursed twangy harp music—and the standoff was shattered by the battle cry of the sergeant of the guard. He flung off his helmet, dashed it to the hearth stones, and charged.

Blocked by the table, the sergeant drove forward anyway and leaped into the air, took two steps across the tabletop, spread his arms, dagger down, and dive-bombed Data where he stood.

Barehanded, Data's arms shot up; he clasped the sergeant's nubby silver uniform with both hands and parried the man over his head. If Data had simply completed the arch, the sergeant would've landed on Crusher, but Data's shock-fast computer brain measured the pivot—angle, force, velocity, energy—and he twisted exactly right. The sergeant bellowed his shock and surprise, slashed downward with his blade—raking Data across the back of the neck—and then flew into the wall as if shot from a cannon. Though it looked as if he had just struck the velvet drapery, his body made a distinct *thok* of bone and armor striking against sheer rock. He crashed onto the corner of the vanity and thence to the floor.

Enraged, the three other guards now charged in unison, vaulting and smashing past the furniture. Data's hands struck out like cobra tongues, skirting the slashing blades of his attackers with such blinding speed that two of the guards cut each other instead of him and stumbled back. The third received a kick in the gut and was thrown off. The first guard now flew from his position on the floor and jumped onto Data's back, clinging and grimacing viciously while trying to position his knife at Data's throat. Data merely turned under them as freely as a weathervane, his expression completely unfazed.

Sentinel Iavo, astounded by what he saw, rushed between the table and the couch, his ceremonial dirk's long blade golden in the firelight, as he drove it forward into Data's ribcage. There the blade lodged.

Data reached over his head with one hand to clasp the clinging sergeant by the hair and down with the other hand, to grip Sentinel Iavo's dirk hilt as it protruded from his chest. Crusher winced as the three men waltzed together.

Behind her, Ansue Hashley's gasps and gulps narrated every move, and he somehow had the sense to stay back, no matter what he thought he saw.

"He'll be slaughtered!" Hashley empathized. "That knife—it's in him!"

Restraining herself from idle boasting, Crusher said, "Don't worry yet. Data's the best concealed weapon around."

In a spin of color and firelight, the sergeant slammed to the floor at Crusher's feet, dazed, his face bleeding, lungs heaving, weapon completely missing. Crusher stooped and heaved him up onto his knees. "There you go. Keep fighting."

She stepped back, watching tensely to see if the seed of guilt she'd planted would sprout quickly enough to turn the tide. Already she sensed a halfheartedness in the Romulans' effort—or was she imagining it?

With a prideful roar, the Romulans surged back into the fight just as Sentinel Iavo and one of the other guards crashed into the couch and drove the whole thing right over backward, dumping them into a stand of shelves, whose contents came shattering down upon them.

"You're making a mess," Crusher commented.

"I shall be happy to tidy everything later, Doctor," Data responded as he whirled and took a blaze of vicious stabbings to the arms and upper body and blocked hard-driven blows that were meant for his face. In return he drove his fists, knuckles, and the heels of his hands into the soft tissues of his opponents. "By the way, I am expecting a communiqué from the empress's first cousin's physician on Usanor Four. Would you mind activating the channel?"

"Oh, sure."

Completely rattled by the casual conversation going on while they were panting like dogs, the Romulan guards let their anger get the better of them. Data's hand-eye coordination was at computer speed, he had the strength of any ten Romulans all equalized throughout his body, and he wasn't getting tired. When the next one came within grasping range, attempting to body-blow Data to the floor, Data instead grasped the man fully about the chest and heaved him into the air, propelling him up and into the corner.

"Data, it's getting out of hand. Wrap it up as soon as you can."

"Certainly."

Sentinel Iavo was poised ten feet from them in an attack stance, staring at the body of his guard. Summoning the commitment he had made, he forced himself to swing once again at Data with his dirk blade slashing. The blade fell on Data's shoulder and glanced off. Iavo stumbled.

In that instant, Data managed to drive off all three remaining attackers at once, just long enough to grasp the dagger hilt that was still sticking out of him. With a firm yank, he drew it from his body. The blade dripped with colored fluid as he turned it toward the charging guards and the Sentinel. He was armed.

His eyes narrowed and his teeth gritted, Data's jaw locked, and there was a flush of effort in his complexion. The Sentinel and two of the guards attacked him as a unit with their blades, met with driving force by Data's weapon. The clang and shriek of metal against metal erupted over the harpsong.

"Uh-oh, he's getting mad," Crusher observed. "And they say he doesn't have those emotions . . . apparently he's got something like adrenaline on his side."

"How can he do this?" Hashley asked. "How can he throw those big guards around!"

"He eats his broccoli. This is what happens to all conspirators, Mr. Hashley. Sooner or later they have to show themselves."

Iavo spun around and glared at her while two of his men lunged at Data and were thrown off. "Conspirators?"

"The Sentinel did it, didn't he?" Ansue Hashley reckoned, taking the topic and running with it while the other men fought their way around the arena. "He poisoned the royal family! He wanted power all the time. He's been close to it all his life, like the prime minister waiting for the queen to die, but he gets impatient. I've heard of that."

Crusher rewarded him with a nod, then accused Iavo with a glare. "I guess he thought he could get away with killing the entire royal family."

In the middle of a dagger-swipe, Iavo let his move be parried without challenge as he sang out, "I did nothing to make this happen! I have no idea why they turned ill at the same time! I thought it was their blood!"

Wondering how good an actor he was, Crusher moved sideways, keeping behind the periphery of Data's slashing weapon. "Who helped you engineer the viral terrorism?"

"I did *not* do it!" Iavo shouted. He actually stopped fighting, backed away from Data, and stood there waving his weapon in a kind of helpless gesture, as one of his guards writhed in pain at his feet and the other braced to charge again. "This was providence working! I had the power to see what could be! I wanted to change the hearts of our people, not this . . . this—stop it!"

He lashed out at the last guard, driving the charging soldier sideways into the table just before the other man would've plowed back into Data's circle of engagement.

"Stop, all of you!" Iavo ordered. "Stop . . . stop. No more . . ."

The other guards—the two conscious ones—clasped at their bleeding and broken limbs and obeyed him. Mindful of Data's dangerous abilities, they shrank back, away, and crouched near the fireplace. Somehow Crusher could tell that they weren't obeying because they were beaten. They were obeying because they knew they were wrong.

Emotionally destroyed, baffled and sickened by the rankness of what he had been tempted toward, Iavo stalked the width of the room, then finally sank into the chair at the center table as if some magical pry bar had opened a valve and let the air out of him. He raised his striking jewel-like eyes to Crusher, and she saw mirrors of anguish.

"A thousand loyalties," he mourned, "a thousand pressures . . . these days have been torment for me . . . I have spent my life in the service of the royal family, never once thinking such thoughts, until along came this miracle, this disease that struck every one of them . . . at first it seemed tragic, soon changing to a glimmer . . . the allure of opportunity . . . to cut away the throne's ancient core . . . change the future of the empire, dilute the power of blood succession that causes these terrible dangers and finally try something new—this might've been the only chance in history to try. But I can't finish it—"

Demolished, Iavo sank back on the vanity, his head hanging, his arm draped across the console.

"I could let them die," he moaned, "but I could never kill them. You must believe me. . . ."

"Data, stand down," Crusher ordered.

The android lowered his weapon, although Crusher was reassured when he did not put it away, and remained poised in the middle of the room, ready to spring in case anybody got any ideas.

"Good work," she said as she came to the android's side. "How badly are you hurt?

"A little lubricant leakage, Doctor."

"I'll fuse you up in a few minutes."

Emboldened, Crusher crossed the furry carpet in three strides and got the dazed Sentinel by the collar, her hands knotted like cannonballs at his throat. She leered into the crumple of his face.

"All right, Iavo. Look at me. I'm willing to have seen nothing here today, do you understand me? Data's not only the devil with a handweapon, he's also got what you might call a photographic memory. We've got a record of everything that's gone on here, but I'm willing to keep it between us if you do exactly as I order. You get your buddies out of here and don't show me another armed guard for the duration of my visit. You're now the empress's one and only bodyguard. Monarchies are stupid, but that little girl didn't do anything except get born into the royal family. It's like a curse, y'know? It's not her fault."

"You must believe me," he beseeched. "I know nothing of the plot to make them all ill. . . ."

"I believe you." She dropped his collar so abruptly that he flinched. "This biological assault's been going on all over the quadrant and it's never involved the Romulans till now. As much as I'd like to hate you right now, nothing points to you. You're just an opportunist. A clumsy one, at that. You think I can't tell that you've never done anything like this before?"

"I never have . . . please forgive me . . . I never expected you to be so brave. We have always been told that humans whimper and sneak, stab in the night . . . I have served loyally all my life, until this opportunity raised it head—"

"And you can still have your coup d'etat someday, I'm all for revolutions, but not while the opposition is lying helplessly ill and I'm around to make them better. If the empire falls this way, this fast, you'll take all the rest of us down the drain with you. You threatened to kill me, so here's the counter offer. You won't kill me, and Data won't have to kill you. I keep treating her and the rest of the royal family, and you and your men pretend none of this happened and quit thinking that this is a good way to change things. You can all keep your positions and get another chance some day to do it right. I'll send you a biography of Benjamin Franklin and you can get some ideas, but until then be patient and do your jobs with some statesmanship. For now, you'll back off and let me do my job without any more theatrics. Simple enough?"

The fire snapped, and the harp chimed.

Chapter Nineteen

"MR. STILES . . ."

The devil's own carnival ride. Hands still tingling. Hate bad dreams . . . Orsova, looming over him while some creepzilla who'd won an auction flayed the flesh off him with bare fists. Arms throbbed. Legs, back . . . wake the dead with that drumbeat.

Leave me alone. Can't go back, can't go back there. . . .

Lips clamped together and teeth gnashed, coming down on gritty slime. Stiles swam back to consciousness. Threads of grit made way between his teeth, the side of his tongue, the back of his throat—he gagged himself awake.

As if something were crawling across his face, he backhanded himself in the mouth and wiped moist filth from his face, then heaved up spitting, weed pods netted with slime sheeting off the left side of his uniform as he rolled.

Someone groaned—he opened his eyes and seemed to see the sound of his own complaint rush into the sky like a bird. Pressing grit from his watering eyes, he forced himself up on both arms and hovered there on hands and knees, as his head battled to clear.

He was kneeling in shoulder-high ferns. The ground was soft, sticky, made of pea-like pods in a great carpet, light green like duckweed on an everglade. And stank like a bilge.

"What's that awful smell?" he complained.

A few yards from him, Spock rose to his knees in the ferns, his hands dripping with green stuff. "The great outdoors."

As if afflicted, Stiles stood up on a pair of rattling maracas. "God, we lived . . . that was the longest beaming I've ever been through. My head feels like a stone."

"The restraint shield they put around us is apparently geared toward weapons energy, fortunately. It allowed us to beam in—is your phaser active?" Spock was holding his phaser, looking at it critically.

Stiles pulled his own phaser. "Drained! These were fully charged!"

"The shield sensed the charge," Spock said, "and neutralized them. Useless." Just like that he dismissed their lack of weaponry.

"Where are the grenades?" Spock slashed at the ferns with his hands, looking for the only thing they'd had time to bring with them—a pouch loaded with heavy-duty shaped grenades normally used by CST crews to blow off an irreconcilably leaking nacelle before the nacelle exploded and took a whole ship with it.

All around and above them, black trees spindled high and low, wretched branches dipping low into the marshy weeds and snaking up again with newly absorbed nutrients. Hands shaking, Stiles dug at the thickly shadowed overgrowth and wished there were more sunlight. Those clouds up there, blocking the light, those were the ones he'd seen displayed on the *Saskatoon*'s screens as the energy from the planet drew the ship deeper and deeper into the atmosphere. The clouds seemed so passive and blanketing, he had to struggle to recall that they were as deadly as venom, blinding his crew as they were sucked closer to being milled to dust.

Seemed like the ship was a million miles away, down here with the peace and quiet and ferns . . . be easy to lie down and take a nap.

"Twelve minutes," Spock reminded. "At this rate, the CST will crash at six hundred ten miles per hour."

"And disintegrate—I know." Stiles pawed furiously through the ferns now. "It's got to be here. It came through, didn't it? What if the envelope let us through and stopped the grenades somehow?"

"The pouch would be here empty."

"Oh . . . right. Here it is!" He came up from the ferns with a weed-matted satchel, and half a bush attached to his hair. Through the pouch's mock-leather skin, he felt the presence of two charges in their canisters.

"We must hurry," Spock urged.

After a moment's clumsy hesitation, clarity struck him that Spock's statement was meant to let Stiles lead the way.

"Right—this way."

The transporter had put them down at the edge of the weed forest. As they broke out of the knotty growth, tripping on hidden roots and fingers of dipping branches coming up again as independent plants, Stiles immediately saw the center of his universe—a blocky gray beam housing nestled in a meadow, positioned so that it had almost 170-degree firing clearance in every direction, even over the mountain range to his right—those mountains sent a javelin through him, which seemed to drive him backward . . . moving his feet to go toward the building caused such physical stress that his legs nearly went numb.

The blocky beam housing was nothing more than a platform of granite blocks and a spidery dutronium arrangement that acted as legs for a conical device standing about thirty feet above the ground. From that device at this moment a blinding blue beam was being emitted, that bellowed like a concert band trying to tune up.

Maybe they could've brought it down with hand phasers, but it would have taken a while to melt, Stiles noted with some satisfaction. At least the right choice had been made there. They hadn't taken the time to get hand phasers out of the security lockers and had brought only the canister charges. A dumb mistake. A dumb midshipman's mistake. Why did his mind always turn to taffy when Ambassador Spock was around?

"Both sides of the base?" Stiles asked as he handed one of the charges to the ambassador.

"Yes."

"These are shaped charges, sir, so be sure to point the open end down so the force'll go into the ground and not up to the ship. *Saskatoon*'s not much more than fifteen miles over our heads by now."

"Twelve point two. These are five-minute charges? No more, no less?"

"That's it. When you're blowing off a nacelle, all the alternatives have been exhausted. The decision's already been made. All you need is a small safety margin. Five's usually enough."

"It will not be enough today." Spock glanced around as he positioned the canister between the bolted fingers of a stanchion. "Other than the trees, there is no cover here."

"Most of those 'trees' aren't even trees. They're tendrils of an ancient root system. They just keep going up and down out of the glade like some giant's sewing them all over the countryside. They're hollow with liquid inside. They'll be blown down and act like a big net on us. The bark'll just crumble and turn into shrapnel."

"Perhaps we should head in another direction, in that case."

"We'll head over that way, on the open meadow. How far can we run in five minutes?"

"Hardly matters, Mr. Stiles. We're unlikely to survive the blast wave. If the ship is freed from this beam, Dr. McCoy can lead a landing party to collect your friend and continue with the medical mission."

Stiles peered through the dutronium spiderweb. "Is that why you left him up there? To lead a second landing party if we got killed?"

"Yes. Two fronts are better than one."

"Hmm . . . I left him because I figured he couldn't run." With feelings appropriately scornful to that little step down, Stiles pressed the charged canister into place. "Ready . . . it's set. Now what?"

"Four minutes, fifty-five seconds."

Ambassador Spock set his own canister, then stepped back from the granite block, his black eyes vibrant with the moment's risk. He was actually enjoying himself.

"I believe the operative phrase," he said, "is 'run like hell.' "

"Three minutes."

How long can five minutes be?

As Spock ticked off the time in thirty-second intervals, Stiles's legs pumped in unison with the pounding of his heart.

The longest Constrictor on record (the last time Stiles had experienced one) was three and a half minutes. The last eruption of Mount Vesuvius had lasted nine hours. A two-minute earthquake was really long. A ten-minute tornado. Minutes stretched into drawn-out experiences that seemed never to end, seemed to make the whole universe turn slower and slower, until a heartbeat itself became a sluggish kettledrum with the drummer falling asleep.

Five minutes of running across a swamp meadow, splashing through rancid fluids, anticipating the platform back there to blow sky-high and sweep him off the face of the planet—that five minutes shot by faster than a snapped finger. What happened to all those stories about minutes becoming hours?

As the five-minute mark approached, they were only a third of the way across the meadow, running toward a blister of stony hills. At thirty-six years old, Stiles could devour some ground, and he had been holding back somewhat because he didn't want to outpace the ambassador in case Spock needed help. Soon that showed itself to be unnecessary—Spock was tall, long-legged, and Vulcan.

They ran. Hindered by the knee-high meadowgrass and the uneven ground beneath, the exercise became a venture into hopping, tripping, sprinting, and catching on thorns and tangles. Another ten feet . . . another . . . each step drew him deeper into misery. His brain shut down, he couldn't think of what to do but keep running. In his periphery he saw the flash of purple and black—the ambassador's clothing moving at his side, the flick of Spock's fists and arms pumping as he forcefully kept up with a much younger man.

Stretching out his right leg to pass over a depression that opened before him, Stiles gasped suddenly as a cramp tore through the bottom of his thigh, wrecking his stride. His foot connected with the upward slope of the depression, but his leg instantly folded and he crammed into the compacted dirt knee-first, down onto his side, skidding on his right cheekbone into the grass. Not the kindly patch of green at the end of the block, this Pojjana idea of grass had serrated edges and left his hands and face reddened as if he'd just shaved with a sawblade. He was on the ground, and the last seconds were gobbled up.

"Keep running!" he shouted into the dirt. "I'll catch—"

But then the landscape opened up and reached for the sky. Black noise concussed between the mountains and the swamp forest, a great stick striking a great drum, and Stiles's skull rang and rang. He tried to rise, to run again, but the flash blinded him and the raw force drove him into the depression, not more than eight inches lower than the level of the ground they'd run across.

Suddenly he was lying in a furnace, pressed down by weight he couldn't fight. He turned his head to one side and opened his eyes in time to see the blast wave blow over him in a single, solid white-hot sheet. The side of his face turned hot and he buried his head in his arms and waited to die.

Into the muffling warmth of his sleeve, he murmured, "Go, Sassy, go, go . . . push. . . ."

The carnivorous shock wave sheeted across his body, raising the hairs on his neck and limbs. He couldn't breathe—he sucked at a vacuum—

And just as the compression was about to crush his chest, Stiles took one more desperate attempt to breathe and got a lungful of warm dusty air. His head cleared almost instantly.

As he maneuvered his elbows, pinned under his chest, and tried to shove himself upward, a weight across his shoulderblades pressed him down and held him. A wave of cool air now flooded over him, replacing the rushing scalded air of the blast sheet.

"Stay down." Spock's voice rang in his ear. "Cover your head."

Drowning out Spock's words, a shattering hail of granite bits and shards of metal pulverized them as they lay crushed to the floor of the depression. Stiles shrank into the smallest crushed-up ball he could manage as his back was hammered by his own success. The wreckage of the beam housing had taken a little tour flight and was now coming to visit the two little elves who'd arranged the trip.

His chest heaving, he finally managed to press up onto his elbows, then to his knees.

Crouched at his side, Spock was slapping him on the back over and over.

As Stiles was trying to figure out a way to tell the ambassador that he wasn't choking and didn't need to be patted, Spock simply explained, "Your clothes were burning."

"Oh . . . thanks. Was that . . . one . . . explosion . . . or two?"

"Two. One concussion wave." Spock spoke as if nothing had happened at all, then coughed. The cough made him seem perfectly mortal and gave Stiles a bit of comfort that otherwise might've slipped on past him.

As a shimmering cloud of debris—the last of the pulverized housing—drifted around them as if it were a theatre curtain lowering, he winced his way to a standing position and had to lock both legs to stay up. His whole body trembled and pulsed with aftershock.

Through the drifting dust, he peered at the mass of wreckage, completely flattened, in fact depressed into a crater. The steel structure that had held the beam's emitter lay in mangled messes all over the grass, which had itself been seared brown.

"Think it worked?" Stiles wondered. "Is the CST okay now?"

"If they veered off at the correct tangent, yes." Spock made moves to stand up, but faltered. Instead he looked at his legs, first one, then the other, in a strangely clinical manner.

Stiles turned to him. "Sir?"

Before he could ask the question that came up, he flinched bodily at what he saw—a shard of metal the size of a writing stylus embedded in the side of the ambassador's left thigh, with a good two inches sticking out.

"Oh, sir . . ." Stiles knelt beside him. The cloth of Spock's pantleg was stained with his blood, and the Vulcan was plainly stiff with pain, although he pretended this didn't bother him much. "How deep in do you think it is?"

"No way to tell," Spock said, and looked around at the sky. "The blast was substantial enough to have alerted the authorities. Someone should be arriving soon."

Shaken by that, Stiles also looked around at the gray sky. "And here we are, out on the lone prairie, with no way to defend ourselves—sir, don't!"

He put out a hand, though he didn't really know what to do when the ambassador abruptly grabbed the protruding two inches of the metal shard and simply slid it out of his leg.

"You're not supposed to pull out something that's sticking in you like that!" Stiles protested. "What if it hit an artery? You could bleed to death!"

"I clot well." Spock tossed the shard into the scorched grass and pressed the heel of his hand tightly to the wound. "I must be able to maneuver, and certainly a metal implement in my leg would be troublesome."

Stiles stood up again and looked around. "They'll be here any minute. We can take cover in those hills . . . I've heard of people digging down a few feet and finding the hollows made by ancient root systems that aren't there anymore." In the blast-flattened grass, he found a large piece of a support strut with the bolt still attached in one end. "We can dig with this. I think I can hide you for a while in there, and after nightfall we can make it into the foothills."

"Commander . . . would you consider—"

"No, I will *not* consider leaving you and going off on my own. That's not even in the picture, so don't think about it. If you'll let me help you up. . . ."

Holding his digger in one hand, he slipped the other arm around the ambassador, who allowed himself to be pulled to his feet. Smeared with Vulcan blood, their clothing scorched, hair filthy, they hitched their way out of the almost invisible depression that had saved both their lives by allowing the blast wave to pass over them instead of deep-frying them into the ground. Any minute now a patrol would show up to investigate the blast, which probably showed up on every scanner on this part of the continent. Obviously, too, the Pojjana must've known they'd caught something in that gravity-weird contraption.

"This way, sir." He drew Spock along, dismayed that the Vulcan seemed not to be helping much. "We'll hide until night, then we can make a bivouac in the hills and figure out a way to defend it. There they are! I see a plane! Come on, before they spot us!"

Chapter Twenty

STILES PRESSED FORWARD, aiming for the shadowy protection of the rocklands ahead. He could hear the distant murmur of the plane's engine, recognized the type of aircraft, and made his bets.

"They're still miles away," he gasped, pulling Spock along, "but even if they spot us they can't land on this terrain. They'll have to send a recon hoverscout with a patrol team to flush us out. If we can make it to the hills—"

"Commander?"

"Don't worry, I can take more of your weight. We can't slow down. If we can make it to—"

"Of course, Mr. Stiles, but I do have a question."

"What's that, sir?"

"From whom are we hiding?"

"Watch that rock—don't trip!"

"From whom," Spock repeated, "are we about to hide?"

"The authorities. They'll be here any time—"

"And to whom . . . did we come here to speak?"

Stiles dragged the ambassador along another five or six steps before this sank in.

As the drone of the aircraft drew closer to the bomb site, he felt his face screw up in a frown of confusion and doubt. Something just didn't seem right about this.

The ambassador tentatively put more weight on his injured leg.

Stiles shifted back and forth on his own feet and finally met Spock's eyes. "I'm doing it again, aren't I?"

Spock bobbed an eyebrow, flattened his lips, and charitably avoided nodding.

While digesting that little nugget, Stiles lowered the ambassador onto the first sitting-sized rock they'd come upon, a harbinger of the fact that they could've made it to cover if logic hadn't gotten in the way.

They remained still, unresisting, out in the open, as the Pojjana aircraft buzzed the scene of the explosion and Stiles thought his arms and legs were going to fall off with the urge to run again, hide, defend—

The plane strafed the flattened beam emitter for several seconds before veering abruptly toward them. His spine shriveled. They'd been spotted.

'They've seen us," Spock said with quiet satisfaction.

"How are we going to explain blowing up their emitter?" Stiles circled behind the ambassador and came around the other side as if stalking the plane on its approach. "We had to do it. I couldn't let it pull my ship down—"

"Of course not."

The plane soared over them, one wing tilted low, and they could clearly see the pilot in his helmet looking down at them. He was contacting the Pojjana security forces.

They'd never get away now. Stiles battled inwardly, wrestling with the idea that getting away wasn't the best idea, wouldn't get them where they needed to be, wouldn't find Zevon.

"You needn't call me 'sir,' " Spock told him, as if they were sitting over a dinner table or playing badminton. "I have no Starfleet rank any longer, and you are the commander of the vessel that matters in our lives today."

"Yeah, well . . . well, it'll be long time before I can think of you as anybody other than Science Officer Spock of the *Enterprise.*"

The plane circled the area, keeping them inside its surveillance area while no doubt calling for backup. Stiles never let his back turn to the plane, moving constantly to stay between the aircraft and the ambassador, a shield of vellum against rockets if they decided to open fire. Each step drove him deeper into his troubled thoughts.

"Do you know," he began, "do you realize how many hours on end I rehearsed calling you 'Ambassador' before that evac mission? I just knew I'd get down to that planet and call you 'Mister' or 'Captain' or 'First Officer' or 'Your Honor' or 'Your Highness'—something stupid was waiting to pop out of my mouth and I could just taste it. All the way in Travis and the evil twins kept saying, 'Eric, will you quit mumbling the word *ambassador?*' I'll bet . . . I just bet Captain Kirk never had that kind of problem."

Spock paused a moment. His eyes never flinched nor did his expression change much. He peered solemnly into the past and seemed to enjoy what he saw.

"No," he said. "He had others. Those were excellent days. But they are passed now."

Despite the circumstances, Stiles found himself sighing. "Maybe for you. Not for the rest of us."

Looking up now, Spock said, "Because you feel you must live up to them?"

Somehow there was no right answer to that question. Damned if he did, damned—

Apparently the ambassador didn't expect an answer, because he kept talking himself. "If James Kirk's mission logs are the barometer against which you measure yourself, you set too high a task for yourself. You must temper your awe. You can never attain so high a standard."

Even though a patrol scout craft now appeared over the mountains and streaked toward them across the meadow flats, Stiles turned to Spock and didn't bother to look at the patroller as he heard its humming engines approaching.

"Oh, is that right?" he challenged. "I always admired you for the things you did and the—I guess 'style' is a good way to say it . . . I never got the idea you were filled up with yourself. Till now, anyway. . . . Why are you nodding? I just insulted you."

"Rather, you just complimented yourself," Spock corrected. "And you must not expect me to argue with the ship's commander."

His tone was somehow cagey, manipulative, carrying palpable ulterior messages. And that eyebrow was up again. Stiles scoured him silently, wondering what to make of the ambassador's expression. Was he being teased?

"Are you feeling ill?" Spock asked him then.

Stiles flinched. "What?"

"You're very pale."

"Well . . . it . . . isn't easy getting needled by a . . . by a . . ."

"A super-eminence?" Spock supplied.

Stiles peered at him, able for a moment to ignore the approach of the Pojjana security scout. Was Spock smiling? Was that a little smile? Was it?

As the Pojjana scout came to a hover over them with its warning lights flashing, its containment field snapped on to enshroud them in red spotlight—they could no more walk out of it than through a vault wall.

"Stay quite still," the ambassador warned. "They will assume we're armed."

With the flat of his hand Stiles shielded his eyes from the containment field's glare. "We should've been. I botched it."

His hands were ice. Emblazoned on the flank of the scout, the Pojjana symbol of a gray lightning bolt crossed by a red arrow seemed alive to him, a swollen symbol of his captivity. Those terrors and miseries rushed back at him. His legs trembled so violently that he could barely stand. Only Spock's steadying presence kept him from bolting, a spontaneity which would've fried him to a flake at the edge of the containment field. Strange—he knew that if he were the senior "eminence" here and his crewmates were with him, he wouldn't be so shaky. He would never let them bolt. How there could be two men in one suit—

"HOLD POSITION!" the scout's broadcaster boomed, so loud it knocked Stiles back a step.

Spock held up both hands in a surrendering gesture. Stiles couldn't manage that. His hands were frozen at his sides, his chest heaving, his leg muscles bound up.

"Relax, Mr. Stiles," Spock called over the scout's hum as the craft nestled into the crusty burned stubble, his dark eyes squinted into shafts.

Without looking at him, Stiles gulped, "Remember what happened last time you told me that?"

The Pojjana craft settled completely and gave off a loud hiss as its antigravs equalized. The sight of Pojjana guards lumbering down the hatch ramp as it crashed down gave Stiles a cramp in the middle of his gut. All four guards and a sergeant came thundering out and leveled firearms at them.

"Our sidearms are completely drained," Spock stated in passably fluent Pojjana to the sergeant who came to face them down. "We wish to speak to the planetary authorities."

"You are aliens," the sergeant said with malice, and confiscated their phasers instantly, drained or not. "This is Red Sector. We're supposed to be left alone."

Beside Stiles, the ambassador struggled to stand despite the fact that everyone could see his leg was bleeding. Spock faced the sergeant at eye level.

"Things change, Officer," he said. "I am Ambassador Spock of the United Federation of Planets, former emissary to the Pojjana Assembly. This is—"

"Don't tell them," Stiles whispered.

Spock instantly revised. "This is the commander of the transport ship you nearly brought down. We destroyed the emitter in self-defense. We have no aggressive intentions. We have a proposal for the provincial exarch."

"We have no exarch anymore. That position was eradicated."

"Who is in charge?"

"The provost of the works."

Spock tipped his head. "That is the supreme authority on the planet?"

"That's right."

"Please take us to this person."

The sergeant shook his head. His helmet reflected light from the clearing sky. "You'll be incarcerated in the provincial prison until you come to trial for invasion."

"We must be allowed to see the senior authority. This is a matter of interstellar importance."

"I'll put you where I want to put you," the sergeant said. "Then I'll wait to be asked what happened."

Stiles beat down a shudder. "Nothing really changes."

"We cannot wait," Spock told the sergeant. "If you withhold us, you will be blunting advancement of a critical mission. Do you wish your name to be prominent when the provost discovers that he was not informed?"

The sergeant stood with an unreadable expression for a few silent seconds, then gestured them toward the scout's ramp and the four other guards waiting to funnel them inside.

"Clear them for energy signals," the sergeant ordered to his men, and one of them came forward.

The guard lowered his firearm, whipped out some kind of scanner, and ran it over Stiles from ears to toes, then over Spock, front, back, and both sides.

"No active energy or signals of any kind," the guard confirmed. "No readings."

"He told you we were unarmed," Stiles complained, knowing that he wouldn't have believed it either.

The sergeant stepped aside and leveled his own weapon. "Go in."

Obviously there wasn't much more to be done here. Stiles's jaw ached to speak up, spit who he was and insist on some kind of instant retribution, but a thousand warnings clogged his throat. He was in command of the ship, not the mission. If they found out who he was, would they take offense or insult? Stuff him back in a cell and start auctioning beatings again?

Stiles started toward the scout, pausing only when the ambassador took a step on his injured leg and crumpled to one knee. The sergeant stepped forward to assist. Stiles met the uniformed guard with a fierce shoulder butt to the chest.

"Back off," he snapped, and took the ambassador's arm himself.

None of the other guards made any attempt to touch them further. Stiles escorted the ambassador into the scout and to the first of only three passenger seats. They were in custody.

Stiles straightened and maneuvered to take the next seat. As he raised his eyes to scan the interior of the scout while the guards came aboard, he found himself no longer seated but rather standing ramrod straight and staring at a mounted photograph in a gilded frame on the port bulkhead.

After a wicked choke, he blurted, "Who in salvation is *that!"*

The sergeant, just coming aboard, glared at him as if he and the ambassador were complete idiots. "That's our provost of the works. He saved half the planet from the Constrictor. He developed a way to predict the waves. He sponsored engineering schools and guided architectural renovations all over the planet. Don't you even know who you came to see? We owe him our lives."

The idling engines of the scout roared in his ears as Stiles stood riveted to the carpet. His voice gravelly, he managed, "I owe him a couple things too. . . ."

Spock surveyed the picture briefly, seeing that something more than a portrait of a guy beside a tiger oak desk was going on here. "Mr. Stiles? Do you have something to say?"

Confused, demolished, Stiles blinked at him, at the sergeant and finally again at the picture.

"Yeah. Yeah, I do. I know how we can get in. Tell the 'Provost' . . . that Eric Stiles is back."

Chapter Twenty-one

"STILES. ERIC STILES. You didn't die. They cured you somehow."

"Orsova. Somehow, it figures."

In one withering instant, all of Eric Stiles's fears and visceral reactions bonded into a single living form. There, behind an enormous orange-and-black desk carved out of that wood that reminded Stiles of tiger oak, except even stronger, backdropped by polished paneling and a dozen plaques and awards, there sat the drunken mess that had represented misery to him for four years.

Orsova was less slovenly than before, indeed had lost weight, though he still carried the wide shoulders and stocky build that came naturally to so many native Pojjana. His black hair was now shot with gold—their idea of getting older—and he no longer wore the uniform of the prison hierarchy but the tweedy suit of a Pojjana planetary official. Stiles had only seen that uniform twice before in person. A long time ago.

Orsova sat behind his huge desk, which had hardly any work upon it, and scoured Stiles with the look of a man who was being shown both the past and the future in one picture.

How could events turn this way? How could a devious slob like that become somebody with a title?

"God in a box," Stiles chafed, "what am I seeing?"

His words barely scratched from his throat. As he stood staring, he thought perhaps that only Ambassador Spock, standing with some effort at his side, had heard him at all.

He felt Spock's peripheral glance. But the ambassador never said a thing to him about his reaction to the person they were both standing before. This was crazy. This was a dream.

Spock stepped forward, favoring his bloody leg, to draw the provost's attention away from Stiles and onto himself.

"Provost, I am Ambassador Spock of the United Federation of Planets. Fifteen years ago I was the emissary to your government. We are here to negotiate the greening of Red Sector. Circumstances have caused the Romulans to need Federation assistance. On an Interstellar Temporary Pass, we have come here to make an offer. The sector can be reopened, allowing for trade, assistance, technological exchange, and limited diplomatic relations without requiring membership. We can help the Pojjana in many ways—agricultural efficiency, technological—"

"We don't want help."

Orsova stood up behind his big desk, and there was something prophetic and distant about him. The desk sprawled like an emblem—tiger oak. That was something Zevon had talked about a long time ago. The memory sparked to life.

"What do you want?" Orsova asked.

"We wish to negotiate for custody of the Romulan prisoner named Zevon."

Please let him still be alive, please let him still be alive, please—

Orsova said nothing about Zevon, clearly determined not to give anything away. Instead, he simply asked, "Why do you want one of our prisoners?"

"Damn you," Stiles grumbled.

Spock looked at him.

In frustration and contempt Stiles wagged a hand at Orsova. "What am I—chopped cabbage? He damned well knows Zevon's not just 'one of their prisoners' to me! Is he alive or not, you bastard?"

At Stiles's single step forward, two of the four guards launched forward from the sides of the office, blocking his way to Orsova. The guard closest to him drove the butt of his rifle into Stiles's stomach, and he was driven down.

Spock grasped the guard's arm, avoiding the weapon, and pushed him back in such a way that somehow the movement wasn't threatening. As Stiles gasped at the ambassador's feet, battling crying lungs and a bruised rib, Spock spoke again to Orsova.

"If the Pojjana strike a deal with the Federation, the Bal Quonott and all others in the sector will be pressured to deal with you on favorable terms. That would give the Pojjana substance beyond just your planet. Indeed, you would be a power to be reckoned with in the entire sector. Certainly that offers some value."

Orsova's round bronze face tilted a little like a ball rolling. Maybe he was trying to think. Looked like it hurt.

Stiles's legs were watery as he waited. He had to force himself to stand still, not flinch or shift around, to bury the cloying nervousness, cloak the haunt of old terrors.

"You'll be held," Orsova ultimately decided, "as part of the foreign ship that invaded our planetary space. You'll be held as hostages until the rest of your ship up there surrenders. The ship is mine now, property of the Pojjana people. The crew will be turned over to your government after a healthy fine is paid for destruction of property, violating our space . . . and any other things I think of."

This was Orsova's playing ground. That showed clearly, as he stood up behind his big fancy desk, made of the wood Zevon had long ago discovered did not compress during Constrictors. He came around the bright orange piece of furniture, touching it only lightly along the edge. At the corner of the desk he paused, only steps from Stiles. His eyes burned into Stiles's eyes.

"Except you," he said. "I'll keep you for the memories."

Cued by some secret signal or habit, two of the four armed guards in the room came forward as Orsova moved out from his desk and paused again at Stiles's side. The guards were close enough to threaten against any attempts to attack the provost, so Stiles was careful to remain perfectly still. Being frozen into place by past horrors helped some.

Orsova's eyes drew tight. "It was an insult to me when they took you away. I promised the planet I would get you back. I kept your cell waiting. Didn't even clean it. Part of the promise."

With eyes flat and still as a doll's, Orsova motioned to the guards.

"Take them away."

"*Orsova.*"

"You brought me back already? Why? I stopped the Federation people. Their ship ran away."

"*Their ship did not leave the solar system. I have been monitoring. They're hiding somewhere. I have discovered why they came here.*"

At these words from the Voice, Orsova paused and frowned. He had been sure the Federation ship had run away. He had the Federation's Vulcan ambassador and Eric Stiles where no one would find them, and the Federation ship had run off. But this person, this ghost who spoke to him in unexplained terms, with impossible knowledge, said otherwise.

"*I have changed my plans. I must have these people alive. The doctors, and Zevon.*"

"And Stiles?"

"Do what you wish with him."

"Why do you want doctors? Why don't you just kill them? We've killed plenty of others—"

"The have found a way to do the impossible, cure the incurable. I must know how. You must capture them and bring them to me."

Trying to make sense of a puzzle when he had only half the pieces, Orsova paced the small chamber of the humming craft as the planet of his birth rotated outside one of the little holes.

"I have something here," the Voice began again, *"that will make the Pojjana supreme in Red Sector. Even the Bal Quonott will shrink before you."*

Suspicious of such a brash statement, Orsova narrowed his eyes. "What will make spaceships bow before our planes?"

"You will have more than planes if you do as I tell you. Look in the space chest."

Space chest . . . this brass case? It had a lock, but the lid opened for him anyway. He looked inside. There was only one thing in there.

"A bottle?"

"A medical vial."

"Poison?"

"Something similar."

Orsova straightened sharply. "Is this biological war? You want me to put a plague on my own people? I won't!"

"No."

"I have no one else to poison."

"You have Zevon."

At this, Orsova paused and grimaced. "Why should I poison Zevon? Who are you to want it?"

"You'll never know me. All these years, and I am still a stranger. You were a jail guard. You became assistant warden, but you would never have grown beyond that but for the day I spoke to you and told you to believe that Zevon could predict the Constrictor. Now, Zevon's usefulness is coming to an end here. Give this to Zevon before he is enticed away, and the galaxy moves forward by a leap."

"Away?" Orsova reacted. "Why should he go away? He hates his own people. We're his people now! He says it every day."

"He is royal family. They need him. He may go."

"He'll never leave. No one could get him to leave now."

"The Federation and the Romulans both have reasons to make him want to go. If he leaves, you lose your power and I lose my chance to have what I want. The vial will end the Romulan threat and make the Pojjana strongest, because it will stop Zevon from leaving."

"Because he'll be dead? What . . . what do . . . if I kill Zevon for you, what comes to me?"

"This will force the collapse of the Romulan Empire. When it falls, you will get Romulan ships."

"Warwings? You'll give me those?"

"And birds-of-prey, and at least one full-sized converted heavy cruiser . . . for the sector governor, so he will become accustomed to flying in space."

"Sector governor . . ."

He discovered a series of small cracks—or were they openings? seams?—in the panels. . . .

"You will get a Romulan fleet, enough ships to control the Bal Quonott and make the Pojjana the power in this sector. Rather than cowering before the Federation, the Romulans, or any other aliens, you will be the winner."

"Winner . . ."

"Stop . . . trying . . . to see me!"

The cabin vibrated with the voice's sudden rage. Whoever this ghostly person was, he would not be discovered.

Orsova felt his curiosity wane and let it go. Some things, he didn't have to know. "Zevon's alien," he protested. "How do you know this will kill him? Are you an alien too? Are you a human?"

"No."

"Are you Romulan, Voice? Is that who you are all these years?"

"No."

"Are you—"

"Zevon will be contaminated. Then the Federation won't have any reason to stay in Red Sector, and Zevon will have no reason to leave. Either way, I will honor my agreement with you."

Standing in the middle of the cabin, Orsova gazed at the reflection of himself. An older man, no longer as fat as the prison guard had been, a glowing copper complexion on his cheekbones and streaks of dignified gold in his black hair. This was the leader of a planet, perhaps the leader of a whole sector of space? Dominion over the Bal Quonott, who had lorded their spacefaring capability over the Pojjana since before he was born?

Liking what he saw, he squared his shoulders and imagined a fur cape. The voice remained silent until he decided to ask a question.

"Every time you speak," he attempted, plumbing for more information, "I still have no reason to believe what you say."

"Believe because you can be in charge of this whole sector instead of just one weak and troubled planet, and I will be in charge of you. You will have more power, more comfort, more stability than ever you dreamed on

the day you were happy to become a jail guard, the day you were astonished to be made warden, or the day you realized Zevon was right about predicting the Constrictor and that he would be silent for you. This is easy for me because you have already seized power here. With Zevon dead or ill, you will be my wealthy, powerful little puppet. Number two is still very high. Do this, and you will be sector governor when the Romulan Empire falls. Don't, and I will kill you now and find someone else. I don't care. Is this difficult?"

"No."

"*Take the vial. You no longer need Zevon. Killing him is better. I will be happier. If you cannot kill him, infect him.*"

The small undecorated bottle was slightly warm, as if it had been kept heated. He noted the temperature and planned to keep it insulated. If he was going to do this thing, he would do it right.

"Needle?"

"*It must go in the body. Skin contact is not enough. Only Zevon's DNA will absorb the virus. Get it into him any way you can. Report to me on this frequency when you have succeeded. The Romulan family dies, you become sector governor and get more than your dreams. You're a small and greedy man, Orsova. But take no insult . . . I need small and greedy men.*"

Orsova tucked the vial deep into his jacket, against the warm skin of his chest, and looked up to the faceless persona that promised him glory.

"Small and greedy governors," he corrected.

"Something weird's going on. Why wouldn't they want help? The Constrictor still comes—that's obvious from the architecture. And that pig's no provost or magistrate. I don't know how he got that kind of power, but he's nothing but a glorified jail guard. You saw how he acted! Nobody runs a planet honesty and forthrightly and then turns down help."

"He did seem somewhat cross-purposed."

"He's got some kind of racket going on here. How else in hell could a brutal superficial lout like Orsova end up in control of a whole planet?"

"How could a corporal become Führer?"

Stiles felt his face pinch. "Who? . . . oh. How's your leg? It's still bleeding?"

"Yes, it seems to be." The ambassador turned his leg for a better look at the wound. "You were right. I should have left the projectile embedded."

"Let me wrap it up."

Forcing himself to put Orsova aside in his mind, at least long enough to open the first-aid kit they'd been given, Stiles knelt beside the cot where Spock was sitting. The smell in here was *so* familiar—that combination of dust and moisture that never quite goes away. . . .

Spock pressed his hands back on the cot, tightened up visibly, and endured the stinging pain as Stiles cut the trouserleg away from the wound. The puncture had clotted some, though blood and tissue still leaked from it. Stiles tried to remember how big the projectile had been. Details failed him. All he could do was apply antiseptic, then pressure, both of which caused Spock to stiffen noticeably. Typically Vulcan, Spock was suppressing both the pain and any appearance of it. Stiles wondered if he could do that well if somebody put an arrow through part of him.

"At least they gave us a medical kit," he muttered as he gauzed the leg.

"They may have an ulterior motive," Spock suggested.

"You mean they want us to escape?"

"Possibly. What do you think?"

Confronted with having to cough up an answer, Stiles felt as if he were back in grade school and hadn't done his reading assignment.

"If anything made sense, I'd have something to think. Orsova as a planetary leader, no sign of Zevon . . . all sorts of technology and architecture that wasn't here ten years ago . . . that composite beam reaching out of the atmosphere and grabbing a ship as big and powerful as a CST—even Starfleet can't mix those properties that way. How could the Pojjana do that in just ten years?"

"From what you tell me," Spock contemplated, "Zevon knew what every civilization needs to make its quantum leap. Energy. Yet, to build and use high energy, he would need to influence the use of resources and manpower on the planet. If somehow he obtained influence, gained trust . . . yet how does an alien, particularly a Romulan, come to gain trust in a culture as xenophobic as this?"

"He couldn't. Something else must've happened. Orsova would never let us get past him to talk to anybody else . . . he kept everything to . . ."

Everything he'd seen, the inconsistencies and irritating facts, stewed under his skin. He thought of those last few hours with Zevon, with Orsova, the last beating that had been auctioned to an alien-hating Pojjana. Bruises nearly rose on his skin as if by habit, summoned by the nearness of those old miseries. Suddenly, as if being tapped on the shoulder, he remembered what he had said to Orsova during that last beating.

"That's it! Orsova as planetary leader makes no sense at all *unless* it finally sank through that iron skull that Zevon really could predict the Constrictor! I told him myself! I tried to convince him! If after I left he decided to check it out and Zevon convinced him, Orsova could've taken that message to the government, succeeded in warning the planet, saved a bunch of people and parlayed that into power—" Grasping his head to keep it from blowing off, Stiles raved, "That's got to be it! Orsova's getting credit for Zevon's work!"

Spock stretched his leg, thinking. "Why would Zevon agree to such an arrangement?"

"Oh, he'd agree in a flat minute," Stiles tossed. The familiarity rushed back. "Zevon didn't want power. He was never afraid for his own life. He wanted to redeem himself in his own eyes by saving more people than he killed when his team's experiments started the Constrictor."

"A composite graviton-traction beam with polarity that high, as well as the phaser-resistant envelope the CST encountered, can only be generated with very delicately balanced quantum charge generation. They plainly have warp energy, but it seems to be planet-bound."

"I know why," Stiles said. "Zevon wasn't interested in space. He'd been there. If he'd had influence and resources, he would've turned all the energy he could control to saving the planet from the Constrictor and other outside threats. Looks to me like the Pojjana turned out to be pretty sharp, at least sharp enough to follow instructions, learn physics and engineering . . . even Zevon couldn't do this by himself. They still don't have massive warships or anything, but in spite of that we were in for a real surprise when we got here."

"If Zevon is the real genius behind the planet's sudden advancement," Spock continued, "and I agree that is likely, then Orsova is in constant danger of his secret's being found out."

Stiles looked up. "He sure wouldn't want you and me blabbing it around, would he?"

"No. Nor would he want Zevon taken away. No deal or favor from the Federation could be as beneficial to him as having Zevon here, with a pact to remain behind the scenes."

Coming to his feet, Stiles paced a few steps. "If all this is right, then if Zevon leaves or dies, the jig is up. Orsova couldn't keep up the illusion of being brilliant all by himself."

"Sounds like a threatening symbiotic relationship," the ambassador surmised. "Zevon has managed to bridge the Pojjana through this period of Constrictors which otherwise would have killed vast numbers of them. Instead, they thrive despite the Constrictor."

"They thrive. Orsova thrives. Zevon's here somewhere, alive, working for Orsova. And we're here, locked in a stone crate."

His words fell to the floor. With nothing more to do for the ambassador's leg, Stiles sat on the other cot against the other wall, and descended into captivity as naturally as into a warm tub. Its arms folded around him. They'd been waiting.

The walls around them, stone and mortar, lichen and leakage, uttered their opinion. All the old perceptions came rushing back. Someone was using an autovac on a floor one story up. Water ran through the pipes.

Other prisoners, probably, taking showers in the next wing. A flicker of the lights. Circuits needed adjustment.

He stared at the opposite wall.

"Somehow I knew," he murmured. "I knew I'd end up back here. It's been like one of those nightmares that won't quit coming back. Look at me . . . I can't breathe right, there's no blood in my hands . . . I used to get like this before academy exams. Or before meeting you."

Across the cell, the ambassador observed him as if he were watching bread dough rise, which annoyed Stiles right to the hairs on the back of his neck. Kicking at a loose stone that had been loose ten years ago too, Stiles vented, "Did it ever happen to you that you didn't know what to do next?"

Spock did not venture an answer to that. Instead of the ambassador's voice, Stiles heard a thousand voices from the past speaking to him, echoing against the hard-learned lessons of a young officer, the struggles of living with crewmates, and finally learning to live with himself. He seldom looked in this kind of mirror any more. He'd never liked the reflection when he had.

Today, though, he didn't look away.

"Funny," he began aloud, "when we were about to die because something grabbed the ship and we had thirteen minutes to live, I wasn't afraid. Standing up there looking at Orsova over the top of that big desk . . . I about crapped my pants."

"I'm glad you restrained yourself," Spock commented lightly.

"Ship disasters don't scare me," Stiles said, keeping on his track. "Disastrous people scare me."

It seemed there was something just around the corner, just beyond his grasp, a whisper in the fog.

After a few seconds, Stiles found himself asking, "Did people scare . . . him?"

The last word, revered somehow all by itself, came out as a pathetic sigh, a comparison that shouldn't be made if any progress was ever to be accomplished. Instantly Stiles regretted that he'd asked.

Spock's answer took some time coming. "Helplessness scared him."

For the first time, Stiles felt a steely connection forged in the cool cell. "Did he ever think of himself the way I think of myself? Like I don't belong where I am?"

Veiled contentment settled over Mr. Spock as the past opened briefly before him for viewing and he enjoyed what he saw. His voice was low, even soft, yet carried a scolding tone.

" 'He' . . . was an exceptional man. He was also my friend. As such, we had our disagreements. We saw each other's uglier moments. The mission logs fail to show those aspects."

Stiles looked up. "Are you saying the logs are inaccurate?"

"Not at all. We simply left things out."

"Like what?"

Spock paused to think a moment. "The logs, the legends, the tall tales, the song and story—these are spirit-charging powers for us all. But legend is selective and usually written by the winners. The legends of the first *Enterprise* . . . they reflect the heroic, not the human aspects, of our life together in those years . . . Jim Kirk, Dr. McCoy, the others, and myself. Legend is a great filter. The traits that shame us most, the ones we leave out of the stories, are often the flaws that give us texture. Without them, we would be only pictures."

Spock leaned back on an elbow, maneuvered his leg to a better position, and considered the past through scopes in his own mind.

"I have come over these many years to understand what it means to be a captain not so much in rank but in manner. There are captains of rank, captains of ships, and captains of crews. A few men are all three. I once commanded the *Enterprise* as her captain. I was capable of giving the proper orders and expecting proper behavior, but I was never captain of the crew's hopes and devotions. That is a different passion. A different manner of man than I."

At first it seemed Spock might be selling himself short, judging the past too harshly—but no. Stiles knew too well the symptoms of that, and didn't see them here. This, instead, was a kind of personal honesty, a stunning depth of self-respect.

He wanted it. He wanted to know how to do that. Spock was so graceful at understanding subtle differences that mattered, and didn't recoil from knowing his talents and limitations.

"Different how?" Stiles asked, somewhat abrasive.

Spock tipped his head in thought. "I see chess," he said. "You see poker."

Broiling with envy and impatience, Stiles rubbed his cracked hands on his trousers. He didn't understand that, exactly, but something about it lit a fire under him.

"We've got to get out of here," he announced. "It's time to go. We've got to do something."

"Then you have decided to act?" Spock asked.

Bitter, humiliated, and angry about it, Stiles held back the answer that bit at his tongue. He looked up, met the ambassador's keen eyes. If only he could slap back the undercurrents of mockery and deserve better!

Spock gazed at him with sharp-eyed significance. "Eric, you underrate yourself and it makes you hesitate."

"I hesitate because I get things wrong so much," Stiles said. "And I don't want to get things so wrong it gets somebody killed. Or a whole lot of somebodies."

"That is what everyone likes about you."

Stiles looked up. "Huh?"

"Your reputation among the captains of front-line ships is well known. Every service commander knows you are a Medal of Valor winner. You could have pushed, jockeyed for position, used your commendation to leap over the heads of everyone on the promotions list. Even in civilian life you might have used your hero status to become a senator or gain other power. You could easily have become one of those people with much rank and little experience, but you chose a wiser and less vainglorious way. You went back out into space for more experience, working your way up rather than forcing your way up. You may not realize it, but you are deeply respected and liked by the people who get all the attention. They speak of you fondly. They hope Eric Stiles is the one who comes to repair their ships."

Astonished to his socks, Stiles gawked in complete stupid amazement. His men had said things like that to him, but he thought that was in-house loyalty and dusted it off with the debris of a day's work.

"Sir," he began, "there's something the history tapes don't show about you."

"What would that be?"

Stiles's voice was low and sincere. "You're a nice person."

Though Spock's face remained passive, his eyes dropped their guard. "A supreme compliment," he said. "Thank you. Now I suggest we vacate this cell."

"I'm ready," Stiles said. "How do we do it?"

Offering a moment to absorb what they had said to each other, the ambassador raised a brow in punctuation. Then he brought his right hand to his ear and pressed the skin just behind his earlobe, and said, "Spock to *Saskatoon.*"

For two or three seconds there was nothing. Then, out of nowhere, the very faint buzz of a voice, unmistakably human, spoke up from thin air, sizzling as if on a grill.

"*McCoy here. What are you clowns waiting for? We've had you located for a half hour! Why'd you wait so long to signal us? You always did have lousy Vulcan timing.*"

Touching his ear in a different place, Spock tilted his head to clear the signal a little more. "The comm link has been charging, doctor."

"*Have you found that Romulan yet?*"

"Not yet. We have been incarcerated, but will be remedying that momentarily and effecting a search. Are you and the ship under cover?"

"*You bet we are. You can track us with this signal, can't you?*"

"Yes. Stand by. No unnecessary signals."

"Standing by. McCoy out."

Astonished all over again, Stiles squawked, "How'd you do that! How could you contact—"

"A micro-transponder embedded in my cochlear cavity." Spock gestured to his right ear as if to display something that couldn't possibly be seen.

"But the guards scanned us!" Stiles asked, "How'd they miss something with a broadcast range?"

"The mechanism was nonactive. Dr. McCoy was under orders to activate a charge by remote after two hours had passed, with short-range microburst—"

"Remote? From the ship? Wouldn't it get interference?"

"The good doctor has many connections on this planet who owe him favors. I suspect he had the signal relayed through several private sources."

"You 'suspect'?"

"He delights in not telling me."

"But can't the Pojjana key in on an outside signal like that?"

"Why should they?" Spock pointed out. "Until today, there were no Federation frequency combinations being used on the planet. Why would they militate against it?"

As he spoke, the ambassador firmly gripped one of the symbolic polished stones on his jacket. The large stone unscrewed as if it were the top of a jar and came off in Spock's hand. He turned it bottom up. In the center of what had looked perfectly well like a real stone was instead a molded chamber, and in that chamber was a black mechanical nugget which Spock plucked out and examined.

Overwhelmed, Stiles stared at the black nugget and recognized it, the little green "charged" light glowing against his skin.

"You've got a utility phaser!"

Surveying the little palm-sized weapon with satisfaction, Spock said, "Like the comm link, it needed time to charge. Enough time for us to beam down and clear all the security scans. If we had allowed ourselves to be captured with the link and weapon charged, the Pojjana guards would've detected the active energy. Also, I supposed the shield might neutralize them if they were precharged—"

"So you're saying you knew they probably wouldn't deal with us. And you knew that ahead of time."

Spock eyed him cannily. "Of course, Mr. Stiles. One hopes for the best, but prepares for the worst."

At the sounds of those casual words, put across so matter-of-factly by one of the last living pioneers of space exploration, shock descended upon

Eric Stiles as if he were under a collapsing bridge. It pressed the breath from his lungs and displayed a shame within him and a smoldering anger that for much more than a decade he had suppressed. Now, today, finally, it sparked.

Prepare for the worst.

He leaned forward on the rusty cot, gazing downward at the empty floor. His knees before him might as well have been distant planets. What had he done all his life? Revere the best, expect the worst, and be prepared . . . for neither.

His skin felt tight, preformed. He drew another breath, huffed it out.

Across the cell, Spock pressed against the brick wall, moving slowly from place to place. He seemed to be listening for outside activity. Listening . . . trying to decide where to aim the phaser, how to break them out.

His own breath rumbled in his ears. Just outgoing, in huffs, short and hot. Dry lips.

As if in a dream he watched Spock prime the freshly charged little palm phaser. Green light, blue, yellow . . .

The Vulcan now stood sideways to present a narrow profile to the blast field, and extended his arm to aim at the portion of the wall he had chosen as their best bet to open an escape route without bringing the building or the Pojjana army down upon them. Orange . . . red.

"Sir!" Stiles bolted to his feet.

The ambassador hesitated and held fire. "Something?"

Shadows lay across Spock's Vulcan features, harsh limited light on the other side, a life-size paper doll of ideals Stiles had thought were bigger than life.

"I'm sorry about this," Stiles announced. He met Spock's gaze without flinching. "From now on I'm thinking ahead."

"What does that mean, specifically?" the Vulcan asked.

"It means you don't have permission to open fire."

This time both of Spock's brows went up. "I beg your pardon?"

Putting out a cold hand, Stiles noted that at least now he wasn't trembling.

"So you've got a phaser. So what? Once we get out of the cell, they've got energy detectors, tiers of fences, guards, weapons. We'll never get through."

"You have a suggestion for me?" Spock asked.

"No, sir," Stiles said. "I have an order for you. This is a military mission. I'm the ranking Starfleet officer here. This is probably the most boneheaded thing I've ever done in my life, and I don't know if . . . yes, I do know. I've been deferring to you for half my life whether you were there or not, and it's time for that to stop. They're expecting us to escape but, sir, we're not here to escape."

Another step brought him right up to Mr. Spock, face to face, man to man.

"I've been acting like a kid ever since I first saw your face on a history screen. It's time for me to start acting like the commander of this mission."

He turned his hand palm up and did not lower it.

Standing before him in what appeared to be amazement and a few other emotions Stiles couldn't quite identify, Spock passed the next few moments without moving so much as a facial muscle.

His eyes moved first, shifting down to the phaser in his grip. He gazed at the nugget-shaped weapon for several seconds as if it were the mean center of the universe.

Then, quite accommodatingly, he placed the weapon in Stiles's open hand. "As you wish."

Stiles found himself in the middle of a prison cell, holding the center of the universe.

Limping back a step or two, the ambassador gave Stiles room to use the phaser. There was a particular quality to his voice as he asked, "What is your plan, Commander?"

As he checked the phaser to be sure it was set where he thought it was, Stiles felt suddenly warm all over, and strong.

"Orsova thinks he's being cute putting me back in the same cell. He's an idiot. I spent years here. I helped rebuild this place after my first Constrictor. I know more about it than he does or any guard ever did. It's his big mistake. I'm not a twenty-one-year-old kid anymore."

"And this is an epiphany for you?"

Stiles blinked at him. *That* look was back on the Vulcan's face, that almost-smile, with the sparkle behind the eyes.

Amusement? Or something else?

"Your men knew their lives were in danger," the ambassador said, "yet you gave them confidence without deception. You marched them past the frozen moment that kills so many, and gave them a chance to fight for their ship and their lives. Against the checklist that counts more than legends, with all flaws and hesitations understood as cells of the whole . . . you are a captain."

Had the lights changed in here? Was it warmer?

Both peeved and flattered, Stiles shifted his weight and waved a hand at the cot. "You mean, all this time you believed in me and you let me sit there and snivel?"

"It was never enough for me to believe in you," Spock said handily. "You had to believe—"

"Please!" Stiles laughed. "Don't finish that! I smell a cliché."

Spock rewarded him with that hint of a smile and a very slight bow. "I stand rebuked."

Bewildered and amazed that he was actually smiling, Stiles sighed roughly and looked down at the utility phaser in his hand. He aimed it, but not at the wall. Instead, he pointed its bluntly conical nose in a completely illogical direction.

The ambassador looked at the concrete floor. "Where are we going?"

"Sir, we're going straight down."

And the cell lit up in a million lights, and the floor blew up, and the ceiling shredded. And Eric Stiles was in charge.

Chapter Twenty-two

BLISTERING HEAT SHOT through the cell. Pressure struck Stiles from all sides and spun him silly. The floor tilted, then disappeared under his feet and gravity dragged him down. It almost felt like a Constrictor.

He struck the griddle of hot rock with his right hipbone and scraped down fifteen feet until a carpet of muck received him up to the ankles. Somehow he managed to stay on his feet, leaning sideways on a nubby slab that was suddenly very familiar. Funny how the years rushed up to remind him of things.

Took out too much of the floor—probably shouldn't have used the full-destruct setting. Too late now.

"Where's the phaser? Oh, I still got it. Couldn't feel my hand. . . ."

No wonder. His whole forearm was tingling. Probably bumped the funny bone. His fingers had convulsed around the utility phaser, luckily, and he still had it. He craned his neck to look up at the hole they'd created. Had anybody heard the cracking and crashing of stone? There hadn't been a blast noise, instead just the whine of the phaser before the rock cracked. If there wasn't a guard on the floor, maybe the crash hadn't been noticed. Please, please, please.

Where was the ambassador?

Not waiting for his eyes to adjust, Stiles glanced around in the dimness, then started pawing at the broken flooring. Six feet away, the rocks shifted. Springing over there, Stiles tripped and landed on a knee. Recovering, he dug until a Vulcan ear appeared, luckily still attached to a Vulcan head.

"Sir!" he called.

Now, how would this look! Eric Stiles, the man who let First Officer Spock get buried alive!

The rubble scratched his hands. Some of the stones were hot to the touch as he pushed them off the ambassador.

"Sir? Are you hurt?"

Dust and pebbles sheeted into the muck and Spock sat up. "Quite well, thank you . . . where are we?"

Stretching off to both sides of them, bending into infinity not far away, the octagonal passageway was lit only by mediocre pencils of light through wrist-width drainage holes. Stiles knew that they could only see at all because the sun was almost directly overhead and the sky had cleared. In another couple of hours, the tunnels would be pitch dark.

"It's a network of tunnels. We built them right after my first Constrictor. The civil engineers thought the gravity effect would be lessened by a layer of planet strata and that maybe people could hide below, but it didn't work. They were deathtraps. Eventually we just gave up and sealed them. I used to imagine using it to escape."

"Why didn't you?"

"And go where?"

"Mmm . . . pardon me."

"I couldn't get off the planet and nobody would help an alien. And I didn't exactly have a way of cutting through the floor either."

Spock accepted Stiles's support as he got carefully to his feet and tested his injured leg. "How long do you suppose our escape will go undiscovered?"

"Depends on whether Orsova wants to auction off a visit now or later. We'll know, because we'll hear the alarms go off. Until then, we can just make our way through to the fresh-water ducts and get out. Darker in here than I remembered . . . looks like the roots are getting in too. Watch your step, Ambassador. With that comm link implant, can you tell me the direction the CST is in?"

"Yes." Spock paused a moment, and even though it seemed that he was doing something psychic, Stiles knew there was nothing like that going on. "East northeast . . . by north. Four miles . . . one eighth."

"East by—four miles from here?"

"Yes."

"Are you sure about that?"

"Very."

"Perfect. I know just what they're doing."

"Why do you ask?"

"Because we're splitting up."

"That may not be wise," Spock protested.

"Well, it wouldn't be my first time," Stiles flatly told him, and left no room for alternatives. "Come this way."

Picking through the crushed flooring into the muck-layered tunnel bottom, even with Spock's bad leg they moved along faster than Stiles expected. The stink was incredible. Heavy roots searched their way down from the surface, hairlike ancillary tendrils unbroken until his hand tore them away, proving that no one had come down here in years. He led Spock in a direction he knew the search would never go if they were discovered gone. That was the plan, all part of where he had told Travis to bring the ship down—away from the mountains, which was the natural place to hide. Hmm . . . been thinking ahead all this time and never knew it.

"Up at that intersection there," he said to Spock, "you go left. You'll be able to get out in about a half mile. That's where the municipal slab ends. I'll go to the right and find Zevon and catch up, and I'll be better alone in case it's a trap. All due respect, you'll slow me down and I'm tired of being slow. I'm sorry if this isn't what you had in mind."

"I had nothing in mind."

What'd he say?

Must be clogged ears. Didn't hear right. Stiles looked over his shoulder, seeing only the gray silhouette of the Vulcan two steps back. As he held aside a thick root for the ambassador to step by, he heard that sentence again in his head and finally just asked.

"You didn't have a plan? I thought the great amazing Mr. Spock always had a plan."

The ambassador tipped his head in a kind of shrug and spoke as they picked their way along.

"You remember what I told you about captains. I know my shortcomings. Discipline can be limiting. This is why Vulcans, with all our stringent codes of behavior, have not generally prevailed as great leaders, and humans, with your elastic spirits, have. I've learned over the years to provide information and opportunity, then step aside and rely upon the more vibrant among us for actual tactics. I hoped you would rise to the occasion."

"Are you saying," Stiles marveled, "you just fake it?"

In a shaft of light from a drain hole, Spock's black eyes flickered smartly. "No. I trusted *you* to fake it."

The ambassador offered that canny look for several seconds without even taking a step. Apparently he wanted a point made.

Overwhelmed, Stiles hovered in the middle of a step. Only a brainless drizzle of water somewhere in the underground system drew him out of his amazement and reminded him of what had to be done, and done soon.

"Said Frankenstein to the monster," he cracked. "Bear left and you'll get out. Once you get outside, keep to the low trail. They'll be looking high first, the way to the mountains. We'll rendezvous east northeast at the lake."

Spock reached out to grasp a root, ready to pull himself forward. "Aye aye, captain."

Flushed with delight and newly emboldened, Stiles looked up and laughed. "Thanks!"

Beverly Crusher took her latest series of biological readings on the shuddering body of the Romulan empress, and compared them with the readings from one hour ago. In the room, only the snap of the fireplace and the bleep of Data's computer, as he processed more information and sent what they had discovered onward to the other physicians across the empire, could be heard. There was not that much more that could be done.

For days now she had kept the empress and dozens of others alive by treating the symptoms. Over the past day, success had noticeably shrunk.

Crusher sat back, exhausted, and pressed her hands to the sides of her head. As she squeezed, her eyes throbbed and her thoughts bundled up into a lump. When she put her hands down, they were holding the only thought left that made sense.

She turned on her chair and sighed. Data noticed the movement and looked around at her. Over on the couch, still battered and bloody from the earlier encounter, Sentinel Iavo sat alone with his own guilts and troubles. He'd hardly moved all day.

"Time for drastic measures," Crusher told him. "She's not making it. She's slipping away. I can't hold on to her life much longer. Are you ready to do what I ask?"

A destroyed man, Iavo's face had paled and his eyes were sunken with weariness. "Anything."

Satisfied, Crusher stood up and strode to him. "This is what I want. You're going to get me a fast ship with an escort battalion. I don't want any trouble at the border. I'm taking the empress into space to hook up with Dr. McCoy and a treatment serum."

"There is no such serum," Iavo protested. "Is there?"

"There may be. If she is to have any chance, we have to go."

"Go where? Who has this serum?"

"I'll give you the course once we're spaceborne. I don't want to take any more chances than that. Once again, Sentinel, you have a choice to make. Whose side are you going to be on for the next few hours?"

Iavo stood up, wavered briefly, and clearly noted that Data also came to his feet behind Crusher.

"Your wisdom and silence have given me a new life," Iavo confirmed. "I will help you save hers. Tell me where you wish to go."

The air seemed a bit too cool in the lab office today. Zevon had thought about turning the heat up several times, but had regularly been distracted by suggestions pouring in from the students at Regional Spectroscopy. He had been reading them all day, between adjustments. The deflectors required almost daily adjustments now. Each adjustment worried him a faction more. The network of deflection stations operated fairly well, though only fairly. He had able technicians working the grid, but not skilled scientists. Several more years would go by before anyone on this planet was skilled enough in quantum physics and space science to replace Zevon's own advanced abilities. He was in a race now, a slow and deliberate race to the next Constrictor.

Some of these students had promise. There were occasional glimmers of hope beyond the daily push and grind. If he had more freedom to move about on the planet—

An old argument. Orsova's reins were tight upon Zevon. Their mutuality was fragile. He dared not jar it.

A long morning. The afternoon stretched before him with a dozen problems. The electrical system in the complex had begun having fits a few minutes ago, and he could do nothing effective with the Constrictor system if the power kept blinking.

Perhaps he could accomplish something by remote while he waited. Yes, that would be better.

His chair rolled slightly under him as he reached to the corner of his desk and keyed the external communications system, touching the autochannel.

"Sykora, are you there?"

"*I just arrived. You nearly missed me.*"

"Did you visit the physician?"

"*They can do nothing for me here. I'll tend myself as I always have.*"

"Sykora . . ."

"*I'm much stronger today. The welts are responding a little to the poultice I made yesterday. If only I had—*"

"You're not a nurse, you know."

"*On this planet, I am all there is for us. Would you like to argue now or later?*"

"Later, I suppose. Would it be possible for you to route yesterday's matter-discharge telemetry readings to Light Geologics at Laateh Mountain?"

"*Are you certain I have them here?*"

"Certain beyond life."

"I suppose that means I have them here. Give me time to arrange the files for relay."

"You'll have it. For some reason, several power centers in the complex have failed. They're tracking the source."

"Why would several fail at once?"

"I hesitated to ask. It's enough that I must handle satellite electrical problems. If I begin solving local ones, I may forget to adjust the deflector grid."

"I would never let you forget."

"I owe you my happiness."

"Yes, you do. Who else would cook you Romulan dinners to keep you from choking on the pathetic Pojjana palate?"

Zevon smiled. "No one on this rock. I shall signal you with the relay channel as soon as the power returns."

"What do they say on a ship?—Affirmative?"

"Affirmative, they say 'affirmative.' Are you—"

He never finished his question. The communications system crackled suddenly as if he'd put his hand into the den of a spitting animal. Almost as abruptly, it went dead.

"Sykora? Do you read?"

Nothing.

He tried a reroute of the local flow.

"Sykora?"

But there was still nothing. The system lay quiet. Someone would get to it.

Ah—there were the alarms from the central bunkers. Would the alarms go off for an electrical power failure? Strange. Power didn't even go off after a Constrictor anymore. He'd made sure of that. Perhaps some work was being done somewhere. He should've been notified.

He thought about calling to ask, but how could he call?

"Possibly the reason for the chill," he murmured to himself, and slipped into the leather-fringed chenille cardigan Sykora had given him at the precinct bazaar last year. The six shades of moss green, brushed soft as moss itself, threaded with dyed leather, comforted him when things went wrong. He liked to see the cardigan hanging on the wall hook next to his desk even better than wearing it. When he had it on, he couldn't see it so well.

However, today it would keep him warm. He pulled it over his shoulders, hitched it into place—awkward, since he was still sitting down and apparently too lazy to stand—and began tying the leather lacings over his chest.

A green chenille Pojjana cardigan with dyed leather lacings, leather lacings threaded through his shoulderlength hair . . . there was so little left of him from that other life, he could no longer find hints of the times before. Only speaking to Sykora occasionally reminded him that he had ever lived anywhere else.

Through the closed window, he could still hear the alarms going off. Possibly there was some trouble. A revolt, perhaps. They still happened sometimes, after a Constrictor, in fear of the next one. He could hide here, in retreat from such mundane troubles, and do his science, battling the next Constrictor in his own way. He hadn't won yet, but the enemy feared him.

Someone was pounding up the stairway down the hall. Through the old walls of his office he could hear the clop-clop of boots on the wooden stairs. Good. That meant someone else was as bothered by the electrical burping as he was. Only when the footsteps pounded up the corridor toward his office did he look at the door in wonder. Why would the maintenance team come to this end of the hall?

The door rattled as if someone had kicked it, but did not open at first. Then, it did. It blew open as if knocked by a hard wind.

A thousand times Zevon had seen this instant in his mind, played out in a dozen ways, and it still surprised him.

"Eric!" he gasped.

The years crumbled and dissolved as they stared at each other, comparing what they used to look like with what they looked like now. Zevon knew he must look different. His hair was longer, thonged with the tiny leather strips many Pojjana wore . . . but as a Romulan, eleven years meant less to him than it had to Eric Stiles.

Zevon's long-ago friend looked like neither a rosy-cheeked boy nor a dying waif, the only two personae Zevon had ever seen. He was a healthy man now, more slender, less clumsy, his blond hair a shade darker, his face clean-shaven. He still wore a Starfleet uniform, but of a new design. There were unborn weed pods stuck to the side of his trouserleg, and drying muck on his boots.

Scarcely able to breathe, Zevon clasped the arm of his chair with one hand and the side of his desk with the other.

Eric's chest heaved from running, from climbing the stairs, and whatever other trials had brought him here. Behind their communion of astonished gawking, the alarms rang and rang in the main complex.

"So I'm a little late," he flipped. "So what?"

Zevon pushed himself around a little more to face him, but still could not find the power to stand up.

Seeing that, Eric simply stepped to him, took his arm, and drew him to his feet. "Let's go."

Zevon came to his feet and gripped Eric's arms in a waltz of amazement and disbelief. "You look—you look—"

"Yeah, got a shave too." Between his fingers Eric spun a piece of the fringe on Zevon's decorated vest. "You look like one of those goofy dancers at the Spring Cotillion when they used to make us work the kitchen. I know you gotta get along here, but do you gotta wear their clothes?"

"I like these clothes."

"Great. Bring 'em along. We're leaving."

Not really surprised, Zevon did find himself startled by the abruptness of the demand. How could he possibly begin to explain?

"No, I can't go."

"Yes, you can. Come on."

"No—I must not leave the planet." He drew back with some force as he realized the serious intentions of what seemed ridiculous. "Eric, I have plans—get your hands off me, Eric!"

"I haven't got time to argue." Eric let go of him, as requested, but instead raised his other hand and aimed a small black device directly at Zevon.

Zevon threw both hands up. "No, no!"

In the same instant a pop of yellow light blinded him. He felt his head snap back and his body convulse. His senses spun wild. His knees buckled, but he never felt the floor strike him. A jostling sensation—his eyes were still open enough to see the ceiling reel, the light flop about, and deliberate movement at his side. His own moan of protest boomed in his head. Voluntary movement sank away.

Through the thickness of semiconsciousness Zevon heard the voice that had come to him so many times in the broken hours of early morning.

"Plenty of seats down in front. Welcome to the opening night of 'Prepare for the Worst,' starring the always effervescent Eric John Stiles. Reset your phasers and enjoy the show."

"Zevon . . . Zevon. Wake up. It's only light stun. Come out of it. You'll feel better in a few minutes."

Some kind of bird cawed in the high tangled roots overhead. The surroundings were ridiculous, an oasis of picnic quality, trying to tell them nothing was wrong and they could just sit here and maybe take a nap.

In the distance, though, more than two miles away, the alarms of the prison still hooted through the open sky. They'd seen airborne patrols sprint from the city toward the mountains, and at least two spotter planes veer toward the valley. None yet angled toward the swamp. Most escapees had more sense than to come in this direction, at least not first.

Stiles glanced around to make sure there was enough root canopy over them that a spotter couldn't easily see them. He knew that if a plane got close enough the infrared scanners would pick up the heat off the tops of their heads. There was nothing to be done about that if it happened.

Zevon lay in a cradle of velvet-coated roots, the kind that were about to plunge into the nearest puddle and release their spores. Till then they were a bony cushion that offered a few minutes' rest. Stiles sat with him, absorbing the leather threads in his head and the Pojjana cardigan, pleased that at least Zevon didn't seem to be starving anymore. They were at least clothing and feeding him for all he'd done for them.

Still drowsy, Zevon gazed at him warmly, with shieldless affection and relief that they were both alive to have this reunion.

"Eric . . ." He smiled again.

Stiles smiled back, knowing the drug of phaser stun was giving them this uncrystallized and uncluttered moment. His hand closed on Zevon's wrist as it had that last day so long ago. For a moment there was nothing around them, no planet, no problems, no past or future troubles to distract them. Certainly nothing to drive them apart anymore.

Gradually, though, inevitably, Zevon's perceptions cleared and he shifted his shoulders. They held onto each other, absorbing the wondrous confirmation that neither was dead, as each certainly had entertained in the troubling hours before sleep.

"I didn't think you'd even speak to me," Stiles attempted. His voice cracked on the last couple of words.

Zevon rewarded him with a kind of glow in his eyes. "Why would I not?"

"Well, I *am* a little late. . . ."

"Yes, you are."

"I swear, I thought they got you out."

"I know you did. Why did you stun me?"

"Oh, because you resisted my charms."

Taking a better grip on Zevon's arm, Stiles helped him sit up and lean against a particularly large and ancient root. Nauseated, Zevon closed his eyes briefly, fielding a wave of dizziness from the change of position.

"Are you okay?" Stiles asked.

Zevon leered at him with unfocused eyes and finally a clearing head. A perception of irony brought the faintest of smiles.

"Yes, Eric, I'm okay."

The buzz of distant aircraft funneled down to them from the foothills. Stiles didn't look away as the awkward moment passed between them.

"So," he began, "how y'been?"

With a grimace of irony and another smile, Zevon sat up and shook pods from his hair. "I've been busy." His face patterned by the shadows of roots overhead, he blinked into the sinking sun. "Where have you taken me?"

"We're out on the swamp flats. Cuffo Lake's a mile or so that way. I was hoping you'd come around so I didn't have to carry you any more. We're under cover, at least."

Another shadow came over them, this one long, crisp, and near. Stiles didn't look around. He knew.

"This is Ambassador Spock," he said to Zevon.

Zevon peered up at Spock, fitted the puzzle pieces into place, and accepted what he saw. He bowed his head courteously. "Your fame precedes you. I am honored."

Spock returned the gesture. "As am I, your excellency."

"Centurion, please."

"As you wish."

As Spock came to sit beside them on a fat root, Zevon said, "Royalty is the mantle I was born to. Centurion is the rank I earned."

"Then Mr. Stiles's report is correct? You are fourteenth in line for the throne?"

"Thirteenth, now."

Spock paused. "Yes, of course. Pardon my error. If you will indulge me for a few minutes, Centurion, I shall explain our problem."

Zevon glanced at Stiles, then back to Spock. "Explain."

"So they're dying. So what?"

A shaft of guilt ran through Eric Stiles at hearing Zevon using affectations of language he had obviously learned during their incarceration. He felt as if he were looking into a curved mirror. Even after all these years, Zevon sounded like Stiles, and it was both nice and weird.

"I understand," Stiles allowed. "They didn't come for you. But it's important, Zevon. And you're the only one."

"I hardly believe that. I am the convenient one."

Stiles winced inwardly. Better let that go for now. "What happened after I left?"

"Once Orsova came sober again that day, he thought about what you said, that we might be able to predict the Constrictor waves. He came to me and wanted to know how. I told him. He understood none of it, of course, yet I suppose it sounded to him as if I understood something. He went to the authorities and warned that a Constrictor was coming."

"I'll bet they listened hard," Stiles chided.

"They hardly listened," Zevon confirmed, his frustration long scabbed over. "Then the Constrictor did come. Millions died. And the people thought Orsova was a genius."

"Ugh . . . what people won't swallow. . . ."

"Orsova used his new influence to get me more equipment. He became the 'head' of the Constrictor project."

Spock clarified, "The science of which he knew nothing at all?"

"Are you kidding?" Stiles said. "He doesn't have a clue."

"Nothing," Zevon confirmed. "He manipulates the power, I tell him what the science can and cannot do."

"You've been working at the pharoah's counting house while he gets the glory."

"I could never have had the glory, Eric. Don't mourn it. If the population had ever found out I was the one who started the Constrictor, they would've killed me. I cannot be replaced in Red Sector. If I am not here to do this, all the Pojjana will suffer. I would gladly slit my own throat if I thought that would stop the phenomenon. Orsova is the umbrella shielding me from the limelight. He can have the attention."

Witness to humility and guilt taken to the extreme and somehow transmorphed into a positive, Stiles glanced at Spock and noted the Vulcan's unmistakable respect for a much younger and much less accomplished scientist. That caught Stiles in a grip between Spock's generosity and Zevon's humility.

Damn, was this confusing.

"Also, one must say," Zevon began again, "Orsova was most tricky and skilled at playing the politics, in which I had no interest at all except what he could get for me. The Constrictors were coming every few months and I quickly became very busy. Everything depended upon my predictions becoming more accurate. The more accurate, the more people thought Orsova was a genius. He developed a network, he controls many resources and lives like a king—"

"And how do *you* live?" Stiles asked.

"That matters not at all, not in the least," Zevon warned, hearing a defensiveness that wasn't necessary for him. "He's welcome to it. My purpose is served. The Pojjana would never have accepted a Romulan as the genius of the Constrictor. Orsova allowed me to succeed much earlier than ever would have been possible. I invented new types of antigravs, compression suits, architectural implements, metallurgy—many things that Orsova has parlayed into a huge Constrictor-survival industry. He has the power to decide where all the resources go, all the revenue, new materials, technology, the buildings—and I tell him what to say. He wields so much power now that he is the de facto head of the government. As he works his plans and I work mine, fewer and fewer people die with each Constrictor. In the last one, only six thousand planetwide. Six thousand, Eric!"

The victory in Zevon's voice and the emotion in his expression cut

Stiles to the core. He pressed Zevon's arm in approval, knowing what that meant to him.

"I knew we had to control energy to survive," Zevon went on. "I have an energy division, a school of physics, a school of mechanical science, defense division, deflection-grid network all over the continent. . . ."

"Why a defense system?" Spock asked. "Have you had problems with the Bal Quonott?"

"Not yet. And they've had no interest in us. Yet. We have no spaceborne fleet with which to defend ourselves. I knew I could never develop conventional weapons sitting trapped on a planet. Instead I've used tricks I learned while trying to read or deflect the Constrictor waves. Using the mass of the planet as an anchor for—"

"The composite beam that almost killed us, I bet."

"Killed you . . . ?"

"Well, how do y'think we got here? Magic? We came in a ship that got sucked into that damned thing!"

"Oh—" Zevon moaned as if he'd just remembered, just realized. A sheet of pallor drained across his face. "I never imagined you might come yourself. . . ."

Now that he'd gotten his pound of flesh, Stiles gave him a light punch in the chest. "That's okay, we got out of it. Come on, let's get moving. We've got work to do."

He pulled Zevon to his feet, while at their side Mr. Spock also stood up and scanned the horizon for trouble.

The trouble, though, was right here.

"Eric, I want to go back to my lab," Zevon announced. "I don't want to go with you."

Stiles huffed out his disbelief. "I'm serious, Zevon. Don't kid around. Lives are at stake. The stability of a hundred star systems are at stake, the Romulan Empire's—"

Zevon squared off before him. "I want to go back to my life. This is where I belong now, where I do good work. I refuse to go."

"Sure, refuse. I'll just stun you again and carry you the rest of the way if I have to."

"Commander," Spock began, "perhaps we should—"

Stiles waved his stun-set phaser demostrably. "Sir, I'm sorry, but there's no time. I want my ship away from this planet. We can talk while we move. That's the direction. Go on, Zevon, unless you want another dose."

"Eric, this is not at all like you."

"Too bad. Ambassador, which way?"

Hesitating only a moment, Spock said, "Follow me, please."

The traipse through the root swamp was messy, tedious, and most of all uneasy. Stiles didn't like holding a phaser on Zevon, but he never let it waver. Whenever Zevon looked at him, he brandished the phaser and made sure his thumb was on the fire pad. How many times did he look at the weapon himself, making good and sure it was set on stun and nothing worse. It had been years upon years since he'd been in a position to use a hand weapon against another person. The idea of making a mistake absolutely petrified him to the bone.

Before him, Zevon's moss-green cardigan flickered in the rays of the lowering sun through the huge twisted roots overhead and around them. He endured delirious joy that Zevon was still alive and here with him, tempered by the obvious tension of Zevon's resistance. He'd been brainwashed or something. He'd given up on being rescued and, surviving any way he could, had conditioned himself to live here, convinced himself it was right.

I'll talk him out of it. Now that I'm back, everything can go ahead and change. I'll walk him through it. He'll like it in a week.

"Eric, I don't wish to go," Zevon attempted again after a half mile. "How can you force me?"

"You're a Romulan, you understand force, right?"

"Orsova will do everything he can to keep us from leaving the planet. If you let me go, I can convince him to allow you to leave Red Sector. He wants no outside—"

"What's wrong with you?" Stiles blazed, pulling up almost to Zevon's side so they could look at each other between steps. "Don't you understand? Of course he doesn't want outside interference! I saw the looks in those soldiers' faces. The Pojjana see Orsova as if they wouldn't survive without him, like he's holding up the planet all by himself. If you or the Federation or anybody manages to stop the Constrictor, suddenly he wouldn't be the great savior anymore. That's why he stuck Mr. Spock and me in a cell and wouldn't deal. He doesn't want anybody to stop it!"

"I have to stay here, Eric, I have to be here every day. We have succeeded in reducing the effect of the waves, but my system requires almost daily adjustment and no one else can do that. I have no one thoroughly trained enough yet to take my place. Every day I breathe, I extend to the Pojjana the chance of someday outdoing my expertise. That has been my goal. I have arranged for Orsova to sponsor engineering and science colleges, apprenticeships and clinics so that some day the Pojjana can go on without me. That day has not come."

"You're taking this self-blame too far, Zevon." Stiles tripped on a cracked root and almost fired the phaser by accident. Ahead of them, Spock glanced back while Stiles recovered, then moved on.

Why didn't he come back here and lay some logic on Zevon? Why didn't he talk about the numbers? The rational analysis of what a collapsing Romulan Empire would do to everything around it? Why didn't he talk about the political and military and trade black hole that would suddenly suck the life out of everything that had been so carefully balanced for so long? What good was a genius hero Vulcan monument if he didn't come back here and lay down a case nobody could resist?

"You've been brainwashed," Stiles said with contempt. "It happens. Prisoners go through it all the time. Sympathizing with their captors' causes, forgetting where they came from, forgetting their native language—"

Zevon grasped a network of root filaments and ripped them from up to down. "I do not wish to leave, Eric! Not for the sake of the royal family or the empire or the Federation. I also do not wish to be exposed. Orsova provides me with cover and lets me work. Every day I can make up a little of what I have done. Do you know I am virtually the only alien this planet trusts?"

Stiles paused as his uniform shirt caught on a thorn and he twisted to disengage it. "Just because you were part of what started all this, you don't owe them your whole life. They can do a few things on their own, can't they? You've become way too custodial about these people. You even dress like a Pojjana!"

Zevon whirled and stopped dead in front of him, enraged and insulted. "I *am* Pojjana!"

They stood in a sluice of muck. Up ahead, Spock stopped and waited, his expression grim, curious.

"And elephants have four knees," Stiles chided. "So what?"

A flurry of anger rose in Zevon's face. "You should know better than anyone! Your own people would never have come for you if not for that elderly physician with so many tricks. Have you forgotten? Since coming here my eyes have been opened. I was stifled in the imperial system. Here, unfettered, unrestricted, with Orsova to field the—"

"I know, I know, you've proven yourself brilliant," Stiles confirmed. "You've kept a lot of people alive. I always knew you could. Even the Federation doesn't have that beam you put on us. If you could be that brilliant and save that many lives and you still have to hide behind Orsova because these idiots are so xenophobic that they won't accept help from an alien, then to hell with 'em. You've done enough. Somebody else needs you more now."

"The royal family? All these years I knew you were not the one who failed. I knew they had simply decided not to bother getting me out. Did you think I had no comprehension of my own blood ties? I have worse than apathy for the Romulans, and their way, and their crown. I have hatred for them. Some day, either the Federation or the Bal Quonott or the Romulans will come and overrun the Pojjana, and when that happens I am determined that my people, these people, will be able to defend themselves, hold their own, and even prevail. I have no prime directive. I am free to help anyone I want to help."

Fired by the depth of Zevon's conviction, Stiles raised the utility phaser. "I won't leave you here a second time. Just turn around and walk. I swear to God I'll stun you."

Zevon did move forward after the ambassador, but continued his point with ferocity. "Even without space infrastructure, we have learned to build and operate survival equipment and refined the barometer so that we not only have warning, but can also predict to some degree the intensity of the waves. My equipment requires almost constant attention. If I leave and intensity is misread, millions could die. Does that mean nothing to you? Have you changed so much?"

"Keep walking. I don't want to hear any more."

He kept it that way. With his manner and his expression he cut off any further discussion, as they made way through the swamp and finally broke out into the open valley beyond. Now they couldn't see the city at all, nor hear the alarms anymore, only hear the occasional drone of a distant search plane. So far, so good.

When Stiles broke out of the ferns and growth, freeing his leg from the last of the grasping roots, Zevon and Spock were already standing on the open meadow, looking out over the elongated expanse of Cuffo Lake. The eternally yellow-green water, rich with biology and nutrients that reflected the sunlight with a nearly neon intensity, was enhanced that much more by the sunset. The sun, resting now on the tips of the faraway mountains, illuminated the valley and showed them unequivocably that the valley was empty. Three hills, a rocky ridge, the meadow flats, and Cuffo Lake. Not so much as a tree more than that.

The ambassador strode a few yards out into the meadow and swept his gaze in all directions. "The CST should be here . . . I'm certain of the coordinates . . . . The directional signal definitely indicates this location, but I see no sign of them."

Zevon turned to Stiles. "You have to let me go now, Eric. Your ship is not here."

"Yes, it is. Ambassador, can you hail them with that implant?"

Spock touched the pressure point behind his ear where the microcom was either situated or had its subcutaneous controls. "Spock to *Saskatoon.* We are at the rendezvous point. What is your location?"

The soft buzz of the tiny mechanism was hard to understand, but good to hear. *"This is Perraton. Is Commander Stiles with you?"*

"Yes, he is."

Stiles said, "Tell him 'Lightfoot confirms.' "

"Mr. Perraton, 'Lightfoot confirms.' "

"*Acknowledged. Here we come.*"

"This is bewildering." Spock frowned and looked at Stiles. "These are the coordinates. The ship should be virtually on this spot. From where are they broadcasting?"

Stiles didn't bother answering. He didn't need to. The answer shimmered on the lake's surface. The still water began to froth, then to erupt as if it were suddenly the center of a resting volcano. Zevon and Spock both looked up into the darkening sky to see if the power were coming from a descending ship, but the sky was still clear.

They looked now at Stiles and saw him watching the lake's surface. They too turned in time to see sharp nonreflective metal formations break the surface and sheet free of the clinging water and the biorich glaze living there. The disruption got bigger and bigger, destroying the beautiful flat lake water with a violent commotion. In the rattle and swoosh of water and engines, the *Saskatoon*'s industrial nose surged furiously out of the water, and the rest of the ship broke free of the suction.

The ship emerged enormously from the water, like a blue whale breaching and not bothering to dive back in. It hovered over the lake while the last of the water drained from its nacelles and spiraled back into the lake, creating a sheen of droplets that sparkled in the setting sun.

"The bottom of the lake," Spock marveled. "Of course. A scan-proof shelter."

"Just thinking ahead." Stiles grinned proudly and eyed him. "You spent too much time on starships."

"Apparently."

"*This is Perraton. We'll set down on the plain directly to your right, on the other side of that ridge.*"

"What's wrong with the transporters?" Stiles asked.

"Is there something wrong with the transporter?"

"*Yup. You broke 'em when you beamed through that reflector envelope. They're under repair.*"

Politely Spock asked, "Permission to grant them permission to land?"

"Permission granted to grant permission," Stiles responded.

The ambassador seemed impressed, maybe a little embarrassed that he hadn't thought of this, and cued his microlink. "You have permission to set down, Mr. Perraton. We shall stand by."

"Let's go over the ridge," Stiles ordered, "and be there when they maneuver down. It'll take us a few minutes to climb over the ridge."

"I don't want to go, Eric."

"My finger's on the button, Zevon."

The ridge was the only rupture on the otherwise pristine meadow landscape, created over a hundred years ago by ambitious roots from the swamp moving below the surface till they hit rock and tried to find the surface again. The roots had grown and grown beneath the crust, fattening and searching and hitting stone, until the stone began to surge upward eight or ten meters. Sometime along the way, the roots had died off, leaving the rocky ridge as the only scar on the meadowlands.

The ridge wasn't very high, only a couple of stories at most, but footing was treacherous and picky. They could hear the hum of the CST as it maneuvered on the other side of the ridge, but could see nothing but the abutments of stone and hard dirt.

Stiles glanced into the sky behind them, fearful that the CST might be picked up on scanners now that it was out of the protective cover of the deep lake. They were only minutes from safety now. Once inside the *Saskatoon* they could buzz away from this forsaken planet and get out there and do some real good. Then he could talk some sense into Zevon. Once Zevon got back into space, saw how wide the galaxy really was, remembered things that Stiles had also forgotten during his incarceration here—everything would be good again. It would be.

Stiles took the rear, holding the phaser where it would do some good as he picked and climbed his way up the rocky slope behind the ambassador and Zevon. He was watching the rocks, nursing out footholds and handholds and avoiding the dangerous sharp edge of the mica-like slabs, when a hard force caught him across the jawbone.

The mighty blow drove him backward and spun him sideways. He skidded onto his side on a sheet of pebbles. As his head rang, he managed to put out an arm and stop himself from sliding all the way down.

"Stand still or die!"

Stiles blinked up through a wave of dizziness.

There above them, taking an attack stance between them and freedom, stood two armed Pojjana assault troopers and an even more heavily armed woman. A Romulan woman!

"Drop your weapon!" The woman aimed her own rifle ferociously at Stiles's head. "Or I will kill you now!"

Chapter Twenty-three

"SYKORA, DON'T KILL HIM!"

Zevon rushed to Stiles's side and put himself between Stiles and the woman's rifle. Spock, luckily, stood aside and let events play out as he watched with attentive interest. He put his hands up, though, so the guards wouldn't arbitrarily open up on him either. A Romulan woman! Or was she Vulcan? Either way, she shouldn't be here at all.

"How can she be here?" Stiles demanded.

From higher on the rocks, Spock agreed. "This is Red Sector. Did the Romulans violate that without the Federation's—"

"The empire has nothing to do with me. I came on my own to protect Zevon," the woman snarled with a toss of her long braids. She was absolutely fierce in her intent. "Anyone who threatens him, I will mutilate!"

As she brandished her weapon at Stiles, Zevon held up a hand to back the woman off. "Sykora, please. This is Eric."

"Eric—" Her tone changed instantly. Her eyes narrowed. "Eric Stiles?"

"Yes."

"What's going on?" Stiles asked as Zevon pulled him to his feet. "What's she doing here?"

"Drop your weapon!" Sykora demanded.

"No," Spock interrupted. "Dropping a phaser could be deadly. If the trooper would simply take it—"

Sykora snapped her fingers at one of the guards, who snatched the utility phaser out of Stiles's hand. That quickly were the tables turned.

Frustrated, Stiles griped, "How'd she find us out here?"

"He is my husband," Sykora said for herself. "I look after him."

"Husband? Since when!"

Zevon nodded. "Sykora is the reason I knew you got the message through to my family. And why I knew they were never planning to come for me."

"I am a subcommander," Sykora interrupted, "in the Imperial Solar Guard. I could never stomach the royal family's abandonment of their prince. I want nothing to do with those disloyal monsters. I confiscated a three-man ship and came to rescue him myself."

"My own defense systems destroyed her ship," Zevon admitted with some sheepishness. "Her two crewmen fought and were killed by the Pojjana planetary guard, but Sykora succeeded in finding me."

"And I will kill any who threaten him," the determined woman said. "Even Orsova fears and respects me."

Even deprived of his weapon and his moment of success, Stiles leered at Zevon in private admiration. "She's pretty tough."

"Yes . . . she is."

"How'd she find us?"

"I actually don't know." Zevon looked at his wife. "How did you?"

A little more agreeable, though no more mellow, Sykora gestured to Zevon's cardigan. "You're always too careless with your own well-being. I take care of you. The fringe is a homing grid."

Zevon touched his sweater, then gazed at her in what could only be adoration. "How kind . . ."

BZZZZZWAP!

Phaser stun! No mistaking that sound!

The Pojjana troopers sprang like stricken cats and flopped to the ground, only an instant before a third beam struck Sykora and she was pitched into a convulsion that left her unconscious in a crotch of stone.

Zevon gasped in anguish and scrambled to his wife's side, but there was nothing to be done for her but wait for the effect to wear off. The tables had turned again.

Over the crest of the ridge appeared a beautiful sight—Travis Perraton leading a landing party that included the evil twins, a handful of security trainees, and Dr. Leonard McCoy.

"We heard the trouble," Travis said. "Ambassador Spock cued his comm link and we heard everything. You all right, Eric?"

"Why? Am I bleeding?"

"Some blood on your neck there."

"I'm okay, Trav, thanks." Stiles accepted a service phaser and looked at the handiwork. "Round up those three and stuff 'em into the equipment locker."

"Even the lady?"

Stiles met Zevon's hopeful eyes, but he had certain decisions to make and certain dangers to consider. "That's no lady. That's a subcommander."

"Uh-huh. Got it. Lock her up, boys."

The Bolt brothers assisted Dr. McCoy down a fairly stable rock incline, where he stopped before Zevon and gave the Romulan prince a good looking over.

"Good evening," he said. "I'm Count Vladimir McCoy. I vant your blod."

"*Orsova.*"

"Again? What do you want now! I tried to put that poison in Zevon, but he's gone!"

"*They have escaped through the root swamp. I will give you the coordinates of their spaceship. You still have a chance to bring them to me. The doctors and Zevon. Alive if you can. Dead if you cannot.*"

"How can I chase them if they go into space? I have no spaceships."

"*You ask too many questions. You will have my ship. I will arrange for you to be close to Zevon. Prepare yourself. You are about to become a spaceman.*"

Chapter Twenty-four

As the two Pojjan guards were heaved off into the waiting CST by the crewmen, Zevon hurried to his wife's side and knelt beside her, touching her face. "I will not even speak to you about this unless you treat her first."

"She'll recover," Stiles complained. "It's just phaser stun."

"No, she's ill. Like you when you were trapped here, we have no way to treat her on this planet. She's not Pojjana. Their medicine has been working only poorly for her since—"

"Uh-oh," McCoy preempted, and immediately came to Sykora's side. "Better check that."

Stiles glanced at Spock. Were they too late? Did Sykora have the royal family thing? He scrubbed the conversation they'd just had to see if there'd been any mention of Sykora's bloodlines. Had he missed something? Did she have this plague that had everybody so worked up?

While McCoy scanned the unconscious woman with some kind of double-built medical scanner, Stiles turned to Travis. "Go back on board. Get ready to lift off."

"Aye aye," Travis said.

"I'll be right there. Go on."

Over the fallen form of the Romulan woman, McCoy let Jason Bolt pull him back to his feet. "She's not royal family. No trace of their DNA at all. She's got hyperplexic myelitis. I've only seen it twice before in Vulcanoids."

Fearful just at the sound of that, Zevon looked at him beseechingly. "Is it dangerous?"

"Eventually, it would be fatal."

"Can you stop it?"

"I need to get her on a table."

The noncommittal answer clearly frightened Zevon.

Stiles watched him. The whole Romulan royal family was sick and dying, and all that meant anything to Zevon was this one woman. He parted his lips to utter some words of assurance, but never got the chance. As the ship sat ducklike on its landing struts, the skin of the CST crackled with an electrical surge that threw sparks all over the people standing on the ridge. For an instant Stiles thought something in or on the ship had exploded; then the culprit came into view. Over the resting form of the CST rose a hovering craft of unfamiliar design, made of dark blue metal and etched with white bolts in an industrial pattern of hull plates. Against the darkening sky, the blue ship was nearly invisible except for the pinpoint etchings of white dots that appeared almost like free-floating constellations.

Would've been pretty if it hadn't been firing on them.

"On board!" Stiles shouted. "On board! On board!"

As Spock and two CST crewmen hustled McCoy down the other side of the ridge and Zevon hoisted his wife's limp form over his shoulder, Stiles aimed his service phaser at the roaring newcomer and opened fire.

His phaser scored the body of the other ship with a great show of noise and sizzling, but the wounds were only superficial.

The blue ship fired again, but not at him. Instead its weapons scored the body of the CST as it had before, leaving steaming gashes on the nose and side of the big tender. As he skittered down the incline, he heard the CST's impulse engines throb to power. In a few seconds, they'd be ready for escape velocity.

That is, if they weren't fried right here on the ground. Gouts of smoke blew across the bottom of the ridge, blinding him to the people running in front of him toward the tender's ramp.

"Keep going!" he shouted, and fired again.

A third time the lumbering blue ship screamed at them. Once more the deadly energy weapons scratched the body of the CST. If that beam hit the defenseless people running toward the ship—

A hard form—metal—slapped the bottom of his boot and tripped him. He skidded forward, almost dropping his phaser. The ramp! In the smoke he hadn't seen how close he was!

"Travis, get us out of the atmosphere!" he called, scrambling on all fours up the treaded surface. "They can't come after us!"

The ramp whined up behind him. He found himself on the midships deck, with Alan Wood pulling him out of the way of the closing ramp.

"Always an English butcher around when you need one," Stiles choked, gagging the last of the smoke out of his lungs.

"Tea's good for that," Alan offered. "I'll get you some. Want cake?"

"I want red alert!"

"Red alert, aye." Alan swung him to his feet and Stiles raced through the hatches to the cluttered little bridge, where Zevon sat on the deck, holding his groggy but awakening wife. Beside them, Dr. McCoy had been planted firmly in one of the anchored chairs at tactical. Jeremy manned the science station, Travis was just ordering full power to the escape velocity thrusters, and the evil twins were at the helm and navigation. Spock was standing beside the helm.

Stiles skidded into place behind the helm and in front of his command chair, but did not sit. "You look good there," he commented.

Spock seemed surprised that he'd even been noticed. "Comforting to know one is picturesque."

Indulging in a nervous grin, Stiles watched the main screen, which showed the thinning atmosphere as the CST powered toward space, and the side monitors, which showed the blue ship with its constellation of white hull buttons moving deliberately after them.

Quite abruptly, the mist on the main screen parted with a nearly audible swoosh, and they broke out into the blackness of open space. Unlike the darkening evening on the planet's surface, here it was once again day, bright and fierce, as they moved away from the protection of the planet with the sun on their port side.

"They're following us!" Jeremy White gulped. "Coming right into space after us!"

Zevon left his wife's side, bolted to his feet, and grasped the edge of the helm and stared at the main screen. "Impossible!"

"Well, here they come anyway!"

The whole CST jolted then with a terrible butt-stroke from the pursuing ship, a blow that peppered the tender with hot energy.

Stiles glanced at Zevon, fielding a bitter distrust. "Shields up. Battle stations."

"I'm not imagining things, am I?" Stiles asked. "That's not a Pojjana ship, is it?"

"No!" Zevon insisted.

"Nor do I recognize it," Ambassador Spock said. "I have never seen that configuration or those markings."

"Neither has the computer," Travis confirmed. "No cataloguing at all."

"Increase speed as soon as you can," Stiles said.

Zack Bolt frowned at his nav controls. "They're hailing us through my nav impulses. Must not be compatible with Federation tech."

"Can you make it so we can hear it?"

"Well . . . attempting." He poked at his controls, and a moment later a completely unexpected sound burbled from the other ship.

"*Surrender. You have no chance against this fighting spaceship. Turn back now and you will live.*"

Rage boiled up in Stiles's head till he thought his hair would blow off. He pounded the right button.

"Orsova! What are you doing in that ship! Where'd you get a thing like that!"

"*Surrender now or be killed. We have more speed and more weapons. I will kill you before I let you leave the sector.*"

"Cut him off!" Stiles roared. "I don't want to hear his voice again! He can't want me back that badly—he can't care about me that much! Travis! What's the gasball got?"

Travis bent again over the tactical scanners. "High shielding . . . full warp capacity . . . strike-force shields . . . weapons are—" He paused and shook his head in worried admiration. "It's a fighting warship, Eric. We're completely outmatched."

"Twins, get us out of this stupid solar system!" Stiles ordered. "Full impulse as soon as you can. Travis, you take weapons yourself. Transfer all the reserve from the cutting phasers and find some distance power. Get ready to use the welding torches if they get too close. I want to skin that bastard!"

At the nav station, Zack Bolt turned to look at him. "We're a combat support tender, not a battleship! We can't beat that thing!"

"We don't have to beat it. He wants us alive for some reason."

Everybody looked at him as if he'd grown feathers.

"You're gonna have to explain that one," Travis said.

"If he wanted to kill us," Stiles told them, "why would he shoot at the CST instead of nice bald helpless people on the ground?"

Unsure of that, Spock tightened his brow and waited for more explanation, so Stiles gave it to him.

"That gives me an advantage. It means I should run harder than I fight. Getting away is more important than beating them. All we have to do is knock 'em down long enough to get away."

The CST hummed and cranked its way toward full speed, chased easily by the constellation ship with Orsova impossibly aboard. Against the pure blackness of night, the enemy ship's blue body nearly disappeared and its hundreds of white plate bolts didn't, so that it looked indeed like a set of stars rushing freely after them in space. But every few moments the other ship made its solid presence known with a full-power blast that shocked the CST to its bones and made everybody grab for something to hold onto.

"How're we doing?" Stiles asked when he thought enough time had gone by.

"Not an inch," Jeremy sourly reported. "In fact, they're closing."

His teeth gnashing, Stiles growled at the side screens. "Maybe if I give myself up, he'll be happy and leave the rest of you alone."

Even in the midst of rocking and rolling, Spock found a way to face him gracefully. "No, Mr. Stiles. That is one decision I will not allow."

"You can't tell me what to do, with all due respect, sir."

"I know. Orsova has no ship like that. Someone is either supporting or manipulating him. That power must have farther-reaching goals than being entertained with your capture. And," he added, rather gently, "once in a lifetime is enough to sacrifice yourself to that man."

In spite of everything, Stiles smiled at the sentimental reminder that Spock knew all the mistakes he'd made, and liked him anyway.

A javelin of weapon power struck the CST and backhanded it across space. The engines screamed. The crew and passengers were throttled, bouncing off the equipment around them. Stiles tried to stay on his feet, but ended up sharing a chair with Jason Bolt at the helm as the ship went howling on its edge through space.

While Jason struggled to recover, Jeremy called, "That was our port engine! We can't make top speed anymore, Eric!"

"Can we have emergency warp?"

"If you don't mind a complete meltdown."

"That's it. No more running. Get ready to turn and fight."

From the glances of the crew, he might as well have ordered them to cut off their hands and throw them in a pot. They were brave enough going into battle situations when necessary to repair the important ships, but it wasn't often that they were the center of the battle—the thing actually being shot at on purpose.

He saw it in their faces. Turn and fight? Fight that warship coming at them at flank speed?

"It's me he wants," Zevon spoke up. He came around the helm to face both Stiles and Spock. "I am the key to his control, Eric, not you. Let him take me. Then you and your ship can go."

"I can't let you go, you know that," Stiles said. "We need you. Your blood—"

"I hate the Romulan ruling family," Zevon claimed bitterly. "I hate the government that flagrantly caused the Constrictor. I hate the relatives who abandoned me. I deride the stupidity of a system that allows birth connections to command important missions. I hate those of my heritage, and now I am told I *must* go save them? I have no interest in saving my philosophical enemies."

"Travis, keep firing on that ship," Stiles ordered. "Just fire at will, any chance you get to hit 'em." That done, furious and frustrated, he barked at Zevon. "So it would be better to go back there and serve a system that allows a scumsucker like Orsova to end up in control of a whole planet? What's the matter with you?"

"My husband is a genius!" Sykora rose from the deck, still pale from the phaser stun, her face a mask of defiance. She moved forward and steadied herself by gripping the back of the command chair. "He has designed a spaceborne barricade that will funnel the Constrictor waves around the planet. If we help you, will the Federation come and build our barricade in space? No! You will go your way and let the Pojjana planet crumble behind you!"

As enemy fire rocked the CST again, the real challenge was right here, right now.

"Why should I trust the Federation?" Zevon confirmed. "After I save the Romulans, you will leave again as you did before."

"We can help the Pojjana," Spock firmly told them both, "but they must be receptive to our help."

Zevon spun to him. "Why should I trust you? Why were you not more persistent? When you saw your presence was good for them, why did you leave?"

"The Pojjana asked us to leave."

"But you *left!*"

Spock seemed to be searching for a way to explain when Stiles took over. "Never mind, Ambassador. Until today, the only Federation citizen Zevon's ever spoken to in his life was me. He doesn't get it." Fixing his glare on Zevon, he forced himself to ignore the pounding the ship was taking. "You're going. I didn't go through this for nothing! We need you to go. If the Empire falls, the whole sector is going with it. Like it or not, you're the last royal family member with unadulterated blood and you're coming with us."

"No, Mr. Stiles. He is not."

Spock's announcement, without a hint of doubt or question, took Stiles completely by surprise. Everyone else, too, from the looks on their faces.

Digesting the words from his idol as quickly as he could, Stiles jabbed a finger toward Zevon. "But he's wrong!"

"He is wrong according to us," the ambassador contradicted evenhandedly. "He has that right."

"Why did we come all this way! Why didn't you say something down on the planet!"

"I entertained the hope that you might be able to convince him."

Setting aside annoyance at being used, Stiles argued, "The Romulans are attacking the Federation for something we didn't do!"

Spock offered only a nod in limited agreement. "I will not force any individual to act against his will."

"Even if it means a war?"

"If that is the price of freedom . . . so be it."

"They're almost in phaser range," Jeremy White reported, a thread of fright rising in his voice.

Stiles didn't blame him a bit. The sight of that dark ship with the white buttons all over it streaking toward them with the posture of an angry bumblebee—it scared him too.

"Jeremy," he ordered, "tell me the two biggest differences between us and them."

With something specific to do, Jeremy concentrated on his instruments while everyone else waited through the tension.

"Their weapons . . ."

No surprise there.

"And shields. Way better than ours."

Unsatisfied with the lack of specificity, Spock leaned over Jeremy's shoulder at the readouts. "High-intensity plasma-fed shielding with direct warp feed. At least four times the power of ours. I must assume their speed capacity and weapons are comparably advanced."

Stiles leered at him. "Situation hopeless?"

"So it seems," Spock said.

"All the odds against us?"

"Correct."

Stiles eyed him. "This is one of those 'leap of creativity' things, isn't it?"

Spock clasped his hands behind his back in a ridiculously casual posture. "That is my hope."

"You wanna just . . . come over here and give me a shove?"

"If you prefer."

From the port side, McCoy offered, "I'll come and push you if you want."

Stiles gave him a floppy wave with his free hand. "Thanks, Doctor, consider me pushed. We need to even things up. Shields first."

"How?" Spock asked.

At the same time, McCoy beefed, "Rhodinium against tissue paper!"

Stiles glanced at them. "Oh, we're a little tougher than that, Doctor. Jeremy, we've got that warp trigger box with the surger for emergency ignition of cold warp cores, don't we? We replaced the last one, right?"

"Always."

"Go back there and take it off the clamps and put it in the airlock, activated. We're going to dump and detonate."

"It'll short out *our* shields!"

"If we're close enough it'll short out his too. He wants us alive—let's use that and play some chicken."

Flushed, Jeremy raced through the hatch toward the aft section.

"Ambassador," Stiles requested, "I'll bet you can take the science boards, can't you?"

"Most certainly I can." Spock moved with fluidity across the bridge and settled at Jeremy's station as if he'd been painted there. Darned if he didn't look happy.

"Travis, fire up the magnetic grapples. Two and four on the port side."

Travis swung full about and gaped at him with his mouth open and eyes like eggs, but talked himself out of asking. "Aye aye," he responded, and got to work.

Stiles stood beside his command chair and watched the screen that showed the approaching blue fighter. "Ready about!"

"Ready about, aye!"

A flurry of activity blew across the bridge, and everybody was suddenly working. Luckily they'd stopped asking what he was up to. Good thing, because he didn't know.

"Helm, you know what to do. Come about and meet him head on, as if we were rafting for a repair."

"While he's moving?" Jason Bolt confirmed.

"Just as if we had to grapple a damaged ship under power. Do it by the numbers. We'll see what happens. Helm over."

"Coming about."

"Then what?" Travis asked—not in challenge, but because to make it work he had to know the next move.

Stiles shook his head and shrugged. "Oh, I dunno, I'm probably about to get us all killed."

Okay, not the greatest slogan to stitch on a banner of war, but there was something to be said for being honest with them. He drew one long breath and held it, watching the forward screen now as the CST turned on its midships keel and the constellation fighter came around. Broad on the bow . . . three points . . . two points . . . one . . . fine on the port bow . . . dead ahead.

Now the two ships were heading at each other in a game that would destroy one of them if somebody didn't flinch.

"Incoming!" Travis called. "They're shooting at us!"

A bright white blast blew from the other ship, looking as if somebody had fired talcum powder out an exhaust port—but when it hit them it didn't feel like powder. The CST shuddered violently but did not turn off her course. Rather than striking them with a single impact, the powder-beam slathered all over the ship as if they'd plunged into a glass of milk, washing along from the prow to midships before dissipating, snapping systems all the way back.

"Hold course!" Stiles called over the shattering of circuits all around them.

"Intentions?" Spock asked. "Do you mean to ram them?"

"We've got an asteroid-cutter prow," Stiles told him. "If they want to try it, I'm game. We can't outrun them. All we can do is make them flinch."

Spock straightened from watching the science panel. "Do you know this man well enough to predict his response?"

"Orsova? Sir, we're willing to die for a cause. Orsova isn't. All we have to do is stand him down."

"Yes, Mr. Stiles, but remember—Orsova has little or no spacefaring experience. It's unlikely he's piloting that ship."

Stiles looked at him. "Who do you think is?"

"I should say whoever provided him with the fighter."

"Oh, good, I love unknown quantities."

Annoyed with himself for not realizing that Orsova couldn't possibly be driving that ship, that he was in fact fighting somebody he'd never met in a ship he didn't recognize, with weapons he'd never seen before, Stiles dealt with a tumbling stomach and a dry mouth as the ships drew speedily closer.

He struck the nearest comm link. "Jeremy, blow that trigger out the hatch right now."

"*Ready . . . it's away!*"

They waited as the octagonal warp trigger box drifted out into space, visible on a side monitor at starboard, floating lazily out there, brainless to what else was going on.

"Distance?"

"Eight hundred kilometers," Spock ticked off. "One thousand . . . twelve hundred . . ."

"Ignite it."

Before his words were even out, space at their side blew bright with disruption and the whole ship was swept sideways away from it. Half the crew was thrown down. Stiles kept his feet only by hanging onto the command chair with both hands. He found himself looking at Dr. McCoy and thanking all the lucky stars out there that the old doctor had been sitting down. Travis was also holding McCoy in place with one hand, himself with the other.

Over the crackle and fume of their own damage, Spock reported, "His shields are losing integrity. They're flickering."

"Ours are down completely," Travis announced, taking the gloss off their victory. "Whatever happens now, we'll feel it hard."

"Enemy vessel is slowing down," Spock announced briskly. There was a clear ring of win in his voice. "You've called their bluff."

"Either that or they're not willing to die for whatever we represent to them," Stiles said. "Doesn't mean they won't keep trying to kill us."

"Incoming!"

Stiles gritted his teeth as they rode out another hit of the powder-beam. Damage reports came chattering in from all sections, none of them good. Stiles ignored them.

"Travis, are the grapples ready?"

"Ready, aye."

"Keep up speed until we're at proximity range. Let me know when we get there—"

"We're there!" Travis said. "We can reach now."

On the main screen, the dark blue enemy ship drew up its braking thrusters and surged upward so they could see its underbelly, just as a rowboat surges up on a swell before settling into the sand. They really didn't want to get hit by the *Saskatoon*'s cutting prow.

Stiles couldn't help a little snicker. "Magnetic grapples two and four—launch!"

wheeeeeeeeeeeCHUNK—CHUNK

"Got 'em!" Travis yelped. "Both grapples are on their hull. Now what?"

"Let you know soon as I think of it," Stiles muttered. "He can't blow us up if we're riding him. Pull up as close as you can, Travis. Zack, heat up the welding phasers!"

"Where do you want me to cut him?"

"Any place you can reach. I want you to connect those white dots into my initials. Right there where I can see."

The Bolt brothers both laughed in spite of the moment's heat.

Heat—yes, it was getting hotter on the bridge, proof that systems were damaged and the ship's computers were selectively saving what they could and sacrificing what they couldn't while waiting for repair. The CST's welding phasers lit up under the viewscreen and scored the blue body of the other ship, leaving trails of white-hot melted metal and snapping circuits exposed to open space. Still . . . how much of this could they do?

As the two ships danced in their locked-together waltz, Spock peered into his monitor. "Reading a power buildup."

"Weapons?" Stiles asked.

"No, sir. Routing shield power, I believe. . . ." He didn't sound sure at all.

Heavy-legged with damage and with the weight of the other ship pulling on the grapples, the *Saskatoon* lumbered around, pushed by the pointless power of the two ships exerting force on each other while going absolutely nowhere.

"Jeremy, can you still hear me?" Stiles called.

"*You're breaking up. Boost your signal.*"

"Forget it." Stiles stalked to the aft hatch, cranked the handle, yanked the hatch open, and yelled through the body of the ship. "Turn on the external hoses! Seal up their impulse ports! Got it?"

"I like that!"

Stiles turned back to the main action, grumbling. "Yeah, I like it too."

Within seconds, the CST's external hoses clacked on. Clear on the main screen, attached to them so closely that they could've touched it if the screen hadn't been there, the blue enemy ship cranked and yanked against the magnetic grapples, trying to break the hold. Now tons of semiviscous compound spewed from the hose nozzles and splattered all over the aft section of that ship, totally clogging the impulse exhausts as if the gods were spewing milkshakes into goblets.

Except this wonderful composite milkshake stuck like glue and hardened chemically within four seconds of contact.

"What's that stuff?" McCoy asked.

"It's chemical fiber bond," Stiles told him. "We use it to coat repairs before putting the hull plates back on. Nasty stuff."

"Their impulse ports are clogged," Spock noted. "They're attempting to fire impulse engines anyway."

On the screen, in the upper corner, they could just see the impulse ports turning yellow, orange, then red with backed-up energy. Volcanic spurts of power blasted through the fiber bond, only to be almost instantly sealed up again. Another kind of battle was going on—between the power of the engines and the strength of a resealing compound that wouldn't take no for an answer.

Flash . . . flash . . . sizzle . . . flash . . . The constellation ship fought with itself, spitting and surging, taking the CST with it on every blurting ride.

The whole CST then began to shake furiously, as if it would break into a billion pieces around them. The sound was horrible, terrifying, the kind of sound that made Stiles wonder what the hell he was doing here in the first place, why anybody would want to come to space when he could stay on a nice solid planet somewhere. Suddenly all the screens flashed a nasty yellow light. A *snap* of electrical surge flailed through the ship, popping everybody's ears.

"What happened!" Stiles called.

"Feedback along the magnetic lines!" Spock called back. "They've thrown us off—power surge is running up the grapples!"

"Damn!"

"What do we do now?" Travis cried. "Surrender?"

"Not since Gabriel's last tea party in hell! Full about! Make some speed!"

McCoy fingernailed Spock in the arm and pointed at Stiles. "I like the sound of that, don't you?"

Still spitting fire every few seconds as the impulse engines coughed through the clinging fiber bond, the enemy ship wheeled clumsily around to face them with its main weapons ports.

"Uh-oh . . ." Stiles's whole body went cold. "Doesn't look like they want to take us alive anymore. . . ."

Spock straightened and watched the ship out there. "Your logic is impeccable . . . we are in grave danger."

His memory nerve tingling, Stiles looked at him. "What?"

"Just a bit of nostalgia. I suggest we distance ourselves."

"Travis, disengage! Jason, full impulse!"

At point-blank range the other ship opened up on them in what could only be described as a fit of anger. Its weapons cut into the CST's unshielded body, blowing systems all around the bridge and all the way through the ship. Stiles agonized as he heard the screams and shouts of his men and knew they would have to see to themselves for now. He hated that—the urge to go back there nearly crushed his chest.

"Speed, Jason," he implored.

"Doing my best."

"Reading power-up on torpedo launchers," Spock warned. "We cannot possibly gain enough distance."

No distance and no shields. No weapons worth spitting back at that ship. Stiles felt his heart sink. He'd bought time, but there was nothing more to do with it. He'd stopped them from maneuvering in space-normal, but the CST couldn't get away fast enough to take advantage.

"Shoot," he ordered. "Fire at will, whatever we can throw at them. At least we'll go out shooting."

The CST's internal systems crackled and complained. His men fired what little working phasers they had left. But they weren't a starship—what could they do? Go over there and rebuild the enemy to death?

As Stiles watched the enemy ship on the screen, pursuing them in fits and bursts with those clogged impulse tubes, he knew that despite its falling behind they couldn't possibly outrun its firepower.

The whole main screen and two lateral ones—the two still working—blasted bright white with incendiary drama. Stiles crimped his eyes, but refused to close them. He wasn't going to die with his eyes closed.

Then he didn't die—couldn't even do that right.

"Romulan bird-of-prey on our starboard stern!" Travis called, horrified. "It's fired on that blue ship! It's driving them off!"

Spock bent over the science station. "Confirmed. Romulan standard warbird . . . in battle mode."

"Now what?" Zack cranked around. "Fire on that one too?"

"No!" McCoy rasped.

"Don't shoot!" Stiles countered at the same time. "Give me ship to ship!"

"You've got ship to ship."

Stiles leaned over the arm of his command chair's comm. "Dr. Crusher, I assume that's you inside that ugly thing."

"It's me, Commander. Everyone all right? Mission accomplished, I hope?"

"Accomplished so far, Doctor." He blinked at the bronze war wing hovering on their flank. "Ugly or not, I'm glad to see that big-eyed bug!"

"It worked." Spock's announcement was reserved, but victorious. "Enemy is moving off at emergency warp one on a retreat vector."

"They're moving off, Commander Stiles. What do you recommend we do? Chase them down?"

Stiles sucked a long breath and heaved it out with a shudder. "No, no, don't chase them. Let them go, Doctor. And . . . stand by."

"Standing by," Crusher acknowledged.

"Do they show any signs of turning back?" he asked his own crew.

"None," Spock congratulated.

Jason's hands shook on his controls. "Think we beat 'em!"

Looking around the deck, Stiles had a hard time believing they'd beaten anybody at all, considering all the wreckage and mess and sparking components. He hadn't even noticed the parts and pieces blowing around him and now cluttering the deck. But the rush of victory was undeniable on the bruised faces of his crew.

"What's that whine?" somebody asked.

"What whine?" Stiles wasn't even sure who asked, and didn't hear anything at first.

Then he did.

"Transporter!" Spock called over the noise that suddenly filled the bridge.

They pressed back, not knowing what was happening until a band of energy crackled into formation in front of the helm and coalesced into humanoid shape. As they stared in amazement, the sparkling form hardened into Orsova.

Stiles opened his mouth to shout an order, but Orsova was already moving, leaping like an attacking lion at Zevon. Stiles didn't see a weapon until the last second before Orsova and Zevon's bodies collided. A flash of metal, as if he were watching a scene from a swashbuckling movie—unmistakably a blade.

For just a flash this made no sense—why would Orsova, who had at his disposal every weapon on a whole planet, use a blade?

Sykora cried out some unintelligible protest, but Spock and Travis managed to hold her back. Zack and Jeremy sprang from their posts, dove forward over the helm, and snatched at Orsova's clothing. It took both of them to pry him off Zevon. By then, Stiles was there.

"Hold him back!" he shouted. He clutched Orsova's left wrist and the metal weapon in it—some kind of spike, polished to a silk finish, with a wooden handle like an ice pick. It's silver surface was spackled with Zevon's blood.

As Jason Bolt joined the effort to hold Orsova, Stiles handed the weapon to Travis and rushed to Zevon. He grasped Zevon by both arms and held him up. Was he hurt? Was he dying?

"Zevon?" Stiles held him and looked for a wound. He found it under Zevon's right hand, pressed to his left side. Pulling Zevon's hand away, Stiles cajoled, "Let me look, let me look."

As Zevon stiffened in pain against him, he found the entry wound, and blessedly an exit.

"It's just a flesh wound, I think." Weakened by relief, he grinned at Zevon. "You just got a good poke!"

Fighting the shock of having been stabbed, seriously or not, Zevon winced and nodded but couldn't manage to let go of Stiles just yet.

Stiles had other ideas. He twisted around and glared at Orsova. "You missed, you filthy ox!"

Orsova slammed an elbow into Jason Bolt and smacked Zack in the face, driving him back. After that, though, he didn't attack anybody, instead crossing to the port panel where the long-range scanner was showing a clear picture of the constellation ship getting smaller and smaller as it ran.

"Voice! Voice, save me!" he cried. "Beam me away, Voice! I did what you wanted! Where are you! Come for me! Voice!"

But nobody came to rescue him.

"Pathetic," Stiles commented.

Apparently just now realizing he was in deep trouble, Orsova cranked around and glared as if trapped in a box. He could do nothing as Stiles closed on him, pressed his fingers into the flesh at Orsova's throat, backed him tight up against the portside scanner panel. "I was afraid of *you?* You're just a quivering little coward when you're standing alone, aren't you?"

"You better not hurt me!" Orsova pressed backward against the panel. "The Voice is coming back for me!"

"Not soon enough." Letting loose a dozen years of frustration—and even anger at himself, that he'd been haunted for a third of his life by the face now crimping before him—Stiles bent Orsova back over the panel until he could push no more. Orsova choked and gagged as Stiles's knuckles kneaded into his throat.

As Orsova's face flushed from copper to almost beet red with strain, quite abruptly, even absurdly, the satisfaction meter began to fall. Stiles glared into the hated face, saw the panic and desperation, and snarled as if looking into a garbage pit.

But he stopped pushing. He even let go a little.

"Damn," he uttered. "You're just a toothache! You're not even worth hitting!"

To the obvious amazement of everybody around him, he pulled Orsova back to his feet and let him reel.

Stiles found himself strangely amused and pleased at Orsova's pitiful display. Over there, Travis was smiling at him in some kind of ironic pride. That felt good.

Shaking his head, he leaned one hip against the helm and commented, "At least I was worth beating up!"

His crewmen rewarded him with a laugh and a round of applause that made him feel like—well, like royalty.

"Just stay there, you puscup," he said to Orsova. "You're as imprisoned as I was. Dr. McCoy, would you have a look at Zevon, please? Zack, escort the doctor around the other side of the helm, away from this mulchy moron."

Playing out his win, he freely turned his back on Orsova as if his former guard were hardly more than a bug on the wall. For the first time, he turned his back on his greatest fear, the ghost of all his nights, and completely dismissed him.

He turned instead to Zevon, as Dr. McCoy probed the Romulan's wound. "How is he?"

"Superficial," the elderly doctor confirmed. "Hardly raising a welt. Punched through the skin, scored the intestines—no ruptures, though. Let me have a better look. . . ."

He drew around his medical tricorder and a scanner and started taking readings.

"All right, Zevon," Stiles began firmly, "you can have what you want. In fact, you can have *more* than you want. I'm going to take you back to that stupid planet and dump you there with your wife, just like you want. And then I'm coming back into space and demonstrate to you exactly what a Federation promise means." Leaning forward with theatrical flair, he announced, "I'm going to build your barricade."

"You, yourself?" Zevon challenged.

From the other side of the bridge, Sykora gasped, "Zevon, can he do it?"

"No!" Her husband flinched as McCoy scanned him. "He certainly cannot possibly do it. The barricade needs raw materials, infrastructure, parts, support—Federation interest will fade before the barricade is built."

"It's not going to fade," Stiles boasted. "I won't let it."

Zevon gazed at him in something like disappointment. "And you have so much influence, Eric?"

"I don't need influence. I have a CST." Stiles swept his hand wide to illustrate the ship around him, and the suddenly proud crew. "We can build it. A combat support tender is a movable starbase, a flying factory!"

"Of course!" Spock breathed. Even he hadn't thought of it, and that gave Stiles a particular zing of pleasure.

"Impossible," Zevon argued. He pointed at Spock, but spoke to Stiles. "You're saying this to get what he wants, because you worship him!"

A rumble of frustration rose in Stiles's throat. Better let that one go. "My crew is packed with trained technicians, mechanics, and engineers. We can build almost anything, darned near anywhere, all by ourselves. And even though you're refusing to help us, we're going to go back there and build it."

Zevon squinted with doubt. "But we have no treaty! Starfleet will not give you permission—"

"I don't need permission," Stiles recklessly sparked. "I'm not even going to ask for it. And on top of that, I'm going to use a few other resources available to me right here and now. For instance, Dr. McCoy over there is going to treat whatever's making your wife sick. I don't have to let him do that, y'see, because I'm in command here and he has to do what I say. But I'm going to tell him to do that anyway, Zevon, because not everything in life is a tradeoff. And then we're going to fly away and leave you alone with your planet and your wife and your barricade, and we'll see if you can forget who did for you what you couldn't do for yourselves." He jabbed Zevon in the arm. "You and everybody on that stupid planet are going to find out what real freedom means."

Across the bridge, Ambassador Spock settled back against the science station and looped his arms into that casual appreciative fold that Stiles had seen so many times on the historical tapes. Stiles got a rush of delight at seeing Spock fold his arms like that, right here on Stiles's bridge, just as if he liked being here.

Astonished, Zevon could do nothing but stare at him with a thousand emotions pushing at him. Stiles did not turn away from that gaze, determined to show that nothing would stop him from doing what he said he could do, exercising both the power of his command and the industrial might of his ship.

Dr. McCoy looked up then, and clicked off his medical tricorder. His face was stiff, his voice rough.

"He's not going to find out anytime soon. There must've been something on the spike." He looked first at Stiles, then at Spock. "It's all over, gentlemen. He's infected."

Chapter Twenty-five

McCoy's words shook Stiles to the bone. Spock too, he could tell, was inexpressibly disturbed. Only seeing the worry on his idol's face caused Stiles to finally absorb just how rare Zevon's uncontaminated blood had been to them all. What would come now? Decades of instability in the galaxy? The suction of a collapsing empire on the Federation's doorstep? Endless struggles and endless repairs, so ships and crews could go back into more endless struggles?

"Call Dr. Crusher to beam over here," McCoy tersely said. "I want a corroborating opinion. Not that it'll change a goddamn thing. . . ."

Wordless, his throat too tight to make a sound, Stiles nodded the order over to Travis, who spoke into his comm. "Dr. Crusher, would you beam over please? Dr. McCoy's request."

"*Acknowledged. One moment.*"

The bridge fell to silence. Except for the snapping of electrical systems that had been violated, there was hardly a sound. The squawk of the transporter beam sent a ripple up every spine. Soon Dr. Beverly Crusher stood right there on the bridge, providing a mere haze of hope. But nobody here doubted Leonard McCoy's diagnosis, not for a moment.

The elegant lady doctor looked around, noted everybody, including the only two Romulans, hesitated briefly over Sykora, then silently concluded that Zevon was the only one who could be the person they'd come here for.

"I think we're too late," McCoy told her in a funereal tone. "Doublecheck me, will you?"

Crusher kept control over her expression, connecting momentarily with Spock as she stepped across the bridge to Zevon and ran her med scanner over him. Then she brought up her own tricorder and compared notes with whatever she had collected while she was gone in Romulan space.

Stiles watched her, worried. Over the doctor's shoulder, Zevon's fearful eyes met his. He stepped to Zevon's side, as if he'd never left, as if his presence alone could protect Zevon from the scourge that was apparently inevitable.

Dr. Crusher shook her head. "It's spreading fast. In forty or fifty seconds, he'll be completely contaminated. How did this happen out here in the middle of nowhere?"

"Hah!" On the other side of the bridge, Orsova bellowed with joy. "You see? You lose! Your civilization will fall apart now! The Voice is coming! You lose now! You can't hurt me now! I'm going to be governor of the sector! I won! I won!"

As retorts reeled in his head, Stiles turned toward his old tormenter. Never got the chance, though.

Sykora, until now still fazed by the effects of the stun, came very sharply and dangerously to life. She shoved Travis harshly off his balance and snatched the bloody spike from his hand. As if shot from a cannon, she streaked to Orsova. Before anyone could think of stopping her, she drove the spike through Orsova's neck with a disgusting pop and a faint crunch of shattered bone.

At Stiles's side, Zevon gasped and jolted with shock, but made no move toward his wife. She was an imperial subcommander, after all.

Orsova gurgled as frothy blood welled up into his mouth and he clasped at his demolished throat with both hands, blinked in surprise, then couldn't suck another breath. No one offered to cushion his collapse onto the deck. There, in a puddle of his own fluids, he died.

Just like that. Over.

And Stiles was glad. And he didn't feel ashamed of it, either. He promised himself he never would. There were more appropriate things in the galaxy to feel bad about.

Even the sight of Orsova bleeding on the deck couldn't raise the pall that suddenly descended on the bridge. They'd failed. After all this.

Dr. Crusher huffed in frustration. "He's right. He won. We don't have any more alternatives for this mutant doomsday virus. We can't even get the empress back to her home in time for her to die in her own bed." Angry, she stuffed her med scanner back in its case and looked snappishly at Dr. McCoy. "Unless you've got a rabbit to pull out of your hat, we're skunked."

"What do you take me for?" McCoy spread his arms and crowed, "I'm going to stop this venom campaign if it's the last thing I do—and at the age of a hundred and thirty-odd, everything I do could be the last thing I do."

"You've got something?" Spock stepped to him. "Another uninfected royal family member?"

Invigorated, Stiles pointed at Sykora and blurted, "It's her, isn't it? I should've known! It's got to be her! Did he marry his own cousin or something?"

"No, he didn't," McCoy denied. "I told you the truth. She's got no royal family blood at all. Not even close. She's peasant stock if I ever saw it. Couldn't be infected if she took a bath in that toxin. But I've got something even better." He looked at Crusher with a winning expression. "You know what they say . . . fetal-cord blood is about twenty times more potent than the ordinary vein stuff. I won't even have to wake the little fella up."

Suddenly the center of attention, Sykora eyed the doctors, then her husband, then Stiles. "What does he mean?"

"You're pregnant, that's what!" McCoy announced.

"You knew?" Stiles accused McCoy as both Sykora and Zevon gawked in undeniable surprise. "You knew that and you still let Zevon be a target for assassination? A decoy?"

"Well, of course!" The elderly doctor nodded proudly. "After the first eight or nine decades, you learn to keep your mouth shut. Now, I know what you should name him, y'see. You've got to pick something flashy and unique. Leonard James Eric Spock Beverly Saskatoon the First. He'll be the only one of his kind. You won't regret it. Wanna see it written down? Hey, kid, got a pen?"

Epilogue

THE CRAMPED LITTLE SICKBAY on board the *Saskatoon* had never seen so much fame. Over a matter of a couple of days, the midsection of a combat support tender had become the center of the universe. Starfleet's Lord High Oracle Leonard McCoy and its state-of-the-art shamanness Beverly Crusher were collaborating with every medical facility within comm range. The first several attempts at synthesizing a serum failed, but only by tiny fractions. Gradually the fractions became smaller, and hope swelled.

Busy as he was with construction, Stiles broke away from his crew on the evening of the second day, and with an admitted rush of nerves went to check on Zevon's progress.

Zevon lay on the portable diagnostic couch that McCoy had ordered brought in. He was clearly in some pain from whatever treatments the doctors were giving him. Sykora was at his side. She hadn't been able to leave the chamber all this time. After all, she was the center of the center of the universe.

In the small sickbay, Dr. Crusher was bending over a cache of tubes, vials, beakers, microprocessors, and analytical equipment they'd had shipped in. Engrossed in her work, she didn't even look up when Stiles came in.

McCoy hovered nearby, peering at a colored liquid in a test tube.

Stiles felt he was interrupting something private as he came to Zevon's side, opposite Sykora, and fielded the obstinate woman's glare, still loaded with suspicion. Oh, well, couldn't win everything at once.

Pressing a hand to Zevon's shoulder, he gained his old friend's attention through the blur of pain.

"Hey, lightfoot," he greeted. "You all right?"

"Oh, Eric," Zevon moaned. "I think I would rather get the plague and die than deal with the cure. . . ."

A smile of empathy broke on Stiles's face. "No, no, you've got your orders. Get better or face the consequences. You don't want the vindictive captain to find out."

"If only . . . he were vindictive enough to . . . put me out of this misery. . . ."

"Not much longer," McCoy said. "Don't make me break out my hip-pocket psychiatry, boy. I'm whuppin' a dragon here."

Even through his discomfort, Zevon managed a smile. Stiles tightened his grip in silent reassurance.

He tried to come up with something more to say but was rescued when Ambassador Spock stepped in over the hatch coaming.

"Mr. Stiles, I thought you might be here," Spock said with not particularly well-veiled contentment.

Stiles instantly saw the undercurrent of success and asked, "How does it look, sir?"

His face expressive—in defiance of legend—Spock spoke almost merrily. "Looks quite well. Your defiant declaration has stirred the resting spirits at Starfleet Command."

"They're not going to challenge me or throw me in a brig or anything?"

"Hardly. The admiralty has a longstanding policy, albeit unspoken, of backing up their captains' flares of caprice. Admiral Douglas Prothero has offered the Zebra-Tango Division of the Starfleet Corps of Engineers and the services of the Industrial Trawler *True North* to assist the *Saskatoon* in building the spaceborne Constrictor barricade. Within a matter of months, the waves will go from deadly to harmless." He turned to Zevon and Sykora, amicably adding, "Your planet will finally be safe."

Battling a rush of deep emotion, Zevon gripped Sykora's hand and took a few moments to gather himself. "I will go before the Pojjana people," he offered, "and convince them of the Federation's integrity. I can do that . . . they will believe me."

"Such a collaboration," Spock said, "will give Starfleet the leverage to stabilize the sector and declare it green."

With both admiration and suspicion, Stiles quipped, "But you didn't have anything to do with that, I'll bet."

"Nothing at all," Spock loftily claimed.

Stiles grinned. "Thanks."

"You're very welcome. And how is construction going?"

"Oh, we've had to modify Zevon's diagrams a few times. Luckily, we're an innovative pack of wolves. Sir, might I say a few things? They're kind of . . . personal."

Spock seemed a little surprised. "Would you like to speak in private?"

"No, I'm not embarrassed anymore. I just wanted to thank you, for everything, past and present. You had faith in me that I didn't have in myself. I'll believe in myself as I am, as I can be—not as my father or my grandfather or Starfleet thought I should be. I'll believe in the Federation, as long as people like you are speaking for it. And I'll never forget something else you taught me. Probably the most important thing."

Spock's dark eyes glowed. It seemed he knew. But he asked anyway. "What would that be?"

As he gazed at his friends both new and old, Stiles absorbed the value of this moment and swore to himself that he would never forget.

"Freedom is never free," he said.

DOUBLE HELIX

QUARANTINE

JOHN VORNHOLT

For E.J.

Chapter One

THE PEREGRINE-CLASS SCOUT SHIP looked much like the falcon that inspired her design, with a beaklike bow and sweeping wings that enabled her to streak through a planet's atmosphere. Her sleek lines were marred by various scorch marks and dents, which left her looking like an old raptor with many scars. Larger than a shuttlecraft yet smaller than a cruiser, she was better armed than most ships her size, with forward and rear torpedoes plus phaser emitters on her wings.

Her bridge was designed to be operated efficiently by three people, allowing her to carry a crew of only fifteen. The engine room took up all three decks of her stern, and most of the crew served there. This proud vessel was state of the art for a scout ship—about forty years ago. Now she was practically the flagship of the Maquis fleet.

"What's the name of our ship?" asked her captain, a man named Chakotay. His black hair was cut short and severe, which suited his angular face and the prominent tattoo that stretched across half his forehead.

Tuvok, the Vulcan who served as first officer, consulted the registry on his computer screen. "She is called the *Spartacus*. The warp signature has aleady been modified."

Chakotay nodded with satisfaction. "I like that name."

On his right, an attractive woman who looked vaguely Klingon scowled at him. "Let me guess," said B'Elanna Torres. "Spartacus was some ancient human who led a revolution somewhere."

Captain Chakotay smiled. "That's right. He was a slave and a gladiator who led a revolt against Rome, the greatest power of its day. For two years, he held out against every Roman legion thrown against him."

"And how did this grand revolution end?" asked Torres.

When Chakotay didn't answer right away, Tuvok remarked, "He and all of his followers were crucified. Crucifiction is quite possibly the most barbaric form of capital punishment ever invented."

Torres snorted a laugh. "It's always good to know that my human ancestors could match my Klingon ancestors in barbarism. Considering what happened to Spartacus, let's not put him on too high a pedestal."

"It's still a good name," said Chakotay stubbornly. Like many Native Americans, he believed that names were important—that words held power. He didn't like having to change the name and warp signature of his ship all the time, but it was important to make their enemies think that the Maquis had more ships than they actually had.

"We've reached the rendezvous point," announced the captain. "I'm bringing us out of warp." Operating the conn himself, he slowed the craft down to one-third impulse, and they cruised through a deserted solar system sprinkled with occasional fields of planetary debris.

"Captain Rowan is hailing us on a secure frequency," reported Tuvok. "Their ETA is less than one minute."

"Acknowledge," answered the captain. "But no more transmissions until they get here."

While Tuvok sent the message, B'Elanna Torres worked her console. "There are no Cardassian ships in scanner range," she reported.

"Still I don't want to be here more than a couple of minutes." Chakotay's worried gaze traveled from the small viewscreen to the even smaller window below it. There was nothing in sight but the vast starscape and a few jagged clumps of debris. This area appeared deserted, but Chakotay had learned from hard experience that it was wise to keep moving in the Demilitarized Zone.

"They're coming out of warp," said Torres.

Chakotay watched on the viewscreen as a Bajoran assault vessel appeared about a thousand kilometers off the starboard bow. The dagger-shaped spacecraft was slightly larger than the *Spartacus,* but she wasn't as maneuverable or as fast. Like Chakotay's ship, her blue-gray hull was pocked and pitted with the wounds of battle.

"Captain Rowan is hailing us," said Tuvok.

"On screen." Chakotay managed a smile as he greeted his counterpart on the other Maquis ship. Patricia Rowan looked every centimeter a warrior, from her scarred, gaunt face to the red eye patch that covered one eye. Her blond hair was streaked with premature gray, and it was pulled back into a tight bun. Captain Rowan had gotten a well-deserved reputation for ruthlessness, and Chakotay was cordial to her but couldn't quite bring himself to call her a friend.

"Hello, Patricia."

"Hello, Chakotay," she answered. "The *Singha* is reporting for duty under your command. What's our mission?"

"Do you know the planet Helena?"

"Only by reputation. Wasn't it abandoned when the Federation betrayed us?"

"No," answered Chakotay. "The Helenites opted for the same legal status as the residents of Dorvan V. Instead of being relocated, they chose to give up their Federation citizenship and remain on the planet, under Cardassian rule."

"Then to hell with them," said Rowan bluntly.

Chakotay ignored her harsh words. "The Helenites have always marched to their own drum. The planet was settled by mixed-race colonists who were trying to escape discrimination in the rest of the Federation. There are some Maquis sympathizers on Helena, and we've been getting periodic reports from them. Two weeks ago, they sent a message that Cardassian troops had arrived, then we lost all contact. There hasn't been a transmission from the planet since then. It might be a crackdown, maybe even total extermination. For all we know, the Cardassians could be testing planet-killing weapons."

"They're not Maquis," said Rowan stubbornly.

Chakotay's jaw clenched with anger. "We can't just abandon four million people. We have to find out what's happening there, and help them if we can."

"Then it's an intelligence mission," replied Captain Rowan, sounding content with that definition.

Chakotay nodded and slowly relaxed his jaw. One of the drawbacks of being in a loose-knit organization like the Maquis was that orders were not always followed immediately. Sometimes a commander had to explain the situation in order to convince his subordinates to act. Of course, fighting a guerrilla war against two vastly superior foes would make anyone cautious, and Maquis captains were used to acting on their own discretion. Sometimes the chain of command was as flimsy as a gaseous nebula.

Captain Rowan's scowl softened for an instant. "Chakotay, the people on Dorvan V are from your own culture. Wouldn't it make more sense to find out what happened to *them* instead of racing to help a bunch of mixed-breeds on Helena?"

Chakotay couldn't tell if Rowan was bigoted or just callous. He glanced at Torres and saw her shake her head. "Good thing there are no psychological tests to join the Maquis," she whispered.

"Did you say something?" demanded Captain Rowan.

Chakotay cleared his throat. "She said the Helenites are not really, uh, mixed-breeds—they're hybrids, genetically bred. I've heard their whole social structure is based on genetics, the more unique your genetic heritage, the higher your social status."

"A facinating culture," added Tuvok without looking up from his console. Rowan grimaced, but remained silent.

Chakotay went on, "As for my people on Dorvan V . . . yes, I'm worried about them. But that's a small village, and they've chosen to live in peace with the land, using minimal technology. They're not much of a threat, and of no strategic value, either—the Cardassians will probably leave them alone. But Helena was a thriving Federation planet with millions of inhabitants and a dozen spaceports. When they go silent, it's suspicious."

"How do we proceed?" asked Captain Rowan.

Chakotay gave her a grim smile. "Have you ever played cowboys and Indians?"

Observing the planet on the viewscreen, Captain Chakotay was struck by how Earth-like it was, with vast aquamarine oceans and wispy cloud cover. Helena had small twin moons that orbited each other as they orbited the planet, and he could see their silhouettes against the sparkling sea. Small green continents were scattered across the great waters, but they seemed insignificant next to all that blue. The lush hues were accentuated by a giant red sun glowing in the distance.

On second glance, Chakotay decided that Helena looked more like Pacifica than Earth. Here was yet another beautiful planet stolen by the Cardassians, while the Federation looked the other way.

"One ship in orbit," reported B'Elanna Torres. "A Cardassian military freighter. They use those for troop transports, too, and they can be heavily armed."

Chakotay nodded and spread his fingers over the helm controls. "Let's keep it to one ship. Tuvok, as soon as we come out of warp, target their communications array with photon torpedoes and fire at will. I don't want them sending for help."

"Yes, sir," answered the Vulcan, who was preternaturally calm, considering they were about to attack a ship that was ten times larger than they were.

"Then hit their sensor arrays, so they have to concentrate on *us*."

"What about their weapons?" snapped Torres. "I hope you aren't planning to take a lot of damage."

"No more than usual." Captain Chakotay smiled confidently and pressed the comm panel. "Seska, report to the bridge for relief."

"Yes, sir," answered the Bajoran. She was only one deck below them, in the forward torpedo bay, and Chakotay heard her footsteps clanging on the ladder behind them. Now if B'Elanna had to go to engineering, they were covered.

The captain hit the comm panel, and his voice echoed throughout the ship. "All hands, Red Alert! Battlestations."

Like the falcon that inspired the *Peregrine*-class, the *Spartacus* swooped out of warp, her talons bared, spitting photon torpedoes in rapid bursts. Plumes of flame rose along the dorsal fin of the sturgeon-shaped Cardassian freighter, and dishes, deflectors, and antennas snapped like burnt matchsticks. Shields quickly compensated, and the next volley was repelled, as the lumbering, copper-colored vessel turned to defend herself.

Phasers beamed from the wing tips of the *Spartacus,* bathing the freighter in vibrant blue light. Although damage to the hull was minimal, the enemy's sensor arrays crackled like a lightning storm. Despite her damage, the freighter unleashed a barrage of phaser fire, and the *Spartacus* was rocked as she streaked past. With the larger ship on her tail, blasting away, the Maquis ship was forced into a low orbit. A desperate chase ensued, with the blue seas of Helena glimmering peacefully in the background.

"Full power to aft shields!" ordered Chakotay.

"Aye, sir," answered Torres.

They were jolted again by enemy fire, and Chakotay had to grip his chair to keep from falling out. From the corner of his eye, he saw Seska stagger onto the bridge and take a seat at an auxilary console. There was a worried look on her face.

"We can't take much more of this," said Torres.

"Making evasive maneuvers," answered Chakotay.

Zigging and zagging, the Maquis ship avoided most of the Cardassian volleys, but the larger ship bore down on them, cutting the distance with every second. Chakotay knew he would soon be in their sights, but his options were limited this close to the planet. He had a course to keep . . . and a rendezvous.

The two ships—a sardine chased by a barracuda—sped around the gently curved horizon and headed toward the blazing red sun in the distance. On the bridge, Chakotay pounded a button to dampen the light from the viewscreen, the glare was so bright. But if he couldn't see, they couldn't either. He felt the thrill of the hunt as he prepared to use one of the oldest tactics of his ancestors.

A direct hit jarred them, releasing an acrid plume of smoke from somewhere on the bridge. The ship began to vibrate as they started into the atmosphere.

"Shields weakening," reported Tuvok.

"Just a little longer," muttered Chakotay. He made another sharp turn, but quickly veered back toward the sun. The Cardassians increased their fire, as if worried that she would escape into the planet's atmosphere. Since the *Spartacus* wasn't returing fire, they had to to assume she was trying to land on the planet.

"They're powering up a tractor beam," said Torres urgently. "Their shields are . . . down!"

"Now!" barked the captain. Tuvok's hand moved from the weapons console to the comm board, while Chakotay steered his craft vertically into the horizon, trying to present a small target. The Cardassians had swallowed the bait, and now the trap snapped shut.

A Bajoran assault vessel streaked out of warp in the middle of the sun's glare. Chakotay knew the *Singha* was there, but he could barely see her on the viewscreen. The Cardassian vessel didn't see her at all, so intent were they upon capturing their prey.

With her shields down, the freighter's bridge took a direct hit from a brace of torpedoes, and lightning crackled along the length of her golden hull. The freighter went dark, but she lit up again as the *Singha* veered around and raked her hull with phasers, tearing jagged gashes in the gleaming metal. The Cardassians got off a few desperate shots, but the *Singha* raced past them, unharmed.

"Aft torpedoes," ordered Chakotay. "Fire!"

With deadly precison, the Vulcan launched a brace of torpedoes that hit the freighter amidships and nearly broke her in two. Chakotay cringed at the explosions that ripped along her gleaming hull, and he made a silent prayer on behalf of the fallen enemy. They were more arrogant than smart, but they had died bravely. Fortunately, that trick always worked on the arrogant. At a cockeyed angle, spewing smoke and flame, the massive freighter dropped into a decaying orbit.

Chakotay piloted the *Spartacus* into a safe orbit that trailed behind the dying ship. "Hail them."

Tuvok shook his head. "Their communications are out, and life support is failing. They have about six minutes left before they burn up in the atmosphere."

The cheerful voice of Captain Rowan broke in on the comm channel. "That was good hunting, Chakotay, and a good plan. What's next?"

"Enter standard orbit and see if you can raise anyone on the planet. We're going to take a prisoner, if we can."

He tapped the comm panel. "Bridge to transporter room. Scan the bridge of the enemy ship—see if you can find any lifesigns."

"Yes, sir." After a moment's pause, the technician answered, "Most of them are dead. There's one weak lifesign—"

"Lock onto it and wait for me. I'm on my way." The captain jumped to his feet. "Tuvok, grab a medkit—you're with me. B'Elanna, you have the bridge. Keep scanning the planet, and try to raise someone. Seska, you have the conn. Keep us in orbit."

"Aye, sir." The attractive Bajoran slid into the vacated seat and gave him a playful smile. "This looks like a nice place for shore leave. What do you say, Captain?"

"I'll put you on the away team," promised Chakotay. He took another glance at the viewscreen and saw the smoking hulk of the freighter plummeting toward the beautiful blue horizon.

The captain led the way from the clam-shaped bridge to the central corridor, which ran like a backbone down the length of the *Spartacus*. He jogged to the second hatch and dropped onto the ladder with practiced efficiency, while Tuvok stopped at a storage panel to pick up a medkit.

Dropping off the ladder, Chakotay landed in the second largest station on the ship after engineering: the combined transporter room and cargo hold. Not that they had any cargo to speak of—every spare centimeter was filled with weapons, explosives, and photon torpedoes, stacked like cordwood.

He drew his phaser and nodded toward the Bolian on the transporter console. The blue-skinned humanoid manipulated some old trimpot slides, and a prone figure began to materialize on the transporter platform. Chakotay heard Tuvok's footsteps as he landed on the deck, but he never took his eyes, or his phaser, off the wounded figure.

It was a male Cardassian, with singed clothes, a bruised face, and bloodied, crushed legs. With their prominent bone structure and sunken eyes, most Cardassian faces looked like skulls, but this one looked closer to death than usual.

"According to his insignia, he's the first officer," said Tuvok.

The Cardassian blinked his eyes and focused slowly on them. When he realized where he was, he wheezed with laughter. "Are you trying to save us?"

"Lie still," answered Chakotay. He motioned Tuvok forward with the medkit, but the Cardassian waved him off.

"Too late," he said with a cough. The Cardassian lifted his black sleeve to his mouth and bit off a small black button. Before anyone could react, he swallowed it. "I won't be captured . . . by the Maquis."

"What are you doing on this planet?" demanded Chakotay. "Why don't you leave these people alone?"

A rattle issued from the Cardassian's throat, and it was hard to tell whether he was laughing, crying, or dying. "You beat us . . . but all you won was a curse."

The Cardassian's bloodied head dropped onto the platform with a thud, and his previously wheezing chest was now still. Tuvok checked the medical tricorder and reported, "He has expired."

Chakotay nodded. "Beam his body back to his ship. Let him burn with his comrades."

"Yes, sir," answered the Bolian. A second later, every trace of the Cardassian officer was gone.

The captain strode over to the transporter console and tapped the comm panel. "Chakotay to bridge. Have you or the *Singha* raised anyone on the planet?"

"No, sir," answered Torres. "But we detected a strong power source that suddenly went dark. It could be a Cardassian installation."

"Are you picking up lifesigns on the planet?"

"Lots of them," answered Torres.

"Pick a strong concentration of lifesigns and send the coordinates to the transporter room. Tuvok and I are going down."

"Okay," answered Torres. "Did you get a prisoner?"

"For only a few seconds—we didn't learn anything. Chakotay out." The captain reached into a tray on the transporter console and grabbed two Deltan combadges, one of which he tossed to Tuvok. The *Spartacus* was so small that they seldom needed combadges while on the ship; they saved them for away teams.

"I've got the coordinates," said the Bolian technician. "It appears to be the spaceport in the city of Padulla."

"Fine." Captain Chakotay jumped onto the transporter platform and took his place on the middle pad. Tuvok stepped beside him, slinging the medkit and tricorder over his shoulder.

"Energize."

A familiar tingle gripped Chakotay's spine, as the transporter room faded from view, to be replaced by a cavernous spaceport with high, vaulted ceilings covered with impressive murals. The captain expected to see a crowd of people, but he expected them to be standing on their feet—not lying in haphazard rows stretching the length of the vast terminal. This looked like a field hospital, thrown together to house the wounded from some monstrous battle. Coughs and groans echoed in the rancid air.

His first impression was that the Cardassians had wreaked terrible destruction on the people of Helena, and he started toward the nearest patient.

"Captain!" warned Tuvok. "Keep your distance from them."

He turned to see the Vulcan intently working his medical tricorder. This caused Chakotay to look more closely at the nearest patient, who was swaddled in a soiled blanket, lying on top of a grass mat, surrounded by filth.

The man wasn't wounded—he had oozing pustules and black bruises on his face and limbs, and his yellow hair was plastered to his sweaty forehead. Although his species was unfamiliar to Chakotay, his skin had a deathly pallor, just like the Cardassian's had. Chakotay took a step away from him.

Another patient finally noticed the visitors. She propped herself up with some difficulty and began to crawl toward them. Others saw the away team as well, and a chorus of desperate voices rent the air. Some of their words were incoherent, but Chakotay could make out a few phrases as the people crawled forward: "Help us! Save me! *Kill* me!"

"What's the matter with them?" he whispered to Tuvok.

"A serious illness," answered the Vulcan with tight-lipped understatement.

Chakotay tapped his combadge. "Away team to transporter room. Beam us up, but on a ten-second delay. Get out of the transporter room before we materialize."

"Yes, sir," said the Bolian, not hiding the worry in his voice. "Is everything all right?"

"No," answered Chakotay as he stepped away from the advancing tide of disease and death. "It's not."

Chapter Two

IT WAS THE MORNING of his twelfth birthday, and his father had promised him something special—a trip to the Yukon Delta National Wildlife Refuge to observe Kodiak bears fishing for salmon. Living in Valdez, Alaska, did have its advantages, and so did having a father who was important enough in the Federation to command his own shuttlecraft and pilot. Will wasn't exactly sure what his father did in outer space—only that it involved diplomacy and lots of traveling. He tried hard not to resent the time he had to spend in boarding schools and living with other families, who were always eager to do a favor for Kyle Riker.

That was why it was so special to wake up in a mountain cabin on the slopes of Mount Waskey and see his dad waving to him from the meadow, where a gleaming shuttlecraft waited. In the distance, snowy peaks shimmered like amethysts and diamonds against a lustrous pearl sky. To the north, the Tikchik Lakes gripped the vast land like fingers of mercury. Will took a breath, delighting in the musky pine scent. The cool breeze carried sounds of trickling water from the snow thaw, along with the calls of terns and geese. And there was his dad, waving to him from the shuttlecraft.

The gangly twelve-year-old strode across the frozen grass, which crunched satisfyingly under his boots, and he watched as his father inspected the small craft. Although it was a shiny new shuttle—with warp drive—Kyle Riker never took the condition of his ship for granted. When something needed to be done, like inspection before a takeoff, he didn't hesitate to do it himself. His dad got things done, no matter what the cost, and Will figured that was his true value to the Federation.

"Hi, son!" he said jovially as the boy approached. Kyle Riker was a tall, robust man with a square jaw, piercing eyes, and a strong handshake. Women loved him, and he was a commanding presence wherever he went, even the Alaskan wilderness. Will was in awe of him.

"Should I wake up the pilot?" asked the boy.

"No, let him sleep. I can fly us for a short jump like this. I'd have to tell him exactly where to go, anyway, and this will be easier." His dad circled the craft one more time, looking for damage to his shiny ship. "By the way, happy birthday."

"Thanks."

"Are you ready to go see the bears? I know a salmon run where they almost always show up. And I packed us a picnic lunch."

"Great!" In reality, Will would be thrilled if they did nothing but sit in the cabin and talk, he saw so little of his dad. But everything that Kyle Riker did had to be an occasion. A mere visit wasn't enough—they had to travel hundreds of kilometers to observe the largest bears in the world.

Dad opened the main hatch of the shuttle. "Jump in. Take the co-pilot's seat."

Will did as he was told, and he was excited to sit at the front of the cockpit, gazing at the amazing array of instruments and sensors. It seemed incredible that they could take off in this small vessel and travel all the way to the stars. More than anything else, that's what Will wanted to do.

His dad settled into the seat beside him and started punching buttons and flipping switches. The instrument panel blinked impressively, and the impulse engines began to hum.

"I wish we had time to hike there, or ride horses," said Kyle. "But we don't, so this will have to do."

"I think it's great," replied Will. The question of time saddened him a bit, because there was never enough of it. "When do you have to go back?"

"Tomorrow." Kyle began his preflight checklist.

"How come you can't stay longer?"

His father scowled, looking slightly resentful of the question. "I'm supposed to be on Rigel II in four days to negotiate with the Orions, and you don't keep Orions waiting. Hang on—here we go."

With a roar of thrusters, the shuttlecraft lifted off the ground and streaked into the pale blue sky, leaving the frozen meadow far below them. They swooped over lakes, forests, and mountains, heading northwest toward the ocean, which glittered in the morning sun like the aurora borealis.

Will knew he shouldn't bother his dad with a million questions, but it might be months before he saw him again. With childlike directness, he pointed to the brilliant sky and asked, "How come you live out there, and I live here?"

"Don't you like it in Alaska?" asked his dad with surprise.

"Sure, it's okay." Will didn't mention that he had never lived anywhere else, so he didn't have anything to compare it with. "I'd like it more if you lived here, too."

"Well, I do live here . . . officially."

"But you're never here."

His dad's scowl deepened. "Are you trying to spoil this trip? I'm here now, aren't I? And I came a long way for your birthday."

Will knew he should shut up, but he had always spoken his mind. And this had been bothering him for a long time. "Dad, why can't I live with you . . . out there?"

Kyle laughed. "On a starbase? In a little five-by-five room, with no scenery at all? It's okay for me, but I'm only there a few days every couple of months. It's just a place to hang my hat between assignments. And the places I go are often dangerous. Believe me, Rigel II is no place for a child. Besides, you need to have some stability in your life, with your school and friends."

"I need to have my dad around," said Will bluntly. "I feel like an orphan sometimes."

"I don't need this," muttered Kyle Riker. "I drop everything and travel twenty light-years for your birthday, and for what? To get chewed out?"

Will hung his head. "I'm sorry, Dad. I'm glad you're here, I really am. But it's just that . . . when you're here, it makes it worse later . . . when you go away."

His father nodded sympathetically, but he kept his eyes on his instrument panel. "You know, Will, I didn't plan for your mother to die when you were so young. The plan was that you would have a home and at least one full-time parent. But it didn't happen that way. When you were little, I stayed close to home and tried to raise you as best I could, but a man only has so much time to make his mark in the universe. This is my time."

Will started to argue that it was also *his* time, that the months they were separated could never be recaptured. But the twelve-year-old didn't have the words or the experience to debate his father. He would often look back and see that his dad had probably decided at that moment to desert him entirely. If it was painful to return home for brief visits and then be separated, he must have figured it would be less painful to never come home at all.

"Lieutenant Riker," droned a voice, "when I clap my hands, you will awaken. You'll feel fine and well rested, and you'll remember what you told me."

A sharp sound jolted the man who called himself Thomas Riker. He blinked at the counselor and remembered where he was—not cruising above the Alaskan wilderness but in a consultation room aboard the *U.S.S. Gandhi.* Dr. Carl Herbert was a skilled ship's counselor, and he had hypnotically regressed Riker to his childhood during the session. It was hard for Tom to come back from that simpler time, before everything had turned to crud.

He mustered a smile. "I'm sorry, Doctor, what did you ask me?"

"You said something about how your father had decided on your twelfth birthday to abandon you a few years later. Do you really think that's true?"

Tom shrugged. "Who knows? That was the only time we ever talked about my feelings. I saw him less and less after that. The last time I saw him I was fifteen years old."

"However, it is true that Will Riker has seen your father since then and made amends."

Riker scowled. "That's not *me.* Although we may be physically identical, we're two different people. You can't compare us."

"Sorry." Dr. Herbert pursed his lips and frowned deeply. "I only meant that perhaps *you* could make peace with your father, too."

"That other Riker has had lots of opportunities I never had, and that was one of them." The bearded man stood and paced. "Are we here to talk about my father?"

"No. We're here to talk about you." The counselor folded his hands in front of him. "Lieutenant, you have some very serious issues with abandonment. First, you fear your mother abandoned you, although you know logically it wasn't her fault. Then your father actually *did* abandon you—an act which you've never forgiven or forgotten. Then Starfleet accidentally marooned you on Nervala IV—for eight years. It could be said that your own double rejected you, and that might be the most devastating of all."

"So you're saying I probably should be in therapy for the rest of my life," grumbled Tom. "I'll agree to that, if you'll just clear me again for active duty."

Now it was the counselor's turn to rise to his feet and begin pacing the nondescript chamber. "Lieutenant," he began slowly, "we're about to patrol the Demilitarized Zone, with a good possibility of seeing action against the Maquis. And you were heard voicing pro-Maquis sentiments."

Riker took a deep breath, trying to stay calm. "In every other mission I've ever been on, we're supposed to discuss the pros and cons of using force. Since when is asking questions a treasonous crime?"

"Since it's the Maquis," answered Dr. Herbert with a sigh. "You're right, they're not like any other enemy we've ever faced. They're *us*—former

Starfleet officers and colonists. We have to be sure that everyone on bridge duty is unquestionably loyal to the Federation."

"And what makes you think I'm not?"

"Your background," answered the counselor sympathetically. "We've talked about your issues with abandonment, and who has been more abandoned than the settlers in the DMZ?"

Tom laughed. "You know, Doc, if Commander Crandall heard you say that, you'd be confined to quarters the same as I am."

The counselor frowned. "Commander Crandall is just doing her job."

Riker sucked in his cheeks, careful not to speak his mind. As far as he was concerned, Emma Crandall had had it in for him since the first day he arrived on the *Gandhi. She thinks I'm after her job, just because that other Riker is the most famous first officer in Starfleet. She's been looking for an excuse to stick me in the doghouse, and this is it.*

"I think I have a way out of this," said Tom, slumping back into his chair. "I want to transfer over to the medical branch. That will get me off the bridge and away from Emma Crandall. It will also allow me to pursue a career that is different than my double's. I won't even be able to help the Maquis, except to heal them if they get sick."

"It will take you years to become a doctor."

Riker sighed. "One thing I learned during my eight years on Nervala IV—patience is a virtue."

Dr. Herbert took a padd off his desk and began to make notes. "I'll recommend your transfer to medical—and your reinstatement—but it will have to be approved by Commander Crandall."

"There's always a catch, isn't there?" replied Tom Riker.

Two hours later, Tom was sitting in his quarters, watching a video log of Kodiak bears fishing for salmon in a wild Alaskan stream. That day with his father, on his twelfth birthday, they hadn't actually seen any bears, although they had hiked several kilometers along a beautiful stream. His dad had been disappointed, but not the boy—he could see bears anytime, but not his father. They had sat on the bank of the stream, eating their picnic lunch, while his dad talked about the far-flung worlds he had visited, and the incredible species he had known.

One thing his father and he could both agree upon: there was no place like outer space. Kyle's enthusiasm had instilled in the boy a burning desire to see those strange planets and people. In fact, the young Riker had outdone his civilian father by joining Starfleet. If possible, he would see even more amazing sights and do more amazing things than his dad had ever dreamed of. Although Kyle Riker hadn't realized there was a competition going on, there was.

Unfortunately, that wanderlust and ambition had been severely dampened by the long years spent on Nervala IV. Now Tom Riker didn't know what he wanted, except to be something different than Kyle Riker or the man called Will Riker.

On the viewer, he watched the great brown bears, who stood almost four meters tall, as they frolicked like cubs in the rushing stream. Catching leaping fish with a swipe of a claw wasn't easy, and the bears often failed. But they looked as if they were having fun. He realized that life wasn't worth it unless fun was involved. Unfortunately, Tom couldn't remember the last time Starfleet had been fun.

A chime sounded at his door, and Riker turned off the viewer. "Come in!"

The door slid open, and a slim woman with short dark hair entered his quarters. Under different circumstances, he could have been attracted to Commander Emma Crandall, but that had never been an option on the *Gandhi.* He jumped to his feet and stood at attention behind his desk, trying not to show the loathing he had for the ship's first officer. She was capable, but she never seemed to have any fun.

"At ease, Lieutenant," she told him in a tone of voice that did nothing to put him at ease.

"Yes, sir." Tom put his hands behind his back and remained standing.

Crandall scowled. "I've seen the counselor's report, and I'm frankly amazed. You want to toss away years of training and bridge experience in order to start a new career in medicine? I don't get you, Riker."

He opened his mouth to reply, but realized that he might make things worse. Then again, how could things be worse?

"Permission to speak freely?" he asked.

Crandall's scowl deepened, because she really didn't like her officers speaking freely. "Very well."

"Commander, you've never understood me, and you've always been wrong about me."

She began to protest, but Riker kept talking while he had the chance. "You think I'm interested in your job, and at one time, I would have been. But I've been through an experience that you can't begin to understand. I had eight years stolen from my life and career . . . and given to someone else. You think I'm a threat; others treat me like an imposter. To everyone, I'm an oddity. Face it, my chances of rising very far in the command structure are dim.

"I need to do something different, something that will make me stop dwelling on my own problems. If I can help other people, maybe I can help myself. In medicine, I'll have a chance to start over, without leaving Starfleet."

Crandall's expression softened a bit, and for the first time in almost two years, she looked at him with sympathy. "You have too much experience to be an orderly in sickbay, but I have a related job you could do. Although it's medical, it also requires command skills."

Riker leaned forward. "I'm listening."

"In addition to our patrol duties, we have to deliver medical teams and supplies to the observation posts along the DMZ. Some of them have been deluged by refugees. The captain thinks it will be more efficient to have a personnel shuttlecraft do these runs instead of the *Gandhi.* So we need a medical courier. You would be in command of a crew of two—yourself and the co-pilot."

Riker smiled gratefully. "Well, we all have to start somewhere. I'll take the job, Commander. Can I have Lieutenant Youssef?"

"Our most experienced pilot?" said Crandall, bristling at the very idea. "I think not. We have a new pilot on board, name Ensign Shelzane—you can teach her the ropes."

Riker nodded. "Thank you, Commander. I won't let you down."

"I hope not. You leave at sixteen hundred hours for Outpost Sierra III. Report to main shuttlebay." Emma Crandall started for the door, then turned back to give him a half smile. "If you want to wear a blue medical tunic instead of a red one, it's okay with me. In a way, I envy you, Lieutenant. Sometimes I think I'd like to make a change."

"You'll be promoted to captain soon," Riker assured her. "Just be patient."

Emma Crandall stiffened her spine and put on her command face again. "One more thing: try not to get into any discussions about the Maquis. I will admit, I made an example of you, so that the talking wouldn't get out of hand. I'm sorry about that, but it was necessary. On this ship, we don't set policy—we follow orders. Like it or not, the Maquis are the enemy until further notice."

"Yes, sir," answered Riker. He hadn't sympathized or thought all that much about the Maquis until recently, when everyone just assumed he must be a sympathizer. This oppressive atmosphere was another good reason to get off the *Gandhi.*

"I'll stay far away from the Maquis," promised Lieutenant Riker.

My first command, Riker thought ruefully as he inspected the squat, boxy craft known simply as *Shuttle 3.* A Type-8 personnel shuttlecraft, she accommodated a maximum of ten people, including crew, in very tight quarters. *Shuttle 3* had warp drive and a transporter, but no weaponry. According to the manifest, they would be transporting six members of the med team, plus the two crew. What worried him were all the boxes of supplies and equipment the shuttlebay workers kept loading onto the small craft. With all that weight on board, he feared she might handle sluggishly in a planet's atmosphere.

Rounding the bow of the shuttle, the lieutenant caught sight of his reflection in the front window. He looked quite dashing in his blue and black tunic, denoting his transfer to the medical branch. A new ship, a new uniform, and a new assignment that would actually do some good in the galaxy—maybe his life was turning around. Tom hadn't felt so hopeful since the day he had been rescued from Nervala IV. He tried not to think about how quickly all those hopes had been dashed.

"Lieutenant Riker?" said an inquisitive voice. He turned to see a diminutive, blue-skinned Benzite female. She was the first Benzite he'd seen who didn't rely on a breathing apparatus hanging from her neck.

"You must be Ensign Shelzane," he said with a charming smile. "Pleased to meet you."

She nodded formally. "Thank you, sir. I've been on the *Gandhi* for a month—it's odd that we haven't met before."

"Well, I've been incognito for a couple of weeks," explained Riker. "You're a shuttlecraft pilot, I presume."

"Class two rating," she answered proudly, "although I haven't logged that many hours of solo flight."

"You will on this assignment, because I intend to get my beauty sleep."

Shelzane forced a polite laugh. "Yes, sir. Are you also a doctor?"

Riker smiled and plucked at his blue tunic. "No, I'm just a . . . a medical courier. Here come the doctors."

He pointed to six more people in blue uniforms who had just entered the vast shuttlebay. They strode briskly between the parked shuttles, and Riker was struck by their youth. Like the young Benzite in front of him, they were just starting their Starfleet careers, and they did everything with self-important urgency. He wanted to tell them to slow down, to live more in the moment. But youth must be served.

Maybe he was a fool to think he could start over at this late stage of his career, but what did he have to lose? Maybe he was nothing but a glorified shuttle pilot, but it felt bigger than that. This mission felt like a step toward destiny, at least personal destiny.

After the introductions were made, Riker and Shelzane shoehorned their passengers into the cramped compartment, then they took their seats in the cockpit. A row of seats had been pulled to make room for the supplies, and the passengers were practically sitting in each others' laps. Every spare centimeter was taken up by crates and boxes. Riker was glad it was only a twenty-hour trip to Sierra III, because they would be at each others' throats if they had to spend any more time in these tight quarters.

During his preignition checklist, Riker tried to think like his father and not miss anything. They weren't over the allowed weight for the craft, but they were darn close. He whispered to Shelzane, "I think we need to compensate for all the weight we're carrying. What if we open the plasma injectors in the main cryo tank to give the impulse engines a little boost."

The Benzite looked at him with alarm. "Sir, that is somewhat unorthodox. It would also cut down our fuel efficiency by twenty or thirty percent."

"As soon as we're away from the *Gandhi*'s gravity, we'll go back to normal," he assured the worried ensign. "Don't worry, I'm used to doing things on the fly."

The Benzite gulped. "I hope you're the one taking us out of dock."

"Yes, and you'll be glad I boosted the engines when I do."

A few minutes later, the preparations were complete, and Riker tapped his comm panel. "*Shuttle 3* to bridge, requesting permission to launch."

"Crandall here," came the businesslike response. "You are cleared for launch, *Shuttle 3.* Lieutenant, I'd appreciate it if you returned in one piece. We've got lots of supplies that need to be delivered. Good fortune to you."

"Thank you, sir," answered Riker cheerfully. His fortune hadn't been all that good, and he was ready for a change in that department. For Commander Crandall, these few words were as close as she had ever come to bubbly enthusiasm. He punched up a wide view of the area on his viewscreen and kept it on during the launch.

The *Galaxy*-class starship hung suspended in space among the dazzling stars, appearing much like her better-known sister ship, the *Enterprise.* Double doors slid open atop the immense saucer section, and a tiny shuttlecraft darted out, looking like an insect escaping from an open window. The Type-8 shuttlecraft cruised to a distance of several thousand kilometers from the *Gandhi,* then with a flash of light, she disappeared into warp.

Chapter Three

LIEUTENANT RIKER CUT impulse engines and slowed the shuttlecraft to a stately drift through a sea of widely scattered asteroids. Some were only a few meters wide, while others were several kilometers wide. Slowly they approached a monstrous rock that was over eight kilometers in diameter. It was as dark as obsidian, yet its center appeared even darker. Riker needed a few seconds to realize that the asteroid had a mammoth hole in its middle, at least one kilometer across. In comparison with the black asteroid and the blackness of space, the chasm looked even darker—like a black hole.

Despite the deserted appearance of this region, these were the correct coordinates. "Open up a secure channel," he told Shelzane.

"Yes, sir," replied the fish-faced, blue-skinned Benzite, working her board with webbed fingers. "Channel open."

He tapped his panel and said, *"Shuttle 3* to outpost, this is Lieutenant Riker from the *Gandhi,* requesting permission to dock."

"Permission granted," answered a pleasant female voice. *"Shuttle 3,* are we glad to see you. Take dock one, the first open dock to starboard."

"Thank you."

"We're lowering shields and force field. Proceed when ready."

With a flash of light, the dark cavity in the asteroid turned into a blazing neon pit. Pulsing beacons guided the way to a mammoth spacedock within, and the walls of the chasm glittered with sensors, dish arrays, and weapons. Trying not to be distracted by the remarkable sight, Riker spread his fingers over the conn and piloted the tiny shuttlecraft into the glowing heart of the asteroid.

"Well, it's about time," muttered one of the doctors behind him.

Riker ignored the crack, as he had ignored so many others during the past twenty hours. Although the ship's sensors claimed that life support was working flawlessly, he could swear that he was beginning to *smell* his passengers.

At least Ensign Shelzane had proven to be skilled, even-tempered, and unflappable. He had to give Commander Crandall credit—she was a good judge of personnel.

As they cruised toward the landing dock, Riker glanced around the cavernous installation. He was somewhat surprised to see several unfamiliar and battered ships docked at the rear bays; they didn't look like Starfleet vessels. This was supposed to be a secret outpost, but it looked more like a junkyard at the moment.

Shelzane noticed it, too, and her pale eyes darted to Riker before going back to her instruments. The lieutenant concentrated on the docking, although a first-year cadet could have hit that huge target. They sat down with a gentle thud, and the umbilicals began to whir.

When Riker heard the clamps latch on to the shuttle's hatch, he sat back in his chair and smiled at Shelzane. "We made it in one piece . . . without killing any of the passengers," he whispered.

The ensign nodded. She couldn't really smile, but her heavily lidded eyes twinkled with amusement. "This job will test my social skills more than my flying."

When the hatch opened, the medical team gathered around the exit, anxious to get off. *Nothing like twenty hours in a shuttlecraft with eight strangers to give one claustrophobia,* thought Riker. *Welcome to Starfleet.*

Without warning, the lights in the great cavern went out, eliciting gasps from the passengers. Once again, the void in the asteroid was as black as space, only without the glistening stars to give it some cheer. Seen from afar, the shuttlecraft glowed like a feeble lantern in a great hall.

A few of the passengers thanked him as they filed out, and Riker nodded pleasantly. He held nothing against them—in many respects, it was easier being a crew member than a passenger on a trip like this. At least he had been occupied. From eight years' experience, he knew how hard it was to pass the time when nothing needed doing and physical activity was difficult.

He and Shelzane shut down all but essential life support on the small craft, then they followed the medical team into the corridor. The last member of the team was just passing through a force-field security gate that demanded positive identification. Riker stepped back to let Shelzane go first, but she stepped back and deferred to him.

Oh, well, there's nothing else I can do, thought Riker. He placed his hand on the security scanner, and the computer's feminine voice declared, "Commander William Riker, access granted."

Shelzane looked quizzically at him. "*Commander* Riker? Did you receive a promotion during the trip?"

"Hardly," muttered the bearded man, making sure the med team was some distance down the next corridor. "It's a long story. On the return trip, I'll tell you about it. Let's just say that Starfleet security systems have a bug in them where I'm concerned."

He walked through the gate and waited for Ensign Shelzane to gain admittance to the outpost. "How long do you think we'll be here?" asked the Benzite.

"Maybe long enough to get a meal," answered Riker. "They're expecting us back as soon as possible for more of these runs. I'm afraid this assignment is going to be hectic but not all that exciting."

"We'll see," answered the Benzite cheerfully.

As the party stepped off the dock, they were met by two officers, both wearing the red uniforms of command. One was a bald-headed Deltan and the other was a tall, antennaed Andorian. Since both were male, neither one could be the friendly female with whom Riker had spoken earlier, he noted with disappointment.

The Andorian conducted the medical team down one corridor, while the Deltan nodded politely to the new arrivals. Two gold-shirted technicians strode into the landing dock behind them, and Riker assumed they would take charge of the cargo.

"Hello, Lieutenant Riker. Welcome to Outpost Sierra III," said the Deltan, with a slight smile. "I'm Ensign Parluna. I believe we met once aboard the *Enterprise.*"

Riker scowled. "That wasn't me."

"But weren't you first officer—"

"You're mistaken," said Riker brusquely. "Now if we could get a bite to eat, and maybe a walk to stretch our legs, we'll be on our way."

The Deltan nodded, but his hairless brow was still knit in puzzlement. "As you wish, sir. However, our commanding officer, Captain Tegmeier, was hoping to meet with you and ask a favor."

"A favor? We're just medical couriers—what could we do for your CO?"

"I'll let her ask," said Ensign Parluna. "But I will show you something on our way. Will you please follow me."

As they walked down a long doorless and windowless corridor, Riker could feel both of the ensigns looking curiously at him, wondering how Ensign Parluna could be mistaken about meeting him. For a while after being rescued from Nervala IV, he had taken the time to explain to people why they didn't know him, even though they had met someone who looked exactly like him. Now he didn't waste words. *Let them investigate his record and figure it out.* He hated being so brusque, but it did no good reliving his misfortune over and over again.

The Deltan took a left turn at a junction in the corridor, and they finally came to a row of doors. He opened one marked "Recreation," and Riker wondered if they would interrupt the CO during her exercise period. As soon as he got a glimpse inside the room, he knew he was wrong.

The room was full of bedraggled, sorry-looking people—men, women, and children—several of them dressed in rags. A few of them glanced at the visitors, but most stared straight ahead with vacant eyes. A handful of children were playing board games and watching video logs, but most of the people looked bored and disillusioned. Riker glanced at Shelzane, and he could see the young officer was deeply affected by the sight. Without saying a word, the Deltan ushered them out and closed the door.

"Refugees," he explained. "And these aren't even the wounded, sick ones—the ones who survived Cardassian torture and starvation. They're in sickbay, which we've had to enlarge twice. That's why we need the supplies and med team."

"I thought this was supposed to be a secret outpost," said Riker.

The Deltan sighed. "So did we. As you can see, the secret is out. They've been flooding in here ever since the treaty drove them from their homes in the DMZ."

"That's terrible!" blurted Shelzane.

"The price of peace," muttered the Deltan. "The awkward thing is that we can't let them leave here, because it's a secret base, even though everybody apparently *knows* about it. I mean, we can't let them leave in their own ships, most of which wouldn't get very far, anyway. So we have to impound their ships and hold them, until we can find official transportation to get them back to Earth . . . or wherever."

Riker crossed his arms. "I bet I could guess what this favor is."

"Let's go to the commissary," said the Deltan with forced cheer, "and you can have that meal you so richly deserve. The captain will join you there."

The lieutenant nodded, knowing he didn't have much choice. If these pathetic refugees were the price of peace, he wondered if it was worth it.

As he gobbled down the finest steak he had ever gotten from a food replicator, Riker watched Shelzane pick at the purple leaves on her plate. He felt sorry for the young Benzite, who evidently hadn't seen much of the cruelty and capriciousness of life. One moment, a person is on top of the world, living high in a Federation colony or on a sleek Starfleet vessel, and the next moment, he's wearing rags, staring at the ceiling, abandoned. Thomas Riker felt sorry for the refugees, but he had seen too much in his own eventful life to be shocked by their plight.

Shelzane glanced up, catching him looking at her. "What's going to happen to them?"

"They're going to start over," answered Riker. "They've lost everything, but they're still alive. A lot of people in the DMZ weren't so lucky. When it comes down to it, all we've got is our wits and tenacity."

"But Starfleet should try to help them," insisted Shelzane.

Riker shrugged. "On most issues, Starfleet employs Vulcan logic: the needs of the many outweigh the needs of the few. You'd better learn that, Ensign."

She peered intently at him. "You're very cynical, Lieutenant."

"Just realistic. I was once idealistic like you. It's good to be like that for as long as you can, but I have a feeling that this assignment is going to break you of that."

Shelzane looked down at her plate and whispered, "They say that some Starfleet officers are going over to the Maquis—to fight against the Cardassians in a hopeless cause. I feel sorry for the refugees, but I can't imagine ever doing something like that."

"Me neither," agreed Riker. "I don't think I could ever feel that strongly about something. As you say, I'm too cynical." He took another bite of steak.

"Around here, cynicism is good," interjected another feminine voice.

Riker looked up to see an attractive blond woman approaching their table. Since she was wearing captain's pips, he jumped to his feet, certain he was about to meet the commanding officer of the outpost. Shelzane did the same.

"Relax," said the captain wearily. "We don't stand on ceremony around here. What good would it do us? I'm Captain Alicia Tegmeier."

"It's a pleasure," said Riker, recognizing her friendly voice from his initial contact with the outpost. "I'm Lieutenant Riker, and this is Ensign Shelzane. Won't you have a seat?"

"Thank you."

"We were a bit surprised to see the scope of your refugee problem," Shelzane explained.

"So were we," answered the captain. "We were hoping the *Gandhi* herself would come, and we could off-load the refugees, but it didn't happen that way. So now I've got to beg—can you take a few of them back to the *Gandhi* with you?"

"Certainly," Shelzane answered quickly.

Riker shot her a glance, and the Benzite lowered her eyes, knowing she had answered out of turn. Riker sounded very cautious as he remarked, "It's not really in the purview of our mission to transport refugees. However, if you ordered us to do so, we'd have no choice."

Captain Tegmeier slumped back in her chair and waved her hand. "Then I order you to take as many as you can. I'm sure I'll get chewed out for that by the admiralty, but I welcome an opportunity to explain the situation to them. Having a secret outpost overrun with refugees is a bit of a security risk."

"We only have seating for six," said Riker. "How will you choose who goes?"

"We have two pregnant women in the group," said the captain. "I'd like to send them first. We're not exactly equipped for dealing with newborn babies here. A young couple showed up yesterday, and they claim they have intelligence to report, but they will only tell an admiral. There are several orphaned children—I'd like to give two of them a break."

Riker shook his head in amazement. "How long can you cope with this?"

"Not much longer, but we've been assured that Starfleet will eventually pick them all up. Then we'll relocate this asteroid. At least now we can cope with the medical problems, thanks to you." Captain Tegmeier gave him a warm smile.

"I wish we could stay longer," answered Riker with sincerity.

"We could use you," replied Tegmeier. "We have to stay on constant vigil—not only are there the refugees, but the Cardassians are experts at sneaking in and out of the DMZ. By the time we've discovered them, they're usually gone."

"We'll report back on the conditions here," said Riker.

"I wish you would."

With her napkin, Ensign Shelzane daintily wiped the tendrils around her mouth. "I'm ready to go when you are, sir."

"Right." The handsome lieutenant managed a smile and pushed himself away from the table. "Is the cargo off the shuttle?"

"Yes, it is," answered Captain Tegmeier. "Do you want to interview any of the passengers you'll be taking?"

"No, I trust your judgment. It's been a short but pleasant visit, Captain."

"I'd like to encourage you to come often. Have a safe journey back, Lieutenant . . . Ensign." She turned and strode through the commissary, nodding encouragment to the officers she passed.

Riker began to think that his new assignment would be a good change of pace. Out here on the edge of the DMZ, he had no bizarre history or hierarchy of command to deal with—he was just a medical courier bringing much-needed supplies. He would make his deliveries and go on to the next post, like the pony express. There would always be new people to meet.

He smiled at Shelzane. "I think I'm going to like this job."

The ensign looked thoughtful. "It's fortunate that Benzites require little sleep."

"Good, then I'll let you take the first shift."

Ten minutes later, they were sitting in the cockpit of *Shuttle 3,* going over the preflight checklist. In the cavernous interior of the asteroid, it was still eerily dark, and the windows of the shuttlecraft looked opaque. Without passengers and cargo, the cabin almost looked spacious, and Riker wished it would stay that way for a while. However, it was not to be.

The hatch opened, and a security officer stuck his head in. "Lieutenant Riker, are you ready to receive your passengers?"

"Sure. I hope they're not expecting a starship."

"This is better than they're used to." The security officer stepped aside, allowing two small Bynar children to enter the cabin. Whether they were actual siblings was hard to tell, but the two of them had bonded in their desperate situation; they held hands as if they were inseparable.

"Sit up front," Riker told them with a smile, "so you can watch Ensign Shelzane pilot the ship."

"Thank you," they replied in unison, speaking so softly they could barely be heard. They both squeezed into one seat, and Riker didn't bother to separate them.

The Bynar children were followed by two females, both obviously in the advanced stages of pregnancy. One was Coridan, judging by her distinctive hairstyle—half of her head sheared and the other half with straight, black hair down to her shoulder. She looked morose, as if resigned to some horrible fate, and she slouched to the back row of seats without a word. He guessed that the other woman was human, until she smiled at him and shook her head.

"Actually I'm a Betazoid," she said.

"I've always gotten along well with Betazoids," he replied.

"I can tell you have great affection for us."

Their conversation was cut short when a young Tiburonian couple entered the cabin, holding hands as tightly as the Bynar children had. With their bald heads and elephantine ears, they looked more alien than the others, and Riker recalled that Tiburonians had a reputation for being brilliant but difficult. These two looked wary.

"We were told we'd be going to a large starship," said the male.

"You will be, as soon as we get there," answered Riker. "I understand you have some intelligence to report."

"But only in a face-to-face meeting with an admiral," insisted the female.

"I've found admirals highly overrated, but we'll find one for you. Have a seat, please."

Once all the passengers were situated, Riker turned to address them. "I'm Lieutenant Riker, and this is Ensign Shelzane. I know all of you have had a tough time, and I would like this trip to be as pleasant as possible. But we don't have many amenities on this shuttlecraft, and the quarters will be tight. In other words, you'll basically have to sit there and not make demands on us. If you do that, I promise we'll get you to our starship as quickly as possible."

"How long will the trip take?" asked the dour Coridan.

Riker glanced at Shelzane, who consulted her computer screen. "If the *Gandhi* stays on course and schedule, it should be about twenty-six hours," she reported.

"The sooner we get going, the sooner we'll arrive." Riker tapped the comm panel. "*Shuttle 3* to operations, requesting permission to leave."

"You are cleared," replied a businesslike male voice. "Please maintain subspace silence in the vicinity of the station."

Beacons suddenly illuminated the depths of the great chasm, and hydraulics whirred as the docking mechanism retracted from the hatch. Riker sat back in his seat and smiled at Shelzane. "Take her out, Ensign."

"Yes, sir," replied the Benzite, sounding eager to prove herself. With considerable skill, she plied her console, and the tiny craft lifted off the dock and moved gracefully through the neon pit. Riker crossed his arms and closed his eyes, planning on getting a little shut-eye.

Once the tiny shuttle had cleared the opening of the chasm, the brilliant lights abruptly went off, and Outpost Sierra III again looked like nothing but a craggy rock floating in the vastness of space.

Thomas Riker laughed and shook his head, then he put the computer padd down. For the third straight time, the Bynar children had beaten him in a game of three-dimensional tic-tac-toe. "You guys are too good for me."

They gave him identical, enigmatic smiles and looked at one another with satisfaction. "We thank you," said one.

"For the game," finished the other.

"Would you like to play each other?" he asked.

"That would be—"

"Pointless."

Riker nodded and looked back at the other passengers on the shuttlecraft. They were a surly lot, except for the pregnant Betazoid, who occasionally flashed him a smile. The rest of the time she sat in contemplative silence with her hands folded over her extended abdomen. He didn't expect refugees who had been driven from their homes to be exactly cheerful, but they might be a bit more grateful for the ride back to Federation space.

Then again, maybe they didn't know what they were getting themselves into. Most of them had probably been born in what was now the DMZ, and they had lived all their lives there. To them, the Federation was a nebulous concept, especially now that it had seemingly deserted them. He wondered whether the two pregnant women had spouses and families to help them, or whether they were as alone as they appeared.

"You're wondering about me," said the Betazoid woman with a wan smile. "I happen to be alone, although not for long." She patted her ample girth.

"I'm sorry," said Riker. With the others watching and listening, he wished he were also telepathic, so they could continue this conversation in private. But privacy was hard to come by on *Shuttle 3*.

"I've never seen Betazed," said the woman. "Have you?"

"It's beautiful," he assured her. "The garden spot of the Federation, with the friendliest people I've ever met." He paused, thinking about Lwaxana Troi. "Even too friendly."

She nodded eagerly. "I always meant to go there one day. I didn't think it would be . . . under these circumstances."

Unable to say or do anything that would change the circumstances, the lieutenant turned to his co-pilot. "How are you doing, Ensign? Getting tired?"

"It's only been three hours," answered the Benzite. "Perhaps in two hours more, I could use relief."

"Just let me know when you're ready. That short nap refreshed me."

The young Tiburonian male rose to his feet. "Is it all right if I stretch my legs?"

"Sure," answered Riker, "but there's not much place to go."

"I realize that." With two steps, he stood behind Riker and Shelzane, gazing with interest at the ensign's readouts. "Where are we, approximately?"

"We have just passed the Omicron Delta region," she answered.

"Then we're still fairly close to the DMZ."

"Yes. That is where the *Gandhi* is patrolling."

"Are you a navigator?" asked Riker.

The Tiburonian nodded. "In a way, I am. I was studying stellar cartography at the university on Ennan VI . . . until the Cardassians burned it down."

"I'm sorry," said Shelzane.

He scowled. "If you two keep saying you're sorry for every wrong committed against us, that's all you'll ever say to us. At some point, we have to stop feeling sorry for ourselves and get on with life."

"That's a good attitude," replied Riker, giving him a sympathetic smile. "We'll do what we can to help you."

"I know you will." The Tiburonian again studied the readouts with a scholarly interest. "Our speed is warp three? That's very fast for a craft of this size."

"Common for a Type-8 shuttle," answered Shelzane.

The Tiburonian sighed. "Where I come from, we only had impulse shuttles. Had we ships like this, more of us might have survived."

"Kanil," said the female Tiburonian, "there's no sense talking about it."

"No, I suppose not." His shoulders drooped, and he turned to Riker. "I don't suppose you have any food on board?"

Before the lieutenant could answer, there came an awful groan from the rear of the shuttlecraft. He whirled around to see the pregnant Coridan gripping her swollen stomach and writhing in her seat. The Betazoid woman staggered to her feet and tried to comfort her, as did the female Tiburonian, while the Bynar children looked on with eerie calm.

Immediately, Riker reached under his console, opened a panel, and grabbed a medkit. His worst fear was that he would have to deliver a premature baby, when he knew very little about delivering babies and less about Coridan physiology. But a groaning, pregnant woman demanded action. He glanced at Shelzane, who gave him a nod, as if to say she would handle the shuttle while he handled the medical emergency.

He vaulted to his feet and muscled his way past the Tiburonian male, who seemed rooted to the spot, unable to move. When he reached the distressed woman, she was panting, and her eyes rolled back in her head. The other women stepped away to allow him room, although what he was going to do for her he didn't know.

"Are you in labor?" he asked urgently. "How far along are you?"

"Not . . . far . . . enough," she muttered through clenched teeth. "The pain . . . the *pain!*"

"I can do something for the pain." Riker opened the medkit and reached inside for a hypospray. While he loaded the instrument with a painkiller, he felt a slight shudder, as if the shuttlecraft were coming out of warp. He turned to tell Shelzane that she didn't need to leave warp—it was better to keep going. That's when he saw the Benzite lying unconscious on the deck, with the Tiburonian seated at the conn.

"What the—"

He never finished the sentence, because the Coridan grabbed him by the shoulders with incredible strength and forced him headfirst into her lap. He struggled, but the young Tiburonian woman also attacked him; the two of them forced him onto his back and jumped upon him like women possessed.

Riker didn't like hitting women, but his instincts took over. He lashed out with his fist and smashed the Coridan in the mouth, sending her oversized body crashing back into her seat. Then he gripped the Tiburonian by the throat and tried to push her away, while she clawed at his face.

From the corner of his eye, he saw the Betazoid fumbling in the arms locker, pulling out a phaser pistol. Whose side was *she* on? Or were they all hijackers! He didn't have time to figure it out.

Riker grabbed the Tiburonian and yanked her around like a shield just as the Betazoid fired at him. The young woman took the full blast of the phaser set to stun, and she fell upon him like a dead weight. With adrenaline coursing through his veins, Riker tossed her off and scrambled to his feet, just as another phaser blast streaked past his head. He saw the Bynar children crouched behind their chairs, watching with wide eyes.

"Don't resist!" ordered the Betazoid, aiming her weapon to get another shot. "We won't hurt you!"

The only weapon at hand was the medkit, and Riker threw it at her with all his might. His aim was good, and the metal box bounced off her head with a thud, causing her to collapse to the deck. Riker dove for the discarded phaser and came up with it just as the Coridan jumped on his back. She was as determined and as strong as a sumo wrestler, and she shoved his face into the deck. Twisting around, he smashed her in the mouth with an elbow, and she slid off his back with a groan.

Riker crawled out from under the dead weight and staggered to his feet. He checked to make sure that the phaser was set to low stun before he fired at both her and the Betazoid.

With all three women immobilized, he turned his attention to the Tiburonian male, who was furiously working the shuttle controls. "Move away from there!" he ordered hoarsely. "Or I'll shoot!"

When the man didn't move immediately, the lieutenant drilled him in the back with the phaser, and he sprawled over the conn. From the stationary stars visible through the window, Riker realized that they must have come to a full stop.

The only ones left to subdue were the Bynar children, and they seemed content to stare at him with a mixture of curiosity and fear. *What kind of world is this?* Panting heavily, Riker stumbled into the cockpit to see how much damage the hijackers had done. He knew the Maquis were desperate, but to hijack an unarmed shuttlecraft was ridiculous!

He bent over Ensign Shelzane to check for a pulse and make sure she was still alive. She was, although a contusion on her skull was staining her blue skin with violet blood. Lying on the deck beside her was a length of metal pipe, obviously the weapon the Tiburonian had used to disable her. At least he had put down the hijacking and gained control of the ship—for the next several minutes. He had to act fast before the attackers came to.

Keeping an eye on the Bynar children, he set down the phaser pistol and grabbed the medkit to attend to his wounded comrade. Just as he loaded a hypospray with a coagulant, Riker felt a peculiar tingle along his spine. In the next instant, he realized it wasn't peculiar at all—it was a sensation he had felt many times. A transporter beam had locked onto him!

Riker reached for the phaser pistol, but his hand had already started to dematerialize—he couldn't close his fingers around it. Helpless, he stared at the Bynar children, and they stared back like porcelain dolls, until everything in the shuttlecraft faded from view.

Chapter Four

Lieutenant Riker materialized not on a transporter pad as he expected, but directly inside an old-fashioned brig, with bars across the door. He charged forward and smashed into the bars, rattling them but not doing any real damage. The outer door whooshed open, and a wild-eyed Klingon woman entered, wielding a Ferengi phaser rifle.

At least she *looked* Klingon, although closer inspection led him to wonder, because her forehead ridges were not very pronounced. But the contemptuous scowl on her face sure made her look Klingon. "Back away!" she said with a snarl.

"Or what?" he demanded. "You'll hijack my shuttlecraft? You've already done that. But maybe you want to torture me—see if I know anything."

"The captain will be here in a moment," she replied. "Just shut up until then."

"What vessel is this? Are you Maquis . . . or something else?"

"This is the *Spartacus,*" said an authoritative male voice.

Riker turned to see a commanding figure in a tan jacket enter the brig. He stared, because it appeared as if the dark-haired man had a maze tattooed on his forehead. Whatever outfit this was, it sure wasn't Starfleet.

"I'm Captain Chakotay," said the man, meeting Riker's hostile gaze. "And, yes, we are Maquis. Despite that, we mean you no harm."

"People keep telling me that," muttered Riker, "but somehow I don't believe it. You cracked open my co-pilot's skull, and you attacked us without provocation."

"Your co-pilot is receiving medical attention right now." Chakotay gave

Riker a grudging smile. "And it sounds like you defended yourself fairly well. I'm glad we backed up our infiltration team, but we can't afford to leave anything to chance."

Riker shook his head in disbelief. "All this to hijack an unarmed shuttlecraft? If that's the scope of your ambition, it's a wonder Starfleet pays any attention to you at all."

"Shut up!" snapped the Klingon woman, threatening him with the phaser rifle.

"Stow it, B'Elanna," ordered the Maquis captain. "He's got a right to be angry. Don't worry, Lieutenant, it's not you or your shuttlecraft we want. It's your cargo."

"What cargo?"

"Aren't you carrying medical supplies?"

"We were, but we're empty on our return trip."

Chakotay scowled in anger and stepped over to a comm panel beside the door. He slammed it with a clenched fist. "Chakotay to bridge. Do we have a report yet on what they found on the shuttle?"

"Yes, Captain," answered a calm male voice. "We found only personnel—our own and the shuttlecraft's co-pilot."

"You're sure of that?"

"Yes, sir. No supplies were found on the shuttlecraft, other than standard-issue medkits. The wounded parties have been transferred to the *Singha* for medical attention."

From the captain's clenched jaw, Riker assumed this was very bad news. "All that trouble for nothing," he grumbled. "Chakotay out."

"Not for nothing," said the woman called B'Elanna. She glared at Riker. "We still have *him* and the shuttlecraft. And he's a doctor."

Riker shook his head. "No, I'm not—I'm just a medical courier who was in the wrong place at the wrong time. But I don't get this—if your people needed medical attention, why don't you just join the refugees? You could turn yourselves in."

With a heave of his broad shoulders, Chakotay stepped closer to Riker. "It's not us. We've got several million people in extreme danger who can't be moved. B'Elanna, open the cell door."

"What?" asked the Klingon in shock.

"Let him out. If we're going to help them, the lieutenant has got to help us of his free will."

Looking as if she disagreed wholeheartedly with this decision, the woman stepped back and pulled a lever on the other side of the room. She kept her phaser rifle trained on Riker as the bars retracted into the bulkhead.

"I'm not joining the Maquis," declared the prisoner as he stepped forward.

"I'm not asking you to," said Chakotay. "I'm asking you to help us save millions of lives. I presume that's why you joined the medical branch—to save lives."

Riker remained tight-lipped, unwilling to admit that altruism had only been one of several reasons, and maybe not the most important. He had already decided to say and do as little as possible, while waiting for a chance to escape.

The Klingon woman scowled. "Do you have a name, Starfleet?"

His lips thinned, because Riker knew he was on shaky ground. Anything he did to help these people could land him in a brig for the rest of his life, but antagonizing them could get him killed. *Better to keep my mouth shut.*

B'Elanna walked over to the comm panel and hit it with her fist. "Torres to bridge. Tuvok, have you tapped into the shuttle's computer yet?"

"Yes, I have," answered the same efficient voice that had answered them before.

"What's the name of our guest in the brig?"

"The computer identifies him as William T. Riker."

Chakotay blinked with surprise and stared more closely at his prisoner. "Are you the same William T. Riker who served aboard the *Enterprise?"*

Riker's jaw clamped shut, and he took a deep breath. Unfortunately, if he admitted to being *that* Riker, his chances of escape from this crew would be nil.

"Come on, Starfleet, answer," said B'Elanna Torres, leveling her phaser rifle at him. "Every prisoner of war is allowed to give his name, rank, and serial number."

"I'm not the Riker who serves aboard the *Enterprise,"* he finally answered. "In a transporter accident on Nervala IV, I was duplicated. My double left the planet and went on to serve aboard the *Enterprise,* while I got stranded there for eight years. I was only rescued two years ago, and now I'm assigned to the *Gandhi."*

"You expect us to believe that?" scoffed Torres.

"I don't really give a damn what you believe!" snapped Riker. "What are you people but a bunch of two-bit space pirates? I find *you* hard to believe."

Torres started to swing the butt of her phaser rifle at his head, but Chakotay gripped the rifle and stopped her. "Calm down! We haven't got time for this. Whether he's William Riker or Santa Claus, it doesn't matter—he's the only link we've got to the medical supplies we need."

Breathing heavily, the woman tried to shake off her anger, but a fire still burned in her dark eyes. Despite his status as her enemy, Riker couldn't help but feel a kinship with this volatile woman. Like him, she harbored a bitterness and anger that couldn't be easily assuaged.

"What race are you?" he asked.

"I'm half-Klingon and half-human," she answered with some resentment. "I guess we're both freaks."

Chakotay waved his hand impatiently. "There's time to get to know each other later. Right now, Lieutenant Riker, I have to show you something."

"What if I don't want to see it?"

"I think you'll want to see it, because after you do, I'll let you go."

"Just like that?"

"Just like that. You can't do us any good stuck in this cell, but you can save a lot of lives if you're free. Let's go." The captain led the way out the door, and Riker followed, conscious of B'Elanna Torres at his back, aiming her phaser rifle at him.

After walking a few meters down a narrow corridor, Chakotay came to a ladder embedded in the bulkhead, and he climbed upward into a small hatch. With a glance over his shoulder at Torres, Riker followed the captain, and they emerged in a longer and wider corridor. Riker got the impression that the *Spartacus* was a rather small vessel, no more than a scout ship or an assault craft.

Chakotay strode down the corridor like a man with pressing matters on his conscience and time running out. He carried himself like a Starfleet officer, and Riker wondered whether he had ever served in Starfleet. Perhaps he had previously captained a merchant ship. What made a proud, competent man like this turn into a rebel in a ragtag fleet? These were the first Maquis he had ever met, and Captain Chakotay, at least, didn't fit his preconceptions.

B'Elanna Torres, on the other hand, was more the kind of person he thought would be attracted to the Maquis. She seemed a bit unstable, low in self-esteem, and angry at life. In short, she was damaged goods. Her Klingon side probably relished the prospect of dying a glorious death battling the imperious and callous Federation.

Riker knew he was damaged goods, too—a freak, as Torres had called them both. But he still had some ambition and loyalty to the Federation. Sure, the Federation was run by fallible beings who could make mistakes, but it was still the greatest hope for peace in the galaxy. He couldn't imagine what Chakotay could show him that would turn him against everything he believed in.

They entered a compact, clam-shaped bridge, and a Vulcan swiveled in his chair to glance at Riker before turning back to his instruments. *A Vulcan Maquis?* Of course, Vulcans could go mad—he had heard of it happening. Maybe everyone on the *Spartacus* was mad, even the dignified Chakotay.

Through the narrow cockpit window, he saw a Bajoran assault vessel off the bow, as well as his own star-crossed shuttlecraft. What could the

Maquis hope to accomplish with these three little ships out here in the middle of nowhere, a stone's throw from the DMZ? Like the attack on his shuttlecraft, this whole thing was surreal.

"Before you show me anything," said Riker, "I want to make sure that my co-pilot, Ensign Shelzane, is all right."

"Tuvok, hail the *Singha,"* ordered Chakotay, "and have them put Ensign Shelzane on screen."

"Yes, sir."

"While he does that," said the captain, "let me ask you if you've ever heard of a planet named Helena."

Riker nodded. "I know it was on a list of planets in the DMZ that were turned over to the Cardassians."

"Yes, but it wasn't evacuated like most of the Federation colonies. The Helenites chose to stay and live under Cardassian rule, but something terrible has happened there."

"I have located Ensign Shelzane," interjected the Vulcan.

"On screen."

Riker turned with interest to the small viewscreen spanning the front of the bridge. The blank image switched to a view of a bustling sickbay, and Ensign Shelzane was lying on an examination table with a fresh bandage around her head. Upon seeing Riker, the blue-skinned humanoid sat up weakly.

"At ease, Ensign," he told her. "Have you been treated well?"

"As well as can be expected, I suppose. What happened to the shuttlecraft?"

"The passengers attacked us, stopped the shuttle, and then we were intercepted by these two Maquis vessels. Cooperate, but remember that you're a prisoner of war."

"Yes, sir. Are we going to be held long? Or exchanged?"

"I don't know." Riker glanced at Chakotay, who stepped in front of the screen.

"You and Lieutenant Riker will be released soon, along with your shuttlecraft," promised the captain. "Please try to rest. I'm sorry that our methods were violent, but Starfleet won't negotiate with *us,* only Cardassians." He motioned to the Vulcan, who ended the transmission.

"Satisfied, Lieutenant?" asked B'Elanna Torres.

Riker shrugged. He wasn't going to argue with someone who was aiming a phaser rifle at him.

"Tuvok," said the captain, "put on the vid log and explain matters to the lieutenant."

The Vulcan tapped his console. On the viewscreen appeared a beautiful, aquamarine planet, sparkling in the vivid light from a distant red sun. The surface of the planet had to be ninety percent ocean, with small green continents scattered across its vast waters. Riker had seen many Class-M planets, but none more lovely than this one.

"Helena," said Tuvok matter-of-factly. "It was a thriving world, inhabited by over four million people, mostly of mixed-species ancestry. The only thing that has protected them so far is the relative isolation of population centers on the various islands and continents."

The image shifted to a modern city street, which appeared to be deserted, despite sunny blues skies and balmy weather. Some kind of dead animal lay in the gutter, and there appeared to be a hunanoid corpse sprawled in an open doorway. Trash and leaves skittered across the empty thoroughfare, borne by a gentle breeze. It was an eerie scene, reminiscent of a planet ravaged by warfare, only without the full-scale destruction.

"This is the city of Padulla," explained Tuvok, "as we observed it four days ago. The streets are deserted, because a devastating plague has struck this continent. The disease is similar to anthrax, only several times more deadly and contagious. It is caused by an unusual combination of three prions, which are transmitted by air, water, saliva, and other bodily fluids."

Now the view changed to the interior of some cavernous hall, where sick people lay in haphazard rows stretching the length of the room. It wasn't a hospital, so Riker had to assume the hospitals were all full. Coughs and groans filled the disturbing scene. Two visitors in white environmental suits moved among the sick like ghosts, or angels. When the video log showed close-up views of dying people with distended stomachs, blackened faces, and open sores, Riker had to look away.

"I get the picture," he muttered. "But the Cardassians must have the technology to deal with this. As you said, it's now a Cardassian planet."

"The Cardassians have abandoned them," answered Tuvok, "except to station ships in orbit to stop any attempt by the inhabitants to leave the planet. Cardassian troops on the ground have destroyed ships and spaceports and shut off all communication with the outside. A quarantine is in effect, and the entire populace has been left to die."

"Maybe the Cardassians did this," suggested Riker. "They're not above using biological warfare."

B'Elanna Torres shoved him in the back with her weapon. "You're a cold fish, aren't you? It *is* biological warfare, only the Cardassians didn't do it."

"How do you know that?"

"Because it's the same plague that nearly wiped them out on Terok Nor four years ago." When Riker gave her a questioning look, she added, "It's now called Deep Space Nine."

Chakotay shook his head. "We don't know that for sure, B'Elanna."

"Oh, don't we? When we've conquered almost every disease known to science, how could an illness with the exact same symptoms pop up again? And look at the way the Cardassians have reacted. They don't want any part of that planet, except to bury it."

"She's right," said another feminine voice.

Riker turned to see a tall, attractive Bajoran standing in the corridor. She stepped onto the crowded bridge, her nose ridges furrowed with concern. "I'm sorry to interrupt, Captain, but I couldn't help but to listen. B'Elanna is right—this is the same plague that struck Terok Nor and the work camps on Bajor, I'm sure of it. I recognized the symptoms the moment I saw them. Only this version seems to spread even faster."

"Thanks, Seska," said B'Elanna with relief. "There's too much at stake here to ignore the past. Going over Starfleet records has made me think that this plague has appeared several times before—in widely separated areas of the quadrant. There was a similar plague on Archaria III, and it affected people who are half-human and mixed-blood. Then came Bajor, and a virus linked to it hit the Romulan royal family just two years ago. What are the chances of that?"

She peered into Riker's eyes. "Ask yourself, why *this* planet? Why *now?* Helena is as advanced as any planet in the Federation, but it's been cut off, abandoned. Nobody cares what happens there. You couldn't pick a more helpless place. But we still have time to help them, because of the distances across those huge oceans."

Riker sighed and held out his hands. "I'm one medical courier with a shuttlecraft. What do you expect me to do?"

"The Maquis are warriors, not healers," said Chakotay. "We're rounding up all the doctors and nurses we've got, but we only have a handful of them. Plus we don't have enough drugs or research equipment to do the job. *You* have access to everything we need."

Riker felt trapped on the cramped bridge, torn between doing his duty and doing what was right. His preconceptions about the Maquis had crumbled even further, and he felt as if he understood them. They were not wild-eyed pirates and opportunists; they were people trying to help other people. The Federation had abandoned the colonists in the DMZ, but the Maquis hadn't—it was as simple as that.

"Is there a drug that's proven effective against this disease?" he asked.

"To a degree," answered Tuvok. "According to Starfleet records, Tricillin PDF can prolong life, but it is not a cure. When the prions combine into a multiprion in the host's body, death can result in as quickly as forty-eight hours. The multiprion can be removed via a transporter biofilter, but that is extremely time consuming. The best way to stop the spread of the disease is to find the transmission vectors and shut them off. That is precisely what the Cardassians are doing with their quarantine."

"What about the Cardassians?" asked Riker. "If they've decided to let everyone die on that planet, won't they fight you?"

"Leave the Cardassians to us," said Chakotay. "They can sneak one or two ships into the DMZ, but they can't send a fleet without alerting Starfleet and violating the treaty."

"At least the treaty is good for something," grumbled Torres. "So will you help us?"

Riker paused before answering, although he knew he would say yes. His first duty was to reclaim his shuttlecraft and his co-pilot and get away from these people. After that, when he had time to think about it logically, he would decide how far to go in helping them.

"All right," he murmured. "Do you have those records you've been talking about?"

Tuvok nodded and pulled an isolinear chip from his console. "This also contains the video log you saw."

Riker took the chip, but as he withdrew his hand, B'Elanna Torres caught his wrist in a tight grip. "Can we trust you, William T. Riker?"

He didn't pull his hand away, because her touch was warm and charged with life. As he gently pried her fingers from his wrist, he gave her a charming smile. "Call me Tom."

"Okay, Tom." She smiled back, but it wasn't a friendly look.

"We'll meet you right here, at these coordinates," said Chakotay. "How soon do you think you can get back?"

He shrugged. "I would guess two or three days. I'll have to fake a requisition or divert supplies going somewhere else."

"If we see anything but a shuttlecraft coming toward us, we'll head into the DMZ," warned Chakotay. "And the deaths of millions of people will be on your conscience."

"I've already got a lot on my conscience," said Riker. "Can I go now?"

Chakotay nodded. "Seska, will you escort him to the transporter room?"

"Yes, sir." The Bajoran motioned to Riker, then led the way into the corridor.

When they were gone, Chakotay remarked to Torres, "Do you know how much help he can be to us?"

"You mean, with medical supplies?" she asked.

"Not just that. If he can impersonate the first officer of the *Enterprise,* he can gain admittance anywhere. The possibilities are endless. We have to try to recruit him."

"I thought we just did."

"I hope so," said Chakotay, his eyes narrowing.

• • •

In the briefing room of the *Gandhi,* Captain Azon Lexen and Commander Emma Crandall sat in stunned silence after viewing the video log and hearing Riker's story. In addition to the three of them, two other people were present: Ensign Shelzane and Lieutenant Patrick Kelly, an expert on the Maquis. Captain Lexen was a Trill joined with a symbiont who had lived six lifetimes, and even he appeared at a loss for words.

Finally Emma Crandall scowled and turned to Shelzane. "Do you corroborate Lieutenant Riker's story?"

The Benzite gingerly touched the small scar on her head. "I can't corroborate all the details, but I know we were attacked by the passengers. Looking back now, I can see that the distress of the pregnant woman was a diversion. When Lieutenant Riker went to attend to her, one of the other passengers must have hit me on the head. I only know that I woke up in sickbay on a Maquis ship with this head wound.

"But I believe Lieutenant Riker must have acquitted himself fairly well, because the passengers who revolted were also receiving medical attention." Shelzane glanced at Riker, and he gave her an appreciative nod.

"I actually regained control of the shuttle," he explained. "But before we could leave, the Maquis ships arrived and transported me directly to their brig."

"And then they showed you this video log and told you about the plague on Helena?" asked Crandall, sounding suspicious.

"After they found out we weren't carrying any medical supplies," Riker added. "That's all they were looking for."

"Did you hear the names of any of these Maquis officers?" asked the captain.

"No," lied Riker immediately. He didn't know why he lied about that, except that he felt oddly guilty about betraying the Maquis' confidence. Perhaps Chakotay, B'Elanna Torres, and the others were known Maquis, but if they weren't, he wouldn't be the one to identify them.

"What can you tell us about their ship?" asked Captain Lexen.

Riker shook his head. "It was small, older, nothing special. They weren't about to show me around. I've told you the truth, sir. I can't imagine that sending a med team and supplies to Helena will give the Maquis any strategic advantage, and it could save millions of lives."

"So you want to collaborate with the enemy?" Crandall asked snidely.

"I want to save lives," answered Riker, appealing to the captain. "If we don't cooperate, they'll just keep attacking our ships until they get what they want. And if any sick Helenites escape from the planet and reach Federation space . . . I don't need to tell you what might happen."

The Trill pursed his lips and rubbed the dark spots on his right temple.

"I'm inclined to agree with you, Lieutenant, but I can't *order* anyone to go on a mission like this. You would have to depend upon the Maquis for protection, not us. We'll brief the medical teams, and if anyone wants to volunteer, you can take them. That is, if *you* wish to volunteer."

"I do."

"Count me in, too," said Shelzane, nodding her fishlike head resolutely.

"Sir, I strongly advise against this course of action," declared Commander Crandall.

"Duly noted." Captain Lexen rose to his feet. "These are strange times, and they require strange deeds. Lieutenant Riker, take a shuttlecraft and strip all the Federation signage; requisition the supplies you need. I myself will brief the medical staff and ask for volunteers."

"Yes, sir," replied Riker. "You should also tell Starfleet to get those refugees off Outpost Sierra III, and give them all a good interrogation."

"Good idea. If you confront Cardassians, say you're on a private, humanitarian mission, or say you're a Helenite. Don't pose as members of the Maquis or Starfleet unless you have to. Wear civilian clothes, and take as many precautions as you need. Dismissed."

After the captain had left the briefing room, Crandall stopped Riker and whispered, "I don't know what you're up to, but I'll break you if you betray us."

Riker stared her down. "I figure there's a good chance you won't ever see me again. I'd love to kiss you before I go."

Crandall stared at him in shock, utterly speechless, but there was a yielding in her eyes that made him smile with victory. "I thought so." He strode away, still grinning.

Gul Demadak laughed heartily as he watched his grandson cling to the back of a Cardassian riding hound. The giant canine galloped around the show ring on the grounds of Demadak's estate, totally oblivious to the young boy who gripped his shaggy fur and screamed. The hound was well trained; the boy was not. The stocky Cardassian looked up, noting that the sky was a beautiful shade of amber, and the breeze was hot and sulfuric. It was a wonderful day on Cardassia Prime, and he wheezed a laugh as he reached for his mug of hot fish juice.

"Hold on to him, Denny!" he yelled, using his grandson's nickname. If the boy fell off, he wasn't too worried, because the ground in the ring was cushioned with several centimeters of black volcanic sand. Besides, Denny could use a little toughening.

Sure enough, the lad slid off the withers of the giant hound and plowed headfirst into the black sand. For the first time, the hound took notice of the boy as he doubled back to lick the sand off his face.

"Get back on!" shouted Gul Demadak from the sidelines. "You can do it, boy!"

He heard footsteps behind him, and he turned to see his servant, Mago, shuffling toward the ring. The old Cardassian looked more bent and cadaverous than usual, and there was a worried look on his scaly face.

Since Demadak had given orders not to be disturbed on his vacation, he rose to meet the old man with a mixture of irritation and concern. "What is it, Mago?"

"Sorry to interrupt, Sir," said the old retainer, lowering his head reverentially. "Legate Tarkon from the Central Command is on the emergency channel."

"Tarkon, eh?" Demadak tried not to show his apprehension over this bit of news. Tarkon was an old friend and comrade, but he was also his superior in the pecking order of the Central Command. He would never say it aloud, but Tarkon had become something of an annoyance since his recent promotion.

"I'll take the call. Watch my grandson, and make sure he doesn't kill himself."

"Yes, sir."

"And get him back on that hound!" ordered Demadak as he strode toward the house.

"Yes, sir," muttered the old man with resignation.

Upon reaching the house, the gul went to his private study and locked the door behind him. Although his wife and daughter were out, there were other servants in the house, and Demadak had not gotten where he was by being careless. Plastering a confident look onto his angular face, Demadak approached the communications console.

On the screen, Legate Tarkon scowled with impatience. "You kept me waiting."

"I'm glad to see you, too," said Demadak with forced joviality. "Thank you for bothering me on my vacation. I was having entirely too much fun."

"This is an emergency."

"What?" scoffed Demadak. "Has the Federation swarmed across the Demilitarized Zone?" The DMZ was *his* responsibility, and he resented anyone telling him how to manage it.

"Nothing quite so dramatic . . . yet. The Detapa Council summoned me this morning—they're very worried about that plague planet. What is it called?"

"Helena."

"Yes. They found out about our losing our troop transport, and they know the Maquis have taken charge."

Demadak laughed out loud. "The Maquis couldn't take charge of a garbage scow."

"The Detapa Council is worried about the civilian population if that plague gets loose."

"It's not going to," declared Demadak irritably. "We have a spy on the lead Maquis ship, and she informs us that they aren't planning to evacuate any of the Helenites. Even the Maquis aren't that stupid. Besides, where would they take them? But they are trying to cure the disease, and it's worth giving them a chance to do that. After all, we still have a garrison of soldiers on Helena, and we'd like to keep them alive."

Legate Tarkon warned darkly, "There's a faction on the council who would like to dispense with halfway measures and just destroy the planet."

"I'm sure there is. There's always a faction who want to destroy things, but in this case it's entirely unnecessary. It could also plunge us back into war with the Federation."

Tarkon shook his head worriedly. "You had better be right about this, my old friend, or no power in the galaxy will be able to protect you."

"Of course I'm right," insisted Demadak with more confidence than he felt. "As we've seen before, panic is worse than plague. The Detapa Council has no business meddling with military policies in the DMZ. Tell them to go back to reforming the nursery schools."

Tarkon chuckled, obviously relieved by Demadak's bravado. "I won't tell them that, but I will tell them that the situation is under control."

"You do that. I'll be back at headquarters in two days, and I'll file a report myself. Demadak out." As soon as the image of Legate Tarkon faded from the screen, so did the smile on Demadak's face.

His bony brow knit with concern, the Cardassian went to his door to make sure that no one was in the vicinity. He closed it and double-locked it. Then he went to his communications console and set it for a low frequency that was seldom used, except for antiquated satellite transmissions. There was a satellite in orbit around Cardassia Prime that was thought to be inactive. In truth, it was a subspace relay employing technology that was far more advanced than anything the Cardassians possessed.

Demadak's fingers trembled as they paused over the console. Even though his transmission would be encrypted and indecipherable to anyone but the intended recipient, he chose his words very carefully:

"Problem on test site. Outsiders present. Will try to delay overreaction from masters. Suggest you proceed to quick conclusion." He signed it with his codename, "Hermit."

When he sent it, a lump lodged deep in his throat. Demadak knew that his message would not be well received, and his secret benefactor would be very angry. Very angry, indeed.

Chapter Five

A CLEAR, GREEN OCEAN stretched before Echo Imjim like the facet of a gigantic emerald. Vast beds of seaweed shimmered beneath the glassy surface, looking like the fire inside the immense jewel. Echo spied a buoy far below them, and small, frothy waves lapped at the alien object floating in their midst. Elsewhere, a school of flying fish broke the surface and arced back into the water like a ghostly ripple. Otherwise, nothing disturbed the glistening calm of the West Ribbon Ocean.

The only sound in the cockpit of the sea-glider was a gentle rush of air through the struts and ailerons. Echo felt as if she could fly forever on this sweet air current, but she knew she had to get lower, even if it meant losing the current. She edged the antigrav lever down, putting the craft into a dive. The sea-glider swooped like a graceful albatross over waters that were now lime colored.

When the seaplane dropped down to about twenty meters above the surface, its pontoons looked liked webbed feet bracing for a landing on the water. But Echo had no intention of landing out here—she was just hoping to avoid Dalgren's sensors by flying below them. At least she still had the easterly wind she needed to stay on course to the west.

As a glider pilot since the age of ten, Echo couldn't believe that she had to sneak from one continent to another. In her opinion, the air currents and the lands they blessed should be as free to travel as the breeze. There had never been borders on Helena before; overnight, freedom had vanished.

Over the rush of air, she called to the back of the cockpit. "Are you all right, Lumpkin?"

"Sure, Mommy!" answered Harper. The ten-year-old boy fidgeted in his seat, but he was content to stare out the porthole at the glistening sea and wispy clouds. He had always been a good passenger, even as a baby, recalled his mother. "We're flying awfully low, aren't we?" he asked.

She laughed nervously. "It only looks that way. Good currents down here." Her son knew too much about antigravity gliding for her to lie to him for very long. He would be suspicious when she didn't go higher to look for faster, safer air currents. She sure hoped they could sneak into Dalgren without anyone throwing a fit.

What is the big deal? We aren't sick, and we don't even live in Padulla! It was only happenstance that they had gotten stuck there while making a private delivery. After all, they *lived* in Dalgren. She knew she had broken the new regulations; but they had their own transportation, and they should be allowed to go home.

Echo shook her antennae and peered out the porthole. Unlike a full-blooded Andorian, her skin was not blue but a wrinkled gray, thanks to her Mizarian ancestry. However, she was much taller and stronger than any Mizarian who ever lived, and she could thank the blue-skinned side of her family for that.

She glanced at Harper, who was also gray but with blunted antennae and smoother features, thanks to the Troyian blood of his father. Ever since she heard about the plague, Echo had been watching her son like a seabird watches the kelp, but she had seen no signs of illness. If anything, he looked like he was going through a growth spurt.

"There's a flock of gliders," said Harper, pointing upward.

"What?" Scrunching lower in her seat, Echo peered into the glare of the reddish sun. High in the sky, at eleven o'clock, came what looked like a formation of snowy egrets, wending their way lazily in her direction. Echo checked her sensors and established that they weren't birds, unless birds had twenty-meter wingspans and were made of cellulose. She counted five approaching sea-gliders.

They must have spotted her, too, but they stayed at their high altitude, riding air currents that carried them toward her. If need be, sea-gliders could use a ripple of antigravity to keep momentum against the wind or in still air, but the constant diving and climbing made even the strongest stomachs revolt. Most glider pilots refused to use antigrav for that, preferring to climb or dive very little, only to find the best currents. It wasn't only a point of pride, although it was that, too. Gliders simply made better time—and the gravity suppressors exhausted less fuel—when they rode the natural air currents. Fuel consumption was a critical factor in a long haul over a vast ocean.

"Climb the wind and ride it," was a popular phrase among glider pilots.

That's what Echo would normally have done, but this trip she was trying to hide. Despite what she saw, she still hoped that the flock wasn't coming after her and her son. With gliders on her tail, she wouldn't be able to go straight to Astar, the capitol of Dalgren. She would have to make for some more isolated port, hoping they wouldn't follow a lone glider for days on end.

Her radio crackled, making her jump. Echo peered at the device embedded in her console, surprised that they would communicate directly with her. It was a terrible breach of etiquette, since neither one of them had waved a wing to indicate a willingness to chat. Of course, this probably wasn't a chatting opportunity.

"Unknown glider, turn back," warned a stern voice over the radio. "Traffic from Padulla to Dalgren is not permitted at the present time."

Echo looked with embarrassment and fear at her son. She had told him that they might have to do some unpleasant things to be safe, and one of those things might include lying. But the scrawny ten-year-old gave her a brave smile, which was all she needed.

She flicked the switch and replied, "Glider *Golden Wraith* to unknown flock, we're *not* coming from Padulla—we're coming from Santos. And we're *residents* of Dalgren, born and raised there."

"That doesn't matter—all traffic has to be rerouted," warned the stern voice coming from the peaceful flock high above them.

Hmmm, this is serious, thought Echo, but she tried not to show how serious it was in her demeanor. "We're not even going to Dalgren," she replied snidely. "We're going to fly right past . . . on our way to Tipoli."

"You're going to turn back."

"Excuse me, but you don't own these skies," she snapped at the faceless voice. "I've been flying this easterly current since you were in diapers! We're not sick—we haven't been in Padulla. We should be free to go wherever we want!"

There came a tense pause, and Echo let her bravado fade for only an instant. She smiled confidently at her son, but he was starting to look anxious. "Maybe they'll see reason," she said, "and do the right thing."

The radio crackled. "You will turn back right now," warned the voice, "or we will force you into the sea."

"Or you'll *kill* me and my son!" she muttered, although she kept the radio mute. They had given her a long pause, and now they were going to get one in return. While they waited, Echo used her sensors to scan the air currents above them. She had already decided to make a run for home before she turned back to a place where everybody was dying.

Before the flock could respond, she activated the elevators on the tail section, turned antigrav to full, and soared upward. The golden nose cone sliced through the clouds, until she found a southernly flow that was fast but wouldn't take her terribly far off course. With any luck, they might conclude that she was turning around, not running.

"Glider *Golden Wraith,* turn to heading—" Echo flicked the radio off before it became even more annoying.

With embarrassment, she shouted back to Harper. "We tried to talk reasonably to them, but they weren't being reasonable. So we'll just go around."

"We're breaking the law," said Harper knowingly. "You said we should never break laws."

"Just this once, because we haven't got much choice." She flashed him a grim smile.

The ocean had turned a teal color directly beneath them, where a cold current made the kelp scarce. As she climbed, Echo could see the rainbows of color in the West Ribbon Ocean. It swirled this way and that in various shades of green and blue for ten thousand kilometers, until it struck the third largest continent on Helena—Dalgren. She could now see land with her superior vision, but it was little more than a bead of rust on the shimmering horizon.

So close, yet still too far! If only we had left right away! Echo tried not to chide herself for getting caught up in events over which she had no control. Yes, she and Harper didn't have to take three extra days to visit friends and relatives in Padulla. Somewhere in that brief period, the plague had exploded and become a major part of life, even supplanting the Cardassians in the news. Padulla was the hardest hit, or so they said. Certainly, the plague had been nothing but distant rumors on Dalgren when they departed nine days ago.

Now vigilantes ruled the skies and waters, keeping away everyone, even native Dalgrens. But that gave Echo hope, because it meant that her home was still relatively free of the plague. If they could just reach it and slip back into the current of life . . . before it was too late.

"They're coming lower," warned her son, who was straining in his seat to get a better look.

"Keep your seat belt on," she ordered him, knowing she might have to make some erratic maneuvers. In normal times, sea-gliders were never armed, but these weren't normal times. Five planes could force one plane from the sky, but they would have to be fools to try that. Then again, fear and panic made people do foolish things, thought Echo, as she continued to flee from the flock of gliders.

After thirty minutes of intense piloting, the prey and the hunters were at the same altitude, about 400 meters above the gleaming ocean. Laterally, only one kilometer separated her from the lead glider. She couldn't hear their pleas over her radio, as she had long ago turned it off, but she imagined that they were now begging her to turn back. Land was getting closer and closer—Dalgren was a spill of brown and dark green across the turquoise horizon.

Echo banked slightly and turned toward the west. Without warning, some kind of missile shot past her window and streaked off into the ocean, leaving a red plume of smoke. Had that been a warning shot?

"Clones!" she shouted, shaking her fist at them. With a cringe, she glanced at her son.

"They're going to shoot us down, aren't they?" asked Harper.

"No!" she answered through clenched teeth. "They're not going to shoot at us, because I know where the pipeline is. Hang on!"

She cut the antigrav and went into a steep dive, being careful to keep her hand near the airbrake paddles and spoilers. There would be no more fooling around, no more running or hiding—she was headed straight for home.

Another missile streaked by the left wing of the glider, coming much closer. She had a feeling that one *wasn't* a warning shot. Warfare had been unknown on Helena for hundreds of years, so she had to hope that these makeshift armaments were none too deadly or accurate.

"Why don't you put out a distress signal?" asked Harper.

His mother nodded thoughtfully. "That's not a bad idea. We *are* in distress, and I'm not going down quietly."

She flipped on the distress signal, on all channels. The gliders pursuing her were probably the Coastal Watchers, the ones charged with answering distress calls at sea. *That's some irony,* thought Echo, *when the rescuers become the attackers.*

Leaning on the airbrakes, Echo pulled the craft out of its dive, and it skimmed the gentle waves of the turquoise sea. She smiled with satisfaction upon seeing the pipeline just under the surface of the shallow water; it looked like a flaw in the great jeweled facet, yet it carried much-needed fresh water. She swooped so close to the pipeline that she felt as if she could lean out the window and spit on it.

As she expected, that dissuaded her pursuers from shooting wildly at her, but her evasions had given them time to close the distance. Two of them were diving toward her position from high altitude. *Maybe they really are going to drive us into the sea!*

Harper looked out the window with awe, having never seen his mom fly this close to the water, except when landing. And then she would be going at a much reduced speed. There was just one problem—the air currents were slower at low altitude, and her pursuers could close the distance by staying in the upper currents. Echo still maintained the innocent hope that just by reaching land she could escape. Once she and Harper were on Dalgren, she rationalized, no one could keep them off.

Flying only meters above the water forced her to concentrate intently, and Echo didn't see them coming until Harper shouted, "Mom! On the right!"

She glanced over to see a large sea-glider swerve into view. Its wing nearly clipped hers, and she had to tap her joystick to edge away from the sky hog. Then she saw the other one crowding her on her left—he shook his fist at her. *Are they so insane that they would wreck themselves to stop us?*

No matter how close those idiots came, Echo couldn't worry about them—the water was still her prime concern. At this speed, she'd be dashed into splinters if she hit it. The three gliders swooped over the smooth jade water, looking like three albatrosses fighting for the same school of fish.

Finally the plane on her right disappeared from view, and she didn't have time to follow it with her sensors. With a thundrous jolt, something hit the roof of her glider. Echo wrestled her controls to maintain altitude and not plunge into the sea; after a struggle, she managed to level her wings.

Seething with anger, she decided, *Two can play at that game! And my hull is stronger than your pontoons.* Tapping the antigrav lever, she rose rapidly and crunched into the struts, floats, and underbelly of the craft riding her. Hanging on to the joystick with both hands, she bucked like a bronco, dumping the unwanted rider.

"Mom!" shouted Harper.

Echo glanced out the window in time to see the attacking glider spin off, its undercarriage badly damaged. Fluttering like a wounded pelican, the glider hit the calm water and sent up a tremendous plume. The plane wasn't completely destroyed, but it looked fairly well shattered. Echo felt a pang of grief, because she had never been the cause of an accident in her thirty years of flying.

"Now we're in trouble," said Harper. It was an accurate assessment.

Echo scowled. "Maybe they'll realize that if we can fly this well, we're not sick."

The other glider on her left now moved away to a respectful distance, and Echo relaxed a bit at the controls. She continued to follow the pipeline toward the shimmering silhouette of land in the distance. At this point, she would normally feel relieved and happy to be so close to home, but today the sight of Dalgren only brought her dread. *What's going to happen to me and Harper? To all of Helena?*

Without warning, a missile slammed into her right wing, shearing it off.

Only her quick reactions on the antigrav lever kept them from plowing immediately into the ocean. Instead the glider shot upward like a leaf caught on the breeze, then it lost its momentum and slowly spiraled downward, a wounded bird.

The glider creaked, trying to hold together, and the air howled ominously in the struts and ailerons. Harper screamed, but the torrent of rushing air drowned him out. Echo tried all of her controls, but none were responsive—the seaplane was in its death dive.

Looking out the window only made her head whirl as fast as the scenery, and Echo shrieked. She tried to reach back for her child, but he was scrunched down in his seat. "Oh, my Lumpkin . . . I'm so sorry!"

Chapter Six

As her sea-glider spiraled toward the pristine ocean, a tingling came over Echo's body. She wondered whether this was the Mizarian Calm of Death she had heard so much about. The woman reached back to grab her son's hand one last time, but his slight body shimmered like a mirage, breaking apart before her eyes. She gasped at the unexpected sight.

The glider plunged erratically into the jade water, striking like a lopsided bullet and spewing a lopsided splash. Splinters from the sleek craft rained down upon the choppy waves, but Echo and Harper weren't aboard.

Mother and son stood huddled together on the transporter platform in what looked like a cargo hold full of medical equipment. The entire room looked like a laboratory, with modular clean rooms and research facilities crammed into its tight confines. They were confronted by four strange creatures dressed in elaborate environmental suits.

Harper shivered and gripped his mother's chest. "Are they . . . are they Cardassians?"

"I don't think so," she answered, unsure about that. Echo tried to stand upright and show some dignity, but she couldn't let go of her son. She remained hunched over his frail form.

"We answered your distress call," said a businesslike male, as he stepped forward and aimed a tricorder at them. He studied the device intently, not about to make any quick pronouncements.

"Federation?" asked Echo hopefully.

"Hardly," snorted a strong feminine voice. "We're Maquis."

Harper brightened instantly. "All right! Can I join you?"

"Harper!" snapped his mother, cuffing him on the antenna.

Another man chuckled. "I hope, by the time you're old enough, the Maquis won't be needed."

"They show no symptoms of the disease," said the man with the tricorder. "They check negative for the multiprions. Either they were uninfected, or the biofilter removed them. They may still be carrying individual prions."

"We haven't been sick!" declared Echo. She hugged Harper defensively. "Look, just beam us down somewhere on Dalgren, and we'll be going. And . . . thanks for saving our lives."

"Please dispose of your clothing," said the officious man. "After your fumigation, we will furnish you with new garments."

"Just a minute!" barked Echo, stepping in front of her son to protect him from these disguised pirates. "What if I don't want to strip naked?"

"You don't have to." The other man stepped forward and removed his hood, showing himself to be a human with odd markings on his forehead. "In our haste, we've gotten off to a bad start. I'm Captain Chakotay, and this *is* a Maquis ship. But we're not here to fight anyone—we're only here to deal with this disease. If you help us with some information, we'll inoculate you and your son . . . and help you get home."

"We don't need—"

"Weren't the other aircraft trying to kill you?"

"Uh, yeah," admitted Echo, scratching her wrinkled gray skull. "I'd heard they weren't permitting people to travel from Padulla to Dalgren, but I didn't really believe it. Now they've destroyed my sea-glider . . . my transportation, my livelihood."

"We've got transportation." Chakotay motioned to the figure with the tricorder. "Tuvok, you had better get to the bridge and check on Riker."

"Yes, sir." The officious man peeled off his environmental suit, revealing himself to be a Vulcan. With several long strides, he dumped the suit in a bin and exited from the cargo hold.

"B'Elanna, you and Dr. Kincaid can help our guests get cleaned up." The captain turned to her, as if expecting her to furnish a name.

"Echo Imjim," she said apologetically. "And my son, Harper."

The boy clicked his heels and saluted sharply. "Permission to come aboard, Captain."

Chakotay smiled and returned the salute. "Permission granted. I'll brief the two of you after you've changed clothes."

The woman named B'Elanna removed her hood, and Echo gasped aloud. Harper only stared. "Oh, by Mizrah!" said the glider pilot. "Are you what you appear to be?"

B'Elanna frowned and put her hands on her hips. "And *what* do I appear to be?"

"Half-human and half-Klingon."

"Good guess," muttered the magnificent female Maquis. "And why is that so special?"

With a start, Echo realized that the other Maquis had no idea what they had in this B'Elanna woman. "It's a rare combination," she explained. "You are very unique. We haven't had any success convincing Klingons to breed with us."

B'Elanna scowled. "My father had no such problems."

Suppressing a smile, Captain Chakotay broke in. "Can we use this to our benefit?"

"Yes! Make sure that she leads any delegation to Dalgren, or anywhere on Helena." Turning her gaze to the unique woman, Echo almost felt like bowing.

"That's exactly the sort of information we need," said the captain, heading toward the door. "We'll have a briefing session after you've changed."

Handsome man—for a human, thought Echo. She had never wanted another child, loving Harper so much and knowing her profession didn't lend itself to family life—but a purebred human mixed with her lineage would produce an admirable child.

Right, she thought miserably. *In another fortnight, we'll probably all be dead.*

When Chakotay reached the bridge, Tuvok glanced at him, and Seska gave him a quick smile. On the screen was a view of the graceful blue curve of Helena's horizon, as seen from orbit. The planet looked serene yet vibrantly alive, kept that way by an enlightened populace. Yet hidden within those wispy clouds, balmy seas, and dimpled land masses was a deadly enemy committed to wiping out all humanoid life.

"Lieutenant Riker has set up Clinic One on Padulla," reported Tuvok. "Visual contact will be possible in seventy-five seconds."

"Bring it up when you can," ordered Chakotay. Like everyone else, he wanted to see some concrete results for all their foolhardy effort. Being in the Maquis often felt like being Sancho Panza in the service of Don Quixote. Would they do some good today? Or were they risking their lives in order to swat at flies on a corpse?

While they waited, Seska leaned back in her seat and looked at him. "You know what I said about wanting to go on shore leave? Never mind. I know where my duty is—right here."

"That's big of you," said the captain with a grim smile. When times got tense, he welcomed the Bajoran's dark sense of humor. In truth, he would need Seska on the bridge, with B'Elanna down on the planet's surface.

"In range," reported the Vulcan. With a flash, the viewscreen revealed a static-filled image with several blurry figures moving about. In a few seconds, the image cleared to make it plain that they were inside a portable geodesic dome. People stood patiently, waiting for inoculations from the efficient medical team. A couple of the medical workers were Maquis, but the majority were Starfleet.

The equipment and facilities were first-rate, thanks to Riker. The lieutenant had gotten everything they needed, but in small quantities, due to the confines of the shuttlecraft. Chakotay still found it hard to believe that Riker had stolen all this stuff, but he wasn't going to question a gift. The man had accomplished his mission, and that commanded Chakotay's respect. The captain couldn't really be sure of the loyalty of those around him, so he had to trust in their character.

Riker sat down in front of the viewer, a satisfied grin on his bearded face. "As you can see, Captain, we're open for business, and it's booming! The word has gotten out in only a few hours. We're offering inoculations of Tricillin PDF and a wide-spectrum antiviral compound—the same thing all of us got. It should prolong onset—and relieve symptoms—until we can do more research.

"If we catch anyone within forty-eight hours of contracting the disease, we're using the transporter biofilter in the shuttlecraft to remove the multiprions."

He was jostled slightly by two confused patients, and Riker lowered his voice to add, "Being on the outskirts of the city was a good idea. We're only getting those people who are still relatively healthy. As soon as I can get away, I want to take the shuttle and find any local doctors who can tell us how this developed."

"Be careful," warned Chakotay. "Wear the suits in the city—it was hit hard."

"We will. What about Clinic Two?"

"We're getting ready to beam down to Dalgren," said the captain, "but it doesn't sound like the plague has hit there very hard. They're more interested in keeping people *out.*"

"Are you sure that's where you want to set up?"

"Yes, because we need a control site with relatively few cases—that's the best way to isolate and track them. At least that's what Dr. Kincaid says, and Tuvok agrees."

"Well, we're swamped here," said Riker, being jostled again. "I'll report in later. Away team, out."

• • •

Tom Riker rose to his feet, feeling very claustrophobic in the crowded dome. Although few of the patients appeared outwardly sick, he was cognizant that they could be. Plus the Helenites were alien in appearance and dress—each one an amalgam of various species, each person dressed in a colorful, billowing costume with ribbons and braids. It was as if they were headed for a masquerade party. Although Riker had served with numerous humanoid species, he found it disconcerting when he couldn't identify people by species. Perhaps that was the point, he thought ruefully.

When he looked more closely, he could see that many of the Helenites' ornate garments were soiled and tattered. In their haunted eyes, he saw that their comfortable lives had been blasted apart. They were either ill, grieving, or in shock; they hadn't yet reached panic, but their dignity was starting to slip. He smiled at them as he passed, but the Helenites were lost in their contemplations of death.

Riker strode out of the portable dome into the golden sunshine and flower-scented breeze of late afternoon on Helena. He took a deep breath of the sun-drenched air, then held his breath when he realized that it probably contained the deadly prions. He reminded himself that he was now in the medical division—his main concern was other people's health, not his own. If he were serving on the bridge in a battle, he wouldn't be worried about his life, only doing his duty. It had to the same here, on this strange front.

Fighting this enemy was harder, he decided, than fighting a well-armed, advanced starship. At some point, a starship would reveal itself and stand to fight—but their tiny enemy would always stay cloaked, if they let it. Now that the clinic was set up and people were being helped, Riker knew he had to find a way to go on the offensive.

He strode toward the unmarked shuttlecraft, formerly called *Shuttle 3,* where people were also gathered. Only they were waiting for friends and relatives to exit the small craft, not enter. He saw Shelzane escort a very weak patient to the hatch and hand her over to her waiting friends. There was much bowing of heads and many expressions of gratitude, and the thin Benzite looked gratified herself.

"Bed rest," she cautioned the patient. "Check back with the doctors in forty-eight hours."

Riker hated to interrupt this heartwarming scene, but he felt the need to keep moving. "Ensign," he whispered to her, "wrap this up, because we have to leave."

"Leave?" she asked in horror. "But I have more people to bring through the biofilter."

"They'll have to wait."

"Some of them can't wait," she insisted. "Tomorrow will be too late."

Riker guided Shelzane back into the shuttlecraft, away from the curious eyes and ears of the patients. "We're logistical support," he reminded her, "not doctors. Don't make me order you."

"Technically, you can't order me," replied the Benzite. "Since we're here on an unofficial, private mission, Starfleet chain of command doesn't apply."

Riker sighed. "Okay, bring through one more. Then we've got to gather information."

"How about *two* more?" she begged.

He nodded with resignation and sunk into his seat in the cockpit. With joy on her rumpled blue face, Shelzane returned to the transporter console at the rear of the craft. Riker could see her quandary—helping individuals gave one the feeling of immediate accomplishment, while research and long-term planning might not help at all. But if they hoped to save Helena, they had to rid the entire planet of the bug, not just a few individuals.

A muscular Helenite with black hair and sharp tusks materialized on the transporter pad. He staggered off, and Shelzane rushed to help him into a seat. For the first time, Riker felt as if he recognized a patient's species, or at least part of it. The man had the bulk and unpleasant visage of a Nausicaan.

"Can you help us?" asked Riker. "Where in the city are the doctors? I mean, where are people going for medical care?"

The part-Nausicaan looked up at him, and the brute actually seemed to smile. "Glad to help. The spaceport and the arena are supposed to be emergency hospitals. But I wouldn't go there—no one ever leaves."

"Where are they doing research?" asked Riker.

The patient shrugged his broad, furry shoulders. "I suppose, IGI."

"IGI?"

"The Institute for Genetic Improvement." He shook his woolly head. "I forget, you're strangers here. Some species do not breed naturally with others, and medical intervention is needed to produce a child. In vitro fertilization, cloning, genetic transplants—whatever is needed—they've done it. There are IGI clinics all over the planet."

Riker turned to his readouts. "Could you show me on a map of Padulla?"

The hulking citizen rose to his feet and moved slowly toward the hatch. "I don't need to—you will see the giant green complex in the center of the city. It's the tallest and biggest. But I've got to warn you—"

"What?"

The Helenite stopped, looking undecided about spreading unpleasant news. "I heard they closed their doors—not letting anyone in or out. Check for yourself."

"We will, thanks." Riker made a note in his log and muttered to himself, "Institute for Genetic Improvement."

He heard a thud, and he turned to see another patient stagger off the transporter pad. Shelzane caught her—a sleek woman with tawny skin and downy white fur on her forehead and neck. While the ensign attended to her, Riker turned reluctantly to his preflight checklist.

As soon as Shelzane escorted her last patient off the shuttlecraft, Riker told her to clear the area. He felt guilty about leaving the medical staff alone, but they knew this was no paid vacation. They could request help from either the shuttle or the *Spartacus,* he told himself.

Ensign Shelzane jumped in the hatch and closed it after her; the Benzite looked energized by the day's work. "Thanks for waiting, Lieutenant. I told them we'd be back soon—there are so many who need help."

"We can help more of them by finding the origins of the infection," he reminded her. "Did you hear anything about how it started?"

"No," she admitted. "I talked to a few people, but they don't know what happened to them. They're still in shock."

"Okay. Prepare for takeoff."

As soon as the area was clear of pedestrians, Riker fired thrusters, and the shuttlecraft rose swiftly from the bluff. It swerved over the ocean and the crashing waves far below and quickly reached an altitude of three thousand meters, where Riker left it. From the outskirts to the center of the city was a short jump in a shuttlecraft, and he wanted to get a good look at everything along the way.

The rolling countryside was startling in its lush growth and natural beauty. The Helenites obviously enjoyed an unhurried but civilized life, with time to walk rather than ride. The only thing out of place was a thin line of sick people wending their way along a footpath to the new clinic. *How had they found out about the medical team so quickly?* wondered Riker. *Maybe hope is also contagious.*

The shuttlecraft flew over a sparkling bay, filled with what looked like seaplanes and small sailing ships, bobbing peacefully in the surf. All that was missing were people. Riker tried to imagine this city a month ago, before tragedy crept up on it. Padulla must have been a bustling paradise, with a populace so confident in their future that they could exchange the Federation for Cardassian rulers. Now their ambitions and dreams were grounded, just like the seaplanes bobbing below him.

The shuttle flew over a rust-colored beach and a picturesque boardwalk lined with quaint two-story buildings. There were actually a few people milling about on the boardwalk, haunting deserted cafés, watching the afternoon sun glitter on the bay. A few pedestrians waved at the shuttlecraft as it passed over, apparently happy to make contact with the visitors. Despite the fact that the handful of people on the boardwalk could plainly see each other, they didn't interact. They obviously preferred their solitude.

The city was large but not oversized, with broad, tree-lined boulevards, ample green belts, and tasteful buildings that didn't dwarf the civic planning. But without any people, it looked like a model of a city, like something on an architect's desk. Riker glanced at Shelzane and could see the Benzite was saddened by the sight of empty streets below them.

"What do they do with the bodies?" she asked softly.

"They may vaporize them with phasers," suggested Riker. "Burn them . . . I don't know." He was about to suggest she help him look for a big green building, when the landmark appeared on the horizon, shaped like a symmetrical tree.

When he flew closer, Riker could see that the jade-green building was actually a massive pyramid built in the Mayan style. It was the central keep of an oval fortress with high, curving walls and billowing battlements. The entrances were minimal—one north, one south, at the tips of the oval. Inside the walls were eight smaller square buildings with the pyramid holding down the center. The sharp angles of the pyramid, and the oval, rounded walls made an odd juxtaposition.

While he circled the complex, looking for somewhere to land, Riker watched for movement within the walls. He spotted none—it seemed to be as deserted as everyplace else. The few romantics on the boardwalk were keeping a lonely vigil for the rest of the city.

There was no landing pad or strip inside the walls, and the spacings between the buildings were just small enough to keep him from landing on the grounds. Outside the northern wall was a landing pad with the wreckage of some kind of vehicle on it. A path led to an archway in the wall and one of the two obvious gates.

As Riker circled, he pressed the comm panel and broadcast on all local frequencies, "Shuttle to Institute of Genetic Improvement. We're a private medical team, here to help you fight this disease. Please respond."

They listened, but there was no response, as Riker circled lower. The shuttlecraft neared the tip of the pyramid when Shelzane suddenly shouted, "Raise shields!"

Riker did so a moment before a beamed weapon shot from the tip of the pyramid and wracked the shuttlecraft. He slammed on the thrusters and zoomed away before the pyramid got off another shot.

"Whew!" He whistled. "Thanks."

"No damage," said Shelzane, still watching her instruments. "We were scanned, then I caught an energy surge. I thought it might be prudent to activate shields—"

"And save our lives. Quick thinking. So there must be someone in there who wants to keep us out."

The Benzite shook her head. "It could be automated. Our drop in altitude may have tripped the scanners, and the scanners tripped the weapon. I'm not reading any lifesigns, but there is a lot of shielding."

"Then let's land outside." Riker banked toward the landing pad outside the northern gate. As he zoomed over, he noticed that the wreckage on the pad appeared to be fairly recent but already scavenged, some of it placed in neat piles. The debris was scattered badly enough to make landing difficult, so Riker looked elsewhere.

He picked a nearby park and landed in a gently rolling meadow of wildflowers and playground equipment. He gazed out the window at the empty swings and slides; although no one was present, he swore he could hear the cries, shrieks, and laughter of the absent children.

"Suit up," he told Shelzane.

"We've already been exposed," she pointed out.

"Yes, I know, but I want anyone who sees us to know we're outsiders." Riker worked his controls. "I'll put on security and enable remote transporter control."

Assisting each other, they put on their environmental suits and armed themselves with phasers. Before the attack, Riker might not have considered a phaser necessary; now he adjusted his weapon from low to medium stun. Despite the apparent desertion of the central city, *something* had given them an unfriendly welcome. He wasn't convinced there was nobody home inside the enigmatic IGI fortress.

As soon as he stepped out of the hatch into the field of wildflowers, Riker was sorry that he couldn't enjoy the late afternoon breeze. He could feel the sun warming the silken fabric of the suit that covered every centimeter of his body, and he wished he could take it off. With a sigh, Riker motioned to Shelzane, and she followed him toward the wreckage on the landing pad.

He didn't step directly on the platform. He prefered to walk around the debris. Maybe he was being overly cautious, but Riker knew that a wrecked spaceship could leave numerous toxins and dangerous substances. He could see exposed fuel tanks and no indication whether they were full or empty. Despite his protective suit, he felt oddly vulnerable in this ghost town, and he agreed with Chakotay—*take no risks that don't have to be taken.*

As Riker passed the wreckage, he mused whether the ship had gotten shot down by the pyramid, or whether they had simply made a poor landing. The debris had been picked through too much to tell him anything.

He saw Shelzane checking the wreckage with her tricorder, and she shook her head. "No lifesigns," her voice boomed in his hood.

"Let's try knocking." Riker motioned to the gate in the circular wall, then took the lead. They moved cautiously down a well-manicured footpath and approached a rectangular archway at the elongated tip of the oval-shaped fortress. The door itself was metal, windowless, and solid, although the wall appeared to be made of a jadelike stone. Riker could see no mechanism that would open the door, except for a small slit for card entry at the side of the door.

In frustration, he knocked, although he doubted whether his gloved knuckles would make any noise whatsoever on the smooth metal. There were no signs or markings, no indication that this complex had once been a vibrant center of commerce and health care. Judging by the variety of hybrids on Helena, the Institute for Genetic Improvement must have been busy night and day.

Shelzane's eyes stayed riveted upon her tricorder, so she didn't see Riker remove his hood. "Hello!" he shouted as loudly as he could. "Is anyone there?"

The breeze whistled ominously through the turrets of the fortress, making it sound like banshees wailing for the dead. But no living voice answered them.

Shelzane shook her head. "Sir, it's highly unlikely that—" She stopped suddenly and stared at her tricorder. "Ten lifesigns approaching rapidly on foot."

"From the complex?" asked Riker, looking at the door.

"No, sir. From the southeast . . . outside the wall."

Reacting quickly, Riker put his headgear back on and stepped away from the gate. He wanted to get a better view of the wall to the southwest, but he didn't like the fact that they were exposed, out in the open. "Start dropping back to the shuttlecraft," he ordered Shelzane.

"Yes, sir."

They scurried down the path, keeping in a crouch, but they didn't move quickly enough. As they reached the landing pad, a squad of infantry jogged around the corner of the wall and dropped into firing position on knees and bellies. A few of them arranged mortars and other equipment.

"Down!" shouted Riker. He and Shelzane dove into the dirt just as the squad opened fire. Their deadly beams raked the brush and twisted metal on the landing pad, causing leaves, twigs, and molten metal to pelt Riker and Shelzane. As he cowered in the dirt, Riker realized that phasers set to stun were not going to do the job.

He squeezed the combadge in his glove. "Riker to shuttlecraft. Two to beam back. Energize now."

When nothing happened, he stared at Shelzane, and she shook her head. She mouthed something, but he couldn't hear her. Since wireless communications had broken down, and Riker didn't like the poor visibility, he ripped his hood off. Then he set his phaser to full.

"Surrender yourselves!" shouted a voice.

Riker looked at Shelzane, who pulled her hood off and pointed to the attackers. "A dampening field."

He motioned to her to keep moving, all the way back to the shuttlecraft. Scurrying on her hands and knees like a lizard, the Benzite darted from one clump of brush and debris to another.

"Surrender? By whose authority?" he shouted back.

"By authority of the Cardassian Union!"

Cardassians! Riker lifted his head from the dirt to peer at the gray-clad soldiers. They were a well-trained unit. They broke from kneeling positions and scattered to cover, moving ever closer to him. Riker glanced around but could see no support ships, then he remembered that the Cardassians had a garrison on Helena.

"We're just a medical relief team!" he called out.

Riker heard a loud whooshing sound, followed by a tremendous concussion that shook the ground like an earthquake. He covered his head as dirt and flaming debris rained down on him, scorching his environmental suit.

"Surrender!" shouted the hidden Cardassian. "Or prepare to die!"

Chapter Seven

SURROUNDED BY A PATROL of well-armed Cardassians, cut off from the shuttlecraft, unsure what had happened to his co-pilot, Riker needed a big diversion. He aimed his phaser at one of the exposed fuel tanks and fired a searing blast. The tank ruptured in a fireball that ballooned high into the dusky sky. Riker was driven to the ground, as more flaming debris rained down.

A dampening field. He recalled the equipment the Cardassians had set up the moment they charged into view, just before they opened fire. While the wreckage on the landing pad continued to burn like a bonfire, Riker scurried forward and found a vantage point atop a decorative mound. Searching for the place where the Cardassians had rounded the wall, he quickly spotted two metal boxes on tripods.

Without time to think, Riker aimed his phaser and opened fire. Despite the beams whistling past his head, he didn't finish firing until he had completely destroyed the two portable dampening boxes. Then he rolled down the hill and cowered in the dirt from a barrage of phasers and concussion mortars, which turned the ground into quivering jelly. He began to sink into quicksand.

Desperately he tapped his combadge. "Riker to shuttle, beam me up now!"

As a phaser beam melted a chunk of his environmental boot, Riker tried to float atop the liquified soil, but he only succeeded in burying himself deeper. The withering fire never stopped, and he was sure death was near . . . until he felt a tingle along his spine. The lieutenant curled into a fetal position until he was certain that he had transported from the fire zone.

Dripping mud, Riker rolled off the transporter pad into the cabin of the shuttlecraft, then he dashed to the transporter controls. Ripping off a glove, he set to work retrieving Shelzane. An explosion sundered the ground just outside the craft, and Riker staggered. His fingers pounded the console as they worked.

With a surprised but grateful look in her eyes, the Benzite tumbled off the transporter pad three seconds later. Riker didn't wait to greet her—he hurried to the cockpit. Even before he got into his seat, he had punched up the shields and ignited the thrusters. He sunk deep into his chair at the same moment that the shuttle left the ground.

Their shields took a direct hit, and the shuttle rocked—but Riker maintained control as he zoomed into the darkening sky. The jade pyramid was lit up like an amusement park by the explosions and light beams hurled at them. With Riker on the conn, the shuttlecraft weaved back and forth through the barrage, unscathed.

Shelzane staggered into the seat next to him. Her environmental suit was scorched and ripped like his, but unlike him she had a dribble of blood on her hip. He recognized that purple color from her previous head wound.

"You were hit?" he asked with concern.

She shrugged, but her blue tendrils quivered for a second. "It's just a scratch—from a rock, not a phaser."

"Let's go back to camp and have the docs look at it." Riker gave her a sympathetic smile.

"We haven't really found out much," said Shelzane with a grimace.

"And we won't until we figure out a way to get into that IGI complex." After making sure they had swung well wide of the pyramid, Riker set course for the clinic. He mused aloud, "Do the Cardassians have control of that place? Or were they just in the neighborhood?"

The Benzite shook her head. "We don't know. With their dampening equipment, they could stay hidden from our sensors. Or they could transport in."

"Maybe later tonight we'll pay them another visit," said Riker with determination.

A huge green pyramid with boxy angles and long staircases commanded the center of the city below them. It glistened in the midday sun like a jewel. B'Elanna Torres had difficulty taking her eyes off the breathtaking landmark. But she had to watch her instruments as Chakotay brought the *Spartacus* down for a rare landing. Following Echo's advice, they had decided to make an impressive landing rather than just transporting down.

Chakotay had agreed to this only because the *Singha* had returned with more medical supplies, scrounged from a dozen Maquis hideouts. The *Singha* was taking their place in orbit, ready to respond to an emergency or fend off a Cardassian attack.

Torres cycled through her checklists as they prepared to land in a fallow field about two kilometers outside of town. She looked out the window to see the quaint streets of Astar swarming with people during the midday break. At least all of them would get a good look at the novelty known as the Maquis.

"The Cardassians destroyed all of our starships," said Echo softly. "So your arrival will be unexpected." The Helenite was seated at the auxilary console in the rear of the cramped bridge.

"B'Elanna, let them know who we are," ordered Chakotay. "But let's keep our shields up."

The Maquis engineer nodded and opened the local frequencies. "To the people of Dalgren," she announced, "this is the Maquis vessel *Spartacus*. We are here to offer medical assistance. Repeat, we are here to help you during your medical emergency. We will land in a field two kilometers northwest of—"

"Don't land!" a voice broke in. "Traffic between Padulla and Dalgren is not permitted."

"We haven't been on Padulla," she snapped back. "We can inoculate your citizens and help you beat this plague."

"We have no plague on Dalgren!" insisted the voice from the ground. "And we don't wish to anger the Cardassians. Maquis vessel, we urge you to turn back!"

Chakotay slid a finger under his throat in the universal sign to cut them off. Torres did so gladly. "Nice, friendly people," she muttered.

Echo looked pained. "They *are* nice people, normally. But they're afraid. They must have seen reports from Padulla."

"They can't hide forever," said Torres. "The disease is airborne, so they'll be exposed to it, anyway."

"Nobody thinks like that," said Echo with a wan smile. "This is the kind of thing that happens to somebody else . . . someplace else."

"So far," added Torres.

Chakotay heaved his broad shoulders and edged the craft into a gradual landing approach. "They haven't fired at us, so I think I'll land. Remember, B'Elanna, you do the talking. You and Tuvok will be the ones who stay and make the arrangements. We need to exchange information, and research any cases they've had."

"What about my son and me?" asked Echo.

"We'd like you to stay on board and advise us. We have to find out the situation on the other continents as well. But we'll beam you directly to your home whenever you wish."

Echo's shriveled brow grew more wrinkled as she came to a decision. "You can send my son to his aunt's place. I'll stay with you—I think you'll need my help."

"Good." Chakotay turned to Torres. "How are we fixed?"

She studied her readouts but found nothing abnormal. "All systems are green."

"Stand by for landing." The attack craft, which seemed small in space but gigantic as it drew close to the ground, dropped into its final approach. Chakotay fired thrusters and set her down in the barren field.

Torres braced for impact, but the landing was surprisingly gentle. The *Spartacus* tilted on her landing legs as she settled into the furrows, but the aged ship held together.

Chakotay smiled at her. "You can let your breath out now."

"Nice landing. That's not what I'm worried about." She looked pointedly at him. "What if they won't listen to me?"

"Just give them a little of that famous B'Elanna Torres charm," replied Chakotay.

"No," interjected Echo. "*Command* them. They'll listen to you."

The captain tapped his comm panel. "Tuvok, meet Torres at the transporter. We'll wait here until you signal that it's safe to leave."

"Yes, sir," replied the Vulcan.

"Good luck," the captain said to Torres.

"If I had any luck, would I be a Maquis?" With a scowl, B'Elanna rose to her feet and strode off the bridge.

Twenty seconds later, she entered the cargo bay, which had been turned into a flying laboratory. A handful of researchers looked on as she crossed to the transporter platform, where Tuvok waited. She nodded to the Vulcan, who handed her a combadge and a holstered phaser pistol. As she added these accessories to her plain brown uniform, Torres glanced again at the researchers and doctors. They looked scared. They had trained all their lives for this battle, but they had never been on the front before. The fight would be until the bitter end, because this enemy took no prisoners.

B'Elanna tossed her short brown hair, prepared to stride out there without an environmental suit. She told herself that she had been inoculated with the best drugs Starfleet had to offer, and the biofilter would remove the multiprions whenever she transported back. But no one could be calm about facing death so squarely.

"Ready?" asked Tuvok.

Torres nodded and stepped upon the transporter platform, her hand resting on the butt of her phaser pistol. Opening and closing the hatch on this old ship was a pain, so they had decided to transport outside the ship. "Energize," she told the operator.

A moment later, she and Tuvok materialized on the other side of the hull, a few meters beyond the *Spartacus*. There was nothing around them but rich, loamy soil piled in rows, awaiting seed. About ten meters away, a spring gurgled in the center of an old artesian well, and an orchard of venerable fruit trees rose beyond the well. In the distance, Torres saw a cloud of dust on the dirt road, and she pointed it out to Tuvok.

The Vulcan checked his tricorder and nodded sagely. "There are three hovercraft headed toward us. Eighteen people, total."

"Are they armed?"

"There are no unusual energy readings. They may have small arms."

She tapped her combadge. "Torres to transporter room. Stand by for emergency beaming."

"Yes, sir," answered the Bolian on duty.

Torres stood her ground as the small craft sped toward them. When they came within range of her sharp eyesight, she could see the fear and anger on their distinctive faces. These Helenites looked wild, almost fierce, in their colorful, billowing clothes, unfurled ribbons, and windblown hair. They were all hybrids she had never seen before, because they had never existed before; and they existed nowhere else outside of Helena.

The three hovercraft stopped at a respectful distance, and six riders in each jumped out and started forward. The garishly garbed welcoming committee didn't appear to be armed, but they did look angry and upset—and uncomfortable with both emotions. As they got closer to the stoic Vulcan and the scowling half-Klingon, their fierce expressions softened, and some of them gawked openly at Torres. Most of them fell back to talk in hushed whispers, and only a handful of them kept coming.

The one in the lead was a tall, dark-haired humanoid with an olive-green complexion and fine golden hair growing down his neck into his gaudy tunic, which had puffed sleeves and golden braid. His age or ancestry would be difficult to guess, but from the way the others fell back and let him approach alone, she assumed he was the one to deal with.

"Hello!" she said, trying to muster some of her allegedly famous charm. "I'm B'Elanna Torres, chief engineer of this vessel."

He stopped and bowed respectfully. "I am Klain, the prefect of Astar, a Royal Son of the Dawn Cluster. I beg your pardon, but we are not accepting visitors at the moment. We ask you to leave."

"We're like the plague," countered Torres, crossing her arms. "You're going to get us whether you want us or not. You can't just cut yourselves off from the rest of Helena and hope it doesn't happen to you. Help us study this disease and find the transmission vectors."

"How do we know *you* aren't carrying the disease?" asked Klain suspiciously.

"We just arrived. We've got tests, inoculations, and Starfleet records about this disease. Our ship has a laboratory and a clinic." B'Elanna shook her head, growing impatient with this begging. "Listen, we just want to combine forces—if we find that we have to quarantine Padulla or someplace else, we will. Just work with us."

Klain smiled and held out his hands. "Let us show you around and prove to you that we don't have this terrible malady on Dalgren."

"Not a single case?" she asked, incredulous.

He shrugged. "Not that I've seen. Granted, I'm not a doctor. Are you?"

"I've said, I'm a ship's engineer. But we have doctors on board—let them examine a few of you. We'll include an inoculation and a trip through our transporter's biofilter, which will take out the fully developed multiprions."

Klain bowed to her, but there was an amused smirk beneath his smile. "As you wish. Lanto! Harkeer!"

Torres watched curiously as two Helenites ran forward to do his bidding. "I've a favor to ask. Would you two go aboard this ship and allow this Maquis medical team to examine you?"

One of them, a tall woman with long, apelike arms, grimaced with alarm at the idea. "How do we know we can trust them?"

"We have their guests here with us," explained Klain, motioning to B'Elanna and Tuvok. "I'm sure there's no danger."

While this conversation was going on, Torres caught sight of another colorfully garbed Helenite training a tricorder on her. When he saw her looking at him, he folded the device shut and melted into the crowd that was gathering.

She tapped her combadge. "Torres to bridge. We're going to take a tour of the city, and we have two locals to beam aboard for tests. They're about two meters in front of me."

"We're locked on," replied Chakotay's voice. "As soon as we get them, we'll head back into orbit. You're doing great—maybe we'll make you an ambassador."

"I'm holding out for admiral," muttered Torres. "Team out."

She and Tuvok stepped away from the *Spartacus* and motioned the others back as well. Still looking frightened, the two sacrificial Helenites clutched hands as they waited to be transported aboard the strange ship. Judging by the welcome given to the Maquis, Torres guessed that the Helenites had already gotten a good dose of Cardassian threats and propaganda. Or maybe they were just cautious people by nature, despite their flamboyant appearance.

When the two finally dematerialized and the *Spartacus* lifted off into the lustrous blue sky, the Dalgrens seemed to relax for the first time. Torres saw Klain talking to the man with the tricorder, and she hoped they had gotten a clean bill of health. For people who didn't believe the plague could touch them, they sure took a lot of precautions.

She glanced at Tuvok, who raised a noncommittal eyebrow. Torres wanted to head back to the ship and keep moving, letting these ingrates fend for themselves. But they had to confront this disease right here, right now, or they might have to chase it over every centimeter of the Demilitarized Zone for years to come.

Prefect Klain walked toward her and held out his arm like a gentleman. His black hair and olive skin glistened with a healthy sheen, and he looked as strong as a Klingon. With a sigh, she took his brawny arm, but only so as not to offend him. Several other Helenites smiled and nodded with satisfaction, as if some event had transpired of which she was not aware.

"Have you ever been to Helena before?" he asked as he led her toward a hovercraft. Tuvok followed closely behind them.

"No," answered Torres. "Why would I?"

"The way you look. Excuse me, but you are half-Klingon, aren't you?"

She nodded. "And half-human."

Klain's dark green eyes twinkled with admiration. "Half-human and half-Klingon. I've seen computer simulations, but never the real thing! And you were conceived naturally?"

Torres bristled. "Well, I wasn't there, but that's what they tell me."

"Remarkable! Obviously, they sent you to Helena because of your unique lineage?"

"No, I'm here by chance. The Maquis doesn't have the luxury of picking and choosing who they send places."

She stopped at the door to the hovercraft, expecting Klain to open it, which he quickly did. If they wanted to treat her like royalty, she would oblige. Torres slipped into the open vehicle ahead of him, and Tuvok followed, keeping a close eye on their hosts. They sat in the back row of seats, allowing a driver and two more passengers to climb into the front. The other locals crammed into the remaining hovercraft as best they could. All three vehicles lifted off the ground at the same time, as if linked, then the caravan glided smoothly down the rough dirt road.

For the first time, Klain turned to Tuvok. "And you, sir, are a full-blooded Vulcan?"

"I am."

"I myself am Antosian/Betazoid on my dam's side, Deltan/Orion on my sire's side. Here we pride uniqueness—the more unique, the better."

He turned to gaze at Torres with unabashed adoration. "You, B'Elanna Torres, are special indeed."

"Aren't there any full-blooded species who live here?" she asked irritably.

"Unibloods, as we call them. Of course, there are." The big man looked wistful for a moment as the hovercraft cruised slowly between rows and rows of flowering vines. The smell of ripe fruit was redolent on the tropical breeze. "Helena wasn't always like it is now—isolated—with all this strife and uncertainty. We used to have many visitors, great commerce, spaceports in every city. A lot of unibloods came here to help us with our breeding programs, and just decided to stay."

"So you are saying that the majority of Helenites are genetically mixed," concluded Tuvok, "while unibloods are a minority, mostly newly arrived immigrants."

"That's right," agreed Klain. "If you stay here long enough, your children will undoubtedly be unique."

"Why is that?" asked Tuvok.

Klain smiled. "You've got to understand where our ancestors came from. They were persecuted all over the galaxy for being of mixed blood. Mixers, they were called in some places. Hundreds of years ago, our ancestors banded together to form a colony that would always be a refuge for persecuted mixbloods, but they did much more than that—they established the Cult of Uniqueness. It became our creed to combine species in as many permutations as possible. And some that weren't possible."

"You employ artificial means of procreation," said Tuvok.

Klain stuck his chin out defensively. "Only when necessary. Most Helenites don't have families and children in the accepted sense. We have clusters, which are communal dwellings . . . a type of clubhouse. For the most part, adults tend to raise their children alone, and the absent parent or parents are regarded as donors.

"We select the genetic traits of our children very carefully, weighing what kind of life we want for them, how much medical intrusion we're willing to allow. And, of course, how attracted we are to the donor." With a glance at B'Elanna, his defensiveness faded. "To be granted such blessings naturally, as you have been, is a great gift."

No matter how attractive the messenger, the sentiments were still disturbing. Maybe it was the Klingon in her, but Torres found the idea of total dependence on genetic engineering to be unnatural. She switched her gaze to the buildings that had come into view: tidy two-story houses with intricate metal fences and spacious balconies. Helenites rushed onto those balconies to watch the caravan of hovercraft as it entered the city. No one waved or shouted, but they didn't throw bricks either. Torres felt like the centerpiece of an impromptu parade before a respectful but fearful audience—the leader of a conquering army.

They passed an open-air market, and the hovercraft had to slow down to accommodate all the pedestrians. It seemed almost like a holiday, with so many gaily festooned Helenites strolling under the cheerful pennants and striped canopies. The goods in the marketplace were bountiful, ranging from fresh fruits and roasted vegetables to utensils, musical instruments, and more gaudy clothing. At first, Torres tried to pick out the different species in the faces and bodies she saw, but the Helenites were such a hodgepodge of different traits that it became impossible. It was easier to consider them all one race that came in infinite varieties.

As they pulled away from the market, she saw a full-blooded Ferengi, who came charging after them in pursuit. But their hovercraft moved more swiftly than a Ferengi on foot, and they skittered around a corner and were gone.

"Where are we going?" asked Torres.

"The Institute for Genetic Improvement," answered Klain, straightening the magenta cuffs on his billowy shirt. "Then to the Dawn Cluster, my home. But I want you to note that the people of Astar do not seem sick, or in a panic. Yes, we have protected our borders from the terrible tragedy on Padulla, but what would you expect from us? You are looking for transmission vectors, and we have sealed off the obvious one."

Torres gazed at the opulent city all around her, with its chic shops, grand commerce buildings, blooming parks, and contented populace. She did find it hard to believe that they were on the verge of annihilation. "You must have some sick people," she pointed out.

"Yes," the prefect assured her. "We are going to IGI now to interview the scientists and the few patients we have. The finest minds on the planet are found at IGI."

He reached forward with an olive hand that was ringed on the wrist with fine blond hair, and he brushed her wrist. "I would consider it a great honor if you would have supper with us at the Dawn Cluster."

"Yes, Tuvok and I will eat with you."

Klain bowed his head apologetically. "We'll make other arrangements for Mr. Tuvok to dine with fellow unibloods at the Velvet Cluster."

Torres glowered at him. "Are you telling me that Tuvok can't eat at this fancy club of yours?"

"He can't even go in the building," said Klain.

While Torres sputtered, unable to find the exact words to rip this popinjay up one side and down the other, Tuvok held up his hand and declared, "I would prefer to eat with the Velvet Cluster. We are on a fact-finding mission, and it would be wise to interview the uniblood community. Perhaps they are not as immune to the disease as the hybrids."

Klain smiled gratefully. "I think Tuvok understands. The Velvet Cluster is every bit as grand as the Dawn Cluster. Ah, here we are."

Torres looked up to see them approaching a gigantic green wall. Behind the green wall loomed the pyramid she had seen earlier, looking like a mountain with intricate steps carved into its gleaming sides. The three hovercraft made a small circle and came to a stop, sinking softly to the ground.

Klain bounded from the hovercraft and ran to the other two vehicles. As they conversed, Torres and Tuvok sat patiently, their eyes moving between their hosts and the incredible structure looming before them.

"They're bigots," Torres whispered to the Vulcan.

He shrugged. "Perhaps. But every culture has a social order, even if it is not as pronounced as this one. It is not unusual for a persecuted group to duplicate that persecution in another form. Otherwise, the Helenites seem to be prosperous and well adjusted."

"At least this place hasn't been devastated by the plague," said Torres with relief. "We're not too late."

Klain returned to their hovercraft, while the other two vehicles lifted off the ground and glided away. "I told them you weren't a security risk," he explained. "That's correct, isn't it?"

"If we were looking out for ourselves," answered Torres, "we wouldn't be here."

The prefect nodded in agreement. "Yes, I suppose, we haven't been fair to you . . . or to our neighbors. But we've fought so hard to keep our home, and our way of life. Our ancestors built this colony from nothing—in the farthest corner of Federation space. The early years were very hard, and our founders suffered greatly—I'd like to show you our histories sometime. We put up with the Federation, we put up with the Cardassians, and now the Maquis—but one thing is certain, we're going to keep our homeworld."

"But you would sacrifice your citizens on the other continents?" observed Tuvok.

"They have the same technical capablities we have," countered Klain. "If they can't cure it, neither can we! And you forget—the Cardassians destroyed all of our long-range vessels. The only way to get across the ocean now is by sea-glider, and that's not the way to move supplies and sick people. We have no way to get off the planet, no way to get help—"

"Until we came," said B'Elanna.

"All right," he conceded, "you came. And how long will you stay here? My guess is that you'll leave the moment more Cardassian ships show up, which could be any minute."

"Then we'd better hurry," said Torres, striding past Klain toward an archway in the green wall. Tuvok walked after her, leaving the Helenites to gape at the audacity of their guests.

Leaving his three comrades with the remaining hovercraft, Klain followed them to the gate. In the archway was a heavy metal door which didn't suit the exquisite green stone of the wall. Beside the door, Torres noticed what looked like a card slot, but their host paid no attention to it.

"Just stand here," he explained. "We'll be recognized."

Sure enough, the door opened, and Klain led the way inside. The walkway sloped downward, with handrails on either side. Torres realized they were headed underground, into a network of tunnels. The lighting came from luminescent strips embedded in the walls, ceiling, and floor of the jade corridor. Their footsteps echoed plain against the dull stone as they descended.

In due time, they came to a shiny metal turbolift, which opened invitingly at their approach. They stepped inside the well-appointed chamber and, following Klain's lead, stood quietly. After a jarring ride that made Torres dizzy, the doors opened, and they found themselves in a sumptuous office, furnished with mementos, plaques, and awards. There were so many chairs arrayed against the walls that Torres decided this was a waiting room, with no one waiting.

A chime sounded, and a small bookcase in the corner spun around. A little man wearing a white laboratory coat stepped off the platform and gave them a crinkled smile. From the riot of spots and bumps on his face, it was impossible to tell what species his ancestors might have been, but it was certain that he was old. White hair sprouted in unruly tufts from his head, eyebrows, and chin, only adding to his gnomelike appearance.

"Hello! Hello!" he said, striding forward. "I am Dr. Gammet. Welcome to IGI." Although he tried to include all of them in his conversation, his pink eyes drifted toward B'Elanna Torres. "Yes, yes . . . remarkable."

"Dr. Gammet," said Klain warmly. "I'm so glad you could see us personally. This is B'Elanna Torres and Tuvok from the Maquis vessel."

"Has their ship left the ground?" asked Gammet.

"Yes, it's back in orbit."

"Good, good," said the little man with extreme relief. He turned apologetically to B'Elanna. "We still worry about the Cardassians more than anything else, and we don't want to give them any excuse to punish us. Although it may not seem like it, I'm glad you're here."

"You people are in denial about this plague," said Torres. "You can't hide from it and hope it goes away."

"I told them we didn't have any cases," insisted Klain.

Gammet scratched his wiry goatee. "I'm not sure of that anymore. It's possible that we could have had some plague cases and not recognized them. People could have died in the countryside without our knowing it. We need to cooperate with these people to find out."

Torres took a isolinear chip from her breast pocket. "I've got all the Starfleet data on the previous outbreaks."

He took the chip and shrugged. "I've seen the data, including some Cardassian files you could never obtain. I didn't tell Klain, but we have samples of the prions, smuggled out of Padulla before the quarantine. We were studying the disease, but it moved too quickly for us to save Padulla."

"Then you know this is serious," said Torres.

The doctor nodded somberly as he paced the quiet library. His shuffling footsteps were the only sound, except for the far-off drip of a faucet.

"It's more serious than you think," he began. "Much more serious. This strain is just as virulent as previous strains—but even more contagious. My theory is that it's a chimera, a genetically engineered combination of two different organisms. In this case, it would be the original virus combined with a less deadly disease that is easy to contract. So we have a disease that was already deadly, only now it's more contagious than ever."

"Who engineered it?" asked Klain, shock spreading across his handsome face.

Dr. Gammet shook his shaggy white mane. "That's unknown. We don't even know what the second organism is, and I've got people in this building who disagree with me—they think it evolved naturally. We've just started looking at this thing, and it could take months, or years, to crack it. And we may not have that much time—either from the disease or the Cardassians."

The little gnome looked into B'Elanna's eyes. "And no one is going to allow us to leave the planet, are they?"

She cleared her throat and returned his frank gaze. "No, we have to fight this battle right here, right now. Win or lose."

"Aren't there drugs that can delay the onset?" asked Klain hopefully.

"Yes, but there is no cure," stressed Dr. Gammet, his pace turning into a nervous jog. "Only by tracking it back to its origins can we hope to snuff it out. Now that we've got a couple of Maquis ships and the means to move quickly around the planet, let's use them."

"I'll get you together with our doctors." B'Elanna tapped her combadge, but nothing happened.

Gammet smiled slyly. "That won't work in here, my dear. No, no. I would suggest that we have as little contact with your ship as possible, in case the Cardassians show up again. In fact, there's a garrison stationed west of here in Tipoli, and they keep a close eye on us.

"So we'll exchange records and personnel as needed, while you two stay with us to coordinate the research. Your ships will do the fieldwork—as they're already doing on Padulla. But direct contact with your ship should be kept to a minimum. Also, it might help if you two didn't go around openly proclaiming your identity as Maquis. Just say you're Helenites."

"With *these* clothes?" asked B'Elanna, pointing to her drab uniform.

"Yes, yes, we'll do something about that." Gammet gave Tuvok a crinkly smile. "You, dear boy, could make a fortune while you're here—in donor fees. Wouldn't require much work on your part—we can induce *Pon farr.*"

While it was not possible to embarrass a Vulcan, Tuvok did manage to look offended. "That is the most unappealing job offer I have ever received."

The little man shrugged. "Not to fear, it is entirely your decision. Romulans are so similar to Vulcans that we've learned to use them almost exclusively. But never mind about that. Are we agreed on how to proceed?"

B'Elanna could feel the leadership of this mission slipping away from her, flowing toward the charismatic little doctor. Then again, they needed help desperately. And he was right, if the Cardassians showed up in force, all bets were off. It was a good idea to make the Helenites self-sufficient, as eliminating this disease was going to be a long, hard job, even if they were successful in containing the outbreak.

She looked at Tuvok, and the Vulcan raised an eyebrow, awaiting her decision.

"All right," she said. "We'll stay with you and coordinate."

Dr. Gammet clapped his gnarled hands. "Excellent! Excellent! I feel very confident that we can fight this chimera. Our people have a lot of natural resistance built into their genetic makeup."

"Do you have biological warfare?" asked Torres.

"No!" squeaked the little man, looking horrified at the idea. "We've never had war of any kind, biological or otherwise. The Cardassians could have wiped us out anytime they felt like it, with conventional weapons. There's no reason they should introduce a disease—or that anyone else should."

Torres nodded, more troubled than relieved by that thought. As she had asked Riker days ago: *Why here? Why now?*

Chapter Eight

A LOUD, WRACKING COUGH sundered the silence of the examination tent, and a thin, naked man shook uncontrollably on the metal table. He looked old and used-up, although that may have been a result of the disease. For all Riker knew, he could have been a young man in the prime of life. This disease attacked every organ at once, bringing on instant aging.

Two medical workers in white gowns and hoods leaned over the old man, conversing silently inside their headgear. Riker stood nearby, waiting to see if the patient had to be transported to the shuttlecraft. Finally one of the doctors turned to him and shook his encased head.

"He's too far gone," said a disembodied voice in Riker's hood.

The lieutenant didn't need any further explanation. He had seen plenty of patients like this one in the last few hours. Although the multiprions that caused the disease could be removed from their bodies by the transporter biofilter, their weakened bodies could not be repaired. Too many other opportunistic diseases had taken over; too many organs were failing; too many healthier people needed attention.

Unable to watch any longer, Riker waved to the doctors. "I have to check something." They waved back and grabbed hypos that would alleviate the man's suffering but not prolong his life.

Feeling constricted inside his hood, Riker stepped out of the examination room into a primordial night. The sky above was sugared with stars, and the dead city cast a boxy silhouette in the distance. The clinic's lights were the only lights between their encampment and the stars.

A clutch of Helenites waited nearby, staring at him. After a moment, he recognized them as the people who had carried the old man in. Their gaily striped and billowy clothes were soiled and tattered, making them look like an impoverished theater company. From their concerned yet hopeful faces, he knew they wanted some reassurance, but he couldn't give them any. It wasn't even his place to talk to them, but Riker knew that if he didn't, no one else would. He removed his headgear and walked toward the people.

"Will the prefect be all right?" asked a female who might have been attractive before worry and tragedy carved themselves into her mahogany face.

Riker looked frankly into eyes that were perfectly round. "I'm sorry, but the doctors say he won't recover."

A man with puckered magenta skin pushed his way through the group to confront the lieutenant. "But the transporter—we saw others being cured!"

"Others who were infected but not that sick," explained Riker. "We have to catch it within forty-eight hours. I'm sorry."

He started to walk away, but the man, who was good-sized, grabbed Riker's shoulder and whirled him around. "That's our *prefect* you're talking about—the chief of the Star Cluster! You have to save him!"

Riker tried to remain calm as he pried the Helenite's fingers off his shoulder. He also tried to ignore the way the man had spit into his face. "We're medical workers, not miracle workers. We're trying to save as many as we can, while we make the others comfortable."

"You'll save him!" shouted the man. "Or I'll tell the Cardassians you're here!"

Riker glanced worriedly into the night sky. "I'm pretty sure they already know we're here. I met a few of them in town, around the IGI building. What are they doing there?"

"You're evading my question!" sputtered the man.

"No, I'm trying to help people in this place . . . and getting shot at, threatened, and exposed to plague for my trouble!"

When the man wouldn't calm down, two of his friends grabbed him in an emotional hug. "Don't make it worse, Jakon," begged a woman. "We knew he was very sick. Let him go."

"They are only trying to help," insisted another friend. "Let's get in line for inoculations."

With lingering anger and denial, the magenta man glared at Riker. The lieutenant knew he should show more sympathy, but death was all around, breathing down their necks, and he wanted to survive. "What are the Cardassians doing around the IGI complex?" he asked again.

The man looked past him, grief finally taking the place of anger, but a pointy-eared lad stepped forward. "They're shooting down any ships that can leave the planet. Those have been their orders for a while."

"And what about IGI? A weapon in that pyramid tried to shoot *us* down."

"That's their regular security," said the boy, sounding proud. "It's to protect trade secrets from their smaller competitors."

"Some secrets," muttered Riker. "Thank you. Once again, I'm sorry."

He hurried off before he could get involved in more grief, sickness, and death. With the *Spartacus* and *Singha* in orbit, Riker wasn't that concerned about an attack from space, but he didn't like squads of Cardassians popping up here and there. If that crack patrol ever decided to attack the clinic, they could wipe them out in less than a minute. It was doubtful the ships in orbit could respond quickly enough to help.

He crossed the flower garden to the shuttlecraft, which was parked on a grassy hillside overlooking the ocean. The hatch was open, and a feeble yellow light spilled into the darkness. In the gloom, the shuttle looked like a panel wagon belonging to a couple of traveling peddlers. It was too dark to see the ocean, but the waves crashed soothingly to the shore; the monotonous sound gave a false impression that all was well.

He stepped into the shuttlecraft, about to blurt orders, when he saw Shelzane sprawled like a limp starfish in the pilot's seat, fast asleep. She looked so peaceful, he didn't want to wake her up, but they were endangering the clinic by being here.

"Ensign!" he snapped, dropping into the seat beside her. "Prepare for takeoff."

Shelzane bolted upright, blinking her blue, hairless eyelids. "I'm sorry, sir, I don't know what happened—"

"I know what happened—you got tired. But don't worry about that. We've got to get out of here. Can you take over the checklist?"

"Yes, sir." The Benzite's hands dropped onto the board, and she was instantly at work.

Riker tapped the comm panel. "Shuttle to *Spartacus.*"

"We hear you," replied Chakotay.

"We're assuming orbit, because I'm worried that the shuttlecraft is endangering the clinic. The Cardassians on the ground are out to get every ship that can leave the planet."

"Understood," said the captain. "But the situation may change quickly, because we're out of contact with Torres and Tuvok on the other continent. We've got no reason to believe they're in danger, but they're not responding to hails."

Riker frowned. "Is there anything I can do to help?"

"No," muttered Chakotay. "They went into a building where there may be shielding. And sometimes those surplus combadges can fail without warning. Let's give them a little longer."

"Okay. After we get in orbit, I'd like permission to beam down to the planet to scout Cardassians and a medical facility."

"Is this important?"

"I think it is. We've got to get records and find out how this thing started. The problem is, Padulla is a ghost town—everything is boarded up. The only ones out and about are Cardassians. How have they avoided the plague? I'd like to know."

"Okay, but keep in touch."

"You've got to take over the transport duties for the clinic," said Riker.

"We just entered synchronous orbit, and the transporter is going full time, no waiting."

"Okay, see you up there. Shuttle out."

Riker punched up the launch sequence, as Shelzane gazed at him with concern. "We're going back to that place?"

"Yes, but we're not going to march right up and knock. Let's launch, and we'll discuss it on our way."

Lieutenant Riker and Ensign Shelzane beamed into what they thought was an empty administration building near the IGI complex. When they shined their lanterns around the dark workroom, Riker was glad he had insisted they wear environmental suits. They were surrounded by hundreds of shrill rodents, interrupted in the middle of dining on two dismembered corpses.

When the rodents advanced, teeth bared, Riker raked the front row with phaser fire; they fell back, squealing. The line of charred rodents pointed the way to a second door, and Riker jogged in that direction, keeping the light in front of him and Shelzane.

The door was automatic and should have opened at their approach, but the power was off. He trained his lantern back on the rats, several of whom were bravely sniffing their footprints, trying to decide if these intruders were a danger or more food. "If they get close, shoot at them," he ordered Shelzane.

"Yes, sir," replied the Benzite with a tremble in her voice.

Riker stepped back and surveyed the area around the door, finding an access panel that might control the mechanism. Since Helenite technology was based on Federation technology, Riker had no trouble opening the panel and determining which circuits he needed to disable to allow it to open manually. He didn't have much hope of restoring electrical power to the building, but he wanted to be able to open a door without blasting through it.

A flash of light caught his attention, and he whirled around to see Shelzane firing at a wave of scurrying rats. "Keep them at bay!" he ordered her.

Riker wormed his gloved fingers into the crack between the two halves of the door. Using every muscle in his upper body, he pried the door open, as Shelzane backed into him. She fired continuously at the rodents, but a sea of fur undulated across the floor, caught in the wavering light of their lanterns.

"Get out!" Riker straightened his arm, forming an archway and holding the door open for the Benzite. When she didn't move fast enough, he grabbed her and shoved her through the door. With a final glance at the frenzied rats, Riker turned the light away and plunged the room back into darkness. With his hold on the door weakening, he squeezed through and let it snap shut behind him.

They found themselves in a deserted corridor, which was fine with Riker, since he wanted to search for the best observation post. He picked a direction and started walking. Shelzane shuffled behind him, keeping an eye on their rear. With no lights except for their portable lanterns, it almost seemed as if they were exploring a mine.

Midway down the hall, they came upon a door that bore the universal pictograph for stairs. Riker gave it a push and found that it wasn't locked or automatic. He held the door open and motioned Shelzane ahead of him, while he took a last look down the length of the bleak hallway.

Once in the stairwell, Riker decided that they might as well stake out the highest ground. He pointed up the stairs, then took the lead. Upon reaching the top landing, he was confronted by another automatic door. While Shelzane held the light for him, he opened the access panel and disabled the circuitry, allowing him and Shelzane to push the door open.

When they stepped onto the flat roof, they were unprepared for the sight that greeted them. Helena's double moons had just risen, casting an eerie blue light upon the dark cityscape. With their intricate wrought-iron balconies, sharp angles, and terraces, the buildings looked like giant mausoleums.

Riker turned off his lantern and motioned to Shelzane to do the same. Then they crouched down and took a good look at their surroundings. Arrayed along the roof were a few communication dishes and antennas, plus some environmental equipment, but little else of interest. Moonlight bathed the pyramid, making it look ebony instead of green.

The two of them dashed to the edge of the roof and peered over a wrought-iron railing at the street below. From a height of about six stories, they had an excellent view over the wall into the IGI complex, where they could now see smaller buildings in addition to the pyramid. They also had a commanding view of the street in two directions. The only disadvantage of having a post on the roof was that they would be visible by air surveillance. But thus far, they hadn't seen any Cardassian aircraft, and Riker didn't think they would have to worry until morning.

He got into a comfortable yet effective reclining position, then removed his hood. After a moment, Shelzane did the same. "What are we looking for?" she asked.

"To see if anybody is in that place. If there's someone home, we have to attract their attention without alerting the Cardassians. Let's just be ready to gather information . . . and move fast if we get the chance."

As the two of them watched the massive pyramid and deserted street, time hung suspended over them like the glittering moons. It seemed as if they were the only people in the universe, keeping a vigil for a long-dead traveler who would never return home. Even though the buildings were standing, and the infrastructure of the society remained in place, this city was dead. Riker wondered if the survivors in Padulla could be relocated somewhere else on the planet, allowing them to start over.

Shelzane tapped Riker on the leg, jarring him out of his reverie, and she pointed to the west end of the street. He peered in that direction but could see very little in the shadows. So he took a small scope from his pack and adjusted it to his eye.

Immediately he spotted a squad of Cardassians strolling down the street, probably the same ones who had attacked them on their last visit. From their movements, it was clear they thought they owned the neighborhood and had nothing to fear. Riker still wondered if they were connected with the IGI complex—or had just discovered a good place to trap unsuspecting shuttlecraft.

Maybe I can find out.

As the patrol drew closer, unaware of the watchers on the roof, Riker turned to Shelzane and whispered, "Remember that payload we talked about beaming into the complex?"

The Benzite nodded. They had discussed transporting themselves directly behind the walls, then had decided to send an inanimate load first. After collecting a few objects to send down, they had finally decided to scrap that plan until they were more desperate.

Riker went on, "I want you to return to the shuttle and beam the package into the complex. Put it on the other side of the wall, where that shrub is. See it? The Cardassians should pass by there in about a minute, but wait for my signal."

"Yes, sir." Shelzane looked for the shrub and checked the coordinates on her tricorder. Then she pressed her combadge. "Shelzane to shuttle. One to transport—now."

With a twinge of dread, Riker watched his cohort vanish into the night like a swirl of dust caught in the moonlight. He had really come to rely on Shelzane, and he didn't like being without her, even for a few seconds.

Creeping along the lip of the roof, Riker peered through the wrought-iron lattice. He could see the unsuspecting patrol, strolling the street with a swagger typical of conquering soldiers. This time, they were wearing some sort of gas masks, although no protective clothing—just their regular gray uniforms. He appreciated the way they skirted close to the green wall in order to avoid a clump of debris in the street.

When they were only a few steps from the shrub on the wall, Riker tapped his combadge. "Energize now."

Gazing down at the complex from above, he saw a blue ripple race along the interior of the wall, as if a force field had rejected an attack. The blue anomaly moved outward in concentric circles, like a ripple in a pool, flowing over the walls and encompassing the unsuspecting soldiers. They screamed in agony, and half-a-dozen of them collapsed to the pavement. The others staggered, although some recovered quickly and aimed their weapons at the wall, which had seemingly attacked them for no reason.

The Cardassians cut loose with a withering blaze of fire, which only carved a minor dent in the impervious green stone. Nevertheless, the defenses of the complex reacted as if a full-scale attack was in progress. A red beam shot from the tip of the pyramid and melted a screaming Cardassian. Now the rest of them stopped firing and beat a hasty retreat, dragging three of their comrades with them.

Riker heard a snort and he turned to see Shelzane watching the curious spectacle. Subconsciously, she rubbed her injured hip.

"Did the package get through intact?" he asked.

"I don't know. The transmitter stopped working, and heavy-duty shields blocked our sensors. We had an isolinear chip in there with all of our data, so maybe they'll take notice."

Riker nodded with satisfaction and turned his attention to the stunned Cardassians. One of them crawled away, but two of them lay completely still, as still as death. They had been the closest ones to the wall, and Riker had a feeling they were not going to get up.

He whispered to Shelzane, "Whoever is in that complex, they're not allied with the Cardassians."

Shelzane started to reply, but a howling noise interrupted her. Screaming out of the night came a missile that slammed into the green wall, exploding with a thunderous concussion that shook the whole street. Shelzane and Riker were hurled away from the edge of the roof into a thicket of antennas. Green hail rained down upon them, and it took Riker a moment to realize that the gemlike pellets were melted bits of the wall.

He crawled to the edge of the roof and peered into the acrid smoke and swirling embers. He was amazed to see a gaping hole in the wall, with sparks glittering around its edges.

Movement caught Riker's eye, and he looked up. From the top of the pyramid, the deadly red beam raked a building farther up the street. Riker was curious about the target, but he couldn't stick around long enough to study it. The heat from the pyramid's weapon was scorching, turning the air into an inferno. He rolled away from the edge of the roof, yanking his headgear back on.

Scrambling to his knees, he spotted Shelzane crouched by the door to the stairwell. He dashed toward her, and the two of them tackled the door; with their adrenaline pumping, they pushed it open in seconds. Just as a monstrous explosion shook their building, they ducked into the cover of the stairwell.

After scurrying down a flight of stairs, Shelzane and Riker finally took a moment to catch their breath and slump against the narrow walls of the enclosure. "I guess they don't like each other," observed Shelzane, panting.

"This would be a good time to get into that complex," breathed Riker. He flinched from another blast that sounded altogether too close, as bits of plaster and dust fluttered down on them.

"Whatever we do next," rasped Shelzane, "I say we get out of here."

"Agreed." He tapped his combadge. "Riker to shuttle—two to beam up. Now!"

They dematerialized just as an explosion ripped off part of the roof, causing beams and debris to cascade down the empty stairwell.

Back on the shuttlecraft, safely in orbit, Riker didn't take time to congratulate himself. He charged to a console and scanned the breach in the wall, while Shelzane slumped into the closest seat.

"That hole goes all the way through," said Riker, "and there's no force field. We could beam right inside—onto a walkway."

"The shooting?" asked the Benzite.

"Has stopped for the moment—both sides are quiet. I'll go by myself if you don't want to go." He checked the other readouts.

"I'll go," said Shelzane, rising wearily to her feet. She pulled the hood back over her head and checked her suit. "We have to find out what's in there."

After making sure that the shuttle's orbit was stable and her status was good, Riker punched in commands and motioned his co-pilot back onto the transporter pad. "Phasers on full."

"On full," she agreed, drawing and checking her weapon. With the lieutenant deftly handling the controls, the Benzite faded into a glittering shimmer. He jumped onto the platform after her, leveled his phaser, and vanished.

The two strangers materialized inside a gloomy walkway that sloped downward. It would have been well lit in daytime, thanks to a ragged hole in the wall about six meters behind them. Riker pushed Shelzane along, because there was a lot of moonlight spilling through that crevice.

As they descended into the walkway, Riker felt a handrail at his side, and he grabbed it. There were enough green pebbles and debris to make walking treacherous. He turned on his lantern and played the yellow beam upon the glistening walls of the corridor. The entire thing was made of the same green material as the exterior. Riker knew he could learn more from a tricorder reading, but he didn't want to take his eyes off his surroundings.

"Ahead," said Shelzane. She pointed her lantern beam straight down the corridor until it glinted off shiny metal. "It may be a door."

He nodded, motioning her to go on. If they both had to return fire, it would be better to have the shorter person in the lead. Suddenly, strips of light glimmered in the floor and ceiling of the corridor, causing the visitors to drop into a crouch.

"They're only lights," Riker said with relief, rising to his feet.

He felt a slight tremble, and he looked back in the direction they had come from. At the far end of the corridor, the green jade appeared to be moving—sliding—and he wondered if it was a trick of the light. Looking closer, he realized that the walls of the corridor were slowly oozing toward the breach, as if they were trying to heal it. He couldn't take time to watch this phenomenon, because Shelzane was already moving toward the gleaming door.

Riker shuffled after her, his booted feet making hissing sounds on the smooth green stone. When they reached the door, it slid open at their approach, revealing a small, conical enclosure within.

Shelzane fumbled for her tricorder, but Riker touched her arm. "It looks like a turbolift."

She looked up and nodded nervously. This time, Riker led the way inside, and Shelzane followed, keeping a watch on their rear. There were no buttons to push, no controls to operate. The doors whooshed shut, and the lift moved so quickly that Riker felt a heave in his stomach and slight disorientation.

The doors opened a moment later, revealing what appeared to be a cluttered waiting room. Diplomas, plaques, citations, and letters hung on every spare centimeter of the walls, while jumbled bookshelves filled the rest. The furniture looked old and comfortable, as if this were a good place to read a paper, have a discussion, or take a nap. By the turbolift was an umbrella stand with two polka-dot umbrellas stuck in it.

Riker stepped gingerly into the room, surveying the walls for other entrances and finding none. Shelzane slowly followed him into the room, her phaser leveled for action. They hardly noticed when the turbolift doors slid shut behind them.

Suddenly one of the short bookcases began to revolve, revealing a small man in a white laboratory coat. His face was a remarkable road map of the most startling traits of half-a-dozen different species, and his broad smile was equally universal. He wore no protective clothing, and his white hair bristled energetically as he strode across the room toward them.

"Welcome! Welcome!" he called, clapping his hands together. "Your perseverance has paid off. I thought we wouldn't be having any more customers for a while, but here you are!"

"We're not customers," said Riker through his speaker. "There's a plague going on out there."

"Let me show you our plans," said the little man. He crossed to a bookshelf and took out a large photo album. "According to our scans, the sire will be uniblood human, and the dam will be uniblood Benzite. Your child will be quite unique, but some intervention will be called for at the fertilization stage. We'll also have to perform lung surgery in the womb, if you want an oxygen-breathing child."

Riker pulled off his hood, thinking the old man couldn't hear him properly. "We're here because of the plague—not to have a child."

The old doctor frowned with disappointment. "You've changed your minds then. That's too bad. It's a big step, I know, but IGI will always be here for you when you're ready."

"Don't you know anything about the outbreak up there?" snapped Riker, losing his patience.

"You're wasting your breath," interjected Shelzane. He glanced over to see the Benzite intently studying her tricorder. "He's a hologram."

Riker peered closely at the little doctor, who gave him a crinkly smile in return. "I haven't had much experience with holograms," said the lieutenant. "I guess this one has been programmed to deal with prospective parents. Are there any *real* people in this building?"

She shook her head. "I can't tell. The shielding is very thick—I can't see anything beyond these walls. I doubt if our combadges would work."

Riker tapped his badge immediately. "Riker to shuttle." There was no response. "Riker to *Spartacus*." The only sound was the bubbling of a small aquarium on a corner table.

The gnomelike doctor chuckled warmly. "If the expense is a problem, let me tell you about our installment plans. Or perhaps you qualify for financial assistance. Let me check."

"We want to see where the procedures take place," demanded Riker. "We want the grand tour."

"Right this way!" chirped the kindly doctor. He started for the turbolift, then stopped and shook a finger at himself. "Sorry, sorry, I keep forgetting. You'll have to remove your weapons. Regulations, you know."

With a scowl, Riker holstered his weapon, and so did Shelzane.

"No, I mean, leave them here." He held out a spotted, white-furred hand. "I'll put them in my drawer—they'll be safe."

Riker's hand hesitated on the butt of his weapon. It seemed unwise to hand it over at this point. "Maybe we'll just be leaving," he said, edging toward the lift. "Just tell us how to get out safely."

The congenial gnome clapped his hands with joy. "The decision is in! You have been accepted as patients on a full scholarship basis. Your pregnancy is completely free!"

"We'll be going now," insisted Riker.

"But it's time for your anesthesia."

Something sharp pierced Riker in the center of his back. He struggled to reach it, but he couldn't in the bulky suit. An instant feeling of well-being spread over him, and he stopped struggling, using all of his facilities just to stand on his feet. Swaying back and forth like a drunkard, he tried to remember why he had come in here.

Riker caught sight of some movement in the room, and he turned very slowly—in time to see Shelzane pitch forward onto the carpet. For the first time he realized that something was wrong.

A throaty chuckle emanated from behind the revolving bookshelf, and he tried to focus his eyes in that direction. A figure in a black environmental suit stepped into the waiting room, trained a phaser rifle on him, and pulled the trigger.

All feeling in Riker's body disappeared, and his head rolled into a black pit.

Chapter Nine

B'ELANNA TORRES LOOKED DOWN at the patient, who showed the strong reptilian traits reminiscent of a Saurian, although in a more muscular body. Through the gauze of a protective canopy, the patient nodded weakly at her, Tuvok, Dr. Gammet, and Prefect Klain. Torres looked around the intensive care unit, impressed with the efficiency and quality of IGI's infirmary. Their tour had been extensive, and they hadn't even seen the obstetrics ward, the biggest wing of the complex.

"This patient is our best in-house possibility for a case of the plague," whispered Gammet softly. "We've had other possible cases, but all of them have recovered. I gather that's not the typical profile. What do you think, Mr. Tuvok?"

The Vulcan studied a large padd containing the man's medical records. "At a glance, it would appear this man has a respiratory infection, not the plague. I would like to have our doctors look at this data, as well as the patient. Can we contact our ship and beam him up?"

The little man sighed, as if this would be possible but inadvisable. "I suppose we'll have to risk it. Why don't you take time right now to go back to the surface, where you can use your communicators."

"How far underground are we?" asked Torres, beginning to dislike this arrangement.

He shrugged cheerfully. "A hundred meters or so, that's all."

"I don't think being cut off from our ship is going to work," she declared. "If this is your only facility, we'll have to move most of the work to the *Spartacus*."

"Excuse me," said Klain. "What about the two healthy people you took earlier?"

"That's another good reason to get in contact with our ship." Torres began to pace the ICU, growing impatient with the time this was taking. The tour had been a good idea, but it still felt as if they were in diplomatic mode, when they needed to be on the offensive.

"Prefect Klain can take you to the surface," said the old doctor reassuringly. "I'll get this patient up there, and we can make all the arrangements we need. I know you understand the need for us to distance ourselves from you, but I also realize the necessity for *some* contact. I do."

"See you later, Doctor," said Torres. "Thanks for all your help."

The diminutive fellow gave her a crinkly smile and waved both hands. Klain patiently herded them away from the intensive care unit.

The prefect looked relieved to get this unpleasantness behind them, and he asked conversationally, "Don't you think it's possible that the disease has bypassed Dalgren? We're a long distance from anywhere."

"I don't know what's possible," admitted Torres, "but if you had seen conditions on Padulla—"

"Helena has awfully big oceans," Klain reminded her. "They give our planet much of its character, and they protect us. You'll grow to love them."

"You sound like we're going to be here for a long time," she grumbled. They paused to let the door open, and the air rushed outward into the corridor; the facility used uneven air pressure to keep contaminants out of patient areas.

"I don't know how long it will take to stamp out this terrible disease," said Klain. "But I know that you can't be a Maquis for the rest of your life, B'Elanna. You'll have to look for peace eventually, and no place would suit you better than Helena. Here you would be worshipped, part of the social elite. You could be whatever you wanted to be."

She scowled. "I'm a ship's engineer, and you don't have any ships."

"Not now, but we're a resilient people. We'll build up our merchant fleet again. You can help us." Klain glanced at Tuvok as they stepped into the jade-green corridor. "In fact, I would say that *all* of the Maquis could blend into our society with ease. You have skills we need to rebuild, and we would welcome you with open arms. Where else can you go? None of you can ever return to the Federation, and most of your homes in the DMZ are gone."

"Your arguments have merit," conceded Tuvok as their footsteps echoed dully in the featureless corridor. "The Maquis do not have a plan to return to civilian life. They lack long-range planning skills."

"Not everyone thinks like a Vulcan," Torres grumbled.

Klain pounded his fist into his palm. "I'm going to bring it up at the next Grand Cluster—sanctuary for any Maquis who wishes to settle here! After you help us save our home, it can become *your* home."

The prefect smiled warmly at Torres, but she was still thinking about what Tuvok had said. "Do you really think we should start planning to get out?"

The Vulcan looked pointedly at her. "Service in the Maquis can only end one of three ways: retirement, imprisonment, or death. I would prefer to see my comrades in retirement than in either of the other circumstances."

"That's very considerate of you," replied Torres dryly.

As usual, she couldn't fault Tuvok's logic—they *should* have an exit strategy from this insane life. *But peace? Retirement? A return to civilian routine?* After the last few months, these notions sounded like pipe dreams. Torres wondered what had brought on Tuvok's sudden concern for the future. The proximity of so much death, she decided, could give anyone a pervading sense of mortality.

The trio finally reached the turbolift at the end of the corridor, and the doors whooshed open at their approach. Klain motioned to his visitors to enter first, then he followed them into the gleaming metal chamber. The doors breezed shut.

Again, an odd feeling of dizziness and disorientation came over B'Elanna, but it was gone a moment later. They stepped into a corridor that sloped upward and was lit with luminescent strips embedded in the green stone. She led the way, eager to get out of the underground complex. There was no reason for the IGI facility to seem so claustrophobic, especially for a person who lived and worked on a small scout ship, but Torres nearly ran for the exit.

The outer door opened as she jogged toward it, and she dashed into the warm, afternoon sunshine. Their hovercraft was parked right where they had left it, and the crowd of onlookers had shrunk but had not entirely disappeared. She tapped her combadge and growled, "Torres to *Spartacus*."

"B'Elanna!" answered the relieved voice of Captain Chakotay. "Are you all right? You've been out of contact for almost an hour."

"I'm sorry about that, but their medical facility is underground, and we had to take a tour." She proceeded to fill him in on everything that had happened to them, including the fact that the bug might be a chimera.

"I'll get our researchers on that," promised Chakotay. "The two people from Dalgren that we examined are healthy, although one of them has one of the prions in his system."

"We've got a sick person we'd like to beam up," said Torres, "along with some records. Also, we'd like to get a couple of doctors down here to go over their files. They claim that Dalgren hasn't had any cases of the disease."

"Let's hope they're right. Maybe this won't be as bad as it looks—a smaller continent to the north appears to be clean, so far."

"One other thing, Chakotay." Torres chose her words carefully. "When this is all over, we may want to lay low for a while. The prefect of Dalgren wants to offer sanctuary to members of the Maquis who would like to stay here and blend in with the populace."

There was no immediate response from Chakotay. "Captain?" she asked.

"I heard you. There are days when that offer would sound pretty good. Ask me again when it's all over. Right now, we've got work to do."

After making arrangements that would keep the transporters and medical teams busy for hours, Chakotay leaned back in his seat on the bridge of the *Spartacus.* He gazed at the watery blue sphere shimmering in the sun and wondered what it would be like to live down there. It had to be better than dodging Cardassian and Federation warships, and hiding out in the Badlands.

With a sigh, he glanced at Seska on the ops console. "Any word from Riker?"

"No," answered the Bajoran.

"Try them again," he ordered. "I'd be a lot happier if we could just maintain contact with all of our away teams."

Seska worked her console for a moment, then shook her head. "Riker isn't responding, and their shuttlecraft is still unmanned."

Chakotay scowled and balled his hand into a fist. "Let's send a pilot to that shuttlecraft, just in case the entire Cardassian fleet shows up."

"Danken is coming on duty in five minutes. We could send her."

"See to it personally that she gets there," he ordered. "Tell her to stand by the comm channels and stay on alert."

"Yes, sir." Seska jumped to her feet and strode off the bridge, leaving Chakotay alone to contemplate the enormity of their mission.

Their first day had gone almost too well, considering the obstacles. Chakotay wasn't a pessimistic man, but he had a strong belief in fate. Something terrible and unforeseen was about to happen—he could feel it. But he wouldn't worry about it. Destiny had drawn them all to this forgotten corner of the galaxy, and maybe this would be the place where their quixotic pursuit came to an end, one way or another.

Legate Tarkon sunk into his chair, a scowl darkening his bony, gray visage. Like everyone else in the conference room, he cowered from the tirade of Legate Grandok, who pounded the table with a beefy fist as he ranted. The object of his wrath was Gul Demadak, who stood watching his old friend, hoping Tarkon would defend him, or at least save his dignity.

No, it's not to be, thought Demadak. He was to suffer this ignominy alone, with Tarkon letting him twist in the wind.

"I cannot believe you let this condition fester as you have!" thundered Grandok, chief of the Detapa Council. "That planet endangers our very existence, and then to let Maquis run wild on it . . . is inexcusable!"

There were grumbles around the room as the other members of the council agreed with their leader. So Demadak let his eyes wander out the large window to the glorious view of the Stokorin Shipyards, high in orbit over the amber clouds of Cardassia Prime. He envied the builders floating in the skeletal frame of a future starship at the next dock. Those menial workers could see the result of their work at the end of the day, while he had to think strategically—decades and centuries down the road. And in this matter, he had kept his own council, so even his friends couldn't speak for him.

"Am I allowed to defend myself?" he finally asked. "Or is it a given that you're going to destroy Helena and be done with it?"

That gasbag Grandok apparently needed to take a breath, because he just waved at Demadak to speak. The military commander appealed to Tarkon and his other allies. "First of all, you act like Helena is in Cardassian space. Technically it is, but it's also in the Demilitarized Zone. We are prohibited by treaty from sending warships in there."

To derisive laughter, Demadak nodded his head. "Yes, I know we often break that rule. However, the Federation *does* monitor us—as we monitor them—so we're very careful. Sending enough ships to fight off the Maquis and kill everything on a planet is bound to bring them running. You've got to ask yourselves—should we start a war with the Federation over this threat? Before we're ready? I think not."

The laughter faded, and they were finally listening to him. "As for the Maquis, we have a spy on their lead ship. We have a garrison of two hundred mobile infantry on the planet—we know exactly what the Maquis are doing. Like the do-gooders they come from, they're committed to fighting the disease and ending the outbreak. That's a job that needs to be done, and we don't really have the stomach for it. According to our reports, they're maintaining the quarantine, keeping the Helenites on the planet. Who knows? They might succeed. We can always crush them later."

"That's taking a terrible risk," warned Grandok, glowering darkly at Demadak. "The Maquis are unprincipled scoundrels who can't even be loyal to their former masters. If they get sick, they're just as likely to pull up stakes as remain there, spreading the disease elsewhere. After we all get the Bajoran plague, we won't be able to punish you sufficiently."

There were grumbles of agreement after that remark, and Legate Tarkon rose to his feet, waving down the others. "I believe my friend Demadak is thinking rationally, but we can't be rational where this plague is concerned. We have to be *irrational.* We should muster enough ships in that region to make sure that the quarantine of Helena holds."

The majority barked their agreement to this remark, and Demadak could see the compromise forming. Tarkon hadn't gotten where he was by being a fool.

The legate lifted his chin confidently. "We must be ready to destroy the Maquis at a moment's notice, if they fail, but not so rashly that we alert Starfleet. If we slowly assemble ships in the region, we'll eventually have enough to scorch the planet into dust and escape before Starfleet can react. A done deed is history, not a threat."

There was polite applause at this remark, and Tarkon looked pointedly at Demadak. "What do you say, old friend?"

The stocky gul knew that he was the military governor and could do as he wished in the DMZ, until they replaced him. Tarkon was right. When people got panicked by a plague—especially *this* plague—they did act irrationally. He could not be sure of holding his post if he failed to seize this compromise, and the compromise would at least buy him time. *I can justify it to myself, but can I justify it to my silent partner?*

Demadak decided to deal with that later. Right now, the entire DMZ was close to slipping from his grip. "I believe that plan is workable," he said with a tight-lipped bow. "I'll begin to assemble ships already in the DMZ, and we'll send another warship through every day, disguised as a merchant ship. We'll use proximity to the Badlands to mask our fleet."

Grandok scowled, not liking the fact that he hadn't gotten credit for the compromise. "I want a list of all the ships in this operation."

Demadak nodded. "That list will be so highly classified that I will entrust it to the keeping of the Obsidian Order."

That should keep your grubby hands off it, he thought to himself.

"Demadak is right," declared Tarkon, clasping his old comrade on the shoulder. "Every detail about this operation is highly classified. Breathe of it to no one, not even your closest mistress."

They all laughed, breaking the tension in the conference room. While the others congratulated themselves on their good sense, the legate whispered to the gul, "I saved your scales this time."

"All the same," grumbled Demadak, "I don't like people telling me how to do my job. I won't forget your interference."

He turned and stalked out of the conference room, thinking very little about Tarkon and all the self-important legates and guls. Demadak was only worried about what he would tell his secret benefactor.

Nothing, he decided. If they could keep this operation hidden from the Federation, the Maquis, and most of Cardassia, perhaps they could keep it hidden from *him.* With any luck, the experiment would soon be over, and Helena would be nothing but a distant, unpleasant memory.

Tom Riker rolled over on the wide, comfortable bed and pulled an armload of silky covers to his chest. Athough it felt natural to remain asleep in this plush splendor, he suddenly realized that he wasn't supposed to be in a bed. He sat up and blinked at the blankets, his silky pajamas, and a large, tastefully appointed bedroom done mostly in white antiques. Sunshine streamed in though the French doors, as did the gentle sound of the surf pounding against the shore.

Riker scrambled out of bed, stepping onto cool, red, rustic tiles. Atop a white armoire, he found a pile of clean clothes; a pair of calf-length black boots stood on the floor. The clothes appeared to be of traditional Helenite design—blousy shirts with colorful stripes and braids, brocaded pants with gaudy buttons and cuffs. Since he seemed to be alone in the bedroom, he stripped off his elegant pajamas and put on the outlandish clothing, which turned out to be warm, well-made, and comfortable.

"Hello!" he shouted angrily. "What am I doing here?"

There was no response, except for a flurry of footsteps that sounded far off but quickly became louder. A moment later, the white door flew open, and Ensign Shelzane stood there, looking very festive in her Helenite ribbons and braids.

He gaped at her. "What's happened to us?"

"I don't know, sir. I woke up in that bed, the same as you. You were still unconscious, so I just got dressed to have a look around."

Riker strode to the door and gazed over her head at a sunny hallway that seemed to open into a large living room. "Where are we?"

"We seem to be in a beach house. I think that's what you would call this place." The diminutive Benzite stepped aside to allow him to enter the hallway.

Riker rushed from room to room, almost thinking he was in a vacation resort on Pacifica. Every room was light and cheery, with comfortable if not sumptuous furnishings. There were two bedrooms, a bathroom, a recreation room with exercise equipment and vidscreens, a compact but functional kitchen, and a living room; his grandmother would have called it a sitting room.

Charging back into the master bedroom, Riker brushed past Shelzane and crossed to the French doors. He threw them open, stepped outside, and felt the sun-kissed, misty sea breeze strike his face. The sun was so bright that Riker had to shield his eyes, but he could tell that he was standing on a white observation deck that commanded a view of a narrow red beach and a few lichen-covered boulders. Beyond the boulders stretched a lustrous sea that looked like blueberry syrup with cream floating on top of it.

Shelzane stepped onto the deck beside him. "What does it mean?"

"Let's think. The last thing I remember is that we were in that waiting room, talking to the little man—the hologram. Then something shot me in the back—"

Shelzane nodded her head vigorously. "Yes, it felt like a dart. We were probably drugged."

Riker scowled angrily. "Before I passed out, I think I remember seeing somebody else . . . they were laughing."

"Who?"

He shook his head. "Someone in a black environmental suit. But who knows, it could've been an hallucination . . . or another hologram. For all we know, *this* could be a hologram . . . one big holodeck."

Shelzane squinted into the bright sunlight. "Yes, but there must be a thousand places on Helena that actually look like this."

"That's true." Riker spotted some stairs going from the deck to the tiny beach, and he bounded down and leaped into the sand. Running, he circled the beach and jogged to the side of the house. To his surprise, the view was virtually identical in every direction—an endless horizon of shimmering ocean.

Off the front door of the house was a small landing pad and a rickety pier that went about ten meters into a picturesque lagoon. Except for three palm trees, there was nothing else.

They were alone on a tiny tropical island.

Riker heard a shuffling sound, and he turned to see Shelzane walking up behind him. Her step wasn't as energetic as usual, and he saw deep furrows on her smooth, blue brow.

"What's the matter?" he asked. "Your injury bothering you?"

She touched her hip. "No, not too much. I just feel a little weak . . . probably a side effect of the drug."

Riker nodded, gazing from the white beach house to the sparkling blue horizon. "I wish I could enjoy the view more. I don't suppose it would do us any good, but we should search the house for a radio, flares, or anything we could use to signal for help."

"We should," agreed Shelzane. "We'll also need food and water."

They returned to the house and soon found that food and water would be no problem. Fresh water ran freely from the faucets, and the kitchen shelves were stocked with freeze-dried food in metallic bags. It was the kind of food that might be found in survival rations, but there was enough of it to keep them alive for several weeks.

Riker was fascinated by the water pouring from the taps, and he traced a pipe under the kitchen sink into the foundation of the house. Going outside, he found a water shut-off valve at the side of the house, and he probed the sandy ground with a stick to find the underground pipe. More investigation revealed that a large pipe lay submerged in the ocean only a couple of meters under the water. Both he and Shelzane decided that this pipe brought fresh water to the isolated isle.

It seemed like an awful lot of detail for a holodeck simulation, and they reached the grudging consensus that their island paradise was real.

Riker dragged two chairs onto the deck off the master bedroom, and they sat there and watched the morning sun rise higher in the sky. This helped them make a guess as to cardinal points, and Riker drew a compass in the sand with an arrow pointing north.

"Why are we here?" he finally asked. "I can guess how, but not why."

"We must have been spared for some reason," answered Shelzane. "It would have been easy enough to kill us. If so, we're probably under observation."

Riker looked around at the multihued expanse of sea and sky. "Under observation? But how?"

"By long-range telescopes or scanners," she said, looking up. "Or maybe there's equipment in the dwelling."

Riker jumped to his feet and charged through the French doors into the bedroom. Over the French provincial vanity table was a mirror, and there was another one in the bathroom. In fact, there was a large mirror in every room.

In the second bedroom, he grabbed the floor-length mirror and tried to yank it off the wall. An electric shock jolted through his body, and Riker flopped to the floor, twitching like a fish in the bottom of a boat. Shelzane rushed into the room and wrapped her arms around him, and he could feel her trembling warmth. Despite the shock and disorientation, he soon stopped shaking, and his head began to clear.

A cheerful chuckle emanated from the doorway, and Riker twisted around to see the gnomelike doctor in his white lab coat. He clucked his tongue at them disapprovingly. "Please don't remove any of the furnishings. No, no. We only *rent* this house."

With a snarl, Riker charged toward the doctor, then he stopped himself. "You're not real, are you?"

"Nonsense, I'm Dr. Gammet. Don't get impertinent with me. Yes, yes, you are the subjects of an experiment, but it has to be done, don't you see? If we can get enough data on the disease this way, then we can spare all the Helenites who aren't already infected. We can step back and let you save the planet. You'll be saving millions of lives by your cooperation."

"How do you know we'll contract the disease?" asked Riker.

The little man pointed a spotted finger at Shelzane. "Because she already has it."

Riker felt as if he had been stabbed in the chest, and he turned to look at his co-pilot. Her startled face went through three expressions: shock, anger, and a dawning realization. He remembered her injury, her recent lethargy, and the way she had been sleeping at odd hours.

"But she's been inoculated," protested Riker. "The same as I've been."

The white-haired doctor scratched his goatish beard. "We were wondering about that. But her physiology has obviously been altered—to allow her to function in an oxygen atmosphere without a breathing apparatus. What about it, dear? Did that affect you somehow?"

Shelzane lowered her head, and the Benzite seemed to shrink into her outlandish clothes.

"You don't have to answer him," said Riker.

Her voice quivered as she answered, "They told me that the procedure might depress my immune system—it's a known side effect. I should have listened, but I've always been so healthy."

"Then you got injured," said the little man. "That was an intervention of fate; it introduced the disease directly into your circulatory system."

"But I'm not infected?" muttered Riker, hating himself for asking.

"No, Lieutenant. So far, the various Starfleet precautions are working in your system, but I can't imagine it will take long, considering your constant, unprotected contact with Ensign Shelzane. How long it will take—that is a question of great interest to us. The two of you are almost perfect subjects for this test."

Riker could contain himself no longer, and he charged the pompous little troll. His entire body passed through the image standing in the doorway, and he crashed into the wall in the corridor.

The doctor reappeared to add, "Please behave normally toward the ensign, just as you would toward any loved one." With a blip, he was gone.

Riker picked himself up from the floor and gazed determinedly at Shelzane. "Listen, we will find a way out of here. All you need to do is go through the transporter biofilter."

"Within forty-eight hours," she said glumly. "It's probably already been twenty-four hours. I'm more concerned about preventing *you* from contracting the disease."

Not knowing what else to do, Riker took a step toward her, and she motioned him back. "No, Lieutenant! You have to protect yourself, even though it's probably too late. I'll be getting sicker and sicker, and you'll have to stay away from me."

"No, I have to get us out of here," vowed Riker. "In time to save you."

Through the open window in the second bedroom, he caught sight of the blue silhouette of the ocean; it seemed as vast as space, stretching into the wavering horizon. Also through the window came the timeless crunch of the surf against their spit of land, wearing it down a few centimeters a year. Time hung heavily on this island, and freedom seemed eons away, in another universe.

It dawned on Riker that *time* was their new enemy.

Chapter Ten

Dr. Gammet and Dr. Kincaid were grinning, and Tuvok, while not grinning, looked satisfied. The patient lying before them in the clean room enclosure was not sick but possessed two of the prions that caused the plague. If the third were present, they would combine to form the multi-prion that brought on the full-scale infection. B'Elanna Torres understood that much.

She had been on the bridge of the *Spartacus,* scanning for Riker and Shelzane, while running computer models for the researchers, when she was summoned to the cargo hold. Starfleet's equipment had meshed nicely with IGI's equipment to produce a state-of-the-art laboratory in a clean room enclosure, and now they had their first success. She could see the excitement among the others, but she wasn't quite sure of the reason.

She gazed through the clear screen at the Helenite lying unconscious on the metal table. "Why is it such a good thing that this woman is almost sick?" she asked Tuvok.

"Because she possesses a prion not previously seen in any of the other Dalgrens we have examined," answered Tuvok. "And her exact movements can be traced. She arrived on Dalgren only three weeks ago, before the quarantine, from a small continent known as Santos. This continent lies east of Padulla, so it may be that the infection is spreading westward."

Torres looked with sympathy at the unconscious woman, thinking she looked mostly Argrathi, with her plump face and high forehead. "So we're off to this other continent?"

"Some of us are going there," answered Dr. Kincaid, a middle-aged woman who seldom smiled but was smiling now. "Dr. Gammet thinks it would be a good idea if you returned to Dalgren with him."

"Why?"

"B'Elanna," said Dr. Gammet with grandfatherly patience, "Prefect Klain was expecting you for dinner, and that was hours ago. It's now the middle of the night. He's been waiting a long time."

"But we've got so much to do—"

"The prefect has complied with all of our requests," said Tuvok. "We should comply with his. This mission has a diplomatic component, and devoting one person to that task is an acceptable use of resources. I would advise you to spend time with the prefect and collect information."

"All right," muttered Torres, tapping her combadge. "Torres to bridge."

"Chakotay here."

"Dr. Gammet wants me to go back to the planet with him and be diplomatic. I'm sorry, but I couldn't find any sign of Riker and Shelzane."

"IGI on Padulla is probably deserted," interjected Dr. Gammet. "People certainly went home to be with their clusters and familes."

"Did you hear that?" asked Torres.

"Yes, we'll keep looking," Chakotay assured them. "They've got to be down there somewhere. You go ahead and be charming, and try to get some sleep, too."

"Sleep? What's that?" Torres strode onto the transporter platform and motioned to the white-haired doctor to join her. "Dr. Gammet, let's go have dinner."

"I shan't be joining you," he said with a twinkle in his eye. "I'm certain that Prefect Klain won't mind."

Torres nodded to the Bolian on the controls. "Put us down in front of IGI."

A moment later, they materialized on the landing pad in front of the immense green pyramid and its protective walls. It was night, and a foggy chill engulfed Torres and made her shiver. She glanced around, expecting the street to be deserted at this late hour, but several onlookers pressed forward, eager to get a look at her. A hovercraft parked on a side street suddenly rose into the air and cruised toward her.

"Good night, my dear!" called Dr. Gammet, as he bustled off to the entrance of the IGI complex.

A whooshing noise grabbed her attention, and she turned to see the hovercraft settle onto the landing pad. At the controls sat Prefect Klain, beaming at her with his perfect teeth, olive skin, and windblown ebony hair.

"They said I was crazy to wait out here, but I knew you would come back." He tempered his joy with a concerned frown. "How goes the battle?"

She walked over to the hovercraft and climbed inside. "The researchers seem happy—they've made a connection with Santos as a possible origin point."

"Oh, really? That's good, is it?"

Torres shook her head puzzledly. "I keep wondering, Why Helena? Why now? It's awfully convenient."

"Convenient for whom? Not us."

"For someone who didn't want much interference." Torres shook her head. "Never mind. It will be good to get some food. Where are we going?"

"My home. The Dawn Cluster." He lifted a box off the floor of the hovercraft and handed it to her, smiling sheepishly. "This is a gift, but it's actually not a gift. It's practical. I promised to give you Helenite clothing, but I don't really see you shedding your uniform. If you wear this, you'll pass as one of us—in case we encounter Cardassians."

She lifted the top of the box and was stunned to see what appeared to be a handwoven coat made of blazing magenta, purple, and green threads, woven together in a tapestry depicting island life. It was at once the most artistic and ostentatious piece of clothing she had ever seen.

"Thank you. This isn't really necessary." She couldn't hand it back—the question was whether she would put it on. Wearing the fantastic robe, she would look like a queen from some old human fairy tale.

She had to admit, it was rather chilly on this foggy night. Not a star was visible in the gray sky, and the marine layer hung in the air like a damp mop. Torres shivered, stood up, and put on the coat. The natural fabrics were surprisingly warm, yet lightweight, and the wrap flowed down to her knees like a purple waterfall.

"It's beautiful," she said, realizing that for the first time.

"No, *you* are beautiful," Klain corrected her. "The coat pales in comparison."

B'Elanna sat down, at an unusual loss for words. "What will we have to eat?"

"Anything you wish," answered Klain, working the controls. The hovercraft lifted gracefully off the pad and headed down the street. For some reason, Torres was glad to get away from the imposing pyramid.

"We're mostly vegetarians," Klain continued. "And of course we eat seafood, but we have replicators if you desire *gagh,* or whatever."

Torres bristled. "I don't eat *gagh.*"

"I see." He piloted the open-air craft down a deserted cobblestone street lined by chic shops and quaint dwellings, topped by ornate walls and roomy balconies. Flowers and vines bloomed from a profusion of pots, boxes, and small plots, and their scents mingled and hung in the fog like incense. Some of the blooms were so vibrant that they glowed right through the fog. Torres looked down at her gaudy coat and realized where the inspiration came from.

In due course, they turned down a street lined with more stately homes—mansions surrounded by high walls. On this street, the fog reminded her of pictures of Earth in the nineteenth century—places like London and Paris. It seemed like ambassadors row, with houses that were too impossibly grand for one person.

They stopped in front of an intricate wrought-iron gate, and a servant rushed from an alcove to open the door for her. Even before the hovercraft had settled to the ground, he was holding the door open and bowing halfway to the ground. After Torres stepped down, the footman remained in this obsequious position until Klain had also exited from the craft. She couldn't help but notice that the servant appeared to be a full-blooded Coridan.

"Any instructions, sir?" asked the servant, staring at the ground.

"Go ahead and charge her up, Janos. I won't be going out again tonight."

"Very well, sir."

Torres wanted to ask Janos how he had fallen to this lowly position in life, but she remembered that she was expected to be diplomatic. This had to be the one job in the galaxy for which she was least suited.

Klain placed his palm against a security scanner, and the gate swung open. He smiled warmly at Torres and motioned her to place her hand on the scanner.

"Why should I be scanned?" she asked curiously.

"All guests need to register," he answered blandly.

Torres nodded. "Oh, it makes sure I'm of mixed blood."

"Due to the late hour, you won't see the club at its finest," said Klain, ignoring her comment. "But there should be a few night birds up at this hour, and hopefully we can roust a cook to make us a meal."

"I don't want to put anybody out," she protested, imagining some poor servant being dragged out of bed to tend to her culinary needs.

"Our cooks would fight for the right to serve you," Klain assured her. To B'Elanna, that thought was more frightening than the idea that they would be forced to serve her.

They walked along a rustic stone sidewalk that meandered through a garden bursting with blossoms and flowering vines. The perfume of the flowers was almost overpowering, and it mingled with the unmistakable scent of food—real food—cooking on a real oven.

"Do you see," said Klain with a smile, "they remembered you were coming. I wouldn't be surprised if the whole house stayed up to greet you."

Looming ahead of them in the fog was the mansion, which had to be four stories tall and a hundred meters wide. The ornate building had giant columns, broad porticos, and balconies on every floor, and it was as large as most government buildings on Earth. The house was certainly big enough to house hundreds of people, not counting servants.

They ascended a wide stone staircase and passed between two massive columns. From the open door came the sounds of laughter and strange music played on a reedy string instrument, like a zither. A doorman bowed politely to them as they entered, and Torres noticed that he was unique, not a uniblood. She recalled what Klain had said about unibloods not even being allowed into the building. They needn't apply even as servants, unless they were content to park hovercraft.

They entered a foyer that was decorated with gaudy velvet furnishings, lamps with stained glass and tassels, and numerous hologram portraits morphing continuously on the walls. From the incredible array of faces on the ever-changing portraits, B'Elanna assumed they were past members of the Dawn Cluster, going back hundreds of years.

Word of their arrival spread quickly through the sumptuous club, and members began to emerge from various dining rooms and bars that opened onto the central foyer. They approached Torres with reverence and joy on their faces, and the music and conversation faded away. B'Elanna wanted to crawl into a shell, or at least a dim engineering room. Instead she was wearing a coat that glittered like the dawn, and dozens of Helenites gathered around her, awe in their eyes.

"Yes, she is as beautiful as we heard!" proclaimed a tall dowager as she gingerly approached Torres. The older woman held out a clawed hand, and B'Elanna had no idea what her ancestry could be. Still she took the proferred appendage, which seemed to be the expected thing to do. At least the other Helenites murmured and nodded their approval.

"The Dawn Cluster is deeply honored," said the older woman with a respectful bow. The others applauded this statement with gusto.

Klain stood behind her, beaming like a proud father. Torres could not believe all this fuss and attention was for *her,* and she fought the temptation to laugh it off or make a snide comment. She had to be diplomatic, which meant bowing and smiling while several dozen strangers gushed over her.

We're risking our lives to save you people! she wanted to yell at them. *But you're hung up on the accidental circumstances of my birth.*

Mercifully, Klain put an arm around her shoulders and shepherded her through the crowd into a plush dining room. Waiters in white uniforms formed a line that led to the best table in the house, one which overlooked a beautiful tile fountain. Torres couldn't get over the feeling that she had stepped into a dream—one that wasn't even hers.

A waiter held her chair for her, and she sat down quickly. At last, the other diners returned to their tables, as if it were proper to resume their merrymaking now that the royalty had been seated.

Klain looked at her, amusement and pride on his handsome face. "You really didn't expect this, did you?"

"Are you kidding?" she whispered. "Most places I go, I get shot at."

Klain looked shocked. "Well, never here. Never on Dalgren or anywhere on Helena. Here, you will always be special—the ideal of uniqueness." He glanced at a server, who was instantly at his side.

"Blood wine?" asked the waiter.

Torres scowled, thinking that the worst thing about being half-Klingon was that she was expected to like Klingon cuisine. "Just water."

"Two waters!" ordered Klain imperiously. "And bring us the fresh fish appetizers."

"As you wish, Prefect," said the waiter, stealing a glance at B'Elanna before he hurried away.

Klain gazed at her and smiled with undisguised pleasure. "I'm certainly glad you came to Dalgren first, and not some other continent. Or else we might have lost you."

Torres scowled. "I'm not something to be won or lost."

"Of course not! I didn't mean that. I only meant that some other continent could have gotten the chance to woo you, and we might have been deprived of your presence."

She shook her head with disbelief. "Don't you even realize that there's a plague devastating half this planet? And you're worried about whether I like it better here or somewhere else!"

"Death and sickness come and go," said Klain, "but a uniqueness like yours has not been seen in centuries. Since your arrival, our morale couldn't be higher—it's as if we have seen perfection."

"Believe me, I am far from perfect."

"Not in our minds," said Klain, reaching across the table and taking her hand. She didn't pull away, only because it seemed cruel to be mean to someone who worshipped her. "We trust in your people and the IGI to neutralize the disease, which means that this day will mainly be remembered for your arrival."

The waiter arrived with two glasses of ice water and a steaming dish full of fresh seafood morsels. Torres had to admit that the smell of real food caused her taste buds to water, and her resistance began to break down a little. Following Klain's example, she speared a morsel with a silver needle and popped it into her mouth. As soon as she tasted the delicacy, expertly cooked in a rich cream sauce, she knew that she wasn't going anywhere for a while—not until her stomach was good and full.

"This could be your life," said Klain, "every single day. You would certainly be elected to the Grand Cluster, but your duties could be light. Or full, as you wish."

Despite her good intentions, B'Elanna laughed out loud. "Are you telling me that, even though I just got here, you would make me a leader?"

"You already are my leader," answered Klain, his black eyes sparkling with sincerity. "I'll gladly spend the rest of my life at your feet, and I won't rest until I convince you to stay."

"Wait a minute. You just *met* me, and you're asking me to *marry* you?"

"Not exactly," answered the prefect. "I'm asking you to have a child with me and join the Dawn Cluster, yes. If you wished to stay with me in a conjugal arrangement, I wouldn't resist, but I don't believe in monogamy."

B'Elanna chuckled as she speared another delicious tidbit. "What if I don't want to have children right now?"

"Oh, you wouldn't actually carry and bear children—that would be beneath you. For that, we would use a vase."

"A vase?"

Klain nodded and looked around the elegant dining room. About a third of the tables were occupied, and all of the diners were surreptitiously watching them. He only had to point to a tall, green-skinned woman with a plume of purple hair for her to stand up and sashay over to their table. Torres didn't know exactly why, but this woman reminded her of the women of easy virtue who followed the Klingon fleets.

"B'Elanna, this is Mila, who works as a vase. The three of us could bond tonight, if you wish. My quarters are large enough."

"I would like that," Mila assured her in a husky voice.

Torres blinked at both of them, realizing that she had just been propositioned for a threesome. Or had she? "Wait a minute. Your idea of a first date is for all three of us to sleep together?"

"The sex isn't really necessary, of course," answered Klain, "but I enjoy interspecies sex. I think I would especially enjoy it with you. Mila, or a vase of your choosing, would carry our baby to fruition. We could raise the child together, or you could be the donor, or I the donor. It wouldn't matter to me, as long as we created a healthy offspring."

He smiled warmly at her. "The physical bonding is just an extra expression of our commitment."

Only hunger and curiosity kept B'Elanna from dashing out the door. "I think I need more food. I'm flattered, but I've got to tell you . . . you move a little fast for me."

"As you point out, we may not have that much time." Klain shrugged and picked up his glass of water. "I could recommend the *ratachouille,* which I understand is a Terran dish."

"I recommend that, too," said Mila, staring vacantly into the crowd of people.

"So you have babies for a living?" asked Torres conversationally.

"Yes, and you fight everybody."

B'Elanna picked up her glass of water. "Well, they're both dirty jobs, but somebody has to do them."

"Excuse me," said Mila, bowing her head. "I'm not myself tonight. Yes, I'm a vase. I've been taking a year off, but I might cut that short for Klain and yourself. Excuse me, I . . . have to be somewhere." The statuesque Helenite dashed from the table and out of the room, into an adjoining café.

Klain looked embarrassed, then regretful. "It hasn't been easy to maintain a standard of courtesy under these circumstances. I suppose you could say we're not coping all that well."

Torres looked around at the gracious dining hall, with its holograms, potted plants, antique lamps, handwoven tablecloths, velvet booths, and plush chairs. Several happy diners smiled back at her, and she had to remind herself that it was the equivalent of two o'clock in the morning. "I think you're coping quite well."

"Do you feel at home?" he asked hopefully.

"No," said B'Elanna with a smile. "But I'm a drifter—I don't feel at home anywhere. One of the ways to my heart is through my stomach, though. So impress me."

In the beach house, Riker stepped back and surveyed the large mirror on the wall of the second bedroom. He had given Shelzane the master bedroom, because it was cheerier, with its big windows and deck. She was sleeping, because they both wanted her to conserve her strength for their escape attempt, whenever it came. Riker tried to tell himself that the inoculations were supposed to delay the worst symptoms, too, but he had seen too much suffering on Padulla. Once the disease took hold, the onslaught was swift and sure.

At least Shelzane was resting and eating. She seemed to enjoy the fish broth, and they had plenty of that in their reserves.

He sighed and looked back at the mirror, which he planned to demolish in order to reach the circuits contained inside. If it was transmitting *out,* maybe there was a way to use the transmitter to signal Chakotay. Riker knew enough not to touch the mirror again, and he didn't want to attack it at close range. That last jolt had almost killed him—but not quite. There was a chance that its defenses were programmed to become even more lethal with repeat attacks.

So Riker stood in a corner of the room with a pile of rocks of various sizes, gathered from the beach and tide pools. Near him was an open window, which was his quickest escape route. It was essential to find out what the mirror was hiding, especially if it was a panel of holodeck controls. Riker picked up a melon-sized rock and hefted it, deciding he had better aim for a corner.

He reared back and threw the rock into the full-length mirror, only his aim was a bit off. It struck more toward the upper center, and the mirror shattered a microsecond before it erupted in a gaseous explosion. Riker dove out the window into a thicket of sand and scraggly bushes just as a wave of heat blistered the windowpanes.

When he lifted his head from the sand, he saw acrid, black smoke billowing from the window, and he heard a shout. "Lieutenant! What happened?"

Riker ran around to the back of the house, where Shelzane was standing on the deck, looking frail and worried. She clutched a blanket around her trembling shoulders, as black smoke wafted over the house, contrasting sharply with the seamless blue sky.

"I was, er . . . inspecting the mirror again," explained Riker.

"By setting the house on fire?"

"Let's see what I did." Riker climbed the stairs to the deck and entered the master bedroom. He stalked across the tile to the bedroom door and felt it with his hand before opening it; there was a bit of heat but not much.

When he opened the door, smoke billowed in, and Riker spent several seconds coughing and rubbing his burning eyes. But a draft blew most of the smoke out the French doors into the crystal sky, and he was able to enter the hallway. Reaching the second bedroom, he glanced cautiously around the edge of the door.

The room lay in ruins—blackened with chunks of glass and some kind of grimy brown residue that covered everything. Nothing was burning. Where the mirror had been fixed on the wall, there was only a rectangular hole, filled with melted residue, shattered glass, and chunks of scorched building material.

"You're not going to be able to tell much from *that,*" said a voice behind him. He turned to see Shelzane, keeping her distance.

"No," said Riker glumly. He stepped into the room and kicked at a pile of debris on the floor. "I've never seen a mirror self-destruct."

Shelzane coughed and leaned against the wall. "Do you have a Plan B?"

"Yes," he answered with determination. "We're going to build a raft with a sail."

"From what?"

"Actually, the raft is already built—it's that small pier out front. If we need more stability, we could lash together some of these doors. I'll look for a pole to use as a mast, and you can gather sheets, blankets, curtains—anything we can use for sails."

Shelzane grimaced and shook her head. "You'll be stuck with me . . . in the middle of an ocean. It might take days or weeks to reach a port. I can't go with you, Lieutenant. You have to try to save yourself—while you're still healthy."

"Nonsense," Riker answered with an encouraging smile. "We got into this mess together, and we're going to get out together. If you feel weak, I'll do the work. We also have to pack food and water. I'd better get started."

As he strode down the hall, Shelzane called after him, "Lieutenant Riker!"

"Yes?"

"Thank you." The Benzite couldn't smile, but her green eyes glittered warmly.

"Thank me when I get you back to the ship." Riker kept a smile on his face until he had stepped outside into the warm sunshine, then he frowned grimly. Shelzane's blue skin looked as pale as the sky, and it had begun to peel on her face and arms. He had no idea what that meant, but it couldn't be good.

Riker's frown deepened as he strode toward the small pier. Shelzane was a young ensign, just starting her career, and he'd had no business involving her in this madness. True, she had volunteered—but without his personal problems, maybe *he* wouldn't have agreed to this foolhardy mission. If he hadn't said yes to the Maquis, Shelzane wouldn't be here—it was as simple as that. All those grandiose ideas about helping people and saving lives, and now he couldn't even save himself and his co-pilot.

He would have liked to blame Chakotay and the Maquis, but what were they but a reflection of himself? Were any of them really out to save the DMZ—or just give some meaning to their misguided lives? Thomas Riker gave a derisive laugh as he stood watching the rickety pier float on the creamy water. Once again, he was stranded—soon to be alone. Somehow he always knew he would die alone, at the end of a pier to nowhere.

You didn't give up before, when you were stranded, came a voice he hardly recognized.

He started to look around for the hopeful voice, when he realized it was inside of him.

Chapter Eleven

B'ELANNA TORRES GASPED when she sat up in bed and saw the size and opulent luxury of her guest room inside the Dawn Cluster. She had seen it the night before in dim light as she staggered into bed in a food-induced coma. Good food was not on the list of perks for a guerrilla freedom fighter, and she had taken advantage of Klain and the Dawn Cluster. If the prefect had thought he was going to take advantage of her, however, he soon realized it wasn't going to happen.

Seen by the golden light of dawn, the pearl-lustre furnishings and pastel drapes and cushions were tasteful and refined. Intricate montages decorated the walls, made from plants, shells, and found objects that must have been gathered locally. Shiny-red flowers blossomed from two vases, giving the soft colors of the room a vivid contrast. It was certainly the nicest room Torres had ever slept in, which wasn't saying that much, she decided.

She staggered out of bed, still wearing the magnificent coat Klain had given her. Several suits of Helenite clothing lay spread on the vanity table, as if awaiting her approval. A silver tray of fruit, toast, and tea graced a flowing desk. B'Elanna had to ignore these offerings for the moment, as she fumbled under her coat for her combadge.

She finally found it. "Torres to *Spartacus.*"

"This is Seska on the bridge," came a friendly voice. "We wondered what had happened to you, but Klain assured us you were okay."

"I was definitely okay," muttered Torres, suppressing a burp that would do any Klingon proud. "I got wined and dined last night, and you ought to see this room they put me in."

"I haven't seen Prefect Klain," added Seska with merriment in her voice, "but I hear he's really something."

"Yeah, yeah, very handsome, and he treats me like a queen. Where's the captain?"

"He's due to wake up in a few minutes. Is it an emergency?"

"No," said Torres, glancing around at her sumptuous surroundings and the pot of steaming tea. "I'm just checking in."

"Chakotay said you should stay on duty there, and help the prefect as best you can. Tuvok is going down to IGI in a few minutes, and Kincaid is on the continent of Santos, tracking down that lead. The clinic in Padulla is busy, but it's tapering off."

"What about Riker and Shelzane?"

"No sign of them," replied Seska. "We're still looking, but there's a growing fear that maybe a Cardassian patrol got them."

Torres scowled. "We know they were going to the IGI on Padulla, right?"

"But it was deserted. Even Dr. Gammet says the workers there were probably sent home. Riker reported Cardassians on foot around IGI in Padulla, but since they've basically left us alone, we don't want to start something on a hunch."

"Those two picked a bad place to disappear," grumbled Torres. "I'll check in later. Out."

As she rifled through the pile of clothing, looking for something at least slightly subdued, Torres heard strains of music come wafting through the open window. At first she thought it was instrumental music from some electronic device, but then she realized it was singing—a choir. A smattering of applause and laughter told her it wasn't a recording but live music.

Torres crossed to the window and peered into the courtyard of the Dawn Cluster. Befitting the name of their lodge, thirty or forty people were gathered around the fountain in the courtyard to greet the dawn. When Torres opened the window to get a better look, several of them caught sight of her. At once, there was a flurry of activity as the chorus formed ranks and came to attention, all staring at her.

Uncomfortable with all the attention, B'Elanna almost ducked out of sight. Then they began singing. Their voices floated upward like an orchestra of horns and strings, an intricate arrangement of soaring harmonies covering half-a-dozen octaves. Passersby gathered in the courtyard to listen, but the concert was directed solely toward B'Elanna in a display of admiration and affection. These people were complete strangers to her, but they seemed to adore her.

So I'm going to wake up and be serenaded, she thought. *My duties can't get any more surreal than this.* Despite the beauty of the music and the velvety voices, Torres wanted to blend into the crowd—she didn't want to be the object of a command performance.

She looked for Klain in the crowd and found him lurking off to the side, under a tree. He was dressed in his finest stripes and ruffles. Upon seeing her looking at him, he bowed rather clownishly and motioned toward the choir. *Yes, they are magnificent,* agreed B'Elanna, and she couldn't help but to flash him a smile. At this, the chorus seemed to sing all the louder and lustier.

These aren't people about to die! she thought with a pang of fear. *They can't be, not people as vibrant and joyful as these. Surely they are right—the plague must be happening someplace else, to someone else.*

Clutching a computer padd in one hand and a case of isolinear chips in the other, Tuvok materialized on the street outside the IGI building in Astar. The Vulcan looked up at the green pyramid, uncertain as to why such an imposing structure was actually needed. His brief forays into the complex had led him to believe that most of the IGI facility was housed underground, not in the ostentatious pyramid.

In most of their buildings and dwellings, the Helenites showed acceptable restraint and taste, but this complex was grandiose for no apparent reason. Its only functions seemed to be to impress the locals and serve as a landmark, and Tuvok preferred architecture that was more practical. According to Lieutenant Riker's report on Padulla, the pyramid probably contained a defense system with a beamed weapon, but even that seemed unworthy of the massive structure and its impressive shielding.

The loss of Riker and Shelzane was troubling, not only because every person was needed, but because they weren't actually Maquis. The moment he saw them, Tuvok knew it was unwise for regular Starfleet officers to be involved in this mission, but he could think of no other way to get the necessary personnel and supplies. He wished he had been able to protect them better, but he couldn't without risking his cover. More than once, the Vulcan had considered telling Riker that he was an operative for the Federation, and warning him to leave. The opportunity had never come, and now it was too late.

In reality, Tuvok decided, having only two people missing in this entire operation was an accomplishment. Still, that didn't prevent him from regretting the loss of two young officers who didn't deserve this fate.

"Sir! Mr. Vulcan!" called a voice.

Tuvok whirled around to see a Ferengi rushing toward him from a storefront across the street. There could be no mistaking those mammoth ears, uneven teeth, and bald pate—he was a full-blooded Ferengi. As he crossed the street, he looked in every direction, as if worried about being followed.

But there were few Helenites on the street at this early hour of the morning, and no one seemed to be paying any attention to them. Instead of approaching Tuvok, he jumped behind a tree trunk and motioned him over. The Vulcan complied.

With his gold-brocaded vest, sashes, jewelry, and bright pantaloons, the Ferengi's apparel rivaled a Helenite's in garishness.

"Thank you . . . thank you for seeing me," he wheezed, out of breath. "I knew you would come back here eventually. My name is Shep. This isn't a very good place to talk—why don't you come with me to the Velvet Cluster? It's not far."

"I have business inside," answered Tuvok, pointing to the pyramid.

"Anything you do in there would be a waste of time. Come with me instead. You'll learn more."

When Tuvok considered this request, he remembered that he had been scheduled to dine at the Velvet Cluster the night before, but hadn't kept his appointment. Information gathering was part of both of his missions—the overt one and the covert one—and their efforts to stem the disease were proceeding as planned. He could spare a few minutes for this Ferengi.

"Very well," answered Tuvok. "I will accompany you."

The nervous Ferengi grabbed his arm and spirited him down a side street. "My name is Shep . . . oh, I already said that. What's yours?"

"Tuvok. Why are you so anxious?"

Shep gave a sour laugh. "Why am I so anxious? Oh, nothing to be anxious about—ship destroyed, profits gone, stuck on a plague-ridden pesthole, surrounded by Cardassians! On top of that, I'm forced to deal with the Maquis, of all people. What's to be anxious about?"

"Your situation is not unusual. Be thankful that you are not on Padulla." The Vulcan continued walking down the narrow street, and the Ferengi had to hurry to keep up with his long strides.

"I'm *grateful,* I really am! Hey, I'm risking my life to see you, and I didn't do it just to complain." Shep looked around the deserted street; the heavy dew of the sea still clung to the lampposts and wrought-iron railings. Choral singing lilted over the rooftops from somewhere in the quiet city, as dawn nudged over the buildings and stole down the streets.

"About a month ago, I brought some laboratory supplies here," whispered the Ferengi. "I didn't know I was going to get *stuck* here because of it."

Tuvok tilted his head and replied softly, "Are you saying that you know who infected this planet?"

The Ferengi smiled, showing a row of crooked teeth; he grabbed Tuvok's arm and steered him toward a row of hedges that ran along the sidewalk. "We Ferengi are businessmen—it would insult our heritage if I were to give you valuable information without getting something in return."

"What do you wish?"

"I wish to get off this blasted planet!" he nearly shouted. "You've got a ship—you could take me!"

"None of us are leaving until this plague is under control."

"Yes, but it's safer up there, isn't it?" The Ferengi pointed into the gray sky. "The transporters cure you, or so I've heard."

"The best I could offer is to take you aboard our ship and let you speak with our captain. It is not a cure, but a trip through our transporter is effective during a certain stage of the disease. You could always be reinfected."

Shep's scrawny shoulders slumped. "So it's hopeless. We're all stuck here . . . for the duration."

Tuvok stopped abruptly and drilled the Ferengi with ebony eyes. "If you know who started this deadly disease, it is your duty to tell us. It could help save the population and the planet, and bring the perpetrators to justice."

"I only dealt with a syndicate," muttered the Ferengi. "Knowing them, I doubt if they even knew who the customer was. The people who removed the cargo were wearing environmental suits—I didn't get a good look at them."

"Then you have no information," said Tuvok curtly.

"I do so," sniffed the Ferengi. "I'll tell you something that none of the Helenites will ever tell you. They're so image-conscious—they always keep up appearances no matter what horrible things are happening under the surface."

Shep took the tall Vulcan's elbow and steered him down the street, their shoes scuffing the quaint cobblestones. "There's a war being waged on this planet, and I don't mean between the Federation and Cardassia, or between the doctors and the plague."

He looked around and stopped, waiting until a small bird fluttered from under a bush and flew away. He breathed heavily and continued, "For centuries, the Institute of Genetic Improvement has controlled the Helenites' reproductive functions, but IGI has gotten too big and greedy. In some places, they put in holographic doctors instead of real ones—things like that. So a few years ago, some wealthy Helenites formed competing companies to do the same work—making hybrids."

Walking once again, the Ferengi continued to glance over his shoulder and around corners. But they seemed to be alone. The air was empty of sounds except for the occasional creak on a balcony. "The competition has been brutal," he whispered, "sometimes resulting in industrial sabotage—if you get my drift."

Tuvok raised an eyebrow. "Are you saying this plague may be the result of industrial sabotage?"

"Well, it has effectively crippled IGI—they're not the monolith they used to be. I'd heard that a few of the smaller companies had gotten together to pull a dirty trick on them. When somebody has a monopoly on reproduction, sometimes competitors will do almost anything to get rid of them.

"If you think about it, the local companies will probably survive this outbreak, but IGI has gotten swamped by plague victims. Most of their facilities are closed, and their operations are shut down. Worse yet, they've had to open their doors to the Maquis and people from outside. Believe me, IGI is the picture of arrogance, and they wouldn't be talking to *you* unless they were desperate."

Tuvok nodded, recognizing an accurate observation. He quickened his pace, a feeling of urgency taking charge of him. "We believe the disease is genetically engineered."

"And who better to do that than genetic engineers?" Shep scowled and kicked a stone in the street. It skittered into the gutter. "I should've gotten off Helena when I had the chance, but they've got the only good restaurants in the DMZ! Even though I'd heard there was a disease on Padulla, I didn't think anything of it. Then *boom!* Without warning, that big Cardassian freighter blasted my ship out of orbit, killing my whole crew. We were told the freighter was a *hospital* ship, for Zek's sake! I'm so glad you shot them down. Luckily for me, I was down here, negotiating a return cargo."

"I am sorry," said Tuvok, abruptly stopping. "I could not enjoy a relaxed meal with this knowledge. I have to act on it."

"But you've got to be my guest at the Velvet Cluster!" insisted Shep. "Later tonight. Please! It would get me more credit. The lodge is right around the corner on Velvet Lane. Just come in and ask for me—Shep."

"I will try to make it," pledged Tuvok with a bow. "You have been most helpful. If the captain wishes to speak with you, I presume you are staying at the Velvet Cluster."

"As long as I can afford to," muttered the Ferengi. "Of course, in these times, who worries about piling up credit?"

"Indeed." Tuvok turned in the other direction.

"And please, bring your captain, too. He's uniblood human, right? And remember, I gave you something for free. You owe me."

As Tuvok strode briskly down the sidewalk toward IGI, it all began to appear very logical. The outbreak could have been a dirty trick gone awry, or even an accident. He had to verify Shep's information and find out who controlled these smaller genetic companies.

He tapped his combadge. "Tuvok to *Spartacus.*"

"Bridge here," came the reply. "This is Seska."

"Is the captain on the bridge?"

He could hear the bristle in Seska's voice as she responded, "No, he's not. Can I help you?"

Tuvok ignored her annoyance and pressed on. "When precisely will he return?"

"Precisely after his flying lesson with Echo Imjim. We think that gliders may be the best way to look for Riker, because the Cardassians don't usually fire on them."

"You're alone on the bridge?"

"Yes, and I kinda like it that way. Want to leave a message?"

"Please hail me when he returns. Tuvok out." He continued walking along the street, but he was suddenly conscious of movement on a roof three stories above him. He whirled around to see something duck into the shadow of a large vent. Tuvok couldn't be sure what he had seen, or if he had seen anything at all. A curtain in a balcony window moved—perhaps that was what had distracted him.

Except for a few lemurlike primates in the rural areas, Tuvok hadn't seen any animals running loose on Helena. He wondered whether a few of those primates sneaked into the city at night, to go through garbage and whatnot. On the other hand, there could be people observing him. The perpetrators of this catastrophe were still at large, according to Shep. Tuvok walked more briskly, keeping an eye on roofs, balconies, and windows, and his hand didn't stray far from the butt of his phaser pistol.

He tapped his combadge. "Tuvok to Torres."

"Hello, Tuvok," she said, her voice lilting, as if coming off a laugh.

"I am sorry to bother you, but I have some important information to verify, and the captain is unavailable. I would prefer not to investigate alone."

"Give me a few minutes, and I'll be there. Where?"

"The IGI building in Astar."

Chakotay beamed with delight as the sea-glider under his command soared over the endless ocean, which looked like blue enamel rimmed in gold from the morning sun. The sun was so bright that it stung his eyes, and the sky looked as endless as space. Chakotay had flown many crafts in his varied career, but never one so responsive and natural. Gliding with the wind made him feel at one with the elements, and the brush of the wind against the fragile hull was like a gentle drumbeat.

"You're doing very well!" called Echo from the co-pilot seat behind him. "But did you notice that you're off course?"

He glanced at the compass and shook his head. "Sorry. It's hard not to get distracted by the beauty."

"Winds shift," said Echo disapprovingly. "You have to watch them. Don't let the wind ride you—you ride the wind."

"Checking sensors," said Chakotay, doing just that. "I've got a northerly wind pattern at three thousand. Should I take it?"

"Go ahead."

Lining up his wings with the horizon to keep level, Chakotay edged the antigrav lever upward. He knew that powerful and sophisticated gravity suppressors were working in the underbelly of the glider, but to him it felt as though a sudden draft had caught their wings and lifted them upward. Since he usually worked in artificial gravity, trying to avoid the problems of weightlessness, it seemed strange to seek safety in weightlessness. The farther he rose above the ocean, the more his sense of wonderment increased.

He glanced back at his Helenite instructor. "How am I doing now?"

"You're a natural!" shouted Echo. "You've got all the basics down. Of course, the hardest part is landing."

"I've had some experience at that. I could fly around like this all day, but I think we should do something useful while we're up here. Do you feel like taking a short flight over Padulla?"

She laughed at him. "Sure, but it would take us days to get there."

"Not when you have friends." He tapped his combadge. "Chakotay to *Spartacus.*"

"Bridge here. Seska on duty."

"Everything under control?"

"Yes, Captain."

"Seska, I want you to lock onto our glider with a tractor beam and carry us over to Padulla. We need to come in near the capital. Let me know when you're ready, because I want to turn off the antigravity and put us at normal weight."

"All right, sir. Give me a moment."

Echo cleared her throat nervously. "Er, Captain . . . remember, the Coastal Watchers are going to want their glider back in one piece!"

"That's my intention," vowed Chakotay. "For my own peace of mind, I've got to look for the missing team. If we see Cardassians encamped around the area where they disappeared . . . we'll assume the worst. We won't take chances. Are you sure they're not going to shoot at us, too?"

"I'm not sure about anything anymore," admitted Echo. "Before, they were only shooting down ships that could leave orbit, not surface craft."

"*Spartacus* to Chakotay," a voice cut in. "We're in range and able to lock onto you with a tractor beam."

He put the lever down to zero, going into free flight at their real weight, which wasn't much. Still, the silver nose cone of the graceful plane started to edge downward.

"Proceed, *Spartacus,*" ordered the captain.

A sudden jolt let them know that the wind no longer controlled their tiny craft. Now it buffeted against them. He tapped his combadge. "Chakotay to Seska! Increase the field to encompass the whole glider."

"Yes, sir. Good thing I started slowly. Compensating—"

When the sea below them began to ripple past like a cascading waterfall, Chakotay sat back and relaxed. It felt as if they were standing still, not moving at all, but he had to look at the sky to keep from becoming disoriented. Like the passengers, the sky appeared to be standing still.

"Ah, this is the way to travel," said Echo, putting her feet up. "Why did I ever bother to go the long way?"

Chakotay looked at the unique Helenite with admiration. "This must be a hard way to make a living, piloting one of these planes across a great ocean."

"I don't hop continents very often," said Echo with a shrug. "Well, maybe more than I want to. If you have a good co-pilot, it's not so bad. That last trip with my son was the hardest of all."

"You risked a lot, including the lives of the people on Dalgren."

Echo frowned, and the furrows in her gray skin deepened. "I know . . . I'm not proud of it. But I wanted to save my son, and I wanted to go home. Those are the things you think about when death is staring you in the face." Chakotay was silent for a moment. He couldn't argue with that.

"Too bad we can't just stay up here," he finally said wistfully. "It's all sunshine and blue sky."

"I always thought I would die on a day like this, plunging into the West Ribbon Ocean," said Echo. "You barely kept me from doing it already. If the plague is about to get me, I think I'll drag myself into a glider and come up here to die."

A voice broke in, "*Spartacus* to Chakotay. We're getting close to Padulla."

Both he and Echo stared into the glittering horizon. "I see it," said his co-pilot, although Chakotay didn't see anything but a blurred ocean.

"Are we close enough?"

"Yes," said Echo. "Why don't I take over?"

He nodded. "Chakotay to *Spartacus,* cut us loose."

"Yes, sir. Happy hunting." With another jolt, they were flying free again, and Chakotay reluctantly took his hands off the controls. Echo knew her way around much better than he did, but it was hard to give up the thrill of flying the sea-glider. He could understand why they were so popular. Not only were they practical transportation, but they kept adventurous, young Helenites at home rather than exploring outer space.

Chakotay checked the sensors, but they were designed to search vertically for wind currents, not horizontally for lifesigns. He had navigation and weathercasting tools, but he already knew the weather was delightful, as Echo Imjim flew by dead reckoning. So Chakotay used his eyes to survey the coastline, picking out the carved bays, green bluffs, white cities, and copper beaches from a distance.

Harnessing the wind, Echo masterfully guided the glider into a low approach that took them directly over the nearest cityscape. "We usually get navigation beacons and landing instructions about this time, but no more."

As they swooped over a sparkling bay, which sheltered a few sea-gliders and sailboats, Chakotay felt like a seagull coming home after a long flight. Only this was a home that was too quiet, too idyllic—the noisy flock had moved on. As they flew deeper into the city, the sight of the empty streets, silent buildings, and deserted courtyards gave him a chill. He didn't know this place or its people, but he could feel their restless ghosts walking beneath him.

Chakotay recalled pictures he had seen of the great pueblos of his ancestors on Earth, deserted even when the white man first saw them. In a thousand years, this place would be like one of those old pueblos—no one would know what had happened to its people, only that they were gone forever.

"We're getting close to the IGI pyramid," said Echo. "How close do you want to go?"

"Close enough to get a good look. Make several passes if you have to." Chakotay could see the green pyramid in the distance, looking alien among the traditional town houses and baroque buildings.

He wished he had told Riker to stay away from the place, but so many operations were going on at once that it was hard to anticipate the risks. Riker had been certain there was information to be gathered here, so Chakotay had let him come back, even after they had barely escaped the first time. Now it was probably too late to do anything to help them. No matter how many ways he justified it, he had lost the one member of his crew who could make a big difference in their struggle with the Federation.

"Captain, is this close enough?" asked Echo.

His troubled reverie broken, Chakotay leaned to the left to view the pyramid as they swooped past. "Yes, this is fine." The jadelike pyramid was impressive, but it couldn't overcome the gloomy pall of the deserted city. It was like the biggest tombstone in a dark cemetery.

He checked his compass. "This is the east side. Let's make a pass on all four sides, gradually moving outward."

"Okay, here we go."

In a slow bank, the glider came around to catch an air current that took them by the north side of the oval complex. Chakotay spotted the landing pad outside the north gate, as well as the wreckage mentioned by Riker. A moment later, they overshot the pyramid and had to dip lower to catch a current that took them by the west wall.

On this pass, Chakotay spotted movement on the street adjacent to the complex. Looking closer, he spotted two gray-garbed figures moving equipment into a dilapidated building. Glancing the other way, he thought he saw a hole in the west wall of the complex, but they soared past before he could tell for certain.

"Make another pass," he ordered. "I saw people down there."

"So did I," answered Echo, sounding worried. "They were definitely Cardassians. And I recognized those launchers they've got—they could shoot us out of the sky in a microsecond."

Chakotay scowled. He knew that Echo was right—they shouldn't push their luck with the Cardassians. Riker had pushed his luck, and now Riker was gone. "Is there any chance we could negotiate with them?"

Echo shrugged. "Well, the Federation negotiates with them. We've seen how well that turns out."

"Yeah," muttered Chakotay. "Head back for the open sea, and we'll hitch a ride home."

"Yes, sir!" answered the Helenite with considerable relief. She shoved the antigrav lever upward, and the glider soared high above the pyramid. Chakotay couldn't tell which she was more eager to put behind them: the Cardassians or Padulla itself.

That's what I have to do with Riker, he finally told himself, *put him behind me.* As they sped away, Chakotay stole a glance at the dead city and wondered whether any of them would get off this planet alive.

Only a hundred kilometers beyond the southern coast of the continent of Tipoli, Thomas Riker swayed uneasily on the deck of the raft he had strung together from doors and the sturdiest planks he cound find on the small pier. Dusk was blanketing the glistening sea, and he feared launching and sailing into the darkness, but he was anxious to test his new craft, with its single mast and sail.

He glanced back toward the house and could see Shelzane seated by the front door, wrapped in a blanket. It was hard to tell if she was even awake. The Benzite had been watching his progress out of support for his plan, although she hadn't been able to help much. Riker still entertained the thought of taking her with him, but it seemed more unlikely with every passing minute. How long would it take them to sail this raft to land? Days? Weeks? That is, if they were wildly lucky and made it at all.

Riker knew, unless they did something quickly, it would be too late to save Shelzane. Even if they were rescued or escaped, she would be too sick for the transporter to help her.

"I'm taking her out!" he yelled. In the gloomy dusk, he thought he saw Shelzane wave back.

Riker checked his rigging, made from curtain cords, then he cast off from the dock and unfurled his sail, made from the curtain. To his astonishment, the wind grabbed the sturdy curtain and dragged him across a stretch of choppy surf. The planks and doors shuddered under his feet, but the raft held together for the first few meters of its maiden voyage.

Two minutes later, he was about sixty meters offshore, where the water was considerably calmer and deeper. Out here, Riker figured he could make decent speed, and he was filled with a giddy sense of accomplishment. Maybe there really *was* hope for them to escape. They would be slaves of the wind, forced to go where it led them, but that was better than sitting ashore waiting to die.

His joy was cut short by a sudden jolt that nearly pitched him overboard. Riker gazed over the side, thinking he had struck a sandbar. When he realized there were dark shapes—huge shapes—moving just under the surface of the water, he got down on his hands and knees for better balance.

Not a moment too soon, as his fragile raft was jarred again, and two planks of wood shattered. This time, he got a glimpse of an elephantine trunk and a spiny fin attached to a huge black form that slid across the water like an oil slick. Maybe these marine creatures were just being playful, he hoped, although this kind of play could have him swimming back to shore.

Suddenly one of the creatures rose out of the water and tried to board his raft, smashing it in half and nearly swamping Riker. He clung to the mast to keep from plunging into the cool, salty brine, and this time he got a close look at the monster before it eased back into the water. It was shaped like a lumbering manatee, but it had a mouth like a lamprey, with rows of jewel-like teeth glittering in its round, sucker-shaped mouth. The giant leech slid back into the water with a final grin, as if to say that dinner looked delicious.

Water sloshed over the sides of the raft, and the creatures began to swim in a frenzy.

Chapter Twelve

WITHOUT THINKING, Riker began calling for help.

He quickly realized how pointless that was, because his shouts only agitated the hellish fish squirming under his raft. They were as large as walruses, but sleek, with sucker mouths ringed by rows of teeth. In their agitation they no longer had the will for concerted attack, but they smashed and jarred the raft until it was little more than a bundle of driftwood tied together.

Riker snapped off his mast and used it as a spear to ward off the beasts, although that had little effect. As the raft broke apart, he curled up on a last door, hoping he would drown before the giant lampreys mauled him to death.

From the shore, Riker heard a cacophony of sounds: high-pitched screams, shrill tongue trills, and the frenzied slapping of water. He turned to see Shelzane, about fifty meters away, standing in the lagoon hip deep in water, making a terrific racket. She ducked her head under the waves, while she continued to slap the surface, and Riker figured she was shrieking underwater.

Whatever she was doing, it was working, as the huge lampreys peeled off one by one to slither in her direction. Riker wanted to shout to her to watch out, but she had to know what she was doing. He quickly grabbed a good-sized plank and used it as an oar to row the door like a boat. He was very careful to ease his oar gently in the water, realizing that movement and sound attracted the creatures. Fortunately, he couldn't compete with the unearthly racket that Shelzane was making.

He watched nervously as she flailed in the water, attracting certain death. "Get out! Get out!" he yelled at her. She managed to crawl out onto what was left of the pier just as black waves roiled under the waters of the quiet lagoon.

Riker lifted his oar out of the water, realizing that he had to be still. But Shelzane dragged herself to a spot on the east side of the island and began to create her diversion all over again. With darkness fast approaching, he could no longer see the awful creatures, so he just kept rowing—slowly, calmly—toward the beach. Incoming waves picked up the door and propelled him the last twenty meters, until he fell off in the surf and staggered onto shore.

"Shelzane! Shelzane!" he called, stomping through the wet sand.

He found her, lying unconscious in the damp marshes near the lagoon. She was soaking wet, her frail body wracked with shivers and burning with fever. Riker picked her up and carried her into the house. He carefully undressed her, dried her, and laid her in her bed. After cleaning up the room, he stood by the French doors, alternately watching Shelzane and the double moons float on the dark sea.

"Lieutenant!" came a hoarse voice.

He rushed to her side. "Are you all right? Can I get you anything?"

"Some broth, in a while," she whispered. "But first, I have a request."

"Anything."

"When I die, please feed my body to those creatures."

"What?" asked Riker, in shock.

"Like most Benzites, I believe in renewal. So give my body to the sea creatures . . . they can benefit from my death. Don't worry, I heard the doctors say that the animal life is unaffected by the plague."

"You're not going to die," said Riker without much conviction.

"You're a bad liar, Lieutenant," she rasped, her voice degenerating into a ragged cough. When she recovered slightly, she added, "My altered lungs will probably fail first. I may die of suffocation."

"You won't—" He stopped. "What do you want me to do?"

Her rheumy eyes looked sick but oddly peaceful. "If my lungs fail in this atmosphere, it should be quick."

Riker looked down, unable to say anything for the lump in his throat. Finally he croaked, "You saved my life . . . I want—" He tried, but he couldn't get more words out of his mouth.

"I know." She nodded her head weakly. "There is one thing . . . you never did tell me why Starfleet security thinks you're a commander."

Riker laughed in spite of himself. "Now that's a story. If you think *this* is a mess, wait till you hear about what happened to me ten years ago—"

• • •

B'Elanna Torres and Tuvok stood outside the gleaming metal door in the northern gate of the IGI complex on Astar. She was literally stamping her foot, because they had been waiting here for fifteen minutes—with no response to their presence. It didn't seem as if the powers within would ever recognize them and let them enter. Tuvok stood calmly at attention, aggravating her impatience even more.

"Let me go get Klain," she muttered. "Maybe *he* can get them to let us in."

"The fact that they are avoiding us is very revealing," said Tuvok.

Torres scowled, "Well, you may want to stand here all day and find that revealing, but *I'd* like to get some work done."

He looked at her and cocked an eyebrow. "Were you getting work done when I hailed you?"

"No," she admitted. "I was eating my way though the Dawn Cluster. These people have real food."

"We must verify the information I received."

Torres scowled. "Do you really think that the Helenites are killing each other with the plague?"

"You are half-human," said Tuvok. "Humans used to inflict biological warfare upon one another with appalling regularity."

"But these aren't humans! Helenites are much more refined." B'Elanna shook her head. "I'm sorry, but it sounds like this Ferengi was just trying to get something out of us—like a ride."

"That is possible," conceded Tuvok. He looked directly at the area just above the door and spoke loudly. "If we cannot verify this information with Dr. Gammet, we will have to contact the smaller genetic companies. Perhaps they will be more open with us. Let us go."

Abruptly the Vulcan turned and walked away. Before B'Elanna could even take one step to follow him, the metal door whooshed open.

"Well, it's about time," she complained as she charged into the complex. Tuvok strode briskly behind her.

They walked down the sloping green corridor, now more familiar than strange, and entered the sleek turbolift. Tuvok surprised Torres by immediately opening up his tricorder. She watched him study the device as she went through the usual disorientation.

"As I thought," said Tuvok. "We have been transported."

"What?" asked B'Elanna. "Are you sure?"

"The shielding makes it difficult to obtain an exact reading, but we are deep under the surface of the planet—*not* a hundred meters, as we were told. If my suspicions are correct, the IGI complexes spread throughout Helena are nothing but empty monuments, with defense systems. There is only one IGI facility, and all the imitation turbolifts feed into it through transporters."

The door whooshed open, and a morose Dr. Gammet stood before them, looking more stooped than he had before. "You are correct, Mr. Tuvok—yes, you are. Except for a few scattered recovery homes, this is IGI. We have fooled and bamboozled our fellow Helenites for over two hundred years, and now we're paying for it. We call ourselves 'miracle workers,' but when our people come to us looking for a miracle, we're fresh out. We're phonies . . . with big buildings and a lot of parlor tricks."

"Somebody on this planet has created and unleashed a very sophisticated chimera," insisted Tuvok.

"Well, it wasn't *us!"* snapped the diminutive doctor. "IGI has been ruined by this thing. We've lost the confidence of the people, and our operations have been exposed to strangers. The pyramid on Padulla is under seige by Cardassians, and we've lost control in half-a-dozen other cities. In fact, our most secure wing—this one—is no longer safe."

"How many rooms are there like this?" asked Tuvok.

"Eighteen. Five of them have been cut off—even I can't get in. We've had serious sabotage."

"Why didn't you tell us any of this before?" demanded Torres.

The little man gulped. "Pride. Disbelief. We've controlled this planet for centuries, and we maintained control even when the Cardassians came in. We bribed them and shared our research with them—they weren't a problem. Yes, we had a few competitors, but nothing we couldn't handle . . . until the plague came. Now, overnight, it's all crumbled down around us."

"So who's doing this to you?" asked Torres.

Gammet shook his head, his spotted forehead crinkling in thought. "I would have said it was our competitors, but I don't think so. The scope of this is beyond them . . . somehow."

"Who are your competitors?" asked Tuvok. "Do you have a list of them?"

The little man nodded and crossed to his stylish desk. From a drawer, he removed a small computer padd, which he handed to Tuvok. "Here they are, plus the information I have about them. I thought about confronting them, but I kept thinking it wouldn't get worse. Well, it has."

As he read the data, Tuvok raised an eyebrow. "One of them is Prefect Klain."

"Yes, yes," said Gammet with a wry smile. "We only tolerate each other. And starting an operation like this, even on a small scale, requires considerable capital. You'll find Helena's finest families on that list."

"This is ridiculous," grumbled Torres. "Prefect Klain is not going to devastate his own planet for a business advantage."

"That's the conclusion I reached," said Dr. Gammet, scratching his unruly mane of white hair. "So who's doing this to us?"

Suddenly, the floor under their feet trembled, and the lights in the waiting room flickered. Dust and paint chips floated down from a crack in the ceiling. Torres and Gammet looked around nervously, while Tuvok closed the padd and put it safely in his belt pouch.

"What is happening?" asked the Vulcan calmly.

"Cardassians!" Dr. Gammet moved toward the turbolift. "We've already evacuated the patients, and there are just a few of the staff left. As you pointed out, our facility is linked by transporters, so once they've breached one of our pyramids, they can attack anywhere. They must be smashing their way from one wing into another."

The little man stopped in front of the turbolift door, looking expectantly at it. When the door didn't open, he pounded on it. "Something's wrong!"

The room shuddered even more violently, and the lights went off and stayed off, plunging them into absolute darkness. A lantern beam finally pierced the blackness, and Torres trained her light upon the turbolift door. It was frozen like a glacier.

"Is there another way out of here?" She strode across the room to the revolving bookcase. "Where does this go?"

Gammet hurried after her. "Yes, yes! Come on!"

Leading the way, the little man in the lab coat ducked into a passage behind the bookshelf. Torres and Tuvok followed, and they found themselves in a featureless corridor that ended in a junction with five similar corridors. At the end of one of the hallways, sparks glittered on the wall. When Torres pointed the light in that direction, it became clear that someone was cutting through the panel with a beamed weapon.

Dr. Gammet whirled around, looking stricken with fear. "They're here!"

"Which way?" she demanded.

"It doesn't matter . . . we're doomed!"

Torres grabbed him by the collar and pushed him down a third corridor, heading in the opposite direction of the sparks. Her light caught colored stripes on the corridor walls, which probably would have told her where to go if she only knew the code. She just moved forward, pushing the diminutive doctor ahead of her. Tuvok drew his phaser and brought up the rear, protecting their escape.

They reached a door, which probably should have opened automatically but didn't. Tuvok applied his tremendous strength and pushed it open, while Torres and Gammet slipped inside. She expected to end up in another waiting room, but a quick flash of her light showed they were in some kind of operating room, with huge metal bins on the walls.

Dr. Gammet shuddered. "The morgue."

"Are those bins empty?" she asked.

"Probably."

From behind them came a clattering sound, as a chunk of metal fell into the corridor. Loud voices sounded, followed by thudding footsteps. Tuvok immediately shoved the door shut, as Torres shined her light around the room, trying to find anything that could help them. Her beam caught the doctor opening a bin on the bottom row. It was empty.

Torres moved her light to the left to reveal a large sign on a pedestal—universal symbols for "Biohazard! Danger!" superimposed over an impressive skull logo. She grabbed the sign and placed it directly in front of the door, so it would be the first thing anyone saw when they opened the door even a crack.

A metallic thud sounded, and she turned to see Dr. Gammet climbing into the body locker. He waved just before he shut it and went into hiding. Tuvok walked briskly around the large room, stopping at a metal door that looked like one of the fake turbolifts. He began fiddling with his phaser; B'Elanna couldn't tell what else he was going to do, because at that moment she heard voices on the other side of her door. She padded across the floor as quietly as she could, turning out her light as soon as she reached Tuvok. In absolute darkness, they flattened themselves on the floor and waited.

These Cardassians have come from Padulla, she told herself. *The plague is bad there, and they may not even know where they are in this labyrinth.*

Grunting, groaning, and scraping sounds issued from the darkness, followed by a clang as the Cardassians slammed the door open. A strong light struck the sign, and from a distance she could see it reflected on their shiny black heads, which were covered with gas masks. They shined their lights around the room, bouncing off the gleaming lockers, but they didn't advance into the morgue. Despite the crisscrossing light beams, the room remained as still as the death promised on the sign.

Nearby an explosion sounded, and the ground trembled. When an officer barked orders, the lights retreated into the corridor. Amid grunting and groaning, the door was pushed shut, and the room was returned to merciful darkness.

Torres rolled over and turned on her light, shining it at Tuvok. He squinted at his phaser, making an adjustment to the weapon. "This will have to do. Please hand me your phaser."

"But they may come back any minute," she protested.

"I need our phasers to supply power to this transporter," he replied. "We will exhaust our weapons, but it may enable us to reach the surface."

Torres couldn't argue with that, and she turned over her weapon. "Do you need a light?"

"No, I have my own. But you can help me get the door open. I have to find the override controls."

Putting her hip into it, Torres was able to help Tuvok get the turbolift door opened. The enclosure was similar to the others, only larger, in order to accommodate gurneys. Tuvok used his tricorder to locate the access panel, then he set up his light. He removed a compact tool kit from his pouch and set to work.

Muttering under her breath about Cardassians, Torres went back into the morgue to unearth Dr. Gammet from his body locker. When she pulled out the drawer, he blinked at her. "Is it over?"

She whispered, "I'm afraid not. But Tuvok is trying to get us out of here. Are the turbolifts the only way up?"

"There are vents, but we're so far down, I'd hate to imagine how long that would take." He whimpered pathetically.

Torres scowled at him. "Is there anything else you haven't been honest about?"

"No," muttered Gammet. "We've reached the end—there's nothing left to protect or hide. Now we're dependent upon you to save us."

"Great. You've got the plague, a mass murderer, and Cardassians running amok—and only the Maquis to save you." B'Elanna Torres offered a hand to pull him out of the body locker. "Let's hope your luck changes, or you're going to need one of these for real."

Gul Demadak laughed lustily at the antics of the Olajawaks, a troupe of comedians who followed centuries-old traditions in their costumes and routines. Although he had seen this troupe before, their clownish acrobatics had the old gul slapping his knee. The rest of the audience was just as appreciative, laughing and applauding in all the right places. Until he had gotten to the theater, Demadak hadn't realized how much he needed this evening of diversion. Considering what he had been through lately, it was understandable.

Besides, he always enjoyed coming to the Primus Theater, an outstanding example of a baroque period in Cardassian architecture. With its numerous statues and busts, thick velvet curtains and chairs, and intricate murals, the Primus looked nothing like most of Cardassia's gray, utilitarian buildings. It always seemed a bit naughty to come here, particularly since the Primus had once been used for more lascivious entertainment. He had a private box, of course, as befitted his station.

He glanced at his long-suffering wife and smiled. It had been her idea to come to the theater tonight, and he was appreciative. Although he mostly ignored the woman these days, she persisted in maintaining the semblance of a marriage. At times like this, thought Demadak, his marriage was comforting. Perhaps he would reward her by inviting her into his bed tonight.

In the middle of a guffaw, he felt a tap on his shoulder. Demadak turned angrily to see a wizened old usher. "What is it?" he snapped.

"Sorry to interrupt you, sir," answered the old man, quaking in his boots. "We have a hail for you on our public communicator."

"That's ridiculous!" snarled Demadak. "Nobody knows I'm here. I'll have your job for annoying me."

The old man gulped and took a step back. "I'm sorry, sir, but he was quite insistent. He knew exactly where you were sitting, and he said that if you refused to come, I should mention a word."

"What word?"

"Helena."

Demadak stared at the old usher, and it would be hard to say which of the two men looked more frightened. He turned to his wife and manufactured a smile. "I'll be right back, my dear."

"What is it?"

"Nothing important." Demadak rose quickly and followed the usher into the ornate lobby. With the show in progress, the lobby was empty, and the usher conducted him to a small booth near the refreshment counter. As soon as he entered the booth and closed the door, soothing lights came on.

"Demadak?" asked a raspy voice that had been electronically altered.

"Yes?" The gul swallowed hard and balled his hands into fists.

"Do you know who this is?"

"I can guess. I don't know why you should be bothering me here. I've sent you all the pertinent—"

"Silence!" roared the altered voice. "You presume to think you can fool *me.* Let this be a warning that I know where you are every minute of the day, and I know everything you do—and *don't* do. Against my explicit orders, you've sent a fleet to Helena—to destroy it!"

Demadak lowered his voice, hardly believing they were discussing these matters aloud. "I am not the entire government of Cardassia," he insisted. "I delayed sending ships for as long as I could, but the Detapa Council is up in arms. All they can think about is the plague and the Maquis—"

"No excuses!" thundered the voice. "I could find a million failures who make excuses, but you were chosen for your independence and ruthlessness. Sending a fleet to Helena endangers the entire experiment and my best operative. Now I will be forced to rescue my operative and end the experiment early—before your ships blunder in and destroy the planet. You had better pray to your gods that our records are recovered as well."

"Or what?" snapped Demadak defiantly. "I don't like to be threatened—even by *you.*"

"I never threaten," said the voice with a steely calm. "I only promise. In fact, I promise you this—when you return home tonight, you will find your prized riding hound dead in its kennel, its throat slashed."

"What!" wailed Demadak with a mixture of outrage and horror.

"And the next time, it will be your grandson, or your daughter. Or *you.* Do I make myself clear?"

The gul started to protest that his estate was protected, under high security—that they couldn't have gotten in and killed his prized hound, Marko. Then he remembered with whom he was dealing. "Yes, it's clear," he muttered through clenched teeth.

"Good. You have to delay the destruction of Helena as long as possible. Exaggerate the number of Maquis vessels, if you must. I'll inform you when it's safe to proceed. And call off your garrison—they're wreaking havoc with my operation."

"Yes, sir," answered Demadak in a hoarse whisper. He wasn't going to mention that he might not be able to hold off the fearful cowards on the council or in Central Command. They could always replace him with someone more amenable. But his benefactor knew that and was counting on Demadak's considerable political skills.

"Don't keep anything hidden from me again," warned the scratchy voice. "Good-bye."

When the gul stepped out of the booth, he finally unclenched his fists and found that his palms were clammy and sweaty. Few beings had such an effect on him.

Still in a daze, he returned to his seat in his private box. His wife smiled at him and pointed to the frantic players on the stage. "You missed the funniest part," she said, "when the harlequin tries to punish the servants."

"Yes, I like that," he replied absently.

When the rest of the audience howled with appreciation at a particularly wild stunt, Gul Demadak turned his attention back to the performers. But he was no longer able to laugh.

A light flickered on inside of the transporter/turbolift in the bowels of the darkened IGI complex. Tuvok motioned to Torres and Gammet to come inside. "Hurry," he urged. "We only have a few seconds."

They did as they were told, although Torres kept her light shining on the empty morgue and the door that they had forced open to get in. Although she hadn't seen the Cardassians since their brief visit, she had heard them ransacking nearby rooms. They couldn't be far away, and this sudden burst of power might alert them.

"Stand in the center," ordered Tuvok, reaching into the access panel. Torres could see their two phasers, jury-rigged to the circuits, with Tuvok about to connect two couplers.

"Are you sure this is going to work?" asked Dr. Gammet doubtfully.

"No," answered Tuvok as he continued to work.

"Then maybe we should—"

Suddenly there was a crash and the sound of angry voices. Torres peered out the door of the turbolift and could see three brawny Cardassians pushing open the door to the morgue. One of them pointed at her, and she quickly killed her light.

"Hurry!" she warned Tuvok.

"That is my intention."

The Cardassians stormed the morgue in force, and their lantern beams crisscrossed the room like a laser show. A phaser beam streaked over Tuvok's head and blasted a hole in the wall, but that didn't stop his nimble fingers from connecting more circuits and wires. Finally finished, the Vulcan took a step to join them in the center of the turbolift just as the lead Cardassians charged into view.

"Raise your hands," ordered Torres, hoping a show of having no weapons would buy them a few seconds.

It did, as the lead Cardassian leveled his weapon but didn't fire immediately. The odd feeling of disorientation gripped B'Elanna not a moment too soon, and the Cardassians were caught by surprise when the dormant transporter suddenly activated. They shouted and fired their weapons, but Torres, Tuvok, and Gammet disappeared in a curtain of sparkling molecules.

A moment later, they found themselves in the same place—the turbolift—only Cardassians were not threatening them with phaser rifles. The door was closed, and the lift was dark, forcing Torres to turn on her light. Tuvok immediately threw his tremendous strength against the door. "Help me, please."

Torres and Gammet also pushed, but the Vulcan did the majority of the work as they heaved the door open half a meter. Torres squeezed through first and dropped into a crouch, warily shining her light into the blackness. With relief, she saw that they were in a jade-green corridor that sloped upward, and she motioned to the others to follow her.

When they reached the next door, Dr. Gammet was able to open it with a pass card. "The outer wall is on a separate circuit," he explained.

Torres pointed her light back down the corridor, but she could see no indication that hordes of Cardassians were chasing them. After Gammet and Tuvok exited into the street, so did Torres, and she decided that warm sunshine had never felt so good.

She glanced around, but the streets appeared deserted. "Where are we?"

"Padulla, I believe," answered Gammet, frowning at that conclusion.

"Let's find some cover," said Tuvok, striding toward a deserted storefront across the street. Torres and Gammet hurried after him.

Once they were off the street, she tapped her combadge. "Torres to *Spartacus.*"

"Seska here," came the reply. "Where have you been?"

"I'm worried more about where we *are,* which is Padulla," she answered. "Three to beam up."

"It will take us a few minutes to get into position. Stand by."

Torres tried the door to the shop but found it locked. She whirled around and kicked the shop door open, and it fell off its hinges with a cracking sound and crashed to the floor. "Let's get to higher ground," she ordered.

She led the way, not pausing until they had reached a stairwell which led to the roof. With a sigh, she halted their mad dash and slumped against the door. Gammet, who was panting heavily, sat on the top step, while Tuvok calmly took out his tricorder.

"I can find no lifesigns in the immediate vicinity," he reported. "We appear to be safe for the moment."

"Thank you for saving me," breathed Gammet.

"You're not safe yet," countered Torres. "How do we find out whether Klain—or any of your competitors—started this disease?"

The little doctor scratched his white whiskers. "I know what Prefect Klain fears the most—that the plague will strike Dalgren. If that happens, his reaction might tell us something."

"Hmmm," said B'Elanna, wiping a sheen of sweat off her forehead ridges. Before she could say anything else, her combadge chimed. "Torres here."

"Stand by to beam up."

"Gladly," she breathed.

All night long and all the next morning, Thomas Riker had been digging a hole on the north side of the island, using pots and pans as shovels. Fortunately, the sandy earth was fairly soft, and his makeshift tools were good enough for the job, if slow. Riker paused every few minutes to catch his breath and listen for sounds from the house. He had found an old dinner bell and had hung it by Shelzane's bed, hoping she would use it to call him, if she needed him.

He felt guilty, thinking he should stay by her bedside until the end. But Shelzane had insisted that he pursue his latest escape plan, although it was the craziest one yet. They both knew that the clock was ticking for him, too, and he was beginning to feel tired. Hours of digging and no sleep were making him feel that way, Riker told himself, because he refused to acknowledge that he was infected by the disease. Nevertheless, a sense of urgency propelled him to crouch on his knees for hours on end, digging this monstrous hole.

The long hours paid off when he reached a metal box containing machinery—the valves, gears, and circuits that controlled the flow of fresh water from the pipeline into the house. While getting Shelzane a glass of water, he had realized that life on the island wasn't static—fresh water came and went everyday. The pipeline came from somewhere, carrying water, then kept going . . . somewhere else. From observing the pipeline in the ocean, he guessed that the pipe itself had to be about two meters in diameter, large enough to accommodate him if it wasn't completely filled with water. He wouldn't find that out until he broke into the pipe.

When he looked up to wipe the sweat from his brow, Riker spotted something in the crystal blue sky. Shading his eyes, he peered at what appeared to be a large white bird, soaring high above him. When he looked closer, he realized it was a sea-glider, similar to those he had seen floating in the bay at Padulla.

He bounded to his feet and waved frantically, yelling at the top of his lungs. The plane, however, never deviated from its course or altitude. Even if the pilot were looking directly at the tiny island, Riker told himself, it was doubtful he could see him from that distance. Nevertheless, spotting the glider gave him hope, just knowing that not everyone on Helena was dead or dying.

As soon as he began digging again, he heard the peal of the bell inside the house. Riker tossed down his tools, jumped to his feet, and rushed inside. Even before he reached the master bedroom, he heard horrible wheezing, and he rushed inside to find Shelzane writhing on the bed, gasping for breath. He rushed to her side and hugged her trembling body.

Somehow his presence calmed her, although her frail chest continued to heave with the struggle to breathe. He felt her hands grip his back, as if trying to hang on.

"I'm here!" he assured her. "I'm here."

"I know," she rasped. Shelzane gave him a final squeeze, then her fingers loosened and slipped from his back. Her entire body went limp, and he gently laid the Benzite on the bed. Despite the ravaged state of her body, she wore a look of peace on her face.

Riker stood up, wiping the tears from his eyes. Enraged, he yelled at the top of his lungs, "Are you happy—you bastards! What did you achieve by killing her?"

He whirled around, half expecting to see the little white-haired hologram, gloating at them. But no one was there—he was alone in the stylish beach house. A breeze ruffled the curtains and blew through the bedroom; despite the warm sunshine outside, the air was strangely cold.

It was time to go.

Riker wrapped Shelzane in her bedcovers and carried her to the lagoon. He unwrapped her body in the waist-high water, then tossed the sopping blankets into the water. As Shelzane had done for him, he slapped the water, calling the creatures. Gazing intently at the surf, Riker finally saw black shapes moving beneath the creamy blue, edging closer to the sounds. He climbed out of the water a few seconds before the sea creatures reached Shelzane's body. The water began to churn, and he turned away.

Fighting back tears, Thomas Riker strode toward the pit he was digging. Before he returned to work, he stopped to look at the endless horizon of two-tone blue. He didn't know who the perpetrators of this terrible disease were, or why they were doing this to Helena, but he knew one thing: he was going to stay alive long enough to stop them.

Chapter Thirteen

AFTER HEARING A REPORT from Torres and Tuvok, Captain Chakotay stroked his chin thoughtfully and looked at Dr. Gammet. "So it's possible that your own people—former colleagues of yours—planted this terrible disease on Helena?"

The little man sunk into a chair in the mess hall of the *Spartacus*. He looked extremely embarrassed. "Yes, it's possible. All of our research would suggest that *somebody* planted this disease on Helena, and I've wracked my brain trying to figure out who. And why. The Cardassians could have done it, but why? If they wanted to destroy the planet, there are more effective means that are less dangerous to them. On the other hand, if somebody wanted to destroy IGI, they've accomplished that."

Chakotay nodded and looked at Tuvok. "Any thoughts?"

"Only that we cannot hope to be successful if unknown parties continue to introduce this disease. Even those who have been treated can contract it again."

"We're fighting an entrenched battle against this thing," said Chakotay, "trying to find a place to draw the line and contain it. Padulla is under control, but the number of people left there is relatively small. If the disease spreads across Dalgren, Santos, Tipoli, and the other continents, we'll be overrun. And now you're saying we don't have IGI to help us?"

"I'm sorry," muttered Dr. Gammet. "None of us were prepared for a disease like this . . . and the repercussions. Most of the people on our staff are already helping you, but the Cardassians have ransacked our facilities. I don't know what else to do."

Torres frowned, as if reaching a very unpleasant decision. "I've got an idea for testing Prefect Klain's honesty, but it's risky. It might cause a panic."

"The whole planet is already an armed camp," said Chakotay. "Dr. Kincaid and her staff were fired upon when they landed on Santos. The Cardassians are liable to pop up anywhere. All in all, I'd say it's too late to worry about panic. While the medical teams do their work, we've got to do whatever it takes to track down this mass murderer."

"Agreed," said Tuvok.

Dr. Gammet nodded solemnly. "B'Elanna and I can go to the Dawn Cluster tonight and try her plan on Prefect Klain. If it's not him, we'll keep looking."

"Captain," said Tuvok, "you and I have been invited for dinner at the Velvet Cluster, a lodge for unibloods. Since the Ferengi already gave us valuable information, we might learn more by going there."

"All right, but let's all be careful and keep in contact," said the captain. "Riker and Shelzane are still missing, and I don't want to lose anybody else."

He looked at B'Elanna and managed a smile. "Where do I get some fashionable clothes like yours?"

Standing in the middle of a large, mucky hole in the ground, Riker looked with satisfaction at an access panel he had uncovered atop the main pipe. It was large enough for him to fit inside, just barely. More important, the panel would mean he wouldn't have to punch his way into the pipeline, an action he didn't think he had the strength to perform. Using a spoon handle as a screwdriver, he opened the access panel to reveal a rapid flow of dark water surging past on its way to some unknown destination.

Although there appeared to be some clearance between the top of the pipe and the water level, Riker wanted as much clearance as possible. So he went back to the control box, where he had already removed the cover. Putting his back into it, he cranked the outlet valve all the way open, siphoning as much water as possible into the beach house.

Then he jogged inside the house and turned on every faucet full blast. Water was soon gushing into the tub, shower, and various sinks at an enormous rate, and Riker laughed, thinking that the exquisite house would be ruined in a few minutes. He felt giddy, slightly feverish, and he tried to tell himself it was mere exhaustion.

Now he needed a float. There was a small wooden table in the living room that he had not used building the doomed raft. With his spoon, he unscrewed the legs from the table and hefted the tabletop, glad it was a fairly substantial chunk of wood. It would have to carry him a long way—how far he didn't know.

Riker gathered some food from the reserves and wrapped them in the waterproof shower curtain. He thought about changing from his muddy clothes into clean clothes, but what was the point? Anything he wore would get soaked. It would also be dark soon, but there was no reason to wait, as day or night would look the same inside that pipe.

With a last glance at the beach house—and final thoughts about his fallen comrade, Shelzane—he walked out the front door of the house and didn't bother closing it.

A minute later, Riker stood astride the pipeline, gazing into the rushing water and thinking he was about to take the ride of his life. There was a good chance he would drown, or get chewed up in a hydroelectric plant, or meet some other such fate, but he couldn't worry about that. It would be a faster death than the alternative. At least in the pipe he wouldn't die of thirst, he thought ruefully.

Taking a deep breath and a firm grip on his tiny raft, Riker plunged into the pipe full of rushing water. The raft was nearly ripped from his hands by the initial surge, but he managed to hold on and right himself. Soon he was speeding along in absolute darkness, and the sensation reminded him of two pursuits from his youth. One was bodysurfing at the beach, and the other was riding the hydrotubes at an aquapark.

Riker was pleasantly surprised to find that the water in the pipe wasn't that cold. Warmed by ocean currents, it was about the same temperature as the lagoon. He had no idea how much clearance there was above his head, which he kept firmly planted on the tabletop. Besides, there was nothing to see but darkness and water—and nothing to do but hang on, stay awake, and ride it out.

As darkness embraced the city of Astar, Chakotay and Tuvok materialized on Velvet Lane, just outside an ostentatious mansion that bore a golden sign proclaiming "Velvet Cluster." A uniformed doorman, who appeared to be Argelian, looked curiously at them, then he broke into a grin.

"Ah, you are the Maquis unibloods," he said with pride at his own powers of observation. "Member Shep has been waiting for you." With a grand flourish, he opened the door and ushered them inside.

For some time, Chakotay had been accustomed to spartan living conditions, and he was frankly amazed by the opulent splendor of the Velvet Cluster. Crystal chandeliers, rich brocaded furnishings, and centuries-old tapestries graced the sumptuous foyer. Several grand rooms opened off the foyer, and Chakotay peered with interest into the open doorways. Laughter and the clinking of glasses came from what appeared to be a restaurant filled with people. In a darkly paneled library, patrons indulged in the quieter pursuits of reading and card playing. A ballroom with a high vaulted ceiling appeared to be empty.

"So this is how the underprivileged live," he whispered to Tuvok.

"It would appear so," answered the Vulcan. "One can only imagine what the Dawn Cluster is like."

"Well, these people are trying to prove something, so it may not be as grandiose as this."

"Mr. Tuvok!" called a voice.

They both turned to see a stocky Ferengi rushing toward them, a snaggletoothed grin on his face. "And this must be Captain Chakotay. What an honor!"

The captain smiled back. "Meeting a Maquis captain isn't usually considered a great honor."

"But you people are heroes. Everyone says so. Without you, Helena would be alone in this moment of crisis." He lowered his voice to add, "Thanks for coming. This should be good enough to get me another month's worth of credit here."

"Glad to oblige," said Chakotay.

"Let me introduce you around." Slipping between them, Shep eagerly grabbed their arms and steered them into the dining room. What followed was a rapid-fire round of introductions with merchants and uniblood dignitaries. Chakotay tried to determine whether any of these people could furnish them with useful information, but most of them asked whether there was any room on the *Spartacus* for passengers.

"Lay off," grumbled Shep to a persistent Andorian named Bokor. "These are *my* friends—if anyone gets off this planet, it's *me*."

"We're not taking on any passengers," said Chakotay. "Believe me, the life expectancy on a Maquis ship is shorter than it is on Helena."

The Andorian laughed heartily, and his antennae twitched. "I suppose it is. But you don't have to worry—the Cardassians like you."

"Why do you say that?" asked Tuvok.

"Because they're letting you operate unfettered here, even after you destroyed their ship," answered the Andorian. "I sell supplies to the Cardassian garrison on Tipoli, and they're under orders to leave you alone."

"What?" asked Chakotay, taking a seat at the Andorian's table. "You're sure of that?"

"Yes. I just flew there myself by sea-glider two days ago, and they don't know what to make of it. Gul Demadak, the military commander of the DMZ, gave the orders himself."

"But they just recently attacked the IGI complex," said Tuvok.

"Well, you aren't the IGI, are you? They don't trust the IGI, and I can't say I blame them."

Chakotay asked, "Did you see two prisoners in the Cardassian camp? Two of our people?"

"Aren't you listening to me?" muttered Bokor. "Although they don't like it, they're under orders to leave you alone. If you've lost two people, somebody else must have them."

The Andorian sipped a tall glass of ale and smiled smugly. "However, they told me something else which you would pay dearly to find out."

"What is that?" asked Tuvok.

He laughed. "When I'm safely aboard your ship on my way out of here, I'll tell you."

"That's not going to happen for a while," replied Chakotay.

"Better not wait too long," warned the Andorian. "Meanwhile, I'll keep looking for some other way off Helena. If you want to do business, you know where I am."

"Come on, let's eat," said Shep, guiding Chakotay and Tuvok to an empty table. He rubbed his hands together. "I don't suppose you brought any latinum with you?"

"No," answered Chakotay. "Being in the Maquis doesn't pay very well."

The Ferengi sighed. "Well, let's see how good my credit still is."

Chakotay lowered his voice to ask, "Is that Andorian trustworthy?"

"Yes, and well connected . . . for a uniblood."

"Can you guess what his information is?"

Shep tugged thoughtfully on a gigantic earlobe. "Let's see . . . he speaks privately to Cardassians, and he wants desperately to get off the planet. Maybe he knows that a big fleet is coming to blow us to smithereens."

"A logical conclusion," agreed Tuvok.

The Ferengi sat down at an empty table and rubbed his hands together. "Who's hungry?"

"All of a sudden, I'm not," said Chakotay.

"Oh, sit down," insisted Shep. "It does no good to die on an empty stomach."

B'Elanna Torres smiled politely at the well-wishers who greeted her when she entered the Dawn Cluster with Dr. Gammet in tow. The two of them were afforded the royal treatment and escorted to Prefect Klain's private booth at the rear of the dining hall.

"The prefect has been notified and will join you in a moment," said the servant, smiling and bowing obsequiously.

"Thank you," answered B'Elanna.

"Can I get you something to drink and show you a menu?"

"No, thank you, we won't be staying for dinner."

The Helenite looked crestfallen. "That's unfortunate."

"We're only here to see Prefect Klain," said Dr. Gammet, looking and sounding very grave.

"I see," answered the confused waiter. "Perhaps I will have the honor of serving you next time."

When he was gone, Gammet whispered to Torres, "I hope you know what you're doing. Klain is a very powerful man."

"I know we can't sit around and wait—we've got to find out who's behind this. There's an old Klingon proverb: You don't know who your friends are until you start a fight."

The conversation in the dining hall rose several decibels, and Torres turned to see Klain cutting a swath through the room, shaking hands and greeting people at every table. With his olive skin, jet-black hair, and impressive build, he was a magnificent male specimen, the finest being that genetic engineering could produce.

"Did you have anything to do with Klain's birth?" she asked Gammet.

"Oh, my, yes," he answered, beaming with pride. "Beautiful, isn't he? But I could combine the same species a hundred more times and not get one like him. I just wish he didn't know how special he is."

The little gnome's eyes twinkled. "Of course, *you* are his equal. The children you two could have, even naturally—"

"Some other time," she grumbled, cutting him off. May-be there would be another time when she could return to Helena to stay—to live in grand style with a perfect man like Klain. Much of that depended on what happened in the next few minutes.

The prefect approached their table, flashing his incredible smile. "B'Elanna, you're looking unusually beautiful tonight. And, Doctor, this is a pleasant surprise."

Gammmet scowled. "It's about to become considerably less pleasant. Please have a seat."

"What's the matter?" asked Klain, slipping into the booth beside Torres. He gazed with concern at the Maquis officer, as if fearing the news concerned her. This made her feel guilty about the lie she was about to tell, but she was committed to her plan.

With her voice a barely audible whisper, she said, "We've found cases of the plague here on Dalgren. I'm afraid there's going to be an outbreak."

"What?" he gasped.

"Please," cautioned Dr. Gammet, "we've got to keep this news secret for now. We don't want to start a panic, and there's a chance that we can contain the disease where we found it."

Klain looked like a man who had been struck by a Ferengi stun whip. "Are you sure they're native Dalgrens? Perhaps they came from Padulla, or Tipoli—"

"No, they're from right here," insisted B'Elanna. "Actually from several outlying villages."

"Several!" Klain buried his face in his hands.

Gammet patted the big man's shoulder. "It was rather unrealistic to think that Dalgren would be spared this malady, but perhaps we've caught it early enough."

"What can I do to help you?" asked Klain nervously.

"For the moment, nothing public," said B'Elanna. "You might want to prepare whatever emergency procedures you had planned to use, but I warn you—the IGI complex is shut down."

"What?"

"It's been ransacked by Cardassians," said B'Elanna. "Tuvok, Dr. Gammet, and I barely escaped with our lives." At least that much was true, she thought ruefully.

Dr. Gammet had been right—Klain looked like a man who had just seen his worst fear become a reality. If it turned out they were wrong about him, and he had nothing to do with this, then her lie would probably come back to haunt her. She could probably forget about any more spectacular meals at the Dawn Cluster.

"You have a genetic company," said Dr. Gammet. "With IGI out of commission, we'll need your facilities."

"But we have only a few beds," muttered Klain. He rubbed his handsome face, still convulsed with disbelief. Torres assumed that he would be upset with this information, but she found his surprise to be somewhat strange.

"I'm sorry, Klain, but we have to be going." She rose to her feet, and he quickly followed suit.

"When . . . when will I see you again?"

"I don't know, but maybe this will hold you over." B'Elanna reached up, wrapped her arms around his broad shoulders, and gave him the kiss he had been desiring for days. His mouth met hers in a bittersweet mixture of passion, sweetness, and desperation. She knew that even if she had lied to him about the disease, there was no lie in her kiss.

He was so distracted that he didn't notice when her hand curled under his floppy collar and affixed a tiny tracking device to his shirt.

Torres pulled away from Klain reluctantly, unsure whether she had made a terrible mistake or had just saved millions of lives. There were hushed whispers in the dining room as the patrons voiced their approval of this fairy-tale romance. Little did they know that the romance had just ended.

She hurried out of the room before her emotions betrayed her, leaving Klain to stare after her in disbelief. Dr. Gammet rushed after Torres, but he didn't catch her until she was in the street, striding down the sidewalk.

"That must not have been easy," he said softly.

"It wasn't." She stepped around the corner into a side street and took out her tricorder. Even in the darkness, she could see the blip that was attuned to the tracking device, and it was moving. "He's going somewhere. He just left the Dawn Cluster."

Gammet peered around the side of a building. "I can see him—he's in a hurry, headed the other way."

She tapped her combadge. "Torres to Chakotay."

"Chakotay here."

"The target is on the move."

"I've got him," said the captain. "We'll meet you en route. Good job, B'Elanna."

"Yeah, real good job," she muttered bitterly.

"You promised me this wouldn't happen!" barked Prefect Klain, pounding his fist into his palm as he paced the back office of a carpet store in the old section of Astar. "You *guaranteed* it."

"Oh, please," came the snide response. "There are no guarantees in an experiment like this. Besides, you got what you wanted—IGI is history."

"We'll *all* be history if this keeps up! Padulla was bad enough, but did it have to happen here? When are you going to deliver the antidote?"

"Soon. We need a few more days." The speaker knew this was a lie, as there was no magic antidote—never would be. "Those idiot Cardassians upset several experiments when they attacked IGI—I wish I knew who caused that. But if the disease is spreading this fast, we'll be done soon."

"*Now!* I demand you put an end to it now!"

"Or what?"

"Or I'll tell the Maquis everything! I'll . . . I'll tell the Cardassians. I'll *expose* you."

The other party's eyes narrowed. "That would not be a good idea. For one thing, you would be ruined."

"I don't care anymore!" snapped Klain with exasperation. "This has got to come to an end, do you hear me?"

"I hear you . . . all too well."

Suddenly a loud beep sounded in the unkempt back office, followed by a pounding on a distant door. A voice broke in over the comm channel: "Intruders at the public entrance!"

"Delay them!" Furious, the speaker turned to Prefect Klain. "You *fool!* You were followed!"

"I don't see how that's possible. I took side streets and watched out for—" Klain's dark eyes widened in horror. "What are you going to do with that phaser?"

"What I should have done long ago."

The phaser spit a red beam, which gnawed a burning hole in Klain's stomach. With a groan, he staggered to the door but collapsed halfway there. His assassin pressed a button, opening a secret panel, and hurried out the exit into the alley.

Chapter Fourteen

"USE YOUR PHASERS!" ordered Chakotay when the door to the carpet store wouldn't budge.

As several Helenites watched with horror and curiosity, Torres and Tuvok stepped back and blasted the metal security door with full phasers. It began to sizzle and melt.

"What are you doing?" demanded one of the onlookers, a burly Antosian/Catullan.

"It's all right," said a small man in a white lab coat. "I'm Dr. Gammet from IGI, and this is official business."

His words appeased the crowd for the moment, although it was unlikely the quiet row of shops ever saw this much excitement. As the door crumbled into molten gobs, a phaser beam streaked from the store, barely missing Tuvok. The onlookers gasped and ran for cover, but the Vulcan stood his ground and calmly returned fire. A groan issued from within.

Tuvok kicked what was left of the door off its hinges and leaped over the molten metal on the ground. Chakotay, Torres, and Dr. Gammet charged into the store after him, and they found a brawny Helenite sprawled across a dozen rolls of carpet, a gaping wound in his chest.

Tuvok knelt down and felt for a pulse, then he shook his head. "He is dead. I regret that my phaser was on full."

"You had no choice," said Chakotay. He turned to Torres, who was studying her tricorder. "Where is Klain?"

"Not far." She led the way through the carpet store to the rear, where she found a door marked with symbols meaning "Private. No

Admittance." Leveling her phaser, Torres pushed the door open and charged into the room.

A moment later, Chakotay wished he had been the one to go first. Lying in the middle of the small, unkempt office was Prefect Klain, crumpled on the floor like a pile of rags. Distraught, Torres bent over the body and put her head to his chest, listening for any sign of life. From the severity of his wound and the pool of blood, Chakotay doubted he was alive.

Still he tapped his combadge. "Chakotay to *Spartacus.* Stand by to beam one to sickbay."

"That won't be necessary," said Dr. Gammet, feeling for a pulse. "He's beyond us now."

"Belay that order," said Chakotay sadly.

B'Elanna jumped to her feet, fierce anger and tears in her eyes. "I killed him . . . as surely as if I had pulled the trigger."

"No, you didn't," said the captain, putting his arm around her trembling shoulders. "But we'll find who did it."

"How could his murderer have escaped?" asked Tuvok, scanning the small room with a tricorder.

"By Mizrah!" gasped a voice. Chakotay turned to see a female Helenite standing in the doorway, her hand covering her mouth and a look of horror on her face.

"What's on the other side of this wall?" he asked, pointing to the wall opposite the door.

"An alley," she rasped.

"Tuvok, you're with me," ordered the captain. "B'Elanna, you'll probably want to stay here and—"

"No!" she said through clenched teeth. "I want to come with you."

"I can handle this mess," muttered Dr. Gammet. "I'll take a look around, too. The three of you go ahead."

There was no time to argue, as Chakotay led the way out the door, through the shop, and into the street. Since they were in the middle of a block of stores, he motioned Tuvok to go one way, while he and Torres ran the other.

An onlooker yelled at him, "What are you people doing?"

"Have you seen anyone suspicious, running?"

"Just you."

Figuring no one at the front of the store had seen anything, Chakotay dashed to the corner with Torres on his heels. They took a right onto a side street and ran to the alley behind the carpet shop. There was no one in the vicinity—not the murderer, not a witness, not anyone they could question.

Chakotay had seen dark alleys before, but none more foreboding than this. He drew his phaser and a handheld lantern, but B'Elanna charged ahead of him, rage in her eyes. The captain almost called after her to wait, but he knew she wouldn't when she was in a state like this.

He tapped his combadge. "Tuvok, where are you?"

"Making my way east down the alley," answered the Vulcan.

"Keep an eye out for Torres—she's headed right for you."

"Acknowledged."

Since the alley was covered from both ends, Chakotay looked around the area, trying to figure out where they were in the unfamiliar city. While in pursuit of Klain's tracking signal, they hadn't paid any attention to where they were going. He had to admit that they were lost.

A cool breeze brushed his face, bringing with it the earthy scents of salt, fish, and rotting seaweed. Chakotay followed the breeze to the end of the block and saw that the street stopped at the wharf. Lights twinkled on the dark water of the bay, where several boats and sea-gliders floated in peaceful repose. Some of the docking slips were empty.

Our prey escaped via sea-glider, he thought to himself. *That's why they chose this place as their headquarters—to be close to the sea-gliders.*

His combadge chirped, jarring him out of his reverie. "Torres to Chakotay."

"Go on."

"We've finished searching the alley—there's no one here."

"I think they escaped via sea-glider," said the captain. "Let's go back to the ship and run some scans—"

"There's a problem," Torres cut in. "Tuvok's been arrested."

When Chakotay got back to the front of the store, he found Torres and Dr. Gammet arguing with two Helenites wearing tricornered hats and blue uniforms with gaudy piping and epaulets. A large hovercraft was also parked in front of the store. Tuvok was nowhere in sight, although several of the onlookers had remained to watch the continuing drama.

"What happened?" asked Chakotay.

"I tried to explain to them," said Gammet with exasperation. "I told them that we were fired on first, and that your man returned fire in self-defense."

"Excuse me," said a stout official, "are you the Maquis captain?"

"Yes."

"We have to arrest you, too."

"Wait a minute," replied Chakotay, trying to stay calm, "are you going to give us a chance to explain?"

"We have accounts from several witnesses. They all tell us that you were trying to break into this shop, and the shopkeeper was trying to protect his place of business. No one denies that you fired first at his locked door, and that the Vulcan killed the shopkeeper. Not only that, but we found our prefect dead inside. In my thirty years of service, this is the worst case of violence we've ever had on Dalgren."

"Do you understand who these people are?" asked Gammet. "And what we're trying to do? We were chasing the people who are responsible for unleashing the plague on Helena!"

The official glowered suspiciously at him. "Are you saying that Prefect Klain was responsible for the plague?"

"I'm afraid so," said Gammet.

"Do you have any proof to back up this slanderous claim?"

"If you'll allow us to search his genetic company, perhaps we can find proof."

"There will be a full hearing," the other official assured him, "and plenty of search warrants. Which one of you killed Prefect Klain?"

"None of us!" shouted Torres. "Oh, this is pointless. People are dying by the thousands, and you're worried about *two* people."

"He was our *prefect,*" insisted the official. "That's the highest office in the land."

"I *know* who he was," said Torres, glaring at him.

Her distress and reddened eyes had some effect on the officials, who evidently knew who she was, too.

"You're not a suspect," the official said with sympathy. "But until we find out what happened here, we have to hold the Vulcan and your captain."

Chakotay briefly considered making a run for it and ordering Seska to beam him back to the *Spartacus,* but they needed cooperation, not more strife. As unibloods, he and Tuvok were obviously at a disadvantage.

"I'll go with you," he told the officials, "as long as you realize that these arrests could further the spread of the plague."

The officials scratched their chins and looked at one another with indecision. Chakotay had the impression that their jobs were mostly ceremonial on the normally peaceful planet.

"Listen to him," pleaded Dr. Gammet. "Captain Chakotay's ship and the medical teams he brought with him are the only things standing between us and disaster."

"But he ordered them to fire their phasers!" shouted an onlooker. "I saw him!"

The stout official, who was the elder of the two, took a deep breath and came to a decision. "Dr. Gammet, if you will vouch for the captain, we'll allow him to remain on his own cognizance until the hearing. But we have to hold the Vulcan, because he admits to killing the shopkeeper."

"I'll vouch for all of them," said Gammet. "They only want to help us."

"Where is Tuvok being held?" asked Chakotay.

"In the Ministry of Public Policy," answered the official. "You can visit him in the morning."

Dr. Gammet strode up to the officials and said, "Right now, we've got to go to Genetic Enhancement—Klain's company—and search it."

"We can't get a search warrant until morning," said the stout official obstinately.

Torres snarled with anger. "A few days from now, when you're lying in bed—dying a miserable death—I hope you'll remember these delays you caused us. Better yet, I hope you come to us to save your life—or the lives of your children—and we say, 'Sorry, can't do anything until the morning.' "

The official's dark complexion paled several shades. He finally motioned to the hovercraft and growled, "Get in."

They could see the fire burning in the night sky from blocks away, the flames rising above the silhouette of the city like rocket thrusters. Helenites were running to and fro, pointing helplessly at the conflagration, and their driver stopped the hovercraft and stared in amazement. The air smelled like burning tar, and sparks floated in the darkness like erratic meteorites.

"That can't be!" he exclaimed. "The automatic sprinklers and transporters . . . the flame retarders . . . we haven't had a fire in Astar in a hundred years!"

He tapped a button on the instrument panel of the hovercraft and shouted over the commotion, "This is Chief Mufanno calling headquarters. There's a fire in section twelve, near the corner of Cosmos and Unity—"

"In the Genetic Enhancement building," said Dr. Gammet, drawing the obvious conclusion.

"Yes," agreed the official, staring at his passengers and realizing that they might have been telling him the truth about Prefect Klain. "Call out the Coastal Watchers and rush them to—"

"I wouldn't do that," cautioned Dr. Gammet. "Don't get anywhere near that building, unless you're wearing an environmental suit. You don't know what might be in there. The safest recourse is to keep people away, and let it burn to the ground."

The official stared in shock at the doctor and licked his blue lips worriedly. "Belay that order. Let's cordon off the block and keep people away. Just let it burn."

"Let it burn?" asked an amazed voice on the comm channel.

"That's right. Don't let anyone get near it, unless they're wearing an environmental suit. There are, uh . . . biohazards."

Chakotay sighed wearily and hopped out of the hovercraft. "I don't think we're going to find any information in that building. B'Elanna, contact the ship and head back as soon as you can. I'm sure Seska could use some relief on the bridge." He started walking away.

"Where are you going?" she asked.

"Back to the Velvet Cluster. There's a man I've got to see. I have a feeling our time is running out."

Gul Demadak breathed a tremendous sigh of relief as he read the coded message on the hidden screen in his library. At last, he was free to do what had to be done. He had also survived the most dangerous partnership he had ever undertaken. If this message hadn't come, he was probably only days, perhaps hours, away from from losing his post as military commander of the DMZ. He would make the Detapa Council and Central Command very happy with his next order.

"Experiment cut short," read the message. "Move in and clear out Maquis. Await my order for final resolution."

Demadak knew what that final resolution was—the end of the thorn in his side known as Helena. Now his place in history and the next great reign of the Cardassian Union was assured.

He quickly sent another message: "Await my arrival, and begin Phase Two. Prepare for Phase Three."

All during the night, Thomas Riker hurtled through the darkness, clinging to a chunk of wood and shivering in his wet clothes. Inside the pipe, he didn't know if it was night or day, sea or land, hell or heaven—whether he was ill or merely exhausted and half-crazed. All he knew was that the instincts for survival and revenge were stronger than the temptation to let go and end it, although that thought was never far from his mind.

Did you survive all those years, put up with all the ridicule and unfairness, give up everything you worked for, and come all the way to Helena . . . just to die?

No! Riker answered the voice within him. *I have to make my life—and my death—mean something. I'm alive for a reason, and there's something I have to do.*

Riker wasn't sure he was destined for success in Starfleet anymore, as he had once been convinced. He thought about the love of his life, Deanna Troi, and how he should never have let her get away. He had given her up for what? A career! What was a career but a bunch of disconnected, often incomprehensible events from which a person tried desperately to make some sense? The only thing in his life that had ever made any sense was Deanna, and he had willfully given her up.

His fingers and legs were painfully cramped as he clung to his board, and he had lost his meager supply of food in the rushing water. But none of that seemed as important as the realization he had just reached. When he got out of this, he would redeem himself. He would no longer let life drag him along like this current—he would bend it to his will.

To his surprise, Riker took comfort from a fact which he had resented bitterly for two years. *I'm not alone. There is another William T. Riker on the* Enterprise. He would let that other Riker scale the heights and have the incredible career that he had always considered to be his due. Tom Riker would be the altruistic and unselfish one—the one who thought and acted for other people.

He had taken the first step by giving up his high-profile bridge position to become a medical courier, then he had gone one step further by shipping out with the Maquis. He wondered what he would do next to further his development as a person.

Without warning, the artificial river dropped away beneath him, and Riker plunged headfirst into darkness. Involuntarily, he yelled and flailed his arms, losing his tiny life raft. At the last second, he ducked his head, put his arms out, and dove into a cold, dark pool of water. He protected his head, certain he would smash into a shallow bottom, but he came out of his unexpected dive in water that was plenty deep enough to swim in. Riker stroked and kicked with all his might, and he broke the surface, sputtering for breath.

Treading water, he looked up and saw a million stars, sparkling like the brightest lights of San Francisco or Anchorage. "Yes," he breathed gratefully, slapping his hand on top of the water. As his eyes adjusted to the night sky and its tiny but vibrant bits of light, he could see that he was swimming in a small reservoir, with a dam looming on one side and a lower embankment on the other.

I made it! Where he was hardly made any difference, as long as it wasn't that damn island.

Knowing he was too weak to tread water for very long, Riker swam toward the low side of the reservoir. He finally found a ladder and dragged himself out of the chilly water. Collapsing on the concrete embankment, he lay there for several minutes, letting the water drip off his shivering body. He was only half-alive, but he was alive.

Riker staggered to his feet and looked around, unable to make out much in the darkness. If anyone was manning the reservoir, he couldn't see them, and no one seemed interested in him. In the distance was a wavering light—it looked like no more than a campfire, but that was enough to give him a new destination. Now he wished he hadn't lost his food.

Picking his way carefully through the dark, Riker walked away from the reservoir and found himself on a dirt path. The closer he got to the wavering light in the distance, the more it actually looked like a campfire, and hope spurred him to walk faster. Soon he heard voices, talking rather loudly, as if they expected no one to be nearby. He couldn't tell if it was friend or foe, but he doubted if his tormentors from the island would amuse themselves with anything as low-tech as a campfire. He was hoping these were Helenites—either rural workers or people who had fled the cities.

As he staggered through the brush, he could see their seated silhouettes huddled around the campfire. With their backs to him, he had no idea who they were, but from their voices, he assumed they were mostly males. Riker figured he had better not charge into their midst without announcing himself, so when got close enough he cleared his throat loudly.

"I'm Lieutenant Riker," he said, his voice sounding hoarse and hollow in his own ears.

The men jumped up as if a bomb had gone off, and he could see them grabbing what looked like weapons. In the dim firelight, he still couldn't see their faces, but he wanted to appear harmless. So he held up his hands and said, "I'm with the Maquis. I got separated from my—"

One of the men charged toward him, rifle leveled at his chest. In seconds, he got close enough for Riker to make out his bony face, black hair, and gray uniform.

Cardassians! Riker thought momentarily about trying to escape, but how far could he run in his condition? In fact, he felt so weak that he didn't think he could stand on his feet for much longer. But he kept his hands raised high and a smile glued to his bearded face.

Unfortunately, Cardassians were not known for responding well to human charm. This one raised his phaser rifle and fired a searing beam that hit Riker in the chest. That was the last thing he remembered before he pitched forward into the dirt.

Chapter Fifteen

"I TOLD YOU, CAPTAIN CHAKOTAY, I won't give you any information until you take me away from Helena. That is my firm price."

The speaker, an Andorian named Bokor, sat stone-faced at his table in the Velvet Cluster dining room. Chakotay sat across from him, his hands folded before him and his face just as implacable as the blue-skinned alien's. The Ferengi, Shep, sat between them, and he was the only one who looked animated, except for the servers who bustled around them importantly.

"Don't agree to anything," Shep cautioned Chakotay. "Let *me* negotiate for both of us."

The Andorian laughed. "What have you got to bargain with, Ferengi? You don't know anything, and you don't have anything. All your goods are floating in orbit around the planet."

"I have my *mind,*" answered Shep, tapping his large frontal lobes. "And a strong desire to get out of here myself. Besides, I was right about Prefect Klain, wasn't I?"

"Yes, you were," agreed Chakotay, his voice barely audible over the clink of glasses and ricochet of silverware. "That's why I came back here—to see what else I could find out."

Bokor arched an eyebrow and waited until an older Catullan couple shuffled past. "Terrible thing about the prefect. Who ever thought *he* could be involved with this tragic disease? Everyone is talking about it. As I told you, Captain, I have a very valuable piece of information, but I won't part with it for free."

"Bokor doesn't know anything," scoffed Shep. "So he talked to a few Cardassians who are also stranded here—big deal. Those boneheads don't know any more than the rest of us! Captain Chakotay is the only one with a starship—he's the only one in a strong bargaining position."

The captain shrugged. "Actually I have *three* ships under my command, all of them in orbit: the *Spartacus,* the *Singha,* and a warp-drive shuttlecraft."

Now the Andorian leaned forward with avid interest. "A shuttlecraft, you say? Now *that* is something worth negotiating for, especially on Helena. How much gold-pressed latinum do you want? Name your price."

Chakotay smiled and leaned back in his chair. "Latinum doesn't do me a bit of good—no place to spend it. Your information isn't all that valuable either, because any fool could guess at it. The Cardassians must be planning to come back here with more ships—maybe a whole fleet. And when they do, we'll run for it, and you'll still be here. If the plague doesn't get you, they will."

The Andorian scowled. "Make your point, Captain. What do you want?"

"Don't hurry him," said the Ferengi, smiling. "A good negotiation must be savored, like good wine."

Chakotay leaned forward and whispered, "I need four things. It would be good to know exactly when Cardassian ships are returning, and in what strength. I also need to know what happened to my two missing crewmen. Just because you didn't see them doesn't mean the Cardassians don't have them. We need to ask them point-blank if they know anything about Lieutenant Riker and Ensign Shelzane."

"What else?" grumbled the Andorian, not enjoying this tough negotiation as much as the Ferengi.

Chakotay's tattoo grew three-dimensional in the furrows of a deep frown. "Tuvok, the Vulcan on my crew, has been arrested for killing a man who was working with the people who brought this plague to Helena. If there is any sort of influence you could bring to bear on the officials, it would be appreciated."

Bokor snorted, and his antennae twitched. "Anything else, while we're at it?"

"Yes. Whoever takes that shuttlecraft has got to return it and the medical team to the Federation."

The Andorian groaned and slumped back in his chair, while the Ferengi nodded with satisfaction. "What will you say to that, Bokor?"

"I'll say that this human wants an awful lot for his shuttlecraft."

"That's all I want from *you,*" said Chakotay. "From you, Shep, I want someone to gather information about Klain's company, Genetic Enhancement. He's still got confederates here on Helena, and we've got to run them down."

"I'm going on the shuttlecraft, too?" asked Shep excitedly.

"Yes, because I reward those who help me." Chakotay rose to his feet and looked at the Andorian, sensing other diners glancing at him. "Bokor, you still have your sea-glider, don't you?"

"Yes."

"Good. I'll meet you at the bay in an hour, and we can take a little flight to look for my missing crew."

The Andorian scowled. "It will take us a day or two to get there."

"I have a shortcut," promised the captain.

"But I haven't agreed to any of this yet!"

Chakotay smiled. "You haven't said no, so I'm taking that as a yes. You might want to load up some supplies to make it look good. See you in an hour."

The Maquis captain strode away from the table, with many of the members of the Velvet Cluster watching him go. Shep nodded his head in admiration. "For a hu-man, he's an awfully good negotiator. Wouldn't you say so, Bokor?"

"A month ago, we would have laughed him out of the cluster." The tall Andorian rose to his feet. "Now I had better put some supplies on my glider."

Tuvok sat in a cell with a force-field grid protecting the open door. There were three other cells linked with his, all of them opening onto a central corridor, but the other cells were empty. His jailers had left him reading material, food, and water, but he ignored these niceties to sit in silence and contemplate the actions that had landed him in this predicament.

He had killed a man. The killing had clearly been in self-defense, but that knowledge didn't assuage his conscience at all. For a Vulcan to take a life was a serious matter, a cause to doubt one's training and commitment to logic. For Tuvok, it was a cause to wonder what he was doing on the Maquis crew—a group of people who lived a life so dangerous that it might be called suicidal.

He realized that he was only here because he was a spy, but that was also an illogical role for a Vulcan. For that very reason, he had been the logical member of Captain Janeway's crew to infiltrate Chakotay's ship. A Vulcan never lied, except when it was more logical than telling the truth, which was very seldom. Until this mission, his role as a spy had never troubled him much, because the actions of the Maquis were both illegal and illogical. But their actions on behalf of the inhabitants of Helena were noble and logical. The absence of the Federation was the only thing that was illogical.

He was not ready to forsake his allegiance to the Federation, but for the first time he questioned the wisdom of a treaty that left innocent people so vulnerable. After recent events, he had no doubt that Helena had been chosen by unknown parties as a breeding ground for this disease for the very reason that it was isolated and vulnerable. A civilized society derived from the Federation, it was a perfect microcosm of the Federation as a whole. If anything, the mixed-species Helenites were more disease-resistant than a typical populace, which made them the perfect proving ground for a biological weapon. If the disease could succeed here, then no Federation planet was safe.

But who would endanger millions of people for an experiment? Not even the Cardassians were so vile.

That question brought him back to the life he had taken. A Vulcan never killed, except when it was absolutely necessary, and he could not say the death of the shopkeeper had been absolutely necessary. Had the shopkeeper lived, he might have furnished valuable information. Dead, he was nothing but a mystery, and a reason for the Helenites to distrust the Maquis. He was also the cause of Tuvok's incarceration and imminent trial.

Try as he might to justify his actions, Tuvok now saw that he had acted rashly. He thought back to his youth, when he had nearly rejected Vulcan philosophy in favor of passion and love. A wise teacher had steered him back onto the proper path, but the doubts always remained. Was he prone to acts of passion and poor judgment?

Tuvok lay back on his narrow bunk, realizing that he couldn't answer these questions himself. Perhaps he wouldn't survive his stay on Helena, which made his introspection moot. One thing was certain—there was nothing like being incarcerated in a cell, awaiting trial for murder, to make a person think.

Thomas Riker squinted into the blazing sun and licked his parched lips, wishing it was still night. He was lying in hot sand on the beach, imprisoned in a crude cage about a meter high and three meters long, made of sticks and wire. Had he any strength, he could probably smash his way out of this handmade cage in a few seconds, but he was extremely weak. His throat felt raw and his glands swollen; he couldn't see himself, but he imagined from his peeling skin that he looked fairly awful.

Riker knew he was dying of the plague.

About thirty meters away, under a canopy that gave them ample shade, a group of ten Cardassians sat in a circle playing a dice game. Every now and then, one of them would look in his direction with a jaundiced eye, noting that he was still there, and still alive. Behind them on the bluff loomed a small fortress, which he assumed was the actual garrison, but it appeared eerily quiet, perhaps deserted.

Riker turned to look at the vast ocean, glistening in the sunshine, incongruous in its beauty in the middle of his personal hell. He had always thought of oceans as a symbol of life and freedom, but this one seemed like a mirage, beckoning him to a freedom he could never attain. It mocked him with its ageless splendor, telling him that it would go on for eons and eons after he was gone. If this was to be the last thing he saw before he died, he almost wished it could be something not so achingly beautiful.

He licked his lips again and rubbed his throbbing head. Riker felt as though he had been unconscious for days, but it had probably only been a few hours since the Cardassians had stunned him and tossed him into this cage. Looking around his enclosure, he figured it was some dead fisherman's lobster trap, or whatever the Helenite equivalent of lobster was. Would they make him die like this, staked out in the heat? Or would they at least give him the succor of food and water? Maybe he could goad them into killing him outright.

"Hey!" Riker shouted, his voice sounding as rough as his shaggy beard. "Give me some water!"

When the Cardassians did nothing but glance at him, he shouted, "Come on, you cowards! Afraid of an unarmed man?"

The guards looked at him and laughed, but one of them stood and shuffled toward him. His phaser rifle was slung casually over his shoulder, as if he knew he needn't fear this prisoner.

He stopped about ten meters away from the cage and sneered. "We're betting on how long it takes you to die. I've got you down for twenty-six hours. Think you can hold out that long?"

"Maybe if I have a drink of water," rasped Riker.

The Cardassian shook his head. "Sorry, but we're not allowed to aid you either one way or another. We can't give you any food, drink, or medicine; and we can't beat you senseless either. This has got to be a fair contest."

"What makes you such experts?" grumbled Riker. "Maybe I'll live for a week."

"I don't think so. I've watched sixty percent of our own garrison die, so I have some experience. I'd say twenty-six hours is just about right, although you look pretty strong. Maybe I should've taken thirty."

The guard laughed, sounding oddly jovial and half insane. "I might not even be here in thirty hours to see you die. It's just as well that I took twenty-six."

"Where are you going to be?" asked Riker hoarsely.

"Far away from this pesthole." He turned and shuffled back to his comrades.

Riker laid his head on the hot sand and wondered if he could burrow into it for some protection from the sun. But the wooden bars extended underneath the cage, and he didn't have the strength to break them. He supposed he could untwist the wires that held the structure together, but his captors were sure to notice him working on it.

Bored, he turned back to look at the endless sky, stretching across the blue sheen of the ocean. Yes, he was going to die—and the way he felt now, he didn't think it would even take twenty-six hours. It was best to sleep, he decided, and conserve his strength, while waiting for a miracle to happen.

Who am I kidding? thought Riker. *Miracles happen to other people, not to me. What did the old blues song say? "If it wasn't for bad luck, I wouldn't have no luck at all."*

Just before he closed his eyes, he caught sight of something in the clear blue sky. Riker rubbed his eyes and peered into the glare, wondering if it was real or only his fevered imagination. After several seconds, the apparition was still there—it looked like another one of those sea-gliders, headed their way.

A sudden babble of voices made him turn to look at the Cardassians under the canopy. They had seen the glider, too, and a few of them rose to their feet and took up arms in apparent defense of this lonely stretch of beach. Others remained seated in the sand, lethargic and apathetic; they looked every bit as resigned to death as he was.

He struggled to listen to their conversation against the gentle flow of the waves to the shore. "It must be Bokor," said one. "Did we order more supplies?" asked another.

Supplies? Riker turned to watch the white glider make its graceful approach. Hope sprang unbidden to his heart, although he knew such hope was pointless. Anyone who dealt with the Cardassians wasn't likely to save him, or even care if he lived or died.

The approach and landing of the seaplane was quite impressive as it glided across the creamy water and set down on its sleek pontoons with barely a splash. Half of the ten Cardassians formed a line in the sand, although they kept a safe distance away from him. There appeared to be two people in the craft, and one of them opened the hatch.

The visitor threw something into the water—it was a compressed-air raft, which instantly expanded to its full size. Riker watched with interest as a gangly Andorian stepped gingerly into the raft, oar in hand, and began rowing leisurely toward the shore. The Cardassians on the beach began to relax, apparently not viewing this new arrival as a threat. Some of them went back to their dice game.

The raft scraped into the sand, and the Andorian climbed out, trying to maintain his dignity as best he could in the tiny boat. As he strolled past Riker, he looked at him with mild interest, although he didn't stop to talk. His destination was clearly the Cardassians and the fortress on the hill.

"Bokor!" shouted one of them with disapproval. "What are you doing here?"

The Andorian shrugged. "Just making my rounds. I thought I'd see if you needed anything. I've got some nice salted fish and a case of Rigelian ale."

"Go away, you scavenger!" yelled another Cardassian, although he didn't sound very angry. "We don't need anything, except to get off this lousy rock."

"I can't help you there," said the Andorian with a resigned smile. He pointed to Riker in the cage. "I see you've found some entertainment."

"Yeah, one of those meddling Maquis. But he's not going to last long—he's got the plague."

"Oh," muttered the visitor. "Are you sure you don't need anything? Your great fleet hasn't shown up yet."

"They will. They're on their way. Now get out of here, before we put you in a cage, too!" At that remark, there was a round of laughter among the Cardassians.

"Okay," said the Andorian, holding his hands up. "I'm not looking for trouble, just customers."

"Who's that in your glider?" asked another guard, peering suspiciously at the sleek craft floating in the surf.

"Just my new pilot. I'm showing him the route."

"Well, there's no sense coming back here again. We'll be gone before we need any more supplies."

"Lucky you," muttered the Andorian, sounding as if he meant it. "I'll cross you off my list. So you're sure?"

"We're sure," growled a big Cardassian, hefting his phaser rifle. "Now if you don't get out of here in ten seconds, I'm going to use your glider for target practice."

"I'm going!" To another round of laughter, the Andorian hurried toward his raft. As he passed Riker, he gave him a wink, which was an odd thing for him to do. *He probably caught a grain of sand in his eye,* thought the prisoner.

"Help me!" groaned Riker, but the Andorian was already pushing his raft into the surf to make his escape.

The lieutenant watched forlornly as the merchant rowed back to his craft and climbed aboard. He hauled his raft in after him, letting out the air as he did. Without further ado, the sea-glider floated majestically into the air; like a giant kite, it caught a wind drift and soared away.

Riker watched the glider sail into the sky, a feeling of despair gripping his chest.

"That's definitely your man down there in the cage," Bokor told Captain Chakotay as the glider cruised away from the Cardassian garrison. "But he's sick."

"How sick?"

"Not that bad—he's still talking."

Chakotay took a deep breath, grateful that they had at least found Riker. "There was no sign of a Benzite in their camp?"

"None. And there's no more time to look for her. They sounded like their fleet could show up any minute."

Chakotay punched some numbers into his computer padd. "Are we out of their range of fire yet?"

"Yes—just barely."

The captain tapped his combadge. "Chakotay to *Spartacus*."

"Torres here," answered a familiar voice.

"I'm sending you some coordinates—it's Riker, and I want you to beam him up immediately. Tell Kincaid that he's got the plague, and she's got to drop everything to save him. Stand by." Chakotay took off his combadge and plugged it into the padd. He watched intently as a stream of lights showed the data transfer.

"We've got the coordinates," said Torres. "Initiating transport." After seconds that stretched forever, she reported, "We've got him!"

The captain let out a long sigh of relief. "Okay, that's two items crossed off our list. Bokor, are you ready to take command of that shuttlecraft?"

"Right now?" asked the Andorian, aghast. "We're flying over an ocean. Who's going to fly my glider?"

"We're going to abandon it."

Bokor gulped, and his antennae twitched. "Abandon it? Right here . . . in the middle of the ocean!"

"If you're leaving Helena, you won't need it anymore."

"All right," muttered the Andorian. "You're a very decisive man, Captain."

"I have to be." He pulled his combadge off the computer padd and affixed it to his chest. "B'Elanna, do you still read me?"

"Yes, sir."

"Lock onto the two of us and beam us up. And alert Danken on the shuttlecraft to stand by for a shift in personnel."

"Yes, sir."

The dour Andorian looked extremely displeased to be losing his fine sea-glider. Chakotay reached forward from his co-pilot seat and patted him on the shoulder. "Think of it as a trade-in for an even better shuttlecraft."

"Right."

A moment later, they disappeared from the cockpit of the sea-glider, while it continued its graceful flight, sailing unmanned into the blue horizon, like a great white albatross.

When they materialized on the transporter pad in the cargo hold of the *Spartacus,* now converted into a sickbay, Chakotay rushed immediately to the bed where Lieutenant Riker lay. Dr. Kincaid and her assistants were working on him with their medical equipment, plying him with hyposprays.

Riker lifted his head and stared at Chakotay in utter amazement. "Have I died and gone to heaven? Or am I dreaming this?"

"Neither one," answered Chakotay with a smile. He looked at the doctor. "Is he going to be all right?"

"We got him not a moment too soon," answered Kincaid. "The biofilter took care of the multiprions, but he has some tissue damage and secondary infections. He's going to be laid up for a while."

"Not too long, I hope. We need him badly." The captain gazed down at Riker. "Where is Ensign Shelzane?"

"Dead," said Riker hoarsely, tears welling in his rheumy eyes. "We broke into IGI . . . and then—"

"Tell me later. Right now, you have to get well." Chakotay patted his comrade on the shoulder.

"I got a miracle," rasped the lieutenant. "I never thought *I* would get a miracle."

"Let's hope for a few more." Chakotay returned to the transporter platform, where the Andorian stood in shocked silence, gazing around at all the equipment and bustle of activity. "You'll take command of the shuttlecraft and fly straight toward Federation space at maximum warp. When they hail you, stop and tell them exactly what's happening here—that a Cardassian fleet is massing to destroy Helena. Tell them the Cardassians are breaking the treaty in a big way."

Bokor gaped at him. "The Maquis are going to call Starfleet for help?"

Chakotay nodded grimly and motioned at the medical teams in action around them. "For some jobs, you can't beat Starfleet—facing down a Cardassian fleet is one of them. That is, if they even bother to show up."

"What about Shep? And the doctors you wanted me to take back?"

"There's no time for that now. Don't let me down, Bokor. The lives of everyone on Helena depend upon you." A metal pan clattered to the deck behind them, as if underscoring the urgency. A weary doctor picked up the pan, then teetered woozily on his feet until a colleague helped him to a chair.

The tall Andorian nodded gravely. "I won't fail you, Captain Chakotay. You have impressed me greatly—I'm glad you drove a hard bargain." He stepped upon the transporter platform and squared his shoulders.

Chakotay turned to the transporter operator. "Beam him to the shuttlecraft, then beam Danken back here. Energize when ready."

"Yes, sir," answered the Bolian on duty.

The Andorian gave him a regal wave as he vanished in a column of sparkling, swirling lights. The captain immediately left the cargo hold and hurried the length of the scout ship to the bridge, where B'Elanna Torres was on duty at the conn. The peaceful blue curve of Helena filled the viewscreen, giving the false impression that all was well on the watery world beneath them.

"Any emergencies?" he asked, slipping into the seat beside her and turning on the sensors.

"The struggle goes on," she answered. "Two members of the medical team on Padulla came down with the plague, and they're being treated along with everyone else. I see the shuttlecraft has just taken off. What's their destination?"

"Federation space. I hate to do this, but it's time to send for the cavalry."

"Why?" asked Torres, with an edge to her voice.

"Because I've learned that a Cardassian fleet is headed this way." He started scanning the land masses on the planet beneath them, looking for kelbonite deposits, or anything that could mask the presence of a small starship. "We've got to find someplace down there to hide this vessel."

"Wouldn't it be easier to run for it?"

"Yes, but we're not going to leave without Tuvok and our doctors. We'll hide this ship and leave the *Singha* in orbit. When the Cardassians show up, the *Singha* can run for it, so they'll think all the Maquis have left."

"That's risky," muttered B'Elanna. She snorted a laugh and gave him an ironic smile. "Maybe this will be our first step toward retirement."

"What do you mean?"

"Prefect Klain offered to let us stay here, remember? Even Tuvok said it was a good idea for us to start planning how to get out of the Maquis. He's right, you know. We can't keep up this crazy life forever. If the Helenites protected our identities, this would be a good place to hide from both the Cardassians and Starfleet."

Chakotay shook his head. "There's too much left to do. Besides, they'll keep hunting us to our graves. Do you think we could go from being Maquis to being law-abiding citizens just like that?" He snapped his fingers.

Torres shrugged. "Maybe. Given the right circumstances."

"It's only a pipe dream," said Chakotay. "But I'll keep it in mind."

"How's Riker?"

"Worse for wear, but he's going to live. But he says Ensign Shelzane is dead. We need to contact Dr. Gammet and see when Tuvok's hearing is."

"Gammet checked in, and he said that the hearing is tomorrow." Torres lowered her head, and her voice sounded far away. "Klain's funeral is in less than an hour. I wouldn't mind going to that."

"You were really starting to care for him, weren't you?" asked Chakotay, knowing that if B'Elanna didn't feel like answering, she wouldn't.

Her shoulders sagged, and the tough facade faded just a little. "It's hard not to like a man who worships you and wants to give you the world. Like most of the men I like, he turned out to be rotten. Why am I always attracted to the rotters?"

"Because you're a rebel at heart. Despite that, someday you'll find a man who deserves you." Chakotay continued working his console, but he scowled when all his scans turned up empty. "Gammet can probably tell us a good place to hide. Let's take this ship down to the surface right now."

"What about the Cardassians down there?"

"The ones who are left are sitting around, waiting to be picked up. They're no threat anymore."

The captain opened a channel and contacted the *Singha,* telling Captain Rowan all that had happened, and all that was about to happen. She was not adverse to the idea of running for it when the Cardassians showed up in force. He also contacted their mobile clinics and filled them in.

That accomplished, Chakotay took over the conn and eased them onto a reentry course.

Captain Chakotay landed the *Spartacus* in the same field they had landed in on their first visit to Dalgren. Although that had only been a few days before, it seemed like several lifetimes ago. Dr. Gammet and a driver met them in a hovercraft, and Chakotay, Torres, and Echo Imjim made up the official contingent from the *Spartacus,* leaving Seska in charge of the grounded ship.

As they rode to the cemetery, Chakotay turned to Echo and said, "You've been a big help to us, and I'm very thankful. But I think you can return now to your son . . . and your life."

The Helenite gave him a warm smile. "Are you sure you don't want to come with us? You could be a very good glider pilot . . . with a few more ocean crossings under your belt. And I've been thinking about having *two* gliders in my flock."

"Thank you, but not now," he answered. "I'll try to come back sometime, after things have calmed down in the DMZ."

"There will always be a home for you here," she assured him.

"I concur," said Dr. Gammet. "After all the effort you've put in, and all the risks you've taken for us, it would be a shame if you had to leave. Stay with us—we'll protect your crew from the Cardassians and the Federation. I know that's what Prefect Klain wanted, too."

"Well, we are going to stay for a while," said Chakotay. "We may have turned the corner, but we're still a long way from conquering this disease. I wanted to ask you if you know of any isolated place on Helena where we could hide our ship for a while. When I say 'hide,' I mean hide from sensors as well as from view."

The diminutive doctor stroked his long, white beard. "Yes . . . yes! I know just the place—Flint Island in the Silver Sea. It's colder there than it is here on Dalgren, but they have kelbonite reefs and silica deposits that would mask your ship completely. So many shuttlecraft and gliders have been lost on Flint Island that it has a reputation for being haunted. But that's good—people seldom go there."

"Sounds perfect," said Chakotay.

Torres took a computer padd from her pack and turned it on. "I've got an atlas here—can you show me where it is?"

"Yes, my dear, I can."

While they consulted and the hovercraft cruised along, Chakotay watched the rolling countryside on one side of the craft and the charming city of Astar on the other. Helena was a remarkable planet—worldly yet unspoiled. Could they actually find refuge here from the turmoil in the DMZ? He had no doubt that the Helenites would accept them with open arms, especially B'Elanna, whom they would probably crown queen. Perhaps it wasn't fair of him to force her to leave when she would never be as warmly accepted anywhere else as she was here. Maybe Tuvok was right, and they should have an exit strategy.

Throughout this entire mission, Chakotay had the urgent feeling that time was running out for them. He didn't know what to do about it, except to plunge ahead with the task at hand. Maybe he needed to slow down and withdraw from the conflict.

By the time they reached a picturesque cemetery on a grassy knoll, Chakotay had nearly talked himself into staying, if their mission proved successful. He saw the hundreds of people waiting to attend Klain's funeral, and he realized that the Helenites were a warm, forgiving people.

When they exited the hovercraft, the crowd parted to let them approach the grave site. B'Elanna took the lead, accustomed to all the attention. Chakotay felt someone tug on his sleeve, and he turned to see Shep, the little Ferengi.

"Captain," he whispered. "I knew you'd be here."

Chakotay stepped aside, allowing the others to walk ahead. "Have you found out anything else?"

"Only that Klain recently got a large infusion of latinum into his company and was poised to compete with IGI. It really would seem that he did all of this for profit, which makes me have some sympathy for him." Shep looked around at the large crowd and whistled. "Imagine how many people would be here if he had been a *good* man."

The captain's combadge chirped. "*Spartacus* to Chakotay!"

"Go ahead, Seska."

"Captain! A huge starship has just entered orbit, and the *Singha* is under attack!"

Chapter Sixteen

In orbit over the shimmering blue planet, a mammoth starship bore down on a tiny Bajoran assault vessel, peppering it with a withering barrage of phaser beams. The *Singha* tried valiantly to return fire while swerving back and forth, but the highly advanced starship had taken her by surprise. The Maquis ship quivered from one blast after another, and her aft sections were aflame, spitting vibrant blue and gold plumes.

"All power to rear shields!" shouted Patricia Rowan on the bridge. Her scarred, gaunt face was haunted with fear. "Continue evasive maneuvers!"

The ship shuddered violently, and the conn officer had to grip his console to stay in his seat. "We've lost all power to the helm. Shields down to six percent!"

"Hail them!"

"They're not answering!" shouted tactical. "We're dropping into the atmosphere—"

Another blast jolted them, and sparks and acrid smoke spewed into the cabin, causing Rowan to gag. The captain dropped to her knees to avoid the worst of the smoke, but she felt herself floating as the ship lost artificial gravity. The deadly barrage never stopped for an instant, and the tiny ship absorbed blast after blast. The scorched, bloodied face of her helmsman floated past her stinging eyes.

"Long live the Maquis!" yelled Captain Rowan with her last breath.

Upon entering the atmosphere, the assault vessel turned into a flaming torch, and a moment later it exploded into a riot of silvery confetti and burning embers. What was left of the *Singha* fluttered through the upper atmosphere of Helena like a gentle snowstorm.

On the ground, Chakotay shoved his way through the crowd and grabbed B'Elanna Torres by the arm. "We've got to get back to the ship—the *Singha* is under attack!"

"What?"

He tapped his combadge. "Seska! Beam us back—now!"

"There's no rush," came a subdued response. "The *Singha* is gone."

Chakotay's jaw dropped, and B'Elanna scowled and ground her boot into the dirt. All around them, Helenites gaped, not understanding what had happened.

"How many Cardassian ships are there?" asked Chakotay, certain that the enemy fleet had arrived.

"Only one ship," answered Seska. "But she isn't Cardassian. At least she isn't like any Cardassian ship we've ever seen before."

"What is she?"

"Unknown. Her warp signature doesn't match anything in our computer."

"That doesn't mean much," grumbled Chakotay, knowing how out-of-date their ship's data was. "What's she doing now?"

"She just beamed one person up from the planet." A tense pause ensued as they waited for more information. "The ship is leaving orbit . . . they're powering up to go into warp. Whoever they are, they're gone."

Chakotay scowled, wishing now that he had kept the *Spartacus* in orbit. "If we had been up there, could we have made a difference?"

"I don't think so. Maybe a Federation starship could have handled them, but not us."

"Well, that's it," said a voice behind Chakotay. He turned to see Shep, the Ferengi, shaking his bulbous head. "It sounds like Klain's murderer has just made his escape."

Anger and frustration surged through Chakotay's veins, and he looked around for the gaudily uniformed officials who had arrested Tuvok. When he spotted the portly one, Chakotay strode toward him and glared at the Helenite. "Klain's murderer—the one most responsible for the plague—has just gotten away in an unknown starship. And they destroyed our sister ship. I want Tuvok released from your prison this instant."

The Helenite looked flustered, but he held his ground. "We can't do that—the hearing isn't until tomorrow."

Chakotay tapped his combadge. "Seska, do you read me?"

"Yes, sir."

"I want you to take off and fly over Astar, destroying buildings at random. In fact, go ahead and level the entire city. You can start with the Dawn Cluster."

"Yes, sir. Preparing to launch."

The Helenite official blanched, paling several shades. "You can't do that! It's . . . it's against the laws of decency!"

"I make my own laws," snapped Chakotay. "I'm Maquis."

The stout Helenite gulped, then he looked around at his fellow citizens, whose expressions made it clear that they didn't want their city destroyed in order to make a dubious point. They slowly backed away, except for Dr. Gammet, who pushed through the crowd.

"Let the Vulcan go, will you!" pleaded the doctor. "These people are *dying* for us. They've risked their lives and their freedom for us. Our own Coastal Watchers are shooting down gliders that try to land here. Our own Prefect Klain was partly responsible for this horrible disease. These are *not* normal times."

After a moment, the official heaved a sigh. "All right, come with me." He motioned them toward his hovercraft.

Chakotay tapped his combadge. "Belay that last order, Seska."

"Yes, sir," she answered, sounding relieved. "What's the real plan?"

"Right now, we're going to get Tuvok out of jail. Stay prepped for launch, because we're taking the ship into hiding. We're going to keep helping sick people for as long we can. Chakotay out."

Dr. Gammet stepped up to the captain and warmly shook his hand. "Captain, I don't think we can ever express our gratitude for what you've tried to do for us. No matter how it turns out, we know you've done all you can. We may not be able to erect any statues to you, but the Maquis will always be heroes to us."

"Hear! Hear!" yelled someone in the crowd. Spontaneous applause erupted, and several Helenites patted Chakotay on the back. He could still see fear and uncertainty in their eyes, but there was also genuine affection.

"I'll keep the clinics open," vowed Gammet. "You leave it to me."

Chakotay nodded, unable to find words to express his own feelings. Moments like this were few and far between for the Maquis, although they were the only reason the Maquis existed at all. When he turned to follow Torres and the official to the hovercraft, he felt a familiar tug on his shirtsleeve. It was Shep.

"What about the shuttlecraft?" asked the Ferengi. "When do we leave?"

The captain looked down at his small confederate and shook his head. "I'm afraid I had to send Bokor in the shuttle already, but you can come with us."

"You'll be the first Ferengi member of the Maquis," added Torres.

Shep thought for a moment, then replied, "No, thank you. I think I'd rather take my chances here. These people aren't so bad after all. Good luck to you, Captain Chakotay."

"You, too," replied the captain.

A moment later, as they settled into the hovercraft, he turned to Torres and said, "So he would rather stay on a plague-ridden planet than join the Maquis. What does that say about us?"

"After what just happened to the *Singha,* I can't say I blame him."

"I'm sorry you didn't get to see Klain's funeral."

"I've got a feeling I'll see more funerals before this is all over," she answered glumly.

Tuvok squinted slightly when he stepped from the huge ministry building into the sunshine after being incarcerated in a dim cell for sixteen hours. "What is our status?" he asked Chakotay.

"Not good, I'm afraid." He told Tuvok about the destruction of the *Singha* by unknown forces, the escape of Klain's murderer, and the imminent arrival of a Cardassian fleet.

The Vulcan raised an eyebrow. "Perhaps I should go back to my cell."

"On the good side," said Torres, "the captain rescued Lieutenent Riker. Near death, but still alive."

"What about Ensign Shelzane?"

She shook her head. "Riker says she's dead."

"I don't know whether it will do any good," said Chakotay, "but I sent the Andorian back to the Federation in Riker's shuttlecraft. Maybe they'll come, maybe not."

"Are we retreating from Helena?"

"No. Our medical teams still have work to do, and we're not deserting them, or the mission. But we are going into hiding." Chakotay tapped his combadge. "Seska, three to beam over. Prepare for launch."

As the *Spartacus* swooped over a dismal, gray ocean with small ice floes bobbing in the pale water, Chakotay knew why it was called the Silver Sea. When the sun caught it, the ocean might have looked quite beautiful, but under a cloudy sky it looked cold and foreboding.

A bleak, rocky island lay ahead of them, and Chakotay knew without looking at the coordinates that it was Flint Island, also aptly named. "What kind of readings are you getting from that island?" he asked Tuvok, who was seated beside him.

The Vulcan studied his instruments and cocked his head. "High kelbonite and silica readings are disrupting our sensors. I presume there must be some vegetation, but I cannot get any readings."

"Perfect. I'm slowing down to make a pass over the island—we'll have to use visual to find a place to land."

Tuvok nodded and sat forward in his seat, ready to use his sharp vision. The *Peregrine*-class starship swooped over a rugged island that looked surprisingly large when seen from close range. Spindly gray mountains rose above rocky bluffs and cliffs, and there were a few scattered clumps of vegetation clinging to the bare stone. In the center of the island was a lagoon filled with brackish water, and a few stunted trees grew there. Flint Island's bays and black beaches lacked the sea-gliders and boats they had seen on the rest of Helena.

"There," said Tuvok, pointing. "Under that ledge."

Chakotay brought the ship around for another pass over the area Tuvok had indicated. Now he spotted it, too—a great ledge carved by crashing waves in the side of one of the cliffs. Under the ledge was a shiny wet chunk of bedrock. It would be tricky to land there, but he thought he could do it. The advantage would be that the ledge would obscure the *Spartacus* from prying eyes, should any of their enemies fly over Flint Island.

The captain hit his comm panel, and his voice echoed throughout the small ship. "All hands, brace for landing. It may be a little rough."

"Allow me, sir?" asked Tuvok.

Chakotay looked at his capable first officer and nodded with relief. "Yes, take the conn."

Under Tuvok's sure hands, the landing was not rough at all. He piloted the *Spartacus* under the ledge and hovered for a second, thrusters blasting away. Then he eased her onto the bedrock like a mother putting her baby down for a nap.

When Tuvok killed the thrusters, Chakotay finally let his breath out. A wave splashed a sheen of water against their front window, and it dribbled down like a veil of tears.

"Now what?" asked the Vulcan.

"Now we wait," answered the captain. "If we put a communications array on top of the cliff, do you think we could monitor subspace transmissions?"

"I believe so. I will attend to it." Tuvok rose from his seat and strode off the bridge, leaving Chakotay to ponder the gray sea that lapped at their precarious perch.

They were safe . . . for the moment.

Eight hours later, Chakotay sat alone on the barren cliff, warming his hands by a small campfire and watching the twin moons of Helena try to shine their way through dense cloud cover. Although the clouds were gloomy, he knew they were keeping the night temperature on Flint Island warmer than it had a right to be. A few meters away, the communications array hummed busily, listening for voices of doom behind the swirling clouds.

The campfire, made from driftwood, was his own small conceit. They had portable heaters that would probably be more efficient, and they could monitor the subspace traffic just as easily from the ship. But Chakotay had felt a need to sit and commune with fire, the ground, and the night. Until this mission, he hadn't realized how much he had missed being on land. He loved space, but he knew he was a visitor there; he felt connected to the land, even this forsaken, haunted island.

Hearing footsteps behind him, he whirled around to see two people approaching. One of them was walking stiffly with a cane, and the other was helping him. When they reached the circle of light from the campfire, he was surprised to see that it was Riker using the cane, and B'Elanna helping him.

"What are you doing up?" he asked Riker, with a mild scold in his voice.

"I couldn't lie in that bed a moment longer," said the lieutenant with a smile. "You look like one of your ancestors, sitting up here by the fire. Except that you used a lighter to start it." Riker pointed at the device.

Chakotay smiled wanly. "I'm sure they would have used more appropriate technology. But however I accomplish the aim, sometimes I need to speak to my ancestors, and this is a good place to find them."

"I don't blame you," said Riker, easing himself to the ground with some difficulty. "I grew up in fairly wild country on Earth, and I miss sitting outside by the campfire."

"Where are you from?" asked Torres.

"Alaska. It's beautiful—forests, lakes, rivers, glaciers, lots of wildlife. Most of the year, it's cold, like this. I miss it."

"Why don't you go back?"

The big man shrugged. "There's not much call for a Starfleet officer in Alaska. Besides, there are some memories I'm not so fond of. But maybe I will go back someday."

Suddenly, the communications array crackled with activity, and several voices broke in at once, overlapping. Chakotay jumped up from the campfire to adjust the equipment, and a moment later they heard a male voice order, "All ships, assume standard orbit, six thousand kilometer intervals. Cruiser *Gagh N'Vort,* coordinate scanning activity. Warship *K'Stek Nak,* coordinate targeting."

"Targeting?" breathed Torres. "They're going to destroy the planet! We've got to get back to the ship."

"Wait a minute," said Riker puzzledly. "Those aren't Cardassian ship names."

"Cloak on my command," the voice continued.

"Cardassians don't have cloaking," said Chakotay. "They're *Klingon* ships!"

A grin spread across Riker's face. "I think the Cardassians are in for a surprise."

Chapter Seventeen

GUL DEMADAK RUBBED his hands together and smiled, thinking how good it would feel to finally be rid of the obstacle known as Helena. Destroying the planet would not only please his superiors and squelch the plague, but it would destroy any trace of his involvement with his secret benefactor. It would also rid the Cardassian Union of a worthless planet that was more trouble to govern than it was worth.

And he would do the deed himself, to achieve the maximum recognition and credit.

"Coming out of warp in thirty seconds," the captain of the *Hakgot* reported to him.

"Excellent," Demadak said with a satisfied smile. He had only been able to scrounge up eight ships on the spur of the moment, but he figured that would be enough to scorch the planet. If they didn't kill everyone and everything with their weapons, the nuclear winter they caused would destroy everything in a few days. From what he knew of the planet, the inhabitants were peaceful and had no working starships, so they wouldn't be prepared for an all-out conflagration. They would have no place to hide.

"Coming out of warp," reported the captain of his flagship.

Gul Demadak rose from his seat and stood before the viewscreen. *What an ugly little planet,* he thought when it came into view—*all blue and watery, like a human's weak eyes.* "Any sign of the Maquis?" he asked.

"None," answered the officer on ops. "There are no ships in orbit."

The gul nodded, thinking that the cowardly Maquis had run for it. Or perhaps they had all succumbed to the plague. It was just as well, because his crew needed all of its firepower for the task at hand.

"What about the garrison?" asked the captain.

Demadak frowned, his bony brow knit with concern. "According to their last report, most of them have already died from the plague, and the rest are getting sick. We have no facilities to care for them, and we don't want to stay here any longer than absolutely necessary."

The captain nodded. Nobody wanted to risk getting the plague, and the whole purpose of this operation was to make sure that the plague died on Helena.

"I'll make sure that they are all decorated for bravery," said Demadak. "Posthumously."

He looked at another viewscreen and could see the other seven ships in his fleet spread out behind him, ready to execute his commands. "Power up weapons," he ordered.

"Yes, sir."

Before they could even fire a shot, his ship was jolted by a powerful blast, and the gul staggered on his feet. "What was *that?*" he demanded.

"Port nacelle damaged!" reported a frightened ops officer.

"Look!" barked the captain, pointing at the viewscreen. A massive Klingon Bird of Prey had materialized from nowhere—dead ahead of them. Behind them, two more Klingon ships came out of cloak.

"Return fire!" yelled Demadak.

"Belay that order," said the captain, fixing a jaundiced eye on the gul. "In total, there are *thirteen* Klingon ships ringing the planet. Gul Demadak, I have to remind you that *I'm* in command of this ship and her crew. I really don't care to die over this stupid planet."

"They're hailing us," reported the tactical officer.

"On screen," muttered Demadak, slumping into a seat. He knew at that moment that his career was over. He would probably be executed.

A rugged, bearded Klingon appeared on the viewscreen. "Cardassian vessels, turn around and leave. I am General Martok, and the planet of Helena is under the protection of the Klingon Empire."

"You . . . you have no right to be here!" sputtered Demadak.

"Neither do you," replied the Klingon.

"This is in direct violation of the treaty!"

"*We* have no treaty with you," sneered General Martok. "However, you are clearly breaking your treaty with the Federation. I have been instructed to deliver a message to you from the Federation. They will overlook this serious transgression if you will leave the Demilitarized Zone immediately. In exchange, they will send a fleet of unarmed personnel carriers to evacuate the population of Helena. This will effectively end your concerns over the disease that has infected the planet. I can see no reason why you should refuse this gracious offer."

"Neither can I," said the Cardassian captain, stepping in front of Demadak. "General Martok, we will take our leave. End transmission."

After the screen went blank, the captain turned to the helmsman and ordered, "Take us home. Maximum warp."

Fuming, Demadak glared at the captain. "I'll have your head for this!"

"No, you won't. They *knew* we were coming. You are responsible for a serious security breach, and I'll make sure Central Command hears about it."

Gul Demadak leaned forward and buried his face in his hands.

A week later, Chakotay and his crew were still hiding on Flint Island, monitoring the evacuation of Helena. They were unable to leave because of all the ships in orbit. Although their mission was a success and most of the Helenites had been saved, there was a bittersweet feeling of defeat. It had never been their intention that a civilization hundreds of years old should be uprooted and taken back to a place from which they had fled. Chakotay could only imagine the sorrow of Dr. Gammet, Echo Imjim, and so many others who had to leave their homes, businesses, and unique lifestyles. In a way, they had won the battle but lost the war.

Also, they were troubled by the knowledge that the real masterminds of this biological weapon had gotten away. Where they would strike again, no one knew; but Chakotay was certain that they *would* strike again.

Night after night, members of the crew sat on the cliff by the campfire, listening to radio traffic from the personnel carriers. At least, thought Chakotay, there was no more talk about B'Elanna or anyone else retiring from the Maquis and living happily ever after on Helena. When the last ship left, Helena would again be the exclusive property of the birds, fish, and animals. Cardassians would be free to settle there, but he doubted they ever would.

He watched Thomas Riker, who seemed to be the most troubled of all of them. The Maquis were used to the Federation messing things up, but the lieutenant had never gotten such a vivid demonstration of its heavy-handed interference before. It had come as something of a shock.

All of the Starfleet doctors had left with the others, but not Riker. He refused to leave the *Spartacus*. One night, Chakotay found himself alone on the cliff with the lieutenant. He hadn't broached the subject yet, but it was time.

"Riker," he said, "the evacuation is almost complete. If you're going back to Starfleet, you've got to go now. We'll beam you over to one of the other islands."

The lieutenant gritted his teeth. "I can't stand what they're doing here. All of it is just to make life easier for *them.* They don't give a damn what happens to the Helenites."

"Why do you think we formed the Maquis? The Federation's appeasement of the Cardassians has destroyed more lives than you can ever imagine. What's a few million Helenites down the drain, as long as it keeps the treaty intact. If you're not going back to Starfleet, are you going to stay with us? Are you ready to join the Maquis?"

The big man nodded slowly. "I can't believe it, but I think I am. What am I going to do in the Maquis?"

"*You* can do a lot for us, since you can impersonate that other Riker. There's a mission we've talked about, but we've never had the right person until now."

"What is it?"

He looked around, just to make sure they were alone. "I think I can trust everybody in my crew, but I'm not entirely sure. So I want you to keep this between you and me."

"That's no problem."

Chakotay smiled. "Ever been to Deep Space Nine?"

DOUBLE HELIX

DOUBLE OR NOTHING

PETER DAVID

SEVEN YEARS EARLIER . . .

I.

Vandelia tried to conceal her astonishment when her rescuer's face fell off.

She had not been expecting a rescuer at all, much less one whose visage suddenly abandoned him. Only five minutes before, her situation had seemed utterly hopeless. Not that it was in Vandelia's nature to admit that any situation was hopeless or in any way outside of her control. It wasn't that she was eternally optimistic. She was just too damned stubborn, not to mention extremely fierce-natured.

She was a sinewy Orion woman, with thick green hair that cascaded about her slim, bare green shoulders. She was scantily dressed, as was the custom of her kind, in a clinging outfit that concealed almost nothing and accentuated that which it hid. Orion females preferred such attire because it made them more formidable fighters. After all, how was an opponent expected to concentrate fully on his own defense when there was so much exposed flesh coming at him? A male never quite knew where to look first, and consequently he never quite reacted properly to an assault. Before he knew it, razor-sharp fingernails would be slashing across his face, or filed teeth would be ripping a chunk of his jugular from his throat. Even Orion men were daunted by their females. Indeed, it explained the serious population problem that Orions were having. Granted, each new generation of Orions was stronger and tougher than the last. That was out of necessity, since only the hardiest of Orion males dared to try their luck with their females. Survival rate of such engagements was roughly 83 percent . . . less if the female in question happened to be in heat, a biological drive that was probably the only reason Orions hadn't vanished from the face of the galaxy centuries earlier.

The sinewy Orion girl pulled with renewed determination at her bonds, but she had absolutely no more luck in severing them this time than she'd had the previous times she had tried to muscle herself free of her imprisonment. Even her formidable fingernails were incapable of severing her restraints. More out of a sense of pure frustration than any true belief that success would result from the efforts, she strained against the bonds, her clearly defined muscles undulating beneath her dark green skin. Still nothing. She was held tight.

Matters might have been slightly improved if she had only had an idea of where "here" was. Unfortunately, she had no clue at all. She had been captured, in her sleep of all things. How cowardly was that? How craven on the part of her captors.

Vandelia was a business woman, a professional entertainer. She danced at parties and social functions, and not only was she very good at it, but she had been extremely canny in investing the financial gains that her performing had garnered her. She had millions of credits stashed away as a result of her seven-plus years of playing to a crowd, plus additional activities on the side.

She had been dancing this night . . . except she realized that she had no reason whatever to assume that this night was the same night. She had no idea how long she had been unconscious. One night, two, five . . . no clue at all, really. The only thing she knew was that when she had woken up, she had been ravenous. Nevertheless, when some flunky had shown up in her bare-bones room to bring her food, she had spat it back in his face. He had cleaned the food off himself without a word. The next time he came to her, he had two assistants along, and they had pried open the woman's mouth and poured the food straight down her throat. Obviously the actions did not endear them to her. They could not have cared less.

The flunky was not of a race that she recognized. He was short and squat, wider than he was tall, bald and jowly and with bright red skin. The assistants he brought with him had similar coloration, albeit different builds. But as far as Vandelia was concerned, if she never saw any members of the entire race again, she'd be the happier for it. She did, however, feel some degree of alarm when she started wondering what the coloration of any offspring would look like. She hoped like hell that she wasn't approaching her heat cycle. Being out of control of her mating instincts was simply not aggravation that she needed.

They (whoever they were) didn't *have* to keep her trussed up. There were, after all, various electronic devices capable of controlling her. Collars, wrist bracelets with shock devices, and many other options. But they had chosen none of those, instead going for something barbaric and debilitating to the spirit such as total immobility through heavy-duty ropes. It was as if her captors were almost daring her to slice her way free. If what they were trying to do was totally muck with her head, then they were succeeding. She was becoming angrier, more frustrated, more of a seething volcano with each passing day. The most frustrating thing of all was that she knew they were doing it just to anger her . . . and yet she couldn't help herself, couldn't do anything to fight back the mounting ire.

On her third day of captivity, she met her host.

He was red-skinned, like the others, but he sported a series of elaborate tattoos on his forehead and also at the base of his throat just above the collarbone. He had high cheekbones and deep set eyes that glittered fearsomely. He dressed primarily in loose-fitting black clothes, with a loose-sleeved tunic and black pants tucked into the top of knee-high black boots. He had an air about him, Vandelia thought, that made it seem as if he didn't care one way or the other whether the individual he was looking at was dead or alive. Furthermore, he didn't seem to care whether he was the one responsible for that death or not. Vandelia was most struck by his hands, which were huge in comparison to his admittedly muscular arms. Every so often, as he spoke to her, his hands twitched slightly as if he was envisioning what it would be like to be crushing someone's windpipe.

"Greetings." His voice was amazingly soft-spoken for one so large and apparently threatening. She had to strain to hear him, and she realized that that was partly his purpose for speaking so quietly. "Have you been enjoying your stay?"

She said nothing, merely snarled at him.

"You are a feisty one. That's what I like about you. There's not enough feisty females in the galaxy."

This time, she spoke. "Come to my home world," she said between clenched teeth. "You'll find more than enough feistiness to keep you busy."

"I daresay." He bowed slightly at the waist as he said, "My name is Zolon Darg. And you are Vandelia."

"And you are dead."

The smile never wavered from his thin lips, but one of his meaty hands swung around so fast that she never even saw it coming. One moment his arms seemed relaxed and at his sides, and the next the hand was smacking her in the face. She lowered her head a moment, trying to compose herself and failing utterly. When she glared back up at him, it was from between strands of hair that lay upon her face, and her lips were drawn back in a snarl revealing her sharp teeth.

"Mind your manners," said Zolon Darg. "This will take as long as it has to take."

"What is 'this'?" she asked.

"Why, to make you mine, my dear," Darg told her. "I saw you dance. I was one of your many customers, your many admirers. But unlike others, I choose not to admire from afar. I wish to draw close, to be . . . personal."

"Go to hell," Vandelia said.

"Yes, yes . . . I'm sure you would like that," he said in a condescending tone that made it sound as if he were addressing a child. "That will not be happening anytime soon, I'm sorry to say . . . for your sake."

"So that is all that this is about?" Vandelia demanded to know. "You kidnapped me because you find me attractive? How pitiful. How mundane."

"You misunderstand me." He smiled, and although he did not have sharpened teeth as Vandelia did, his smile looked no less threatening than hers. He looked perfectly capable of biting a piece out of her if it suited his purposes. "It is not simple attraction. You are a challenge. There are few enough true challenges in this galaxy, and I take mine where I can find them. When I saw you dance, I knew instinctively that you'd be impossible to tame. But I thrive on impossibilities."

"Then think about some impossible things you can do with your own anatomy." Then she spat at him.

He hit her again. And again. The smile never wavered, his pulse never sped up. Three, four, five times and more, and again and again, across the face with those huge hands, first one cheek and then the other. The first couple of times she tried to voice, at the very least, a snarl of inarticulate rage, but when he'd slapped her the twentieth time, she'd stopped. She simply sat there, her head hanging, trying to breathe and laboring because of all the fury that had tightened her chest. She couldn't get a sound out. He folded his arms and stood there with a quietly smug expression. He had the air of someone who was utterly confident as to precisely who was in charge.

"I'm sorry, my dear," he told her, although he didn't sound especially sorry. "I very much wish that I could tell you that there is some deep, greater meaning to your being here. That in fact you have something I need, or that you've actually got a microchip with secret information hidden beneath your skin, or you're actually a long lost princess, or perhaps you and you alone are capable of finding the cure for a terrible disease. But it's none of those things. You're an amusement, a diversion." He crouched down then, going to one knee so that he could regard her at eye level. "A pleasant diversion, granted . . . but that's all."

"Is this what you do?" Her lips were starting to swell up a bit from the pounding she'd taken, but she was determined not to acknowledge the pain. Even so, when she spoke her voice sounded thick and a bit uneven. "Divert yourself? Is this how you . . . pass your days?"

"Not at all," said Zolon Darg. He straightened up and then bowed slightly at the waist as if presenting himself in most courtly fashion. "I will have you know that I am one of the premier weapons suppliers in the territory."

"Are you now." She didn't sound impressed. "So what. You help people kill each other. As if that makes you someone of consequence."

"You do me a disservice, woman. You oversimplify. I have supplied freedom fighters who battle for their crippled rights. I have supplied governments who fight to protect themselves from evil and unappreciative mobs of rebellious ingrates. I am always, always, on the side of those who are in the right."

"And what makes one right and one wrong?"

"Money, my dear girl," he smiled.

She spat in defiance once more. But this wad didn't even manage to cover the distance before it splattered impotently to the floor. Darg didn't give it a glance. "You amoral pig," she growled.

"The moral high ground, my dear Vandelia, belongs to whomever can afford to pay the toll."

She said nothing, merely glowered at him. He smiled thinly, clearly finding the entire encounter very amusing.

Since she was seated, he naturally towered over her. But he took the opportunity to crouch and bring himself to eye level with her. He studied her thoughtfully, and then said, "Let me tell you what's going to happen. We're going to start putting you on a somewhat erratic eating schedule, for starters. Sometimes you will find yourself starving, your belly aching so pitifully that you'll feel as if it would gladly rip through your body and go off in search of food on its own. Other times we will suddenly feed you in such copious amounts that we will literally be shoving it down your throat. The five or so gentlemen who have been overseeing your trips to relieve yourself in delicate lady-like fashion will be assigned other duties. We will simply leave you tied up at all times, so that you can wallow in your own waste products. When you begin to fall asleep, loud noises will be blared at you, blinding lights shined directly into your face. We also have one or two fairly belligerent empaths at our disposal . . . individuals who will be able to project into your mind whatever emotions it amuses me to have you feel. You have a very strong mind, Vandelia. At the outset, you'd likely be able to resist them. But that will only be at the outset, and we have a very long time available to us. We will, in short, do all that we can to disrupt you, discommode you, and utterly break you."

"And once that's done?" she asked levelly.

"Why then, at that point . . . you will be reeducated. Reprogrammed. The personality, the attitude that you have now . . . that will be like a bad dream. It will go far, far away where it can never be of any harm to you again." As he spoke, his voice almost seemed soothing in its confidence. "Instead, it will be replaced by a calmer, more loving personality. Oh, but don't worry. You will continue to dance. But you will perform your seductive dances . . . only for me."

She looked at him with utter contempt. "You have no idea, do you."

"What do you mean?" His head was tilted in a curious manner.

"My dancing. You think somehow that's separate from who I am. That is, after all, what attracted you to me. You poor, pathetic fool, Darg. When I dance . . . that is an expression of my personality. And that personality holds you, and all your kind, in the utmost contempt. When I dance," and she lowered her voice to an almost sultry tone, "I know that you all caress me with your eyes. I know that you think of what you would like to do to me. How each of you envisions possessing me. But you're all too stupid to realize that in my gyrations, I'm letting you know just how little I think of your desires. I don't dance to seduce. I dance to let you know what you can never, ever have. Let us say," she continued as if warming to the topic, "that you somehow manage to break my personality. Make me less than I am. Do you seriously think that if I'm even capable of dancing again, it will bear the slightest resemblance to anything you saw before? You will sit there and shake your head in frustration, wondering what happened to the passion, the fire, the sheer raw sexuality that drew you to me in the first place. And when you sit there in discouragement, when you mourn the loss of something that you truly adored . . . why then, my friend, you will have only yourself to blame. Only yourself. And even if you manage to have your way with the body you see before you now . . ." She grinned ferally. "Even if you manage that . . . you will never have me. I will be long gone, beyond your ability to touch or harm or seduce or even interest. Do we understand each other now, Zolon Darg? Have I made things sufficiently clear for even a brainless pig such as yourself?"

He smiled mirthlessly. "Abundantly clear, yes."

"But it is still your intention to hold me here?"

"Yes. You see . . . it doesn't particularly matter to me if you wind up being destroyed as part of my endeavors. At least I'll know that I was able to bring you down, and I will allow myself to take some pleasure in that."

Then he slapped her several more times. There seemed to be no particular reason to do so. But he did it anyway. Vandelia, for her part, couldn't even muster the ability to spit.

That was when the alarm went off.

Vandelia was positive that that was what it was the moment she heard it. The loud, screeching klaxon jolted Darg, and he looked around in confusion as if he weren't quite certain that he was in fact hearing the noise that was threatening to deafen the entire place. For the first time, Vandelia saw a momentary bit of uncertainty pass across Darg's previously smug face. She was extremely pleased to see it. Her only regret was that she wasn't the cause of it.

He tapped a comm unit that he wore on his wrist and said, "Central. This is Darg. Report: What is the cause of the alarm?"

"We have an intruder, sir," came back a voice crisply.

"How do we know that, Kapel?"

"We found Dikson down on level three. Apparently he'd been in a fight. Someone broke his neck, and they did it very cleanly and very efficiently."

Clearly, it took a lot more than the discovery of a corpse to throw Zolon Darg off his stride. "Will you shut that damned alarm off? How is anyone supposed to concentrate on anything with that godawful noise howling in our ears?" A moment passed and then the alarm, obediently, was shut off, although the lights were still rapidly dimming and glowing. Vandelia viewed the flickering with grim amusement. Since the alarm had likely made everyone in the area deaf, dimming the lights was probably the only remaining means of alerting all concerned to the fact that there was a problem.

"Now then," Darg said slowly, once he seemed satisfied that the alarm was no longer going to assail his ears, "We don't know absolutely for certain that Dikson's death means that we have an intruder. He had a history of gambling, as I recall. Could this be retaliation of some sort for money owed?"

"Sir," came back the voice of the one who'd been addressed as Kapel, "his debts were his protection? Who's going to kill someone who owes them money? Rather difficult to collect."

"Hmm. Yes. Yes, you're right," Zolon Darg said after a moment's consideration. "All right, then. I want everyone throughout the base on full watch. Have all shifts report in. I want tech teams scouring level three. Perhaps Dikson discovered this possible intruder performing some sort of sabotage act. If so, it has to be found and rooted out immediately. Is that clear, Kapel?"

"Yes, sir."

"I will be right up."

"Yes, sir."

He clicked off his comm unit, and then turned to Vandelia. "I have to leave, darling. But rest assured, we will have time together. Not only that," and he ran a finger along the line of her jaw, "but you will dance for me . . . and only for me."

Her head struck forward like a serpent's, her sharp teeth clacking together, but he deftly moved his hand away lest he lose a finger. "Feisty," he said once more in approval . . . and then swung a vicious roundhouse punch. He connected with her on the point of the jaw with such force that it knocked her completely over. The chair crashed heavily to the floor. Vandelia's head lolled back, her eyes closed.

He turned and walked away from her. When he got to the door, it slid open . . . and standing there waiting for him was another of his race. The new arrival was slightly shorter than Darg, and slimmer. He seemed momentarily startled, apparently not having expected the door to open right up. "Zolon Darg," he said, recovering quickly. "The . . . the alarm . . ."

"I heard it," Darg said impatiently. His eyes narrowed as he stared at the other Thallonian. "What is your name again?"

"Qadril, sir," said the Thallonian. "We met not long ago. I'm a friend of—"

"Yes, yes, I remember. Qadril . . . attend to her."

"To her, sir?" He looked uncertainly in Vandelia's direction. "Are you sure—?"

"Of course I'm sure," Darg told him, his temper not becoming any gentler with the constant need for repetition. "Haul her chair upright so that she's not simply lying about on the floor like that. And keep your fingers away from her teeth, would be my recommendation."

"Yes, sir."

With that, Darg headed out.

Qadril glanced right and left. Vandelia knew this since she was watching him carefully. Her eyes were narrow slits as she saw him draw closer, closer. She suspected that he would be of no more use in freeing her than anyone else, but she looked forward to sinking her teeth into him during an unwary moment. His howls of pain would bring her great pleasure, and be a further reminder to Darg that she was going to make every moment that he held her captive as much of a living hell as she could manage.

Qadril hesitated a few feet away, and then he went around her and gripped her chair from behind. She was mildly surprised when he did not grunt under the weight of hauling her back into an upright position. He didn't *seem* all that strong. Obviously he had some muscle, although one wouldn't have known it to look at him.

But, just as obviously, he was remarkably stupid, for the poor fool was actually in the process of exhibiting something akin to concern for her. He walked in front of her and took either side of her face in his hands, tilting her head back so that he could try and see into her eyes. "Can you hear me?"

When he said that, there was something different in his voice. He sounded rougher, more brusque than he had mere moments ago when speaking to Darg. Darg he had addressed in a manner that was fairly simpering. But not now. Now he sounded more dynamic, more confident and sure of himself.

It was probably, she assumed, because she was unconscious. In fact, he was probably trying to determine if . . . yessss. Yes, that was it. He wanted to see if she was still out cold so that he could have his way with her with impunity. Oh, and wouldn't that be something for him to boast to his friends about. She could practically hear his weasely voice bragging of how he had "tamed" her, made her beg for his attentions. Her fury began to bubble over the imagined liberties that he was about to take.

He had momentarily distracted her from her purpose with his feigned concerns as to her well-being. She was annoyed with herself that she had allowed that to happen, no matter how short a time her determination had actually wavered. As if to make up for it, she attacked with speed and viciousness that would have done any Orion female proud.

Just as he was making another inquiry as to her wakefulness, her head whipped around and she sank her teeth into his left forearm. She had envisioned chomping through his flesh, all the way down into the bone if she were lucky. If not, then at least she would take some pleasure in tearing out a large, dripping hunk of the man's arm and spitting it back into his face while his blood trickled down the sides of her face.

But she did not come into contact with flesh or bone. Instead her teeth bit through the cloth of his sleeve and hit metal.

"No!" he shouted.

What in the world? The thought flashed through her mind even as she quickly yanked her head back. Perhaps, she thought, he was some sort of cyborg or android.

Sparks flew from the section of his arm that she had mutilated, and she saw a few quick sparks dancing along his shirt sleeve. He tore at the sleeve, pulling off some sort of device that had been strapped around his arm.

It was at that moment that his face fell off.

Vandelia gaped in confusion as the red skin cracked and crumbled away, cascading to the floor in a powdery heap. Not only was his skin color different, but the very shape of his visage had altered.

The man who only moments before that been calling himself Qadril had gone from having a fairly round face to one that had a good deal more definition to it. His chin was cleft, his nose somewhat irregular, as if it had been broken. Instead of being bald, he had a thick mop of black hair. His skin was no longer red, but instead a paler shade that was more evocative of human beings. Even his eyes had changed color, going from a sort of pale blue to a vivid purple. Most striking about him to Vandelia, however, was a scar that ran the length of his right cheek. Considering the skin graft and dermaplast techniques that were so readily available, Vandelia couldn't recall ever having seen a facial mutilation that was quite so severe.

She found it rather attractive.

"Perfect," he growled, dusting away the remains of the red material that had been obscuring his true features. "Just perfect. You had to do that. You just had to."

"Who are you?" she demanded.

"The one who was going to get you out of here. At this point, though, I'm half-tempted to leave you." He made an impatient noise, blowing air from between his clenched teeth, and then he seemed to make up his mind. "All right," he sighed, "we'll just have to make the best of it. If I free you, will you give me your word that you won't attack."

For a moment, despite the fact that he was offering her aid, she couldn't hold back a contemptuous sneer. "Are you that afraid of me?"

"No," he said reasonably. "But you're a splendid looking woman, and I try to minimize the number of splendid looking women I kill in the average day."

The words were light, the tone quite flip, but she looked into his eyes and there was something in there, a flat, cold stare that caused her to realize that there was nothing cavalier about his attitude. He really did believe that he was capable of killing her. Moreover, she began to get the impression that he might actually be able to accomplish it.

"You would take the word of an Orion?" she asked after a moment.

"Look," and it was clear from his tone that his patience was starting to wear thin, "I'm not interested in passing judgment on a species just now. I'm asking you, personally, if—"

"Yes, yes, all right, you have my word I will not attempt to hurt you," she said at last.

He had a knife hanging from his right hip. He pulled it out and briskly cut through the ropes that bound her. "You use that knife as if you really know what you're about," she commented.

He said nothing, but instead simply slid it back into its sheath. He glanced around the room they were in as if he were trying to see if anything could be used as a weapon.

"What was that device you were using to disguise yourself?" she asked.

"A Zynterian Camouflage Field," he replied as he went to the wall and ran his fingers along it. He seemed to be probing for something. He had been wearing gloves, which one would have thought was simply for ornamentation, but now she realized it had been to hide the true color of his hands.

"Zynterians? They're a passive race. They have no espionage interests that I've ever heard of," said Vandelia. She was busy rubbing her wrists, trying to restore circulation to them. She was a bit unsteady on her legs as well, but was determined not to let the weakness show.

"True enough. But they don't use it for espionage. It's a sex aid."

"A what?" She didn't quite think she'd heard him properly.

He cast an impatient look at her, as if he couldn't quite believe that he was wasting time explaining it to her. "They believe sex in any form is inherently evil, and so they use the camouflage field to disguise themselves as members of other races when they're . . . involved. That way they can pretend that they themselves are remaining pure. It's a sort of ritual."

"I see." She didn't, actually, but it seemed the thing to say.

"Generally Zynterians are the only ones who can use them. Other races who have tried to employ the device for other pursuits—such as espionage, as you mentioned—find that the device tends to sear the flesh from their bones. However, we Xenexians are close enough biologically to Zynterians that we can get away with using them. It causes considerable pain, but otherwise no lasting damage."

"Pain? You were in pain the entire time you were using that thing? I couldn't tell."

"I'm very stoic," he said, never taking his eyes from the wall as he continued his probe of the room. "For instance, my impulse is to throw you to the ground and take you like an animal right here. But you'd never be able to tell."

His voice was so flat, so lacking in inflection, that it was impossible for her to tell whether he was joking or not. She felt a headache coming on just trying to keep up with him. "Who are you?" she demanded.

"Call me Mac," he said over his shoulder. "Ah."

"Ah?"

He had his hand against a section of the wall that looked no different from any other. However, he pushed it and suddenly the wall swivelled around, revealing what appeared to be some sort of passage. She couldn't quite make out any details, although she did see small, flickering lights lining the upper section.

"Come on," he told her.

"But . . . where does this go?"

"Away from here. For the moment, that's good enough."

She mentally shrugged as she realized she had nothing to lose. This strange individual, whoever he was and wherever he was from, at least seemed to have some idea as to what he was about. She really couldn't be much worse off than she'd been a few minutes ago.

They headed down the narrow passage. Moments after they'd entered, the wall had slid back into place on noiseless hinges. The action dimmed the corridor slightly, but not significantly.

"How did you know that was going to be there?" she asked. "That false wall, I mean."

"I didn't. Not for sure. But we've done a good deal of research on Darg, and it seemed a reasonable guess. He had a similar hideaway on Estarcion IV, and he'd laced it with catacombs with similar entrances. He likes to get about unobserved and show up unexpectedly. He feels it keeps his people on their toes."

"It probably does." She paused and then said, "Who are 'we'? I mean, the 'we' who did this research?"

"You don't need to know that either," he said brusquely.

"Listen," and her temper started to flare, "I'd better start getting some answers, or—"

"Or what?" He turned to face her there in the confines of the passage, and there was unmistakable danger in his tone. "Look: You weren't in the plan. I found out that you were here when I was already inside. You're an innocent bystander who's in the wrong place at the wrong time. I decided that it wouldn't be right to simply leave you to die. So I am risking myself to save your neck. I didn't have to. I still don't. If you want to go off on your own and take your chances, go right ahead." He flattened against the corridor wall so that she could pass by him. "My guess is that it branches off just ahead. You can go on and take your chances. I'll give you a five . . . no, three . . . minute head start. You'll go your way, I'll go mine, and that'll be that. Or tell me now if you're going to stick with me but are going to continue to irritate me, because if you are, then I'll put you down right now and be done with it. I don't need the distraction or the grief. Life's too short and on the verge of getting even shorter. Your only other option is to shut up so I can get both of us out of here in one piece. Once we're out of here and safe, you can be as arrogant and irritating as you wish. It won't bother me then because you won't be putting us at risk. Now have I made myself clear?"

"Yes," she said tightly.

"Now are you going to be quiet?"

No reply.

"Good."

She took some small measure of satisfaction in the fact that he actually appeared surprised that she had quieted down.

As she followed him, she said softly, "May I ask a less inflammatory question?"

"If you must."

"You've been talking as if we have a deadline. Why is that?"

That was when a massive explosion rocked them.

She stumbled against him as the passageway vibrated uncontrollably around them. He steadied her and muttered, "Idiots. They must have found it and tried to defuse it."

There was now an unmistakable rumbling all about them, and he grabbed her wrist and yanked. "Come on." There was urgency to his voice, but he didn't sound close to panic. Clearly this was someone who was accustomed to handling difficult situations with aplomb.

She picked up speed and now they were heading at a full dash down the corridor. There was the sound of a second explosion, and a third, and they staggered as they ran. From a distance they could hear shouts and the sounds of running feet, and voices being raised in alarm.

There was a sensation of heat from directly behind them. "I wouldn't look back if I were you," the man called Mac warned her.

She looked back.

A gigantic ball of flame was roaring down the passage behind them.

She looked forward once more, suddenly wishing that she'd done as he suggested.

The seam in the wall that indicated a door barely had time to register on her and then Mac was pushing both of them through. They stumbled out into a main hallway that hardly seemed to be much better in terms of being a safe haven, for men were running about in total panic and any one of them might notice the escaping prisoner. Giving no heed to the danger that being spotted presented, Mac slammed the door back into place just as the jet of flame caught up to them. The wall instantly became superheated, but Mac had blocked off the passageway just in time, and the flames within passed them by harmlessly.

"Come on," and he pulled her roughly. "We've got to get to our ride. This place doesn't have much longer."

It was the first opportunity that Vandelia had had to see anything of her place of capture aside from the one room in which she'd been imprisoned. The place was massive, stretching upward as far as she could see. There were crosswalks and catwalks far overhead and then, when she looked down she saw that they descended to a great depth as well. Everything had been constructed so that everything was visible to some degree from elsewhere within the complex. It was all rather clever; it meant that Darg could keep his eye on just about everything from any point.

Under ordinary circumstances, she and Mac wouldn't have had a prayer of getting ten feet without attracting attention. But these circumstances were far from ordinary. She continued to hear explosions, some further away, some closer, and the entire place had spiralled into chaos. "What did you do?" she cried out over the shouts of others who were running around without noticing them.

"I'll tell you later, provided there is one!"

"*You!*"

Vandelia's heart sank. She recognized the voice immediately, of course.

It had come from behind them, and they turned to see Zolon Darg. He was on a catwalk above them, looking down, and he had half a dozen men with him. He had spotted Vandelia, and more, he obviously realized that it was Mac who was the intruder. Perhaps it was the fact that Mac was wearing the same clothes as the supposed red-skinned guard had been sporting a short time earlier. "You did this! You! Stay where you are!"

"You don't have time for this, Darg!" Mac shot back. "These explosions you're hearing so far are nothing! A chain of bombs to distract you from the real threat: the fact that I set two of your main boomers in your central weapons room to overload. Once those go, you can say good-bye to this entire place! You've got only a couple of minutes to get clear! Are you going to waste them coming after me, or are you going to save your own neck?"

The choice seemed fairly straightforward to Vandelia. Unfortunately, it was less clear-cut to Darg, who did not hesitate to aim a fairly lethal weapon squarely at Mac and fire.

Mac yanked Vandelia forward, barely getting them clear of the shot. "Get them!" they could hear Zolon Darg shout after them, but they didn't look back. Instead they bolted as quickly as they could along the catwalk. "Get back here!" Darg's voice came, and a disruptor blast exploded just ahead of them, missing them but blowing the leg off a hapless individual who was trying to save his own skin. He hit the ground, crying out as he clutched at the stump of his knee. Mac and Vandelia did not slow down, but instead simply vaulted over him and kept going.

They angled left, then a quick right, and they were on a rampway that was heading downward. Vandelia had no idea whether Mac truly knew where they were going, or if he was simply guessing with sufficient confidence to allay her concerns. But she was quite certain that the source of the explosions which were wracking the entire area was below them, and heading toward that source was the height of folly. She yanked her hand from his. He turned and looked at her in confusion. "Come on!" he called to her.

"We're going the wrong way! We're heading towards the explosions! It's suicide!"

"There's no time for this!"

But she wasn't listening. Instead she turned and ran.

Her legs moving like pistons, she charged back up the ramp, found another turn-off, and took it. Someone tried to get in her way. She didn't even slow down, didn't take time to look at his face. She just slashed out with her fingernails and ripped across his face. He doubled over, blood welling up from between his fingers, and she shoved him aside and kept going.

Suddenly she was hit from the back, a flying tackle as someone took her down. She hit the floor, taking most of the impact on her elbows which sent a shock straight up her arms. But she did not cry out, instead keeping the pain within. That was how she was going to get out of it, she had decided. She would focus all her anger, all her agony, and it would drive her forward to safety. At least, that was the theory.

Unfortunately, the weight of the person atop her was such that, not only had the wind been knocked out of her, but she couldn't get the leverage to thrust upward and knock him off her back. She struggled, she snarled, and then rough hands grabbed her by either arm and hauled her to her feet. She tried to angle her head around to bite one of her captors, but another pair of hands came in behind her, grabbing her by the back of the head and snapping her skull back. Her attempts to pull her head forward simply resulted in her nearly tearing her hair out by the roots.

Zolon Darg stood in front of her. He was staring at her with enough cold fury to peel the skin off her face just with the force of his glare. "Where's your friend?" he demanded.

"What friend?" From closer than she would have liked to hear, an explosion sounded. Several of Darg's men flinched or looked about nervously. Darg didn't even glance in the direction of the noise.

"I understand now," he said evenly. "Very elaborate. Very clever. You trick and seduce me into bringing you here so that your mysterious associate could follow you and track you to our hidden location."

"You idiot! I'm the victim here! You're giving me entirely too much credit. You've created some elaborate conspiracy theory where none exists!"

Darg circled her. "Then why did he stop to rescue you?"

"I don't know! Ask him!" She tried in futility to pull free. "I don't know if you've noticed, but this entire place is going up!"

"I have my best people on it," Darg replied confidently. "They will locate whatever further boobytraps your partner has laid and dispose of them. As for you . . ." And he aimed a disruptor squarely at her forehead. "Call your partner. Summon him, right now."

"He's not my partner!"

"Call him." His tone didn't waver.

"He's probably long gone by now, because you've been too busy playing games with me!"

He fired a warning shot to her right. It grazed her upper thigh. To her credit, she still didn't cry out, as much as she wanted to. The bolt almost struck the man who was standing behind her, holding her immobile. Aware of the near-hit, he cast a nervous glance at his associates.

"Last warning." This time he aimed it straight at her face. The man who was holding her head steady angled around so that Darg would have a clear shot.

Realizing she had nothing to lose, Vandelia called out, "Mac!"

"That's better. Call him again."

"*Maaaaac!*"

"Mac what? What is his full name?"

"I have no idea."

He activated the disruptor's energy feed, preparing for another shot that would take her head off.

"Mac Morn Michelity," she said without further hesitation, reasoning that they likely weren't going to be around long enough for Darg to learn that she had no idea what she was talking about.

Suddenly there was a brief clatter from further down the rampway. Vandelia couldn't help but notice that Darg and his men were well-trained: Half of them looked in the direction of the noise, but the rest of them looked instead behind them, just in case the noise was a diversion to allow Mac to get in behind them.

Nothing, however, seemed to come from either direction.

Darg waited impatiently for another noise, and when none was forthcoming, turned back to Vandelia and said—with very little trace of sadness—"It appears your friend has deserted you. Farewell, Vandelia." He levelled the gun right at her face.

That was when the deafening roar sounded from behind them.

As one, they turned just in time to see a monstrous creature, reptilian in aspect, with leathery skin and a huge mouth filled with teeth that seemed capable of rending or shredding a shuttlecraft. It was poised above them on its hind legs, its whip-like tail snapping about with such ferocity that anyone within range of it would have been crushed instantly. When it roared, the hot, foul vapor of its breath washed over them, and the sound drowned out yet another explosion in the near distance.

The response among Darg's men was instantaneous. With a collective shriek of terror, they broke and ran as the creature advanced on them, each stomp of its massive feet causing the rampway to shudder beneath it. In doing so, they released their hold on Vandelia. Her immediate instinct was to try and attack Darg, but the shot he'd taken at her leg had done her more damage than she'd first realized. It went out from under her and she found herself barely able to walk, much less capable of lunging to the attack.

The only one who did not break and run was Darg himself. He stood precisely where he was, utterly paralyzed. His mouth hung open, his eyes were wide and looked almost lifeless as he stared at the monstrosity before them.

Suddenly Vandelia's view was blocked . . . by a rope which had just dropped directly into her line of sight. She glanced up and saw, on a rampway above her, Mac. He was holding the other end and mouthing the words, "Hurry up!"

She did not hesitate, but instead grabbed the rope with both hands and held on as tightly as she could. Mac pulled, and she was surprised how quickly and effortlessly he hauled her aloft. He had looked rather unprepossessing, but there was clearly more than ample strength in his arms if he was able to yank her upward so easily. He drew her upward, hand over hand, one foot braced against the hand railing, his mouth set and his eyes burning with a quiet intensity. He did not grunt, nor make any sound to give away any strain he might be feeling.

Darg still hadn't budged. He was indeed so frozen by what he was witnessing that he didn't appear to have noticed that Vandelia was no longer there. The monster roared once more, a particularly high-pitched shriek, and something in the piercing nature of the howl caused Darg's finger to tighten spasmodically on the trigger. The disruptor ripped out a shot and it went straight through the creature without the monster even acknowledging that it had been hit.

It took a moment for Darg to register for himself what he had just seen. Then his eyes narrowed and he fired again. Once more the creature was utterly unharmed by the disruptor blast.

He shouted a profanity and suddenly looked around . . . and then up. He did so just in time to see Vandelia being pulled over the railing of the overhead rampway, and he caught a glimpse of Mac looking down at him. Vandelia saw the two of them lock eyes, two enemies truly knowing each other for the first time.

"*Get back here!*" bellowed Darg, and he fired. Vandelia and Mac ducked backward as the blast sizzled past them.

"Come on! And stick with me this time!" Mac admonished her. The last thing Vandelia wanted to do was admit that her thigh was throbbing, so she gritted her teeth and simply nodded. Mac grabbed her wrist and they started to run. It was all that Vandelia could do not to limp in a most pronounced fashion. "What was that monster?" she called out.

Without glancing behind himself to address her, Mac said, "Holo unit. Pre-set monster, emanating from a disk about the size of my palm."

"That was the noise we heard . . . you activated it on a time delay and then tossed it down—"

"You're going to hear more noises than you'll want to hear if we don't hurry—"

The rampway shook beneath their feet. There seemed to be a series of seismic shocks building, one upon the other, throughout the structure. Mac glanced around. There was a network of ramps some thirty feet away from them, and between them was a deep well that seemed to fall away nearly into infinity. The ramp trembled once more.

Suddenly there was a screech of metal and the ramp started to twist at an angle. "Hold on," Mac said with a sort of resigned calm. He yanked off his belt buckle, twisted it, and suddenly he was holding a device that looked like a small gun. He tapped a button on the side and the end of the device was ejected, trailing a cord behind it. It "clacked" onto an upper rampway across the well.

At the far end of the ramp that they were upon, Darg was suddenly there. He was howling with fury, heedless of the chaos around him, as he charged straight toward them. He was firing his disruptor indiscriminately, no longer aiming but instead just shooting in their general direction. He lurched toward them, gripping the handrail, apparently not even aware that the ramp was in danger of collapsing.

Mac didn't even bother to glance at him. Instead he gripped the device in his palm, threw an arm around Vandelia's waist, and launched off the rampway. Vandelia had a brief glimpse of the ground, unspeakably far below, but it was all a blur, and suddenly they were on the other side. Mac snagged his legs around the railing and shoved Vandelia onto the ramp.

Zolon Darg brought his disruptor to bear, aiming at them across the divide, and then with a roar of metal the rampway that he was standing upon gave way. He tried to clutch onto something for support, but couldn't find anything. The sounds of the tearing metal drowned out Darg's shrieks as he tumbled downward and landed with a thud on the rampway below. He had about a second's respite before the falling metal of the upper rampway landed on him. The last that Vandelia saw of him was his face twisted in fury before he was completely obscured by the mass of twisted metal that crunched down atop him.

Mac, for his part, didn't appear to give it any notice. He seemed far more concerned about other things, such as survival. "This way," he said, and pulled her wrist. She limped after him.

"But we're heading toward the explosions!" she cried out to him, the same objection that she'd been raising before. But she was at that point somewhat resigned to her fate, convinced that she had only moments to live anyway. As if to underscore the point, there was another explosion, even louder than before.

"Here. Right here!" Mac called out to her. He hauled her over to a spot near a wall that was quivering from the most recent explosion. Then he stood perfectly still. "Don't worry," he said confidently.

"Don't worry!"

"That's right. Don't worry."

From deep within the well that the rampways surrounded, there was an explosion that was so loud Vandelia felt her teeth rattle.

Orion beliefs had one aspect in common with human theology. They shared a belief in an afterworld for the evil that was a scalding pit of torment. At that moment, Vandelia was suddenly convinced that she was within that very pit, for the air around her started to sizzle. She found it impossible to breathe, the air searing her very lungs. The entire area seemed bathed in light. She looked down into the well around which the rampways hung, and she saw a massive fireball roaring up toward them. Within seconds it would envelop them.

Part of her wanted to scream, to curse, to agonize in loud misery over the hideous and unfortunate set of circumstances which had brought her to this pointless end of her life. Instead, somewhat to her surprise, all she did was turn to Mac and say, sounding remarkably casual, "Can I worry now?"

He sighed. "If you must."

And she saw a flash of amusement in his purple eyes . . . at which point his eyes abruptly started to haze out in front of her. Then she realized that she, too, was disappearing, as the entire area around them demolecularized. Considering the circumstances, it was understandable that she didn't quite realize at first what was happening. *So this is what death is like* went through her head before she truly had a chance to register that she was not, in fact, dying, but that instead she was in the grip of a transporter beam.

Then the world reintegrated around her and she found herself in the back of some sort of small transport vehicle. Somewhat larger than a runabout, it seemed like a small freighter more than anything, designed for short runs with cargo that was generally contraband. The smaller the vessel, the less chance there was of attracting attention. Then she fell, for Mac was no longer supporting her. Instead he had moved quickly off the transporter pad and was at the helm. "Hold on!" he called.

"Hold on! To what?!" she cried out. Ultimately it didn't matter; the freighter suddenly leaped forward, sending Vandelia tumbling backward, her feet up and over her head. She clambered to her feet, her leg still throbbing but starting to feel improvement.

She could see that they were on the surface of a planet, but the freighter was already firing up and leaping skyward. Vandelia lurched to the front and dropped into the copilot seat next to Mac. He barely afforded her a sidelong glance as he checked readings on the control dash. "How's the leg?" he asked. Considering the circumstances, he sounded relatively calm.

"Getting better."

"Good. Let's see if we can keep the rest of you intact."

He urged the freighter forward, and it rocketed upward, faster and faster.

"That place you had us stand. It was a preprogrammed transporter point," she said.

"Yes," he said tersely. "I didn't know the exact layout of the place, but I knew they had scanners that would detect transporter homing beacons or comm units, as well as any beam-ins. So I had to sneak in on my own, and make a guess as to coordinates when I set a time and place for a beam-out."

"You could have explained that."

He didn't reply. The chances were that he wouldn't have done so anyway, but he was actually handed an excuse for not continuing the conversation as several explosions around them caused the freighter to rock wildly.

"*Oh, now what?*" demanded Vandelia.

"We have company," Mac muttered. "Computer, rear view."

A section of the screen in front of them shifted. It was only then that Vandelia realized they weren't looking through a window, but instead through a computer-generated representation of what was outside. Most of that view remained, but now part of it had altered to present the view from behind them. Three small vessels were approaching them most rapidly. They were so small that they appeared to be one-man fighters each, but because of their diminutive size, they were fast and very maneuverable. The odds were that they would be able to catch up with the freighter in short order.

But that wasn't the only thing that attracted Vandelia's attention. What she noticed in particular was a tall tower in the distance. It was surrounded by rich and green forest, but stood high above it, almost a mile high, it seemed. It had a wide base, becoming progressively narrower as it got higher. It was silver and gleaming and would have been far more impressive if it hadn't been for the huge gusts of black smoke wafting out of a number of places. Then, as Vandelia watched, the lower third of the tower was engulfed in flame. She saw the upper two-thirds start to wobble, teeter, and then tumble over in excruciatingly slow motion.

"Impressive," was all she managed to say.

Then the pursuing vessels began to fire. Mac's fingers flew over the board, handling the freighter's course with astonishing confidence, sending it zigzagging one way and then another, dodging a number of the blasts with facility even as he continued them on their upward course. Nevertheless, the freighter shuddered as several of the shots got through.

"Rear deflector at eighty percent and dropping," the computer informed him.

"Concentrate all deflector power to rear shields. Shore it up," he ordered.

"We're not going to make it," Vandelia said.

The vote of no-confidence didn't seem to perturb him. "Then we don't make it."

"You seem rather sanguine about the prospect."

"Would you rather I started to panic?"

"No."

"Then shut up."

She opened her mouth to reply, but came to the realization that perhaps shutting up would indeed be the smarter course of action.

The freighter angled down abruptly. The ground seemed to be approaching them at horrifying speed and Vandelia was certain that there was no way, absolutely no way, that they were going to forestall a crash, at which point the freighter zoomed upward once more. Mac tapped the control board again, and Vandelia was surprised to see on the rear view that a suddenly great gust of white was billowing behind them. "Are we hit? Are we leaking something?"

"No."

For a moment she could see nothing on the rear view, and then the pursuing vessels burst through the mist and continued after them. But then Vandelia noticed something: Their hulls were starting to change colors.

"What's happening to them?"

"Watch," he replied. He hadn't taken his eyes off the front view, but she could see a touch of amusement at the edges of his mouth.

The vessels that had been pursuing them were slowing, and then Vandelia looked on in amazement as she saw their lower hulls start to be eaten away. Huge spots of corrosion appeared on them and then rapidly spread. With each moment it spread faster and faster, eating through the exterior of the ships with the greed and velocity of a hungry child being handed a handful of sweets. Breaking off the pursuit, the three vessels dove as quickly as they could for the ground, but they didn't quite make it in time. Within seconds the ships had fallen apart completely, and Vandelia watched with smug delight as the erstwhile pilots of the vessels tumbled toward the ground, waving their arms and legs in a most entertaining manner. She felt as much remorse and pity for them as they likely did for her . . . which was to say, of course, none.

Seconds later, the freighter tore loose completely of the planet's surface, spiralling into space. "We're clear of the planet's atmosphere and gravity," Mac announced. "Taking her to Warp One."

"This ship has warp capacity?" Vandelia said in surprise. But then she reined in her surprise with clear amusement. "Well, why shouldn't it? Apparently it packs some sort of gas that eats ships."

"Only unshielded ships. We were lucky. Vessels that small don't pack enough power or equipment to generate anything beyond the most minimal of shielding. They count on their speed to avoid attackers. Leaves them vulnerable. Warp on line."

Space twisted slightly around them and the ship leaped into warp space. Vandelia leaned back in her chair, shaking her head in amazement. "I still can't believe it," she said. "An hour ago, everything seemed hopeless."

"An hour ago, it was. Things change."

She turned to face him. "I owe you my life."

"Yes," he said matter-of-factly, without even looking at her.

"And what do you want."

At that point, he did afford her a glance. "Want?"

"Yes. Want." She cocked an eyebrow.

To her surprise, he seemed to laugh slightly to himself, and he shook his head. "It's some world you live in. People do things because they want something in return. Everyone's out for themselves. No one does something for the common good."

She seemed puzzled by what he was saying. "That's right. That's my world. Yours, too."

"And it's impossible that I could have helped you just because it seemed the right thing to do at the time."

She sat back in the chair, her arms folded tightly across her breast. "Everyone wants something in exchange. No one does anything if it doesn't serve their interests, first and foremost."

"You're probably right," he said with a sigh.

"Which brings us back to what you want."

He appeared to give it a moment's thought, and then said, "There's a changing area and hypersonic shower in the back."

Now here was something she understood. In a way, it was almost comforting to her. Her entire world view was predicated on the selfishness of all those around her, particularly males. The last thing she needed was someone coming along and shaking up the very foundations of her philosophy. "So . . . you want me to strip and shower, is that it?"

"Yes. You've been slapped around, tortured, shot at . . . you've worked up quite a sweat, and it's detectable. So please shower it off. And there's a jumpsuit you can change into."

She was stunned. There was no interest in his voice at all. He wanted her to stop smelling. Beginning, middle, end of interest.

Then, of course, she understood.

"I see. You prefer men."

Mac looked at her, and then laughed. He didn't even reply, but instead continued to laugh softly to himself while shaking his head.

Without another word, Vandelia went to the shower and washed herself thoroughly. Even though it was merely a hypersonic shower, it was still a tremendous relief to her. It was particularly soothing for the injured thigh, the hypersonics caressing it so that, by the time she was done, there was not the slightest hint of pain in her leg.

She put on the jumpsuit, and walked back into the main cabin. Mac didn't even appear aware that she was back. Instead he was finishing issuing some sort of report as to the completion of the "mission." When he did notice she was there, however, he ceased the recording, or perhaps it was a transmission. Vandelia couldn't be sure.

"Who are you?" she asked as she dropped into the seat next to him. "Are you some sort of spy?"

"If you wish," he said.

"Who do you work for?"

"Myself."

"Someone must be sponsoring you. You must report to . . ."

"Get some sleep. We'll be at Starbase 18 before too long. I'll be dropping you off there. There'll be a connector flight there which will take you wherever you wish to go."

"I . . . do not know what to say."

" 'Thank you' will suffice."

She considered that a moment. Then she rose from the chair, went to his, and draped herself across his lap, straddling it.

"What are you doing?" he inquired.

"Saying 'thank you.' " She undid the fastenings of the jumpsuit and slipped it off her shoulders. It dropped to her waist, leaving her nude from the waist up.

He stared at her. "Apparently it's cold in here," he said.

"We'll warm it."

"Vandelia . . ."

She put a finger to his lips, and grinned in a most wolfish fashion. "I'm going to return the favor you've done me, Mac. And when I'm through," and she put her hands behind her head, arching her back, "you'll never think about having sex with men."

"That's probably true," Mac said.

And she began to dance. And for the first time in her life, she danced only for one person . . . only for him.

It was not possible that anyone should be able to haul himself from the wreckage of the tower. Not possible that anyone should have been able to survive. Particularly when one was considering that the candidate for survival had had his body crushed by falling metal.

All this, Zolon Darg was most aware of. Nonetheless, as he lay there on the ground, staring up at the twilight sky that was rapidly becoming night, it was impossible to overlook the fact that he had, in fact, survived.

It was also impossible for him to move. Sheer fury, pure force of will, had pulled him from the flaming wreckage that had been his headquarters. That, and the memory of a green woman with a defiant gleam, and a man . . . a man with purple eyes and a scar on his face. A man he would never, ever forget.

He tried to feel something below his neck, but was unable to. Nothing would move, nothing would respond to the desperate commands that his brain was issuing.

He drew in a breath, and it was an agonizing effort. But it was worth it, for it allowed him to exhale, and when he did so, what he breathed out were the words, "I'll . . . kill them . . ."

Then he lay there, a sack of broken bones and bloodied meat, and wondered when the dark gods he worshipped would see fit to do something about his condition.

He remained that way for three days before he received his answer . . .

Now . . .

I.

DOCTOR ELIAS FROBISHER was forty-three years and one day old, and he couldn't quite believe he had made it. When he woke up, he had to pinch himself to make certain that he had really managed to accomplish it. When someone had lived under a bizarre death sentence for the last decade or so, as he had, the achievement felt particularly noteworthy. He lay in his bed, breathing in the filtered air of the cone-shaped space station, but never had that air felt quite so sweet. It felt like a glorious day. Granted, concepts such as day and night were entirely subjective, created and controlled by the computer core of the station. There was neither sunrise nor sunset, and this was something that had taken Frobisher some time to get used to. He had been planet-bound most of his life, and the curious and unusual life which existed in space was a difficult adjustment that Frobisher had made because he'd really had no other choice.

Quite simply, he'd had no other choice. He'd had to get away from the Guardian.

He took a long shower that morning, and felt that he had earned it. It was pure water rather than hypersonic, a rarity that Frobisher was revelling in that morning. As he did so, visions of the Guardian came to him unbidden, as they were wont to do. Frobisher shuddered, thinking about the hideous shadow he had lived under all these years.

Then he started to tremble more and more violently. He had lathered up his thinning brown hair, and the shampoo dribbled down into his eyes, but it barely registered upon him. The soap slipped from his hands, his legs went weak, and he sagged to the floor, still unable to control the spasms which had seized him. Paradoxically, he began to laugh. It was a bizarre sound, that choked laughter, a combination of chuckling and sobbing that grew louder and louder, so much so that it could be heard in the hallway outside his quarters. His assistant, Dr. David Kendrow, heard it, and started banging on the door. Normally Kendrow, a thin, blond man, was overly mannered and reserved in his attitudes, but one wouldn't have known it at that point as he was fairly shouting, "Doctor Frobisher? Are you all right, sir?"

"Yes! Yes," Frobisher called back to him. "Yes, I'll . . . I'll be fine." It was all that Frobisher could do to pull himself together. He hadn't expected to react in that manner, but really, it was inevitable when one looked at it with hindsight. The amount of anxiety that had built up as he approached his forty-third birthday had been truly horrific. The knowing, and yet not knowing. That insane combination of certainty and doubt, warring within him as each passing day had brought him closer and closer to the inevitable . . . except, maybe not.

And he had made it. He had survived his birthday. It really was true, what they said: Today is the first day of the rest of your life.

He emerged from the shower and, as he towelled off, looked at the gut that had been building up on him. As the dreaded day had approached, he hadn't been bothering to exercise or take care of himself. He'd had a fatalistic attitude about him, and that was certainly understandable. But now the joke was on him, as was the extra flab. He was going to have to do something about working that off. After all, it wouldn't be particularly attractive to women.

Women. His face lit up as he dressed. Relationships. He had been afraid to begin any, because the prospect of condemning some poor woman to become an early widow. Oh, certainly he could have had a string of casual relationships that went nowhere. Love them and leave them, and rationalizing that, since he was a walking dead man, it was the only way that he could conduct his life. But he was a highly moral man, was Dr. Frobisher. Highly moral, and more than that: He knew that one woman after another, used and tossed aside, was simply not for him. He wanted companionship, he wanted someone who, he knew, was going to be there for him. He wanted someone to wake up to, someone who would cheerfully kiss him in the morning and loved him so much that it wouldn't bother her if he hadn't had a chance to brush his teeth yet. Someone he would be able to look at across the breakfast and smile at. Someone who wanted to spend a lifetime with him . . . a real lifetime, not the truncated thing that had been handed him.

Oh, and someone who was a brilliant engineer in the field of artificial intelligence and computerization, of course. That was a must as well.

There were a few likely possibilities, actually. To give himself some vague bit of hope, something to cling to even though he was certain that it was hopeless, Frobisher had had the Omega 9 run a scan of potential mates. It was unbelievably quaint, even absurd: Using a creation as infinitely advanced as the Omega 9 for the purpose of, essentially, computer dating, seemed absurd on its face. But he had done so nonetheless, and the list that had been drawn up had been quite impressive. Now that the dreaded day had passed, he was looking forward to trying to act upon the possibilities. As he headed to the lab, having had his customary quick breakfast, he patted the data chip in his pocket to which he had copied the information that Omega 9 had obtained for him. His mind was already racing with possibilities. He would pick the most likely prospect, "likely" being derived from personality profile, shared interests, age, background, etcetera. He'd subtly do some checking to see if she was otherwise involved and, if not, he would find a pretense to begin a correspondence with her. Hopefully, he would be able to develop it into something substantive and sufficiently personal that she would be prompted to come out to the Daystrom Station where he worked and meet with him.

And then . . . who knew? Who indeed knew?

"I knew," he said rather cheerfully to no one. "I knew, but I didn't know. But now I know, and it's great knowing and not knowing!"

He entered the lab, his lanky legs carrying him across it with a jaunty speed. Kendrow was already at work, but he was casting a watchful eye upon Frobisher. "Good morning, David!" called Frobisher.

"Good . . . morning, sir." The surprise in his voice was unmistakable. He wasn't used to Frobisher sounding so cheerful in the morning . . . or ever.

Frobisher glanced over the station log, and frowned slightly. "Some sort of glitch in the standard running program?" he asked.

"Yes, sir, I just noticed it. It's minor systems failures . . . so minor that we hadn't even been noticing when they'd been going down. I'm running diagnostics checks on them, sir. I'm hoping to get it locked down by this afternoon."

"Oh, you'll get it sorted out, Kendrow." He patted him on the shoulder. "I have the utmost confidence in you."

"Th—thank you, sir." Kendrow stared at him as if he were concerned that Frobisher had been replaced by a lookalike, lighthearted alien.

"Not used to seeing me this chipper, are you, Kendrow?" asked Frobisher.

"To be blunt . . . no, sir. I'm not."

Frobisher laughed, and then sighed to himself. "Between my attitude now and what you heard earlier . . . you must be somewhat puzzled, eh, Kendrow?"

"Yes, sir. I am, sir."

"Sit down, Kendrow."

Kendrow looked down at himself. "I am sitting, sir. Already, I mean."

"Oh. Yes, of course." Frobisher leaned against a console and smiled broadly. "I'm sorry, Kendrow," he said earnestly. "The truth is, this last week, leading up to the day I've dreaded for so long, seemed almost to fly by. Now I know I've been out of sorts the past few days . . . weeks . . ."

"Try months," Kendrow muttered, but then looked immediately apologetic.

Frobisher waved it off. " 'Months' is probably more accurate, to be honest," he admitted. "And yesterday was probably the worst of all."

"Well, I have to say, your behavior was rather pensive considering it was your birthday. I know that some people become daunted by the prospect of turning forty or fifty . . . but forty-three." He shrugged. "It seemed . . . odd. You seemed to want to do everything you could to ignore it."

"Believe me, I did want to ignore it. Although I'm surprised that my parents did. Usually they send me a greeting on my birthday, but this year . . . nothing."

"Had you told them not to?"

"No. No, I kept my unease to myself . . . or at least I thought I did. But perhaps they picked up on unspoken signals nonetheless. Ah well . . . no use worrying about it now. You see . . . there's been a reason for my concerns. Do you know what I used to do, Kendrow? Before I joined Daystrom, I mean, to work on the Omega 9."

"You were involved in some sort of archaeology project, I think, sir."

"Not just some sort. This was THE project. The Guardian of Forever."

Kendrow blinked in surprise. "The time portal? I'd heard about that, but I'd almost thought it was a myth."

"Oh, it's not a myth, I assure you. It's real." Despite his newly achieved state of bliss, Frobisher shuddered slightly as he recalled the image of that cheerless place. It wasn't just the Guardian itself that so spooked him. He couldn't get out of his head that eerie, mournful howl of the wind that filtered through the remains of the ruined city around the Guardian. It was as if ghosts of a race long lost still haunted the place, laughing and taunting. "It's . . . all too real."

He was silent for a moment. Prompting him, Kendrow said, "And you studied it?"

"People . . . tend to come and go there," Frobisher told him. "Oh, they're excited at first. Word spreads, after all. And it's an irresistible proposition: Studying the past, seeing it unspool before you. How can anyone pass that up? And yet . . . people burn out, very, very quickly. Six months, a year at most, and suddenly you see complete turnover in the staff there. I didn't understand why. But now I do." He laughed softly to himself. "Now I do. It just . . . gets to you after a while."

Kendrow tilted his head slightly as he regarded the doctor. "What happened there, sir?"

"I . . . saw my future. At least, I thought I did."

"The future? But . . ." Kendrow shook his head. "I thought that the Guardian only shows the past, not the future."

"That was my understanding as well. That's what they told us, at any rate. But I will never forget it, nonetheless. I had been there two months . . . well," and he smiled ruefully, "two months, seven days, eighteen hours. I was monitoring a playback on the Guardian. No two are exactly the same, you know. Even if you ask for the exact same scenario to be replayed, there's always slight variances in the scene. Some of them can be extremely minor . . . but they're there. That's one of the things we study: The reasons for it all. It truly supports the notion that time is in a constant state of flux.

"In any event, I was monitoring . . . and there was a rather fearsome ion storm overhead. Not low enough to be of any direct danger to me, but I was getting apprehensive just the same. In fact, I was even considering packing it in for the day. Still, I was doing my job, my tricorder picking up the events as they hurtled past on the time portal's screen.

"Suddenly, overhead, there was this . . . this burst of ionic energy. Despite the awesome artificial intelligence that the Guardian displays, it's still just a machine. Perhaps the most sophisticated machine that ever existed . . . aside from the Omega 9," he smiled, and then continued, "but a machine nonetheless. Perhaps the ion storm interfered with its working for just a moment . . . or perhaps it was my imagination all along . . . I couldn't be sure. But the screen flickered in a way I'd never seen before, and then I . . . saw it . . . or at least, thought I saw it . . ."

"Saw what?" When Frobisher didn't immediately continue, Kendrow repeated, "Saw what, sir?"

"A report. A news report . . . a printed one, actually. It flew by so fast, my eye barely registered it. And it said . . ." His mouth suddenly felt dry. He licked his lips. "It said, 'Elias Frobisher Killed on Forty-third Birthday.' "

"You're joking."

"Do I look like I'm joking?" Even though the awful day was behind him, he still couldn't keep that feeling of dull terror completely out of his thoughts. He had lived with the knowledge for so long . . . and had never shared it with anyone. How could he have, after all, inflicted that upon another human being?

"No, sir, you certainly don't." He let out a low whistle. "That's . . . truly awful. To be carrying that with you all this time. Are you sure of what you saw . . . ?"

"No. That's the worst part. I wasn't sure, not completely. It happened so quickly and then it was gone. Not only that, but no matter how many times I played back my tricorder record of the event, there was no trace of it. My tricorder hadn't picked it up either. Then there was the 'knowledge' that the Guardian only played the past, not the future. Every credible, scientific measure that I had available to me only served to underscore the impossibility of what I was sure I'd witnessed. And yet . . ."

"You couldn't be sure."

"Could you?" he asked. Kendrow shook his head. "Well, neither could I. I couldn't help but wonder if I'd been given this . . . vision . . . for a purpose. Except what that purpose might have been, I could only guess. Was it a warning? A random attempt at torture? Was it something avoidable, or was I supposed to surrender to fate? I remember . . ." The recollection was painful to him, even after all this time. "My last day there, I stood in front of the Guardian and just screamed and kept on screaming, wanting to know what the purpose to all of it had been. And the thing just sat there, replying in one of its preprogrammed ways that it was there to be my guide. No man should know his fate, Kendrow, or the time of his demise . . . even the possible time.

"The events that I experienced on that world shaped—'distorted,' might be a better word—the way in which I handled the rest of my life up to this point. I had no idea whether I had imagined it, whether it was to happen irrevocably, or whether it was one of the assorted possibilities that trickled through the Guardian but wound up being swept away by the rivers of time. I spent about six months barely functioning as a human being before I pulled myself together enough to carry on with . . . well, with whatever it was that I was going to be left with.

"But you know what, Kendrow?"

"What, sir?"

Slowly he walked over to the interface console of Omega 9. The flashing pad blinked its hypnotically entrancing lights at him. The pale blue pattern was rather soothing to him. "If not for that experience . . . it's possible the Omega 9 might not exist. When your mind reaches a point where it can't function in its normal patterns, it seeks out new patterns. And my thoughts eventually brought me in the direction of the Omega 9. I saw . . . possibilities," he whispered the word. "Circuits, possibilities, revealed themselves to me, one unfolding upon another. And when I saw them, ignoring them was not an option. That's what brought me to the Daystrom Institute. The years hurtled past, Kendrow. I almost didn't notice them, because I was so busy working to produce the Omega 9."

"I just wish . . ." Kendrow began to say, but then he stopped.

"No, it's all right, Kendrow." He folded his arms and leaned back against a console. "What's on your mind?"

"Well . . . the top secret turn this entire project has taken." He gestured around him, at the banks of computer circuitry and nannite growth technology that was in place. "It's . . . well, this outpost is fairly remote, sir. Somewhat lonely."

"I prefer it that way, Kendrow. My theories, my work is off the beaten path. I'd prefer that I remain that way as well. The fortunate thing about the Daystrom Institute is that they understand and respect the concept of creative vision. Once they're convinced that they're dealing with a true visionary . . . such as myself, I modestly admit," and he laughed at the obvious pretentiousness of the viewpoint, "then they're willing to provide as much or as little help as required, as much or as little in terms of equipment as needed. And the precise working environment to foster the best work. I wish . . ." and he shook his head, "I wish I could have met Daystrom himself. Poor fellow. What a tortured genius he was. That incident with the *Enterprise* a hundred years ago . . ."

"Sir . . . about this working environment . . ." He coughed politely. "To be honest, I haven't spoken to you about it since I first came here six months ago because of, well . . . your attitude, and the tension that seemed to, frankly, ooze from every pore. But since we're being open and straightforward now, I feel inclined to ask . . . doesn't our presence here make us something of a target, sir? The Omega 9 . . . ?"

"Of course not." Frobisher laughed at the notion. "The work we've developed here is going to be made available to all. There's nothing for anyone *to* steal. And even if we did . . . we have enough internal defenses here to hold them off until help comes. And those defenses were built by very paranoid Daystrom executives who have the exact same mindset as you, Kendrow. You should be pleased . . . or maybe you should be afraid, I'm not quite sure." He clapped Kendrow on the shoulder. "Be of good cheer, Kendrow. I feel like I have a new lease on life. Tell you what: Let's track down that glitch you were talking about, and then we can actually take the rest of the day off from work. Have you put Omega 9 on the trail of this glitch?"

"Oh, sir, that's kind of like using photon torpedoes to kill an insect. It's just some sort of elusive little bug. Why waste the O-9's time on it?"

"Kendrow, for all its advancement, for all the potential it displays . . . it's still just a machine. It's not as if we're going to hurt its feelings or insult it by asking."

"Sir, perhaps . . ."

"Kendrow, for crying out loud, cheer up! Life's too short." He walked over to the Interface station and placed his hand against it.

"Interface activated," came the calm tone of the Omega 9. Despite the ominous name of the computer itself, the machine's voice was that of a young female, not more than ten years old. One of the scientists back at the main institute, in the early days of the computer's development, had patterned the voice on his daughter's as a sort of birthday surprise for her. He had intended to change it subsequently, but Frobisher felt it was so charming that he opted to retain the voice for the Omega 9.

"Interface prepared," said Frobisher. "Activate nannotech for link."

He felt the familiar tingling along his palm. The most difficult thing he'd ever had to accomplish in the early days of the Omega 9 was develop the confidence to allow the machine to work as intended. It had taken something of a leap of faith for him, and he still saw it as the one possible drawback in the widespread acceptance of the Omega 9. But he hoped that that, too, would pass.

"Nannotech on line," the computer informed him. Already he could sense the computer's voice not outside of his mind, but within. "Link established."

"Doctor . . ." Kendrow seemed to be trying to get his attention.

But it was too late. Frobisher's mind was already deep within the Omega 9. He felt the usual, intoxicating rush that came to him at such times. It took an act of will for him to steady himself, to avoid being swept away into the morass of the complex machine's innermost workings. The nannotech helped keep his mind focused, and then he turned the Omega 9's formidable abilities to the fairly minor task at hand.

His mind plumbed the depths of the machine, information coming in from all over, giving Frobisher a link to every part of not only the computer, but the entire station.

At times such as this, Frobisher rarely had any true sense of time. Usually, he felt as if he were inside the machine for at least an hour, perhaps more. Invariably, though, he was there for less than a minute.

This time it was only seconds. But when he emerged from the machine, his eyes were wide and his face pale. Slowly he turned his gaze toward Kendrow. "What . . . have you done?" he whispered.

"Done, sir?" Kendrow appeared politely confused.

"You've . . . taken down our defenses. Slowly, gradually, subtly . . . done it in such a way that the computer detected no attempt at sabotage. Rerouted systems, drained away energy . . ."

Kendrow started to voice a protest, but one look from Frobisher was enough to silence him.

". . . and your work . . . affected the chronometers," Frobisher continued, as if speaking from a place very far away. "You probably didn't even realize it. It was an accident, an unexpected side effect of your tampering. It sped the chronometer up. That's why time seemed to fly by. It wasn't just subjective. The computer core was actually malfunctioning, shortening hours and minutes, eventually days over the past week or so. At night, while we were sleeping, we lost even more time. At his point, we've misplaced about twelve hours. Which means . . ."

Kendrow's expression was one of frightened understanding. "I'm . . . I'm sorry . . ."

"Which means . . . today is still my birthday," Frobisher said tonelessly.

At that moment, the entire station shuddered as something smashed against the exterior. Frobisher, at one with Omega 9, felt the shock as if it had happened to him personally. Alarms screeched throughout the station, and the Omega 9 registered that a group of unknown beings had just materialized in one of the station's upper sections. There was a ship, a massive war vessel of some sort with utterly unknown markings, in orbit around the station. The sensors and early detection devices had all been taken off line, as had communications and weaponry.

So . . . here it was. His destiny, staring him in the face.

Oddly, he had never felt more calm. He had spent so many years worrying, wondering, angsting over his known-but-frightening future, that now that it had arrived, all the fear dissipated. Instead he marshalled his concentration and dove into the Omega 9 with all the speed and precision that he could muster. All the damage that Kendrow had done was laid out before him, and he had only seconds to choose what would be the most effective thing to undo. Shields? Too late. Weaponry? Likewise. That was all created to deal with potential intruders while they were still outside, but they already had unknown enemies rampaging through the station.

Communications. That was the only hope. Again, seconds were what remained to him . . . but a second for a computer is quite unlike a second for anyone else. Frobisher envisioned himself within the Omega 9, saw his hands moving through the circuitry like an electronic ghost. Like a father gently kissing a scrape on a child's knee in order to make it feel better, Frobisher untangled the knots of interference that Kendrow had tied. Kendrow, good lord, how could Kendrow have done this to him? He had hand-picked the man out of a field of twenty-seven applicants as the man who seemed most capable, most intelligent, who had the most on the ball. And Kendrow had betrayed him to these . . . to whoever these people were.

He had allowed his mind to wander. That was pure foolishness, something he should not be permitting himself to do. He had little enough time as it was.

Using the Omega 9, he punched through the comm snarl that Kendrow had created and immediately sent out a distress call. He didn't have to record it, didn't have to speak. His mind shouted into the computer, "This is Daystrom Station, we are under attack, repeat, we are under attack. Any Federation vessel in the area, please assist. This is Doctor Elias Frobisher of the Daystrom Station, we are under attack, please assist . . ."

A comm message suddenly sprang into existence within the computer's program. That was fast, miraculously fast. Perhaps there might be a hope in hell of salvaging this situation yet. Frobisher's mind opened the message . . .

It was from Earth. It had been sent hours ago. There was an elderly couple, smiling at Frobisher. The man looked like an older version of Frobisher himself.

"Elias, darling! It's Mom and Dad! Happy birthday, son! We ran a little late, but this should still get to you in time, and we wouldn't want you to think we forgot your very special day!"

And suddenly Frobisher felt himself yanked out of the Omega 9. He fancied that, from very far away, he heard the alarmed cry of a young girl's voice . . . the voice of the Omega 9, pleading with him to come back, asking that she not be left alone.

Frobisher staggered, the nannites slipping away from him, scurrying back into their techno hidey-hole. The world around him appeared flat, one-dimensional, as his senses fought to cope with reintegrating themselves with reality. The world snapped into two-dimensions, then three, and Frobisher found himself handled roughly by an alien being of undetermined origin. His skin was brown and leathery, and he had thick tusks jutting from beneath his upper lip.

There were several others nearby, a mixed bag of races, and one being from a race he did recognize, for they had been very much in the news lately. It was a Thallonian. He was very oddly built, however. His head seemed smaller in proportion to his massive body than it should have been. Frobisher attributed it to body armor.

Beg for your life, the suggestion came into his head. *You might still get out of this. Beg. Beg to live.*

Frobisher was not a fighter, not a hero, and not particularly brave. But he felt an anger, implacable and unstoppable, bubbling up and over. And he realized that all these years of living in fear, all the years of frustration, he had carried incredible resentment within him. The problem was, he had never had anyone to be angry with. No one had done anything to him. No one had forced the knowledge upon him. He had simply stumbled upon it, like a scientist out to probe the secrets of the universe and inadvertently finding more than he had bargained for.

But he resented it nonetheless. Why had the fates done this to him?

What in the world could he have possibly done to deserve this awful foreknowledge of the time of his demise? He had been a good person his entire life. Never cheated anyone, never tried to hurt anyone that he knew of. And yet he had been handed this hideously raw deal.

For years, for more years than he cared to think about, he had wanted someone, anyone he could strike against. A target upon which he could vent his anger, anger which had grown exponentially as years had passed. Wasted, wasted years . . .

The being who was leering over him was bigger, broader, infinitely stronger than he. It was the kind of situation where, under normal circumstances, Frobisher would have put up his hands, surrendered, and prayed . . .

. . . and given over control of his life one more time.

In his mind's eye, he saw the Guardian staring at him. That thing, that monster, that machine had cast a long shadow over so much of his life. Built by beings unknown, functioning in ways no one knew. The Andorians had their own name for it: The T'Sh'Iar, which meant "God's Window."

God had looked through the window, seen Frobisher peering through, and had punished him for absolutely no reason at all. Taken away his destiny by sadistically handing it to him.

Frobisher saw the blaster hanging at the hip of the alien with the brown, leathery skin, the being who looked like a giant serpent. There was a throbbing in Frobisher's head. The tall red alien nearby was addressing him, but the pounding in his head drowned it all out. All the rage, all the anger, everything that had ever infuriated him over the hopeless wreck that his life had become as time's inexorable march had carried him unwillingly toward his doom, it all exploded from him at once.

There was no way that Frobisher should have been a threat to the serpent man, no way. The serpent man was paying so little attention to the possibility of Frobisher as a threat that he never even saw the trembling fist that Frobisher's fingers had contracted into. Furthermore, his skin was so hard that even if Frobisher were to land a punch, he shouldn't even have felt it.

Frobisher's years of anger congealed into that fist, and without listening to a word that the red-skinned alien was saying, he spun and swung his fist into a powerful roundhouse. In his entire adult life—for that matter, throughout his childhood and adolescence—he had never thrown a punch in his life. The roundhouse was his very first.

It was perfect.

It caught the serpent man squarely in his lantern jaw. The impact immediately broke Frobisher's knuckles. It didn't matter. Frobisher never even felt it. But the serpent man most certainly felt the blow as his head snapped around and he let out a startled squeal that seemed totally at odds with his hulking demeanor. He staggered, and that was all the opening Frobisher needed. He yanked the blaster out of the holster at the serpent man's side, swung it around and aimed it squarely at the red-skinned man who was clearly the leader.

The red-skinned man looked mildly surprised.

It was the single most exultant moment in all of Frobisher's life. Given a half second more, he would have fired the blaster.

He never saw the blow from the serpent man coming. The alien swung his fist like a club, and it caved in the side of Frobisher's head. His arm swung wide. His finger squeezed spasmodically on the trigger and the shot went wide, exploding harmlessly against the far wall. Frobisher collapsed, his head thudding to the floor. He heard a sort of distant buzzing, saw a thick liquid dripping in front of his eyes that he did not recognize as his own blood. He reached out a hand, and it touched something warm. He couldn't tell what it was, but a female voice seemed to be singing to him.

His lips puckered together. He drew in a breath with effort, and then with even more effort expelled it. It rattled from his throat and out through his mouth, and in his mind's eye he saw candles flickering in front of him. With the gust of breath from his lungs, the flames disappeared. All out at once.

I hope I get my wish, thought Frobisher as he died.

Zolon Darg stared at the corpse on the floor, and then slowly levelled his gaze at Shunabo. Shunabo, for his part, seemed extremely irritated with Kendrow. The brown-skinned, leathery Shunabo approached Kendrow with a stride that was an odd combination of swagger and slink. "You said he wouldn't be a problem," Shunabo said, his irritation causing him to over enunciate every syllable. "You told us—you told *me*—that he was a quiet, reserved, run-of-the-mill human who wouldn't offer up the slightest resistance." His soft voice began to get louder. "Oddly, you didn't happen to mention that he had a punch like a berserker Klingon, or that he was capable of coming within a hair of *shooting Zolon Darg's head off!*"

In point of fact, Zolon Darg knew that Shunabo was right. He had been caught completely flat-footed, and this little scientist, this no one, this weakling, this nothing, had nearly succeeded in accomplishing what some of the greatest and most accomplished bounty hunters in two quadrants had not. Darg had gotten sloppy, very, very sloppy, and Shunabo had saved his ass.

It was a situation that had to be addressed immediately.

In two quick steps, Darg was directly behind Shunabo. He slapped a hand around Shunabo's chest, yanked him backward, grabbed the top of his head and twisted quickly. The sound of Shunabo's neck snapping echoed through the suddenly silent lab.

There was still a flickering of light in Shunabo's eyes as Darg snarled in his ear, "I was in no danger. I could have handled him. And you were under specific instructions to keep Frobisher alive." That last, at least, was accurate, and really, in the final analysis, one point was all that was necessary. Zolon Darg spread wide his arms and Shunabo sank to the floor. Before Shunabo even landed, Darg turned away from him disdainfully. He towered over Kendrow, and he could see that Kendrow's legs were trembling. Kendrow appeared to be keeping himself standing by bracing himself against a table.

"Are you going to be able to do the job in Frobisher's place?" he demanded.

Kendrow's mouth moved, but nothing audible came forth. Darg scowled in a manner that seemed to suck the light right out of the lab. "Well?" continued Darg. "Are you capable of speech at all?"

"Probably not at the moment, Zolon."

The voice behind them, in contrast to the increasing bellow of Darg, was remarkably mild. The individual to whom it belonged likewise seemed mild in appearance. He was a Thallonian like Zolon, but whereas Zolon Darg was massive, the newcomer appeared quite slender, although it was hard to tell since he was wearing fairly loose black and purple robes. He had a neatly trimmed, yellowing beard, which indicated his age to anyone who happened to know that Thallonian hair tended to yellow with age rather than turn gray or white, as occurred with humans. His face was carefully inscrutable. Only his eyes seemed to burn with an inner light. The rest of his presence was so minimal that one's gaze could easily have passed right over him.

"Is that a fact, General Thul?" Darg said. But despite the defiant sound of the words, there was nothing in his tone that was challenging. It wasn't out of fear, of course. It was more from a sense of respect. And it was quite possible that General Gerrid Thul was the one individual in the galaxy for whom Darg was capable of showing that sort of deference.

"Well, look at the poor man," Thul said. He crossed the room toward Kendrow, and didn't seem to walk so much as glide. "You seem to have scared him terribly. Am I correct, sir?"

Kendrow slowly nodded.

"There? You see?" The General clucked sympathetically. "You know, Darg . . . you used to be a much calmer, understanding individual. The difficulties you've encountered in the past years have not mellowed you. You must learn to be calmer. You will live longer."

Darg smiled in a rather mirthless way. "I shall be sure to remember that."

"See that you do. Now, Mr . . . Kendrow, is it?" When Kendrow nodded, the one called Gerrid Thul continued, "Mr. Kendrow . . . you have been paid a significant amount to cooperate with us, have you not."

"Yes, sir. I have, sir."

"Articulate speech. You are capable of articulate speech. That is good, that is very good. Now then, Mr. Kendrow . . . since the good Doctor here," and he tapped Frobisher's corpse with the toe of his boot, "is not in any condition to provide assistance to us, it is important to know whether you are going to be able to continue in his stead."

"I'm . . ." He cleared his throat. "Do you really want an honest answer?"

General Thul smiled in an almost paternal fashion. "Honesty is always to be preferred."

"Truthfully, I'm not sure. I tried to familiarize myself with all aspects of his work, but the Omega 9 was such a uniquely personal, and truly amazing, piece of work . . . I can't pretend that I know or understand all the parameters and aspects that he brought to it. I know and understand the basic interface options, I can program the—"

Thul stopped him with a casual gesture. "It is not necessary to go into details, Mr. Kendrow. Your honesty is appreciated. Is it safe to assume that you can aid us in transporting the key components of the Omega 9 to our ship, and that you will, at the very least, give us your best effort in adapting and understanding the possibilities this amazing device provides?"

Kendrow's head bobbed so eagerly that it seemed as if it was about to tumble off his shoulders. "Yes. Yes, absolutely, sir."

"That is good. That is good to hear. So, to summarize," and he placed a hand on Kendrow's shoulder, "you will help us . . . and we will allow you to live. And if you cease to help us, either due to lack of cooperation or lack of knowledge, why . . . you shall meet the same fate as Doctor Frobisher. Except your demise will be far slower, much more protracted, and will involve an impressive array of sharp objects. Do we understand each other?"

Kendrow gulped deeply.

Zolon Darg, for his part, smiled. For a moment there, he had been concerned that Thul was going to be entirely too sympathetic. He realized that he should have known better. After all, when someone was interested in obliterating almost all sentient life, as General Thul was, such an individual was not about to be concerned about sparing the feelings of one insignificant little scientist.

"Well, Mr. Kendrow?" General Thul prompted once more. "Do we understand each other?"

Kendrow nodded.

"Well, then!" Thul said, and he clapped his hands and rubbed them together briskly, "let's get to work, shall we?"

And as they got to work, the distress call continued to issue forth, searching for someone . . . anyone . . . who might be able to save what was left of the day . . .

II.

COMMANDER WILLIAM RIKER felt as if all the eyes in the Ten-Forward lounge were upon him. He kept telling himself, however, that he was probably imagining it. He found a table off in the corner and signalled to the bartender that he'd like a drink. One was quickly produced and he proceeded to sip it in relative peace that lasted for a whole seven seconds.

He glanced up as Lieutenant Palumbo looked down at him. Palumbo was half a head taller than Riker, with black hair slicked back and a rather open manner that Riker wasn't quite sure how to react to. Palumbo clearly considered Riker something of a curiosity; one might even have said that Palumbo came across as being in awe of him, as if not sure how to respond to the presence of the Great William Riker aboard the *Starship U.S.S. Independence.*

"So . . . what's it like?" asked Palumbo without preamble.

" 'It,' Lieutenant?" Despite the breach of protocol, Riker couldn't help but feel some amusement at Palumbo's manner.

Palumbo promptly dropped down into a chair across from Riker. "Being related to one of the original signers of the original Resolution."

"Well . . . Lieutenant," Riker felt constrained to point out, "the Resolution of Non-Interference was signed nearly two hundred years ago. Granted, I'm related to one of the original signers. But it's not as if Thaddeus Riker was someone that I spent a good deal of time with. In point of fact, he died more than a century before I was even conceived."

"Even so. Even so," Palumbo's head bobbed as if he were furiously agreeing and disagreeing simultaneously. "It must make you proud, right? Am I right?"

Actually, Riker had never given the matter all that much thought. Riker had always considered himself somewhat self-sufficient. He was determined to carve his own career and obtain his own notoriety, and he wasn't the type of person who rested upon the achievements of those who had come before him.

Still . . . he had to admit that there was something to be said for it. He'd done a good deal of reading up on Thaddeus Riker as the bicentennial had approached, and the more he'd learned, the more impressed he'd been.

"You're right," agreed Riker.

Palumbo slapped the table. It shook from the impact. "See, I knew I was right!"

"Is this guy bothering you, Commander?"

Lieutenant Mankowski had come up behind Palumbo. During their shift, Palumbo operated conn while Mankowski was at ops, so they were accustomed to working tightly together. When Mankowski spoke, it was with a faint southern drawl. Riker couldn't help but notice, to his amusement, that Mankowski was keeping one eye on his reflection in the observation glass nearby, running his fingers through his wavy brown hair to make sure that it was "just so."

"No, Mankowski. No bother at all."

"Thanks for being so concerned, Joe," Palumbo said in obvious irritation. "What, you trying to embarrass me in front of the Commander here?"

"Oh . . . please. You needn't concern yourself about that, Lieutenant," said Riker. "Really. It's not a problem. To be perfectly honest, if I were in your position, I'd probably be reacting in exactly the same way."

"Well, that's good to hear, sir. Very understanding of you." There was one other chair at the table, and Mankowski sat in it. Riker chuckled softly to himself as he saw that Mankowski straddled the chair in the same manner that Riker habitually did. "Look . . . to be honest, sir, there's a goodly number of people on this ship who would love to bend your ear about all manner of things. Not just about your ancestor, but about you yourself. You've had a hell of a career, after all."

"It's been . . . interesting."

"You're being too modest, sir."

"Oh, yeah. Way too modest," echoed Palumbo.

"Now me," and Mankowski tapped his chest, "I'm not that kind of person. The hero-worshipping sort, I mean. I think people have a right to be proud of their accomplishments, but that's no reason to elevate them to some sort of bigger-than-life status. In fact, I was just saying the other day to—"

From across the lounge, a crewman called, "Hey, Joe! Joe! Got a second?"

"Hey!" Mankowski shot back, clearly annoyed. "Can't you see I'm talking to Commander William T. Riker here? *The* William Riker?"

The crewman held up his hands, palms out, in mute apology for butting in.

Riker put a hand in front of his mouth and laughed into it.

"It's just that," Palumbo jumped in during the momentary lull, "it's just that, well . . . the truth is, I've been a fan of yours ever since I was a kid."

"A *kid?"* Riker couldn't quite believe his ears as he stared at the young officer. "Lieutenant, for God's sake, I'm not *that* old."

"Well . . . not a little kid," Palumbo amended hastily. "Just since, well . . ." He considered it a moment. "Since I was a teenager."

That still seemed a hideous age discrepancy to Riker, and he said, "That can't be right. I haven't been at it that long . . . have I?" His voice trailed off on the last two words.

"Oh, sure," Palumbo said with a cheerfulness that Riker couldn't help but find disturbing. "My dad was—is—in Starfleet, and he talked about officers who were on the fast track. He especially thought the crew of the *Enterprise* was top-notch."

Riker quickly did the math in his head and realized that Palumbo was exactly right.

"Those were the good old days, huh, Commander?" Palumbo asked.

"Ohhhhh yes. The good old days." Riker was suddenly starting to feel as ancient as Thaddeus Riker.

"Mike . . . I think you're making the Commander uncomfortable," Mankowski said cautiously, glancing from Riker back to Palumbo.

"Nah! Am I? I didn't mean to . . ."

"It's . . . all right," Riker said. He generally had a fairly ready smile and it didn't fail him this time either as he was able to appreciate the more amusing aspects of the situation. "It's just that, well . . ." and he tapped his chest, "in here I feel like I joined the Fleet only yesterday. I'm not entirely sure at what point I went from eager young cadet to gray eminence. It's a disconcerting transition, that's all."

"Do you think Captain Picard went through the same thing?"

"The captain?" Riker smiled puckishly. "Absolutely not. The truth is that Captain Picard was born forty years old. He didn't have the time or patience for child or adolescence. He simply went straight to the status of 'authority figure.' "

"I believe it," said Palumbo. "He came and lectured to one of our classes once. He scared the crap out of me. But . . . don't tell him that next time you see him, okay?"

"My lips are sealed," Riker assured him.

They chatted for a few minutes more, although Palumbo and Mankowski seemed more and more interested in crosstalk between the two of them, leaving Riker serenely to his thoughts. And, naturally enough, those thoughts turned to Thaddeus Riker.

The truth was that the Resolution was indeed one hell of an accomplishment, and Thaddeus Riker had been one of the main architects. The Resolution of Non-Interference had been a sort of United Federation Bill of Rights. It had pulled together a number of fractured members of the United Federation of Plantets into a basic position paper that put forward, in language so plain and firm as to command their assent, the basic philosophies that the UFP hoped to pursue. Many historians felt that the Resolution was not only the turning point in the UFP's early development, but the basics for some of the Federation's most fundamental philosophies—including, most notably, Starfleet's Prime Directive—had its roots in the Resolution of Non-Interference.

Thaddeus Riker, one of the principal drafters of the Resolution, had affixed his name to it along with some fifty other representatives of assorted worlds, outposts and colonies. That important event had occurred nearly two hundred years ago, and a major celebration on Earth was in the works. Indeed, that was the reason for Riker's presence on the *Independence.* The starship was en route to Earth anyway, and the ship had been instructed to pick up Riker and bring him along. For other officers, the easy assignment would have been considered something of a paid vacation. That was not the case with Riker. He thought it a colossal waste of time, and tried to convince Starfleet that this endeavor was worth neither the time nor the effort as far as his presence was concerned. He could think of a hundred more constructive things he'd rather be doing than putting in an appearance at some high-profile function, no matter how historically important that function might be. Unfortunately, as so frequently happened in cases like this one, Starfleet wasn't able to come up with any.

Which was how Riker had wound up aboard the *Independence,* being made to feel old by two young officers who seemed bound and determined to worship Riker to bits. They chatted on with Riker barely listening, and hoping against hope that something—anything—would distract them from the unwanted attention they were lavishing upon him.

That was the moment that the yellow alert klaxon went off. Without hesitation, Mankowski and Palumbo high-tailed it out the door, as did the other patrons of the Ten-Forward. Within moments the place was empty, leaving a disconsolate Riker staring at the glass still in his hand. His very soul cried *"Foul!"* as he thought of where he was during an emergency as opposed to where he'd prefer to be.

On the other hand . . . he was a guest. Guests should be, and are, accommodated whenever possible. And perhaps he was a guest who could lend a hand, presuming the captain was interested in the extra help.

Couldn't hurt to ask him, Riker reasoned. Couldn't hurt at all . . .

Captain George Garfield, a man of modest height but booming authority, looked surprised to see Riker striding onto the bridge. Garfield's face had a craggy ruggedness about it, and his gray hair was so tightly curled that some felt it was possible to slice one's finger open on it. "Is there a problem, Commander?" he asked.

"No problem at all, sir. I just . . ." On the face of it, it seemed absurd to make the offer now that he was there. It was an insult, really, an implication that the captain was unable or unwilling to handle the situation on his own. First officer Joe Morris was watching Riker warily. He was a lean man with thinning hair and a foxlike face. He tended to smile a lot for a first officer, and he had a habit of taking pains to display his perfectly arrayed teeth whenever possible.

Garfield smiled grimly and nodded in apparent understanding. "When there's a red alert, you don't exactly feel comfortable with the prospect of hiding down in your quarters, is that it?"

"Exactly it, sir."

"Very well. As long as we remember whose ship this is."

There was a bit of a ribbing quality to the comment, but at the same time, a very clear, somewhat territorial warning. Riker didn't have to be told twice. "I'm just a spectator, captain."

"Spectate from there," Garfield said, indicating the vacant counselor's chair. The ship's counselor, Lieutenant Aronin, hadn't been feeling particularly well as of late, and had been confined to sickbay under orders of the ship's CMO, Doctor DiSpigno. "And don't you worry. Once we attend to whatever's going on, I assure you we'll give you a smooth ride to your destination."

"Much obliged, sir."

Riker promptly slid easily into the chair.

"Talk to me, Mr. Palumbo," Garfield said.

Palumbo scanned the board and reported, "Distress signal, sir. I believe it's coming from the Daystrom Institute Outpost."

From the tactical board, Lieutenant Monastero called, "Confirming, sir. Putting it on screen."

The image of a gentle-looking man appeared. But the background behind him was extremely strange. It didn't seem to be an actual place so much as an environment of pulsing energy.

"Good God," said Morris. "What's that?"

"This is Daystrom Station, we are under attack, repeat, we are under attack," said the man on the screen. "Any Federation vessel in the area, please assist. This is Doctor Elias Frobisher of the Daystrom Station, we are under attack, please assist . . ."

"It appears to be computer generated," Mankowski said. "Not an actual image, but one composed by a computer. Question is, why?"

"No, Mr. Mankowski, that's not the question at all," Garfield told him in no uncertain terms. "The question is, 'How fast can we get there?' "

"At maximum warp . . . ?" Mankowski did some rapid-fire calculations. "Three hours, eighteen minutes."

Morris had stepped over to the ops station and was glancing over Palumbo's shoulder. "We appear to be the closest ship in the area, sir."

"Lieutenant, best speed to Daystrom."

"Aye, captain." Mankowski immediately punched in the course, and the *Independence* angled sharply away from its then-current heading and headed with all possible alacrity toward the scene of the distress call.

The captain shifted in his chair and looked at Riker with mild apology in his eyes. "Seems we're going to be late getting you to your appointment with fame, Commander. Regulations clearly state . . ."

"That any Starfleet vessel capable of responding to a distress call must lend assistance whenever possible," Riker recited with a smile. "Captain, there's a number of regs that I would be the first to dispute . . . but that is most definitely not one of them. The only question is, is there going to be anyone or anything left by the time we get there."

"I don't know," Garfield admitted. "We can only do the best that we can do, Commander. The thing is, a science station such as Daystrom's outpost isn't like a planetary treasury or some such, where you just go in, raid the riches and depart. Whatever these possible raiders want—whether it's technology, files, information, what-have-you—it's probably going to have to be handled with delicacy. That means they'll have to take their time extracting it for fear of damaging it, and if they take enough time," and he nodded grimly, "then we've got them."

There was little talking for the remainder of the trip. Riker watched the crew of the *Independence* going about their business. It was an odd sensation for him. He was, after all, part of his surroundings and environment. And they were all Starfleet, after all. They might be spread out among various ships, but they were a unit nevertheless, each capable of helping one another and functioning as a team.

But just as he was a part, he was also apart. He had his rank, certainly, but he had no place on this vessel. He was simply a passenger, with no more intrinsic importance to the ship than cargo being carted down in the hold. It was a very, very strange feeling. Every so often Garfield or Morris would engage him in polite conversation, but it seemed to Riker that it was more a matter of form than any real interest in him. Then again, he might simply have been imagining it.

"Approaching Daystrom Station," Mankowski announced finally. "Sensors indicate that the company hasn't left the party yet."

"Magnify," ordered Garfield.

The screen rippled briefly, and then the conical shape of Daystrom station appeared in front of them. Sure enough, in orbit around the station was a vessel the likes of which Riker had never seen before. It was low slung, built for speed but, at the same time, clearly heavily armed . . . an assessment that Monastero confirmed a moment later from tactical.

"Disruptors, phasers . . . and some sort of plasma weapon as well. They're well armed, all right. Nothing our own weaponry and shield can't handle, but I don't think I'd care to face them in anything less than a starship."

"Thank you, Mr. Monastero. Open a hailing frequency, please."

"Open, sir."

Garfield leaned back in his command chair, crossing his legs in a rather casual manner as if he were having a comfortable chat in his living room. "This is Captain George Garfield of the *Starship Independence.* Please identify yourselves immediately and prepare to be boarded. Thank you."

"Captain," warned Mankowski, "they're powering up their weapons."

"Didn't their mothers teach them that 'please' and 'thank you' are the magic words?" said Morris.

"I know mine did," said Garfield. "Shields up. Maintain hailing frequency. Unidentified ship, please stand down your weapons immediately, or we will be forced to defend ourselves."

"They've opened fire!" Mankowski said. Sure enough, plasma torpedoes were hurtling across the void and spiralling straight toward the *Independence.*

And both Garfield and Riker called, "Evasive action!", the latter doing so by reflex. Immediately realizing his error, he looked with chagrin at Garfield. Fortunately, Garfield seemed more amused than usurped.

Mankowski spurred the mighty ship forward, and the *Independence* gracefully angled down and away from the brace of torpedoes. "Return fire," ordered Garfield.

"We're not yet at optimum distance for full effectiveness."

Garfield glanced over his shoulder. "Indulge me."

Monastero nodded as his hands flew over the tactical array, and the phaser banks flared to life. But the distance was indeed too great, and although the phasers scored a direct hit upon the opposing vessel, the damage done to their shields was virtually nonexistent.

"They're moving off!" Mankowski said.

Riker realized that Garfield was faced with a dilemma. If he attended to the space station, took the time to send down an away team, then the delay might give the other vessel time to get away. But if there were wounded or dying people at the station, then a chase after the attacker might delay the *Independence* for so long that no aid to the station personnel—should there be any surviving—would be possible.

An obvious solution immediately presented itself to Riker, and out of reflex he was about to suggest it. But as Riker opened his mouth to speak, Morris said, "Captain, I've readied the shuttle bay in case . . ."

"You read my mind, Number One. Bridge to security."

"Security. Petronella here."

"Mister Petronella, scramble a security team and med unit and get yourselves down to the shuttle bay. Attend to whomever needs help aboard the station and remain here until we return."

"Aye, sir."

Garfield noticed Riker's still-open mouth out of the corner of his eye and asked, "Is there a problem, Commander?"

"No, sir. Obviously no problem at all."

"Good."

"Enemy vessel preparing to go to warp, sir," Mankowski announced.

"Stay on her, Lieutenant," Garfield said calmly. "Mr. Monastero, fire a warning shot. See if we can persuade them to stay and chat."

As the *Independence* hurtled toward the station, closing the gap, Monastero fired the phasers. One blast coruscated against the enemy ship's shielding, while the other went across her bow, intercepting the vessel's momentary trajectory. But the unknown vessel spun out of the way and moved away from the station, picking up speed with every passing moment.

"Shuttle away!" called Palumbo.

"Chase them down, Mr. Mankowski," said Garfield.

"Aye, sir." Mankowski grinned in a slightly devilish manner. If there was one thing he liked, it was a pursuit.

The *Independence* darted straight toward the alien vessel, but the other ship immediately kicked into high gear. It was a burst of speed that was a bit surprising to those on the bridge of the starship, for it hadn't seemed as if the other ship had that much power to her. But they were only momentarily daunted. "Looks like we're in a race," observed Riker, and no one disputed that.

The "race" continued for some minutes, and then for an hour. Every so often, the opposing vessel would scatter something behind them: A plasma torpedo, or a bomb. But the *Independence* adroitly kept out of the way.

Unfortunately, the starship wasn't drawing close enough to do any serious damage with her own array of weaponry.

"Sir . . . we're approaching Thallonian space," said Mankowski. "I know that she's been opened up ever since the collapse of the Thallonian Empire . . ."

"But there's still an 'approach with approval only' mandate on it. I know, Mr. Mankowski. But this is likely where they were heading in hopes that we were going to break off pursuit. Are you interested in quitting the chase, Mr. Mankowski?"

"No, sir," Mankowski said with a grim smile.

"Maintain course and speed, then."

Riker found the give and take between the captain and his crew to be a bit amusing. Garfield was older than Picard, and yet he seemed to take a somewhat paternal air with his crewmen. It was a very different command style, and certainly not Riker's own during the times when he'd been in command, but it was certainly a viable one nonetheless.

"Engineering to bridge." A formal British accent came over the comm unit.

"Bridge. Garfield here," replied the captain. "Go ahead, Mr. McKean."

"Captain . . . may I inquire as to whether we will be reducing velocity in the near future? I am uncertain whether I will be able to maintain maximum thrust for all that much longer."

"No promises, Mr. McKean."

"Sir, I'm not asking for a commitment. But I do wish to be able to provide the velocity you require if and when you require it. As things stand, I am unable to guarantee said velocity will be yours for the asking. The warp core is, if you'll pardon my poetic language, complaining bitterly. All the velocity in the galaxy will be irrelevant if the ship has exploded."

"Understood, Mr. McKean."

"Captain!" Mankowski suddenly called. "The other ship is slowing down."

"Is she turning to fight?"

"Doesn't appear to be turning, no, sir. Perhaps their engines are overtaxed."

And from down in engineering, McKean could be heard muttering, "Perhaps their bloody captain listens to his engineering officer and reduces speed when reasonable."

It was all Riker could to do repress a grin. It was comforting to know that there were some universal constants, and chief engineers appeared to be one of them. For his part, Garfield kept a poker face as he said, "Mr. McKean, we still have an open channel."

"Oh." There was a pause, and then another, "Oh. Uhm . . . McKean out," and the connection was broken.

Turning back to business, Garfield said, "Bring us ahead slow, Mr. Mankowski. Let's see what we've got. Monastero, open a channel."

"You're on, sir."

"Unidentified ship, this is the *Independence.* Please respond."

On the screen, the vessel they'd pursued all that way had come to a complete halt. She wasn't dead in space, but she wasn't taking any action at all. She just sat there.

And Riker couldn't keep his mouth shut. "Sir, I don't like this. With all respect . . ."

"No apologies necessary, Commander," Garfield said, rubbing his chin thoughtfully. "I'm not sure I like it either. Smells like some sort of set-up."

"My thoughts exactly, sir."

"We can't exactly go running away from a ship we chased down this far, and which isn't even firing at us. But still . . ." He thought a moment and then said, "Sensors on maximum. Sweep the area."

"Sweeping, sir," said Mankowski. "Not picking up anything."

"Nothing on tactical sensor scans either," Monastero affirmed.

"Checking the . . ." Suddenly Mankowski's voice caught. "Picking up an energy discharge, sir. Consistent with the patterns detected . . ." He turned and looked straight at the captain. " . . . detected when a Romulan shp is decloaking, sir."

"Where?" demanded Garfield.

"To starboard, sir. At 813 Mark 2."

A moment later, everyone on the bridge saw that Mankowski was correct as a Romulan vessel shimmered into existence to the ship's starboard . . .

. . . and then, a moment later, to her port. In the meantime, the ship they'd been pursuing had come around. "Enemy ship approaching. They're weapons hot, sir," said Mankowski.

"Captain . . ." Riker said in a tone of warning.

Garfield surveyed the situation arrayed against them and nodded his head. "I believe it's time to make like a shepherd and get the flock out of here. Reverse course, Lieuten—"

And then two more ships materialized, one forward and one after. They were now completely surrounded by Romulan warbirds, all of them combat-ready with their weapons prepared to discharge.

Despite the fact that they were overwhelmingly outnumbered, Garfield did not appear the least bit perturbed. Instead, acting as if he still maintained the strategic advantage, he called out, "Attention all ships. This is the starship *Independence.* The vessel we have been pursuing has illegally entered, and attacked, an outpost in Federation space. This is not your concern, and I strongly advise you to veer off before it's too late."

And then, to their surprise, a voice crackled back across the channel. It was a female voice, and the moment Riker heard it, a chill went down his spine. The voice said, in a mocking tone, "Too late? Too late for whom? For us? Or for you?"

"This is Captain George Garfield. Identify yourself, please."

The image of the ships around them momentarily vanished from the screen, to be replaced by the face of a female Romulan. She had tightly cut blonde hair and an expression that seemed to radiate contempt. "Very well," she said. "We are the ones who are going to kill you. Is that sufficient identification . . ."

Then her gaze flickered toward the officer seated in the counselor's chair, and her eyes went wide with sadistic delight. "Well, well. It's been ages, Will Riker."

"Sela," Riker said tersely.

Garfield didn't even pretend to understand what was going on. "Commander, do you know this . . . individual?"

"Her name is Sela. She's the half-Romulan daughter of a deceased woman from an alternate time line."

"Oh, well, that clears things up," Palumbo could be heard to mutter.

"If you know this individual, then I suggest you advise her against any rash actions."

"You heard the man, Sela. Don't look for a fight where there need not be one. It's not as if you're in the best of relations with the Romulan government at the moment. You can't afford any more military disasters."

"How kind of you to care about my well-being, Riker," Sela replied, "considering that all of my past 'disasters' can be placed squarely at your door. But," she added thoughtfully, "you're right. I don't need more blemishes on my record."

"As I said . . ."

"Instead, I need to blow you all to hell. All vessels," she called out, "you're tapping into this communication. Directly in the middle of us is one Will Riker. Let me tell you, I've been waiting to say this for ages." Her lips drew back in a feral smile of triumph. "Fire at Will."

And as the Romulan ships, as one, opened fire, Riker felt the world explode around him.

III.

It was the weekly poker game, and all the usual suspects were grouped around: Deanna, Data, Worf, and Geordi. As Riker studied his hand, Geordi leaned forward and said without preamble, "So there's this mighty sailing ship, a British frigate, cruising the Seven Seas, and one day the lookout shouts down from the crow's nest, 'Captain! Captain! There's two pirate ships heading our way! They mean to attack! What should we do?' And the captain, he says, 'Bring me my red shirt.' So they bring him his red shirt, he puts it on, and leads his men into battle. It's difficult, and there are a number of casualties, but they manage to beat back the pirates. That evening, after the survivors have gotten themselves bandaged up, they ask the captain why he called for his red shirt. And he says, 'Because if I'm wounded and bleeding, I wouldn't want the sight of my blood to destroy the morale of my men. But if I'm wearing my red shirt, no one will see it.' Well, the crew thought, 'Wow. What a captain.' "

By this point, every eye at the card table was on Geordi. He continued, "So the next day, another shout, even more worried, comes down from the crow's nest. And the lookout says, 'Captain, my captain! There's ten pirate ships heading our way, and they mean to board us! What should we do?' The frightened crew turns to their captain, but he doesn't flinch. He doesn't hesitate. And he calls out, 'Bring me . . . my brown pants!' "

Laughter echoed around the room, although Worf was naturally somewhat restrained. Even Data, thanks to his newly installed emotion chip, was able to laugh in appreciation. Suddenly Geordi immediately stopped *laughing as he looked at something over Riker's shoulder. Riker turned and promptly fell silent, as did the others.*

Jean-Luc Picard was standing there. It was impossible to tell how long he'd been there, for he'd entered fairly quietly and everyone had been engrossed in the joke. It was also impossible to tell what was going through his mind. He had a small, enigmatic smile, but that was no indicator. Picard had a standing invitation to join them for poker, but he almost never took them up on it. And of all times, that was the moment he had chosen to make an appearance at the game.

They all waited.

And at last, without the slightest change in expression, he said, "I don't think jokes about cowardly captains are very funny." With that observation hanging in the air, he turned and walked out.

Then the room jolted under Riker, tossing Troi, Worf, Data, and Geordi to the floor, and the recollection dissolved into reality.

It took Riker a few more moments to sort the confusing real world from his recollection of times past. The jolt had been rather sudden and, when Riker had been thrown from his chair, he had hit his head rather severely. It had dazed him and sent his mind spiralling back to a time with his shipmates where, somehow, things had seemed simpler. But then, didn't times past always seem that way, no matter how complicated they were?

His lungs began to ache. He wondered why, and then the full realization of his situation imposed itself upon him. The bridge was thick with smoke.

The flame-retardant chemicals were already being released and were controlling the fire adequately enough, but that still didn't help the wreck that the bridge had become. It had all happened so fast, so decisively, that it was difficult for Riker to fully grasp.

Then he saw Palumbo's unmoving body slumped backward in the chair, with half his scalp torn away and a huge metal shard buried in his skull, and the full reality of it sank in quite quickly.

His immediate impulse was to stop, to mourn, to dwell on how just hours before he had been chatting in relaxed and casual fashion with this young man who had considered Riker someone to emulate. And now he was gone, just like that. No more aspirations, no more dreams. Nothing.

And the others, my God, the others. First Officer Morris was also gone, buried under a pile of debris that had broken loose from overhead.

Then Riker, from long practice, pushed such sentiments and concerns aside. There would be time enough later to mourn . . . presuming there was, in fact, a later.

Mankowski wasn't moving either, tilted back in his seat, his head slumped to one side. But he seemed to be breathing at least, albeit shallowly, and he was moaning softly. There was a streak of red down the side of his face, but apparently the wound was under his hair because Riker couldn't immediately discern it.

As for the captain . . . Garfield was unconscious. He was slumped over the ops console, and Riker realized that Garfield must have tried to take over when Palumbo went down. But there was only a blackened shell where the ops console had been. Apparently the entire thing had blown up in Garfield's face. His uniform was torn, his face was blackened, and there was blood everywhere. That Garfield was breathing at all was nothing short of miraculous.

"Commander . . ."

The voice came in a croak. Riker turned and saw Monastero, the security chief, rising from the wreckage like a ghost. "We've . . . got to get them out of here . . ."

"Report, Lieutenant," Riker said through cracked and bleeding lips. "Where are the attackers."

"We have to get out!" Monastero repeated.

"Give me an update, Mister!" Riker was starting to become irritated. Monastero appeared to be in shock.

"A report." Monastero pulled himself together and then fired a dark glare at Riker. "Sensors are down. We're dead in space. Impulse engines off line. Emergency distress signal has been activated. And thirty seconds ago, we got word from engineering that there's a warp core breech."

"What? Riker to engineering." He wasn't quite sure that Monastero, who had a dazed look in his eye and appeared to have gone several rounds with a brick wall, was fully reliable. On the other hand, he was the only person still coherent on the bridge.

There was no response to Riker's hail. But at that moment, the computer voice of the *Independence* said with its customary *sang froid,* "Warp core breech reported. Four minutes, eighteen seconds to final detonation. Evacuation of ship proceeding . . ."

Monastero spread his hands in a "Told you so" gesture.

It was not a situation that gave Riker a warm, squooshy feeling. Outside the ship was an array of Romulan vessels, and he was quite certain that they weren't about to be sporting about the emergency situation. The only hope they had was that the Romulans had moved off upon detecting the rupture of the warp core. The explosion was going to be rather intense, and nobody wanted to be in the vicinity when it happened.

Of course, that included the crew of the *Independence.*

"Are the turbolifts functioning?" Riker asked. Monastero's look said it all. "No, of course not. That'd be too easy," Riker continued, answering his own question. "All right then." He hauled Mankowski out of the chair and draped him over his shoulders in a fireman's carry. "The captain. Get the captain."

Monastero was already ahead of him. He draped Garfield over his shoulder and headed for the emergency exit. Riker followed quickly, while the computer calmly informed them that in just four minutes, the ship they were presently residing in would be nothing more than a large patch of space dust.

When the *Enterprise* had suffered a warp breech, they had been able to separate the saucer section from her and make their escape that way. But that option was not open to the *Independence.* With the impulse drive down, the saucer section would have no means of propelling itself away from the blast area. They'd go up in a ball of fire the size of Topeka. The only hope they had was the individual escape pods which would be able to hurtle away from the ship with sufficient speed to reach a safe distance from the explosion. At least, that was the theory.

Riker just prayed they were still functioning. The escape pods were on a separate, emergency system from the mainline computers, just for this sort of emergency. Still, with everything else down, who knew for sure? But there was no other option. It was either the escape pods or blow themselves out the photon torpedo tubes and pray that they suddenly developed the ability to breathe in a vacuum.

Climbing through the emergency hatchways under ordinary circumstances was problematic enough. Doing so with the slumped body of Mankowski over him was particularly challenging. Every so often Mankowski would flutter on the light side of consciousness, muttering something incoherent—once it was something about a beautiful waltz, another time it related to triangles—before passing out once more.

Monastero, for his part, was utterly stoic. He hauled his captain to safety without complaint or even the slightest grunt. One would have thought he was carrying a bag of katha chips for all the effort he was displaying. He was definitely stronger than he looked.

They arrived at the lower deck which led to the nearest set of emergency pods. "Let's hope there's some left," said Riker.

"Let's hope a lot of things," replied Monastero.

They stumbled down the corridor, and Mankowski had recovered enough of his wits to be able to haul his own weight. Garfield was still out cold. His color—what was discernible of it beneath the burns—did not look good. Riker was no doctor, but he gave Garfield a fifty-fifty chance at best. Then he spotted the sign, glowing in the half-light of the hallway, pointing the way to the escape pods. "There! This way!"

"I know that! It's my damned ship!" shot back Monastero.

They made it to the pods. Other crewmen were hurriedly launching themselves into space, but when they saw the captain was there, several of them stopped what they were doing and helped load him into a pod. It was a gesture that Riker couldn't help but appreciate. They were placing the survival of their commanding officer above their own. That was a true measure of the mettle of Starfleet officers, particularly in a time of crisis. Riker wished that the remaining pods allowed for more than one person; in his condition, the captain could really have used someone with him. But it simply wasn't an option.

"Captain away!" called Monastero. But rather than jump into a pod himself, he helped Riker load Mankowski into an escape pod. Only after that had been fired off into space did Monastero turn to head for his own means of escape. He paused for a moment, however, turned to face Riker, and—despite the fact that such gestures were all-but-unknown anymore—snapped off a crisp salute to Riker. The commander returned the gesture and then climbed into his own pod. He ran through the launch protocol as fast as he could, trying not to think about the dwindling time left to him. The seal slid into place, and Riker engaged the "eject" sequence. Seconds later, the escape pod shook violently around him, and the next thing Riker knew, he was watching the *Independence* spiral away from him.

Through the small viewing porthole of the pod, he couldn't believe the damage he was seeing once he was outside. There was scarcely a section of the ship that hadn't been scored or ruptured. Warp core breech? The amazing thing was that the starship had held together for as long as it had. One warp nacelle had been blown away completely, and was hanging like a severed limb nearby the ship's hull. Air was venting into space, the seals having failed. Even the ship's name, etched proudly on the saucer, was covered with carbon scoring and was barely visible.

"Bastards," breathed Riker.

Then he saw the ship begin to tremble violently, and he realized that the moment of total destruction was very close. Unfortunately, so was he. The escape pod was moving quickly, all right, but he wasn't confident that it was quick enough to put enough distance between himself and the ship.

And then, with a final shudder, much like a death throe, the engineering section of the *Independence* erupted. Riker looked away, partly from the emotion involved in seeing such a magnificent vessel destroyed, and also simply because such a detonation was blinding.

The unleashed energies of the all-consuming warp core enveloped the remains of the *Independence* like a high-speed cancer, and seconds later the ship was gone. In its place was a massive, dazzling blast, with a shock wave radiating from the midst of it that was overtaking Riker's escape pod with horrifying ease.

Riker braced himself, and then the wave overwhelmed the escape pod.

It propelled him, faster and faster, and Riker set his jaw and didn't cry out. He wasn't entirely certain why he felt the need to keep it in. It wasn't as if there was anyone around. But he kept his mouth sealed just the same, closing his eyes against the spin of the pod.

Throughout all of it, he was struck by the silence of it all. The blast happened in relative silence, and as he spun about in space, caught up in the force of the detonation, the main sound he was able to hear was that of his own breathing . . . and possibly the pounding of his own heart. He braced himself within the pod, grasping the grips on either side to steady himself. He felt his gorge rising and pushed it back down. The last thing he needed to do was vomit in the confined space of the escape pod.

The momentum continued to carry him as he rode the crest of the wave, tumbling end over end, and the incandescence was simply overwhelming. He was shoved along, a pebble at the edge of a wave. Images flashed before him, people he loved, people he'd worked with, people long gone and people he wondered if he'd ever see again. He realized his life was flashing before his eyes and all he could think was, *How terribly cliché.*

It was only belatedly that he realized the light was fading. He peered through the viewport and saw that the explosion was dissipating. He had made it, had tumbled beyond the blast range. There were some other pods within his field of vision, but it was impossible to tell who it was or how many of the crew had survived.

Now that he was clear, he activated the pod's propulsion system. It wasn't as if the escape pod had a ton of maneuverability. To be specific, when compared to the propulsion and maneuver capacities of a starship, the pod was equipped with little more than a pair of oars. Then again, since the pod really was a glorified lifeboat, that was fairly appropriate.

The problem was, there wasn't really any place for Riker to head *to.* He wasn't situated near any planet . . . and even if he was, there wouldn't be any guarantee that it would have been hospitable. Up to that point, he'd been more reacting than acting. The idea had been to get away from the dying starship rather than be concerned about getting to someplace. Now his main concern was steadying himself and returning to the other pods. If there were a hospitable planet in the area, then the smart thing to do would be to head there as quickly as possible, touch down, and wait for rescue. But with nothing around and Riker uncertain precisely where they were, the only reasonable thing to do was keep together as a group and hope that a ship responded to the rescue call that had been sent out . . .

Just as we responded to a rescue call, Riker thought ruefully. Well, this rescue mission had turned out just wonderfully, hadn't it.

He saw a cluster of escape pods floating to his right, and was about to try and open up a comm channel so that he could discern who it was . . .

. . . and that was when a huge burst of light detonated. Reflexively he shielded his eyes. He didn't even have to look, though, to know what had just happened.

They were moving in, vultures converging on a wounded and helpless herd. Two Romulan cruisers were coming in. *Only two,* he realized. Obviously the *Independence* had not gone out without giving a good account of herself. The other warbirds, as well as the ship they'd been pursuing, had either been destroyed or else so badly shot up that they had had to return to home base—wherever that was—for repairs.

Unfortunately, two warbirds were going to be more than enough to handle the life pods. In fact, considering that the pods were for life maintenance only and contained no offensive capacity, a single Romulan warrior with a phaser cannon could probably dispose of them handily. So two warbirds, in this instance, was overkill.

They were taking their time, the damned sadists. They began fine-tuning their shots; instead of disposing of a group of pods, as one of the ships had just done, they started picking them off one at a time. *Target practice,* thought an infuriated Riker. *They want to drag it out, have some "fun."* Naturally they weren't interested in rescuing any of them. Romulans habitually did not take prisoners. The only time they had that Riker knew of was the imprisonment of Tasha Yar which had resulted in the birth of Sela, and apparently that had been a rather unique set of circumstances.

He wondered if Sela was aboard one of the ships now, or whether she had been on one of the ones that was crippled or destroyed. "She's there," Riker muttered. "She's definitely out there, taking her time, making us suffer. That's her style."

Another pod picked off, and another still. There was no way for them to know who was in which pod. There was no mission to try and seek out particular individuals. It was simply an exercise in barbarism.

"*Selaaaa!*" Riker shouted, even though she couldn't hear. Even though no one could hear. "Sela . . . I'll find you! Even after I'm dead, I'll still find you, and drag you kicking and screaming to whatever hell you're destined for!"

One of the Romulan warbirds slowly started to turn in his direction. A more fanciful turn of mind would have prompted Riker to think that Sela was in that ship, and that she had heard him. And that she was about to give her reply in the form of phasers aimed right down his throat. At that moment, he thought about the joke. About being faced with a situation where the odds were utterly hopeless.

Never, in all his career, had Riker been as close to death as he was at that moment. A Romulan warbird staring at him, her weapons fully charged and ready, and he had no means of escape, no ability to defend himself. Nothing. He was a sitting duck. And it was just he in the pod. He was faced with the moment of his death, and if he cried out, or sobbed, or broke down in frustration, or shouted out curses at the unfair universe that had left him in such dire straits . . . no one would ever know.

He levelled his gaze straight at the warbird's gunport . . . and then he straightened his uniform jacket, tugging down on the bottom to smooth it.

"Farewell . . . Imzadi," he said to one who was not there. Then he tilted his chin slightly, like a prize fighter daring a challenger, and he said, "Take your best shot."

It wasn't a phaser that the warbird fired, as it turned out. It was a photon torpedo, and it streaked from the ship's underbelly straight at Riker. There was absolutely no way that it could miss. Through the silence it came at him, and within a second or two, it would blow him to bits.

At least it would have . . . had not a phaser blast lanced down from overhead, spearing the photon torpedo with surgical precision and detonating it while it was still a good five hundred yards from the pod.

"What in the—?" said a confused Riker, which was no doubt what they were saying aboard the warbird as well. A shadow was cast over them as something blotted out the light from the nearest star.

Down the starship flew, normal space twisting and roiling around it as the mighty vessel leaped out of warp, firing as it came.

If the warbird could have let out a shriek of surprise, like a genuine bird, it would have. The warbird literally backflipped out of the way as the new arrival unleashed another phaser barrage that clipped the warbird's warp nacelles. Riker was impressed at the precision. Whoever was manning tactical aboard the starship unquestionably knew what he was about.

The other warbird peeled off from its steady annihilation of the life pods and opened fire on the starship. The warbird's phaser blasts danced around the starship's shields, even as the starship returned fire with a photon torpedo barrage that bracketed the warbird, leaving it nowhere to go, keeping it in position for another well-placed phaser blast.

The first warbird tried to move upon the starship, operating in tandem with its mate, but the starship would have none of it. In what had to be the most insane maneuver that Riker had ever witnessed, the starship actually barrel-rolled via thrusters. As it did so, it unleashed phaser fire that pinwheeled around it, tracing such a bizarre arc that the warbirds didn't know where to maneuver in order to avoid them.

"*Who the hell is flying that thing?!*" Riker said in shock.

The first warbird moved in the wrong direction and paid dearly for it as the phasers sliced straight across her underbelly, slashing through what remained of the warbird's shields. A plume of flame blossomed from the ship's lower decks. Naturally the vacuum of space quickly snuffed it out, but it didn't matter as the interior of the ship blew apart. Pieces of warbird scattered everywhere, all in eerie silence.

The second warbird, seeing the fate that had overtaken the first one, apparently didn't need to see anymore. It whipped around and, seconds later, had leaped into warp space and was gone. If it had so chosen, the starship could have gone after it, but much to Riker's relief, it chose to stay and attend to the floating life pods.

The ship slowly cruised over him, and he was finally able to make out the name of the vessel as it drew near enough: *U.S.S. Excalibur.*

"I should have known," Riker said. Indeed, he should have. The *Excalibur* was the primary starship that had been assigned to Thallonian space. Still, considering they weren't *that* far into Thallonian territory—indeed, that they were relatively close to the borders of Federation space—the rescuer could have been anyone. However, it was cosmically ironic that it was the *Excalibur* because it meant that, any moment, he'd likely be hearing the voice of—

"All lifepods, this is *Excalibur,* Commander Shelby speaking," a familiar voice came over the pod's speaker system. "We'll be beaming you all aboard momentarily. Please be patient."

"Shelby. Naturally it would be Shelby," Riker said.

To his surprise, her voice came right back at him over the comm. "Commander Riker . . . is that you?"

He blinked. He'd been unaware that the two-way was on, but he realized somewhat belatedly that it was. Still, considering that Shelby had likely gotten numerous responses to her opening hail from other escape pods, it was nothing short of amazing that she'd been able to single out his voice.

"It's me, Commander."

"Hold on." Clearly she was busy getting a track as to which pod his transmission was coming from. "My God," she said after a moment, "you're in the one that we intercepted the torpedo for."

"That would be me, yes. Kudos to the timing of you and your CO."

"I just wish we could have gotten here sooner."

"So do I," he said regretfully, thinking about the crewmen who had been lost.

Suddenly the pod seemed to dematerialize around him, and then he found himself standing on a transporter pad with a number of other shaken-looking former crewmembers of the *Independence.* Elizabeth Paula Shelby, who had served under Riker as his second-in-command when he'd captained the *Enterprise* against a Borg invasion, was standing in the transporter room with her hands draped behind her back. "Welcome, all of you," she said briskly. "Please report to sickbay immediately. We have a medteam just outside who will escort you down."

There were murmurs of "Thank you" as the crewmen filed out. The last one out was Riker, who stopped within a foot or two of Shelby. "Be certain to tell me as soon as you have Captain Garfield's status confirmed . . . whatever that might be."

"I certainly will. It shouldn't take too long to find out. We're utilizing all the transporter rooms to bring the rest of them aboard even as we speak," she said.

He nodded.

She actually smiled. "It's good to see you again, Commander," and she sounded like she meant it. Considering that she and Riker had spent most of their time at each other's throats the last time they'd served together, he considered that a genuine compliment.

"Good to see you too, Commander," he replied. "For a little while there, I thought I wasn't going to be seeing anyone again."

"It must have been terrifying when that thing had you targeted."

He gave it a moment's thought and then said, "Well . . . at least I didn't need my brown pants."

She stared at him. "Oh. Well . . . good. That would . . . clash with your uniform top."

He nodded and walked out, as Shelby stared after him and scratched her head in obvious confusion.

IV.

Captain Mackenzie Calhoun was sitting behind his desk squeezing two small, green rubber balls together when Commander Shelby entered. She stared at him for a short time and then asked, "What are you doing?"

"Relieving tension," he said.

She watched him for a moment longer. "Squeezing those relieves tension?"

"Absolutely. A friend got them for me, many years ago. Would you care to try?" He held up his hands, and there was a green ball in either one. They were fairly small, but the rubber was sturdy and was able to withstand pressure with relative ease.

"No. Thank you."

"Because you look tense."

"I'm not tense."

"You look it."

"Mac . . . I'm not tense."

"All right." He leaned back in his chair. "So . . . bring me up to date."

"We managed to rescue 374 crewmen. The rest either died during the initial Romulan attack, or else when the two ships returned and starting picking people off. Starfleet has been informed and has told me that they'll be sending a transport. We're supposed to be hearing back from them once they've firmed up the rendezvous point."

Calhoun shook his head. His face was fairly impassive, which was not unusual for him; he didn't tend to keep his emotions up near the surface for casual display. But the disgust was evident nonetheless. "Not honorable. Picking off helpless people. Not honorable at all."

"The Romulans don't particularly care about such things as honor."

"They used to." He put the balls down on the desk and tapped his computer console. "I've been doing some research. They've always been in opposition to the Federation . . . but they used to be far more honorable than they are now. It's very odd. The Romulans used to focus on honor, while the Klingons were the dastardly race you wouldn't dare turn your back on. But they've switched places in their racial conduct. Curious."

"You can find it curious if you want. What I want to know," and she sat down opposite him, "is what they were doing out here in Thallonian space."

"So would I." He considered the question. "The *Independence* was lured here by that unknown ship they were chasing. The Romulans were waiting for them. Which suggests one of two things: Either the vessel they were chasing signalled ahead, picked this area at random, and instructed the Romulans to rendezvous here. Or else . . ."

"Or else the Romulans have a base somewhere hereabouts, and this was a pre-arranged rendezvous point," finished Shelby. "If that's the case . . . we should find it."

"Excellent idea. Considering that space is infinite in all directions, which way do you suggest we look first?"

"I never pretend to have all the answers, Mac. I leave that to captains."

He smiled thinly and then shifted gears. "Speaking of that . . . how is the captain of the *Independence?* Or at least what was the *Independence?"*

"He'll live. He was one of the lucky ones, actually, to have survived that shooting gallery from the Romulans."

"They'll pay for that," Calhoun said with quiet conviction.

"It's not the job of the *Excalibur* to carry out acts of revenge."

When he'd spoken earlier, he had been staring off into space, but now Calhoun swivelled his head so that the gaze from his purple eyes was squarely levelled upon Shelby. "Don't kid me, Eppy," using the nickname—a collapsing of Elizabeth and Paula—that he knew so irritated her. "If we find ourselves in a battle situation with the warbird that got away, or that ship they were chasing, you'll be hoping I blow them out of space. You know it. I know it."

"That's the difference between us, Mac," she said softly, even a little sadly. "I wouldn't revel in it. Two wrongs don't make a right."

"Yes. They do."

"But—"

"They do," he told her firmly. "Someone commits a wrong, a wrong is committed against them in turn . . . that comes out right."

"I'm speaking from a moral point of view, Mac."

"So am I," he said mildly. "That's the joy of morals. They're not absolute."

"There are absolute standards of right and wrong, Mac."

"You should know better than that, Eppy. Physics are absolute. But anything that man can conceive from his own skull is up for debate."

"You see, Mac . . . you would think that. Because you're someone who thinks that rules apply to you when you feel like it, but can be discarded when you consider them an inconvenience."

"Not always."

"No. Not always. Sometimes you have your moments. Sometimes you realize the importance of regs. I like to think that I've contributed to that somewhat. But most of the time . . ." She shook her head and let out a long, exaggerated sigh. "Sometimes, Mac, I just don't know."

"Fortunately enough, I do. But then again, I am a captain. As you said, either I know, or pretend that I do." He paused and eyed her in a slightly amused manner. "So . . . getting reacquainted?"

"What?"

"With Commander Riker."

"Oh. Him." Shelby absentmindedly picked up one of the green balls and started squeezing it. "There's not that much to get reacquainted about."

"Really." He drummed his fingers on his desk. "From what I've heard, the two of you had some interesting chemistry together."

"Chemistry? We didn't have chemistry, Mac. We had fights. Riker is . . ." She shook her head and squeezed the ball tighter.

"Riker is what?"

"Oh, he's an arrogant ass. So self-satisfied, so smug. Spends his entire career hanging onto Jean-Luc Picard's coattails. Now Picard, there's a quality officer . . . as you well know. And Riker, he thinks he's the moon to Picard's sun, basking in the reflected glory."

"Very harsh, Commander. From what I've read, he handled himself in exemplary fashion during the Borg encounter when Picard was assimulated."

"He had his moments, I suppose. But it's . . ."

"It's what?" He cocked an eyebrow. "Eppy?"

"He's got potential, all right? Potential. There's something there. Possible greatness." She was speaking all in a rush, the words tumbling one over the other. It was hard to tell whether she was angry or frustrated or sad or some combination of all those. "I can tell. I can tell these things because I've just got a knack for it. He could be one of the great ones, one of the truly legendary captains . . ."

"But I thought you said—"

"He's got to come out from Picard's shadow, though!" she said in frustration, as if Mac hadn't spoken. "I don't know why he's so satisfied to hide there! And when you talk to him about it, he gets all defensive and his jaw gets so tight and his eyes get all hard while the edges crinkle up . . ."

"Oh, do they?"

"But he's just so . . . so . . . so . . ." Her voice became louder and a bit more shrill with every word. " . . . so . . . so . . ."

The ball popped.

Shelby jumped back in her chair, startled by the sound and reflexively her hand flipped the broken rubber shell away from her. It "thwapped" onto Calhoun's desk rather pathetically. Calhoun stared at it and then, as if handling a rotting carcass, he picked it up delicately between his thumb and forefinger. "I've had the set for nine years. I didn't think it was possible to do this."

When Riker entered sickbay to check on Captain Garfield, he was momentarily surprised to see Doctor Selar checking over one of the *Independence* crewmembers. He remembered her from her time on the *Enterprise,* and hadn't been aware that her new assignment was the *Excalibur.* He remembered that he'd always been quite impressed with her. She didn't have the most delicate bedside manner, but she was a superb diagnostician and extremely efficient. Plus, because she was a Vulcan, she had the customary Vulcan reserve.

He walked up behind her and said, by way of greeting, "Doctor Selar . . ."

"*What do you want?!*"

He had never, in his life, heard a Vulcan speak above normal conversational tone, much less have one bellow at him. And it had been, to put it delicately, completely unprovoked. And the oddest thing was probably the fact that no one in sickbay seemed to feel that this was behavior that was remotely unusual for a CMO, let alone a Vulcan.

Remembering the accelerated strength that Vulcans possessed, to say nothing of such techniques as the Vulcan nerve pinch, Riker suddenly felt that it would probably be wiser for him to take a few steps back. He promptly did so. Selar had now turned to face him and was staring at him with no hint of recognition.

"Doctor . . . Selar? Commander Riker. Will Riker. We . . . worked together."

"I am aware of who you are, Commander," she said. "I am also aware that we served together aboard the *Enterprise.* I am further aware that I have been working steadily since the arrival of the survivors from the

Independence. Fortunately I do not require rest and relaxation as humans do. Lack of sleep has absolutely no effect on me whatsoever. What does have an impact upon me is people engaging me in pointless discussion, social niceties, and significant wastes of my time. If you consider it a possibility that you fall into any of those categories, you might want to reconsider your apparent interest in engaging me in extended social intercourse."

"Doctor," Riker said slowly, "I know this isn't my ship. I know I'm a visitor here. But nonetheless . . . I still outrank you . . . and that rank, to say nothing of simple common courtesy, should afford me a degree of respect. Respect that I don't see happening here. Now I'm not entirely sure what you think I've done to deserve this sort of brusque and, frankly, rude treatment. But I suggest you either tell me what's going on, or—"

"I am not interested in your ultimatums, Commander. Nor do I wish to discuss my personal affairs. Kindly tell me what you desire by coming here, or please leave."

"I'm looking for Captain Garfield."

"There." She pointed to a bed in the far corner and, sure enough, there was Garfield lying there, looking somewhat battered and bruised but most definitely alive. His eyes were closed, his chest rising and falling regularly.

Riker was about to say a curt "thank you" but Selar had already moved off. Shaking his head, Riker walked over to Garfield and stood over him.

"That you, Commander?" Garfield's eyes opened to narrow slits. His voice sounded raspy.

"Yes, sir."

"Sorry . . . we weren't able to give you that smooth ride I promised you."

"Don't worry, Captain. I won't hold it against you."

Garfield stared off into space.

"Captain . . . ?"

"I once met a captain . . . in a place . . . a special place," and he didn't quite smile, but it seemed to bring back pleasant memories. "A place for captains. Perhaps you'll go there sometime. We would sit around . . . tell stories . . . and one evening . . . the subject became losing a command. Different captains talked about it . . . but it wasn't addressed with the usual enthusiasm that usually involved discussions at this . . . particular place. And eventually . . . it got rather quiet. Quiet throughout the entire place, as it never had been before. And someone turned to me . . . and asked me if I'd ever experienced . . . such a loss. And I said I hadn't. That I was totally ignorant of what it was like. They looked at one another, the other captains did, and then they raised their glasses and, almost as one, they chorused,

'To ignorance.' They hoped that I would never have to go through it. But I'm afraid that I've had to disappoint them."

"Sir, it wasn't—"

He held up a cautionary finger to silence him. "If the next two words out of your mouth are going to be 'your fault,' I would suggest you keep them to yourself. It's always the captain's fault, commander. Always. No matter what boards of inquiry may decide. No matter what others may say. Do you know why captains are supposed to go down with their ship? It's so we don't have to listen to well-meaning individuals telling us it's not our fault. Because it is always . . . the captain's . . . fault."

It was as if he'd expended all his remaining energy just to get those words out. Then his head slumped back and he closed his eyes. For just a moment, Riker was about to shout an alarm, but then he glanced up at the scanner mounted on the wall and he saw that the readings were steady. He had simply fallen back to sleep.

"He appears to be resting comfortably."

Riker literally didn't recognize the voice at first as he turned to see Dr. Selar standing at his arm. "Yesss . . ." he said cautiously.

"It was very traumatic for him. We have him slightly medicated to ease him through . . . but not excessively."

He tilted his head slightly as if needing to make sure that he was talking to the same person he'd been addressing before. "Doctor Selar . . . ?"

"Yes? Is there a problem, Commander?"

Her attitude and disposition had completely changed. Gone was the edge of anger, the snappishness, the impatience. Now she was a standard-issue, matter-of-fact Vulcan.

"I . . . don't know. *Is* there a problem?"

For answer, she looked not at Riker, but at the bio-readouts over Garfield's bed. "No," she said after studying it a moment. "There does not appear to be. However," and she looked back to Riker, "if you believe there is one, please do not hesitate to inform me. Good day." All-business, she moved on to the next diagnostic table, leaving an utterly perplexed Riker literally shaking his head.

The doors to the Medlab hissed open, and Commander Shelby entered. "Commander Riker," she called.

"Yes, Commander?"

"I was just informed by the captain that we're receiving an incoming message from Starfleet, and apparently our presence has been requested."

"And you came down to get me yourself?"

"I was in the neighborhood and thought I'd drop by."

"I see. Very considerate of you." He headed for the door, stopping only to nod slightly to Doctor Selar and say, "Doctor."

"Commander," she nodded in acknowledgment as she went about her business.

Riker and Shelby headed down the corridor and into a turbolift. Waiting until the door had slid shut and they had privacy, Riker turned to Shelby and said, "Would you mind telling me what the hell is Doctor Selar's problem?"

"Problem? Oh," she said as if just realizing, "the mood swings."

"Is that what those were? It's not Bendii, is it?

"No. Pregnancy. And when the father is a slightly flighty Hermat, with whom the doctor has formed a close psychic bond due to their intimacy which has permeated her entire personality, well . . ."

"Wait a minute. She's pregnant?"

"Yes."

"But the father is a Hermat?"

"That's right."

"Hermats . . . that race that has both male and female—"

"Correct again."

"And they've formed a psychic bond because . . . ?"

"Of reasons too complicated and, frankly, delicate to go into."

"I'm afraid that's not good enough."

She had looked amused at the situation up until that point. But now she studied Riker as if he were a single-celled organism under a microscope and said, "I'm afraid it's more than good enough. I remind you, Commander, that Captain Calhoun is in charge of this vessel, and not you. You are simply a visitor . . . a refugee, if you will. Captain Calhoun obviously feels that Doctor Selar is capable of carrying out her duties. His judgment is not only to be respected, but particularly in your case, it's not to be second-guessed. Do I make myself clear, Commander?"

"Commander," and he folded his arms across his broad chest, "I am not about to try and undercut a CO. But by the same token, I will speak my mind where I see fit."

"You do that. And of course, if you wish to show us the best way to go about running a ship, you can just head back to the ship that you're commanding . . . oh! Wait!" She slapped her forehead with her open palm as if she had just recalled something fairly crucial. "That's right. You don't have a command of your own. Do you? Perhaps the next time one is offered you, it would be in your best interests to take it, because sooner or later, they'll stop offering."

Riker said nothing, but he couldn't help but feel that the temperature in the turbolift had just dropped rather precipitously.

Calhoun glanced up as Riker and Shelby entered the captain's ready room. They walked in several feet, both stopped, smiled gamely in perfect unison, and stood at parade rest. He looked from one to the other.

"Have a tiff, did we?" he inquired.

"Simply a spirited discussion, sir," Shelby said. Riker nodded slightly in affirmation.

"Mm hmm." Believing that it would probably be wiser not to pursue it, he called out, "Bridge to Lefler. We're ready. Put the comm through."

When the face of the Starfleet officer calling them came on screen, no one could have been more surprised than Calhoun. He hadn't been expecting anyone in particular, and yet, despite that, this was the last person he was expecting.

One would not, however, have had any inkling of his astonishment from his voice. Instead, without blinking an eye, he said, "Admiral Nechayev. A pleasure as always. I wasn't expecting to hear from you. This business is a bit outside your normal purview, isn't it?"

Nechayev looked a bit older than when he'd last seen her. A little jowlier, a little grayer. He'd always been impressed how little the strains of her job seemed to weigh on her, but he had to assume that time caught up with everyone . . . even the Iron Woman of Starfleet. "My purview tends to expand as the need arises," she said drily. "Commander Riker, it's good to see you hale and whole. Your loss would have been a terrible blow to the public relations plans for the bicentennial."

Riker bowed slightly at the waist. "I appreciate your concern, Admiral."

"There's humanitarian concerns as well, of course, plus Starfleet's interest in the money they've invested in you as an officer . . . but those worries would likely be outside my purview, and I wouldn't want to tempt Captain Calhoun's wrath."

Calhoun noticed Shelby hiding a smile behind her hand, but he chose not to comment on it.

Quickly becoming all-business, Nechayev said, "And how is Captain Garfield?"

"I believe Commander Riker was the last one to speak with him." Calhoun half-turned in his chair and looked to Riker.

Riker nodded briskly. "If anything, I'd say he's somewhat in shock."

"If he weren't, I'd think there's something wrong with him. Poor George. A good man. He, and his crew, deserved better than this." She shook her head, a grim expression on her face. Then she continued, "A transport is under way, Captain, as promised. You will leave Thallonian space and proceed to Deep Space 4, where you will discharge your passengers. And you, captain, will join them."

There was a brief moment of unspoken confusion in the ready room. "I'm sorry . . . say again, Admiral?" said Calhoun. "I'm joining them on Deep Space 4?"

"That is correct."

"And the *Excalibur* is to remain on station for how long?"

"She is not to wait for you. I will be meeting with you on DS4, to discuss a matter of some urgency. The *Excalibur* is to return immediately to Thallonian space and continue the investigation of this Romulan attack. We've put our best people on it, and they've come up with one or two possibilities: Either it was random chance that the Romulans intercepted the *Independence* where they did, or else there's a secret Romulan stronghold somewhere in Thallonian space."

"Thank heavens we had the best minds in Starfleet to come up with that," Shelby commented. The remark was, of course, not lost on Calhoun. He knew perfectly well that Shelby had come to the exact same conclusions all on her own. It was probably Elizabeth's greatest curse, he decided, to feel that she was consistently undervalued as an officer. Not only was she hungry for her own command and feeling thwarted that she hadn't received it yet, but he knew that she still felt a certain degree of "exile" in her current post as second-in-command to Calhoun. She believed she was ready for a command of her own, and truth to tell, so did Calhoun. That didn't stop him from valuing her contributions and presence as first officer. There was probably no one else in Starfleet whose advice Calhoun would readily listen to, even though he frequently gave Shelby the impression that he was hardly attending to anything she said.

"Either way," Nechayev was saying, "we want the *Excalibur* to look into the matter and see what you can discern either way."

"How long will I be away from her?" Calhoun asked.

"Impossible to say at this point."

But Calhoun wasn't really listening to what she was saying. Instead he was attending to what she wasn't saying . . . and it spoke volumes.

Some years earlier, Calhoun had departed Starfleet under rather acrimonious circumstances. It had been Nechayev who had seen a potential waste of material and had drafted Calhoun to work freelance for The Division of Starfleet Intelligence, that she oversaw. Her connection to SI was not widely known. She had other, more prominent and promoted duties to which she attended, most of which simply served as cover for her SI responsibilities. After all, it wouldn't do for any communiqué from Nechayev's office to immediately carry with it a likelihood that there was something going on with Starfleet Intelligence. Notoriety is counterproductive to secrecy.

But Calhoun, who had done a number of jobs for her on "his own," knew all too well. He also knew that DS4 was an outpost station for SI, another fact that was neatly hidden from the public at large. If Nechayev was meeting him there, it was because she wanted to assign him to something. He wasn't especially sanguine about it, considering those days long behind him. But he was also aware that if Nechayev had targeted him for an SI assignment, then there had to be a pretty damned good reason. She wouldn't be removing him as captain merely on a whim. He trusted her judgment that much, at least. Still . . . he was beginning to wonder whether this might actually be a precursor to an extended departure from the *Excalibur,* or even a permanent loss of command as Starfleet arbitrarily decided that his talents could better be served elsewhere than the bridge of a starship.

As if reading his mind—which he was convinced Nechayev was actually capable, on occasion, of doing—Nechayev smiled and added, "Don't worry, captain. It won't be indefinite. Simply a matter that needs to be attended to. You'll be back with your ship as soon as possible."

"Very well." Although his next remark was addressed to Nechayev, he was looking at Shelby when he said it. "I have every confidence that the *Excalibur* will be in good hands during my absence." Shelby inclined her head slightly in response as if to say, *Thank you.*

"As are we," Nechayev said. "Commander Riker has proven his capability time and again, and we are certain he won't disappoint us this time, either."

The words hung there. Of everyone in the room, it was Riker who seemed the most astounded. "Admiral . . . I assumed that I would be departing on DS4, to head back for the bicentennial . . ."

"Never assume, Commander. It makes an ass of 'u' and 'me.' Well . . . not of me, in this case, but you get the idea. Did they never teach you that at the Academy?"

"Yes, they did, but I . . ."

"The simple fact, Commander, is that we're taking advantage of your presence there. You not only have more experience with Romulans than does Commander Shelby, but you're certainly the most familiar with the operative named Sela. You know how she thinks, how she plans . . . you can likely second-guess her strategies. You will receive a field promotion to 'captain' for the duration of your stay aboard the *Excalibur,* and assume command as soon as Captain Calhoun has departed."

"But Admiral, I . . ." He glanced at Shelby, whose face was a mask, and said, "it's my belief that Commander Shelby is perfectly capable . . ."

"That is my belief as well. But I believe you to be more so, and intend to exploit that. Commander Riker," and there was just a hint of warning in her voice, "are you turning down a command . . . *again?"*

There was a momentary silence, and then Riker drew himself up and said crisply, "No, ma'am."

"I'm glad to hear it. Captain Calhoun, I shall see you shortly. Captain Riker . . . good luck and good hunting. And if you have any difficulties, I know we can count on Commander Shelby to give you full back-up."

"Absolutely, ma'am," Shelby said without hesitation.

"Starfleet out."

No one said anything for a time, and then Calhoun said, "Commander . . . I'm sorry, *Captain* . . . Riker . . . since apparently you'll be here for a time, I suggest you go down to ship's stores and obtain some things you might need, considering that whatever possessions you were travelling with were blown up. Some off-duty clothing, toothbrush, that sort of thing. I'll have Miss Lefler give you a more detailed tour of the ship at your earliest convenience, and introduce you to some of the key personnel. We're a rather . . . relaxed group around here. I'm sure you'll fit right in."

"I'm sure I will, sir."

"Dismissed."

Riker turned and left. Shelby didn't even glance after him. Instead her gaze was focused on the now-blank screen that Nechayev had been on moments later.

"Are you going to be all right, Elizabeth?" he asked with as much genuine concern as he could get into his voice.

"Not . . . immediately. In a while, perhaps . . . but not immediately."

She stopped talking and simply stood there, still staring at the screen. She didn't seem to show any inclination to leave, but she appeared so seized with contained rage that she couldn't quite figure out the best way to move.

Calhoun picked up the remaining green ball. "In point of fact," he said slowly, "it was Nechayev who gave me these . . . well . . . this. Would you care to . . . ?" He extended the ball to her.

She took it from him, stared at it for a moment. Then, her face twisted into a picture of silent fury, she cocked her arm, and let fly.

The ball struck the monitor screen, ricocheted back, and Shelby had to duck to avoid being struck in the head. The ball bounced back from the far wall and landed squarely in Calhoun's hand.

Slowly Calhoun stood up from behind his desk and stared down at Shelby, who sat, shaking her head. "I actually assumed you were simply going to squeeze it. But, as the lady said, never assume." He waited for response and, when he didn't get one immediately, ventured to add, "Not your day, is it, Eppy."

"Not my lifetime, Mac. Not my lifetime."

V.

The pubs of Argelius II were reputed to have the absolutely best dancers in the entire quadrant, and it was there that Zolon Darg had journeyed as part of what had become his eternal quest. He was looking for a dancer who would expunge the memories of . . . her.

After all this time, the recollection of Vandelia still remained with him. When he closed his eyes, he could see the curves and lines of her body. He could see her breasts upthrust. He could see the saucy smile, the come-hither look in her eyes, the temptation and raw sex that radiated from her body with the clarity of light from a star. And most important of all, he could see his hands at her throat, strangling her for the way that she had turned on him, tricked him, brought down his entire operation in flames around his head. Her and that friend of hers, that "Mac."

Darg had many friends and a long reach, but Vandelia was still just one person, and it was a big galaxy with lots of places to hide if one was so inclined. She had probably changed her name, perhaps even left the quadrant entirely. Who knew for sure? If she'd taken it into her head, she might even have booked passage on a ship and gone through the Bajoran wormhole into the Delta quadrant to explore new territories and possibilities there. Who knew? Who cared?

He cared. She was a dangling loose end that he hoped he would one day be able to tie off, and he would do so by tying it off around her neck.

In the meantime, this dancer that he was now watching was a pleasant enough diversion.

She was not Orion, by any means. Her skin was milky white, for starters, and her long black hair managed to tantalizingly cover her bare breasts at all times. It was somewhat amazing, really. She went by the name of Kat'leen, and her gyrating body was a joy to behold. Her stomach was remarkably muscled, and her legs seemed to go on forever. She kept time in her dance with small finger cymbals, and an enthusiastic drummer pounded away nearby. Darg found himself unconsciously keeping time with a steady beat on the table.

He fingered the glass on the table and realized, with a distant disappointment, that it was empty. "Shunabo, get me another drink," he ordered to his second-in-command, and then came to the hazy recollection that Shunabo wasn't there, mostly due to the fact that—in a fit of pique—he had killed him. The action seemed rather harsh, in retrospect. Shunabo had served him well, and it was just remotely possible that he did not, in fact, deserve what had happened to him.

"Well . . . so what," Darg growled to no one after a moment's thought. " 'Deserve' has nothing to do with it. He was becoming full of himself. A danger. If a man's going to watch my back, I have to be sure he's not going to stick a knife in it. I don't need a man who's going to openly defy me." Whether, in fact, Shunabo had openly defied him was a bit fuzzy in Darg's mind. The drink wasn't helping to keep him clear.

Kat'leen's dance drew to its enticing climax, and then she sprawled on the floor, her legs drawn together, her arms spread wide, her hair once again strategically placed in such a way that Zolon Darg began to wonder if the damned stuff had a life of its own. All around him, lights were clicking on and off furiously on the table tops, which was the standard Argelius means of showing approval.

The one exception was a human over in the corner. A heavyset, gray-haired, mustached man, he was pounding on the table and whistling shrilly between his teeth. He had a large bottle of some liquid that appeared to be green positioned in front of him, and he had clearly been at it for a while. His raucous behavior drew glares from some of the more reserved patrons who liked everything "just so." Darg watched in amusement as the owner of the establishment approached the gray-haired gentleman and clearly, with some polite gestures, indicated that perhaps it was time he take his business elsewhere. With a growl and a burst of what was likely some sort of profanity—but spoken with such a thick terran accent of some sort that Darg couldn't even begin to comprehend it—the gray-haired man swayed out of the pub and into the street.

Darg promptly forgot about him, instead deciding that now would likely be the most opportune time to approach the young lady. Kat'leen was just in the process of drawing a type of shawl across her shoulders. Darg found it rather charming in a way. When she danced, it was with complete lack of inhibition as she practically basked in her sexuality. But now that the dance was over, she seemed almost shy. Not in a shrinking, frightened sort of way. Just a bit more . . . modest . . . than she had been.

"Yes?" she said, one eyebrow raised as Darg approached.

"You dance magnificently," he told her.

"Thank you." She seemed to be looking him up and down, trying to get a feeling for the type of man he was.

"I have two questions for you, if you don't mind."

"Not at all."

"First . . . have you ever heard of another dancer . . . an Orion girl . . . named Vandelia?"

"Not that I can recall," she said with a smile that seemed rather mischievous. "Why? Wasn't I enough dancer for you?"

"Oh, yes, you were superb. The second question is, Would you do me the honor of accompanying me for the rest of the evening?"

She sized him up once more, but before she could respond, another voice said, "She's mine."

Zolon Darg turned and looked up . . . and up. Darg was certainly no slouch in the height department with his massive build, but the individual confronting him was, incredibly, a head taller and also wider. He had one eye, having apparently lost the other in a fight . . . or, for all Darg knew, in a card game. His head was shaven, his nose crunched in so stylistically that it was difficult for Darg to tell whether he was an alien who normally sported a nose of that style, or whether an opponent had simply crushed it. His lips drew back in a sneer to reveal a neatly pointed double row of sharp teeth. This was not an individual who appeared likely to back down.

Then again, neither was Darg.

"Calm down, Cho," Kat'leen said to the behemoth, and then looked apologetically at Darg. "I'm sorry. Cho is a regular . . . customer. And he gets a bit possessive sometimes."

"I understand," Darg said calmly.

"So you also understand," Cho growled, "that you better back off."

"I will on one condition."

Cho was clearly puzzled. "Condition?"

"Yes. Condition. A simple enough word. I'm sure it's even in your vocabulary."

"What . . . condition."

"I will back off," Darg said calmly, "if you would be good enough to take a step or two back, bend over, and shove your own head up your own nether bodily orifice."

Kat'leen rubbed the bridge of her nose in obvious pain and took several steps back as if to try and get as clear of the area as possible. It was rather evident she didn't anticipate matters going particularly well in the next few minutes.

Cho digested Darg's requested stipulation for a few moments before fully grasping just what it was that Darg had said to him. Then, with an infuriated roar and no other warning, he came straight at Darg. He wielded no weapon. Apparently he didn't feel that he needed one.

Darg, on the other hand, was quite prepared. He extended the fingers of his right hand, and vicious-looking blades snapped out of the tips. Each of them wasn't more than an inch long, but it was not their length that was the main problem for Cho. Rather, it was the fact that Darg's hand moved so quickly that the word "blur" wouldn't even have begun to cover it. One moment his hand was at this side, the next it was across Cho's throat.

Reflexively, Cho grabbed at his throat, and seemed quite surprised when a thick red liquid began to seep from between his fingers, pumped through the gaping wound in his neck that Darg had just put there. Kat'leen looked from Cho to Darg and back again in confusion. She had blinked when the strike was made and had literally missed it because of that. So she didn't fully grasp what was happening at first. But when Cho sank to his knees, his hand still at his throat and an expression of total bewilderment spreading across his face, that was when Kat'leen understood.

"I believe you're now free for the evening," Darg told her calmly. The blades were still in evidence on his fingers, but they were tinted with red.

Kat'leen let out a shriek, and that was when Darg came to the realization that Cho might have been many things, but what he was most definitely not was friendless.

They started coming in from all sides, bruisers big and small, advancing on Darg. Darg, slightly impaired both by drink and by the headiness of a blood strike, wasn't quite sure where to look first.

Cho burbled something incomprehensible and then fell forward like a great tree, hitting the floor with such impact that the entire establishment shook. That was all that was needed for the attackers to converge on Darg at full bore. Darg readied himself for the attack, and couldn't help but wonder if perhaps, just perhaps, he might have gotten himself into a bit more trouble than he could reasonably handle this time.

Suddenly the man was next to him.

It was no one that Darg knew, no one that he had ever seen. It wasn't one of Darg's entourage, certainly. He'd made a point of leaving them behind for the evening, saying that he wanted some time alone. They had obediently given it to him, and it had seemed for a few moments there that the decision was going to cost him dearly. Not that he wasn't sure that he could have ultimately handled all comers.

The question was rapidly becoming moot, however, thanks to the newcomer. He appeared to be a human, but he wasn't particularly tall, not even all that impressive looking. But he seemed to exude a confidence, display a sort of pure magnetism and force of personality that could not be ignored. He had a neatly trimmed gray beard, and a head of silver hair that was smoothly combed back. His brow jutted forward a bit, and it was his eyes that were the most interesting to Darg. They seemed cold and pitiless. They were the eyes of a man who could easily kill you as soon as look at you. He was dressed mostly in black, and was sporting a long coat that seemed to whip around him like a cape whenever he moved.

In either hand, he was holding a disruptor. In a rather flamboyant gesture, he crisscrossed his arms in front of himself, putting the disruptors at odd angles to one another, and then he started shooting. He did so with such precision that Darg couldn't quite believe what he was seeing.

The instinct when a mob is bearing down upon one from all sides is to fire blindly into the midst of the crowd and try to take out as many as possible. But that wasn't the case with the newcomer. Instead he was targeting one person after another, blasting out precision strikes that were taking opponents in the shoulder or upper arm or thigh. They weren't even being knocked unconscious. They were simply being incapacitated.

"Not the most elegant of weapons," said the newcomer in what seemed an almost conversational tone. "Very restricted settings. There's 'kill' and 'kill some more.' One has to be precise if one doesn't feel like killing. Hold on, please." He fired again and another attacker went down.

The floor was now covered with moaning, groaning individuals who were clutching assorted parts of their bodies. Darg nodded, impressed with the marksmanship. Still, he felt the need to ask, "Why not just kill them all?"

"And leave a big mess for the owners to have to clean up? I'm a regular customer here. I don't need to get the owners mad at me. All right, let's go."

There were still some individuals on their feet, but they were slow to approach. It was hard to blame them, considering the substantial number of people who were scattered about, crying out in agony. No one seemed particularly interested in shoving their faces into the buzzsaw. In fact, a few were even looking down at Cho's unmoving body with what appeared to be grim assessment, as if trying to determine whether or not he was worth their risking their necks for.

One apparently decided that it was, and he tried to pull a weapon. But the silver-haired man moved so quickly that Darg didn't even see it. All he knew was that suddenly there was a man clutching his hand and screaming profanity, while his weapon lay on the floor. He made as if to move for the weapon with his other hand, but the silver-haired terror simply said, "I wouldn't." The wounded man froze.

"As I was saying: Let's go."

Darg glanced around. Kat'leen was nowhere in sight, apparently having ducked out when the trouble started. There didn't seem to be anything to be gained by remaining. "I couldn't agree more," Darg said readily. They moved out back-to-back, the silver-haired man covering their rear while Darg watched in front of them. Moments later they were out the door and halfway down the street, the silver-haired man holstering his disruptors with a brisk and slightly flashy twirl.

They put a couple more blocks between them and the place before they slowed down to a casual stroll. Around them were the sounds of music and laughter, people sauntering about and having a good time. Over just inside an alleyway, a couple was engaging in the galaxy's oldest pastime with lusty abandon. The silver-haired man modestly averted his eyes; Darg watched with unabashed glee for a few moments before turning his attention back to his unexpected companion.

He stopped walking and said, "What's your name?"

"Kwint," came the reply.

"Kwint. Do I know you?"

"Not to my knowledge. Well . . . good evening to you." He turned and started to walk away.

"Wait!" Darg looked at him with open skepticism. "Why did you help me just now? Because I could have handled them myself."

"I have no doubt that you could have."

"Then why?"

Kwint shrugged. "I didn't like the odds. One of you against all of them. Didn't seem right."

"What are you, some sort of hero?"

"No," laughed Kwint. "Just looking to enjoy myself. Get some relaxation."

"And you do that by getting into fights."

"Sometimes, if the mood takes me."

"And it doesn't matter to you what the fight was about?"

Kwint appeared genuinely puzzled. "Should it?"

"Shouldn't it?"

"I don't see why," Kwint said reasonably. "A fight is always between two sides, both of whom think they're right. Usually, they both are . . . from their point of view. So it really doesn't matter which side you take, because it's never really about who's right. It's about who wins."

"Yes. Yes it is." He paused. "You didn't ask my name."

"You didn't offer, I didn't ask. A man introduces himself or doesn't. Makes no difference to me."

"The name's Darg. Zolon Darg." He waited to see some flicker of recognition . . . and got it. "You've heard of me."

"Yes. I have. Weapons runner, correct?"

"Correct."

Kwint studied him skeptically. "I'd heard you were dead. That your operation crashed and burned some years back, and you went with it."

"Obviously not. Whereabout did you hear my name mentioned?"

"I worked with a fellow named Gazillo. Secondary distributor. Bought a shipment of Tolasian night slicers off you about five years back."

"Yesss . . . yes, Gazillo." He stroked his chin thoughtfully. "I heard Gazillo died ugly."

"He did. Because of me."

"You killed him?"

"No," sighed Kwint. "But he wanted to deal with some people who I knew were going to doublecross him. I tried to convince him of it. But he wouldn't listen to me, no matter what I said. He smelled money and lots of it. When he refused to pay attention to what I was telling him, I walked out on him. Within two days, his body turned up . . . or at least, what was still identifiable as his body. If I'd stuck with him, tried harder . . . hell, if I'd just shot and wounded him, prevented him from going to the rendezvous . . ." He closed his eyes for a moment as if reliving it, and then visibly shrugged it off. "Can't change the past. Well . . . good evening to you, Darg."

Once more he started to walk away, and Darg said, "You seem to be in quite a hurry to leave."

"You served my purpose," Kwint said matter-of-factly. "I saw an opportunity to even some odds . . . the opportunity is done . . . and I'm out to enjoy the rest of the evening. Unless, of course," he said, apparently struck by a sudden thought, "you intend to get into some more uneven fights. Then I suppose I could just follow you around, save myself some time. Not have to start from scratch every time."

"It's entirely possible." Darg had to admit it to himself: he liked this Kwint fellow. There was a remarkable devil-may-care attitude about him. In some ways, he very much mirrored Darg's own philosophies, but in others, he was clearly his own man. For one thing, Darg wouldn't have given a second thought to Gazillo's fate. If the man was fool enough to ignore sound advice, then he deserved what he got. But Kwint still regretted Gazillo's loss . . . while at the same time, showing an admirable lack of interest in such niceties as the righteous high ground. He was a cheerful combination of morality and immorality. In short, he was someone that Darg could very likely use.

Suddenly the loss of Shunabo seemed less unfortunate and more an instance of good timing.

He clapped a hand on Kwint's shoulder and said, "You know, Kwint. There's more to life than fights. Let us not forget that which Argelius is most renowned for. Why," and he lowered his voice conspiratorially, "I know a place around here . . . where the women are sooo . . ."

He didn't have to finish. Kwint promptly nodded eagerly and said, "I know the place."

And they headed off into the night.

VI.

"HELLO, MAC. Ready to have the fate of the entire Federation in your hands?"

Calhoun shrugged indifferently as he sat down opposite Nechayev in her office. From the corner of his eye, through the large viewing window in Nechayev's office, he caught a glimpse of the *Excalibur* just before she leaped into warp space and vanished. Calhoun had made a practice of being self-sufficient. When one witnessed as much death and destruction as he had, it seemed the best way to go about keeping one's head screwed on. And yet, as his ship hurtled away into warp, he had the feeling of someone cut off from their family.

Family. Is that what they had become to him? How very, very odd. It was not something he had remotely anticipated, for some reason.

"A shrug? I ask you a question like that, and a shrug is all I get?" There was an element of teasing in her voice, but there was an undercurrent to her tone that was deadly serious.

"My apologies, Admiral. It's just that . . . this came out of nowhere. I simply never expected to be back in this situation before."

"I know, Mac," she said earnestly, "and I wish I didn't have to put you in it. But I think you'll see that, when it comes down to options, you're our best shot."

"I suppose I should be flattered."

"Don't be. You may very well be sorry by the time this is done." She paused and then said, "You look well. Command has agreed with you."

"Well, command and I have had a few arguments along the way. But I think we've got mutual wrestling holds on each other by this point. So," and he leaned forward, attentive, "let's not dance around. What's happened. What's going on."

"Down to business. Good. You haven't changed. All right . . . we've received the findings from the Away team that the late *Independence* left behind at Daystrom Institute. It appears that whoever our friends are that attacked the place made off with the Omega 9."

"*No!*"

"You've heard of it, then."

"No."

She winced slightly. "Walked into that one, I suppose." She folded her hands on the desk. "The Omega 9 could easily be considered the next major breakthrough in computerization: a computer that enables its user to interface with its data base through pure thought alone."

"Thought? You mean like telepathy?"

"The brain sends out electrical impulses, Captain, just like any other machine. The only difference between the brain and a computer is that the brain is generally smaller, but the computer is faster and has more capacity. The Omega 9 is more than simply a computer. It's a gateway, if you will, that simplifies the communication of mind-to-computer. For all the sophistication that we've brought to computers throughout the centuries, one barrier has never been truly broken down. We still have to talk to the damned things, and the information that we draw out of it is only as good as the questions we put into it."

"And with the Omega 9, that's no longer necessary?"

"Correct," she nodded. She held up her palm. "The Omega 9 bypasses conventional speech. Instead the user simply puts his or her palm against an interface padd. Sensors, combined with Nannite technology, form a temporary bond between user and database so that the user is able to extract information literally with the speed of thought, and can also supply instructions to the computer in the same way. It's taken a long time to perfect the technology. In the initial stages, there was a tendency for the computer to flood its user with so much information that the human brain would simply collapse. Poor devils, those test subjects. They could barely think coherently at all after their exposure to the Omega 9. Eventually, we—"

"Made them into admirals?" suggested Calhoun.

Her eyes narrowed in her best "we are not amused" expression. As if he had not spoken, she said, "Eventually, we were able to help them recover their normal thinking process. But it was a near thing."

"And now the computer is gone."

"Yes. It's not as if the work is irretrievable. Daystrom has duplicate material at its main headquarters. But building another one would take time, and besides, that's only the tip of the iceberg.

"You see, the Daystrom raid was not an isolated incident. There have been a number of thefts in recent weeks, raids on various labs and such belonging to assorted members of the Federation. The common thread is that most of them have to do with some aspect of research on AI . . ."

"Artificial Intelligence," Calhoun said. Slowly his demeanor changed. He seemed harder-edged. There was something in his eyes that no one who had an affinity for breathing would want to see aimed at them. "All right. Go ahead," he said.

"So . . . there seems to be an excessive interest in artificial intelligence research, of which the Omega 9 might well be the most advanced. There has been one individual who has been spotted at the scene of several of them, however. An old friend of yours: Zolon Darg."

"Darg. You're joking."

"Do I look like I'm joking?" She punched in a code on her computer and Darg's picture appeared on it. It was clearly a picture taken by a hidden security camera somewhere. Apparently it was the last shot that particular camera had taken, because in the picture Darg was turning and pointing straight into the shot. No doubt a few seconds later, the observation camera had been blown to bits.

"No. No, I don't think you're joking at all." He couldn't take his eyes off Darg's massive form. Darg had hardly been a weakling when last they met, but he hadn't been the colossus that he was now. "There had been rumors that Darg had survived our encounter a few years ago, but I had no idea he'd gone this active again." He considered the implications of the news. "So Darg is behind these raids—"

"I didn't say he was behind them; merely that he's involved. We believe that the person who is actually behind them is this individual . . ."

A Thallonian whom Calhoun did not recognize appeared on the screen. It was an older individual, with yellowing beard and a surprisingly gentle look on his face.

"He is General Gerrid Thul. He's a Thallonian noble. We don't have any visual proof that he's connected directly to Darg. If he is, then he's been either too lucky or too clever to be caught on camera."

"Then why do you think he is connected?"

"Because the report came in from an intelligence officer who subsequently wound up dead."

"Dead." He frowned. "Who?"

"McNicol."

This prompted a gasp from Calhoun. "McNicol. He was good. He was damned good. He's dead? Are you sure?"

"There was barely enough left of him for a genetic trace, but yes, he's dead."

The news caused Calhoun to look even more intently at the image of General Thul which sat on the screen. He could almost imagine a look of contempt in Thul's expression. Whatever it was that Thul was playing at, a personal face had suddenly been attached to it: the face of Jack McNicol, a dedicated and clever agent who had paid the ultimate price in his pursuit of keeping the Federation safe.

Nechayev, for her part, didn't seem to be giving McNicol any further thought. It was as if she needed to move on to the next crisis immediately. "Thul has had a rather rocky career. He was imprisoned for a while on charges of treason and attempted murder, but served his time and was released. At the tail end of his tenure in prison, he managed to convince the powers that be that he was a changed man. It's possible he is . . ."

"People don't change."

"You did," she pointed out.

He fixed a gaze on her. "No, I didn't. At heart, I am as I always was. I've simply gotten better at covering it, that's all. Watch . . ."

And just like that, he seemed to relax his guard. Nechayev looked into his eyes, and there was a world of hurt and anger and cold, calculating fury, all warring for dominance behind those eerie purple eyes.

Then, just as easily, he "veiled" his eyes once more. They went to half-lidded, and he seemed so relaxed that he might have been mistaken for a sleeping man . . . or possibly a corpse.

"You see?" he said softly. "It's all still there. M'k'n'zy of Calhoun, the warrior, the slayer of Danteri, the liberator of the planet Xenex. The barbarian who had no place in Starfleet. I keep him locked away . . . for when I might need him. So . . . my point remains. People don't change."

"I could still endeavor to argue that, but I don't see the need right now," she said diplomatically. "You see, in this instance, I happen to agree with you. I don't think he's changed either. From what we were able to gather from McNicol before he was lost to us, Thul has some sort of personal grudge against the Federation. McNicol was a bit unclear on it, and didn't have the opportunity to clarify it before he died. But apparently someone dear to Thul died under unfortunate circumstances which he blames the Federation for."

"And is he right to do so?" asked Calhoun. "Was the Federation responsible for the death of this individual?"

"Considering that the whole of the Federation, every world with sentient races, certainly wouldn't deserve to suffer if that were the case, do you really think it matters?"

"It might. To him."

"And does it to you?"

Once again that veiled look passed over his eyes. He didn't answer, but instead simply said, "What do you want me to do, Admiral?"

She bobbed her head slightly, as if acknowledging Calhoun's having skipped over a potentially problematic part of the conversation. "Despite his being an outspoken critic of the Federation in the past, Thul has now positioned himself as a supporter of the UFP since the thawing of relations between the Thallonian Empire and the UFP. He's got a good deal of personal charm; he's managed to make some rather high-placed friends. And that means I can't use my normal channels of support in investigating this. You're uniquely qualified for this situation, Mac. You've had more experience with Thallonians than anyone else in the Fleet." She paused and glanced at her computer screen. "There's going to be a reception in San Francisco to launch a week's worth of festivities in connection with the bicentennial . . ."

"The one Riker was supposed to attend."

"Precisely. Thul is going to be there; he's on the guest list. I've arranged with Admiral Wattanbe—who shares my concerns—that you will be there as well. I want you to get close to Thul, find out what he's up to . . . and once you do . . . stop him."

"You're forgetting something, Admiral: There's the matter of Zolon Darg. Even if I do manage to work myself close in with Thul, sooner or later I'll be face-to-face with Darg. He'll recognize me. Perhaps I should go in some sort of disguise . . ."

"Thul's too cautious. If his plans, whatever they are, are coming to fruition, he might not be so quick to welcome a complete stranger into his ranks. But you have a reputation as a maverick, Mac. You've had a publicized 'falling out' with Starfleet before. Dissatisfaction and a willingness to break the rules will be believable coming from you. The fortunate thing is, if you do run into Darg, he has no reason to assume that you were working with SI or had any Starfleet or UFP agenda."

"Meaning I can always pretend I was acting in a freelance capacity for a rival, so that he won't automatically assume that my presence now is part of a covert operation."

"Precisely."

"That's all well and good as far as it goes. But even as a 'freelancer,' I did happen to blow his operation to hell and gone. He might be the sort who carries a grudge."

"Perhaps. But I have every confidence that you'll be able to handle him."

"I'm flattered."

"Report to research and development, two decks down, room 18. The

Professor will provide you with some specialized tools and weaponry that might be of use to you."

"It's starting to seem just like old times, Admiral. Of course, we're both a little older . . ."

"But probably no wiser, else I wouldn't be sending you into this." She sighed. "Mac . . . be careful. I'd hate to lose you."

"I'd hate to be lost," he replied, and as he started to walk out, he stopped at her door, turned and said, "By the way . . . I'll want my vehicle. And this time I'll want to keep it, rather than returning it to SI. Signed over to me, so no matter what happens in the future, it will go with me rather than being part of Starfleet equipment."

"That shuttle isn't your property, Captain."

"That's somewhat the point, Admiral. I want it. Think of it as an incentive bonus."

"Think of yourself," replied Nechayev, "as a Starfleet officer who does what he's told."

"I've tried that. It doesn't work."

They locked gazes . . . and then Nechayev fought to hide a smile as she said, "Fine. I'll put through the paperwork."

"Thank you, Admiral."

"In all probability," Nechayev added, "the entire question will be moot, since you'll probably wind up dead as a result of this mission."

"So you win either way."

"Well," and she shrugged, "being an Admiral does have its perks."

The room was empty. Calhoun checked the markings just outside to make certain that he'd come to the right place. There were some counters, table tops, a few cabinets. But nothing was laid out, and there didn't appear to be anyone around. "Hello?" Calhoun called out. And when no reply seemed forthcoming, he called once more, *"Hello?"*

"You don't have to shout. I'm not deaf."

Calhoun turned and looked in utter confusion at the man standing behind him. He could have sworn that there had been no one else there, but this fellow had simply seemed to show up out of nowhere. He was wearing a Starfleet uniform. He had a somewhat long face, and dark, curly hair, but the thing that Calhoun noticed the most about him was the singular air of arrogance that hung thick around him.

"I didn't see you here," Calhoun said. "Are you the Professor?"

The man looked at Calhoun oddly. "Why do you want to know?" he asked.

"I'm here to get weapons. That sort of thing."

"The survival of Galactic civilization is hinging upon you, you know," the presumed Professor told him. He spoke in a rather strange manner, as if he were lecturing from a very great distance.

"So I've heard."

"Perhaps you have, but I don't think you yet fully appreciate the magnitude." He shook his head, seemingly amused with himself. "I must admit to being somewhat intrigued to see where it all winds up, providing humanity—and the rest of the Federation—is allowed to continue through to its natural conclusion rather than an aborted one. That would be something to see."

"I couldn't agree more," Calhoun said, deciding it'd be best to humor him. "So . . . what have you got?"

"Well, there's some interesting things here. There's also some things that can be improved upon." He started opening cabinets and pulling out an assortment of materials, looking each thing over and inspecting it closely. "The trick is going to be enabling you to avoid whatever weapons detection devices they might have. But such devices are only as good as their programming. That is to say, if they don't know what to look for, they won't find it. Here."

He held up what appeared to be a tooth, but when he tilted it, Calhoun could see that it was hollowed out inside. "Here. Slip this over one of your molars." Calhoun did as he was told, and then the Professor said, "Now press the back of it with your tongue."

He did so, and to his surprise, three identical replicas of himself appeared around him. They did not simply mirror him, however. Instead each one moved and reacted in its own, individual manner.

"Portable holo-generator. It generates hard-light holograms, just as you have in holodecks. So not only can they serve as distractions, but you also triple your manpower in one shot. Push it again with the back of your tongue to shut it off."

Calhoun did so, and then the Professor handed him a scar. Calhoun took it and stared down at it. It was an exact replica of the scar on his face.

"It's an explosive," said the Professor. "Hide the weapon in plain sight."

"Am I risking blowing my head off?"

"Not at all. Nothing can set it off as long as the circuit isn't completed. You simply take the two ends and twist them around each other. That engages it, and the chemicals inside it begin to interact and build toward detonation. Once the chemical reaction has begun, there's no stopping it. You'll have about fifteen minutes to clear the area before it blows."

Calhoun held the scar gingerly. "Oookay," he said slowly. He lined it up with the scar on his face and pressed it against it. He heard a small hiss of air and a seal was promptly engaged, adhering the fake scar to his face. The metal of the cabinet was highly polished, and he was able to see in his reflection that the blend was perfect. If he himself had not known, he wouldn't have been able to tell.

"This is almost standard issue by this point," said the professor. He extended a fairly nondescript ring which contained a round emblem at one end. "Push it firmly against someone's skin, and it injects a subcutaneous transponder which sends out a homing signal. You'll be able to track anyone."

"Convenient. No woman will dare brush me off again."

The professor didn't seem amused. "Now . . . this next thing is a pip."

"What is it?"

"It's a pip." And sure enough, he held up what appeared to be a standard-issue pip that indicated rank. "If you're not in uniform, you can still easily attach it to a collar or other article of clothing."

"What's significant about it?"

"Put it on." When Calhoun had done so, the Professor said, "Now say, 'Activate transporter, right.' "

"Activate transporter, right," Calhoun said, wondering why he was doing so. Then, to his astonishment, he suddenly heard a familiar hum around him . . . and an instant later, he was standing on the other side of the room.

"Short range personal transport device. Moves you ten feet in whichever direction you indicate you want it to go. Just be careful, though. You wouldn't want to move into the middle of a solid object."

"Definitely not." He studied the pip. "I didn't think Federation technology had anything like this."

"Officially, It doesn't. Now . . . here. You can probably use an offensive weapon as well. He produced from a cupboard a pair of boots that were exactly Calhoun's size. He turned them over and, from the right one, removed the heel. He proffered it to Calhoun for closer examination, and Calhoun immediately saw the small, tell-tale barrel of some sort of phaser weapon inserted neatly into the inner edge of the heel. "Squeeze the middle with thumb and forefinger top and bottom, that'll produce a stun blast. Squeeze in at the sides, that'll get you level two power. It will only respond to your DNA imprint, so you actually have to be holding it."

"You mean I don't have to worry about stepping down too hard and shooting myself in the foot."

"Something like that," said the Professor. "The left heel contains a communications device. I'll show you." He tapped the middle of the heel and a small, palm-size device slid out. He removed it and held it up. "Under normal circumstances it would only get you standard range, but I've improved it."

"Improved it . . . how?"

"Total security bypass."

"Total security bypass?"

"That's correct, yes. Plus its broadcast will piggyback on any other signals it detects giving it almost unlimited range."

"Oh really." He tapped the comm button and said, "Calhoun to Admiral Jellico, Starfleet headquarters, San Francisco. Come in please. Admiral . . . my men are under attack by a squad of berserk Amazon women and I can't get them to leave. Please advise."

He smiled wanly at the professor, and then the smile froze as back over the communicator came the unmistakable, and clearly irritated, voice of Admiral Jellico. "This is Jellico. Amazon women? Who the hell is this? Calhoun, is that—?"

Stunned, Calhoun said in a high-pitched voice, "Sorry," and shut down the line. Then he gaped at the professor.

There was no smile on the professor's face, not a hint of amusement or triumph. He simply stared at Calhoun impassively.

"That's very impressive," Calhoun said slowly.

The professor took a step toward him, and in a low voice tinged with warning, said, "Yes it is, isn't it? Apparently you have been selected to be the champion of the galaxy. I've decided to give you a slight edge. The rest is up to you."

Calhoun stared into those implacable eyes for a long moment. "Who are you?" he demanded.

"Me? I'm simply the fellow in research and development who hands out the weapons." With that, he turned and walked out the door. Calhoun quickly followed him out . . . but saw no sign of him.

VII.

"I WILL ATTEND TO IT, Captain Riker," Si Cwan said with confidence. The Thallonian noble made a few more notes as he looked across the desk of the captain's ready room at Riker. "I have certain . . . avenues . . . I can check. If there is a hidden Romulan base, I might very well be able to get some indication of where it is."

Seated next to him was Robin Lefler, who was also taking notes. In addition to her position at Ops, Robin had taken on the additional duty of personal aide to Si Cwan. Riker felt himself to be something of an aficionado of the ways in which the human heart moved, and as he watched Lefler try—perhaps a bit too hard—to be all business with Cwan, he had the funny feeling that there might be more motivating her than simply trying to be a good officer or find ways to fill the day. Then again, it wasn't really any of his business or his place to comment. So, rather wisely, he kept his opinions on the matter to himself.

"Do you want me to send out the messages?" Lefler asked him.

Si Cwan shook his head. "No . . . no, I think it'd be best if these came directly from me. Thank you for the offer, though."

"And thank you, Lord Cwan, for your assistance in this matter," Riker said.

" 'Lord' Cwan." He smiled slightly at the title.

"Did I miss a joke?"

"It's simply that I cannot recall the last time I was addressed with the title. Here on the *Excalibur,* they tend to address me simply by my name."

"And you tolerate that?" Riker asked in amusement.

He shrugged slightly. "I tolerate the familiarity. They, in turn, tolerate my presence. A philosophy of mutual tolerance, I suppose you'd say."

"I am rather pleased to hear it, Lord Cwan . . . particularly considering the rather incendiary nature of our last meeting."

"Incendiary" had hardly been the word for it, as Riker recalled. The first, and last time, that he had seen Si Cwan was right around the time that the Thallonian empire was beginning to crack apart. Si Cwan, exiled but still imperious, had sought out the Federation for aid, and Riker had been present at the meeting where that aid had been decided upon.

"I have not forgotten, Captain," Si Cwan said with a measure of respect in his voice, "your contribution to that meeting. You not only took my side in the discussion . . . but it was you who recommended the assignment of this vessel to Thallonian space. If not for you none of this would have been possible."

"Someone else might well have suggested it," Riker said, "but nonetheless, I appreciate the thanks. Although as I recall, your being posted to the ship was not part of the plan."

"There was a change of plan," Si Cwan said with a combination of dignity and deadpan.

"Yes, and he changed it," Lefler put in with a slightly teasing tone.

"I was invited by Captain Calhoun to serve as a sort of guide and lead diplomat in Thallonian space."

"After he was caught as a stowaway."

Si Cwan turned in his chair and looked at Lefler with something approaching disapproval. "In my opinion," he said slowly, "you are deriving far too much amusement from the situation." He turned back to Riker and said, "I admit, my arrival on this vessel was not the most . . . dignified. But I am here now, and there are no regrets." He fired Lefler a look. "Although I am beginning to have one or two in regards to certain personnel."

"This is all very interesting, and I would certainly like to hear all about it at some future date," Riker said readily. "However, at this point, I do have other matters to attend to . . ."

"And we shall be more than happy to allow you to attend to them, sir." Si Cwan rose, and seemed to keep rising. Riker was impressed, not for the first time, by the sheer presence of the man. He seemed someone who was genuinely entitled to be referred to by the term "noble." He bowed slightly, a gesture which the now-standing Riker returned, and then he turned and left. Lefler, however, remained where she was. "You told me earlier I should stay after the meeting?"

"Yes. There's a matter I wish to discuss with you. A matter regarding one of the bridge crew . . ."

"Shouldn't you be discussing it with Commander Shelby, sir?"

She had a perfectly valid point. In fact, Shelby was probably the person he should really be dealing with. The problem was, he wasn't entirely certain that Shelby would be anything other than defensive, no matter how diplomatically he tried to handle the matter.

He had no desire to say that, though. So instead he said coolly, "Actually, I thought it best to speak with you first since you work with him fairly closely."

"Ahhh." She sounded as if she knew precisely what was going to be said. "You're talking about McHenry."

"Yes. That's right. When you and Si Cwan came in here, I caught a glimpse of McHenry out the door and it appeared he was . . . well . . ."

"Sleeping. At his post."

He nodded. "Lieutenant, I admit I feel a bit like I'm walking on eggshells here." That was no exaggeration. Riker still remembered, all too clearly, the time that Admiral Jellico had taken command of the *Enterprise.* Despite the fact that the assignment was purely temporary, Jellico had wasted no time not only imposing his command style upon others, but going head to head with the senior staff in a manner that was unnecessarily harsh and certainly aggravating. At that time, Riker had made a solemn promise to himself that if he ever found himself in a similar position, for whatever reason, he would do everything he could not to disrupt the pre-established routines of the vessel. It was one thing when one was coming aboard as permanent commander, but Riker was not about to lose sight of the fact that he was a visitor. Still . . . when he saw something that so set his teeth on edge as a crewman displaying total lack of professionalism, he couldn't keep silent. Delicately, he continued, "I'm aware that Captain Calhoun's command style is somewhat different than mine . . . or Captain Picard's . . . or, in fact, anyone that I can think of offhand. Very much a 'live and let live' philosophy, a tendency to celebrate the little differences in people. And by all means, there is much to be said for that. But there is also such a thing," and his voice hardened, "as maintaining at the very least a bare minimum of acceptable preparedness. And having the helmsman asleep in his chair simply doesn't fit that criteria."

"He's not asleep," she said with the air of someone who was not explaining this for the first time. "It only seems that way. Actually he's just deep in thought, but he's completely attuned to everything that's going on. One hundred percent alert."

"I see."

"Also, I admit. . . . he's probably a bit worn out. I still don't think he's sleeping on the job. But his exhaustion is understandable. He's been through something of an emotional wringer."

"How so? Unless you feel it's none of my business."

"Well, sir . . . probably it's not your business, no." With that mandatory disclaimer out of the way, Lefler quickly and eagerly sat down, elbows propped on her knees.

Riker noted with quiet amusement that she was displaying one of the oldest mindsets of young humans, stretching back centuries: the slightly guilty joy of dishing gossip. No matter how advanced humanity became, no matter how many horizons were explored, no matter how many adventures were pursued, no matter how great and noble the race aspired to be . . . there was simply something irresistible about chattering about people behind their backs. Riker, the older, wiser, cooler head, was relieved that he himself was above such things . . . and then leaned forward so as not to miss anything.

"Okay," continued Lefler, "the fact is that for a while McHenry and Burgoyne 172 were quite the couple, if you catch my drift."

"Not really."

"Well, Burgoyne is a Hermat."

"Hmm. A Hermat." He understood why she said it that way. Not since the Deltans had there been a race whose sexual mores and practices had engendered more interest than the Hermats. He stroked his chin thoughtfully. "There aren't all that many in Starfleet. It's somewhat amazing that two were assigned to this vessel."

"Two?" The tops of her eyebrows knitted together in quiet surprise and confusion. "What two?"

"Well, the Hermat who is involved with McHenry, and the one who is involved with your CMO. At least, I was told the father . . . mother . . . whatever . . . that that individual is the father of Doctor Selar's child."

"Right. That's Burgoyne. Same person."

Riker stared at her. "The . . . *three* of them are involved . . ."

"No, no. You see . . . well, yes, kind of," and she started ticking off major elements on her fingers. "Burgoyne was interested in Selar. But Selar wasn't interested in Burgoyne. At least, she was trying to pretend that she wasn't interested, but she really was, but part of it was as a result of this whole Vulcan biological thing. They don't like to talk about. There's all kinds of different stories about it. It's a personal, private cultural thing and far be it from me to pry.

"Anyway, Selar apparently changed her mind, but Burgoyne was involved with McHenry by that point. So Selar approached the captain about 'accommodating' her. Apparently he said okay . . ."

"He said *what?"*

"He said okay. Apparently it was part of his Xenexian duty to be accommodating about something like that." At Riker's shocked expression, she quickly added, "It's a life or death situation."

"Apparently so." For some reason, Riker was suddenly relieved that Calhoun hadn't been in command of the *Enterprise* when Lwaxana Troi had shown up with a quadrupled sex drive. He was sure that Lwaxana would have convinced Calhoun that hers was a life and death situation as well. "You seem to be rather up on everything that's going on around the ship, Lieutenant."

"A starship is like a small town, Captain. Everybody hears everything. Fortunately enough," she said with a touch of irony, "there's some of us who work hard to make sure that accurate information is being disseminated."

"Bless you."

"Thanks," she said, with a grin. "Anyway, some other stuff happened, and Doctor Selar wound up with Burgoyne after all. Now she's pregnant."

"I see." He was intrigued in spite of himself. "And how does McHenry feel about all this?"

"Well, he was okay with it, but really stunned when he found out that Burgoyne was pregnant too."

"*What?*" He felt his head starting to spin.

"Yeah. At about the same time that Selar announced she was pregnant with Burgoyne's child, Burgy announced that s/he was pregnant with McHenry's child. Poor Mark. Passed right out. Fainted dead away. Since then, he's just thrown himself into his work. I don't think he knows quite how to approach Burgoyne about it. He feels embarrassed about fainting, I know that, and I sure don't think he was prepared for the notion of being a father."

"Well, he's going to have to deal with it sooner or later."

"I think he's angling for later, sir."

"Computer . . . service record of Burgoyne 172. I think," Riker said slowly, "that I very much want to meet Burgoy—." His voice trailed off as he stared at the screen, and his eyes widened. "Burgoyne is the *chief engineer?*"

"Yes, sir."

"Is this individual *stable* enough?"

"Oh yes," Lefler said cheerfully. "S/he's as stable as the rest of us."

Riker wasn't sure if that was a good thing or not.

They walked out of the Captain's ready room. Shelby was seated in the command chair, and made as if to stand up and give way to Riker, but he waved her off. "That won't be necessary, Commander. Presuming everything is calm here, Lieutenant Lefler is going to help familiarize me with the ship."

"As you wish . . . Captain."

There was just that moment of hesitation, and Riker wondered if something vaguely insubordinate was meant by it. But there was nothing about Shelby's attitude or deportment that seemed to indicate it, and Riker chalked it off to his imagination.

His gaze shifted to Mark McHenry. McHenry was exactly as Riker had seen him before. He was tilted back in his chair, his eyes closed. He wasn't snoring. He didn't even quite seem alive. No one else on the bridge, however, was taking notice of it.

Shelby noticed what had caught his attention, and she smiled slightly. "I went through the same thing," she said. "Trust me . . . it's fine. He's completely attuned to the ship. Check if you want."

Riker paused, wondering how one could possibly "check" such a thing. Then a thought occurred to him. He walked over to the tactical section of the bridge, quietly gesturing for the man on duty there to step aside. He did so and Riker glanced over the array. He tapped a control . . . and the ship's primary defense shields snapped on. There was no signal of an alert, although there was a slight rerouting of energy that was part of the natural defense systems process.

The effect on McHenry was instantaneous. He sat bolt upright, glancing at his board and looking at the main screen at the same time. "Are we under attack?" he asked.

Riker couldn't believe it. He looked to Shelby, who shrugged in a "told you so" manner.

"He'll do," Riker said after a moment, and then walked out of the bridge with Lefler right behind him, leaving a puzzled McHenry checking his readouts.

They walked briskly down the corridor, Lefler saying, "Ensign Beth down in engineering said that Burgy is down in the holodeck, working out. She checked with Burgy, though, who said we should feel perfectly free to come by."

" 'Burgy' is what you call him?"

"That's what everybody calls *hir*. Hermats have their own pronouns. 'Hir (H,I,R)' and 's/he.' "

He shook his head. "Hard to be—"

Then he stopped as a woman headed down the hall toward him. She was a dark-haired, older woman, with a rather aristocratic air about her. And she looked stunningly familiar.

"Hello, honey," she nodded to Robin.

Lefler kissed the woman lightly on the cheek. "Mom . . . this is Captain William Riker. He's in temporary command of the ship while Captain Calhoun is on another assignment. Captain, this is my mother, Morgan Lefler."

"An honor." She shook his hand firmly and then tilted her head in polite confusion. "Is something wrong, Captain?"

"It's just that . . ." He couldn't take his eyes off her. "You just . . . you remind me of the mother of someone else I know."

"It's entirely possible, I suppose. I have gotten around quite a bit."

"Mom's very long lived," Robin said cheerfully.

"Aren't they all," Riker said. He couldn't take his eyes off her. "I'm . . . sorry, Mrs. Lefler. It's just . . . the resemblance is uncanny."

"Yes, I'm sure it is. Well, you go on about your business; I'm sure you have far more important things to do than standing around, ogling me. I'll see you for dinner, Robin," and with that, she headed off down the hallway.

"Incredible," Riker said as he watched her go. "They could be twins. It's like looking at the same woman. Voice, attitude, everything."

"Captain—?"

He shook it off. "I'm sorry. I shouldn't allow myself to get distracted by things that probably don't mean anything."

They chatted about assorted other matters as they walked to the holodeck. When they arrived, Riker leaned close to the door, frowning. He could have sworn he heard something that sounded like . . . growling. "What is Burgoyne doing in there?" he asked.

"Let's find out." She tapped the control padd on the doors and they obediently slid open.

The sight that greeted them upon entering was a rather astounding one.

Burgoyne was dressed in a skintight workout suit, and s/he was surrounded by a forest environment. There was a vista of trees as far as the eye could see. The ground was uneven around them, with dirt and gravel that made traction difficult. At that moment, Burgoyne was perched in a tree, crouched on a branch, and s/he had hir mouth drawn back in a feline snarl like a cornered cat.

Below her was roaring a massive creature with thick white fur, leaping up at hir and swinging its clawed hands, trying to get a piece of hir and drag hir down from the branch.

"Lieutenant Commander Burgoyne," Lefler said, "this is—"

Burgoyne leaped from the branch, seeming not to have heard Lefler or even noticed her presence or that of Commander Riker. Hir speed carried hir between the outstretched arms of what looked to Riker like a white furred monster, and drove the creature flat onto its back. They rolled across the floor together, hissing and snarling at each other. Then the monster braced itself and twisted, hurling the lighter but more agile Burgoyne back. S/he landed on hir feet, and the way that s/he had her hands poised, s/he looked for all the world as if s/he had claws.

Riker had had enough. "Lieutenant Commander, I hate to break in on your exercise . . ."

And suddenly Burgoyne was flattened from behind.

What looked to Riker's surprised eyes like a white furred creature was atop hir, roaring its fury. Burgoyne twisted around within its grasp and grabbed it by either wrist. S/he managed to get the creature's hands from around hir throat, but apparently it was everything s/he could do to stop it from tearing hir to pieces.

"*Computer, freeze program!*" shouted Riker. Burgoyne, intent on hir opponent, didn't seem to hear him.

The creature was straddling Burgoyne, and appeared to be doing its level best to kill the struggling Hermat.

Believing there to be a holodeck malfunction, Riker didn't hesitate. He charged toward the creature and leaped onto its back. He braced himself, putting all his strength into trying to haul the monster off Burgoyne. It didn't seem to be paying any attention to him at all, focusing all its efforts on annihilating its chosen prey. For that matter, Riker wasn't entirely sure what he was going to do in the event that the monster actually noticed him, because the odds were that it could kill Riker without any great effort. But Riker was determined that he wasn't going down without a struggle.

He saw Lefler standing there . . . and she was shaking her head, looking more bemused than anything. He couldn't understand it. Here she was faced with a clear emergency, and she didn't seem to have a clue how to react. "*Security! Get security down here!*" Riker shouted.

"Commander," Lefler began, "this is—"

Burgoyne snarled, trying to fight back, but s/he seemed to be losing the struggle.

"*I gave you a direct order, dammit! Now follow it!*"

With a troubled frown, she tapped her comm badge. "Security, this is Lefler, in holodeck 4A. Get someone down here, fast." But there was absolutely no sense of urgency in her voice.

Is everyone around here insane? Riker wondered as he redoubled his efforts to haul the creature off Burgoyne. And if he did manage to accomplish that feat, his only hope then was that Burgoyne would recover quickly enough to aid him in subduing the creature. Or at the very least, they could hold out long enough for security to get there. And why was Lefler just standing around? Granted, she was rather slight in comparison to Riker and Burgoyne, but dammit, she could certainly find something to do besides just watching it happen.

The doors slid open and a walking land mass entered. The security guard took up the entirety of the door frame. When he moved, it was slow and ponderous. He had no neck, his head apparently attached directly to his shoulders, and his skin in the dim lighting of the holodeck looked like solid granite.

"Hi, Zak," said Robin.

"Hello. You called?" he rumbled.

Riker couldn't believe it. They genuinely *were* all insane. A security officer had just walked into the middle of what was clearly a life-and-death holodeck malfunction, and he didn't seem quite clear on what had to be done.

"*Stop this thing before it kills someone!*" shouted Riker.

The guard called Zak stood there for a moment, taking in the situation. He didn't move. Instead he spoke four words:

"Janos." Zak shouted, "Janos! Knock it off." Zak's loud voice almost shook the moon.

The white furred creature stopped in its tracks. Then, with a sigh, it stood fully upright rather than in the hunched position it had been using until that point. Riker was still hanging on its back, dumbfounded.

"Sir? If you don't mind?" asked the creature, and the question was clearly addressed to Riker. "Apparently, this exercise period is over." Riker, feeling as if sanity was slipping away from him, released his grip and dropped to the floor. Burgoyne, for hir part, was picking hirself off the floor and dusting hirself off.

Zak looked back to Lefler. "Anything else?"

"No, that should about do it."

He inclined his chest slightly, which was his equivalent of nodding, and then he turned and walked back out the door.

VIII.

Gerrid Thul was eminently pleased as he looked around the room of dead men.

That might not have been the most accurate of terms, he reasoned. Not all of them were men, for starters. A goodly number of males of the species were there, yes, but there was a vast array of females as well. All equally deserving, equally titled, equally dead. And to be absolutely, one hundred percent correct, he would have to admit that none of them were actually, in point of fact, dead.

Yet.

Never had the word "yet" been so delicious, held so much promise. Yet. Definitely, indisputably, yet.

As he walked through the grand reception hall that hosted the first of what was intended to be a number of gatherings celebrating the bicentennial, he couldn't help but be satisfied, and even amused, at the way that others within the Federation were reacting to him. There were nods, smiles, a polite wink or two. And many, ever so many requests for "just a few moments" of his time that invariably expanded into many minutes.

He had been careful, so very careful in making his contacts. And what had been so elegant about the entire matter was that those poor, benighted fools in the Federation had a tendency to side with the underdog. And that was something that Thul had very much seemed. A man who was once great, who had lost everything, and who was now trying to build himself back up to a position of strength and influence. He had come to people seemingly hat in hand, unprepossessing, undemanding. And he played, like a virtuoso, upon one of the fundamental truths of all sentient beings: Everyone liked to feel superior to someone else. It made them comfortable. It made them generous. And best of all, it made them sloppy and offered a situation that General Thul could capitalize upon.

Of course, Vara Syndra had helped.

"Where is Vara this fine evening?" assorted ambassadors and high muck-a-mucks in the Federation asked. But Thul had held her back, and not without reason. Best to build up anticipation, to get them to want to see her, ask about her, look around and try to catch a glimpse of her. Vara knew her place, though, and also knew that timing was everything. She would remain secreted away until the appropriate time had presented itself, and then he would send for her.

He had a feeling that the time was fast approaching.

"Thul! General Thul!" came a hearty voice that Thul recognized instantly. He turned to see Admiral Edward Jellico approaching.

He did not like Jellico. That, in and of itself, was nothing surprising; he didn't like any of them, really. But Jellico was a particularly pompous and officious representative of humanity. Thul hoped against hope that he might somehow actually be able to see Jellico when the death throes overtook him, but that didn't seem tremendously likely. He would have to settle for imagining it. Then again, Thul had a famously vivid imagination, so that probably wouldn't present too much of a difficulty.

"Edward!" returned Thul cheerfully, perfectly matching the pitch and enthusiasm of Jellico's own voice. He had to speak loudly to make himself heard over the noise and chatter of the packed ballroom. Furthermore, all around him the scents of various foods wafted toward him. Thul had a rather acute sense of smell, and the array was nearly overwhelming to him. Some seemed rather enticing while others nearly induced his gag reflex, so it was quite an effort to keep it all straight within him. "It is good to see you again, my friend."

"And you as well, General." He gestured to those who were accompanying them. One was another human, a tall and powerfully built human female. The other was a rather elegant-looking Vulcan with graying hair, and that annoying serenity that Vulcans seemed to carry with them at all times. "This is Admiral O'Shea," he said, pointing to the female, "and this is Ambassador Stonn. Admiral, Ambassador, General Thul of the Thallonian Empire."

"The late Thallonian Empire, I fear," said Thul. He bowed in O'Shea's direction, and then gave a flawless Vulcan salute to Stonn. "Peace and long life," he said.

"Live long and prosper," replied Stonn.

One of us will, thought Thul.

"I'm familiar with your good works, Thul," said O'Shea. "As I recall, you were working just last month to seek more humanitarian aid for refugees from Thallonian space."

"Actually," Thul told her, "I have been looking into expanding my efforts. You see, in exploring what needs to be done to help our own refugees, I have stumbled upon other races that could use aid as well. Aid . . . which is sometimes hampered by the Federation."

"Hampered? How so?" asked Stonn.

"It is . . . ironic that I would bring this up now," Thul said, looking quite apologetic. "We are, after all, here to celebrate the signing of the Resolution of Non-Interference, one of the keystone documents of the entire Federation."

"Yes. So?"

"So, Admiral O'Shea . . . it may be time to revisit the entire concept of the prime directive. All too often . . . and I truly do not wish to offend with my sentiments . . ."

"Please, General, say what you feel," Jellico urged him.

"Very well. It seems that, all too often, the intent of the prime directive is corrupted. The letter is followed when the spirit is violated." He noticed that several other people had overheard him and were now attending his words as well. Superb. The larger audience he had, the better he liked it. "The fact is that the prime directive was created specifically so that more advanced races would not *harm* less developed races. But too many times, we encounter situations where it is specifically cited as a reason not to *help* those races. Starfleet stands by, watches them fumble about, and simply takes down notes while observing from hidden posts. Think, my friends. Think, for example, of a small child," and his voice started to ache with imagined hurt, "a small boy, dying of a disease . . . the cure for which is held by those who look down from on high. But do they help? Do they produce a medication that will save him? No . . . no, my friends, they do not. They bloodlessly watch, and take down their notes, and perhaps they'll log the time of death. And who knows if that child might not have grown up to be the greatest man, inventor, thinker, philosopher, leader of that race. The man who could bring that race into a golden age, cut off . . . in his youth. What would it have hurt . . . to help that child? And what tremendous benefit might have been gained. Who among you could endorse such a scenario . . . and believe it to somehow serve a greater good?"

There was dead silence from those within earshot. Finally, Stonn said, "A very passionate observation, Thul. At its core, there may even be some valid points. However . . . interference invites abuse. It was an earthman who stated that power tends to corrupt . . . and absolute power corrupts absolutely. For all of the positive scenarios that you can spin, I am certain that I would easily be able to create plausible hypotheticals of abuse of that selfsame power."

"What Ambassador Stonn is saying," said Admiral O'Shea, "is that if the non-interference directive is, as you postulate, an error . . . isn't it better to err on the side of caution?"

"Two hundred years ago, perhaps. I will certainly grant you that. But of what use is experience if one does not learn from it," replied Thul. "There are people who need help and don't even know that they do. Besides, is not human history rife with such 'interference'? Were there not more advanced members of the human race who went to less-developed, undernourished or undereducated areas and brought them technology . . . advancement . . . even entire belief systems?"

"And in many instances did as much harm as good," Jellico said. "There was also conquest, to say nothing of entire races of people who were annihilated by germs and strains of diseases that their own immune systems were completely unequipped to handle."

"Ultimately, however," and Thul smiled, "things seem to have worked out for you."

"Yes, because we found our own way."

"Or perhaps in spite of finding your own way. Think, though. If older, wiser, more advanced races such as yours, and all those represented in this room were to use their experience, their knowledge of the mistakes that they themselves made to avoid mistakes in the future . . ." He shook his head. "Don't you see. But when there is want and need by other races who have never even heard of the Federation, and who could benefit so tremendously by the help . . ."

"You're saying that perhaps it's time to abolish or reframe the prime directive?" said Jellico.

"At this time? On the anniversary the signing of the document that was its genesis? Yes, that is exactly what I am saying."

There were thoughtful nods from all around, like a sea of bobbing heads. Finally it was Jellico who said, "You may . . . have some valid points there, General. Obviously I can't speak on behalf of Starfleet, and certainly not the Federation . . . but perhaps some serious study should be done as to whether it's time to rethink our intentions and perhaps expand upon—"

"You hypocrite."

The voice had come completely unexpectedly, and the words were slightly slurred. As one, everyone within earshot turned and saw the rather remarkable sight of a Starfleet captain, holding a drink and glaring at Admiral Jellico with as open a glare of contempt as Thul had ever seen.

"You are some piece of work, Admiral. You are really, truly, some piece of work." He took another sip of the blue liquid that was swirling about in his glass.

Thul couldn't quite believe the change that had come over Jellico's face. He had gone from thoughtful to darkly furious, practically in the space of a heartbeat. "Captain Calhoun . . . may I ask what you're doing here?"

"Listening to you reverse yourself," replied Captain Calhoun. "The number of times I've had to listen to you pontificate and talk about the sanctity of the prime directive . . . of how unbreakable the first, greatest law of Starfleet is . . . and how you've used that selfsame law to second-guess and denounce some of my most important decisions. But now here you are, all dressed up at this extremely important gathering," and he added exaggerated emphasis to the last three words, "and this . . . person . . ." and he waved in a vague manner at Thul, ". . . suggests the exact same thing that I've been saying for years now . . . and suddenly you're ready to listen. You act like this is the first time you've heard it."

"Perhaps General Thul simply has a way of expressing his concerns that is superior to the belligerent tone you usually adopt, Captain," said Jellico. Quickly he said to the others around him, "General, Ambassador Stonn, Admiral O'Shea . . . I'm terribly sorry about this. I'm not entirely certain what this officer is doing here . . ."

"I'm here because I was ordered to be here," Calhoun said. A number of other guests were noticing the ruckus, which wasn't difficult since Calhoun's voice was carrying.

"That's strange. My office should have received a memo on that," Jellico said, his eyes narrowing with suspicion.

"Really. Perhaps someone simply forgot. Or perhaps you were too busy getting ready for this little get-together that you didn't have a chance to stay current with your memos. Look, Admiral," and Calhoun swayed ever so slightly. Thul could tell that this rather odd individual had clearly had a bit too much to drink. "Make no mistake. I'd rather be on my ship. But I was ordered to be here because I'm supposed to be representing the Federation's interests in Thallonian space. One of the new frontiers that we brave individuals are exploring and protecting. Here's to us," and he knocked back more of the drink, leaving about a third of it in the glass.

"Of course," said Thul in slow realization. "Captain Calhoun . . . of the *Excalibur.* Am I correct?"

"Correct."

"I am very aware of your vessel's humanitarian mission. It is also my understanding that Lord Si Cwan is among the personnel of your brave ship. I met him once, when he was a very small child. I doubt he would remember me."

"Captain Calhoun was just leaving," said Jellico, "weren't you, Captain?"

"Oh, was I?" Calhoun smiled lopsidedly. "But Admiral, this is a party. Why are you so anxious to have me leave?"

"Captain," O'Shea spoke up, "I'm well aware that you have some . . . issues . . . with Admiral Jellico. But I submit that this is neither the time nor the place . . ."

"Or perhaps it's the perfect time and place," Calhoun shot back. Thul quickly began to reassess his opinion. Calhoun wasn't a bit drunk. He was seriously drunk. Not in such a way that he was going to fall over, but certainly whatever inhibitions he might have about speaking the truth were gone. "The fact is that the good Admiral here has had it out for me for years now. Just because he got it into his head that I was some sort of super officer, and then I didn't live up to the place that he'd set for me. I saved his life, you know," he said in an offhand manner to Thul. "This man would be standing here dead if not for me."

"And because of that, I protected you as long as I could," Jellico said, his body stiffening. "But you're the one who allowed the *Grissom* incident to get to you, Calhoun. Accidents happen, bad things happen to good people. True leaders manage to rise above that."

"And leave their consciences behind?"

"I didn't say that. Look, Calhoun," said Jellico, his ire clearly beginning to rise, "you said you're here because you were ordered to be here. If you're actually obeying orders, it's going to be the first time that I can recall in ages . . . perhaps ever. That being the case, here's another order: Get the hell out of here before you embarrass yourself further, if that's possible."

"Gentlemen," Stonn said, "perhaps you might wish to take this conversation into a private area . . ."

It seemed to Thul that, at that point, everyone in the place was watching them. He also saw several men dressed in UFP security garb threading their way through the crowd.

"I'm sure he'd like that," Calhoun said. "That's how his kind best operates: in the dark, in private, alone, like any fungus."

"*That's enough,*" said Jellico, the veins on his temples clearly throbbing.

"You sway with the wind, Jellico," said Calhoun. "To your superiors and your pals, you say what you think they want to hear. And to the rest of us, you step on us like we're bugs. That's all we are to you. And you can't stand me because I actually stood up to you. Stood up! That's an understatement. I flattened you. I flattened him," Calhoun said to O'Shea. "One punch. I resigned from Starfleet, he tried to get in my way, I warned him, and one punch, I took him down."

"It was not one punch." Jellico looked around, clearly embarrassed. "Not one punch."

"It was. One shot to the side of the head, and you went down on your ass, right after you grabbed my arm . . ."

"All right, that's it. Security!" called Jellico . . .

. . . and he grabbed Calhoun by the arm.

Calhoun's smile went wolfish, and to Thul it seemed as if all the inebriation, all the fuzziness about the man, dissolved in a second. Whatever the man might have had to drink, he was able to shunt it aside in a split second. His fist whipped around with no hesitation, and caught Jellico squarely in the side of the head. Jellico went down amidst gasps from everyone surrounding him.

"That will suffice," said Ambassador Stonn, stepping between Jellico and Calhoun. At that moment, despite the superior strength of the Vulcan, Thul would not have wanted to place bets on just who would win an altercation between the Vulcan and Calhoun.

But Calhoun didn't display the least interest in fighting off Stonn. Instead he simply grinned and said, "See? Told you. One punch."

"Get out of here!" Jellico said, rubbing his head. His eyes weren't focused on anything; Thul could practically hear Jellico's head ringing right from where he was standing.

Calhoun seemed to be enjoying Jellico's disorientation immensely. "One-Punch Jellico, they should call you. That's all it takes," Calhoun called. "That's all it takes to puncture a pompous windbag."

O'Shea helped Jellico to his feet, asking after his health solicitously, but it didn't seem as if Jellico even heard her. Instead, across the room that had now become completely hushed, Jellico shouted, "I'll have your rank for this, Calhoun! Do you hear me? This is the last straw! I don't care who your friends are! I don't care what you've accomplished! I don't care if Picard backs you up! I don't care if the words, 'Calhoun is my favorite captain' appears on the wall at Starfleet headquarters in flaming letters twelve feet high! You are gone! You are finished! Do you hear? Finished!"

"I hear you, Admiral!" called Calhoun as he stormed out of the room. "And I heard you when you said it years ago! And I came back, didn't I? I keep coming back!" He turned and walked out of the room.

"Not this time, Calhoun! Not this time!" Jellico shouted after him.

There was a long silence after Calhoun left from the room. Jellico was flushed red in the face, clearly utterly chagrined at the turn of events. "You've nothing to be embarrassed about, Admiral," said Thul consolingly. "Obviously he was a madman."

"I could tell you horror stories, General, I really could," said Jellico. "Mackenzie Calhoun represents . . . I'm sorry, I should say 'represented' . . . everything that's wrong with the 'cowboy' breed of captain. No respect for rules or for authority. No respect for the chain of command. No . . ."

"No respect, period?" offered Thul.

"Yes. Yes, that's exactly right. He left the fleet once before . . . went freelance . . . did dirty work for whomever would pay him. The only reason he was brought back into the fleet was because he had well-placed supporters, but after this debacle, even they won't back him. Believe me, we're stronger without him."

"And he certainly seems to have no love for Starfleet . . . or even perhaps the Federation," Thul said slowly.

"The Mackenzie Calhouns of this world love only themselves and care about their own skins, and that's all. We were speaking of abuse of power before, General? He's exactly the type that the prime directive was created to ride herd on. Good riddance to him, I say." Jellico rubbed the side of his face. "Let him be someone else's problem."

"Excellent idea," said General Thul. "A most excellent idea."

Mackenzie Calhoun sat at curbside outside the great hall. From within, he could hear the music and voices building up to their previous levels.

He shook out his hand and squeezed it into a fist. It hurt. That was very annoying. His hand shouldn't be hurting. And it seemed to him that Jellico had fallen much faster, and bounced much harder, when he'd struck him years earlier.

"I hope I'm not losing my punch," he said to no one.

"I hope not, too," came a sultry voice, indicating that he had not quite been speaking to no one as he had previously thought.

He turned and looked up.

She was, quite simply, the most beautiful Thallonian woman he had ever seen. She had absolutely no hair, except for two delicate eyebrows that were carefully sculpted. Her neck was long and elegant, her bosom in perfect proportion to her hips. Her legs seemed to go to somewhere up around her shoulders, and when she smiled it was incandescent.

Calhoun automatically rose to his feet.

"Hello," she said.

"Hi. I'm . . ." He thought for a moment, then recalled the information. "Mackenzie Calhoun."

"I'm Vara Syndra," she purred, displaying a remarkable facility for recalling her own name. "Gerrid Thul is interested in speaking with you."

"Will you be there?"

"Yes."

"Then so will I."

IX.

"APOLOGIZE, ENSIGN. RIGHT NOW. You too, Burgoyne."

They were in the conference lounge. It was Shelby who had just sternly addressed Burgoyne and Ensign Janos, while a somewhat chagrined-looking Robin Lefler looked on. Riker's face was expressionless. Janos had changed to the Starfleet uniform that he usually wore, albeit uncomfortably, when he was on duty.

"My apologies, Commander," Janos said sincerely. "When . . . exercising . . . my Hermat friend and I can get quite intense. We simply did not hear you call for the program to freeze. Then, when you attacked me, we thought you were joining us. Captain Calhoun does, on occasion."

"My apologies as well," Burgoyne put in.

"Well, then," Riker said, smiling, "a simple mistake. No hard feelings."

"Thank you, sir," Janos said. "But . . . permission to speak freely?"

"Of course," Riker said.

"I am aware that my appearance can be quite startling, even frightening, to those unprepared for it."

"All right," Riker suddenly spoke up. His face was still inscrutable. "I see where you're going, and you're right. I shouldn't have made assumptions about you . . . even a 'hologram' of you, based solely on your physical appearance. We in Starfleet are supposed to be above the concept of making judgments based on surface impressions. Therefore, Janos . . . I apologize for jumping to the conclusion that you were a threat and not a Starfleet officer. Perhaps if you were wearing clothing . . ."

"I was, a white jumpsuit."

"I didn't notice. Again, my fault, I apologize."

"Thank you, Captain."

"Sir," Robin Leffer put in at that moment, "I apologize for not taking firmer control of the situation. I could have done what Zak did. I should have been more take-charge, instead of allowing myself to be carried away by the avalanche."

"Yes, you should have," Riker said. "Just try to be a little more aggressive in the future."

"Aggressive. Yes, sir."

"Well, that wraps that up," Riker said, smiling again. "Oh, one more thing. Burgoyne, I understand that you're pregnant. Is exercise of this nature a good idea?"

"Wait, wait a minute," Burgoyne said. "Where did you hear I was pregnant? I'm not pregnant."

Lefler looked utterly confused. "But you are, aren't you?"

"No, I'm not. I think I would know that."

"But . . . you told McHenry . . ."

"What, in sickbay the other day? That was a joke! He knew I was joking."

"Uh oh."

Now both Riker and Burgoyne was staring at Lefler. In unison, they said, "Uh oh?" Janos and Shelby looked at each other in confusion.

"Well . . . McHenry didn't know," said Lefler. "You weren't there when he came to, after he passed out."

"Yes, I know that. While he was unconscious, that's when I was called down to engineering. Worked the eighteen straight hours, as I said. When I finally got back to my quarters, though, there was a message from him. We got together and I let him know it wasn't true. That it was just intended to be a joke."

"You told him that?"

"Yes. A few hours ago."

"Uh oh."

"Why does she keep saying 'uh oh'?" Burgoyne asked Shelby. Shelby shook her head, not knowing the answer.

"Well . . . the thing is, you see . . . McHenry told me. And I sort of told, well . . ." She shifted in her seat, looking extremely uncomfortable.

"You just sort of told, well . . . who?"

Wincing as if she were preparing to duck back from a punch, she said, "Uh . . . everybody."

"*What?*"

"Yeah, I'm afraid so. How the hell was I supposed to know?" she said defensively.

"You mean everybody on the ship?"

"No, everybody in the quadrant," she shot back. "Yes, on the ship. And not really *everybody*. Just . . . a lot of people."

"Perfect. That's just perfect," moaned Burgoyne. "One casual remark, and suddenly . . ."

At that moment, the doors hissed open and Si Cwan entered.

"Excellent," said the Thallonian noble. "I'm glad you're all here."

"Ambassador, could this possibly wait . . . ?" asked Shelby.

"Narobi II."

Shelby and Riker exchanged looks. "Pardon?" asked Riker.

"I've received word from one of my sources that the Romulans are going to be attacking Narobi II. He's reasonably sure that it's the same pack that you're talking about. The Renegades we'd hoped they return to Romulus to help rebuild after the Dominion War."

Instantly everyone at the table was alert. "How does he know this?" Riker asked.

"He's the type of individual who makes it his business to know such things. In this instance, someone with whom he was connected apparently aided in repairs on one of the vessels that the *Independence* engaged in battle. And this individual happened to hear about one of the next intended targets."

"I'm not sure I like this. It's too pat," said Shelby.

"I agree," Riker said.

"Perhaps. Perhaps not," said Si Cwan. "When you deal with a large operation . . . and this apparently seems to fit that description . . . there's large numbers of people who let things slip. In any event, Captain, you wanted me to try and bring you information. If you're going to dismiss it out of hand, then why am I bothering?"

Slowly Riker nodded. It was, he thought, a valid enough point. "Narobi II. Tell me about it."

"It's a rather unique world in Thallonian space. It's populated entirely by a race who has converted itself into beings of a sort of living metal. They created ultra-durable bodies for themselves that last for hundreds of years. In essence, they've made themselves immortal. They are utterly peaceful, but fully capable of protecting themselves should they be under attack. I'm not entirely certain why the Romulans would choose to target them."

"Neither am I. But we can't afford to let the possibility go. Commander . . . set course for Narobi II."

"Aye, sir."

As they got up from the conference table, Si Cwan suddenly turned to Burgoyne and, to hir surprise, placed a hand on either side of hir face. "What are you—?" s/he began to say.

Si Cwan proceeded to utter a lengthy chant, the performance of which stopped everyone in their tracks. Cwan had a surprisingly melodious voice which floated up and down the register. It was so lovely that no one dared to interrupt as Cwan continued that way for about forty-five seconds, murmuring, chanting, and swaying back and forth slightly as he did so. Then he lowered his hands and smiled.

"What was that all about?" demanded Burgoyne.

"That," Si Cwan said in a booming voice, "was the ancient Thallonian prayer for a smooth and uncomplicated pregnancy, which can only be delivered by one of the Noble house upon an expectant mother. Congratulations, Burgoyne. May you have a child which brings glory to your name."

"I'm not pregnant," Burgoyne said testily, and s/he walked out of the conference room.

There was silence for a moment and then, non-plussed, Si Cwan decided, "Well . . . it's probably for the best. It's been a while, and I was out of practice. Instead of the pregnancy chant, I may have accidentally prayed for hir not to contract root rot."

"Smashing. So the odds of it being effective just went way up," said Janos cheerily.

I've got to get off this ship, thought Riker.

X.

Zolon Darg was rather pleased with the turnout.

The place that he had chosen for the rendezvous on Argelius was somewhat out of the way, well off the beaten track of most of the places of entertainment and merriment which drew in most of the tourists. Darg, for the get-together that he had been busily arranging, had selected a rather disreputable place which was in violation of at least three Argelian health codes.

He was also drawn by the name of the place: "Kara's," in commemoration of some hideous event which had occurred on Argelius nearly a century ago during which a number of women were slaughtered . . . rather nastily, at that.

Kwint was looking around with open curiosity. They had been out drinking much of the night, but Kwint didn't seem particularly daunted by the amount of alcohol they had been putting away. Zolon Darg was impressed by that. As a Thallonian, he was more than capable of imbibing considerable amounts of alcohol without displaying, or even feeling, the ill effects. Kwint was obviously just a human, yet he didn't seem to be displaying any ill effects at all. Darg wondered if one of Kwint's limbs wasn't actually hollow, enabling him to store vast quantities within.

There was a permanent layer of dirt on the walls of Kara's. Many of the chairs seemed rickety, and the tables weren't much better. There was a large mirror behind the bar. It was cracked. There were also signs that there had been a fight in the bar not too long ago. Darg wondered absently what had started it, who had won . . . and if anyone had actually survived.

Behind the bar, a surly Tellarite bartender named Gwix poured out drinks. Gwix wasn't the type of bartender one poured their heart out to . . . at least, not unless one was a masochist. Gwix had little patience for anything except serving the drinks, getting the money, and closing up for the night. Nonetheless, even Gwix was aware when Darg came in, and tilted his pig-like head in acknowledgment.

"Nice place," Kwint said at length. "Come here often?"

"Often enough."

"You want to tell me what's going on?"

"You'll find out soon enough. Come here." He moved around one of the tables and indicated that Kwint should sit. Kwint did so. Darg, however, continued to stand, and as he leaned on the back of one of the chairs, it was quickly evident why. Just leaning on it would have been enough to break it.

Darg seemed to be assessing Kwint for a long moment, stroking his chin thoughtfully. Finally he said, "You have a lot on the ball, Kwint. I've seen that tonight. First with the way that we met. Then we went to that gambling place, and you immediately nailed the guy who was trying to cheat us. Then we went to the brothel, and you immediately nailed—"

"What are you saying, Darg?" Kwint asked, cutting him off.

"I'm saying that I think you have potential in my organization. An organization that's only going to let larger." He glanced over Kwint's shoulder. "Ah. I see some of our guests have arrived."

They were filing in, one at a time, regarding each other with obvious distrust. Then again, that wasn't all that surprising. The dozen or so beings who had shown up at Kara's were not accustomed to trusting anyone or working together, for they were all from races who were outside of the Federation. Races who, for whatever reason, considered the alliance of the UFP to be suffocating to their own interests. There was an Orion . . . a Kreel . . . a Tan'gredi, all ooze and nictating membranes . . . a Capitano, growling deep in its chest, its eyeless face gazing around with its internal radar taking in the parameters of the room . . . an assortment of others.

"Thank you all for coming," Darg said once everyone was settled. He was all too aware of the suspicion that focused on him from every direction. That was perfectly fine. He could handle that. "Since this is a matter of some delicacy, I know that I can count on all of you for your discretion."

"We're not interested in your compliments or your kudos to our discretion, gun runner," said the Kreel. "We all have other matters to attend to. Say what you have to say."

Darg didn't reply immediately. He'd learned that some extended silence could often be more useful than simply leaping straight into discourse. So he allowed the quiet to hang there a short time before he said, "All of you have grudges and difficulties with the Federation. They, and the races that they represent, have stifled you, interfered with you, operated in manners that are contradictory to your interests. And I'm not speaking of you as individuals, of course—although that much is certainly true—but also for the races that you represent."

There was that slightly nauseating "slurping" sound that always preceded a Tan'gredi before it spoke. "Races do not operate as whole, Darg. There are always different factions. Some of my people—the radicals—speak of joining the Federation at some point."

"True enough," Darg said smoothly. "But let us say that I have contacted you—singled you out as individuals—because I thought that you would be most amenable to the cause I represent."

"What cause is that?" The Orion was idly stabbing the table top at which he was seated with his curved dagger.

"The cause that involves . . . a new time to come. A new era that we think of as the post-Federation era."

"Who is 'we'?" The Kreel, as quick-tempered as most of his type, clearly wasn't interested in vagueness. "And what exactly will make this era of yours 'post'? The Dominion war is over; the Federation is not going anywhere anytime soon."

"I . . . choose at this point not to focus on the specifics."

There was a skeptical groan.

"What I am here to tell you," continued Darg as if they had not made a sound, "is that there will come a time—soon—when the Federation will not be a consideration. At that point, it's going to be a whole new galaxy . . . and whoever has the greatest technology, the most formidable weapons, and the strongest allies . . . will come out on top. What we—those I represent—are seeking are those who are interested in buying into our vision."

" 'Buying in.' Here it comes," said the Kreel, sneering. "And what exactly does that entail?"

"One hundred thousand bars of gold-pressed latinum from each of you . . . on behalf of the races that you represent."

There was a roar of mixed laughter, disbelief, and outright contempt. Through it all, Darg simply stood there, taking it in, his face immobile, his manner patient. He acted as if he had all the time in the world.

"And if we don't buy in?" asked the Capitano in that remarkable voice that seemed to originate from somewhere in the ground beneath his feet.

"Then you will die."

It was not Darg who had spoken, however. It was Kwint. The attention promptly switched to him, and even Darg was clearly surprised to hear the relative newcomer speak so boldly.

"Is that a threat?" asked the Kreel quietly.

Kwint half-smiled and walked in a slow circle around the gathering. "If someone offered you safe haven from a supernova . . . and you displayed lack of interest . . . and that someone informed you that you were going to die . . . is that a threat? Or is that simply a prediction?"

"Does this human speak for you, Darg?" inquired the Orion. He had stopped sticking the knife into the table, his interest caught by the shift in the atmosphere.

Darg sized Kwint up for a long moment. In point of fact, he had told Kwint absolutely nothing about the plan. Kwint was speaking entirely from conjecture, bluff . . . and attitude. It was, however, an attitude that Darg found most intriguing. "He speaks for himself," Darg said slowly, "but I choose not to contradict him. Make of that what you will."

Apparently feeling that he'd been given a tacit endorsement to continue, Kwint promptly did so. "Yes . . . I am human, as you noted. And there have been any number of times in human history where people were offered an opportunity by those who had vision . . . and the will, drive and resources to bring that vision to life. At the time that these visionaries presented their views of things, there were always those who were skeptical or derisive. Who would gladly turn their back and walk away, not realizing that they were leaving greatness behind. Zolon Darg is connected to that vision. He has seen the dream. He sees a place where there is a galaxy that is unstifled by the rules of the Federation, striving ceaselessly to create a perfect realitv that exists only in the minds of those who have an interest in maintaining the status quo. You deserve to come into your own . . . and Zolon Darg, and those he represents, are the ones who bring you there."

There was silence for a long moment. And then the Kreel representative stepped forward and said, "I'm out."

"As am I," said the Orion, "although I'll have another drink first . . . if our generous host doesn't mind."

"Of course I don't mind," said Darg calmly, but his attention was focused on the Kreel. "My friend . . . I understand your concern. And I wish you well in your future endeavors."

He gripped the Kreel by the forearm and nodded firmly. The Kreel eyed him suspiciously, apparently tensing for Darg to make some sort of sudden move. But then Darg stepped away, nodded and said, "Good-bye," and then turned to the others. "I would ask you others to consider the matter a bit more carefully and deeply than our Kreel friend here."

As the Kreel headed out the door, the Capitano rumbled, "You have to at least meet us halfway here, Darg. At least give us some idea of just why you are so certain that you will be able to dispose of the Federation in such a—"

There was a sudden scream from just outside the bar. The voice and tone was unmistakable. It was the Kreel, and to say that he sounded in distress would have been to understate it.

There was a rush for the door. The only ones who didn't move in that direction were Zolon Darg and Kwint, the latter glancing at the former in silent query. Darg simply nodded and became extremely engrossed in studying his fingernails.

As the others peered out the door, there were gasps of disbelief, a number of profanities, several quick prayers offered up to respective gods, and the sound of the Tan'gredi becoming physically ill . . . although considering the somewhat disgusting noises they customarily made, it was admittedly hard to distinguish.

What they saw was the Kreel representative, collapsed on the ground and trying with all his might just to stand up. His skin had become a distinctive shade of green, and gaping pustules had opened up all along his body.

And then the Kreel slumped forward, hit the ground once more, and fell silent. His body twitched spasmodically, but that was all.

There was deathly silence in Kara's. Then Darg moved among them, handing out small rectangles with coordinates engraved in them. "If you are interested in learning more of what I've said . . . if you are interested in participating . . . and if," and he glanced at Kwint in acknowledgment, " . . . if you are someone of vision . . . then show up at these coordinates precisely five Federation Standard Days from today. We might as well use their units of time measurement," he added in amusement, "for as long as they're vaguely applicable."

"What did that to the Kreel?" the Tan'gredi burbled. "I've seen fast-acting poisons before, but—"

"That wasn't a poison . . . was it," said the Orion slowly. "That was some sort of . . . of virus. A disease. You gave it to him somehow. What was it? Have you passed it on to us somehow?"

"My dear fellows," Darg said soothingly, "I assure you that you are perfectly safe." And then he added, rather significantly, "for the time being. As Kwint stated, those supernovas can be rather vicious, and I would hate to see any or all of you incinerated."

The Capitano looked at the coordinates and growled, "I know this section of space. There's nothing at these coordinates. Nothing at all."

"There will be," Darg said with a small smile. "There will be."

And with that, Darg made it quite clear that the meeting was over. One by one, the assorted representatives departed, stepping rather gingerly around the remains of the Kreel. "Worry not," Darg said with remarkable cheer, "he'll be attended to shortly enough. I wouldn't advise getting too close for the time being, though." The representatives took care to attend to his advice.

"Well," Darg said once he and Kwint were alone. "That went about as well as could be expected."

"You suspected that someone was going to doubt you . . . to walk out . . . didn't you," said Kwint.

Darg shrugged. "There's always one. Frankly, I was hoping it would be the Kreel. Insufferable race." Then he regarded Kwint more closely. "You spoke out of turn."

"Yes, I did. I considered your proposal intriguing, and seeing skeptical and even disrespectful looks from those . . . individuals . . . was bothersome to me."

"And if something strikes you as bothersome, you feel an obligation to do something about it. Is that it?"

Kwint nodded slightly. "Something like that."

" 'Something like that.' I see." Darg looked Kwint up and down. "You know, Kwint . . . you have potential."

"Potential as what? You mentioned bringing me into your organization before . . ."

"Part of what I was doing during this meeting was keeping an eye on you. Trying to determine what one can expect of you. But you know . . . I'm still not sure. Your speaking up was not particularly wise on your part . . . but on the other hand, it took nerve. I suppose you simply felt you had to 'equalize' things once more."

"In a way."

" 'In a way' is another means of saying 'something like that.' Yes, Kwint, definite potential. If you seem worthwhile, you might definitely be in line for my number two man."

"Me?" Kwint looked like he couldn't believe it. "But we've only known each other for a few hours. Are you sure?"

"I work on instinct a good deal, Kwint. That's how I judge people, and most of the time, I'm right."

"What happened to your previous number two man?"

"I killed him."

"Oh." Kwint didn't seem to know what to say.

Darg, for his part, couldn't have cared less. "I said most of the time, I'm pretty reliable. Everyone has setbacks."

And suddenly his hand was on Kwint's chest, and he was lifting the smaller man up and slamming him against a wall. The pressure on Kwint's chest was such that, not only had the wind been knocked out of him, but he couldn't get any air into his lungs. He pulled in futility at Darg's immovable hand.

"Have a care," Darg said quite softly, "that you do not have a setback of your own." Then his hand opened wide and Kwint slid to the ground, coughing violently as he gulped down air. "Do we understand each other?"

Kwint nodded, still coughing.

"Now . . . you can attend to your first duty as a member of my organization." And he handed Kwint a large sack and a thick pair of gloves. Kwint, having managed to recover his breath, looked in confusion at Darg. Darg simply pointed in the direction of the remains of the Kreel. "Kindly clean that up. That is the first rule of my organization: We pick up after ourselves."

Kwint looked none too thrilled.

"Setbacks," Darg reminded him in a slightly singsong voice.

Kwint promptly did as he was told.

XI.

NICE NIGHT TO BE SEDUCED, thought Calhoun.

Indeed, it was a splendid night, one that seemed to be filled with promise. However, Calhoun couldn't be entirely sure just who was going to be seducing whom, or what precisely was going to be promised.

This "Vara Syndra" was unlike any woman he'd ever encountered. She was pure sex. Calhoun found it difficult to concentrate on the matter at hand, or even remember what the matter at hand was. But that wasn't what he needed to do at all. He had to stay focused, remember what his—

Grozit, look at those hips. The sway of them, and the arch of her back . . . the way she swivels when she walks . . .

He nearly had to slap himself across the face to try and bring himself back in line with what he was doing.

Vara Syndra was talking as she walked, and he came to the abrupt realization that he hadn't heard a word she said. At one point, though, she smiled at him in a way that seemed to indicate that she not only knew the effect she was having, but that she was accustomed to it. He wondered why she was suddenly so much further ahead of him, and suddenly noticed that he'd stopped walking. He was just standing there and admiring her.

Stop it. This isn't funny, he snarled at himself, and forced his feet to go back into motion. It was incredible to him that this female appeared to be an associate of General Thul. One wondered how in the world the man got any work done. Then again, she was certainly eminently capable of making slacking off appear to be the single greatest pastime known to man.

They had been strolling about, apparently aimlessly, for more than an hour. But now they had arrived in a section of San Francisco that had been restored to much of the late twentieth century architecture. It was an architecture which had made that city so unique before the massive earthquake and fire had practically levelled the place in the first half of the twenty-first century. Vara Syndra was guiding him to one of those townhouses. It had an old-world elegance and charm to it, but at the same time it also had an air of dark foreboding. Calhoun allowed the possibility that he might just be projecting his own concerns upon it. There was the further possibility that, when compared to the vision that was Vara Syndra, *everything* had an air of dark foreboding.

"In here," she said, stopping at the door and gesturing that Calhoun should precede her.

Calhoun had a fairly reliable sixth sense for danger. So if there was an ambush of some sort waiting inside, for whatever reason, he would likely have been alerted to it. Then again, considering how distracted he was by Vara Syndra, it was possible that an entire regiment of Danteri nationals, thirsting to avenge themselves against the fabled liberator of Xenex, were concealed within and Calhoun still wouldn't know the difference. Still, there was enough of the cautious and experienced warrior about him that he was prompted to say, as suavely as he could manage, "After you, Vara."

"How very gallant," she said, and entered without hesitation. Calhoun followed a moment later.

There wasn't a single Danteri, or other such soldier, in sight.

There was, however, a full-size portrait of Vara Syndra decorating the portico, and she was gloriously nude in it. She was also discreetly positioned, but still . . .

"Oh," said Vara Syndra in a teasing voice as she saw where his gaze was drawn. "That old thing. Do you really think it captures me?"

"I don't think a hundred big game hunters could adequately capture you," said Calhoun.

"Aren't you sweet." She ran a finger teasingly under his chin, and then sashayed up a long, winding flight of stairs. Calhoun took them two at a time.

At the top of the stairs she went through a door that Calhoun followed her through, which in turn led to a large suite of rooms. And seated rather comfortably in the elaborately furnished suite was General Thul. He was holding a drink, swirling the contents around casually, and he gestured to a cart nearby which had an assortment of beverages arrayed on it in assorted decanters. "Greetings, Captain Calhoun . . . or is it accurate to call you 'captain' anymore?"

"Simply 'Calhoun' will do for the time being."

"Really. Your friends, so I understand, address you as 'Mac.' I was hoping that we might become friends."

"Interesting that you should be aware of that. Been checking up on me, have you?"

"It wasn't all that difficult, Calhoun. After your rather unceremonious eviction from the gathering, you and your past 'antics' were very much the talk of the party for some time afterward."

"Indeed. I'm flattered."

"You needn't be. Much of it wasn't particularly complimentary. Still," and he stroked his yellowed beard thoughtfully, "even those who were less than flattering clearly had a measure of grudging respect for your . . . curious talents."

Calhoun said nothing.

"M'k'n'zy of Calhoun," continued General Thul. "A young Xenexian who watched his father beaten to death in the town square by Danteri oppressors, and was inspired by that incident to free his home world from Danteri rule. By the age of twenty, he had accomplished this rather remarkable feat, achieving the rank of warlord and becoming possibly the most admired man on his world. All of Xenex was at his feet, but he instead walked a different path at the behest of one Jean-Luc Picard. He joined Starfleet, developed a reputation as an independent thinker whose sheer bravery and resourcefulness got the job done, and then resigned after an incident that resulted in the death of his commanding officer aboard the *Grissom.* Spent a number of years doing whatever jobs he could for whomever he could before rejoining Starfleet and being assigned command of the *Excalibur,* presently on extended assignment to my dear Thallonian space. And now . . . ?" He waited, but Calhoun still said nothing. "Now . . . what, Calhoun?"

"I don't know," Calhoun admitted. "I wasn't expecting this to happen. Then again, in retrospect, I suppose it was inevitable. Starfleet and I have never exactly been a smooth fit."

"I've thought as much myself." General Thul rose from his chair and slowly walked in a circle around Calhoun. Calhoun, for his part, simply stood where he was, his hands draped behind his back. "I may be able to make use of a man like you."

"Give him my regards."

"Who?" Thul seemed momentarily puzzled.

"The man like me."

The confusion remained for a second longer, and then Thul allowed a smile. "Very witty. That was very witty, Calhoun."

"Not really. But my head's a bit foggy. Give me about three hours, I'll have reduced you to helpless giggles."

"What do you think of this one, Vara?" Thul said.

Vara had draped herself over a nearby chair. Calhoun suddenly found that it was all he could do not to jump out of his skin. "I think a good deal of him, General."

"So do I. Then again," and he returned to his seat, "caution is always to be preferred. These are, after all, dangerous times."

"Not for you, I'd think," said Calhoun. "General Thul, doer of good works. Darling of the Starfleet upper rank. What danger have you to fear?"

"Oh, I'd rather not speak of such things. After all, we wouldn't want to upset Vara. Would we, Vara?"

Vara Syndra fanned her face with her hand as if she were a southern belle fighting off an attack of the vapors. "I should certainly hope not," she said.

Every movement, every gesture she made, even the rising and falling of her chest as she breathed, was alluring to Calhoun. *I must be losing my mind. She must be doing something. But I have no idea what. Moreover, I don't care all that much, which is even more disturbing.* "What things," he forced himself back on track, "should we speak of, then."

Thul didn't answer immediately. Instead he strolled with slow, measured steps toward a skylight that provided a splendid view of the starlit sky. He stood under it and gazed heavenward. "I have a small matter that I need attended to. You may very well be just the man for the job, and it would fulfill an old debt."

"I see," Calhoun said neutrally.

"You see, I've recently managed to track down a certain individual who is a 'guest' of the Andorian government." The contempt was evident in his tone. "They're holding him on trumped-up charges of espionage."

"But certainly a well-connected individual such as yourself would be able to have him freed through the use of your considerable contacts."

"I have my friends, Calhoun, but make no mistake: My influence is not quite as wide and all-encompassing as you obviously think it is. Andorians, you see, are members of the United Federation of Planets, and the UFP will not involve itself in how member worlds conduct themselves. However," and now he turned back to face Calhoun, "I was hoping you might be able to aid this individual's . . . recovery."

"You want me to break him out of wherever it is the Andorians are holding him?"

"Nothing goes past you, I see, Calhoun. That's very comforting to know. You should be aware, though, that participation in this matter will likely be the end of your association with Starfleet, particularly if they learn of your involvement."

"That association doesn't appear too promising at the moment anyway," said Calhoun.

Thul openly scoffed. "You mean that business with Jellico? Calhoun, I have enough contacts to know that Jellico has not earned himself quite as many friends as he would like to think he has. There are some who would probably applaud that you struck him. Although serious black marks on your record might appear as a result of the incident, that wouldn't necessarily spell complete doom for your career. My mission, however, likely would. So the question is, do you worm your way back into Starfleet? Perhaps apologize to Jellico in the hopes of smoothing matters over? Or do you acknowledge where your talents would best be suited?"

"And when I accomplish this mission of yours . . . ?"

" 'When.' Not 'if.' 'When.' Very confident, aren't you."

"When it seems warranted. If I didn't go into risky situations confidently, I'd never come out of them."

"Very well . . . when you accomplish the mission . . . then you and I shall speak again. We shall speak of things of . . . great importance. So . . . what say you, Calhoun?"

Calhoun found himself staring at Vara Syndra once more. She wasn't even looking at him at that point. Instead, in rather leisurely fashion, she was trailing her fingers along the curve of her leg.

"What does the job pay?" asked Calhoun.

"A man after my own heart," Thul said with a smile. "What would you consider to be adequate compensation for your time?"

Calhoun looked at Vara. Vara looked at him. Thul looked at both of them, and his smile widened.

"Everything," he said, "is open to negotiation."

XII.

BURGOYNE BURST ONTO THE BRIDGE, which was an unusual enough event in and of itself since s/he didn't tend to hang about the bridge all that much. Even more unusual, s/he went straight to Shelby and stood in front of her, hands on hir hips. "May I speak with you, Commander?" s/he asked.

Shelby was a bit surprised at the urgency to Burgoyne's manner. Granted, s/he was one of the more flamboyant individuals aboard the ship, but s/he never displayed the sort of outright consternation that s/he was now showing. Also, Shelby couldn't help but notice that McHenry was making a determined effort not to look in Burgoyne's direction. The normally near-comatose helmsman suddenly seemed extremely interested in checking over his instrumentation.

Riker, who'd been standing next to Zak Kebron and going over tactical relays in preparation for possible battle, looked up in confusion. "Is there a problem, Burgoyne?" he asked.

"Nothing that Commander Shelby can't handle, sir."

Riker took a step down from the upper ring of the bridge. "Indulge me. What's the problem?"

"All right," Burgoyne said after a moment's consideration. "I want to know why I just got a reassignment."

"What?" Riker said, glancing at Shelby. Shelby shrugged, not knowing what Burgoyne was referring to. "Are you no longer chief engineer?"

"Oh, I'm still that, yes. But I've been rotated to a desk job. Instructed to remain in my office or work at the engineering station here on the bridge."

"But why . . . ?"

"I don't *know* why," said a clearly exasperated Burgoyne. "I got the message over my computer, and the computer simply said it was orders. I thought they were yours." Some of the ire was being replaced by simple confusion. "Because of . . . you know . . ."

"Payback, perhaps," suggested Riker. "For our little misunderstanding in the holodeck?"

"The thought did cross my mind."

"I don't operate that way, Lieutenant Commander. I had nothing to do with this reassignment."

"Lefler," Shelby called to Robin at ops, "run this one down, would you? See what's going on?"

It took Lefler only a few brief moments to track down the origin of the orders. "Captain Calhoun," she said, punching up the transfer records at her station. "It came from Captain Calhoun."

"*What?*" said a stunned Burgoyne.

"Hold on. There's a notation here . . . oh," Lefler said after another moment's checking. "According to his log, he was concerned about keeping you in engineering, in proximity to potentially high levels of radiation. Because of, well . . ." She cleared her throat. " . . . you know."

"No, I don't know."

"Because of you being pregnant."

"I'm *not pregnant.*" Burgoyne waved hir arms about in clear exasperation.

"Well, yes, but the captain didn't know that when he put in for the reassignment. Apparently he did it right before he left, and there hasn't been the opportunity to clear it up yet."

"Perfect," sighed Burgoyne. "Just perfect. Mark, tell them I'm not pregnant." When McHenry didn't answer immediately, Burgoyne repeated, "Mark?"

Shelby couldn't help but notice how strange McHenry's voice sounded when she spoke. Usually the most carefree-sounding of individuals, this time he came across as a bit stressed. "So you've told me, Lieutenant Commander. Then again, you also told me you were pregnant in the first place. I guess even in this high-speed age, it's hard to keep up."

Quickly Shelby stepped in. "I'll expunge the orders immediately, Burgoyne. Sorry for the confusion."

"That . . . would be appreciated, Commander," said Burgoyne, but s/he was looking with open curiosity at McHenry. "I hope I didn't come across as too belligerent."

"No, not at all."

"Mark," Burgoyne continued slowly, "is there something you wish to discuss?"

The entire bridge crew was watching, but McHenry didn't give any indication that he was aware of the scrutiny. If he was aware, he didn't seem to care. "No, Burgy. Nothing at all, thanks. If you'll excuse me . . . I'm kind of busy . . ."

Without missing a beat, Burgoyne turned to Shelby and said, "Commander, I have a few navigational issues that need to be attended to. May I borrow Mr. McHenry for a few minutes?"

"That sounds like it might not be a bad idea," Shelby said readily.

McHenry turned in his chair, looking slightly betrayed. "Commander . . ."

But Shelby simply said, "Go," and her tone of voice made quite clear that no dispute was going to be welcomed in the matter. With a heavy sigh, McHenry rose from his station and headed into the turbolift.

"Commander, a moment of your time, please," Riker suddenly said. Shelby frowned, because it was clear to her from his tone of voice that something was bothering him. She nodded and followed him into the ready room. Once they were inside, he didn't sit, but turned to face her and said, "I don't know if you've noticed, but there's a tendency among the crew to speak directly to you on all matters."

"No, I hadn't noticed," said Shelby.

"I doubt that, Commander, although perhaps you're just being too tactful to say so."

"I try not to let tact stand in the way of doing my job, sir."

"In that, you succeed admirably," Riker said dryly. "The point remains that I've been noticing it repeatedly, on all matters great and small. And it's something that you've been encouraging."

"Encouraging? You mean I've been answering questions and dealing with problems? Is that your definition of encouragement?"

"You could, on occasion, make a point of consulting me, instead of acting as if I'm not even on the bridge."

"Permission to speak freely, sir," Shelby said stiffly.

"If I said 'no,' would that stop you?"

"Probably not."

"Permission granted, then."

"This isn't about the crew, Captain. This is about your ego. You're the cock of the walk on the *Enterprise* and you feel that now, as captain here, you're entitled to get the same sort of treatment."

"What I am entitled to get, Commander," he said hotly, "is the respect that is due the rank."

"A rank you've made no effort to obtain. You've practically had to have it shoved down your throat," retorted Shelby. "Will Riker, the reluctant captain. How is anyone here supposed to take you seriously."

"You listen to me, Shelby," Riker shot back. "I've been through enough battles, through more life-and-death situations than you can even begin to count."

"Not with us. I've been here. You haven't. Besides, how do you expect this crew to warm to you? You make it clear that you think they're all vastly inferior to the *Enterprise* crew."

"I've done no such thing."

"Oh, please!" she rolled her eyes. "With gestures, with looks, with tone of voice. You make it clear just how second-rate you think this crew is. Well, I'll tell you something, 'Captain,' this is one of the best crews I've ever dealt with. And they deserve better than to be condescended to."

"Don't tell me you've never felt separate from this crew yourself, Commander," Riker said. "That you weren't accepted, that you didn't fit in, weren't respected . . ."

"I don't know what you're talking about."

"Your log clearly stated—"

"My log?" That stopped the conversation dead. "My log?" she said again. "I never said anything like that in my public log. Only my . . . personal log . . . when did you read my personal log?"

"It . . ." Riker suddenly looked a bit uncomfortable. Falling back on regs, he said, "Captains and chief medical officers reserve the right to review all records of their command staff."

"That doesn't give you the right to read my personal log." She felt her cheeks starting to flush.

"Actually, it does. I was trying to familiarize myself with this crew and with all the pertinent attitudes. If I'm going to be leading you into potentially hazardous situations, I want to know where everyone's mind is. So a few hours ago, I reviewed entries relevant to—"

"You bastard," said Shelby.

"Watch it, Commander," Riker said. "Speaking freely or no, you're pushing it. The bottom line is that you've had a serious attitude problem with me for years, and I can't be in a position of having to tolerate . . ."

"Position? What do you know of positions?" she demanded. "The only position you know is standing in the cooling shade of Jean-Luc Picard's shadow. What is it with you, anyway? Getting in behind him and staying put. What are you, just lazy?"

"Not that it's any of your damned business, *Commander,* but have you considered that, after the *Enterprise,* command of another ship might be something of a come-down?"

"Nice little theory . . . except the *Enterprise* you were aboard for over half a decade blew up. So what's the new excuse? Oh, I know, maybe it's the name. Or maybe it's just that Picard fills some sort of need in your life that you didn't get elsewhere. What is he, some sort of father figure that you've just attached yourself to and can't let go, no matter what, because you'll feel like you're abandoning him or something . . . ?"

Her voice trailed off as she saw Riker's face become more darkly furious than she'd ever seen. For a moment, just the briefest of moments, she actually thought he might haul off and belt her.

"At least I've been offered command of my own vessel," Riker said with barely contained rage. "Perhaps before you start analyzing *my* problems, you might want to turn that piercing vision of yours inward and see just why it is that you *haven't* been given the same opportunity."

Then, slowly, through sheer force of will, he composed himself. He drew himself up to his full height and, as if speaking from high on a mountain, he told her in a flat, even voice, "Until further notice, all decisions and matters that are put forward in my presence are to be addressed to me. I will not be treated as if I'm not there. Is that clear, Commander?"

"Crystal," said Shelby.

"Turbolift, all stop."

The turbolift that had been carrying McHenry and Burgoyne came to a halt in immediate compliance with Burgoyne's directive. McHenry looked around, mildly puzzled. "This is going to make it take much longer to get to engineering."

"Okay, Mark, what's going on?" Burgoyne faced him, arms folded across hir breast. "You've been avoiding me."

"No, I haven't."

"Yes, you have."

"No, I haven't."

"Yes, you . . ." S/he shook hir head. "This isn't getting us anywhere."

"Yes, it is."

"No, it isn't."

"Yes, it is."

"No, it . . . *nyarrrh!*" snarled Burgoyne. "Stop it! Just . . . stop it! You're trying to make me crazy!"

"How am I doing?"

In the question, in the attitude with which it was asked, there was a flicker of the puckishness that had always characterized McHenry in the past. Burgoyne was extremely relieved to see it, if only for an instant. "You're doing quite well," s/he admitted. "Mark . . . is this about Selar and me? Because you said you could take it in stride. Nothing fazed you, is what you said. You said you were happy for us."

"Yeah . . . I know."

"What, was that true?"

"It was when I said it."

"But now . . . ?"

He leaned back against the railing of the turbolift. "I don't know."

"What don't you know?" S/he put a gentle hand on his shoulder. "Mark, above everything else, we've always been able to communicate. I don't want to lose that."

"I'm just . . ." He sighed heavily. "Look . . . Burgy . . . the truth is that I'm not in touch with my feelings, okay? If you know anything about me, you should know that. There's just so many other things to think about, and wonder about . . . and if I have to start putting everything through the filter of how I 'feel' about it, I'll go kinda crazy. So I sort of like to live for the moment."

"All right. But it would be nice if, every once in a while, it was somebody else's moment as well. You do tend to go off into your own world, Mark . . . and it's hard for anyone to know what's going on in there."

"I know. It's . . ." He seemed to steady himself, and then the words all came out in a rush. "It's just that . . . I was very angry with you. There. I said it. Don't hate me."

"Hate you?" s/he said, bemused. "Why would I hate you? What were you angry about? Because I made a joke to see if I really could throw you off kilter, and it worked more than I could have hoped?"

"No, that's not it. It's that . . . well . . . after I came to, I had plenty of time to think about the whole idea before you wound up telling me it wasn't true. And during that time, I just . . . well . . . I got to like the idea. It seemed fun . . . and . . . I dunno . . . grounding, somehow. And that didn't seem to be such a bad thing . . . particularly the notion of having one with you, because you're so . . ."

"Maternal? Special? Intelligent?"

"I was going to say 'weird,' but those others apply too, I guess." He shook his head. "And you know me, I start thinking . . . and I just go off in my own world, and think of things, and I was building up this whole life together. I even had this whole weird family unit built up in my head, with you and Selar and that baby, and me and you and that baby, and maybe even the three of us working together . . ."

"Now *that* would be weird."

"I know. That's what I kind of liked about it. But that's not going to happen anymore. I mean, when it was just you and Selar and you guys having a baby, I had no trouble with that. I could handle that, accept it, even step aside. But for a while there, I just saw something different, and kind of liked it, and now it's gone, and I'm back to being an outsider again."

"Oh, Mark . . . you'll never be an outsider with me. You—"

"But I'll never be her," McHenry said with a sad smile. "I'll never be

Selar. I was always a second-place choice to her, I understood that. And I thought that was okay. And it should be. But for a while I . . . ohhhhh . . . never mind."

"Mark, you keep saying 'never mind' and shutting things off . . ."

"Yeah, I know. That's the way I am. I kind of like me that way."

"Do you?"

They looked at each other levelly for a moment that seemed to stretch out for quite some time. Finally he said firmly, "Yeah. I do. Turbolift, resume."

The turbolift promptly started up once again, and the two of them rode the rest of the way down to the engineering deck in silence. Burgoyne turned to McHenry. He didn't move. "I assume you didn't really need me down in engineering."

"No. Not really. But I do need you to be a friend—"

"Always. Well, I guess this is your stop then," he said a bit too quickly to sound sincere.

"I guess it is."

S/he disembarked, then started to say something to him, but he put up a finger to shush hir. "It's okay. Relationships are like turbolifts. Sometimes you just have to know when to get off."

"Yellow alert," Riker ordered. "All handles, battle stations."

As the *Excalibur* approached Narobi II, Riker stroked his chin as he contemplated the scene before him and came to two conclusions: First, Si Cwan's "tip" might have been groundless. And second, he really, really missed his beard.

"No Romulan vessels detected, sir," announced Zak Kebron from the tactical station. "But if they're cloaked, they're harder to pick up."

From the science post, science officer Soleta said, "Sensor scan to pick up emissions will take time."

"Understood," Riker said. "Proceed with scan. Hailing frequencies, Mr. Kebron?"

"Open, but we're not getting a response from Narobi."

"That could be a definite indicator of a problem," said Riker thoughtfully.

Abruptly Soleta looked up from her science station. "Two vessels with cloaking devices detected uncloaking, at 352 and 367 Mark 2."

She was absolutely correct. On the far side of the Narobi homeworld, two Romulan warbirds wavered into view.

"That," Shelby observed, "could be an even more definite indicator of a problem."

"Red alert. Shields up," Riker ordered crisply. "Weapons systems?"

"We are at weapons hot," Kebron said. "Good to go."

"Try to hail them. Warn them off." He leaned forward in the command chair, fingers interlaced, trying to determine what it was the Romulans were up to.

"Attempting to do so now, sir. No response. It is my belief that the warbirds are jamming transmissions from the planet."

"I suspected as much. Mr. McHenry, target both warbirds. Report on warbird readiness?"

"They are running weapons hot . . . but they are not targeting us, sir," said Kebron.

Riker turned to Soleta. "Can we confirm that?"

"Confirmed," Soleta said without hesitation. "They're ready to shoot if need be, but they're not doing so."

"Some sort of Romulan game," Riker said thoughtfully. "Trying to make us guess what they're up to."

"I don't like this," said Shelby.

"What's to like?" muttered Kebron.

"Bring us in slowly, Mr. McHenry," said Riker. "Let's get them to move off. I want them clear of that planet."

"Sir," Shelby said, turning to face Riker, "something's wrong here."

"Specify."

"They're just sitting there, as if they're daring us to get closer. Why would they do that?"

"Romulans are like cats, Commander. They like to arch their backs and hope that larger and more formidable enemies will be thrown by it," Riker told her confidently. "They have their weapons on line, but they won't target us because they know that'll provoke us into firing. They want to see if we'll hesitate to engage them. If we don't hesitate, if we don't show fear, they'll move off. If we do . . . they're that much more likely to attack. Except that most likely the ones they will attack will be the planet in an attempt to strong-arm us into surrendering. No hesitation, Commander, and no fear. It's all based on an old earth game called 'chicken.' "

"Captain, as much as I appreciate the assorted barnyard analogies, I maintain that something doesn't seem right. I suggest we hold our position. Make them come to us."

"I've had a lot more dealings with Romulans than you, commander, with all due respect," Riker said firmly. "I know how they operate."

"What if they've changed their method of operation?"

The eyes of the bridge crew were going back and forth, from Shelby to Riker and back, as if they were watching a tennis match. McHenry, meantime, operating on his last instructions, kept the starship moving forward.

"Sir, I'm telling you, they're up to something. I can feel it," Shelby said.

"And how would you suggest we find out just what it is they're 'up to,' Commander?" Riker tried to keep his voice even, but it was difficult to refrain from sarcasm.

"For what it's worth," offered McHenry, "we may be able to ask them face-to-face. At this course and speed, if they don't back down, we're going to collide with one of them in two minutes, ten seconds."

"It won't come to that," Riker said. "Even if they open fire, it won't be with anything our shields can't handle. We'll do far worse damage with return fire. They can't afford a pitched battle. They won't want to, either. It's not the Romulan way."

"Captain . . ." Shelby said, with clear exasperation in her voice.

But the more annoyed Shelby got, the calmer Riker felt. "Commander . . . we're not going to run from two Romulan vessels who don't even have us targeted. That would send a message that none of us wants to send. Understood?" he said in a tone that indicated no further discussion would be appreciated.

Shelby straightened up in her chair, moved her gaze solidly to the screen, and without looking at Riker, said, "Aye, sir."

The *Excalibur* drew closer, closer still. And still the Romulans weren't moving.

"Contact, one minute," McHenry said.

"Fire a warning shot across the lead ship's bow."

Kebron promptly did so, a phaser lancing out and narrowly missing the lead Romulan warbird's bow section. Still, the vessels didn't move.

"Attention Romulan vessels," Riker said firmly over the open hailing channels. "We are not turning off course, repeat, we are not turning off course. You are instructed to vacate the area immediately. If you do not, we will fire, repeat, we will fire. Reply."

"Sir!" Soleta informed him. "The ships are moving off. They are powering down their weapons."

McHenry, who was not particularly looking forward to the prospect of slamming the *Excalibur* into a Romulan warbird, let out an audible sigh of relief.

Riker turned to Shelby and said, "I would have to say that constitutes a reply, wouldn't you, Commander?" But Shelby said nothing in response. Riker could only chalk it up to being a poor sport. All-business, Riker turned to McHenry and said, "All right, Lieutenant . . . let's remember that the purpose of this is to track them to whatever base they may be operating from. They'll likely go into warp, and that's when we'll have to—"

And that was when McHenry's board shut down completely.

McHenry gaped at the sudden loss of his instrumentation. It wasn't as if he needed it, but nonetheless the fact that it had abruptly gone south was disconcerting. "Uhm, sir . . . we may have a problem . . ."

"Tactical systems down," Kebron announced.

"All sensors, all scanners down," Soleta said.

"Lefler, what the hell is going on with shipboard?" Riker demanded.

Lefler desperately tried to make sense of it, but the answer she was coming back with was virtually incomprehensible. Her fingers flew over the control padds, but nothing was coming back at her. "Sir . . ." she said with a tone of pure incredulity, "our computer's crashed."

"*What?*"

The entire bridge was promptly plunged into total blackness. The front viewing screen went blank. Moments later, the emergency lights came on, giving the ship's command center an eerie Halloween-esque glow. Riker was on his feet, leaning over Lefler's ops station. He couldn't believe it. "Our power is done . . . ?"

"Not a power loss, sir. Power's all still there. But the computer routes everything, unless we tell it otherwise," Lefler said. "The only thing that's functioning at the moment is the emergency life support system. That's a bottom line fail safe. But otherwise we're dead in space. No guidance systems, no weaponry, no shields . . . nothing!"

"Find a way to get us out of here," Riker ordered.

"Quick, let's crack out the oars," suggested McHenry.

"Stow it, lieutenant!" Shelby said, also out of her chair. "We have got zero time before the Romulans move in on us. Lefler, try to reroute via manual . . ."

Suddenly the air in the bridge began to shimmer, and an all-too-recognizable hum sounded within the confined area. And Riker knew, even before they materialized, what he was going to see.

A Romulan raiding party, fully armed and ready to annihilate anyone who opposed them, appeared dead center of the bridge. And standing foursquare in the front, with her finger on a trigger and a smirk on her face, was Sela.

"Hello, Will," she purred. "Miss me? Because this time, I won't miss you." And she aimed her phaser straight at his face.

XIII.

LODEC LOOKED AT HIS REFLECTION in the polished wall and barely recognized himself.

Naturally he still possessed the bronze skin that marked him as one of the Danteri race. But his hair was dirty and matted, his beard thick and scraggly. Oddly enough, it may have been that, even more than his imprisonment itself, that was the most depressing thing with which he had to contend. For Lodec had once been a soldier, and his training, his very essence, cried out for a neat and trim presentation to the world. Servitude, lack of freedom . . . these he could handle. But being reduced to looking like a slob? It was more than he should have had to bear.

Somehow, though, he suspected that those who were running the Andorian prison ship that he was being held upon weren't going to be sympathetic to his plight.

Lodec coughed again, but none of the other prisoners who were in the cramped barracks with him paid any attention. He felt a deep rattling about in his throat and would have been most grateful for some sort of medication to ease the congestion before it grew into something far worse. But nothing was forthcoming from the Andorians.

Gods, did he hate the Andorians.

The blue skin was almost hurtful to his eyes, it was so glaring. When they spoke, the Andorians did so in a sort of whisper that almost made them seem the most polite of races. But the ones who were running the vessel were among the most sadistic bastards that Lodec had ever had the opportunity of dealing with. They would deprive the prisoners of food for days on end, and when they did give them sustenance, it was so wretched that it became almost impossible to hold it down. In many instances it was, in fact, impossible, and the stench of the heaved food would hang in the air of the cells for ages until the hideously slow filtration system finally expunged them.

The worst thing of all was that there was really no need for the transportation of the prisoners to take so damned long. The transport was equipped with warp drive, and could easily have gotten to its destination within a few days. Instead, it was taking its own sweet time, proceeding mostly on impulse drive, utilizing warp only every so often when proceeding through areas of space where prolonged travel might result in jeopardy to the crew (since the crew didn't give a damn about the cargo). There were a couple of theories among the prisoners as to why it was taking so damned long. One was that the prison for which they were bound was overcrowded, and they were waiting either for prisoners aboard the transport or prisoners at the receiving end to die in order to free up space. Another theory was that it was simply part of the softening-up process. Prison officials didn't want to have to deal with prisoners who might have some fight left in them. So their spirits were battered and broken along the way, making them nice and malleable when they arrived.

And so one day stretched out into another for Lodec and the others who had been luckless enough to transgress against the Andorians.

He lay on his bunk in the cramped quarters that he shared with a number of other prisoners and murmured to himself, "This is not how my life was supposed to turn out."

Suddenly the door to the quarters slid open, the glare of light from the hallway outside nearly blinding as his eyes tried to adjust. Standing in the doorway was Macaskill, the transport commander who was exceptionally softspoken—even for an Andorian—and exceptionally ruthless—even for an Androian. He was an older Andorian, his skin a more pale blue than the others, but that made him no less deadly.

"I'm looking for volunteers," he whispered, so much so that Lodec had to strain to hear him. As the prisoners blinked to get the sleep from their eyes, Lodec glanced around and then pointed at several in rapid succession: "You," he said, "and you . . . and you. And you." And one of the ones he chose was Lodec.

Slowly, Lodec sat up. He rubbed at his wrists which, as always, had the electronic manacles secured to them. He let out a long, unsteady sigh, but knew better than to ask what was so important that they had to be rousted from bed at that time of night. He wasn't likely to get any sort of answer in any event, and far more likely that he'd simply get a major shock pounded through him. That was certainly not aggravation that he needed. Besides, when one got right down to it, what did it matter if he knew what was going on or not? He was still going to have to do what he was told anyway. His life was not his own, and had not been for some time.

Then, to his surprise, one of the other prisoners asked the very question that he hadn't seen fit to risk punishment over: "What's this all about?" It was a Pazinian, a very small and harmless-looking species, with a perpetually wistful look on its vaguely avian face. His voice was high-pitched and reedy.

To his even greater astonishment, Macaskill answered without hesitation. "We've come upon a small freighter in distress, and will be requiring your volunteered aid to unload its cargo," he said. "We are not in the salvage business, of course. But it turns out that the pilot's carrying a shipment of gold-pressed latinum. Naturally, in good conscience, we could not turn away from a sentient being in need."

"Or from the latinum?" asked the Pazinian.

"Naturally," Macaskill said. "That goes without saying." Macaskill then tapped a small control device on his wrist . . . and energy lanced through the Pazinian, his arms flying out to either side as if he'd been crucified. He let out a shriek and collapsed to the ground, quivering and spasming as Macaskill continued calmly, "On that basis, you probably should not have said it."

He then turned to another prisoner, pointed, and indicated that he should take the Pazinian's place. "The freighter is presently in our main bay. We're drafting you to help unload it. May I safely assume there will be no further questions?"

It was an eminently safe assumption. And as they filed out, Lodec couldn't help but wonder if the Pazinian had simply been that anxious to get out of helping with the shipment. It seemed a rather extreme thing to do just to get out of some work. On the other hand, as the Pazinian lay there insensate, Lodec mused upon the fact that at least the Pazinian had gotten to go back to sleep.

They trudged down to the main bay in silence, several Andorian guards falling into step alongside them. In point of fact, they weren't really needed. The manacles were more than enough to keep the prisoners from fighting back or even, absurdity of absurdities, escaping. But their presence helped to pile on the feeling of hopelessness. Talking was actively discouraged, under all circumstances. The Andorians had means of eavesdropping even when the prisoners were by themselves. The captors didn't want to take any chances that the captives might put together some sort of breakout strategy. Lodec tried at one point to stifle a loud yawn, but was unable to do so. This got him a fairly fierce scowl from one of the guards, but no further recriminations, and he considered himself extremely lucky.

They arrived in the main bay, and sure enough, there it was: A reasonably small freighter. There was nothing particularly impressive-looking about it. In fact, it seemed rather old and worn out, the hull distressed and pockmarked with years of service in the harsh vacuum of space. The obvious captain of the ship was standing just outside the main door of the freighter, engaged in what appeared to be a fairly animated discussion with one of the Andorian guards.

The freighter captain turned and looked at Lodec with what appeared to be bottomless purple eyes. In a heartbeat, Lodec knew the man was a Xenexian. Then he saw the scar that ran down the side of the man's face . . .

. . . and he knew exactly which Xenexian it was.

He had absolutely no idea how to react. He had heard many conflicting reports about the life of the rebel outlaw who had broken Xenex from the control of Danter. Lodec had never had the opportunity to come face to face in battle with M'k'n'zy of Calhoun, but he had certainly heard enough about him. Moreover, he had lost a number of friends to Calhoun's fabled sword, strength and resourcefulness.

Ostensibly, he had heard that Calhoun had then left Xenex once freedom was established and joined Starfleet. But his awareness of Calhoun had eroded over the years. There had been rumors that he had left Starfleet, that he had taken up an aimless, freelance life. It seemed a rather pathetic existence for one who had once been the warlord of Xenex and one of his people's greatest heroes. Lodec had always thought, though, that people such as M'k'n'zy were simply destructive types at their core. When they turned their destructive tendencies outward, they could accomplish amazing feats that left enemies stunned. But when they had no opponents before them, that selfsame destruction often wound up turning inward, and they would slowly diminish themselves until their greatness faded to nothing.

And now here was evidence that all that he had heard was true. The great M'k'n'zy of Calhoun, reduced to being a common freighter pilot. Probably an underhanded one at that, transporting gold-pressed latinum. For all Lodec knew, Calhoun was even in the process of stealing it.

Macaskill had stridden up to M'k'n'zy, and in his customarily soft voice, he said, "So . . . I understand your name is Calhoun."

Calhoun nodded. Obviously he wasn't going by an assumed name. How very foolish.

"I am Macaskill . . . your savior."

"I appreciate the help," Calhoun told him. But there was an expression in his face that indicated he knew that the help would not come without a price. Sure enough, he said, "So . . . I assume that you'll be seeking some sort of finder's fee."

"We did find you," agreed Macaskill. "We have taken the time to expend our resources in aiding you. Your ship is not functioning; you will require us to repair it, I trust."

"How much are we talking about?" asked Calhoun, clearly resigned to the inevitable.

"Does ten percent seem fair to you?"

Calhoun looked surprised. "It . . . does indeed. I have to admit, I thought you'd be looking for much more than that. But a ten percent commission seems more than fair."

"No . . . you don't understand," Macaskill said. His smile displayed a perfect row of white teeth. "Ten percent of your cargo . . . is what you will be left with."

"*What!*" Calhoun clearly couldn't believe it. He stomped back and forth a few feet, shaking his head and gesticulating wildly. "*What!*" he said again. "Look, you don't understand! This isn't my latinum! I'm just transporting it! A ten percent loss, at least I can cover that by giving up a portion of my fee . . . *grozit,* probably all of my fee. But if you walk off with ninety percent of the cargo, the people I'm supposed to be delivering it to aren't going to be happy! To be specific, they're going to be rather angry, and they'll be taking out that anger on me! If you gut me that much, I'm dead!"

"No. If we toss you into space, you're dead," the Andorian politely corrected him. "If we fix your ship and leave you ten percent of your cargo, we are giving you a fighting chance. But if you do not wish to have that chance . . ."

And he extended a hand in the general direction of the airlock.

"I will give you precisely two standard minutes to make up your mind," said the Andorian, "although I strongly suspect what your answer will be."

Calhoun, looking stunned, walked in the general direction of the prisoners. He was shaking his head in disbelief, clearly unable to deal with what had happened. The pity that Lodec felt for him grew and grew. Poor devil, indeed, to have fallen this low.

And then, as Calhoun drew within a few feet of the prisoners, his gaze shifted—ever so slightly—in Lodec's direction. And something seemed to come alive in his face, an almost fearful determination that Lodec had no idea how to interpret.

Then Lodec saw Calhoun's mouth move silently, addressing the mute question to him: *Lodec?*

Lodec nodded imperceptibly. He had no clue as to what to expect.

Calhoun mouthed two more words: *Hold on.*

At which point, Lodec forgot himself. Out loud, he said, "Hold on? To what?"

The confused comment drew a puzzled look from Macaskill. "Prisoner . . . who told you you could speak? Calhoun . . . it's time for you to admit the hopelessness of your situation. If you will cooperate, perhaps we can be generous and provide you with an additional five percent of—"

Calhoun turned to face Macaskill, and his attitude had completely changed. He was standing straighter, more determined, and utterly confident. And he called out, "Freighter! Execute offensive preprogram one!"

"What are you—?" Macaskill demanded.

He didn't get the entire question out as the freighter—which had previously been thought dead in space—roared to life.

From the sides of the vessel, white mist blasted out in all directions. Lodec stared, still not grasping what in the world was happening, and suddenly Calhoun was at his side. He was slapping some sort of unit on Lodec's face, a breathing device with goggles attached. Calhoun already had an identical device affixed to his own face. "Come on. We're leaving," Calhoun told him curtly.

"But—" Lodec had no idea what to say, no clue as to what was going on. Something screamed a warning though in his mind, and the warning said, *The deadliest Xenexian who ever lived is trying to make off with you.* To Lodec, there could only be one reasonable conclusion. For whatever reason, M'k'n'zy of Calhoun had decided to hunt down, kidnap, and murder Lodec of Danter.

It wasn't as if a prison world such as the one that Lodec was being transported to was any great place to be, but at least he would be alive there, and where there was life, there was hope. But if Calhoun got away with him, he'd have no hope at all.

Blind panic seized Lodec, and as Calhoun tried to drag him forward, Lodec abruptly began to struggle. "What are you doing?" demanded Calhoun. "Will you come on!"

All around them, people were dropping. Macaskill, who had been closed to the ship, went down first. Others were tumbling just as fast. As they lay on the ground, Lodec saw that they were virtually frozen in position. They weren't frozen in the sense of people covered with ice. Rather, they were paralyzed, every muscle in their bodies apparently completely taut.

Lodec struggled all the more, trying to claw the mask off Calhoun's face. "You idiot!" snapped Calhoun, and he punched Lodec just once on the side of the head. Lodec sagged, not lapsing into unconsciousness, but the fight momentarily knocked out of him. From that point on, he had no choice at all. Calhoun half carried, half dragged him to the freighter. The engines of the freighter were roaring to life; obviously the entire business about the ship being helpless had been a ruse.

"Let me . . . go . . . you'll kill me . . ." Lodec managed to get out, although his voice was muffled by the mask.

"Fool! If I wanted to kill you, I'd just do it here and now! Snap your neck and rip your head off as proof!" Calhoun said angrily as he approached the freighter. The main door automatically swung open and Calhoun shoved Lodec into the main cabin. Calhoun continued, "I wouldn't be going to all this trouble if your murder was my only concern!"

"Oh . . ." The panic was beginning to slip away from Lodec, even though he still didn't comprehend just what was going on. "That . . . hadn't occurred to me."

"I bet it hadn't. Hard to believe your kind ruled my world for years."

The door slammed shut as Calhoun swiftly operated the computer interface on the control panel. "What are you doing?" asked Lodec.

"Ordering the transport's computer to open up the bay doors . . . there!"

The massive main bay doors of the transport ship began to open wide. The stars beckoned as the freighter lifted off.

Then Lodec heard shouting from outside, and several shots ricocheted off the freighter's hull. "Damn," muttered Calhoun.

The doors began to slide shut again.

"Hold on," Calhoun said, and gunned the ship forward.

Lodec gasped. The doors were closing far too fast, and there was absolutely no way that the freighter was going to make it. He looked to Calhoun . . . and saw what he could only describe as a demented grin on Calhoun's face. Either the man was utterly suicidal . . . or else he simply really loved a challenge.

With astounding dexterity, Calhoun manipulated the controls and the freighter leaped forward even faster, half-turning sideways and sliding out just before the bay doors slammed shut.

"You did it!" shouted Lodec. "That . . . that white stuff! That mist! What was that?"

"Cyro-mist. Put them into temporary suspended animation . . . uh oh."

"Uh oh? What is . . . uh oh?" Lodec asked, scrambling to the front of the freighter.

Then he saw it. There, tracking on the screen, were two plasma torpedoes, coming in fast. They'd been launched by the prisoner transport, and they were going to overtake the freighter in no time.

Calhoun didn't appear to be the least bit concerned. Instead he flipped open a panel and tapped a blue square inside.

The freighter shuddered slightly and an alarmed Lodec said, "Are we hit?!"

"If we'd been hit," snorted Calhoun, "you wouldn't be here to ask that question. Those were torpedo counter-measures. Watch," and he tapped another panel.

The viewscreen showed a rear view of the vessel, and the transport was clearly in evidence. And then, to his astonishment, he saw the plasma torpedoes that had been pursuing them . . . streaking straight back toward the transport. "There's something small . . . leading them . . ." Lodec said after a moment.

"You've got good eyes," Calhoun admitted. "That's the counter-measure. It's a false beacon. Draws the torpedoes away from the intended target and toward one that I far prefer. Such as . . ."

The torpedoes slammed into the rear of the transport. The ship shuddered under the horrific impact. The transport had shields which it had barely managed to get up in time, but it was not designed to be a combat vessel and the shields were minimal at best. The first of the torpedoes didn't get through, but it did damage the shields sufficiently that the second one blasted into the hull. Plasma tore through the bulkhead, and the ship sparked furiously. All along the transport vessel, the lights went out and within seconds the entire ship was dark.

"That should take them some time to repair," Calhoun said calmly. "If it's repairable at all, that is. In the meantime, they'll be the ones who are floating in space. Let's hope that anyone who comes upon them will be a bit more generous than they were going to be with me."

"There was never any latinum on this ship," Lodec said.

"That's right."

"And you were never actually crippled. This ship, I mean. It was a lure to get aboard the vessel."

"Also right. You pick up things quickly."

"So all of this . . . was to get me out of there." He paused and then asked, with a sense of dread, "Why?"

"Because someone wants you out. That's all you need to know at the moment. That, and the fact that we rendezvous at Wrigley's Pleasure Planet."

"A desirable rendezvous point if ever I've heard one."

The freighter, under Calhoun's guidance, surged forward and leaped into warp space, leaving the crippled prison transport far behind.

Out of range of the transport, the manacles were no threat to Lodec. He looked around the interior of the freighter with interest. "Is this your ship?"

"It is now," said Calhoun. "I've used it from time to time, but it's been out of commission for a while. It's good to be back, though." He patted the console in what almost appeared to be the type of gesture that a person would use with a pet.

"Listen . . . I suppose I should—"

"Don't." As if reading his mind, Calhoun briskly cut him off. "Don't thank me. Don't give me gratitude. I don't want it, I don't need it. I know who you are. What you are. Just as you know who and what I am."

"M'k'n'zy the Destroyer," Lodec said softly. "M'k'n'zy the monster."

"Those and many other names," Calhoun agreed readily. "I'd like to think I earned them all. And I do not suggest you press me about old times, because I assure you the years have not made me think more kindly about your race. There's little forgiveness in my heart."

"In your heart?" scoffed Lodec. Part of him screamed a warning, that engaging in discourse with this man could result in a very quick and painful death if Calhoun were so inclined. But Calhoun was clearly operating on someone else's behalf, and it was obviously in Calhoun's interest to bring Lodec back in one piece. That gave Lodec a certain amount of boldness. "In *your* heart? You were personally responsible for the deaths of friends of mine. Good friends, good men, who deserved better than to die on some damnable foreign planet at the hands of barbarian heathens. Do you think that we . . ."

"*What?*" Calhoun cut him off, and there was danger in his eyes. "Do I think what?"

Lodec laughed softly to himself and shook his head. "Do you think . . . that we wanted to be there? Most of us didn't give a damn about Xenex. We did what we were told. We followed orders."

"The oldest excuse in the universe."

"It works for Starfleet officers."

"Yes. It does. Notice that I'm not one," Calhoun pointed out.

Lodec's back was against one of the bulkheads. Suddenly feeling all the strength ebbing from his legs, he allowed himself to slide to the floor. Drained, he said, "It was all . . . a very long time ago. And I suppose none of it matters anymore."

"No," said Calhoun. "I suppose it doesn't."

And then, after a long pause, Lodec said, "Thank you anyway. For getting me out of there." And after a hesitation, he added, "You don't have to say 'you're welcome.' "

Calhoun didn't.

XIV.

THE SITUATION IN THE ENGINEERING ROOM of the Excalibur had not come close to panic . . . but it wasn't all that far away from it, either.

Burgoyne 172 and Ensign Beth were sorting through the isolinear chips with a finely controlled franticness. Throughout the engine room, the rest of Burgoyne's people were checking every circuit, every possible route that might explain what in hell had just happened to cause the ship's computers to come tumbling around their ears.

S/he held a stack of the thin, hard chips in hir hand. "These things are useless . . . *useless,*" Burgoyne said, the "s" in "useless" extending to a snake-like hiss. "The only way we're going to get things back on line is to bypass the computer altogether. Everything's got to be done manually." S/he glanced in the direction of the warp core. The power emanating from it was still comfortingly humming away. "At least power still exists in the ship. Thank the Great Bird for that. If the engines were out and we had to do a cold start . . ."

"If there's power, then why isn't it getting to the rest of the systems?" Beth said, her frustration mounting. Even as she complained, though, she was rerouting systems to get around the stalled computer. "Henderson! Camboni! Punch this pulse through subsystems A1 through A7!"

"It's like a body that's had a stroke," Burgoyne said as s/he started reracking the isolinear chips in hope that s/he could find some sort of short cut s/he hadn't spotted before. "The brain is functioning fine. The rest of the body may be in perfect shape. But the connectors have been cut. If we can—"

Suddenly they heard the sound of transporters. And there, materializing not ten feet away from Burgoyne, were four Romulans, heavily armed and clearly ready to take possession of the engine room.

Burgoyne had no weapons on hir. S/he hadn't been expecting trouble. The Romulans, for their part, looked prepared to start shooting the moment they finished their materialization. Immediately what came to the forefront for the Hermat was concern about the safety of hir ship and the safety of hir people. Hir crew, hir engineers who looked to hir for guidance and leadership. And these no-good Romulans were going to show up and wreak havoc in hir engine room?

Not bloody likely.

At first glance, Burgoyne did not look particularly daunting. One would not readily appreciate hir strength and speed until one found oneself in a dire situation . . . which was more or less what the engineering crew of the *Excalibur* had on its hands. Burgoyne, however, did not hesitate.

S/he snatched an assortment of isolinear chips from their receptacles. And the moment that the Romulans materialized, s/he let fly, one after the other, in rapid succession.

Several years ago, Burgoyne had seen a magician, a card master who billed himself simply as Jay, entertaining at a local pub during one of hir pubcrawling expeditions. His mastery of simple pasteboard cards had been nothing short of astounding. Claiming to be descended from a long line of master cardsmen stretching back centuries, the most impressive stunt that he had pulled was hurling playing cards with such velocity that they had actually lodged in solid objects, such as fruit. Burgoyne had been incredibly fascinated by the stunt, and with hir long fingers and quick-snap wrists, had long felt that s/he would be eminently capable of imitating the act. And so s/he had taken up card flipping as a hobby, developing superb accuracy so that s/he had been able to hit a target from a reasonable distance away.

S/he had never, however, been able to get sufficient velocity for the cards actually to pierce anything . . . even a fruit. However, s/he had never had quite the incentive that s/he had at that moment. Furthermore, isolinear chips were harder and nastier than playing cards.

Consequently, as s/he tossed the chips with a vicious sidearm snap of hir wrist, the things shot across the distance like bullets, and had about the same devastating effect. The chips were relatively harmless when they were stationary. When they were hurtling at high speed, however, they were astoundingly nasty.

One Romulan took one square in the base of the throat. He choked on his own blood while the second turned and got one right in the eye socket, and went down, shrieking. The third took a step in Burgoyne's direction while bringing up his gun, which proved to be a mistake . . . not the motion of the gun, but the movement toward Burgoyne, because the increased proximity resulted in the thrown chip literally cleaving straight into the Romulan's skull. He went down without a whimper. It had all happened to fast, all within split seconds, that the fourth Romulan's jaw dropped open in amazement. This proved to be a spectacular blunder as the chip sailed through his open mouth and lodged in the back of his throat. He went down gagging.

Four appeared, four dropped, in less time than it took for the engineering staff to fully comprehend that they were under attack. Beth turned pale as she saw the Romulans piled up, one atop the other on the floor. The only one who was still alive was the one with the chip in his eye, and then he stopped moving a moment later, apparently dead from shock.

Burgoyne regarded them with remarkable calm and then glanced at the chips remaining in hir hand. "Hunh. I was wrong. These things were useful after all." Then, without hesitation, s/he shouted, "Shields and warp drive, first and second priorities! We want to stop these bastards from beaming on, and we want to get the hell out of here! Move!"

The largest raiding party, composed of about twenty Romulans, had materialized in deck 10. There had followed a furious pitched battle with an *Excalibur* security team which had resulted in casualties on both sides. The security crew, which had been far outnumbered, had managed to whittle the Romulans down to twelve, but the *Excalibur* team was hurt far more badly, and with only three of them still alive, had gone into full retreat. The Romulans, sensing victory, had gone in pursuit, and the trio of badly wounded, barely alive security guards had been certain that their time was up.

They had rounded a corner, hearing the pounding of the Romulans right behind them . . . and then they had come upon Si Cwan. The Thallonian noble was simply standing there. His palms were pressed together, his eyes closed, and he looked as if he were delving deeply into some sort of inner strength.

"Go," he said softly. "I will hold them."

The security team was in no shape to argue. One of them tried to thrust his phaser into Si Cwan's hands, but Si Cwan waved it off. "I don't like weapons," he said. "One tends to rely on them too much. Go. I will be fine."

Moments later, the attacking Romulans came around the corner, and Si Cwan was still standing there, just as calm as he'd been moments ago. The fact that a dozen Romulans had weapons angled squarely at him did not seem to bother him particularly.

He put his hands over his head in complete surrender. "I'm not one of them," he said, walking slowly toward the Romulans. "I'm just a passenger. In fact, I'm . . ." he started to stammer. "I'm a rich passenger. Rich and influential. See? I've . . . I've no weapons. No way of hurting you. Please . . . don't kill me . . . please . . . take me prisoner . . ."

"Romulans," said the foremost one in the group, "don't take prisoners." And he aimed his weapon at Si Cwan.

Si Cwan, hands over his head, was still several feet away. It did not, however, matter. He leaped straight up, swinging his legs upward as he did so. In one smooth movement, both of his feet caught the closest Romulans squarely in the pits of their stomachs. They doubled over. He had barely landed before he jumped again, this time nailing them squarely in the face. Both of their weapons flipped into the air, and Si Cwan caught them on the way down. He crisscrossed his arms and opened fire.

It was true. Si Cwan generally preferred not to use weapons. However, he prided himself on his adaptability.

Within seconds, six more Romulans were lying strewn about the floor. The remaining half dozen opened fire on Si Cwan, but he grabbed up the fallen body of the nearest Romulan and used it as a shield. A disruptor shot disintegrated the top half of the Romulan, and then Si Cwan hurled the remainder of his carcass, knocking down two more of the Romulans.

And then Si Cwan laid into the remaining Romulans. They fired at him, point blank . . . and missed. He scrabbled across the floor, moving like a gigantic spider, and then forward-rolled and came up with his feet planted in their faces. Just that quickly he was back on his feet, and he snapped the neck of another without slowing down, grabbed yet another and smashed him against the wall with such force that his face was little more than a red smear.

Blood jetted from his opponents as Si Cwan waded into them. His hands like spears, his movements economical and with machine-like precision, he bobbed and weaved through the increasingly frantic—to say nothing of diminishing—crowd of Romulans.

When Sela aimed the phaser at William Riker, she did not for one moment think that there was any question of missing.

She was also under the impression that the four Romulans she had with her would be able to handle matters. They were, after all, heavily armed. The average bridge complement was usually less than a dozen, and only one of them—the on-bridge security guard—was ever armed. Plus, she was all too familiar with the ways of the Federation. They liked to talk, to discuss, to debate. When they appeared on the bridge, "What do you want!" would be the first defiant words to leap from the throat of the ship's commander—in this case, as delightful luck would have it, Will Riker himself. After that would follow a dialogue, a back and forth, vituperation, sneering and cutting remarks, and so on.

A substantial threat, though? That truly didn't cross Sela's mind. That was why she knew that she could execute Will Riker with impunity. The boldness, the viciousness of her act would be enough to completely paralyze the battle-unready crew. As his lifeless body tumbled, so would their resistance. She was absolutely positive of that.

Which was why it was all the more confusing to her when she heard the sound of tearing metal. She had no idea what the cause was. She didn't have long to wait to find out.

As hard as it was to believe, she had not noticed the Brikar when she had arrived on the bridge. He had been crouched behind his tactical board. For a large individual, Zak Kebron had a surprising way of coming across as less substantial than he truly was. Now, however, he made no such effort. He emerged from behind his station, gripped the hand railing that ran across the upper section of the bridge . . . and pulled.

The railing tore out of its moorings. It took the Brikar no more than an instant to be clutching the massive piece of metal, and the instant the Romulans were turning to see what in the name of the Praetor had caused that ear-splitting racket, Kebron was already swinging the railing like a baseball bat.

Sela saw it coming and ducked. The Romulan standing directly behind her was far less fortunate. The railing struck him squarely in the head. The humanoid neck is actually one of the weakest links in the body, the flexibility of the neck coming at a high price. Romulans shared the same weakness as humans. Consequently the Romulan's head was sent flying from his shoulders. Sela jumped back, emitting a most un-Romulan shriek, and even as the horrified Romulans tried to react, Kebron took a step forward and shoved the jagged-ended metal railing squarely forward into the chest of another Romulan. A third Romulan let out yelp that was actually higher-pitched than Sela's as the impaled Romulan crashed into him.

It had all happened within seconds, and Sela had been so distracted that she had actually forgotten about Riker. But she had a forceful reminder as Riker lunged forward, grabbed her gun hand, and shoved the phaser straight up.

He was strong, but she was no slouch either. Giving as good as she got, the two of them struggled hand-to-hand, and then with a grunt, Riker shoved Sela back. She tripped over one of the fallen bodies, sprawled . . . and that was when Riker spotted what appeared to be a small comm device on Sela's wrist. He noticed that all of them were wearing similar equipment. "Get that thing off her!" shouted Riker.

At that moment, the fourth Romulan managed to open fire with his disruptor. He nailed Zak Kebron squarely in the chest. Kebron rocked back on his heels and then announced, "Ouch," before getting the Romulan to drop the gun through the simple expedient of crushing his hand so that he couldn't hold it ever again.

Shelby, meantime, moving with remarkable speed, literally hurled herself atop the fallen Sela. With a snarl, she got a grip on Sela's arm and received a punch in the head for her trouble.

"Ha!" shouted Sela right in her face.

In response, Shelby slammed her fist down against Sela's head. She heard a satisfying crunch of bone; it would have been far less satisfying had it actually been her own bone.

"Ha!" Shelby shouted right back, and tore the comm device from Sela's wrist. "Zak!" she shouted as she tossed it in Kebron's direction. It landed on the floor at his feet, and Zak simply stepped on it. The Romulan communications device . . . and her locator for beaming . . . crunched rather pleasingly beneath the massive foot of the Brikar.

The other Romulan who remained alive had already hit his comm device, and he was shouting, "Get me out!" As Kebron tried to grab at his comm link as well, the other two Romulans, along with the corpses, vanished in a haze of molecules. Sela, without her communicator link which would have enabled them to home in on her, didn't go anywhere.

But she was hardly finished. From the folds of her tunic, she pulled a long-bladed knife and lunged straight at Riker. At that moment, a slim hand clamped down upon her shoulder. Sela's head snapped around, her eyes rolled up into the top of her head, and she sank to the floor without a sound. Standing directly behind her, Soleta simply shook her head. "If you had simply allowed me to get close enough to apply the nerve pinch," she said to Shelby and Riker with mild reproof, "we could have terminated this violence far more quickly."

"Captain!" Lefler suddenly called from her station. To her credit, she had never budged from it even as chaos had unleashed itself on the bridge. "We've got shields back on line . . . and engines, too!"

Riker, who was envisioning the warbirds moving in on the still blind and weaponless starship, allowed a quick sigh of relief. "Bless you, Burgy!" he called to the engineer who obviously couldn't hear him. "McHenry, take us out of here!"

"We can't set coordinates," McHenry replied. "That's run through the computer. Of course, I could probably . . ."

The ship suddenly shuddered under a blast to her starboard, and then another to port. Obviously the warbirds were moving in, and it was impossible to fire back. Although shields were back on line, that was hardly going to save them for an extended period of time.

"McHenry, I know we'll be flying blind, but at this point if we wind up in the middle of a supernova, we won't really be much worse off than we are!" Riker told him.

"True enough," admitted McHenry. "Hold on."

He closed his eyes. Riker found that disconcerting for a moment, and then realized that it didn't make all that much difference. Not only did they have no instrumentation, they didn't even have the viewscreen.

The warp engines flared to life, and seconds later the wounded, but still active, *Excalibur* leaped into warp and was gone.

"We were set up! That's got to be what happened!" Shelby said furiously.

Shelby, Riker, Soleta, Sela, Lefler, and Kebron were in the conference room. Kebron was there mostly to keep Sela in line, and he did so through the simple expedient of keeping one hand firmly on her shoulder with his hand on her. The handbinders were simply a formality. This was more effective than one might have thought, because every time Sela tried to stand or shrug Zak's hand away, she failed utterly. She had, by that point, given up, and was just sitting in place with a rather irritated expression.

"Set up," Shelby continued, and she looked angrily at Lefler. "Si Cwan should have known."

"We don't know that we were 'set up,' Commander, and even if we were, there was no way that he could have known. He's only as good as his information," Lefler said defensively.

"Then his information should have been better," Riker said, no happier about the situation than Shelby. "Mr. Kebron, where is Si Cwan?"

"Intraship communications are still down," rumbled Kebron. "I've sent a security team to find him and bring him to this meeting, since you said you wanted to see—"

The door slid open. Lefler's gasp could be heard immediately. The others contained themselves, but just barely.

Si Cwan was covered with blood, and since it was for the most part green, it obviously wasn't his. Blood on his tunic, on his face, and on his hands. He had clearly been in a massive pitched battle with the Romulans. Seeing all the Romulan blood on him, Sela visibly paled.

Riker half rose from his chair. "Lord Cwan . . . are you all right?"

Si Cwan seemed puzzled that Riker would even have to ask. "Of course. Why?"

"Uhm . . ." Riker hesitated a moment, looked at the others in the room who nodded silent assent with what was clearly going through his mind. "Why don't you head back to your quarters . . . get cleaned up, relax . . . you've . . . clearly had a rough time . . ."

"You said you wished to see me. You sent a security guard to escort me here for that purpose."

"We'd heard that you'd been in a fight, that's all," Shelby said quickly.

"That is true. Is that all you wished to know?"

"Yes," said Riker.

"Very well." With that, he turned and left the conference lounge.

Somewhat more sedate in her tone, but still with no less conviction, Shelby continued, "These Narobi natives . . . Si Cwan said they were machine beings. And our computers went down. That certainly suggests . . ."

"That it was not a coincidence," Soleta agreed. "I have been doing further research since Si Cwan brought them to my attention. Their cybernetic make-up would appear to give them some sort of affinity for computers. That would put the odds of their involvement, and a possible alliance with the Romulans, at 83 percent."

"I had heard that 92 percent of all statistics are made up," Kebron observed.

This small attempt at levity actually drew smiles from several people in the conference room which, considering the circumstances, was quite the achievement. But then, turning serious once more, Riker turned to Sela and said, "It's more than that, isn't it, Sela. A lot more."

"Scamper back to the *Enterprise,* Riker," Sela said contemptuously. "Without Picard to show you how it's done, you're no threat . . . and certainly of no interest to me."

Riker didn't rise to the bait, keeping his cool. "You're going to tell us, Sela. You're going to tell us everything that's going on. About the Romulan involvement, about the raid on Daystrom . . . everything."

"Over my dead body, Riker."

And there was something in Riker's voice that caught Sela's attention as he said very deliberately, and very menacingly, "If necessary, Sela. Only if absolutely necessary."

XV.

THERE WERE FEW WORLDS in the galaxy that were more of an assault on the senses than Wrigley's Pleasure Planet. Actually, Calhoun really couldn't think of any, now that he put his mind to it.

They walked through streets that were in perpetual celebration. Lights garishly flickered on and off all day and all night, loud music blared from buildings all around them. Calhoun couldn't help but wonder when the natives slept, and came to the conclusion that the likely answer was "never."

Wrigley's Pleasure Planet was entirely a manufactured world, bought and paid for by one Horatio Wrigley several centuries ago and run by his family after his death . . . a passing, it was rumored, that resulted from an extended stay upon his own world. Supposedly he went with a smile on his face. There were certainly, Calhoun reasoned, worse ways to go.

Ostensibly, Wrigley had taken the hedonistic lifestyle that he had found on such worlds as Argelius and Risa and decided to heighten it, jack the level up to an unprecedented degree. Wrigley's was the only world where you could see spotlights shining while in orbit.

Calhoun and Lodec were not exactly allowing themselves to be swept up in the perpetual celebratory mood. Calhoun observed the gaiety around him as if he were watching from outside himself. It didn't seem to have anything to do with him or with his life. What underscored that the most for him was that he was walking down the street with a living reminder of the oppression his people had suffered under. A Danteri, right there, right next to him, and he himself had freed him. He would just as soon let him rot, and yet he had risked himself to set the man free.

It was all . . . a very long time ago. And I suppose none of it matters anymore.

Those had been Lodec's words, and the thing was, Calhoun couldn't help but wonder if Lodec was correct. Two decades. Could it have been that long? Two decades since he had spearheaded the liberation of Xenex. He hadn't really dwelt on what that passage of time meant, not really. Twenty years. There were Xenexians who were adults now who had absolutely no recollection of a time when Xenex had been anything other than free. For whom the name M'k'n'zy of Calhoun was simply a name in a history book (plus a name attached to several statues which dotted the Xenexian landscape, none of which he thought looked a damned thing like him). Indeed, there were Xenexians to whom the Danteri meant nothing in any threatening sense.

The fact was that the leadership which had come in after Calhoun had itself made many inroads and wound up working quite closely with the Danteri—a leadership that had been spearheaded by Calhoun's own brother. That alliance, that willingness to work with their former oppressor, had driven a wedge between Mac and his brother that continued in force more or less to the present day.

Do you think . . . that we wanted to be there? Most of us didn't give a damn about Xenex. We did what we were told. We followed orders.

. . . And I suppose none of it matters anymore . . .

That wasn't how he wanted to think of the Danteri. It didn't fit into his view of the universe at all. The Danteri were uniformly oppressive monsters who wanted nothing but to reestablish their chokehold on Xenex and hated all things connected with that world. They were heartless bastards who would just as soon kill Calhoun and his kind as look at them. They weren't allowed to come across as simply . . . mortal. Fallible mortals, tired of fighting, or perhaps grateful to a Xenexian, or even friendly . . . it simply wasn't allowed.

None of it matters . . .

Should it? Should it matter? Was there a statute of limitations on hatred? Was Calhoun being unreasonable, intransigent? Truthfully, Lodec seemed a decent enough sort. Once he'd gotten rested, cleaned up, he actually came across as a man of quick wit and ready tongue, a man who took a slightly skewed view of the universe.

And his crime against the Andorians? If he was to be believed . . . and he had, at that point, no reason to lie . . . it had nothing to do with crimes of violence, or spying, or anything that one would normally have expected in such a situation. No, Lodec had made the hideous mistake of having an affair with the wife of an Andorian high government official. He had not taken kindly to being cuckolded, and when he'd learned of the involvement, had Lodec brought up on charges of high crimes against the state. Lodec would have been more than happy to tell his side of the story, had he not had an electronic gag slapped across his mouth during the trial. And so a casual tryst by Lodec, who had just been passing through the homeworld of the Andorians, had turned out to be the beginning of a fifteen-year prison sentence. Granted, absconding with the affections of someone's wife was hardly an act that warranted having a medal pinned on you, but losing one's freedom for fifteen years because of it seemed a bit excessive. Even Calhoun had to admit that. But part of him wanted to feel that anything bad which happened to any Danteri was deserved and not to be mourned. That any ill fortune which befell any Danteri was something he had coming to him . . .

Except . . . that didn't hold up, either. After all, if there were Xenexian adults who had never been the slaves of Danteri, then it was also an inevitable conclusion that there were Danteri who not only had never been party to the oppression of Xenex, but had no inherent interest in Calhoun's world in the first place. Hell, if one could believe Lodec, he never "gave a damn" about Xenex to begin with. Of course, he didn't know for sure just how much he *could* believe Lodec, for the Danteri had been deliberately vague about what he himself had done during the war. He had basically admitted to being involved on a military level, but he had not gone into specifics. As near as Calhoun was able to determine, militarily Lodec was not much above a grunt.

None of which explained why in the world he was of such interest to General Thul.

Then Calhoun suddenly became aware of the fact that several Thallonians were following them.

Mentally he chided himself. That had been unforgivably sloppy. He had no idea how long they had been behind him. Had they just shown up? Were they there for several blocks? No way to tell. And he had been too wrapped up in his own musings to pay attention.

His first instinct was to confront the Thallonians following him. If nothing else, the notion pleased his ego. The thought of anything believing that they could tail Mackenzie Calhoun without his knowledge was galling to him.

But then he reconsidered. The fact was that they weren't making any aggressive moves against him. Furthermore, Thul had given Calhoun an address to which he was supposed to bring Lodec. It was possible that the Thallonians were there simply to observe, and report any questionable behavior back to Thul.

If one were to follow that reasoning, one would also assume that anything construed as being on Thul's side would likewise be reported.

With that notion in mind, Calhoun abruptly draped an arm around Lodec's shoulders. Lodec was clearly startled, and looked at Calhoun in surprise. "Is something wrong?" he asked.

"You're right. It was a long time ago," Calhoun said. "There's no need to hold grudges."

Lodec let out an obvious sigh of relief. "You can't believe how glad I am to hear you say that," he told Calhoun. "You've seemed to be wrapped up in your own thoughts since we got here . . . I have to admit, I was getting worried. I felt as if you were trying to figure out the best way to kill me or some such."

"No, no," and Calhoun laughed heartily. If one had looked closely, one would have seen that there was no touch of humor reflected in his eyes, but Lodec didn't look closely at all. "No, that's just my way. I've just been considering the situation, and concluded that there's nothing to be gained by obsessing about the past. We should only be concerned about the future, correct? That is, after all, where we all intend to live."

"I know I do," said Lodec, and he laughed. The noise was almost painful to Calhoun's ears, but he maintained his outward appearance of good humor, anyway. He took pains not to glance back at the Thallonians who were pacing them, since he didn't want to take any chance of giving away to them that he knew they were there.

They arrived at the prescribed address, and were promptly escorted upstairs to a private suite. There, in somewhat the same environment as he'd seen him on earth, was Thul. He was dressed far more festively than he had been on earth, much more in keeping with the general atmosphere of Wrigley's.

Vara Syndra was also there. Draped alluringly across a chair, winking at Calhoun, she was wearing an incredibly skintight yellow . . .

No. She wasn't. Calhoun's eyes widened. She was wearing body paint. That was it.

He promptly zoned out of the first minute and a half of the conversation, and only managed to re-enter it through sheer force of will as Thul was pouring drinks for all of them. Calhoun, cautious as always, mimed sipping from it but actually left the contents intact. Thul and Lodec were seated opposite each other, and appeared to be catching up on old times. At that moment, Thul was busy speaking directly to Calhoun. It was fortunate that he'd managed to get his head back on track, as it would have been rather embarrassing if Thul had asked him a question and Calhoun had been too busy staring at the thimbleful of paint which constituted the entirety of Vara Syndra's present wardrobe to answer.

"Lodec here was a close friend of my son, Mendan Abbis," Thul was saying. "As such, I had promised Mendan that Lodec would remain under my protection. Up until recently, that promise was merely words, as Lodec here," and he patted the Danteri's knee, "had always been more than capable of taking care of himself."

"Oh, yes," Lodec said with amused sarcasm. "I certainly was doing a wonderful job of caring for myself, wasn't I. If it hadn't been for you and Calhoun, Thul, I'd still be en route to the Andorian prison world right now."

"Everyone needs assistance from time to time in their lives, my dear Lodec," Thul said.

"The thing is, Thul . . . poor Mendan is gone," Lodec said, and there seemed to be genuine sorrow in his voice. "If you had not assisted me . . . if you had left me to my fate . . . then Mendan would never have known."

"Granted," admitted Thul. "But I, General Gerrid Thul, made a promise to my son nonetheless, and our family name has always stood for integrity. Whether Mendan Abbis is alive or not, if my word is not to be trusted, then truly, what kind of Thul am I?"

"True. Very true." Lodec held up his glass after a moment and said with quiet conviction, "To Mendan Abbis."

"To Mendan Abbis," echoed Thul, and so did Calhoun.

"So," Lodec continued, "what now? You have obtained my freedom for me. Your debt is fulfilled . . ."

"Hardly," laughed Thul, although there was an odd undercurrent to that laugh. "If my promise of protection is to be seen through, then I am personally going to have to attend to your safety in the times ahead."

"The times ahead? What is that supposed to mean?"

"It means, good Lodec, exactly what it means. I am going to assure that you survive all that is to come." He rose. "Attend, then . . . we will pass the night here, enjoying the hospitality this world has to offer. Tomorrow we will depart, rendezvous at my headquarters . . . and all will be made clear. Calhoun . . ." and he extended his hand. Calhoun shook it firmly as Thul continued, "You have done well. Extremely well. No one could have done better. Vara," and he inclined his head toward her, "will see you to your room. I can count on you to depart with me tomorrow?"

"Absolutely," Calhoun said. And as he shook Thul's hand, his ring implanted a transponder directly into Thul's palm. Calhoun was taking no chances; the last thing he needed was for Thul to depart during the night, leaving Calhoun high and dry.

The next thing Calhoun knew, Vara Syndra was hanging on his arm. "Come along, Mackenzie," she whispered softly in his ear. "Let me take you to your . . . room . . ."

At which point every hormone in his body completely stopped paying any attention whatsoever to whatever it was that Thul wanted to do or had in mind. Without hesitation he followed Vara out the door.

The moment they were in the hallway, out of sight of Thul, she began to kiss Calhoun. He did nothing to stop her. It was doubtful he could have done anything to stop her. He returned the kisses with equal passion, and hungrily locking lips with one another, they sidled down the hallway to the room that had been reserved for Calhoun. They eased in through the door, which obediently slid shut behind him.

It was a perfectly serviceable room, although nowhere near as opulent as Thul's. Somehow, though, opulence was not at the top of Calhoun's concerns at that particular moment. All he was concerned about was whether or not the place had a bed. Actually, it didn't matter all that much. The odds were sensational that the room had, at the very least, a floor, and the way he was feeling, that was all that he was going to need. But as luck would have it, there was indeed a bed there, large enough for an entire security team to wrestle with Vara, were such needed.

He ran his hands along the length of her body as they tumbled onto the bed, kissed her hungrily. Then he stopped long enough to look her in the eyes and say, "Why? Why me?"

She smiled at him. "Why not you? Don't you deserve it? Aren't you brave and heroic? Aren't you," and she ran her hands across his chest, "aren't you remarkably handsome?"

"And it doesn't have to mean more than that?"

"Of course not. Do you think it has to?" She actually seemed amused by the notion.

"No. No, it doesn't." He kissed her again, and his entire body was screaming at him to just get *on* with it already, she was wearing *body paint* and she was ready, willing and eager, how long should this possibly *take.* She pulled his shirt over his head. Naked from the waist up, he pressed against her. He groaned as she ran her tongue under the line of his chin, and he whispered her name . . .

"What's an 'Eppy'?" she asked.

He stopped, stared at her. "What?"

" 'Eppy.' Just now." There was laughter twinkling in her eyes. "You said, 'Eppy.' "

"I . . . said I was . . . happy. I whispered the word 'happy.' "

"Oh. Okay." She shook her head and chuckled once more. "Thul said you would be an interesting one. He had no idea, though, did he?"

"Thul. You're . . . here because Thul told you to be here," Calhoun said slowly.

"I'm here because I want to be here," Vara Syndra said firmly. "I'm here for my own reasons. Thul is part of it, yes. But you," and she fondled the lobe of his ear, "you are the main part of it. You rescued Lodec. You rescued . . . so many people, I'm sure."

"Yes. Yes, I did. I have."

She ran her fingers down his back, and he trembled from her touch. "Thul kept talking about how important it was to save Lodec. Kept talking about how he'd met Mendan Abbis, back in the days when Lodec worked for some man . . . Faulkner, I think, or Falcon, something like that . . . they'd stayed so close, and when Lodec was captured, Thul just knew that you'd be the man to get him out. Just like I—" She gasped. "You're hurting me!"

And he was. Because he'd had his hand on her wrist, but suddenly he was gripping it tightly.

"I'm . . . sorry." He let go of it immediately. She sat up, looking far more irritated than seductive. "Falkar?"

"What?"

"The man he worked for . . . was his name Falkar?"

She frowned a moment, concentrating, and then her eyes widened. "Yes!" she said, eager and cheerful, the momentary pain on her hand apparently forgotten. "Yes, that's right. Falkar. He worked for a man called Falkar. Lodec was apparently his main lieutenant, did all the tough jobs for him. That sort of thing."

His mind reeled as he sagged back onto the bed.

"Mackenzie? Are you all right?" She looked down at him with genuine concern. "Do you know this 'Falkar' person? What's happened? What's wrong, you seem so upset . . ."

Slowly, absently, Calhoun ran a finger down the scar on his cheek. The scar that a Danteri general named Falkar had left there, as if it were a gift to wish him luck as an adult. And in his mind's eye, he called up images long buried, recollections of his father, strapped to a post in the public square, being beaten by a Danteri officer at Falkar's direction.

Twenty years unravelled in an instant, and he put a beard on the then-beardless youth with the whip, and he aged him in his mind's eye . . .

"Mackenzie!" she called loudly.

Before, it had taken him tremendous effort to focus on anything besides Vara Syndra. Now it was a formidable task to concentrate on her. "What?" he said in confusion.

"What's going on? Can you tell me what's going on?"

"I . . ." He couldn't find the words.

No. No, he knew the words. *That man I rescued . . . that man I almost started to like . . . that man who was a friend of Thul's son . . . that man executed my father. He beat him to death in the town square, and the man who ordered the beating is long dead by my hand, but the man who actually did the job is right down the hallway, tossing back drinks with your boss and if you'll excuse me now, I've got to go kill him . . .*

He started to rise from the bed.

"Mackenzie," and for the first time, there was a sound of warning in her voice. "I don't appreciate the notion of men walking out on me. It's never happened before. It had better not happen now."

He turned his attention back to her and realized that the last thing he needed was Vara Syndra complaining to General Thul that the merest mention of Lodec or his former employer was enough to send Calhoun over the edge. He was trying to get himself on Thul's good side, after all. Besides, what was he going to do? Kill Lodec? Run in there screaming his father's name, announce that Lodec would pay for his deeds, rip out his beating heart and show it to him? The idea had some merit, granted, but ultimately it was counter-productive. Calhoun still had no true idea what it was that Thul was up to, and no certainty of where he was hiding, what it was he was hiding, or who it was he was hiding it from.

The only thing he knew for sure was that if he didn't give Vara Syndra what she wanted, it was going to look bad for him. Very, very bad.

So he looked at her for a moment as if appraising her, and then he forcibly rolled her onto her back and brought his mouth ruthlessly down upon hers . . . and then proceeded to give her what she wanted.

But he didn't enjoy it.

Not especially, at any rate.

XVI.

"I WILL NOT DO IT."

There was nothing in Doctor Selar's attitude that suggested she was going to change her mind anytime soon. Nonetheless, Riker did not appear remotely prepared to back down. Standing with him in Selar's office were Shelby and Soleta. Soleta kept her face, as always, impassive, while Shelby looked concerned and uncomfortable. She was no more happy with what Riker was proposing than Riker himself was, she had made that quite clear. But, to her credit, she was there as a sign of support for the commanding officer.

"Doctor," Riker began again, "it's not as if we have a great deal of choice here."

"You, Captain, may not have a choice. I, however, do." She shifted her gaze to Soleta, and there was a hint of disapproval in her eyes. "And you have agreed to this . . . proposal?"

"It is necessary," replied Soleta, sounding rather formal. "The Romulan woman, Sela, knows information that is potentially of great importance. The Romulans are not in the habit of acting in a capricious or haphazard manner. The raid on the Daystrom Institute, their presence in Thallonian space, their possible alliance with Narobi . . . they are pieces of a puzzle that Sela apparently knows."

"And that gives you the right," Selar said to her, "to forcibly thrust your mind into hers?"

"No," Soleta admitted. "It does not give me that right. It does, however, make it an obligation."

"If you must do this thing, and are committed to this deplorable course, then that is your own consideration," Doctor Selar said. "But to seek to involve me in the matter is adding insult to injury . . ."

"I have performed initial probes into her mind. Very mild. However, I can already sense that she has had training in psychic combat."

"So you believe that you alone cannot accomplish the job?"

"That is correct."

"And you would have me disgrace myself because you are incapable of doing so yourself."

"Doctor," Shelby said impatiently, "it is not a 'disgrace' to do something on behalf of a greater good. Furthermore, when you're in a service, such as Starfleet, it's your duty."

"Duty. Duty." Selar shook her head. "Commander . . . throughout history there have been those who were presented with situations where they were asked to make a choice that was morally repugnant to them . . . usually during a war when they were 'serving' the interests of their country in some way. More often than not, they went ahead with those repugnant efforts, even though they knew them to be wrong. Even though the cost may have been the purity of their very *katra* . . . their soul. And the excuse they invariably fell back upon was that it was their duty. The duty I attend to, Commander . . . Captain . . . Soleta . . . is the duty to do no harm. As a doctor, that is not only my first priority, it is my only priority. I will not force myself into the female's mind. You will have to find another way, or Soleta will simply have to do it alone. But that is my final word on the subject. Now, will there be anything else?"

"Doctor," Soleta said slowly, "a moment of your time . . . alone? If you please?"

"Lieutenant . . ."

"It will be all right, Commander," she said to Shelby.

Shelby seemed no more thrilled than did Riker by the situation, but finally she nodded and she and Riker walked out of the room, leaving Selar and Soleta alone.

"Do you desire to have me talk you out of this course?" Selar asked calmly.

"Doctor . . . there was a time some months ago when you needed me. I am telling you now that I need you."

"Soleta . . ."

Soleta leaned forward on the edge of Selar's desk, and the careful reserve that she maintained, with effort, slipped somewhat. " 'I believe I am ill. Mentally ill. And I require your services to ascertain that.' That is what you said to me, Selar, when you needed my help. When you were so convinced that you could not possibly be undergoing Pon Farr that you asked me to help you. No . . . no, you begged me. You asked me to grant you succor, you were so wretched . . ."

"I know that," Selar said. "I was there. I know what I did. I know what I went through. And you helped me, and for that I shall be forever grateful. But this is a different situation . . ."

"It would be, to you. I'm the one asking for help this time. Selar," she said in a lowered voice as if someone were eavesdropping, "I am not full Vulcan. You know this. I am impure, my mother Vulcan but my father a Romulan. They are expecting me to meld with a half Romulan woman, against her will, who is quite likely capable of resisting me. And she has had training . . . what if she turns it back against me? What if she uncovers my background? The risk to myself, the—"

"You are scared." Selar almost sounded sympathetic.

"Yes. I admit that freely. I am afraid of what I am being asked to do."

"Then do not do it. I am refusing."

"The difference is," Soleta said, "that you are refusing based upon moral principles. If I refused, however, it would be predicated purely on fear."

"Not necessarily. When you granted me succor, realized that it entailed a mind meld that you did not wish to perform, and further realized that I was just desperate enough to force you to do it anyway, you were morally and ethically repulsed by the notion. You felt that forcing one to perform a mind meld was repellent."

"Yes. I did. I still do."

"Then that is the basis upon which you can refuse. For is it not a small step from being forced to perform a mind meld, to having one forced upon you. The woman, Sela, does not want to have her mind probed. On the basis that such matters are best left to personal choice, you can and should refuse."

And then, to Sela's complete astonishment, Soleta let out a low roar of fury and, with a sweeping gesture, knocked everything off Selar's desk and sent it scattering to the floor. The clatter grabbed the attention of everyone in sickbay, and whatever anyone was doing came to a complete halt as all eyes turned to Selar's office.

Selar's eyes were wide with astonishment; not even her Vulcan training could repress that. As for Soleta, she was gripping the edge of the desk and trying to restore her breathing to normal. "Have you lost your mind?" Selar asked her, recapturing her customary calm.

"I need you," she said in a low voice. "And I need Starfleet. I am an impure bastard offspring of a violent rape. I have nowhere else to go in this universe where I can be at home except Starfleet."

"You are not limited or defined as a person by the circumstances of your birth, Soleta . . ."

"Yes. I am. And I have been asked by Starfleet, by my commanding officers, to do this thing. They believe that there may be something very terrible at stake, and Sela holds the key. I care about Starfleet. I care about people possibly being hurt or killed by the machinations of this woman. I have asked for your help. When you asked for mine, I provided it; as much as it cost me, I provided it. The short-term result was your coming to terms with, and understanding, what was happening to you, and the long-term result is the baby you carry in your belly. You owe me," she said in a low and angry voice. "You owe me, Selar, and if you won't help me, then to hell with you."

Selar did not even hesitate. "I cannot help you. It is a question of principle. For what it is worth, however . . . I am sorry."

Soleta drew herself up, her facade of reserve firmly back in place. "No. You're not sorry at all. What you are . . . is Vulcan."

She turned and walked out of Selar's office.

Shelby and Riker were standing in the corridor just outside sickbay, and Shelby was saying, "I don't know about this. I'm . . . uncomfortable about it."

"Truth to tell, I'm not happy with it either."

"Really?" Shelby seemed surprised. "I wouldn't have known it. If you ask me, you seem perfectly sanguine about it."

"I know I do. If there's one thing I've learned, it's that whether you make a good decision or a bad decision, what's just as important—if not even more so—is making a decision and sticking to it. You can't be a commanding officer and not be committed to your commands."

"Yes, well . . . that would explain why some of the CO's I've worked with should be committed."

They both laughed at that, and then Riker turned to Shelby with mock astonishment and said, "Why, Commander. Did we just have a moment there?"

"I don't think it was a whole moment, sir. Maybe half a moment."

"Half."

"Three quarters at most."

"I see." He paused. "You were right about the Romulans."

"I know. But then again, in retrospect, so were you."

He raised an eyebrow. "What do you mean?"

"I mean ninety-nine times out of a hundred—hell, maybe nine hundred ninety-nine times out of a thousand—the way you played it was absolutely right. Who knew that they had some bizarre scheme or ability to break into our entire computer system and cause the kind of havoc that they did?"

"You knew."

She shook her head. "No. I guessed. I had a gut feeling . . . which, I have to tell you, is damned peculiar for me. I've always been by-the-book, follow-the-rules."

"Perhaps you've been hanging around with Captain Calhoun too long. You're starting to pick up some of his seat-of-the-pants method."

"Perhaps. Or perhaps it was just, with you here, my inclination was to second-guess what you were doing. Maybe . . . that's my basic nature. I've never thought about it before, but maybe it's the way I operate. When Mac is here and being all gut-feeling, I'm all rules and regs. When you're here, doing things by the numbers, I'm suddenly advocating acting on impulse. Maybe . . ." and she sighed deeply. "Maybe that's why I've never gotten command. Maybe I don't have my own command style, but instead I simply react to other people. But a captain needs to be a leader, to set the tone. Maybe I just don't have that in me."

"Nonsense," Riker said. "You're selling yourself short, Shelby. Way short."

"Oh really. And why do you say that?"

He grinned readily. "Call it instinct. Hey . . . even I have to go by it sometimes."

She returned the smile, but before she could reply, Soleta walked out into the corridor. She had never seen the Vulcan science officer look quite that deliberately stone-faced before. "Soleta . . . ? Are you all right?"

"I am perfectly fine, Commander . . . Captain," she took in both of them with a glance.

"Is Selar going to help you? Give you back-up?" asked Riker.

"No. And I will endeavor to respect her decision. So . . . let's get this over with." And she headed toward Sela's cell.

Soleta didn't like the look of things from the moment she got to the cell.

Sela was sitting there looking infinitely smug and infinitely composed. There wasn't the slightest flicker of fear in her eyes. "Well, well, little lieutenant . . . going to take a shot at visiting the dark side, are you?"

Riker and Shelby were standing on the other side of the security field, as was Zak Kebron. But for all that their presence mattered, they could have been on Mars. The struggle, on all levels, was purely between Soleta and Sela.

"I will give you one last chance to cooperate," said Soleta.

"That's very gracious of you," Sela replied in a throaty voice. "Ever so gracious. But I don't need your chances."

"You may not have as much luck with resisting a mind probe as you think you will," Soleta warned her. "You are, I understand, half human. That will hamper you."

"And you are a fool, so that will hamper you."

Soleta did not rise to the obvious bait. Instead, she nodded her head in Kebron's direction as she extended her hands in preparation. "I feel it necessary to warn you that if you resist my making physical contact, Lieutenant Kebron will enter this room and hold you down. That will be most uncomfortable for y—"

"Resist? Why? What possible reason would I have? Do you think I'm afraid of you?"

"I am simply . . ."

Sela was on her feet, and in two quick strides she was directly in front of Soleta. She grabbed Soleta's wrists and, with that confident grin of hers, said, "Take your best shot." And she slammed Soleta's hands onto either side of her own head.

For the briefest of moments, Soleta hesitated, but she knew that way lay utter defeat. So she cast away her doubts and plunged headlong into Sela's mind.

Sela had not overspoken when she talked of walking on the dark side. Soleta felt completely overwhelmed by darkness. Darkness all around her, impenetrable and chilling. Somewhere deep in the distance, she was sure she heard Sela laughing at her. The contempt irritated Soleta, fired her forward, and she plunged further, further on.

Run while you can, little Vulcan, came the warning, but still Soleta moved forward. All round her reality shifted and twisted, because there was no reality, there was only the subjective aspects of what she was perceiving within Sela . . . and within herself. For a meld was not simply a one-way connection. She was risking making herself as vulnerable to Sela as Sela was to her . . .

. . . except Sela didn't seem vulnerable at all.

Soleta crashed into something.

It was huge and black and unmoving, and now the laughter was coming in from all around. She pulled back, withdrew her perspective, and she saw it in her mindscape. It was a gigantic image of Sela, a mile high it seemed, her face reflected in some sort of gargantuan mirror. The world twisted and turned back on itself around her, and still the image of Sela loomed over all. The blackness with which she had collided was the gaping maw of Sela's mouth, wide-open and laughing at her.

There was no delicacy, no finesse to Soleta's probe. She simply hurled herself with brute force against the image of her opponent. She slammed into it and she felt a painful shudder throughout her body, except of course she had no true body there, the pain was all in her mind and somehow that made it worse. But she could not go back, nor could she go around, she had to go through.

Having problems, Lieutenant? The image of Sela sneered at her, and then added, *Here come a few more problems.*

Black tendrils seemed to expand from all around, wrapping themselves around Soleta, and she did everything she could to shake them off. For a moment she was free and then once more she crashed into Sela's massive face, and once more there was the pain of collision, and once more she got nowhere, and this time she was a bit more tired, a bit more frustrated, and even a bit more—

Frightened? Are we having problems, Lieutenant? What's frightening you? The prospect of failure? Or the prospect of something more? Her voice was everywhere, not just all around her but inside her, inside her head, there was nowhere to go, nowhere to escape.

Escape? Is that your concern? Why would you want to run away? Is there something you are concerned I'll learn? Come, come, Soleta, you wanted to find out my secrets. You should be willing to trade some of yours in turn. This is just girl talk, after all . . .

And the tendrils were back, and this time there was no shaking them off. Sela's training had been too thorough, and it was more than just training, she burned, she burned with a dark and fearsome intensity that was painful in and of itself. And Soleta tried to pull away, tried, but Sela was everywhere now, penetrating and violating her, and she was thinking of what her mother must have suffered except she didn't want to think of that because that way lay madness, and there was Sela's face as huge as a star, filling up everything . . .

. . . and suddenly Sela's face changed. It went from smug triumph to alarm. Soleta didn't understand at first, but as the tendrils slipped away from her, she saw the first cracks appearing in the mirror image of Sela.

And a voice said, *Calmly, Soleta. Calmly. That is what is needed here. Calm and focus.*

She did not see the image of Selar next to her, did not perceive her in that way. But she sensed her, sensed the steadying presence.

Sela discerned the cracks that were appearing in her image, and a snarl of animal fury that carried psychic repercussions blasted out from her. *Get out! Both of you! Get out while you can!*

Are you with me, Selar? Soleta asked.

I am here. My hands are upon your brow. Our minds have merged. Do as you need.

GET OUT! Sela howled, and that howl translated into winds so massive, so deafening, that they threatened to blast Soleta right out of the mindscape.

But she drew strength from Selar's presence, drew focus. And more, she began to draw upon herself. For she knew that Sela's heritage was hers too.

The fires of fury that burned within Sela raged within her as well. It was that pure, raw, fierce emotion that she drew upon now. *Not calm, Selar,* she thought, *not just calm. You bring the calm . . . but it's the calm before the storm.*

And she summoned that rage, then, the rage and pure emotion that was part of the Romulan make-up, the rage that she felt over the circumstances of her own birth, the rage from the confusion and frustration and sense of desolation and separation that she had carried with her for year after year. All that she pulled to her, clutching to herself, and then she hurled herself forward straight toward the mirrored image of Sela.

Sela screamed in protest, but it was too late, far too late as Soleta smashed through. The image, the psychic shield that Sela had created, cracked and splintered and fell completely apart. And it poured out, it all poured out, images, awareness, facts, tumbling one over the other, and Sela was desperately trying to prevent the strip-mining of her thoughts; however, not only could she not slow it down, but Soleta was enjoying it with a primal fury that was terrifying to perceive.

Tell me what I want to know! Show me! You have no choice!

GET OUT!

Tell me, you Romulan bitch!

And it was there, everywhere, the Thallonian and the plan and the location and she just needed a few more details to help it all fit together and then she saw a horrible, horrible landscape, bodies, bodies piled up in mountains stretching so high that they blotted out the sun hanging in the sky, except it wasn't the sun, it was something glistening and metal . . .

And then the world crashed in around Soleta.

Her body collapsed, and the only thing that stopped her from hitting the ground was Selar. It wasn't that Selar caught her; Selar also collapsed, but as it turned out, Soleta fell on top of her so that her fall was slightly cushioned.

There was nothing to prevent Sela from hitting the ground, though, which she did with all the elegance of a sack of rocks.

Shelby and Riker were through the door in a heartbeat, Riker helping up Selar while Shelby attended to Soleta. "Soleta . . . are you all right?" she called to her.

Soleta stared at her, trying to focus her eyes. "You don't have to shout, Commander. I'm right here."

"Oh, thank God. I . . . I heard this shriek . . . and . . ." Shelby turned to Riker. "Did you hear it, too . . . ?"

He nodded. "In my head. Nothing spoken."

"Psychic backlash," Selar now spoke up. Riker was helping her to her feet. "Even those who have no telepathic leanings can sense such an event."

"What happened to her?" Although Shelby was propping up Soleta, she was now looking at Sela. The Romulan was lying flat on her back, staring up at nothing. Her eyes were glazed over. "Doctor . . . ?"

The doctor was already tapping her comm badge. "Selar to sickbay."

"Sickbay," came Maxwell's quick response.

"We need a team up to the brig, immediately." She was checking Sela over briskly even as she was speaking to Maxwell. "Blood pressure, vital signs all appear minimal but within safety limits . . ."

"What's happened to her?" demanded Riker.

"Brain fried," Soleta said tonelessly. They all looked at her, and she noticed that Selar was nodding. She continued, "To put it in human terms . . . we strip-mined her. Forced our way in, took what we needed. She fought . . . valiantly . . . but realized that she was losing the fight. So she . . . burned herself out."

"You mean deliberately?" said Shelby, appalled.

"In a manner of speaking, yes. It wasn't that difficult, really. Everything that she was turning outward for the purpose of resisting us . . . she turned inward instead. Like burning the crops so that the attacking forces can't use the food."

"Will she recover?"

"I . . . don't know," Soleta said. "I've never actually seen this technique used. I've heard whispers about it, stories of people who had done it to themselves as a sort of mental suicide out of extreme depression . . . but I've never witnessed it myself. I have absolutely no idea of what to expect in terms of her recovery."

"And as long as she's like this . . . we can't find out anything from her?" asked Riker.

Selar shook her head. "It would be like trying to read a book with blank pages. She has done to herself what her people did to us: She has crashed her computer."

"Which leaves us right back where we started."

"No, Commander Shelby," Soleta said. "Not quite. I . . . learned some things. Some terrible things. Saw visions of what's to come . . . saw those involved, or at least some of them . . ."

"Do you know where they are? Where to find them?" asked Riker.

She nodded, but then added, "What I don't know . . . is whether we can do a thing about it."

XVII.

Calhoun stared out at empty space and tried to figure out what in the world it was that he was supposed to see.

In his freighter, he had arrived at the designated coordinates at the same time as General Thul, who was piloting his own vessel, a sleek mini-cruiser that looked as if it was more than capable of handling itself in most combat situations. Truth to tell, Calhoun had been concerned if, once he was out in space, he might be subject to some sort of sneak attack or ambush arranged by Thul or his minions. That was why he was somewhat relieved that Vara Syndra was with him.

She was wearing something a bit more substantial than body paint this time, but the clothes were still extremely tight and rather revealing. She positioned herself in the co-pilot chair in such a way that he wondered if he would ever be able to look at anyone else sitting there in quite the same way.

"Why are we sitting here?" Calhoun said after a brief time. "There's nothing out here. What's the point?"

"Oh, you'll see. The General likes to be mysterious," and she said the word 'mysterious' in a deliberately dramatic manner. "That's just his way. You know," and she leaned forward, displaying her ample cleavage, "instead of simply complaining, I can think of ways in which we could pass the time."

He looked at her, regarded her thoughtfully. He'd had a lot of time to think about her. When he had woken up in the middle of the night, she had been lying on his shoulder, snoring softly. He had studied her for some time, giving matters a good deal of consideration. He knew himself. He knew what others were capable of. And he had come to some rather interesting conclusions.

"Pheromones," he said.

He got precisely the reaction he was hoping he would get: startled. He'd said something that she had not remotely anticipated. "Wh-what?"

"Pheromones. You generate them in such a way that I, and any other male, couldn't help but be affected by them. You can regulate it however you wish, 'turn on the charm,' as it were. You can crank it up to high heat, which is what you did with me, depending upon what it is that Thul wants you to do. Problem is, you did too good a job on me. You made it so that I couldn't think straight. Except I can always think straight."

"I . . . don't know what you're talking—"

"Yes, you do." When he interrupted her, he did so with no rancor. Indeed, he sounded a bit sad. "I don't know whether you come by it naturally, or if it's somehow been implanted into you. Don't know, don't care, really. The most depressing aspect of all is, I have absolutely no idea whether I would have been attracted to you just because of you yourself, or whether you need something like being able to artificially stimulate male hormones in order to function. If I had to guess, that's probably a bit depressing for you, too. Not to know, I mean. Considering the way you look, it's somewhat sad to think that you would have to depend on something chemical. Or . . . do you really look that way . . . ?"

She turned away from him, then. "Here's my back," she said with far more anger than he would have thought she was possible of generating. "Just stick a knife into it and be done with it."

"Vara," he said softly, "listen—"

"No," she snapped, looking back at him. "God, you're all the same. The surface is all that matters to you. And you know what? I thought you were different. I thought you'd know me. That you, of all people, would know me. But you don't know anything. You know what I wanted to do after you fell asleep last night? Leave. That's what I usually do. But not with you, no. With you, I stayed. I totally, totally let down my guard with you . . ."

"Why?" he asked.

"Because I thought I could. Because I thought we had connected on a deeper level than simply the physical. Because . . ." A tear trickled down her cheek and she wiped it away angrily. "It doesn't matter," she said finally. "None of it does, I guess."

"Why are you hooked up with General Thul?" he asked. "Look what he's doing to you. He uses you."

She stared at him with eyes that were glistening. "And I use him.

Everyone uses everybody else, Mackenzie. And anyone who says otherwise is probably one of the biggest users of all."

"Vara . . ."

Suddenly Calhoun's ship-to-ship comm channel flared to life. "Calhoun. Are you still with us?" Thul sounded particularly jovial.

"I'm here, yes. Although I'm wondering why, exactly. Is there some deep, hidden meaning to the fact that we're sitting here?"

"Just being cautious. I generally like to do a detailed scan of the area before going home, just to make sure that there's no one about who shouldn't be here. But I'm pleased to report that the area is clear."

"It's certainly clear of anything that could possibly be called 'home,' " Calhoun observed.

"You should not always believe what your eyes tell you, Calhoun. First appearances do not necessarily mean anything."

"Yes, I think I've heard that occasionally," he said with a sidelong glance at Vara. She was looking resolutely away from him.

"Welcome to my home, Calhoun."

Calhoun still had absolutely no clue what Thul could possibly be talking about.

And then, in the near distance, space began to ripple. At first Calhoun thought it was something dropping out of warp space, but then he realized it was a ship dissolving its cloaking field. His immediate instinct was to prepare for battle, for when Romulan vessels dropped their cloak, it meant that they were about to open fire.

Then he realized that the dissolution field was too wide. It wasn't just one ship, it was a fleet of ships. A huge fleet . . . but . . . there was no space between the ships . . . it was one, big, solid, wavering mass . . .

"*Grozit,*" whispered Calhoun.

It was a gigantic sphere, massive beyond belief. The thing could have contained the entirety of Starfleet within itself and had room left over for the Klingon fleet and a few others as well. It blotted out everything. Calhoun had his viewscreen on maximum reverse magnification, and he still couldn't make out the whole thing. He prodded the freighter into reverse.

"Don't run away, Calhoun, it won't bite," came Thul's voice.

"I'm not running away," said Calhoun, "I'm just trying to get a better view of the thing."

Within moments he'd backed up far enough away so that he could see it in its entirety. "It's a Dyson Sphere," he said.

"I believe that is what terran technology refers to such a structure as, yes. Call it what you will. As I mentioned, I call it home."

"But it's impossible! Cloaked? How can you possibly cloak something that big?"

"I've been working with the Romulan empire for some time now, Calhoun. You would truly be amazed what a few people with determination, resources, and sufficient hatred for the Federation can accomplish. Follow me, if you please."

Thul's ship moved toward the sphere, and Calhoun fell in behind him. The closer he got, the bigger it got. His instrumentation gave him readings as to the size, but knowing it intellectually and seeing it up close were two entirely different things. "How did he build it?" he asked Vara. "How long did it take? How—?"

"You can ask him," Vara Syndra replied. "I'm just here for my looks."

Calhoun rather wisely decided not to press the point.

They moved through the massive entrance bay, passing through to the interior of the sphere itself. It was, to all intents and purposes, hollow. This hardly meant that it was empty, however. For starters, there were dozens, perhaps hundreds of ships, parked within. Furthermore, the walls of the sphere itself were lined with walkways, residences, work areas. Toward the top and bottom of the spheres, Calhoun spotted hydroponics growing fields where fresh food was being cultivated. And straight down the middle of the sphere was a huge, pulsing device that Calhoun immediately recognized as an infinitely larger version of a Romulan cloaking device. He saw that it was feeding off a core that was a modified version of a warp core. The Dyson sphere had no means of propulsion, however. It simply utilized the combination of matter and anti-matter explosions to feed its energy needs. He also saw workers casually walking vertically along the outside of the core, getting from one point to the other, and he realized that the sphere was creating an artificial gravity by the simple expedient of rotating on an axis.

"Incredible," he breathed.

"Follow me, please," came Thul's voice over the comm. "You'll see a docking beacon flashing. That will guide you in."

Calhoun did as he was told. It wasn't particularly difficult maneuvering, really. If it had been remotely difficult, they probably would have had a computer come on line and handle it for him. As it was, he followed Thul's lead across the vast interior and locked into position at a docking bay on the far side.

Moments later Vara and Calhoun had exited the freighter and were in what appeared to be a large reception area. People were walking briskly about on their business, but every single one of them paused in their stride to nod and acknowledge Thul's presence. It was an impressive variety of races represented there . . . and Calhoun noticed that the vast majority of them were not members of the Federation. Of those individuals who were, Calhoun recognized a number of them from records that had been circulated to all Starfleet captains, warning about individuals who posed a hazard to life and liberty.

"This way," said Thul. Lodec was next to him, and as Vara and Calhoun joined them, they made their way to what appeared to be some sort of turbolift.

As they walked, Calhoun found it more and more difficult to so much as look in Lodec's direction. Every time he did so, he risked betraying the depth of fury that the merest proximity to the Danteri provoked within him. One of the few things that Calhoun had never been able to accomplish was to learn from the Danteri government the name of the individual who had wielded the whip that killed his father. Intellectually, he had always known that it was Falkar who had ordered the deed. That gave him the responsibility, and that scale had been balanced. But part of Calhoun had always wanted to crush the throat of the man who had actually done the deed. He longed to feel that pulse beneath his fingers, struggling and beating its last before falling forever silent.

And now, after all these years, he had the motherless scum at arm's length. But he couldn't touch him. The object was to stay in Thul's good graces, and slaying the best friend of Thul's late son was hardly going to accomplish that goal. Calhoun was anxious to learn what it was that Thul was up to, and determined to stop it. But now he had an additional incentive, something that—perhaps not surprisingly—gave him something more personal at stake than simply the entirety of the Federation's survival.

At one point, Lodec seemed to sense that Calhoun was eyeing him. He glanced in Calhoun's direction, but by that point Calhoun was looking off somewhere else. Lodec shook his head slightly, as if endeavoring to sort out his imagination from reality, and Calhoun simply watched him through half-lidded eyelids, like a great cat waiting in the high grass.

They stepped into the turbolift car. The doors hissed shut as Thul said, "General Thul, command level." The turbolift immediately started moving, sliding noiselessly toward the instructed destination. The lift was situated on the inside wall of the Dyson Sphere, which meant that they had a dazzling view of the entirety of the place as they moved downward.

"What do you think of my little endeavor, Calhoun?" he asked. "I noticed you studying some of the other residents of my home quite carefully."

"Well . . . if you're really asking me . . ."

"Oh, I am. I am," Thul said sincerely.

"As near as I can tell, a goodly number of the individuals here are . . . how should I put this delicately . . ."

"Scum?"

"Yes. Thank you. That's the word I was looking for. And the problem with filling a place with the scum of the galaxy, with some of the least trustworthy individuals around, is that you're going to have a hell of a time watching your back."

"I could not agree more, Calhoun," Thul said readily. Calhoun could feel the lift slowing to a stop. "On that basis, I've taken great care to have the best people watching my back. Here's one of them now."

The doors slid open and Calhoun stepped out, looking around.

Zolon Darg was standing there.

Clearly he had been waiting for Thul to show up. Perhaps Thul, in a rather perverse bit of amusement, had requested that he show up and meet them there. Whatever the occasion might have been, the fact was that Darg was there and it took him all of two seconds to recognize Calhoun.

For his part, Calhoun couldn't believe how massive Darg looked. Bigger, wider than when Calhoun had last seen him, with arms, legs and chest so thick that one could only conclude that he had rippling muscles beneath his clothes, the likes of which no one had ever seen.

"Darg, this is—" began Thul.

That was as far as he got. With a roar of inarticulate fury, Darg charged forward and grabbed Calhoun by the front of the shirt. He slammed the Starfleet officer against the far wall with such fury that Calhoun felt every bone in his body rattle. His eyes felt as if they were ricocheting off his brain.

"Miss me?" he managed to get out.

Darg howled again and threw Calhoun to the floor. When Calhoun crashed into it, he barely managed to absorb the impact with his arms. If he hadn't pulled it off, the impact would likely have broken his neck.

Calhoun couldn't believe his strength; it surpassed understanding. Darg would have given Zak Kebron a run for his money, and perhaps even beaten him. Then there was no time to think as Darg drove a boot straight down toward Calhoun's face. Calhoun barely managed to roll out of the way as Darg's foot crashed down where Calhoun's head had been moments before.

"I'll kill him!" Darg shouted, which was the first coherent thing he had managed to get out since he'd first seen Calhoun. All things considered, it was a somewhat wasted pronouncement. His actions had already spoken far more loudly.

"Stop it, Darg. Right now," said Thul, and there was an iron sense of command in his voice that snagged even Darg's attention.

Darg rounded on Thul, and he looked like a barely contained nuclear detonation. "He's mine, Thul! Mine to kill! Mine!"

"That's enough, Darg. The idea! Throwing a guest of mine around," and he helped the shaken Calhoun to his feet. "Are you all right, Calhoun?"

Calhoun was woozy, his knees starting to buckle. "Well . . . fortunately, I'm still alive. Except . . . that might be a bit unfortunate, too, because I don't really feel like being alive at the moment."

"I'll remedy that!" snapped Darg, and he started to advance on Calhoun once more. " 'Calhoun,' eh? So that's the name you're going by. I've never known it . . . but by God, your face has been seared into my memory long enough! And I'm—"

"I said enough!" and if there was any doubt until that moment as to who precisely was in charge, that strident bellow more or less demolished it. Darg froze where he was, in mid-step, as he had been advancing on Calhoun.

"I warn you, Darg. Do not cross me on this matter. Calhoun has done me a great service. Because of that, he is not to be harmed."

"He nearly killed me," Darg said slowly, as if addressing a child. "He . . . tried to kill . . . me . . ."

"Yes, he did. And the only reason that you're still alive is because of me," Thul reminded him. This appeared to be getting through, and he continued, "Because of Calhoun, Lodec stands with me now."

"I could have gotten Lodec for you," Darg said with contempt, as if the feat of freeing Lodec was a simple conjuring trick that could be performed by the average eight-year-old with a home starter magic bag.

"You were busy elsewhere. You cannot be everywhere, Darg, and I need others I can count upon."

"You would put . . . that . . ." and his finger quavered as he pointed in Calhoun's direction, " . . . that . . . thing . . . on the same level with me? You would depend on both Calhoun and myself equally? That is madness!"

"Grow up, Darg," Thul said, and he certainly sounded as if he meant it. "What is past is past. Reliving grudges and offensive acts taken toward one another is a fool's errand. And I am no fool. Now . . . Mackenzie Calhoun . . . Zolon Darg . . . you will work in tandem with each other, in a spirit of cooperation. I do not want to hear rumors of either of you trying to kill the other one. That would be unacceptable. And a mysterious midnight poisoning . . . ? That would be unacceptable as well." Calhoun wasn't sure, but he thought perhaps that Darg had looked a bit crestfallen upon learning of the further edict. "You will work together. You will trust each other as much as can possibly be expected. If there are any disputes, they will be mediated through me. And gentlemen . . . think of it this way . . ."

"What way?" Calhoun asked, still rubbing the parts of his body that had been badly bruised while being tossed around.

"It will be in both your best interests to lead a long, healthy, and productive life here in the Thul Sphere. Because if either of you dies, I will automatically assume that the other had something to do with it, and act accordingly."

"Wait a minute," Calhoun said, "you can't hold us responsible in such an open-ended manner. What if one or the other of us dies of natural causes?"

"That might be almost impossible to determine," Thul said reasonably. "There are too many drugs and poisons that can simulate demise from a certain cause . . . and the poisons themselves are undetectable within minutes after doing the job. Therefore, we would likely err on the side of caution, decide that the means of death was actually murder, and act accordingly."

"You can't do that!" protested Darg.

"Darg . . . Calhoun," Thul said slowly, with tremendous warning in his voice, "this is my place. I cannot suggest strongly enough that you do not tell me what I can and cannot do. Understood?"

Calhoun and Darg looked at each other. Calhoun did not think for a moment that Darg was going to let it drop quite that easily, and was fully aware that he was going to have to watch himself every waking minute—and, even more important, those minutes when he was not awake. Still, he simply nodded and said, "Understood."

"Understood," muttered Darg.

"Good. That's settled then."

"Mackenzie Calhoun," Darg said slowly. "I know that name. You are with Starfleet. I've heard your name bandied about in Thallonian space. There are some who worship you as a god."

Calhoun shrugged indifferently. "Some. I don't encourage it."

"You're not wearing a Starfleet uniform. What is a Starfleet man doing here, anyway?"

"He is late of the fleet, Darg," Thul assured him. "This is a place where new lives are started. All I care about is what a man brings with him, not what he leaves behind. Now then, Darg . . . the recruitment drive on Argelius. How did that go? We are running short on time, and are rapidly drawing to the 'now-or-never' moment."

"It went quite well, actually," said Darg, casting one more sidelong glance at Calhoun before continuing his comments to Thul. "Of the twelve representatives I met with, nine showed up in force several hours ago, bringing the required payment along with the people they represent. The population of the Thul Sphere has increased exponentially."

"Perfectly acceptable," smiled Thul. "That is perfectly acceptable. The resources of the sphere have been carefully built up. You see, Calhoun," he continued, turning back to the officer, "this has hardly been an overnight project. I have labored many years to bring this to fruition."

"You must be very proud."

"Very, yes. And who is this?"

Calhoun didn't understand the question, and then realized it wasn't being addressed to him. Someone else was walking toward them from behind him, joining the group. It was Darg to whom Thul had been speaking.

"This fellow," Darg said, "was of tremendous use to me on Argelius. I have taken the liberty of inviting him to join our operation. General Thul . . . this is Kwint. Kwint, this is our glorious leader, the great General Thul. And this is Thul's glorious associate, Vara Syndra, and Lodec of Danter, and . . ." he growled the name reluctantly, as if hating to acknowledge that it needed to be spoken, "Mackenzie Calhoun, late of Starfleet. Gentlemen, lady . . . this is Kwint."

Calhoun turned and saw a man with silver hair and beard, but a face that otherwise he recognized instantly. His voice caught in his throat as he found himself staring straight into the eyes of Jean-Luc Picard.

XVIII.

"WE WERE SET UP, SI CWAN. I'm sorry, but that's one of the things I drew from her mind," said Soleta. She looked around a conference lounge that was occupied at that point by Shelby, Riker, Selar, and Burgoyne, and Si Cwan. Cwan's face, in particular, was deathly serious. "This ostensibly 'peaceful' race you spoke of had actually allied itself with the Romulans. Because of their machine make-up, they were apparently the perfect tools to help put into place the final elements that were needed for Thul's plan. And they decided to test those elements on our computers. They were simply able to take our computer system over with no problem, punching through all the safeguards and security codes as if they weren't even there."

"So their plan is to try and take over computers of starships?" asked Burgoyne. "But why? It sounds somewhat abstract to me."

"You mentioned Thul. That would be Gerrid Thul," Si Cwan said slowly.

"You know him, then," asked Riker.

"More by reputation, although I seem to have a vague recollection of meeting him when I was quite young. A rather power-mad individual. At the time he was a second-level Thallonian nobleman. Very eloquent, but that eloquence helped to cover a ferocity of ambition that was rather chilling. My father once said that Thul is a man who uses lies the way a surgeon uses a scalpel, and assigned him to be in charge of one of the farthest-flung of our outposts. But Thul craved power, and decided that the best way to go about it was to court the emperor's sister, my aunt. My father thwarted that, feeling that Thul wasn't good enough for her. This infuriated Thul. Then there was a rebellion . . . Thul's son was killed, I believe . . . and then one thing led to another, and Thul wound up in prison."

"Well, he's out, and apparently he has no love for the Federation. What I managed to draw from Sela's mind before she collapsed is, unfortunately, spotty at best," admitted Soleta. "Thul has been experimenting with some sort of virus . . . a virus that apparently is one of the most devastating that the Federation has ever dealt with."

"Dealt with? You mean it's surfaced before?" asked Riker.

"Apparently it has, yes," said Soleta. "The *Enterprise* first encountered it several years ago on Archaria III. It then resurfaced on Terok Nor a few years later. A variation was used to attack the Romulan royal family, and finally, just before his defection, Tom Riker reported dealing with the virus on a planet in what was then the demilitarized zone between the Federation and Cardassia."

"But what's been the point of it all? These repeated attempts at a virus . . . ?" But then Shelby realized it. "He's planning to unleash it on the Federation, isn't he."

"Apparently so," said Selar. "From what I have garnered, this virus crosses races with the ease that we cross warp space. If Thul does manage to unleash it somehow, it could annihilate every living organism it comes in contact with."

"But a virus can't travel through space. How can he possibly do it?" asked Si Cwan.

There was dead silence for a moment as they looked at one another.

Then Riker's eyes widened. "I get it. Good lord . . . I get it."

"Get what?" asked Shelby. "I don't understand . . ."

Riker leaned forward, his fingers interlaced. "Federation races share technology. That's one of the fundamentals of the alliance. That technology includes such standard items as holotech . . . computers . . . and *replicators.*"

"So?" asked Shelby . . . and then she understood. "Oh, my God."

Riker nodded. "Replicators work via computers. They tap into a data base and use that information to replicate food, clothing, whatever's needed. It's one of the underpinnings of our way of life, because as long as replicators exist, no one wants for anything. With the aid of the artificial intelligence equipment and research that Thul has stolen, via such catspaws as Zolon Darg, and the help of the Narobi, Thul has found a way to access any and all computers throughout the Federation. Because computers are the connecting tissue of the entire Federation."

"Thul has come up with the ultimate computer virus," Soleta said, comprehending.

"That's right," said Riker. "He's going to take over the data base of every computer in the Federation, just as easily as he took over ours. Every homeworld, every colony, every starship, everything in the shared computer environment. Once he's 'in,' he's going to program the replicators to produce this virus of his."

"But replicators can't create living things," said Shelby. "Aren't viruses partly alive?"

"Partly, yes. But there are ways around it," Soleta said. "I can think of several."

"So can I," said Riker, "And either it'll put the virus right into the food, or the clothing, or he might just pump it right into the air. We should consider ourselves damn lucky that he didn't decide to try and replicate the virus aboard the ship or we'd all be goners."

"We can probably thank the Romulans for that, ironically enough," Soleta said. "I know them, I know how they think. We did them some serious damage. They probably wanted to beam aboard first and obtain some personal vengeance for the ships of theirs that we destroyed. Once done with that, they likely would have started pumping their virus throughout the ship after they left . . ." Her voice trailed off.

All eyes turned toward Burgoyne. But s/he shook hir head quickly. "No. No, nothing like that's been done. We got out of the area fast enough to avoid any such stunts."

"But we might be carrying something within the computer base . . ."

"No, that's the problem. We're not carrying anything in the computer base. When they got into our mainframe, they wound up erasing all the data. Everything. This ship is a damnable blank slate. All of the fundamental material and information needed for its running is gone."

"Gone? Completely?"

"Information is never gone completely from a computer, Captain. It's there somewhere. But when it's wiped clean, what basically happens is that we can't get at it. I'll find a way . . . but it'll take time."

"How much time?"

"I don't know," s/he admitted. "I have all my people working on it, but I simply do not know. And that's not all."

"What, it gets better?"

"That's an understatement. Our preliminary probes reveal imprints of mental engrams left behind, like fingerprints. This wasn't simply a virus or a machine wipe. A mind . . . an actual mind . . . entered the computer and nearly wiped it, and us, from existence."

"The Narobi. It has to be," said Si Cwan.

"Perfect. So what have we got?" asked Riker. "In terms of capabilities, I mean."

"Minimal, being routed through manual control. We've got life support systems on line. Warp drive is up, as you know, which is how we managed to throw ourselves to . . . wherever the hell it is that we are."

"Have we got coordinates as to our present location?" asked Riker.

Shelby nodded. "McHenry says he knows where we are. I have no reason to doubt him."

"We jumped blind through warp space and he knows where we came out?"

She nodded again. "He's rather talented that way."

"So I hear. All right: life support, warp drive . . . what about communications?"

"Not yet," said Burgoyne. "Besides, even if we did have communications up and running and could get through to the Federation . . . what would we say? '*Excalibur* to UFP: Shut down everything throughout the entire Federation. We're celebrating the bicentennial by reverting to the Stone Age. Cease and desist in your entire way of life until you hear from us again. And by the way, we have no proof.' Oh, that's going to go over very well, I can assure you. They'd probably shunt the message over into a committee which would debate about it for three weeks before resolving to tell us that we're idiots."

"You've made your point, Burgoyne," Riker said. "Is anything else functioning around here?"

"Manual guidance control just came back on, and we've got the viewscreens up and running. Basically, we can move, at warp speed if we need to. But navigation is still off-line. It would be like trying to steer in the dark while blindfolded. It's impossible. Besides, we have no idea where we would go anyway."

"Yes. We do," Soleta said. "That was the one other piece of information I . . . we," she amended with a glance toward Selar, " . . . managed to get out of Sela. The coordinates of where Gerrid Thul is."

"But as Burgoyne said, trying to plot, to navigate without the computers . . . unless these coordinates are practically next door, it's just not possible," Riker said.

"I wouldn't be so quick to say that," Shelby told him. "I suggest we run it past McHenry."

"Are you sure?" he asked.

She smiled thinly. "Trust me."

"All right," he nodded slowly. "I don't see that we have much of a choice. Let's do it, people."

As they cleared out of the conference lounge, Soleta found herself momentarily alone with Selar. She moved toward her and said, "Doctor . . ."

But Selar shook her head. "Lieutenant . . . do not."

"I was just . . ."

"Going to thank me?"

"Yes."

"Do not," she said again. "I do not wish to be thanked. You have done me service in the past. I found that I could not turn away from you when you were in need. But I compromised myself . . . my sense of ethics . . . my very morality. I did harm, Lieutenant."

"For the greater good, Doctor. That should make it easier."

"It should. I agree. But . . . it does not. If you will excuse me," and she walked out of the conference room.

Mark McHenry stared out at the stars. So many. So many of them. Riker stood behind him on the bridge, as did Shelby. "They are gorgeous, you know," McHenry said softly. "I see them in my head last thing before I go to sleep . . . and first thing when I wake up. I know them. Know them all."

"And you know where we are in relation to them right now?"

"Yes, sir."

"And these coordinates that Soleta has given you . . . you know where those are, as well?"

"Yes, sir."

Riker found it hard to believe. He had been treading the spaceways for over half his life, but like virtually everyone else he knew, he required star-charts, computer-generated readouts, and whatever else could be provided for the purpose of making his way around the vastness of space. To just . . . *know* . . . to be able to look out into the galaxy and have that clear an idea in one's head of exactly where one was . . . it was astounding.

"And you can get us there?" Riker said.

McHenry closed his eyes a moment. It seemed as if he'd gone to sleep. Riker started to say something, but Shelby touched him gently on the arm and shook her head. Then McHenry opened his eyes once more and said, "Yes, sir. Not a problem."

"All right, then. Lay in a course—" His voice trailed off, and he corrected himself, because it was impossible to plot a course. All the steering would have to be done manually. "Take us out, Mr. McHenry. Warp factor . . ." He hesitated and then shrugged. "Whatever you feel comfortable moving at. And let's hope to hell that Burgoyne has the weapons on line by the time we get there."

"Aye, sir. May I ask a question, sir?" he inquired as he urged the ship forward.

"Absolutely."

"What's going on? I mean, I can get us there, but it's not without risks. Without navigation on line, it's going to be a bit trickier avoiding, oh . . . black holes, asteroid fields and the like. I can do it, mind you . . . but it's trickier. The smart thing to do would be to remain where we were until everything is back up and running. So what's the rush? What are we trying to do?"

"Fair enough." He glanced around the bridge and said, with sufficient graveness of tone to put across the gravity of the situation, "A deadly virus is threatening to wipe out the lives of everyone we hold dear . . . and only the good ship *Excalibur* has a hope of stopping it. Does that answer it?"

"Yes, sir."

"You're frowning, Lieutenant. I hope you're not feeling daunted."

"No, sir," said McHenry. "Just the strangest feeling of déjà vu, that's all. Don't worry. It'll be gone soon enough."

XIX.

CALHOUN HAD BEEN in his quarters for all of two minutes when Kwint showed up at the door. He entered without a word and they faced each other as the door slid closed.

"Are you out of your mind!" Calhoun fairly exploded the moment they were in private. "What the hell are you doing here? You almost gave me a heart attack!"

"Calm down, Mac," Picard said stiffly. "Having apoplexy is not going to help the situation."

"That's putting it mildly! It was everything I could do not to react when I saw you! Why are you here? With the hair? And the beard? And Darg?"

"I was sent in by Jellico . . ."

"*Jellico?* But he was working with Nechayev! He helped stage an entire confrontation at the big diplomatic reception to make it seem as if I was storming out of Starfleet! It's how we got Thul's attention!"

"So it would seem. I was unaware of that. Jellico called me in, summarized the situation for me, and sent me on a mission to get in good with Zolon Darg. He chose me because Jack Crusher and I had dealings in the past with Thul. Jellico had heard the rumors that Thul was involved and wanted to make certain, one way or the other."

"But if he knew about—" Then Calhoun actually half-smiled to himself. "He didn't trust me. He didn't trust me not to screw things up. So he sent you in as back-up, without telling Nechayev or me."

"Charming," said Picard.

"And this disguise," and he tugged slightly at the beard, "was supposed to fool him? It didn't fool me."

"First, you've seen me far more recently than Thul. He hasn't laid eyes on me for a good many years, and Darg has never met me. Second, you're Xenexian. You have a heightened sensitivity to such things. Besides, I didn't know for sure that I would wind up face to face with Thul. In any event, he hasn't recognized me, nor has Darg. So we're safe enough . . . for the moment. We have to stay steady, though . . ."

"That was easy until this got personal," said Calhoun, tightly.

Picard looked at him in confusion. "What do you mean?"

"Lodec . . . the Danteri that you saw . . . ?"

"Yes? What about him?"

"He killed my father."

Picard's eyes widened in concern. "Are you certain?"

"Absolutely. Absolutely positive." He paced the room like a caged tiger. "The longer this goes on, the more I think of my father crying out . . . think of what he did . . . Picard . . . there's so many people here now. It could be covered."

"What could be covered?"

"I could kill him, make it seem as if it was a random act of violence. There's enough disreputable individuals that the suspicion wouldn't fall on me, and—"

"Mac," and Picard grasped him by the shoulders, "you can't lose focus. Letting feelings get in the way is not a luxury we can afford."

"Laying my father's soul to rest is not a luxury, Picard. It's a mandate. It has to be done."

"Not here! Not now!" Picard said harshly. "If you do anything to jeopardize the mission we're on now, Mac, just out of a personal sense of vengeance, I will . . ."

"You will what? Have me busted in rank? Slap my wrist? Give me ten lashes? Do you think I seriously give a damn what happens to me?"

"Probably not. But I would hope you give a damn what happens to everyone else. Mac . . . I appreciate your anger and your frustration. But you simply cannot indulge in those feelings at the moment. It could be ruinous for everyone and everything. We have to determine what Thul is up to and stop him. The Mackenzie Calhoun I know wouldn't elevate his need for vengeance over the needs of those who are depending upon him."

"Maybe you don't know Mackenzie Calhoun, then."

"Maybe I don't. But the brutal, simple truth, Mac, is that killing Lodec won't bring your father back. . . . and it could result in the death of many more. Are you prepared to take that chance? Or are you going to do what's right?"

"And who knows what's right, Picard. You?"

"Not always. But in this instance . . . yes."

Slowly, Calhoun sat. He rubbed the lower half of his face in thought, and finally said, "All right. For now . . . for now I do nothing against Lodec. But I'll tell you something, Picard . . . I never thought that doing nothing would be a hundred times more difficult than doing something. Do you have any idea what it's like, Picard? That there's someone you hate so much . . . that with every fibre of your being, all you want to do is hold their head in one hand, their neck in another, and with one quick movement, break it?"

For a moment, Picard saw the skinless, gleaming skull and spine of the Borg queen in his hands, and the cathartic cleansing that came with that glorious snap.

"Believe it or not . . . I do," said Picard.

The summons had come.

Everyone had been informed that they were to come to the grand hall, and come they did. The lifts were operating at peak capacity throughout the sphere as the entire populace converged on the main meeting area.

There had been those who had doubted. Even though they had shown up with the one hundred thousand bars of latinum as promised, still there had been doubts and discord. But the revelation of the sphere's existence, in and of itself, was enough to quell their initial concerns. They knew, beyond question, that they were now part of something special, something incredibly significant in the entire history of the galaxy. There were still questions, still worries, but there was also enough faith that Gerrid Thul actually had a plan. That he knew what he was doing.

And now they were going to find out. All their questions were to be finally, ultimately, answered.

Calhoun and Picard had resolved that going together would not be the brightest move. There was no intrinsic reason for them to be especially friendly with one another, and so it was advisable that they keep their distance, at least until such time as it was unavoidable. So Calhoun headed toward the turbolift on his own upon receiving word of the summons. He stepped into the lift, and froze.

Lodec was standing there. It was just the two of them.

Calhoun couldn't believe it. What was this, some sort of perverse joke that the cosmos was playing on him? He forced a smile as he stepped onto the lift and the doors shut behind him.

"Impressive set-up, isn't it," Lodec said after a moment.

Calhoun managed a nod. He pictured himself with his sword in his hand, plunging it into Lodec's heart. It gave him a minuscule amount of satisfaction, but not much.

And then Lodec said, “I’m sorry.”

“Sorry.” Calhoun repeated the word tonelessly. “Sorry . . . for what?”

“You were right. My saying that I was simply following orders . . . that was just an excuse. A nice, tidy way of shirking my responsibility. The things that we did . . .” He shook his head. “Inside . . . I was screaming. Screaming. But Falkar—that’s who I was connected to—Falkar was the liege-lord of our family. Our patron, as he was to a number of us. So when he selected me to serve him, I had no choice. At least, that’s what I told myself. My family sent me off to war, and I’ll never forget my father looking at me so sternly, giving me the admonition, ‘Don’t dishonor us, son. Don’t dishonor us.’ And me, young and foolish . . . I would have done anything to make my father proud. Do you know what that’s like?”

“No,” Calhoun said hollowly.

“Oh. Well . . . that’s all I cared about. Pleasing him, pleasing my family. But I hated every moment of it. It got so bad . . . there was a time there where we were posted to Xenex, and I thought of leaving the camp and walking into the nearest Xenexian town and picking a fight, and then allowing myself to be killed. That way . . . that way it would have been over. I didn’t have the nerve, though. I didn’t want to throw my life away because part of me kept saying, ‘Stay steady. Things will get better. You won’t have to live this way forever.’ Except the problem is . . . even when you’re not living it . . . it stays with you for as long as you live. The things we did,” he said again, shaking his head, looking lost. “The helpless people we killed . . . the beatings . . . lord . . . they put me in charge of whippings, can you believe that?”

“Indeed. Why you?” Calhoun’s voice was strangled. But he saw that Lodec was so far in his recollections that he wasn’t noticing.

“I’d practiced with whips ever since I was a kid. To me, it wasn’t a weapon. It was a tool of skill. I could knock over a particular rock from thirty paces without disturbing anything around it. Falkar saw me showing off one day, and on the spot, stated that I was his new whip master. He had me beat people . . . the screams . . . the blood . . .”

“Beat them to death, did you?”

“Sometimes,” he whispered. “Sometimes, yes. I’d be there, torturing the poor devils, and in my head I was taking myself away, somewhere far away . . .”

“What are you telling me this for?” demanded Calhoun abruptly. “What do you want from me? Absolution? You want me to tell you that it’s okay, you’re forgiven?”

“Perhaps. You were their warlord. If you said you understood . . . if you . . .” Then he saw the look in Calhoun’s hard purple eyes. “No. No, I suppose not. My apologies. It was foolish of me even to try.”

The door slid open and he walked out, leaving Calhoun drained in the turbolift, his hands shaking.

The viewscreen was massive, and on it, everyone could see the celebration of the bicentennial well under way. It was in the great plaza of the United Federation Headquarters, and it was a wonder to behold. a veritable sea of races and faces, smiling or doing whatever their respective physicality allowed them to do when it came to expressing pleasure. Calhoun even fancied that he could make out Jellico's face somewhere in all that hubbub.

Gerrid Thul was standing upon a raised platform, looking down at the assemblage that he had gathered. He looked stronger, more vital than he had before. "Thank you, my friends," he said. "Thank you for coming. Thank you for . . . believing. For many months now, you have heard the whispers . . . you have had revealed to you, in small amounts, the truth of the time to come. And you see there, now, on this screen, on the planet earth, the United Federation of Planets celebrating its own birth. As it so happens, we shall be celebrating as well. We shall be celebrating . . . its demise.

"It is ironic somehow that we are witnessing a celebration on earth. Earth has many interesting and intriguing end-of-the-world myths from its many cultures. The details differ, but the outcome remains the same: The old is washed away, while the new rises to take its rightful place.

"The time has come for a new cleansing. The Federation has become too huge, too insensitive, interested only in maintaining its own existence and status quo rather than attending to the true needs of various sentient beings. There is too much need for commonality, and there is a loss of individual identity. You see on that screen a dazzling array of species . . . but as year upon year has gone by, they have slowly lost that which made them unique, special. The Federation must pay for that loss. And the Federation must, and shall, pay for the disservice that it has done to you. You, the outcasts, who for whatever reason, do not fit in with the Federation's grand scheme of the way things should be. Rejoice, my friends, for the days of your living in a galaxy that attends to the Federation's beck and call are soon over."

Thul gestured to his right, indicating that someone should join him on the podium. In the meantime, Calhoun looked around, trying to catch a glimpse of either Picard or Vara Syndra or, most particularly, Zolon Darg. Darg was the only one he managed to spot, but that wasn't too surprising. With his bulk, he towered above everyone around him. Picard might have been standing right next to him, but thanks to the crowd, Calhoun couldn't possibly see him.

A rather unassuming human was now standing next to Thul on the podium. "This . . . is Doctor David Kendrow, one of the premier computer scientists in the quadrant. Wave to the good people, Kendrow." Kendrow obediently waved. He seemed none too thrilled to be there. "Doctor Kendrow," continued Thul, "has been instrumental in aiding us. He has helped us to coordinate an astounding amount of information about artificial intelligence. His greatest aid has come in helping us to understand a remarkably advanced computer called the Omega 9 . . . a computer which sets new advances in the art of interfacing with existing mainframes. Working in tandem with the Omega 9, assorted other research, and dissident residents of a world called Narobi II, we are going to accomplish what no one else in the history of the Federation has managed to do: We are going to connect, at one time, with every computer mainframe through the entire UFP.

"The very commonality which has made the UFP into such a tightly-knit organization is going to be used against it. But we are not simply going to use the Omega 9 to destroy the computers, oh no. Far from it. You see, the computers are tied in with, and control, food replicators which are common technology on all the member planets. The Omega 9 is going to cause all the computers to replicate a virus which I call the Double Helix, which I have spent years perfecting. Now . . . replicators are limited. They cannot create something that is alive. They can, however, create a string of chemicals which will replicate the disease, and as the disease is introduced into the food or textiles that the replicators generate, that—I assure you—will be more than sufficient.

"But that is too slow. Oh yes . . . too slow, my friends, and too inefficient. So what will, in fact, happen, is that at the precise same moment, all replicators everywhere will go active, and a gas will be issued by them. That gas will contain the Double Helix virus, and will spread as an airborne menace in no time at all, over every single planet.

"The Federation representatives are scheduled to re-enact the signing of the charter. That will be the moment when the virus will be released on all the Federation worlds simultaneously via the replicators. It will be galaxy-wide, and the entire Federation will be obliterated in one stroke. Those worlds which are not part of the Federation will naturally survive . . . as will anyone who is safe within the Thul sphere." He smiled out at the crowd, spreading his arms wide. "And that will be that. In one grand, glorious stroke, the entire United Federation of Planets will become a thing of the past!"

A huge buzz of conversation had been building and building as Thul had continued, and when he stopped and waited for a reaction, he very much got one. There was a gigantic cheer, a roar of approval so loud that

Calhoun thought he was going to go deaf. The applause and huzzahs seemed to go on forever, and when it finally did subside, it was only at Gerrid Thul's urging as he clearly had more to say.

Calhoun, in the meantime, was endeavoring to drift toward the back of the room. He had no problem making sure that no one was watching him; every eye in the place was riveted on Thul. He tapped the inside of his left heel, and the long-range communicator slid smoothly out of the heel and into his palm.

Thul started to speak again. His voice was amplified, and it was so loud that Calhoun knew he was going to have trouble getting anyone to hear him.

"Yes, my friends. The Federation has become weak," said Thul. "The Federation has become stupid. And the most insulting of all . . . the Federation thinks that we, ourselves, are so stupid, that we will easily be fooled by whatever pathetic plan they might come up with. See for yourself the pathetic spy that they have sent into our midst."

Calhoun's head snapped around . . . and he saw himself. To be precise, he saw his face on the gigantic screen behind Thul, having replaced the image of the UFP celebration. There he was, right in the midst of the crowd, palming the device that he was about to speak into.

Those who were standing around him naturally recognized him immediately and lunged toward him. Calhoun tried to fight his way out, but it was hopeless before he even began. Innumerable hands surrounded him, shoving him toward the floor, and the communicator flew out of his hand. It skidded to a halt several feet away and he could see it, just out of his reach.

And then it was trampled, simply crushed beneath the stampede that was converging on the spy who had been named by Gerrid Thul.

Calhoun was hauled to his feet, still struggling. Even as he did, though, he knew that it was futile. It was almost more out of misplaced pride than anything else, because in point of fact, he didn't stand a chance.

"Up here, my friends! Bring him up here!"

They shoved Calhoun forward, laughing and shouting, and within moments he had been thrown at the feet of Gerrid Thul. He started to get to his feet, and then an immense foot came down on his back. He knew who it was immediately, even as his spine creaked under the weight.

"Zolon Darg," Thul said conversationally to Calhoun, "has been asking for this opportunity."

"I'm not a spy—" Calhoun began. Then he couldn't get another word out as Darg increased the pressure, chortling as he did so.

"It is possible," Thul allowed. "On the other hand, that is merely a possibility . . . whereas I consider your being a spy to fall far more into the realm of likelihood. Darg . . . do as you like."

"As I like?" Darg said, and made as if to slam his foot completely through Calhoun's torso. Then he paused and said, "No. Why should I keep the fun to myself? You know . . . there are many things I can do with you, Calhoun, after you're dead. So why not give others the opportunity to actually escort you to the other side." He pulled his blaster from his holster and called out, "Kwint!"

Kwint appeared at his side, his face one big sneer. "Yes, sir?"

"Here," and he handed the blaster to Kwint. "Execute him."

Calhoun, very carefully and very deliberately, did not look up at the disguised Picard. To do so would have come across as pleading, and that was not something he could risk. Calhoun was done for, he knew that. But if Picard foolishly attempted to save him, they would both be finished. One of them had to complete the task. And if Calhoun was going to be the one to fall, then so be it.

He just prayed Picard wouldn't be so foolhardy as to try some insane rescue ploy. Surely Picard had to know that it was hopeless, that Calhoun had to be sacrificed. That was simply the way it had played out. No offense, no foul, see you next lifetime.

In a way, it was almost a relief. At that point, Calhoun had absolutely no idea what to do about Lodec. At least dying first would resolve that quandary.

He had always understood that, when one is about to die, one's life flashes before one's eyes. He waited for that to happen.

There was no flash. There was no life.

This made him edgy, as it seemed to indicate that he wasn't about to die. If that were the case, then it was most unfortunate because that meant—

"Nobody move!" shouted Picard.

"Oh, hell," muttered Calhoun.

Picard considered, for a moment that was in fact brief but, to him, seemed endless, the option of shooting Calhoun. There didn't seem to be any other options being presented to him.

His finger even started to squeeze the trigger . . . and that was when Picard knew that he simply couldn't do it. If one was dealing with sheer numbers—the death of one man, Calhoun, versus the potential death of trillions of beings—obviously there was no choice. But Picard refused to accept that it was that simple. There had to be other choices.

Moving with surprising speed, Picard vaulted the distance between himself and Thul and put the blaster straight at Gerrid Thul's head. Darg didn't budge. Neither did Thul. The crowd started to converge, to surge forward, and Picard called out, "Tell them to back off! We're going!"

"Are you?" Darg asked calmly. "And if you're prevented from doing so . . . ?"

"Then Gerrid Thul dies," Picard said firmly. "I'll kill him . . ."

"As you killed my son?" Gerrid Thul asked.

The words froze Picard. Did Thul actually know him? What was that possible? But if he did, then that meant—

"Go ahead," Darg was saying. "Shoot. See if I care."

That more or less clinched it for Picard. He looked down at the energy indicator on the blaster he was holding, but was reasonably certain about what he was going to find.

It read "empty." The blaster was completely out of power.

Picard looked up and saw that he was ringed by half a dozen blasters, all aimed squarely at him.

"Now these," Darg said conversationally, "all work."

Slowly Picard put up his hands, knowing there was no choice. He was grabbed from all sides, and he saw Calhoun being hauled to his feet as well.

"I never trusted you for a moment, 'Kwint,' " Darg told him. "So I had a DNA check run on you from scrapings taken off a glass at Kara's. By the time we arrived here, Gerrid Thul was already quite aware that the man who killed his son was going to be making a return visit."

"I was not responsible for the death of your son, and you know it," Picard said to Thul.

"You can believe that, if it pleases you to do so," Thul said. "I, however, know otherwise. Darg . . . take them away. Put them in lock-up."

"What? Why? I'll just kill them . . ."

"You'll do no such thing," Thul admonished him. 'I want them in lock-up, with a screen that broadcasts the Federation ceremonies. I want them to witness their Federation's fall. I think . . ." and he smiled broadly, "I think my son would have liked it that way."

XX.

"WHAT DID YOU EXPECT me to do?" demanded Picard.

From within their cell, Calhoun glowered at him. "I expected you to pull the damned trigger, that's what I expected you to do."

"And kill you in cold blood."

"If it meant preserving the mission, yes."

Just outside the cell, two guards were visible through the force field that was blocking the door. They appeared to be smirking as the two captains disagreed rather vocally about the direction that Picard should have followed in the given situation.

Calhoun was sitting disconsolately on one of the hard benches that constituted the entirety of the furniture in the cramped cell, while Picard was standing and facing him. "So you expected me to shoot you down?"

"Absolutely," said Calhoun. "I knew there were hazards to this mission . . ."

"For God's sake, Mac, there are hazards to any mission. But this was . . ." He paused and then said, "If the situation were reversed, would you have shot me."

"With the safety of the entire Federation on the line?"

"Yes."

Without hesitation, Calhoun said, "In a heartbeat."

They stared at each other for a long moment, and then Picard said softly, "And if it were Shelby?"

Calhoun looked away. "This is a stupid discussion. It's all moot anyway. The game was up before they even handed you the blaster."

"True."

"So . . ." Calhoun slapped his thighs and stood. Then he walked over to the forcefield that barred the way and he stroked his chin thoughtfully. The guards outside watched him through narrowed eyes. "Here's what we have to do. We have to get out of here, destroy their computer system, take down Gerrid Thul and Zolon Darg, and do it all before they have the signing ceremony back on earth that's going to signal the beginning of the end."

The guards clearly thought this to be a hilarious proposition. They laughed out loud as Calhoun stared at them. "Is something funny?" he asked quietly.

"No, nothing at all," said one of the guards. "We'd be most interested in seeing you get out of here. Wouldn't we, Benz?" he said to the other.

"Absolutely, Zeen," said Benz.

"I just need to warn you," Calhoun said calmly, "that if I do get out of here, the first thing I'm going to have to do is kill the both of you. Nothing else to be done for it, I'm afraid. I can't take the chance of either of you recovering and sounding an alarm prematurely."

"Oh, we understand that perfectly. We won't hold it against you. How are you going to kill us, by the way? Weapons scan revealed no weapons on you."

"I'll just have to do it with my bare hands."

"Very well. You go right ahead," grinned Zeen.

"You're sure you won't be upset?"

"Not at all. We understand you have a difficult job to do. Far be it from us to resent you for it."

"That's very kind of you. Activate transporter, right."

The grin remained on their faces for another moment or two . . . and then, to their shock, Calhoun vanished in a burst of molecular rearrangement.

"What the hell!" the one called Benz roared.

They were both facing the cell when Calhoun rematerialized directly behind them. They spun, faced him.

Benz was closer. Calhoun's right hand speared out, nailed Benz in the throat, crushing his windpipe. It was effectively over for him at that moment as he collapsed to the floor, unable to breathe.

Opening his mouth to shout out a warning, Zeen brought up his weapon at the same time. Calhoun didn't even slow down. Moving with incredible calm, he grabbed Zeen's gun, angled it backward and fired. The blast struck the forcefield, ricocheted, and hit Zeen in the back. Zeen's eyes went wide as his spine sizzled, but he didn't feel the pain for long as Calhoun grabbed either side of his head and twisted with brisk efficiency to the right. Zeen's neck broke with remarkable ease and he sagged to the floor.

As he fell, Calhoun pulled the gun from his lifeless fingers and glanced down at Benz, gasping on the floor, unable to draw in air. Calhoun fired off a quick shot into his head and Benz stopped thrashing about.

From the moment he'd reappeared outside the cell to the moment that the guards were dead, the entire incident had taken no more than four seconds.

Calhoun shoved the blaster into his belt, picked up Benz's, which he'd never even had the chance to pull out, and then tapped the controls deactivating the cell forcefield. Picard stepped out and looked down in astonished horror at the unmoving guards . . . and then up at the cold purple eyes of Calhoun.

"Let me guess," he said coolly to Picard. "You wouldn't have done it."

"I would have found another way, yes."

"I guess you're not a savage, then."

There was an element of pity in Picard's eyes that Calhoun found most annoying, "I guess not."

He handed one of the blasters to Picard. "That's too bad. It's a savage galaxy. Let's go."

Suddenly they heard a footfall behind them, someone else coming down the corridor. Calhoun spun, levelling his weapon and fully prepared to annihilate almost anyone who appeared around the corner.

Vara Syndra, however, fell into the "almost anyone" category, and so it was that when she came into view, she did not immediately die. Instead she looked at the fallen bodies, and up at Calhoun, with a remarkable lack of surprise.

"I should have known," she said, and for some reason her voice sounded different. Less airy, less seductive, more hardened. "I show up to free you, and you're already out."

"Free us? Why?" demanded Picard.

"Because I owe him," she said, indicating Calhoun, "and I always pay my debts."

"You don't owe me anything," Calhoun said. "I mean, granted, it was good, I thought, but—"

"This isn't about sex, you idiot!" she said in exasperation. "Don't you know anything? Don't you—?"

And then, from behind Vara, came three guards. Like the fallen ones, they were Thallonians. Unlike the fallen ones, they had their weapons up and they were ready to start firing. Picard and Calhoun had their blasters up, but Vara was squarely in the way.

"Hold on a moment," she sighed, and then she spun and she was holding a knife in either hand. Before the guards were even aware they were under attack from her, they were already dead. A thick pool of blood began to spread from their fallen bodies as they lay on the floor, one piled atop another, dark liquid pouring from the vital arteries that Vara had effortlessly cut.

Vara grinned. There was nothing seductive about her. The woman who had been radiating sex not so long ago had changed into something completely different. Feral, wild, brutal and—

And Calhoun laughed.

"What," Picard asked him stiffly, "is so damned funny?"

"She knows what's so funny," said Calhoun. "Don't you, Vandelia."

"It took you long enough, you Xenexian jerk," said Vandelia of Orion.

In the main computer lab, Kendrow studied the final link-ups very carefully. The last thing he wanted at this point was for something to go wrong, because he knew all too well that any sort of failure at this point would be the end of him.

He kept glancing, equally nervous, at the Narobi who was standing nearby. His name, loosely translated, was simply Silver, which was his color. He had another designation which was used to distinguish him from other Narobi, but since there were none others around at that point, he had seen no need for its use. When it had been made clear to him that human interaction almost required that he be called *something,* he had chosen simply "Silver" and recommended that that be the end of it.

Silver was the leader of the dissidents of Narobi. Normally a peaceful people, it had been Silver who had felt most strongly that they were capable of so much more than simple peace, and he had been more than accommodating when he had been approaching by Gerrid Thul. Silver, like all his people, was tall and glistening and almost entirely machine. There were some small elements of the mortal left within him. Those were doubtlessly the ones that made him dissatisfied with the Narobi philosophy of peace.

When he spoke, his lips did not move, for the simple reason that he had none. No mouth, for standard food was not a requirement; he was solar powered. No nose, for of what interest was scent. He did, however, have eyes, not so much for sight as it was that the Narobi had discovered other races like to have eyes they could look into when they were talking.

Standing nearby, observing the final preparations, were Gerrid Thul and Zolon Darg. "Everything will be ready, will it not, Kendrow?" asked Thul in that silky voice he had that was half pleasantry, half warning.

"Yes, sir."

"Good, Quite good. We wouldn't want anything to go wrong, would we?"

"Definitely not, sir."

There was an observation window in the computer center that opened up onto the grand square. The screen was up and running, once again focused upon the events at the Federation gathering. Many of Thul's followers who had gathered there were still there, watching the drama unfold that was going to spell the end of the Federation. Thul smiled down at them. His people. His followers. He very much liked the sound of that. And Mendan Abbis would have liked the sound of it, too. The thoughts of his son momentarily saddened him, and he pushed them away. Now was not the time for distractions.

"Darg . . ." he glanced around. "Have you seen Vara? She seems to have disappeared."

"No, sir. I have not."

"See if you can find—"

And suddenly there was a *breep* that came over Darg's comm unit. "Yes. Go ahead," he said brusquely into it.

"Sir! The prisoners are out! We found the cell deactivated! Five guards down!"

Darg looked at Thul in a most accusing, "told you so" manner. "Alert the security force. But do it quietly. We don't need alarm bells howling, getting everyone upset and also letting the prisoners know that we know they're out. I'll be right there." Then he stabbed an angry finger at Thul. "I told you this would happen! I told you I should have killed them immediately!"

"I simply have endless confidence in you, Darg, that you'll be able to handle them. In fact, you should thank me. You see . . . you made a muddle of attending to Calhoun last time you faced him. If I hadn't found you and . . . attended to you . . . you'd be long dead by now. So I'm generously giv-ing you an opportunity to get it right this time. Do not disappoint me, or yourself."

With an irritated growl, Darg headed out. Thul, meantime, turned back to Kendrow and said calmly, "Don't slow in your preparations, Kendrow. Timing, after all, is everything."

At the site of the great Federation assemblage, Admiral Nechayev, in full formal dress, felt a tap on her shoulder. She turned and saw Admiral Jellico behind her, with his customary polite-but-pained expression. "Greetings, Admiral," he said. "I don't usually see you at such functions, particularly at such crowded ones."

"I know that, Admiral. But even an office-bound old thing like me likes to get out every now and then. Mingle. That sort of thing."

"So," and he folded his arms, "your boy Calhoun staged quite an exit, didn't he, Alynna?"

"You cooperated admirably, Eddie."

"Cooperated? He hit me! In the head!"

"He was simply improvising."

"In the *head,*" repeated Jellico.

"Oh, well, Eddie, it's not as if you were using it for anything."

"You're a riot, Alynna. We were supposed to stage an argument. Not get physical."

A slightly tipsy Tellarite bumped into her. He grunted an apology and moved on. She shook her head in annoyance, although she was more irritated with Jellico than the Tellarite. "And how convincing do you think it would have been if you threatened to throw him out of Starfleet after a simple argument. I don't blame Mac for slugging you. It all serves a higher purpose, Eddie, just remember that."

"So you say." He looked around. "Except I don't see him here. In fact, I don't see any danger of anything at the moment."

"That's why he's involved, Eddie. To attend to whatever it is we don't see."

"And maybe he's not needed. Maybe there are others who are attending to it just fine."

She looked at him askance. "What is that supposed to mean?"

"Nothing." He smiled enigmatically. "Not a thing."

Rolling her eyes, she said, "Fine, Eddie. Whatever you say. It means nothing. Oh," and she pointed toward the front of the room. "They're starting."

"Starting what?"

"The re-enactment of the Resolution of Non-interference. Come along, Eddie. We're about to see history."

XXI.

ALL THOSE YEARS AGO, even after Calhoun had freed her, Vandelia had lived in fear of Darg. For she had heard rumors that Darg had somehow survived the destruction of his headquarters. That he was back in the business, building up his strength, making his connections once more. That he was more powerful and nastier than ever. And that he had never, ever, given up the notion of tracking down Vandelia and the mysterious man who had freed her, and making them both pay. On at least two occasions, Vandelia had narrowly missed him, arriving at a performing spot mere days after Darg had been there.

Vandelia was a brave and fierce woman, as was typical of Orions. But even she had her breaking point. Night after night she would lie awake, listening, wondering whether this would be the night that Darg tracked her down. She had no interest in facing him and teaching him one final lesson, nor did she desire to track him down first so she could put an end to him. For Vandelia had had the most uncanny feeling that she had gotten off quite luckily the first time, and to encounter Darg again would be to tempt fate in a manner that would ultimately rebound to her detriment.

She saw only one way out . . . and she took it.

Vandelia disappeared . . . and Vara Syndra was born.

It had not been all that difficult, really. The changes were mostly cosmetic. She hadn't really been transformed into a Thallonian. Shaving her head, changing the pigmentation of her skin from green to red, all had been fairly simple. Her physicality, however, and the ability to give off waves of sex appeal in the same way that stars gave off light was another matter, however.

For that, she had turned to a supplier of all things exotic, questionable and, for the most part, illegal. His name had been Brace Carmel Mudd, and the first time that she had encountered him, she had felt unclean. Purported to be a "family business," it had been his name which she had heard bandied about most often when she'd made inquiries as to obtaining Venus drugs. She had managed to track him down and, for a healthy price (not to mention a substantial loss of her self-respect), had obtained the drugs.

The drugs had been around for nearly two centuries, and the core suppliers—whose real names were unknown to all but a handful, Mudd included—had spent much of that time perfecting them. In the old days, their effects had been fairly temporary, and the alterations they made relatively modest. They had simply enhanced those features that the users felt were their strongest. But it had been as much in the mind as in the body.

Not anymore. The Venus drugs of the modern era were far more sophisticated. They had put inches on Vandelia in all the right places, reconfigured her into an absolute sexual magnet. They had even altered the shape of her face, to the point where she was unrecognizable. Mudd had given her a ten-year supply and gone on his way, and Vandelia had used it extremely well. She had gone into Thallonian space, which on the surface of it seemed insane. It was, after all, the native territory of the one man she never wanted to encounter again. But she had decided to play the concept of hiding in plain sight to the hilt. If Darg was busy checking the far reaches of the galaxy for Vandelia, it would never occur to him to look in his own backyard. And even if he did, he wouldn't think at all about a sultry Thallonian woman who went by the name of Vara Syndra.

Everything had been going fine . . . until the drugs had run out prematurely. For Mudd, as it turned out, had not exactly dealt fairly with her. The ten-year supply was, in reality, half that, the rest of it simple colored gelatin. It meant that she had overpaid significantly. It also meant she was in tremendous danger.

It was around then that she had fallen in with Gerrid Thul. Thul had taken an immediate liking to her. He did not know her true name, or even that she was originally an Orion. What he did know, however, was where to obtain the Venus drugs which she now desperately needed as her supply of the real drugs was dwindling to nothing. It became an eminently workable arrangement. She became his full-time aide, generating her considerable sex appeal whenever he needed it, and he kept her in supply of the Venus drugs. It worked out rather nicely.

Nonetheless, she nearly panicked when Zolon Darg came on the scene.

At first she couldn't believe it was he when Thul "introduced" them, he had become so huge. Then she waited for some glimmer of recognition from him. She had steeled herself for this possibility for many years, but once it arrived, it was everything she could do not to run screaming from the room.

Darg grunted.

That was it. End of encounter. He grunted. Whenever he would see her in the future, it would always be the same terse acknowledgment of her. She couldn't believe how fortunate she had been; he had no idea who she was. In fact, at one point, he even asked her if she knew of an Orion dancer named Vandelia. It was all she could do not to scream the truth in his face to display her contempt for him. That, however, would not have been a wise move, since he would then have killed her in short order, so she managed to restrain herself.

"Vandelia? Never heard of her," she had said, wide-eyed, and he never inquired again.

He also never displayed any physical interest in her. For the first weeks after encountering him, she had dreaded the day that Gerrid Thul might tell her that she was required to "entertain" the formidable Zolon Darg. But it had never happened. He wasn't remotely drawn to her. She couldn't quite figure out whether she should be relieved or insulted. Ultimately she opted for the former.

Thus had her life gone, hiding in plain sight. Living the life of Vara Syndra, adored by more males than she had ever known. It was artificial, it was a shadow, but at least she was alive and enjoying herself.

But every so often she would think about her dancing . . . and also about the scarred man who had rescued her back when she was another person entirely . . . the scarred man who had, amazingly, not immediately succumbed to her charms as an Orion dancing girl, even though the pheromones that she generated (as did all of her kind) should have made her irresistible. She was sure, though, that the Venus drugs enhancing her pheromones would prove irresistible even to Calhoun.

She'd proven right.

She was, for some reason, a little disappointed . . .

Calhoun, Picard, and Vandelia headed down the corridor as quickly as she could. "Down this way," she said. "We've got to get you out of here."

"We can't," Picard said. "We have to stop Thul's plan."

She was about to try and talk them out of it, and then she mentally shrugged. "Yes. You would have to, wouldn't you?" Calhoun was staring at her. "Well? Any questions, Mac?"

"No," he said after a moment's thought. "Shaved the head, retoned the skin, Venus drugs, hid in plain sight. Correct?"

She blinked back her astonishment and then said in the most bored tone she could muster, "Wrong. Completely wrong. Now come on."

"Where's the central computer room. He must be programming it from somewhere," said Picard.

"Up," she said. "It's up at the top level. Here," and she suddenly walked over to a computer station that was built into the wall. She tapped in an identification code and, moments later, a schematic of the sphere appeared on it. "Here it is," and she pointed out the location.

"Are there laboratory facilities?" asked Picard.

"Yes. Here. Two levels below the top. Why?"

"Because if we don't manage to stop the initial launch of the virus, and it does get loose, we need to know if there's some sort of cure for it," Picard said. "And if he was doing research on it—"

A blaster bolt struck the computer station and smashed it apart.

The three of them whirled, just in time to see a squadron of Thul's men charging toward them.

Picard and Calhoun immediately fell back, firing as they went, desperately trying to keep their pursuers off balance. Vandelia, who had lifted a blaster from one of the Thallonians who had tried to take them down earlier, was also firing. They picked off several of their pursuers, and the others ducked for cover. "Come on! This way!" shouted Picard, and they bolted down the corridor.

Blasts ricocheted off the walls around them as they ran. One of them struck an overhead pipe, and coolant blasted out, filling up the entire walkway with thick, white smoke. Vandelia took a deep breath of air before it became impossible to do so, and then she couldn't see anything. There were forms, shadows ahead of her, and she ran after them. She went around another corner, and then another.

And suddenly she was alone.

She looked around, tried to figure out where she had become separated from Calhoun and Picard. There were no sounds of pursuit; perhaps they had decided to go around another way, she must try to catch up with them. Even so, retracing her steps would not be the best idea. So she decided to keep going forward.

As she did, she mulled over the fact that she could easily have ducked out of the situation. She could have pretended that Calhoun and Picard had just now taken her hostage. The guards that she'd killed were dead, so they weren't going to talk. The Federation men would certainly have played along so that she wasn't at risk. She could have kept her life going . . .

Except it wasn't her life, not really. It was Vara Syndra's life, and she realized that she had grown rather tired of her. She missed the woman she was. She wanted Vandelia back. And this was the only way to recapture her.

She saw a figure ahead of her in the mist, turning and looking at her. "Mac!" she called. "Mac! Over here!"

The figure suddenly seemed to stand up, looming large in front of her. Zolon Darg emerged from the mist and looked at her as if seeing her for the very first time.

"Hello, Vandelia," he said.

Then he killed her.

XXII.

Picard had absolutely no idea how he had become separated from Calhoun, but there was no time to worry about it at that point. What was of far greater concern were the men who were pursuing him.

He turned quickly, spotted an open lift, and charged toward it. He ducked, weaved, ran as fast as he could. A blast bolt singed his shoulder and he staggered, but he tumbled into the lift, losing his grip on his blaster as he did so. "Level 3A!" he called, which was how he had seen it demarcated on the schematic.

The doors slid closed . . . but just before they did, a Thallonian leaped the distance and fell into the lift car atop Picard. The car started up.

The Thallonian snarled into Picard's face, tried to bring his blaster up. Picard gripped his wrist and they struggled furiously as Picard tried to aim it away from himself. The blaster discharged, blasting through the clear backing of the lift that overlooked the dizzying interior of the sphere.

Picard and the Thallonian struggled to their feet, pushing and shoving against one another. The blaster went off again, ricocheting and striking a glancing blow against the Thallonian's heavily armored back. It wasn't sufficient to hurt him. It was, however, enough to knock both the Thallonian and Picard back and out the gaping hole in the back of the turbolift.

For a moment, there was nothing between Picard and a drop except air, and he was floating in the zero-G environment. Then he snagged the shattered exterior of the lift. It sliced up his hand fiercely, but it held firm.

The Thallonian was less fortunate. He tumbled away from the lift, but he did so in extreme slow motion. He tried to make it back to the lift, looking for all the world as if he were swimming in the air. But he simply drifted backward, faster and faster, heading toward the core of the sphere where the massive cloaking device was.

Picard knew immediately what was going to happen. When he hit the gravimetric center of the sphere, he was going to make a fairly significant splat. And if Picard didn't manage to haul himself back into safety, he was going to go the same way.

The slicing of his hand was excruciating—it was like massaging broken glass—but Picard had no choice. Setting his jaw determinedly, he dragged himself into the lift, fighting against the zero-G which seemed so buoyant but was, in fact, so deadly. In a moment he was tumbled to the floor, and then looked up as the door opened on the level that he had requested.

He picked up the blaster that he had dropped on the floor of the turbolift and staggered out. His blood-covered palms made it difficult to grip the gun securely, but he had to do the best he could. He looked around desperately and saw signs pointing to the lab. How exceptionally convenient.

He followed them quickly, got to the lab, and just as he arrived, ran into another squadron of guards. They had their weapons out, he was ten feet short of the door to the lab, and they absolutely had him cold.

At that point, Mackenzie Calhoun ran by.

And another. And another still.

"Get him!" the lead attacker shouted, but they had no idea which "him" to get. "And him!" he added, and pointed at Picard.

Several of them indeed fired right at Picard, and he would have been dead if Calhoun had not thrown himself into the blaster's path. The shot took him down from the back, and Calhoun collapsed into Picard's arms.

"Mac!" Picard cried out.

At which point, Calhoun abruptly got to his feet and started running back the other way.

By then, everyone was so confused, that they totally missed it when Picard charged into the laboratory.

There were workers and people whom Picard presumed to be scientists within the lab. They were milling about in confusion, clearly concerned over the shots that they were hearing just outside. One of them, not realizing that Picard was the target of those shots, demanded, "What's going on out there? Are you people insane! We can't have blasts flying around here! We can't—"

Picard aimed his blaster squarely at the scientist's face. "You can't . . . what?"

He froze. They all did. When he spoke again, it was with a stammer.

"We . . . there are dangerous chemicals . . . things here that can't . . . that mustn't . . ."

"Things such as the Double Helix virus?" Picard said, his blaster never wavering. His hands were throbbing. It was everything he could do to hold his weapon steady.

There were apprehensive nods from everyone in the room.

"And that means it would be very, very bad if something were to be broken . . . wouldn't it . . . because it might release something that you don't want released. . . ."

At which point, he swung his blaster around in a sweep of the room. He didn't fire . . . he just aimed. But when he was pointing to one corner in particular, that caused an alarmed jump by nearly everyone in the room.

A-ha, he thought as he crossed quickly. Several of the scientists made a move toward him, but he held them back with a glance that spoke volumes.

There were vials, samples lining the wall where he was standing. "Which one?" he demanded. "Which one is the Double Helix? And which one is the cure?"

"There is no cure!" one of the scientists said, and the others bobbed their heads in agreement.

It was too spontaneous a reply to be a falsehood. Picard's heart sank when he heard it, but then he reasoned that if the Federation got their hands on a pure sample of the virus, perhaps their researchers could find it. "A sample. A sample of the virus. I need it, now."

"But . . ."

"*Now!*"

They pointed to one of the tubes, and he snatched it up.

"No, that's the wrong one! It's not the standard virus . . . that one's highly concentrated!" one of them said. "Ten times more virulent! You—!"

Suddenly the pursuing guards burst in through the door, their weapons ready to blast holes into anything and everything.

Considering the inflammatory nature of the moment, Picard was remarkably calm. He simply held the vial up and said, coolly, "You would not like me to drop this?"

In spite of themselves, the guards cast a glance at the scientists. There were rapid and very anxious shakings of heads from all of them, verifying the notion that shooting at Picard at that moment in time would be an extremely bad idea.

Slowly Picard moved toward the door, holding the vial in front of him. "That's it. That's fine. Everyone stay right where they are," he said. "My hands are slippery enough with blood, you see. Wouldn't want me to be even more clumsy, would you? Now, clear the way." They didn't move. His voice dropped even lower, so low that one would have been inclined to check and see if he still had a pulse. "Clear . . . the . . . way," he said very slowly, very methodically, and very dangerously.

They cleared the way.

Calhoun had run to the upper levels and no one stopped him.

He had done so through a rather crafty subterfuge that he was, in fact, rather proud of. He had circled around to where Vandelia had dispatched the group of guards, torn off a piece of cloth from one of them, soaked it in the widening pool of blood, and then held it up to the right side of his face. He then proceeded to run as fast as he could, using stairwells and ladders rather than the lifts which he felt would be watched more carefully. He kept the cloth pressed against his face.

The first time he encountered a squadron of guards, he said nothing, but simply pointed and gesticulated while groaning. What the guards saw was a man who had clearly been badly injured by the escaped prisoners who were somewhere behind him. They promptly ran right past Calhoun and, grinning to himself, he kept on going. It happened three more times as he made his way up the sphere, and each time played out in exactly the same manner.

The fourth time, while on the third level, it didn't work.

It worked at first as they started off down the hall. But then around the corner came Lodec, and he and Calhoun froze, face to face. Lodec wasn't fooled for a second, but for a moment—just a moment—doubt seemed to play across his face.

Calhoun brought his blaster up, operating completely on instinct, ready to shoot Lodec down. And he, likewise, hesitated for a moment.

And then Lodec shouted, "Calhoun! He's here!"

The guards, as one, turned and charged back.

Calhoun shoved his tongue against the replicator inside his mouth, and suddenly multiple versions of himself sprang into existence and started running in all directions. The guards were frozen in confusion, and when they did start opening fire, it was too late. As for the real Calhoun, he paused only long enough to swing a roundhouse punch that flattened Lodec. He hoped he had broken his jaw, and would have liked to do more, but it was all he had time for.

Just ahead of him, on the uppermost floor, was the computer room. He braced himself, holding his blaster firmly, and then he thrust himself in, coming in low, getting ready to fire . . .

There was no one there.

That wasn't entirely true, actually. Vandelia was there, her body tilted back on the chair, blood trickling from her mouth. Calhoun could see from across the room that she was dead. God knew he had seen it enough.

Even so, he didn't want to believe it was true. He approached her slowly, hoping against hope that somehow she would just get up, come back to life. That it was all some sort of a sick joke. Then he heard her voice, and she was whispering, "I wanted to dance . . . for just you . . . Mac . . . one more time . . ." And then her voice rattled in her throat.

And then she repeated it . . . and died again . . . and again . . .

He turned and saw Darg's image on the screen. He was smiling. It was not a pleasant expression.

"Those were her last words, Calhoun. I recorded them for you. I knew you'd want to hear them. If you're hearing this . . . which I assume you are . . . I can further assume that you're in the main computer room. That's where you would naturally come to try and head off Thul's plan. That is naturally where we would be . . . if we didn't mind being easy targets for you. We're secured in another part of the station, I assure you, preparing for the great moment. I'm afraid there's nothing you can do to stop it. It would be most appreciated, however, if you would kindly . . . die."

At that moment, Calhoun had no idea where to go.

At that moment, Calhoun didn't care.

The door to the computer room slid open, as he knew it would. Darg was standing there, as he knew he would be. He was empty-handed, and he waggled his fingers toward Calhoun. Pressing in around him, from all sides, were armed guards. They had their weapons trained on Calhoun. The slightest move and they could easily blast him to free-floating atoms.

"If you drop the weapon . . . you have an opportunity at me . . . man to man. If you don't drop the weapon . . . my men drop you." He paused and then said softly, "Come on, Calhoun. You know you want it."

Calhoun allowed the blaster to drop from his fingers. At that moment, they could easily have killed him where he stood.

They didn't. Instead, they simply watched and grinned. Clearly they were all of the opinion that Darg was in absolutely no danger at all. But at that moment, Calhoun didn't give a damn what they thought. Instead he charged toward the far bigger man, building up speed with every moment, and he slammed into Darg with everything he had.

And bounced off.

His head spun around him as he hit the floor. He had no idea what had just happened. It had been like crashing into a bulkhead at full tilt. His eyes crossed and then uncrossed and he looked up at Darg who was coming right toward him, his fist cocked and ready to slam home. He barely managed to roll out of the way in time as Darg smashed the floor where he'd just been and made a hole in it the size of a watermelon.

Calhoun stumbled out the door. Darg's men made no effort to stop him. They seemed to be having too good a time. Darg lumbered after him, coming toward him like a tidal wave, just as easy to reason with, just as unstoppable.

"A little different this time," he rumbled. "Come back here, Calhoun. We have old scores to settle."

He closed on Calhoun, swung an uppercut that could have taken off Calhoun's head had it connected. Calhoun barely dodged it, moved out of the way of a second thrust, dodged a third. "Stay still!" snarled Darg, but Calhoun did not feel inclined to oblige.

Once more Darg swung, and once more Calhoun got around him, and this time Darg was slightly off balance. Calhoun moved quickly and drove a punch to Darg's jaw. Darg let out an angry yelp and staggered, and Calhoun hit him in the head a second time, staggering him. But then he pressed his luck and this time Darg caught his hand, yanked him off his feet, and slammed him against the wall as if he were a beanbag.

Calhoun felt his face starting to swell from the impact of hitting the wall face-first. He saw Darg advancing on him. Trying to stall for time, he pushed his tongue against the false tooth to activate it. Nothing. Instead he felt the broken shards of the device crumble in his mouth. The impact had shattered it. He spit it out and made a mental note to write a memo to Nechayev about the durability of SI devices.

Darg extended his hands . . . and razor-sharp blades snapped out of the ends of his fingers. He swiped at Calhoun, slashing across his tunic, and Calhoun barely managed to avoid more serious injury. He stared at the blades uncomprehendingly.

"You still don't understand, do you," Darg said. "All right. I'll make it clear for you." He turned the blades toward himself and slashed open his shirt. It fluttered to the ground in several pieces, to reveal Darg's glistening metal silver torso.

"Thul found me, damned near dead. He was impressed I'd survived that long on sheer hatred. He kept me alive and took me to Narobi. They built me this body. My head, my brain's all that's left. I'm not a man anymore. I'm a walking weapon, a machine that pretends it's vaguely alive. A freak. And it's your fault, Calhoun. *Your fault!*" Upon the last words, he succumbed to total rage and charged at Calhoun.

Calhoun twisted loose the heel of his boot. It came clear and he aimed and fired. The phaser blasted out, smashing Darg squarely in the chest. It knocked him back and he fell with a startled grunt.

Calhoun did the only thing that seemed reasonable under the circumstances. He turned and ran.

One of Darg's men tried to fire after him, but Darg slapped the weapon from his hand. "No! He's mine! After all this time, he's mine!" He charged after Calhoun, the floor trembling under his footfall.

In the back-up computer room to which they had been relocated, Kendrow was making the final adjustments under the watchful eyes of Silver and Gerrid Thul. "We're running out of time, Mr. Kendrow," Thul said. He didn't sound nearly as jovial as he usually did.

"I'm very aware of that, sir," said Kendrow nervously. "But I'm getting some odd readings off the Omega 9. Having a bit of trouble locking down some of the neural nets . . ."

"I have far too much riding on this, Kendrow." He pointed below him at the masses who were watching the ceremony about to start. "When one makes the sort of announcements that I have made, it is incumbent upon me . . . for the purpose of my sustained credibility . . . to see them through. I do not need last-minute glitches ruining my plans."

"Neither do I!" Kendrow shot back, sounding rather nervous. "Do you think I don't know what you'll do to me if I—"

"Steady, Kendrow, steady," said Thul gently. "Just do your job. Silver . . . are you prepared?"

Silver was seated in front of the interface panel. He had his palm flat, prepared for the process to begin. "I am ready," he said in that flat and rather unappealing voice of his.

"Excellent." Thul's eyes glittered with anticipation.

Calhoun found an access port directly in front of him, and then he heard the thundering footfall of Darg coming in fast behind him. He ripped open the access port and dropped through.

He landed lightly on a narrow maintenance bridge and made the hideous mistake of looking down.

"Down," in this instance, went on forever. Because he was at the uppermost point of the sphere, standing on a very small bridge which ran across the top of the gigantic column that fed energy into the cloaking device. It was anchored to the top of the sphere by support struts overhead.

Far, far below him, in the center of the great sphere, the cloaking device hummed powerfully.

Clutching onto the railings, Calhoun started running the length of the maintenance bridge. He had almost made it to the far end when he heard a tearing of metal, and then Zolon Darg dropped onto the bridge in front of him. Darg looked utterly confident. There was no reason for him not to be.

"Shoot me again," Darg challenged him. "Go ahead."

Calhoun aimed for Darg's head and fired. But Darg easily blocked the shots by raising his huge metal arms in front of his face and deflecting the blasts. Quickly, Calhoun squeezed the sides of the heel-shaped phaser instead, increasing the intensity of the blast. This actually caused Darg to stagger under the barrage, but it also seemed to anger him more. Despite the sustained assault, Darg advanced step after steady step. His arms outstretched, he was within five feet of Calhoun, then four and then three, and the phaser blast was starting to falter. Calhoun realized that he was reaching the limit of the small phaser's energy capacity.

Calhoun backed up, further and further, and cast a desperate glance behind and up. He saw Darg's men clustered at the access port above and behind him. They didn't seem about to let him climb out. Instead they grinned and pointed and clearly were waiting for the inevitable moment when Darg would get his mechanical hands on him.

He glanced up at the support struts . . . levelled his phaser, and fired.

Darg's smug grin of triumph flickered and then vanished as he saw what Calhoun was doing. "Wait! Hold it, you idiot! Stop!"

But it was too late. The phaser blast tore through the support struts, weakened it sufficiently, and the entire thing tore loose. The maintenance bridge, with a groan of metal, angled wildly downward, affixed to the ceiling only by the struts behind Calhoun. Calhoun clambered toward the section that was still secured, holding on to the railing for dear life as the bridge slanted wildly beneath him, threatening to send them both tumbling off.

Darg leaped forward and upward toward Calhoun, trying to forestall sliding down and off. Calhoun tried to swing his legs up and clear away from Darg's desperate grasp, and almost managed it. But Darg, at the last second, snagged Calhoun's leg. Calhoun let out a yell as he felt his leg practically being torn right out of its socket. Then he lost his grip on the railing and both of them slid off the maintenance bridge and fell.

Gerrid Thul grinned in triumph as the Narobi named Silver pressed his hand flat against the interface board. "Contact processing," announced Silver.

Suddenly a clipped voice called from behind him, "Disconnect him."

He whirled, and couldn't quite believe what he was seeing.

It was Picard. He was standing there with a blaster and an extremely irritated expression. The insensate bodies of a couple of guards could be glimpsed out in the corridor. "You," he said, "have been a very difficult individual to locate."

"Indeed," said Thul slowly. "How did you do it?"

"I asked around. I believe you will find that several of your guards are no longer functioning at full capacity. Have him back away from the computer. Shut it down."

"That's not going to happen, Picard," said Thul.

"I think it will." Picard aimed the blaster and fired almost point blank at Silver.

The blast coruscated around Silver. He paid it no heed.

Picard couldn't quite believe it. Thul, however, didn't seem the least bit thrown. "Very dense material that the Narobi are made from," he said mildly. "Resistant to blasters, phasers, disruptors . . . just about anything. And you'll find that the exterior of the computer bank is coated with the same material. Just one of the several contributions that the Narobi provided. You see, Picard . . . I tend to think ahead. I was not *expecting* that some foolhardy Federation idiot would come charging in here at the last moment and try to disrupt it . . . but I *anticipated* it. I try to anticipate everything."

Picard swung the blaster around and aimed it at Thul. "You," he said sharply, "are not blaster proof. Shut this down, now, or I'll—"

"You'll what? Kill me?" There was no longer any trace of amusement in his voice. "You already killed me, Picard. You killed me years ago, when my son died because of you." Slowly he started to walk toward Picard. "You know . . . when I considered the possibility of the Federation sending someone . . . when I contemplated, imagined that I might find myself facing a desperate emissary trying to stop me . . . I always fantasized it would be you. Isn't that interesting? No one else. Always. In my mind's eye, I saw it just this way, with the two of us face-to-face, and you standing there feeling the same sort of helplessness as Double Helix was unleashed that I felt when I lost my son. Lost him because of you. Because of your damnable Federation."

"And everyone, every man, woman and child is to suffer because of your loss?"

"That's right. That is exactly right."

"You won't live to see your triumph."

"Don't you understand? *I don't care!* Do your worst, Picard! I assure you it will pale next to what I have already done to myself! But in the meantime, nothing you will do will matter one iota, because in the final analysis, I will still win! And there's absolutely nothing you can do to—"

That was when the lights when out and the sphere was rocked by a massive explosion.

In other sections of the Dyson Sphere (or the Thul Sphere, as it were) the gravity was zero, as Picard had learned. But in the center the gravity was near normal. Calhoun tumbled, end over end, trying to find something that he could grab onto, but there was nothing. Far, terribly far away to his left, was the docking port where his ship was comfortably anchored. It operated on voice recognition, but it had to hear him to respond, and he was simply too far away.

Then Calhoun slammed into something. He landed badly, wrenching his shoulder, and he lay there a moment, stunned. He realized that he had struck the outer edge of the cloaking device. He could feel the power of the mighty machine humming beneath him.

He slid a few feet but then managed to halt his skid. Slowly he tried to push his way back up toward the center of the cloaking device, in the meantime looking around and trying to catch a glimpse of where Darg had gone to. His main hope was that Darg had not landed quite as fortunately as he had. That he had instead clipped an edge and bounced off, or perhaps missed it entirely, and was sent tumbling the rest of the way to the bottom of the sphere.

Suddenly he felt the surface of the cloaking device tremble beneath him in a manner that was in excess of the power rumbling beneath it. He craned his neck around and saw Darg charging him.

The top of the cloaking device was slightly angled downward, and Calhoun did the only thing he could: He stopped fighting the pull of gravity and allowed himself to skid toward the edge. Darg was right after him. Calhoun got to the edge of the device and saw a yawning drop beneath him. He also saw that the side of the device was not smooth: There were handholds, or at least protruding surfaces that could be utilized as handholds. The only hope he had was that Darg's metal fingers were so thick that he wouldn't be able to utilize them.

Calhoun swung his body over the edge. His toes sought and found something to break his fall. He started clambering down the side like a monkey scaling a mountain. He just couldn't help but wish that he had some clear idea as to just where the hell he thought he was going.

And in the meantime, his mission was still unfulfilled. He knew that he had almost no time before the Double Helix was unleashed. He had to stop it, somehow.

There was absolutely no choice.

He reached up to his face, grabbed the fake scar that was adhering to his own, and pulled. It came loose with a soft tearing sound, and he slapped the adhesive against the side of the cloaking device. He twisted the edges around each other, and he realized that he had no idea as to whether it was actually activated or not. Well, within fifteen minutes, he'd know for sure . . . and if the thing really were as powerful as claimed, it would wind up being the last thing he knew.

He then continued his descent, and he'd made it fifteen feet, moving quickly in the slightly lighter-than-normal gravity when he saw Darg reach the edge and look down at him with cold, implacable fury. But it would still take Darg time to find a way to come down after him.

Darg jumped.

Son of a bitch, thought Calhoun.

Darg's hand lashed out and he snagged a crossbar, halting his fall. The bar held. Damned sturdy devices these Romulans designed. He was clinging, bat-like to the surface of the cloaking device, only a few feet to Calhoun's right. He advanced on Calhoun, and Calhoun looked around frantically, up and down, trying to determine if there was a direction he could go fast enough that would carry him out of Darg's reach. Nothing presented itself.

Darg was closer, closer, and the blades were fully extended on his hand. Within less than a second, he would be close enough to slash out at Calhoun and cut him to ribbons. Beneath Calhoun's fingers, he could feel the power of the cloaking device surging beneath him. If there were some way to disrupt it, maybe . . .

Too late. Darg's fingers lashed out, trying to slice through Calhoun's grip. Calhoun desperately shifted handholds, swinging his body out of the way, buying himself perhaps another second or two. But Darg had him cold, they both knew it.

And then Darg spotted the explosive that Calhoun had affixed to the surface of the cloaking device. He didn't recognize it for what it was, clearly, but he didn't like what he saw. With one glance at Calhoun's expression, he could tell that Calhoun wasn't happy about his noticing it either. That was more than enough reason for him to reach for it and start to peel it off. As he did so, he said almost conversationally, "Any last words?"

"Actually . . . yes. Three, to be exact," said Calhoun. He yanked the pip off his shirt where he had secreted it and slapped it on Darg's arm. "Activate, transporter right."

Darg looked at him in confusion, and suddenly he dematerialized. He let out a roar and lunged at Calhoun, but his now-phantom hands went right through him, and then Darg vanished. Seconds later, he materialized in the heart of the cloaking device.

Calhoun had no real idea what would happen when that occurred. The energies required to power a cloaking device that big were like nothing that Calhoun had ever encountered before. He didn't know what powered it, nor did he know what powered Darg's robotic body. All he knew was that he was combining two elements, and hoping for the best.

What he got was far more than he had bargained for. For he felt a violent rumbling beneath him, and he heard, or thought he heard, a truncated scream from Darg before the energies within the cloaking device ripped him apart, even his powerful mechanical body not impervious to the power and energy that was buffeting him.

And then Calhoun heard an explosion, muffled but huge, and he suddenly realized that the explosive adhesive had been stuck to Darg when he rematerialized, and he had the further flash of understanding that the explosive had been detonated prematurely thanks to the forces roiling within the cloaking device.

He did the only thing he could. He hurled himself off the cloaking device into mid-air, hurtling down and away from the immediate blast area.

A split second later, the cloaking device erupted.

XXIII.

THERE WAS ALARM throughout the sphere as the cloaking device erupted in flame. The entire manufactured world trembled from the detonation.

Thul saw it from a distance and couldn't believe it. From his vantage point he could see the crowd that had been milling about in the great square, waiting to witness the signing of the document that would be the cue for the annihilation of the Federation. Except the picture on the huge screen had disappeared as systems shorted out and went down all over the sphere. Not only that, but they could see and hear, as he just had, the terrible explosion that had originated at the very core of the sphere.

Silver stood up, gingerly pulling his hand from the surface of the computer.

"What are you doing!" said an alarmed Thul in the now-darkened room. "I need you to interface with the Omega 9! The job's too big for a normal human mind! You have to—"

"I have to do nothing," Silver said calmly. "I have analyzed the present situation, including the obvious sabotage to this sphere. It is my belief that, within three minutes, at the present rate of destruction, this sphere will be destroyed. I have no desire to accompany it. So . . . I am leaving."

And suddenly there was a fearful looking weapon in Thul's hand, pulled from the folds of his cloak. "Get back there, Silver!" he snarled.

"I am leaving," said Silver.

Thul fired.

• • •

Picard watched the entire scene unfold with a sort of distant disbelief.

Thul fired upon the being whom he called Silver. But the blast from Thul's own weapon was no more effective upon Silver than anything that Picard might have wielded. The blast ricocheted harmlessly off Silver . . .

. . . and struck Kendrow.

With a howl of agony, clutching at his blackened chest, Kendrow went down. He flopped about on the floor like a just-landed marlin, making incoherent babbling noises.

Thul paid him no mind. Instead he fired once more at Silver, and had no more luck than he'd had the previous time. Silver walked past him, completely ignoring him.

Everything forgotten except his boiling rage and desperation to carry out the final demise of the Federation, Thul charged at Silver. All pretensions of dignity, all of his superiority, were gone, vanished, boiled away by pure fury. It made him a very easy target. Picard reversed his gun, bringing the butt-end around, and as Thul passed him, Picard slammed him across the side of the head. Thul collapsed at his feet.

Silver paused a moment to cast a glance at Picard. "I would leave here if I were you," he said simply, and then the silver-metal being turned and walked away.

Picard turned quickly and headed over to Kendrow. He knelt down next to him, saw the severity of the wound, saw the despair in the man's eyes. Kendrow clearly knew he was dying . . . and yet he was looking up at Picard with heartbreaking despair, silently pleading for him to help hm. Picard hesitated, unsure of what he could possibly do . . .

And that was when Gerrid Thul leaped upon his back.

A huge piece of metal, buffeted by the shock wave, slammed into Calhoun as he hurtled through mid-air. His head rang from the impact, but then he quickly realized that it was the single luckiest thing that could have happened to him.

The shock wave from the explosion hit, radiating outward, propelling Calhoun toward the far edges of the sphere. He tumbled end over end, but because he was clutching with all his strength at the large shard of metal, his body pressed flat against it, he managed to avoid losing consciousness altogether. He was like a crazed surfer riding out a massive wave.

Before he knew it, he slammed into the interior surface of the sphere. He lost his grip on the metal shard and it spiralled away from him. Once again in a zero-G area, Calhoun hung there for a moment, dazed, banged up, barely able to string a coherent thought together.

Then he started to float back toward the center, toward the massive conflagration which was building upon itself exponentially.

It was at that moment that he saw his freighter, docked and waiting. It was some distance away and he prayed his voice would carry as he shouted at the top of his lungs, "Freighter! Voice response activate! Pick up!"

For a moment he was certain that it hadn't heard him, and then the running lights suddenly flared to life. Wasting no time, the freighter pulled away from its moorings and angled obediently down toward its pilot.

Another explosion roared from within the heart of the sphere as the lower half of the cloaking device went up in flames.

Calhoun was now plummeting toward it, and then the freighter was there, main door open. Calhoun tumbled into the cabin, kept rolling and slammed into the far wall. He lay there for a moment, stunned, muttering, "I'm not getting paid enough."

Then he stumbled to his feet and seized the controls of the freighter . . .

. . . and was abruptly faced with a very difficult choice.

Picard tried to stagger to his feet and barely managed to do so. Thul was on his back, howling in fury, and Picard barely managed to shove him off. They faced each other, both their weapons fallen. Thul had a look of dementia in his eyes.

"It's over, Thul. We have to get out of here—!"

"No." Thul was shaking his head like a man deep in denial. "No . . . they have to die . . . you have to die . . . the Double Helix . . ."

"I said it's over! Snap out of it, man! Nothing is going to be accomplished by staying here and being incinerated!"

Thul didn't listen. He was beyond listening, beyond caring. Instead he came right at Picard, his attack so sudden that Picard barely had time to defend himself against it.

And Picard abruptly found himself in the hands of one of the most devastating hand-to-hand combatants he had ever encountered.

One wouldn't have known it to look at Thul. The Thallonian was clearly an older man, older than Picard. He wasn't all that tall, not especially wide. But in close-quarters combat, he was a terror, an absolute terror. Picard wasn't exactly helpless in such situations, a fair hand-to-hand combatant himself, with some good moves and a rather nasty right hook, if he said so himself. But he couldn't even begin to mount a defense against Gerrid Thul.

Thul's hands were lightning. Picard would try and block a punch, and even before he had time to realize it was a feint, Thul had landed two blows, a third and a fourth. He struck Picard at will, doubling him over, straightening him up with an uppercut. Picard never even laid a hand on him.

Thul picked him up and threw him out into the main corridor, advancing on him mercilessly. All around them, panicked residents of the sphere were running like mad, trying to get to whatever ships were nearest so that they could get the hell out of there. Thul didn't seem to notice any of them. He was focused, with laser-like efficiency, on Picard.

Picard felt the world swimming around him, tried to get to his feet, and then Thul was there and he kicked Picard in the gut, causing him to curl up like a fetus, and he kicked him over and over, howling, "You, Picard! It's all your fault! You're the living symbol of everyone and everything that destroyed my life! But you're not going to be living much longer!"

David Kendrow's desperate, questing hand stretched out toward the hand padd for the Omega 9. His body trembled from the exertion, and he was certain that he wasn't going to make it. But then, at the last moment, like a gift from God, he had a small surge of energy that was small, ever so small, but it was enough. He lunged forward and his hand came into contact with the padd.

He trembled as the nannites, careless of the environment that was crumbling around them, did their job. They joined with him, penetrated his mind, his body, and seconds later his consciousness was pulled from his body and sent hurtling into the depths of the Omega 9.

What he had, at that point, was a plan that could most charitably be called a long-shot. What he was hoping was that his consciousness would survive the passing of his body if it was buried deep within the Omega 9. The problem was that, all too soon, the Omega 9 would be dust, gone with the rest of the sphere.

But the intention had been for the Omega 9 to interface with computers on other worlds. Granted, it had been too massive a job for Kendrow to do himself. Silver was supposed to bridge that gap with his machine mind. But Kendrow was still capable of at least projecting himself to some other computer data base . . . earth, perhaps, or another world. And perhaps . . . just perhaps . . . he could use the replicators wherever he wound up to fashion himself some sort of body. There were other possibilities as well, but before he could explore any of them, he had to survive.

He plunged into the heart of the Omega 9, the glistening circuitry singing gently to him. It was the first time that he himself had done it, and it was glorious, it was like nothing else. He floated there, feeling as if he had somehow managed to return to his mother's womb. There was peace, there was security, there was . . .

Darkness. Something was moving in around him, something that seemed alien to the Omega 9. Kendrow's consciousness looked around, tried to perceive, tried to understand . . .

And a voice echoed all around him, a voice that said, *I'd been trying to get your attention, David. Causing glitches here and there, doing what I could in my own small way . . . how kind of you to finally brave the interior of the Omega 9 . . . it took you quite some time, didn't it . . . but you always were a bit of a coward at heart, you know that, don't you, David . . . ?*

Kendrow looked around frantically. It was everywhere, the dark and cold, and he called out, *Who is it? Who's there?!?*

I brushed against the Omega 9, David . . . with Darg and the others standing there, and you, and all you bright people, and you didn't spot it. Didn't spot the final connection. What did you think, Dave . . . that you were the first person to hit upon the idea of putting his consciousness into the Omega 9? You always were more of a follower than a leader . . .

And then he understood. *Fro . . . Frobisher . . . but . . . but you're dead . . .*

Yes, Dave. I was dead. But you know, Dave . . . I'm feeling a lot better now . . .

The laughter was everywhere and Kendrow screamed as the darkness enveloped him.

Picard rolled over onto his back and then Gerrid Thul was upon him. He was straddling Picard, his hands at Picard's throat, and he slammed the captain's head against the floor. Stars exploded behind Picard's eyes, and Thul wasn't letting up, not for a second.

"I made a son . . . and you destroyed him. I created the perfect virus . . . and you destroyed my plan to implement it," and as he spoke the pressure of his hands upon Picard's throat was steady and unyielding. "You call me the destroyer? It's you, Picard! You are the bringer of pain! You are the slayer of dreams! You!"

The test tube rolled out from Picard's pocket.

It made a gentle, tinkling sound as it rolled. Thul cast a confused glance in the direction of the tube . . .

And the distraction was all Picard needed. He broke Thul's grip and shoved as hard as he could, sending Thul off-balance as he gasped and drew in air. Thul tumbled to the side, hit the floor hard.

Picard heard something break.

He clambered to his feet and saw Thul, on his back, starting to tremble. Instantly Picard understood. Thul had landed atop the test tube and crushed it . . . and the Double Helix virus was rampaging through his body. But it was doing so in highly concentrated form.

Gerrid Thul, creator of the Double Helix, writhed in the grasp of his own creation. His back arched, his tongue lolled out, and his eyes went wide with horror as he realized what had happened. For all his speeches about not caring about life, about being dead already, he certainly seemed to have the expression of someone who was suddenly terrified about being hurled into oblivion. Or perhaps it was simply the way that it was occurring.

Thul's eyes shrivelled, collapsed into their sockets, his tongue began to blacken even as he voicelessly screamed his terror, the skin started to pucker and blister, pus oozing out from sores that had appeared spontaneously all over.

Picard was transfixed, and then it suddenly occurred to him that if the damned thing became airborne, this was going to be the perfect time to get the hell out of there. He tore his gaze away from Thul and ran like mad.

His legs and arms pumping, Picard dashed down the corridor. He hoped that he remembered where the docking area was, and also prayed that he would be able to find a means of escape once he got there. The sphere rumbled around him and he knew there wasn't much time left as the systems ate themselves, one explosion feeding upon another. Bleakly, he wondered what had happened to Calhoun and Vara Syndra, or Vandelia, or whatever her name was. He could only pray that they were all right and that somehow they were going to manage to get themselves clear.

He saw a sign marked for one of the docking areas, turned right, and saw huge double doors that were just sitting open, which led to the docking ports. He dashed out into the vast docking area which opened out to the interior of the sphere. From that viewpoint, he could see flame erupting from spots throughout the sphere. The far side of the sphere was already a massive wall of flame, and it was spreading wildly. He was witnessing the death of a technological marvel. From a purely scientific and even aesthetic view, it was a tremendous waste and tragedy.

All this he saw from where he was standing. What he did not see were any ships. He spotted the last of the small transports moving away, and there was nothing left in his immediate area. There were other docking ports, but they were too far away for him to get to in time.

He saw the firewall racing toward him from either side. There was nowhere to go.

He took a deep breath, faced his death, and thought about a book his mother had read to him several times in his youth: *Peter Pan.* He thought of the time that Peter was crouched on the rock, having just been stabbed by Hook, unable to fly, unable to save himself, and he had looked at the rising tide and mused philosophically about his impending doom.

"To die," Picard whispered, "would be a great adventure."

At which point he promptly disappeared in a haze of sparkles.

Seconds later, he materialized in what appeared to be a small freighter. He looked around in confusion . . . and then a smile broke across his face. "I should have known."

"Yes, you should have," Calhoun said reprovingly from the control panel. He hadn't even bothered to turn around. "I was on my last sweep of the place looking for you. You certainly took your sweet time getting somewhere that I could see you. Thanks to you, I've had to cut this a lot thinner than I would have liked."

"It's getting thinner still. Where's the woman?"

"Dead," Calhoun said tonelessly. "Darg killed her. But considering there's not two molecules of him left to rub together, I doubt he'll be hurting anyone else. Where's Thul?"

"The same, but more grisly. Get us out of here."

"That's why you've been captain longer than me. You know how to make the tough decisions."

Even as he spoke, he was sending the freighter hurtling toward one of the few areas that was not completely aflame. The sphere was collapsing on itself, gigantic flaming shards smashing into one another. Calhoun coolly maneuvered the shuttle between the debris, dodging left and right as he called out, "Hold on. This is going to be a little tricky."

He saw an escape route and went for it, and the freighter darted forward just before a huge piece of debris could smash into it. Then they were clear of the sphere, moving away from it faster and faster as the last of the explosions utterly consumed it.

Other ships were all around, scattered, confused, unsure of where to go or what to do. Then, after a few moments, they slowly started to move away from the area of the destruction. Picard watched them go, shaking his head, and—like an old-time policeman—he said, "Show's over. Nothing more to see here."

"Yes," Calhoun said slowly, "yes . . . there is."

He was angling his freighter toward one particular ship. "What is it, Mac?"

"That's Thul's ship. But you said he's dead."

"He is."

"Then I'm going to take a shot in the dark," Calhoun said.

He touched several controls and Picard heard the distinctive whine of phasers powering up. "What are you doing?"

But Calhoun had opened up a ship-to-ship channel. "Lodec. I have you targeted. I'm coming in at 273 Mark 2. This is it, Lodec."

There was dead silence as Picard looked in puzzlement at Calhoun . . . and then Lodec's voice came back over the channel. "Hello, Calhoun."

"Do you want an opportunity to fight back . . . or should I just blow you out of space?"

"Calhoun, back off," Picard said sharply, "this is absurd—"

Calhoun looked at him with blazing eyes and said, "No. This is personal. Well, Lodec?"

Again a moment of silence, and then Lodec said, "I was going to let you go, you know. In the corridor. I saw you there, and I was all set to keep my silence. And you had to draw on me, so that I thought you were going to shoot me. You left me no choice. But it's all about choices, isn't it, Calhoun? So fine. I leave you the choice you didn't leave me. Shoot or don't. It's of no consequence to me. Death will just silence the voices that have been crying out in my head for so many years. Do as you like."

With that, he cut the connection.

Picard said nothing. He simply watched Calhoun, who stared out at the ship that was hanging there, a huge target. It offered no defense. It would have been so easy.

And then, unmolested . . . the ship moved off. A moment later, it kicked into warp space and was gone.

Picard let out a slow, relieved breath, and he patted Calhoun on the back. "Mac . . . believe it or not . . . I know how difficult it is to let go of the need for revenge. But—and I don't mean to sound patronizing here—I think you've taken a tremendous step forward in your personal growth and—"

"The phaser banks are empty," Calhoun said.

"What?" Picard leaned forward and looked. It was true. The phasers had powered up, but had been unable to sustain it.

"They're empty. And it's not just them. Thul must have drained the ship's systems. Engines, life support, all going. He had quite a knack for thinking ahead. Here was a man who thought, Well, just in case Calhoun and/or Picard escape, I'll leave them just enough power to get away. To make them think they're safe. And then all the systems will . . ."

The lights in the freighter suddenly went out.

". . . cut out," he concluded.

On earth, the closing ceremonies for the bicentennial went without a hitch. As they did, Jellico turned to Nechayev and said, "Well, well . . . it would appear that we got all concerned for nothing."

"Apparently so. Unless, of course, someone just saved the galaxy as we know it from total disaster and we're simply unaware of it."

"I doubt it," Jellico replied. "I mean, I think I'd know if something like that had happened."

"Yes," said Nechayev. "It'd be fairly difficult to slip something like that past you, Eddie."

Picard and Calhoun spent the next several minutes seeing what they could possibly do to reverse the situation, but nothing seemed to present itself. Furthermore, all the other ships had moved out by that point. Not that their being present would have offered any great options. Calhoun and Picard had already been named as traitors and enemies by Thul. Finally, options expended, they simply sat there, looking at each other.

"Had you already decided not to kill Lodec before you saw the phasers were out? Or did you notice that the phasers were out and realize that the decision was out of your hands?"

Calhoun said nothing.

"You're not going to answer, are you."

"Picard," Calhoun said slowly, "you are probably one of the brightest men I've ever met. You've known me for twenty years. You know my background. You know what I stand for. And you know that, ultimately—even if there are some bumps along the way—I'm going to end up doing the right thing. So I think you really know the answer to that question, don't you."

"Nice try, Mac."

"All right . . . I suppose I knew I wouldn't get away with it that easily. The truth, Picard . . . is that I was in the same situation once before. The indecision led to my resigning from Starfleet because the universe was very black and white to me. This time around . . . I have to admit that, once again, I don't know what I would have done. I still might have given in to the impulse for vengeance. Or I might not. I'm just not sure. But at least this time, I'm not going to let the lack of knowledge get to me. It took me a long time and a lot of learning to realize that it's all right not to know everything . . . including every aspect of oneself. That it's acceptable to live within the shades of gray on occasion. Good enough?"

"Not really. But I suppose it will have to do."

They sat there for a time more, and then Calhoun said, "What are you thinking about?"

"All the people I've known. All the opportunities I've had in my life, and whether I would do it all the same. About Thul's son, and whether his death could have been prevented . . . whether I could have done anything differently, for if I had, all this could have been avoided. Lives wouldn't have been wasted and lost, and incredible forays of ingenuity wouldn't have been dedicated to such a useless endeavor as a hollow need to destroy in the quest for useless revenge. I'm thinking about the universe in general, of free will, and of man's place within that universe and whether we really have a place at all, or how much we matter in the grand scheme of things. I'm wondering . . . what the ultimate answers to all reality are, and whether we'll ever get to know them." He paused, feeling the chill of space beginning to work its way into his bones. "And you? What are you thinking about?"

"I'm thinking about how nice it would be if the *Excalibur* showed up and rescued us."

Picard laughed softly to himself, starting to feel a bit lightheaded as the carbon dioxide began to build up. And at that moment, space in front of them rippled, a hole in the space-time continuum opened up, and the starship *Excalibur* dropped into normal space a mere five hundred kilometers away.

Picard gaped at the sight and then turned to Calhoun, who maintained an absolute deadpan as he said, "I don't know about the ultimate ones, but I guess some answers come more quickly than others."

XXIV.

CALHOUN AND SHELBY were escorting Picard and Riker to the transporter room. "Sela's already been beamed aboard the Enterprise, as per your request, Captain," said Calhoun. "I'm afraid there's been no change in her condition."

"I'm hoping that Starfleet will be able to give her the help she needs," Picard said. "Perhaps even leave her better than when she started. No matter what it is that she's become . . . she remains the daughter of an old, dear friend. If there's any way to salvage the influence of the good person that Tasha Yar was, then we have to take it."

"Looking for the best in people. It's comforting to know that some things about you don't change, Captain," Calhoun said.

"It is equally comforting, Captain, to know that some things about you do change," Picard replied with a carefully neutral expression, which drew a wary grin from Calhoun. Picard continued, "Number One . . . how went your temporary assignment to the *Excalibur?"*

"Good question," seconded Calhoun. "Commander Shelby, did you two get on with each other? Or were there any problems I should know about?"

Shelby and Riker cast a glance at each other, and then Shelby said, "Actually . . . it went about as expected."

"It was a learning experience . . . for all concerned," Riker added.

"It would appear, Captain Calhoun," Picard said, "that the crew here is beginning to imitate your rather enigmatic way of expressing yourself. Perhaps you—"

He stopped in his tracks.

A dark haired woman was approaching him. And she looked like . . . but . . . it couldn't possibly be . . .

"Leaving, Commander? I hope you enjoyed your stay. Well, have to rush. Good day to you," said Morgan Lefler as she breezed past.

Picard gaped after her, then looked back to Riker. "What was . . . was that . . . how?"

"Captain," Riker said in a firm but understanding voice, "I've learned that around this ship . . . it's best not to ask too many questions."

"Is it finished yet?"

Burgoyne lay on the examination bed in sickbay while Doctor Selar studied the readouts. "Almost, Burgoyne. But let me see if I understand this. Medical scans and similar procedures are privileged information . . . but you want me to post this scan publicly? To everyone on the ship?"

"Yes. That's correct," Burgoyne confirmed. "I'm tired of everyone congratulating me on my pregnancy. It's gotten very old, very quickly. And some of them even think I'm being coy when I deny it. So if I just publicize it in one shot, with the scan confirming that I'm not pregnant, that should put an end to it."

"That sounds like a commendable plan. I wish I could oblige."

"But Selar, I told you, I'm waiving the confidentiality—"

"It is not a matter of that. But if you wish to circulate this scan as proof of what you are claiming, that is not going to be possible."

"What?" Burgoyne was completely confused. "What are you talking about?"

"You are pregnant."

"What?" The blood drained from Burgoyne's face. "But . . . but I can't be . . ."

"You are. Look for yourself."

Burgoyne took one look at the readout and fainted dead away.

Selar stood there and regarded hir with very mild amusement. And then McHenry emerged from hiding nearby and grinned down at the unconscious Hermat. "Well, well, Burgy. You told me you were pregnant, except you really weren't . . . and I passed out . . . and you teased me about it. So now, with the good doctor's help here, you get told you're pregnant, except you're really not . . . but you handled the unexpected fake news as well as I did. For some reason, I find that very comforting. Don't you think that's comforting?"

"I think you are all insane, and I think I am just as insane for cooperating," sniffed Selar. And she turned away to hide the slight smile that she couldn't quite repress.

DOUBLE HELIX

THE FIRST VIRTUE

MICHAEL JAN FRIEDMAN
&
CHRISTIE GOLDEN

Prologue

As Governor Gerrid Thul walked through the heavy wooden doors and entered the throne room of his emperor, Tae Cwan, he reflected on how different the place looked.

After all, the three prior occasions on which Thul had visited were all elaborate state gatherings of nobles and high-ranking officials in the empire. He was only a small part of them, though his standing had grown surely and steadily over the years from a respected general to the governorship of an outpost.

But this, the governor told himself, looking around at the cavernous, high-ceilinged hall and the splendid furnishings . . . this was different. He frowned. He was all alone now, without a crowd to hide him.

And at the end of the rich, blue carpet that bisected the chamber's white stone floor, the illustrious Tae Cwan himself waited for Thul. The blue-robed emperor sat between two armed guards on a chair of carved night-wood that had given his forebears comfort for more than a thousand years.

It was daunting. Or it would have been, if the governor were one who allowed himself to be daunted. But he hadn't risen to a rank of esteem and power by being timid.

Lifting his chin, Thul set foot on the carpet and approached Tae Cwan's presence. The chamber magnified every sound—the flutter of his cape, the padding of his feet on the blue path, even the drawing of his breath—as if the room weren't filled with simple air at all, but something infinitely more sensitive and unstable.

Finally, the governor reached the end of the carpet and stopped. His emperor gazed down at him from the height of his chair, his features long and perfect, his expression a tranquil one.

Thul inclined his head out of respect—or at least that was the nature of the gesture. Then he smiled his best smile. "I believe you know why I have come," he told Tae Cwan, his voice echoing in the chamber like stormwaves on a rocky beach.

"I believe I do," the emperor replied without inflection, though his voice echoed just as loudly.

Abruptly, he gestured—and a door opened behind him. A couple of attractive handmaidens came through, followed by someone else in the deep blue color that could be worn only by imperial blood. It was Tae Cwan's younger sister, Mella.

The resemblance was difficult to ignore. However, as often happens in a family, the clarity of feature that made the brother a handsome man made the sister look plain and austere.

Nonetheless, the governor turned his smile of smiles on Mella Cwan, and the woman's eyes lit up in response. Dark and vulnerable, her eyes were by far her best attribute.

"Proceed," said the emperor.

Thul inclined his head again. "As you wish, Honored One." He paused, as if gathering himself. "I have come to profess my love and admiration for your sister, the Lady Mella."

A demure smile pulled at the corners of the woman's mouth. Unfortunately, it didn't make her any more pleasant to look at.

"I ask you for permission to make her my wife," Thul continued.

Tae Cwan considered the governor for a moment. He had to know that nothing would make his sister happier than the prospect of marriage to Thul. And yet, the governor noted, the emperor hesitated.

It was not a good sign, Thul knew. Not a good sign at all.

"I withhold the permission you seek," said Tae Cwan, his expression stark and empty of emotion.

To the governor, it was more than a disappointment. It was like a blow across his face, with all the pain and shame such a blow would have awakened in him.

The Lady Mella, too, seemed shocked by her brother's reply. She stared at him open-mouthed, her face several shades paler than before.

Still stinging from Tae Cwan's words, Thul asked, "Is it possible you will change your mind in this matter, Emperor? Or perhaps reconsider my request at a later date?"

Tae Cwan shook his head from side to side, slowly and decisively. "It is *not* possible," he responded flatly.

Thul felt a hot spurt of anger, but managed to stifle it. After all, it was forbidden to show excessive emotion in the presence of a Cwan.

"I see," he said as calmly as he could. "And am I permitted to inquire as to the emperor's thinking in this matter?"

"You need not inquire," Tae Cwan informed him. "I will give you the insight you want."

The emperor leaned forward on his throne, his features severe and impassive. But his eyes, as dark as his sister's, flickered with what seemed like indignation.

"I do not wish you to be part of the royal family," he told Thul. "Certainly, you have been a dedicated and efficient servant who has made considerable contributions to the Empire. However, there is also something dangerous about you—something I do not entirely trust."

The governor's teeth ground together, but he said nothing. After all, it was he who had requested Tae Cwan's response.

"Beyond that," said the emperor, "you are well inferior to my sister in station . . . a former military man, unworthy of the royal family. No doubt, she would be willing to overlook this difference now. But in time, she would come to see it as a problem, as I do."

Mella averted her eyes, her brow creased with disappointment. But like Thul, she was forced to keep her emotions in check.

"These are my reasons for disallowing your request," Tae Cwan finished. "I assume I have made my decision clear."

"Eminently," said the governor, though he felt something twist inside him as he said it. "And though I have not been granted my request, I remain grateful for the audience, as befits a loyal servant of the Empire. May you continue to reign in splendor, Emperor."

Tae Cwan inclined his head, his eyes sharp and alert, though the rest of his features were in repose. "Go in peace, Gerrid Thul."

The governor cast a last, wistful glance at the Lady Mella. But with her brother's pronouncement still hanging in the air, she didn't dare return it.

Thul cursed inwardly. As his wife, the woman would have brought him immeasurable power and prestige—more than enough for him to overlook his lack of attraction to her. But with a few words, the emperor had taken away that dream of power and prestige.

Enduring his loss—one that was no less painful for his never having had the thing to begin with—the governor inclined his head a third time. Then he turned and followed the length of blue carpet to the doors and made his exit.

But as soon as the doors closed behind him and he was left alone in the hallway outside, Gerrid Thul turned and glowered in the direction of Tae Cwan. Emperor though he might be, the governor reflected bitterly, he had gone too far this time.

He had humiliated one of his most determined servants—one who had risked much and accomplished much on behalf of the Empire both as a soldier and as a politician. He had told Thul in no uncertain terms that he would never be more than what he was—the administrator of a farflung outpost.

The governor swore again. Maybe he couldn't ascend to power by marrying the Lady Mella, but he was still no beast of burden to wallow in self-pity. He was intelligent. He was resourceful. And he was every bit as Thallonian as the feared Tae Cwan.

For some time now, Thul had toyed with an alternative to marrying the Lady Mella—one that would allow him to enjoy the prominence he craved without the need to seek the emperor's blessing. With his first option closed to him, the second came to the fore in his mind.

And the more he thought about it—the more he considered how badly he had been treated by Tae Cwan—the more inclined he was to pursue it.

Chapter One

THUL ENTERED THE REGGANA CITY tavern by one of its several revolving doors, his Thallonian commoner's clothes and attached hood uncomfortably rough against his skin.

The place was loud with jangling music and crowded with a surprising number of aliens. Squinting to see through the dim lighting and the acch'ta smoke, he took a look around.

At first, he couldn't find the one he was looking for. Then he heard a familiar laugh and traced it to its owner—a tall, lean Thallonian youth with an antic sparkle in his eyes and a mouth that seemed ready to break into a grin at any moment. He had clearly had too much to drink.

His companion was an Indarrhi of about the same age. Like most every member of his species, the fellow was slender and as dark as carbon, with deepset silver eyes, a fleecy mop of silver-white hair, and three thick fingers on either hand.

The Indarrhi also had rudimentary empathic powers. Or so it was said of them in the empire.

Spotting an unoccupied table, the governor pulled out a chair and sat down. Then he sat back and watched the Thallonian and the Indarrhi.

"Drink?" asked a gruff but feminine voice.

Thul turned and looked up at a triangular face with a single bifocal eye in the middle of its leathery forehead. A Banyanan, he mused. And this one had even fewer manners than most.

He considered the question that had been posed to him. "Thallonian ale," he decided. "Room temperature."

The waitress grunted. "Room temperature." She sneered, as if it were not very likely his request would be met. Then she turned her angular body sideways and made her way back through the crowd.

Halfway to the bar, she passed the young Thallonian. Winking at the Indarrhi, he grabbed the Banyanan around the waist and drew her to him. But the waitress was stronger than she looked. With a push, she freed herself and continued on her way.

It didn't anger the youth in the least. In fact, it might have been a game he had played with the female before. Laughing out loud, he clapped his companion on the back and lifted a mug to his lips.

The contents, a frothy liquid as dark and scarlet as blood, dripped down the youth's chin and spattered the table below. Wiping himself with the back of his hand, he swung his arm around the Indarrhi's shoulders and whispered something into his friend's rounded ear.

Yes, Thul thought disapprovingly. The Thallonian had *definitely* had too much to drink.

Suddenly, the youth thrust the Indarrhi away and laughed even more loudly. His companion smiled, appearing to enjoy the joke—but not with the fervor of the Thallonian. The governor frowned.

The youth was a misfit—an embarrassment to his species. Whoever had raised him had done a stunningly bad job of imparting Thallonian manners to him. Were it not for his ruddy skin and his size, one might have wondered if he was Thallonian at all.

"Thallonian ale," said a by-now familiar voice.

Thul glanced at the serving woman as she put his drink in front of him. Then he reached into his pocket and produced an imperial disc. "This should be enough," he said.

The Banyanan eyed it, then plucked it from the governor's hand. "It should at that," she responded. Then, with her overly generous payment in hand, she disappeared again.

With the waitress gone, Thul returned his attention to the youth. He was just in time to see the fellow thrust his leg out in the path of a green-skinned Orion trader.

The Orion, who had a mug in his hand, never saw the danger. With a curse, he tripped on the Thallonian's foot and went flying. So did his drink—into the lap of another Thallonian, a brawny specimen with a scar across the bridge of his nose.

Outraged, the victim rose from his seat and seized the Orion's shirtfront in his fists. With a surge of his powerful muscles, he lifted the trader off the floor.

"Orion scum," he spat.

Releasing the trader with one hand, the Thallonian drew it back and struck the Orion in the face. Thul heard a resounding crack as the trader's head snapped back. A moment later, it lolled on the Orion's shoulder, and the Thallonian let him drop to the floor.

When the trader woke, the governor mused, he would have a headache. A rather *considerable* headache.

"Damn you!" bellowed the youth, leaping to his feet. "That was my friend you hit!"

The Thallonian with the scar glanced at him warily. "The fool spilled his drink in my lap!"

"Only because you tripped him with your big, clumsy feet!" the youth roared at him.

It was anything but the truth, Thul noted inwardly. But, of course, the fellow with the scar had no way of knowing that, and neither did anyone else in the establishment.

"Who are you calling clumsy?" the man with the scar snarled.

"You!" the youth snarled back. "Why? What are you going to do about it, you bulging sack of excrement?"

The older man's eyes popped and his hand went to his hip. "Sack of excrement, is it?" With a flash of metal, he slid a blade out of its scabbard. "How would you like me to cut your tongue out and shove it down your scrawny throat?"

The youth grinned as he whipped his own sword free. "I would like to see you *try!*" he shot back.

Seeing what was about to take place, the other patrons cleared a space for the two antagonists. The Orion, who was allegedly the cause of the youth's indignation, was the only one who remained in the vicinity—and that was only because he was still unconscious.

The governor sighed. The youth's behavior was worse than embarrassing. It was despicable. He had actually gone out of his way to pick a fight with an innocent man.

Still, Thul didn't do anything to stop the impending combat. He just sat there like everyone else in the tavern, drinking his ale and wondering who the victor would be.

"Serpent!" boomed the Thallonian with the scar.

"Rodent!" came the youth's reply.

Suddenly, they were at each other, their swords clashing in a blurry web of bright metal. The scarred one thrust and the youth parried it. The youth countered and the scarred man knocked his sword away.

Back and forth they went, knocking tables and chairs aside, slashing away at each other with wild abandon. The scarred one was stronger and steadier, but the youth seemed more skilled. In time, the governor mused, skill was likelier to win out.

His theory was borne out a few moments later. The scarred man saw an opening and brought his sword down at his adversary's head, but what seemed to be an opening turned out to be a trap. The youth sidestepped the blow, then swung his blade at his opponent's shoulder.

The metal cut deeply, eliciting a spray of blood and a cry of pain from the scarred one. Then his enemy struck again, battering the sword from the scarred one's nerveless fingers.

The older man stood there, waiting for the deathstroke that did not come. Instead, the youth smiled and knelt beside the Orion, who had been all but forgotten in the melee.

Some of those present might have expected the youth to drag the trader to his feet, since he had claimed the fellow as his friend. But he didn't do that at all. He merely used the Orion's tunic to wipe his blade clean.

Finally, he stood up again and addressed the scarred one. "Next time," he said grimly, "be careful whose wine you catch in your lap." Then he tossed his head back and howled with laughter until the rafters rang with it.

The scarred man, who was clutching his wounded shoulder, just glared at his adversary. He glanced at the sword he had left lying on the floor, no doubt wondering if he might have a chance at revenge if he moved quickly enough. But in the end, he thought better of it and slunk away.

Remarkable, Thul reflected sourly. The youth had made an art form of arrogance and braggadocio.

Downing the remainder of his ale, the governor got to his feet and crossed the room. When he was halfway to the swordsman, the Indarrhi took note of him and said something.

The youth turned to cast a glance at the governor over his shoulder, his eyes intense in the hollows of their sockets. At the same time, his hand wandered to the hilt of his weapon.

Thul stopped in front of him. For a moment, the youth seemed ready to gut the older man where he stood. Then the governor tossed his hood back, revealing his identity.

Slowly, the fire in the swordsman's eyes dimmed. His features softened and his hand left his hilt. "Father," he said, humor and surprise mingled in his voice—along with something like distrust.

Thul gazed at him. "Strong drink does not agree with you. You have looked better, Mendan."

The youth grunted scornfully and cast a sidelong glance at his companion. "Have I really?"

"And you have exhibited better manners," the governor went on, unperturbed. "Was it really necessary to create a scene? To wound an innocent man? And all to prove your valor for the hundredth time?"

His son sneered at him. "Among Thallonians, is the first virtue not courage? And are you not the one who taught me that, before I was old enough to eat with a fork?"

Thul nodded. "I did," he conceded. "But one truly confident of his courage does not pick fights to demonstrate it. He knows life will give him plenty of opportunities to show how brave he is."

The youth shot a conspiratorial look at his companion, the Indarrhi. "You see how it is, Wyl? The man is a font of wisdom." Then he turned back to the governor. "I will try my best to remember what you've taught me, Father. I have *always* tried to remember what you taught me . . . even if I *am* only your bastard."

Thul shook his head, knowing Mendan had no intention of remembering anything. "You are my son . . . the son of a high-ranking Thallonian official. It would be a pleasant surprise if you acted accordingly."

Mendan eyed him. "Why have you come slumming, Father? Do you know how far you are from anything resembling the imperial court?"

Thul's hands clenched into fists at the thought of what had happened at court. With an effort, he unclenched them. "I have come," he said, "because I have a mission for you—one that cries out for a man who can navigate the underside of society."

The youth's eyes opened wide. "So, naturally, you thought of me. Mendan Abbis, the benighted product of a drunken revel twenty-two years ago. And you dare lecture *me* about making merry!"

"If you perform this mission," the governor continued evenly, "you will be rewarded beyond your wildest dreams."

That seemed to get his son's attention. "My dreams may be wilder than you think," he said warily.

"I doubt it," Thul said with the utmost confidence. He leaned closer, grasping the back of his son's chair. "If all goes well, Mendan, you will become the crown prince of a brand-new empire."

The bastard looked at him. "You're joking."

The governor shook his head. "I'm not."

Mendan considered the answer for a moment. Then he said, "Let's talk," and pulled over an empty chair.

"Outside," Thul insisted.

The youth gestured for the Indarrhi to come along. Then he got up and led the way out of the tavern.

The alley outside was cold and wet, but it had the very important virtue of being private. Thul pulled up his hood against the weather and watched wisps of white steam emerge from his son's mouth.

"Well?" Mendan asked, his eyes alive with curiosity. "How do you intend to make me heir to an empire? And why would that pompous windbag Tae Cwan allow such a thing to take place?"

The governor glanced at the Indarrhi. "He can be trusted?"

The boy nodded. "With our lives. Now answer my question."

Thul's jaw clenched at his son's audacity. Clearly, Mendan had a lot to learn. "Why would Tae Cwan tolerate the formation of an empire that would rival his own?" the governor asked. He didn't wait for an answer. "He wouldn't—if he knew about it."

The bastard's mouth pulled up at the corners. "I see."

"I won't lie to you," said the governor. "It won't be easy to keep this from the emperor. And there are a number of other problems as well . . . which may not loom quite so large if you are successful at your task."

"My . . . task?" Mendan echoed.

Thul shrugged. "Did you think it would all be placed in your lap?"

His son shook his head. "I suppose not."

The governor imparted the most basic details of his plan. It didn't take him long—only a few minutes. When he was finished, he eyed Mendan and waited for his reaction.

The bastard seemed hesitant. "Why should I trust you?" he asked his father. "You've never spoken to me this way before, like an equal instead of an inferior."

"An oversight for which I apologize," Thul told him. "Before, I was blinded by ambition. Now, my eyesight is a little sharper—and I see more clearly who is important to me and who is not."

Mendan's eyes narrowed as he considered the proposition. Finally, he nodded. "All right. What do you want me to do?"

The governor told him.

Captain Jean-Luc Picard of the *U.S.S. Stargazer* was looking forward to a most rewarding day.

His vessel was about to become the first to conduct an in-depth study of the long-vanished civilization of Zebros IV, in the Archaidae sector. Briefly charted about six years before and ignored ever since, the planet was reported at the time to have little to offer in terms of either strategic importance or natural resources.

The only entry, made by one Captain Philip Terrance, was a brief, almost disparaging comment. "The ruins on this world," it said, "are testament to the fact that this was once a thriving society."

But nothing more . . . nothing to whet the appetite of the Federation Council. That was why it had waited such a ridiculously long time to authorize a proper exploration of the place.

To each his own, Picard reflected, as he stepped onto his ship's raised transporter pad in his Starfleet-issue envirosuit, his helmet in hand. The few images taken by Terrance's vessel might not have inspired Terrance himself or the council, but they were enough to make the *Stargazer* captain's heart beat a little faster.

And the fact that the Federation had chosen to ignore Zebros IV for so long? That was quite all right as far as Picard was concerned. He and his crew would have an even better excuse to pick through the ruins at their leisure, as the first sentient beings in a millennium or more to handle long-buried examples of Zebrosian art and architecture.

But then, wasn't time one of the perquisites of lengthy deep-space missions like the *Stargazer*'s? If Picard and his people were really fortunate, they might even discover some bit of information that would cure a disease or enhance a Federation technology.

But even if they didn't, Picard thought, even if all they did was gain an appreciation of Zebrosian culture, that would be all right. He would still be perfectly content with the result.

After all, he had been in love with archaeology for a long time now. Since his days at the Academy, actually. And that love hadn't dimmed in all the years that had gone by since.

Yes, the captain thought, donning his helmet and locking it into place, it would be a rewarding day indeed. And eventually, if Zebros IV was as intriguing as it appeared, it might be a wonderful month. It was difficult not to smile at the prospect, but he managed.

His away team, he noticed, was less circumspect about its enthusiasm than he was. Tall, gangly Lieutenant Cabrini, for example, was grinning almost ear to ear in the transparent dome of his helmet, and darkskinned Lieutenant M'ketwa was chuckling with pleasure. Ensigns Kirby and Moore looked—and acted, Picard thought with a bit of a frown—like Academy cadets on leave as they joined him on the transporter platform.

"I realize today's mission will be of extraordinary interest to all of us," the captain told them, his voice muffled slightly by the confines of his helmet, "but let us conduct ourselves as scientists and not as schoolchildren, shall we?"

They sobered up at once, causing Picard to regret the sharpness of his words. These were some of the brightest and most eager young people Picard had ever had the privilege of working with. Of course they were excited. They relished the opportunity to get at those ruins, just as he did.

"After all," he added on impulse, "scientists are not compelled to come in from recess."

His quip was rewarded with a surprised but pleased smile from Ensign Kirby as they dematerialized.

Chapter Two

BIN NEDRACH COULDN'T HAVE asked for a better day.

The pale green sky that arched over Melacron V was clear and bright. The planet's two moons, Melia and Melusha, were easily visible near the horizon. There was no wind to speak of, no precipitation, no thermal inversions . . . and the dark cloud, the meteorological phenomenon called Lai'bok that scoured the surface of Melacron V from time to time, was not supposed to appear for several more weeks.

He had timed it brilliantly.

From his perch on the roof of a commercial edifice slated for demolition, Bin Nedrach shifted his position. He had been in the same spot since well before dawn. However, having rehearsed his task repeatedly, he was familiar with every inch of the old building.

There were three different ways he could swiftly flee once his task was completed, and four places where he could effectively hide himself in the unlikely event that all three exits were blocked. It had been a long time since he had had so many escape options.

Calmly, his two hearts beating slowly and regularly, Bin Nedrach examined his long, shiny energy rifle again. He had checked it thoroughly already, but the Melacron had learned it was always a good idea to double- and triple-check one's equipment.

The trilanium barrel was unmarred, nor was there any debris inside it which might clog the passage of the energy beam. The red safety keypad glowed softly and invitingly.

Bin Nedrach pressed it with a long, sharp-nailed finger and it changed color to yellow, indicating that the safety was off. Then he fingered it again and the safety was restored.

Good, he told himself. Working perfectly.

Faint sounds of activity wafted up from the plaza below. It was very convenient for Bin Nedrach that the officials of Melacron V had clustered all their important buildings around the same square. Of course, once his assignment had been carried out, it was entirely possible that the government would rethink that policy.

Street vendors were setting up shop, their little tents creating a colorful parade of cloth. The sweet scent of roasting shu seeds wafted up to Bin Nedrach's single wide nostril and he inhaled deeply. The more pungent aromas of grilled trusk flesh and pastries filled with a variety of berries mingled with the heady smell of the shu seeds.

They made Bin Nedrach hungry. He could do with a hot stick of grilled trusk or a bag of roasted shu seeds, he told himself. But with the iron discipline that had gotten him to the top of a dark and dangerous profession, he put aside his body's needs.

Time enough for food—good, exotic food—when his pockets bulged with latinum, he mused. For now, he had to concentrate all his faculties on the work at hand.

Little by little, the day grew brighter. There was more activity in the square below. Talk and laughter floated up to Nedrach's small, furred ears and they pricked upward, listening for more significant sounds.

There was the patter of the scarf seller, as usual. But then, he was setting up for what promised to be a brisk business with the holiday of Inseeing just around the corner. And there was the laughter of the little girl, dancing for a few coins like a leaf borne on the wind while her father played tunes on an old, battered p'taarana.

Everything reeked of normalcy. Everything was just where it should have been. And that was very much to Bin Nedrach's liking.

Abruptly, he heard the soft hum of an approaching hovertran. The sound made Bin Nedrach's hearts race. His black tongue snaked out to moisten thick, dry lips.

The hovertran, an official vehicle that could transport up to eight people at a time, shuddered to a halt and floated while the passengers disembarked. They were right on time—punctual, as all Melacron, including Bin Nedrach himself, were punctual.

As a youth, he had not realized how predictable his people were. Then, at the age of twenty, he began to plan his first assignment and he saw how everything ran by the clock.

The revelation had caused him to change his habits . . . to scramble his own comfortable routines. It would make it harder for someone to do to him what he was about to do to someone else.

One by one, in the same order as the day before and the day before that, the various heads of the Melacronai government descended into the square. The G'aha of Medicine, an older but still attractive female, headed right for the dancing girl. No surprise there.

As part of his job, Bin Nedrach had researched all the G'ahas in detail. He knew that the G'aha of Medicine had made it past her childbearing years unCompanioned and without children of her own. As a result, her weakness was her fondness for children.

It would have been simplicity itself for Nedrach to capitalize on that tendency, that vulnerability. However, the G'aha of Medicine was of no importance to him today.

He watched, noting everything, as the G'aha tossed the little dancer the same number of coins she had tossed the day before. Then the G'aha patted the child on the head and moved toward the tall, spired government building that dominated the square.

The G'aha of Finance, who could stand to lose a few kilograms, bought a big bag of shu seeds and dusted them with a pinch of blue pepper. Then he too made his way to the government building.

Chances were, in a few seasons or so, nature would do to the G'aha of Finance what people paid Bin Nedrach to do to others. Food was the fellow's great love, his ultimate indulgence.

Parties given at his home for other high-ranking Melacron were said to be extravagant, unforgettable. What's more, his Companion and children were every bit as rotund and unhealthy as he.

But to Bin Nedrach, the G'aha of Finance was no more important than the G'aha of Medicine. They simply weren't on his agenda.

Next, he turned his attention to the G'aha of Laws and Enforcements, a slender, handsome individual who seemed rather young for his position. As Bin Nedrach watched, the G'aha stopped to purchase an embroidered scarf from the scarf vendor.

Bin Nedrach frowned deeply as his boyhood superstitions threatened to get in the way of his duty. For a moment, his mind raced, caught up in an unexpected struggle.

The rite of Inseeing was the most revered celebration among his people. It was a time to stop, retire to the peace of one's own domicile, fast for three days and think about one's life. During this period, all attention was directed inward. The ritual Inseeing scarf, translucent enough to permit vision yet sufficiently opaque to perform a symbolic blindfolding, covered one's head and face at all times.

It was said to be the height of evil to harm someone while they wore the

Inseeing scarf . . . or even held it in their hands. Bin Nedrach set his jaw. *Then call me evil.* The G'aha of Laws and Enforcements had a Companion and children, he knew. Perhaps the G'aha was thinking about them as he admired the scarf, wondering about their futures.

But for the G'aha of Laws and Enforcements, there would be no wearing of the sacred scarf this year. There would be no fasting, either. Any insights he might have would come in the next few seconds, and he would regrettably have no time to act upon them.

Steadily, Bin Nedrach lifted his energy rifle. It clicked and buzzed as it automatically locked in on its target, saving him the trouble of aiming the weapon manually. He took a deep breath and pressed the safety pad, releasing the triggering mechanism inside.

The G'aha of Laws and Enforcements paid the vendor for the scarf, admired its workmanship a bit more, and reverently folded it as he headed for the black stone steps of the government building. He was the only potential customer in the plaza now, Bin Nedrach noted. The other G'ahas had already made their way inside.

No innocent bystanders would be harmed today—that was very important to Bin Nedrach. He was a professional, after all, and professionals were economical.

Still holding his breath, with a feather-light touch, Bin Nedrach's finger brushed the rifle's firing pad. Instantly, a stream of seething blue energy exploded from the weapon. It struck the G'aha of Laws and Enforcements at the base of his neck—the place where the assassin's people were most vulnerable to attack.

The G'aha arched in agony but did so silently, as Bin Nedrach had intended. He fell an instant later and tumbled down the black stone steps like a child's stuffed toy.

Bin Nedrach heard screams and wails from the square below, but he was already halfway down the rickety steps of the abandoned building. He did not have to wait to make sure the G'aha was dead. No Melacron struck with such force at the base of the neck could have survived.

The assassin's long legs flew and he jumped the last few steps to safety. By the time the stricken scarf dealer had pointed to the top of the building from whence the attack on the G'aha had come, Bin Nedrach was ensconced in his private hovertran and well and safely away.

He allowed himself a smile as he began to dismantle his weapon, just in case someone stopped him. *Mission accomplished,* he thought. *And if I am fortunate, the gods will have pity on my soul.*

The ruins of Zebros IV turned out to be unlike any Picard had ever examined. In fact, they couldn't even properly be called "ruins."

Nearly every edifice he encountered was comprised of an extremely hard, extremely durable blue material, which seemed to exist in great abundance on the planet. The result was that few of the buildings showed any significant signs of wear.

Cabrini scrutinized his tricorder readings against the backdrop of an intense orange sky. Then he looked up at the captain. "This stuff is approximately twelve times harder than diamond," he said. "We won't be able to cut it with traditional implements."

Picard nodded. "Which confirms my theory that this civilization enjoyed advanced technology, despite the deceptive simplicity of the construction." He found himself warming to the subject.

"That building there seems to be the most complex," Cabrini observed. "If we were to—"

"Ben Zoma to Picard," came the deep voice of the *Stargazer*'s first officer, interrupting the ensign's suggestion.

The captain hid a grimace. "Picard here," he said in response. "What is it, Number One?"

"You're not going to like it, sir."

"Try me," said Picard.

Gilaad Ben Zoma's voice was full of regret. "You've got a message from Starfleet Command. An Admiral Ammerman from Starbase Three is champing at the bit to talk to you."

Picard felt his heart sink in his chest. The message had, of course, been heard by his away team. They knew as well as he did what it meant and they looked at their captain sympathetically.

Don't waste pity on me, thought Picard. Unless I am mistaken, *none* of us will get to enjoy this trip.

"Understood, Mr. Ben Zoma," he said aloud. "One to beam up."

"Aye, sir," came the response.

Stepping away from the group, the captain eyed each of his people in turn. "Unfortunately," he told them, "you may not have much more time here. If I were you, I would make it count."

The next thing he knew, Picard was standing in his transporter room again. His operator regarded him.

"Short trip, sir?"

The captain scowled as he removed his helmet and pulled away his suit's collar flap. "*Too* short."

Stepping down from the transporter platform, he tucked his helmet under his arm. Then he headed for his ready room, which adjoined the *Stargazer*'s bridge.

In just a few minutes, Picard was sitting down in front of his desk, his helmet resting on the smooth, black surface beside his monitor. He thumbed the controls on his workstation and the admiral's blue-eyed, blond-haired visage filled the screen.

"Hello, Jean-Luc," said Ammerman.

The admiral was an old acquaintance. He and Picard had met at the Academy, where the older man was serving as an instructor, and continued to stay in touch over the years. Picard had been best man at Ammerman's wedding and godfather to his eldest daughter.

The fact that Starfleet had chosen Ammerman, who had such a lengthy history with the captain, to deliver what was clearly going to be an urgent message did not bode well. At least, not in Picard's mind.

"Hello, Admiral," said the captain, leaning back in his chair. "It's been a long time. How is Julia?"

"She's great, just great," said Ammerman. "And she sends her love, of course. But to be honest, I didn't contact you to talk about my family." He frowned a little as he took in the sight of Picard's envirosuit. "Hauled you out of an away mission, did I?"

The captain eased farther into his chair and began fiddling with the suit. "As a matter of fact," he replied, "you did. An exploration of some ancient ruins on Zebros Four."

"Damn." Ammerman looked sincerely regretful. "I hate to do this to you, Jean-Luc, but—"

"Duty calls." Picard smiled a little. "So . . . what shape has my duty taken this time, Admiral?"

The other man's expression turned sober. "How familiar are you with the Melacron-Cordracite situation?"

Picard shrugged. The names sounded familiar to him, but he couldn't place them right away. Then it came to him.

"Two powerful, unaligned species in the Kellasian sector," he said. "As I recall, they have been engaged in bitter territorial disputes over the last several years. Their governments have been trying to work toward a peaceful resolution, though there are some radical factions on both sides who don't share that goal." Something else occurred to the captain. "Unless I'm mistaken, Admiral, those factions have been responsible for some rather vicious incidents of terrorism."

Amerman nodded grimly. "That's essentially correct. Now jack up the viciousness of the attacks by a factor of ten and thin out the patience of both governments, and you've got an accurate picture of how badly things have fallen apart there."

Picard ceased fiddling with his suit. "When did all this happen?" he asked the admiral.

"Over the last couple of weeks." Ammerman rubbed his eyes. He looked tired. "It's bad, Jean-Luc."

"What about the Benniari?" the captain asked, referring to a neutral species in the sector. "It was my understanding that one of their number was acting as a mediator . . . that he had gotten the Melacron and the Cordracites to sit down together at an intrasector congress."

"That's right," said Ammerman. "His name is Cabrid Culunnh, first minister of the Benniari."

"Can't he make any headway?" Picard wondered.

The admiral sighed. "It's Culunnh himself who has contacted us, requesting Federation assistance. He tells us that the Benniari are starting to fear for their lives."

Picard was disturbed by this, but kept his expression neutral. Had the Benniari been official members of the Federation, Cabrid Culunnh would have become a highly respected ambassador by now.

Word had it that he had singlehandedly prevented war in the sector by proposing and overseeing the Kellasian Congress. For him and his government to ask for official Federation aid made it clear to Picard just how dire the situation was.

"Interestingly," said Ammerman, "it's Culunnh's opinion that this fresh wave of terrorist incidents isn't the work of the Cordracite and Melacronai groups who've been responsible for the violence until now."

That surprised Picard. "Who then?"

Ammerman shook his head. "He's not certain, but he feels pretty strongly about it. I don't know if it's wishful thinking or what. If some third party *is* involved, flushing them into the open might help put negotiations back on track. But as it stands, the situation is pretty dicey."

Picard nodded to himself. The Benniari were a peaceful, intelligent people, but their planet was not a wealthy one. They didn't have the resources to search for an elusive third-party terrorist group—if it was even true that one existed.

"Unfortunately," the admiral told him, "your ancient civilization will have to wait a while, Jean-Luc. We want you to take the *Stargazer* to the Kellasian sector immediately."

The captain had already resigned himself. "I understand," he answered.

"Assess the situation and cool things down if you can," said Ammerman. "If you can't . . . well, the Benniari are our allies. You're authorized to do everything necessary to keep them safe."

"Acknowledged," Picard responded.

"And while you're there," Ammerman added, "see if you can find anything out about this third party. Identifying and exposing it could be the key to peace in the sector."

And, perhaps, thought the captain, the key to opening the door to Federation membership as well. But he kept that observation to himself.

"I'll have my navigator set a course for the Kellasian sector," he assured his old friend.

A somber smile played about Ammerman's lips. "Not quite yet. You need to come to Deep Space Three first. You're scheduled for a passenger pickup—someone who has firsthand knowledge of the sector."

"Cabrid Culunnh?" Picard guessed. At the same time, he wondered what the Benniari would be doing on a starbase.

Ammerman shook his head. "No, Jean-Luc. An ensign, currently serving on the *Wyoming*. Seems he's the only one in the whole damned fleet who's ever spent any time in that part of space."

The captain sat back in his chair, a little perplexed. "With all due respect, sir, why don't you simply send the *Wyoming* on this mission? Why do you need the *Stargazer?*"

The admiral sighed. "Don't you remember who's commanding the *Wyoming* these days, Jean-Luc?"

Picard remembered all right—and he could see Ammerman's point. The *Wyoming* was captained by a fellow named Karl Broadnax, whose pugnacious personality had given rise to a host of colorful nicknames—among them, "Broad-Sword" and "Battle-Ax."

To date, no one had dared inform Captain Broadnax of any of these nicknames. It wasn't considered to be worth the risk. While Picard could think of no one he would rather have at his side in the heat of battle, Broadnax's naturally confrontational attitude would be the last thing they needed in such a touchy situation.

"Karl Broadnax," said the captain, searching for words, "may not be precisely the individual the situation calls for."

The admiral smiled without reservation for a moment. "And with those words, you prove that you are becoming one of the best diplomats we have in Starfleet. Congratulations, Jean-Luc. You're the indispensable man."

Picard grunted. "We'll be there as soon as we can, sir."

Ammerman turned serious again. "Make your best speed, Captain. The Benniari will be grateful. Ammerman out."

A moment later, the screen went dark. Picard stared at his reflection in its shiny blackness for a moment.

It seemed it was not going to be a rewarding day after all.

Chapter Three

PICARD WOULD HAVE LIKED to spend an evening on Deep Space Three with Admiral Ammerman and his wife, sampling the admiral's wines and talking about old times. However, he thought—as he made his way to the Stargazer's transporter room—the urgency of his mission required that he pick up his passenger and depart at once.

Partway to his destination, he saw Lieutenant Commander Jack Crusher emerge from a turbolift and fall into step alongside him. The commander was tall and cleanshaven, with a wide forehead and deepset dark eyes.

"Jack," the captain said by way of acknowledgment.

"Sir," Crusher responded.

During their off-duty hours, the younger man had become Picard's best friend. But while they were on duty, Picard preferred for them to act as captain and second officer. That way, no one would ever have reason to question Picard's objectivity.

"So," Crusher remarked, "an ensign serving aboard the *Wyoming* is the only person in Starfleet to have firsthand knowledge of this sector?" He turned to the captain. "An *ensign?"*

"Which seems a little strange to you," Picard suggested.

"That it does," the commander agreed.

The captain smiled. "It might not seem that way if you knew that this is not the first time this ensign has been in Starfleet."

The other man made a face. "What do you mean? He resigned and then joined up again a few years later?"

Picard nodded. "Precisely."

"That's strange."

"But not unheard of."

"Any idea why he quit?" Crusher asked.

"None," the captain informed him. "But you'll soon have an opportunity to ask him yourself."

They turned a corner and a set of doors hissed open ahead of them, revealing the *Stargazer*'s transporter room. Picard nodded to the transporter operator, who deftly manipulated the controls. The mechanism whirred softly and a brightness appeared in the air above the platform.

Crusher frowned a little. "Exactly how long has this individual been out of the mix, Captain?"

Picard spared him a glance. "Fifty years."

The commander looked at him. "Did you say . . . fifty *years,* sir?"

"I did," the captain confirmed. "He served under the twenty-third-century captain Hikaru Sulu."

Crusher's forehead creased. "Then he's got to be—"

"A Vulcan," said Picard.

At that moment, the ensign in question finished materializing on the transporter pad. His erect bearing, calm eyes and cool demeanor proclaimed him a true son of his hot and hostile planet.

"Welcome aboard, Ensign Tuvok," said Picard. "Your expertise on this mission will be most useful." He indicated Crusher with a gesture. "May I present my second officer, Lieutenant Commander Jack Crusher."

Crusher was a naturally gregarious fellow. Picard could see him struggling not to step forward with hand outstretched. Instead, imitating their new temporary crewmember, he inclined his head.

"A pleasure, Ensign Tuvok," said the commander. "I must say, I'm looking forward to hearing about your service on the—"

"Captain," Tuvok cut in smoothly, "our mission, as it was described to me, is one of the utmost urgency. I suggest we dispense with"—he straightened, unable to hide his contempt for the word—"pleasantries, and call an immediate meeting of your senior staff. It will be necessary to share information and plan a strategy."

Picard was a bit surprised. Vulcans were certainly not ones for idle chitchat, but most were not quite as . . . prickly . . . as Tuvok seemed. Courtesy was actually a logical concept, as it improved relations between species and individuals, and most Vulcans practiced it religiously.

Tuvok, on the other hand, seemed to be more Vulcan than any of his fellow Vulcans. His posture had not relaxed a single iota.

"Very well," said the captain. "You make a good point, Ensign. Let's go to my ready room and we can bring everyone up to speed."

Without further ado, Tuvok crossed the room and preceded Picard out the door. As the captain and Crusher followed, their eyes met—and the commander pretended to shudder with cold.

Picard didn't want to smile, but he couldn't help himself.

The world officially known as Debennius VI had the intimidating nickname of "the Last Stop to Nowhere." Entering the shoddy establishment where he and his employer were scheduled to meet, Bin Nedrach had to admit that the ancient label was well deserved.

Debennius VI was the outermost planet in a system that in itself was not exactly a well-known destination for space travelers. Any hint of a thriving community was manifested on the other planets, with the main cultural center located on Debennius II.

Out here on the sixth planet, only the lost, the poor, and the incurably antisocial were welcomed. Bin Nedrach allowed himself a passing worry about how he was going to get out of here with both his latinum and his skin, but he quashed the thought.

After all, his employer had seen to everything thus far. No doubt, he would see to Bin Nedrach's safe departure as well.

The establishment in question—if one could dignify it with that name—had none of the orderly precision of a Melacronai equivalent. It was dark and smoky inside, and patrons were visible only as dim shapes. Apparently, the owner of the place could not afford proper lighting. That, or else he or she simply didn't care to install it.

Reflexively, Bin Nedrach's wide single nostril clamped shut against the stench of the place. He was mildly irritated by his body's automatic response, but resigned himself to breathing through his mouth until he could get out of there. It was a small enough inconvenience, considering the amount of latinum he was about to collect.

Finally, his eyes adjusted to the light. But once he got a good look at the place's "customers," his six-fingered hand fell automatically to the weapon at his side. For the first time since undertaking the mission, Bin Nedrach experienced a genuine flash of doubt.

Was it possible that someone as powerful as his employer truly enjoyed a place like this? Or, the Melacron wondered, was this whole meeting some kind of set-up?

Nedrach knew it would be easy enough . . . hire a hungry assassin, let him undertake a dangerous mission for you, and then lure him to this "Last Stop to Nowhere." (Now that he thought about it, the nickname *did* have an ominous ring to it.) And finally, while your hungry assassin is salivating at the thought of how rich he's about to become, have another assassin dispatch him.

And who would suspect? No one.

With that in mind, the Melacron looked around some more . . . but couldn't discern any real threats. Finally, his gaze fell upon two humanoids in a dark, almost hidden corner of the room.

Ah, he thought. *He's here.* Relief flooded Bin Nedrach as he made his way as unobtrusively as possible in the direction of his employer.

By the look of him, Mendan Abbis was already half-drunk. That, Bin Nedrach had to concede, was an improvement over the first time he had met Abbis—when he was *completely* drunk.

The Thallonian's eyes sparkled as they fastened on Bin Nedrach, and he smiled a lopsided smile. Heedless of who might see, Abbis beckoned to the assassin enthusiastically.

The cold, silver eyes of the youth's Indarrhi companion seemed to bore right through Bin Nedrach. He knew that the dark-skinned, white-haired Indarrhi possessed empathic abilities.

Abbis had never introduced Nedrach to the Indarrhi, so the assassin had never learned his name. But not for the first time, he wondered how much the empath was picking up from him. Just to be safe, he calmed his thoughts, put even the most remote notion of treachery out of his mind, and approached the Thallonian with a smile on his face.

"You," slurred Abbis, making a stab at Bin Nedrach with a ruddy index finger, "are my favorite person in the entire galaxy!"

"Am I?" Bin Nedrach asked.

"Well," the Thallonian amended, pouring himself another drink from a dirty pitcher filled with a potent-looking black liquid, "at least today."

"I'm delighted that my work pleases you," said Bin Nedrach.

The Indarrhi didn't say anything. He just stared. It was unnerving, even to a hardened assassin like Nedrach.

"Your mission was a complete success." Abbis took a long drink, then wiped his mouth with his sleeve. "Even better than I had hoped. Not only was the G'aha of Laws and Enforcements an important figure, he was a very popular one as well. I'd almost go as far as to say beloved."

That was Nedrach's understanding as well.

"His murder," said Abbis, "has upset all Melacron everywhere. They're starting to murmur about going to war with the Cordracites, even the most peaceful of them."

Suddenly, he grinned and leaned in toward Bin Nedrach with an air of conspiracy. "And do you know what the best thing about this is? The most delicious thing of all?"

The assassin shook his head.

"The G'aha of Laws and Enforcements was adamantly against war with the Cordracites. Isn't that ironic?" asked Abbis. He began to laugh.

"Quite so," said Bin Nedrach.

The Indarrhi was still staring at him, his thick fingers twitching. The assassin wondered what that meant.

"You were hired with the intention of sparking a war," said Abbis. "I'd say you succeeded."

Not for the first time, Bin Nedrach wondered why Mendan Abbis, a member of a species that had nothing to do with the conflicts between the Cordracites and the Melacron, so desperately wanted to spark war between those two civilizations. Clearly, Nedrach reflected, the Thallonian had something to gain from it . . . but what could it be?

The Indarrhi's glittering eyes narrowed slightly . . . and Bin Nedrach hastily redirected his thoughts to the latinum for which Mendan Abbis was fishing in his tunic pocket. That, after all, was the assassin's only real interest in being here.

And as the Thallonian's latinum began to appear on the table in significant amounts, Bin Nedrach found it easier and easier to put the question of Abbis's motives aside.

In fact, he soon forgot about it altogether.

Crusher at first thought the lounge was empty.

After all, it was dark except for the dim glow that manifested automatically when the room wasn't in use. If any of the commander's colleagues had been there, they would have called for some real illumination.

He called out, "Computer, lights."

When the room lit up, revealing another uniformed humanoid there, Crusher nearly jumped out of his uniform. Then he saw who it was, and he forced himself to relax.

Tuvok fixed the human with his cool yet somehow piercing gaze. "Commander," he said simply.

"I'm sorry," said Crusher. "I thought the room was unoccupied. I mean . . . there weren't any lights."

The Vulcan arched an eyebrow. "Obviously," he replied with what was clearly forced patience, "you were incorrect in your assumption. I prefer soft lighting whenever possible."

The commander felt a little awkward. He had never managed to be all that comfortable around Vulcans, and this one was . . . well, as Vulcan as they came. Even so, the man was a visitor on a ship full of strangers, and Crusher didn't want to make him feel unwelcome.

He caught sight of a cup of steaming beverage on the table. From the aroma, he judged it to be Vulcan spice tea. Crossing to the replicator, he asked Tuvok, "Care for a refill?"

"No," the Vulcan said. "Thank you." His voice was every bit as icy as when he got off the transporter platform.

The commander shrugged and ordered his own drink—key limeade, extra pulpy. He'd have a synthale for his second drink, but this one made him think of Beverly. She had introduced him to it on their second date, back on Earth. He had fallen in love with key limeade and her simultaneously.

Bev, he thought. His bright, stable, yet passionate redhead. God, how he missed her. And little Wesley . . . he wondered what irretrievable moment of the toddler's childhood he was missing today.

Turning around, drink in hand, Crusher saw that Tuvok was still staring at him. He held a padd in his hands and seemed, even in his Vulcan calm, to have a shadow of annoyance on his face.

"Care for some company?" the commander asked.

"I would prefer to be alone," replied Tuvok.

Crusher ignored the comment. How was he going to get to know the ensign if they didn't speak at least a little bit?

He gestured to the padd. "Research?"

Tuvok's long fingers closed about the device ever so slightly. "No. I am fashioning a private message for my wife back on Vulcan."

The commander's eyebrows shot up. Family? *This* iceberg?

Well, it just went to prove the adage that there was a cover for every pot. Intrigued, Crusher decided to ignore Tuvok's request for solitude for a few more seconds.

Hey, he mused, everyone likes to talk about his loved ones. Could a Vulcan be any different in that regard?

"I've got a family myself," said Crusher, slipping into the chair beside Tuvok. "A wife and a little baby boy named Wesley."

The ensign didn't say anything.

"Beverly is a Starfleet doctor," the commander continued. "I'm hoping that after my stint here is wrapped up, we can work together on a starship. It'd be nice not to have to say good-bye to the wife and kids all the time, wouldn't you think?"

Tuvok's expression didn't soften, but he did put the padd down on the table and regard Crusher steadily. "I am a father as well," he said. "I have three sons and a daughter."

Crusher smiled a gratified smile. Now we're getting somewhere, he told himself. "Miss 'em, do you?"

"Your statement implies sorrow or loneliness," said the ensign. "You should know that I experience neither."

Spoken like a true Vulcan, thought Crusher. He sighed, wondering how to get past the brick wall that had been thrown up in front of him.

"However," Tuvok went on abruptly, "I do find that I am aware of their absence. I was fortunate enough to be with my children during their formative years. It is . . . regrettable that you are on such a lengthy mission and cannot be with your son."

Surprised, the commander regarded him for a moment. By Vulcan standards, the man was positively gushing.

Crusher tried to conjure an image of Tuvok dandling an infant on his knee . . . and failed. What were Vulcan children like? Were they born with this level of control, like tiny, emotionless adults? Or were they as wild as human children—maybe even wilder, if the ancient Vulcan heritage of violent emotion was still present in their genetic code?

It was an interesting question—and one that had never before occurred to the human. He asked the ensign about it.

Tuvok shrugged. "Control must always be learned," he said flatly. "That is the primary responsibility of a Vulcan parent. However, to most of our offspring, it comes as second nature."

Crusher nodded. "I'll bet," he said sincerely, "that you're an excellent father, Tuvok."

The ensign cocked his head just a millimeter or so. "I am indeed," he replied simply.

The commander chuckled. There was no bragging in the statement, just a flat proclamation of fact.

Impulsively, he leaned forward. "I'd like your opinion on something, Tuvok. That is, if you don't mind."

The Vulcan inclined his head. "Certainly."

"I hate being away from Beverly," said Crusher. "I mean, I *really* hate it. And Wes—damn it, he's practically growing up without me. I have these nightmares about going home and finding out he's graduating from the Academy, and there I am holding a stuffed Circassian cat and looking like an idiot."

Tuvok's expression remained impassive.

"Anyway," the commander went on, "it struck me that there could be a way to accommodate crewmembers with families."

The Vulcan's brow creased ever so slightly. "Explain."

Crusher shrugged. "I thought maybe we'd take them with us."

What little openness there had been about Tuvok's features closed up.

"Think of the psychological benefits to the crew," the human went on. "We would be living full lives instead of just carrying out our assignments."

The Vulcan frowned. "It would not be wise," he said. "Starships are military vessels. They are often involved in battle and other dangerous activities. They are not places for children."

Crusher found he was eager to win Tuvok's approval—though why that might be, he couldn't exactly say. "Well, not right now, they're not," he answered reasonably. "We'd have to plan for their presence . . . take advantage of the ship's ability to separate into a primary hull and a stardrive section. Then, if we anticipate danger, we can deploy all non-essential personnel to the primary hull and get them out of harm's way."

The Vulcan's dark eyes narrowed slightly as he considered the plan. But the commander couldn't read him at all, couldn't tell if Tuvok liked the idea or thought it foolish.

Damn it, Crusher thought, I'm actually nervous! I feel as if I were standing up in front of my third-year class back at the Academy, presenting my thesis again. . . .

"I see no flaw in your logic," Tuvok concluded suddenly.

The human felt a grin begin to spread over his face. He tried to stop it, but he didn't stand a chance. After all, it wasn't every day that one received a compliment from a Vulcan.

"I'm glad you approve," he said.

"Your approach will need some refinement, of course," said Tuvok. "And you should be aware that others may have certain emotions tied up in their analysis of your plan—unlike myself."

Crusher stood up. "But . . . it would be nice to have the family with you, wouldn't it?"

The Vulcan hesitated, then met the commander's eyes. "Yes," he said. "It would be . . . nice."

Crusher grinned again. "I've enjoyed our conversation, Tuvok. Maybe we can talk again sometime." He shrugged. "I guess I'll leave you to your message. Sorry to have interrupted."

Before he realized what he was doing, he had clapped the Vulcan on the shoulder in a display of camaraderie. Tuvok stiffened slightly—and inwardly, the commander cursed himself.

Physical contact was a violation of a Vulcan's privacy. He had just committed a terrible *faux pas.*

Oh, well, he thought, it was done.

Of course, the commander still felt an impulse to apologize. But in the end, he thought better of it. It would only make things more awkward. Instead, he turned and walked out of the lounge.

Despite his unintentional error in interspecies courtesy, Crusher felt pretty good about the conversation. In a peculiarly Vulcan way, Tuvok clearly loved his family. So did the human.

It was a start.

Chapter Four

AS PICARD ENTERED the five-sided Grand Council Chamber on Debennius II, he decided that it was as beautiful as any venue he had ever seen. And yet, as he had been told, beauty was not its chief virtue.

After all, the chamber had been built to allow opposing forces to clash over and over again without violent incident. In that respect, it had to be a lot more than easy on the eyes.

Looking up, the captain saw the overarching, transparent dome that let the natural light of the sun shine in, albeit through a glare-softening filter. When debates continued into the evening, it was Picard's understanding that artificial illumination would be employed—but that it mimicked the sun's light so well as to be completely non-distracting.

Soft, muted colors were the rule in every aspect of the decor. Pale blues, delicate greens and purples seemed to dominate, but there was a hint here and there of a metallic hue such as silver or gold. Still, the overall effect was profoundly soothing.

Even the chamber's walls were constructed of sound-absorbing materials. And its thick carpeting was designed to feel soothing to the feet—for those diplomats and observers who had such appendages.

Picard smiled appreciatively. It was a wise collection of decorating choices for a chamber in which so many disparate voices were liable to argue over so much.

However, it wasn't just the decor that impressed the captain. Plainly speaking, the place was enormous. It easily sat the several hundred Benniari, Melacron, Cordracites and other interested species who were taking their seats for the morning's peace talks—including a few avian visitors who perched on pedestals of native woods along the walls.

The captain was impressed with the power and ingenuity of the Benniari's vision. It was for good reason, it seemed, that they were known all over the quadrant for their sensibilities in art, architecture, and music.

"Some place," commented Ben Zoma, who had accompanied him there along with Commander Crusher and Ensign Tuvok.

Picard's first officer was dark and lanky with a rakish smile. He had a way with women the captain couldn't help envying and loved a good joke, but was all business when he had to be.

"Indeed," said Picard.

Jetaal Jilokh, aide to First Minister Cabrid Culunnh, looked up at the captain. At a meter and a half in height, the Benniari was somewhat on the tall side for one of his people.

"Our council chamber meets with your approval?" he asked, his Benniar voice soft and breathless to human ears.

Picard nodded. "Very much so."

"I am pleased," said Jilokh. He looked about the room with what was clearly a flush of pride. "Both the Melacron and the Cordracites were extremely generous in donating funds to build this hall. However, the design is strictly a Benniar invention.

"Before it was built," the aide went on, "the sector was headed for war. Despite the obstacles, which were many and varied, we managed to craft a foundation for peace within these walls . . . a foundation that until recently seemed as solid as bedrock." He shook his head with obvious sadness. It was an oddly human gesture, the captain thought.

"Unfortunately," Jilokh concluded, "that foundation is proving to be as fragile as blown glass."

"But that's why we're here," the captain said assuringly. "To see to it that that foundation becomes rock-solid again."

Jilokh looked at him. "Of course," he responded. With a clawlike hand, he gestured to the two-level speaker's platform at the other side of the chamber. "Let us proceed. The First Minister awaits us."

The universal translator built into Picard's communicator badge translated the Benniari's voice as thin and reedy. That, combined with his typically Benniar appearance—evocative of a small, furry Earth animal known as a koala bear—might have made those who didn't know his people dismiss them as docile and ineffectual.

The captain, of course, knew better. "By all means," he told Jilokh, "lead the way."

Turning to face the speaker's platform, the Benniari trundled down the chamber's central aisle with a rocking gait. Picard and his people followed, glancing with curiosity at the assembled delegates as more and more of them filled the chamber.

The captain noted the presence of not just Melacron, Cordracites, and Benniari, but Denesthians and Shera'sha-sha and Banyanans as well. There was even a Thallonian official, a tall, poised individual dressed in expensive-looking clothes that marked him as a man of high station.

He met Picard's gaze and their eyes held for a moment. Then the Thallonian nodded cordially and took his seat.

Commander Crusher leaned closer to the captain. "Seems the Melacron-Cordracite situation has many interested observers."

"I was just thinking the same thing," Picard noted.

Jilokh looked back over his furry shoulder and chirped a couple of times—the Benniar equivalent of a chuckle, if a dry one. Obviously, he had overheard the commander's remark.

"Many interested observers indeed," he said. "Not the least of them you yourselves, representing the Federation. And each one has his own peculiar reason for monitoring our proceedings."

"No doubt," said the captain, "they are all a little concerned."

"*Quite* concerned," Jilokh confirmed.

By then, they had reached the two-stage speaker's platform. Ascending to the first level and then the second, the Benniari led them to a door in the far wall. Then he touched a pad beside the door, causing it to slide into a pocket aperture.

"Please," said Jilokh, indicating with a gesture that his companions were to enter.

Picard complied . . . and found himself face to face with the renowned Cabrid Culunnh. The First Minister of Debennius II was seated behind a sleek, rounded desk made of dark wood. As he rose, the captain could see evidence of the Benniari's considerable age.

"Captain Picard," said Culunnh, as Jilokh slid closed the door to the room. He held his hands out, leathery palms exposed. "I rejoice that you were able to answer my summons."

Always aware of protocol, Picard mimicked the palms-out gesture. "I only regret we were not able to arrive sooner," he replied. He indicated his companions with a sweep of his hand. "Commander Ben Zoma, my first officer. Commander Crusher, my second officer. And Ensign Tuvok."

The First Minister took special note of the Vulcan. "You are the first of your people I have ever had the pleasure to meet," he told Tuvok. "I wish it were under different circumstances."

"As do I," said the ensign.

Picard regarded Culunnh. "I understand you are in need of some assistance, First Minister."

The Benniari chirped. "To say the least."

Reaching down under the surface of his desk, he manipulated some kind of control. A moment later, a section of wall beside the door turned transparent, affording them a view of the council chamber—although the captain had a feeling the transparency was a one-way effect.

Culunnh looked past Picard and regarded the assemblage of diplomats. "As you know," he said, "this congress's stated goal is still to try to resolve disagreements over territory. However, there are moments when it would be difficult to discern that."

"There's been discord, I take it," said Picard.

"To say the least," the First Minister responded. "Every day, we see more shouting matches, more veiled threats and accusations flung back and forth. Unless we do something, and quickly I might add, I fear we are headed for the war we built this chamber to avoid."

The captain absorbed the information. Obviously, Admiral Ammerman hadn't exaggerated the seriousness of the situation.

"If I may ask a question or two?" Tuvok suggested, asking permission of Picard and Culunnh simultaneously.

"Of course, Ensign," said the First Minister.

The captain nodded. He still felt strange hearing someone address Tuvok in that fashion, considering the Vulcan's age and experience. And yet, that *was* his official title.

"You have said," Tuvok began, "that you do not believe that this fresh wave of terrorist incidents was caused by either the Melacron or the Cordracites. However, the intervention of a third party seems unlikely, given the history of the various races in this sector."

"You wish to know if I have any proof?" asked Culunnh.

"I do," the Vulcan responded flatly.

The First Minister regarded him with a faint, hissing whistle. "You have an incisive mind," he told Tuvok. "A wonderfully Vulcan mind, I would guess. As to your question . . . I have no *real* proof. However, the methods and equipment used in the terrorist assaults are clearly not in keeping with the methods and equipment used before."

"The terrorists could be dealing with arms merchants," Crusher suggested. "If war really does break out, weapon dealers would be the first ones to reap the benefits."

"A possibility, Commander," admitted Culunnh, "but a rather unlikely one, I am afraid. We have seen weapons in these assaults from nearly every sector in the galaxy, well beyond what our local arms merchants would normally have available to them."

It was an interesting point, Picard conceded. And it seemed that Culunnh wasn't finished speaking.

"The two established terrorist presences—the Cordracite Qua-Sok and the Melacronai Me'laa'kra—have traditionally incited fear in their enemies, but have seldom actually killed anyone. They have demonstrated a preference for destroying property rather than people."

"But that has changed?" asked the captain.

"Yes," said Culunnh. "Now we are seeing brutal acts perpetrated upon beloved public figures. Public figures with families . . . even young children, I might add. This is a level of barbarism to which neither the Me'laa'kra nor the Qua-Sok ever stooped."

"I see," Picard replied.

"Previously, the terrorists wanted sympathy for their causes," the First Minister noted. "They wanted allies. None of these more recent attacks has stirred up anything but anger and hatred."

The Vulcan nodded. "And that is why you believe there is a third party involved in the attacks?"

"Correct," Culunnh told him. "Mind you, as I said, I have no hard evidence to back up my belief at this time . . . nor do I have any suspects in mind. I just look at the data and cannot help feeling as I do."

Tuvok frowned. "I understand."

Culunnh eyed him. "But you still have your doubts?"

The Vulcan nodded. "I still have my doubts."

Ben Zoma gave the captain a look. "I guess we've got our work cut out for us, sir."

"That we do," Picard agreed.

Suddenly, a gong rang loudly enough to be heard in Culunnh's office. It seemed to reverberate in the captain's bones. He looked inquiringly at the First Minister.

"That was the three-cycle bell," Culunnh explained. "It means the morning session will begin shortly."

Jilokh spoke up. "I have set aside seats for Captain Picard and Commander Ben Zoma, First Minister."

Culunnh picked up a metal medallion on a chain and hung it from his short, furry neck. Then he glanced at Crusher and Tuvok. "And his other companions?" he asked his aide.

"They merely wished to meet with you," said Jilokh.

"That's correct," Picard chimed in. "Commander Crusher and Ensign Tuvok will be beaming back to the *Stargazer* to take the lead in our investigation."

The First Minister seemed to approve. "Our hopes go with you, gentlemen. May your endeavor be a successful one."

"Thank you," said Crusher.

Tuvok merely inclined his head.

Culunnh turned to Picard and Ben Zoma. "As you observe our meeting," he told them, "you will see for yourselves the passions raging on both sides. I think you will agree, they are considerable."

The captain nodded. "Thank you for the warning."

He watched as Culunnh toddled off on his bowed Benniar legs, followed closely by Jilokh. Both Benniari exited the room. Then Picard turned to Crusher and Tuvok.

"What I've heard from Cabrid Culunnh," he told them, "leads me to believe his theory of a third party is worth investigating. He mentioned that the methods and equipment used in the recent terrorist incidents were different from those employed by the Qua-Sok and the Me'laa'kra. I want Joseph, Vigo and Simenon to take a look at this. And Dr. Greyhorse as well."

"Aye, sir," said Crusher.

Joseph, Vigo, Simenon, and Greyhorse were individuals of uncommon intelligence and insight. The captain had no doubt that they would be able to confirm or refute Culunnh's suspicions in no time.

"Work closely with them," Picard said. "I want at least *some* useful information by the time I return to the ship."

"Aye, sir," Crusher replied again.

The captain turned to his new, rather aloof ensign. "Mr. Tuvok, I don't believe you've met our chief engineer, Mr. Simenon. You'll find he's a bit outspoken, but he certainly knows his business."

The Vulcan raised an eyebrow. "Then we should get along admirably."

Beside Picard, Ben Zoma hid a grin. Like the captain himself, he was no doubt trying to picture the tall, elegant Vulcan working alongside the cranky, arrogant, lizardlike Gnalish.

Picard held the image in his mind for a moment—the long gray face, the mobile tail, the bright ruby eyes fastened on Tuvok's implacable visage. Simenon would no doubt consider it a personal challenge to get some kind of rise out of the ensign.

The captain glanced at his second officer again. "See you back on the *Stargazer,* Mr. Crusher."

"Aye, sir," said the commander. Then he tapped his comm badge. "Crusher to transporter room. Two to beam up."

"Ready, sir," came the response.

"Energize," Crusher ordered.

Almost instantly, the commander and Tuvok were enveloped in the shimmer and sparkle of the transporter effect. A moment later, they were gone as if they had never been there in the first place.

Nodding approvingly, Picard tapped his own comm badge. "*Stargazer,* this is the captain," he said.

"Asmund here," came the voice of his efficient young helm officer. "I trust you're making progress, sir?"

"A bit," Picard told her. "Ensign Tuvok and Commander Crusher have beamed back up. As I noted before I left the ship, Commander Ben Zoma and I will stay down here in the—"

"Gladiator pit," Ben Zoma quipped with a hint of a smile.

"—Benniari's Grand Council Chamber," Picard continued evenly, without missing a beat.

He glanced at his first officer. Ben Zoma had a sometimes inconvenient sense of humor, but he was a damned fine first officer. The captain didn't begrudge him a witticism now and then.

"Acknowledged, sir," said Asmund.

"Picard out," said the captain.

Chapter Five

"RECORD MESSAGE," SAID JACK CRUSHER, leaning back in his chair.

"Recording," came the response from his workstation.

Crusher smiled at the monitor screen, imagining his wife's face there instead of a Starfleet insignia. "Hi, honey. It's me. I hope everything's working out for you and Wesley."

The commander hated like the dickens to talk to a computer screen. Unfortunately, it was the only way he could get a message to Beverly, so he put up with it.

"We're out here in the Debennius system," he said, "trying to stop a run of terrorist attacks that are bringing a couple of species called the Melacron and the Cordracites to the brink of war. My job is to check out a theory that some third party is responsible for the attacks—presumably, someone who wants that war to happen."

Crusher knew he didn't have much time. After all, the captain wanted results—and quickly—and the fact that his shift had ended an hour ago was hardly an excuse.

"I'm working with a Vulcan named Tuvok, who's had some experience in this neck of space. He's a little stiff—not unexpected, I know—but deep down, he seems like a good guy. A family man, too. I told him my idea about bringing families aboard a starship and he seemed to like it."

The commander recalled Tuvok's reaction and smiled to himself. It had given him a good feeling.

"I've never really had a lot of contact with Vulcans. Few people have. You know . . . they keep to themselves a lot." He shrugged. "But I like this guy. I think if he sticks around a while, we could become friends."

The Starfleet insignia on the screen stared back at Crusher, despite his attempts to see his wife there instead. It seemed to be reminding him that he had work to do.

"Got to go now," he said with a sigh, "but I'll send you another message as soon as I can. Love you, honey. And give Wes a hug for me. Tell him his daddy can't wait to see him."

This was the part the commander hated the most. However, he managed to get it out before the lump formed in his throat. Guess I'm getting better with practice, he told himself.

"Bye, Bev," he concluded.

Crusher instructed the computer to end the message and send it with the next subspace packet intended for headquarters. Then he got up from his chair and headed for the door.

The lounge awaits, he mused.

The sound of a gong filled the council chamber, then died.

Sitting in a seat on the second level of the speaker's platform, Picard watched First Minister Culunnh rise from his ornately carved wooden chair and approach a small lectern.

By then, all the delegates had presumably taken their seats. To the captain, the chamber looked absolutely full. There were even a few observers standing in the back.

Culunnh's small, furry head poked over the top of the lectern. His large violet eyes blinked solemnly, his shiny metal medallion glinting in the filtered sunlight.

"The four hundred and forty-first session of the Kellasian Congress is now in session," intoned the Benniari. "First Minister of Debennius II Cabrid Culunnh presiding. May I remind you that this is a place for discussion and debate—nothing else."

Ben Zoma leaned toward his commanding officer. "Not a good sign when you have to say that right off the bat."

"No," Picard breathed, "it's not."

Culunnh consulted a small screen built into his lectern. "The chamber recognizes Sammis Tarv, Chief Delegate of Cordra Four."

Tarv, a pale-skinned insectoid with Andorian-like antennae, stood up and faced the congress. "Once again," he said in a rasping voice, "I would like to address the matter of the Melacronai colony on Tebra Six. It must be clear by now that—"

He was interrupted by a warbling cry of protest from a Melacronai throat: "I speak for the dead!"

As Picard scanned the assemblage to determine the origin of the high-pitched protest, he saw a Melacronai female come down the central aisle. She wasn't alone, either. There was a small child in her arms, an infant really, and one more on either side of her.

"G'aha Avriil cannot decry the manner of his death," the female shrilled, "but his widow can!"

"I must protest!" Sammis Tarv grated loudly. "First Minister, this woman was not properly presented to this body, nor have children ever been allowed to enter this chamber!"

Before he finished, the entire delegation of Cordracites was on its feet, adding their objections to his. Their voices sounded like a collection of rocks grinding together.

The translator installed in Picard's comm badge squealed in protest. Both the captain and his first officer winced and removed their badges. Picard scowled, having been warned that this might happen if too many of the delegates decided to speak at once.

"Silence!" demanded Cabrid Culunnh.

The Cordracites fell silent as he asked, though they continued to gesticulate with great vehemence. But the Melacronai female chose not to heed the First Minister.

"First Minister Culunnh!" she cried out. "It seems to me that the Companion of a murdered G'aha ought to be honored within these precincts, not silenced like an unruly ta'pur!"

Her children stared wide-eyed at Culunnh. The smallest of them began to weep, his single nostril flaring and then sealing shut.

Ben Zoma shook his head. "Why do I have a feeling she and the kids didn't come here on their own?"

Picard knew exactly what his exec meant. He had no doubt the female was what she appeared to be—the spouse of a murdered Melacronai official. However, her presence there was so incendiary as to raise questions.

"More than likely," the captain whispered, "the Melacronai delegation arranged her passage here."

"To show the congress how the Melacron are suffering at the hands of the Cordracites," Ben Zoma suggested. "So in the end, everyone will sympathize with Melacronai territorial claims."

And the congress hadn't been in session for more than a minute or two. Picard had to wonder how often this type of thing occurred.

A sharp buzzer sounded, interrupting the G'aha's widow. Cabrid Culunnh's tufted ears lay flat against his round head, a sure sign of irritation. "Madam," he responded, "I grieve for your great loss—"

A roar of protest went up from the Cordracite delegation. However, the First Minister barreled on.

"—and I am certain everyone here does the same. We have never condoned and *will* never condone the assassination of an elected official under any circumstances at all."

He glared at the entire assembly. Picard hadn't thought it possible for a Benniari to glare, but Culunnh was doing it.

"However," said the First Minister, "it is true that you did not petition to be heard, and that your children are not permitted at these debates. I levy two rounds of silence against the Melacronai delegation as a penalty for violating the established rules of conduct for this congress."

"I object!" trilled a Melacron. "We had no more warning than you did that this female would seek to address the Congress!"

"Perhaps not," Culunnh allowed, whether he believed it or not. "However, it has long been a policy here to hold delegates responsible for the actions of their people. The decision stands."

The Melecronai delegation warbled their complaints, but to no avail. The First Minister buzzed them a second time and a third. Eventually, they sat down and fell silent.

"Sammis Tarv," said Culunnh, "you had the floor before the proceedings were interrupted. Please go on."

However, when the Cordracite got up again to speak, he was shouted down by a group whose species Picard was unable to identify. And when they were silenced, the Melacronai delegation objected, citing some obscure and seemingly useless rule of protocol.

The First Minister denied the Melacron their objection, but they continued to voice it loudly and at great length. Culunnh buzzed them; it didn't help. Then the Cordracites began to speak at the same time, their deep, scratchy voices grating on everyone present.

Before long, it was a free-for-all.

The captain scanned the crowd, trying to discern who was attacking or defending whom. However, alliances seemed to shift from moment to moment, making it impossible for him to learn anything.

He did make one intriguing observation, however. The Thallonian nobleman appeared to remain silent throughout the conflict. He sat back in his seat observing the ebb and flow of charges and accusations with eyes that didn't seem to miss a thing.

Ben Zoma grunted. "You know, I'm amazed that war didn't break out a long time ago."

"That makes two of us," Picard muttered.

"Captain Picard?" said a soft, fluttery voice.

The human turned and saw that it was the First Minister who had called his name. The Benniari's large, violet eyes looked at him pleadingly, though Picard didn't have any idea what would be asked of him.

But he wouldn't have to wait long to find out.

"Yes, Minister?" the captain replied.

Culunnh turned to the congress. "Captain Picard of the Federation has agreed to honor us with his advice on these matters."

Picard blinked, but otherwise did nothing to reveal his surprise. He had believed that he and Ben Zoma were there to observe the proceedings, not make speeches to the congress.

However, he had been charged with reestablishing the peace in this sector in any way that made sense. If the First Minister of Debennius II thought he could help to calm this assembly, who was he to refuse?

For a moment he wondered if some faction or other would object, saying that the captain had not been properly "presented." However, the shouting appeared to die down as soon as he stood up and approached the lectern. Clearly, at least some of the delegates wished to hear what a Federation official had to say for himself.

"I would be honored to address this august body, First Minister," Picard said in his smoothest, most diplomatic-sounding voice. He straightened the red tunic of his dress uniform and approached the lectern. At the same time, Culunnh took a few steps back.

The captain was concerned that he would look silly standing behind a meter-high lectern. However, as he got closer it automatically rose to the height of his chest, removing at least one problem.

It was a good thing, Picard reflected soberly. After all, there were so many other problems to deal with.

He gathered his thoughts as he surveyed the sea of people sitting before him. From the insectlike Cordracites to the small, fuzzy shapes of the Benniari to the long, tentacled forms of the Shera'sha-sha, every sentient race in the sector seemed to have a representative here.

That was good, the captain told himself. He would start there.

"My name is Captain Jean-Luc Picard," he said, "of the Federation starship *Stargazer.* I was invited to this planet, this congress and"—he smiled a little—"to this podium by the First Minister of the Benniari. May I take this moment to salute Cabrid Culunnh for his tireless efforts to secure peace in this sector."

The sounds of accolades followed. Culunnh nodded slightly, receiving Picard's compliment with grace and dignity.

The captain's ears strained for sounds of resentment from the audience, but none came. It was a good sign. When parties in conflict turned their attention to attacking their mediator, whether verbally or physically, it was usually time to prepare for war.

"I am pleased to be present at these historic talks," Picard continued, "and pleased to see that, unless I am mistaken, every species in the Kellasian sector has a representative at this congress. What that tells me is that everyone here cares deeply about avoiding an armed conflict. That gives me, and the United Federation of Planets I represent, reason for optimism that a peaceful conclusion will be achieved in due time."

"Not until those who murdered my Companion are caught and punished for their crime!"

The outburst from the widow of the Melacronai G'aha was unexpected. So was her sudden rush toward the stage. After all, the female had already been escorted from the chamber with her children.

Picard didn't think she posed a threat, however. So he stayed where he was and let the Benniar guards deal with the woman.

Under different circumstances, the thought of Benniari guarding anything effectively might have seemed ludicrous. Fortunately, they didn't have to rely on their physical size. A touch of a button on their baldrics immobilized the woman's limbs, if not her voice.

"Justice, Picard of the Federation!" she screamed. "Justice! Help us find the Cordracite killers of my Companion!"

The captain swallowed. "Those responsible for the terrorist attacks will be caught and punished, I assure you," he said in the most tranquil voice he could muster, hoping desperately that fate would not prove him a liar. "But so far we have no proof that the Cordracites—"

"Who needs proof?" came the gurgling, hissing voice of one of the Shera'sha-sha. Its pale green tentacles waved frantically. "We all know what the Cordracites are! We all know what they do!"

"The Cordracites defend themselves against the aggressions of the Melacron, nothing more." The flat voice of the skeletal-looking Tikraat who had spoken made the words a statement more than a defense.

No translation device ever devised could convey the emotions of the Tikraata. The best they could do was serve up the words, uttered in a mechanical, atonal voice. "It is the Melacron who—"

"Let us have order in this hall!" Picard cried out. His voice carried and the arguments ceased. For the moment, he thought darkly.

"Listen to yourselves!" he told the assemblage. "Squabbling like children tearing at a new toy! You are diplomats, every one of you. You represent the highest virtues your people have to offer. I understand that tempers are running high, but let us move forward with our eyes open—so that we may truly see and understand what is taking place!"

"The Melacronai murderers are getting away with it, that's what's taking place!" someone shouted.

Picard felt his jaw muscles clench. He held his hands up in a call for quiet, but no one would pay any attention to him. Abruptly, the clear, pure sound of the Benniari gong sliced cleanly through the melee.

"Let us recess for a few cycles," said Cabrid Culunnh, who had taken up a position beside the captain. "As Captain Picard sagely counsels us, it is wiser to proceed thoughtfully and deliberately than to rush forward in the heat of emotion."

The congress muttered its dissatisfaction, but it was obvious that nothing more could be accomplished that morning. The delegates rose and dispersed, still arguing among themselves.

The First Minister turned to Picard. "Thank you for trying, Captain," he said in a soft, resigned voice. "Now you have some idea of the obstacles that confront me here."

"Indeed I do," Picard replied sincerely. He shook his head. "I doubt that Hercules had a more difficult time."

"Hercules?" Culunnh echoed. He cocked his head, obviously curious about the captain's reference.

"A great hero from one of my world's mythologies," Picard explained. "He was charged with seven supposedly impossible tasks. But in the end, he managed to complete them all."

Understanding flitted over the Benniari's furred face. Culunnh chirped once, and then again.

"Your Hercules," he said dryly, "never had to get a Melacron and a Cordracite to stop arguing. Otherwise, he might still be at it."

Picard acknowledged the truth of the comment. "Perhaps he would at that, First Minister." He watched the delegates continue to filter out of the chamber, still contending bitterly. "Perhaps he would at that."

Chapter Six

PICARD HAD NURTURED A HOPE that the afternoon session of the Kellasian Congress would be more productive than the morning session. That hope was dashed when the Cordracite delegation announced that it was absenting itself from the afternoon proceedings.

"For what reason?" Cabrid Culunnh asked.

"To protest the repeated admission of the Melacronai female," was the indignant answer supplied by Sammis Tarv.

The captain sighed as he watched the Cordracites file out of the chamber with their heads bowed, to the disgust of some observers and the rather vocal approval of others. Clearly, they would not solve a territorial dispute with only one of the disputants present.

"Those Cordracites sure know how to ruin a party," Ben Zoma observed in a voice only Picard could hear.

The captain nodded. "I imagine they've had lots of practice. But then, the Melacron seem no better."

The afternoon session went ahead without the Cordracites. But as Picard had predicted, it didn't get very far. In fact, it seemed to him that it took a few steps backward.

Tempers were running too high, the captain observed. Racial hatreds, some old, some new, had replaced rational objectives. No one was listening, everyone was talking, and poor Cabrid Culunnh seemed to get older and more exhausted by the minute.

The Kellasian Congress had become a joke. He could see that clearly now. Perhaps it had been effective before this latest wave of terrorist attacks, but it was effective no more.

Picard sincerely hoped his research team aboard the *Stargazer* was making headway. He and his first officer certainly weren't.

At the midafternoon recess, the captain and Ben Zoma departed the podium. Their intention was to use the allotted seventeen cycles—approximately a half-hour of Earth time—to stretch their legs. Debennius II was a lovely planet, after all. Picard believed a brief walk beneath a soft blue sky might clear their minds a bit.

It was not to be, however. No sooner had Picard descended to the chamber's central walkway than the large Thallonian he had observed earlier appeared suddenly at his side.

"Captain," said the Thallonian in a smooth, cultured voice.

The human turned to him. "Yes?"

"Permit me to introduce myself," the delegate told him. "I am Governor Gerrid Thul, here at the congress representing the interests of the Thallonian Empire." Thul extended a large ruddy hand, demonstrating that he was familiar with human customs.

Picard shook the Thallonian's hand. His grip was strong and firm, a rarity among aliens who attempted the handshake ritual.

"Jean-Luc Picard," said the captain, though by now he was certain everyone knew precisely who he was. He indicated his companion. "And this is Gilaad Ben Zoma, my first officer."

Thul shook Ben Zoma's hand as well.

"We have seventeen cycles before the war of words begins again," Thul told Picard. "Might I have a moment with you?" His eyes flickered to the first officer, then back to the captain. "In private?" he added.

Picard turned to Ben Zoma.

"Go ahead," said the dark-haired man. "I should call up to the *Stargazer* anyway. I need to check on some things."

The captain nodded, aware of at least some of the matters Ben Zoma would be checking on—all mundane but necessary aspects of ship's business. Then he turned to the Thallonian. "Very well. Shall we speak outside? Or do you have somewhere else in mind?"

"Outside will be fine," Thul told him.

Together, they made their way through the doors of the Grand Council Chamber and walked out into a beautiful, sunny day. Picard had to blink as his eyes adjusted to the brighter light.

In front of them, white stone steps led down to a circular pool with a fountain. The Thallonian approached it and peered into the sparkling depths. As the captain followed suit, he caught a glint of color—some kind of marine life, he realized.

A small bowl filled with some gray-green, crumbly matter stood on a nearby pedestal. Thul reached a big, red hand into it and began to sprinkle the surface of the water with the gray-green stuff. At once, the fish—if they could be called that, for they resembled no fish Picard had ever seen—darted to the surface and snatched at it.

The captain laughed as he realized what the stuff on the pedestal was. "Fish food," he said.

The Thallonian glanced at him and smiled. "Indeed," he said. He finished feeding the aquatic creatures, meticulously dusted off his hands, and turned to face Picard again.

"You asked to speak with me," the captain noted, acutely aware of how little time they had before the session resumed.

"I did," Thul agreed. He held his hands out, palms up. "Let me be blunt. How much do you know about our problems in this sector?"

Picard replied with equal bluntness. "Very little, I'm afraid. Only what's generally known to all those assembled. But I assure you, I intend to learn a good deal more."

The governor clasped his hands behind his back and stared into the depths of the fish pool. "Truly," he said, "it is a shameful spectacle. Supposedly, it is over territory. But of course, it has become a great deal more than that in recent weeks."

"You've been here that long?" asked the captain.

Thul nodded. "Too long, as you can imagine. I would much rather be back at my outpost, doing some real work. I need not tell you that attending these sessions has taken its toll on me." He glanced at Picard. "But then, I'm sure there is somewhere else you would rather be as well."

The captain grunted, thinking of the ruins on Zebros IV. "The same could probably be said of everyone in the congress . . . except perhaps the Cordracites and the Melacron themselves."

"Except them," the Thallonian agreed. "And they are closer than ever to an armed conflict—one which would take place precariously close to my emperor's borders. As you can imagine, the revered Tae Cwan does not wish to see such a conflict. That's why I'm here, a loyal servant of my master—to see to it that a war never takes place."

Picard was glad to hear that at least one delegate was approaching the matter with a cool head. He said so.

"One delegate, by himself, can do very little," Thul pointed out. He eyed the captain. "However, judging by what I heard from you this morning, it sounds as if your Federation and my Empire seek the same sort of outcome to these talks."

"It does at that," Picard agreed. By then, he could see where the

Thallonian was going with his comments. "You're suggesting that we join forces, I take it?"

"I am," Thul confirmed, his dark eyes blazing resolutely. "Let us work in concert, Captain. Then perhaps we can put an end to this war of words before it becomes a war in truth."

"We could pool our knowledge," Picard said.

"And back each other up during the talks," said the governor. He smiled. "Certainly, we have nothing to lose."

The captain hesitated a moment before replying. He didn't know very much about the Thallonians. Hardly anyone in the Federation did.

However, Thul seemed genuine in his desire to end the enmity between the Melacron and the Cordracites. Nor had it escaped Picard's notice that the governor was one of the very few delegates not crying out for blood in the Grand Council Chamber.

The one thing the captain knew for certain was that the Thallonian Empire was a powerful entity. Perhaps if he and Thul worked together here and now, their unity would not only improve the present situation but influence future negotiations with the governor's people.

"You make a compelling case," said Picard. He smiled as well. "From now on, we'll work together as closely as possible."

Thul clapped him on the shoulder. "I am pleased," he told the captain. "I am pleased indeed."

Crusher leaned back in his seat and surveyed the faces of the others who had joined him in the lounge.

Phigus Simenon, the ship's lizardlike chief engineer. Pug Joseph, the baby-faced head of security, who was straddling a chair in front of the room's computer workstation. Carter Greyhorse, the big, broadshouldered Native American who served as chief medical officer. Vigo, the strapping blue Pandrilite in charge of the *Stargazer*'s weapons systems.

And, of course, Ensign Tuvok, who was standing off to the side with his arms folded across his chest.

"Well, Ensign Tuvok," said Simenon, eyeing the Vulcan with slitted, blood-red eyes as he switched his scaly tail from one side to the other, "you're the expert on the Kellasian sector. Why don't you tell us who this mysterious third party is already, so we can all go have a nice snack and put our feet up?"

Caught off balance, the ensign looked quizzically at the Gnalish. "I beg your pardon?" he said.

The engineer stopped and returned Tuvok's scrutiny. "We backtracked all the way to Starbase Three to pick you up, didn't we? I thought that you might know something."

Tuvok frowned ever so slightly. "I know quite a bit. However, it will require considerable investigation to determine if there is a third party—and if so, to uncover his identity."

"Investigation," Simenon hissed, his eyes gleaming with humor. "Now why didn't I think of that?"

"Pay no attention to him," Greyhorse told the Vulcan.

"The doctor's right," said Joseph. He had turned around to face his workstation and was tapping away. "Our friend Simenon doesn't always work and play well with others."

"Doesn't *ever,*" Greyhorse amended.

Crusher knew that the Gnalish could be irascible in the extreme. The human had long since given up trying to beat him in a game of one-upmanship, since he never seemed to get anywhere.

Simenon smiled to himself. "My apologies, Mr. Tuvok. I didn't know your feelings were hurt so easily."

The ensign's brow creased. "I do not have feelings," he shot back. "I am a Vulcan. And if it is your intention to bait me, I would advise you to spend your time in more gainful pursuits . . . for instance, adjusting the magnetic switching controls in the plasma distribution manifold."

The Gnalish's head snapped around. "What are you talking about? There's nothing wrong with the magnetic switching controls."

The Vulcan lifted an eyebrow. "That is correct. It was merely . . . an example," he said archly.

It took Simenon a moment to realize that the tables had been turned on him, but when he did he hissed with delight. After all, he liked nothing better than when someone matched him blow for blow.

"Thataway," he told Tuvok with a surprisingly paternal tone in his voice. "Don't take guff from anyone—even me."

Crusher nodded approvingly. It seemed Tuvok was going to be able to hold his own on the *Stargazer*—even against the likes of the Gnalish.

"Now," he said, as the ranking officer in the room, "let's put the sharp part of our wits to the problem instead of each other."

"Here's a start," Joseph told them. He swiveled around in his chair again. "I've taken the liberty of pulling up all pertinent information on terrorist incidents in the sector."

"You mean the latest wave?" asked Greyhorse, his expression a characteristically grim one.

"No," said the security chief. "All of them, including the ones attributed to the established terrorist groups."

"The Quack-Socks and the Melly-Craw," snorted Simenon.

The Vulcan opened his mouth to correct the Gnalish's deliberate mispronunciations, but Crusher caught his eye and shook his head. Realizing he was being baited again, Tuvok remained silent.

"Gather 'round," Joseph advised his colleagues. "Don't be shy."

They all complied. Even Simenon.

"Now, as I understand it," the security chief went on with his colleagues looking over his shoulders, "the First Minister has two reasons for suspecting the intervention of a third party. One is a change in the methods used by the terrorists. The other is a change in the equipment they used . . . in other words, the weapons."

Crusher nodded. "That's right."

"Okay," said Joseph, tapping his monitor screen with a forefinger. "This is a catalogue of the terrorist incidents that took place between a year and six months ago."

One by one, scenes of carnage filled the screen, lingered for a moment, then faded . . . only to be replaced by others. Crusher shook his head as he looked at a bombed-out building in one scene, the desecration of a graveyard in another, the remnants of some ancient statuary in a third.

What a heartbreaking mess, he reflected. He couldn't understand how people could be so bent on destruction.

"All right," Joseph told them. "Now let's take a look at the incidents that took place in the last couple of weeks."

Again, scenes of carnage filled the screen. As Crusher watched, a series of dead Cordracites were pulled from a ragged hole in the ground. A moment later, a bound Melacron was executed with a directed-energy weapon. More Cordracite corpses, scattered across a playground. More Melacron corpses, floating on an expanse of blue-green water.

"I would say these are of a distinctly more bloody nature," Greyhorse noted with an air of disapproval.

Simenon slid a ruby-red eye in his direction. "Is that your professional opinion, Doctor?"

Greyhorse frowned at the Gnalish. "If you like."

"So," said Crusher, "so far, Culunnh seems to have a point. The terrorists' methods *have* changed."

"What about their weapons?" Vigo asked.

"Coming right up," said Joseph.

With that, he pulled up a set of objects depicted against a white background. They included hand weapons, blades of various shapes and sizes, and a couple of undetonated bombs.

"Each of these was used in a terrorist incident between a year and six months ago," the security chief remarked.

"They're all rather standard," Vigo observed.

"Nothing from outside the sector?" asked the Gnalish.

"I'd be surprised if it were," said the weapons officer.

Tuvok pointed to one object in particular—a long, scimitarlike affair. "What is this?" he inquired.

"Have you seen it before?" Greyhorse asked him.

The Vulcan shrugged. "I am not certain."

Joseph magnified the weapon and the legend beneath it. "It's the ritual slaughter blade of the Me'laa'kra," he explained. "All the sacred burden beasts in the incident on Cordra Four were killed with it."

"Twenty-two in all," said Simenon, reading off the screen. There was no hint of sarcasm in his voice anymore. "Absolutely sickening."

"Twenty two?" Tuvok asked. "Are you certain?"

Joseph looked at the ensign. "Positive. Why?"

"Twenty-two is a lucky number in the view of the ancient Cordracites," Tuvok informed him without emotion. "It is associated with the acquisition of wealth and power."

The security chief looked impressed with the observation. "Interesting, Ensign. But why murder burden beasts?"

Tuvok considered the question for a moment. Then again, he spoke dispassionately. "In primitive times, the Cordracites used these animals to sow their fields. In some regions, they were elevated to the status of harvest gods—deities who presided over the cultivation of land."

Crusher nodded. "So these animal slaughters might have been symbolic—a ritual objection to the Cordracite drive for territory."

"A drive matched meter for meter by our friends the Melacron," Joseph pointed out with a frown.

"Which, in a naaga shell," said the Gnalish, "is why they're at each other's throats all the time."

"More significantly," the Vulcan went on, "it seems the Me'laa'kra see their activities as a holy crusade, striking at the mystical symbols of the Cordracite belief system—and not at the Cordracites themselves."

"Indeed," said Simenon.

"But as we've already seen," Crusher noted, "recent incidents have clearly been designed to generate Cordracite fatalities."

"Which lends a bit more support to the third party theory," the chief medical officer told them.

"At least among the Me'laa'kra," said the Vulcan. "Perhaps we could examine a Qua-Sok weapon."

The security chief reduced the ritual slaughter blade to its previous size and gave them a view of the entire collection. Tuvok studied it again, but nothing seemed to pop out at him.

"Pick something anyway," Greyhorse encouraged him. "We had good luck with your last choice."

Vigo planted a big, blue forefinger on the screen. "Here," he said. "I'll do it for him."

As before, Joseph magnified the object—a small, black undetonated bomb. He glanced at the Vulcan. "Anything?"

Tuvok shook his head. "No. Perhaps if we were to see the aftermath of the incident, however . . ."

"Your wish is my command," the security chief told him. As Crusher watched, he tapped out the requisite command on his keyboard.

A tableau came up showing a half-destroyed power relay station on Melacron VI. The ensign extended a dark index finger and pointed to a scrawled message on a broken wall.

"Would you please magnify this?" Tuvok requested.

Joseph did as he was asked. Abruptly, the message became large enough to take up most of the screen.

"What does it say?" asked Crusher, who had no idea.

"I do not pretend to be an expert in Cordracite languages," said the Vulcan, "but I believe it credits the destruction of the relay station to the 'fierce and terrible Qua-Sok,' who only acted in 'the most upright and justified' fashion. Or something to that effect."

"Worried about their image, are they?" asked Simenon.

"Culunnh said they were," Crusher pointed out.

"What's more," Tuvok added, "they claimed responsibility for the incident. We should determine if anyone claimed responsibility for any of the more recent crimes against the Melacron."

Vigo nodded. "Good idea."

They went over each of the incidents—three of them in all. There was no sign of any scrawled messages at any of the sites. In fact, the perpetrators seemed to have gone out of their way to avoid leaving traces of their having been there.

"Another significant difference," Simenon noted.

Finally, Joseph tried to call up a visual inventory of the weapons used in the previous two weeks. But after a moment, he sighed and sat back in his chair, an expression of bemusement on his pugnosed face.

"What's the matter?" asked Greyhorse.

"They don't have any pictures of the weapons employed recently," said the security officer. "Whoever used them took them along with them."

"Sounds like the work of professionals," Vigo observed.

"But the Melacron must have speculated as to what was used," Crusher suggested.

Calling up the data, Joseph nodded. "They did. Unfortunately, they weren't able to get very specific. They weren't familiar with the energy signatures they found."

The Pandrilite weapons officer grunted. "Even *more* like the work of professionals," he maintained.

"Well," said Simenon, "the evidence—or lack of it, in this case—seems pretty clear. The First Minister is right. There *is* a third party involved in these attacks."

"Trying to pick up where the Qua-Sok and the Me'laa'kra left off," the security chief expanded.

"That would be my guess as well," said Tuvok.

Crusher recalled that the Vulcan had disagreed with Culunnh's conclusions down on Debennius VI. However, he now seemed quite willing to agree with them. *I guess that's one of the benefits of being without emotions,* the commander mused. *You never get too attached to a particular point of view.*

He could see how the Vulcan's bland yet somehow arrogant demeanor might seem a bit unsettling at times. But if Tuvok knew the Kellasian sector as well as he appeared to know it, Crusher would put up with his quirks from morning to night.

"Of course, that begs a question," Vigo pointed out.

Joseph nodded. "If there's a third party . . . who is he? And what does he hope to gain by killing innocent people?"

No one answered him, at first.

Then the Gnalish spoke up. "Arms merchants?" he suggested.

"I mentioned that as a possibility," said Crusher, "but the First Minister told us he didn't think so. He seemed to think the incidents involved weapons from all over the galaxy—a wider variety than arms merchants could get their hands on."

The Vulcan nodded. "Let us dismiss them for the time being."

"So," said Simenon, rephrasing the question, "who's busy killing all those Melacron and Cordracites?"

The six of them exchanged uncomfortable looks.

"Aye, there's the rub," the engineer commented cheerfully, as if nothing made him happier than pronouncing doom. "Your Shakespeare did have a way with words—especially violent ones."

Crusher stroked his chin. "Let's try another angle. I'm willing to bet that whoever killed the G'aha on Melacron Five wanted to get away as quickly as possible. Let's call up a list of everyone who left the planet between the time of the assassination and today."

Joseph provided them with a list on his monitor screen. "Unfortunately, it's pretty long," he told the others.

Crusher inspected it and fought back a sigh. "So it is."

"Exactly what are you hoping to find?" inquired the Gnalish, his crimson eyes bright with curiosity.

Crusher shrugged. "I just thought something might—"

But Tuvok stopped him with a gesture, his eyes locked onto the screen. "Fascinating," he murmured.

"What is?" Vigo asked him.

The Vulcan pointed to one of the names on the screen. "That is." Then he looked at Crusher. "I believe I may have something, Commander."

Crusher smiled. "That's great. But what is it?"

Tuvok told him.

Chapter Seven

NEARLY TEN HOURS after his away team first beamed down to Debennius II, Picard tapped his communicator badge and contacted the *Stargazer.* "Two to beam up," he told Crusher.

"Aye, sir," said the second officer.

The captain regarded Ben Zoma, noting inwardly that his exec looked as weary and frustrated as he himself felt. It took its toll, sitting in a room full of angry, argumentative people. What's more, the food offered them by the Benniari had been less than appealing. Neither of them had been driven to eat very much of it.

"I don't know what I want to do first," said the first officer, "gorge myself or find someplace quiet to collapse."

Picard frowned. "Unfortunately, we're not going to get the opportunity to do either, Gilaad. We need to discuss the progress of our investigative team as soon as we get back."

Ben Zoma grunted goodnaturedly and turned a weary smile on his superior. "Slavedriver," he said.

Then they were surrounded by the transporter effect. A moment later, they materialized in the *Stargazer*'s transporter room.

Glancing at the transporter console, the captain noticed that his chief engineer was working the controls. Simenon's sharp, lizardlike face split into a grin that showed pointed teeth. What's more, his tail lashed back and forth in what Picard had come to learn was an expression of eagerness.

"Progress?" the captain asked.

Simenon shrugged his narrow shoulders. "Some," he replied, almost perverse in his terseness. "We're all waiting for you and Commander Ben Zoma in your ready room, sir—though I should warn you, none of us is dressed as nicely as the two of you are."

Picard pulled down on the front of his dress tunic and gestured to the sliding doors. "Lead the way, Mr. Simenon—and be glad I didn't ask you to beam down as well."

The engineer hissed to show his amusement. Then, complying with the captain's command, he made his way out into the corridor and found the nearest turbolift. In less than a minute, the three of them were walking out onto the *Stargazer*'s bridge.

As Picard turned right and passed the communications station, he nodded to Cadwallader. The young woman smiled and nodded back—and didn't say a word, vituperative or otherwise. It was good to be out of that damned council chamber, the captain reflected.

The doors to his ready room slid aside for him. Crusher, Tuvok, Greyhorse, Vigo, and Joseph were clustered inside, no doubt discussing some element of their investigation.

"Sir," said Crusher, turning to acknowledge Picard, "I—"

The captain held up a hand for silence. Then he crossed to the room's only replicator and punched up two plates full of bread, fruit, and cheese, along with a couple of glasses of sparkling water.

Ben Zoma, who was right behind him, smiled as the orders materialized. "Thanks," he said. "I don't think I could have lasted another minute."

"Think nothing of it," Picard responded.

Bringing his plate over to his desk, he laid it down on the sleek, black surface and sat down beside it. Then, slicing an apple and a piece of sharp cheddar, he downed them both at a single bite.

At the same time, Ben Zoma dug into his own food. Watching him, the captain believed his exec really *couldn't* have lasted another minute.

Picard's officers waited patiently for their superiors to finish. But the captain didn't want to wait that long. He signaled for the team to proceed with their report.

As the ranking officer on the assignment, it fell to Crusher to outline their progress. "As far as Culunnh's theory about a third party goes, sir . . . we seem to have found some corroborative evidence."

Picard was interested. "Go on."

Crusher described the weapons found at the sites of the earlier incidents—and the dearth of weapons found at the later ones. He also spoke of the relative levels of violence.

The captain nodded. "So the First Minister wasn't too far off base after all, was he?"

"We don't believe so, sir," said Crusher.

"What's more," Simenon added with a grin, "our friend Mr. Tuvok has come up with a lead as to the identity of the third party."

Picard turned to the Vulcan. "Tell me more, Ensign."

Tuvok's forehead wrinkled. Obviously, he was more than a little discomfited by the Gnalish's attitude. "Unfortunately," he said, "it is what you humans might call a long shot."

"If I may say so," Joseph chimed in with undisguised eagerness, "it's better than a long shot, Captain. It's a legitimate lead."

With his upturned nose and close-cropped, sandy hair, some people often tended to underestimate Pug Joseph. Picard wasn't one of them.

Crusher smiled at the security chief. "Maybe we should let the captain decide for himself, Mr. Joseph."

The chief nodded, chastened. "Whatever you say, sir."

The captain regarded Tuvok. "Ensign? Is someone going to tell me about this or not?"

The Vulcan's nostrils flared as he began. "A Melacron named Bin Nedrach was listed as a passenger on an intrasystem transport vessel departing Melacron Five approximately two point four hours after the assassination of the G'aha of Laws and Enforcements."

Picard turned to Ben Zoma, who was washing down his hastily eaten food with some sparkling water. "That would be the spouse of the female we saw in the council chamber this morning?"

The first officer nodded. "I'd imagine."

The captain returned his attention to Tuvok. "Go on."

"At first glance," said the Vulcan, "it may appear that Nedrach's departure was merely a coincidence. After all, he had no criminal record. There would be no good reason to suspect him of wrongdoing."

"Except?" Picard supplied.

Tuvok remained as deadpan as ever. "Except that fifty-five years ago, when I was visiting this sector for the first time, there was an infamous Melacronai crime clan in existence. It had all but claimed the furthest planet in the system, Debennius Six, controlling who came and went, who was allowed to open and run businesses—everything. It was during this time that Debennius Six became known as 'the Last Stop to Nowhere.' "

"I see," said the captain, "but—"

The Vulcan went on as if Picard hadn't opened his mouth. "One of the clan's top 'bosses,' " he noted, "if I am using the term correctly, was an individual named Bin Nedrach."

The captain's eyes narrowed. "The same man who departed Melacron Five on that transport?"

"He would have to have been pretty advanced in years," Ben Zoma remarked between bites. He glanced at Simenon. "And the Melacronai don't live as long as *some* species do."

"I wondered about the same things," said the ensign. "Digging a little more deeply into the passenger manifest, I discovered that it was not the Bin Nedrach who had held the Melacronai in an iron grip fifty-five years earlier. It was his grandson."

Picard was growing more and more interested. So much so, in fact, that he pushed his plate of food aside.

"The fact that Melacronai crime clans place a high value on familial relationships," Tuvok continued, "and that this younger Bin Nedrach left less than three hours after an assassination, suggests that this may be a worthwhile lead." He lifted an eyebrow. "And if I may speak frankly, Captain, at the present moment, it is the only lead we have."

Joseph chuckled, obviously proud of the Vulcan's deductive abilities. In fact, it seemed to Picard, he couldn't have been prouder if Tuvok were a long-standing member of the crew.

"What a memory!" said the security chief.

Tuvok glanced at him. "I am a Vulcan, Mr. Joseph. Please do not attribute to skill what is merely the result of genetics."

"Still," the chief rejoined, "to remember a name for that long—and to be able to link it to this Bin Nedrach—all I can say, Ensign, is it's too bad you're not a security officer. You'd make a damned good one."

Tuvok appeared to take the compliment in stride. "I will keep that in mind," he told Joseph.

In the meantime, Picard thought, they had something to go on. It wasn't a great deal, but it was something.

The captain stroked his chin, mulling over their next step. "Do we know where this Bin Nedrach is now?" he asked.

Joseph shrugged. "We can make a guess, but—"

"I cannot afford to guess," said Picard. He turned to Crusher and the Vulcan. "Jack, Tuvok—I'm putting you two on this. I want you to go undercover and try to locate Bin Nedrach."

"And when we find him?" the second officer asked.

The captain shook his head. "Don't bring him in immediately. One man, even if he is an assassin, could not be doing everything by himself."

"Someone's pulling his strings," Ben Zoma translated.

"That is right," said Picard. "And that's the someone I want."

"Aye, Captain," Crusher and Tuvok responded at precisely the same time.

The captain saw them glance at each other. They were good men, both of them, he reflected. They would work together just fine, despite the essential differences in their natures.

At least, he hoped so.

"In the meantime," Picard said, "Commander Ben Zoma and I will continue to monitor the situation on Debennius Two."

The first officer grunted. "I think Crusher and Tuvok have the easier assignment by far."

Picard allowed himself a hint of a smile. "We will see about that." He considered the second officer and the ensign. "Dismissed, gentlemen." He turned to Simenon, Joseph, Greyhorse, and Vigo. "You too."

He waited until the six of them had left his ready room through the sliding doors. Then he regarded Ben Zoma. "I know what you're thinking," he told his exec. "Tuvok seems like the type who works better on his own."

Ben Zoma dismissed the suggestion with a wave of his hand. "That may be so, Captain—but we don't know Tuvok the way we know Jack. We couldn't very well have sent him out there by himself."

Picard nodded and pulled his plate closer again. "I suppose not," he said. And as he sliced another piece of apple for himself, he focused on what lay ahead in the council chamber.

It was midafternoon on Cordra III.

Dar Shabik knew that his face would appear calm and composed if anyone happened to glance in his direction. After all, he had spent many years learning to keep it that way.

Not a twitch of an antenna, nor a dilation of his faceted pupils betrayed him as he hurried through a sea of his fellow Cordracites, looking like any other worker heading home to his family after a long day in the capital city of Kiwanari.

This was the busiest hour. By law, every business shut down at the same time, though opening times were permitted to vary widely. The public transports were always crowded now. No one paid much attention to his fellow commuters. Everyone had one goal—getting home.

Except for Shabik.

He was dressed as the other workers were, in the long black mantlecoat that served a purely decorative function on bodies sealed and protected with a chitinous shell. And like many of the others, he was carrying a small collection of packages.

Many Cordracites purchased foodstuffs from the vendors who set up shop near the major business centers. This was especially true during the harvest season, when fresh fruits and vegetables were at their peak.

Of the three sacks in Shabik's arms, one was full of the delicious, juicy fruit of the jaami tree. The second contained an assortment of leafy green vegetables; he had been careful to allow their tops to peek out of the bag, allaying any suspicions that might have arisen.

The third bag was full of death.

At a corner he had chosen ahead of time, Shabik stopped and waited for the hover shuttle. There were seven other Cordracites in line ahead of him already, females as well as males, but he wasn't concerned about securing a place on the vehicle.

He had spent more than a week planning this, accumulating all the information he might need and then some. He knew how many seats were likely to be available on the shuttle this afternoon. He knew when it was likely to arrive at this corner—in another minute at the outside. He even knew the color of the driver's eyes.

His fellow commuters didn't need to be concerned with such things. However, Shabik did. Because, in truth, he wasn't one of them. His actions were dictated by an entirely different agenda.

Twenty seconds after he began waiting for the shuttle, it turned a nearby corner and headed his way. Forty seconds after he began waiting, it stopped and allowed additional passengers to board.

And as luck would have it, there was a seat available for each and every one of them.

Shabik sat down in one of them. Then he leaned back and went over what he had to do. It was simple, really. But then, even simple plans had the potential to go awry.

Less than a minute later, the shuttle began to slow as it approached its next stop. Shabik rose. As the vehicle lurched to a halt and the door opened, he made his way through the thick press of bodies.

In the process, he exaggerated the awkwardness of his packages. Unfortunately, he played his part too well and he got himself wedged between one of the other commuters and a vertical bar.

"Excuse me?" he said pointedly.

"Oh! Terribly sorry," the female apologized, turning her body so that Shabik could get by.

For an instant, their eyes met and he got a good look at her. She was lovely, her flesh a delicate shade of gray, her eyes as large and as yellow as their world's magnificent sun.

Pity, Shabik thought. But what he said was "Thank you."

As he made his way toward the door, the third package slid down his body and plopped onto the floor of the shuttle. He pretended not to notice, of course. As quickly as he could, he exited and disappeared into the crowd on the street.

But as the shuttle doors slid closed, he heard the female cry out. "Wait!" she said. "You dropped something!"

Shabik looked back again—and again, their eyes met. Silently, he cursed her. If her comment gave him away—

No, he assured himself. It won't. There won't be enough time. Turning and picking up his pace a little, but not too much, he buried himself more deeply in the safety of the milling throng.

Shabik didn't look back at the female or the shuttle, but the muscles beneath his shell were tight in anticipation. Come on, he thought. It should happen any—

Suddenly, there was an explosion.

Like everyone else, he stopped for a moment and watched the shuttle go up in a ball of wild, red flame. He allowed the heat of it to lick at his face like a lover. Then he drew a breath, put the cries of terror behind him and made his way to his private vehicle . . .

Mission accomplished.

Chapter Eight

"MELACRONAI BEASTS!" RASPED SAMMIS TARV. "Is there no depth to which you will not stoop in your madness?"

On the two-level podium, Picard winced at the Cordracite delegate's choice of words. They were not the sort he had hoped to hear at the Kellasian Congress's morning session.

A moment later, the insult was joined by others. It was several cycles before Cabrid Culunnh could get the room silent enough for everyone to understand exactly what had happened.

There had been another terrorist attack. This time it was a bomb, not a political assassination—and it was on Cordra III, not Melacron V. However, the captain reflected, it was essentially the same old story.

His hopes sagged as he scanned the chamber. All he saw were angry faces. Frightened faces. Under the circumstances, he supposed they had a right to feel that way.

Picard hoped that Crusher and Tuvok would find what they were looking for—and quickly. Otherwise, the Congress was in danger of deteriorating into a name-calling competition.

"Innocents!" another Cordracite voice grated. "Workers on an afternoon shuttle, going home to mates and offspring—"

Another voice trilled to meet it and clash with it. "And our G'aha was not innocent?" asked a Melacron. "He had no Companion? No children?"

"Order!" Cabrid Culunnh demanded.

But the accusations didn't stop. In fact, other voices rose up to support the first bunch.

Picard's jaw clenched. Out of the corner of his eye, he caught a glimpse of someone standing amid the chaos. It was Gerrid Thul, the Thallonian. And he was glaring at the captain, obviously as unhappy about this turn of events as Picard was.

"What is it?" asked Ben Zoma from the seat beside him.

The captain frowned. "It's time to see whether our alliance with Governor Thul is going to get us anywhere."

"Order!" the First Minister called out—again, to no avail.

Making sure the Thallonian was still paying attention to him, Picard jerked his head in the direction of Cabrid Culunnh. Thul's eyes narrowed. Then, as understanding seemed to set in, he nodded.

A moment later, the captain of the *Stargazer* left his seat and positioned himself beside the First Minister. At the same time, Thul advanced to the podium and ascended to the higher level, then placed himself on the Benniari's other side.

"Order!" Picard called out, speaking as one used to having his commands obeyed. "We will have order in this room!"

Something in his tone of voice pierced the chaos. The cries of outrage subsided. And before the turmoil could begin again, the Thallonian added his voice to the captain's.

"We have no proof that the Melacron were responsible for the bombing," he thundered, "any more than we have proof that it was a Cordracite who assassinated the G'aha!"

Like Picard, he had a way of getting people's attention. The captain gave Thul room to maneuver.

"We don't even know yet what kind of bomb it was!" he went on. "Are we nothing but frightened children, to leap to such conclusions? Or are we the bearers of wisdom our people trusted we would be when they dispatched us to this momentous congress?"

Picard suppressed a smile. He couldn't have put it better himself. In the wake of the Thallonian's remarks, Culunnh stepped forward. There was dignity in every line of his small body.

"This is our sector," the First Minister said quietly, but in a voice that carried throughout the chamber. "These are our planets. Our people. And yet, see who must remind us of our mission here—a Federation starship captain and a Thallonian governor. I, for one, am ashamed."

The assemblage had the grace to look embarrassed by Culunnh's words—embarrassed and repentant. For the first time that day, they gave the Benniari their undivided attention.

"See what fear and hatred have done to us," he said, "that only outsiders can see our problems clearly." He lifted his head. "Rest assured, reports will come in throughout the day. We will be able, I hope, to trace the origin of the bomb, and perhaps that will give us the answers we seek. In the meantime, let us conduct this congress like the civilized beings we are!"

Picard glanced at Thul. The governor nodded, obviously as relieved as the captain was that the congress had settled down.

Culunnh turned to the two of them. "Gentlemen, I thank you for your intervention. Please take your seats again. I trust I can call upon both of you to speak later in the session."

Picard nodded. "Of course."

"It would be my great pleasure," said Thul.

As the Thallonian left the podium for the time being, Picard returned to his seat as well. He saw that his first officer was impressed.

"Quite a performance," Ben Zoma whispered.

"For the governor too," the captain noted.

His first officer quirked a smile. "Actually, sir, it was the governor I was talking about."

Picard chuckled a little. Then he leaned back in his chair and watched the First Minister try to move the meeting forward. Even with order restored, it wasn't an easy task.

Find something, Jack, the captain urged silently. Find something before we run out of tricks.

Sitting cross-legged at the navigational controls of his new space vessel, Jack Crusher wished the Benniari were just a little bigger and a little more humanoid-shaped.

Not that he was complaining. It had been generous of the First Minister to lend them a ship in which to travel to Debennius VI. It would be a whole lot less noticeable than one of the *Stargazer*'s shuttles, and would therefore raise fewer questions.

However, because the Benniari were small and . . . well, differently shaped than either humans or Vulcans . . . some emergency retrofitting had been necessary. Actually, quite a bit of emergency retrofitting. For instance, while the Benniar ship—a compact vehicle by any standard—granted them enough room to stand up, the seats had needed to be completely removed for Tuvok and Crusher to access the controls.

The second officer had to laugh. "I feel a little silly," he confessed to the Vulcan.

Tuvok didn't even favor him with a glance. "We were able to make this ship serve our needs. There is nothing silly about that."

It seemed to Crusher that his companion spoke with a touch more severity than was required—a little extra dollop of dignity, as if he too were somewhat unsettled by the position he was forced to assume.

Methinks the Vulcan doth protest too much, the commander reflected.

But in the end, of course, Tuvok was right. They had been able to make the ship work for them, and that was all that really mattered.

"We are now entering orbit around Debennius Six," said the ensign.

"The Last Stop to Nowhere," mused Crusher.

Tuvok frowned as he worked at his controls. "That is the sobriquet by which it is known, yes."

"And this is where we'll find Bin Nedrach," said the commander.

"That is indeed our hope," the Vulcan rejoined.

Fortunately for them, Nedrach hadn't bothered to cover his departure from Melacron V. With no criminal record to set him apart from the other passengers, he apparently hadn't believed it necessary to obtain a pseudonym or a set of falsified documents.

But then, Nedrach hadn't taken the estimable Ensign Tuvok into account. It helps to have someone with a ridiculously long memory on your side, Crusher told himself.

Because of the nature of this planet's "society"—or lack thereof—there was no one to contact for permission to land. The commander was reminded of Earth's late nineteenth century, the "wild, lawless West," where a gun was all a man needed to get where he wanted to go.

The ease with which they found a place to land and hide their small craft, all within a few kilometers of a main city, was actually rather unsettling.

"Any disreputable type can sneak onto this planet," Crusher said.

"But then," Tuvok told him as they concealed their ship with loose foliage, "so can a team of Starfleet officers."

The commander looked at him. "In other words, I shouldn't look a gift horse in the mouth."

The Vulcan appeared perplexed—and maybe a little annoyed as well. "The reference escapes me," he said.

"What it means," Crusher explained, "is that you shouldn't question good luck. You should just run with it."

Tuvok sighed a little. "I see."

"Don't you have any colorful Vulcan expressions?" asked the human.

The ensign glanced at him. "No," he said flatly. And he dragged a few last branches full of leaves up against their vessel.

Crusher brushed off his hands. "Looks like we're done."

"Indeed," said Tuvok. He gestured. "The city is that way." And he began to walk toward it.

The human had no trouble catching up with him. "Impatient, aren't we?" he asked his companion.

Tuvok stopped and turned to him, obviously a little surprised. "Not really. I simply saw no reason to delay."

Crusher smiled at the ensign's expression. "My fault. You're absolutely right—there isn't." And as he started walking again, he reminded himself that he couldn't joke with the Vulcan as he might Joseph or Simenon—not even about the clothes they had to wear.

Gone were the tailored, maroon tunics that marked them as members of Starfleet. Also gone were the ribbed, white turtleneck pullovers they were used to wearing underneath.

Crusher was now clad in a multicolored vest and black trousers—both of them made of high-quality material and pleasant to the touch, marking him as a man of means. And the style, he had been assured, was the most up-to-date for the system.

Unfortunately, the boots were new and pinched him a little, and the voluminous red shirt he wore beneath the vest made him feel a bit like a pirate from Earth's turbulent fifteenth century. But on the bright side, the full sleeves of his shirt actually turned out to be a bonus; Crusher found they were handy for concealing pouches bulging with latinum, not to mention a small, handheld phaser.

Tuvok was clad in a tight-fitting jumpsuit of black and gray. His belt bristled with weapons, none of them Starfleet issue—but unlike Crusher, he made no attempt to hide them. The unforgiving cut of the garb accentuated his lean, powerful muscles, pointed ears, and dark skin.

People would talk to Crusher—but they would be wary of his grim-looking companion. At least, that was the plan.

"Fascinating," said Tuvok as they came in sight of a low, dark building that seemed on the verge of falling apart.

"Fascinating?" the human echoed. For the life of him, he couldn't see what the ensign found intriguing about the place.

"Yes," said Tuvok. "Last time I visited this sector, this was a gaming establishment called The Den."

Crusher grunted. "Lovely."

The Vulcan spared him a glance. "At the time, Commander, it was a well-known meeting place for the members of the crime clan to which Bin Nedrach's grandfather belonged." He eyed the ramshackle structure again. "Although the Melacronai species is short-lived in comparison to my own, this edifice has changed little in more than fifty years."

"It *always* seemed to be on the verge of collapse?" Crusher wondered.

"Indeed," came the reply. "I must confess, I marvel that it has not completed the process."

"That makes two of us," said the commander. "Well, come on, Sulak. It looks like we've found our first stop."

Tuvok frowned at the use of his pseudonym. "Of course . . . Marcus."

As they approached The Den, Crusher took a deep breath. Relax, he thought. If there's trouble, you'll be able to handle it. That was what the phaser was for, though he wouldn't use it if he didn't have to.

Assuming an air of boldness, even arrogance, the commander pushed open the door. It was dark and musty inside The Den, and he had to pause for a moment to let his eyes become adjusted to the light. Then he went in. Naturally, his companion followed him.

Noise that was undoubtedly meant to be music assaulted Crusher's ears. Smoke from various burning substances attacked his nose, his eyes, and his mouth. But instead of giving into an urge to choke on it, he forced himself to inhale deeply and fashion a grin.

The commander was glad of Tuvok's solid presence behind him as he made his way through the room. The place was a lot bigger than it had looked from the outside, he reflected.

"Dabo!" came a cry from some corner, followed by a chorus of groans and cheers. "All right, everyone," said the same voice, "double down, double down, let's get this game going!"

In another corner, a handful of Orion traders were playing a heated game of dom-jot, which was similar to Terran billiards. The Orions looked up at Crusher and the Vulcan as they passed by, their sparkling green eyes wary in their green-skinned faces.

Casting about for someone to speak with, the commander spied a gangly, beetle-browed humanoid standing behind a bar, busy pouring drinks for patrons and wiping away spills. The fact that he had four long arms made his task a bit easier.

There didn't seem to be anyone else in charge, so Crusher made his way through the crowd and slipped into a wobbly chair at the bar. He gave the bartender a dazzling smile.

"What'll it be?" asked the four-armed specimen, training a dark, protuberant pair of eyes on the human and Tuvok.

"Information," Crusher said. "I'm looking for a Melacron named Bin Nedrach. Seen him around lately?"

The dark eyes narrowed to slits and the alien paused for a moment, indicating to Crusher that he wasn't all that quick on the uptake. "Who wants to know?" the bartender rumbled warily.

"Someone who wishes to offer him employment," the Vulcan replied.

His clipped tone made the commander wince a little. "Lucrative employment," Crusher added quickly.

The bartender stared at Tuvok for a moment, his brow creased down the middle. Then he began to wheeze alarmingly. It took the commander a few seconds to realize that the alien was laughing.

"You want to employ Nedrach, do you?" he asked, exaggerating the words in a mocking tone of voice. "Well," and his voice dropped to an unfriendly growl, "you won't find Nedrach around here. Go find someone else."

Crusher didn't like the way the conversation was going. He had to do something about it, he told himself, or he and his Vulcan partner would soon find themselves stymied in their investigation.

Before the bartender could turn away from them, the commander reached up with a casual bravado he didn't feel and seized the grimy material of the alien's tunic front. Then he hauled the bartender's face down to within an inch of his own.

Silence fell all around him. By that, Crusher knew everyone present was taking in the scene. It was fine with him. In fact, it was exactly what he had been hoping for.

"I don't think you understand," Crusher growled, smiling a wolfish grin. "My friend Sulak here said we wanted Nedrach. We don't want anyone else." The human tugged harder on the bartender's shirtfront. "Only Nedrach will do. Maybe you understand that now?"

The alien was big enough and muscular enough to pound the commander to a bloody pulp. However, as Crusher had gambled, he was also too slow-witted to be sure of his chances in a fight.

Crusher held the bartender's gaze for just long enough before releasing him with an air of disdain. Then, flicking his wrist, he let a few pieces of latinum slip from his sleeve onto the wooden bar.

Staring into the alien's dark, angry popeyes, the commander repeated, "Do you understand now?"

The bartender's thick, hairy brow lowered at the sight of all that latinum gleaming on his bar. This much, at least, he clearly understood. He reached out a thick-fingered hand for the latinum, the slender slips of yellow-white metal looking tiny in his big mitt.

But before he could close his fingers about the latinum, Crusher deftly plucked them from his palm.

"Hey!" the bartender exclaimed indignantly.

"I don't give something for nothing, friend," the human told him.

For a moment, the alien looked as if he was about to vault over the bar and do some pulping after all. But Crusher stood his ground as if he weren't the least bit concerned about that possibility.

At last, the bartender jerked his massive head. "Back here," he said, lowering his voice so only the human and the Vulcan could hear him. "Too many eyes and ears out here, you know what I mean?"

Crusher knew what he meant, all right. It seemed that everyone in the Den was watching as they followed the alien's hulking figure to a tiny, smelly back room. The barkeeper opened the door, closed it behind the three of them, then glanced around carefully before speaking.

"Like I said," he grumbled at last, "Bin Nedrach doesn't come around this place anymore."

"Do you know where he *does* go?" the commander inquired.

The alien shook his head from side to side. "No idea."

Crusher glanced at Tuvok. The Vulcan shrugged. Turning back to the bartender, the commander said, "In that case, I fail to see the purpose of this conversation—which means no more latinum."

Again, a reference to the precious metal seemed to work wonders with the alien's powers of concentration. "Wait!" he howled, holding up all four of his long-fingered hands. "I don't know where Nedrach is, but I can tell you who *would* know."

"And who's that?" asked Crusher.

"His rider," came the reply. "And *him* I know how to find."

The commander wasn't familiar with the term "rider," but it wasn't difficult to guess what it might mean. A steed or a mount, a beast of burden who did the work, needed someone to tell him where to go and what to do.

"And where can we find Nedrach's rider?" Crusher asked.

Languidly, keeping his eyes on the bartender's face, he again shook out the three slips of latinum—this time, into his palm. He ran his thumb over the shiny metal and waited for the alien to speak.

"There is a klaapish-klaapish'na house not far from here," said the bartender, his dark popeyes glued to the latinum. "The name of the place is The House of Comfort."

Jack kept his expression as neutral as possible. He wasn't sure what a klaapish-klaapish'na house was, but with the name The House of Comfort, he could make a pretty good guess.

Already, he was formulating his next message to Beverly: Hi, honey. Hope you and Wes are well. My most recent assignment took me undercover to an alien brothel. Hope you understand the sacrifices an officer has to make in the line of duty. . . .

"You'll want to find a Melacron named Pudris Barrh," said the bartender. "You tell him you know he's Nedrach's rider and he'll have to be the one to tell you yes or no."

Crusher nodded. He had gotten what he came for. With a flourish, he dropped two slips of the latinum into the alien's outstretched hand.

The barkeeper looked up with an angry expression on his face. "There were three on the counter," he snarled.

"Three to put me in touch with Nedrach," the human said, conscious of maintaining the hardnosed reputation he had established minutes earlier. "You didn't do that. You only told me how to find his rider."

The alien seemed about to object. Crusher smiled up at him. "Two slips of latinum—and keeping your pretty face from being rearranged. I'd call that good for a few moments' work." He bowed almost insultingly. "Thank you for your time. Nice place you run here."

Then, without another word, the commander opened the door and stepped back into the main gaming room. With a last glance at the sullen bartender, Ensign Tuvok followed.

"So far, so good," the human muttered.

The Vulcan didn't comment.

Some of the customers shot them bold, appraising glances as they crossed the floor. But Crusher met each of the looks with equal boldness. Then he and Tuvok opened the front door and walked outside.

"Progress," the commander said triumphantly as they strode away from The Den. "Now we . . ."

He noticed that the Vulcan was giving him a look that could only be classified as a glare.

"What?" asked Crusher.

Tuvok didn't answer.

"Come on," said the commander, "you're obviously upset about something. What is it?"

"I am not upset," came the reply. "I am a Vulcan."

Crusher rolled his eyes. "All right, then. Let's just say you seem to disapprove of something."

Tuvok frowned at him. "I *do* disapprove."

"Well, why?"

"You took a clearly unnecessary risk with the bartender," the ensign explained with a hint of annoyance in his voice. "Your implied threat and your extravagant display of latinum accomplished nothing except to draw unwanted and perhaps dangerous attention to us."

The commander was stung by Tuvok's disapproval. "That's not true at all," he said. "It got us exactly what we wanted—information on how to get hold of Bin Nedrach."

"Perhaps," the Vulcan responded. "However, we could have obtained the same information in a far less public and confrontational fashion. Surely there were others here who know of Nedrach and his rider. We could have approached them quietly. Subtly."

Crusher stifled an impulse to put a comradely arm around Tuvok's stiff shoulders. "That's a logical approach, all right," he admitted. "Damned logical. Just one problem—hardened criminals and the dregs of society seldom appreciate that kind of logic."

The Vulcan grunted scornfully.

"All they respect is force and power," the commander explained. "Back there, I let everyone know that I had both. I was willing to rough up the barkeep if I needed to, and I had the latinum in my sleeve to give the impression that I had connections."

Tuvok still didn't look convinced.

"People form impressions very quickly," said Crusher. "When you spoke to him politely, the bartender laughed at you. If we'd let him get away with that, don't you think every two-bit thug in the place would have treated us the same way?"

The Vulcan turned away.

"Nobody would have been willing to talk to us," the commander continued. "We would still have gotten noticed, but for an entirely different reason. Your way, we would have been objects of ridicule, pariahs. My way, they couldn't help thinking we were just like them." He paused. "Do you see what I'm talking about?"

Tuvok regarded him again, but refrained from speaking. Crusher's explanation had satisfied him enough, apparently, for him not to pursue the matter any further.

But the frown remained.

Chapter Nine

TRICIA CADWALLADER EYED the heaping plate of sturrd across the rec room table from her and tried not to grimace.

Vigo, who had brought the sturrd to the table, looked at her face and winced in sympathy. "Sorry, Cadwallader," he said in his deep, rich voice. "I forgot the effect that sturrd has on you."

The ensign dismissed the need for an apology with a wave of her hand. "It's what you eat, Lieutenant. I mean, you don't complain about watching me eat barbecued shrimp."

The weapons officer shrugged. "That's because I don't mind the sight of barbecued shrimp."

Cadwallader smiled at him. "But even if you did, you wouldn't say anything because it wouldn't be polite. That's why I'm not going to say anything about your sturrd . . . even if it does look like beach sand and ground glass with maple syrup thrown over it."

Vigo studied her for a moment. Then he got to his feet and picked up his plate. "I'm going to get something else," he told her.

"No!" said the ensign, drawing stares from her colleagues at other tables. "Don't you dare get rid of that. I want you to sit here and enjoy it." Suddenly, she remembered the difference in their ranks and blushed. "I mean . . . enjoy it, *sir.*"

The Pandrilite frowned as he considered his course of action. It must have seemed to him that he would trouble her no matter what he did.

"Please?" Cadwallader added.

With a sigh, Vigo put his plate of sturrd back on the table and sat down again. "If you insist," he told her.

"I do," the ensign confirmed.

For a while, the two of them sat and ate in silence, and Cadwallader managed not to listen too hard to the crunching sounds in her companion's mouth. Then Vigo spoke up again.

"Care for a game of sharash'di later?" he asked.

The ensign looked at him askance. "You know your problem, Lieutenant? You've beaten everyone on the ship so many times that no one wants to play with you—including me."

Vigo tapped his fork on a particularly hard piece of sturrd. "Commander Crusher plays with me every chance he gets."

"If I may say so," Cadwallader replied, "Commander Crusher sometimes finds it difficult to let go of something once he's sunk his teeth into it—which, I suppose, is one of the qualities that makes him a good officer."

The Pandrilite gave it some thought. "He does tend to hold onto a single sharash strategy too long, now that you mention it."

The ensign smiled. "There you go."

Vigo shook his head. "I wish I was out there with him."

Cadwallader could empathize. "Me, too," she said. "Sitting up here in orbit is the worst part of being in the fleet."

Actually, the worst part was watching the Pandrilite eat his lunch. However, she refrained from returning to that topic.

"It's not just that," Vigo told her. "It's that they're working undercover in a place they don't know very well. I'd feel a lot better if the captain had sent me to watch over them."

The ensign nodded. "We all would. However, big fellows like you tend to attract attention. Besides, Tuvok's a Vulcan. From what I've been given to understand, those people can take care of themselves."

The weapons officer smiled without much enthusiasm. "You're talking about that neck pinch they use?"

"That," said Cadwallader, "and other things. I'm just saying that Tuvok will be able to provide all the muscle they need. And if it comes to that, Commander Crusher's no slouch either."

Vigo grunted. "I suppose you're right." He paused. "So there's no chance at all that you'll play a game? Not even one?"

The ensign shook her head. "I wouldn't be much competition, sir. I figure I'm beaten before I start. Look, why don't you find someone you *haven't* played yet? Someone who doesn't know how badly they're going to lose?"

The Pandrilite nodded his big, blue head. "Maybe you're right."

Just then, someone came to stand by their table. Looking up, Cadwallader saw that it was Gerda Asmund with a tray of food in her hands.

"Do you mind if I join you?" asked the tall, blond navigator.

"Not at all," said Vigo, his eyes narrowing craftily.

"Have a seat," the ensign told her.

Gerda put her tray down on the table and pulled out a chair. Then she glanced at her companions. "So," she asked with her usual blunt efficiency, "what are we talking about?"

The Pandrilite considered his words for a moment. Then he said, "Tell me, Lieutenant . . . have you ever played sharash'di?"

Picard sat back in his ready room chair and sipped appreciatively at his hot, steaming drink.

"What is the name of this delightful beverage?" Thul asked from the other side of the captain's desk.

"Earl Grey tea," Picard replied. "It is named after the man who crafted this particular recipe."

"Wonderful!" the Thallonian remarked. "When these talks are concluded, I must negotiate with you to bring a supply back to my Emperor. I am certain he would enjoy it as much as I do."

The captain smiled at his ally's enthusiasm. "Governor," he said, "if you and I can manage to conclude these negotiations without any blood being spilled, I will replicate and send you more tea than your entire Empire can consume in a year."

Gerrid Thul chuckled at that. Then he sat his cup down in his lap and regarded Picard with a sly smile.

"Despite the drama in which you and I find ourselves embroiled," he said, "I must say getting to know you has been an unexpectedly pleasant turn of events. We work well together, I think."

The captain returned the smile. The delicate, tart aroma of the bergamot in the tea teased his nostrils.

"I agree, Governor. Perhaps our teamwork on this matter will translate into something more momentous . . . say, a diplomatic relationship between your Empire and my Federation."

"Perhaps," Thul replied pessimistically, "but I would not place a very large wager on the possibility. My Empire is—shall we say—a good deal more insular than I am."

"That is a pity," Picard told him. "Still, I am pleased by the way the talks are going now. Did you see the G'aha of Finance and the First Elected of Kiwanari Province actually laughing together?"

It was the first real sign of hope that the captain had received since his arrival on Debennius II. It is difficult, he mused, to sit down and share a laugh with your enemy and fire upon him the next day.

"The improvement is remarkable," the governor agreed. "And it's your efforts that have made it so."

"*Our* efforts," Picard amended. "There are those in the congress who couldn't care less about some distant Federation. But the Thallonian Empire . . . that appears to be a different story."

Thul shrugged. "And in some cases, the reverse is true. Perhaps we should say we have both contributed and leave it at that."

The captain nodded. "I would agree to that."

For a moment, the two of them sipped their tea in silence. Then the governor spoke up again. "You have a fine ship here, Picard. I wouldn't mind seeing a bit more of it."

The captain sighed. "And I wouldn't mind showing it off. Unfortunately, Starfleet regulations prevent me from doing that."

Thul's brow furrowed. "Regulations . . . ?" Then understanding dawned. "I see. It is a security matter."

Picard nodded. "I'm afraid so."

The Thallonian dismissed the apology with a flip of his hand. "It's probably a wise policy, now that you mention it. You must have all sorts of visitors on your vessel from time to time. You can't be expected to discern the honest from the dishonest."

"Then you take no offense?" the captain asked.

"None at all," his guest assured him. He reached into a vest pocket and removed a flat, latinum-plated chronometer. "But if there's no guided tour today," he said, consulting the device, "we should probably return to the planet's surface. It's impossible to tell how many brushfires may have begun in our absence."

"Done," Picard responded.

Taking a last sip from his tea cup, he got up and retrieved Thul's as well. Then he brought them both to the replicator.

"This way," he told the governor, indicating the exit.

"After you," Thul told him.

Together, the captain and his guest left his ready room and walked back to the *Stargazer*'s transporter facility. En route, Picard wondered how Crusher and Tuvok were doing.

He hoped they were all right—and that they were making some kind of progress in their quest for the truth.

Ulassi's heart pounded hard in her chitin-shelled chest.

The daughter of a high-ranking government official, she had been indulged and cosseted and sheltered all of her young life. However, she had never done anything even vaguely significant or lasting. Though others envied her and she had taken a bit of pleasure in that, her station in life had always felt like a burden to her.

Now, at last, Ulassi was acting on her own. She was doing something she believed in, instead of something she was expected to do. It was a remarkably heady sensation.

She opened her mouth as she climbed, panting to release some of the body heat she had built up. Her body, slim and attractive but unused to such exertion, would ache the next day. She was sure of it.

But that was all right. In fact, the prospect was thrilling to her in a way. Until that moment, she had only used her physical form for her own selfish pleasure. The stiffness she would feel tomorrow would be a welcome reminder of the worthy work she had performed today.

Finally, muscles quivering from the strain, Ulassi reached a plateau. She sat there for a moment, trying to catch her breath, and surveyed the terrain below. The perspective was impressive to say the least, but Ulassi was in no mood to appreciate the natural beauty of the place.

Mountains, forests, the pure expanse of water that stretched out beyond them . . . what good was any of it when her people were enslaved? How could she find joy in the view when she knew the price her father and others had to pay for it?

Once, Cordra III had been independent, able to sustain its people with the bounty of its fields and its forests. Now, the once-proud Cordracites needed trade, negotiation, commerce. And with whom?

With Melacron V. The very thought was revolting to her.

Some Cordracites, Ulassi's well-born father among them, were still trying to bring about peace with the Melacron. They were trying to smooth over their considerable differences. But the notion made Ulassi's stomach roil like a giant grubworm.

Peace, she thought, with that ugly, violent, inferior race? How could anyone in their right mind even consider such a thing?

Spurred by the thought, Ulassi resumed her climb down the treacherous rock face. Halfway to her destination, her feet slipped and she gasped in fear. Stones tumbled beneath her, striking off the cliff walls as they fell and finally splashing in the water below.

She had almost been killed, she realized. She had almost lost her life in the pursuit of something noble. By the gods, she thought, this was exciting! This was living!

Trembling with fervor, trepidation, and joy, Ulassi finally made her way to the rocky outcropping she had been aiming for all along. Only then did she stop to rest.

For a long moment, she gazed into the water just below her. She studied her gray, antennaed reflection, found renewed faith in the determination that was plain on her own golden-eyed face.

Armed with it, fortified with it, Ulassi closed her eyes for a long moment. Then slowly, almost reverently, she brought forth the vial of death that she had safely packed in her waist pouch.

Strange, she thought, holding it in the sunlight. It was so small a thing—just a few milliliters of liquid—and yet it would eventually bring about the deaths of thousands . . .

And in time, a great and terrible war.

Squatting, Ulassi opened the vial and poured its contents into the water. Only a few drops per thousand liters of water were necessary to achieve the desired goal. There was something sacred in the potency of the poison, she thought dreamily. Something wonderful and outrageous, like the judgment of a wronged, angry god.

For now, sadly, it was her own people, the Cordracites, who would have to perish. She was sorry about that, but there was little she could do about it. Sacrifices were needed if she was to bring about the changes that would save her planet as a whole.

And soon enough, Ulassi thought . . . soon enough it would be the disgusting, single-nostriled Melacron who would be dying. Then Cordra III would disentangle itself from the grip of Melacron V and stand, proud and whole and independent once more.

As the thick black poison dissolved into the city's water supply, she said a prayer . . . for herself, for her father, for all those whose deaths would bring about her world's liberation. She prayed that they would die quickly and without pain.

"Long live Cordra III!" Ulassi whispered aloud, tears filling her eyes at the righteousness of her cause.

Then, with a start, she realized what she had become. She was a hero now, wasn't she? A hero like Risaab of Golluk or the Sisters Noraddis or the Ten Warriors of Hitna'he. Someday schoolchildren would sing songs about her and old people would write her name in their graves.

The thought made Ulassi smile as she climbed back up the face of the cliff and started back to her father's domicile.

Chapter Ten

"WELL," SAID COMMANDER CRUSHER, mainly to break the uncomfortable silence into which he and Tuvok seemed to have fallen, "there she is, in all her bacchanalian glory."

"The House of Comfort," the Vulcan observed warily.

"The House of Comfort," the commander confirmed.

"It does not," said Tuvok, "look very comfortable."

For the briefest of seconds, Crusher wondered if the ensign had made a joke. Then he dismissed the notion. As usual, it seemed, Tuvok was simply being literal.

Viewed from outside, The House of Comfort looked every bit as dark, dilapidated and unappealing as The Den had looked—maybe even more so, though he wouldn't have thought that possible. The commander hoped that the interior would prove more attractive.

Like an actor assuming a role, Crusher set his jaw and again began looking at things as "Marcus" would. A Starfleet officer might feel uncomfortable about entering a house of prostitution, but Marcus wouldn't hesitate. Marcus, if he actually existed, would probably be comfortable in this sort of environment.

At the very least, he wouldn't have a wife and a small son back in Federation space, the thought of whom made him feel guilty. Putting the thought aside, the commander walked forward and flung open the door.

A wave of moist, warm air rushed out to meet him. It was saturated with a variety of alien scents—many of them surprisingly pleasant, some a good deal less so.

Crusher wondered at the high level of humidity in the place, but chalked it up to the idiosyncrasies of the patrons. The same for the soft, cloying music of unknown origin that seemed to waft its way around him. In any case, he had to admit that the ambiance was a welcome change from the rank, hostile environment of The Den.

"Welcome to The House of Comfort," said a soft, husky voice.

The human turned and saw where it had come from—an attractive female half a head taller than either himself or Tuvok, with a tight-fitting golden gown and skin as purple as the lush carpeting underfoot.

The proprietress? he wondered.

As she moved closer, Crusher got a better view of the golden eyes and thick, indigo hair, the high cheekbones and the full lips. The female lacked a proper nose and had a set of ears three times the size of a human's, but he didn't imagine she would have any problem getting someone to buy her a drink at a starbase lounge.

"Do you have a room reserved or is someone waiting for you?" she asked him and Tuvok.

The commander felt the betraying heat of a blush in his face. He hoped the woman would attribute it to the warmth of her establishment, or perhaps a flush of anticipation at the "comforts" to come.

He didn't speak immediately, wanting to make certain his voice was under control. And when he did speak, he chose his words carefully.

"We're here to meet someone," he said. "I was told that a Melacron named Pudris Barrh enjoyed visiting this establishment."

The alien smiled. "Oh, I see . . . you're one of Barrh's boys," she remarked with a knowing lilt.

Barrh's boys? Crusher asked himself. What did she mean by that? He experienced a moment of alarm but kept his composure.

"If you can get past Old Scowly there," the female continued, "you can join Barrh at his pleasures if you like." She raised a long, slender arm and pointed to a gilded door to her right.

Standing guard there was one of the biggest, ugliest, most dangerous-looking humanoids it had ever been the commander's misfortune to see. The moniker "Old Scowly" seemed more than appropriate. The fellow was three meters tall if he was a centimeter.

He only had two arms, but they were heavily muscled and covered with skin so callused that Crusher wondered if a phaser would do it any damage. Twin sets of horns, one at his temples and one protruding from a mouth crowded with yellow teeth, had been sharpened and decorated with carvings the commander had never seen before.

Small, porcine eyes glittered beneath an overhanging brow ridge as Old Scowly turned his oversized head in their direction. Large, round nostrils flared with a grunting sound.

The commander glanced at Tuvok, whose expression—naturally—had not changed an iota since they entered the establishment. Forcing a grin, Crusher swaggered over to Old Scowly and took the bull by the horns—figuratively speaking, of course.

The commander wondered how they would ever get past such a specimen. With an effort, he banished the thought. After all, failure was not one of their options. Inside that room, at his so-called "pleasures," was the man they needed to see—and see him they would.

"We're here to meet with Pudris Barrh," Crusher told Old Scowly.

The behemoth scowled, his lips writhing in a way the human had never seen before. "I do not know you," he rumbled, his voice both exceptionally deep and exceptionally ominous.

Crusher continued to smile, undaunted. "But you *will* know me," he assured the alien. "You see, I'm here to conduct some mutually profitable business with your employer."

Expertly he flicked a slip of latinum down from his sleeve into his palm. He was getting pretty good at it, too.

"Extremely profitable," the commander emphasized.

Old Scowly's face twisted even more. Crusher would not have thought it possible, but there it was.

The enormous alien straightened to his full, imposing height. "I serve Barrh for reasons other than profit," he rumbled.

"Really," said the commander. He wondered what those reasons could be. Loyalty? Fear? Debt? Unable to figure it out, he shrugged and the latinum disappeared again up his sleeve.

"Whatever you say," he responded casually, "but I still think Barrh would be interested in seeing me."

The tiny eyes peered at him.

Ensign Tuvok was not pleased.

He had disapproved of his companion's flamboyant methods from the outset. The Vulcan had accepted the necessity of their charade in deference to Picard, but it seemed to him that Crusher drew far too much attention to himself and their mission.

Of course, the human was still a youth by the standards of Tuvok's people. No—less than a youth. An infant. And yet, in the eyes of Starfleet, Crusher was his commanding officer.

His *superior.*

Inwardly, Tuvok shivered. Humans, he thought.

He had been around them far too long in situations that were far too volatile. He longed for the crystalline stillness of Vulcan's deep meditation chambers, the tranquility of a walk in a sunwashed, crimson desert, the sense of balance and well-being that enveloped him when he sat down to harmonious meals with his family.

And yet, after so many years, something had pulled inexorably at Tuvok to rejoin Starfleet. Duty had struggled with duty, and no entity living could win such a battle.

He watched with a mounting sense of apprehension as the conversation between Crusher and the guard called Old Scowly unfolded. Clearly, he told himself, the commander's scheme was leading them into trouble.

Finally, Old Scowly agreed to approach his employer. With some difficulty, he slipped his hulking frame inside the gilded door—whereupon Crusher leaned closer to Tuvok and spoke quickly and quietly.

"I don't know for certain what kind of establishment this is," said the commander, "but I can make a pretty good guess."

"Unfortunately," the Vulcan whispered back with sincere and undisguised revulsion, "so can I."

"Still, we may have to go along with it." Crusher regarded Tuvok. "Would that . . . pose a problem?"

"Naturally," the Vulcan replied.

The commander grunted. "I was afraid you would say that."

"And knowing what I do of human marriage customs," said Tuvok, "I would imagine it would pose a problem for you as well."

Crusher looked lost. "Maybe we could just play along for some of it . . . for the sake of—"

"My master will see you now," said Old Scowly. He had reappeared before the Vulcan knew it. "You may enter through the changing room, remove your clothes, and join Pudris Barrh at his pleasures."

Tuvok kept his disgust to himself. His companion maintained control over his expression as well, though the visible darkening of his cheeks seemed to betray him. The Vulcan hoped that Old Scowly was unfamiliar with the physical manifestations of human emotions or, as Crusher might be inclined to phrase it, "the jig" would be "up."

"Excellent," Crusher replied heartily. He turned to Tuvok. "Sulak, you'll accompany me."

"You will divest yourselves of your weapons as well, of course," growled Old Scowly.

The commander winked knowingly. "Of course."

The gilded door opened again and they went inside. As the door closed behind them, the Vulcan saw that they were in a dressing room of some sort—or more accurately, an *un*dressing room.

The walls were paneled with dark woods and there were lockers made of the same material. The only other pieces of furniture in the room were a couple of long benches.

Crusher uttered an earthy human phrase with which Tuvok was not unacquainted. "What the hell do we do now?" he sighed.

The Vulcan didn't answer, of course. The question was clearly a rhetorical one.

Frowning, the commander sat down on one of the benches and began to remove his boots. He didn't look happy.

As it happened, Tuvok wasn't happy either. If he didn't know better, he would have said that the uncomfortable sensation in the pit of his stomach was apprehension. Of course, that was impossible. His control over his emotions was impeccable.

And yet, the sensation remained.

"There must be another way," said Crusher.

"There is no other way," the Vulcan told him. "This is the situation in which your plan has placed us." He knew his words sounded biting, but he didn't wish any of them back.

The human ran his hands through his thick, dark hair. "Damn it," he said, "if Beverly ever . . ."

"Finds out about this?" the ensign suggested.

Frowning, Crusher nodded. "But as you say, there's no other option open to us. I guess we'll just deal with whatever comes as best we can." He grunted. "The things we do for king and country."

Tuvok looked at him. "We do not pay homage to a king, nor does Starfleet ally itself with any provincial governments," he pointed out as he unstrapped his weapons belt.

Crusher darted an amused glance at him. "I'm glad you're along for the ride, Ensign."

This was not a ride, but a mission. Nonetheless, the Vulcan saw no point in correcting his companion at this juncture.

He remained silent while he and Crusher disrobed. It was not a particularly pleasant experience for Tuvok.

Vulcans, after all, were intensely private people and he was no exception. While it was illogical to be ashamed of the way one's body happened to have formed, neither was Tuvok in the habit of divesting himself of his clothing at the drop of an invitation.

He went through a quick mental exercise to quiet his unusually charged thoughts and reestablish calm. It helped, though not as much as the ensign would have liked.

When both he and Crusher had finished undressing, they glanced at each other's face—carefully avoiding the possibility of glancing elsewhere. The commander cleared his throat.

"Well," he said, "let's go." Then he crossed the room and opened the door in the far wall.

Steam rushed out and enveloped them, and for a moment Tuvok couldn't see. Then he made out some shapes in the warm mist and realized what he and Crusher could expect there. A wave of relief washed over him.

The House of Comfort was not a house of prostitution, the Vulcan told himself. It was a *bathhouse.*

The man he presumed was Pudris Barrh was lounging in a steaming pool of what appeared to be green slime. However, as the Melacron shifted his position in the pool, it became obvious that it was merely water that had been treated with something—Tuvok couldn't be certain what.

When the air cleared for a moment—a byproduct of their entrance—the Vulcan was able to get a better look at their host. He was rather corpulent for a Melacron, it seemed, and more pale-looking than most.

As thick, sludgy ripples made their slow way outward from Barrh's generous torso, he waved to Tuvok and Crusher. "Please, gentlemen, join me. We've not met yet, but there are few better places to get to know someone than in The House of Comfort!"

Barrh threw back his head and laughed loudly at his joke. The commander laughed as well.

"No weapons, of course," the Melacron told them, wagging a chubby forefinger in their direction. "No distractions of any kind. Just good fellowship, engaging conversation, and business."

"Of course," Crusher responded.

He and Tuvok exchanged a quick glance. Taking a deep breath, the human walked up the carpeted stairs and placed first one foot, then the other, into the hot, liquid muck.

The ensign had little choice but to follow suit. He assured himself, as he sank up to his chest in the thick, surprisingly pleasant-smelling stuff, that there was really no logical reason T'Pel ever had to become acquainted with this misadventure.

Besides, he reflected, there was quite a good chance that the majority of his and Crusher's actions would be classified. He had to confess that he found some comfort in the prospect.

"Now," said Barrh, surveying them with slitted eyes, "my associate says you have something profitable to offer me?"

"That's our hope," said the human. He let the liquid lap at his chin for a moment before continuing. "My name is Marcus. I'm told by someone who should know that you're the rider of one Bin Nedrach."

The Melacron rumbled deep in his throat. Casually, Tuvok lifted his arms out of the water and placed them on the back of the tub, just in case he had to reach for Barrh quickly.

"If you had come a few weeks ago," said the Melacron, "you would have been right. I am no longer the bastard's rider."

"Problem?" Crusher was almost cheerful.

"You could say that," Barrh replied with a note of bitterness in his voice. "We had a little . . . disagreement over a commission. I don't keep steeds I can't control, Marcus. Surely you understand that?"

Crusher nodded. "Naturally. Still, it's a pity."

"But he's not the only steed in my stable," their host continued. "I've several who will—"

The commander affected a look of disappointment and shook his head. "No, I'm afraid it's a special job. It's got to be Nedrach."

Barrh shifted his considerable bulk in the water. "Then you might as well enjoy the soak, friend Marcus. You're out of luck."

Crusher chuckled and fixed the Melacron with a look—alerting Tuvok that they were in for more of the same nonsense displayed at The Den. He felt the familiar sensation of disapproval stir within him. Humans were irksome, no question about it.

"No, I don't think we *are* out of luck," the commander told Barrh.

The Melacron looked at him. "What do you mean?"

Crusher shrugged. "Someone's got to be riding Nedrach. Who would let a steed of that caliber go unsaddled for long?" He leaned toward Barrh. "I'm willing to bet you can tell me who that someone is."

The Melacron laughed out loud at Crusher's brazen behavior. Tuvok thought of Old Scowly, standing just behind the gilded door, ready to burst in at a moment's notice. It would be bad enough for them to be shown the door, he reflected. To be shown the door without the benefit of their clothing would be even less acceptable.

"It is obvious to me, friend Marcus," said Barrh, and this time there was a distinct edge to his words, "you don't place much value on your life or the life of your friend, or you wouldn't be threatening a fellow who handles assassins for a living."

Crusher fell still for a moment. He smiled easily, but his eyes had gone quite hard and cold.

"It is obvious to me, friend Barrh," he replied, "that you don't place too much value on your life either, or else you wouldn't be threatening a man with the wealth to hire assassins in Nedrach's price range . . . not to mention the precaution of a Vulcan bodyguard."

Tuvok was startled by the comment and the sudden hard look Barrh gave him, but he played along with the commander's charade. He tilted his head and cast a sidelong look at the Melacron. Let Barrh make of the gesture what he will, he thought.

The Melacron looked from the Vulcan to the human and back again, his eyes sharp and alert. Finally, he sighed.

"Bin Nedrach has caused me sufficient irritation," he said. "He's not worth ruining a good, hot soak over."

Crusher nodded. "That's the spirit."

"The fellow you want," Barrh continued, "is Bidrik Onaggh. He's a Benniari. He runs a dance hall on the other side of the city—just the thing to entertain a gentleman after spending some time at The House of Comfort."

"Onaggh is Nedrach's rider?" the commander inquired.

"No," said the Melacron. "But he speaks with him from time to time. He'll know more about Nedrach's whereabouts right now than anyone."

Tuvok was surprised to hear that a Benniari was involved with crime on this depressing planet. The Benniari were known for their culture and gentleness, after all.

Then again, he reminded himself, even a Vulcan occasionally forsook logic and turned to unsavory pursuits. Given that, Barrh's revelation wasn't necessarily all that surprising.

Crusher rose from the pool. Green slime clung to his body for a moment, then oozed off and plopped back into the clogged bath water. As he reached for a large towel on a nearby wall rack, he said, "Thanks, friend Barrh." Wrapping the towel around him, he turned around slowly to meet the Melacron's gaze. "Of course, if you've lied to us, we'll be back."

"Naturally," said Barrh.

The commander gave his host a perfunctory smile, tucked the loose end of the towel into the area around his waist, and nodded brusquely to Tuvok. However, the Vulcan hesitated for a fraction of a second before he followed Crusher out of the pool, and therefore saw what the human did not: a subtle change in their host's expression.

It had started out as affable as when they entered. But for a moment, it was clearly filled with scorn.

Making note of it, Tuvok rose, secured another towel and wrapped it about himself, then trailed Crusher out of the room. Before long, he found himself back in the dressing facility—and relieved to be there indeed.

To his dismay, the commander seemed inordinately pleased with himself. "We got what we came for," he crowed, discarding his towel and reaching for his clothing. "Now it's on to the dance hall."

"I wonder," the Vulcan replied stiffly. "You shamed our host—and he appears to be a proud man."

"I didn't *shame* him," Crusher responded, stepping into his trousers and belting them. "I just called his bluff. We talked business."

"On the contrary," Tuvok said, "it is my belief that we have made a powerful enemy in Pudris Barrh."

The commander frowned. "Look, I'm only doing what needs to be done. These people play rough."

The Vulcan raised an eyebrow. "That is precisely my concern."

Crusher began to pull on his boots. "Trust me, Tuvok—I know what I'm doing. Barrh and his colleagues treat each other like yesterday's garbage." He jerked a thumb at the door that led to the bath. "Look at how they refer to their employees. They call them steeds—as if they're fit for nothing more than getting them where they want to go."

"The reference did not escape me," said Tuvok.

"If we don't act as tough and dangerous as they are," the commander went on, "they won't show us any respect. If you want to worry about something, worry about that."

The Vulcan disagreed. He said so—to Crusher's surprise and chagrin, apparently. "You have put us in unnecessary danger," Tuvok observed. "When this assignment is completed, I will make note of that in my report. And I will add that you are motivated, at least in part, by the pleasure you take in acting out your role."

The human stared at him. "You think I enjoy this?"

"I do," the ensign replied honestly.

Crusher turned an angry shade of red. "That's fine," he said, glancing at the doors to make sure no one was eavesdropping on them. "You can think what you want. You can even report what you want. Just remember that while this mission is in progress, you follow my orders—no matter how many years you've got on me. Is that understood?"

Tuvok was inclined to retort, but he refrained from doing so. After all, the human was correct in his assessment of the Vulcan's responsibilities. Tuvok had voiced his objection—he could do no more.

"I will do as you say," he agreed at last.

That seemed to take the edge off Crusher's anger. Taking a breath, the human continued getting dressed. But now and then, he threw a searching look in the Vulcan's direction.

Crusher wished to be his friend, Tuvok noted. He had recognized that from the moment they met. The Vulcan had even acknowledged that he and the commander had something in common—families they cared for a great deal, though they were far away.

However, every move Crusher had made on this planet had irritated and alarmed Tuvok—and placed their mission in jeopardy. Mentally, the ensign began drafting his report.

He only hoped that he would live long enough to record it.

Chapter Eleven

MENDAN ABBIS WAS A HAPPY MAN.

The Thallonian ale in his goblet was surprisingly good today. It had even been served at room temperature to bring out the tartness in it. Even his Indarrhi friend Wyl was in a pleasant mood, having had his fill of Mephylite pleasure pods.

But most importantly, thought Abbis, Melacronai and Cordracites were dying in obscene numbers, and no one had the slightest idea why. Everything was going just as he had planned.

Abbis had even learned to like Debennius VI, the irreplaceable "Last Stop to Nowhere." For the rest of his long and exceedingly powerful life, he would look upon these days and this place with great fondness.

Even The Den had its good points, he reflected as he looked around. It was almost always dark and crowded, and people left one alone. It smelled a bit, of course, but what was that but a minor inconvenience?

"He's here," said Wyl in his high, nasal voice.

Abbis straightened a bit. The Indarrhi's empathic abilities might be rudimentary, but the Thallonian trusted him to be able to pick out a single Cordracite in a crowd. Wyl's silver eyes were fixed on the door, and by concentrating Abbis could make out the pale, insectoid form half-hidden by bodies and smoke.

Smothering a grin, the Thallonian waved down a waiter with a tray full of empty ceramic drinking vessels. "Another goblet!" he demanded.

A chipped specimen was plunked down on the dirty table in front of him. With great anticipation, Abbis uncorked a new bottle of Thallonian ale and poured to the goblet's brim. Then he poured some more for himself as well, spilling a little.

He chuckled at his clumsiness. No doubt, his reflexes were dulled a bit by the liquor and—

"You're an easy man to find," came the rasping voice of the Cordracite, his faceted eyes blinking at him.

Abbis glanced up at him. "I have no reason to hide . . ." *What was the name?* he asked silently.

He is called Shabik, Wyl supplied just as silently.

"No reason at all, my good friend Shabik. Sit down and join me in a celebratory cup!" Abbis demanded.

He tried to push the overfilled goblet of ale in the Cordracite's direction without spilling it. It wasn't a very successful maneuver. *Oh, well,* he thought. *I can afford another bottle or three.*

"Thanks, but I don't drink," said the Cordracite. He didn't make any move to sit down, either. He just stood there, blinking. "I'll take my money now, if it pleases you."

"It would please me if you would do me the honor of sitting at my table," said Abbis, his voice rising.

The Cordracite frowned at the remark. Still, he sat down on the crude bench opposite his employer.

"There," the Thallonian said approvingly, "that's better." He fumbled in his pocket and produced a pouch full of the agreed-upon sum in slips of latinum. "Your work was excellent, incidentally."

"Of course," said Shabik.

His tone was supercilious; it grated on Abbis's nerves. He watched as the Cordracite opened the pouch and counted the slips of latinum. Then he looked up at his employer.

"Will there be additional jobs?" he asked.

Abbis took a sip of his Thallonian ale. "Not at the moment," he said. Recalling something he'd just learned, he couldn't help chuckling. "Actually, you may be out of business soon."

Shabik blinked again. "What do you mean?"

Abbis shrugged. "I guess you haven't heard. The water supply of the capital city on Cordra Three was poisoned by a fanatic—and for free!" He laughed again, this time with greater vigor. "If this keeps up, it may be I won't have to part with latinum anymore!"

Shabik didn't look amused. His antennae bent forward, as rigid as lances. Leaving his ale untouched, he got up from his seat. "If you change your mind, let me know. If not, we've never met."

And he left without another word. For a moment, Mendan Abbis watched the assassin make his way through the crowd. Then he grunted, drained his goblet, and reached for the one the Cordracite hadn't bothered to taste.

"It *is* remarkable," he told his companion. "Now even the victims have victims. Truly, war can't be far away."

Wyl narrowed his eyes as he smiled. "I am pleased for you," he remarked. "I hope you are pleased with yourself."

The Indarrhi had a habit of spouting cryptic phrases that meant nothing to Abbis. Was he pleased with himself? He sprawled in the chair, the alcohol warming him, and thought about it.

Yes, he decided, he was *very* pleased. He was pleased with Bin Nedrach, he was pleased with Shabik, and he was pleased with all the other professionals busily executing his orders.

He was doing the job he had set out to do. He had chosen his henchmen well. His timing had turned out to be impeccable. So what was there *not* to be pleased about?

Abbis drained the goblet that had been scorned by Shabik and filled his own again. His world was growing warmer and fuzzier around the edges when a big, ungainly-looking alien brushed against his table and knocked over one of his ale bottles.

An empty one, the Thallonian noted. But it didn't keep a spurt of anger from filling his throat. He was on his feet and his sword was in his hand even before he realized he'd drawn it.

"Oaf!" Abbis bellowed at the alien. "In your clumsiness, you knocked over an entire bottle of Thallonian ale!"

Though large, the alien clearly wasn't the belligerent sort. He shrank away from Abbis, lifting appendages that were not quite paws and not quite hands in front of his mottled, nearly shapeless face.

"Humblest apologies!" he wheezed. "The room is crowded, you see. I was jostled and I—"

The Thallonian felt his whole body thrumming with excitement. It had been too long since he'd had the pleasure of an all-out fight. Brandishing his blade like the expert he was, he rose and closed the distance between himself and the alien.

Abbis could smell his victim's terror. It was a heady perfume, and his drunkenness only seemed to magnify it.

"I did not see your table, I swear it!" the alien moaned. "Please, sir, allow me to repay you for your—"

"I'll say you're going to pay!" cried the Thallonian. In an instant, the naked tip of his sword was at the alien's soft, fleshy throat.

One quick push, he thought—ah, so easy—and The Den's manager would have a very large and bloody body to haul away. The alien closed his eyes and whimpered softly, no doubt seeing the same end for himself.

But before he could make his thrust, Abbis felt his anger begin to cool. And cool some more. There was no challenge for him here, he realized, nothing to be gained. Not even a little fun.

The alien's toppling of the bottle had obviously been an accident. And even if it weren't, the Thallonian told himself, the thing was empty. So what was the point of taking offense?

Abbis thought of his last conversation with his father, and what Thul had said about true valor. He thought of all the assassins who answered to him. He thought of war, only another incident or two away.

He had accomplished a great deal during his short stay on Debennius VI. There was no need for him to prove his manhood by taking the life of a fat, defenseless fool.

The Thallonian stuffed his sword back into his belt and looked down his nose at the alien. "Yes," he repeated, "you'll pay. Another bottle of The Den's best and we'll call it even."

The alien opened his eyes, saw that he was not going to die and exhaled a huge, trembling sigh of relief. "Yes, yes, of course," he breathed. "Thallonian ale, was it? Happy to do so, sir, happy, yes, happy!"

Abbis withdrew and lowered himself onto his bench again. The silence that had descended when he first unsheathed his sword began to fill in with sound. The buzz of conversation and the clicking of ceramic goblets resumed. Little by little, the erstwhile customers and staff of The Den turned their worthy attention elsewhere.

Wyl, however, was staring at him. It bothered Abbis.

"What are you looking at?" he asked his friend.

"You," came the reply.

The Thallonian snorted. "I might have guessed that. But why?"

"You have never walked away from a fight in all the years that I've known you," the Indarrhi observed.

Abbis scowled. "Is that a problem?"

Wyl smiled. "Quite the contrary, I would say. I see a bright future ahead of you, Mendan Abbis. After all, the only thing that ever really stood in your way was yourself."

Just then, the waitress came over with another bottle of ale. Without a word, she plunked it down on the table and left. The Thallonian looked around. Finally, he caught the eye of the big alien. Pointing to the bottle, he nodded. The alien seemed happy, yes, happy.

"A bright future indeed," said the Indarrhi.

The Thallonian shot him a look of disdain. "You're telling fortunes now? Stick to what you do best."

But Abbis's words belied the pride he felt. And his companion being what he was, he would know that.

Wyl leaned back in his chair. "Sometimes," he said, "predicting the future is not all that difficult."

Picard was sitting on the Council Chamber's podium in his usual spot, watching a Melacronai diplomat address the afternoon session, when Jetaal Jilokh entered the room with a look of anxiety on his furry, round face. The Benniari's ears were pressed flat against his head and his violet eyes were enormous.

By that, the captain of the *Stargazer* knew that the news was bad. Of course, he had no idea *how* bad.

Culunnh's aide trundled down the central aisle and ascended the podium. Then he approached the First Minister, who was seated against the wall opposite Picard, and whispered something into his tufted ear.

As he listened to the message, Culunnh's mouth opened and he seemed to shrink in size. He muttered something in return, but the captain couldn't make it out.

From his seat next to Picard, Ben Zoma leaned over and whispered a grim "This is not a good thing."

"I'm afraid you're right," the captain sighed.

The First Minister waited until the Melacron had finished, then took his spot at the lectern. "I have some distressing news from Cordra Three," he said, his voice solemn and hushed.

The chamber fell silent.

"I have just been informed that . . ." Culunnh swallowed. ". . . that more than two thousand Cordracites in the capital city of Mailoc have been poisoned by a contaminated water supply. Four hundred have already died. The city council suspects . . ." He winced. ". . . tampering."

Picard was already on his feet when the silence was shattered by long wails of grief and fury. Before it could get any worse, he joined the First Minister at the lectern.

"We do not know for certain that it was an act of terrorism!" The captain had to bellow to be heard above the din. "We need to learn the results of the investigation first!"

He glanced down at Culunnh. The little Benniari looked broken. In his soft violet eyes Picard read the truth: the city council of Mailoc was not ready to officially announce that the reservoir had been deliberately poisoned, but everyone involved knew that was the case.

Suddenly Gerrid Thul was by the human's side, his towering presence a reassurance. "Captain Picard has the right of it," the Thallonian thundered. "Let us give the city council a chance to do their jobs."

There were cries of protest from the Cordracites and their allies. And to Picard's consternation, they were just as loud as before.

He conceded that the Cordracites had reason to be angry. Indeed, he would have been furious if he were in their place. But he couldn't allow that anger to sabotage the proceedings.

"We cannot act without reliable information," the captain said.

"Let us resume our talks tomorrow," Thul advised. "By then, we should have a better understanding of what took place."

"We have come so far," Picard told the delegates, appealing to their reason with a voice that rang through the chamber like a bell. "We have made so much progress here in the last few sessions. We must not let something like this undo the work we have done!"

For a long, tense second or two, he had a feeling that their pleas to wait, to be rational, would be ignored by the assemblage. The captain would not have been shocked if the delegates rose, picked up their chairs, and hurled them at the podium with murderous intent.

But they didn't.

To Picard's surprise, the congress of diplomats—for that was what they surely were, in that moment—began nodding in agreement. Slowly but surely, the sentiment spread from one end of the chamber to the other.

Then Sammis Tarv rose to speak for the Cordracite delegation. "We will postpone any radical action until we have a better understanding of the tragedy," he announced gravely.

"Thank you," the captain said earnestly.

"A wise decision from a wise delegation," the Thallonian added with a hint of relief in his voice.

Unfortunately, it wouldn't take more than a day for the official report to come in from Cordra III. The captain didn't want to think about what would happen then.

He turned to face Thul. "Time is running out," he observed in a low voice, with unavoidable solemnity.

The governor didn't disagree.

Chapter Twelve

AS CRUSHER AND TUVOK APPROACHED the entrance to the dance hall, the commander was feeling pretty good about their chances of success.

It seemed to him they were a hair's breadth from locating Bin Nedrach. And once they did that, they would be able to get some idea as to who was behind the terrorist incidents.

Of course, Tuvok's criticisms back in the dressing room still rankled a little—not to mention his threat of filing a report. It was too bad, Crusher thought. At the outset, he had liked the Vulcan and valued his opinions. But now he saw that Tuvok was more of a hindrance than a help.

After all, what did someone of the Vulcan's background know about bluff and bluster, or what motivated scum like Barrh? When had one of Tuvok's people ever won a hand of five-card draw?

Crusher glanced at the Vulcan, but Tuvok didn't glance back. He seemed to be in a world of his own.

Now that the commander thought about it, it had probably been a mistake to have the Vulcan accompany him in the first place. In fact, any of the *Stargazer*'s command officers would have been better suited than Tuvok to achieving their objective—even if the ensign *did* have some experience in this star system.

Like The Den and The House of Comfort, the dance hall looked slovenly and run down from the outside. Even the wooden sign by the door was so weathered as to be illegible.

With all the money that seemed to be floating around Debennius VI, the commander wondered that the owners of these establishments were so willing to let their places look dilapidated. Then again, for all he knew, it might be a sign of status, some kind of peculiar Benniar ranking system. Perhaps the more wealth you had, the worse you let your place appear—an indication that you didn't have to go to the trouble of courting any new customers.

Or maybe the people who owned these places just didn't give a damn. That was a possibility as well.

Before Crusher or Tuvok could open the door to the dance hall, it opened for them and a gangly Shaidanian pushed his way out. All four of his eyes looked bleary and red-rimmed with too much alcohol, including the two on the long, slender stalks protruding from his forehead.

Music, slow and sultry and played by someone who knew what he was doing, floated out of the place. The commander was more than a little surprised. Maybe the floor show would be of the same quality, he mused, though he certainly wasn't counting on it.

He and Tuvok walked inside, allowing the door to slam shut behind them. The dance hall was dark and crowded and filled with alien smells—in many respects, a first cousin to The Den.

On the rounded center stage, however, illuminated by brightly colored lights, a lithe Orion slave girl danced. And contrary to Crusher's expectations, her performance was a compelling one indeed.

The slave girl's long, lean muscles rippled smoothly under her green skin, which changed color as she moved in and out of the lights. Her cascade of black hair seemed to coil and uncoil as if it had a life of its own, and the smoke swirling about the place caressed her body as she moved in time to the slow, sensuous pipe music.

Breathtaking, the commander thought. It was almost impossible for him to take his eyes off her. But then, she had been bred from birth to achieve just such an effect.

At one point, the slave girl bent her knees and, arms undulating, bent backward so far that her hair swept the floor. As she writhed, beads of perspiration glistening on her skin, she arched her belly upward and flexed her abdominals with uncanny control.

Abruptly, her bright green eyes fixed on Crusher, sending a jolt of electricity up and down his spine. No, he thought, she can't be looking at me. Not with all the lights blinding her.

And yet, the slave girl's gaze seemed to linger. Well, the commander mused, maybe she can see *despite* all the lights. But why was the Orion looking at Crusher in particular? Or was it just part of the show for her to meet a customer's gaze now and then?

The latter, no doubt. Still, part of the commander wanted desperately for it to be otherwise.

Suddenly, the slave girl broke eye contact and turned her attention elsewhere—to another patron, he imagined. Crusher felt vacant, oddly disappointed. Then she returned to an upright position again and moved away, disappointing him even more.

Breathtaking, he thought again.

"Commander," said a familiar voice.

Crusher turned and saw Tuvok standing next to him. Somehow, he had managed to forget that the Vulcan was there.

"Let's find someone in charge," Crusher said, shaking off the effects of the slave girl as best he could.

He looked about for someone who might have some authority. As in The Den, no one popped out at him, so he went to the bar. The Vulcan followed dutifully, as always. Seating themselves, they ordered drinks.

As he partook of his beverage, the commander scanned the crowd. His eyes fell on a tall, sallow individual with an elongated head and a narrow thread of dark fur that ran from his crown down the back of his neck. Crusher wasn't familiar with the species, but the being appeared to move through the throng with confidence, greeting several people and occasionally leaning over to whisper in someone's ear.

This individual might or might not have been in charge of the place, the human acknowledged. However, it was a good bet that he could steer them where they wanted to go.

Crusher pointed out the alien to Tuvok. "Let's go," he said, starting in the requisite direction.

The Vulcan didn't seem particularly enthused, but he didn't lodge any complaints either. He simply got off his seat and followed the commander through the crowd.

When Crusher reached the being with the elongated head, he tapped him lightly on the shoulder. The alien turned gracefully, fastening small, emerald-green eyes on him.

"You are not regular patrons here," he observed in a high-pitched whistle of a voice.

The commander smiled affably. "No," he conceded, "we're not. But from what we've seen," and he indicated the Orion on the stage with a tilt of his head, "we'll be sure to come back some time. At the moment, however, my friend and I are here on business."

"Oh?" said the alien.

"That's right," Crusher told him. "I'm looking for a Benniari named Bidrik Onaggh. I believe this is his—"

The commander felt the threat of moving bodies before he actually turned and saw them emerge from the shadows. There were six or seven of them, he counted at a glance, all big and dangerous-looking. Lousy odds at best, he told himself.

It was obvious now to Crusher that their arrival had been expected. It was also obvious that this reception had nothing to do with sharing mutually beneficial information about steeds and riders. It had to do with the way he had treated Pudris Barrh.

Tuvok had been right, it seemed. The commander had made a mistake. He only hoped it wasn't too late to make up for it.

Making eye contact with the Vulcan, he shook his phaser pistol out of its hiding place in his voluminous sleeve. It fell with easy convenience into his waiting palm.

Unfortunately, Crusher didn't get a chance to fire it. The big blue hand of a Pandrilite clamped down suddenly on his wrist, its thick, blue fingers squeezing his bones like a metal vise. Groaning in pain, the human dropped the energy weapon.

But as he did so he also launched a kick at his captor's knee. It must have struck with considerable force, because the Pandrilite screamed and let go of Crusher's wrist.

Grunts, curses, and the sound of bone striking bone told him that Tuvok was fighting hand-to-hand beside him. The commander saw at least two bodies hit the floor in quick succession—one a Melacron and the other someone from the same species as Old Scowly. Clearly, Crusher reflected, the Vulcan nerve pinch had been employed with at least some success.

But he didn't take the time to think anything more. Not when his phaser was lying on the floor, still up for grabs.

Diving for it, the commander reached out and closed his fingers around its barrel. Then he flipped over onto his back and began firing. In this press of bodies, he reasoned, he was bound to hit someone. He did. Twice, in fact.

But before he could hit a third adversary, an exceedingly ugly Banyanan sprang on him with a yell. Crusher tried to spear his adversary with a phaser beam, but the alien was too quick for him.

Knocking the commander's weapon hand aside, the Banyanan raised a dagger that was as unsightly as he was. For an instant, Crusher could almost feel the pain of the serrated blade penetrating his unprotected throat.

But remembering his training, he shot the heel of his hand into the alien's angular chin, making the Banyanan's head rock back. And before he could recover, the human had wrested control of the knife.

The alien grunted in surprise, unsure of what to do next—giving Crusher all the opportunity he needed. Clenching his jaw, he drove the dagger into the side of the Banyanan's neck.

As the alien clutched at his wound, trying to draw the bloody dagger out, the commander pushed him away and made an attempt to get to his feet. Halfway there, something hit him.

Hard.

Peering up from the bottom of a deep, red well, where the sounds of battle seemed much too far away, Crusher tried to make out his adversary. A being who could have been Old Scowly's twin hauled him upward, nearly yanking the human's arm out of its socket in the process.

For a moment, he stood there, his knees too weak to support him for long, and attempted to fire his phaser—only to realize that he had managed to lose it again. Bad, Crusher thought. Very bad.

Then he saw the alien's mammoth fist come at him in what seemed strangely like slow motion. He watched, fascinated, as it made inexorable progress in the direction of his face.

Very bad, the commander repeated inwardly, bracing himself for the inevitable, devastating impact.

Lir Kirnis was bored.

A master scientist, she was the head of a small band of Melacron who had dared to leave the worlds of their home system to explore the frontiers of science—which was little more than a fancy way of saying they were stuck out here on a distant rock, far away from friends and kin, and had been for a long, long time.

Sitting in her lab above the colony's enclosed, hundred-meter-long main thoroughfare, Kirnis could see the comings and goings of her colleagues and their families. Somehow, they always seemed happier than she was.

But then, her colleagues had been wiser than she, bringing along their Companions and their children for company. Lir had always been Companioned to her work, not to another living being.

Back on Melacron V, that had been enough to sustain her. But here at this lonely outpost surrounded by a forbidding landscape and volatile weather, there were no fields through which she could stroll while puzzling out a problem. There were no restaurants with good food and wine to satisfy her physical needs, no entertainments to divert her mind.

Nothing but dark, barren mountains and her fellow scientists and the microscopic organisms that continued to elude her scrutiny.

Kirnis heaved a sigh. The creatures had been such a lure at first, such an irresistible temptation. The G'aha of Medicine had approached her with the first findings, taken from an unmanned Melacronai probe. The tiny life forms embedded deep within the rocks boasted a gene sequence that no scientist had ever observed.

Preliminary tests indicated that there might be a way to turn these microscopic entities into instruments of medicine in much the same way that, some three hundred and fifty years earlier, her people had been able to turn common bacteria into cures for a variety of diseases.

The whole prospect was wonderfully exciting. And of all the master scientists at work on Melacron V, Kirnis had been asked to head the expedition.

That was four years ago, she reflected. Four long, frustrating years. Where in the gods' names had the time gone?

Sighing again, Kirnis called up the latest report and watched it appear on her monitor screen. The log indicated that sample 857230-KRA, obtained from the heart of the volcanic range located at forty-two point four degrees latitude and thirty-seven point zero degrees longitude, had been just as disappointing as all the other samples taken before it.

It simply refused to survive in laboratory conditions. How could one study a microscopic organism if it refused to live any longer than a day—and for no reason anyone could discern?

Four years here, she thought, and all their efforts had been in vain. It wasn't a record Kirnis was proud of, especially in light of the high expectations that had accompanied her voyage here.

She glanced over at her bright green-and-scarlet scarf, folded reverently, awaiting her. At least Inseeing would begin at sunset tomorrow; she could console herself with that. It was her favorite holiday.

Normally, a Melacron purchased a new scarf every year and wore it only for the period of Inseeing. Then it was burned in accordance with the ancient sacraments. She and her team, however, had already been stuck at their outpost two years longer than they had planned. As a result, they had been unable to purchase new scarves.

Tradition held that it was bad luck to preserve the scarves and not burn them. But Kirnis had always held a sneaking suspicion that "tradition" had been started by scarf-makers. Besides, she couldn't bear the prospect of having no scarf at—

Behind her, the colony's advance warning monitor began to beep. Apparently, she told herself, the sensor mechanisms orbiting the outpost had detected the approach of something.

Adrenaline flooded Kirnis. She hadn't expected a Melacronai vessel to show up for several months yet. Whirling, she checked the monitor. Then her eyes went wide as she read the information couched there—the impossible, heartstopping and yet undeniable information.

Status: vessel approaching. Bearing: two six four mark two. Vessel type: Cordracite warship third class, weapons systems armed.

"No," she breathed. Of course there had been a history of bad blood between the Melacron and the Cordracites, but that was no reason for an armed warship to bear down on an isolated outpost.

"There's nothing here," she complained, though none of her colleagues was in the room to hear her.

Gritting her teeth against panic, Kirnis flipped a switch on her communications console. Abruptly, the image of the approaching vessel appeared on her screen. It was indeed a Cordracite warship, bristling with weapons ports and full of terrible purpose.

She would contact them, she decided. She would convince them that they were making a mistake.

"Master Scientist Lir Kirnis to Cordracite vessel," she said in a voice that shook. "This is a Melacronai research outpost populated only with scientists and their families. Repeat, this outpost is populated only with scientists and their families. The results of our research are available to all. There is no need for an attack." She swallowed in a painfully dry throat. "Please respond and we will discuss the situation further."

Then Kirnis punched a brightly lit button on the console and waited for the Cordracites' answer. To her horror, none came.

Trembling, her two hearts thumping, she repeated the message, adding, "We have no weapons here, no tactical systems. Ours is a purely scientific venture. Please respond, Cordracite vessel. Your orders to attack this facility must be in error."

There was silence across the vastness of cold space. Nor did the ship turn away. It continued to bear down on them.

Kirnis glanced at the main thoroughfare, where her colleagues and their families continued to make their way from place to place. Clearly, they were oblivious of the danger facing them.

She wondered if she should tell them what was about to happen. She wondered if she would want to know, if their positions were reversed—and decided not to say anything.

If these were their last moments, as seemed increasingly likely, why tear them apart with fear? Why not let the Melacron there go on as though nothing were wrong, enjoying each other to their last breath?

Kirnis turned to the monitor again. Numbly, disbelievingly, she watched the vessel's weapons stations flash a bright green—and being a scientist, knew what that meant.

"This can't be happening!" she shrieked into the console's communications grid. "Hold your fire! Cordracite vessel, you've made a mistake! There are no weapons here, nothing of value." She felt her stomach muscles clench. "There are children . . . children, damn it! Come down and see for your—"

Then it was too late to protest, too late for anything, because the sky was ablaze with a hideous emerald fire. The last thought that went through Kirnis's mind was, absurdly, that not burning her Inseeing scarf for two years in a row had brought her very bad luck indeed.

Chapter Thirteen

"THIS CAN'T BE HAPPENING!" Lir Kirnis screamed. "Hold your fire! Cordracite vessel, you've made a mistake! There are no weapons here, nothing of value." She licked her lips. "There are children . . . children, damn it! Come down and see for your—"

Jean-Luc Picard watched in horrified silence—along with the rest of the Kellasian Congress—as Melacronai Master Scientist Lir Kirnis frantically tried to dissuade the attack that ultimately destroyed her.

Kirnis stared up at something, her eyes wide, her face bathed in a sickly green light. Her mouth moved, but it didn't produce any words. Then the image on his screen went blank.

The captain's teeth ground together. After all, he had seen the terror in Kirnis's expression. He had seen the damning sensor data downloaded from the colony computers, which somehow survived the attack. And he had seen the list of those who had perished.

As Kirnis had indicated, there had indeed been children at the outpost—a great many of them, it seemed. And they had all fallen victim to the Cordracite war vessel.

"There can be no error!" shrilled the Melacronai G'aha of Finance, his eyes wide with fury. "On the eve of our most sacred and holy time, the Cordracite monsters appear like demons out of legend to massacre the young, the helpless and the innocent!"

"No!" countered Sammis Tarv, on his feet now, his antennae bent forward with indignation. "This is not just an error—it is a cold, calculated attempt by the Melacronai government to blame the Cordracites for their tragedy! These—these *creatures* murdered their own scientists and made it look as if we did it!"

"We would kill our own?" The G'aha was stunned by the accusation. "And we would do this on the eve of Inseeing? Trust a Cordracite to think of something so irrational . . . so abominable!"

"Trust a Melacron to *do* something so abominable!" came a rasping reply from one of the Cordracites.

And then it happened. The assemblage's carefully built foundation of diplomacy and reason shattered like fine crystal under the impact of a level-ten phaser barrage. The Cordracite Elected One charged the Melacronai G'aha, his jaw pincers extending from his mouth as he hissed the ancient blood cry of his people. Just as eager for a confrontation, the G'aha bellowed and met the Elected One halfway.

Picard couldn't allow it. Leaping down from the podium with Ben Zoma on his heels, he made a beeline for the combatants.

As it turned out, Gerrid Thul reached them first. He threw his body between them and struggled to keep the delegates from killing each other—no easy task. Fortunately, others arrived to help, the captain and his first officer among them.

The Cordracite was the more formidable of the delegates. His pincers and his clawlike fingers tore clothing and flesh alike.

"Peace! Peace in these halls, I beg you!"

Cabrid Culunnh's voice was shrill with grief—over the murders of innocents, over the violence displayed in a hall meant to nurture peace, over the looming specter of war and even more death. He hastened down from the stage, his small, round face expressing his apprehension as eloquently as any words he might utter.

"The First Minister is right!" said Picard, raising his voice to be heard over the uproar. "These halls are meant for dialogue, not defamation . . . debate, not indictment!"

The combatants glowered at each other, their chests heaving and their faces flushed with emotion. But it seemed that, for the moment at least, the fight had gone out of them.

"You are right, Captain Picard," said Sammis Tarv. There was blood on the front of his tunic—though the captain couldn't tell whose it was. "This chamber is for discourse. It is not for combat."

Then, before anyone could stop him or even guesss what he was about to do, the Cordracite darted forward and slashed the G'aha's face with his hand. And as quickly as he had attacked, he stepped back.

"That is an informal declaration of hostility," Tarv spat at the Melacron. "Rest assured that a formal declaration will be dispatched from my government in due time."

"Cordracite excrement!" howled the G'aha, clapping his hand to his wound. His eyes were enormous with anger. "And to think I once believed that peace with your people would be a worthwhile goal. The Sakari area of space is ours—and if we have to take thousands of your worthless lives to claim it, then so be it!"

The Cordracite made a rasping sound in his throat. "You took the words out of my mouth," he said.

Picard shook his head. His worst fear had come to pass. Despite his best efforts, it seemed, there would be war.

There was no more fighting after that. The two delegations simply turned away from each other and marched out of the hall. The other species represented in the council chamber muttered and exchanged glances, no doubt mulling their options.

Some seemed to stream after the Melacron. Others appeared to follow the Cordracites. Before long, none of the delegates remained.

Only a few lost souls still stood there in the mammoth chamber, looking shellshocked and perplexed: Picard, Ben Zoma, Gerrid Thul, Cabrid Culunnh, and a few of his Benniari attendants. The place seemed to ring with ghostly cries and threats even after those who had uttered them were gone.

"It will destroy us," Culunnh said softly.

Picard didn't have the wherewithal to argue with the Benniari, though he wished it were otherwise.

"At first," the First Minister went on, "it will only be a conflict between the Melacron and the Cordracites. But one by one, the other species in the sector will choose sides."

"Perhaps . . ." Jilokh began.

Culunnh held up a hand. "No . . . don't hold out false hope, Jilokh." He eyed the captain, Ben Zoma, and then Thul. "You have all seen the beginning of it today. Caught in the middle, as always, the Benniari will be the victims." He shook his head. "We have failed. I am ashamed."

"You did everything you could," Picard assured him. "You kept both sides talking far longer than anyone had any right to expect. I would not consider that a failure."

"It does not matter what went before," said Culunnh. "The Cordracites and the Melacron have left with the heat of war in their hearts."

"Which may yet cool," the Thallonian put in.

The First Minister smiled wanly at him. "I did not know Thallonians were such optimists."

"Not optimists, no," Thul conceded. "But the first virtue among my people is courage, my friend. And that means more than how well you conduct yourself in a fight."

"Once the first official attack begins," said Culunnh, "courage will be needed by all of us. I pray that we find it."

Picard sighed. He had hoped to make an optimistic report to Starfleet Command. He had hoped there would be some good news. It didn't appear that that was a possibility anymore.

Commander Jack Crusher had once had a headache more painful than this one. But only once.

He was young back then, only twenty-two, attending a bachelor party for a fellow cadet. There were women and dancing and loud music, and some remarkably smooth Romulan ale that had been smuggled to Earth somehow.

Crusher had drunk too much and danced too much and his friends had tried to convince him that he had done other things as well. Unfortunately, he didn't remember any of them. What he did remember, and would never forget, was the exquisite torture of a hangover that had all the force of a Klingon disruptor barrage behind it.

This headache was a close second.

He tried to push himself up into a sitting position, and it was only then that he realized his hands had been tied behind his back. He winced as pain awakened unexpectedly in his face.

His nose hurt worst of all. It felt flattened so badly he probably could have given Old Scowly a run for his money in the ugly department. Then again, he doubted it was anything Greyhorse couldn't fix in his sickbay.

Unfortunately, the commander wasn't *in* Greyhorse's sickbay. He looked around the room he *was* in, trying to ignore the bruises and the dried blood and the stiffness in his limbs. The place was small, cold and dingy, he observed. There were no windows and only a single door.

A silhouette beside him, dark against the greater darkness, had to be Tuvok. His face was turned away, so Crusher couldn't gauge the extent of the Vulcan's injuries. But from what he could tell, Tuvok was breathing all right, and that was the most important thing.

Abruptly, the human heard a ripple of voices from outside, though he was unable to make out the words, and a harsh, quick burst of nasty laughter. It was probably at his expense, he told himself.

Crusher cursed softly. He supposed he deserved some abuse. Though it was too late to do anything about it, he remembered the strange look the Orion dancer had given him. He had flattered himself into thinking she was just appreciative of his boyish good looks. He realized now that it had been the woman's way of warning him about the impending trap.

"You are awake," came Tuvok's voice, remarkably crisp despite the beating he had taken.

The commander glanced at the Vulcan, who had turned to face him. His features too were swollen and caked with dried blood, but the dark brown eyes were as implacable as ever.

"I wish I wasn't," Crusher told him. "And how did you wind up? No serious injuries, I trust?"

"Nothing life-threatening," Tuvok reported disdainfully.

"Me either," said the commander, though he was well aware that the Vulcan hadn't asked. "I don't suppose you've used your remarkable powers of observation to find a way out of here?"

"There *is* no way out except through the door," Tuvok informed him coolly and efficiently. "It is undoubtedly locked and there appear to be two guards. Escape will be difficult if not impossible . . . unless, of course, an opportunity presents itself."

He didn't sound hopeful that it would.

Crusher flexed his fingers. They were all but numb and the attempt at movement set sharp pains rushing through their joints. Despite them, he tried to twist his wrists and loosen his bonds, but the knots held.

"We'd better start working on that unexpected opportunity," he said.

His companion cast him a withering look. "There would be no need to depend on the unexpected if you had taken my advice to heart."

The commander didn't like the tone of Tuvok's voice. "I'd say that's water under the bridge, wouldn't you?"

"You humans have a saying," the ensign noted. "Those who do not learn from history are doomed to repeat it."

Crusher felt a surge of resentment. "In other words," he said, "you'd rather look back than ahead."

Tuvok's eyes narrowed. "In other words," he responded coldly, "one cannot look ahead with confidence until he has gained an understanding of what came before. In the current instance, for example, I warned you that you were taking unnecessary risks. However, you chose to ignore me. You decided to intimidate Pudris Barrh in his home territory."

The human frowned. He had to admit that it wasn't the best idea he'd ever had—but only to himself.

"Had you exercised restraint," the Vulcan went on, "he would not have arranged to have us beaten and bound." He sighed. "You are careless, Commander Crusher—careless with your life, with your mission and with the subordinate officer under your command, not to mention the requirements of your wife and your young child . . ."

The mention of Beverly and Wesley caught Crusher off guard. "My wife and child . . . ?" he echoed.

"When you exchanged vows with your mate," Tuvok explained, "you made a commitment. When you impregnated her, you made a commitment to your son. By pursuing an illogical, reckless course of behavior, you have violated both of those commitments."

The commander made a face. "Now wait just a—"

But the Vulcan forged on, undeterred. "If you die here," he said, "your spouse will no doubt grieve your loss. However, she is a mature adult; she will recover from the experience. Your child, on the other hand, may not. Humanoid offspring require input from both parents to achieve their full potential. Your actions here have all but ensured that your son will be deprived of your input."

Crusher was getting more annoyed by the minute. "We're not dead yet," he reminded Tuvok. "And don't accuse me of not caring about my wife and son, all right? They're the most important people in the universe to me."

"One would not know it from your actions," the Vulcan insisted.

The commander's jaw clenched. "Listen to me, dammit. I'm a Starfleet officer. So's my wife. And for that matter, so are you."

He glanced at the door. He had to be mindful of the guards outside it, despite the wave of emotion he could feel crashing over him.

"When we accepted our commissions," Crusher went on, "we accepted everything that goes along with them—the bad as well as the good. As a Starfleet captain said a long time ago, risk is our business."

There was a flicker of recognition in Tuvok's eyes. Obviously, he too had heard the reference.

"Now," said the commander, forcing himself to put the matter in perspective, "I'm not saying you don't have a point . . ."

The ensign raised an eyebrow.

"In this particular instance, I mean," Crusher added quickly. "I maintain that my overall strategy was a good one. After all, it worked on the bartender at The Den, didn't it? It just didn't work on Pudris Barrh."

Tuvok frowned.

"All right," said the human, "it backfired horribly when I tried it on Pudris Barrh. But that doesn't mean I'm going to stop taking chances if I think they're reasonable. And it doesn't mean—"

He stopped abruptly and gazed at the Vulcan. Suddenly, he realized what was going on. The revelation chased the heat of indignation out of him and left only compassion in its wake.

"Oh, man," said Crusher. "I'm sorry. I understand now."

"Understand what?" asked Tuvok.

"You're a Starfleet officer," the commander explained. "You feel that responsibility as intensely as anyone. But you're also a family man, with a wife and children—and you don't think you're going to make it home to them. You think that you've somehow let them down."

The Vulcan didn't confirm Crusher's observation. On the other hand, he didn't deny it.

"And since it's not appropriate for one of your people to feel guilt, you're projecting that feeling—that conflict—onto me," the commander concluded. "You're accusing me of abandoning my family because you can't contemplate the idea of accusing yourself."

Still, Tuvok said nothing. He just stared.

"But there's no need to beat yourself up about it," Crusher insisted. "You did what you had to do—just as I did. And we're both going to have to hope our loved ones understand that."

For the first time since the beginning of their conversation, the Vulcan looked away. The commander saw that Tuvok needed some time to think. He gave it to him.

Finally, the Vulcan turned back to him and spoke again. "I was . . . as you humans put it . . . out of line."

Crusher didn't reply right away. He sensed there was something more Tuvok wanted to say.

"It is unsettling indeed," the ensign continued, "to consider that your interpretation of my actions may be correct in some respects. I cannot deny that there is a conflict within me between my duty to Starfleet and my duty to my family, and it is certainly possible that this conflict has colored my view of the situation."

It was a truly remarkable admission for a Vulcan. Tuvok might as well have admitted a yen for cotton candy . . . or the Romulan ale that Crusher had run afoul of as a cadet.

"However, we should be concentrating our efforts on escape," the ensign pointed out, no doubt hoping to change the subject. "After all, we *do* have a mission to complete."

The commander smiled, though it hurt him to do so. "All right," he said. "What about that unexpected opportunity you mentioned?"

Chapter Fourteen

Captain's log, supplemental. Despite the efforts of myself, Commander Ben Zoma, and others, including First Minister Culunnh and Governor Thul of the Thallonian Empire, we have failed to hold the peace talks together. The congress on Debennius Six has disbanded, perhaps for good. Also, we are no closer to discerning who is behind the terrorist assaults than we were before. All we know is that they are cold-blooded murderers, acting with a purpose and a plan—as evidenced by the fact that each incident is more brutal than the last. First a political assassination, then the bombing of a commuter vehicle, then the poisoning of a reservoir . . . and now the destruction of an entire colony, damn their—

PICARD PAUSED. His anger at the atrocities was beginning to color his log. Taking a deep breath, he deleted the last two words.

As he was about to resume his report, the door to his room chimed softly. Looking up, the captain wondered what new bit of bad news Ben Zoma might be bringing him.

"Come," he called.

Then he remembered that he wasn't in his quarters back on the *Stargazer.* He was in a suite First Minister Culunnh had obtained for him on Debennius II so the Benniari could reach him at a moment's notice, and the door mechanism wouldn't respond to his voice.

Rising from his chair, he crossed the room and touched a pad built into the wall beside the door. A moment later, the panel moved aside with an exhalation of air, revealing his visitor.

It wasn't Ben Zoma, either. "Governor Thul," said Picard.

The governor smiled. "Captain . . . may I come in?"

"By all means," Picard responded, moving to one side so the Thallonian could enter the room.

"I've become persona non grata among both the Cordracites and the Melacron," Thul observed as he came inside.

"As have I," the captain noted, as the door hissed closed again. "Which makes it rather difficult to talk sense into them."

The Thallonian took the seat against the wall, opposite the one where Picard had been sitting. "I'm afraid that peace-mongers are not much appreciated at the moment."

Picard grunted. "So it would appear." He indicated a transparent decanter full of bright yellow liquid sitting on a wooden endtable. "Would you care for some wine, Governor?"

"Wine?" Thul replied wonderingly. "I thought tea was your beverage of choice, Captain."

Picard smiled without humor. "Cabrid Culunnh had this sent up here a couple of hours ago. He said he hoped it might give me some consolation."

"And has it?" asked the Thallonian.

The captain shrugged. "I've barely touched it."

"Then let us rectify that oversight," said Thul.

Picard nodded and poured two glasses of the stuff. Then he gave one of them to his visitor.

"To peace," the Thallonian noted. As he raised his glass, it sparkled in the light.

"To peace," the captain agreed, raising his glass as well. "May it be more than the empty illusion it seems at the moment."

Together, they sipped the dry, tart beverage in silence. The wine wasn't to Picard's taste, exactly, but it wasn't awful either. His father's vineyards back on Earth had occasionally produced worse.

Staring into the depths of his wine, Thul spoke. "I cannot get it out of my head, Captain. There will be war soon. So many millions of innocents . . . what a waste of life."

Picard didn't answer. His mind's eye was filled with images of the soft-spoken, wise Benniari. Because of their presence in the disputed territories, they would no doubt be among the first to perish—just as the First Minister had predicted.

"I'm tempted to intervene," said the governor. "To stop it, somehow. And not just on behalf of Culunnh's people. After all, there are Thallonians in danger as well—those who serve the Emperor in various ways outside the borders of the Empire."

"I envy you that liberty," the captain answered sincerely. "Unfortunately, my hands are tied."

Thul looked at him. "What do you mean?"

"You spoke of the first virtue among your people," Picard said. "We of the United Federation of Planets have a central tenet as well. We have vowed not to intervene in conflicts among other civilizations, unless we are asked to do so by one of the combatants—and clearly, neither the Cordracites nor the Melacron have asked for our aid."

"The Benniari have," the Thallonian pointed out.

"Yes," the captain agreed, "and we will protect them if they are attacked. But beyond that . . ." He shrugged again.

"That must be terribly frustrating," said Thul.

Picard smiled wryly. "You have no idea. But those are my orders and I will obey them."

The governor finished his wine, then got to his feet and stretched. "I thought we might come up with something . . . an idea. But I find I'm too tired to do much thinking. Maybe I should just call it a night."

"As you wish," said the captain.

"Thank you for the wine," Thul tossed back over his shoulder as he crossed the room.

"Anytime," Picard told him. "May it help you sleep better."

The Thallonian stopped at the door. "I'll see you tomorrow," he said, "assuming the council chamber is still standing then."

"Tomorrow," the captain replied.

And with that, Thul made his exit.

Picard watched the doors slide closed behind him. Then he raised his glass again and watched the way the light filtered through the wine. The stuff wouldn't help *him* sleep better, he remarked inwardly. At that moment, he doubted anything would.

But he poured himself another glass, just in case.

After what seemed like an eternity of wrestling with his bonds, Jack Crusher arrived at the frustrating conclusion that they had been tied by the all-time expert.

"I've been at this forever," he growled, half to himself.

"You have only been conscious for one hour, twelve minutes and seventeen seconds," Tuvok corrected him. "And you have only spent seventy-six percent of that time attempting to free yourself."

The commander opened his mouth to make a less-than-pleasant retort, when he heard scuffling sounds on the other side of the door. He glanced at Tuvok, who had obviously heard them too. They fell silent.

A moment later, they heard the grating sound of a bolt being lifted. Then the door was pushed open.

Crusher recognized the alien who stood in the doorway as a Thallonian, though he had never spoken to one before. The tall, red-skinned being surveyed them with bright eyes.

"My name is Mendan Abbis," he said haughtily and incautiously. "I understand you've been sniffing around my steeds. Tell me, my friends—what do you *really* want with Bin Nedrach?"

"Ah," said the commander, trying to act as if he weren't in such a disadvantageous position. "So you're the elusive rider we've been hearing about. I can't say I much like the way you do business."

The Thallonian didn't smile at the jest. "I asked you a question," he reminded the human.

"What would *anyone* want with him?" Crusher replied as nonchalantly as possible. "We want to hire him, of course. We've got a job for him—if he's the best assassin around, as people say."

Abbis's gaze never left Crusher's face. "That sounds plausible. If it's true, it'll be confirmed soon enough. Then perhaps we can do business." He tossed a look over his shoulder. "Wyl!"

A tall, slender figure stepped into the room. His skin was dark, his hair white and tightly curled, and his deepset eyes glittered like silver. He seemed to look to the Thallonian for guidance.

"My friend Wyl here is an Indarrhi," said Abbis. "Perhaps you've heard of what they can do." A satisfied pause. "Rest assured, he'll get the truth out of you."

"Torture?" asked Crusher as calmly as if he were inquiring if the Thallonian took milk and sugar in his coffee.

Their captor chuckled. "You can resist torture, if your will is strong enough. Wyl has . . . other ways."

He nodded in Tuvok's direction and the Indarrhi approached him. Kneeling beside the ensign, he extended a hand and placed thick, ungainly fingers on Tuvok's temple. The silver eyes closed in concentration.

Though his expression remained utterly neutral, it was clear to Crusher that the Vulcan didn't like the idea. However, under the circumstances, he could hardly put up a fight.

"Now then," Abbis told Tuvok, "I ask you again—and you'd better answer if you value your life—what do you want with Bin Nedrach?"

His voice flat and lifeless, the Vulcan replied: "We wished to hire him to perform an assassination."

The Thallonian turned to his friend. "Wyl? Is he lying?"

The Indarrhi shook his curly, white locks. He looked confused, his dark brow creased. "I . . . I can't tell!"

Abbis's eyes narrowed. "What?"

Wyl rocked back on his heels, looking at Tuvok with a look of mingled awe and annoyance on his face. "This one," he said, "doesn't seem to have any emotions. At least, I can't sense any."

Abbis frowned—rather petulantly, Crusher thought. "Curse him," he said. "Try the other one, then."

As the Indarrhi knelt beside him and stretched his fingers out to touch his face, the commander called on all the techniques for mental calm he'd ever known. He tried to think about something, anything, other than the true reason he and Tuvok had come . . .

A thick rare steak. A good beer. A hot fudge sundae with sprinkles. Kissing Beverly for the first time.

The pain in his bladder right now.

"Can you feel *his* emotions?" asked the Thallonian.

The Indarrhi nodded. "He'll do."

Abbis turned his attention to Crusher. "What do you want with Bin Nedrach?" he demanded.

The commander tried to feel irritation. "How many times do we have to say it? We want to hire him!"

The Thallonian tilted his head to one side, still wary. "Tell me who you want killed," he said.

Fear thrust up a white wall in Crusher's mind. Then he asked, "Why should I tell you anything before we've struck a deal? When you find out who it is, you might jack up the price."

Abbis's lip curled. "What is your relationship to this other man?" he inquired, indicating Tuvok with a flick of his wrist.

Damn it, thought the commander, he was merciless.

"He's my bodyguard. Can't be too careful in my profession." Crusher forced a laugh; it sounded false, even to him. "I can see you have an appreciation for such things."

"He's lying," said the Indarrhi firmly. "He and his friend are most definitely not here in search of a steed."

Abbis approached the commander and towered over him. "If you're not here to hire Bin Nedrach . . . why are you here?"

Crusher didn't utter a word in response. He simply met the Thallonian glare for glare.

Abbis sighed. "Under the circumstances," he said, sounding reluctant, "I'm afraid I'm just going to have to kill you both. Though I confess to a great deal of curiosity about your true mission, I can't afford to indulge it. It would be too risky."

Casually, he reached for a directed energy weapon at his belt. With a quick flick of his fingers, he had it in his hand—its business end pointed at a spot between the commander's eyes.

I love you, Beverly.

"Wait." It was Tuvok. "There is no need for bloodshed. I will freely tell you what you wish to know."

Abbis hesitated for a second. Then he lowered his weapon.

Crusher glanced at the Vulcan, trying to keep his expression neutral. He wondered what kind of elaborate fantasy Tuvok was about to weave to throw their enemies off the trail.

"My name is Ensign Tuvok," he said. "This is Lieutenant Jack Crusher. We are officers in Starfleet, operating under the aegis of the United Federation of Planets."

Surprise and anger flared in the commander. What the hell did Tuvok think he was doing?

"We are attempting to find Bin Nedrach," the Vulcan went on, "because we believe him to be responsible for the assassination of the Melacronai G'aha of Laws and Enforcements."

The commander couldn't believe what he was hearing. He wanted to cry out, to tell Tuvok to shut his mouth, but that would only confirm the truth of the Vulcan's statements.

Tuvok continued gamely with his confession. "We are operating in a clandestine mode under orders from our captain. Our mission is to identify and stop those who are behind the incidents of violence on Melacron Five and Cordra Three—incidents which are propelling the Cordracites and the Melacron toward war."

"In other words," Abbis concluded, "you're trying to keep this war from taking place?"

"That is correct," said the ensign.

Hurt and anger flooded Crusher. He wished Tuvok had never returned to Starfleet. Clearly, he didn't belong there.

"This is the truth?" asked Abbis.

"The truth," Tuvok agreed. "If you do not believe me, you are free to have your Indarrhi friend examine Commander Crusher again. He will confirm what I have said, whether he wishes to or not."

The commander could only stare in dismay. He wasn't looking forward to dying, of course, but he would have embraced death if it meant carrying out their mission. After all, this wasn't just a walk in the park. Millions of innocents in the Kellasian sector would die if the Melacron and the Cordracites went to war.

Earlier, Tuvok had said he was torn between family and Starfleet. Clearly, the traitorous bastard had chosen the former. His life for millions of lives—damned poor logic, in Crusher's opinion.

The commander was so full of righteous anger, he almost didn't hear what Tuvok said next. And even when he did, he didn't have the slightest idea what the Vulcan was talking about.

"Your father is playing you for a fool," Tuvok told Abbis.

The Thallonian looked at him. "What did you say?"

"Your father is playing you for a fool," the Vulcan repeated evenly.

Clearly, the words had hit home. Abbis's face was even ruddier than usual, his eyes screwed up small and tight.

"Explain yourself," he told Tuvok, "before I punch a hole in your skull and let you watch your brains spill out."

"We know all about him," the Vulcan said calmly.

Crusher listened as intently as the Thallonian. *What* do we know? he wondered. *And how the devil do we know it?*

"We have discovered that your father, Governor Gerrid Thul, is the one behind the assassinations and the other terrorist incidents," Tuvok continued. "He is acting through you, his illegitimate son."

Abbis looked shocked—but he didn't seem able to deny it. Therefore, the commander figured, it was true.

"We also know his goal," said the Vulcan. "He wishes to set himself up as Emperor of a new empire, made up of the systems situated between the Thallonian worlds and the Federation."

The Thallonian exchanged glances with the Indarrhi. The one named Wyl shrugged his shoulders.

"Such a goal," Tuvok noted, "will be far easier for Thul to accomplish if most sentient life in the sector is eliminated. Hence, a war between the Melacron and the Cordracites, instigated by your father and attributed to terrorist groups on both sides."

Abbis's expression was one of respect. "I'm impressed," he said.

So was Crusher.

"It is an ideal plan," Tuvok observed, "nearly flawless in its logic. The Kellasian sector will destroy itself, each species thinking the other one responsible, and the Thallonian Emperor will have no idea that it is all your father's doing."

Abbis nodded. "Yes," he said slowly. "It *is* an ideal plan. And I'm proud to be part of it."

"However . . ." the Vulcan added, letting his voice trail off as if he had thought better of revealing something.

"However *what?*" the Thallonian spat.

"What you do not know," Tuvok continued unperturbed, "is that Thul is only using you. Once you have done what he wishes you to do, you will no longer be a necessary component of his plan. Indeed, you will be a hindrance—which is why he plans to kill you."

Abbis's brow creased in disbelief. "You're insane," he breathed.

"Thul is nothing if not logical—and logic clearly indicates that you will be a danger to him," the Vulcan maintained. "After all, you know too much. You could betray him to the Thallonian Emperor." He shrugged. "Why would he let someone like that continue to live?"

"Because I'm his son," Abbis told him, trying to affect an air of confidence, even disdain. "I'm his flesh and blood, damn it." But the tremor in his voice gave him away.

"In addition," said Tuvok, "your father has dreams of founding a new imperial line. He does not want a bastard for his heir. He craves a son of pure and noble blood. Surely that is why he asked for the hand of the Emperor's sister in marriage."

For the briefest of moments, Crusher found himself feeling sorry for the young Thallonian. He had a mercurial face, and it was difficult for him to conceal his emotions.

Then he remembered the weapon in Abbis's hand, and how he had planned to kill the commander with no more remorse than he might feel squashing a bug. Abruptly, Crusher's pity evaporated.

"You asked for the truth," the Vulcan told the Thallonian. "I have given it to you."

Abbis's mouth twisted with anger, and for a wild moment Crusher feared the youth might use his weapon after all. But instead, he turned his back on his captives and went to the far wall.

Leaning against it, he took long, slow, deep breaths. He looked as if he was trying to calm himself, trying to come to terms with the devastating impact of what Tuvok had revealed to him.

His Indarrhi friend joined him and put a hand on the Thallonian's shoulder. But with a snarl, Abbis batted it away. Shrugging, Wyl withdrew to the center of the room.

Just then, a slight rustling sound caught Crusher's attention. He glanced at the Vulcan and realized what it meant—that Tuvok had freed himself from his bonds. But the Thallonian seemed to have heard it too, because he turned back to them with widened eyes.

What happened next took only a fraction of a second, but it seemed to the commander that it occurred in slow motion.

As Abbis raised his hand weapon and took aim, the Vulcan launched himself across the room and grabbed the shocked Indarrhi. Then he spun Wyl around and used him as a shield against the blue bolt of energy the Thallonian unleashed at him.

The bolt struck Wyl in the chest and the Indarrhi spasmed horribly under its influence—then slumped in Tuvok's arms. There was no question in Crusher's mind that Wyl was dead.

"Wyl!" Abbis cried out, horror etched into his every feature.

The hurt in his voice made Crusher's chest ache in sympathy. He suspected, if even part of what Tuvok had said was true, that the Thallonian had just murdered the only being who ever really liked him.

Before he could fire again, Tuvok was on him like a panther. A quick contraction of the Vulcan's fingers on a nerve in his adversary's neck and Abbis crumpled without a sound.

Tuvok recovered the Thallonian's weapon and tucked it into his belt. Then he listened for an intrusion from outside. When none materialized, he came around behind Crusher and began loosening his bonds.

"An unexpected opportunity," he remarked casually.

Crusher thought he saw a glint of humor in the dark brown eyes. "Is that a joke, Ensign?"

Tuvok looked at him, as inscrutable as ever. "Vulcans do not joke," he pointed out.

At last, Tuvok crossed the room again and placed his pointed ear to the door. "Abbis must have dismissed the guards for the moment," he noted. "I still do not hear anyone out there."

As Crusher got up and rubbed his wrists, restoring circulation to them, he said, "Can you tell me what the hell just happened? For a second I thought you were turning traitor or something."

"A necessary ploy," Tuvok noted.

"And that business about Abbis's father . . ." the commander asked. "Where did you get all that?"

"The Indarrhi's empathic connection worked both ways," the ensign explained—though it seemed that only half his attention was focused on the explanation. "When he attempted to sense my emotions, our minds were linked. It was not difficult to examine his thoughts and extract something useful from them. And the rest—" He hesitated.

"The rest . . . ?" Crusher prodded.

Again, Tuvok's dark eyes seemed to glimmer with the faintest hint of mischief. "The rest," said the Vulcan, "I made up."

Crusher grinned at him. "Tuvok, you son of a mugato. I didn't know you had it in you."

The ensign's brow wrinkled ever so slightly. "There is much you do not know about me, Commander. Perhaps we will have the chance to rectify that at a later time. For the moment, however, I suggest we address ourselves to the question of regaining our freedom."

He had barely gotten the words out when a series of loud grunts and other noises beyond the door alerted them to the guards' return. Thinking quickly, Crusher whispered an idea to Tuvok.

The Vulcan nodded his approval, changed the setting on the Thallonian's hand weapon, and turned it over to his companion. Then they returned to the chairs to which they had been tied, sat down and placed their hands behind their backs.

Here goes nothing, thought the commander. "They killed each other!" he cried out at the top of his lungs. "Somebody help us! Oh, God, the blood—get them out of here!"

At once the door was flung open and Old Scowly's twin—the one whose mammoth fist had pounded Crusher's face—rushed into the room. He was brandishing a weapon that seemed puny in his hand.

Behind him, glaring at the prisoners with his single eye, was the Banyanan. He, too, was armed.

"There!" the commander yelled, his voice high and—he dearly hoped—filled with convincing terror. "The two of them killed each other right in front of our eyes!"

Crusher watched as Old Scowly's twin knelt beside the bodies. Then he exchanged glances with Tuvok. There was a brief instant when both alien guards took their eyes off the prisoners in their desire to see what had become of Abbis and his friend.

"The Indarrhi's dead," snorted the Banyanan. "But the Thallonian doesn't even look injured."

A tribute to Tuvok's skill, the commander thought.

Then he whipped his weapon out and fired it at the Banyanan. At the same time, the Vulcan sprang for Old Scowly's twin.

Struck squarely in the chest, the Banyanan went flying backward and hit the wall behind him. He was unconscious before he slumped to the floor. Old Scowly's lookalike took a bit more attention, but in the end Tuvok was able to disable him as well.

Crusher and the Vulcan looked at each other, gratified that their plan had borne fruit. All their differences, it seemed, had been put behind them.

As Tuvok stripped his adversary of his weapon, the commander dropped down at the side of the Banyanan and did the same.

"Two down, a few dozen more to go," he said.

"Indeed," was the Vulcan's only reply.

A few moments later, armed with three directed energy pistols and a couple of sharp, wicked-looking daggers, the Starfleet officers were ready to pursue their escape. Cautiously, Crusher advanced to the door, twisted its archaic-looking metal knob, and pushed it open a crack. Then he craned his neck and peered out of the room . . .

Into the splendid, knowing eyes of the Orion slave girl.

Chapter Fifteen

THE GOLDEN-HUED SHACKLES on the slave girl's arms and legs gleamed luxuriantly against the rich green of her flesh. Stunned by the sight of her, Crusher couldn't think of anything to say.

Fortunately, he had the presence of mind to pull the Orion inside the room. Her skin felt warm and supple to the touch—unnervingly so.

"So," she said in a husky and not unpleasant voice. She took in the sight of the fallen Thallonian and his friend. "It seems you are Federation spies after all. They thought you might be."

"You . . ." said the commander, finding his voice again. "You tried to warn us, didn't you? When you were dancing?"

She tossed her black mane of hair and smiled, pursing her dark, full lips. Crusher was uncomfortably aware of the fact that the girl's outfit didn't cover very much.

"Yes," she said in answer to his question. "But you were too absorbed in your charade to notice."

The human's first inclination was to object, but he didn't think he would get very far. "Yes," he conceded, "I was."

"Commander . . ." said Tuvok.

Crusher held up a hand. His gut was telling him that this girl might be useful. She'd already tried to help them once. . . .

"That was risky," he said, trying to sound her out. "What you did on the stage, I mean."

She laughed softly. "Not that risky. No one would suspect me of being intelligent enough to betray my master. I know what we are called, after all . . . Orion *animal* women. I also know that in Federation space, the kind of slavery our masters practice is illegal."

The intensity of her stare was doing something to Crusher's stomach—and regions slightly lower. The slave girl moved closer to him on her bare feet and gracefully raised her chains to the level of his face.

"I can help you escape," she said invitingly, whether she had intended that kind of effect or not. "Take me with you. Free me."

Her eyes, he thought, were pools of obsidian, the kind a man could get lost in forever. And that mouth. . . .

"Commander," Tuvok repeated, this time in a slightly more forceful tone of voice. "We only have so much time at our disposal."

"I know," said Crusher. He regarded the girl. "What's your name?"

She looked surprised. "I—I don't have one," she replied. "The Master simply calls me . . ." and she uttered a word that was a local epithet regarding certain female body parts.

The commander winced. That did it.

"From now on . . ." he said, recalling how beautifully she had moved, how strong and graceful she had been, "from now on, you're Grace. That is, until you choose a name for yourself."

The slave girl seemed delighted. Her eyes shone gratefully. "Grace," she repeated as if it were a toy.

Crusher couldn't help smiling a bit as well. "So what kind of plan did you have in mind . . . Grace?"

She told him.

As the door to his guest quarters on Debennius II hissed shut behind him, Gerrid Thul smiled to himself.

After all, the foolish human captain had told him everything he needed to know. The Federation was a toothless beast unless asked to fight, and right now, both the Cordracites and the Melacron were hot for each other's blood. They would not ask anyone to help them stop it.

Everything was going splendidly, the Thallonian told himself. There was only one more thing that needed to be done before the Cordracites and the Melacron went hurtling over the edge into a full-blown war.

Thul removed his oval-shaped communicator from his tunic and spoke into it. "This is the governor," he said.

"Kaavin here," his second-in-command replied crisply.

"I wish to return," he told her.

A moment later, the air around him with filled with swirls of golden light. The next thing the Thallonian knew, he was standing on a raised pentagon in his vessel's transporter facility.

The transporter technician inclined his large, hairless head. "My lord," he said dutifully.

Thul didn't say a thing. But then, he didn't have to. On his ship, as in the colony he governed, he could do anything he liked.

As he descended from the pentagon, the doors to the room whisked open and Kaavin entered. Tall, slender and elegant, she stopped and inclined her head as well.

"Accompany me," said Thul.

He walked out into the corridor, Kaavin at his side. Like any good Thallonian second-in-command, she would remain silent until he demanded something of her.

"Report," the governor told her.

Kaavin glanced at him, all polish and efficiency. "Everything proceeds according to plan, my lord. No one appears to suspect our role in the massacre of the Melacronai colony."

He nodded. "Good."

Naturally, he thought, the Melacron had only seen what Thul wanted them to see—a Cordracite warship bearing down on a defenseless research outpost. That was what their sensors had picked up, what their now-deceased master scientist had screamed into her communications system before she was obliterated by the vessel's energy fire.

Of course, if the Melacron hadn't been so ill-disposed toward the Cordracites to begin with, they might have been more skeptical of the circumstances surrounding the attack. They might have looked beyond their loathing, beyond their species-hatred, and analyzed the colony's sensor data with more sophisticated instruments.

If the Melacron had done that, they would surely have been in for a surprise—for they would have discovered that the aggressor vessel's ion trail was different from the kind left by Cordracite warships. They would have seen, then, that it wasn't a Cordracite vessel that attacked and destroyed Lir Kirnis and her esteemed colleagues after all, but another kind of ship entirely, its appearance altered to make it seem like a Cordracite vessel.

The Melacron didn't have the wherewithal to disguise a spacegoing vehicle. Neither did the Cordracites or any other species in the sector. The Thallonians, on the other hand, had perfected magnetic-pulse imaging technology years earlier.

Granted, it was seldom used. But people only saw things where they thought to look for them. And what would the Thallonian Empire have to gain by exacerbating hostilities in the Kellasian sector?

Nothing. Nothing at all.

So instead of insisting on the truth, the Melacron shouted and screamed and raged at the top of their lungs, accusing the hated Cordracites of destroying a colony full of innocents. And the Cordracites, who of course knew they hadn't done anything wrong, believed that the Melacron had simulated a massacre to set off a war.

And in both cases, Thul's purposes were served.

The governor had always prided himself on his poise, his equilibrium. But as he and Kaavin approached a lift, he had to fight the urge to whoop with glee. It was going to work, he reflected, and work perfectly. The fools were going to destroy each other.

All it would take was one more outrageous, intolerable affront to tip the scales in favor of war, and Thul was about to see to it that that one final affront would take place.

"Bridge," he said, as he and his second-in-command entered the lift compartment. A moment later, the doors whispered closed behind them and the compartment began its journey through the ship.

"When this is over," the governor told Kaavin with a surge of generosity, "you will be amply rewarded."

She looked at him, no doubt wondering in what shape the reward would come. After all, Thul's second knew nothing about his ambitions—only that he wanted to spur a war in this sector. And being a loyal subject, she hadn't questioned that ambition.

"I am honored," Kaavin told him.

You don't know *how* honored, the governor thought.

Then the lift doors opened and his ship's bridge was revealed to him. At the sight of their lord, his officers leaned back in their seats and thrust their chins out.

Thul smiled at them as he emerged from the lift compartment. They were Thallonians all. There was no mixture of inferior aliens here, such as could be seen on Picard's Federation vessel. They were warriors, professionals. And whether they admitted it to themselves or not, they hungered as he did for something more than what their blood-rights had granted them.

Soon, the governor reflected, these steadfast souls would become the lords of his new empire. They would serve him as he presently served Tae Cwan and they would reap the benefits accorded such service.

Thul eased himself into his center seat and turned to his helmsman, a stocky fellow with a dueling scar down the side of his face. "Set course for the fleetyard on Cordra Three."

He recited the coordinates from memory. He had been looking forward to this for a long time.

"Aye, lord," replied the helmsman, and entered the course. The governor settled back to mull over the final stage of his plan.

His own vessel was now equipped with the same magnetic-pulse technology as the one that had destroyed the Melacronai outpost. Like the scientists at the outpost, the Cordracites at the fleetyard would never know it was a Thallonian ship that had attacked them.

As he watched the stars streak by at impulse speed on his forward monitor, Thul tried to picture the destruction of the fleetyard in all its brutal, explosive glory. It was difficult for him to do it justice.

But the results . . . those were easier for him to imagine. The war would get under way instantly, of course. And the first victory—thanks to his crippling of the Cordracites' shipbuilding capabilities—would be claimed by the slightly weaker Melacron.

What's more, he told himself, there would be several hundred fewer Cordracites for the Melacron to kill. And it would no doubt spur the victims' kinsmen to violence unmatched in the history of the sector.

The governor smiled and thought of his son . . . his loyal, efficient, infinitely clever son. What Thallonian in his right mind would have imagined that Mendan Abbis could prove so useful to Thul's cause? Who, indeed, but the governor himself?

Once he understood his father's scheme, once he embraced it, the boy had risen to the challenge. He had executed each and every step of the plan flawlessly, knowing whom to contact for a particular assignment and how to make the most of their talents.

That alone would have been enough, Thul reflected. No—it would have been more than enough. But in addition, Mendan Abbis had demonstrated a flair for the dramatic.

The assassination of the Melacronai G'aha, the bomb that slew the Cordracite commuters, the poisoning of the reservoir on Cordra III . . . all these things were accomplished with a sense of theater and spectacle that would have been a credit to the most skillful Thallonian courtier.

Thul sighed. He had not done right by the boy as a child; he knew that. He recalled showing up for a visit at his humble home every so often, handing Mendan's mother a small pouch full of latinum and regarding the fruit of their reckless union with patrician distaste.

Whose fault had it been, then, that Abbis had grown up with a chip on his shoulder—with a sense of inferiority and a need to prove himself at every opportunity? Whose fault but that of his father?

But that was over, the governor promised himself. He'd given the boy a chance and Mendan Abbis, bastard, had seized it better than any privileged Thallonian whelp ever could have.

Thul himself had been snubbed by his Emperor because he wasn't high-born enough to marry Mella Cwan. The governor would never make that mistake when he sat on a throne. His Empire would be based on merit, on skill and talent, not on accidents of birth.

As for Mendan Abbis . . . he would get what his father had promised him: a seat on Thul's right hand, the time-honored place of the Emperor's rightful heir. And why not?

The boy had earned it.

The commander and his Vulcan companion stumbled into the heart of the dance hall, clad in the filthy, smelly garb of their guards, which they had liberally sprinkled with alcoholic beverages.

Crusher hoped no one noticed how poorly Tuvok's clothes fit—an unfortunate but unavoidable problem given the differences between the ensign's spare physique and that of Old Scowly's lookalike. With luck, any potential observer would be more interested in Grace, who walked between the Starfleet officers with her arms linked through theirs.

There was a Pandrilite on the stage and the loud music that accompanied her gyrations thundered in the commander's bones, more primal than the subtle, sultry sound of the flute to which Grace had danced. The place was significantly more crowded as well, though Crusher wouldn't have believed such a thing was possible.

He laughed and pretended to fall in his drunkenness, then called something to one of the other dancing girls. But that was only what would have been expected of him. And Grace held her head high, saying without words that she had two customers who wanted her favors tonight, and wasn't she just glorious enough to deserve it.

Thus they walked unnoticed and unchallenged to the private quarters where more intimate business was transacted, and Grace closed the door. Inside were a few beds covered with rank-smelling linens, and a couple of candles that represented a pathetic attempt at ambiance.

Grace's feral face shone in the yellow light. "No one suspected anything," she told the commander.

He nodded. "Excellent."

"Indeed," Tuvok added.

Grace went to the room's only window and opened it with an effort. The soft sounds and hard, pungent smells of the night wafted to them on cool, moist drafts of air.

"If you have access to this room and this window," asked Crusher, "why haven't you run away before now?" He found he was a little suspicious at how easy their progress had been to this point.

The slave girl gestured to her shackles. "I have these on all the time, except when I dance. And this," she said, pointing to a tiny box that flashed red and blue and was suspended from the shackles, "will not permit me to leave the building."

The commander decided that he believed her. Wordlessly, he drew the energy weapon formerly owned by Mendan Abbis. Understanding his intent, Grace held out her hands and stood still.

Crusher's objective was to destroy the control box without hurting Grace—not as easy as it sounded with an unfamiliar weapon in his hand. His eyes met hers and she nodded trustingly, clenching her jaw.

The human took a breath to steady himself. Then he placed the weapon's nose within six centimeters of the box and pressed the trigger. The weapon spit out a dark blue stream of energy.

Grace gritted her teeth against the heat. Sparks flew haphazardly. But after a few seconds, there was a satisfying crack and the box clattered to the floor in two pieces. Grace laughed wildly from her belly.

"Free!" she whispered, and savagely kicked at the box, sending it scuttling along the floor.

"We will only remain that way if we make haste," Tuvok warned them, and this time Crusher wasn't inclined to argue with him.

They helped Grace out the window first—though with her catlike agility, she didn't need much assistance. The Vulcan went next and the commander brought up the rear.

As Crusher poked his head out, he saw that his companions were standing in a narrow alleyway alongside the dance hall. Clambering through the window opening and swinging down, he landed in something that squished and smelled awful. Fortunately, the darkness prevented him from analyzing the substance too carefully.

"We must return to our ship," Tuvok told Grace.

"Where is it?" she asked.

"In the foothills west of town," said the commander. "Don't worry, we know the way."

The Orion snarled softly beneath her breath. It was a sound Crusher had never heard before.

"What is it?" he asked.

"We are on the easternmost side of the city," she pointed out. "By the time we reach your vessel, they will have found Mendan Abbis and his friend and realized that I am gone."

"And they will overtake us," the Vulcan concluded.

Grace nodded—and even that small gesture was alluring. "Can you not purchase passage on a—?"

"No," Tuvok said emphatically.

Crusher shrugged, apologizing for his friend and agreeing with him in the same gesture. "I'm afraid it's not an option."

"Very well," the Orion told them. "Follow me." And she started off down the length of the alley.

"We came from the other direction," the commander told her, plodding through the muck to catch up.

"I am aware of that," Grace replied. "However, if you take the direct way back, we will almost certainly be caught. I know a more winding route that may get us there safely."

Crusher looked back at Tuvok. The ensign looked concerned about the change in plans, but he came along.

Grace turned out to know the streets rather well for someone who had to that point in her life been prevented from leaving the dance hall. What's more, she seemed to have an instinct for when to duck into the shadows and when to slip boldly out into the moonlight.

The commander asked her about it.

"I have many hours," she whispered back. "I talk with the men who come to me. They tell me much, not thinking that I am truly listening to them. They even show me maps—pointing out their businesses, their homes, where they like to eat." Her voice dripped contempt.

And Crusher didn't blame her one iota. It couldn't have been an easy life she had led.

Later, when they were sitting in the lee of a building waiting for a band of drunken revelers to make their way across the street, he asked her another question. "How long have you been on Debennius Six, Grace?"

The slave girl turned to look up at him. Her face was cloaked in deep shadow, but her bright green eyes caught the light of a streetlamp and glittered like distant stars.

Crusher had heard all the rumors about Orion "animal women," how no man could resist them, how they were all heat and allure and violent sexuality. He knew now that the rumors were true. Like a witch out of Terran folklore, Grace had already cast a spell on him.

"My mother was known for breeding fine female stock," she said. The words hurt the commander as if they were weapons. "I was bought as a child, and I have lived most of my life here on the Last Stop to Nowhere."

"It's not *your* last stop," Crusher assured the Orion. "You're free now, Grace, and we're going to take you to a place where you'll be safe. I promise you that."

"Commander . . ." said Tuvok.

Crusher returned his glance. "Yes?"

"It is unwise to make promises you may not be able to keep," the Vulcan advised him solemnly.

The human was about to respond when Grace said, "Your friend is correct, Commander Crusher. We may not even live long enough to get back to your ship. But you are right about one thing . . . I am free now."

Crusher found that his mouth was dry all of a sudden, and decided not to say anything more.

Chapter Sixteen

EVEN AFTER TWO GLASSES OF WINE, Picard found he couldn't sleep. His mind was filled with violent, haunting images: flashes of red and blue, of exploding ships, of murdered people—Melacron, Cordracites, Benniari—all of them floating bloodily in the void.

Had Culunnh been wrong about third-party intervention, after all? Was this simply the logical if tragic progression of relations between two firmly entrenched adversaries?

If only he had heard something from Crusher and Tuvok, he might have had an answer. However, they had yet to report in. In fact, the captain was beginning to wonder if something had happened to them.

Finally, he decided that enough was enough. He crossed the room to the communications cube that sat on an endtable and tapped it. It lit up instantly, filling the place with a gentle blue radiance.

"This is Culunnh," came the Benniari's reedy reply.

"Sorry to disturb you at this hour," said Picard.

"Ah, Captain Picard," said the First Minister, and his voice grew warm and sad at the same time. "It would not be possible for you to disturb me. How may I assist you?" he asked. "Or," and Culunnh sounded more hopeful suddenly, "do you have news to impart?"

Picard sighed before replying. "No news, First Minister, save that I feel I must return to my ship. I appreciate your hospitality, but I have to question if there's anything more I can accomplish here."

"I see." The Benniari's voice was soft . . . resigned.

"I think the wisest course of action," said the captain, "may be for me to brief Starfleet Command on what has taken place here . . . and to advise them to prepare for the worst."

Culunnh made a whistling noise. "I cannot help agreeing with you," he replied, "though I wish it were not so. The Melacronai and Cordracite delegations have alerted me that they will depart in the morning, sooner than I expected. And most of the other diplomats will leave as well, as soon as they realize the Melacron and the Cordracites are gone."

"I am sorry to hear that," Picard said sincerely.

"There will be a formal breaking of fast in the morning for whoever has remained," the Benniari continued. "But at this point, I think there will be so few left that I may be able to host that meal in my quarters."

The captain sighed. "I hope it fills the council chamber," he told the First Minister, though he hadn't the least expectation that his wish would come true.

"Shall I see you off?" asked Culunnh.

"No," said Picard, "that won't be necessary. I've bothered you enough tonight as it is. We will be in touch, however, I assure you." He paused. "I only regret we were unable to be of more help."

"You staved off an armed conflict for several days," the First Minister told him. "As you yourself pointed out, that was an accomplishment. Travel safely, Captain Picard."

"Thank you, First Minister. It has been a genuine honor to work with you." Then something else occurred to him. "Say good-bye to Governor Thul for me, will you? Tell him I enjoyed working with him as well."

"I will do that," Culunnh promised.

Unfortunately, there wasn't much more either of them could say. "Good night," the captain added.

"Good night," came the reply.

With that, the cube went dark. Frowning, Picard tapped his communicator badge. "Picard to Ben Zoma," he said.

A pause. Then, "Ben Zoma here. What can I do for you, Captain?"

"A change of plans. I won't be staying the night here after all," Picard informed him.

"Nothing more for you to accomplish?" asked the first officer.

"Nothing," the captain agreed. "Alert the transporter room, will you? I'm ready when they are."

"Aye, sir. Ben Zoma out."

Picard had time to look around his quarters one last time and wish he were leaving Debennius II a happier man. Then there was a shimmer in the air and he found himself back in the *Stargazer*'s lone transporter room.

• • •

As Crusher watched, Grace slunk out of the shadows and took off, leading the way again.

He and his Vulcan companion followed her through a labyrinth of dark alleys, backstreets and, once, even into a sewer tunnel. Then, as if by magic, they were outside the city limits, on a lonely, unpaved road that wound its way through the hill country.

The commander was thoroughly delighted to leave town. The dirt felt good underneath his boots and the air smelled cleaner. He glanced now and then at Grace, both of them doing their best to keep up with the rapid pace Tuvok was setting for them, and his heart lifted.

They had done what Captain Picard had asked of them. They had identified the elusive third party responsible for the attacks of terrorism in the Cordra and Melacron systems.

Now that the quarry had a name, he could be tracked down and stopped. And they had accomplished this while doing something else exceedingly worthwhile—freeing a woman from a life not fit for a—

"There they are!" came a deep-throated cry.

Crusher turned in time to see blue energy blasts light up the night, striking and pulverizing the stones at their feet. As one, he and Tuvok dove for cover behind some larger rocks.

The commander had imagined that Grace would do the same, lithe and athletic as she was. He thought she would be the least of his troubles. But she continued to stand there in the line of fire, her body taut, her head thrown back in a defiant howl.

"No!" she snarled. "You will not take me back!" Bending, she took hold of a stone and lifted it over her head, ready to hurl it at her attackers in a useless but valiant gesture.

Crusher clenched his jaw and went back out after the slave girl. But before he could get to her, there was a hideous flash of blue light and she crumpled to the ground.

"Grace!" the commander cried out.

She was writhing on the ground, moaning in agony. And what he could see of her abdomen didn't look good.

Anger coursing through him, Crusher raised his weapon and fired. He heard himself shouting something—he didn't know what. But he kept shouting and firing and shouting and firing . . . until Tuvok put his hand on the commander's arm and told him there was no one left to fire at.

Crusher took a deep, shuddering breath and lowered his weapon. Then he went to Grace, dropped down at her side and slipped his hands underneath her, so he could pick her up.

"Hang on," he urged her, even as his eyes told him that her wound would be fatal. "We'll take you to our ship and—"

"Liar," she said, wincing at the pain in her blackened, bloody belly. "I am dying. We Orions know such things. I—" Before she could say any more, she went rigid with a sudden surge of torment.

"Grace . . ." he hissed.

A slender green hand covered with blood reached up to grasp the commander's filthy shirt. The Orion's expression was a defiant one, even now. She bared her teeth as she spoke.

"I . . . die . . . free. . . ." she moaned, her eyes blazing with an inner fire. "Not a slave . . . *free.*"

Then, with a pitiful expiration of breath, Grace's hard-muscled body went limp in his arms.

Crusher gazed helplessly at the Orion, his vision blurring. Damn it, he thought miserably. They had been so close to escaping, all of them. Why did she have to make a stand all by herself? Why couldn't she have gone for cover the way he and Tuvok did?

He knew the answer, though, didn't he? All her life, Grace had been trained to act on instinct—and that was what she had done this time as well. But this time, her instincts had led her astray.

Gently, the commander released the Orion and shut her bright green eyes. Then he stood and turned to the Vulcan, who had been checking on the bastards who had murdered her.

"There were only four of them," Tuvok reported. "Barrh must have split up his henchmen into small groups to improve his chances of finding us."

Crusher gazed at Grace. "We met her, what . . . a couple of hours ago? And yet I feel as if I've lost one of my best friends."

"Commander," said the Vulcan, his voice unusually soft, "do not allow Grace's sacrifice to be wasted. We must hurry before we are again apprehended by Barrh's men."

Crusher blinked to clear his vision. "I hear you," he said.

They would find their captain, he vowed, and tell him of Thul's treachery. War would be averted, and millions would be saved.

And who would ever know how big a part an Orion slave girl had played in it? Who would ever understand how brave she had been?

Only he. And Tuvok.

And what had she gotten for her trouble? Just a small taste of freedom, the commander reflected. But for her, maybe that had been enough.

"Come on," he told the Vulcan.

As Tuvok had advised, Jack Crusher would make sure his friend hadn't died in vain.

The sight of his transporter room was unexpectedly comforting to Picard. However, it didn't make up for the discomforting outcome he had brought back with him.

He had hoped to report another diplomatic success to Starfleet Command; it would have been a nice prelude to a few days of rest and relaxation at Starbase Three with Admiral Ammerman and his family. But it was not to be. The captain bore a message of war, not peace, and the future looked grim for this small sector of space.

Picard nodded his thanks to the ensign who had transported him up. Then he crossed the room, meaning to head for his quarters.

"Cadwallader to Captain Picard," came a summons, stopping the captain in his tracks.

The comm officer's voice, upbeat at the worst of times, was now positively bubbly. Wondering simultaneously what she was doing at her post at this late hour and what had caused her excitement, he replied, "Picard here. What's going on, Ensign?"

"A message for you, sir," said Cadwallader. "It's from Commander Crusher. Ears only, it seems."

The captain's heartbeat sped up. "I'll take it in my ready room."

"Aye, sir," said the comm officer.

A minute later, he emerged from a turbolift compartment onto his bridge. His officers—Ben Zoma in the center seat, the Asmund twins at helm and navigation, and Cadwallader at communications—all turned to him with expressions of relief on their faces.

What's more, Picard understood why. They had been worried about their friend Jack. A message meant that he was still alive.

Without a word, he made his way across the bridge and headed for his ready room. As the doors slid apart for him, he called back to his comm officer. "Patch it through, Cadwallader."

"Acknowledged, sir," she told him.

Circumnavigating his desk, the captain sat down and eagerly faced his monitor. Then he tapped in the command that would play the message for him. As it was a simple audio transmission, the Starfleet insignia remained on the screen throughout.

"This is Commander Crusher," said the second officer's voice. He sounded pleased and weary at the same time. "Sir, we're en route to your position in our Benniari craft. It seems First Minister Culunnh's hunch was right—there *is* a third party behind these attacks. They were instigated by a Thallonian governor . . . a man named Gerrid Thul."

Picard felt a cold like that of the vacuum of space settle in his stomach. "Thul?" he muttered, bewildered.

The Thallonian had seemed so concerned about the situation, so determined to avert a war. However, Crusher didn't sound as though he harbored any doubts—and Tuvok, a Vulcan, would have argued with his conclusion if he had. If they said Thul was responsible for the attacks, they must have discovered proof that it was so.

Thul, the captain repeated inwardly.

He listened as Crusher went into the details of the governor's plot and his motivation. Each word Picard heard served to infuriate him a little more. By the time he heard the last one, his face was crimson with rage and indignation and his hands had clenched into fists.

Thul was fortunate he wasn't on the *Stargazer,* the captain told himself. He was fortunate indeed.

"Cadwallader," Picard barked, getting up from his chair and heading for the exit, "locate Thallonian Governor Gerrid Thul on Debennius Two."

As he strode out onto the bridge, still filled with righteous ire, the ensign was manipulating her controls. She spoke softly into her headset for a moment, listened, then turned to the captain.

"You're not going to like this, sir," she told him. "The Benniari report that Governor Thul left Debennius Two an hour and a half ago."

Picard swore under his breath.

"What's going on?" Ben Zoma wanted to know.

"Our quarry has been here all the time," the captain informed him, "right under our noses. It seems our good friend and ally Governor Thul was behind the attacks."

The first officer's eyes widened. "Thul . . . ?"

"Yes. And now he's disappeared. We have to catch him before he makes the situation worse than it already is."

Ben Zoma thought for a moment. "Sir," he said, "a Thallonian ship leaves a distinctive ion trail . . ."

"Which we can follow," Picard noted crisply. "Quite right, Number One." He turned to Gerda Asmund, his statuesque, blond navigator. "Find that trail for me, Lieutenant."

"Aye, sir," said Asmund.

The captain regarded Idun Asmund, Gerda's twin. "When we find it," he told her, "pursue at full impulse." At least until we leave the planet's gravity well, he reflected.

"Full impulse," the helm officer repeated.

Finally, Picard addressed Cadwallader. "Send the following message to Commander Crusher and Ensign Tuvok," he instructed. "Message received, quarry has departed. We are following the trail, bearing—" He raised an eyebrow as he regarded his navigator.

Gerda Asmund frowned for a moment as she analyzed the sensor data. At last, she looked up. "Bearing three two four mark nine," the lieutenant said with the utmost confidence.

The captain nodded, grateful for the quality of his bridge personnel. It was hard for him to imagine having a more efficient officer in charge of his navigation console.

"Bearing three two four mark nine," he repeated for Cadwallader's benefit. "Make your best speed to intercept. Picard out."

He watched Idun Asmund out of the corner of his eye as she set a course in accordance with the Thallonian's escape route. Like her sister, she was as proficient as they came.

"Course set," the helm officer announced when she was finished.

"Thank you," the captain told them, "one and all."

He took his center seat and trained his eyes on the viewscreen, where the field of stars wheeled by as Idun Asmund brought the *Stargazer* about. Ben Zoma came over to stand at his side.

"That old fox Thul has led us on a merry chase," the first officer noted without any of his characteristic good humor.

Picard nodded. "Yes," he agreed, "that he has. But the hounds are finally on the right trail."

He imagined the Thallonian's vessel centered on his screen, in his phaser sights. Now, the captain added silently, it's just a matter of how fast the old fox can run.

Chapter Seventeen

JACK CRUSHER FINISHED LISTENING to Picard's return message through his Benniari headset. Then he turned to Tuvok, who was seated beside him. "They want us to rendezvous with them," he said.

"Our Benniari vessel cannot match the speed of a Constellation-class starship," the Vulcan observed.

The commander shrugged. "I know. I guess we'll just have to do our best."

Tuvok nodded and tapped in their new heading. The ship came about smoothly under the Vulcan's direction.

Crusher leaned back and unfolded his long legs, which were starting to cramp. There was nothing to do now, he reflected, but activate the warp drive when they escaped the gravity well of Debennius VI—and hope they were in time to be of some help to their captain.

"Commander?" said Tuvok.

Crusher looked at him. "Hmm?"

"I have been spending a great deal of effort reviewing this mission . . ."

The human smiled wanly. "Me too."

"And I have come to two conclusions," the ensign announced. "First, that I was insubordinate to a superior officer. And second, that I was incorrect in my assessment of his methods."

Crusher realized his mouth was agape. He closed it. "You're kidding, right?" And then, before Tuvok could correct him, he added, "Don't say it. Vulcans never kid."

"That is true," Tuvok remarked.

"But how can you say that about my methods?" the human asked. "All I did was manage to get us captured by Barrh's men. As you yourself said, I put us in unnecessary danger."

"Nonetheless," the Vulcan insisted, "we obtained the requisite information and survived to report back to our captain. If we are in time, and it is my sincere hope that we are, we will have averted a catastrophe from which the Kellasian sector might never have recovered."

"But that was all your doing," Crusher insisted. "If you hadn't read the Indarrhi's mind and discovered what Thul was doing, we would still be on square one—or worse."

Tuvok arched an eyebrow. "I would not have had the opportunity to read the Indarrhi's mind, as you put it, if you had not led us to Mendan Abbis. Had we proceeded as I wished, we might still be in The Den drinking what passes there for alcoholic beverages."

The commander couldn't challenge the Vulcan's statement. After all, Tuvok was right.

"Your methods were . . . unorthodox," the ensign allowed. "However, our mission was an unqualified success—and as Surak himself once said, it is illogical to argue with success."

Crusher shrugged. "Surak . . . ?"

"The visionary leader who introduced the philosophy of logic to Vulcan. He was nothing if not practical."

Then something else occurred to the human. "What about Grace?" he asked. "I didn't do her any favors, did I?"

"You took calculated risks," Tuvok conceded. "But you did not force her to take them with you. You simply made the opportunity available to her. I believe she would thank you for that, if she were able to."

Crusher's throat constricted. "Maybe." He peered at his companion. "Anyway, thanks for saying so."

"No thanks are required," the ensign assured him dispassionately. "I am merely stating the obvious."

The commander sighed. "Well, maybe I needed to hear the obvious as stated by a Vulcan."

Tuvok considered the possibility. "Perhaps you did," he said.

In the dark brown depths of the Vulcan's normally implacable gaze, Crusher could have sworn he saw a flicker of warmth. It was gratifying to know that he had helped put it there.

"So," the human said as they streaked toward their rendezvous with the *Stargazer*, "tell me about your kids."

Thul considered his viewscreen, where the Cordracite fleetyard sprawled across several kilometers of orbital space. He wondered if he had ever seen a more lovely sight.

There they were . . . a hundred or more Cordracite vessels, from the powerful Predator Class warships with their sharp and unattractive angles to the quicker, more delicate-looking Racer Class reconnaissance vessels. They hung in space as if they didn't have a care in the world.

The governor savored the moment. He scanned each vessel in turn, deriving pleasure from its vulnerability, delighting in the knowledge that it wouldn't be there much longer.

Finally, he turned his attention to the cavernous drydock facility, where various ships were in the process of being repaired or upgraded or simply maintained. His intelligence reports had told him there were more than two hundred Cordracites manning the station.

And none of them had registered the Thallonian's presence. After all, Thul's ship was outside their rather primitive sensor reach. His intelligence reports had enlightened him in that area as well.

"Activate the magnetic-pulse envelope," he said. "Then move into their sensor range. Full impulse."

"Full impulse, my lord," his helmsman confirmed.

On the viewscreen, the fleetyard gradually loomed larger. The governor smiled. He was enjoying this immensely.

To this point, it was his agents alone who had planted the seeds of chaos in which his empire would take root. Finally, the Thallonian had an opportunity to plant some seeds of his own.

There was something exciting about that, something that appealed to the aggressor in Thul. It was the same instinct that had raised him from his modest origins to the leadership of a large and important colony.

"My lord governor, we have entered the Cordracites' sensor range," his navigator announced crisply.

Thul nodded. Any moment now, he told himself.

Nakso, his comely communications officer, turned to him. "My lord, the Cordracites are hailing us."

Ah, there it was . . . the first challenge. The governor sat up straighter in his chair. "Put it through," he instructed Nakso, "but on an audio channel only, as we discussed."

"Complying, lord," the communications officer responded.

A moment later, the rasping voice of a Cordracite filled Thul's bridge. "Fleetyard Commander Yov to approaching Melacronai vessel. State the nature of your business in our space."

The governor glanced at Nakso again. In accordance with their plan, she made no attempt to respond. After all, they didn't want to puncture the illusion that they were Melacron.

"Maintain speed," said Thul.

The Cordracite commander spoke again. "Our ships are armed and ready to defend themselves, Melacronai vessel. If you come any closer, we will assume hostile intent and fire."

The governor chuckled. "Please do," he whispered.

He knew that the Cordracite was bluffing. Had any of those ships been as "armed and ready" as he pretended, at least some of them would have been deployed already—and of course, they hadn't been.

Thul had caught them totally unaware. It was an exhilarating feeling, one that raised his senses to a fever pitch. And of course, the best part was yet to come.

"Repeat," snapped the Cordracite, and this time there was a hint of urgency evident in his voice, "if you come any closer, we will fire."

The governor could almost smell the terror floating rank and musky off the Cordracites at the drydock facility. "Maintain speed," he said again. He turned to Ubbard, his burly weapons officer. "Range?"

"Momentarily, my lord," came the reply.

Thul eyed the fleetyard. There was still no response, no movement among the ships, though he was sure the Cordracites were scrambling to organize a defense. Unfortunately for them, they would be too late.

"Range," his weapons officer reported.

The governor smiled, anticipating the taste of victory already. "Target weapons," he said.

"Targeting," responded his weapons officer, working at his control panel. He looked up. "Ready, my lord."

Now, Thul thought.

He was about to give Ubbard the order to fire when his navigator spoke up again. "Governor . . . a vessel is approaching."

A vessel? Thul wondered. He turned to Nakso. "Put it on the screen," he told her.

A moment later, their view of the vulnerable Cordracite fleetyard gave way to the image of a single ship. What's more, the governor recognized it—recognized it all too well, in fact.

It was the *Stargazer.*

Cursing under his breath, Thul whirled to face his helmsman. Fortunately, he had taken great care to arm his vessel to the teeth. "Bring us about and prepare for engagement."

The helmsman nodded, already implementing the order with admirable efficiency. "As you wish, my lord."

The governor turned to the forward viewscreen again. Picard would find himself at a considerable disadvantage, he reflected. He hadn't learned very much about the armaments of the *Stargazer,* but what he *had* learned told him the captain didn't stand a chance.

"My lord," said Thul's communications officer, "the Federation vessel is hailing us."

The Thallonian smiled grimly. "Answer their hail and establish a communications link, Nakso."

"As you wish, my lord," came the officer's reply.

Before Thul could draw another breath, he found himself face to face with the image of Jean-Luc Picard on his viewscreen. The human didn't look at all pleased with the situation.

"Captain Picard," the governor said in an affable tone. "What a surprise. I had not expected to see you again so soon. Tell me . . . did you finish the rest of that delicious wine?"

Picard came forward until his face seemed gigantic on the screen, the muscles working in his jaw. "I know what you're up to, Thul," he told the Thallonian in a voice that cracked like a whip. "In fact, I have been apprised of your entire scheme."

The governor felt the blood drain from his face.

"I know about the hired assassins," said the human, "about your grandiose plan to build an empire of your own, about the treason you intended with regard to your Emperor."

Thul absorbed the information. It unsettled him, he had to admit, to know that his intentions had been laid bare. After all, he hadn't been apprised of any security leak.

However, he reminded himself, he still had the upper hand.

"And you are here . . . why?" asked Thul, allowing a note of disdain to color his voice. "Not in an attempt to stop me, I hope."

"That is *precisely* why I am here," Picard confirmed, his resolve evident in his eyes. "The game is over, Governor. Stand down and surrender, or I warn you, I will have no compunction about destroying your vessel."

The Thallonian lifted his chin. "Forgive my ignorance," he said with studied calm, "but I thought your hands were tied. Did you not tell me it was the Benniari alone you were ordered to look out for?"

The human frowned. "Under the circumstances," he answered, "I don't think the Cordracites will object if I save their fleetyard and their base crew from obliteration. Do you?"

Thul chuckled dryly. "I see your prime directive is subject to your convenient interpretation of the circumstances."

"No," said Picard. "It's subject to reason alone—and reason dictates that only a fool would stand by while you do to this fleetyard what you did to that Melacronai research colony."

The Thallonian shook his hairless head. The human had been thorough, hadn't he? "I will miss your mind, Captain, and that's not something I find myself saying very often. It's a shame you and I came down on opposite sides of this conflict. In another life, another set of circumstances, we might have been allies . . . even friends."

The captain shook his head as well—but more firmly. "No, Governor. You and I could not have been friends in any life. You see, I don't tolerate the company of *murderers.*"

Thul was stunned by the boldness of Picard's invective—not to mention the ringing sincerity behind it. For just an instant, hot shame coursed through him . . . but it rapidly became anger.

"All right," he told the captain, doing his best to keep his voice free of emotion. "Have it your way." Then he glanced at his weapons officer again. "Target the *Stargazer,* Ubbard. Weapons to full intensity."

"Aye, sir," came the obedient reply.

The governor turned to Picard, wishing to see the human's face as he gave the order. "All stations . . . fire!"

Abruptly, the *Stargazer* was buffeted by twin blasts of fiery blue energy. Her shields absorbed the brunt of the impact, but Thul knew that they couldn't do that indefinitely.

"Fire again!" he snarled.

But this time, the Federation vessel was on the move, veering to the Thallonian's right. As a result, Thul's azure bursts missed their target and vanished into the vastness of space.

The governor smiled thinly. "All right, then," he said. "I like a game as well as the next fellow."

But he was confident that it wouldn't go on for long.

"Red alert!" Picard ordered, leaning forward in his center seat. "Lieutenant Asmund, evasive maneuvers!"

They wheeled as the red glow of the alert lights filled the bridge. A blue burst of energy glowed for an instant on the viewscreen, but the *Stargazer* managed to avoid the impact this time.

"Shields down twenty-four percent," said Vigo, his face grim as he bent his massive frame over a control panel.

He barely got the words out before another volley struck the ship, sending it lurching dizzily to starboard. It was only the armrests on the captain's chair that kept him in his seat.

"Fire phasers!" he bellowed.

Twin shafts of red fury sped toward the Thallonian vessel. As Picard watched, they slammed savagely into the enemy's shields.

"Direct hit," said Vigo.

But in the same heartbeat, another barrage from the Thallonian sent the *Stargazer* staggering to port. One of the aft consoles blew up, spewing sparks and billows of thick, black smoke across the bridge.

"Report," Picard demanded.

"Shields down fifty-eight percent," the Pandrilite told him, hanging onto his console for all he was worth. He glowered at his monitor, his face bathed in its ruddy glow. "But we barely made a dent in their deflectors, sir. We can't match their firepower."

The captain nodded as Idun Asmund wove her way through an elaborate maneuver, eluding another series of devastating energy discharges.

"Hard to port, Lieutenant Asmund," the captain said. "Mr. Vigo, prepare to fire photon torpedoes on my command."

The *Stargazer* dove to the left under the skillful hands of her helm officer. A moment later, the blue blaze of a Thallonian energy blast passed harmlessly beside them.

The ship was still in the roll as Picard shot a glance at Vigo and cried out, "Now!"

A rapid volley of photon torpedoes struck Thul's vessel dead on, detonating when it hit the Thallonian's deflectors. Picard didn't need his weapons officer's report to know he had made the right choice. He could see how quickly the enemy withdrew in the wake of his assault.

"We made some headway that time," Vigo reported. He grinned at his monitor. "Their shields are down thirty-eight percent . . . and we seem to have taken out one of their weapon ports."

The captain decided to press his advantage. Given the disparity in their weapons systems, Thul wouldn't be expecting it.

"Bear down on them," Picard told Idun Asmund. "Mr. Vigo, ready phasers and torpedoes. Full spread."

"Aye, sir," said the helm officer.

"Aye, sir," said the Pandrilite.

The governor's ship was still looping about in an almost casual manner, her flank very much exposed. The captain's eyes narrowed eagerly as she loomed on his screen.

"Fire!" he barked.

Suddenly, the *Stargazer* hammered her adversary with all the might at her disposal. The Thallonian seemed to recoil from the barrage, ruby-red phaser beams ripping hungrily at her shields, photon torpedoes exploding around her to spectacular effect.

If Picard was going to win this battle, he told himself, he would do it now or not at all. "Fire!" he barked.

Again, Vigo unleashed a hail of phasers and torpedoes, tearing apart the enemy's defenses with overwhelming efficiency. The Thallonian tried to escape, but to no avail. No matter how Thul's ship tried to elude her, Idun clung to it like a predator worrying her prey.

One more volley, the captain thought, and it would all be over. One more volley and the enemy vessel would be crippled.

"Fire again!" he told his weapons officer.

But no sooner had the words left his mouth than the Thallonian turned the tables. Instead of trying to shake his pursuer, he did the last thing Picard had anticipated . . . he came about and fired back.

All the captain saw was a blue-white burst of brilliance on his viewscreen. Then he was catapulted out of his chair like an ancient cannonball. The next thing he knew, he was pulling himself up off the deck, a distinct taste of blood in his mouth.

He looked about—and didn't like what he saw. The *Stargazer*'s bridge had been transformed into a scene out of hell. Control consoles blazed and smoke gathered in dark clouds under the low ceiling. All around Picard, his officers were struggling to get to their feet, trying to shake off the bludgeoning effects of the Thallonian's counterattack.

"Casualties on decks six, seven, ten and eleven," Ben Zoma bellowed, waving smoke away so he could see one of the aft consoles.

"We've lost weapons," Vigo announced sharply, wiping some blood from his forehead with the back of his hand. "Shields as well."

"Propulsion and helm control are offline," Idun observed grimly.

"So is navigation," Gerda added.

The captain turned to the forward viewscreen. Through the thick, acrid smoke, he could make out Thul's ship. She seemed to be hanging in space, her portals dark.

"What about the Thallonian?" he inquired as he made his way back to his center seat.

"Looks like he's in bad shape too," Ben Zoma reported, checking his sensor readings. "No shields, no weapons, no propulsion . . ." He turned to Picard. "That killer's in the same boat we are."

The captain grunted at the irony—not that he wasn't grateful for it. "Picard to engineering."

"Aye, sir?" came Simenon's response.

"How does it look down there?" he asked the Gnalish.

"Like we've been turned inside out," came the answer. "I've got half my people working on restoring propulsion and the other half on the EPS system . . . unless, of course, you've got a better idea."

"No," Picard sighed. "Can you tell me how long it will be before the shields are restored?"

"A couple of hours?" the engineer ventured.

"Make it thirty minutes," the captain told him. He could hear Simenon hiss a curse. "Picard out."

Next, he turned to Cadwallader. Her strawberry-blond hair was in disarray, but outside of that she looked all right.

"Hail the Thallonian," he told her.

She nodded. "Aye, sir."

A moment later, the ruddy face of Gerrid Thul graced the viewscreen, replacing the sight of his crippled ship. Picard took the opportunity to survey the enemy's bridge. There was damage there, though the Federation vessel had suffered worse.

"Ready to surrender, Captain?" asked the governor. He was grinning like a damned jackal.

Picard feigned surprise. "That's odd," he retorted. "I was about to ask the same thing of you."

Thul glanced at his bridge and shrugged. "A small setback, I assure you. In the long run, it won't help you a bit."

"We will see," said the captain, "won't we?"

The governor's smile faded. A moment later, he severed contact. Once more, the image of his damaged ship filled the viewscreen.

Picard turned to Ben Zoma again. "We know so little about Thallonian technology," he said ruefully. "If only I had some idea of how quickly they can effect repairs . . ."

His first officer grunted. "I know how long it's going to take *us*." He looked at the viewscreen less than optimistically. "Of the two of us, sir, I would put my money on the Thallonians."

It wasn't what the captain had wanted to hear.

Chapter Eighteen

THUL SAT BACK IN HIS CHAIR and tried to control his anger. "You're certain?" he asked his sensor officer.

"Quite certain, my lord," said the Thallonian. "They are just as helpless as we are."

The governor eyed the *Stargazer,* which was hanging in the void like a crippled bird. Without shields, she was utterly defenseless. One good energy barrage would destroy her.

But the Thallonian vessel couldn't muster an energy barrage. With its weapons systems offline, it couldn't muster a single shot.

"Make the weapons systems operational!" he demanded of Ubbard.

"Yes, my lord," said the weapons officer, placating him as best he could. "As soon as possible, my lord."

The governor scowled. He didn't want obeisance. For the love of the Twelve, he wanted *results.*

"Governor," said his sensor officer, "another ship has entered the vicinity of the fleetyard."

Thul looked at him, trying to absorb the unexpected information. "A . . . Cordracite ship?" he wondered.

That could prove disastrous, the governor reflected. To think he had had the entire fleetyard at his mercy not so long ago . . . and now he was worrying about a single vessel!

"No, my lord," said the sensor officer, scrutinizing his monitors. "It appears to be a Durikkan vessel. But its commander identifies himself as Mendan Abbis . . . a Thallonian."

Thul's brow creased. Mendan . . . ?

What was the boy doing there? Certainly, he had known of the governor's plan to attack the fleetyard, since Thul had held nothing back from him. However, they had made no plans to rendezvous here.

The governor stroked his chin. "Answer the vessel's hail, Nakso. And establish a visual link."

"Yes, my lord," came the woman's response.

Abruptly, the image on the viewscreen changed. Thul found he was no longer looking at the crippled *Stargazer,* but rather the familiar visage of his bastard son.

"Why are you here?" the governor asked, intensely aware of the questions Mendan's presence would raise among his command staff.

"Why?" the boy echoed, smiling a thin smile. "I've been informed that you lied to me." His voice was strangely cold, strangely distant.

"What?" Thul couldn't believe what he had heard. "Lied . . . ?" He glanced at the faces of his bridge officers, who looked stunned. After all, they had never seen their lord receive such an affront.

Mendan's eyes narrowed. "I encountered some Starfleet officers on Debennius Six," he said. "They knew everything . . . and I mean *everything* . . . though I still have no idea how."

The governor felt the scrutiny of Kaavin, Ubbard, and the others. His face flushed. "This is neither the time nor the place for this discussion," he told his son.

"I beg to differ," Mendan replied. "These Starfleet people . . . they said you had no intention of making me heir to your new empire, Father." He leaned forward in his seat. "They told me that once you had gotten what you wanted, you were going to kill me—that you wanted a son of noble lineage, not some poor, stupid bastard."

The boy fairly spat out the word, making Thul feel as though a knife had been twisted into his gut. And now his officers were exchanging wide-eyed glances, putting the pieces together for themselves.

But then, they would have found out his intentions eventually, the governor told himself. If it came a little sooner, what difference did it make? None at all, Thul reflected.

More importantly, Mendan's vessel was well-armed for its size, and the governor's ship was an easy target at the moment. If the boy acted out of anger and resentment, without thinking . . .

Thul shook his head. "No, Mendan," he said, hoping his sincerity would come through in his voice, "it's not true. I don't know what these Starfleeters told you, but they are the liars—not I."

He searched his son's face, to see if his protest had had any effect. But the hardness in Mendan didn't seem to have gone away.

The governor swallowed away a dryness in his throat. "I swear on my life," he said. "I could never betray my own offspring."

Still the boy remained silent, inscrutable.

"You have earned your place at my side," Thul assured him. "More than earned it. You know I will not live forever. Who better to guide my empire after I am gone than the only son of my flesh?"

Mendan continued to stare at him—and for the space of a heartbeat, the governor was certain that his bastard would destroy him after all. Then, finally, the boy nodded.

"I believe you," he told his father in a more animated voice. "In fact, I never doubted you for a moment."

Thul's eyes narrowed. "Then why . . . ?"

"Why did I tell you all this?" asked Mendan. He smiled, and for just a moment, the governor thought he saw the child he had shunned and neglected shining through the eyes of the adult. "Because I wanted to hear the truth from your own mouth, Father."

The governor was relieved, to say the least. "And now you've heard it," he told his son. "The truth entire."

"I thank you," said Mendan. "But there's another reason I wanted to tell you about the Starfleet officers, Father. You see, I need to make amends—and I wanted you to understand why."

Thul tilted his head. "Amends . . . ?"

The bastard frowned. "These Starfleet people—they were able to surprise me, to get themselves free and . . ." He paused. "And kill my friend Wyl. Then they escaped and warned this starship." He jerked a thumb over his shoulder to indicate the *Stargazer.*

The governor grunted. He was beginning to understand why Picard had tracked him there.

"You would have arrived here unopposed if it weren't for me," said Mendan. "You would have been watching this shipyard burn by now. As it is, the Starfleet beasts were able to stop you." His mouth twisted with what was clearly a thirst for revenge. "But now they're helpless, unable to defend themselves. This is my chance to even the score."

"Abbis's ship is coming about," Kaavin announced. "It is approaching the Federation vessel." She looked at the governor, clearly uneasy with this turn of events.

He's going to attack it, Thul realized numbly.

"My lord," said Kaavin, "it is inadvisable for our . . . ally to fire on the enemy ship, even in its crippled state. He will need to let his shields lapse in order to power an effective disruptor burst, and the Federation vessel may still have some tactical capability of which we are unaware."

They hadn't severed contact with Mendan, so he had heard Kaavin's warning. But it didn't seem to faze him—far from it. The reckless grin that was so sickeningly familiar to the governor spread across the youth's face.

"I'll take my chances," he chuckled.

"No!" Thul was out of his seat and striding in the direction of the screen, as if his son were standing there on the bridge and could be stopped by physical means. "Please," he counseled, "there is no need for haste, Mendan. At least take some time to probe the enemy before you fire on her."

The younger man turned his attention to his control panel. "I'm targeting her now," he announced.

"Mendan!" Thul barked, a drop of cold sweat making its way down the length of his spine. "I know your worth. I know your courage. You do not have to demonstrate it anymore . . . not to *me*."

His son's laughter had an unnerving strain of bitterness in it. "Perhaps not to you, Father. But I allowed those Starfleet officers to slip through my fingers and Wyl is dead as a result. That leaves me with a need to prove something to *myself*."

"Damn your stubbornness!" the governor roared. He had a bad feeling about this. "Listen to me, Mendan! You have *time!*"

But his son wasn't heeding his warning. He was working feverishly at his control console, determined to gather all the power his tiny vessel could bring to bear.

Suddenly, Mendan looked up, his eyes alight with anticipation. "I hope you enjoy this, Father. I know *I* will."

Picard eyed the Durikkan vessel that had appeared scant minutes earlier and established contact with the Thallonian. "Anything yet?" he asked.

"No, sir," Cadwallader said. "However they've protected their communication, I can't seem to break through."

The captain scowled, wary of the newcomer. "And the Durikkan still won't answer our hails?"

"That's correct," the communications officer responded.

Picard swore beneath his breath. "Keep trying," he told Cadwallader. Angrily, he thumbed a control. "Engineering, this is the captain. We may need those shields in a matter of moments."

"I wish I could give them to you," the Gnalish answered, his voice drenched with frustration. "Unfortunately, sir, we're not even close."

"Then what about weapons?" asked the captain. "Would a single port be too much to ask?"

"I'll see what I can do," Simenon promised dryly.

"Sir," said Ben Zoma, who was sitting at one of the peripheral stations, "the Durikkan is coming about."

Picard regarded the viewscreen again. As his first officer had warned him, the newcomer was indeed turning away from the Thallonian vessel . . . and pointing its bow at the *Stargazer.*

"Open a channel," the captain told Cadwallader, not knowing what other option to exercise.

"Aye, sir," she answered. "Channel open."

"Durikkan vessel," Picard snapped, "this is Captain Jean-Luc Picard of the Federation starship *Stargazer.*"

The smaller vessel began to close in.

"State your purpose here," the captain demanded.

Cadwallader shook her head. "Still no response, sir."

"Captain," said Gerda Asmund, duranium in her voice, "the Durikkan is dropping her shields and directing all power to her weapons."

Picard bit his lip. The *Stargazer* had no protection. One good barrage would split her end to end like a walnut in a nutcracker.

"Mr. Simenon," he said in a chill voice, "if I don't get a functional weapons port very, very soon, all of this will be academic."

"We can't work any faster, Captain," the engineer replied, his voice high and strained.

"You'll have to," Picard told him.

But even as he uttered the words, he already suspected that it was too late. Modestly equipped, the Durikkan would have been no threat under normal conditions. Given the situation, however, the *Stargazer* was little more than the proverbial sitting duck.

Inexorably, the enemy approached.

Picard realized that his hands were clenched into fists and relaxed them by force of will. This was a hell of a way to go down, he told himself, a hell of a way to perish. It was one thing to succumb in the heat of battle against a superior adversary, defending a fleet of innocents from destruction. But to bow to this little ship, a vessel a fraction the size and sophistication of the *Stargazer . . . ?*

He didn't even know who was at the controls. An ally of Thul? A rogue? A mercenary? He would never find out, would he?

And it irritated him.

"Captain!" Gerda Asmund's athletic body was taut as she turned suddenly in her seat, her eyes ablaze with excitement.

"What is it?" he asked.

"There's a vessel approaching!" she told him. "A Benniari vessel!"

Picard knew instantly what it meant. "Jack," he breathed. "And Tuvok." They had followed the ion trail, albeit more slowly than the *Stargazer*—but the important thing was that they were *there.*

"Sir," said Ben Zoma, "the Benniari vessel is powering up *her* weapons!" The first officer paused. "She's firing, Captain!"

Picard studied the viewscreen, where the Durikkan was so close it seemed it would ram itself down their throats at any moment. But before it could send a volley at the *Stargazer,* the Benniari ship sliced into the picture and unleashed an energy barrage of its own.

Caught by surprise, the Durikkan had no time to put her shields up. She had no time to do anything but take the full impact of the other vessel's assault. For a moment, the Durikkan heeled under the force of it and glowed with an eerie blue fire.

Then her warp engine tore itself into atomic particles in a savage fit of white-hot splendor.

Thul stood there in front of his center seat, refusing to believe the evidence of his eyes, denying what he had witnessed with every shred of strength in his body. Mendan, he thought. My son . . .

My son is *dead.*

Feverish with rage, robbed of his ability to reason, he staggered over to his weapons officer. "Fire!" he bellowed at the top of his lungs. "Destroy the *Stargazer!* Destroy Picard!"

Ubbard looked up at him helplessly. "My lord, our weapons are still offline. We are incapable of firing."

"No!" cried Thul, slamming his fist down on the weapons console. "You will fire, do you hear me? You will annihilate Picard and his crew!"

Ubbard held his hands up, palms exposed. "My lord, I—"

Before the governor knew what was happening, a blast of blue energy struck the officer and he went flying backward out of his seat. When he landed, there was a smoking hole where his chest had been.

And Thul's pistol was in his hand, still hot from use.

He rounded on the officer who sat at the next console. "You!" he thundered, pointing his hand weapon in the Thallonian's face. "Fire the weapons! Do it now, damn you!"

The officer gaped at the pistol, stricken with fear. He moved his mouth, but nothing came out. Worst of all, he didn't move a muscle to comply with his governor's command.

Abruptly, he too was driven out of his seat by a dark blue beam. And like his comrade before him, his chest had become a blackened ruin.

Thul whirled and saw the wide-eyed expressions of the others. They were backing off from their consoles, hands held in front of them, begging for their lives. But not a single one of them offered to blow the *Stargazer* out of space for him.

What kind of bridge officers were they? he wondered wildly. Why could none of them carry out a simple command?

He would have to punish them as he had punished the first two. He would have to hammer them with one crushing energy beam after another until they remembered who was in command of this vessel.

Maybe then he would get some—

"Thul!" said a voice, taut with urgency.

It wasn't Thallonian, but there was something familiar about it nonetheless. The governor turned to find out who had had the gall to call his name and saw Picard standing in front of him.

Picard! he seethed.

But before he could aim his disruptor pistol, before he could do anything at all, he felt something smash him in the face. As he stumbled backward, it occurred to him that his weapon had slipped from his fingers.

Then his head struck something and consciousness flickered. When his senses stabilized again, he saw that he was slumped on the deck at the base of a control console, the taste of blood strong in his mouth.

Thul spat it out, grabbed the edge of the console, and pulled himself up. He had to fight back, he told himself. He had to regain his ship and get his revenge on the bloody, interfering human.

Suddenly, the object of his hatred loomed in front of him again, his eyes hard and determined. "Don't move," said Picard, the governor's pistol clenched firmly in his right hand.

He wasn't alone, either. Four of his security people had beamed over with him and were pointing their weapons at Thul's surviving officers.

A howl of pain and fury erupted from the Thallonian's throat. "My son!" he grated at Picard, his fingers opening and closing as if of their own volition. "You murdered my son!"

"He attacked my ship," the human told him, his tone flat and expressionless, his eyes colder than Thul had ever seen them. "My people had no choice but to fire back at him."

"You lie!" the governor shrieked, and flung himself at Picard.

But the human was too quick for him. He sidestepped Thul's lunge and let him crash to the deck. Once again, the Thallonian found a console to latch onto and dragged himself to his feet.

"You think you've won," he told Picard. "You think you've heard the last of me. But you haven't."

The human didn't try to silence Thul. He just frowned and let the governor go on.

"Remember this day," Thul raged at him, wiping bloody spittle from his mouth as he eyed each Starfleet officer in turn. "Remember my promise, damn you. One day, I will have my revenge on you, Picard—you and your entire Federation!"

He was still shrieking, still cursing the captain and everything he stood for, as the human officers wrestled him away.

Chapter Nineteen

PICARD AND BEN ZOMA were sitting in their customary seats on the podium when Cabrid Culunnh took his place at the lectern.

For days, the captain had been trying to convince the intrasector congress to maintain order, to observe decorum. Yet now, when every delegate and observer in the place made a clamor that shivered the Council Chamber to its foundation, Picard was far from displeased.

In fact, he was quite happy about it. After all, the delegates weren't bickering or threatening or accusing each other, as they had in the past. They were unanimously cheering the Benniari First Minister, who had cajoled and prodded and warned them into postponing a war.

By making them wait, by keeping the sparks of hatred from becoming a conflagration, he had bought time for his Federation allies. As it turned out, it was all the time they had needed.

The captain would not have wagered on this outcome when he last left the Council Chamber. And yet, here it was—a phoenix peace, risen from the ashes of acrimony and discord and suspicion.

"My fellow Kellasians," Culunnh said in a soft, breathy voice, barely audible over the roar of accolades, "please . . . if I may . . . I would like to say a few words to you."

Little by little, the applause died down. Finally, it was quiet enough for the First Minister to be heard. He chirped lightheartedly, his medallion gleaming in the filtered sunlight.

"You are much too kind," he told the assembly, "but I am an old man and I will take my recognition where I can get it."

Again, the congress broke out into a tumult of praise for Culunnh.

And again, he had to wait until it faded before he could speak.

"We were duped," he said, "all of us in equal measure. We were set upon each other like ravening animals, pawns of a stone-hearted power seeker . . . a Thallonian who will find it a lot more difficult to seek power in the imperial prison he now calls his home."

Though the First Minister hadn't mentioned Thul by name, everyone knew whom he meant. The reference was met with a wave of hoots and catcalls and other assorted sounds of derision.

"What's more, he came close to accomplishing his objective," Culunnh went on. "Perilously close. He almost had the war of devastation that he sought." He turned to Picard. "Fortunately for us, he underestimated our friends on the Federation starship *Stargazer.*"

By then, every being in the congress had heard the story. At once, they rose to their feet or whatever analogous appendages they stood on and raised a thunder that exceeded what had come before. It was a staggering spectacle, a stunning tribute.

Picard turned red in the face. Despite his embarrassment, the First Minister beckoned for the captain to take the lectern.

"Gilaad," the captain told his first officer, "I don't know if it is such a good idea for me to go up there. They're liable to tear me limb from limb."

"Don't worry, sir," Ben Zoma chuckled in his ear. "I'll bring your remains back to the ship."

Picard turned to him. "How thoughtful of you."

"I try to please," said the first officer. "Besides, I've always wanted to be *Captain* Ben Zoma."

Picard grunted. "I suspected as much."

Taking a deep breath, he stood and pulled down on the front of his tunic. Then he confronted the members of the Kellasian Congress with all the dignity and humility he could muster, and he tried not to think about how much his executive officer was enjoying his discomfort.

Gradually, as the captain stood there, the applause gave way to a respectful silence. Picard cleared his throat.

"I accept your gratitude," he said, "on behalf of all those under my command who helped to stop Gerrid Thul and stymie his grand ambition. Prominent among them were Commander Jack Crusher, my second officer, and Ensign Tuvok, on loan to us from the starship *Wyoming.*"

Again, cheers erupted from hundreds of alien throats. And again, they died down in time.

"However," the captain continued, "I am told—and I must take my colleagues' word for it, because I was not there—there was another who played a critical role in this effort . . . someone who had nothing to do with the Federation or the Melacron or the Cordracites, yet contributed nothing less than her life to seeing peace restored to them."

He paused, noting the intrigue expressed in the faces of his audience, and recalled what Crusher and Tuvok had told him of this person. "Her name," he said with due regard, "was Grace . . ."

Bin Nedrach was thirsty.

After all, the sun was hot on Melacron II. And as good as its rays felt on one's naked skin, they had a tendency to dry one out.

Fortunately, there was no shortage of beverages on Melacron II—especially for a man with latinum. And thanks to his recent labors, Bin Nedrach possessed a great deal of latinum.

Suddenly, he felt a band of cool shadow cross his chest. "Ah," he said, "you're just in time. I was getting thirsty."

It was no secret that Sulkoh Island had the most attractive female attendants on the planet, if not in the entire Melacron system. In the last couple of days, Bin Nedrach had discovered that they were alert as well. Whenever he even thought of needing a drink or a warm-oil rubdown, they were there at his side.

It was almost as if they were mindreaders, like that Indarrhi who had dogged Mendan Abbis's tracks. He shuddered at the memory. From now on, he vowed, he would steer clear of mindreaders.

"I'll have another Sulkoh Sunset," he said.

"I beg to differ with you," a decidedly masculine, decidedly *un*-Melacronai voice responded.

In a heartbeat, Bin Nedrach was on his feet, assessing his situation, deciding which of the many unarmed combat maneuvers that he had mastered would allow him to escape his predicament. Unfortunately, none of them seemed to fit the bill.

"Go ahead," said a human Starfleet officer, one of four who stood with their hand weapons trained on the assassin. "Try to get away. This phaser may only be set for stun, but it's got a kick like a Missouri mule."

"If I were you," said the only Vulcan in the group—the one who had roused Bin Nedrach in the first place—"I would surrender. My colleague's assessment is as accurate as it is colorful."

"Don't badger him, Tuvok," said the human. "He's a grown assassin. Let him make up his own mind."

"Very well," the Vulcan replied with an air of resignation. "You *are* the ranking officer here."

Bin Nedrach glanced about. To his back was the pool, to his left the featureless, white wall of the indoor recreation center. Neither direction was an option. That left the areas directly in front and to the right of him, both of which were blocked off by the Starfleet people.

The Melacron knew what would happen to him if he were put on trial. The G'aha of Laws and Enforcements had been an exceedingly popular figure—and Bin Nedrach had cut the fellow down while he was inspecting an Inseeing scarf. Without question, he would receive the maximum penalty.

Call me evil, he had mused at the time. And they would.

Anything was better than a lifetime spent in a Melacronai penal colony, the Melacron told himself. Avoiding such a fate was worth any risk, any effort, any amount of pain.

"Well?" asked the human, the muscles working in his temples. "What's it going to be?"

Taking a deep breath, Bin Nedrach lashed out with his bare foot and knocked the weapon out of the officer's hand. Then the Melacron pushed past him and tried to make a break for it.

He didn't make it.

Picard was sitting at the desk in his ready room, going over one of a great many repair reports filed by Phigus Simenon, when he heard a chime. Looking up from his work, he said, "Come."

A moment later, the doors to the room slid aside with a hiss, revealing Jack Crusher and Ensign Tuvok. They entered one after the other and crossed the room.

"You asked to see us, sir?" said the commander, when both he and the Vulcan were standing before the captain.

"Indeed," said Picard. He sat back in his chair and smiled. "I believe congratulations are in order. Your good work saved the lives of everyone at the fleetyard, not to mention the millions who likely would have perished if the Cordracites and the Melacron had gone to war. What's more, you did an admirable job working with local law enforcement agencies to apprehend the assassins we were able to identify."

Tuvok inclined his head ever so slightly. "Thank you, Captain."

"But it was all in a day's work," Crusher said dutifully. He glanced at the ensign, his expression suddenly becoming sterner and more severe. "Figuratively speaking, of course."

Tuvok glanced back, perhaps just a touch less deadpan than when Picard had seen him last. "Of course."

Clearly, thought the captain, the two men had developed something more than a working relationship. It pleased him to see it. But then, it was the rare sentient being who couldn't get along with Jack Crusher.

Picard was also glad to see how much more comfortable the Vulcan looked on the *Stargazer.* Tuvok was a fine officer. It would be very much to Starfleet's advantage if he were to stay on this time.

"Apparently," he told the ensign, "undercover work agrees with you. I'm sure Captain Broadnax will be glad to hear that."

The Vulcan frowned. "Actually, sir, I believe I am more effective serving on a vessel than off it. However, if I am again required to go undercover, I am certain this experience will serve me well."

The captain nodded, still smiling. "No doubt."

Tuvok cast a sidelong look at Crusher—the kind of look that might be meant to dissuade someone from revealing something. If that was what it was, it seemed to work. The commander took a deep breath, but ultimately kept his mouth shut.

"That will be all," Picard told them. "You're dismissed, gentlemen."

Crusher nodded. "Thank you, sir."

And with that, the two of them turned and departed, leaving the captain curious as to what their conversation might be once they were by themselves in the nearest turbolift.

Tuvok waited until the lift doors closed in front of him. Then he turned to Jack Crusher.

"I am grateful," he said, "that you refrained from describing to the captain our misadventure in The House of Comfort."

The commander shrugged. "It didn't seem necessary."

"Though," the Vulcan went on, "it no doubt would have made for a very humorous story, by human standards."

"A *very* humorous story," Crusher agreed. He glanced at Tuvok. "Are you going to tell your wife about it?"

The Vulcan sighed. "I vowed to share everything with T'pel when she and I were linked in marriage. I cannot make an exception . . . as dearly as I would like to."

The human grunted. "Me either."

Tuvok nodded approvingly. As it turned out, he and Crusher had much in common after all.

For a moment, they stood there in companionable silence. Finally, the commander broke it.

"You know," he said, "you took quite a chance when we were Abbis's prisoners back on Debennius Six."

The Vulcan cocked an eyebrow. "Explain."

"That story you told about the treachery Thul intended and how we had discovered proof of it . . . Abbis could have had his Indarrhi pal read my emotions to see if you were telling the truth. And even if he didn't, he could have chosen to discount your claims about Thul and simply told his father that Starfleet was onto them."

"Thereby endangering not only our mission, but the *Stargazer* as well," the Vulcan finished. "I can see where an individual of your species might reach that conclusion."

"Let's not bring species into this," Crusher told him.

"However," Tuvok went on, undaunted, "what you fail to consider is that we, our mission, and indeed this entire *sector* were already very much at risk. It was only by applying native ingenuity that we were able to remove ourselves from Abbis's grasp and eventually turn failure into success."

The commander frowned and wagged a finger at him. "Uh-uh. You don't get off that easily. You still had no idea how Abbis would react."

"On the contrary," said the Vulcan, "I had a very good idea. Remember, I had previously experienced mental contact with the Indarrhi—a link which permitted me to search his mind even as he was searching mine. As a result, I had come to know Mendan Abbis through his associate's impressions of him, and therefore could predict with reasonable certainty how our captor would react to my ploy."

Crusher sighed and shook his head. "I should know better by now than to argue with a Vulcan."

Tuvok shot a look at him. "For once," he commented, "I find myself agreeing with you."

The commander smiled. "I won't tell anyone if you won't."

The Vulcan maintained his composure, despite an inexplicable impulse to smile. "It is a deal," he said.

Jack Crusher basked in the grins of his beautiful bride and his impish baby son. "And since our rendezvous with the *Wyoming* was so close to Earth," he continued, "I saw my chance and booked some time on subspace."

"You couldn't have been the only one," said Beverly.

"That's true," the commander agreed. "But rank has its privileges." He shrugged. "Actually, I didn't take any more time than anyone else with family in the sector—I just went first."

His wife chuckled and shook her head. "You're always thinking of others, aren't you?"

"Right now," Crusher told her, "I'm thinking about you. And about Wes. And about how much I miss the two of you."

Beverly sighed. "Any prospect of shore leave?"

"None right now," he said. "But you never know. Just keep hoping." He paused. "Honey, there's something I want to tell you about."

She must have sensed something in his voice, because her eyes narrowed. "Is something wrong, Jack?"

"No," the commander said, "nothing like that."

Then he brought her up to date about his mission on Debennius VI. He started with the explosive diplomatic situation the *Stargazer* had sailed into and proceeded through the beginning of his adventures with Tuvok.

"Sounds dangerous," Beverly said, clearly none too thrilled about the idea but resigned not to say too much about it.

"Maybe a little," Crusher conceded. "But the worst part . . ."

She looked at him. "Yes?"

"Was at a place called The House of Comfort." And he went on to tell his wife all about it.

The commander wasn't sure what reaction he expected—but it wasn't the one he got. When he had finished with his description of what happened in the bathhouse, Beverly broke into peals of laughter—so much so that little Wesley gaped at her, startled.

"Jack," she exclaimed when she was able to catch her breath, "that's the funniest thing I've ever heard!"

"It is?" he blurted. "I mean . . . of course it is. Absolutely. That's why I . . . er, wanted to share it with you, because it's so funny. And you're not . . . upset or anything, right?"

His wife looked at him askance. "You mean . . . am I angry that my husband was willing to go to any length in that place to get the information he needed?" She thought about it for a moment. "Yes, I guess I *am* a little angry. But you were doing your duty, Jack."

"That's right," Crusher confirmed.

"And for a very worthy cause."

"Right again," he told her.

"And if our positions were reversed and I had to do what you did, you would understand too . . . wouldn't you?"

The commander was about to agree again when he realized just what he would be agreeing to. Suddenly, he didn't know what to say.

Again, Beverly broke into laughter—and this time, Wesley laughed along with her. "Honestly, Jack, you must be the most predictable man in all of Starfleet. Don't you know when I'm kidding you?"

Crusher blushed. "Um . . . sometimes?"

"But what happened after that?" his wife asked. She stifled a snicker. "After you and Tuvok got out of the bath, I mean."

He told her the rest—about the fight in the dance hall and their ensuing imprisonment at the hands of Mendan Abbis. About Grace, whose violent end saddened her. About his warning to the captain, and about his timely arrival with Tuvok at the Cordracite fleetyard.

Beverly smiled. "Then the good guys won?"

The commander nodded. "This time."

"And what about Thul?" she asked.

He shrugged. "As I understand it, the Thallonians are pretty intolerant when it comes to treachery. No doubt, Thul will be placed in prison for a long time. Maybe the rest of his life."

Beverly sighed. "Wherever he is, I hope he never gets a chance to carry out that revenge he was ranting about."

Crusher shook his head. "Don't worry, honey. I think we can be pretty sure we've heard the last of Gerrid Thul."

Epilogue

In his nightmare, he was once again standing on the bridge of his ship, watching the hideous, blinding flash of his son's vessel as it reduced itself to subatomic particles on his viewscreen.

"Thul!" someone said.

He looked about at the faces of his officers. They stared back at him, uncertainty etched in their every feature.

"Thul!" someone said again, louder this time.

But the summons hadn't come from anyone on his bridge. He turned to his viewscreen. There was no one there either.

"Thul!" someone growled.

With a shock, the governor bolted upright—and saw that he wasn't on his ship after all. He was on the hard, uncomfortable pallet that had served him as a bed for the last several months, ever since he became an inmate of the Reggana City Imperial Prison.

Rubbing sleep from his eyes, willing his heart to slow down, Thul swung his legs over the side of the pallet and stared through the translucent energy barrier that separated him from the corridor beyond. There was a guard standing there . . . and someone else. Someone wearing a dark, hooded robe.

Someone whose bearing was vaguely familiar.

"A visitor," the guard spat.

A feminine hand emerged from the robe and deposited something in the guard's big hand. Quickly, he stuffed it into a pocket of his tunic, but not before Thul saw the distinctive glint of latinum. Then, with a glance at the prisoner, the guard walked away.

Thul was alone with his guest. "Who are you?" he asked as he approached the energy barrier—though he had a feeling he knew the answer.

"It is I," the hooded one said in a soft whisper. Pulling back her hood, she revealed herself as Mella Cwan.

The prisoner had forgotten how plain the emperor's sister was, how flatly unappealing. Nonetheless, he managed to put all that aside and smile his most fervent smile.

"My lady," he said breathlessly.

Mella Cwan smiled back at him, affection and sadness illuminating her eyes. "Lord Governor . . . how it grieves me to see you like this."

No more than it grieves me, Thul thought bitterly. But what he said was, "Please, my lady . . . I am no longer a governor; that exalted position has been stripped from me. I am once again General Thul. It is the penalty for ambition."

Her brow knotted over the bridge of her nose. "And a long penalty it is," she replied. "A lifetime . . ."

"Is very long," he agreed. "But the worst part of my imprisonment is not its length in years, but the knowledge that I will never share any of them with you—as I surely would have if my plan had borne fruit." He heaved a heavy sigh. "If only your brother had not been so stubborn when I came to him in his throne chamber . . ."

"He *is* stubborn," Mella Cwan agreed. "But he is also the emperor. No one can oppose his wishes."

That wasn't what Thul wanted to hear. "True, you can't oppose them," he began, "but surely, there is a way for you—*us*—to have our hearts' desire short of actual defiance."

The emperor's sister tilted her head, a hint of wariness in her eyes. "What do you mean?"

Careful, he thought. You won't get another chance like this one. "Why," he said, "only that not every flower flourishes in sunlight. Some live in shadows, and smell that much more sweetly for it."

Her dark eyes widened as understanding dawned. "You speak of an illicit affair? Between you and me?"

Thul smiled sadly. "Only in the absence of the marriage I would have preferred. But if that is denied to us, must we give up everything? Do we not deserve some small measure of happiness?"

Mella Cwan drew a shuddering breath as she considered it. "You ask much, General."

"I *dare* much," the prisoner said, coming within a hair's breadth of the energy barrier to prove it.

"If we were ever exposed . . ." she said, her voice trailing off into the grimmer realms of imagination.

He held up a hand. "Don't think about that," he insisted. "Think about us, my dear. Think about our being together at last."

The Emperor's sister frowned. "You're right," she told him. "I cannot live in fear. I must think about my happiness."

"Exactly," Thul replied.

"I must think about the two of us."

"Yes," he said encouragingly.

Mella Cwan's expression became resolute. "I must think of a way to free you," she decided.

He nodded. "I would never have asked it of you, my lady . . . but clearly, it is the only way."

She bit her lip in a very unimperial way. "It will take time. I have never done anything like this before."

"I could make suggestions," Thul offered. "I know people who can arrange almost anything for latinum."

The emperor's sister smiled. "Latinum will not be a problem." She reached a hand lovingly toward his face, almost touching the energy barrier herself. "As long as I know that when you get out, you'll be mine."

"I'll be yours," he told her. It wasn't the first promise he had ever broken, nor would it be the last.

A sound came from the far end of the corridor. It was the guard, no doubt, telling them that he didn't dare give them any more time—not even for all the latinum he could carry.

Mella Cwan pulled her hood up. "Have courage," she said.

Thul smiled a thin smile. He thought again of his bastard son, whose death at the hands of the Federation cried out to him for vengeance. "I will," he assured the emperor's sister. "For is courage not the first virtue?"

And I am nothing, he thought, if not a virtuous man.